Uwe Tellkamp was born in 1968 in Dresden. After completing his military service, he lost his place to study medicine on the grounds of 'political unreliability'. He was arrested in 1989 but went on to study medicine in Liepzig, Dresden and New York, later becoming a surgeon. He has won numerous regional prizes for poetry, as well as the Ingeborg Bachmann Prize for *The Sleep in the Clocks*. In 2008, he won the German Book Prize for *The Tower*.

Mike Mitchell is a former lecturer in German at Stirling University and has been a freelance translator since 1995. He has translated over eighty books from German and French.

THE TOWER

Tales from a Lost Country

Uwe Tellkamp

Translated by Mike Mitchell

PENGUIN BOOKS

PENGUIN BOOKS

UK | USA | Canada | Ireland | Australia
India | New Zealand | South Africa

Penguin Books is part of the Penguin Random House group of companies
whose addresses can be found at global.penguinrandomhouse.com.

First published in German as *Der Turm: Geschichte aus einem versunkenem Land. Roman*
by Suhrkamp Verlag 2008
This translation first published by Allen Lane 2014
Published in Penguin Books 2016

001

Copyright © Suhrkamp Verlag Frankfurt am Main, 2008
Translation copyright © Mike Mitchell, 2014
The moral right of the author and translator has been asserted

Set in 11.13/ 14.21 pt Fournier MT Std
Typeset by Jouve (UK), Milton Keynes
Printed in Great Britain by Clays Ltd, St Ives plc

A CIP catalogue record for this book is available from the British Library

ISBN: 978-0-141-97925-0

For Annett and for Meno Nikolaus Tellkamp

The plot of this novel is fictional.
The characters that are depicted live in my imagination
and have as little in common with living people as a
sculptor's clay has with a sculpture.

Contents

Contents

Contents

BOOK 2: GRAVITY

Contents

Overture

Searching, the Great River seemed to tauten in the approaching night, its skin crinkled and crackled, as if it were trying to anticipate the wind that arose in the town when the traffic on the bridges had thinned to a few cars and the occasional tram, the wind from the sea surrounding the Socialist Union, the Red Empire, the archipelago riven, reft, rent by the arteries, veins, capillaries of the Great River, fed by the sea, the Great River that in the night carried the sounds and thoughts on its shimmering surface, the laughter and the gravity and the merriment, into the gathering dark; suspended matter down into the depths where the watercourses of the town mingled; in the deep-sea darkness the swill from the sewers crept, the dripping discharge from the houses and the VEBs, the state-owned factories, in the depths, where the wraiths dug, there was metallic sludge, heavy with oil, from the electroplating shops, water from restaurants and brown-coal power stations and large-scale industrial plants, streams of foam from the factories that produced cleaning products, effluents from the steel works, hospitals, iron foundries and industrial zones, radioactive outflow from the uranium mines, toxic waste from the Leuna, Buna, Halle chemical plants and the potash works, from Magnitogorsk and from the high-rise tenements, toxins from fertilizer plants, sulphuric-acid factories; in the night the Great River, the rivers of mud, slag, oil, cellulose branching out in all directions, fused into a huge ribbon, sluggish as pitch, on which the ships sailed through the rusty spiders' webs of the bridges into the ore harbours grain harbours tropical-fruit harbours the harbours of the thousand little things

— And I remember the town, the country, the islands combined by bridges

into the Socialist Union, a continent of Laurasia in which time was encapsulated in a geode, closed to the Othertime, and music rang out from the record players, crackling under the tone-arms in the billowing black of the vinyl, spindles of light pulsating across to the yellow label of Deutsche Grammophon, to the Eterna and Melodia lettering, while outside winter froze the country, piling clamps of ice on the banks of the Great River that squeezed it to a standstill between their jaws, as they did the hands on the clocks . . . but the clocks struck, I can hear, as if it were today, the Westminster chimes in Caravel when the living-room window was open and I was walking down the street, I can hear the chime of the grandfather clock from the apartment on the ground floor of Wisteria House; the delicate ring of the Viennese clock from the Tietzes' music room, the melodiously rising ta-ta-ta-taa, snapping off with the last note, after the piercing sawing-sound of the West German Radio time check, which, at the beginning of the eighties, the Tower-dwellers of the Island of Dresden no longer listened to under their bedclothes; now the voiceless hand of a Japanese quartz watch that, from the wrist of a State Orchestra double-bassist, joins in the gonging and pinging, clinking and cuckoo calls in the shop of the clockmaker Simmchen, known as Ticktock Simmchen, in the deep hour-chimes of the grandfather clocks, the full-voiced repetition of the wall clocks at Pieper's Clocks, 8 Turmstrasse; the coloratura soprano of an elaborate porcelain clock at the widowed Frau Fiebig's in Guenon House, the hoarse rebellion of a pilot's watch on the second floor of the Steiner Guest House, in the apartment of the former general staff officer in Rommel's Afrika Korps; the Pekingese snarl in the apartment at the end of the hall where a man by the name of Hermann Schreiber lived, once a master spy in the tsarist Okhrana and the Red Army; a clock with the Tsar's coat of arms rescued from the storming of the St Petersburg Winter Palace in 1917; I can hear the croak of Dr Fernau's pocket watch, as if I were sitting in his surgery or standing in the X-ray van for one of the annual TB checks and looking at the black-and-white screen over which the grey-haired doctor is bent; the Meissen porcelain bells of the Zwinger join in, undistracted by

*footsteps, people hurrying along corridors, telephones ringing, the course
of events, the noise of the paternosters moving on, I can hear the clocks
in the buildings of the State Planning Commission, formerly the Reich
Aviation Ministry*

*— Searching, searching, in everlasting night, on the sea, the dark ocean
that branched out into the Great River and the lesser rivers that creep round
the Inhabited Islands*

*— And I heard the clocks of the paper republic ringing sounding striking
across the arms of the sea, Scholar's Island: a spiral cone that rose up to
the sky, a helix drawn on the table in Auerbach's Cellar, apartments linked
by steps, houses screwed together by staircases, auditory canals designed
on drawing boards, spiders' webs, the bridges*

*— In the night the rusty bridges, attacked by the mildew of sleep, eaten
away by acids, guarded, wreathed in brambles, trapped in verdigris, the
Prussian eagle firmly wrought, bridges releasing their eavesdroppers on the
stroke of midnight, craning their hundred-eyed periscopes, focusing lenses,
bearing flags, sulphurated from the chimneys, feigning lines of music, steam-
rolled with bitumen, rotting with dripping, seeping, sweating damp, creeping
through mouldering files, braided with barbed wire, leaded with clock faces;
what was ATLANTIS, which we entered at night after pronouncing the
magic word, 'Mutabor', the invisible realm behind the visible one, which
only, not for tourists and not for the dreamless, broke out of the contours of
the day after long stays there and left rifts behind, a shadow among the
diagrams of what we called The First Reality, ATLANTIS: The Second
Reality, the Island of Dresden/Coal Island/the Copper Island of the
government/Island with the Red Star/the Ascanian Island where the
disciples of Justice worked, knotted, spun, crusted into ATLANTIS*

*— The second hands of station clocks in the branching tracts of the Ana-
tomical Institute crawled, hesitating at twelve, until the minute hand woke
from its paralysis and dropped into the next slot, where it seemed to throw
out adhesive anchors, in which, as if stunned, compressed by the buffers of
the previous and coming minute, it stuck; Omnia vincit labor, insisted the*

bell on the Kroch high-rise building, struck by two giants with hammers, and the scholars, the players of the socialist glass-bead game, the ludi magistri at the university, floating on the sea as an open stone book with Karl Marx as a totemic figurehead, bent over the spirit of the age of Goethe, invited the revolution into the witness stand, proclaimed the Principle of Hope, held forth on the legacy of Classicism in lecture room 40, dissected the human body in the rooms under Liebigstrasse: here is death in the service of life, Anatomy: the key to and rudder of medicine

— Searching, in the night the Great River, a weary, sick animal, dreaming in a sleep-case with the cold rising round it, and veined streets on the islands, sparsely lit, squeezed in between the frost and the silence, people with supple shadows hurry across the boulevards where the banners wave on the first of May, marches spiral out of the loudspeaker membranes like metal shavings from a work-piece in a lathe, explosive charges, chisel bits, pneumatic hammers drive galleries into the mine, pare the fingertips of the river forward, the Stakhanov-, the Henneke-Movement, the tunnel borers dig beneath the islands, carpenters insert the props, the river opens ear trumpets

— The Great Clock struck and the sea rose up in front of the windows, the rooms with the fern-pattern wallpaper and the frosted chandeliers, the stuccoed ceilings and fine furniture, inherited from a vanished middle-class past hinted at by the berets of the monument curators, the measured gestures of ladies eating cakes in the Italian cafés, the florid and chivalrous greeting ceremonies of the pursuit of art in Dresden, the hidden quotations, the mandarinesque, pedagogical, allusive rituals of the Friends of Music, the stately free-skating programmes of middle-aged gentlemen on the rinks; left over in the gently rolling hills of the Elbe valley in houses under the Soviet star, left over like the pre-war editions of Hermann Hesse, the cigar-brown Aufbau Verlag volumes of Thomas Mann from the fifties, jealously guarded in second-hand bookshops, where the undersea light commanded reverence from every customer that entered, paper boats that housed fossils slowly poisoning themselves with memories, tended pot-plants and

kept the compass over the creaking floorboards unwaveringly pointing to Weimar, left over in the roses growing round the island, across the faces of the clocks that were rusting away, their pendulums cutting though our lives between the poles of silence and non-silence (it was one or the other, mere 'noise' or 'sound' it was not). We listened to music, the records were called Eterna, Melodia, they could be bought from Herr Trüpel, in the Philharmonia record shop on Bautzner Strasse or in the Art Salon on the Old Market Square . . . the Great Clock struck

— Dresden . . . in the muses' nests / the sweet sickness of yesteryear rests

— Searching, in the night the Great River, woods turned into lignite, lignite formed seams beneath the houses, the pit-moles burrowed their way forward and dug out the coal, conveyor belts carried it to the stokers, to the power stations with their volcanic vents, to the houses, where the acid smoke went up out of the chimneys, eating away walls and lungs and souls, transforming wallpaper into toad's skin; the wallpaper in the rooms, peeling off and blistering, yellowed and criss-crossed by the excrement threads of the bugs; when the stoves were lit, the walls seemed to sweat, secreting nicotine that had been collecting there since the old days; if it turned cold the windowpanes froze over, the wallpaper was covered in rime, ferny smears and oily ice (like fat in an unwashed frying pan banished to an unheated lumber room). A golden bird, which sometimes croaked in our dreams, watched over everything, the Minol oriole, and when the clocks struck, our bodies were stiff and captive, the roses grew

wrote Meno Rohde,

the Sandman sprinkled sleep

BOOK I

The pedagogical province

I
Ascent

The electric lemons from VEB Narva decorating the tree were faulty, flickered on and off, erasing the silhouette of Dresden downstream. Christian took off his mittens, which were damp and covered with little balls of ice on the wool of the palms, and rubbed his almost numb fingers rapidly together, breathed on them – his breath a wisp of mist dispersing across the blackness of the entrance, hewn out of the rock, to the Buchensteig, which led up to Arbogast's Institutes. The houses of Schillerstrasse disappeared in the dark; a cable ran from the nearest, a half-timbered house with bolted shutters, into the branches of one of the beeches that grew over the passage through the rock, where an Advent star was burning, bright and motionless. Christian, who had crossed the Blue Marvel – Loschwitz suspension bridge – and Körner-platz, continued on his way out of the city, towards Grundstrasse, and soon reached the cable-car railway. The shutters were down over the windows of the shops he passed – a baker's, a dairy, a fish shop; half in shadow already, the houses were gloomy and had ashy outlines. He felt as if they were huddling together, seeking protection from some-thing indefinite, as yet unfathomable, that might float up out of the darkness – just as the January moon had floated up out of the darkness over the Elbe when Christian had stopped on the deserted bridge and looked at the river, the thick woollen scarf his mother had knitted pulled tight round his ears and cheeks against the icy-keen wind. The moon had risen slowly, detaching itself from the coldly sluggish mass of the river, which looked like liquid earth, to stand alone over the meadows with their willows wreathed in mist, the boathouse on the Old Town bank of the Elbe and the range of hills disappearing in the direction of Pillnitz. The clock on a distant church tower struck four, which surprised Christian.

He took the path up to the funicular railway, put his travel bag on the bench by the gate that closed off the platform and waited, his mittened hands in the pockets of his military-green parka. The hands of the station clock over the conductor's shed seemed to move forward very slowly. Apart from him, there was no one waiting for the funicular, and to pass the time he examined the adverts. They hadn't been cleaned in a long time. One was for the Café Toscana on the Old Town bank of the Elbe, another for Nähter's, a shop farther along towards Schillerplatz, and a third for the Sibyllenhof Restaurant by the station at the top. In his mind Christian began to go through the fingering and melodic line of the Italian piece that they were going to play at his father's birthday party. Then he looked into the darkness of the tunnel. A faint light was growing, gradually filling the cavity of the tunnel like water rising in a fountain, and at the same time the noise increased: a slate-like crackling and groaning, the steel-wire guide cable creaked under the load; jolting, the funicular approached, a capsule filled with an undersea glow, and two headlight eyes lit up the line. The hazy outlines of individual passengers could be seen in the carriage with, in the middle, the blurred shadow of the greybeard conductor – he had been on this section for years, up and down, down and up, always alternating, perhaps he closed his eyes to avoid the sight of the all-too-familiar scenes, or to see them with his inner eye and then repress them, to exorcize ghosts. But he could probably see by hearing, every jolt during the journey must have been familiar to him.

Christian picked up his bag, took out a groschen and spent the remaining moments contemplating the coin: the oak leaves beside the crudely cut ten, the tiny, worn year with the A underneath it, the obverse with the hammer, compasses and the wreath of grain, and he thought back to how often they, the children of Heinrichstrasse and Wolfsleite, had copied the embossed surface of these coins by placing them under a piece of paper and rubbing them with a pencil – Ezzo and Ina had been more skilful at it, and keener than him, back in the days of their childhood dreams of adventurous lives as forgers and robbers, like the heroes in the films at the Tannhäuser Cinema or in the books of Karl May and Jules Verne. The funicular, braking softly, came to a halt, and the doors, graded in height and sloping, released their passengers. The conductor got out, opened the gate and a narrow entrance beside it for the passengers who were going up. The gate had a coin-box attached, and Christian dropped his fare in and pulled down the lever on the side; the ten-pfennig piece slipped out of the rotating disc and joined the others on the bottom. Instead of the groschen, the local children sometimes put in flat stones that had been ground smooth by the Elbe and which they called 'butties', or buttons – much to the annoyance of their mothers – who were sorry to lose them, for the little aluminium coins were easy to get while buttons, on the other hand, were difficult to find. The doors were closed; if you wanted to get into the carriage in the winter, you had to pull a cable to open them; they closed as soon as you let go. The conductor had gone into his shed, poured himself a coffee and watched the passengers hurrying off, disappearing like shadows round the corners to Körnerplatz or Pillnitzer Landstrasse.

After a few minutes a weary-sounding voice came from the loud-speaker above the adverts and said something in a Saxon accent that Christian couldn't understand; but the conductor stood up and carefully closed the door to his shed. Slowly, the round leather change-bag dangling over his well-worn uniform, he went to the driver's cabin at the front – its many control buttons seemed pointless to Christian, since the funicular was steered by the cable and rollers and was brought to a halt automatically, if the cable should tear, by a sophisticated clasp mechanism. Perhaps the buttons were there for some other reason, perhaps for communication or for psychological purposes: the buttons must have some meaning, a function, and would demand knowledge, guard against monotony and work-weariness; moreover, halfway along, one of the cars had to move onto a siding to allow the other to pass. The cabin door closed behind the conductor with a crash; it was opened with a box spanner and was not connected to the cable for the other doors.

'The train is about to depart,' said the voice from the loudspeaker. The carriage remained motionless for a moment, then smoothly started moving, gliding out of the station. Christian turned round and watched the path and platform grow smaller, until all that remained was the oval of the tunnel entrance against the flinty green of the sky; gradually that grew smaller as well, and darkness pressed in from either side. For a short while, before the exit came into view, the only light was provided by the dim tunnel lamps and the headlights. Christian took a book out of his bag; his Uncle Meno had given it to him. He had hardly had time to look at it during the previous week: the pre-Christmas mood had spread round Waldbrunn, and though the lessons weren't as strict as usual, preparations for the birthday party, and the daily bus journeys home to rehearse the Italian piece with the others, had taken up his time. Christian intended to read the book more thoroughly during the Christmas holidays. It was a fairly fat tome, printed on fibrous paper and bound in coarse linen; he knew the picture on the cover from a facsimile edition of the Manesse Manuscript he had seen in his uncle's library and at the Tietzes', in a particularly handsome and well-preserved example – Niklas, Ezzo's and Reglinde's father, often read it. The picture showed the legendary figure of Tannhäuser, a man with long red hair in a blue robe with a white cloak, a black cross on his breast; on either side above him were his coat of arms and a winged helmet, both black at the top and yellow below, above stylized tendrils with leaves; 'Tanhuser', as his name was written above the plate, had raised his left hand to ward off, or perhaps cautiously greet, someone or something; his right hand was holding his cloak. Christian opened the volume – *Old German Poems*, selected and edited with notes by Meno Rohde – and returned to the legend he'd been reading on the journey from Waldbrunn to Dresden. The lamp on the ceiling above him started to make a rasping noise, the page the book was opened at had a pale, grainy look and, with the gentle vibration of the carriage, the letters started to blur before his eyes. He couldn't concentrate on the story of the Knight of the Golden Spur who had set out with seventy-two ships to free Queen Bride. The lamp went out. He put the book back in his bag, and felt for the barometer, a present for his father that he had collected from the former lodge of the Association of Elbe Boatmen. It was safely packed and cushioned in the bundle of dirty laundry that filled his bag.

In its slow but steady upward climb, occasionally jolted by unevennesses between the rollers, the funicular reached Buchensteig, the path that ran alongside the track, and continued parallel to it for a while, a few metres above the ground. You could see into lighted windows; an outstretched hand could easily have touched the passing carriage. At the top the Sibyllenhof restaurant, which had been closed for several years, came into view beside the second tunnel; its terraces stuck out like school slates that had been forgotten there by giant children years ago. The carriage would head straight towards the restaurant, only turning off into the entrance of the tunnel that led to the station shortly before it reached the bottom terrace. On some journeys Christian had dreamt of bygone banquets in the dark, uninviting rooms: of gentlemen pursuing cultured conversations, wearing starched shirts with jet buttons and watch chains over the pockets of their waistcoats; of flower sellers in pages' uniforms, called to a table with the hint of a click of the fingers, to present ladies, wearing masses of jewellery which gave off fiery sparks under the bowls of the crystal chandeliers, with a rose; of dances for which the band struck up, the pale violinist with pomaded hair and wearing a chrysanthemum in his buttonhole . . . The light of

7

the January moon slid over the roofs of the houses that sloped steeply down to Grundstrasse, making the ridges shine and giving the snowy gardens patches of powdery brightness which, with the white highlights of isolated, snow-covered sheds or stacks of wood, merged at the edges with the shadows cast by the bushes and trees.

Christian realized they were above the painter and illustrator Vogelstrom's house, a grey castle that Meno called 'Cobweb House', sparking off in Christian's mind a vision which, as he looked out of the window, his face close to the cold glass, lurked behind the everyday sobriety of the unapproachable windows and tall trees. In the towering mass of the Loschwitz slopes, on the other side of Grundstrasse, which was partly visible as a pale ribbon winding in the depths, the needles of moonlight were sucked into the darkness in front of the watch towers of East Rome and faded at the bridge, across which soldiers were heading for the checkpoint on Oberer Plan. The garden of Cobweb House was in darkness, sheltered from eyes and events, and Christian could hardly even see the tops of the pear and beech trees, with their dusting of snow and their filigree branches hanging like wisps of smoke over the depths; it flowed into the contours, the narrow cleft between the Buchensteig path and the battlements, like brightness in the cross-hatching on old, unfinished drawings. He saw the fountain, the almost completely overgrown driveway that curved round the weathered stone catfish on the fountain and led up over mossy steps; the beginning of a poem had been chiselled into the panel over the catfish, but the letters were blurred, already half erased. However hard he tried, Christian couldn't remember how the poem went, but he could clearly picture the broken-off barbels of the catfish, its sightless eyes and the dark covering of moss; he remembered his superstitious fear of the beast, and also of the long-defunct fountain that gave off a graveyard chill when he went to see Vogelstrom with Meno, and his almost childish fear, which was only made greater by the strange conversations that took place between Meno and the gaunt painter in

Cobweb House. But it was less the words and topics themselves that had seemed strange than the atmosphere of the house; with his childish understanding, the little that had been comprehensible to the boy of eleven or twelve seemed right and appropriate for the adult world that bent down to him from its heights. He could remember words such as 'Merigarto' or 'Magelone', words which, in his awakening surmise, seemed more like conjurations than concepts that meant something in the real world, words that touched him in a curious way and that he was never to forget, even though they had seemed less mysterious than the paintings in the gloomy hall of the house: idyllic landscapes, garden scenes with flute-playing fauns and naiads flooded with bright blue light, a Dutch-brown series of ancestors, serious-looking men and women with a flower, a nettle or – he had looked at this for a long time in astonishment – holding a golden snail. These paintings, fading away in the hall, which Vogelstrom and Meno only rarely glanced at as they passed them, seemed to have much more to do with those two words: the one for the island and the other the name of a girl who appeared out of the depths of time and disappeared back into them; he had noted them and repeatedly savoured their long-forgotten euphony in murmured soliloquies. Sound, too, had stayed with him from their conversations, like the babble of a stream from Vogelstrom's studio, which was so cold in the winter that frost sent out tentacles towards the easels and the lozenge-patterned wallpaper, and the two men, Meno with Vogelstrom's coat over his shoulders, Vogelstrom himself in several pullovers and shirts, hurried round the room with steaming breath, their voices scarcely distinguishable when they were in the library and Christian was looking at one of the ancestors' portraits in the hall and listening; now and then there was the sound of cautious laughter, expressions of praise for, or disgust with, the tobacco they happened to be smoking. Sometimes Meno would call out and show him steel or copper engravings in musty-smelling tomes, the painter cautiously turning the pages, and it was probably then that they uttered the strange words that stuck in his ear, words he had never heard before, words like those two magical names.

The lamp above him flickered on again. From above, out of the darkness below the tunnel and the Sibyllenhof, the descending funicular crept towards them, reaching the loop where the track split and one could move out of the way of the other. The driver was a motionless shadow in the passing capsule, which had no passengers, and he replied to the greybeard conductor's greeting with a brief nod before the carriage continued down and disappeared from view.

Christian remembered that it was in Cobweb House that he had first heard something about Poe; Meno and Vogelstrom had been looking at illustrations to one of Poe's stories. He particularly remembered one print – Vogelstrom's needle had etched an elaborate picture of a castle rising up into the darkness of the nocturnal countryside; then one of Prince Prospero and his retinue of a thousand ladies and knights in the castle with the welded bolts on the doors; he saw them again, as he had all those years ago under Vogelstrom's thin, slim-fingered hand, strolling and chatting, as if the company were alive and playing their merry games, while outside the plague was raging, devastating the land, as if Prospero were passing through the rooms amid the frenzy of a masked ball – music swelled, and the chimes of the ebony clock in the black chamber echoed and faded in the vastness of the castle, and in the six other chambers the people were dancing, for Prince Prospero would not countenance sadness, and the cries of the despairing populace could no longer be heard over the music, the singing and laughter, the barking of the dogs outside the gates.

The carriage was slowing down, coasting the last few metres. Lost in his thoughts and memories, Christian had hardly noticed it enter the upper tunnel, which, with its whitewashed walls, was brighter than the lower one, he had merely glanced automatically, but without really taking anything in, at the upper station with its cheerful bright paint and gracefully curving roof, the red-brick building with the neon sign:

Funicular Railway, the machine room and the waiting room where you could examine photographs of earlier models and technical details in a glass display case. The funicular came to a halt, shuddering gently. The doors opened with a clatter. Christian slung his bag over his shoulder and, still immersed in thought, went up the shallow steps of the station towards the exit gate.

The conductor shuffled off in the direction of the waiting room, felt for a button concealed in the wall; there was a buzz, the gate opened and Christian went out. He was home, in the Tower.

2

Mutabor

'Great that I caught you. I was thinking I'd have to come back again.'

'Meno! You've come to meet me?'

'Anne has had to find somewhere else for Robert and you to stay tonight. You're sleeping at my place.'

'So many guests?' Christian only asked so that he could hide his delight behind a casual-sounding question. He already knew. The vast amount of baking ingredients that had been procured during the last few weeks and piled up in the larder of Caravel indicated the number of guests they expected for the birthday party – and had convinced him that coming home to stay in Caravel, except to take part in the rehearsals that would take place mainly at the Tietzes', would be ill-advised; that is, if he didn't want to irritate Anne, in her nervous state, by hanging about, or risk exposure to her suspicious gaze and end up, once excuses were no longer possible, being sent off to Konsum or Holfix larded with shopping lists, or to face never-ending stacks of dishes in the kitchen.

'There were at least thirty of us for coffee this afternoon and the official celebrations only start later; more people are sure to be coming then.'

They were walking along Sibyllenleite.

'And where's Robert sleeping?'

'At the Tietzes'.'

So his brother would be spending the night in Evening Star. Christian put his mittens back on and thought of the House with a Thousand Eyes, where he would be spending the night, in a quite different atmosphere from that at home in Caravel.

'I decided to come and meet you so that you didn't go home first. Anne has already taken your cello with her to the Felsenburg.'

Christian nodded and looked at his uncle, who had taken his hat off and removed the snowflakes with a few flicks. 'Since when have you been wearing that?'

'Anne bought it for me in Exquisit. Said it ought to suit me. A good style too.' Meno looked at the writing on the sweatband. 'A delivery arrived from Yugoslavia. Anne said people were queuing all the way back to Thälmannstrasse, at least fifty metres. They didn't have one for your father.' He put his hat back on. 'Did everything work out with the barometer?'

'As agreed. Two hundred and fifty marks. Lange even cleaned it up and polished it again.'

'Good. Shall I take your bag?'

'Oh, it's not that heavy, but thanks, Meno. Apart from the barometer, it's only dirty laundry.'

They came to Turmstrasse, the main through-road of the district, and from which it derived its popular name of the 'Tower'. Meno walked with more measured steps than Christian; he had taken out a briar pipe with a curved stem and a spherical bowl and was filling it from a leather pouch. Christian raised his nose and sniffed, sucking in the vanilla fragrance that mingled with the aroma of figs and cedar-wood.

Alois Lange, a former ship's doctor and Meno's neighbour in the House with a Thousand Eyes, got a box of the tobacco every year from the deputy chairman of the Copenhagen Nautical Academy, and he gave half to Meno – the ship's doctor had once saved the deputy chairman's life and thus, to the annoyance of Lange's wife, Libussa, there was never a shortage of tobacco in the House with a Thousand Eyes. A match flared up, illuminating Meno's lean, pale features and bluish five-o'clock shadow; the reflection flickered in his brown eyes, which were warmed by a few flashes of green – they were Anne's eyes, and those of her other brother, Ulrich, the eyes of the Rohdes; Christian had inherited them too.

'Did you get through all right? The Eleven was cancelled this morning. It was an hour before the replacement came. The curses at the stop' – Meno sucked at his pipe to get it going – 'would have been something for "Look & Listen". And the Six had a diversion.' His pipe still wasn't going, he lit another match.

'I noticed.'

'Anne was going to ring you, but the lines didn't seem to be working or something, I don't know what was broken again – she couldn't get through at all.' His pipe was finally going, and he blew out puff after puff of smoke.

'Yesterday it snowed like mad higher up, the snow's more than a metre deep in Zinnwald and Altenberg, I was getting worried the bus wouldn't go. Near Karsdorf we had to get out and help the driver shovel the snow away. The brushwood barrier in the fields had fallen over, and all the new snow had been blown onto the road.'

Meno nodded and gave his nephew, who was almost as tall as he was and was tramping through the powder snow a little in front, a thoughtful look. 'How are things at school? Are you managing?'

'Pretty well so far. People stare at me a bit because I'm from Dresden. Civics is as usual.'

'And the teacher? Is he dangerous?'

'Hard to say. He's also our principal. If you just regurgitate what he says, you're left in peace. The Russian teacher's pretty devious. One of the quiet types, very observant, a Party fanatic. There's something feline about him, he creeps round the corridors and checks on us in the hostel. Today he turned up in white gloves and felt in all the corners to see if they were really clean. I'm sure everyone in the next room missed their bus – he found an apple core under the lockers, and they had to clean the place again.'

'Is he provocative?'

'He certainly is.'

'Be careful. They're the worst. I know the type. You always have the feeling they can see through you – you can't look them in the eye, you become nervous, make mistakes. And that's the mistake.'

'That's true, about being seen through. He has such a piercing look, whenever he looks at me I always think he can read my thoughts.'

'But he can't. Don't let tricks like that make you nervous.'

'"A wise man walks with his head bowed, humble like the dust."'

Meno looked at Christian in surprise.

'I made a note of it, Meno.'

The snow, criss-crossed with sledge tracks, reflected the sparse light from the lamps; it covered the garden walls, and the roofs of the few cars that were parked by the pavement, with thick caps. On the left, the houses of Holländische Leite appeared, almost all of them belonging to the Baron's Institute: Baron Ludwig von Arbogast, who in the district was generally called by his inherited title and whose huge premises on Unterer Plan, to which Holländische Leite led, were referred to, half admiringly, half suspiciously, as 'the Institute'. The Baron was the sponsor of the school Christian had attended until the previous summer, and whenever he had seen the Baron, he recalled a conversation between Meno and his father: how to reconcile Arbogast's *soigné* appearance – he wore bespoke suits and carried a stick with a silver handle – with the weathered and grey, but still clearly legible, inscription over the central building of the Institute: FOR SOCIALISM AND PEACE; and 'baron', the title that was clearly written on the boards and signposts in the Institute gardens, with the workers' state. It was a question Christian would have liked to ask his civics teacher.

The lights were still on in the Institute buildings on Turmstrasse. Arbogast's little observatory, which had not been open to the public for ages, even though a sign in front of it promised a 'People's Observatory', was shielded by a sweet chestnut that stretched its branches far out over the footpath. A sundial with its gnomon was rusting away in the ivy that covered the crumbling plaster. Meno was the person Christian would have thought most likely to have had a look inside the door at the rear of the observatory; he had often observed him when astronomy and astrology cropped up in conversations: his uncle adopted an attitude somewhere between latent amusement and concealed interest and scrutinized the newspaper cuttings and pamphlets the guests had brought, quietly leaning against the wall in a corner, his round-bowled pipe in his mouth, listening to his brother, Ulrich, animatedly discuss astronomy in Far Eastern antiquity.

'I was reading your book just now.'

Smoke rose in thick clouds from the bowl of his pipe. 'Strange old things,' Meno muttered at the crossing of Turmstrasse and Wolfsleite. 'Hardly anyone knows them any more. The censors, probably, and the Old Man of the Mountain. The book brought me a thumping great letter from him, from East Rome to West Rome, so to speak. Took three days to arrive when all the old man needed to do was to walk across the bridge. But they said he was ill. – Otherwise people tended to look askance at me because of it.'

'The book doesn't provide an answer to the question of how the steel was tempered.'

'Eisenhüttenstadt doesn't appear in it.' Meno waved his pipe. 'Nor does Parsifal represent a clear revolutionary proletarian standpoint, and in general the class-consciousness of the knights leaves much to be desired.'

'And the Merseburg Charms are much too formalistic?'

'It's not *quite* that bad any longer.'

'The Lay of Hildebrand, the beginning?' Christian gave his uncle a pleading look. Meno took another suck at his pipe and began to recite. Fascinated as always, Christian listened to the pleasant timbre of his voice, the stage diction; he was strangely moved by the ancient language and its power, especially the 'I heard tell / that in single combat / two warriors did meet' of the beginning and by the 'sonandfather' of the fourth line. As they walked on slowly, Meno continued to recite beyond the opening, had already reached the thirteenth line, 'all great folk I ken in this kingdom'; as he walked on, nodding his head to the rhythm of the lines, he spoke of the wrath of Odoacer, of Theoderic and the torc wrought of the Emperor's gold that had been given to him by the king, the lord of the Huns, and how father and son fought 'till their shields were shattered, slashed by their swords'. A light breeze had sprung up, and the trees on either side of the street began to sway, snow drifted down from the branches. They had now reached Wolfsleite, and the broad bulk of Wolfstone lay there like a ship with lights ablaze; in the 'bassoon', as the octagonal extension was called, the 'story-lamp' was smoking: so they'll be telling each other stories, Christian thought, and in his mind's eye he saw his uncle, the toxicologist Hans Hoffmann, explaining monkshood and woody nightshade, which he grew in the 'bassoon' himself, to Fabian and Muriel; he thought of Malivor Marroquin, the white-haired Chilean who ran the fancy-dress shop and a photographic studio next door – when he was fourteen, Christian had had to go there to have his photograph taken by Marroquin, for his ID card; quotations from Lenin's works lined the walls of the staircase that led up to the heavy Ernemann plate camera, and they were mutely scrutinized by the queue of boys and girls with their neatly combed hair; at the top the Chilean shouted, 'Plizz lukk at liddel gold-finsh, plizz lukk naow', at which one had to direct one's gaze at a little red bird that was clipped to the edge of a screen with a clothes peg.

'There's a soirée tomorrow,' Meno said, pointing to Dolphin's Lair, the house opposite Wolfstone, which looked delicately and flimsily built, with the curve of the roof like an upper lip and the large scroll over the coving of a wall. 'Soirée' meant that Frau von Stern had sent out invitations in copperplate script on hand-made paper, invitations to share her memories of the Winter Palace and Dresden Castle, for she had been a lady-in-waiting.

The Italian House was on Wolfsleite as well; Ulrich, Christian's other Rohde uncle, and his family lived there. Ulrich was a director of one of the state-owned companies; his wife, Barbara, worked as a furrier and ladies' tailor in the Harmony Salon on Rissleite. Sometimes Christian would go to see the Rohdes, for some more or less valid reason, so that he could have a good look at the staircase and landing, and the art nouveau details in their apartment. No side of the house was like any of the others. The stairwell stuck out at the front, like the bow of a ship, the shape emphasized by four windows, a single one higher up and three a little lower down, as in a gallery. The lone upper window, over which the roof described an elongated curve, was like an oversized keyhole. Christian put his bag down and went in through the double doors, each shaped like the prow of a gondola, to switch the light on. The portico, an Oriental-looking pavilion set in the masonry, was lit by the hall windows, which had been decorated, as in Dolphin's Lair, with flowers and plants. Dame's violets wound their way up the storeys as far as the keyhole window, interrupted by a key-stone between the floors that was adorned with two facing sandstone spirals. And to the left, on the side of the jutting-out stairwell that faced Turmstrasse, a decrepit oriel was squatting on its corbel; it belonged to the Rohde apartment. In many places, the plaster revealed the bricks that had been eaten away by time and rain.

'Shall we ring? – No,' Meno murmured. 'Come on.' They continued on their way, Meno head bowed, hands in his coat pockets, hat pulled down over his face.

On Mondleite the elms were stretching out their skeleton branches against the sky. It began to snow. The flakes gusted and drifted across the road, which hardly had enough room for the Ladas, Trabants and Wartburgs that squeezed up against the very edge, here and there shouldering aside the broken, weather-beaten fences, overgrown with brambles. The mantles of the lamps that were still working began to flutter, reminding Christian of the visions he'd had during evening walks of carriages appearing outside the silent houses that had withdrawn into the past, emerging from the nocturnal haziness of Mondleite and Wolfsleite on winter evenings such as this and driving up or away, inaudible in the snow – ladies with ermine muffs got out after a zealous servant had opened the carriage door, the horses snorted and shuffled in their harnesses, scenting oats and sugar, their home stable, and then the gate with the two sandstone balls on the pillars and the spiral lady's tresses ornament carved on the arch opened, cries rang out, a chambermaid hurried down the steps to take the luggage . . . Christian started when he heard a barn owl screech. Meno pointed to the oak trees by the House with a Thousand Eyes, which had come into view, half hidden behind the gate and the massive copper beech. It stood at the side of a wider stretch of road, into which Mondleite led, and which, where the oak trees grew, formed a sharp bend between Mondleite and Planetenweg. Meno took out the key, but the house still seemed far away to Christian, inaccessible, woven into the beech tree branches as if in a large coral in the night. The shriek of a barn owl came from the park that fell away steeply from Mondleite and was separated from the garden of the House with a Thousand Eyes by a line of Bhutan pines, whose resinous fragrance mingled with the metallic smell of the snowy air. 'Here we are, then.'

And Christian thought, Yes, here we are. This is your home. And when I go in, when I cross the threshold, I will be transformed. The Teerwagens across the road seemed to be having a party; a clatter of laughter came from the physicist's apartment in the house that Christian and Meno called the 'Elephant' – massy, yet elegantly proportioned, undulating at the rounded corner of the façade with oyster-like balconies and rusty flowers sitting on its art nouveau railings like large-winged, melancholy moths. Meanwhile, Meno had scraped out his pipe, chewed a few mints, then gone on ahead, down the path of broken sandstone slabs that were bordered by hedges of sweet briar. He opened the door with an ornate key that had been stained with brazing solder. Christian would often see the key in his mind's eye when he was lying in bed in his boarder's room in Waldbrunn and think: the House with a Thousand Eyes. As he adjusted his bag over his shoulder, he felt warmed by Meno's 'here': it took in the whole district, the villas all around in the darkness and snow, the gardens and the barn owl still calling in the depths of the park, the copper beech, the names. Meno switched on the hall light; the house seemed to open its eyes. Christian touched the sandstone of the arch; he also touched – a superstition, the origin of which was lost – the wrought-iron flower on the gate, a strangely shaped ornament that could often be seen up here: petals curving out in snail-like whorls round a curving stem which was also encircled by several coils of an elaborate spiral; a plant that, with its aura of beauty and danger, had already fascinated Christian as a child – sometimes he would spend half an hour contemplating the bee lily. The name came from Meno. Christian followed his uncle into the house.

3
The House with a Thousand Eyes

The door, rounded at the top, with wrought-iron hinges, fell shut. Meno didn't take his coat off. In a vase on the table below the hall mirror, there was a bouquet of roses; Meno carefully wrapped it in paper that was waiting there. 'From Libussa's conservatory,' he said proudly. 'You just try to get something like that in Dresden at this time of year. Just see what the others have to offer: Centraflor only has funeral wreaths, poinsettias and cyclamen.' Meno picked up a slim package that was beside the vase.

'Anne's brought a few things for you, up in the cabin. What shall we do with the barometer? I promised Anne I'd be there a bit before things start.'

'Have you any wrapping paper?'

'In the kitchen.'

'Then I'll take some weather all wrapped up with me.'

'Nicely put, my friend. Before you go, will you please check the stove? Towels are upstairs. You can have a shower if you want, the boiler's on.'

'Had one already, back at the hostel.'

'I'll leave the key here for you. I've also told Libussa, in case there should be a problem.'

Meno went into the living room. Not long after, Christian, who had taken his shoes and parka off, heard the clatter of the stove door and the thump of briquettes. The tongs clanged against the ash-pan, Meno came back. There was a gurgle of water from the kitchen. 'And don't give in to Baba if he comes begging, he's had enough already, the fat beast. Leave him in the hall, the heat will all be gone if the living-room door's left open, and I don't want to see a disgusting mess like we had the day before yesterday ever again.'

'What did he do?'

'Calmly did his business behind the ten-minute clock. And I was only away for an hour!'

Christian laughed. Meno, checking his appearance and adjusting his tie in the mirror, growled, 'Such a lazybones. I didn't feel like laughing, I can tell you. And the stench! . . . Ah, well. Please bear that in mind.'

'How are things at work?'

'Later,' said Meno at the door and, holding the slim package and the flowers he'd put in a bag, tipped his hat.

Christian took a pair of felt slippers out of the shoe cabinet by the door, started, and quickly looked round. He'd heard a creak, perhaps from the kitchen, perhaps from upstairs, where the cabin was – that was what Meno and the ship's doctor called the bedroom where Christian was going to sleep. Perhaps the floorboards under the worn runner were moving. Christian waited, but there was nothing more to be heard. He slowly took in the familiar but still astonishing things: the dark-green, slightly faded fabric wallcovering with the plant and salamander motifs in the hall; the oval mirror, whose silvering was tarnished in places and had taken on a leaden tone; the wardrobe by the unseasoned pine stairs – as a child, he'd sometimes hidden there, among cardboard boxes with spare bulbs and work clothes, when he'd been playing 'cops and robbers' with Robert and Ezzo; and the hall light with the green clay toucan, which hung from it motionless and could perhaps, with its sad-looking, painted button eyes, see as far as Peru. That was where Alice and Sandor had brought it from years ago – 'Aunt' Alice and 'Uncle' Sandor, as Christian and Robert called them, although that wasn't quite correct: Sandor was the cousin of their father, Richard Hoffmann. Christian remembered that he would see them again later that evening – they were visiting from South America; they lived in Quito, the capital of the Andean state of Ecuador; he was looking forward to it; he liked them both. So as not to disturb something for which he had no other name than the 'spirit of the house', the djinn with a thousand eyes that were never all asleep at the same time, Christian quietly placed the slippers in front of him on the floor, put them on and went into the living room.

As far as he could tell from a quick look round, nothing had changed since his last visit. Even the fat, cinnamon-coloured tomcat, Chaka-mankabudibaba, welcomed him in the same way as he had on that evening two weeks ago: blinking one eye, then yawning and showing his claws as he stretched, as if the light suddenly going on had woken him from dreams of murder. He sniffed Christian's hand and, finding nothing edible in it, rolled over lazily onto his side to let his tummy be scratched. Christian murmured the cat's full name, at which it made growling noises. Chakamankabudibaba, the name Meno had found in one of Wilhelm Hauff's fairy tales, was not one you could use to call him for a long time in the evening or morning. But since the dignified feline did as he liked, a curt, crisp name, which could be called out repeatedly with no great effort, was no use anyway – if Chakamanka-budibaba was hungry or, as now in the winter, wanted to sleep in the warm, he would come, if he wasn't hungry, he wouldn't. When Christian turned him over on his back to scratch his expansive tummy, the cat gave a grunt, of disgust, and chattered angrily, but he was far too listless to do anything about it. His four paws remained stuck up in the air, like the legs of a roast goose; the cat graciously stretched his neck and already his eyes were clouding over; he would presumably have fallen asleep in that pharaonic posture if Christian hadn't given him a little prod so that he sank back onto his side.

The yellow curtain was drawn over the door with the pointed arch. It led out onto a balcony that seemed to dream over the grounds of the House with a Thousand Eyes in the summer, like a fruit on a tall plant bending with motherly pride over the garden blooming all around; then the doors and windows of the room would be left open until it was dark to let the light and odours pour in from the garden. Christian looked at the clock: four forty-six; soon, five sonorous chimes would drift round the room and the whole house. Ever since he was a child, Christian had been fascinated by the strange design of the clock; he'd often stood looking at it as Meno explained the mechanism of the pendulum and the movement: the clock struck every ten minutes, once at ten past, twice at twenty past, three times at half past and so on; six times for the full hour, which struck momentously after a short pause; at midnight or noon, eighteen chimes rang out. But what impressed Christian most was the second dial below the clock face: a brass ring, tarnished in places, with the signs of the zodiac engraved round the edge; a symbol of the sun travelled round the zodiacal circle, indicating sidereal time. Constellations had been embossed on the ring, and the engraver had made the main stars somewhat larger than the others and connected them by needle-point lines. The Serpent-Bearer, the Hair of Berenice, the Northern Crown, the Whale – Christian remembered how enchanted he'd been by the names and their Latin translation when Meno recited them in a low, almost wistful voice, pointing to the engraved signs as he did so – for the first time one evening about ten years ago, the names had trickled into his seven-year-old's ear like some indeterminate but pleasant substance, and they had given him his first sense that in the adult world, which was also the world of the incomprehensible giant that was standing beside him, a giant who lived in very different regions and whom his mother called Brother dear or Mo, that in the adult world there were very interesting, very special things, secrets; and in his child's mind something must have happened or, hidden away, have grown and suddenly burst open: since that day, Christian had never forgotten the words, their strange, peculiar sound. Ophiuchus. Coma Berenices, Corona Borealis, Cetus. He quietly repeated the names. The clock struck four fifty. It'll only take a few minutes to get down there, Christian thought, there's still plenty of time, the party only starts at six, no need to rush. – He only found out that Meno had been using Latin later, from Ulrich, he thought, or from Niklas, on that evening at the Tietzes' when they were talking about legends.

He went to the table beside the crammed bookshelves his father had made out of plain boards, examined the books and periodicals piled up on top of each other. Even here there had hardly been any changes since his last visit: an issue of *Nature* with a newspaper wrapper was still lying beside several specialist biological periodicals, all covered with a fine layer of dust, and a few fairly well-thumbed copies of *Weimarer Beiträge*. Beside them was that day's edition of *Die Union*, the paper of the CDU, neatly folded, the grainy paper smelling of newsprint. Curious, Christian fingered a leather-bound book, opened it and read the title: *The Ages of the World*, F. W. J. Schelling; the book beside it had the same author and was also bound in leather: *Bruno, or On the Natural and the Divine Principle of Things*. Christian picked it up; it was a quarto volume, and a cloud of dust rose from the marbled edges when he blew on it. It still wasn't clean, so Christian took out his handkerchief, but as he was trying to hold both covers, the pages suddenly fanned out and a few pieces of paper escaped; as he bent down to retrieve them, the book fell onto the floor. Chakamankabudibaba shot up as if he'd had an electric shock and looked at him with green eyes. Christian hastily picked up the scattered pieces of paper and put them back in the book. But they might now all be in the wrong place, so he put the volume back on the table and tried to rectify his clumsiness by opening the book at random: when you did that a book would often open at frequently consulted pages. That didn't seem to be the case here: it was virgin paper, with none of Meno's usual underlinings or notes in the margins. Despite that, Christian inserted one of the slips of paper, repeated the process, several times opening the book at the page where he had just inserted the first note, but finally he had all the pieces of paper back in. Feeling apprehensive, he replaced the books in their original positions.

The cat had closed its eyes again and put its head back on its paws, just the tip of its tail was slowly curving to and fro, as if there were another cat inside the visible, cinnamon-coloured Chakamankabudib-aba, one that was not yet asleep and was watching the young man, who was listening anxiously by the table, with intense concentration. The six bulbs radiating from the cone-shaped lamp spread a canopy of diffuse brightness over the desk and the cat in its chair. In the distant gloom, the books on the shelves that went up to the ceiling, the plants in the corner by the stove, seemed to be looking at Christian, as if even at this late hour they had been called up from an Otherrealm and who-ever had called them had forgotten to say the magic word that would allow them to return. The clock too seemed to be looking at him with both its time-circles. There was no sound to be heard, apart from the regular tick-tock, the rattle of the shutters when the wind got under them and the draught in the stove. Christian went into the kitchen and took a pair of work gloves out of the coal box under the oven, checked whether the bolts on the damper and the ash-pan were closed properly and tightened up the screws a little. He could feel the heat of the metal, even through the heavy material of the gloves; he couldn't touch the tiles around the stove door without having to draw his fingers away immediately. Yet it was still only moderately warm in the living room; the House with a Thousand Eyes was old – the windows didn't fit tightly any more, there were cracks in the wood, and the heat seeped out into the corridor.

His father had made the desk, as a wedding present for Meno, with all the meticulousness and attention to detail he showed in matters of craftsmanship. The wood still seemed to smell of the forest, even though the desk had been under the large window for seven years and had absorbed the odour of tobacco. Richard had built it across the corner; the desktop was more than three metres long, and he had managed to make it fit both the cramped proportions of the room and the space by the window – to the right was the arched door leading out onto the balcony, to the left a solid larch cupboard that the previous owners had left because it was simply immovable: it wouldn't go through the door, it had originally had to be lifted in through the window by a crane. Meno had arranged two workplaces on the desk: one for his slide preparations, dissecting instruments, specialist periodicals and microscope; the other for his typewriter and manuscript folders. Christian switched on the table lamp but didn't touch anything, and he was careful not to get too close to the desk, Meno's holy of holies. He looked at the photos: the three Rohde children in their parents' lounge in Bad Schandau; Meno dissecting in the Zoological Institute of Karl-Marx University, Leipzig; as a boy of eleven or twelve, already wearing his hair with a parting, collecting botanical samples with his father, the ethnologist, near Rathen; a photo of Hanna, Meno's ex-wife. Beside them were piles of letters, newspaper cuttings, writing paper covered in Meno's fine, flowing, yet difficult-to-read handwriting – for many of the letters he still used the old German script which had not been taught nor generally used for a long time. Christian saw a few books published by Dresdner Edition, for whom Meno worked. It was an imprint of the Berlin Hermes-Verlag and published books the like of which could not be found on the shelves of any of the bookshops Christian knew: leather-bound de-luxe editions, hand-printed on the best-quality paper, of works such as *The Divine Comedy*, *Faust* and other classics, most with illustrations. The larger part were earmarked for export to the 'Non-Socialist Economic Area'. Many of the few remaining copies went to acquaintances and friends of the managing director or to book collectors in the higher reaches of the Party; Christian had never seen one of these books on sale in a Dresden bookshop, and even if he had, they would have been well beyond his means – the copy of *The Divine Comedy* that Meno possessed cost as much as a doctor's monthly salary.

For quite a while Christian stood looking at the things on the desk, things he automatically connected with the House with a Thousand Eyes, and with Meno, when he thought of him from far away, during one of the long bus journeys to and from Waldbrunn or at school.

He switched the light off again, stood there for a few minutes in the gloom, listening, and then took Chakamankabudibaba into the kitchen and put him down on the kitchen bench, which annoyed the cat – it wasn't as cosy there as in the living room next door. Chakamankabudibaba arched his back, meowed plaintively and jumped down to his feeding bowls. The milk in the dish beside the food bowl was sour, and there was a piece of meat floating in it. Christian poured it all down the toilet, washed the dish and filled it. Then he fetched the barometer and wrapped it in the gift paper.

As he went upstairs he suddenly heard voices. Perhaps Libussa, Lange's wife from Prague, had visitors; but then he recognized the voices of Annemarie Brodhagen and Professor Dathe, the famous director of the East Berlin Zoo – Libussa had switched on the television and was watching *Zoos round the World*. For a moment Christian felt a twinge of envy: hearing the popular professor with the clear enunciation reminded him that the last episode of *Oh, What Tenants* – a Danish series in which many of the 'Olsen gang' appeared – was on that evening, a series he loved and had grown up with. He frowned as he switched on the stair light – a bronze flower with a bulb in it; the petals were bent.

He didn't like big celebrations, as his father's fiftieth birthday that evening would in all probability be; he preferred to be alone. It wasn't that he was unsociable – his dislike of company was connected with his appearance. If there was one thing Christian felt ashamed of, it was his face, precisely what people looked at when they looked at you. Although his face was basically attractive and expressive, it was covered in acne and he felt horribly embarrassed at the thought of all the people who would give him searching, mocking or even revolted looks. It was precisely that expression, revulsion, which he feared; he had seen it often enough. Someone would turn round, look at him, and, unable to conceal their shock, or even repugnance, would openly show their reaction for a fraction of a second. Then they would control themselves, realize that Christian would presumably feel hurt if they gawped at him like that and quickly select a different expression, one that was as incurious as possible, from the stock of expressions people use when they meet someone they don't know. But in fact it was precisely this incurious expression that hurt Christian even more; for him it was the admission that the other person had seen his disfigurement and was now ignoring it. Christian usually felt these slights so deeply that he burnt with shame. He tried to divert his thoughts from that as he slowly went up the stairs, but the closer he came to the cabin, where his dark suit and, certainly, his good English shirt would be awaiting him, the more and more uneasy he felt at the prospect of the party: all the questions people were bound to ask, mainly just for form's sake, about how things were going at school, the well-meant advice that would follow, but above all playing his cello; even though he knew his part well, the mere thought of appearing in public made him uncomfortable.

The lamplight spread out palely over the worn stairs, hardly reaching the lower ones. The disagreeable questions and the attention focused on him were one thing, he thought, as he felt the banister, the irregularities and the grain that had been familiar since childhood. The other was the delicacies he was looking forward to, and not just since his breakfast in the hostel that morning – the same eternal constipating bread made of wheat and rye flour from the Konsum in Waldbrunn, spread with Elbperle mixed-fruit jam, syrup or black pudding – but ever since it had been agreed that the party would be held in the Felsenburg; after the small Erholung, it was the best restaurant for miles around. It wasn't easy to even get a table in the Felsenburg, never mind to reserve the room for a large birthday gathering – as so often, it had only been made possible through connections: not long ago, the chef had been a patient of Christian's father's.

The ten-minute clock struck twenty past five. Professor Dathe's voice had sunk to a low mumble; perhaps Libussa had only opened the living-room door for a moment, to see who had come into the building or to get something out of the kitchen. Since the new tenants in the top-floor apartment had arrived, the 'Alois?' or 'Herr Rohde?' that she unfailingly used to shout downstairs, however quietly you opened the door, was no longer to be heard. Christian stopped half-way up the stairs and imagined that he could hear Libussa's high, rather husky voice, the rolled 'R' when she spoke his uncle's surname, the slightly palatal 'O's which caused most visitors who didn't know her to wonder where she came from. As far as he knew, she had worked as a secretary for the VEB Deutfracht shipping company and had moved to Dresden with her husband many years ago. The two of them could be seen together on some of the photographs on the staircase walls: a tall woman with a bony physique, shoulder-length hair and dark, fragile-looking eyes that seemed too big for her slim, heart-shaped face, and which regarded the observer with an expression somewhere between irritation and weariness; the lean man in the white uniform, with a searching look, hands casually stuck in his pockets and half turning away, so that the bright light of a summer's day in Rostock harbour, some time in the fifties or sixties, left a patch of dazzling brightness on his shoulder, blending it into the background. In that picture, Christian thought, they looked like lovers who had been caught out, but perhaps they were both standing stiff as a poker because they were trying to fit in with the photographer's idea of what a snapshot for the work team's diary or the local section of the *Baltic News* should look like. On the picture beside it they were laughing, both had ruck-sacks slung over one shoulder and their hair was already grey; Libussa was pointing with her trekking pole into the vague distance: *To Špindlerův Mlýn* was written in thin handwriting on the mount; Christian had leant forward a little to decipher it. The edges of the photos were perforated, like postage stamps, and they all had the mildly dusty, shallow exposure that one got with ORWO black-and-white film.

The photos on the opposite wall, on the other hand, were quite different, and they had always aroused Christian's admiration, and Robert's and Ezzo's when they were here: they were familiar with their sepia tones from the UFA film programmes that were hidden in a suitcase in the loft at Caravel – in those you could see film stars, hair precisely parted, surrounded by a faint nimbus, looking up confidently at wild mountainsides; there was no Piz Palü on the stairs, however, no dashing Johannes Heesters, but the Gulf of Salerno; the Naples coast road, the Posillipo; and Genoa harbour with the tall, massively castle-like lighthouse above it. In the past, the second flower lamp at the bottom by the entrance had worked, so that there was good light for looking at the pictures; there must be a fault in the wiring somewhere under the plaster since it still didn't work with new bulbs. When he had been staying here, Christian had often crept down during the night to look at the photographs with a torch, sometimes with one of the miner's lamps that were lying unused in the shed. He especially liked the three Italian ones and would marvel as he looked at them again and again, would stand there, as he did now, and let his eye wander over patches of light, houses and ships that seemed to have sprung from the sea. He went up the rest of the stairs to the top, each one creaking with a different, familiar sound. There was a dead bulb in the flat ring of lights on the upper landing as well, and the others flickered when he turned them on briefly, so as not to stumble over the coal boxes beside the Langes' kitchen and the cabin. A strip of light could be seen under the door to the Langes' living room; Professor Dathe had fallen silent, and a measured male voice, perhaps an announcer, had taken his place.

It was cold in the cabin; the tall cylindrical stove beside the door was only lukewarm, so Christian went to fetch a few briquettes and put them in. They clattered down the cast-iron shaft, flames shot up. In the bathroom next door, which the Langes, the Stahls and Meno shared – only the top-floor apartment had a small bathroom of its own – he washed his hands and shaved with the chunky Bebo Sher razor he had been given by his father. Then he changed, leaving his bag, still with all his things in it, on the bed where Anne had laid out linen, blankets and pyjamas for him, looked round the room once more and drew the curtain over the bullseye window before going downstairs.

He fetched the bag in which he'd put the barometer, left the kitchen door ajar for Chakamankabudibaba, checked his tie in the mirror. Now it was quiet; he could no longer hear Libussa's television. He picked up the key and put out the light. As he closed the door, he heard the ten-minute clock strike five times; the chimes seemed to come from far, far away.

4

In the Felsenburg

'The beautiful, refined Felsenburg, hot and cold running water in every room,' he read on the enamel sign by the entrance. Brambles and roses cast shadows across the pavement, which had been swept and gritted as far as Vogelsang's butcher's shop. In the street the cars were closely parked – Christian had even seen the Opel Kapitän belonging to the director of the Surgical Clinic.

In the foyer, facing the stairs that led up to the rooms, there was a sign on an easel: PRIVATE PARTY – PLEASE DO NOT DIS-TURB. A bit of a cheek, Christian thought; after all, the Felsenburg did also offer accommodation and even though he knew from what his parents said that there was a direct connection between the goodwill of the restaurant staff, encouraged perhaps by repeatedly rounded-up bills, and the availability of certain tables close to the stove – especially now in winter – or clearly in the waiter's field of vision, he could still, as he slowly walked towards the restaurant door, put himself in the place of one of the poor people who were staying the night but otherwise weren't to disturb the private party. So there! But what had they had to eat?

'Ah, the Herr Doktor's eldest son, if I'm not mistaken?' A half-smile flitted across Herr Adeling's cheeks. 'Of course you are, you've been here before, I remember. But you've grown since then, oh yes, tall oaks from little acorns grow, as they say. This way, please, your father's birthday party has almost commenced.' Herr Adeling hurried out through the flap in the reception desk and calmly took Christian's coat. He was wearing classic waiter's tails and there was a badge on his chest with his name engraved in clear, legible letters. He was against the decline in standards in the catering industry. One of Reglinde's friends was in training with him and she had told Christian what that meant for the 'bu-bils en-drusded to my kare'. That he only fell into the Saxon dialect in places where any genuine Saxon venturing out onto the slippery ice of High German would fail hopelessly could perhaps be explained by the fact that Adeling was still, as Reglinde's friend, full of understanding, had told them, a 'worr-k in bro-kress'. Because of his centre-parting and manner of speaking, the trainees had nicknamed him 'Theo Lingen' – like the film actor, Herr Adeling was also fond of pursing his lips, clasping his hands and, after briefly rocking on his immaculately polished shoes, gliding across the dining room, his head tilted to one side and swinging his arms gracefully. He was, as he said, 'just one lin-g in the chain', and for him the PLEASE DO NOT DISTURB sign could well be just one more example of the declining standards in the catering industry.

Christian entered the restaurant as the wall clock at reception was striking six. Herr Adeling followed him and stood by the door, hands clasped. All heads turned at Christian's appearance and, feeling a blush spread over his face, he tried to make himself smaller. He was annoyed with himself. He had delayed setting off by having a look at Meno's desk, so that the others wouldn't have time to stare at him – but because he'd arrived on the dot, that was exactly what was happening and the feeling that the eyes of everyone in the room were on him was torture. Without looking at anyone in particular, head bowed, he nodded a greeting in the general direction of the tables, which were arranged in a rectangle and at which there must have been forty or fifty people sitting. On the right he saw the Tietze family, Meno beside them, Uncle Ulrich with his wife Barbara, Alice and Sandor. Anne was at the head of the table, between his father and the director of the Surgical Clinic. As he squinted, red as a beetroot and frowning in embarrassment, towards those seated at the tables, he also spotted Grandfather Rohde and Emmy, Robert's and his grandmother on their father's side. Had there been any possibility of going unseen to the empty seat between Robert and Ezzo at the lower end, of simply and suddenly *appearing* on the chair without anyone noticing, he would have chosen it without hesitation. He was, therefore, grateful that Professor Müller, the short, portly director, stood up at that moment and tapped his wine glass with a spoon, at which all heads turned towards him. By this time Ezzo had carefully pulled the chair back and Christian, on whose face the blush was gradually fading, sat down with a sigh of relief and, having clearly seen Anne's look of disapproval, made a great show of leaning over to the side and hanging the bag with the barometer over the back of his chair. As he turned, he saw the mildly ironic expression in Meno's eyes, for it was only recently that he had told Christian about the behaviour of the ostrich: 'It sticks its head in the sand and waits – believing no one can see it because it can't see anything itself. But that,' Meno had added, 'is not something for your civics teacher. Comparisons between humans and the animal kingdom are only permitted in limited cases, as sure as I've studied biology.'

Professor Müller took a step back and stood there, head bowed so that his double chins bulged out over the collar of his snow-white shirt, meditatively rubbing his cheeks, which were so closely shaven they shone like slabs of lard, and making his thick, black, owl-like eyebrows hop up and down. His cuff, standing out against his midnight-blue suit, slipped back, releasing a tuft of stiff black hair that continued down the back of his hand to the base of his fingers; he wore a signet ring on the little finger of his right hand. He took a piece of paper out of his pocket, clearly the notes for a speech, glanced at it briefly and put it back with a weary flap of the hand. It didn't go right in but stuck, like a blade, several centimetres out of his pocket, so that Müller had to push it down with a delicate but firm tap. He cleared his throat, patted his upper lip with his signet ring.

'Ladies and gentlemen. Goethe himself said that in the life of a man his fiftieth birthday is one of special significance. We take stock, look back on what we have achieved, consider what is still to be done. Our time of storm and stress is over, we have found our place in life. From now on, as my teacher Sauerbruch used to say, there is only one organ we can count on for continued increase: the prostate gland. Exceptions, of course,' he said, stretching out his hand and waggling his fingers, 'only serve to prove the rule.'

Laughter from the surgeons: the roar of dominant males; their wives lowered their heads.

'The ladies will, I hope, forgive me this short excursion into the uro-genital tract – I can see I will have to cut out these jokes; for a surgeon the unkindest cut of all.' He nodded to the group of doctors and patted his upper lip with his signet ring again. 'You will note, gentlemen, that I am borrowing the principle of covering myself from our beloved colleagues in Internal Medicine.' A hint of mockery flashed across the faces of some of the doctors. Christian had worked in hospitals as a nursing auxiliary often enough to know about the differences between the two main branches of medicine. Müller became more serious.

'Born the eldest son of a clockmaker in Glashütte, a small town in the eastern Erzgebirge, Richard Hoffmann grew up during the years of Hitlerite fascism and as a twelve-year-old – he was an auxiliary in an anti-aircraft battery – experienced the Anglo-American air raid on Dresden. On the night of the air raid, he suffered severe burns from phosphorus bombs and had to undergo lengthy treatment in Johannstadt Hospital, the present Medical Academy – in the same clinic, moreover, which he is in charge of today. It was then that his desire to study medicine took shape. Now it is true that such youthful dreams are often not realized. I remember, for example, that twenty years ago' – he wrinkled his brow and pursed his lips – 'all the boys suddenly wanted to be astronauts, Gagarin and Vostock and Gherman Titov; not me, I was too old already, although my wife is always telling me that the training in Baikonur, together with anchovy paste out of a tube' – he looked down at his body and spread his arms in mock incomprehension – 'would have done me no harm, but I think that is the too one-sided view of a dietary cook.' Müller's wife, who was sitting next to Anne, sent embarrassed looks in all directions and blushed sufficiently. Wernstein, one of the junior doctors in the clinic for trauma surgery, leant over with a grin to a colleague and whispered something.

'Ah,' Müller cried with an ironic undertone in his voice, stretching out his arm theatrically, 'at least our junior colleagues do not take the view that I would interpret a relaxation of their attempts to restrain the risorius as disrespect for, or even mockery of, my physical constitution. Very bold, gentlemen. Thank you. And others among us perhaps wanted to be atomic scientists, an Indian chief like Winnetou or, dear ladies, a second Florence Nightingale, but as the years passed, elementary particles and the struggle for the rights of the Apache nation were perhaps no longer so interesting. However, surgery, the youthful dream of the man whose birthday we are celebrating today, retained its interest and since that stay in hospital he never – this I have from his own lips – lost sight of his goal of becoming a surgeon. He attended the high school in Freital, completed an apprenticeship as a fitter and then went to Leipzig to study medicine in the hallowed halls of the *alma mater lipsiensis* that for some of us was, to use a good old Prussian expression, the seedbed of our medical career. It was there, in the unforgettable anatomical lectures of Kurt Alverdes and later in the *Collegium chirurgicum* of Herbert Uebermuth, that his decision to become a surgeon was strengthened and confirmed. However, the great clinician Max Burger almost made him reconsider, which would have robbed us of one of the best trauma surgeons we have in the country, when he became aware of Richard Hoffmann's exceptional talent for diagnosis and suggested that he should do his doctorate under him. Not that our friend was unfaithful, in his heart, to surgery. It was above all the after-effects of his injuries during the air raid on Dresden that made him hesitate; deformities of his right hand made it difficult, at times impossible, for him to clench his hand – and that is, naturally, a fundamental problem for a person who wants to specialize in the surgical field. It was only a second operation, performed by Leni Büchter, a true magician in hand surgery, and the devoted care of a certain Nurse Anne, née Rohde' – he made a slight bow in the direction of Anne, who looked away – 'that removed this obstacle and finally secured Richard Hoffmann for our field . . .'

'My God,' Robert whispered to Christian, 'does he have a fancy way with words! I should get him to go over my German essays, that would certainly be something for Fräulein Schatzmann.' Fräulein Schatzmann – she expressly insisted on being addressed as 'Fräulein', even though she was on the verge of retirement – was the German teacher at the Louis Fürnberg Polytechnic High School Robert attended. Christian had also been one of her pupils before he transferred to the senior high school in Waldbrunn and he could well remember Fräulein Schatzmann's strict lessons, which were full of tricky grammar exercises and difficult dictations. With a shudder he recalled the Schatzmann 'ORCHIS' rule, which she would always write on the blackboard in red chalk, to remind the careless and forgetful pupils whenever there was an essay to be written: Order – Risk – Charm – Interest – Sense; eventually Christian, on some vague suspicion, had looked the word up in his father's medical dictionary and then, together with other pranksters in the class, had stuck a photo of a naked blonde together with a fairly explicit drawing on the blackboard before the next essay was due . . . Fräulein Schatzmann's reaction had been unexpected; in a steady voice she told the class – which was waiting on tenterhooks; some of the girls were giggling, of course, and had flushed bright red, as always – that there were clearly some pupils in 10b who had learnt something in her classes, and to a certain extent had taken the ORCHIS rule to heart . . . Unfortunately Fräulein Schatzmann had confiscated the picture of the blonde – 'that, gentlemen, comes under number two of my rule' – much to the chagrin of Holger Rübesamen, who had swapped it for a high price: two football pictures of Borussia Dortmund . . .

'I'm hungry,' Ezzo whispered. 'Is this going to go on for long?' But Müller seemed to have got into his stride, speaking with expansive gestures, stepping back- and forward, sketching things in the air, making his owl-eyebrows hop up and down and patting his lips with his signet ring whenever he got a laugh.

'When are we on?' Christian asked.

'Your mother will give us a sign.'

'And our instruments?'

'In the next room.'

'I can't see a piano.'

'There, just behind your uncle.' Indeed, there was a piano in the corner behind Meno.

'I haven't even had a chance to warm up, you were already all seated when I arrived, damn it. I thought there'd be the usual chit-chat to start with and then things would gradually get going . . .'

'You can play that at sight, Christian. But remember the sforzato

37

on the A when Robert comes in the second time. I'm starving, and there's all those lovely things over there . . .' Ezzo nodded towards the cold buffet that had been set up along the opposite wall.

'What? Have you had a look?'

'Yummy, I can tell you. Loin steaks, cut very thin and fried till they're crisp, you can see the pattern marks of the grill, and then rice' – Ezzo pointed furtively at three large dishes with stainless-steel covers – 'but not Wurzener KuKo stuff, I'm sure it's from the other side.'

'You've already had a taste?' Robert, who had leant back a bit, whispered to Ezzo across Christian's back.

'Mmm, yes.'

'You have? Didn't you say earlier that you had to go to the loo?'

'Shh, not so loud . . . I did . . . But when I came back I discovered the fruit bowl, and there happened to be no one around – look, just an inch to the right of my father and you'll see it . . . Can you see it?'

'The big blue one?' Christian and Robert whispered with one voice.

'That's the one . . . there are apples and pears in it, proper yellow pears with little bright-green spots and oranges –'

'Sour green Cuba oranges?'

'No . . . Nafal, or something like that. Mandarins and plums and, yes, you've got it: bananas! Real bananas!' There was a tremor in Ezzo's voice.

'Hey, Christian, that parcel from the other side we lugged in last week, I bet the old folks have guzzled it all already.'

'Perhaps Aunt Alice and Uncle Sandor brought that stuff . . .'

'It's a possibility . . . And what else did you see? Tell me' – Robert leant back a little more; he'd spoken rather loudly, so Christian put his finger to his lips and hissed 'Shh!' at his brother – 'tell me, did you just look or did you . . .'

'No, I didn't, there wasn't enough time, just a few grains of rice and then Theo Lingen appeared and glared at me as if I were a criminal, really, Robert.'

'How are things at the Spesh?'

Ezzo went to the Special School for Music in Mendelssohnallee. 'Oh, as usual. School's a bore. Physics is the only subject that's fun, we've got Bräuer, you two must know him.'

'Why?'

'Of course you do, Robert, he's the strict guy who visited us a couple of years ago. The one that looks a bit like Uncle Owl, you know, on kids' TV, in *Pittiplatsch und Schnatterinchen*.'

Ezzo smirked. 'Yes, that's the one. But he's great. Does fantastic experiments. Apart from that . . . Christmas is coming.'

'And the Wieniawski?'

'Hellish difficult piece. Don't make me think about it. On Tuesday it's my major again, I've really got work my arse off.'

'. . . my father gave me strength and height, my earnest application, my mother dear my humour bright and Fromme – not only him – my joy in operations . . .' Müller declaimed, earning a round of applause. 'I hope the literary specialists in the audience will forgive my distortion of Goethe's famous lines; all I can say in my defence is that it is in a good cause. But to come to the point – and what's the point of birthdays if not presents – we in the clinic, Herr Hoffmann, spent a long time thinking about this. We are all, of course, aware of your love of classical music – when the nurses see a trolley heading for your operating theatre, where you are about to operate to, say, a violin concerto, they say the patient is "going to face the music".' He cleared his throat, seeming to expect applause which he then waved down. 'Since, as your wife was good enough to divulge to me, we will have the opportunity to enjoy a piece of classical music later on, we, that is your colleagues, the nurses and I, have thought of something different. Your love of painting and the fine arts is also well-known in the clinic, so we organized a little collection, the result of which is the object which I now ask these gentlemen to please bring from the adjoining room.'

Two junior doctors went into the side room and returned with a large, slim, carefully tied-up parcel.

'Dad on the throne of trauma surgery,' Robert whispered to Christian, 'and instead of a sceptre he's holding a scalpel . . .'

Herr Adeling brought in the easel. By this time Wernstein had unpacked the picture, apart from a last layer of tissue paper, and he placed it on the easel that Herr Adeling, furiously wielding a gigantic duster, had cleared of chalk powder. Wernstein stepped back. Müller thrust out his chin and pursed his lips in a raspberry-coloured pout – a pose, well known to every junior doctor in the Surgical Clinic, with which Professor Müller would conclude the moment of hesitation to which all surgeons are subject before they make the first incision into the still-inviolate skin lying before them, pale in the glare of the spotlight. With solemn tread he made his way over to the easel and, with a vigorous but well-calculated tug, at the same time giving Richard, who had stood up and was beside him, a malicious smile, pulled the tissue paper away from the picture. It wobbled a little, but Herr Adeling, who probably knew the easel well and had followed Müller's actions with raised eyebrows, had unobtrusively positioned himself behind it and, with a sideways twist with which one avoids giving offence during a fit of coughing, he surreptitiously supported the easel with his left hand, now in a white glove, during Müller's revelatory tug, while simultaneously covering two dry coughs with his still ungloved right hand before urgent business sent him hurrying off in the direction of the foyer.

'A watercolour by one of our most important painters, who unfortunately died too young: Kurt Querner. There you are.'

Richard Hoffmann, almost a head taller than Müller, had slumped in on himself, his dark-blue eyes, which Robert had inherited, were staring in disbelief.

'His *Landscape during a Thaw* – Professor, that can't be . . . so it was you?'

'Herr Wernstein was so good as to travel to Börnchen for us and acquire this watercolour.'

'But . . . I'm flabbergasted. Frau Querner told me that this picture was only to be sold after her death . . . It meant so much to her husband . . . And then it wasn't there any more, we were told it had been sold after all . . . Anne, come here, our favourite picture.'

'Our surprise for you.'

'But' – in his agitation Richard ran his fingers through his short, sandy hair; it had a blond strand at the crown, which Christian also had in the same place – 'but Professor, colleagues, that must have cost a fortune! I can't possibly accept it.'

'As I said, there was a collection, so it was spread among us. By the way, there is an interesting perspective to the picture when it is seen *à contre-jour* as you might say . . .'

'*À contre-jour?*' Taken aback, Richard walked round the picture.

'For Richard Hoffmann – gratefully, Kurt Querner,' Müller read out loud. 'He knew that this was the picture you liked best. You and your wife had "crept round it too often", as he put it. If he wanted to give it to anyone, it was you, and when Frau Querner heard about our plan, she allowed herself to be persuaded.'

Most of the guests had stood up and were crowding round the picture. As his father shook the hands of his colleagues from the Academy in thanks, addressing each by their first name and hugging them, Christian could see that he was moved.

'Just accept it, Richard,' said Weniger, a senior doctor from the Gynaecological Clinic. 'You can hang it up in your living room, next to that bird in the buff with the magnificent horse's arse,' he went on, deliberately falling into a local accent, 'that's a kind of landscape too. Pardon my French, Anne.'

The doctors, many of them surgeons or orthopaedists, were amused.

The women turned away or put their hand or a handkerchief over their mouth to hide their giggles.

Anne had given Ezzo and Christian a sign. They slipped past the throng round the picture, fetched their instruments from the adjoining room and set up their music stands in front of the piano.

'Your father's happy as a sandboy,' Ezzo whispered to Christian.

'He's been after that picture for years, I can tell you.' Robert sucked calmly at the cane blade of his clarinet. 'And you can imagine what it was like when he heard it had gone. National mourning, lousy mood, frosty evenings. Well, I can see everything's hunky-dory for the old man again. I'm sure that means there'll be another Sunday trip out there or a visit to an art gallery . . . Oh God, art galleries.'

Reglinde, Ezzo's eighteen-year-old sister, was already sitting at the piano and had opened her score. She shook her head. 'You really are crazy. The way you talk!'

'Just give me an A,' Robert replied, unmoved, taking the reed out of his mouth and slotting it into the mouthpiece.

'Did you see it? Even framed!' Christian, warming up with a few runs on the cello, looked across at the picture; Niklas Tietze, Reglinde and Ezzo's father, the local GP, emerged from the group round it. He had chosen the Italian piece and was taking the viola part.

'The money they must have in the Academy!' Robert muttered. 'Always assuming they didn't quietly take it out of the Solidarity Fund or the account of the Society for German–Soviet Friendship. But if I want a new fishing rod, there's no way it can be afforded. "Go and collect waste paper and bottles, you get ten pfennigs apiece for them at the SERO collection point, and anyway, when we were your age . . ."'

'Hi, you guys, everything OK?'

Christian embraced 'Uncle' Niklas, as he was called by the Hoffmann children, like 'Aunt' Alice and 'Uncle' Sandor, although Niklas Tietze was Richard Hoffmann's cousin on his mother's side.

'We'll have to play everything *presto*, Uncle Niklas. Ezzo and I are starving.'

'Your mother's baked a fantastic cake. You must have a piece of it afterwards.'

'But I'm sleeping at Meno's tonight. – Apple cake?'

'And a cherry pie – with a marzipan base and meringue topping, very thin and the cherries lovely and sour . . .' Niklas sucked his upper lip and gave an appreciative 'Mmmm . . .' He picked up his viola, which Ezzo had brought from the adjoining room, and put it on the piano.

'Right, Anne will give us the sign any minute now. Then, as agreed: first the fanfare, then "For He's a Jolly Good Fellow", then off we go.' Niklas rosined his bow, played over the open strings and adjusted the tuning slightly while his eyes, behind the immense spectacles he always put on for playing, quickly ran over the notes.

'Tatata-taa!' rang out from the instruments as Anne came and sat down next to Reglinde. When they played 'For He's a Jolly Good Fellow', even Herr Adeling, who had reappeared by the door, joined in; as he sang he tapped the tips of his fingers together precisely in time to the music and at the final 'and so say all of us' his falsetto even outdid Müller's trained guttural voice.

Then they played the Italian piece, a suite from the baroque period, originally for flute but Niklas has arranged the flute part for clarinet. Christian was tense. Once more he could feel the eyes of everyone on him. Reglinde had switched on the wall lamp over the piano and, since he was sitting diagonally behind her, the strong light fell on his face, revealing with merciless clarity the very thing he most wanted to hide. During the previous week's rehearsals, everything had been calm and secure, but playing here, in front of an attentive, though probably well-disposed audience of fifty, was a quite different matter from practising in the Tietzes' quiet house, where 'Aunt' Gudrun had brought sandwiches during the intervals and he and Ezzo had got so high they'd tried to play the piece at double the speed. There were three pairs of eyes that weighed especially heavily on him: his father's, Meno's and those of his cousin Ina, Ulrich and Barbara's pretty nineteen-year-old daughter . . . He curled up inside himself and kept his eyes focused on the music. He mustn't let himself be distracted. – Where did she get that dress? Pretty daring, those bare shoulders, he thought, before he stormed up the mountain of semiquavers at the beginning of the courante – Oh yes, the dress she'd made together with Reglinde, pause, legato, da-da-dada . . . Strange: while during rehearsals his greatest fear had been the fast, technically difficult passages and the slower, more melodious ones had come out better, now the opposite was the case: he was happy when the furioso bars came, he played almost every one securely, as if in a dream, and his heart started to pound at every harmless sequence of minims and crotchets. At a piano passage his bow began to tremble, the note was 'frayed', as his cello teacher would have said, which brought him a glance from Ezzo, who, as the best in his class in the Special School, was impeccably positioned and playing with the luscious bowing that had already attracted attention among experts . . .

'I can do that too,' Christian told himself in irritation; he stretched a tenth and slammed his bow down on the string. A trickle of rosin floated down. – Yes! Sounds like a cathedral bell, does my cello . . . There was a 'Ping!' Ezzo and Robert started, which made Robert look odd, as he was in the middle of a cantabile passage, and at the same moment Christian realized that the A-string of his cello was bobbing up and down in a huge corkscrew spiral and he had no time to replace it. Niklas looked at him over the rim of his glasses and improvised while Reglinde, the only one who was completely relaxed, began to reduce the tempo imperceptibly . . . Christian had never been in such a tight situation. All the passages that, before his misfortune, he could have played fairly comfortably had suddenly turned into technical hurdles. Out of the corner of his eye he saw that Ina had her head in her hand and her shoulders were twitching with suppressed laughter.

Silly cow! he roared inwardly, and in his fury he swept through a passage at such speed that Ezzo and Niklas looked up in alarm, and even Reglinde, who had her back to him, half turned round. – Yesyesyes! he exulted when he managed to play a passage on the D-string alone, in a position he hadn't practised for this piece. In the surge of melodies he saw Niklas's aquiline nose glow redder and redder, and tiny beads of sweat had started to gather on Ezzo's forehead, just as they had on his waxy-pale, fleshy nose; Ezzo was adjusting his violin on its chin rest much more often than he had during rehearsals and the fiery red violinist's mark on his neck became visible – both, as Christian knew, unmistakable signs of nervousness. Anne, who was turning the pages for Reglinde, behaved as if nothing had happened. He wasn't bothered about anything any more – it was bound to end in disaster – and strangely enough, it was just at that point, in the middle of the rather rocking bourrée, that the title of an obscure book from his parents' library came to mind: *The Gallant Blundering in the Labyrinth of Love* – the A-string sundering in the labyrinth of music was what his overwrought mind made of it before he set his fingers dancing over the remaining three strings and, remarkably and unexpectedly, everything went well apart from a couple of little slips. Applause.

'Phew.' Ezzo nodded, waggled his hand, wiped his brow and fiddled with the nut on his bow. They bowed. Niklas, who was standing behind Christian, gave him a complimentary tap on the shoulder with his bow.

Robert snorted. 'That looked really funny! I kept telling myself, just keep your eyes on your music, man . . .'

'I'd like to see you if one of your keys flew off, but that can never happen with your *wind* instruments,' Christian hissed back, putting profound contempt into 'wind'. The feud between strings and wind was an age-old rivalry that would never be resolved.

'That was close,' said Reglinde. 'When you suddenly accelerated in the allegro, I thought I was never going to get into it. And that on this jangly old piano.'

5

The barometer

Anne took Meno and Christian to one side. 'I think we should give it to him afterwards, when there's just the family. I don't know a lot of the guests very well; I don't want it made that public. Agreed?'

Richard made a short speech of thanks. His final words brought a grin from Christian and Ezzo: 'But now, colleagues and friends, eat your fill.'

'You can rely on that!' Ezzo chortled, already on the edge of his chair. But still he hesitated – because everyone else was hesitating. Clearly no one had the courage to be the first at the buffet and therefore liable to be suspected of a lack of good manners. Müller, playing delicate trills in the air with the fingers of his right hand, was already jutting out his chin purposefully and pouting his lips when Emmy got up and set off for the buffet with short but nimble steps – forgetting the walking stick that Richard took over to her. 'Thank you, young man,' she cried, but the last word was drowned out by the noise of chairs being pushed back. Very few, Christian observed, replaced their chairs at the table – Niklas did, demonstratively taking his time over it, carefully placing his long, slim hands on the exact point of the chair back that precluded any misunderstanding; Niklas even had to lift the chair slightly, the calm and precision of his orderliness in stark contrast to the precipitate and distasteful rush of the others; he even replaced Gudrun's and Ezzo's chairs and nodded to Christian, who had also stood up. Then Niklas strolled to the buffet; Ezzo unobtrusively shifted his weight, leaving a gap between himself and Gudrun, who was standing in front of him. If you closed your eyes for a moment, you could still see the thirty-centimetre gap well to the front of the queue, and when you opened them again, the gap was filled by Niklas. Either as the result of a general tendency to observe successful manoeuvres or of an unconscious but necessary part of the atmosphere, the phenomenon was repeated when Müller too left his seat. He moved no more quickly than his position permitted – a position that had, so to speak, vanished into thin air, though not because he was not on official business – and after elegantly and, with an obliging smile, giving his wife his arm, he first headed back to *Landscape during a Thaw* rather than towards the buffet. Wernstein and another junior doctor at the buffet exchanged glances and the doctor in front, who worked more closely with Müller, took his time moving forward, thus allowing Professor Müller and his wife, Müller patting his lip with his signet ring and bending his ear to his wife, to join the queue . . . Christian had gone to say hello to his father and wish him a happy birthday and was now standing behind him, pretty near the end of the queue. Adeling and another waiter had taken the lids off the dishes and the room was now filled with enticing aromas. There was the clatter of crockery and cutlery, muted conversation. Weniger, a senior doctor in his late forties with receding hair and red, shovel-like hands, and a slim, grey-haired doctor called Clarens, with glasses and a sparse beard, were standing with Richard discussing medical matters, the main topic being the forthcoming 'Health Service Day'.

'When you're awarded the title of Medical Councillor, my friend, you can open a few more of these foreign bottles for us. We know you – you've only sent part of them into battle here, the rest are keeping cool in your cellar. You've still got your supplies, you old desert fox.' Weniger filled his glass to the brim and had difficulty raising it to his lips without spilling some. Clarens laughed. 'Don't drink so much, Manfred. Think of the drive home.'

'Don't worry, my wife's driving.'

'What's all this about supplies! I haven't a drop left in the house. I wouldn't let my friends go thirsty on my fiftieth birthday. But what's all this about a Medical Councillor? What does it matter anyway? – Or have you heard something?'

'Oh, come on, Richard, it's common knowledge. From what one hears you're going to get a Med Councillor or the Hufeland Medal, Pahl the Hufeland Medal or perhaps even the Fetscher Prize.'

'Really? One hears that, does one? I don't.'

'But my boss did. At the last directors' conference.'

Richard lowered his voice. 'Much more important than all this frippery would be if we finally didn't have to beg for every drip bottle and every lousy bandage! If they could sort out their structural problems so that we could work efficiently! They can keep their gongs, for God's sake. That's just a sedative to stick on your chest . . . If we butter up the directors and the consultants now and then, the rest'll sort itself out – that's the way they think!'

'Not so loud, Richard.' Weniger had become serious and was looking round nervously. When he caught sight of Christian, his expression brightened. 'Well done, that sounded just like a concert. How long have you been playing?'

'For . . .' Christian screwed up his eyes as he thought. '. . . for about eight years.' He felt embarrassed because it wasn't just his father and the two doctors who were looking at him but all those waiting in the queue, in front and behind.

'Do you want to take it up professionally? As a cellist?'

'No. Graduate from high school.'

'Ah.' Weniger nodded. 'Then you can follow in your father's footsteps?'

'I'd like to study medicine, yes.'

'A good decision.' Weniger pursed his lips and nodded vigorously. 'And, if I may ask: your grades?' Before Christian could answer, he made a dismissive gesture. 'If I had my way – good grades in themselves don't make a doctor. If I think of some of the young ladies who come to us . . . Nothing but "A"s for their studies, but no feel for it, fingers like thumbs to put it crudely, and they keel over at the first post m—'

'Oh, my grades are quite good. Apart from maths . . .'

'Oh yes, the medic's old problem. My God, in maths your father and I were a real pair of duffers. Don't you worry about that. There is less mathematics in heaven and earth than is dreamt of in your philosophy . . . Hmm, it's all very well for me to talk. Just do your best. But how are things otherwise . . . a girlfriend?'

Christian, who by now had a plate and cutlery, carefully helped himself to some rice and cleared his throat in embarrassment. 'Hmm, no, not yet.'

'Well, that'll come, you'll see. And don't worry about those little pimples on your face, they'll go of their own accord, and a girl who sees nothing but that's not worth bothering with, young man.'

'How's your lad?' Clarens asked the medical director from gynaecology. Christian had gone bright red.

'Matthias? He's doing his military service at the moment, signals. Spends all day running round the countryside laying telephone lines. But he's no idea yet what he wants to do afterwards. "Don't panic, Dad . . ." is all I get from him whenever I have the temerity to ask a question or drop a hint. At one point he wanted to be a stage technician, then a radio presenter, then a forester . . . Gesine and I were thinking that was something definite, forester, when he applied for a place at the forestry school in Tharandt last year; but then he withdrew his application. What will be next – who can say? All he knows is what he doesn't want to do: study medicine. "I don't want to be rummaging round in the holy of holies like you, Dad," the brat says that to my face and smirks.'

The laughter was something that Christian found irritating.

'Come on, Manfred, you'll need to tuck in after that. Take one of these splendid stuffed peppers . . .' Clarens looked at Weniger over the top of his glasses. 'Oh, I was going to ask you – you know the boss of that car repair shop in Striesen, Mätzold or whatever he's called . . .'

'Pätzold. Yes, what about him?'

'You performed the abortion on his daughter last year, didn't you . . .?' Clarens leant over to Weniger and murmured something. What Christian could hear sounded like 'cavity seal' and 'carcass' but he couldn't imagine what a dead body could have to do with a Moskvitch.

'. . . a Friday car, I can tell you. It's already starting to rust through at the front, where the passenger puts their feet. I told my wife: "Once it goes through you're really going to have to run fast" . . . and the brakes, soft as butter. I'd like to know how the Russians manage that. But probably nothing happens over there because there's only five cars on the road, or they just don't worry about it . . . The armour plating on their Volgas is just the same. Oh, this looks good, I'm going to have some of this . . . So, Manfred, could you set something up with this Pätzold . . . ? You know that departmental head at VEB Vliestextilien, the fabrics company from Chemnitz? Well I'm still treating him. He says the targets in the economic plan have given him a nervous break-down. I managed to get him a place for a course of treatment in the spa at Bad Gottleuba; at the same time I made it clear to him that a psychiatric clinic needs an incredible amount of dressing material . . . an *incredible* amount. Just like a gynaecological clinic. I assume I'd have to send you what you might call a referral form for this, er, patient?'

Weniger stuck his tongue in his cheek as he thought. 'I'll give Pätzold a call on Monday. But I can't promise anything. There's a problem there, you see – he threw his daughter out when he discovered who the father was. The son of some guy on the Party District Committee. And Pätzold's had about as much as he can take from them, I can tell you. The guy's son was in the clinic too. Always the same. Hit the booze then get your oil changed and pull your dipstick out of some stranger in the morning, then have kittens at the result of the pregnancy test and collapse into the capable arms of Nurse Erika . . . You didn't hear any of that, Christian.'

The queue moved forward slowly. Adeling was at the other end of the buffet, serving consommé with meatballs; he had his left arm behind his back, the ladle in his white-gloved right hand, and each time before he served the soup, with a smile and a twitch of his nostrils, he briefly closed his eyes in acknowledgement of the guest's wishes.

Weniger leant forward to Richard and Clarens with a conspiratorial expression. 'Since the District Committee has cropped up, have you heard this one: The teacher says: "Make a sentence with the two nouns, Party and peace." Little Fritz puts up his hand. "My father always says: 'I wish the Party would leave me in peace.'"'

'Hahaha, very good. But yesterday Nurse Elfriede told me a great one during an operation: Why does *Pravda* only cost ten pfennigs and *Neues Deutschland* fifteen? – "I can explain that," the assistant at the newsagent's says, "for *Neues Deutschland* you have to add five pfennigs translation costs."'

'Now then.' Weniger slapped Richard on the shoulder with his shovel-like hand. 'You'd better not tell Herr Kohler that one.'

'An idealist and a schemer,' Richard replied. 'And not a bad doctor, either.'

'The worst are the ones who really believe in what they believe in. And have enough energy for the professional doubters.' Weniger gestured diagonally upwards with his thumb. 'Doubtless you laughed.'

'Wernstein laughed so much the forceps in which he was holding the disinfection swab fell open . . . But I've got another: The General Secretary is on the breakwater in Rostock watching the ships being loaded. He asks the sailors, "Where are you going?" – "To Cuba." – "And what are you carrying?" – "Machines and vehicles." – "And what are you coming back with?" – "With oranges." He asks the sailors on another ship, "Where are you sailing?" – "To Angola." – "What are you carrying?" – "Machines and vehicles." – "And what are you coming back with?" – "With bananas." – And he asks the men on a third ship, "Where are you going? – "To the Soviet Union." – "What are you carrying?" – "Oranges and bananas." – "And what are you coming back with?" – "With the train."'

Clarens whispered, 'Listener's question to Radio Yerevan: "They say a new history of the Communist Party of the Soviet Union has been published for the sixtieth anniversary of the October Revolution?" – Answer: "Yes, illustrated even! With cuts by Brezhnev."'

'That's a good one! We could put it up on the Party Secretary's noticeboard.'

'I know one too.' Having filled his plate with fruit, crisply fried hamburgers and loin steaks, bread and rice, Christian joined in the conversation, his face burning. 'Brezhnev is visiting the USA. On the second morning President Ford asks him what he dreamt of. – "I dreamt of the Capitol in Washington, there was a red flag flying on it!" – "Strange," says Ford, "I dreamt of the Kremlin and there was a red flag flying on that too." – "But of course, you can always see that." – "Yes, but there was something written on it." – "What?" – "I don't know, I can't read Chinese."'

'Careful,' Clarens warned. Müller came over, a forced smile on his face and a plate with kebabs and peaches in his left hand. 'What is it, gentlemen? May I share the joke?'

'We've just heard a new one, Herr Professor,' Weniger said in a provocative tone. Müller raised his eyebrows.

'A banana machine has been set up in Berlin, on Alexanderplatz. If you put a banana in, a mark comes out.'

Müller pursed his lips. 'Hmm, yes. Well, gentlemen, I have to say I don't think that's a particularly good joke.' His eyes narrowed, his lips became thin. 'Certain circles would be delighted if they knew they'd managed to make so much progress here . . . And I find it all the more regrettable, Herr Weniger, when I see that you have a banana on your plate . . .' Müller's eyes narrowed to thin slits. 'We bear a responsibility, gentlemen, and it's all too easy to join in cheap jokes about our country . . . But it doesn't change anything, you know, it doesn't change anything . . . And you above all, gentlemen' – he shook his head disapprovingly – 'we, we should be aware of our position.

With or without bananas . . . And above all we ought' – he pronounced it 'ouought', softly and drawn out, his head still slightly on one side – 'to refrain from mockery of a great man whom our Soviet brothers have lost. Don't you agree?'

Weniger swallowed and looked to one side. 'Of course, Herr Professor.'

'I'm glad we are of one mind.' Müller gave a gracious smile. 'By the way, Herr Hoffmann, your wife is a quite superb cook. She prepared the steaks and the soufflé together with the restaurant chef, I believe? Excellent, really excellent. I've already expressed my appreciation to her and asked her to let my wife in on the secrets of a few recipes, above all the cherry pie at your house this afternoon. Superb!' He slowly walked back to his seat, chatting to some of the doctors on the way. Weniger and Clarens, pale-faced, watched him go.

'How on earth can you stand it with him, Richard?' Weniger hissed through his teeth. 'The slimy devious bastard.'

'Manfred.' Richard raised his hand to calm him down.

'Oh, leave it. Goes around like Lord Muck. "We had a collection, we bought the picture." – Shall I tell you something: he didn't lift a finger. The idea came from your senior nursing officer, and it was Wernstein who put his back into it. That's how it was. Then the Herr Professor came along once the matter was taking shape and took everything under his aegis.'

'Forget it,' said Clarens. 'We mustn't let him spoil this splendid meal for us.'

A look of determination flashed across Weniger's face. 'I've got another one. How can you work out the points of the compass with a banana? Place it on the Wall. The end that gets bitten off is pointing east.'

When everyone was sitting down, Müller proposed a toast. Christian and Ezzo were not the only ones to set about the food ravenously;

to get it all together Anne and Richard had had to start months ago, spending a fortune in the Delikat shops. And without his secretary's brother, who drove special consignments of fruit, including citrus and tropical fruits, to supply Berlin, they would have had to make do with the two sorts of apples that were available in a normal greengrocer's: brown, too-sour Boskoop and green, too-sweet Golden Delicious. In exchange for the loin steaks, the ground meat for meatballs and hamburgers and the beef for the kebabs from Vogelsang's, the butcher's, Richard had had to sacrifice one of the two sets of snow chains Alice and Sandor had given him two years ago. The Felsenburg restaurant had made the least contribution to the buffet: just the kitchen, crockery and premises had been made available for the party.

Most of the guests left around eight. The official part of the birthday celebrations was over. Frau Müller put away the few recipes Anne had written down and attempted a smile that looked to Christian like an attempt at an apology. Adeling and the other waiter brought hats and coats, helped the ladies put them on. The guests who remained took advantage of the break to stretch their legs a bit.

The seating plan was abandoned. Some chairs were moved over to the stove. The surplus crockery and cutlery was taken away, the flowers – with Meno's roses a red magnet among them – were placed beside the table with the presents.

Outside, Christian helped his father and a couple of junior doctors push Müller's Opel Kapitän to get it started and out of the snowdrifts. The professor himself was pushing, at the front, on the passenger side. 'Take your foot off, Edeltraut, take your foot off,' he shouted as the wheels started to spin.

'We're pushing, Herr Professor; you give us the command, Herr Doktor Hoffmann.'

'You're learning, Herr Wernstein. Always delegate responsibility,' Richard replied with a laugh. 'Right then: heave-ho, one – two – three – and away she goes. Watch out, Christian, you're standing by the exhaust –'

Müller jumped in and the car slithered off.

'Hope you have a quiet day at work tomorrow, Manfred. So long, Hans, hope you get home OK. And thanks a lot for everything.' Richard shook Weniger and Clarens by the hand as their wives said goodbye to Anne. With astonishment the two men realized they were both wearing the same winter coat from VEB Herrenmode.

'They had them on Tuesday, my wife got it for me.'

'Mine too, queued for five hours. I wasn't supposed to get it until Christmas, but my old one was worn out.'

'How are you two getting home, Hans? Can we give you a lift?'

Delighted, Clarens nodded.

Christian was freezing and went inside. Kurt Rohde, Meno and Niklas were standing in the foyer listening to Herr Adeling: '– by Kokoschka, I assure you, I'm certain of that. The chambermaid who used to look after the guests told me herself . . . She kept a record of her tips in a notebook, with the sums the guests gave, and I saw Herr Professor Kokoschka's tips, they were some of the biggest. It's one of the Herr Professor's easels, yes, he left it to the hotel in memory of the many nights he spent here and naturally we treasure it, yes indeed.' He looked up, rocked on his heels, the chalk-white napkin over his arm, casting a severe eye over one of the younger of the waiters who were still tidying up or clearing away.

'Interesting, very interesting what you've told us there.' Niklas had taken out his pipe and was filling it with vanilla tobacco from Meno's pouch. Matches flared up; Meno had filled his pipe too, a different one this time, a short, broad one made of some purplish-brown wood. Kurt Rohde had lit one of his cheroots. 'And you've never had any problems with it? I mean, I'm sure this easel is very valuable and there are perhaps people interested in it, people who would like to see it somewhere else, rather than here in your hotel . . .' Kurt Rohde said, puffing away at his cigar. Adeling raised his eyebrows and gave him a suspicious look. 'No, we haven't had any problems so far and we at the Felsenburg Hotel would be very grateful for your discretion in this matter. If you would now excuse me . . .' Adeling fluttered off.

'You played beautifully, my lad. Come here and give me a squeeze, we haven't said hello properly yet.' Christian embraced his grandfather, who had taken his cheroot out and was holding it well to one side. Kurt Rohde was shorter than his grandson, and Christian leant down a little so his grandfather could kiss him on the forehead. He furrowed his brow – not because he was uncomfortable at being kissed by his grandfather but so that the pimples would disappear in the furrows. His grandfather's familiar smell: his hair, combed back straight, still thick and full despite his sixty-nine years and only white at the temples, and the skin under his trimmed beard smelt of eau de Cologne, the coarse material of his suit of tobacco and naphthalene.

'Christian, Anne would like us to give him the barometer now, once we're all back inside,' Meno said between two puffs on his pipe. 'Would you be so good as to get things ready?' Christian, sensing that he was in the way, nodded and went back into the restaurant, where Ezzo, Reglinde and Robert were busy at the buffet again, Ezzo and Robert smacking their lips and rolling their eyes with pleasure.

'Where's your clock-grandfather?' Reglinde asked as she chewed.

'Since he and Emmy got divorced they've come to an agreement: he doesn't want to be where she is and vice versa.'

'Oh. Have you seen Ina?'

'Perhaps she's gone to the loo. Fantastic dress she's wearing.'

'We made it at the Harmony. Barbara helped, of course.'

Christian could picture the little furrier's on Rissleite, the glassed door, the paint peeling from exposure to the elements; it had become a tradition in the spring and summer, when the furs for the winter were delivered, for the children of the district to gather there and ask for the scraps that were left over after the furs had been made up. They collected the scraps and once they had collected enough, their mothers made them into warm jerkins, mittens and caps.

'Actually, she had intended to wear it the first time for the college of education's end-of-term ball. Did you see? The doctors on the other side of the table had their eyes popping out.'

Christian shrugged. Reglinde, who was studying to be an organist and choirmaster, told him news from the college for church music, but Christian was only half listening. He was still cold, he put his hands in the pockets of his best suit – Richard had passed it on because it had grown too tight for him – but took them out again when he remembered that it was impolite to stand there like that. He was embarrassed. When he looked at Reglinde for too long, her eyes strayed away from his and ran over his untidily combed, light-brown hair and its cowlicks and, when he smiled, the dimples in his cheeks – his bad skin. She had Gudrun's high, beautifully domed forehead, also her delicate, translucent though not pale skin with the blue veins visible; her cheeks and mouth came from Niklas. Her natural chestnut ringlets, which she kept short, were not typical of the Tietzes, who, like the Rohdes, all had fairly dark, straight hair. People who didn't know the family always took Robert for Ezzo's brother – apart from his eyes, Robert was much closer in appearance to the Rohdes than to Christian.

Reglinde, probably sensing his embarrassment, concluded the conversation and went over to join Ina, who was waving to her from the doorway.

Christian went over to the table with the birthday presents. Meno had not only made a contribution to the cost of the barometer but had also given Richard – so that was what had been in the parcel – a record: Beethoven's late quartets, by the Amadeus String Quartet. Beside it was the gift from Ulrich Rohde and his family, a book. Christian read the title page: Bier / Braun / Kümmell: *Chirurgische Operationslehre*, edited by F. Sauerbruch and V. Schmieden, Johann Ambrosius Barth, Leipzig, 1933. He knew the book, a well-preserved antiquarian edition with many coloured illustrations; it had always had a special place in his uncle's library, for it was the famous edition of a famous book and, on top of that, had handwritten dedications by Sauerbruch and Schmieden; Richard always admired it and held it in his hands with a certain envy when they visited the Italian House. Ulrich Rohde had a large collection of such books.

Grandfather Rohde had given his father an odd present: an egg-shaped stone, about the size of a person's head, that stood in the hollow of a smoothly polished wooden cube.

'Careful if you pick it up, it's sawn through in the middle,' he suddenly heard Meno say beside him. 'It's called a druse or a geode, they're found like that in the rock. Be careful, it's valuable.'

Crystals glittering blue, crimson and purple, prisms, such as Christian was familiar with from rock crystal, arranged close together; some as long as his little finger and so precisely formed they seemed shaped by human hand.

'That's an amethyst,' Meno said, the blue and purple reflections of the crystals flitting to and fro across his eyes.

Emmy had contributed to the barometer and Christian had heard about the Tietzes' present from Ezzo, it was at home in Caravel: one of Niklas's lovely nickel-plated stethoscopes from St Petersburg.

'And what are the two of you looking at? My God, Gudrun, and people talk about the impoverished East,' Barbara broke in, drumming on the table with her gaudily painted fingernails. 'What d'you think of Ina's dress? We got her hairstyle from one of Wiener's magazines, you can forget what's in ours. Should I arrange an appointment there for you?'

'I went to the hairdresser's yesterday, Barbara. To Schnebel's.'

'To be perfectly honest, Gudrun, I'm afraid you can tell. Send Reglinde round some time – her measurements are about the same as Ina's and no one can have anything against more attractive funeral hymns.'

'The success of a dress is measured by the number of proposals a woman receives, as Eschschloraque says in his latest play. A bit sexist, I mean, for God's sake, Barbara, but we're putting it on just at the moment. And Ina is getting to the age when off-the-shoulder is a bit risky.'

Barbara ignored that. She picked up the book on vintage cars, the present from the Wolfstone-Hoffmanns. 'Richard and his little hobbies . . . That's enoeff.' The English word, though in Saxon pronunciation, was one of Barbara's favourites. 'Men need something to keep them busy, otherwise they start getting funny ideas. You remember that, Christian. Did you drop in on Hans on the way here? After all, it is his brother's fiftieth, to be honest, that's not the way an English gentleman . . . enoeff.'

'Iris called,' Meno said. 'They've got the measles.'

'What?!' Gudrun stepped back in horror. 'And you only tell me now? The measles! For adults that can . . . be fatal! I read recently that these viruses are terribly infectious. And they'll be on that book now!'

'Muriel assured me she only touched it with gloves on and Hans even disinfected it,' Meno said to calm her down.

'Muriel? That little Miss Head-in-the-clouds?!'

Christian thought of his cousin. She was quiet and decisive but certainly didn't have her head in the clouds. He took the barometer out of the bag and gave it to Anne as she came in with the others. He was keen to see how his father would respond to the present and whether it could hold its own alongside *Landscape during a Thaw*.

A simultaneous 'O-oooh' came from Richard, Emmy and Ezzo, who had elbowed his way to the table.

'Lord love us!' said Emmy in her thick Saxon dialect, clapping her hands together. 'That's the real McCoy!'

'Indeed, it is that.' Richard cautiously stroked the barometer. The mechanism was cased in carved oak with, above it, a thermometer marked in both Réaumur and Celsius scales. 'Aneroid barometer' was written in Gothic script on the white face of the capsule, under it the name of the manufacturer: Oscar Bösolt, Dresden. Over the air-pressure indicator was a manually set needle for measuring changes in pressure. The wood, which Lange had oiled and polished up, had a rich gleam. Round the capsule were stylized aquatic plants that, at the lower part, turned into two dolphins crossing their tails, their mouths swallowing the arrow-shaped leaves of the plants. Growing out of these leaves and framing the thermometer in a lyre-like motif were two slim stems that gradually broadened as they rose, again seamlessly turning into two dolphins, the bodies of which, each under a pair of reeds, framed the top of the barometer. In the middle, above the thermometer, was a bird spreading its wings; its body was worm-eaten and one or two pieces of the wooden feathers had broken off.

Meno told them how they had discovered, and eventually managed to buy, the barometer. 'It belonged to the landlord who runs the bar in the former clubhouse of the Association of Elbe Fishermen. Lange knows him. At first he didn't want to sell it, even though he'd advertised it. But Lange persuaded him; Christian went to see him today and that's how we got it.'

'But – it must have cost a packet, you can't do that. How much . . . I mean, how much did you pay? I'll put something towards it myself, that goes without saying.'

'We're not going to tell you. Anne said you've always wanted a really nice barometer. Well, there it is.'

'Meno . . .'

'We all chipped in,' Anne broke in. 'It's a present from the family to you. Everyone gave what they could afford and if we hang it up in the living room, on the wall over the television, I thought, we'll all get something out of it, won't we?'

Richard embraced Emmy and Meno, kissed Anne, then his two sons, who both made a face – it was embarrassing for them in front of all the others, above all in front of Reglinde and Ina.

'Well, thank you, thank you, all. Such a beautiful present . . . Thank you. And I thought I was going to get a pullover or two, a tie or something like that . . . You've all gone to such expense for me . . .'

'Come on, everyone, sit down,' Anne said. Meno carefully packed the barometer in the bag and put it down on the table.

'A fine piece, delicate work.' Niklas nodded in appreciation. 'Now you'll always know what the climate's like, Richard.'

'Landscape during a thaw?' Sandor asked with a grin; so far he had hardly taken part in the conversation at all.

'Hm, we shall see.' Niklas wiped his massive aquiline nose, on which the red mark of the bridge of his glasses could still be seen. 'We shall see,' he repeated, nodding and furrowing his brow.

The conversation split up into little groups. Ulrich and Kurt Rohde talked together quietly; Emmy, Barbara and Gudrun were listening to Alice; the two girls had gone into a huddle, whispering and giggling. Adeling, the only waiter left in the room, brought some wine, Radeberger and Wernesgrüner beer, mineral water and glasses; Anne, bowls of biscuits and nuts. Ezzo and Robert were talking football, chatting about some of Dynamo Dresden's recent matches; Christian was listening to the men, who, as almost always on such occasions, were talking politics. Richard especially was in his element there.

'When you think about what that Andropov said . . . Did you read it? It was splashed all over the newspapers . . . The usual blah-blah, of course. Sandor, Alice, do you fancy a crash course in "How to fill three pages of a newspaper – Berliner size – without saying a single word that means anything"? You have to pick out the juicy bits and make sense of them yourself. I recommend you have a look at our sausage- and cheese-wrapping papers, namely the *Sächsische Neueste Nachrichten*, the *Sächsisches Tageblatt* and, above all, the *Sächsische Zeitung*.'

'Not so loud, Richard,' said Anne, looking round anxiously.

'OK, I know. Have you read it?'

'You couldn't miss it,' Niklas growled. 'I tend to avoid the dreary acres of newsprint, but it did strike me that he intends to continue the course prescribed by the Twenty-Sixth Party Conference.'

'Did you expect anything else?'

'No. In the band they've made various jokes about it – for example, that he should have said, "Keep going forward on a quite different course . . ."'

'And away from hard liquor. Just look at the guys marching past Brezhnev's coffin. The puffy faces! All alcoholics, I swear. Twenty-five years on nights. Socialism equals ruined livers, varices of the oesophageal veins.'

Anne grasped Richard's arm. He lowered his voice so that they all had to lean forward, even though he was speaking clearly.

'Varices of the oesophageal veins? What's that?' Reglinde was trying to change the subject and when Richard started out on a detailed explanation, Christian thought it was stupid to go into it out of politeness, since going into it looked like falling for her diversion.

'I also took the trouble to read it,' Meno said. 'I thought it was interesting that they didn't say that Comrade Andropov was head of the secret service,' he went on reflectively.

'And why should they? Look, it's self-evident. Brezhnev ruled for a good twenty years. Now he's dead. Who's going to be his successor? The one who knows the country best, of course. The head of the secret service.'

'Be careful, Richard, not so loud, who knows, perhaps even here . . .' Anne glanced suspiciously at Adeling, then waved him away when he looked as if he were about take a step towards them. 'No, it's nothing, I don't need anything, thank you.' She shook her head. 'But all of you? Perhaps you'd like . . . ?' She looked round. 'There's still ice-cream sundaes.'

'Oh yes!' Ezzo and Robert cried simultaneously.

Adeling tapped his fingertips, rocked on his heels and nodded to Anne. He and another waiter brought the ice cream.

'But tell me, Alice and Sandor,' Niklas murmured in a conspiratorial voice, lifting his long spoon, on which a piece of Neapolitan ice cream the size of a plum glittered, 'what about this Helmut Kohl? All we hear is lies.'

'Yes, he's . . . better, wouldn't we say, Alice?' Alice blinked in irritation when she heard her name, adjusted her glasses and nodded vaguely in Sandor's direction. Emmy was talking about her many health problems with such eloquence that Gudrun, Barbara and Alice were spellbound. The men listened attentively as Sandor, in his mid-forties with an olive complexion and a full head of very grey hair that ran across his forehead in a tight wave, told them about the events in the West German parliament that had led to the vote of no confidence in Helmut Schmidt and his fall as chancellor. He and Alice had been living in South America for twenty years, which meant that he sometimes had to search for words when he spoke, and he hardly ever left the pauses between the harsh consonants that the German words ended with; instead he would soften them by adding an 'eh' that joined the words together. No one would have taken him, neither from his appearance nor from his accent, for a man who had been born in Dresden.

'The development-eh-will not suit-eh-your superiors and-eh-I think-eh-that Kohl will make-eh-radical changes to the policy of rapprochement to which the Social Democrats-eh-had committed themselves . . .'

'I hope so,' said Niklas with a meaningful nod. His left hand twitched nervously as he stuck the long spoon into the strawberry layer of the Neapolitan ice cream with his right. 'It's about time there was an end to the policy of seeking change by ingratiating themselves that the gentlemen over there pursued and that Brezhnev and his gang just laughed at. The way they went crawling to the Russians and their henchmen was embarrassing to see. Peace was what they wanted to bring, and détente – I ask you!' Niklas brushed away a few drops of ice cream that his vehemently outraged pronunciation of the 'ch' in 'henchmen' had sprayed over the table.

'Wimps, Niklas, wimps the whole lot of them! Middle-class revolutionaries from '68 who're still pursuing some daydreams or other but have no idea about the real world . . . They should come over here and live with us, or in beautiful Moscow, if the reality of socialism is that wonderful. But that's not what these gentlemen want either, they're not *that* blind.' Richard had flushed red with anger and slapped his forehead several times. 'They want to recognize the GDR, for God's sake! We have to accept the division of Germany, they say, it's a historical fact, they say, and the GDR is a legitimate state like any other! Don't make me laugh! This state, huh, whose only legitimacy comes from the Russian bayonets holding it up. A state that would collapse at once – at *once* I tell you – if there were free, genuinely free elections . . .'

'Richard, please.'

'You're right, Anne. But I do get worked up about it. These doves who're soft on communism – against those hardliners! Reagan's got the right idea, he has no illusions, tough talking's the only thing the Russians understand . . . force them to keep up the arms race till the country collapses.'

'But – Richard, the arms race . . . what if one side cracks up and presses the red button? Is what Reagan is doing right then – even at that price?' Meno, a reflective look on his face, was poking around in his sundae. Reglinde, Ina, Ezzo and Robert, who were familiar with this kind of discussion from many family gatherings, were talking among themselves without bothering to follow the course of the argument. By this time Emmy had got to her hip operation, though the only one listening now was Gudrun, while Alice was showing the Rohdes, whom she hadn't seen yet, photos of their four sons and their last holiday.

'Yesyes, the red button, that's the argument that's always used by our hypocritical press. They write that because they're afraid. They're well aware that they're starting to run out of steam. What are the four main enemies of socialism? Spring, summer, autumn and winter. Or why do you think they keep feeling it's necessary to urge us to increase our productivity . . . Without competition nothing works, that's what I've always said.'

'But, Richard, surely you're not disputing that the more weapons are stockpiled – and they're here, all those rockets, they're deployed in our country – the greater the danger of war. When there are no weapons, war is impossible. All your talk can't make that go away.'

'Oh, war.' Richard made a dismissive gesture. 'That's what I'm talking about, Meno. I don't think anyone really wants one. They're not all idiots. Our media always draw a parallel between stockpiling armaments and war. And conversely between disarmament and peace. However, the paradoxical thing about it is – man has clearly been carved from such crooked timber that he'll use his fingernails to scratch people's eyes out if he has no other weapons. If, on the other hand, he possesses rockets and knows that the other tribe, over there behind the palisade, also possesses rockets – he'll calm down and go and till his field. Odd but true.'

'No, I'm sorry, that's not true, it's nonsense, Richard.' Meno frowned and shook his head. 'No weapons – no war, and that's that. Fingernails, to stick to the terminology, could be weapons or, if you like, could be used as such. I would like to emphasize that. But what does surprise me is that you of all people, as a doctor, a surgeon, are speaking in favour of the arms race –'

'Just a minute. I'm speaking in favour of humanity. And I'm wondering what is the best way of getting out of an inhuman system. These systems have their own laws . . . Once they've been set up and are firmly established, the principles of common sense are turned upside down in them! You don't get rid of dictators by sucking up to or even hobnobbing with them. For that kind of person there is only one law: the law of force, my friend.'

'But, I repeat, increasing the stocks of armaments only increases the danger of war breaking out, and where the *danger* of war is increased, then the danger of something actually happening is increased, you surely won't deny that . . . A rocket heading in our direction will put an end to all discussion! Is that what you want – as a doctor?'

Richard was getting worked up. 'As a man who thinks about politics, my dear brother-in-law! And one who doesn't switch off his common sense and his observations when he puts on a white coat.'

'What worries me,' Ulrich interjected – he was sitting beside Christian and was presumably trying to calm things down a little – 'is what Chernenko and Andropov said more or less in the middle of their speeches. One can't beg peace from the imperialists, only defend it by relying on the strong power –'

'Invincible,' Niklas broke in raising his ice-cream spoon, 'invincible power! I underlined it in the *Tageblatt*.'

'Right, then. By relying on the invincible power of the Soviet forces. Sounds pretty bellicose. That worries me.'

'You see. So there you are,' the triumphant look Richard gave Meno seemed to say. His dish was empty, even though he'd had a large helping of ice cream and spent more time speaking than concentrating on eating it. Christian suspected that in the heat of debate his father hadn't noticed what he was eating. Richard waved his spoon. 'And what that means is crystal clear. That Moscow intends to continue to keep us on a short leash and that there will be no relaxation, quite the contrary. I read both speeches very closely. Anyway, Meno, it's not true that they didn't say Andropov had been head of the secret service. They did say that, only between the lines. Chernenko said . . . let me think a moment . . . yes: Yuri Vladimirovich had experience from his varied activity in domestic and foreign affairs in the field of ideology. In the field of ideology, I ask you, what's that supposed to mean? Domestic and foreign affairs, if you put the two together I can see three fat Cyrillic letters shining: K, G and B . . . Moreover Chernenko says that Andropov has done great work in the consolidation of the socialist community and in the maintenance of the security – as a man sensitive to language, Meno, what do you think of the repeated genitives? – of the security of our state. And where do you think he performed that service, certainly not on a collective farm . . . This Andropov will not deviate one millimetre from official dogma, I can tell you. And Chernenko!'

'He says that all the members of the Politburo are of the opinion that Yuri Vladimirovich has mastered Brezhnev's style of leadership well,' Christian replied. The adults looked at him in astonishment. 'We went through the article at school, in civics. However,' he added with a smile, 'not with your deductions.'

'We keep those to ourselves, Christian, d'you hear?' Anne warned him in a low voice.

'Yes, exactly. Mastered well, that's what it said. In a word: a hard line! And when I read what else this Andropov said, what was it now, oh yes, something like: "Each one of us knows what an invaluable contribution Leonid Ilyich Brezhnev made to the creation" – to the creation, oh dear me, these abstract nouns always seem to crop up in the rubbish they write, sometimes you get the impression they do it deliberately to discourage people from reading on, and then they put the bit that matters in the last third . . .'

'I know what you mean, Richard, it left a nasty taste in my mouth too.' Niklas gave an outraged nod.

'". . . to the creation of the healthy moral and political atmosphere that characterizes the life and work of the Party today" . . . that is the worst kind of cynicism you can get, if you exclude Mielke's call to the comrades in the Stasi, that really takes the bacon, Chekists, he calls them, Chekists, it makes you feel sick; that's the justification for the camps . . .'

The political discussion soon subsided once Anne, realizing that the tension was increasing and Richard was getting more and more worked up, had given Niklas and Meno a sign and changed the subject. Moreover Christian could see that as hostess she was unhappy that the party had split up into three or four groups that were pursuing quite separate conversations. So Alice had to take out her photos again and Sandor had to tell them again about the Galapagos, where they had been on a cruise; Niklas then talked about the Dresden State Orchestra's tour of West Germany, on which he had been the accompanying doctor.

'A great success, great success . . . and all the grub they laid out for us poor starving Zone-dwellers! . . . further proof for us of what a thoroughly decadent society imperialism is and how magnificent its death-throes are . . .' Niklas waved his hand dismissively, and when they asked him what exactly they'd had to eat, his only reply was to close his eyes and give a real Dresden 'Ooooh', an expression that combined wonderment and stupefaction with acknowledgement of the limited nature of local catering. 'But no one's going to match what you've put together this evening that soon, even if it's the boss of VEB Delikat himself.'

Then Niklas talked about *Il Seraglio*, which had been performed recently in the Dresden theatre. Here he was in his element, going into detail, vivid detail, imitating the gestures of the Japanese conductor, who, according to the withering verdict of the majority of the orchestra, had no idea about music; he also recounted anecdotes that were going round the theatre. The ice cream and desserts had all been finished; everyone was cheered up by the good food, the company and Niklas's stories. They left at around eleven.

The left-over food and drink were packed up.

'I'll make up a special parcel for Regine and Hansi, they'll be hungry.'

'Yes, good idea, Anne. I'll see to the presents.' Richard went to the easel. Meno helped Anne and Adeling pack up the food. 'How are things with Regine?'

'Not very good, I think. She doesn't say that, but she doesn't look well. They're giving her a lot of hassle, Hansi gets it at school as well.'

'How long's she been waiting now?'

'Since nine this morning. When I left, around five, the call hadn't come, nor when Richard left. They won't have managed it since then either, otherwise they would have come.'

'What should I do with the cold meat? Have you any wrapping paper?'

'Wait a minute.' Anne went over to Adeling, who went out and reappeared shortly after with a roll of greaseproof paper.

'How long is it since Jürgen went?'

'Two and a half years. Terrible. When I imagine what it would be like if Richard were in Munich or Hamburg, Mo, and I was stuck here all by myself with the children . . . No, I just don't want to think about it.'

Outside it was bitterly cold. The air seemed to be grasping their cheeks and the tips of their noses with sandpaper fingers. It had stopped snowing. Canopies of light hung over the crossings, the only places where the street lamps were still on; the pavements lay in darkness, with a touch of faint moonlight here and there; the houses were black blocks with glassy outlines. Meno supported Grandmother Emmy and was carrying most of the presents in a bag; Richard, walking alongside Anne, had the picture, she the barometer, Christian his cello; the Tietzes were far ahead of them, each with some kind of bag containing wrapped-up food over their shoulder.

'Well, little nurse, who tended me with devoted care?' said Richard, teasing his wife. 'Didn't you blush!'

'And he bowed to me into the bargain, your well-informed Herr Professor Müller. He could at least have asked you how things were before confusing me – at your birthday party in front of fifty people! – with that Nurse Hannelore.' Anne shook her head in outrage. 'I wasn't even a student nurse at that time and certainly not in Halle.'

'It was well meant, as a compliment.'

'Well meant, compliment – you know what you can do with your compliment . . .' Angrily Anne kicked a snowball that was lying on the path out of the way.

'Aren't you angry! Come here, my little lambkin.' Richard grabbed her and gave her a kiss.

'Watch out with the picture . . . And don't call me your "little lambkin" – you know very well I can't stand it. Of course I'm annoyed. I just hope he gets stomach ache from all the cakes he stuffed himself with.'

Anne looked across at the children, who were running in the road and laughing as they threw snowballs at each other. Emmy and Meno were some distance behind, then came Kurt Rohde with Barbara and Ulrich; Alice and Sandor were behind them.

'There's one thing I ask of you, Richard: you mustn't talk so openly when there are so many people present, some of whom we don't know very well. We know, of course, what the Tietzes' views are, and Meno's. But you know that Ulrich is a Party member.'

'Yes, and why? Because otherwise he wouldn't have been made managing director. He didn't join from conviction. He's got eyes in his head, he's still in his right senses.'

'Still. You've a tendency to get louder and louder the more you get worked up about a subject. Can you vouch for every one of your colleagues? You see.'

'Müller showed a dangerous reaction to a joke Manfred made. We were at the buffet, Christian had just told one about Brezhnev and along came Müller to give us a slap on the wrists: that mockery of a great man whom our Soviet brothers had lost was uncalled for and that we should be aware of our position and stuff like that.'

'You see, that's just what I mean. And he was standing quite far away, I was watching you. You must think of things like that, Richard, promise me that. You must learn to hold your tongue. You encourage Christian and you know what he's like, that he takes after you in this respect. The boy's bound to think: If my father thinks he can get away with it, so can I.'

'I don't believe that's what he thinks. You underestimate him. But you're right, my feelings keep running away with me. I'm not one of your devious lickspittles and I don't want to bring up my boys to be like that, goddammit,' Richard said in a voice strained with fury.

'Don't swear. You know, I'm not that worried about Robert. He's quieter and somehow . . . more sensible. At school he says the things they want to hear, keeps his thoughts to himself, then comes home and switches over. But Christian . . . Your boss mustn't hear that Christian has told a joke about Brezhnev, especially now, when he's hardly been dead a month and they don't know whether they're coming or going and fly off the handle at the least thing . . . You know all that. And Christian does too. But sometimes I really feel it's like talking to a brick wall. And then you don't even know whether that restaurant's been bugged all over the place . . .'

'Oh, you can be sure of that.'

'So why don't you behave accordingly, then? I did have a word with you about it only this afternoon, and Christian yesterday! But I can talk till the cows come home, it's still no use. The boy's old enough, you say, but when you and your friends encourage him like that . . . He's only seventeen, for God's sake, he must feel it's a challenge when he listens to you lot . . . But I think he's not yet old enough to assess such situations properly.'

'You're right, Anne. I should have been more cautious. Oh . . . all this ducking and diving . . .'

'Moaning won't change it.'

'That Müller . . . I saw very clearly that he was boiling with rage

71

and didn't kick up a big fuss only because he was our guest. Manfred will have to watch out too. I know for a fact that his boss and Müller can't stand each other, but . . . A comrade's a comrade, and when it comes down to it, dog doesn't eat dog. Oh, Anne, I've been living in this state for thirty-three years and I still don't know when it's time to keep my mouth shut.'

Anne looked at him, gave his arm a squeeze.

'That's why I love you. Come on, then, it's too late to do anything about it now.'

Richard sensed that she was depressed and wanted to change the subject. 'Hey, what are we going to do about sleeping arrangements? I thought Sandor and Alice could stay in the Little Room . . .'

'My dear, we sorted that out ages ago.' She shook her head in amusement. 'You men always think of these things in such good time, don't you? It's amazing. If these things were left to you, we'd be in chaos in no time at all. Alice and Sandor are going to have to sleep with Kurt in the children's room, they can move back into the Little Room tomorrow. Regine and Hansi in the living room, Emmy in the Little Room. Your mother needs to sleep by herself and anyway, you can't expect her to put up with the hard sofas in the living room; it doesn't bother Regine and the young lad. And they'll have the telephone in there, in case the call comes very late. Hey, Robert, Ezzo, stop that, you almost hit us. I don't want anything to get broken, d'you hear?'

'Yesyes,' the two shouted happily, sweeping snow off the top of the walls into each other's faces.

Christian was thinking about Regine, who was a friend of his parents. Jürgen Neubert, Regine's husband, had left the country illegally two years ago to go to Munich. Since then they could only meet in Prague, once a year, after great difficulties, Jürgen always afraid of being arrested. Regine had applied for an exit visa, and since then her telephone had been cut off. She had to use Anne and Richard's line to speak to Jürgen. The call might be put through at four in the morning, you never knew when beforehand, which was why Anne had taken the precaution of making up beds for Regine and her son.

'Aha,' Richard murmured outside Caravel, taking the key out of his coat pocket. The light was on in the living room, the windows of which, with their flying buttresses, could be seen from the street. That was the sign that Regine was still waiting for her husband's call.

6
'Prek-fest'

The first light of day was crouching at the window when Christian woke. He listened. Everything was quiet in the house, but he knew that Meno liked to get up early and spend lauds – as, like the monks, he called the hour between five and six – at work or meditating in the gradually waning darkness of the living room, which was still reasonably warm from the previous evening. In the summer Meno would sit on the little balcony watching the return of the garden, the branches and flowers being outlined in the flush of dawn, Lange's pear trees still dark, the pears still not released from the twilight; watching and perhaps listening as he, Christian, was listening now. The rusty tick of Meno's Russian заря alarm clock, the faint green glow of the fluorescent lines under the numbers and on the hands. It was shortly after seven. Christian got up and put on the dressing gown Anne had laid out for him. The stove had gone out during the night; the room was so cold his breath came out like a cloud of smoke and there were ice patterns on the window. The light was on in the bathroom, and he heard Libussa singing one of her Czech folk songs; when she sang, her voice sounded like a little girl's. On the landing it was even colder than in the cabin, there was a glitter of frost on the coal box. He hurried back into the room, swung his arms round, did knee bends, then some shadow boxing with an invisible opponent who, in his mind's eye, took on the features of his Russian teacher, and then, after a blow full in the face, the puffy red face of his civics teacher, a jab, a straight right, a straight left, a right hook and then one to those thick, always slightly parted lips with the curve of the red-veined jug-like nose above them – there was a knock at the door. 'Krishan,' he heard Libussa shout, 'the bathroom's free now, breakfast' – she pronounced it 'prek-fest' – 'is in the conservatory, d'you hear.'

Kri-shan. That was what Libussa called him; he liked it. The civics teacher had burst under the force of his punches. Panting, Christian flung open the window. It had continued to snow during the night; the garden, which fell away steeply below the window, lay under a thick white blanket, and the summerhouse, where Meno often used to work, sometimes even sleep in the warmer seasons, looked as if it were covered in icing; the sandstone balustrade on either side, which separated the upper garden from the lower, wilder part, just peeked out of the snow; a stone eagle was perched on the balustrade and its wings, delicately carved and elegantly outspread, seemed to be carrying a pile of folded white towels. Fresh animal tracks criss-crossed the snow. A flock of crows was busying itself about the huge stack of wood that Meno, the ship's doctor and Meno's next-door neighbour, the engineer Dr Stahl, had piled up the previous autumn. In front of the rhododendrons, which covered the left-hand side of the balustrade almost completely, several bird feeders were hanging from some clothes poles; countless birds were fluttering round and squabbling. He closed the window and went to the bathroom.

At weekends they had a communal breakfast in the House with a Thousand Eyes. It was Libussa, who was very sociable, who had introduced the custom. They took it in turns to provide rolls, butter, milk and jam; in the summer they often had breakfast in the garden, in the lower part, at a table in the middle of a wild, romantic tangle of bushes, out of sight of prying eyes; a weathered set of steps led down to it.

A jet of boiling hot water shot into the tub with the lion feet. There were fine cracks in the enamel. There were traces of black mould in the joins between the tiles, on the ceiling with the layers of peeling paint, on the wood of the windowsill, which had been leached grey by soapy water; the mould was an intruder in all the houses Christian knew up there, and it was impossible to eradicate entirely, no matter how much time people spent airing rooms, brushing on fungicides or painting white lead or spar varnish over it

Soon the bathtub was steaming. He refilled the boiler with water, thinking about the conservatory. Whenever Christian said anything about the conservatory, or about the House with a Thousand Eyes – in the school hostel after they'd finished their homework for the evening and the three of them were sitting in the lounge together and it was difficult to stay out of the exchange of information, the 'who-are-you-then?' and 'where-do-you-come-from-then?' – the response would be disbelieving looks, sometimes unconcealed doubt. He quickly sensed their scepticism and would change the subject before he got onto the details that really sounded fantastic and magical, didn't mention Caravel, East Rome, Meno's name for the house where he lived and where there was a room that could be reached both through the Langes' apartment and by a spiral staircase that was hidden behind the salamander wallpaper in the hall, with chessboard tiles and light coming in through a sloping overhead window that the Langes, like the original owners, used as a conservatory. – 'Oh come on now, with the shortage of accommodation, you don't seriously expect us to believe that. Hasn't your ship's doctor had someone allocated to one of his rooms?' Christian could hear his fellow boarders in Waldbrunn say as he got out of the bath and went back to the cabin, dressing as quickly as he could, the cold was so biting. – He hasn't, but my uncle has. He shares the lower apartment with an engineer and his family; my uncle has one large room and two smaller ones. It's an old villa, built by a soap manufacturer around the turn of the century; one family lived in the whole house then, and there were a few attic rooms for the maids. He would have had no idea that he would be expropriated one day – otherwise he might have made better arrangements to suit the Communal Housing Department. 'Well now, isn't he a little mocker, our Dresdener?' It was Jens Ansorge who said that. The son of the general practitioner from Altenberg, he was in 11/2, Christian's class, and sat right at the front of the row by the window; a little shorter than Christian, his hair blow-dried into a slightly dishevelled style, he had spoken with a conspiratorial grin and tugged at his large beak of a nose with relish. That meant: Don't try to fool me, OK? Sometimes Jens watched him during classes; they both sat at the front, though Christian was alone in the row by the door, and he could feel Jens's blue eyes, openly scrutinizing and challenging, going over his face, the clothes he was wearing, the Swiss walking boots that had been handed down to him by his father.

Christian was already on the stairs. He intended to go to the conservatory by the concealed door, but Libussa was just coming out of the kitchen, where she'd been warming up some rolls – the odour filled the hall. 'Just come right in, Krishan, and help me carry the things into the conservatory. You know where everything is, the salt's on the right in the wall cupboard.' Libussa, holding the basket of rolls, her hair gathered in a bun, nodded to him. 'The door's open, but close it behind you or we'll lose all the heat.'

Christian picked up the tea tray. The Langes' apartment smelt of vanilla tobacco; the smoke seemed to have seeped right into the yellowing wallpaper and faded curtains that were hung over the doors for extra insulation. Christian lowered his head to go through the wooden-bead curtain into a little vestibule in which were a shoe tidy, key hooks, a hat rack on which were several of Libussa's large hatboxes. The ship's doctor, who was just coming out of the living-room door with the ash pan in his hand, blinked behind his horn-rimmed glasses when he saw Christian, but not in surprise at seeing him in their apartment, for he immediately said, in his tobacco-smoky voice, 'Did it go well, did it go well, was your father happy with it?' He said 'fadder', almost swallowing the 'r' – Lange came from Rostock. 'Very happy, even.' Christian then wished him a slightly embarrassed good morning, for Lange was in a rather strange get-up: striped pyjama trousers and a tweed jacket with a cigar peeping out of the breast pocket. 'Right then, let's get on with it, my son.' Muttering to himself, he looked for a key on the hooks, the goatee on his chin and upper lip – which had retained its light-brown colour, in contrast to the rather tangled hair on his head – bobbing up and down as he did so.

The teacups were steaming; they were also heavy and the ball of his hand was touching the hot teapot; despite that, Christian didn't go straight into the conservatory but cast greedy eyes on the pictures on the walls, mostly photographs of the ships on which Lange had been the doctor: the *Oldenburg*, a proud and tall full-rigged ship – when Christian asked about it Lange would growl, 'She were a good ship' in his Low German dialect, jutting out his chin and puffing smoke from a pipe that was curved like an upside-down question mark; passenger ships of the Hamburg–America Line; then, during the war, destroyers, menacing grey iron hulks. Harbours, the Torres Straits, the rocky coast of Patagonia, taken from a ship of the Laeisz shipping company's nitrate line; a U-boat crew in the Second World War, the submarine surfaced beside a battleship, its sailors waving, the hatches open, the crew fallen in on deck, pennants, illustrated with the number of gross register tons they had sunk, fluttered above the bearded faces, and the captain was saluting, his hand raised casually and, as it seemed to Christian, slightly sceptically to his hat with its armed-forces eagle hanging askew. *Scapa Flow – Captain-Lieutenant Prien salutes Rear Admiral Dönitz CUB –* 'Commander of the U-Boats,' Lange had replied to Christian's question about the abbreviation, and he stroked his thin beard, going on in his Low German, 'An' I knew Prien as well. 'e were the great hero back then. A German U-boat sinks the *Royal Oak* in Scapa Flow. Reception in the Reich chancellery, the Knight's Cross, red carpet an' all that. An' then? Lost at sea for Führer, Folk and Fadderland. All lost at sea, my son. The seventh from t'left, on the big tub, that's me.'

Beside the photos were sailors' knots, carefully drawn by Lange on black cardboard and framed: bowline, clove hitch, carrick bend and bunting hitch. The ship's doctor had taught him some of them – they were useful for fishing. The television, a Raduga, reflected the growing light and seemed to be staring at him. The stove gaped wide, the surround was spattered with ash – Libussa would go round later with the vacuum cleaner and wipe the bottles on the shelf beside the stove in which Lange's ships dreamt of long voyages. Christian went into the conservatory.

'Good morning, young man.' The engineer turned up the right corner of his lip; it was perhaps intended to seem cool and detached, but to Christian it just looked funny since Stahl had a moon-face and just a few strands of hair on his head, which he combed straight back and plastered down with hair lotion. To make up for it, his eyebrows and the hair on his chest, sticking out like wool from his lumberjack shirt, were all the more bushy. Lange often used to tease him: Gerhart Stahl, he would say, was like a Soviet actor who played a sunflower-seed vendor on the runway of Baku airport in a TV series. A sly clown and an inventive rogue, he would always shake his head dubiously and waggle his eyebrows when the Moscow celebrities, who were returning from their summer holiday, took off in an Ilyushin – 'I do not waggle my eyebrows,' the engineer would object irritatedly. Dr Gerhart Stahl didn't like the Soviet actor because he didn't like the Soviet Union.

'Slept well.' It was a statement, not a question. He crushed Christian's hand in his engineer's paw, then leant down to the oil radiator and turned the control knob. Although the tall windows were no longer perfectly insulated and the conservatory was fairly big – there was plenty of room in it for the breakfast table, and they could sit round it without the palm trees in the tubs getting in the way – it was noticeably warmer there than in the Langes' living room. The conservatory had a stove of its own, and the ship's doctor would stoke it up before going to bed; it continued to heat the conservatory until after breakfast, by which time the stoves in the other rooms were going.

'What a lovely prek-fest!' Libussa clapped her hands together with joy. 'Krishan, Gerhart, let me remind you of that before you start eating like horses. We can thank God that at least we can get enough rolls and bread in this country. When I think back to the war . . .' She went round filling their second cups with hot milk that she got from a collective farm beyond Bühlau, on the Schönfeld plateau; very little fat had been taken out of the cow's milk – it was more like white soup than milk and Christian found it nauseating; but Libussa thought he didn't have enough muscle, and that he was at the stage that would decide 'whether he would turn into a man or a pencil'. Therefore she refused to be put off by his expression and filled his cup.

'Thanks again for the roses, Libussa.' Meno, who had switched on Radio Dresden, bent over a tub with Maréchal Niel roses. 'All the wives were envious of them and insisted I give them the address of the market garden. Did I perhaps get the flowers from the Rose Gorge or from Arbogast's greenhouses? How did I manage to bribe the grower?'

The ship's doctor came in. He'd put on a dressing gown and was carrying Chakamankabudibaba, who blinked in the light, arched his back and climbed into a basket that was next to a magnificent sago palm. Lange and Stahl rubbed their hands expectantly and licked their lips. There was the smell of tea, coffee, freshly made cocoa, there were preserved quinces and cherries, plum jam and forest honey, and beside the basket of rolls covered with a cloth was one of Libussa's specialities: apricots that had been dried to make a kind of firm pastry and cut into thin strips that Christian (who kept squinting over at the plate, bringing a grin from Stahl, whose chair was much closer to the delicacy) thought would do a lot more to promote his growth and physical development than hot cow's milk. Libussa and her husband put their hands together for grace: 'By Thy hands we all are fed, give us, Lord, our daily bread.' Radio Dresden was broadcasting a poem by a senior functionary of the Writers' Association who had fought valiantly for socialism. Meno listened, a pained look on his face, while Christian and the others, unmoved, helped themselves to what was on the table. The poem was about ideals, a bright future, Lenin and Marx, about heroic deeds on the building site of tomorrow, about shaping communism and 'About you, comrade, blithely breakfasting, / free of the cares of those / on guard!' Stahl paused as he was cutting his roll open. 'Tell me, Meno, do you have to read that kind of stuff every day? O blithely breakfasting book-editor . . .'

'Theodor Fontane?' the ship's doctor suggested, pursing his lips as he looked for his Heilpunkt digestion tablets. Meno still had the pained look on his face. The engineer put his knife down and, his elbow on the table, rested his chin on his hand to listen, chortling now and then, the sides of his nostrils quivering. Seizing the opportunity, Christian speared two slices of apricot with his fork.

'That's what those in East Rome like to hear. If it was up to them, writers would only produce that kind of stuff.'

'Do they have to broadcast it? So many verses from blithely breakfasting bureaucrats per month? For once they could' – Stahl looked round, searching – 'celebrate something quite ordinary in their verse. We have to do it! Four fuel engineers fashion fire from faeces. Celebrate the common things, comrade.'

Meno laughed, picked up his roll and examined it for a while, a glint of mockery in his eye. He stood up, stretched out his hand with the roll in a histrionic gesture:

'Thee will I sing, O thoroughbred Dresdner bread roll,
Splendidly chubby-cheeked promoter of gluttony.

But, tell us, cam'st thou from Elysium's Konsum?
Did Bunn, the baker, take thee out of a state-owned oven?
Cam'st thou from Wachendorf's cosily floured emporium?
Or from Walther's or George's baskets, morose in the dawn's early
light?
But tell me, O dough-born culinary marvel from Dresden,
How should the bard's greedy-gluttonous mouth name thee,
He whose longing lips laud thee in lustful lines?
Pert and pliant as a young girl's bosom thou lurest
To taste thee, but is it merely a taste thou wilt grant
When the bard's one desire is to sink
His teeth into thee as deep as a ravenous wolf,
To tear, with beastly maw and howling, juicy lumps
Out of thy flavoursome flanks – O how!
How shall I name thee, freshly baked, toothsome bagpipe,
Taste-buds tickler, O Dresdner dulcimer,
Manna of the muses, who suffer in silence
The oven's hellish heat, thou acme of Saxon genius,
O bread roll?'

Their laughter broke off abruptly as applause came from the door
to the spiral staircase and the hall. They all turned their heads. The
two young men who lowered their hands and slowly put them in their
trouser pockets looked by no means unsure of themselves. The flush
on their cheeks seemed to come from participation in the amusement
rather than from embarrassment, and Christian, who kept looking back
and forth between the twins and those sitting round the table, would
never have managed the lack of inhibition with which they, giggling
and praising the condition of the plants on either side, sauntered towards
them. They were identical twins, and they added to their confusing
similarity of appearance by wearing the same clothes: white, fine-gauge,
cable-stitch roll-neck pullovers, rather worn jeans and trainers.

'This is a private room, Herr . . . Kaminski?' Stahl was the first to recover from his surprise and pointed round the conservatory with his knife, which had a little blob of butter on the tip.

'That is correct, Kaminski is our name. And to distinguish between us, I'm René and this is Timo.' The closer of the two jerked his chin in the direction of his brother, whose cheerful expression turned into an inviting smile at the words 'distinguish between', which his brother had accompanied with an explanatory, but not mocking gesture. No one returned the smile or interpreted it as the invitation to a friendly response, as it might have been intended; Libussa and her husband sat there, stiff and silent; Meno, who was still standing, blinked in irritation then, after an exchange of looks with the ship's doctor, sat down as Kaminski, perhaps in order to get over the oppressive silence, came towards him. The news was on the radio now; Christian heard the ten-minute clock chime in Meno's living room. Chakamankabudibaba had woken up and was eyeing the two brothers suspiciously; their blond hair, combed this way and that over several cowlicks, was struck by the irruption of light and looked like frothy sunshine.

'Oh, you've got two more chairs, that is nice.' The twin whose name had been given as Timo pointed to two folded garden chairs that were leaning against the tub of roses. Stahl cleared his throat and dropped his knife on his plate with a clatter. The bafflement on Lange's face had given way to outrage. 'This is a private room, as Herr Stahl said, and I cannot remember having invited you to join us for breakfast. Would you be good enough to explain your behaviour, gentlemen? You are in the apartment of Alois and Libussa Lange and I am not aware that the Communal Housing Department has made any new decrees or amendments –' The ship's doctor broke off as Kaminski quickly raised his hand. 'New decrees or amendments are not necessary, Herr Lange. At least not insofar as you are referring to existing tenancy agreements.'

'This is home invasion!' thundered the engineer. Timo Kaminski had unfolded the chairs and placed them on the chessboard floor under the sago palm. His brother took out a packet of Jewel cigarettes, sniffed the air and asked, with a suggestion of a bow in Libussa's direction, whether he might smoke. She nodded, speechless with surprise, as it seemed to Christian. Kaminski flicked his lighter, lit the cigarette, drew on it with relish. 'No, it is not a case of home invasion, Herr Stahl. The concept doesn't apply here . . . We are the new tenants in the attic apartment in this building. We were very pleased to be allocated that apartment . . . You know the difficult housing situation. And then we are assigned the attic apartment in a quiet house on a slope with excellent views . . . Can you not imagine our delight? And can you not imagine that in such a case one does not simply move in, as into any old accommodation, but makes enquiries about the conditions here, finds out as much information as one can in city departments, in documents at the land registry, and about you as well, of course, our future neighbours? That is right and proper, is it not? We're not moving just anywhere but here, into this district above Dresden, to Mondleite, into the former property of a manufacturer of fine soaps whose renown, in his day, had spread far and wide beyond the confines of the country . . .'

The ship's doctor interrupted him: 'What do you want?'

'Us? Nothing at all. Except to introduce ourselves, make ourselves known in the hope that we will be on good terms with our neighbours.'

'And for that you break into someone else's apartment, into our conservatory? What kind of behaviour is that?' Libussa shook her head in indignation.

'Breaking into someone else's apartment?' René and Timo, who had already sat down and spent the conversation pushing back the cuticle of his fingernails with a knife, looked at each other in astonishment. 'Breaking in? Home invasion? My dear neighbours – is that how you respond to our attempt to be friendly, to introduce ourselves? That isn't very fair. It doesn't show goodwill. As I said, we have gathered information, my dear Frau Lange. And in no lease, no document in the land registry, in no tenancy agreement does it say that this conservatory belongs to your apartment and is thus for your own private use. It is not written down anywhere and that is a fact. You don't need to go and check now,' René said, raising his hands as Lange stood up. 'But if you don't believe me – well, go and check in your documents. You will see that I am right. And that means this conservatory belongs to all of us who live in this beautiful house, that is to you, Dr Stahl, and your family, to you, Herr Rohde, to the Langes and to us, since we now live here – and for that reason, then, prohibitions, claims of established rights and so on have no relevance. No more than those misleading expressions you used previously and which we beg you not to repeat. As good neighbours.'

7

East Rome

Snow, snow was falling on Dresden, on the Mondleite where Meno, as he came back from his walk in the dark, could see the shadows of the inhabitants in the lit windows, the worried face of Teerwagen, a physicist in the Barkhausen Building at the Technical University, who waved to him from the balcony; snow was falling on the district, was caught on the branches of the trees, lay there like strips of candy floss, transforming the rhododendrons into white bells, piling up on the footpaths, covering the tracks of birds, deer and cats in the front gardens with a sheet of fresh, glistening damask, burying in a few hours the cars, which had been laboriously scraped clear, in thickly spun layers, huge cocoons in which shapeless organisms slept through their metamorphosis.

On Monday morning Meno got up earlier than usual, yet he could hear the engineer already bustling about in the kitchen.

'Morning, Gerhart.'

'Morning. Baba's back outside. I've already given him something.'

'Can I have a bath?'

'It's free. The boiler will take a few minutes.'

'Did Sabine ring?' The House with a Thousand Eyes had a telephone; Lange had finally had a line allocated after waiting for fifteen years. The tenants used it communally.

'Her train should arrive at Neustadt Station at half five. Nine-hour delay because of snow drifts. I'll go and collect her, that's why I'm up already. The Eleven's still not going, but should I try with the car in this weather? What d'you think?'

'They were gritting Bautzener Strasse yesterday, it should be fairly clear by now.'

'But the stuff is so corrosive, it'll absolutely ruin the bodywork.'

Stahl went to the refrigerator, took out bread and butter, started to butter a few slices. 'Sylvia will be really tired. And hungry. After Berlin there was nothing to eat in the buffet.'

'Give both of them my best wishes.'

After his morning wash Meno went to his living room to look through the papers for the Old Man of the Mountain again. Christian had lost his place markers in the Schelling books but hadn't mentioned it, presumably confident that he, Meno, immersed in thought, self-absorbed and dreamy, as he probably appeared to most people, wouldn't notice. Oh but he did! His father had encouraged him to observe things precisely; he had often gone walking with him in the hills of 'Saxon Switzerland' and his father had always subjected botanical or zoological finds to detailed scrutiny; he hadn't been satisfied with a quick glance but tried to bring out the specific characteristics of any living thing, whether plant or animal, ordinary dandelion or rare lady's slipper, to familiarize Meno with it. Precise observation, quiet, devoted faithfulness to the large- and small-scale phenomena of nature, daily routine and yet tireless seeking, digging, the capacity for amazement. Meno thought of his university teachers – Falkenhausen: choleric, obsessive attention to detail, running round the institute in Jena, white coat fluttering out behind him, by day wearing a magician's blue bow tie with white spots, by night sleepless in his pyjamas and dressing gown; he had a room in the basement of the institute, where he lived surrounded by snakes, white mice and spiders, making coffee in Erlenmeyer flasks, frying eggs for supper in platinum crucibles which were iridescent with the remains of chemicals, setting off firecrackers, left over from New Year celebrations, to counter the oppressive silence of all the stuffed and prepared animals in the nocturnal corridors of the institute; Otto Haube in the Leipzig Institute, which had two massive stone bears by the entrance and labyrinthine staircases and laboratories where alchemists would have felt at home; Haube, who had escaped from the concentration camps in the Third Reich and wanted to develop a socialist zoology – before the beginning of the term, he sent all the students out into the fields round Leipzig to help in the fight against the Colorado beetle, which had been dropped there by the imperialist class enemy – but who could also, after hours of an inquisition-like viva, suddenly push his spectacles up onto his scholar's forehead with the duelling scars and, faced with a fruit-fly that the candidate, as a last resort, had had to make out of modelling clay, quote Goethe: 'Nature and art, they seem to shun each other'. It wasn't easy with either of these teachers, they were merciless in their fight against imprecision, and Haube, the socialist zoologist, once even had an assistant transferred because he had twice, in a short space of time, recorded imprecise data, saying he had no sense of the dignity of his work, that was what he, Haube, had been forced to conclude from the results of these experiments, which had been carried out inadequately out of sheer laziness, whereas a scientist expressed his love in the strictest precision. Such assistants were no use either to him or to socialism.

Meno picked up the manuscript the Old Man of the Mountain had submitted to Dresdner Edition. There were going to be problems with the book, that was clear to Meno; that was clear to Josef Redlich, Meno's superior at Dresdner Edition; that was clear to the managing director of the firm, Heinz Schiffner, who read a few pages, raised his ice-grey bushy eyebrows and slowly lowered them, closed the book and shook his head sadly; and that was clear to the Old Man of the Mountain himself. A tale about a mine into which the 'hero' descended, enticed into the depths by the siren song of a silver bell. Problems less of an artistic than of an ideological nature; the old story Meno had become sick of hearing over the last few years. Editor's report, external report from an editor not employed by the publishing company with a recommendation for publication, Yes or No, together with the grounds for the decision, then the whole lot went to the censor and, if he was unsure, which had been happening more and more recently, the dossier went to the Minister for Books or even higher. A time-consuming process, injurious to one's self-respect. He wondered how the Old Man of the Mountain dealt with it, and whether one of the reasons that had prompted him to try Dresdner Edition was precisely these problems with the censors and the hope that he could avoid them in a branch of Hermes-Verlag that was outside Berlin. That would be a mistake, as he would have to make clear to the old man; after all, he had been in the business long enough not to harbour any illusions. Meno knew that it was a delicate mission he was about to undertake. Schiffner didn't like these conversations with his authors and would send his editor, Meno, in his stead. Meno felt that there was something dishonest, perhaps even obscene, in these conversations – he'd once mentioned this to Schiffner, but the only result had been an outburst of rage from his boss, which to him seemed to suggest a guilty conscience. You explained to the author which passages would, in all probability, be objected to and then left it to him to decide whether, and to what extent, he was prepared to accept censorship, that is self-censorship. Some called that fair dealing; but on top of the humiliation that the manuscript would not be printed as it had been written came the humiliation that the author had to mutilate it himself, bit by bit. That meant he was left without the opportunity to defend himself against certain criticisms – he had given the book the shape in which it had appeared himself. This was standard practice with all publishers, but it gave Meno palpitations, and he felt sorry for the authors, and not just because he was an author himself. It was taking away part of their dignity. Meno hated these conversations just as much as Schiffner did, but Schiffner was his boss. He hated them above all when the authors themselves – and this did happen – had no problem with the practice, when, on the contrary, they were grateful that the publisher was so cooperative and discussed desired changes of an ideological nature with them.

Meno thought of Lührer. With the most unconcerned expression, he would pick up the red pencil and cross out whole paragraphs of his text, which wasn't badly written at all, would change the interpretation of a character with two or three sharp cuts, would turn a pensioner non grata into an acceptable policeman, an undesirable allusion to our Polish brothers into a pat on the back for Bulgaria; he knew the most important people in the Ministry of Culture who were responsible for publishing, knew their characteristics, preferences and little foibles, and took them into account in his writing. What he didn't know was the 'state of the weather': the guidelines of the binding ideology that could change from week to week, sometimes from day to day. What was acceptable, what was no longer acceptable and, even more important, what would soon be acceptable. Lührer would rewrite his manuscript according to the way the managing director or Meno interpreted the prevailing mood; recently he had even gone over to working from the outset with variants that would fit in with the most common, the most likely developments, such as had been seen often enough since the sixties and seventies. Meno would sit there with this man, who once, long before the Bitterfeld writers' conference in 1959, had written some outstanding stories and been one of the most talented writers of the East, saying nothing and staring into space while Lührer talked about the compromises 'Schiller and his comrades' had had to accept to get their works performed and printed at all. Eventually they would drop the topic of literature and examine the entrails of various Party Conference resolutions, commentaries on them and circulars from the secretaries of the different levels of the Writers' Association. Perhaps it would be different with the Old Man of the Mountain, perhaps he would be confronted with a fit of rage and a plain refusal to distort his manuscript until it fitted in with some kind of ideological concept. Perhaps. Meno was looking forward to the meeting with a kind of sporting thrill of anticipation. He was acquainted with the Old Man of the Mountain as an author, in fact very well. But as far as this side of literary work was concerned, he didn't know him at all. In a somewhat excited and apprehensive state, Meno shut the briefcase in which he had put the papers and books and stood up. The clock was striking half past six as he left the house.

When the wind freshened, blowing the snow along in thick clouds, Meno had to hold on to his hat. The park was swathed in fine crystalline veils; icicles were hanging from the branches of the copper beech beside the House with a Thousand Eyes, the massive trunk looking as if it were made of black glass in the half-light. By the park, where Mondleite turned off, a pair of headlights were edging their way closer. Meno saw that they belonged to a dustcart that was approaching cautiously, slithering on the street, which was slippery under the layer of new snow; the men jumped down from the top and, swearing, trundled the dustbins, so full the lids wouldn't close, to the lorry and stuck them in the clips, at which the bins were tipped up by the hydraulic mechanism and shaken several times to empty them. Meno turned onto Planetenweg. The street lamps were swinging and cast their metallic white light in swaying cones onto the roadway, on which gravel, grit, ash and frozen snow had been crushed to a grey pulp. Professor Teerwagen was at the wheel of his Wartburg, turning the key in the ignition – the engine kept making pained whirring noises but didn't start – while Frau Teerwagen was busily brushing the snow off the bonnet and scraping the ice off the windows. There was a light on in the garage of Dr Kühnast, a chemist in the pharmaceutical factory; the sound of a hairdryer could be heard, Kühnast was probably using it to defrost the windscreen of his Škoda. Teerwagen's Wartburg gave a howl, he was clearly revving up in order to try and knock some sense into the stubborn vehicle. The houses on either side were dark and silent. On Querleite, which connected Planetenweg with Turmstrasse and Wolfsleite, the characteristic winter-morning sounds could be heard: the scrape of wooden snow shovels on garden paths and pavement, the shovels being knocked to clear them at irregular intervals, the rasp of the clumps of snow that had fallen off being cleared away. Herr Unthan, the blind man who ran the communal baths in the house called Veronica, was carrying in coal. Meno turned up his coat collar and walked more quickly. It had become appreciably colder overnight; the thermometer in Libussa's conservatory had gone down to zero. He waggled his fingers in his pockets, the tips stinging in the frost despite his good leather gloves – Richard had received a 'quota' through a grateful patient and passed them on to friends and relatives.

Meno thought back to the birthday party. All the doctors and their wives, with their more or less self-confident bearing and loud voices, had disturbed him. Discussions in which the Hoffmanns, Rohdes and Tietzes were involved would quickly grow more and more heated, threatening to turn into pulse-raising declarations of principle . . . There was a strange ferocity at work there, an absolute sense of being right came through in those discussions, giving them a sharpness outsiders must find disconcerting, though sometimes, once they had a sense for it and could stand back, pretty funny as well . . . Meno smiled and gleefully kicked away a ball of snow. The way Richard and Niklas waved their arms about, making grand gestures and shouting, their faces red as beetroots: 'Gilels is a better pianist than Richter!' – 'No! Richter's better!' – 'No!! How can you say that?' Meno gave a quiet laugh: at that point the gesturing hand, as was only logical, would turn to the forehead and tap it, which usually led to a further entrenchment: 'Gilels! In-du-bit-ably! Just come over and listen to this, surely you can't seriously maintain . . .' – 'Well come on then! Now we'll see that your o-pin-ion is lack-ing all found-a-tion!! I tell you . . .' Niklas didn't get worked up about all this hot air and was astonishingly good at dealing with it; Richard . . .

But Meno, who had turned into Turmstrasse, didn't hear any more of what the opponents in his imaginary dialogue had to say. He started back in alarm – a silhouette appeared out of the driving snow and bounded towards him in furious leaps. It was a black dog the size of a calf, and it halted abruptly about three feet in front of him, slithered clumsily closer in flurries of snow Meno didn't dare brush off his coat, and started to howl. He clutched his briefcase and, in order to try and assess the moment a possible attack might come, stared the beast in the eyes, which had a green glitter and looked as big as saucers when they were struck by the light of a street lamp. He looked all round. A few windows lit up in the Anton Semionovich Makarenko teacher training college where Mondleite crossed Turmstrasse; a whistle sounded, broke in the icy-cold air and continued a fourth lower, a kind of 'heigh-ho'; the door of the college for cadet teachers opened and a bunch of sullen-looking students in brown army tracksuits with yellow and red stripes down the sleeves appeared and were ordered out into the street for their morning exercise by a man in a bobble hat. But he wasn't responsible for the whistle; the 'heigh-ho' fourth sounded once more but from a man in black with a fedora whom Meno recognized as Arbogast. 'Kastshey,' the Baron shouted in an indignant voice, the whistle still in his hand. In the other he was holding a stick with a silver gryphon handle clenched under his arm. 'Kastshey, heel.' The dog flattened its ears, blinked and ducked out of the way. 'Good morning.' The Baron raised his hat a few centimetres above his high, emaciated-looking skull and sketched a smile that was perhaps intended to be soothing or friendly but was oddly crooked, almost like a mask on his pale face. 'Heel,' he repeated in a strict voice. Kastshey whimpered when the Baron gave him a tap on the head. 'Was he a nuisance? He's still very young and inexperienced, and almost completely untrained. Do forgive the annoyance.' The Baron adjusted his steel spectacles. 'By the way . . . I've read your study . . .' He hesitated and his smile broadened. 'What do you call it? I presume it's not a novel? . . . of our friend Arachne. A very good piece of work, I like to see monographs like that . . .' He hesitated again, put the whistle in his pocket. 'I've long been fascinated by spiders. Would I be right in assuming this book is part of a more extensive work?' The dog was sitting up on its hind legs and following the conversation attentively, panting now and then with its pink tongue hanging out. 'Probably,' Meno replied, nonplussed and not with great presence of mind, as it seemed to him. To be asked in the street, by a person with whom he wasn't very well acquainted, about an article that had been published in an out-of-the-way scientific periodical, and a few months ago at that, seemed as strange as it was pleasing. Apart from the editorial committee, which had spent some time undecided as to whether it wasn't more suited to a literary magazine, no one seemed to have noticed its publication. 'Yes, probably,' he said reflectively, 'I've got some more material.' Arbogast nodded, looked up again at the sky, which seemed to consist entirely of falling shrouds of snow, dirty grey in the dawn light. 'We will invite you some time, I think. Do you know the Urania Society?'

Meno said yes.

'It will be at one of their meetings. We will contact you. Two Mondleite, isn't it?' Again the smile appeared and again Meno had the impression it was a foreign body hanging on Arbogast's waxen features. 'Or do you have a telephone?'

'Only one that is used by all the tenants.'

'Then we'll write. We have nothing free for the rest of this year or next January, if I have remembered aright. But there should be some-thing in February and certainly in March.' Arbogast waved his stick up and down and clicked his tongue at Kastshey, who shook himself vigorously, sending out a whirling spray of white that plastered Arbogast's face and spectacles with patches of snow. Then Kastshey dashed off. The Baron waved his stick angrily at his departing rear and left Meno without saying goodbye.

Our friend Arachne? An odd choice of words, and Meno, who was walking on, confused but also pleased by the meeting, would have spent a long time thinking it over had a squad of soldiers not appeared out of the snowstorm when he was level with Arbogast's observatory. A corporal with a thick Saxon accent was in charge. 'Right wheel! – March!' The squad turned off the street onto the path that led to the bridge, followed by the bored and arrogant look of a first lieutenant. A few cars, which Meno only noticed now, were held up behind the soldiers. The soft snow absorbed the echoes of the noises, the voice of the corporal and the tread of the boots seemed to be packed in cotton wool.

'Detachment – halt!' the first lieutenant ordered. 'Get the men to repeat the manoeuvre, Comrade Corporal. That wasn't a precise right wheel. That was as slack as an old tart's tits.'

More cars joined the queue, pedestrians too who had come out of Sibyllenleite and Fichtenleite and were on their way to work. They waited in silence as the squad performed an about-turn, stamping across the whole width of Turmstrasse as they did so. Meno watched them. Some of them waited with their chins jutting out aggressively, watch-ing the soldiers' manoeuvre out of eyes screwed up into narrow slits. Most, however, stood there with heads bowed, hands buried in their coat pockets, making patterns in the snow with the toes of their shoes. The driver of the car at the front of the queue looked at his watch irritatedly several times, drummed with his fingers on the steering wheel. One of the cars behind sounded its horn impatiently. The lieutenant broke off the manoeuvre again and strolled, clapping his hands together behind his back, as if undecided what to do, towards the car whose horn had sounded. A brief exchange could be heard, imperious on the part of the lieutenant, abashed on that of the driver. The lieutenant returned, putting a notebook back into the inside pocket of his coat, nodded to the corporal, at which the squad continued the right wheel. When the soldiers set off down the path to the bridge, the traffic jam was released. Intimidated by the behaviour of the lieutenant, whom he would meet again at the control point at the end of the path, Meno checked the papers in his briefcase again: ID card, invitation from the old man, certified hectographic copy of the contract. He had a quick look around – anyone setting off along the path to the bridge was going to East Rome and there was very little that was regarded as more suspicious in the district than a visit 'over there', as they would say, their scorn expressed in the avoidance of its real name. People had no great opinion of that district, or of anything connected with it – in general people avoided Grauleite; it was on the corner of Fichtenleite and Turmstrasse and it was where the barracks for the guards stood – they were called 'the Greys' after the street name; there also, hidden behind some trees, was a concrete bunker with tall directional antennae on it. People said they oversaw all those who marched along Grauleite, they saw through all those who walked along Grauleite.

Three-metre-high walls ran along either side of the path to the bridge. After twenty metres there was a gate, the surrounds of which reached as high as the walls, and, beside it, a red-and-white-striped sentry box; the guard had shouldered his Kalashnikov as soon as Meno appeared and shouted, demanding to know what Meno wanted and to see his identity card. Then he pressed a bell push in the sentry box and the door opened.

'Who are you going to visit?' The lieutenant gave Meno, who was standing at the window of the checkpoint holding his hat, an appraising look and, with a casual gesture, took off his gloves.

'I have an appointment with Herr Georg Altberg, eight o'clock.' Altberg was the real name of the Old Man of the Mountain, but hardly anyone in the literary world in Dresden used it when they talked about him among themselves. Meno was surprised at how strange the name sounded, unfamiliar and oddly unsuitable. The lieutenant stretched out a hand for a binder that he was given by a corporal who was sitting at a telephone table below a board with light diodes. Rumour had it that the binder listed every one of the inhabitants of East Rome, with their name, address, function and photo, making them easy for the duty officer to identify, so that no unauthorized person could slip in. The lieutenant ran his finger down the page and showed something to the corporal, probably a telephone number, since the latter immediately drew one of the beige phones to him, dialled and handed the receiver to the lieutenant, who, after a short exchange, nodded and pushed Meno's identity card back out on the little turntable. 'That's in order, you may pass. Make out a permit for him Comrade Corporal. How long will your visit last?' the officer asked, turning to Meno.

'I can't say at the moment, it's a business meeting.'

'Take a one-third form,' the lieutenant ordered. The corporal took a form out of a pigeonhole that was full of neatly ordered papers, inserted it with a carbon and a sheet of paper in the typewriter and started to hack out the permit, letter by letter, on the machine beside the red telephone, which was on the far right, below the light-diode board. There were one-eighth, one-quarter, one-third, one-half and full permits; they were for fractions of twenty-four hours. As far as Meno knew, only residents had unlimited permits. He waited. The two-finger system of the corporal, a well-fed, sandy-haired lad with peasant's hands, did not seem very efficient. If he mistyped a letter the whole process would begin again, and he would be given another chance to watch the typist's tongue gradually make his cheek bulge and the lieutenant twitch slightly every time the corporal hit a key. The officer was standing there quietly, sipping coffee out of a plastic mug, and observing Meno. The corporal then began to fiddle with the light-diode board. Behind him were a shelf with keys, a sealed cabinet, a portrait of Brezhnev with a black ribbon across the upper left corner. On the table beside the lieutenant was *Snow Crystal*, a volume of short stories by Georg Altberg.

'Signature, one-third permit, eight-hour stay.' The corporal rotated the form and a ballpoint pen through the window. 'In the box under "Permit-holder".' Meno put his hat back on, picked up the pen but was so agitated that his signature came out as a scrawl. He folded the carbon copy and put it in his briefcase with his identity card. The barrier beyond the checkpoint was raised.

At the other end of the bridge a few soldiers were engaged in shovelling snow and knocking off ice. Meno pulled his hat down tighter and kept his coat collar up by fastening the button to the loop on the lapel; there was a bitter, raw wind, constantly blowing snow over the studded cast-iron plates on which he was walking, playing with the bare bulbs that hung down from the wires between the railings, which were well over six-foot high, plucking at the steel hawsers that secured the arch between the slopes as if they were harp strings, and producing a dark, singing sound, now and then shot through with a violent crack, as when ice breaks.

The milky early light over the point where the valley opened out in the direction of Körnerplatz and the Elbe had risen as far as the flanks of East Rome, casting a reddish glow over the ridge, which was saw-toothed with the tips of spruce trees; the citadel of the suspension railway towered up from it like an ancient triumphal arch. The light also revealed the funicular, where the cars were just going through the manoeuvre at the loop half-way up, the queue of cars on Grundstrasse below, Vogelstrom's house, gardens covered with snow and the black blobs of the wood-stacks. Dirty grey smoke came from the chimneys on most roofs; torn away by the wind, the fumes drifted through the air like scraps of dishcloth. Now and then the fog would open up and Meno could see the queue of cars creeping slowly towards Körnerplatz, a 61 bus wheezing as it struggled up the road, could make out the ice brush bristling with jagged prongs into which the White Nun over the wheel of the disused copper mill had frozen. Was anyone watching him from below? Recognizing him from his hat or his build? The railings were high and the bridge itself was over sixty feet above the ground, so it seemed unlikely. However, he still started to walk faster. The soldiers stood to attention and saluted as he passed. That alarmed him. Did he look like someone from East Rome, like an influential functionary with his briefcase, hat and coat? Had they recognized him? It wasn't the first time he had been there, though his last visit had been almost two years ago – when he and Hanna had got divorced. If the soldiers had been recruits then and had been called up again as reservists, they might remember him. Or did they salute everyone who came across the bridge – just in case and out of fear of the vanity of some important or self-important man? Reflecting on this, Meno passed through the second checkpoint. A captain waved him through without asking to see his identity card. Perhaps the lieutenant had informed him and the captain, knowing him to be reliably alert, had decided he didn't need to bother with a second check. Still, Meno was surprised. This laxity was something new. Even when he'd gone out with Hanna and they'd come back over the bridge, they had had to submit to two checks, and neither of the two officers had ever been put off by Hanna's maiden name, under which she appeared in the binder and was careful to state. At that time the bridge had been the sole access to East Rome – the suspension railway had been out of use for months because of a structural defect – and it was only when Barsano himself, First Secretary of the local Party organization, had been double-checked every time he went across the bridge that the repairs to the suspension railway were carried out at undreamt-of speed.

Meno was on Oberer Plan. The railway clock over the checkpoint clicked onto a quarter to eight. It wasn't far to Oktoberweg, where the Old Man of the Mountain lived. The snowflakes were falling less thickly; the wind had eased off; the flags on the poles to the right of the checkpoint flapped sluggishly: the red flag with the hammer and sickle, the black-red-and-gold flag with the hammer and compasses in a wreath of grain, a white one with stylized portraits of Marx, Engels and Lenin. Guards were standing by the flagpoles, staring straight ahead, presenting their Kalashnikovs; the expression on their faces was impassive and yet, as he knew, they were watching his every move. He could feel the captain's eyes behind the reflective glass of the window that looked out onto the square. He turned right, into Nadezhda-Krupskaja-Strasse, sticking close to the railings beyond which Oberer Plan fell away steeply, allowing a view of the lower parts of East Rome. Coal Island was wreathed in haze; a railway line ran along beside Majakowskiweg and its House of Culture; a squad of soldiers was busy shovelling snow off the track; clouds of steam were already coming out of the tunnel at the bottom of Majakowskiweg; in a few moments the narrow-gauge train would emerge from the cavity, give two brief whistles, presumably for the switchman at the little thermal power station on German-Titow-Weg, cross the valley in a curve and disappear into the other tunnel, which was not visible from Meno's viewpoint. The driver was leaning out of the window; he straightened his railwayman's cap and pulled his head back in as he passed the soldiers, who were now standing beside the track, smoking and leaning on their shovels. A man was squatting down on the tender, his face smeared with ashes and wearing a fur chapka with the earmuffs tied under his chin; smiling, his teeth gleaming, his hands in shapeless mittens that made them look like bears' paws, he waved up to Meno. He felt uncomfortable about it and glanced at the soldiers, who had noticed the gesture and were now staring up at him as well; he stepped back a little, not only to get away from observation but also because at that moment the engine was right underneath him, and he would otherwise have been standing in the thick cloud of steam full of particles of soot from the smokestack. So it was still the same: the 'Black Mathilda', as the train was called, supplied the power station and the households of East Rome with coal – a separate line that came from Coal Island for that district alone, from a mine that had officially been closed down but was secretly still in operation, as Hanna's father had once told him. It was the same driver as well; he'd recognized his walrus moustache.

Nadezhda-Krupskaja-Strasse wound its way gently up to the top of the steep ridge. Yew hedges, trimmed into vertical walls, screened a row of two-storey detached houses, all with the same light-grey roughcast, each with a garage and, on the garden fence, a letter box in the form of a cuckoo clock decorated with sprigs of fir and little 'year's-end-winged-figures' – as they supposedly said up here instead of 'angels', Meno recalled with a snort of laughter. Beside the neatly cleared and gritted garden paths each property had a Douglas fir, and each tree had one bird feeder and one fat-ball hanging from it; peering out of the snow round the trunk were garden gnomes, the three versions with pipe, with wheelbarrow and with spade – that gnome was balancing on the spade with both feet and a roguish smile on its face. There were two flags over the front door of each house: on the right the flag of the GDR, on the left that of the Great Socialist October Revolution. This had not changed either, was familiar to him from his time with Hanna. It was something else that was new. He stopped for a moment and listened. Muted, many-voiced barking could be heard, turning after a few seconds into loud howls. He had noticed the noise earlier, as he was watching the soldiers from Oberer Plan; the arrival of the narrow-gauge train had drowned it out. It sounded like the barking of young dogs, but he couldn't be sure. When he reached the top of the ridge, he had a view of almost the whole of the district: the House of Culture with, in front of it, the massive sculpture of *Upright*

Fighters for Socialism brandishing their granite fists in the morning light; the avenue, paved with sandstone flags and lined with traffic cones, leading from the House of Culture to Engelsweg, a dead end with chestnut trees in which there was an HO supermarket, a chemist's, a florist's and an electrical store – for the East Rome housewives to do their shopping – and a men's and a ladies' hairdresser. The two chimneys on Gagarinweg belonged to the Friedrich Wolf Hospital and the Ivan V. Michurin restaurant complex, both of which were for the exclusive use of East Rome. Rising up from the wooded range of hills on the other side of the valley were the box-shaped storeys of Block A, a restricted area within the restricted area of East Rome; there, in the spacious bunkers protected by a company of guards, were the apartments of the top nomenklatura. The barking came from a kind of sports field below Block A, something he had not seen before. What, at his first, cursory glance, he could have taken for a teeming mass of black leeches turned out, when he had gone a little farther to a place where he had a better view, to be a cluster of black dogs, which, from that distance, looked no bigger than puppies. But the men beside them, wrapped up in protective clothing, armed with truncheons and blowing commands on referee's whistles, were no bigger than children – it was just the perspective that made everything look smaller; the dogs' hindquarters came up to the men's hips. He would have liked to have had a pair of binoculars. But it was unthinkable to stand up here looking round East Rome with binoculars. In no time at all a squad in uniform would have appeared beside him, or a car would have detached itself from the shadow under one of the trees; he would have been asked what he was doing there, would have been invited to a shorter or longer interrogation in Block B, which, like the thermal power station, could not be seen from that viewpoint. The binoculars would have been confiscated; the two duty officers would have been reprimanded for not having noticed such a hostile, negative piece of equipment and impounded it. Laxity had appeared there too. He was surprised that they had not demanded to inspect his briefcase at either checkpoint. Was that no longer necessary? Had they developed technology that made such crude methods unnecessary? Meno went on. Even without binoculars he was still being observed – he had spent too long staring at the dog-training field, a suspicious individual with a hat, coat collar turned up and a briefcase; it was uncertain whether the powers-that-be would react to his little bit of spying, but he certainly had no desire for closer acquaintance with Block B, nor for encounters with unknown men at work or at home. As he made his way to the Old Man of the Mountain, he took with him in his memory the runs that radiated out from the training field in all directions, the barbed-wire fences round it and the kennels underneath, the wooden puppets with arms spread wide into which the dogs – they seemed to be of the same breed as Kastshey – leaping up, sank their teeth, the climbing walls with the window slits that had been cut out of the scratched and splintered wood six feet above the ground. The dogs could reach them easily.

On the dot of eight he was at the garden gate of 8 Oktoberweg and rang the cracked bell that was held on with sticking plaster.

8

Picture postcards

The nights, Christian felt, were far too short. He had just hit the stop button on his alarm clock to switch off its rattle, that burst of machine-gun fire in the world of a beautiful dream; but then there was the cold of the room in the grey half-light of dawn, the sound of Falk Truschler's unmoved snoring in the lower bunk across from him – when would he learn to be on time? Never, Frau Stesny, the manager of the hostel, had said – the bed, table, a few chairs appeared, Arturo Benedetti Michelangeli's ecstatic face on the black-and-white calendar that the girls and the boarders from the twelfth year in the room next door envied him for. From the other side! Jens Ansorge had assumed a crooked grin and waved his index finger. Schnürchel won't like that at all. And indeed, during his round of the rooms Schnürchel, the Russian teacher, had demanded the calendar be removed. Christian left it there and only took it down on Saturdays, before Schnürchel came sneaking along to stick his face, chafed raw from his razor, into matters that, unfortunately, did concern him. It was Verena above all who was interested in the calendar and even more in the musicians whose pictures were on it. Verena the unapproachable, the mocker, the beauty. Christian had dreamt of her. Perhaps it was her hair, its colour the brown of instruments, that was what he had first noticed about her in the summer work-week that the future pupils at the Maxim Gorki Senior High School had had to complete; perhaps her eyes, darkly shining like the cherries on the gnarled tree in the garden of his clock-grandfather in Glashütte when they were overripe and their skins would burst open in the next shower of rain. It was probably a movement, however; she had dried her hair in the school library, where half of the boys were housed during the work camp; that afternoon he had been there by himself, lying on his camp bed; she had come in and asked if she might use the socket, the one over in the girls' accommodation wasn't working; and then, through the whine of the dryer, she'd wanted to know why he was lying there in the murky room, shutting himself off from all the things the others were doing. He lowered the book he was pretending to read, it was Goethe's *Elective Affinities* and he found it deadly boring but it was far above the stuff the others read – if they read at all – and left no doubts as to its quality. She stared at him; he stared back, confused by her finely drawn, dark-red lips that were swelling into a provocative pout under his gaze, by the index finger with which she scratched her neck, by the fingernail blackened by a hammer blow that missed its target. The girls had been in the schoolyard repairing the desks, while the voice of Tamara Danz of the Silly rock group was bellowing out from the radio that Herr Stabenow, the boyish physics teacher, had set up by the flagpoles; suddenly the cry of pain and all the boys, apart from himself and Siegbert Füger, dashed over to Verena, who was sobbing. 'Too dumb even to knock in a nail, these women,' Siegbert had said, wrinkling his nose. 'And look at them all running. And her, she's going to make some man's life a misery, I can tell you. Much too pretty. And sure to be as conceited as they come. My mother always says: "You can't build a house with jewels, my lad." And my mother knows what's what.'

Christian peered down at Falk again. He was still snoring, though now he'd pulled his pillow over his ears.

He'd been struck by her at the very first meeting of the future pupils of the senior high school. The pupils had come with their parents. The Dacia with the Waldbrunn numberplate had parked beside the Lada from Dresden; Richard had noticed the first-aid kit on the rear shelf and the doctor's special parking badge on the dashboard of the Dacia and immediately started a chat with his colleague: 'Hoffmann.' – 'Winkler.' – 'Pleased to meet you.' – 'The pleasure's all mine.' – 'Blahblah.' – 'Blahblahblah.' Verena had waited, scrutinized the Dresden numberplate, the paved corner with the flagpoles and bust of Maxim Gorki, then cast Christian a quick glance so that Robert, with a grin, whispered, 'Just look at that peach, man', in his ear. The multipurpose room in the basement had been set up for the meeting. There was a piano, a Marx–Engels–Lenin poster in front of a lectern draped in red cloth, a table behind it, at which a few teachers were talking to each other, ignoring the chatter of voices. Most of the pupils knew each other already. Christian felt as if they were all looking him over, for he seemed to be the only one no one knew. When he came in there was just one seat left, by the entrance; sitting there was like being on show, which didn't seem to bother Robert in the least, he just brazenly chewed his chewing gum and cast his eyes over the girls. Christian, on the other hand, was embarrassed; his acne had to choose that day of all days to blossom like a willow in spring. Verena's family had sat in the back row, under the high tilt windows, so that Christian could observe Verena. She greeted some of the others in a friendly but, as it seemed to him, distant manner. The babble of voices gradually subsided. Furtive glances. Christian lowered his head and didn't dare look at anything apart from his fingernails, his new watch or Baumann, the white-haired maths teacher who, from the lectern far away at the front, was giving an introduction to socialist education for young people; as he spoke, his apple-cheeked face seemed strangely roguish – as if he himself didn't believe everything he was saying. But Christian sensed that one should trust that friendly appearance less than the flash of his clear and sharp rimless spectacles . . . Christian suspected he would never be in the good books of that archetypal schoolteacher with the flashing spectacles. His ability at maths was too awful. The dark-haired girl by the windows at the back, he thought, would definitely be good at maths, she would definitely be good at everything in school. A swot, no question.

'So why do you shut yourself off from everything?' the swot had asked on that afternoon during the summer work camp, in the school library, the hair dryer in her hand; only she and he in the room. 'I suppose everything we poor benighted village kids do is too boring or too ordinary for a boy from the big city of Dresden?' He wanted to make a quick-witted reply, but nothing occurred to him and that made him even more furious when immediately afterwards Verena, without waiting for an answer, shrugged her shoulders and went out.

A boy from the big city. How they'd secretly – and sometimes less secretly – mocked him, made remarks about his strange habits. He didn't go for a shower with the others but always arranged things so that he was by himself; nothing in the world would have persuaded him to display his puberty-stricken skin to others; he didn't go with them to the swimming pool in Freital and he preferred to pursue his own thoughts or dreams rather than seek out the company of the other boys. He only sensed something like understanding from Jens Ansorge and Siegbert Füger; at least they left him in peace. He had been pleased when he learnt he was to share a room in the boarders' house with them. Even though he didn't go with them when they went into the town, he did also look round Waldbrunn, by himself and in the evening, when he could be reasonably sure he wouldn't meet the other pupils. Waldbrunn, the administrative centre of the eastern Erzgebirge; the F170 motorway wound its way above the school, descended into the river valley of the Rote Bergfrau, cut through the central district as it headed for the ridge of the Erzgebirge and the Czech border, which it reached just after Zinnwald. Simple, low houses, church and castle, each with a tower; in the distance, when you came by bus from Dresden, drove over Windhaushügel and down into Waldbrunn and the new housing appeared on the right, you could see the gleam of the Kaltwasser, the reservoir that dammed the second Waldbrunn river, the Wilde Bergfrau. To the left of the motorway was a potato field, during the work camp they'd picked potatoes, they got ten pfennigs a basket, hard work, they were picking the potatoes on piecework, their backs ached from all the bending and he, the boy from the big city, had been one of the worst, even a lot of the girls had managed more baskets than he did. In the evening of the two potato-picking days, he had crept into his camp bed completely exhausted; he'd had to put up with a few teasing, sarcastic, even contemptuous remarks. From the beginning he felt there was a gap between himself and the other pupils of that senior high school.

He had a collection of postcards that he would often look at in the evening, by the light of his reading lamp. They were sepia and coloured views of distant places with exotic-sounding names that stimulated his imagination: Smyrna, Nice. You could see the white horses of the Mediterranean as it broke on the Promenade des Anglais, a clay pot with an agave on the left, on the right edge the row of fashionable hotels along the Promenade lined with palm trees. 'Salerno, Piazza M° Luciani' on a photograph that at the edges merged into the yellowing white of the postcard; as if wiped away by the erasing fingers of time. However, the ones that led to the profoundest daydreams, farthest removed from reality, were a series of views of Constantinople that he had been allowed to select from duplicates in Herr Malthakus's stamp and picture postcard shop in Dresden. A leaden blue sea: 'Vue de l'Amirauté sur la Corne d'Or'; 'Vue de Beycos, côte d'Asie (Bosphore)'; 'Salut de Constantinople'; 'Le Selamlik. Revue militaire' with a crowd of black, cube-shaped carriages dotted with the red fezzes of the crowd. Those were the places where one ought to be, to live. When he looked at the cards Christian dreamt, dreamt of adventures, of conversations between pirates overheard in harbour taverns that would enable him to save beautiful women who had been abducted. Constantinople. Salerno. The Bosphorus. And 'la Corne d'Or' was the Golden Horn. That was where heroes lived, that was where adventure was. And what did he have? Waldbrunn. He would walk round the little town but with the best will in the world he couldn't find any sailing ships such as there were on the pictures of Constantinople, the fairy-tale city. No muezzin called from the dark, bastion-like church on the market square and Herr Luther, in blackened sandstone on which the pigeons perched and left white theses, proclaimed, 'A safe stronghold our God is still' in chiselled letters. None of the women queuing at the butcher's or the baker's on the market square were anything like Princess Fatima, who, in gratitude for her rescue from the hands of the negro Zurga, would marry the adventurer Almansor – that was Christian's alias in the Orient. But to get married: Christian, standing on the bridge over the Wilde Bergfrau as it foamed over smooth round stones the size of footballs, shook his head. He would never get married, never, never, as long as he lived. An adventurer had adventures, a hero was solitary; with Fatima he had an affair that, as in the films he saw at the cinema, ended in the sunset, wild, painful and sadly beautiful. He looked across at the tannery: in the past the Wilde Bergfrau had powered it with its steely clear water; now it housed a museum. In the autumn he had enjoyed following the course of the Wilde Bergfrau, had thrown red maple leaves into it and, head bowed and hands clasped behind his back, watched them bobbing up and down; had Verena seen him like that, a glint of mockery at his poses would have crept into her eyes again. It seems that in the big city people mature earlier, she would have cried, as she had on the afternoon when their unit had gone to the cinema at the end of the street that ran along the bank of the Wilde Bergfrau, beyond the castle that now housed the local Party headquarters. Her eyes had flashed and she had rolled her hair round her index finger, and he, in his fury, had thought: You don't understand, you silly Waldbrunn goose; I've just come from Constantinople and not from your east Erzgebirge dump with its paved marketplace and ten hunchback houses round it; it's the flutter of Sinbad's sails I can hear, not that of the wings of the few provincial Trabbis puttering past us. If you only knew that Sinbads don't drive Trabbis.

9

Everyday life with Asclepius.
The sorrow of a houseman

'Knife.'

The operating-theatre nurse handed Wernstein the scalpel.

'Adjust light, please.'

Richard was enjoying himself: he had handed this operation over to Wernstein and taken the role of assistant himself and now he was actually treating him as a junior physician. If you're going to do something, you might as well do it properly. He reached up and focused the light of the lamp on the operating area that was framed in green cloths. 'There you are, sir.'

Wernstein cut open the fascia. He didn't respond to the joke; his tension was evident as he tried to widen the cut with his finger. The houseman, Herr Grefe, who was standing at the other side of the operating table holding the retractors, grinned behind his mask; the movement of his mouth that stretched the material of his mask and the wrinkles at the corners of his eyes indicated it.

'I bet you anything you won't manage the fascia with just your finger.'

'We'll see.' Wernstein took a deep breath, asked the anaesthetist to add the antibiotic drop by drop.

'Which fascia are we actually talking about here?'

Grefe, whom Richard had asked, started. 'Fascia . . . er . . . the fascia . . .'

'Lata,' Wernstein said after a while. 'The fascia lata. But that's not the entire truth. What I'm trying to force apart here with my fingers but am never going to manage to open like a can of beans is . . . the tractus iliotibialis. Where did you do your preliminary study?'

'In Leipzig.'

'There's a motto over the entrance to the anatomical lecture theatre there.'

You had to know that if you were working under Dr Hoffmann. The anaesthetist, who was just looking over the edge of the guard cloth, smirked.

'Anatomia – clavis et clavus medicinae.'

'The key and the rudder of medicine,' Nurse Elfriede, who handed the operator the instruments, translated in a dry voice. 'Young man, for the last fifteen years all Leipzig students have been asked that question in this operating theatre.'

'Are you suggesting I'm starting to bore you?'

Nurse Elfriede rolled her eyes. 'I'll give Dr Wernstein the scissors rather than answer that. You know that you're our guiding light, Dr Hoffmann.'

Muttering, Wernstein got down to work and started to cut open the fibrous tissue. – How difficult he finds it to admit I was right. Now he's sawing away at it after all. But, dammit, I was just the same. Smiling to himself, Richard staunched the flow of blood. At the same time he was irritated by the houseman. These young people, they came to an operation and had no idea! If we'd dared do that in the old days . . . He thought of a few of the surgeons under whom he'd developed his technique, eruptive characters inclined to outbursts of rage if things didn't go precisely the way they expected; most of them came from the operating bunkers and field hospitals of the war, from the mills of unimaginable carnage. With Grosse the assistants had to prepare everything; once they'd finished he would make his way, godlike, eyes half closed, unapproachable, as if in a trance, gently waving his hands still moist from disinfection, to the operating table, have someone help him into his gown and gloves before silently holding out his hand for the scalpel that the operating-theatre nurse placed in it with due reverence. Woe to any assistant who was unable to answer one of the questions he would suddenly fire off into the silence. The boss wouldn't look at him again, his career with him was over.

'Thread.' Richard tied off a bleeding vessel. With decisively made cuts Wernstein deepened the incision, felt for the fracture. His every movement, the elegance and assurance with which he handled the instruments, his finely gauged sense of when it was necessary to proceed with caution and when he could work more purposefully, his feeling for the hidden dangers of an operation, for all the deviations from operational and anatomical theory when, suddenly reduced to a blind man in a pitch-dark tunnel, you had to rely on instinct alone – all that spoke of the talent, intuition and outstanding technical ability of a born surgeon. Richard had always been surprised at how varied things could be in his profession. As a student he had assumed there was no difference between one doctor and another, more specifically between one surgeon and another. Everything was done according to the textbooks and surgery seemed to be something like ticking off boxes in a catalogue: every patient was a human being and what the human being the surgeon was interested in was could be seen in the meticulous drawings in Spalteholz's and Waldeyer's handbooks of anatomy. That's where the problem lies, these are the anatomical conditions, off we go. Practice had taught him otherwise. There were surgeons who worked incredibly slowly, who were afraid of every vessel, every little mucous membrane and, as they operated, transmitted this sense of fear to all those around them and who yet, for all their caution, had no better, sometimes even worse results than their apparently more casual colleagues. Richard remembered Albertsheim, his fellow assistant with Uebermuth in Leipzig. Albertsheim, whom they called Guarneri, for when he had a good day his intuition and his speed combined with perfect technique were as astonishing as a Guarneri violin. At such times Albertsheim would reach heights that Richard never reached, and presumably never would reach, and that had drawn cries of admiration even from Uebermuth. If he had a bad day, however, he operated 'like a drayman' and it was said that on his bad days Guarneri had also made 'drayman's violins', which had led to the nickname, which didn't even annoy Albertsheim – on the contrary, he cultivated his artist's pose. On the other hand he had never managed to develop even an average feel for diagnosis, he could hardly distinguish crepitations in the lung from a pleural effusion, the slightly metallic rasp over a tubercular cavity from the wheeze of an asthmatic lung. But those were clinical skills, they were the business of the Internal Medicine specialist, of whom he would speak, like many a surgeon, with mild condescension – as if clinical knowledge were superfluous for a surgeon. Nor was he interested in further developments. 'Great surgeons make great incisions,' Albertsheim had said, mocking Richard, who had his doubts about this absolute principle of these surgical monarchs, since he had found that great incisions can also cause great infections. Wernstein was not like that. What was it Albert Fromme, the first rector of the Medical Academy, had said? A surgeon has the heart of a lion and the hands of a woman. And now the houseman was moving the retractors of his own accord. Wernstein and Richard looked up simultaneously.

'It's the operating surgeon who moves the retractors, not you,' Wernstein growled indignantly. 'Now I can't see anything. You must tell us if you can't hold them any longer.'

Richard felt angry. The young man was far away from them in age and training, and certainly they ought to remain matter-of-fact, treat him like a colleague, but . . . The truth was, he couldn't stand this houseman. He knew that that was connected with the fact that Grefe was the son of Müller's sister and the Professor had, in an embarrassingly formal conversation, 'asked' Richard to send a houseman who had already been given the post to another clinic. True, Grefe could do nothing about these machinations, probably didn't even know about them; one had to try to remain objective. And the lack of specialist knowledge would sort itself out. If he was honest, as a houseman he himself had paid more attention to the nurses than to surgery; moreover the idea of housemen was for them to acquire practical experience. Despite that, the pedagogue inside him broke through: 'What characterizes pertrochanteric fractures?' Again Grefe started to hum and haw. 'I . . . er . . . I've only been with you for two days . . .'

'But you did a degree in surgery; did you skip trauma surgery?'

'Should I get them to put a little music on, Dr Hoffmann?'

Nurse Elfriede was well acquainted with her senior traumatologist's angry outbursts. But he didn't feel like music. This fellow might perhaps tell his uncle that the trauma surgeons were listening to music during an operation again, which, for his uncle, was an expression of a casual attitude and the Professor had no time for 'bohemian' surgeons.

'That's for Herr Wernstein to decide, he's performing the operation. Let me have the retractors.' He took the retractors out of Grefe's hands and with a curt nod ordered him to come round to his side. 'Be careful you don't touch the image intensifier and make yourself unsterile. Let him feel it,' he said to Wernstein, using the familiar 'du' without thinking, as if he were an equal colleague. 'Can you feel the fracture?' Grefe poked about in the wound.

'The fracture line is between the greater and the lesser trochanter, almost directly on the neck of the femur. You do know where we're operating here?'

'Oh, yes, I've got it now. Basically at the hip joint, I thought?'

Wernstein had stepped back and was waiting, hands dripping with blood raised.

'Good. We'll change over again. In grown-ups at what angle are the femur and the neck of the femur to each other?'

Grefe, who was back on the other side and raised the retractors, gave the wrong angle.

'Fractures of the neck of the femur – how are they classified and why?'

His knowledge was sketchy.

'Five wrong answers to my questions, Herr Grefe. We have a rule here. For each wrong answer the person asked has to cut a hundred swabs or fold a hundred compresses. That's five hundred swabs for you. Report to the duty operating-theatre sister after we've finished.'

That hit home. Wernstein was continuing his preparations in silence. Richard's anger subsided as quickly as it had arisen. He sensed that he had reacted too harshly and that he was punishing Grefe for his uncle's methods. Now he felt sorry for the young guy. You're doing just the same as the communists! he told himself. That reminded him that in Grefe's file he had discovered a request to be accepted as a member of the Socialist Unity Party . . . So what, he decided. If something was to be made of them, you had to be hard on them. The plus side was that Sister Elfriede had 500 more swabs in her sterilization unit, swabs that the run-down socialist economy couldn't manage to manufacture. If he wants to join the Party that determines all our lives, he should get to know the kind of world that it has produced.

'Spherical cutter,' Wernstein demanded, reamed the bone. 'A Lezius nail on the handle grip. – Who was Lezius?' This time it was Wernstein who asked. But Grefe knew the answer and proudly gave a little lecture. There was no addition to his 500 swabs.

After the operation Richard went to the Academy Administration. He took the route through the hospital. Wernstein had taken just three-quarters of an hour to perform the operation on the patient, a woman of sixty who had slipped while cleaning the stairs and broken her femur as she fell. The atmosphere in the clinic was something that had been familiar to Richard since he had started to study medicine, when, after his apprenticeship as a fitter, he had got to know the work of the hospital from the bottom upwards, first of all as a nursing aux-iliary, then during the university vacations, as a student and a professor's assistant: the morning rounds had finished in the wards on the north side, nurses were rushing to and fro, doctors were bent over patients' notes or X-rays. 'Morning, Dr Hoffmann.' – 'Morning, Nurse Ger-trud.' – 'Morning, Dr Hoffmann.' – 'Morning, Nurse Renate.' Familiar faces, some he had known for twenty years; he knew the people behind their routine masks, knew about their major and minor worries that you didn't hear about during the day, in the hectic rush of the wards, but during night shifts when the city was asleep and the acute cases had been settled for the night. Nurse Renate, who, even after twenty-two years, still trembled like a schoolgirl when faced with the senior nurse and whose first husband had died in this ward, the surgical cancer ward. Richard sidestepped a mop that a nursing auxiliary was swinging across the PVC floor-covering in vigorous semicircles. The smell of disinfectant – Wofasept – how familiar it was; how it brought every-thing back: the nurses with their blood-pressure gauges and intravenous-drip stands, the clatter of scissors and glass syringes in kidney dishes which were just being put into the sterilizer in the ward he was passing. He went into the vestibule. Food carts clattered by the lifts, a haze of voices came from the swing doors of South I, Müller's powerful, precisely articulating voice: the consultant was doing his round of the private ward. Richard hurried out past the bust of Carl Thiersch. He had actually intended, before going over to Administra-tion, to look in at his own ward to check on things, but he would probably have run into the gaggle of doctors, and he wasn't in the mood for that, especially not for an encounter with Müller. Wernstein had done North II and Trautson, Richard's fellow senior doctor, North III, together with Dreyssiger, who had been on duty and would see the outpatients. He could rely on Wernstein and anyway, when he'd done the round of North II today everything had been in order. With Dreys-siger you had to be more careful; he was good as a scientist, and as a teacher the students liked him; but in general the senior nurse knew better than he what was going on in his ward, North III, as the young houseman Richard would have liked to have kept often did as well.

He left the clinic and set off for the old Academy section where the Administration building was. The air, fresh after the snow, did him good, he took deep breaths. He had an uneasy feeling about the meet-ing he was about to attend. The eternal struggles for dressings, swabs, drip-feed bottles, plaster. Trifles. On the one hand. On the other, Administration had asked him to hand in his Christmas lecture to be checked. He had deliberately not brought it with him. How had Wern-stein put it just now? We'll see. Although he was freezing, he didn't regret having taken this route and not the one through the subterranean tunnel system that appealed to his old sense of adventure and that he had known like the back of his hand since his days as a nursing auxil-iary, but he preferred not to breathe its air, which was stale with the smell of cigarettes and rats' urine, after an operation. A few electric carts were bumping along the Academy road; far ahead, by the porter at the kiosk beside the Augsburger Strasse entrance, which was flanked by frosted-glass cubes with the red cross, patients were queuing for newspapers. A few doctors were coming from Radiology, which was in sight of the massive block of the Surgical Clinic. Richard went across the park, past the Dermatology Clinic and the equipment store, where thermophores were being loaded. Taking cover behind a hedge, he did a few jump squats to warm up.

10

Veins of ore. The Old Man of the Mountain

'Dear Herr Rohde, I can't get our discussion out of my mind. I became agitated and you, or so it seemed to me, remained unimpressed in a way that disturbed me because I am familiar with it from situations that make me seem powerless and the person facing me fairly powerful. You had to reject my pieces, you said, and left it to me to read, between the lines and behind the reason that was clear to both of us, a different one, less edifying for the modicum of author's vanity that remains to me, for you did not state it expressly and, on the one hand, I don't know you well enough to see your restraint as other than reserve, on the other you are an author yourself; and an author who, as far as I am aware, works precisely, so you know how, at this sensitive stage – the book is finished but not yet out – one weighs every word. I would like to tell you again, this time in writing, what your ability to listen at our meeting instigated (I apologize that that turned it largely into a monologue); it is important to me that it should not remain in the

transient medium of the spoken word. A story that I, rather presump-
tuously, do not call my own for the sole reason that, with variations,
it applies to so many people of my age. – No. I must break off. Please
excuse me. I will not continue this letter . . . I'm so tired, I find all this
so exhausting . . . Yet I will still post this letter to you; I know that
sounds confused but, to be honest, I hope you will visit me again . . .
Do you really consider the book a failure?'

Meno lowered the letter. He thought. The Old Man of the Mountain
had not had a fit of anger, Meno hadn't noticed the agitation he mentioned or it had arisen after he'd left. On the contrary, the old man had
nodded and put on a dreamy smile which had given his face with the
high, Slav cheekbones a mischievous touch; the parchment-pale skin,
creased with many wrinkles, had even started to glow as if the old man
had not merely expected but had hoped for Meno's restraint. Yes, Meno
thought, it was as if he had hoped for Schiffner's shake of the head – like
an accolade, an honour. 'You . . . don't regret that a year's work has
been for nothing?'

'Well, Herr Rohde . . . no. Of course I suspected it might happen,
you know that, your words, so carefully chosen to break it to me gently, tell me that . . . And now you're wondering why I'm laughing?
Because once again I've noticed how much vanity there still is inside
me. How the rejection rankles, despite the tactfulness with which you
step delicately round it, how it gnaws at me and festers. Festers, yes,
that's the right word. It was three years' work, by the way, hard work;
I'm pretty exhausted. And then I have to laugh. Just laugh. At myself,
at my face, that's staring at you, at my head, that looks as if it's made
out of papier mâché, a real rag-and-bone ghost's head fit only for the
puppet-theatre, with fluffy bits of wool instead of hair – don't you
think?'

'Please, Herr Altberg, I'm . . .'

'Yes, yes, I know, you're sorry. Incidentally, so am I. I can imagine
how hard it must be to have to come and tell me . . . Who enjoys being

a bearer of bad tidings, eh? But I'm forgetting my duties as host. Would you like coffee or tea?'

'Now I am able to continue the letter. I don't want to send it as it is. I've had a temperature, I had to stay in bed when it was at its worst. Dr Fernau, my GP, will make a house call, but after that he won't come again if it's under forty degrees. Mere trifles, he says, up to that limit the body can help itself. I was tired and exhausted, had to think a lot. Now I've more or less recovered and I don't want to give up that soon. Your questions have brought so many things back to mind . . .

'Am I outside, with no one to watch over me? In a landscape of deep snow? For I dig my hands into the white and see myself sink to my knees trying to match my father, who lifts up the ball and carefully places it on top of the other one, giving the snow-woman a torso; with a large wooden comb she made herself, my sister has already traced the pleats in her skirt, now she's waiting for the third ball, mine, to fix straw hair into it, make the eyes with little lumps of coal, stick a carrot nose in and cover it with a battered pot that's usually in the shed and full of bulbs in the summer. The enamel has split off in several places, the patches look like black islands, which makes me say: Gundel, we'll sail to the South Sea in it. With no one to watch over us. No one to keep a watch on us. But Father's standing beside me, my face is still stinging from the smack he gave me, because it won't do that I, the son of the district pharmacist Hubert Altberg, do not have the strength to lift a measly little ball of snow up onto two others. His big red hand. On the back of his hand dry skin from freckles, tufts of sandy hair on his fingers, thick; Father's fist (just catch a sniff of that, one tap and you're done for, eh?) looks as if it's got fur on. Education with cats: he throws the kittens in the rainwater barrel behind the house – either they manage to scramble out of the water, which is so good for the flowers in the beds in the front garden, or they're sucked down into the depths, in which soft shadows play for minutes on end. The kitten that managed it is grasped by the scruff of the neck and held over the water again; Father looks seriously at the struggling paws, seems to be wondering whether my sister and I, who have to stay by the barrel, understand what he's telling us; finally he swings his arm out to the side (but not always; sometimes he throws the kitten back in and holds it under water with his thumb until the end), opens his fist over the ground and only then may we pick the cat up and rub it dry.'

Meno was impressed by Altberg's ability to transform his look. The thousands of wrinkles and creases seemed to be there for the sole purpose of producing every possible facial expression with the precision of a woodcut; the light in the spacious study, which cast imperious shadows, only served to intensify that impression. A piece of acting? That was not how it seemed to Meno; every emotion that appeared on the old man's face seemed to be genuinely there at that moment and every one was unmistakable. Essences of emotion: at those words he could see in his mind's eye the walnut pharmacy cabinets beside which the old man had walked up and down, the brown and white phials with their many-coloured contents, labels with rounded corners and ornate inscriptions in iron-gall ink, the precision balance on a shelf above the desk. The old man threw the manuscript into a drawer, muttering something in a tone of contempt rather than resignation that alarmed Meno. The housekeeper came, bringing coffee, hot milk and a basket with biscuits, reproachfully held out to Altberg a scarf that he wound round his neck with an expression of disgust, took a china mortar and pestle off a shelf, ground tablets. 'Your medicine, you haven't taken it again,' the housekeeper said in a voice weary of reminding him, of her fruitless struggle with the old man's obstinacy. He grimaced, waved her away, went over to the window, slurped the milk after having tipped the contents of the mortar into his cup.

'I'm not supposed to get up yet, that's why she was so short with you. My doctor has forbidden it. She's his ally and begrudges me the pleasure of having a visitor,' the old man croaked with a conspiratorial expression. 'But you can only believe half of what doctors say and if they write something down you should be extra suspicious.' He laughed quietly to himself. 'It was my father who said that, the owner of the Sertürn Pharmacy in Buchholz, a little town in the Riesengebirge. Unreadable prescriptions, outrageous potions! "Quacks with degrees the lot of them!" was his stock phrase. Of course, it was partly jealousy. Fernau sounded my lungs, tapped me on the chest and back: "You've got pneumonia, Altberg, you should be in bed, right? You're wheezing like an old alarm clock." And I said, "Yes, sir, Major Doctor, sir!"'

'A tactful man,' Meno remarked.

'He knows how to treat me, that's all. His gruff manner cheers me up. Moreover I imagine a gruff doctor can deal with illnesses better, but that's probably an old wives' tale, but I tell myself: he's not taking the illness seriously, so it can't be serious. Oh, look.' The old man pointed out of the window to a bird table standing alone on the steep downslope of the garden where the snow, perhaps from the power station, perhaps from Black Mathilda, had traces of soot here and there.

'Sparrows, inevitably,' said Meno. 'Hawfinches. A pair of gold-finches.'

'And there a crossbill, if I'm not mistaken!' Altberg was pleased. 'They've become rare. Next to the chaffinch, do you see? But let's sit down.'

'I will pick the smooth yarrow . . . And Grandmother's gestures, her wood-pulp voice: You shall have some soldiers, my lad, hussars in dolman and jerkin with mother-of-pearl buttons and braiding, drawn swords and horses from the Puszta, and during the night the wind will tell you stories of the rivers, of the Neisse in the country round Glatz as it winds its way through our Silesia, and it will tell you about a girl, my lad, who is waiting for you and whose picture you carry in your hussar's coat, and when the smoke comes from the great Silesian Railway her eyes will not be sad. The train, the fiery horse with smoking nostrils and blazing red hair behind the tender, will carry me off, on a winter's morning like that the air is soapy, the snow wheezes under your feet, a rickety zinc-white suit of armour and the knight inside it is breathing heavily, as if he were combing hessian when he takes a breath. Yarrow, yarrow . . . And sage and arnica – that the old women in the little town call mountain wolverley – meadow kerses and devil's spoons, horsetail for cleaning silver and the Aesculapian snake in the glass cylinder, Rübezahl, the spirit of the Sudeten Mountains, smiles down from an enamel advertising sign promising healing power from the Riesengebirge and when the doorbell has stopped ringing after the butcher's wife has left, there are no more customers in the shop and Father is stomping upstairs, puffing and panting, with the sausages that he's been given in exchange for Glauber's salt, an infusion of bittersweet, a specific to lower blood pressure and Altberg's Genuine Digestive Herb Mixture, patent pending in Breslau, the light in the room pauses, has to get used to the silence again, has to peek out of its hiding places in the medicine cabinets, phials, chemical ampoules, has to grow again, to unfold on the writing engraved in the frosted glass of the shop window before it starts to flirt with the wall mirror, with the brass banister going up to the living quarters, before it gets sleepy again and stretches out on the polished mahogany on which Father checks prescriptions and puts them together; then it starts to trickle out of the clouds on the ceiling on which a Silesian heaven, as Aunt Irmelin derisively puts it, has been painted. The driver grasps the cord of the steam whistle.'

'You despise me, don't you?' The old man raised his hands in a protective gesture when Meno made a movement. 'You won't admit it, of course. But when you're by yourself, what then? You'll take an image of me away from here, of Altberg's doleful countenance and his hundred pathetic paste pots, with the contents of which he sticks feathers on his paper birds, and of that there' – he pointed to a manuscript on the desk, a jumbled heap of interleaved sheets of paper and photos all stuck together; but the gesture could also have been directed at the sketches hanging beside the desk, tangled lines full of cryptic symbols, numbers and arrows in different colours. That must be the mountain project, Altberg's magnum opus. 'This thing,' he murmured, 'that I've been hacking away at for eight years and it still refuses to take shape. Ten days for one page, and every page has to be of the same glass on which even the hardest and most malevolent reader's eye cannot leave a scratch. But you . . . You'll go home and despise me, secretly, perhaps without even realizing yourself that you despise me . . . An old man who still believes in a just society – after the events you have read about in the manuscript your publishing house has rejected! A perfect fool, yes? As to your rejection – I know Schiffner. An honest man, a publisher of the old school and that means one who knows how to find a way; but he's also a bit self-important and timorous . . . Self-importance and fear, that, by the way, is the typical German mixture. Expressed in externalities: sentimentality and the barracks yard . . . they love songs and munitions do the Germans . . . Well, I'm a dead man, Rohde, I'm not fooling myself. But the thing that I've believed in is alive . . . What do they think of us over there?' the old man asked, abruptly and with an eager expression, leaving it to Meno to interpret 'over there' as the district to which the funicular railway went. 'Not very much,' Meno said after some hesitation. 'They don't like East Rome. Anyone who lives here is despised by those over there, without exception.'

'So I'm right.'

'I don't despise you.'

'But you will! Times change and we are asleep . . . Didn't the gnomes smile at you as you came up the street?'

'I too believe in the improvement of mankind, Herr Altberg . . .

That it is possible to build a society in which everyone can live a decent life.'

'But that is not this society, Herr Rohde!' the old man said in a voice that made Meno shudder.

'Rübezahl's helpers come steaming out of the engine's chimney, on the window ice-patterns form that my breath makes transparent, makes disappear so that I see the marketplace of Buchholz gradually float out of sight; on a hillside the train goes past the valley in which the town lies, the church tower with its weathercock and fire bell, the Hagreiter House of the Rebenzoll brothers, the richest merchants in the town, with its arched façade and half-timbered upper storey on which a fresco painter from Obersalzbrunn has painted hunting scenes; his father's pharmacy with its turret and the statue of Friedrich Sertürner holding a snake and a balance, then comes the bend and Buchholz is memory; the flood-sprite is booming, the ebb-sprite is looming, the sand-sprite entombing, I can hear Grandmother whisper as she soothingly strokes my fevered brow; the snow-sprite . . . The train stopped on the open line, a man in uniform got on the train, held up a lantern and ordered us out, one suitcase per boy, "Off the train, at the double, cases on the sleigh"; we were to follow him. Snow slipped off the branches of the spruce trees, hobgoblins were crouching in nests of shadow, pointing malicious fingers at us, the uniformed man strode on ahead of us at a speed we could hardly keep up with, on the left a gorge opened up, a menacing eye with lashes of bizarre branches; I was the last in the line, not daring to turn round, Woodwose would have given me a wolf's foul form, Banshee howl till I was lost in the storm; how I started as a heavy bird flew off with a clatter of wings. The Löschburg came in sight, the former robber baron's lair in the Eulengebirge, now a school and educational establishment for "useful future recruits for the state service", as it was called and where Father had decided I should go, Aunt Irmelin could sigh and Gundel weep as much as they liked: Georg has to be broken, it will be for his own good, one day he'll thank me for it and you'll see that I was right. He dreams too much, and anyone who dreams too much will end up as food for the crows. – A room in which a hundred pupils sleep. An iron bedstead, a bedside table, a locker, unlocked because, the principal tells us at roll-call: Anyone who steals from a comrade should be cast out of the community of the school and from the community of the German nation. Obedience, Order, Honesty, Loyalty are demanded by an inscription in the refectory, where at six in the morning we say prayers with our breath steaming in the cold before we eat nettle soup and a crust of bread. We, ten-year-old boys with cropped hair, had the honour of being selected, from among all those in Silesia, for the Löschburg, the brightest minds in the country, as Father said; I see his name scratched on my desk. Stand up when answering, thumbs on your trouser seams, sit down when required to, sleep to order, lists of Latin vocabulary, a smack with the cane on the palm of your hand for every word you forget. Motto: pain makes you remember. The boy in the bed and desk beside mine, he's called Georg like me, is bold enough to contradict the teacher; a month's detention in the castle with lessons to catch up on makes him hold his tongue and sends me, who also have to undergo the punishment, into despair, to the sick-bay, full of hatred, fear and introspection. I had done something, as the rector announced at punishment roll-call, that was worse than Georg's contradiction: I had supported him, I was loyal to the deviant, not to the school; I had not obeyed the undisputed authority of the teacher, expressed in the silver braid on his epaulettes, where we, the pupils, only had a cloth number. I get a month in the detention cell instead of being expelled because Father goes to see the principal and agrees with him that I need a firm hand. I avoid being expelled. I get a thrashing with a cane soaked in water and am allowed back in the dormitory where Arthur, my personal servant – whom I, like the other pupils with their servants, never address by anything other than by his first name – will once more empty my chamber pot and washbasin for me, who have returned to join the young elite of the future model German state, to join those whose resistance to the silver braid will consist in gaining it.'

'By the way, I've read your piece about spiders. Arbogast was good enough to make a hectograph copy for me. I assume he's invited you to one of our Urania meetings? He intended to do that, he said so in the accompanying letter.'

'I ran into him this morning and, indeed, he did invite me.'

'What do you think of him?' At this question the Old Man of the Mountain gave Meno a quick, cold glance.

'I don't know him and I don't think one should draw any half-baked psychological conclusions from the fact that he sets store by his "von", has a walking stick with a silver gryphon handle and an untrained dog. They're just labels.'

'And that, you think, is the same as the Spreewald pickled gherkins the label on the jar promises us, without the piece of paper telling us how they taste! A good answer. A cautious answer.' The Old Man of the Mountain laughed quietly. 'You don't trust me. You secretly despise me and react like a fox that has scented the hunter.'

'What you are insinuating is not the case, Herr Altberg,' Meno replied indignantly. 'Why should I despise you? What would make me do that? Please believe me.'

'I know that earlier on you said you consider a better society possible . . . the fair social order in which people can be happy. *Égalité, Fraternité* . . . the ideals of 1789, in other words the socialist kingdom of heaven. It comes from Paris, as we see. In Antiquity hope was an evil . . . *Égalité*, hmm. Soon it'll be the year of people who are more equal than all the rest.'

'You read Orwell?' Meno said with a faint smile. 'If you're trying to test me –'

'It would be a poor testing technique to quote the class enemy first of all in order to lure you out of your reserve; as it happens I've had a sniff of that as well. You have a sense of humour, Herr Rohde, I like that. Humour is an unmistakable sign . . .' Of what? Meno didn't ask when the old man broke off abruptly.

'1940, the official letter with swastika and stamp. Romanticism and bureaucracy, there's nothing worse, Herr Rohde. Conscription papers for those born in 1922, of which I am one. Report to the barracks; I was delighted to do it, I was an unconditional supporter of National Socialism, blond, blue-eyed and six foot tall, I had nothing to fear from it, I belonged to the race of the chosen ones, that was setting out to conquer the world . . . and would conquer the world, for me there was no doubt about that. And that was quite right for the others were inferior; it had been hammered into us that they did not share our beliefs, our values: decency, loyalty unto death, honour. I was part of it, a hussar a hussar thou shalt be with dolman and sabre and sword-knot, the villages will burn, but thou but thou, my little Guards officer . . .'

The old man walked up and down in front of Meno, giving him reflective, searching looks. He sat down at the desk and opened the manuscript. Then he started to talk, with many a 'well then' and 'act-u-al-ly' ('act-u-al-ly you should never say act-u-al-ly, no, not ever') and, something at which Meno was quietly amused, 'No, that ain't it, nope' with a nod whenever he was trying to remember a line from a 'book poem'. 'Wrong quotation . . . here I am trying to spice up my account and, to stick to the image, have picked out cardamom instead of salt again, you must forgive a man who lives like a monk as far as culinary matters are concerned.' As he spoke he twisted his mouth in a wide grin. His housekeeper brought a tray with a bottle of Nordhäuser schnapps, frosted with the cold. Meno said no thanks, Altberg filled both glasses with trembling hand.

*

'Let's go.'

'But you're an ill man, Herr Altberg.'

'Just a failure, Herr Rohde, just a failure.'

They got out at Neustadt Station, stood there in the station forecourt watching the pigeons and the trains. Perhaps Altberg was hoping the noises would accept him even if the ground wouldn't; he pressed the soles of his shoes into it, perhaps to trigger off recognition or at least a greeting in the putty-grey humps, cracked like elephant skin. Perhaps. Soldiers walked past, travellers with the weary, hostile memories they had of the uniforms and of those they seemed to mark: Meno sensed that in the eyes of these other people the uniform and those wearing it were not – perhaps: could not be – two different things. 'But how proudly the colours fade,' said Altberg; Altberg said, 'D'you know, Herr Rohde, I sometimes used to think that, in order to be less alien, I ought to find something even more alien, and that could only be a place where, from the memories of somewhere I'd travelled through in one of my daydreams, I'd often wished I could be. You will know it, but walk with me for a while.'

Meno took the letter about the *Old German Poems* from the shelf beside the ten-minute clock, put some more coal in the stove, read both letters once more before sitting down at his typewriter.

II

Moss-green flowers

– *The very fragility of the vestibule*, Meno wrote, *frightened me, we waited, even though the worn banister still seemed to be the same, the foot scraper, the grating with the steel slats that spring round, the sign above it Please wipe your feet; the damp patches on the walls, the high door shielded*

with dulled white lacquer. Suddenly you seemed changed to me. P. Diene-
mann, Succrs. I read but, while I was listening to you, I had nothing to say
to someone good enough to hide their own name behind a philosophy of life
going by the name of Succrs. White-haired, cigar-puffing Herr Leukroth
certainly did have a taste for it: a few photos over his daughter's desk showed
the antiquarian bookshop on König-Johann-Strasse before the air raid,
showed letters with Dienemann's letterhead that had gone round the world
under exotic postmarks and returned, showed a signed portrait of Gerhart
Hauptmann, the writer from Obersalzbrunn, that you kept on looking at.
Perhaps Leukroth would even have hung over the Local History section a
'Dresden Succrs.' sign, as you insisted on calling it, handwritten, of course,
in the iron-gall ink that was rusting through the index cards on which his
staff (just for his sake?) kept track of their stock. For the present, sir, I
thought I heard the voice of Herr Leukroth say, is nothing yet. And I saw
him shaking his head as he took the books of the old man in the beret, who
had gone in through the door marked No Entrance in front of me and now,
at the remarks of the old man chewing on his cigar as he roughly leafed
backwards and forwards through them, hunched his shoulders or, rather,
let them slump, like a collapsing soufflé, in resignation. What do you say,
young man? Herr Leukroth grouched to you, making a dog-ear in a page
that had been given a dismissive wave. – Right then. – So. You can take
'em home again, Dresden, Herr Leukroth declared, can manage without
your presence. At this the old man shook his head, muttered Ye gods and
turned to leave. One moment, Herr Leukroth, waist-high on a ladder,
gestured, tell me, do you really want to lug those all the way home? For
five marks you can leave them here with me, books to books, since you're
here already. And with trembling fingers (he had Parkinson's disease) he
took a coin from a jar of five-mark pieces with a strip of adhesive tape on
it on which Taxi Money was typed. Behind cotton curtains with a pattern
of moss-green flowers cans of food were sleeping, pyramids of floor polish
towered up, writing paper from the VEB Weissenborn paper factory was
turning yellow and slumbering away on one side were cardboard boxes full

of handmade, deckle-edge Königstein paper which Herr Leukroth printed owls on and sent, covered in his Parkinson's handwriting, with Christmas greetings to good customers; you showed me examples on which was written To be prepared is everything, Your antiquarian bookshop P. Dienemann Succrs. Herr Leukroth revealed to me one day that the assistant in the chiffon blouse with a paper rose on the collar (always a similar one, never the same), who wrings her hands with a careworn look, is in the habit of coming to the shop by taxi every morning and he is in the habit of leaving by taxi. The five-mark piece (the beret-hatted gentleman gladly clenched it in his fist) gave most of his clients the feeling they had got away with something again; it was a heavy, handsome coin, minted to celebrate the XXth birthday of the Republic and, like the twenty-pfennig piece, was not made of aluminium. You and I, Herr Altberg, were still in the vestibule, the matt-white lacquered door in front of me, beneath my feet the foot scraper that didn't have any steel slats, instead there was a coconut mat that was covered with a floorcloth in the damp season and steamed all day long when the bookshop was open. Please wipe your feet carefully. The carefully was carefully underlined. Fräulein Leukroth, the daughter of the current owner, would certainly be sitting at her desk in the corridor between the two rooms of the bookshop, writing, now and then dipping her steel nib into a little pot of iron-gall ink from VEB Barock and carefully wiping off the superfluous drops on the glass rim. I suspected she was in contact with important minds of the past, for the scratch of her pen on the paper, which was yellowing at the edges, and the ink would be bound to seem familiar to the souls of the dead, residing perhaps somewhere in the wide expanses of the void, more probably, however, here, in the steps between and inside the books, and have the power to call them up; it must be possible to get them to leave the heavens above Dresden and swirl back down into King Solomon's bottle, and then all that would be needed would be a cotton curtain, with a pattern of moss-green flowers (Fräulein Leukroth had a dress of the same material), over the light from the window for the soberly effective conjuration; in the twilight and the night, when the woodcut Book Fool in the corner of the adjacent room would come to life and, together with his employees, take over the bookshop, Fräulein Leukroth would, so I thought, have no choice but to disappear with the ghosts that had been conjured up. That was until one day when the assistant at the elderly cash register in the front room of the shop, opposite the No Entrance door, waved me over and, raising her eyes to the heavens, accidentally on purpose let me see a note from Fräulein Leukroth: It would be welcome, gratifying even, if you would be good enough to see to it that the porcelain flower gets one over the eight to drink. For some particular reason the water, with which, despite the request, she had nonetheless to be economical, had to be stale. — We stood in the vestibule, listening. It must have been a Monday, for all that I could hear behind the matt-lacquered door was the murmur of my memories, not the voice of the lady with the paper rose telling a customer off for not treating Rororo paperbacks with due care and attention, Herr Leukroth shuffling along beneath the sacrosanct dimensions of a plaster cast of Goethe's Jupiter head enthroned above the bookcase doors with little filigree keys in the locks that also wore adhesive-tape ties, also with typed inscriptions — Classics! Apply at counter to inspect! The command was obeyed, for an unauthorized touch would have created a different kind of silence; also, I thought, the keys must be linked to an invisible alarm: to Fräulein Leukroth's nervous system turned inside out and stretching into the bookshop, perhaps also to the whispering of some telltale benign spirits conjured up by the scratch of a pen. It must have been a Monday, for Dienemann Succrs. was 'Private' and 'Private' shops were closed on Mondays, I knew that from Walther's and Wackendorff's bakeries, Vogelsang the butcher's and the cobbler Anselm Grün. The floorcloth wasn't steaming; deliberately ignored, it was drying out into the grey of a shark's fin that had been washed up on the coconut mat. No icy silence from within when someone interrupted Fräulein Leukroth in her inky activity to ask about the books in the glass-fronted case beside her desk: behind a curtain with a pattern of moss-green flowers were, guarded by pharmacists' bottles, Hermann Hesse books of the old S. Fischer Verlag, linen-bound in faded blue with gold-embossed lettering, Unger Gothic typeface, and those of the GDR Aufbau Verlag, linen in artificially faded lime green, sand-coloured wrappers, Garamond typeface, and when a train went past, the pharmacists' bottles took over the trembling that sent out its jagged rays from the core of Fräulein Leukroth's silence: Books by Hermann Hesse, sir. And for Fräulein Leukroth, who didn't even turn her head, no further explanation was necessary. – Oh, Hermann Hesse, the potential customer insisted: – Most certainly! and: I will tell you straight away, Fräulein Leukroth said; – I presume you're not selling them? – Listen, said Fräulein Leukroth, terminating the discussion, after Hermann Hesse! there is! no more literature! then carefully, while the prospective customer shrugged his shoulders, realizing he had not passed one of the usual Dresden tests of worthiness, wiped off a superfluous drop of ink from her steel nib on the rim of the Barock jar. And you, Herr Altberg, were listening. And I was watching as you opened the books, chatted with the assistants, advised Fräulein Leukroth about pharmacists' mixtures for skin problems and illnesses caused by radiation from outer space, as you gave Herr Leukroth, who approached, withdrew, approached again with one of your volumes of essays in his hand, a signature; you seemed confused, perhaps you hadn't imagined you yourself could be an object of interest for P. Dienemann Succrs.; I found it touching that I could observe you, one of my stern teachers, in a carefree moment. There is much that you have taught me – without realizing it, I have never had the courage to tell you; for I cannot pretend that I understand you. I suspect that our impressions of life, which I am unwilling to call experiences, since I don't know whether anything is ever repeated, lie too far apart. I see us standing in the vestibule outside Dienemann's antiquarian bookshop, you told me about the beginnings of the German Democratic Republic, about your hopes and dreams, about the dawn you greeted joyfully and for which, after the thousand-year darkness, you were prepared to do, to give, everything. You fell silent; I was listening. Gramophone records had eaten their way into the walls. Voices did not come together. The line from the fishwives' song: Shark thou sea-green officer, slipped through the matt-lacquered and the connecting portal, disappeared into the bookcase beside Goethe's Jupiter head, behind the table whose overhanging offerings of books worried the wooden fool. There was a little key in that case as well: Romantics, ditto! was typed on the tape. And as you remained silent, Fräulein Leukroth raised her head and listened on her part: even if no one was 'rooting round cluelessly' (as the assistant in the chiffon blouse would quietly groan after she'd followed a customer to see what he was up to, only to find, manically and fearlessly rummaging in the second rows, behind eternal revenants such as Karl Zuchardt's Stirb du Narr! *— never read, notoriously in stock — or Sienkiewicz's* Quo Vadis? *ditto, an intellectual robber baron by the name of Georg Altberg); could there be someone who wasn't standing the accepted Dresden viewing-metre away from the books, head respectfully tilted to one side in order to examine the titles, chin in his right hand and that supported by his horizontal left arm? Fräulein Leukroth listened. Was it time for her medicine? It would be welcome, if the staff of this establishment were more economical in their use of brown paper; old newspapers are just as good for wrapping books, for which reason I, as you are aware, always bring a supply. The subjunctive 'were' was carefully underlined.*

12

Rust

You had to learn your lessons, relentlessly, tirelessly, endlessly, if one day you wanted to be one of the great ones – that, too, was a lesson Christian had learnt. Niklas, Ulrich and Richard had little time for anything but the best and the most significant; Ezzo, when he played a piece, was told that this or that violinist had done it better, that he still lacked this or that 'in order to really move the listener, not just to play the notes but to fill them with life; there's still no depth to it'.

Christian had learnt this when Richard had taken out his old school reports and silently tapped an A grade in a subject where Christian had a B; a C was already a minor disaster and he didn't dare imagine what would happen if he got a D, or even an E, the maximum credible catastrophe. Nor did he dare imagine what would happen if he didn't get a place at medical school.

'Being a doctor,' Richard said, 'is the best, the most wonderful profession there is. It's a clearly defined, beneficial activity, the results of which can be seen immediately. A patient comes with a complaint. The doctor examines him, makes a diagnosis, starts the treatment. The patient goes home healed, relieved of pain, able to start work again.'

'If he hasn't died,' Ulrich retorted. 'Has it never struck you that hospitals are often next to graveyards? And next to ones where the gravediggers are shovelling out holes all the time, at that. – It's the economy where the best jobs are, my lad. There you're creating things of material value. Let's say you're producing lavatory seats. You don't have to grin, it's time someone undertook a defence of the lavatory seat. Despised it may be, but everyone needs that oval, even if no one talks about it. By the way, did you know it's called *le couvercle* in French? You won't be in the limelight if you manufacture kuverkles, definitely not, but woe betide you if they're out of stock. The economy is real life. And you'll make a packet there!'

'You and your stupid jokes, don't confuse the boy, Snorkel,' Barbara said reproachfully. 'The economy! Which one are you talking about? The socialist economy? Don't make me laugh.'

'You may laugh, my little ball of fluff, but I tell you that the economic laws also operate in . . .'

'Richard's not that far off the mark. The boy has to learn something solid. I always thought he should be a tailor. I think he has a natural talent for tailoring. A feeling for material seems to run in the Rohde family . . . Meno has a feel for it too. – Just don't be anything connected with books, Christian. That's all crap, isn't it, Meno?'

'Not entirely. Though there's a certain amount of shit there too.' Meno hardly took part in these discussions at all, concentrating on his supper while the others argued.

'Rubbish! I know writers, they come and moan to me. They want to write that the sky is blue, but they have to write that the sky is red. A suit always has two sleeves, here just as in the West. And it has buttons. One of these . . . scribblers! asked me whether I knew the people who make buttons, he'd like to make buttons, nothing but buttons.'

'As a doctor you really are a *general* practitioner. You have to be able to do everything. You even have to know a bit about the economy. And lots of doctors I know are artistically inclined. Art, craftwork, culture: everything comes together in the doctor. You can go into research, as Hans has. Toxicologists are always needed. You can even, if you study history along with medicine, become a medical historian, we have a chair in the Academy. A well-paid professor, with a nice situation in the Faculty of Medicine, well away from the ideologists. He sits there writing books all day.'

'Well I think the nicest thing of all is still music,' said Niklas.

When he was staying with his parents, Christian liked to go for a walk by himself in the evening. He didn't see many people, mostly the district lay in profound silence. More clearly than ever he sensed the melancholy and solitary atmosphere of the old villas with their pointed gables and steep roofs, lit by the Advent stars on the balconies and in the oriel windows, by the meagre light of those street lamps that were still working. Snow fell, snow melted, sometimes it rained as well. Then he would hear his steps echoing on the wet flagstones of the pavement and feel that these houses concealed something, an insidious disease, and that this disease was connected with the inhabitants.

He often went to see Niklas, whom he liked very much, and he would look forward to the visit to his uncle well in advance, during the last class, during the monotonous sway of the journey from Waldbrunn to Dresden. If they had agreed on eight o'clock, he would be walking restlessly round the streets an hour beforehand, looking at the lights and asking himself what the inhabitants behind the windows might be doing, whether, at the sound of the bells from the city, at the striking of the clocks, which was audible through the windows, they too might be thinking of the disease, for which he could still not find a name, however hard he tried. He'd once talked about it with his Uncle Hans. Hans had given him a surprised look, shrugged his shoulders and answered, with an ironic smile, 'We're being poisoned, that's all', had added, 'And Time, how strangely does it go its ways', and placed his index finger to his lips. Christian had not forgotten that. It was a quotation from *Der Rosenkavalier*, it was sung by the Marschallin; and Christian believed that this Marschallin was still alive, somewhere here in one of the houses, and was whispering about time, even possessed it, like an essence, and fed it into the clocks in the slow, patient manner of a spinner at her spinning wheel from which there went a thread: time, dripping, trickling in the wallpaper, scurrying in the mirrors, time weaving its visions. On one of these evenings with Niklas in the music room of Evening Star, the needle of the record player kept jumping out of the groove and playing the same passage again and again, Tannhäuser, Christian imagined, kept raising his arm and singing the praises of Venus in her mountain grotto, at which point the needle would go no farther, seemed to hit a barrier that knocked it back and made it mechanically repeat the same melody to a rustle of tremolando violins, rippling harps and the crepitation of the record, that had been made during the Third Reich, a probe into a long-vanished theatre, scratched and, as Christian sometimes thought when he was sitting listening with Niklas, pervaded with the crackle of air-raid warnings on the wireless and the radar of the bombers approaching Dresden. But in the same way as the needle kept jumping back, until Niklas got up and put an end to the echoes, multiplying the minnesinger's earnestness so that he slipped into ham acting, copy after copy thrown out like a jiggling marionette in an endless loop, so the days in the city seemed to Christian, repetitions that made you want to laugh, each day a mirror image of the previous one, each a paralysing copy of the other. Then he thought of Tonio Kröger, the bourgeois from the city with the draughty, gabled streets, the warehouses and churches, the Hanseatic merchants with a cornflower in their buttonhole and the ships sailing past their counting houses up the Trave. He had no idea what had made him think of that, the sight of the house called Dolphin's Lair perhaps, or his happy anticipation of a musical evening with Niklas. It was a long time since Christian had read the story. Meno thought highly of it; sometimes, at their soirées, they would talk about Thomas Mann. As Christian walked round the sparsely lit streets that smelt of snow and the ash from lignite, he felt as if he were Tonio Kröger himself; true, he didn't quite have the right style, since he wasn't the son of strait-laced Lübeck patricians. He would presumably have had to go in and out of the Gothic vaults of the Kreuzschule in Dresden as well. Yet he still had that feeling and the longer he walked, the more Tonio Kröger seemed to take possession of him, as if he were the right mask for the district up there, protection against something Christian couldn't define but that seemed to cause the morbid atmosphere of the houses all around, their silent decline, their sleep.

Niklas . . .

'*Salve*, Christian, come on in, I've got something for you.' It was mostly Niklas who came when he rang the bell at the door with the peeling light-grey paint and the crooked 'Tietze' sign covered in verdigris. Gudrun seldom went to the door and when she did Christian knew it wasn't a good evening to visit Niklas; then he would often see him already in the hall adjusting his beret in the mirror with the curving frame and silhouettes of Reglinde and Ezzo on the right and left (Zwirnevaden Studios, Steiner Guest House), putting on his coat and gloves, checking his midwifery bag, his car keys – then he had a house call, would wave him away: another time, as you can see, today's not on.

'You can always go and see Ezzo,' Gudrun would say, 'though he has to do his practice and you mustn't distract him; when you're there he doesn't complete his daily quota. And I have to go out soon as well. – But there aren't any pears for you to gobble up,' she explained and Christian, feeling slightly awkward, wondered whether she meant it seriously or whether it was intended as a kind of hearty joke, which to his mind didn't go with Gudrun's delicate features (Niklas said he'd recognized them in drawings by Dürer) and her stage voice (she was an actress at the theatre), with her smell of preserved rhubarb, ears of corn and deer tallow cream. Or she said, 'Use sea-sand and almond bran for your acne, I don't want you to infect Reglinde or Ezzo', and when Christian replied that his pimples weren't infectious, gave him a sceptical look, as if he were knowingly telling a lie, but anyway certainly didn't know enough about such matters to have an opinion that was worth listening to. Sometimes there were better-eyesight weeks when the Tietzes fed mainly on carrots, since Gudrun had read in a magazine at Schnebel's, the hairdresser's, or heard from a colleague at the theatre, that carrots contained a lot of vitamin A and that vitamin A was good for your eyesight; during those weeks their eyes were sharp but their stomachs rumbled. Gudrun discovered that sliced carrots absorbed the taste of the meat that was cooked with them in the frying pan – the better-eyesight weeks were followed by the weeks of carrotburgers. She was told that butter was harmful and read something in an old magazine about an outbreak of margarine disease: 'Professor Doktor Doktor aitch see Karl Linser of the Charité Hospital in Berlin gave an interview, so there must be something to it', and she immediately threw away all the margarine she had in the house. ('Carcinogenic! You turn yellow!') Every year, shortly before Christmas, a scientist ('a specialist!') would announce in the newspapers his discovery that bananas were harmful and oranges (except for those from

Cuba) contained certain substances that could inhibit children's growth and lead to constipation in adults ('he describes it precisely, you can peel them as carefully as you like, there's always a bit of pith left on the piece, it's deposited at the pylorus in your stomach and eventually you're completely blocked up, for the pith of the orange doesn't get digested!'). No one apart from Gudrun believed these specialists and to the annoyance of her family she gave the West bananas in the yellow packets away to the Hoffmann children. 'You'll see what they do to you, you'll grow up like little dwarves; go on then, eat them, if you don't believe me, go and catch cancer. You'll all be eaten away by cancer! You always have to know best.'

'Oh, do stop your nonsense,' Richard said, 'it's just a very obvious ploy. They don't want to use their hard currency for tropical fruits, and to avoid criticism, they put this rubbish about. And you fall for it! If it really were true, all monkeys would die soon after they're born, given the amount of bananas they polish off.'

'Oh yes, you always know best. The man in the newspaper was a proper scientist and you're not even a proper doctor.'

'Oh, come on now!'

'You just hack people about!'

'Despite that, I do understand something of these matters,' said Richard, hurt.

'Because you get everything out of books, just out of books, most of the stuff in them is pure fabrication, just to get people so they'll believe anything and so the writers can collect their royalties.'

'Is that true, Meno?' At such moments Richard would fold up the newspaper.

'Physicists and medics are the worst,' said Meno in a matter-of-fact tone. 'They fabricate like nobody's business and have no idea, none whatsoever. And moneygrubbers! Suck the publishers dry like vampires.'

Gudrun was not to be moved. 'You two can make fun of me if you like, but I know what I know. I read recently that monkeys are monkeys because they eat nothing but bananas. You can let your children grow up into monkeys. Not me. And you, Meno, you haven't even got any.'

'*Salve*,' said Niklas. 'I've got something for you.' Christian was eager to see what it was this time, a new record from Philharmonia, Trüpel's record shop, picture postcards from Malthakus or a piece of Saxon sugar cake from Walther's on Rissleite? Niklas loved surprises and put on a mysterious air, shuffled along in tattered slippers, one hand in the pocket of his baggy trousers, vigorously playing an air piano with the fingers of the other (or was he trying out fingerings on an imaginary viola fingerboard?), over the soft PVC of the hall to the ground-glass living-room door, illuminated with seductively warm light. Gudrun withdrew, either to the bedroom to learn her lines or to darn stockings, eight thimbles on her fingers making a soft, castanet-like noise, in the kitchen, where the cupboards hung crookedly and the window ledges were eaten away with black mould, where the paint on the pipes was blistering and embroidered recipes for Salzburg soufflé, pumpkin soup and a dish called 'industrial accident' (an exceptionally fragrant, disgusting-looking hotchpotch the children stirred with long spoons) could hardly cover the damp patches on the walls.

Then there began another session of what Christian was unwilling to call 'teaching', although there was a teacher, Niklas, and a pupil, Christian (only occasionally Ezzo or Reglinde as well, sometimes Muriel and Fabian Hoffmann, the children from the house on Wolfsleite); even though it was mostly the pupil who asked the questions and the teacher who gave the answers, 'teaching' didn't describe it, that would have reminded Christian too much of Waldbrunn. The evenings with Niklas – and with the other Tower-dwellers Christian visited – had little in common with the lessons there. When Ezzo and Reglinde had time, Christian would bring his cello and they played string quartets, sometimes Gudrun would take the piano and they would go through a Mozart quintet or the 'Trout', the lilting theme of which would regularly send Gudrun into ecstasy and, humming along, she would get the utmost possible out of the yellowed keys of the Schimmel piano, which occasionally stuck in the top and bottom registers.

'*Salve.*' In the living room the tiled stove was pumping out regular rings of heat, briquettes rumbled onto the grating, the wind howled in the chimney. Sometimes sparks flew out onto the metal plate under the stove door. The windows rattled and banged even when it was snowing and there was no wind outside; the wood in the frames had cracks, the old-fashioned bascule bolts were covered in verdigris and, as in many of the apartments up there, thick draught excluders made in the Harmony Salon workshop from remnants of wool and clothing were stuck between the windows on the sill. Niklas poured a glass of mineral water for Christian and a Wernesgrüner Pils for himself, stroked the threadbare corduroy of the three-piece suite, leant back and said, 'Aah' and 'Right, then' to the plaster frieze round the ceiling, to the paintings by Kurt Querner on the walls: stolid scenes from the Erzgebirge done in earthy colours, the Luchberg in melting snow; a lane in Börnchen with gnarled trees; one of the famous portraits of Rehn, a peasant farmer, bringing out his pinched features with the rich blue of his eyes, his hands, crooked and knotted like roots, that had always impressed Christian. As did the portrait of Reglinde in the corner with the honey-coloured wing chair: it was one of the painter's last works, Reglinde at eleven or twelve, in a plain dress, a few dolls beside her that Christian remembered from winter theatre evenings at the Tietzes' and the Wolfsleite Hoffmanns' years ago; as he walked home Christian often wondered about Reglinde's alarmed eyes in the picture.

Niklas talked about productions from the past. The sound of the 'abbot's clock', of Ezzo's violin exercises in the adjoining room, of Gudrun declaiming, 'Oh, who is the villain, speak', of the chimes of the grandfather clock with the brass face fading away over the carpet, in front of the ceiling-high bookcase with Dehio art books, alphabetically arranged biographies of musicians and volumes of correspondence from Europe's past, all mingled with names from the heyday of opera and music, which for Niklas was a German art, with all due respect to the Beatles and ABBA, about whom he could talk knowledgeably at the evening meetings of the Friends of Music. 'The pentatonic scale . . . now, when the orchestra plays in Japan, they can't get enough of our music. Mozart on the pentatonic scale, well, OK. America has its dschezz and Dschordsch Görschwin, it has Börnschtein's *West Said Schdori* and Nyu York . . . Great, great. People are always saying the Germans are the nation of poets and philosophers, I would say they're the nation of musicians. In no other area is the Germans' contribution so unique as in music. Leaving aside Verdi and Berlioz, Puccini and Vivaldi . . . there's not much left! A few Russians, Tchaikovsky, Mussorgsky, Borodin, but that's a special case, that's already peripheral. Shostakovich as well and Prokoviev, Stravinsky, but he's too abstract, it comes from his head, not his heart . . . No, music is a German art and that's that.'

Niklas talked about the singers of the Dresden Opera, about the great conductors of the past. Outside the rain would beat against the windows, the snow swirl, the flakes, a hundred eyes sticking to the panes, slowly melt. In the summer Christian and Niklas would sit on the veranda, beside the music room. It smelt of the white-painted wooden furniture that came from Gudrun's parents' house, of the tobacco from Niklas's pipe that he would smoke with relish on mild evenings with open windows, the humming of the bees, orange and blue sunset streaks and the call of the blackbirds. In the winter Christian would listen to Niklas, to the wide sweep of his memories bringing the past to life again, in the living room and the music room, where Niklas would first of all sit by the telescope table, then, when it was time to listen to music, on the chaise longue in front of the mirror that had turned a watery grey. The record on the turntable of the hi-fi machine with the imitation beech veneer would start to revolve and they listened to the singers Niklas had been talking about. Then, Christian felt, something happened to the room: the green wallpaper with the pattern of protozoa and diatoms seemed to open up; the Viennese clock acquired a human face; the yellow artificial rose under the glass cover on the escritoire in the corner where Niklas wrote his letters in ink on hand-made, deckle-edge Spechthausen paper, seemed to grow rampant and branch out, the way it happened in silhouette films in the Tann-häuser Cinema in which shadow plants (roses? thistles? neither Muriel nor Christian nor Fabian knew) twined round a castle; the photos of the singers on the walls were no longer close, looked as if they had floated up from the cabins of ships that had sunk; the rasping sound of the stylus sounded like the swell of the sea. Niklas sat leaning forward, tense, caught up in the sweep of the melodies, the entries. Christian observed his uncle surreptitiously; he too seemed to be part of the world of the tides, the murmur of the sea from days long past, not the present; sometimes Christian was even slightly startled to hear his uncle talk of everyday matters such as snow chains for the Shiguli or Dynamo Dresden's last game; in this world of the thousand little things and the curse of climbing the stairs to the offices of public officials he seemed to be merely a visitor, wrapped in the cloak of a kind fairy. Christian had to feel his way back into his everyday world when he said goodbye to Niklas, had to find his way back as he went home (Caravel was diagonally opposite), often taking detours, his head full of the names of singers and composers, anecdotes from the life of the State Orchestra during previous decades, full of pictures of German cathedrals and features of pre-war Dresden.

And with Malthakus it was the stamps, the historical postcards with the landscapes, that the dealer's narrative commentary turned into little living tableaux; the albums with stamps from distant countries: 'papillons, 100 différents', 'bateaux, 100 différents'; butterflies from Guyana and Réunion, Gabon and Senegal; ship motifs: 'République du Bénin', Indochina, São Tomé e Príncipe; triangular stamps from

Afghanistan joined by a perforated line at the hypotenuse that the dealer patiently explained: 'The ship here with the red-and-white striped sails is a cog of the Hanseatic League' (Christian knew it from an engraving on the glass door of the staircase at Caravel); 'the one on the other side, with the blood-red sails, a Venetian merchantman'; then he rotated the globe and tapped his finger on the places that sounded legendary to the ears of the Heinrichstrasse and Wolfsleite children – Benin, previously the Kingdom of Dahomey, a narrow country on the west coast of Africa, capital – capital? I ought to know that. Quick, open the atlas. What is the capital of Benin called? But they got stuck in Togo, a former German colony bordering Benin; Togo was interesting too and then they discovered countries such as the Ivory Coast and Upper Volta, the capital of which (they all loved its name and could remember it later when they played 'name – city – country': Ouagadougou; Sinbad and his crew would certainly have been to Ouagadougou; everything was different in Ouagadougou).

Knowledge, knowledge. Names, names. Brains soaked it all up like sponges until they were dripping with knowledge that they didn't release since these sponges couldn't be squeezed. Knowledge was what counted; knowledge was the closely guarded treasure of those who belonged up there.

Those who knew nothing seemed to count for nothing. There was hardly any insult that was worse than 'ignoramus'. At weekends there were anatomy lessons with Richard (he particularly enjoyed testing them on the bones of the wrist, having taught them a mnemonic verse: 'A tall ship sailed in the moonlight bright – lunate – Triangulated a pea-shaped rock one night – triquetral, pisiform – The captain and his mate, each on a trapeze – trapezium, trapezoid – Dived head over heels, caught the hook with ease – capitate, hamate') and talks on famous doctors: Fabian, Muriel, Robert and Christian, who intended to study medicine, sat in Richard's study and revised their notes: 'When did Sauerbruch start to work in Munich? – Late summer 1918. – Name three forerunners of surgery of the chest and one of their achievements. – Bülau. Bülau drain. Rehn. First open-heart operation. Mikulicz. Mikulicz line, clamp; operation on the oesophagus in the chest, made possible by Sauerbruch's low-pressure chamber. Sauerbruch's teacher in Breslau.' Muriel and Fabian seemed to join in more out of habit (there was also tasty food from Anne); Christian admired Sauerbruch, was fascinated by the stories about Robert Koch's heroic rise, dug his way through *Ärzte im Selbstversuch*, Bernt Karger-Decker's book with its scary bright-orange wrapper about doctors who tried remedies out on themselves, through the many volumes of the biographical series *Humanisten der Tat* that took up a whole shelf in his father's bookcase, opened, full of trepidation, the anatomical atlases, where thousands of Latin names indicated meticulously described parts of the body – 'Do we have to learn all this at medical school?' – 'That's on the syllabus in the first two years, in addition you get biochemistry and physiology, chemistry, biology, biophysics, mathematics for doctors and, unfortunately, Marxism–Leninism still,' Richard replied. Christian refused to be put off by Anne's concerned objections ('Let them go out and play, Richard, you're stuffing them full of books; you're going too far and I don't think it's good for them') and devoured as much knowledge as he could. He too wanted to be famous and recognized by Richard and Niklas, Malthakus and Meno, the Tower-dwellers, his name too must shine out: Christian Hoffmann – the great surgeon, the man who conquered cancer. The first person from the GDR to win a Nobel Prize, applauded in Stockholm. After that he would probably get out, accept the offer of an English or American elite university. Or study economics and become director of a concern after all, like Ulrich? A clear desk every morning, the secretary brings papers that can determine the future state of a whole country, your signature, please, Comrade Director. Comrade – unfortunately that was unavoidable. Christian examined his own feelings about it: no, no scruples. If it meant you could become a director. Or a scientist like Meno. An insect specialist and umpteen insect species will end in H for Hoffmann. A physicist puzzling over the foundations of the world! Ezzo saw himself as an astronaut. Sinbad and Tecumseh were good. Chingachgook, the big snake. To be a trapper like Leatherstocking. To be a cellist on the world stage, to thunderous applause – but Christian sensed, and his teacher had indicated, that his talent wasn't up to that; it was enough to get by with, certainly; you could surprise the presidents of countries when, as the Nobel Prize winner for . . . (whatever) you picked up your cello and played one of Bach's suites. Fabian, much taken with Lange's stories, was drawn to the tropics, wanted to become a ship's doctor and a second Albert Schweitzer. Robert would say, 'You've all got a screw loose', and go fishing or to watch football with Ulrich. Muriel was getting difficult, talked more about love than about science and art. Christian read.

And when he wasn't reading, he sometimes started to laugh.

When he was younger he'd enjoyed Jules Verne, Jack London, Friedrich Gerstäcker's novels set in exotic countries, had read Mark Twain's *Huckleberry Finn* and *Tom Sawyer* again and again. He loved stories of adventure, Stevenson's *Treasure Island*, Defoe's *Robinson Crusoe*, stories of spies, musketeers and agents. When he had started at the senior high school, however, Meno had given him a book that impressed Christian in a way he couldn't explain; it was *The World of Yesterday* by Stefan Zweig, a book that told about an age that had long since disappeared, the Belle Époque in the Vienna of the turn of the century. It was teeming with names, allusions, quotations that Christian recognized from having heard them from Meno himself or from Niklas, an effect that delighted him. Not only that, there was a casual remark by Zweig he couldn't get out of his mind: that in Europe before the First World War you didn't need a passport to travel wherever you liked; that you could attend university in Paris or Florence, if you wanted (and, of course, assuming you had the money). In that book he found wide horizons he had not yet come across, even with the Tower-dwellers.

In the 'Camp for Work and Relaxation' he had read Goethe's *Elective Affinities* more in an attempt to impress Verena than out of interest; now this book by Zweig gave him a sense of what the concept of 'world literature' meant. World literature – they'd talked about that at school as well (Goethe, *Faust I*: but at the time Christian had preferred to play battleships or handball); he had only had a vague idea of what it meant: it was the grey-linen rows of dignified books behind the glass of the bookcase in the living room of Caravel that seemed to stare at Christian with an expression that said: You're too young, too stupid for us. Out of a sense of disdain that already had a touch of curiosity, he had occasionally taken a book out of the row, leafed through a few pages here, read a paragraph there (dialogues between lovers, that too), then carefully weighed the book in his hand and replaced it. He had to read, he had to learn more. He told himself that his models had been much farther on at fourteen, fifteen, than he was now, at seventeen; he told himself that, if some day he really was to become one of the great figures of science, he would have to at least double the daily quota he'd set himself. Every day in Waldbrunn he longed for the end of lessons so that he could finally get down to his own work. He studied like one possessed, eight to ten hours a day, both coursework and his own, but only as much coursework as he needed to get an A grade in class and oral tests. His own work consisted of fifty words each of English, French and Latin vocabulary a day together with further topics in chemistry, physics and biology. Christian swotted day in, day out, to the point of bitter despair that arrived by midnight at the latest because by that time he usually started confusing all the vocabulary, had forgotten the word for the biochemical cancer cycle (a complex of thistly formulae intended for second-year medical students), which was almost unpronounceable and ended in -ate or -asis, and no longer knew what the difference between an enzyme, a vitamin and a hormone was. He was dog-tired but he hadn't done enough yet. He now forced his brain, which was already generating delusions, to read at least one chapter of world literature. Woe to anyone who dared to disturb his daily routine; Christian had already once driven off Frau Stesny, the middle-aged head of the pupils' hostel, with a fit of rage; astonishingly she hadn't complained to Engelmann, the principal. The other pupils in the hostel looked askance at him because he shut himself off from everything. Svetlana Lehmann tapped her forehead, Verena shrugged her shoulders, Jens mocked. Only Siegbert said nothing, Siegbert, with his little desk full of matchstick ships and sailing manuals, who knew all the ranks in the People's Navy (and also of the Nazi navy, but no one was to know that), the types of ships, classes of cruisers and tonnages, Siegbert Füger, who wanted to go to sea and liked stories of the sea, especially Hugo Pratt's Corto Maltese comic books; Christian had given him a few, ones of which Lange, the ship's doctor, had spare copies. He even read the *Odyssey*, Apollonius of Rhodes's saga of the Argonauts, the reports of Pharaoh Necho's captain, of Herodotus.

When Frau Stesny, not knowing what to do next, locked the door of the classroom where Christian studied in the evenings (he disturbed the quiet of the building, and not only when, at two in the morning, his overwrought brain had the idea of relieving the strain by playing his cello or the school piano) – well, if Frau Stesny locked the rooms, Christian would just go on working in the toilet. He didn't get much sleep, just four or five hours, and went with glassy, red-rimmed eyes to classes where he only realized the teacher had asked him a question from the gleeful giggles of the rest of the class. The books were beginning to become attached to him, as he called it, for the others they were something like his emblem. He seldom went anywhere without having a book with him. He read during break, while the others ate their rolls, or, during the lunch hour, went out into the yard, where the girls swapped cassettes and the boys played cards, argued about rock bands or discussed the latest football results. He even arranged his books into different categories: reading for the bus he took to Dresden, reading for the lessons he found boring (English with Frau Kosinke, geography with Herr Plink, who kept waving his pointer at the maps hanging on the walls), reading for his free time (his daily chapter) and reading for the break. Soon he was no longer satisfied with reading one chapter of world literature a day and set himself 100 pages. His day extended well into the early hours of the next. During the autumn break, when he naturally continued his study, he increased his quota to 400 pages a day, with the result that he sometimes read for fourteen, fifteen hours on end and then got up off the couch eyes rolling, pale and wan as a potato sprout. Sometimes he read two or three books in a day and afterwards all he knew about Tagore, for example, was that during the previous week he had got through five books by him. He ploughed his way through the Waldbrunn library, returned the complete editions of Max Planck, Rutherford, Albert Schweitzer after three weeks, in order to take out the next enticing pile for the next week, and the longer the book, the better! Christian loved long books. A novel wasn't a real novel unless it was at least 500 pages long. At 500 pages the ocean began, anything less than that was paddling in a brook. It was in vain that Meno shook his head and pointed out that there could be more of the world in a short story by Chekhov, more of life and art than in many a fat, blubbery tome. But Christian went for the blue whales, as he called the epic novels of Tolstoy, Dostoevsky, Thomas Mann, Robert Musil and Heimito von Doderer, he loved Thomas Wolfe, from the pages of his books came the sound of ships' sirens, music from the steamers in the Southern states, the whistles of the American transcontinental trains. He read that Eugene Gant (that is Wolfe himself, he thought) had read 20,000 books in ten years (which seemed absolutely unimaginable to Christian), a real logodipsomaniac, then.

'Now Christian's really flipped his lid,' Verena said.

On free days it had to be 500 pages, so for that he didn't bother with physics and chemistry. Now the following happened: Robert had got really hooked on some Balzac novel and, out of the blue, worked his way through 555 pages in a single day. That mustn't be allowed to happen; as far as reading and studying were concerned, Christian was the boss, Robert's record had to be broken. One day Christian got up at four in the morning, washed, had not too full a breakfast and started to read. He wasn't going to study that day, it was to be entirely devoted to breaking the new record. He read uninterruptedly from 4.30 a.m. until 12 p.m., though with two very irritating breaks for lunch and supper that Anne forced him to take. On the stroke of midnight he'd read 716 pages – and forgotten them, but what did that matter, he'd broken the record.

He had to become famous, then those at home would recognize him.

One evening in Waldbrunn, in a dark corner of his brain, over-wrought with vocabulary and formulae, the plan for stage-by-stage progress appeared. Christian switched off the light and went to the window. Now the classroom was in darkness, just the metal of the chairs in the window row, which had been put up on the tables, wearily slurped the light from the lamp in the yard. He had no idea how late it was. The street lamps had come on long ago, the contours of the new district of Waldbrunn merged with the waves of the hill above Kaltwasser reservoir. Behind the two sports halls, low, standardized, glass-and-concrete buildings, was the ridge along which the F170 ran. The yellow headlamps of the long-distance lorries rummaged around over the rye-field on the ridge, the way from the school into the town.

The Great Man. Stage 1: Learning, studying, educating the mind – that was the stage Christian was on at the moment. Being highly educated was the first requirement for becoming a great man. A great man was, moreover, highly cultured as well and so when classes were over for the day (usually around 1 p.m.) Christian, instead of having lunch, would go to the club room and occupy the communal record player for an hour. It didn't bother him in the least if others wanted to use the record player. Apart from him that was mostly only Svetlana – and she was an enthusiastic socialist, wanted to go to Lomonosov University in Moscow and listened to red singer-songwriters, for Christian 'the pits'. Every minute the record player was on without that 'nauseating stuff' (as Christian, Jens and a couple of boys from the twelfth grade said) was a gain for culture. He saw himself as a serious, mature man and as such listened to classical music, though he was pretty much alone among the boarders with that point of view. Christian didn't let that bother him: the others were philistines, how could they, coming from villages as they did, appreciate the profundity, the seriousness of a Bach, the serenity, the comic detachment of a Mozart, the emotional power of a Beethoven. Since Svetlana was a bit feeble-minded (an opinion he shared with several boys in his class), she didn't need a record player. When listening, Christian would sit leaning back in his chair, with his legs up, a *profoundly serious* expression on his face when, for example, he was listening to Beethoven. Christian *understood* Beethoven's outbursts of suffering . . . Like Christian, this titanic personality must have found himself surrounded by uncomprehending philistines and have had to struggle against them, his whole life long! Beethoven was a Great Man and Christian understood him, for he was cast in the same mould, definitely. Added to that, he really was affected by the music. He didn't show it; it confused him and when he had the feeling that Svetlana or Siegbert was observing him, he would jump up and switch the record off, furious (leaving the record there, though – he was counting on their curiosity).

Stage 2: University studies. Naturally he would have to abandon them. A trifling university course could not satisfy him, the young scientific genius, the irrepressible hothead and tomorrow's benefactor of mankind. He would even get poor grades at university: was that not the way it was, had he not read in many biographies of Great Men that they didn't fit in? Did university courses not cover familiar territory – and wasn't the reason a Great Man was great precisely that he broke new ground? Something that the simple-minded professors, trying to drum their long out-of-date knowledge into the ordinary minds of their students, could not of course see.

Stage 3: Nervous breakdown. That went with it. The tension the

young Great Man is under is just too much. Even Mozart had sometimes gone off his rocker, so it was quite normal. Christian would have
to go through terrible crises and consider suicide four times a day (it
had to be four times, once or twice was too little, that happened in
almost every family, three times sounded like a cliché, at four, Christian concluded, it somehow seemed more serious).

Stage 4: The Great Achievement, finally completed. Honours, prizes,
applause would be heaped upon the young Faustian seeker after knowledge. Now the important thing was to remain modest (because of
those who envied him and of the capricious deities of moments of
inspiration) and not let himself be dazzled by all these externalities.
The Great Man continues his research, restlessly, selflessly. He doesn't
care about the applause, all he cares about is his WORK. He makes
a further discovery, even more revolutionary, more profound than
the previous one. Petty-minded rivals who had begrudged him his
success and shouted from the rooftops that the Great Hoffmann would
soon be finished would crawl back into their holes. Remorsefully they
would recant, shamefacedly admit their limitations. Triumphant
jubilation.

So: down to work.

Love, Christian thought, would distract him from his studies.

13
Those we do not know

Little touching habits, he hadn't forgotten them and he would presumably always associate them with their childhood: back in the fifties, in
the sandstone hills by the Elbe. Meno was waiting, among the crowds
doing their Christmas shopping, outside the Intecta furniture shop in

the Old Market arcades on the corner of Thälmannstrasse, and recognized Anne at once from a distance; the way she threw back the orange scarf with a will of its own that she wore over her coat and that kept slipping down off her shoulders as she hurried along, that spot of orange in the turbid swell of the shopping-bag-laden throng; then the way she nibbled at the fingertips of her gloves while still walking, as if she were trying to take them off; that she always ran the last bit, once they had seen each other, embraced him passionately with all her shopping, her net bags with vegetables, her packages dangling from strings (had he ever, since she was married and the boys were beyond kindergarten age, seen her with her hands unencumbered – he couldn't remember), embraced him unconcerned at what others might think, Meno's colleagues at the publishers, when she met him there (Dresdner Edition looked out onto the Old Market, Meno just needed to cross the square to get to the furniture shop), or her colleagues from Neustadt Hospital whom she sometimes gave a lift to do their shopping. Anne never introduced him, the women would nod and swarm out at the hurried, well-trained pace of mothers who, after the morning shift, their first job, were setting off in the few hours remaining until closing time on their second job, there must have been something in the newspaper, or the bush telegraph had spread a rumour about deliveries: 'Attention, housewives, the Centrum store has preserving jars in stock' (they were needed in the autumn, but they arrived during the winter, what should one do, wait? You always regretted it), on another day the rings for the preserving jars; 'hairdryers have arrived' (the particular kind shaped like flounders with the blue plastic casing and black muzzle that after a few minutes of jet-engine noises smelt of burnt flies), or 'Everything for the Child': baby bottles of Jena glass that didn't crack when heated, nappies that would survive no more than three or four washes, pans for boiling nappies, thermometers for checking the water while boiling nappies, Milasan baby food, dummies, two or three of the priceless modern prams that, actually intended for export, had managed to find their way to a department in a store on the edge of town that was now under siege . . .

'Mo.'

'Anne.'

She kissed him on the cheek and took his hand, waving it merrily up and down as if they were a couple that had just fallen in love. The list: in his mind's eye he could see Anne's rough-looking handwriting, a dozen lines, of which a couple at the beginning had been deleted; but he liked going shopping with her, he was interested in all the apparently trivial little things that were needed to make daily life troubleproof: shoelaces, vacuum-cleaner bags, buttons, a darning mushroom (he had seldom seen a new one in the families he visited, everywhere he went the ones he saw were the bread-brown darning mushrooms from the pre-war Müller sewing-machine works in Dresden, riddled with the holes of countless needles), and Anne liked to have him with her, since he never grumbled on their expeditions that took them all round the city, he was able to summon up an interest in coffee filter papers or the varying quality of materials for suits, she trusted his judgement of dress patterns (she had done that, he recalled, when she was still a little girl) and she asked his advice when she needed to buy presents. It was Advent now and when he looked at the faces of the women in the Centrum store or the poorly stocked shops along Prager Strasse, he thought that they hated this time of the year: all the running round after a few ridiculous articles of, in general, mediocre quality, the hustle and bustle of the Christmas Market with its brass bands, the chimney-sweep figures made of prunes, the baked apples, hot, strong grog, moaning kids clinging on to their hands and men who didn't have to bother with all that because they had to work (but the women had to as well) or were sitting with a beer in their local bar watching *Sports Report* or playing cards. Robert, for example, wanted some new football boots, the ones with screw-in studs, and Anne told him as they crossed the Old Market, heading for Prager Strasse, that she had asked

Ulrich where she might find boots like that, 'he says the best place would be in Dům Sportu in Prague, they have Bata boots, they're better than ours, but to go all the way to Prague for a pair of football boots . . . ? But when I think about it, why not? Perhaps I'd find something for Richard there and perhaps a decent shirt for Niklas, he's always wearing the same ones and the cuffs are already frayed, I'm surprised Gudrun doesn't say something about it, and his trousers ought to be let out a bit, they're much too short for him . . . We'll see. Perhaps I'll manage to get to Prague. You could come too, we'll go in the car and have a nice day out. And you can speak Czech.'

'Only the little Libussa teaches me, Anne. But I don't know if I'll have the time.'

'Then we'll just have to go one Saturday.'

'Imagine what things'll be like at Hřensko. And at all the other crossings. We'd have to get some crowns as well.'

'We've still got two thousand. Two thousand unreturned, illicit crowns. And they say Dům Sportu's got a very good angling department. That'd be something for you. And for Christian.'

'How's he getting along? I was talking to him about the senior high school and he seems to be managing all right.'

'He's difficult at the moment, he's not easy to deal with, sometimes he can get quite abusive . . . He absolutely has to have a new pair of shoes and there's nothing out there in Waldbrunn. And then the school, you know, he has a lot of work to do; sometimes I think they're demanding too much – or he does of himself, he's very ambitious and Richard keeps on at him too . . . I often wonder whether he's not too strict with Christian, everyone ought to do what they can and if they can't, then it's no use forcing them. Oh, look at these, they're pretty' – she held up a few embroidered oven cloths, but shook her head when she saw the price – 'and he needs some new cello strings as well, do you remember how one snapped at the party? That was a great success, don't you think? Richard keeps playing your records over and over again.'

'Does he still want to be a great, famous doctor?'

'Christian? Oh yes, he talks about it sometimes. I don't like the way he puts so much emphasis on the "great and famous"; I mean, being a doctor's enough, surely? Why great and famous? And if he doesn't become great and famous, will his whole world collapse? Well, he doesn't get that from me . . . Now just look at those stupid rotary eggbeaters. Scandalous it is, really scandalous. Listen,' she called out to the assistant who was standing behind a pile of lurid plastic products *for the modern housewife*, frozen stiff, 'I'll show you something.' She picked up one of the appliances, which consisted of three intermeshing whisks on a revolving plate with a crank-handle at the side, and set the whisks whirring. Anne turned the handle faster, the whisks got caught up in each other and whichever way she turned the handle, they still didn't move. Eventually one of the whisks broke off. Anne dropped the broken machine on the counter. 'And you sell this trash?' The modern housewives who were standing round started to mutter dangerously.

'You've broken that, you'll have to pay for it,' the assistant said. 'Hey, you, don't you dare run off, help, police!'

A District Community Policeman came. 'What's going on here, citizens?'

'Comrade DCP, that woman there wrecked this eggbeater and now she's refusing to pay for it.'

'There's no way I'm going to pay a single pfennig for this rubbish, it's outrageous, I just thought I'd try out your goods so that you can see what your modern housewives have to make do with. A rotary beater, huh, turn it five times and it's beaten itself to bits.'

'Citizen, you've damaged the goods, the citizen assistant has a right to compensation.'

'Did you hear that!' The modern housewives who were gathered round expressed their indignation. 'That crap costs a pile of money – and it's not even any use for cracking your old man on the head.'

'But this is riotous assembly!' The D C P took out his notebook. 'On the other hand . . . let me have a look.' The assistant handed him a beater. Then another. One after the other they broke. The assistant was furious and started swearing at the custodian of the law. He lost his temper as well and started shouting that his wife too needed a reliable mechanical eggbeater for her pre-Christmas baking; Meno drew Anne away.

Well, really, she would say. Well, really, he would answer. They were already laughing.

There was a long queue outside the Heinrich Mann Bookshop on Prager Strasse; Anne, sniffing an opportunity, an unusual, unannounced delivery, immediately asked what they had. The man in front of her shrugged his shoulders and said he'd only joined the queue because there were so many in it already, he was just going to wait and see.

'Some important novel, an illustrated art book?' Anne asked Meno, then someone shouted that hiking maps had been delivered.

In the window of the music shop next to H O Kaufhalle a few violins were hanging, shining like wet sweets, together with a screaming-gold violin and a ukulele; inside they had guitar strings, double-bass end pins and a good dozen recently delivered Czech violin chin rests (of which Anne took one for Ezzo, you never knew), but no cello strings, though there was an implement for cutting clarinet blades that Anne, since Robert had only one, bought immediately: Robert's clarinet teacher had a brother who was an oboist and he, as Anne knew, corresponded with a cellist in the Berlin Philharmonic, perhaps they could wangle something through him.

They headed back towards the Old Market, swept along in the crowds coming from the main station and from Leninplatz. The women wrapped in headscarves, many of the men wearing Russian fur chapkas, pedestrians dressed in grey and brown, hurrying along, hunched up, towards the city centre, to the shops under the concrete slabs of the

Königstein and Lilienstein luxury hotels. There were groups of people waiting outside the Round Cinema, which looked like a powder compact with vertical stripes. Meno looked across at the display cases in the promenade outside the various cinemas: Bud Spencer was flexing his biceps on the posters, seeing that justice was done with a smile on his face, *Flatfoot on the Nile* was being shown. The boys wanted to see it, Robert had asked Meno to go with them and had enlisted Ezzo and Reglinde as well, while Muriel and Fabian were going to wait until it was on in the Tannhäuser Cinema. The clock on the Church of the Holy Cross struck five. Meno looked up at the windows of Dresdner Edition in the massive bulk of one of the buildings on the east side of the Old Market; the light was still on in the office of Josef Redlich, the senior editor, in the little room of the proofreader, Oskar Klemm, as well, Schiffner's window was dark.

A number 11 arrived, the red-and-white, mud-bespattered Tatra cars discharged people going to the cinema and the Christmas Market, women, like Meno, with bulging shopping bags in either hand. Anne was carrying a duffelbag full of clothes that had to be taken to the dry cleaner's to be mended; it was Friday, the VEB Service Combine in Webergasse was open until 7 p.m. but there was only one hour left to buy things needed for the weekend and to hunt for Christmas presents. Anne suggested they should split up, she gave him the duffelbag, she wanted to look for some socks for Arthur, who lived out in the deepest backwater as far as the supply of goods was concerned, and Emmy had asked for a wheeled tote for shopping, 'and of course we'll give her some money as well, her pension's nowhere near enough, and have you any ideas about something for Gudrun? I did want to get some gloves for Barbara; there were some in Exquisit, but I didn't get them right away and they'd gone, well, I'll just have to see if I can get them somewhere else. I've already got something for Uli, and for Kurt. At the dry cleaner's it's the express service and if they're difficult, I've made an appointment, Mo, the number's pinned to one of the pieces of clothing. The umbrella needs a new cover and the two pairs of scissors need sharpening. Where shall we meet?'

'This end of Webergasse, in an hour?'

'See you then', and she was off. Just like the old days, he thought, when we were kids playing cops and robbers and she would disappear in the woods; just a few branches swaying, a dusting of pollen from the spruce trees, an alarmed bird; an invisible door had opened and swallowed her up.

He sometimes thought about their childhood, perhaps he was getting to the age when, amazed at the way time had quietly passed, you start to look back and in the evening, alone with shades, open the photograph album that is full of frozen gestures, you can still smell the aromas round them, they've just happened and not, as the date under the photo claims, one day twenty or thirty years ago. See: that apple at the top right of the picture, scarcely visible, but you know that it's there, that it will be picked in a couple of minutes; the way the juice dripped off Anne's chin as she bit into it and Ulrich tried in vain to take it off her, and look: Father waving from the window of our house, it's 1952, not long since we got back from Moscow, when the Peace Race came through Bad Schandau and the crowds on the road beside the Elbe cheered the cyclists, or is he going to play us one of his Hans Albers records, 'In a Starry Night by the Harbour', an orange headband, Albers with a Sherlock Holmes pipe is looking up at the sky and Father says, as he takes the record out of the sleeve with the black Decca ellipse: 'Did you know that the first time he appeared on the stage was here in Schandau, nineteen hundred and eleven?'

And then Anne, on some evenings in his mind's eye he could see her face at that moment, her furrowed brow, her brown eyes wide with astonishment as she held out the apple to Ulrich; he was just as amazed as she was at this, for he had hesitated to touch the apple, had, embarrassed, pointed at the tree where there were other apples, then put his hands in his pockets and scuffed up the sand with the toe of his shoe . . .

Anne: you can have it, if you want – but at that moment, with the suddenness of a bird of prey striking, Ulrich's hand shot out of his pocket and grasped the fruit, leaving Anne stunned, as if the gesture had cut through her like a sword and nothing could undo it; Ulrich ran off with shouts of jubilation.

In the Service Combine in Webergasse Meno joined the queue and observed the way the staff went about their business, moving with fluent slowness and emphasizing every syllable when they spoke. Below a sign saying 'Using Every Mark, Every Minute, Every Gram of Material with Greater Efficiency' shirts were drying out on frames, billowing and bulging like a jazz trumpeter's cheeks, stretching out plump, tube-like sleeves. Not all the drying dummies seemed to be working: now and then the air came hissing out, the shirts spat the sealing clips away and gave up the ghost with a grunt.

After he'd been served Meno sat down in the waiting area of the New Line hairdresser's, which was on the same floor as the dry cleaner's. Anne's shirts would be ready in half an hour.

Sometimes he thought back to the years in Moscow. He remembered the autumn of 1947, the 800th anniversary of the founding of Moscow. He had been seven, Anne just two, Ulrich nine. A dark, untidy sky above the people in their Sunday best; in the parks there were brass bands, people selling candy floss and military bands waiting in the avenues.

Parked outside the Krasnaya Zvyozdochka kindergarten were the black limousines in which the Kremlin children were brought and picked up; the chauffeurs waited, smoking.

Girls in school uniforms with white aprons trotted past, chattering excitedly, holding little flags, they turned into the 'Street of the Best Workers', posters as high as the walls smiled down on the lines of demonstrators. Heroes of the Great Patriotic War, Heroes of Labour, of the Soviet Union. The girls had classes in the afternoon, in the second shift. The pupils from the first shift, which started at half past nine, were streaming out of the schools. Trolley buses, trams, lorries with slogans and decorated with flowers; the heavy Podeba and ZIS limousines came from the Arbat, jaunty marches rang out from the loudspeakers, everywhere red flags were fluttering. Portraits of the 'most human of human beings', attached to balloons, were swaying over Moscow. Meno recalled songs, fragments of lines drifted to the surface, he murmured the Russian words: 'Stalin is a hero, a model for our children, / Stalin is the best friend of our youth'; 'Our train goes full-steam ahead / and stops in communism' . . . the starved faces of the people, Meno thought, Father's emaciated hand holding mine, I ask about Mother and he answers, as he has for several months, that Luise is abroad, she sends the children her best wishes and hopes we are working hard at school. One day he takes Ulrich with him to the prison: Father waits until his letter of the alphabet is called. He goes to a counter to pay in money. If the official accepts the money, Mother is still alive.

14

Josta

Richard parked the Lada outside the 'House of German–Soviet Friendship' on Pushkin Platz and decided to walk. Leipziger Strasse was bustling with the evening throng, the lamps cast weary light over the traffic. A number 4 tram heading for Radebeul rattled past, swerving on the rails, Richard saw the cluster of passengers holding on to the straps sway to and fro. He crossed the road, but so slowly and immersed in thought that a military-green Volga stopped and a Russian soldier, driver for a senior officer whose gloves Richard could see making impatient gestures in the interior, stuck his head out of the window and shouted a hoarse but not unfriendly sounding 'Nu, davai' to him. Richard got out of the way, the Volga, a big limo, slithered off in the slush.

Cries came from the Paul Gruner Stadium, they were playing handball; there was still a league, mostly made up of workers and employees of the state concerns Robotron, Pentacon, Sachsenwerk. Indoor handball had long since taken over but here, in the suburbs, it still went on. Richard knew the changing rooms in the Paul Gruner Stadium, the photos of old sporting heroes: the Dresden footballer Richard Hofmann, known as the 'Bomber' because of his shot; the German and Hungarian teams of 1954, with signatures; the boots of players for Dynamo Dresden who had played in the youth teams here. The breeze freshened, bringing along smells: there was the brackish smell of the nearby Pieschen harbour, coming from the old arms of the Elbe in which the river water was stagnant and even in a harsh winter only formed soft ice. The fumes from the slaughterhouse in the Ostragehege district on the other side of the Elbe added a revoltingly sickly-sweet element to the river smell, then the wind changed, bringing the smells of the industrial district: vehicle exhaust fumes, metal, the acidic chimney smell of inefficiently burning lignite. Night was falling swiftly. How quickly the days pass, Richard thought. You leave the house in the dark and you go back home in the dark. And he was struck by the thought that he was now fifty and that there was something incomprehensible about it, for the day when he'd found a bird's nest in his father's garden and leant down in astonishment over the eggs with their green and rusty-red spots didn't seem that long ago and yet it was forty years. He watched the people. The way they drifted along in the darkness wearing grey or brown coats, only now and then was there a little colour, pale blue, beige, a cautious pink, and everyone deep in thought and cogitation, no one with their head raised, looking at other people with an open expression: all this filled him with sadness, with a feeling of inevitability and hopelessness. Fifty years – and it was only yesterday that he'd kissed his first girl! She was older than him, nineteen or twenty, almost a woman for him at twelve. Her name was Rieke, a quiet girl who'd graduated from commercial college and was doing community service as a nurse, her firm having been completely demolished in the air raid. What beautiful hair she'd had: light brown with a few blonde strands; sometimes, when he looked at Christian or stroked his hair, he had to think of Rieke – and to repress a smile no one else would have understood; an explanation would have ended in a bad mood all round. How light and gentle the touch on his skin had been as she smeared on ointment or rubbed his back with cognac, and he could feel her breath as she sat on the bed, bending down behind him, and a rebellious strand of hair that she kept blowing back. She leant back before something that was aroused in him, giving him a presentiment of something previously unknown, throbbing, forbidden, could no longer be seen as mere chance, as an incidental contact that kept occurring during this kind of treatment. One evening, when they were alone, it lasted too long for his senses, erect, over-sharp antennae, and he turned over, not knowing himself what he was doing, or why, or where he found the courage, just that something was driving him beyond his fear and stuttering pulse to take her nonplussed face in his hands and kiss her on the lips. She didn't pull back, didn't give him a slap. Afterwards she sat there in silence, looked at him, began to smile and, with a shy gesture he found strangely arousing, pushed back her hair, which had fallen over her face. 'Well, you are starting young,' she murmured and he thought, What comes next? as his mind was swamped with a flood of scraps from books he'd read on the sly, hints and dirty jokes from older anti-aircraft auxiliaries, obscene pictures in magazines. Then an expression that he didn't recognize appeared in her eyes, a kind of tender and respectful mockery; she lifted up his pyjama trousers: 'Well, you are a one. Only twelve and already you can see the effects.' He said nothing, she laughed quietly. 'Come back later, you need to feed yourself up a bit first.' At the time he'd felt insulted, he could very well remember the dull, vague feeling of shame mixed with indignant sadness; now Richard had to laugh. Thank you, Rieke, you tender young woman with your smell of cognac and soap. Tell me, has life been kind to you? I hope it has – I still lust after you! Richard gave a little leap and then, when an approaching passer-by looked at him in astonishment, pretended he'd just managed to avoid a dog turd on the pavement. He went past the Faun Palace and remembered some of the films he'd seen in the cinema that used to be a dance hall and meeting place for the workers. A building full of nooks and crannies, the seats with threadbare upholstery; on the walls of the vestibule were dusty silhouettes of Hans Moser, Vilma Degischer, Anny Ondra and other stars of UFA or Wien-Film. Framed signed portraits of DEFA actors were hung either side of the wooden kiosk housing the ticket office that, with its projecting front and brass fittings on its rounded corners, looked like a stranded carriage of the Orient Express. On the post of the wide, curving staircase with the worn fitted carpet was a snake plant some long-departed owner of the cinema had brought back from the tropics. Richard called it that because it had white and green speckled leaves hanging out of the pot like a bunch of sleeping snakes. He reminded himself to ask Meno its proper name when the opportunity arose. He saw the long queues outside the swing door of the cinema, the flickering greenish light in the display cases with the posters of Progress Film Distributors: a man in a trench coat with the collar turned up, behind him the tower of Lomonosov University, with the red star on the top stretching up into the evening sky, and facing him a woman whose wide-open eyes expressed disappointment, a last remnant of love and farewell. She looked like Anne, Richard turned his head away. He was overcome with sadness, melancholy; Rieke's smile, the cheerful mood that had brightened his day only a few minutes ago, had vanished, vanished so completely it was as if it had never been. He tried to repress the thoughts that came to him, but it was impossible. Anne, he thought. Fifty, he thought. You've been made a Medical Councillor, just as Manfred prophesied at the birthday party:

speech, thanks in the name of the people et cetera, certificate opened, certificate closed, handshake, applause, speech of thanks, one-two, buckle my shoe, just like marionettes. And Pahl did get the Fetscher Prize . . . a good surgeon, someone ought to tell him that at our age we should be beyond these little vanities. Fifty, he thought, and memories. You're full of memories, but where has your youth gone? The laughter, the exuberance, the ready-for-anything energy . . . ? The wind, the wind blowing through your hair. He'd read that somewhere recently, probably in one of those magazines the nurses read during the night shift; perhaps it was a line from a pop song, one of those trashy songs they played on TV in shows with titles like *Variety Bandbox* or *Your Requests*, songs he couldn't listen to without a feeling of distaste and revulsion. But sometimes it was these simple, sentimental and often all-too-calculatingly naive tunes that contained a phrase like that, a single line that stuck out from the rest of the concoction and touched a nerve in him that many of the serious, complex and harmonically much richer scores in the concert halls missed, leaving him cold. They rang out but they didn't go through the seventh skin to his innermost heart . . . Where the secret lay, unfathomable to all, even those closest to him.

He had hardly rung the bell for a second than Josta was embracing him, kissing him. 'You're late.'

'No reproaches, now.'

She grasped his shoulders and, as so often, he was amazed at how undisguised the emotions that could be read on her face were. A changing flush of hurt, pride, anger, defensiveness and the hunting urge of a hungry cat flitted across her face that was a Mediterranean brown with black-cherry eyes.

'Ah, Count Danilo is in a bad mood again. As he came up the stairs to see his mistress that old hag Frau Freese watched him through her spyhole. In the lobby it smells of wet washing and –'

'Oh, do stop it!' he broke in grumpily. 'And give up these silly nicknames, I'm no Count Danilo.'

'Well, what are you then? My little spoilt darling.' Josta threw her head back and laughed so that he could see the single amalgam filling in the row of her teeth, took his hand and stepped back.

'Your eyes, you . . . witch!'

'Ooh, I can see it,' Josta cried merrily, lifted his hand to her mouth and took a vigorous bite at the ball of his thumb.

'Stop! that hurts.' She bit even harder, undid his belt.

'Daniel,' he murmured.

'Playing football. He knows you're here. At the moment he has no great need to see you. Unlike me.'

'Where's Lucie,' he whispered as Josta knelt down.

'Don't worry, the apple of your eye is fast asleep.'

He looked at the bite marks on the ball of his thumb, dark red and deeply incised. His desire, which had flared up so abruptly, subsided as he looked through the corridor door into the living room, where the television he'd got for Josta through connections was on. He was overcome with resentment and a sudden feeling of disgust at the sight of the gas meter in the corner of the hall behind the sliding door into the kitchen and, on a shelf beside the key rack, the two dolls with loving smiles holding out their hands in a tender gesture. Josta stood up and embraced him, remaining silent. He released the ponytail that stuck out sideways; it looked pertly determined to go its own way and had caught Richard's eye the first time they'd met, in the Academy photocopying office, of which Josta was the head.

'Happy birthday,' she said quietly.

'Fifty, for God's sake.'

'For me you're younger than many a thirty-year-old.' They went into the living room. Richard switched the television off. It was one of Josta's idiosyncrasies to leave it on while they were talking.

'I've got nothing for you – apart from myself,' she said with a kind of furtive coquettishness. 'You've forbidden me to give you anything.'

'A tie I pretend I bought myself? Scent?' Richard smiled sarcastically. 'I can't take it home.'

'You could leave it here?'

He looked up. A slight undertone of bitterness in her reply told him she was trying to challenge him again.

'Josta . . .'

'Your family, I know. Oh, don't keep using your family as an excuse. You've got a family here just as much as there. Your daughter's here, your son's here —'

'Daniel isn't my son.'

Josta came up to him, twisting her lips in a mocking grin. 'No, he's not your son. But he calls you Dad.'

'He despises me. I can feel how he always goes on the defensive when I'm here and try to get closer to him.'

'No, he doesn't despise you! He loves you . . .'

'What?'

'I know he does, I can sense something like that, I know him very well. That penknife you brought him is sacred, and recently he got into a fight because of you, the mother of one of his classmates was a patient of yours and supposedly was treated badly . . . supposedly on your ward . . . He's coming up to twelve . . .' Josta turned away. 'I was so looking forward to your visit. You're the one who's cold, not Daniel!'

Richard went over to the window. This grey sky over the district and tenements opposite with straw stars and sad washing fluttering stiffly in the wind . . . Down below, a fenced-off playground illuminated by lamps with well-wrapped-up mothers keeping an eye on pale children who were shooting at each other with toy cap pistols. Along the wire fence of the playground was a row of overfull dustbins, the snow round them stained by piles of ash that had simply been dumped beside the bins because of a lack of space. 'I can't come at Christmas.'

'No, of course not.' Josta clenched her lips in a forced smile. 'But Lucie's made a present for you. You can't forbid her to do that. Oh, she's woken up now after all.' Lucie came in, a teddy bear under her arm. Her hair was sticking out all over, she looked pale and tired. When she saw Richard, she ran straight over to him without a word. He knelt down, she wrapped her arms round his neck, a gesture that suddenly made him feel easy and free, as if Lucie's embrace had broken the dejection he had felt even on the way to Josta's.

'Tummy ache,' she said. 'Daddy, make my tummy ache go away.'

'My little girl.' He stroked and kissed her. 'My little girl's got tummy ache . . . Let's have a look.' She lay down, Richard carefully palpated her stomach. The abdominal wall was soft, there was no point of pain and Lucie didn't have a temperature either. Nothing serious. He asked how long she had had stomach ache, what she had eaten, how her digestion was. Josta waved his questions away. 'She has that quite often.' Richard kissed Lucie's stomach and covered her up again. The little girl laughed. 'Better now, Daddy.'

'There you are.'

'Do you want to see the drawing I made for you.'

'Show me.'

It was a sheet of paper covered with numbers. They had arms and legs, happy and sad faces, a seven was wearing a hat, a fat-bellied five was smoking a cigar and had a little, chubby, sheep-like eight with dachshund ears on a lead.

'Lovely! You've drawn that beautifully. Is this for me?'

'Because it's your birthday.'

'What made you think of the numbers?'

'I saw them. When Mummy takes me to the kindergarten, we always go past a seven.'

Josta laughed. 'It's a poster for 7 October. They're learning the numbers in the kindergarten just now, that's why.'

'And are you staying here now, Daddy?'

Richard turned away from the bright little face looking up at him so trustingly; it hurt, and all the gloominess that the sight of Lucie had driven away came back. 'Not today.'

Richard left. Josta stood at the window and didn't return his farewell wave.

He went down the stairs in the darkness. It seemed not only to sharpen his eyes, he felt he perceived the smells and sounds more intensely than when he had come up the stairs half an hour ago. The smell of ash, damp washing, unaired beds, moisture and mould in dilapidated masonry, potato soup. From an apartment on the second floor – Josta lived on the fourth, the top floor – came loud voices, cries, bickering, the crash of crockery. Frau Freese on the upper ground floor, the block supervisor's apartment under the Nazis, must have heard him, for even on the half-landing above it, where the door of a shared lavatory was open, letting out a pungent smell of Ata scouring powder, he could see that her spyhole was open: a yellow needle of light pierced the darkness of the staircase and disappeared immediately as soon as he tried to creep past on tiptoe – Frau Freese had either closed the spyhole or greedily glued her beady eye to the opening.

The front door snapped shut behind him. The air was cold as iron. He went down to Rehfelder Strasse and turned towards the Sachsenbad, where he kept his swimming things. The pool attendant knew him as a regular and had even offered, in return for a doctor's certificate that kept him out of the army reserves, to give him a key, in case he should want to go swimming later because there were too many people doing their lengths. That he went swimming after work every Thursday, when he wasn't on duty, was his alibi for Anne and the boys. Anne had accepted that once a week he needed some time to himself and firmly rejected all suggestions that they use the time together. Anne, he felt, would not spy on him. Richard feared the boys, most of all Robert. During the week Christian was at the senior high school, so he was unlikely to meet him here. Moreover he tended to stay at home. Robert was different. He was adventurous, thought nothing of trailing all round Dresden with his pals, of getting on the city rail system or one of the suburban trains and, to Anne's amazement, bringing home some bread and fresh rolls he'd bought with his pocket money from a baker's in Meissen. Moreover he enjoyed swimming as much as he, Richard, did and there weren't that many swimming pools in Dresden. Also he had the feeling that Robert sometimes watched him, scrutinized him sceptically when he came back from swimming on those Thursdays. Was he imagining things? He had assumed the rapid gait, sniffing for danger on all sides, of a timid person who feels observed. It was not only Anne and the boys he had to fear, there might be acquaintances he knew nothing about – Frau Freese might be the aunt or grandmother of one of Robert's pals. Or of the boy Daniel had had a fight with . . . Chance, pure or not, loved such unfortunate encounters. Or one of his colleagues from work, a nurse or a physiotherapist who happened to live in the area, might see him and wonder what Dr Hoffmann was doing in the building where Frau Josta Fischer, the attractive – and divorced – secretary in the Administration department of the Medical Academy, lived alone with her two children in a two-and-a-half-room apartment on the top floor, even that was suspicious given the shortage of accommodation . . . And he couldn't be certain that Josta kept to her part of their agreement with the same strict rigour, the same constant, never-slackening caution as he did . . . Were there questions regarding Lucie? Did Daniel keep his mouth shut? He felt miserable and would have given a lot to get out of the tangle of lies. Five years ago he'd tried to end his affair with Josta, but then she'd got pregnant; his immediate reaction was to suggest an abortion but she had refused categorically, even used the word murder to him. Do you want to murder your child? Even today her reproach made him shudder. If he'd had his way, Weniger would have carried out an abortion, the box for 'child's father' in the case history would have been left empty. His Lucie, his daughter whom he loved more than anything! Richard leant against a wall. What have I become . . . ! A beggarly scoundrel, a cheat who creeps through the town every Thursday, caught in a net of falsity, lies, nastiness . . . Sometimes he couldn't look Anne in the eye, sometimes he was tormented by fear when he met Meno or Ulrich and they greeted him as their brother-in-law . . . What would they think of him, if it were to come out? That he was a swine, definitely, a vile wretch . . . who couldn't get away from Josta. When her eyes flashed, as they had just now, when she threw her head back challengingly, especially when she had that ponytail on the side of her head, that for others was probably no more than a quirky detail – it aroused him, almost took his breath away, had aroused him the first time he saw it, that time when he'd taken the typescripts of his lectures to the office to be hectographed. She was twenty-five and in the prime of womanhood. She was aware of it and used it. Not like a girl who is flirtatious but doesn't really know where it might lead because she doesn't yet really know either the other sex or herself; but like a mature, experienced woman, and when you were alone in a room with her, it crackled with tension – every time he would be reminded of the plastic rods the physics teacher used to rub with a cloth and you couldn't touch them without getting an electric shock. When he slept with her, he felt young, it wasn't followed by the sadness that had overcome him with other women. She clutched him and whimpered and screamed, drove him to efforts he had hardly been capable of as a thirty-year-old. Josta was insatiable and made no secret of her sexual appetite and the pleasure it gave her. Everything about her was violent: her physical reactions, her desire, once it had been aroused – sometimes he thought it was like a powder keg and when you went past, all it took was a bit of friction to set it off – her fury, her muscles, her demands and her hatred. Wild rage, feverish desire, what he thought of as her witch's fury urging his blind scattering of seed on to the very last drop: that was how he had fathered Lucie in seconds of unimaginable happiness. His daughter! He thought of her hair, her large brown eyes that gave him such an intelligent, questioning look, the child's calm, attentive quickness to learn, her unobtrusive curiosity and touching imagination. She'd given him a picture with numbers that had eyes, ears and clothes, numbers, 'I saw them, we always go past a seven.' He'd left the sheet of paper at Josta's, but it was his best birthday present. He would really have liked to take it with him and show it to everyone! Sometimes he felt the urge to take the girl home with him, to present her proudly to Anne and to say, Isn't she marvellous. My little daughter Lucie! Simply so that Anne could share the joy, this exhilarating feeling with him, so that he could give some of it to her and not selfishly keep it all to himself. Do you know what great happiness, of which you have no idea, there is in my life, come here and have a look at it, it's called Lucie, Lucie, I can't keep it to myself or I'll burst, I'm crazy with happiness; I have to share it round liberally otherwise it will tear me apart! That was how he saw it in his mind. My God, am I really so naive, Richard thought, that's impossible. Could I really do that to her? – You've already done it to her, he heard himself say. You've already done it to her.

15

Who has the best Christmas tree?

It was clear that Scheffler, the Rector of the Medical Academy, didn't know exactly what course to set: on the one hand Comrade Leonid Ilyich had died, scarcely two months ago, and the great ship of socialism was drifting along, leaderless. On the other, Christmas was approaching – and every restriction beyond a certain limit would be interpreted not as respect for the dead, but as weakness, and an expression of paralysis. Richard glanced round the Rector's office, Brezhnev's gorilla face, with the sly look in his deep-set eyes beneath his bottle-brush brows, the black lines across the corner of the photograph, next to it the Comrade Chairman of the State Council in a grey suit before a sky-blue background, a *winning* smile on his lips; then the series of Scheffler's predecessors.

'So you're rejecting my lecture?'

'Please, Herr Hoffmann.' Scheffler made a gesture of irritation. 'You must understand my position. It's bad enough that this stupid battle of the Christmas trees is starting again.'

'We hardly have any painkillers, Rector.'

'Yes, I know. The pharmacist came to see me this morning. There's one thing I'm asking of you Herr Hoffmann – don't panic. We'll find a way to deal with it. This very day I've an appointment with Barsano. His wife will be there. I'll ask for the Friedrich Wolf to help us out.' That was something that hospital had never done, Scheffler knew that, Richard knew that. 'Don't panic, that's the most important thing at the moment. There are enough rumours as it is. And what we've discussed is just between ourselves, yes?' Wernstein said, as he and Richard were washing their hands outside the operating theatres: 'They say the Internal Medicine people have found a beautiful Christmas tree.'

'And ours?'

'The senior nurse was at the Christmas Market, the Christmas tree stall: just the halt and the lame.'

That meant that the Surgical Clinic was in danger of losing the competition for the best Christmas tree, and to Internal Medicine of all people! That, it was decided in a specially convened meeting, must not be allowed to happen. In the Orthopaedic Clinic Wernstein had seen a rachitic specimen that had probably grown to maturity in the dry sand of Brandenburg; in the Eye Clinic a well-proportioned, charming tree, but scarcely five dioptres tall; in Urology a hulking great Douglas fir, ten foot wide at the bottom but only eight high, moreover it ended in a three twigs arranged like a whisk. Neurology was entering one from the Christmas Market, three foot wide at the bottom and twelve foot high, thin, brittle and touchy, for it had immediately started to shed its needles and still hadn't stopped.

That evening Richard went to Planetenweg. Kühnast didn't have a telephone at home and the porter at the pharmaceutical factory hadn't been able to put him through. Richard had rung the House with a Thousand Eyes and asked Alois Lange to put a note on the chemist's door. All over the district there were boxes on the doors, with a pencil on a string, for that kind of message. Please knock, bell not working, it said under Kühnast's nameplate.

'Ah, Herr Hoffmann, do come in. I saw Herr Lange's note. – No, no, you can keep your shoes on. This way, please.' They went past bookshelves, with gas and electricity meters ticking between them, and into the living room. Ground-glass doors, damp patches on the hall ceiling, fine cracks, plaster flaking off. 'My wife's made a few sandwiches.' Kühnast pointed to a tray. 'What would you like to drink?'

'One of your liqueurs, if you don't mind.'

A pleased expression flashed across Kühnast's face. 'Of course, we're only at the trial stage. Has it' – the chemist adjusted his glasses, which had been mended with adhesive tape – 'got round to you then? I can recommend the peach.' Kühnast poured him a glass and watched Richard as he tipped the liquid – it was a lurid sunset-red – down his throat. 'Strong.'

'Isn't it?' The chemist sat down, crossed his legs. 'Right then. What can I do for you, Herr Hoffmann?'

Richard described the problem. '. . . so I thought that you, being in the pharmaceutical factory . . .'

'At the source.' Herr Kühnast nodded and, after a while, took off his spectacles and dangled them by the mended earpiece. It would soon be Christmas, he said, in measured tones. Richard didn't quite understand. The Dresden Christmas stollen was famous, and justifiably so, Kühnast went on. Butter, sugar, flour, candied peel, sultanas – and every year it was becoming more and more difficult to get hold of the exotic ingredients; Walther's bakery was increasingly compelled to only bake them if the ingredients were supplied. Sultanas, where could you get those? And the stollen ought to be rich in fat, when you squeezed it, the cut end should be damp, the stollen should be heavy, nourishing, rest comfortably in your stomach for a while, sweet but not sickly-sweet company for the digestive enzymes, the stollen should be rich in sultanas, the stollen should be from Walther's bakery. 'Twenty of them, Herr Hoffmann. All my relations, you know.'

With Wernstein and Dreyssiger, the most enterprising of the younger doctors, Richard went to Malivor Marroquin, the costumier's; each of them hired a Father Christmas outfit. 'A bit uncomfortable, but it'll work. And we need camouflage.'

They parked the car with its trailer on the edge of the heath. The moon peered through the tops of the trees, making the snow beside the forest track shine like corrugated zinc. Dreyssiger shouldered the saw, Wernstein took the axe, Richard the bolt cutters.

'As long as nothing goes wrong,' Wernstein said. 'If we're caught, we've had it.'

'Nah, we'll manage it,' said Dreyssiger, who was in high spirits. 'Who dares wins. Or are you going to chicken out, Thomas?'

'If only this stupid beard wasn't so itchy. I'd guess it's been stored in tons of moth powder. That's what it smells like too.'

'Careful from now on,' Richard cautioned them. 'It's about ten minutes to the plantation from here. It's guarded. By Busse, the forester, in a raised hide, and a soldier. The local pastor told me that. Busse will probably have his dog with him.'

Grinning, Wernstein help up half a blutwurst.

'Excellent.'

'I hate blutwurst, boss.'

'The best tree is in the middle, slightly apart from the rest. It's said to be clearly visible from the hillock before the plantation.'

'Pretty well informed, your pastor.'

'No one can stop him combining his woodland walks with observations. But let's get on. The plantation's fenced off, Busse's hide is about fifty metres from the track; the soldier patrols the fence. We'll creep up cautiously – and then this here.' Richard held up the bolt cutters. 'Snip, snip, snip and we're through. Herr Dreyssiger, you and I will crawl over to the corpus delicti and saw it down. Herr Wernstein will keep a look-out. Can you imitate an owl?'

Wernstein put his hands together and blew into the gap between his thumbs.

'Sounds OK.' Richard gave a nod of approval. 'Two hoots if things get dicey. From now on not a sound unless it's absolutely necessary. And in a whisper.'

The baker's mother had a heart condition and Walther was in principle sympathetic towards Richard's request. But he had a bakery to run and a private one at that. 'The taxes' – he raised his floury hands – 'the taxes, Herr Doktor. We have to have a new oven but the taxman takes all our profits.' Richard gave him the sultanas from Alice and Sandor's parcel.

'I'll make you the twenty stollen, Herr Doktor. But I need medicines for my mother.'

'I'll write you a prescription.'

'No, no, they're special ones from Dr Tietze. From over there. Made over here but for over there. And sent back from over there.'

They waited behind a tree on the top of the hillock overlooking the plantation and watched. The hide wasn't to be seen, but the soldier was; he was wrapped up warmly and, Kalashnikov on his shoulder, was walking up and down in front of a gate in the fence. Now and then he flapped his arms, switched on a torch to illuminate the surroundings and rubbed his hands. He looked at his watch. On the hour he set off on his round.

'I estimate he'll be back in a quarter of an hour.' Richard wet his index finger and held it up. The wind was against them, so wouldn't carry their scent to Busse's dog. Once the soldier was out of sight, Richard gave the sign; Wernstein stayed behind. In the shadow of the track he and Dreyssiger slipped across to the fence; Richard checked the tension of the wire and cut it apart almost soundlessly. A criminal act! he thought. But the tree has to go through it. I hope it's not visible and I hope the idiot in uniform doesn't shine his light on that spot when he comes back. They crept into the plantation, stood up with some difficulty among the closely planted trees. They hung up their Father Christmas coats on a branch – they'd only be a hindrance in there and get torn – and worked their way through to the middle of the plantation. The trees were thinner there and a white rectangle was dangling from every tree. Dreyssiger shielded his torch, cautiously shone it on them. The signs bore names, all of them those of high Party functionaries; the finest blue spruce was labelled with the name 'Barsano'. It was about ten foot high and completely regular in growth.

The nurses on North Ward 1 opened the last batch of painkillers. Kühnast was sympathetic towards Richard's problem – in principle. 'We could run a special shift. The problem is that I wouldn't have any staff. It's only possible on a Saturday, our big shots are never around then.'

Richard rounded up his students and arranged a *subbotnik*. He loved the kind of extra-curricular activity that this Saturday voluntary shift would be. His opinion as a university teacher was that his students ought to know where they were studying, what they were studying and why they were studying. Germany had once been the world's pharmacy and Dresden the cradle of pharmacology. The pharmaceutical factory, created by the amalgamation of the firms Madaus, Gehe and the von Heyden Chemical Factory, where acetylsalicylic acid – the basic material for aspirin, the most widely sold medicine in the world – was first produced on an industrial scale, had its main site in Leipziger Strasse, in Gehe's former drugs and chemical finishing plant. The gutters hung crookedly, the windows wore cravats of ash, the smiles of award-winning workers on the photos along the works entry were eaten away by sulphuric cancer, as was the chalked 'labourers of all kinds' on the 'We are looking for' board hanging beside the porter's lodge.

'Psst!' Dreyssiger held up his hand. They heard the cracking of the undergrowth and immediately scurried into cover.

'Well, just look at that, it's Magenstock!' Richard ducked down. 'Magenstock in person with one of his sons.'

The two of them headed straight for the best blue spruce, listened for a few seconds, during which Richard and Dreyssiger didn't utter a word, and started to saw. Richard thought: should they jump up and say, Stop, we were here first? Dreyssiger was already doing that and striding over towards Pastor Magenstock. 'Who are you?' the pastor grunted. Dreyssiger shone his light on their faces. They had black make-up on, a kind of Indian war paint. 'We were here first.' Dreyssiger could hardly control his anger.

'Oh, Herr Hoffmann,' Pastor Magenstock murmured, pressing his hand to his heart. 'So your questions were not without ulterior motive.'

With a wave of his hand Richard told Dreyssiger to switch his torch off. Hearts pounding, the four men listened. There was nothing to be heard apart from the whispering of the trees.

'Herr Hoffmann, what you are doing is . . . in the interest of a clinic?' Pastor Magenstock was breathing with difficulty. 'You see, I'm doing this in the interest of my faith. The custom comes from the womb of Christianity.'

At that moment Wernstein's warning hoot sounded. The men pulled themselves to their feet. Magenstock and his son ran over to Barsano's spruce and furiously completed their sawing. A dog started to bark. 'Come on, let's go,' Magenstock croaked with remarkable coolness. Dreyssiger grabbed the saw, in his panic Richard left the bolt cutters on the ground. Already they could see the swaying beam of a torch through the branches of the young trees. The four of them crashed unhesitatingly through the lower branches. 'Stop there! Stop!' and 'Get them, Rudo!' came the cries behind them. Magenstock's son bent the twigs back as he dashed on ahead, and sent them smacking into his father's face. The dog was barking, interspersed with Wernstein's nonstop owl cries; how pointless, Richard thought, it sounds like a drugged cuckoo. 'Stop there! Stooooop!'

'It just won't do, Herr Kühnast. You can't let just any old people in here. There are hygiene regulations, there's a schedule for machine running time –'

'They would only have done non-skilled work,' the chemist said. 'We've had problems in packing for months.'

'Nevertheless. If something gets broken or an accident happens, what then? Anyway, you should have agreed it with me first.' The expression on Kühnast's superior's face changed. 'On the other hand, you're here now. Just come with me a moment, Herr Hoffmann', and he took him to a broom cupboard full of typewriters. 'All faulty! I've been trying to get a technician from your brother's firm for eighteen months now. You'll get your medicines. Once our machines have finally been repaired. And give your brother my best wishes.'

*

'I'll let you go, gentlemen. On one condition. One of you must play Father Christmas for my boys,' the forester growled. 'The little rascals don't believe me any more.' They tossed for it. Wernstein lost.

Richard took the First Party Secretary's tree to Ulrich, who had agreed to send a technician to the pharmaceutical factory if he was given a Christmas tree with which his department won the coveted challenge cup in the socialist 'Who has the best Christmas tree?' competition – and the considerable money prize that went with it.

'Will Dr Hoffmann please go to Professor Müller,' came the announcement over the clinic's Tannoy. Müller was walking agitatedly up and down. 'If only Reucker wouldn't give me those triumphant looks during meetings. I have to control myself, Herr Hoffmann, and I don't like having to control myself.' He twisted his lips in a sulky raspberry pout. 'But it's no use. I suppose we have to admit we've been beaten by the Internal Medicine lot this year. It's beyond belief that Reucker is also the chairman of the Christmas Tree Inspection Committee.'

'What? Not the Rector?'

'Exactly. That's the scandal.'

'We've not given up yet.'

'But as far as I can see all that's left is the Christmas Market.'

'They've got nothing but walking sticks that would make us the laughing stock of the Academy.'

Müller's face lit up as an idea came to him. 'And twigs, Herr Hoffmann, and twigs.'

But, at the inspection, with a cool gesture Reucker, the head of the Internal Medicine Clinic, took a screwdriver out of the pocket of his snow-white coat, searched for a while, during which Müller's lips pressed together until they were no more than a slit, then screwed off one branch of the proudly upright, symmetrically built surgical tree.

The nurses, doctors, diet cooks, nursing auxiliaries stood there, heads bowed; the crackle of their coats was audible. 'The screw-tree does not grow in our land,' said Reucker and he dropped the screw from high up into the hand of an assistant, who, engaged to a nurse from Surgery, gave a smug smile. In the house on Planetenweg they ate the best stollen in the world that evening.

16
The blank sheet

The Christmas holidays were over. Alice and Sandor had returned to Ecuador, amazed at the ashes and snow, as they had said; amazed at an excursion to Seiffen, where the toymakers turned hoops of wood and cut sheep, cows and the pack animals of the Three Kings out of them, painted them and sold them, bright and new, at the Christmas Market. They'd seen a miners' procession, breathed in the smell of 'Knox' incense cones and punch and, adding the East German marks they'd been forced to exchange to their West marks, they'd bought one of the tall, plain pyramids that were not sold at the Dresden Christmas Market but for which they had to knock at the low door of an Erzgebirge cottage and overcome the suspicion of the carver's wife, who opened the door and regarded them in silence. And Dr Griesel, who lived on the upper ground floor of Caravel and kept the house register, said to Christian, with a sour expression on his face, 'You can tell your father that it just won't do . . . He told me nothing about that trip and his visitors are staying longer than intended. I shall have to report it.'

'Oh, the clown can go to hell, he just moans all the time because he didn't get our apartment. Yesyes, Herr Hoffmann, we're always helping to heat your apartment,' said Richard, imitating Dr Griesel's fretsaw voice. 'But he's always leaving his Trabbi in my parking space.'

Their neighbour's gaunt knuckle tapped the register with Griesel's entries in his engineer's script. 'I am the house supervisor and it is my duty to keep this register. The declared length of visit has been exceeded. And recently you left the front door and the cellar door open and all the cats of the neighbourhood came in and shat on the sand, the next time you'll clear it up yourself with your bare hands. And we don't heat the whole neighbourhood, either.'

At school the pre-Christmas torpor had vanished. A hum of tension, of hectic activity, had returned. Upstairs and downstairs the new building, which, compared with the old school, a concrete block for almost 1,000 pupils, seemed full of light, was abuzz with pupils repeating vocabulary and theorems. In the corridors the PVC reduced the sound of hundreds of pairs of slippers – Waldbrunn was the smallest senior high in the GDR – to a soft shuffle. Maxim Gorki's eyes glittered on a photo in the display case on the first floor, below it were a trumpet, a Pioneer's neckerchief, a copy of a letter from Gorki to young people, a letter of greeting from the Wismut workers to the new senior high school and, something a lot of pupils stopped to look at, an agate, the polished surface of which was covered in milky rings and fiery patterns. It came from Schlottwitz, not far from Waldbrunn, where many such stones were found.

For Christian the classes with Herr Baumann turned out to be the fiasco he had feared. 'Well, Christian, thinking again, are we?' Herr Baumann would say sympathetically, his rosy-cheeked face under the scholar's brow crinkling in amusement when Christian pondered an exercise on the following model: Calculate where A and B will meet when they are building a road towards each other with A laying concrete slabs of size α at rate x; B concrete slabs of size β at rate y. To hell with those exercises! To hell with mathematics and its five lessons a week! What if B was a boozer and deviated from the set line . . . Of course, there was no boozing in maths.

'Thinking again, are we?' Baumann smiled quietly and didn't rate any of the busily scribbling pupils more highly than was necessary. 'I'm giving you a B, Svetlana,' he'd said recently when Svetlana Lehmann had to go up to the blackboard and, concealed behind one of the wings, wrestle with a vector calculation. 'I'm giving you a B because I have to. A B means: good. So that means you're good at maths. So sit back down. D'you know who was good at maths? René Gruber, he was good at maths.' With that Baumann shrugged his shoulders and softly announced, 'Now we're going to put our folders in our desks and take out a piece of paper.' The class sat there, paralysed with fear; only Verena had shining eyes. Yes, she was good at maths as well. When she did exercises, Herr Baumann didn't smile and when, at the blackboard, she found another way of solving an equation and, in the middle of a tangle of formulas and unbelievably complicated-looking integrals and square roots, looked for help from Herr Baumann, who was sitting on the edge of the desk at the front, following, the rings of his blue irises, now devoid of gentleness, like two metal discs, he would answer, 'What you were trying there was really elegant, Verena, but look at this', then take a piece of red chalk and insert numbers in his copperplate handwriting in the gaps in Verena's spiky lines. There were only two pupils whom he always addressed by the familiar 'du' – Verena and Heike Fieber, who sat next to Jens Ansorge at the front desk of the window row and during maths lessons held her freckled face in the sunshine that trickled over the hill with the motorway into the classroom. At such times Baumann would ask her, like a kindly grandfather asking his little granddaughter, 'Well, Heike, dreaming? Or are you counting lorries?' adding, 'René Gruber could have looked out of the window. But, do you know, he didn't.' People didn't talk about René Gruber at the Maxim Gorki Senior High School, it was an unwritten law. On the one hand René Gruber was undoubtedly a mathematical genius who had won both the GDR and the Eastern Bloc Mathematical Olympiad in Moscow – and that, as some malicious

Waldbrunners said, despite the fact that his mother was on the check-out at the local Konsum, next door to the angling club, and his father a simple forestry worker. On the other hand when they sent René, on the basis of his achievements, his political reliability and his family background, as a working-class child to the International Mathematical Olympiad in New York, where he won a special prize for the most elegant solution, he did not return but accepted instead the offer of an American university. From then on he was regarded as an illegal emigrant and traitor. Baumann never used that word when he talked about René Gruber, and that struck Christian. The closer he came to retirement, the more exclusively Baumann's interests were directed towards mathematics, the pure sphere of conclusive proofs and irrefutable, crystal-clear conclusions.

During classes in the laboratory cubicles Verena sat on the bench beside Christian, only separated from him by the row of instruments. Siegbert Füger teased him: 'Hey, Christian, you seem impressed by Fräulein Winkler.'

'Nonsense!'

'You keep looking across at her.'

If even Siegbert Füger, who sat in the window row, noticed, then he'd have to be more careful. It meant Verena would probably have noticed too. That would explain her curt and tart remarks when he said 'Good morning' to her for the second time in a day – which, as he admitted to himself, he did out of both politeness and a certain maliciousness . . . Of course, the politeness was exaggerated and since Verena would nod the first time he said it, she couldn't be deaf or not have noticed him in the throng of pupils. He wanted to hear her voice, for her voice, an alto whose vibrations already had undertones of a mature woman, fascinated him; he tried not to let it be obvious. His fascination was such that when she was nearby, he would tell dirty jokes to make Falk Truschler or Jens Ansorge laugh but in reality were directed at Verena in order to provoke her to protest or express her displeasure, and that he got to hear often enough . . . Sometimes then a particularly quick-witted reply would occur to him – at least he thought it was quick-witted; the way Jens and Falk fell silent seemed to confirm that. Verena would also fall silent and scrutinize him and he felt this eye contact, this deep shadow that had no coldness, as something delicious that far outweighed his embarrassment at his pimples. Stop, stay there! his eyes flickered, but he couldn't interpret her look: had he, Christian, just thrown away his last chance and condemned himself to appear an incorrigible idiot in her eyes . . . ? And after one such look Jens had the effrontery to tell him he should take advantage of the moment of stunned silence between them and kiss Verena. 'You'd do that?' Christian asked in disgust.

'Of course, you idiot. Anyone can see the girl fancies you,' Jens roared.

'Not that big-city peacock,' she retorted.

Christian flared up. 'How do you know that?' he demanded. How pretty she looked now.

'You play the cello in the cellar, everyone can hear it, you . . . poseur! Our gifted artist always immerses himself in his music just as 11/1 has finished and he can achieve the greatest effect, especially on Kerstin Scholz!'

It was true. Christian often found himself thinking of Kerstin Scholz, especially of her figure, when he was practising in the cellar. And that brought a certain intensity to his exercises.

'Oh, how I suffer,' Verena mocked, 'but only in front of the others.'

'So you do listen?'

'Don't kid yourself!'

He found her sauciness impressive . . . 'Oh, you know, you . . . pretty little thing,' was his lame retort. Jens pretended he was going to be sick. Verena went bright red. Falk grinned. She turned away without a word.

*

Herr Schnürchel was strange in a way that made Christian go along with Schnürchel's games. Christian thought, in the evening: he smiled when you finally got the Moscow pronunciation of the letter shtsha right. Creamy like a soft ice. On the one hand Herr Schnürchel crept round the hostel and school corridors with suede-soft steps, put on his dusting gloves with pleasurable meticulousness and with an expression of dismay turned up lots of dirt, complained about Christian's black-and-white calendar and Jens Ansorge's magnetic tapes with suspiciously invisible music – Christian knew that Jens listened to the German New Wave music from the West – on the other hand Schnürchel would have nothing to do with the linguistic slovenliness of previous Russian teaching and came to every lesson with a pannier brimful of Russian words that he would tip out at his hard-pressed pupils' Heiko fountain pens. Christian was intrigued by this other side of Schnürchel, his ambition was aroused. Every morning – Russian was generally one of the first two classes – his eye would survey Schnürchel's cheeks, so closely shaved they looked gangrenous, the horse nostrils of his narrow nose with the red ball at the tip, his black hair that he smoothed down with sugar water; it was divided by a parting as precise as the edge of a folder. Herr Schnürchel would sit at his desk, ready to pounce, his eyes wide open with a look that was too penetrating for seven o'clock in the morning and made even Svetlana Lehmann lower her eyes. Herr Schnürchel wore Präsent 20 suits with razor-sharp creases, his shirts and ties were striped and always had a badge pinned to them, a pennant with the hammer and sickle on it. When he sat down, he crossed his feet and tilted his chair impatiently so that the white flesh of his calves could be seen above his striped socks and garters.

One day in March, during the history class, he wrote a question on the board and told them to put their books and folders away in their desks. An unannounced class test. 1983, the Karl Marx Year. Wall newspapers had been covered with articles on the prophet-bearded

philosopher, gradually obliterating the black-edged Brezhnev portraits.
On 1 May, International Workers' Day, there was to be a 'Karl Marx
procession of the pupils of the high school and senior high school',
Principal Fahner had announced at assembly. Schnürchel's question
was: 'By what can we tell that the victory of socialism over capitalism
proceeds according to certain laws. Base your argument on Marx's
theory of history.' Without hesitation the pens started to scribble. Christian was annoyed; he was badly prepared. Every grade was important – the
final grade was the average of all the individual grades and anyone
who, like Christian, wanted to study medicine had to be close to an A
at the end of the eleventh year, since it was that year's report with
which you applied for a place at university. He started to break the
question down into its component parts. 'By what' and 'according to
laws' and 'Marx's theory of history' seemed to be the key words. Marx's
theory of history . . . Nothing came to mind, however hard he tried.
He remembered the history room at the Louis Fürnberg High School
where a few pictures on the wall, with an arrow underneath running
from darkness to light, showed the history of humanity: primitive men
with raised spears facing a mammoth, hairy women gathering fruits,
the boys sharpening arrows or chipping hand axes; then Roman heads,
slaves bowed low under the yoke, the glint of the Spartacus uprising
already in their eyes . . . In the Middle Ages peasants in revolt bran-
dished their scythes; then the picture from the days of the French
Revolution with the bare-breasted figure of Liberty storming the bar-
ricades (her breasts had been worn flat by pupils who liked to get
physically to grips with history); then came the age of the bearded
heads: Marx, Engels, Lenin, and then nothing more, there was no wall
left, the arrow of time stopped at the corner. There were always lots
of pieces of chewing gum there . . . When someone asked the question
'What next?' a dreamy look would come over Frau Dreieck, the history teacher and principal of the high school, and she would give an
answer containing a lot about light and air, making Christian think of

Pioneer camps . . . the transition of imperialism, the orchid stage (flourishing on decaying ground) of capitalism, into socialism that somehow switched to or somehow softened into communism . . . He regularly pondered that 'somehow'. The word 'switched' made Christian think of 'setting the points', a concept that frequently occurred in civics lessons; and now he had to set his points, in the direction of writing down his thoughts . . . Somehow. But what thoughts? Should he describe his amazement at the arrow of history ending in the corner of the classroom? Or would he be on the right lines (to continue the image), if he thought of a very ripe pear in his grandfather's garden in Glashütte? Was history like the fruit, hanging proud and heavy with juice before the eyes of a humanity thirsting after water and sweetness? You could make excellent fruit brandy from pears like that . . . So was socialism the pear and communism the brandy distilled from it? Fruit brandy for everyone. And the hangover the next morning . . . ? Did that follow according to some law? The pear ripens, pests nibble at it and hollow it out, maggots leave a capitalist parasitical trail of waste matter, but then . . . If you ate you had to go to the bog, that too was a law of nature. Marx's theory of history. Christian looked around for help, but he was sitting by himself and couldn't crib from anyone. Herr Schnürchel was sitting, feet crossed, at the teacher's desk, rocking back- and forward in his chair, his basilisk stare fixed on Verena. Verena wasn't writing. She seemed to be taking a break or pursuing some thought that her pen would record in a few seconds. Verena was staring out of the window. As far as Christian could tell, the sheet of paper in front of her was white. Her neighbour, Reina Kossmann, was squinting over at her irritatedly. Verena wasn't writing. When the bell rang, Christian had gleaned four pages from the treasure-house of memory. Verena handed in a blank sheet.

17

Long-distance calls

Spring had arrived quietly, its pale fingers of sunshine had wiped away the snow along the F170 so that the fields round Possendorf and Karsdorf seemed to be covered in dirty sheets. There were still days of cold, but they merely suspended the rout of winter; the snow was sickening, beneath the crust there was a dripping, sintering, trickling, water-druses formed, quicksilvered, licked away at bridges between hollows, sought each other out, wove rivulets. Icicles hung from the school roof, like rows of glassy eels hung up to dry, drops tocked, pinged and clacked in melodious antiphony; Jens Ansorge would have liked to record it and work it up into a 'Song of the Thaw'. What he had in mind was Tomita's music based on Mussorgsky's *Pictures from an Exhibition* that the Japanese sound artist had arranged in the witches' kitchen of his synthesizer and published with Amiga. How the others envied Jens that record! It had just come out and could not be bought in any record shop in the whole area, not even in Philharmonia. The owner, Herr Trüpel, had anticipated Christian's request and told him even as the 'clong' of the shop-door bell was still sounding that 'Herr To-mitta's disc' was no longer in stock, not even 'for the freaks'. As he spoke he had given Christian a blank stare from blue eyes that were much enlarged by gold-rimmed glasses with round lenses. Not even under the counter? That was asked more out of naivety than cheek; Herr Trüpel simply raised his left eyebrow and hesitated a moment before he looked under the counter, stood up ramrod-straight and said, 'No.' One had to make do with cassettes. Without a word Herr Trüpel placed one on the counter in front of Christian. 'That will do.' And collected the retail price of 20 marks – for an ORWO magnetic tape cassette.

Thaw in the Erzgebirge. The grey of the shingle roofs emerged like a stony skin, old and worn out, dulled by the lashing of wind and rain. The air lost the metallic smell of snow. In the higher villages the roads often became impassable, washed away by torrential mountain streams. The bark of the fruit trees lining the tracks across the fields was black and shiny with the moisture; the trees on the slopes of the Windberg and the Quohrener Kipse were like peasant women hunched from work.

When the class went on a study outing on Tuesdays during the double biology lesson with Dr Frank, Christian kept apart from the other boarders in his house in order to avoid having to talk to them. He kept his senses awake to all impressions: this was his father's and Uncle Hans's country, this was where Arthur Hoffmann, his clock-grandfather, lived. And it was Verena's country. They walked along the banks of the Kaltwasser, the Wilde Bergfrau, explored the upper reaches of the Rote Bergfrau with the tributaries that washed out the earth from underground veins of copper that gave it the reddish colour from which its name came, and Christian would think: she's seen this, she went for walks here, perhaps she learnt to swim here, perhaps just here where the bank curves. He never asked her, didn't dare to, fearing one of her tart or dismissive answers. But he observed her all the more closely, stared at every plant she looked at for any length of time, registered every whispering huddle, every outburst of laughter when the girls got together, casting mocking glances at the boys scattered around. Most often, he imagined, he seemed to be the target of these secret conclaves so that for a while he kept away from Verena, even sought out Dr Frank, their class teacher, as if he could think of nothing more interesting than the flora associated with a stream in the eastern Erzgebirge. He was familiar with most of the plants from his many walks with Meno and Grandfather Kurt. Dr Frank asked cautious questions about him. If Christian seemed about to say too much, he left him in peace. Then Frank would walk on by himself, well ahead of the pupils, and come back when he found something interesting. He would never force it on them or explain it just to show off his knowledge but seemed almost shamefaced in asking the pupils to pay attention. Dr Frank was a calm man with medium-length, grey-ing hair that looked shaggy and had a half-hearted parting – less, so it seemed to Christian, because Dr Frank felt the need to have his hair combed than because it was usual and you had to have your hair done in some way or other anyway. He had grown up in Schmiedeberg, a small town to the south of Waldbrunn that huddled up against the Erzgebirge motorway, low, nondescript houses set in the delightful countryside of the catchment area of the Wilde Bergfrau dominated by the factory buildings and chimneys of VEB GISAG Ferdinand Kunert, where most of the inhabitants of Schmiedeberg worked. Frank had not only completed a PhD but a DSc as well, the only schoolteacher in the whole country with that qualification, so it was said. The Tech-nical University of Dresden had even offered him a professorship but, since he wanted to abandon neither his pupils nor Schmiedeberg, he had declined. Christian knew that his father had spoken to Frank and that it was Frank's intervention with the district education department that had led to an exception being made to the usual selection proced-ure. He ought to have attended one of the senior high schools in Dresden but since those had the reputation of being particularly dogmatic ideo-logically, Richard was happier to see his son in Waldbrunn.

Frank was a Party member. In one of their first chemistry lessons he remarked that if he should meet someone who had attended the school and his classes at the expense of the people of the German Democratic Republic but then gone to the West, he would cross over to the other side of the road. As he spoke, he had given Christian a look of veiled melancholy with flashes of shy warmth.

Frank was doing research into left-handedness. The days when left-handed pupils were rigorously made to write with the right hand were not long since past. Frank himself was a left-hander who had had his 'polarity' reversed and it seemed to disturb him, for he mentioned it several times, paused, broke off. Sometimes he would pick up a piece of chalk with his left hand, turn away as if he had been caught out, and when he turned back to the blackboard, the chalk was in his right hand.

Frank knew plants and animals, the wooded gorges as far away as the Karl-Marx-Stadt district, showed the pupils the abandoned tin mines outside Altenberg, the boggy Georgenfeld moors where the sundew grew. He knew the Kahleberg, from where you could see the ČSSR and on which, as on the whole ridge, the only trees were isolated, damaged spruces. The class went for several walks there, for just a few hours each time since the wind, which swept the yellowish fog over the Erzgebirge, grew stronger in the afternoon. At first the fog caused an irritation in the throat and difficulty swallowing, then coughing and red-rimmed eyes. Dr Frank, who also taught chemistry, knew where the fog came from.

One Tuesday at the end of March the history tests were handed back. Herr Schnürchel meandered round the room, giving out their essays, briefly commenting on them: 'Svetlana, nice, clear class standpoint, very good deduction, A', 'Siegbert, confused the Gotha Programme with the *Anti-Dühring*, still a C', 'Christian' – Schnürchel's eyes fixed on him and he felt as if he were being cut open by their oxyacetylene-torch look – 'too many empty words but you bring out Marx's theory of history well, B minus', then he sat down, intertwined his fingers and contemplated the remaining sheet of paper. Christian looked out of the window so that he had Schnürchel's profile in view but avoided eye contact; Heike Fieber was playing with her fuzzy hair, Reina Kossmann had placed her hands on her desktop, her shoulders hunched up, her face and Verena's two bright patches in the light flaking from the neon tubes in this still misty early morning that would probably brighten up into a sunny day. Schnürchel's voice flashed out and seemed to hit Verena physically, as gently as a lizard's tongue: 'Why didn't you tell me you didn't feel well?'

'I . . . didn't feel unwell.'

'No.' Schnürchel nodded, as if he'd expected that answer, but Christian could see neither satisfaction nor irritation in his expression. 'If there is something you have to tell me . . .'

The whole class seemed to be concentrated round Verena's seat, a chorus of intense silence not daring to ask, What's going to happen?, crouching now in expectation of a blow, straining every nerve to absorb its force. Suddenly Christian could hear Uncle Niklas's voice: In this country you have to be able to afford everything, see him turn round unhurriedly in the music room of Evening Star and take a sip of coffee. What he had said lodged in his mind, continued to work, returned as a vivid, nasty thought that took root when Verena's face showed no signs of unease, was just paler than usual, which could come from the neon light; her coal-black eyes, alert, almost cold, fixed on Schnürchel's. Could she afford it? No, that was absurd. If she could, it would be the equivalent of exposure, and They could have no interest in that, no more than in stupidity. Pupils who were involved supposedly had certain gaps or nonsense entries in their column in the class register. Their parents' professions were not entered if they belonged to Them, or just the bare name was there. But that was not the case with Verena. Father: Johannes Winkler, doctor, District Clinic, Waldbrunn; Mother: Katharina Winkler, organist and choirmaster, Protestant church, Waldbrunn; Siblings: Sabine, librarian, District Library.

Verena an informant . . . He sought her eyes, he must have given her a horrified look, her eyes slid away.

'Perhaps you want to tell me afterwards.' Schnürchel's words were not a question but a closing statement. His stripy socks, his crossed feet – not funny at all.

'I didn't feel unwell.' Verena's voice was jagged, she had to clear her throat.

'Verena.' This time Schnürchel answered quickly, Christian sensed the surprise in the class at the restrained warmth of his tone. 'Then

I will have to call a meeting of the FGY leadership and inform your class teacher.' Verena remained silent, and Christian couldn't understand her, turned his head towards the door and whispered, 'Why? Why?' with a pointless intensity. He felt another burst of suspicion and thought he could also see it in Jens Ansorge's expression, in Siegbert Füger's thin smile, Reina Kossmann's now chalk-white face.

The meeting of the FGY committee was arranged for three o'clock, after the last class, in the Russian room surrounded by pictures of Sputnik and the Artek Pioneer camp on the blackboards, sponsorship letters from their related Komsomol organization and a plaster bust of Maxim Gorki. The rest of the class waited outside.

Agenda, taking the minutes – Falk Truschler took out a pencil and paper – Dr Frank's freckled hand opening and closing. 'Go on, please.' He nodded to Verena, who was staring to one side, the sheet of paper, blank apart from her name and the exercise, before her. 'I didn't know what I should write.' Her voice was clear, tone curt, with a touch of contempt; Christian looked up but only met Frank's eyes, the light brown of which he for some inexplicable reason now found disagreeable, as he did his helplessly opening and closing hand. 'Then you had a blackout.' Frank stated it in a murmur, it wasn't a question. 'That can happen.'

'In this case you will have to be given an E.' Schnürchel had spoken hesitantly but before Frank had stopped speaking. Again there was the silence, like something that couldn't be switched off. Christian was wearing the blue Free German Youth shirt, as were Falk Truschler and Siegbert Füger and Svetlana Lehmann: Herr Schnürchel had asked all the boarders in the class to put them on.

'I don't agree with the way this discussion is going. In my opinion Verena has a negative attitude to the question set and didn't answer it for that reason. It wouldn't be the first time.'

Verena looked up and scrutinized Svetlana with startled fascination.

'Yes, you got up to the same kind of thing back at the high school. Just like your sister.'

'Svetlana –'

'In my opinion it's deliberate provocation, Dr Frank.'

'I don't believe that.' Reina Kossmann, the treasurer on the committee, shook her head. 'She said something to me beforehand.' Verena had felt ill because of something that happened once a month –

'She said she didn't feel unwell,' Svetlana insisted. 'I'd be interested to know what standpoints the two of you have. My view is that the committee should pass a resolution and present it to the principal.' Svetlana thought for a moment, tapped her lips with her finger. 'To both principals. And to the Party committee.'

At this Siegbert Füger joined in: Svetlana couldn't simply say 'I don't believe her'; in that case not only Verena, Reina too, would be under suspicion of lying, he himself didn't know Verena from the high school but from sports lessons with Herr Schanzler here, there'd been a collision when they were playing dodgeball. Her lip had bled, but she hadn't fainted, as usually happened, Verena was the kind of person who would just grit her teeth, as she had before the history test.

What did he mean by 'as usually happened', Reina wanted to know, straightening her back, it was the boys who were the quickest to start moaning and wailing, for example at the potato harvest. Christian remained silent because he could see in his mind's eye Verena's face contorted with pain after she'd hit her thumb with the hammer, but since Falk Truschler said nothing – he had to take the minutes – Svetlana fixed her eyes on him, while Dr Frank folded a piece of paper up small and Schnürchel took a tube out of his briefcase, squeezed out an inch of transparent cream and rubbed it over his hands. There was a pleasant smell of herbs.

'Your position, Christian?' At that moment he found himself thinking of Svetlana's curly hair. It was beautiful and of a brown colour he couldn't quite find a word for. 'She isn't in condition to do a test if she feels ill.'

'She should have said so beforehand, of course. – That was her mistake,' Schnürchel said reflectively. 'We can't withdraw the E grade. Not a good start, but I think that in your case it will just be a blip. There are oral tests as well and apart from this you're good to very good.'

'That's all you have to say?' Schnürchel's contribution seemed to have gone right past Svetlana, like an insect you ignore because you're concentrating on something. She fixed her eyes on Christian and it seemed to him that she was having to make an effort, her eyelids were fluttering almost imperceptibly, her look wasn't steady. 'Pity that the best positions were already taken, hm? The deputy Free German Youth secretary, the clerk and the treasurer. That would have done for acceptance at medical college, wouldn't it? But the way things are . . . As agitator you'd have to show real commitment, wouldn't you? Nail your colours to the mast.'

'Svetlana, you're not being objective. We can't work together like that.' It was Dr Frank who said that, his lips grey, and Reina Kossmann hissed, 'To suggest I accepted an easy position just to get a few extra plus points in my file –'

'But it's the truth! The most important thing for you lot is getting to college, your career, that's why you join the Free German Youth committee. Not as secretary or agitator, where it really matters, of course . . . Would you be here if it didn't bring any plus points? What we're trying to realize in this country is a matter of complete indifference to you!'

'Svetlana! We'll get nowhere like this. Dr Frank is right, that is not objective. It is not correct. Not correct. To conclude we should hear what Verena has to say. Please calm down.' It was remarkable how gentle Schnürchel could be, fatherly, as if he had to save an unruly favourite daughter from herself; his left hand had shot forward: as if he wanted to grasp something, Christian thought. Perhaps it was a situation he had come across before, one he recognized.

'What Reina said is right. I . . . had problems.' Verena was pale now, she spoke quietly, her face turned away.

That evening Christian rang home. He had walked a long way, past the city castle, where there were still lights on, and past the cinema, along the embankment beside the Wilde Bergfrau to the tannery. The foaming, thundering river did nothing to calm him down, he kept seeing scenes from the afternoon in his mind's eye and couldn't clear his head. On the bridge he leant over the parapet and looked at the dark eddies with metallic spindles gliding through them at irregular intervals, but after a while he felt cold and the darkness was becoming a problem. A single lamp was hanging like a white pot above where the road along the embankment crossed the main road leading out that started at the bridge. He headed back into the town, towards the market, but went the wrong way and after an empty time found himself outside the cinema again, which confused him; but then he saw the telephone booth beside the path outside the porter's lodge of the castle. The porter eyed him over a copy of *Morgenpost*. Christian strolled over to the telephone booth. That seemed to be enough for the porter, he turned back to his newspaper. The telephone in this booth was probably monitored. Nothing that might get us into trouble on the telephone, Anne had drummed into him. But perhaps things were different with this telephone . . . It was outside the Party headquarters. On the one hand. On the other there must be more telephones in the rooms of the dilapidated castle than anywhere else in Waldbrunn, so why would they need another one here . . . Was that not precisely the trap? They knew how people thought: hardly anyone used the telephone on the market square, in fact so far Christian had never seen anyone using it – everyone assumed that the booth would be monitored and since Security knew the way people thought, knew that even when someone made a call from there, aware it was being monitored they would only say harmless things, Security might perhaps regard that booth as useless and leave it untapped, while here, smiling at how clever they were, people walked straight into the snare.

Or was the booth outside the castle perhaps after all a free space that the Party leadership could keep for themselves? Christian thought it over. How would he act if he were one of Them . . . He'd simply tap every line without further ado. Richard had often played 'Think like your enemy' with him and Robert and had said, 'That's unlikely, they can't have so many people to listen in, they would need three shifts a day and that on every line, and even if they had the personnel they would hardly have the technology and tapes. There must be a few untapped lines in this country. That of the Comrade Chairman of the State Council will definitely not be one, nor that of the head of Security.' – 'Nor those of the telephone booths either,' Christian had replied. – 'Why not? It's precisely those that are not very promising for them since no one says anything on a public line. Only idiots and foreigners would do that and they're kept under surveillance round the clock anyway.'

Christian continued to think about it. There was just one reason to call from here and not from the phone at the market. This booth would probably be in working order.

'Hoffmann?'

Christian could hear laughter in the background, his father's voice, the Westminster chimes of the grandfather clock striking the quarter.

'Hi, Mum, it's me.'

'Oh, is there something special, since you're calling?'

Christian closed his eyes, so strange did those voices sound, as if they were sloshing round in an aquarium. 'No . . . No.' He couldn't speak, not now, not on the telephone and, especially, not to his mother. When he'd had problems he'd never gone to his mother. Nor to Richard.

To Meno instead, whom he could hear in the background. That meant he couldn't ring him either.

'Has something happened, Christian?' Now she was suspicious; he knew the concern in her voice.

'No, not at all. I . . . just wanted to ask Robert something, is he there? It's about the Tomita record . . .'

'No, he's gone to Uli's with Ezzo.'

'It can wait until the weekend. Is Niklas there?'

'Yes, and Wernstein.'

'All the best, Mum.'

'Are you coming at the weekend?'

Christian gave a vague answer, but brightened up and told her about the history test and his B minus and how annoyed he was, told her about the reasons for that moderate grade, so that when he'd finished he had the feeling Anne wouldn't ask any more questions.

18

Coal Island

Ridged like a karst landscape, a deposit of jagged piled-up ice floes, Coal Island lay before the four visitors, of which three showed their permits to the guard on the bridge before setting off – Richard took little Philipp down from his shoulders so that Regine could take him by the hand – across the Kupferne Schwester bridge to the government offices. Fog lay over East Rome, the whistle of Black Mathilda as it turned out of the tunnel and announced its approach to the power station sounded muffled. Even at this early hour the snow on the bridge had been trampled by many pairs of shoes; it was the first Thursday in the month, the day the offices were open to the public. Meno shaded his eyes, the white was dazzling and he saw that it was the first sharp rays of the March sun setting off sparks on the steeply sloping, frost-encrusted roofs of the buildings and on their windows, now clear as water, now a confusing swirl, bursting apart like dewdrops on a cobweb, suddenly frozen in a multiple prismatic glare, sparks flickering up as a tangle of light and finding countless echoes in the deep fault-lines between the buildings: this had recalled the picture, the piled-up quartz slabs, yokes, ice crystals.

They had arrived before the offices opened and joined the queue that stretched from the portico of the entrance to where the Marx–Engels Memorial Grove, empty, an almost insurmountable obstacle for the human voice, spread out its concrete grey. Marx and Engels had bronze books in their hands and seemed to be reading them. Crows were perched on their heads and the soldier on sentry duty, who wasn't allowed to move, kept trying to drive them away by clicking his tongue. A few of those waiting clearly felt sympathy for him and raised their hands to clap, but acquaintances who were less sympathetic and had their eyes fixed on the portico pushed them down. At 'one hundred' Richard gave up counting, opened his briefcase, checked that the report was still there (but who would have taken it away from him anyway, he'd packed and checked the briefcase himself before he left the house); Meno too had opened his worn attaché case and was rummaging around in the papers. Regine clutched the violin case to her and let go of Philipp, who immediately went over to the sentry at the Memorial Grove, who, as the clocks in the office building began to chime, stood to attention, shifting his machine gun with angular movements, staring fixedly in front of him from under his steel helmet and for the following hours, until he was relieved, would give no indication of whether he saw the queue, which was dispersing at the front, growing at the back, whether he saw anything at all: Philipp plucked at his uniform, made faces at him, but the only response was the restrained amusement of a few of those waiting. The queue moved forward. There was a play of bluish, crimson and purple iridescence over the pepper-and-salt granite of the vestibule. A cord controlled access to the kiosk-like lean-to where a porter was sitting surrounded by telephones on retractable arms that were sliding out and back with deliberate slowness, like the tentacles of a sea anemone. Perhaps a faulty control, Meno thought.

The members of the public stated their business, opened their bags to be checked and were allowed through. Behind the porter's lean-to there was a wall with clocks showing different times around the world; the name of the place was written on the clock face in black lettering: Jakarta, New York, London, Valletta, Moscow, Vladivostok, Lima, Peking and many others; little Philipp listened to the clicking of the hands and wanted to know who lived in all these places. The offices' paternoster lifts opposite the clock-wall started to move.

'We have to separate here,' Richard said, pointing to the clocks. 'Shall we meet at twelve?'

'There's a public-address system,' said Meno. 'If one of us has to wait longer they can put out a call for the others.'

'So second floor, F wing,' Regine reminded herself. 'Come on, Philipp.' She took the boy by the hand; he headed straight for one of the lifts. On the second floor they looked down from a rotunda into an air well. Employees in grey coats were hurrying to and fro, some pushing files in carts trundling along quietly; worn carpets swallowed up the footsteps, the clearing of throats behind the doors, the distant murmuring. Corridors radiated out from the rotunda, which had a glass chandelier in the Kremlin's beloved icicle style hanging down into it.

'Touch the knight,' Philipp demanded and Richard lifted him up so that he could reach the stone figures on the balustrade of the rotunda. Men with shields and raised swords; most of the finely chiselled features expressed amazement, perhaps at being caught by surprise, that the sculptor had mixed, as if strained through a muslin cloth, with more profound liquids: a clear conscience, new negotiations seen in older light, traces of a comic love of haggling; the weathered armour had strange spines on the shoulders and breastplates, they made Richard think of a rare disease through which the poor patient's skin had developed horny spines, he tried to remember the name but only the prefix 'ichthyo-' occurred to him. Philipp couldn't break off the spines and said with a laugh, as if to be on the safe side, 'Ouch,' when he touched one with the tip of his finger. The sculptor must have gone to great pains to make the stone so pencil-sharp. Now something was ticking, like the pendulum of a large metronome set at a slow tempo. Richard looked out of the window, it must be coming from outside, from the derricks beyond the offices, in the prohibited part of Coal Island.

Second floor, F wing. Corridors enlivened by threadbare red runners and smelling musty. The distant roar of a vacuum cleaner, the clatter of typewriters behind closed doors, queues outside open ones.

The thud of stamps, whispering, the creak of thick piles of paper having holes made by office punches, the hum of sewing machines. Certain files were sewn into the binders, something that had been taken over from the Soviet Union, where it had been the custom of the Okhrana, the Tsarist secret police, as Richard had learnt from a patient who worked on Coal Island.

'And you think we can go straight to this office?' Richard asked doubtfully. 'Normally you have to go to Central Registration first.' 'The invitation is direct and I know where I have to go, I don't need to go to Central Registration for that,' Regine said. The official at the desk at the entrance to F wing knew better, however. 'You've no slip from Central Registration, you can't be allowed in just like that, Citizen Neubert –'

Regine protested that this registration was a pure waste of time, why should she register downstairs when her appointment was up here –

The official reminded her of the regulations, which she, as a citizen, had to observe!

Regine shrugged her shoulders. Richard followed her, she hurried on ahead, unfazed by the junctions that led to other corridor systems, all of which looked the same. Not even the indoor plants on the window ledges were noticeably different: well-fed exotic plants with spoon-shaped, carefully dusted, fleshy leaves. One little copper watering can with a spout like an ibis beak per floor.

They passed a rotunda and Richard was already thinking they'd lost the way and gone back to the first – the same icicle chandelier with thousands of bits of opaque paste frippery dangling from it, the same pillars on the rotunda's balustrade, the same threadbare reddish-pink runner – but the statues, although similarly armed with swords and shields, had different expressions on their faces. Amusingly, one of the stone knights had stuck his sword between his knees and was blowing his nose on a handkerchief. The sculptor, in whose name Richard was now interested, had done the folds with delicate meticulousness and kept them as thin as a communion wafer.

Central Registration was a hall with counters all round buzzing with voices, Job-like patience, the noise of conveyor belts. In the middle a Christmas tree, still decorated with snail-shaped decorations, Narva lemons and little wooden horses from Seiffen, was quietly shedding its needles and in cordoned-off solitude, which didn't seem to bother the overalled messengers pushing their carts through the queues without looking anyone in the eye. Regine joined the queue at the counter with the letters 'L, M, N', Richard that at 'H' and when he looked round he saw Meno, who, like them, had been overhasty and had to register at the 'R' counter, which had the second-longest queue after 'S, Sch, St'.

After an hour it was Richard's turn. He had two pieces of business: in the first place he had to collect a second medical report on the case of a car tyre repairer who, although he was the sole specialist of that type in the southern area of Dresden, had been sent his call-up papers (upon which Richard, at the behest of Müller, whose Opel Kapitän was sorely in need of such a specialist, had written a first report attesting the man's absolute unfitness for military service because his left leg was ten centimetres shorter); in the second, the gas water-heater in Caravel was nearing the end if its life and Richard wanted to apply for a new one.

'Fourth floor, E corridor, HM office – Housing Matters – forward slash, Roman two,' the man behind the counter informed him. Regine also had two things to see to: firstly she had to get a certificate attesting that Hansi's violin was not part of the state's cultural heritage and that its export would not damage the interests of the state in any other way, secondly she had an invitation to a 'personal discussion' with the official in charge of her matter. 'The valuation section is also on the fourth floor, though in B corridor, but we can go up together,' Regine said. In the HM – Housing Matters – office Richard was told that the employee at Central Registration had made a mistake and that the office for requesting communal gas water-heaters was on the eleventh floor, G corridor, CHA – Communal Housing Administration – office, Arabic five. He went back to Regine. She was looking nervously at the clock. She had an appointment at nine thirty and there were about two dozen people waiting at the Valuation Section. Could Richard get the violin valued for her?

'But you'll have to get a certificate confirming that, my dear lady,' a man in front of them in the queue warned her. 'Firstly you'll have to get a certificate confirming that you are the person requiring an article to be assessed, secondly that it belongs to you, thirdly that you have given this gentleman here the power of attorney. – I speak from experience.'

After he came back from the certification procedure Richard remembered that recently there had been certain rumours circulating about this valuation section. Wernstein had told him about one case that he had heard from a nurse who was engaged to an assistant doctor in Internal Medicine. A technician in the department had inherited a

Guarneri violin, but wasn't sure if it was genuine and had had it examined here, at the Valuation Section. The instrument was actually a genuine Guarneri, a rarity on which her late aunt had quietly and modestly bowed her way through several decades in the ranks of the second violins in the Dresden Philharmonic; no one apart from the aunt, who was single, had known what a special instrument it was; the first mention of the name of the Italian instrument maker was in her will. In the Valuation Section a man in a grey suit had appeared who, after the evaluator had pored over a few catalogues, repeatedly looked inside the violin with a dentist's mirror and, for safety's sake, consulted a colleague, picked up the telephone and had a long conversation. A few days later the technician, who thought her worries were over, was sent a letter from the Coal Island finance department. She couldn't pay the sum that was demanded in inheritance tax and so the violin was taken away from her. That was the story Wernstein had told; but Niklas Tietze, whom Richard asked, had also heard about it; as had Barbara, who had picked it up at Wiener's, the hairdresser's.

The evaluator glanced at Richard's power of attorney, shuffled back to his table, which was covered in green billiard cloth, and started to study the violin.

At first he twisted and turned it with jaunty, elegant movements, the violin whirled, stopped – a look through a lens; more turning, a few pencilled notes; more turning. He didn't look inside the body, didn't open a catalogue. Scroll, pegbox, fingerboard, shape of the F-holes; then he put the violin under his chin, took the bow out of the case and began to play Bach's Chaconne. He let its solemn, stately tones ring out clearly for a good minute, so that the other officials of the Valuation Section interrupted their work and listened to him. The muttering in the queue stopped, the crackle of sandwich wrappers, the rustling, the shuffle of feet. But no one clapped when he put the violin down. Richard observed his crisp, precise movements; there was no superfluous nor even jerky action; in his mind's eye he could see his father repairing a clock at his workbench in Glashütte, Malthakus sorting postage stamps, the same precise, finely adjusted movements, and that made him think.

The evaluator put a form in the typewriter and typed a few lines. Then he replaced the instrument and closed the lid. However much of an effort the violin maker had made – he spoke the name with mocking contempt – who, as far as the secrets of the ribs and purfling were concerned was at least more than just an amateur, his violins would never be part of the cultural heritage of the German Democratic Republic. There, he had it in writing. The evaluator stuck a revenue stamp on the certificate and pushed it across the flap in the door. Richard paid, was about to leave.

'One moment.'

'Yes?'

The evaluator removed his glasses and took his time cleaning them. 'As you will be aware, the bow goes with the violin. I have only certified that the violin is not part of our country's cultural heritage. You have to get that certified for the bow as well.'

'Oh, right.' Richard fiddled with the violin case, was going to take the bow out there and then.

'Sir,' the evaluator said, 'I am a certified specialist for string instruments and bows; according to regulations, however, string instruments and their bows are to be submitted for assessment separately.'

'But I'm here and you could, I mean it would save time, and there are other people waiting behind me –'

'According to regulations string instruments and bows are to be submitted for assessment separately.'

Richard lost his temper. 'Now listen . . . what nonsense! You've just played the violin yourself. – And to do that you used the bow, otherwise you wouldn't have been able to play it. Please have a look at it and put your stamp on the bumph –'

'Are you threatening my colleague?' another official asked, looking

Richard disparagingly up and down. 'In our state all citizens are equal before the law. Are you demanding special treatment? Who do you think you are?'

'Just check his bow, this is ridiculous,' a man behind Richard muttered. 'I've got nothing against all citizens being equal and that, but I've got a violin and a bow to be assessed as well, so I'll have to go to the back again too, and who knows how many others will be in that situation today. A load of nonsense!'

'Yes, nonsense,' Richard agreed. 'I'm going to make a complaint.'

'If you want to have the bow certified, please go to the back of the queue,' the first evaluator said with official politeness. There was no point in continuing to object; if he did so Richard would have only been inconveniencing Regine, who would have had to come back another day. Richard stood aside, took a sandwich out of his briefcase, thinking about a bomb, and joined the queue at the back.

After the bow had been checked ('not one of Tourte's, not one of Pfretzschner's, not one of Schmidt's'), Richard went to the second floor, F corridor, to find Regine. Going up and down the stairs, he encountered acquaintances, said hello to Frau Teerwagen here, to Frau Stahl from the House with a Thousand Eyes there, had a brief chat with Clarens.

'Not on duty either, Hans?' Clarens shrugged his shoulders in silent impotence. 'What're you here for?'

'Gas water-heater, report, favour' – Richard waved the violin. 'And you?'

'Vehicle licensing office, increased coal allocation, burials office.'

'Who's died?' Richard shouted from one staircase to the other. The psychiatrist waved his question away. 'Let's just say: hope, my friend, hope!' and, smiling and waving goodbye, he slid back into the stream of supplicants, applicants, messengers and officials.

'Where are you going?' The attendant outside F corridor asked to see Richard's identity card.

'I'm waiting for someone.'

'This is solely for people wanting to emigrate, those are the only ones I can let in.'

'But as I said, I'm just waiting for someone, surely that isn't forbidden?'

'Hm. Who are you waiting for?'

'Frau Regine Neubert.'

The attendant leafed through his documents. 'Your name? — We could sort the matter out in the following way: I give you an entry permit. You leave your identity card here, you'll get it back when you leave. You have one hour, then you must come and report to me again.'

Richard looked up, it was rare to be addressed in such a friendly manner here.

'Hmm, Dr Hoffmann.' Immersed in thought, the attendant riffled through the lists of names, one sheet after the other.

In F corridor the sewing machines were buzzing behind the doors. Here the queue stretched out into the rotunda. Richard, not finding Regine, stood by a window and waited, not without receiving suspicious, not to say hostile, looks – a man with a violin who didn't join the queue, what was he doing here?

'Hey, you there,' a woman barked, 'there's no jumping the queue here. We all want to get out.' Richard was about to reply that he had no intention of jumping the queue when a door was flung open and a woman stormed out, swearing and cursing loudly. 'I'm Alexandra Barsano, you've presumably heard the name, this will cost you dear,' she shouted back in through the open door. Soothing words were to be heard from inside. The waiting queue observed the scene that was being played out in front of them in silence. Richard remembered: years ago there had been photos in the press showing the powerful Party Secretary of the district, one arm proudly round the shoulder of his daughter; but the young woman, who was getting more and more worked up, swaying as if drunk and waving her arms around, clearly had nothing to do with the young girl in the old photos any more. A few shaggy black strands were hanging down either side of a Mohican hairstyle, the spikes of which were a lurid yellow, otherwise her head was completely shaven. Her eyes ringed in black, skull-rings on her fingers, a slashed leather jacket with a 'Swords into Ploughshares' symbol sewn on the back, leather trousers, studded belt; over her shoulder Alexandra Barsano had, attached to clinking silver chains, a chimney sweep's weight. As she turned round, Richard saw the Party badge on her lapel. A man in a grey suit approached.

'You'll hear from me,' Alexandra Barsano snarled. The man in the suit drew her to one side, talking to her quietly all the time. The door to the office slammed shut, opened briefly, someone hung an 'Office closed' sign on it. Alexandra Barsano ran to the door and hammered on it with her fists. Two men in uniform appeared and led her away, she didn't resist, the chimney's sweep's weight hit her in the back. The man straightened his suit, ran a comb through his hair, jutted out his chin to the queue: 'The office is closed.'

The muttering from the people in the queue grew louder.

'I will have any troublemakers arrested for resistance to the authority of the state. Is that clear? This office is closed, shut, for the rest of the day.' The man in the suit strode off. In disbelief, those in the queue waited for a while longer, then dispersed, grumbling and cursing. The daughter of our District Secretary at the office for exit permits, Richard was thinking, still dazed by the scene, when the office door opened and Regine came out, pale and tear-stained. Beside her was Philipp holding a packet of Ata out of which there came a trickle of white scouring powder. 'Come by yourself the next time, Citizen Neubert.' During a long discussion, in the course of which she had been strongly advised to divorce her husband, since he was a traitor and they had 'proofs' that he went to brothels in Munich, Philipp had wandered over to the washbasin of the soundproof discussion cubicle and, with scrubbing brush and duster, set off an Ata snow-fest in the whole room. The door slammed shut; as he walked away Richard could hear coughing inside.

The first censor, Meno thought, as he adjusted his tie in the mirror over one of the washbasins there were at regular intervals along the corridor. He was somewhere in the depths of the east wing of Coal Island. Up there, on the top floor, it was quiet; it was an area one needed a special permit to enter. Schiffner had made one out for Meno and signed it.

'Come on in now,' the writer Eschschloraque called, roguishly beckoning Meno with his index finger from the end of the corridor. Although the reddish wood of the purlins allowed a soft, reassuring light to filter into the corridor, Meno was somehow reminded of a visit to Frau Knabe, his dentist; in her practice, at least in the vestibule, there was the same forbearing, forgiving, peach-soft brightness (the mistake was that time passed, Meno had the impression that the ministering spirits, who camouflaged the anterooms of the pain-inflicters, knew this); even though the smell of coffee and cigarettes dribbled out of the keyholes of the doors he passed, the feeling of having to go down a tunnel with no turn-off came just as promptly as in Frau Knabe's practice – only Meno had not expected the *dramaticus* (Eschschloraque wrote mostly plays). Today, on Schiffner's behalf, he was supposed to be seeing all four senior assessors of the Dresden branch of the Ministry of Culture's publishing section; he had previously only negotiated here with two of them, Albert Salomon, whom people called 'Slalomon' because of his reports that took account of every twist and turn of political developments, and Karlfriede Sinner-Priest, who was known as Mrs Privy-Councillor.

'Do come in, Rohde. Do you like tea? – Good to hear. Tea drinkers are mostly good people to talk with. They're intelligent murderers into the bargain and they mostly have something to say. I need that for one of my plays, you should know. Is it not much more effective when a torturer sips a cup of tea than when he just downs a beer?'

'Aren't you making it too easy for yourself if you have the said torturer drinking tea. The critics will say, "Oh God, a torturer drinks beer, a proletarian touch! How does a crafty author avoid that? He makes him drink tea. That is such an unsurprising surprise, Herr Eschschloraque, that it's become a cliché."'

'You may well be right, my dear Rohde. Should I go back to beer, then? What our critics don't realize is that this beer has been through all the pipes of the directorial drinks department and has reached a second innocence, a higher innocence so to speak. I would avoid the cliché by renewing the cliché . . . Hm. Interesting tactic, but you'd have to get the torturer to deliver a soliloquy on the innocence of beer. Despite that, I feel I can manage a tea. I can give you Earl Grey.'

'I've brought a lemon, Herr Eschschloraque.'

'Is it to have an acid taste? Acid corrodes but you don't make anything wrong with it. I could have my torturer drink cocoa instead . . . Or a fizzy drink. Lemonade. I prefer people who love lemons to those who love melons, for example, basically a melon is nothing more than sugar and water and despite all the seeds is only the principle of the bellows transferred to horticulture. Anyway, you don't need to offer me anything apart from arguments, up to now I have nurtured the illusion of being incorruptible. Sit down and let's continue.'

Eschschloraque made the tea and started the 'Conjuration of Snakes' as the presentation of manuscripts and discussion of reports was called among the editors. Meno looked round, listened and observed Eschschloraque. He asked which manuscripts Meno was thinking of fighting for. Meno knew the ritual, made a gesture that could mean everything and said nothing: keep your cards close to you chest, editor. If you name a writer, the other person might hate him and finish him off with a smile. If you deliberately name a wrong one, in order to mislead them, the other person might be happy with that and confirm the name with a smile. Cover your flanks and protect your king – and be aware that your queen can never be brought into action too soon. Sacrifice a pawn, if it's a knight or bishop that's threatened, sacrifice your queen so that the last pawn can checkmate the king. And remember, the other person has studied your wiles and knows your ruses.

'Right, then I will give you two names for which I will fight in the publishing plan. Let's not fool ourselves, Rohde. You have fourteen titles, twelve of them are' – Eschschloraque glanced through the telescope by the window of the room that was stuffed full of books and papers – 'the way they are. Two will cause offence: Altberg's essays and Eduard Eschschloraque's slim volume of writings full of wittily mendacious truths and classic pesticide for the romantic rodents gnawing away at the vineyard of literature. You know just as well as I do that one of these projects has to die.'

But Eschschloraque's smile vanished when he continued. Meno left his tea untouched and let his eyes wander round the room while the playwright, who seemed to Meno like a mixture between a clown and a sharp-witted old woman, exercised his wickedly mocking tongue on the more or less characteristic qualities of those colleagues whose manuscripts he had reported on in his quality of assessor. A copper engraving of Goethe on the wall, the old Weimar edition of his works in a glass-fronted bookcase, a bust of Goethe on the dramatist's desk between a Soviet pennant and a signed portrait of Stalin; in front of them two neatly aligned typewriters: a black Erika and beside it a sign, like those saying 'Reserved' in restaurants, bearing the inscription 'Mortal'; a second sign, beside the other typewriter, made by Rheinmetall, with 'Immortal – when I'm fresh'; by this time Meno had shifted sideways up to the table and didn't need to bend back much as the playwright strode up and down. 'Hoary expressions, Rohde! And always with heartfelt' – Eschschloraque drew the exclamation mark in the air with his finger – 'good wishes . . . why not liverfelt or lungfelt once in a while? We all have to breathe, why should good things always have to come from the heart? Most people's ticker is a clock, not a heart. The liver: the body's chemical factory. Its potions and juices are much richer.'

His sarcastic thrusts broke off as if he'd hit a barrier when Eschschloraque got round to the Old Man of the Mountain's book.

Meno was astonished at the seriousness, the knowledgeable, almost solemnly expressed love that warmed Eschschloraque's remarks on those essays; he wouldn't have believed Eschschloraque capable of it, wouldn't have expected it of him. 'Do you know what I see, my dear Rohde, when I look through this telescope? I see a classical land and Altberg is one of Goethe's children. Goethe. Goethe! After all, he's the father – and all the criticism merely the twitching of frogs' legs.' He had never, Eschschloraque went on, read such essays on writers and their works. That was European, indeed world, class.

Meno couldn't believe his ears. Eschschloraque, that captious critic, that occupational shadow who ruthlessly pursued every careless slip, who openly spoke up for Stalin and the Stalinist system, for whom Richard Wagner's music was a crime, the man was standing there by the door, disarmed, all his mockery, his caustic wit gone. 'Don't gawp like that, that's your blasted lemon. Hm. So we'll live and pray and sing, and tell old tales and laugh at gilded butterflies . . . but he misunderstands matters when he says that their relationships with each other are always created by people alone. Have you never encountered lifeless people? Have you never thought about the idea that you might have different shadows that take alternate shifts? – Now you know,' Eschschloraque said brusquely, 'or at least you think you do. The manuscript submitted by Eschschloraque needs to be revised and improved. It cannot be recommended for publication at the present moment. And now out you go, you've stolen enough of my precious time as it is. You'll have it all in writing – and no sly tricks, Rohde.'

'Left leg shorter by twelve centimetres,' Dr Pahl wrote on the form and closed the handbook on assessing fitness for military service. 'The man is entirely unfit for military service. At ten centimetres he could have been conscripted as a naval wireless operator or staff clerk without having to go through basic training. Of course, that leaves the question of what we do if there's an appeal or if the orthopaedist for the regional military command should read the file. He'd immediately want to know what remedial measures were being looked at. Are there orthopaedic shoes with the soles built up by twelve centimetres?'

'I don't think so,' Richard said. 'We'd have to add that an operation to shorten the other leg is being planned.'

'Hm.' Pahl thought for a moment. 'A bit thin. That would be a matter for Orthopaedics and at least I do know some colleagues there that we can trust. But what will happen if some overzealous military bone setter should simply summon this tyre repairer to have a look at the leg.'

'And would he not also want to know how the man had managed to walk up to now? Twelve centimetres, Herr Pahl!'

'Yes, he's not just got a limp. Well, we'll just say he's made himself raised soles for his shoe out of old tyres. It's crazy to conscript this man! We have to stop it. Do you know the orthopaedist for the local military command, Herr Hoffmann?'

'Unfortunately not.'

'Me neither. – Shall we risk it?'

'Let's risk it.'

Meno almost exclaimed, 'You!?' when he saw the Old Man of the Mountain come out of the door. The old man invited him into his room. 'What would you like to drink? Tea, mineral water, lemonade? No, I know what you drink.' Altberg reached under the desk and, with a sly grin, fished out a bottle with an oily, amber liquid. 'Home-made, the recipe comes from my housekeeper. Nectar of the Gods. Please . . .' Waving away Meno's protests, Altberg poured some of the nectar into two glasses. 'Prost!'

Meno took a sip: shards of fire went tumbling down his throat, merging into a fire-eel that slowly, bristling with spines, filled his gullet; Meno felt he was on fire and as if his eyes were being forced out of their sockets from inside. Then the blaze splashed back in a surging wave that went to the roots of his hair, to the tips of his fingers, electrified his nostrils and brought peace. The Old Man of the Mountain poured himself a second glass, tossed it back, chewed on the drink like a slice of bread. Then he took the reports out of the drawer and his friendliness vanished.

The old man tore, ripped, slashed almost the entire publishing plan to pieces. He made holes in a novel by Paul Schade that left it like a Swiss cheese; he made the pieces between the holes sound as if they had the taste of a rubber eraser, designating them ideologist's puree, he crossed out the holes, sliced them lengthways, chopped them up crosswise, drew, after he'd downed a third glass of nectar, the slats of a blind in the air and shut them.

'Do you know what would have happened to you in the past, after the Eleventh Plenary Session of the Party Central Committee, if you had ventured to present such a plan, such deviations from the Party line? Just ask your colleague Lilly Platané in Editorial Office 1 . . . A financial penalty in the form of a reduction in salary, a serious charge of endangering the targets of the plan, self-criticism before the editorial board . . . Just be glad I'm not attacking you personally. You can look over the cuts I prescribe when you get home.' He put his reports in a folder and tossed it over to Meno.

'But there's something else. Herr Eschschloraque's manuscript. That, my dear Rohde,' the old man said, 'I'm going to finish off for you well and good. My volume of stories is going to be chucked out, a good thing then that I've got a few more essays as well; and in place of that you want to publish this crap, this stilted celery, this . . .' He struggled for words to drive his contempt for Eschschloraque, who was a blowfly, incapable of flight, crawling over plaster casts of the classics, forcibly into Meno's ear while he, pale, was contending with the consequences of the nectar. Meno wondered if he should make the Old Man of the Mountain aware of Eschschloraque's attitude but, stunned, he decided not to.

Three o'clock. Richard checked his wristwatch as the gong echoed. Regine had said goodbye, she had bravely and defiantly decided she was going to come back there in a fortnight's time. No hysteria à la Alexandra Barsano, that only led to trouble and got you nowhere. Obstinate insistence, unwavering chipping away until you found the weak spot – 'even if I have to spend the night here'. Richard leant against the wall, looked out of the window, wondered whether to steal one of the little copper watering cans or at least a sucker from one of the fleshy leaved plants, ate his last sandwich. The violin evaluated, the report with Pahl finished – a sensible and experienced man, you never knew which assessor you were going to get . . . That left the gas water-heater. The strange ticking noise there'd been this morning had gone. Meno had not turned up at twelve and the porter had refused to send out a call for 'any old citizen, we're not at the football stadium'.

Or the racecourse, Richard thought. Flurries of snow started. The derricks in the prohibited area of Coal Island were just visible, as if sketched with faint pencil lines. Crows winged down from the Marx–Engels memorial; the sentry in front of it, whom Richard could see obliquely from behind, stood there motionless, covered in snow, rifle at attention. A clunking meandered down the heating pipes that ran, uncovered, along the walls. Richard folded his sandwich paper, washed himself in one of the hand-basins and set off for the eleventh floor, G corridor, office CHA/5.

Meno looked at the clock: his next appointment was for 3.30 p.m. Ravenous, he ate the apple and the two pieces of cream cake he'd packed in his briefcase in the morning. *Slalomon.* He was the only one who still wrote his reports – extensive free-skating programmes with a scatter of cut flowers – by hand. His handwriting was clear and flowing, as in official letters from the nineteenth century. They looked strange among the office files, like jetsam from a long-ago age, and when he read Albert Salomon's reports, with the roundabout style avoiding anything too direct, Meno had the same feeling as with the pre-war telegrams he saw at Malthakus's, lines that read as if put together laboriously and against considerable resistance, arousing in him the urge to write an essay on the attraction of the 'just-about'; it must have something to do with being saved, an innate desire for protection, that made such a document, rescued from the crypt of time, seem more valuable than modern, easy, newsy letters which gave the impression that neither their preparation nor their distribution had taken much effort.

A lengthy part of Salomon's reports consisted of apologies: apologies for having to make a judgement; for recommending a cut here and there; for inconveniencing the author and editor; for the fact that he, Albert Salomon, existed.

Mrs Privy Councillor: Eschschloraque, in his role as dramatist, had once taken the liberty of making a joke and given himself a speech in one of his plays: 'Censors! Who is it that becomes a censor if not someone / whose head is largely empty / even if the fellow's read this line' – that was what the whole play was like had been Karlfriede Sinner-Priest's sole comment on this salutation from a fellow socialist. Meno was afraid of her. She was unpredictable, her opinion outweighed all others in the Ministry of Culture, she had been on Coal Island since time immemorial, her reports were looked upon as an ideological litmus test. No Hermes editor had ever managed to get a book accepted that she wanted to refuse 'entry into literature'. She was gaunt and looked as if she'd been turned on a wood lathe, a doll that never laughed, who, depending on her mood, would kill off a book or a person with a single sentence, sharp as a sliver of glass, or go off on sparkling, sometimes self-ironic purple passages enthusiastically scrambling over each other. Her authority was Lenin, her interest free of prejudice. She had pencils stuck like Japanese pins in her wig that was always askew and made her face seem unnaturally long, giving her the look of something extinct; Meno sometimes imagined her at a castle ball, dancing ceremoniously to the sound of a spinet. She had been given one of the SS's travel scholarships. She had survived Buchenwald.

Richard was astonished to see Albert Salomon at the office of the Communal Housing Administration. He was waiting on the sixth floor, C corridor, office H/2; office CHA/5 in G corridor on the eleventh floor was only for heating problems, insulating material, pumps and the maintenance of gas meters, but not for gas water-heaters, they were a sanitary problem, as Richard was informed. Albert Salomon kept looking at the clock above the office window and appeared to be getting increasingly nervous. Richard knew him, he was one of his patients. Before 1933 Albert Salomon had worked for Meissen Porcelain as a pattern maker and design painter but someone had informed on him and he had ended up in a Gestapo prison, then in Sachsenhausen concentration camp, where he was tortured and both his arms were crushed. His right arm, the one he used to paint and write with, had had to be amputated in the concentration camp. Only once, as far as Richard could remember, had Salomon talked about the camp: commenting on a passage in a Soviet novel in which he thought a detail was wrong – the boot-testing track with different surfaces along which prisoners had to go at a forced march for days on end to test out various materials for the soles of army boots; every surface 'a city I thought about'.

A shrill bell sounded. 'Closing time!' The office window rattled shut.

19
Urania

The ten-minute clock struck twenty to five; once more Meno checked his manuscript, key, the letter of invitation written by Arbogast's secretary, took the rose for Arbogast's wife out of the water, wrapped it in paper and left. He went down Wolfsleite, waved to Herr Krausewitz, who, puffing away at his Mundlos cigar, was busy in the garden of Wolfstone: 'Oh, good evening, Herr Krausewitz, isn't it a little early for flowers?' – pointing at the garden tools in Krausewitz's wheelbarrow.

'For flowers yes, Herr Rohde, but it is time for the fruit trees, and the branches of the old apple trees are too thick, I'll have to thin them out, otherwise we'll only get little apples in the autumn.' – 'Pretty cold, isn't it?' – 'Oh,' said Krausewitz, waving the comment away, 'fear ye not the cold March snow, a good warm heart doth beat below, as the farmers say. And the caterpillars have to be dealt with as well. Look' – he pointed to several branches – 'I put some glue-bands on – and now the blasted creatures have laid their eggs underneath the strips. The winter moth especially, it was a real pest last year. The bands aren't sticking on any longer, I'll have to renew them. Otherwise the caterpillars will crawl up the branches and that'll be it for the fruit and everything that goes with it.'

'In our garden the trees have lots of splits in the bark.'

'You mustn't leave them open, Herr Rohde. No wonder given how cold it's been. The bark splits like dry skin. I recommend you cut away the edges smoothly and then seal them with a proprietary product. Frau Lange should still have some, I saw her getting in a good supply in the pharmacy last October. Otherwise just come and ask.' – 'So cut away smoothly?' – 'Like a surgeon, yes. These trees are living beings too. And they have a character of their own as well. But, as I said, don't forget to seal the splits.'

How were things at the airport, Meno asked. Krausewitz worked there as a controller. Same as ever, routine you know, they tried to transfer him from the tower to ground control, after all he had turned fifty-eight, hadn't he? But in the tests he'd outperformed two younger colleagues and then there was the experience, so he was still slotted into the cycle of four-hour shifts like all the rest. Give the Langes my best wishes, won't you. With that, Krausewitz tipped his angler's hat and dug the spade, which he'd been leaning on while they talked, into the soil, which was still dappled with snow.

Meno had gone home rather earlier than usual that day, which was easier on a Friday since the publishing section in the Ministry of Culture didn't call after one and Schiffner left at that time when he'd come from Berlin: not to start the weekend but for his beloved visits to artists' studios where he hoped to find up-and-coming young artists. 'Until this evening, Herr Rohde, we'll see each other then at Arbogast's, I'm very much looking forward to your talk. You could have told me what your hobby is, after all we can do something for that sort of thing – you just sit here quietly pondering over literature and keeping yourself to yourself.'

Meno really ought to have done some more work on a manuscript by Lührer, an urgent task, but he wanted to read his paper out loud again and had gone to see his colleague Stefanie Wrobel, known as Madame Eglantine. 'Off you go,' she'd said with a resigned smile, 'and all the best for this evening.'

'Thanks. I owe you. If I can do anything for you –'

'You could put on a pot of water for my coffee before you go. I'd also like a copy of your talk, a detailed report of course – and an honest explanation.'

'Of what?'

'Of how you managed to saddle me with our classical author's latest opus.' She pointed at Eschschloraque's manuscript.

'He's threatening me.'

'Who is he not threatening?' Madame Eglantine shrugged her shoulders and hurriedly downed the last of her coffee.

Darkness was still falling quickly, the lights above Wolfsleite and the Turmstrasse crossroads drifted into view like moons. A white Citroën turned into Wolfsleite and stopped outside the first house after Turmstrasse. That had to be the car of Sperber, the lawyer. Meno kept in the shadow of the trees on his side of the road. The lawyer got out, there was a jangle of keys, the gate at the end of the wrought-iron fence opened and Meno watched Sperber, about whom there were many rumours circulating in the Tower: that during the week he worked in a lawyers' chambers on the Ascanian Island, where he also had an apartment and a mistress, whom his wife not only knew about but had selected for him herself from among the throng of female students in the law faculty, where he also gave lectures; that he was a fanatical supporter of Dynamo Dresden – Meno had that from Ulrich, who had often met him in the stadium – and that he was ready to listen to anyone who was in political difficulties. Sperber turned round, fixed his eyes on Meno, waved: 'Good evening, Herr Rohde, it doesn't start until seven, if I'm not mistaken.' Does that mean Sperber's part of Urania as well? Concealing his surprise, Meno went over to Sperber, trying to appear unselfconscious, for he was embarrassed at being discovered in his attempt to hide. But he'll be familiar with that, he told himself with amused irritation, it'll be the behaviour pattern of his clients. Sperber said it was good they'd finally got to know each other, he was a fan of Dresdner Edition, a subscriber, you might almost say, and since the name of the editor was always given in the imprint, he had in a way already made his acquaintance, assuming one could take a person's approach to their work for the person, as he also had that of Frau, 'or Fräulein?' – Sperber gave a charming smile – Wrobel, who, however, ought to be more strict with some authors, there were errors, naming no names, of course. – Of course. – Some of our living

classical authors are quite unsure about punctuation. For prices you
need an em dash, not a two-em dash nor a hyphen. Recently he'd come
across a word division he'd immediately made the subject of his lecture: surg-eon instead of, correctly, sur-geon! Sperber chopped down
with the side of his hand and screwed up his right eye. Schiffner was
one of the old school, couldn't he . . . But more of that later. Sperber
laughed and took Meno's hand in a limp handshake.

Turmstrasse was busier, a squad of soldiers was marching in the direction of Bautzner Strasse, perhaps heading for the Waldcafé or the
Tannhäuser Cinema or, more likely, to a dance in the Bird of Paradise
Bar in the Schlemm Hotel; no, thought Meno, when he saw that the
leader had a net of handballs slung over his shoulder, and recalled a
plain notice on the advertising pillar on Planetenweg: a friendly between
the German and Soviet brothers-in-arms in the sports hall in the
grounds of the sanatorium. People were coming out of Sibyllenleite,
from the funicular, some familiar faces among them; Meno nodded to
Iris Hoffmann, who worked as an engineering draughtswoman for the
VEB Pentacon combine, she nodded back. And there was the sweet
chestnut outside Arbogast's Institute already, there was the People's
Observatory behind the wall, the wide gate on rollers with the flashing
light at the cobbled drive to the Institute buildings on Turmstrasse,
there the modern cube of the Institute for Flow Research at the beginning of Holländische Leite, into which Meno turned. On Unterer Plan
he waited at a high, wrought-iron gate; the elaborate Gothic tendrils
combined to form a black gryphon; the top of the gate was in the shape
of a bee lily.

Arbogast Castle appeared in all its glory. Castle wasn't the official
designation; the Baron preferred the more modest 'House' and that was
what was written in high relief on a metal plate over the main entrance
with the sweeping flight of steps. Many of the Tower-dwellers called
it 'Castle', a designation that another property up there had: 'Rapallo
Castle' below Sibyllenleite. But Rapallo Castle looked Mediterranean,

had the bright lines of the south, a Riviera building in northern exile with stone scrolls and an elegantly curved roof, not a palace jagged with pinnacles and needlepoint ridge turrets like the one Meno was facing that made him think more of prehistoric animals, extinct dinosaurs with armoured scales and dragon's spikes, than of a home with hot and cold running water.

Lights were going on and off, cutting changing stage sets out of the garden: the three flagpoles beside the steps appeared: the Soviet flag in faded red, the black-red-and-gold one with the hammer, compasses and wreath of grain, and the third flag, a yellow one with a black retort. Meno had never seen that flag before, perhaps it bore the coat of arms of the Lords of Arbogast. When windows in the east wing lit up, they illuminated the large Arbogast observatory, which, clad in white stone, looked like an owl's egg in the sloping part of the garden. There were still a few minutes to go until five o'clock, the time for which Arbogast had invited Meno. He grasped the wrought iron of the gate, unsure whether he should ring now. At that moment an alarm bell began to blare, sirens joined in with their wail; lights burst on in the garden, flooding the paths with white brightness. A camera on a tubular stand rose like a ghost out of a flap in the ground, searched for a moment, then shot a flash at his face that looked as baffled as it was terrified. He staggered back, and it was a good thing too, for at the next moment two snarling bodies thumped into the gate; Meno thought, once he had recovered his sight, he recognized one of the two dogs as Kastshey. The camera hummed back into the ground. Once more Meno heard the shrill 'heigh-ho' boatman's whistle, the dogs immediately left the gate and raced back with long bounds into the depths of the garden, where, after a few seconds, they silently disappeared. An intercom beside the gate crackled and a rusty female voice said, 'Baron Arbogast is delighted you have come. Please use the little door in the wall beside the intercom.' Until now Meno hadn't noticed this door; it was less a door than a heavy steel bulkhead that slid up like the blade of a guillotine. Clutching his briefcase with his manuscript to him, Meno leapt through the opening. At the entrance he was received by a female dwarf in an apron, the pockets of which were packed full of clothes pegs. 'Good evening, Herr Rohde. My name is Else Alke, I am Baron Arbogast's housekeeper. He apologizes for not being here to welcome you himself and for keeping you waiting a little while. An important meeting. For Baroness Arbogast?' The housekeeper pointed to the rose, which Meno quickly unwrapped. 'Give it to me.' She took the paper, raised her head and stared at Meno out of toad-green eyes. 'The Baroness loves roses.'

I thought she would, Meno said to himself. While Alke was taking his coat and hat and putting them away, he looked round. He had taken his best suit out of the wardrobe, put on the best of the few shirts he owned, but the polished chessboard floor, the flame-patterned columns to the right and left separating gallery corridors from the hall, the heavy oak table: a black dragon carrying the top on its outspread wings, two solid-silver candelabra the height of a man on it flanking an oil painting, the rock-crystal chandelier filling the hall with soft light – all that made it clear to him that he was poor. He had also had that feeling when he had visited Jochen Londoner, Hanna's father, but it wasn't as strong as here, this was wealth that shouldn't exist in socialism. Meno had already seen a few apartments of big-selling authors, of Party functionaries – never a house like this, however. The Party functionaries mostly had dubious taste, clearly deriving from their lower-middle-class background; it had also struck him that Party functionaries had no time for comfort without recognizable usefulness. The poor food at Barsano's was notorious and the apartment he had furnished for himself in the extensive Block A complex was spartan. Here on the other hand . . . A door banged at the end of the left-hand colonnade, a man in a white coat came out and went, with echoing footsteps, bent over papers, without taking any notice of him, to the staircase. It was made of white marble with black spots, like a

Dalmatian's coat, and split into two wings that rose in an elegant curve to the first floor, where they came together in a balcony with a balustrade. On a thin-legged stand, like an easel, was a mirror that, as Meno realized when he went closer, was not made of glass but of metal. Meno adjusted his tie.

He heard the housekeeper's rusty voice behind him. 'The Baroness.' Hurriedly he looked round at her, Else Alke nodded to him and pointed to the staircase. At the top a door opened and a woman in a hunting outfit came down to him.

'Frau von Arbogast.' My God, I really did sketch a kiss on the hand.

'Herr Rohde. What a beautiful rose.' She was visibly pleased.

'Thank you very much for your invitation.' How old can she be, fifty, sixty? Older? A face as brown as leather, a tough, supple figure. I wouldn't want to go through the fires that have melted away every superfluous gram. And she does indeed have lilac hair.

'It's my husband you must thank. We're delighted you've found the time to come and see us.' Could she offer him something? Her husband was unfortunately still occupied, an urgent unscheduled meeting such as often cropped up in the stages of the formulation of the five-year plan. He had asked her to express his regret at his lack of punctuality, all the more so as he had explicitly requested that Herr Rohde be there as early as five o'clock. Would Herr Rohde be happy with her company until then? 'Can I offer you something?' They were standing at the bottom of the stairs and when he nodded, she made a gesture that he only understood when the housekeeper appeared. 'Please put the rose in a vase and in my room. Something to drink for Herr Rohde.' She raised her brows questioningly.

'A glass of water, please.'

'Oh, Herr Rohde. A glass of water. I'd like to give you something especially delicious. Bring us two glasses of pomegranate juice, please.' They had been sent the fruit from the Black Sea, from Georgia, the Institute still had connections there. 'There are various stories about us going round the district here. We are aware of that. The truth is that we worked in Sinop for ten years. It was good work and it was right that we did it.' Was there anything else he wanted. He said no, observed her. How concerned she is. She's like a ringmaster while the bareback riders are performing. That suit she's wearing didn't come from Exquisit. 'That picture.' He pointed to the oil painting over the dragon table. Frau von Arbogast couldn't say. She handed Meno a glass and filled it and one for herself out of a carafe of blood-red pomegranate juice; the housekeeper held the tray and stared straight ahead as the Baroness drank with little hurried sips. Meno drank some, praised it. The juice was icy cold, of a velvety consistency and tasty; Meno closed his eyes, it was as if his throat were being coated in metal. The man in the white coat walked past again. 'Herr Ritschel.' The man stopped and turned round slowly, as if in slow motion or like someone who has to control an old rage, to face the Baroness. 'Would you please tell my husband that I'm going to show Herr Rohde round the house for a while.' Herr Ritschel turned round again, slightly more quickly, and plodded up the stairs.

'By the way, I hope the dogs and the alarm system didn't give you too much of a fright? It's one of my husband's passions, you know. He earned the money to set up his first firm by making cameras and alarm systems. The first camera went to me and burnt out, but that was intentional, Ludwig wanted to see me again . . . He's so proud of his skill at making things.' She examined her fingernails, took Meno's empty glass and placed it beside her own on the tray that the housekeeper had left on the dragon table. 'Yes, the picture. It's very old. I brought it with me.' The frame was square with sides of about six feet. The picture itself was in a circle that touched all four sides of the square but left the four corners free; they were painted over with copper paint and had an inscription with lots of flourishes that Meno couldn't decipher. In a colonnade with stairs leading up to it, four men in long togas were quietly talking. In the foreground a man was sitting at a

microscope; two men in green were standing by a telescope, one pointing up at the sky, the other observing an astrolabe with the seven
planets; they looked like fruits ripening on his outstretched hand. A
man with white hair was holding a carline thistle. A woman was doing
calculations. In a meadow a child was playing; a wolf and a stag were
drinking from a spring. A girl was holding a balance, a boy was drawing. Standing in the corner was someone with bad eyes. 'Do you know
what I always think when I see that man?' The baroness pointed to a
man in red with arms outstretched and face raised. 'That he's just about
to invent the piano. Old Dutch school, that's all I know; Ludwig says
it's a piece of good painting and I think he's right, since most people
who come to see us are interested in the picture. Fräulein Schevola,
however, doesn't think much of it . . . Too many old, learned men and
if there has to be a woman, then a mathematician . . . She doesn't like
unjust pictures.'

'Unjust?'

'Pictures with totalitarian colours which are so strong that they
demand humility *and* love, as she says. – You know Judith Schevola?'

'From her books,' Meno said, avoiding a direct answer.

'She is a stimulating element in the circle of old debauchees who
want to put the world to rights, some of whom you will meet this
evening.' She gave Meno a hard smile. 'Let's go. Ludwig would like
you to see a few things before the others arrive. Ah, but he can show
you them better than I.' They went to meet Arbogast.

'Herr Rohde. I'm delighted you've come. Please excuse my delay.
Is there anything I can do for you? – Did you have some of our pomegranate juice brought out for him?'

'Of course, Ludwig. – We were just looking at the picture. Herr
Rohde was asking who painted it.'

'You're keen on painting? Oh, that is a pointless question to someone from Dresdner Edition.' The Baron let go of Meno's hand, which
he, still standing on the bottom stair on which he was a good two

heads higher than Meno, had been giving a weak but unceasing handshake.

'I'll go and check the preparations again. I'll leave you two alone now.'

'Of course, my jewel.' Arbogast sketched a bow to his wife. She gave Meno a wink and left.

'You must forgive my limp handshake, it's what happens when you put your right hand in the one-million-volt electron-beam of a Van de Graaff generator. Do you know what that is? – Doesn't matter. It corresponds to the ionizing effect of a hundred-kilogram radium source, which is, of course, purely hypothetical. Marie Curie had one gram at her disposal and for radium that is a considerable amount. So,' Arbogast said coolly, looking at the blotchy burnt skin of his hand, 'for the rest of my life as a physicist I'll know what I'm talking about when I discuss radiation damage. My fingers are still a bit stiff . . . It's something of an advantage at tennis. And Trude has never complained. My wife.' Arbogast looked at the clock. 'We still have fifty-two minutes and sixteen seconds before the official part of the evening begins. I would very much like to have a chat with you. If you're agreeable?' Arbogast spoke with a slightly nasal tone and a hint of a North German accent, which Meno had only just noticed from the way he pronounced the 'st' of stiff as 's-t' rather than as the 'sht' usual elsewhere.

On the first storey the floor was made of smoothly polished clay-coloured stone with sea snails and ammonites that had been deposited in it; most were the size of a one-mark coin, a few had the diameter of a standard alarm clock, some that of a plate with the compartmentation clearly visible. Noticing Meno's interest, Arbogast waited at the glass double door that had a proliferation of ferns engraved on it, bizarre plants with something of ice needles about them, very elaborately worked. The door handles were bronze sea horses.

Arbogast led Meno through a room with a conference table, at which Herr Ritschel and a few other white-coated assistants, without looking up, were slowly leafing through periodicals, to his study, quietly waving away Meno's attempt at a general greeting. His study adjoined the conference room and was very plainly furnished: a large desk with two telephones, two chairs at an obtuse angle to each other, bookshelves that Meno scrutinized with curiosity the moment he went in: novels by Karl May stood beside handbooks of optics, a few Dresdner Edition volumes beside leather-bound annual numbers of physics journals. Meno couldn't work out the system by which the books were ordered until he noticed that the books on any one shelf were all of the same height.

'It looks better, I like this order, that might seem barbaric to you but, you know . . . Let's sit down. Do you smoke?'

'Now and then,' Meno lied, 'rarely and . . . not here, Herr Professor.'

'We can abandon the formalities, Herr Rohde. Feel free as far as smoking is concerned, I've breathed in a fair number of substances.' A thin smile appeared behind his steel-rimmed spectacles. 'Be my guest.'

From his chair Meno could let his eye roam round the room unobtrusively. He had the impression that Arbogast noticed his curiosity and even approved of it, despite the fact that it wasn't very polite to have a good look round while they were talking. Meno briefly wondered whether the chairs were deliberately placed at that angle to each other in order to allow guests to look round unobtrusively . . . At least it didn't seem to bother Arbogast that Meno took advantage of the opportunity and that his answers were rather monosyllabic. Arbogast talked about Urania and the usual course the evenings took. He had crossed his legs and jiggled his foot in time to his words, and waggled his toes so that the leather of his snakeskin slippers was constantly undulating; in addition, though slightly out of time, Arbogast underlined his words with gestures of his long hands; Meno could see the black scarab slipping up and down on his ring finger. On the wall behind the desk were some framed tables and a coloured representation of the human organs of vision with the eye, suspended from fine ligaments, shown in various sections and perspectives. They were, as far as Meno could tell, physical and mathematical tables, but he couldn't make head or tail of the one in the middle. Arbogast noticed what he was looking at. 'That table is, in fact, only related to the others in general terms. I have been keeping it since I was young, since the inflation period, to be precise. On the left are the individuals I have got to know. On the right the amount of money needed to bribe each one.' The Baron smiled. 'I was always expensive, you know. Very expensive. To be able to afford that is part of an idea of freedom that is unfortunately mis-understood nowadays. You should tell me where you come some time.' There was a knock at the door. Herr Ritschel came in. He pushed a cart with rubber tyres across the floor. With a gesture of apology Arbogast stood up, Meno as well, when Ritschel turned his head slowly in his direction. His eye sockets were unusually deep and shadowed, did he have eyes at all . . . ?

'The models, series D,' Herr Ritschel murmured, giving each syl-lable the same emphasis. In the cart were several A4-size blocks of some transparent synthetic material, all veined with coloured lines.

'You're a zoologist, Herr Rohde,' said Arbogast, waving him over, 'you will be interested in this.' There were eyes with nerve fibres and visual pathways each leading to a piece of the cerebral cortex, coloured light blue, the visual cortex where the brain creates an image of the world from the optical impressions pouring in.

'Dingo, dogfish, dolphin, donkey, dove, dromedary, duckbilled platypus,' said Herr Ritschel in his strange, equal-emphasis tones. 'The donkey's eyes are strikingly similar to those of the Minister of Science and Technology.' Arbogast picked up one of the blocks and turned it over and over, scrutinizing it. 'I can't help it, Ritschel, but I'm sure these eyes have looked at me quite often. You did do them from real life . . .'

'Of course, Herr Professor. They are from Bileam, our pet donkey that unfortunately died last summer. I asked to have its eyes as a model.'

'He's my best man for synthetic materials, Herr Rohde, invaluable.'

Ritschel bowed slightly.

Meno had never before seen anything like these eyes in the transparent blocks, even in the zoological institutes of Leipzig and Jena, where outstanding specialists were working. The preparations had been cast with the greatest precision in the blocks of synthetic material, though not to scale, however, for they were all the same size, the pupils looked like table-tennis balls with a colourful glaze. In each a single eye had been let in beside the visual pathway, sections showed the internal arrangement: iris ring, control muscle for the iris, corpus vitreum, retina, choroidea and from that a further section with rod and cone.

'One of my hobby horses.' Arbogast had sat down again and was looking at the stick with the gryphon handle; he nodded to Ritschel, who put the blocks back in the cart and trundled it out again. 'Another is, as you will have noticed, the physics of alarm systems. Do you know, even I have felt what it is like to have to earn your daily bread – even if it doesn't look like that. I grew up during the inflation years. It was with alarm systems and cameras I'd constructed myself that I earned enough to gain the knowledge I needed to build my physics laboratory. I started off in a lumber room, in the bad years around 1923 in Berlin. I was just sixteen, Herr Rohde, and an independent entrepreneur. If you like I'll show them to you afterwards. But, Rohde' – Arbogast spread out his arms and invited Meno to sit down again as well – 'let us talk about you instead. When I do have guests, I like to get to know them better. One gets too caught up in one's daily work and I enjoy evenings such as this, look forward to them weeks in advance. What do you say to Ritschel's skills?'

'Amazing, Herr Arbogast.'

'Well, *von* Arbogast. Yes, you're right, it really is amazing. Ritschel is a master of his art . . . As a former zoologist you will know how much as a scientist one is dependent on one's craftsmen. They it is who construct our apparatuses and what would even a Röntgen have been without his laboratory mechanic . . . These eyes: they are looking at us, Rohde, my friend. It is the eyes that see and are seen. "What is most decisive happens in our looks," said the optical illusion – a little physicist's joke in passing. It is a particular delight for me in the evening, after the day's work is done, to stroll round my eye-room and feel my heart start to pound at the hundreds of mute questions . . . Not a pleasant feeling, certainly not, but helpful. It seems to set off certain synapses, cause an increase in hormonal activity, I've had my best ideas there lately. – But let's talk about you. You come from the countryside south-east of here?'

'From Schandau.'

'Any brothers or sisters?'

'One sister, one brother.'

'We've had business with your brother-in-law . . . An open-minded man. We have certain projects that require cooperation with a clinic. We'll contact him again at some point. – You like my pencils?'

Meno had been staring at his desk, trying to count the pencils, which were arranged precisely according to size, in one of Ritschel's transparent blocks, a battery of sharply pointed little lances.

'There are precisely three hundred and fourteen. Pi, you understand. Three point one four pencils would have been too few for me, so I moved the decimal point back two places. But unfortunately I can't give you a pencil. There always have to be exactly three hundred and fourteen, the Ludolphine number, the relationship between circumference and diameter. And it must always be these same pencils. Genuine Faber pencils. The dark green is soothing, it's a real little pine forest I have before me here, the colour is fresh and young, too; the Czech ones you can buy in this country use poorer-quality wood, it splinters and breaks. Moreover they're yellow. That never happens with these. I don't want to be confronted with an autumnal deciduous wood. That's why I have a special standing order with Faber . . . I could put you on our list of potential pencil-recipients, if you like.

'Very kind of you.'

'My deputy, my two sons, and the head of our gas discharge laboratory are in front of you in the queue, however. – As a zoologist how did you manage to end up as editor in a literary publishing house, if I might ask. That's something I wondered about.'

Yes, Meno thought, that was in Leipzig, 1968. It's the little things you remember first before they let what's behind them shine through: a match, perhaps, a swimming cap with something written in ballpoint pen on it, a pattern on a piece of clothing. Perhaps the match with which the Party Secretary lit his cigarette – was it an F6 or a Juwel, or did he smoke Karo, which was considered a worker's brand? – and then his voice, matter-of-fact, slightly disappointed: As long as you're a member of that society you can forget about your PhD, Rohde. Socialist zoology demands people who are committed to it. You're one of Professor Haube's students, you should take him as your model in that respect too. That gang of Protestant students is a collection of counter-revolutionary subversives, keep away from them! We'll soon have eradicated them. Just think what's going on in Prague! – I wasn't the only one thinking of that, nor the students and assistant professors at the Institute; Talstrasse and Liebigstrasse were abuzz with the whispers, the cafés, it was what people were talking about wherever you went. Socialism with a human face . . . It was what we all wanted.

'There were problems. I was in the Protestant Student Society, in Leipzig, in '68.'

'I understand. Yes, those regulations. They were not necessarily to our advantage. When you remember how many valuable people, talented scientists . . . I know there's this stipulation that the mark for your degree dissertation must not be more than one grade higher than that in Marxism–Leninism. That, I would say, is not very productive. But perhaps it was necessary at the time . . . We have largely overcome that now. You must put yourself in the mind of the decisionmakers at the time, we were threatened on all sides, the situation was getting out of control in Czechoslovakia, drastic measures had to be taken. Which is not to say that in individual cases, probably in yours as well . . .'

Meno remained silent.

'There were misunderstandings and overheated reactions, and yet . . .' Arbogast made a conciliatory gesture. 'You know how it is. I can understand you. And I have been told that you are an excellent editor. So you were expelled from the university?'

'Not actually. But a scientist without a PhD, at a university—'

'Yes. These are things that happen to people. But take comfort from me, my friend. I was only able to attend a few lectures at university and I'm only an honorary doctor. But I hope that I can say that despite that I have made something of myself, hmm? – Then you joined Insel Verlag?'

'You are well informed, if you don't mind my saying so.'

'An experiment is only as good as its preparations.' Arbogast twisted his lips. 'Which is not to say that I regard you as an experiment. Yes, and now I remember – before Insel you were with Teubner's, the scientific and academic publishers that also brought out my volumes of tables for electrophysics. You were a bit out of the firing line there, so to speak, but not far from your original field.'

He'll have had his informants, Meno thought. B. G. Teubner, where I found work, Haube got me the position. A course at the Bibliographical Institute, evening classes. The bears at the entrance to the Zoological Institute . . . The light and the rooms come back into memory and if you see them again, they've become strange and have nothing to do with you any more – and yet they did belong to me, just as I belonged to them. The stockily built, bald Party Secretary of the Institute, in the conference room in Talstrasse; my mentor, who's present at the summons; my fellow assistant, who has to take minutes and with whom I share a room in the student residence . . . The empty-looking pieces of furniture reflecting Haube's idea of socialist functionality – he hated flourishes, hated the baroque, the Catholic Church, hated Vienna, where he had grown up and we didn't know and of which he, a large illustrated book in his hand, would speak in a tone of revulsion, hacking at the black-and-white photos with his index finger, the Theresianum, the Ringstrasse, the Capuchin Vault, the Hofburg: that had been the breeding ground for Hitler and his gang – the shit-brown criminals, ladies and gentlemen, there's no other word for it, you will have to get used to my strong language in this respect.

'Your eye collection is very impressive, Herr von Arbogast.'

Write it down, Hanna had said, and then perhaps you can get it out of your system. Those years in the sixties when we were young in Leipzig and carried two cards round with us in our wallets: one with a number, that was the *butter number* you had to give in the shop to get some of the rationed butter – or not to get it when the ration had all been used up: there's none left, Herr Rohde, but I can give you a bit of margarine; and the *house fire basic card 1*, the coal card that you needed for your fuel allocation. – The Café Corso in Gewandgässchen, the decayed splendour of the cloth merchants, with its landlady who spoke in a Bavarian accent, its buffet on the first floor and sitting opposite it the fat ladies, who were worthy of a place in Heimito von Doderer's *Demons*, the cream-cake-ladies as they were called; the hum of voices upstairs in the preserved Art Deco room: the sea-green fabric wallpaper behind which the Geiger counters ticked and the auriculate jellyfish listened, so people said; where, when the windows were open in the summer, the bellowing voice of the Regional Party Secretary was squeezed out of the pillars with the city radio loudspeakers; the Café Corso: Ernst Bloch would come and talk about Marxism; the university Rector, Mayer-Schorsch, with the fraternity duelling scars he was said to have acquired on the same duelling floor as Haube, would order half a dozen glasses of Hornano vermouth for himself, drink a toast to the goateed Chairman of the State Council on the wall, stand a round for *his students* and argue about Brecht with the principal of the Institute of Literature, while we at the tables at the front would whisper about Sartre and Anouilh, Beckett, the poems of Yevtushenko and Okudzhava till our heads were spinning; to get that out of my system —

Arbogast had been playing with one of the pencils and staring pensively out of the window. Giving Meno, who was sitting slumped in his chair, a brief glance, he said, 'Well, Rohde, I won't keep you in suspense any longer. I'm writing my autobiography. Your publishing house has approached me, the book is something they'd like to see. What I need is a critical eye, an opponent I can take seriously . . . I read these pages to my family at weekends, they all nod, but I have the feeling this acceptance comes either from cluelessness or from a mistaken idea of love; perhaps they also want to spare my feelings . . . It could be that Trude is to a certain extent lacking in that respect . . . To put it in a nutshell: I need a partner. I've made enquiries about you, as I said, and you have an outstanding reputation.'

There was a knock at the door.

'We'll talk about this another time. Think it over carefully. Should you say no, you will be forfeiting a fee that would be, well, appropriate. If you say yes, you will have a large amount of work ahead of you, at an unusual hour now and then. I'll call you tomorrow evening, at eight sixteen. Come in.'

'The guests are arriving, Herr Baron.'

'Thank you, Frau Alke.' Arbogast picked up the gryphon walking stick and ushered Meno out of the room. They went down into the hall. Meno recognized Vogelstrom, who was talking to Dietzsch, a sculptor who was a neighbour of the Hoffmanns in Wolfstone, Lothar Däne, the music critic of the *Sächsisches Tageblatt*, the physicist Teerwagen in conversation with Dr Kühnast from the pharmaceutical factory, the dentist, Frau Knabe, who had the apartment above Krausewitz in Wolfstone. Her husband, who worked in the Cabinet of Mathematical and Physical Instruments in the Zwinger, was standing with Malthakus, the stamp dealer, and a woman: Judith Schevola. Meno had heard rumours about her that were going round the literary scene and read a few remarkable stories by her in *Sinn und Form* . . . One of the most gifted young writers, she wrote with a passion that was rare in German literature. He had seen her a few times at meetings of the Writers' Association, also at the Leipzig Fair, but had never spoken to her. She had grey, close-cropped hair, but seemed to be in her early or mid-thirties at the most. Everything about her face looked displaced and distorted, as if it had been put together out of many other faces. Only her eyes seemed to belong to her. She scrutinized Arbogast, then Meno, taking sips from a glass of pomegranate juice. The men were standing facing her, on the other side of the hall as well. Alke opened the door, letting in Sperber, the lawyer, Schiffner, the publisher, and a man with a slightly hunched walk and a fleshy lower lip hanging down, whom Meno knew all too well; he started back and grasped the banister, which the woman with grey hair seemed to register with simultaneous curiosity and hostility, then she looked up and followed Meno's reactions; he thought: like an entomologist pulling a fly's leg off to see how it will deal with the new situation. The man – who had noticed him and surreptitiously raised his arm – was Jochen Londoner, his ex-father-in-law.

'Please make your way to our television room.'

'One moment, Ludwig.' Giving her husband a polite smile, Frau von Arbogast introduced Meno to the other guests. Judith Schevola's greeting was brief: 'We know each other. At the last Association conference you showed a great talent for falling asleep.' Arbogast led the company to the door out of which Ritschel had emerged. Judith Schevola, Malthakus, the stamp dealer, and Frau Knabe, the dentist, stood looking at the painting over the dragon table and only came when Arbogast rang a little bell.

After his talk and the subsequent discussion, Meno went upstairs before the others; a buffet had been set up in the conference room. Alke and

Ritschel were busy at the table with the white cloth. A youngish physicist, who had sat behind Arbogast during the talk, gave Meno a friendly nod. 'If there's anything else you'd like to see . . .' He opened a little door that led out onto an oriel running round part of the building.

'Thank you, Herr . . .'

'Kittwitz. I work at the Institute for Flow Research. And don't worry, they'll find you soon enough, Herr Rohde. I enjoyed your talk. The way the garden spider makes its nest – remarkable parallels to the buffet-encirclement behaviour at physics conferences . . . But I'll leave you in peace now.'

Rohde went to the edge of the balcony. The cool air did him good, his face was burning and he was glad that Kittwitz's friendly gesture had enabled him to have a few moments to himself. He was shaken by hot and cold shivers alternately, the excitement was gradually dying down, for a few seconds he was in a state between profound tiredness and cool alertness, like a clock spring, he thought, that is being squeezed tight by the fingers of a clockmaker but can slip out and fly open at any moment; this blasted stage fright, I didn't speak well. In his mind's eye he saw the face of his ex-father-in-law, bright, with the expression of concentrated listening that he knew and in which his lower lip drooped and was drawn up with a start at regular intervals, then Londoner became aware that he was being or could be observed; he would grasp his chin between index and middle finger and clear his throat; those nails that were always too long, Meno thought, the thick signet ring – master's ring, Londoner used to say – like a yellow frog on the bottom joint of his index finger: one of those tropical amphibians with warning colours; but this one seemed to be asleep in a state of metamorphosis, especially when Londoner, as during his talk, let his hand dangle down and crossed his legs, kept his heavy eyelids closed and his nose – Hanna's nose, too small for his full-fleshed face – became covered in drops of sweat. Arbogast's introduction; Schiffner's eyes, unfathomable under his white bushy brows, variable: sometimes cool, sometimes concerned, sometimes with a kind of fatherly benevolence that fascinated and oppressed Meno in equal measure; and Madame – in his thoughts he used that instead of the 'Fräulein' that seemed inappropriate – Schevola, cold, head proudly thrown back: Do you think what you have to say is of any interest to me? Get it out of your system, Meno told himself, and that strange television room . . .

He searched for his cigarettes, Arbogast wouldn't see that he smoked, but even if he did, he was presumably allowed one now. He hadn't brought any with him and remembered that he had left the yellow packet of Orient at home, between his typewriter and an issue of *Sinn und Form* that Schiffner had given him to have a look at. The city lay dark below him, with sparse lights scattered round the edges, Kleinzschachwitz and Pillnitz upstream, above them, near Pappritz, the television tower with faintly phosphorescent antennae; the Elbe water meadows and the hills towards the Czech border mere inky-black surfaces; farther downstream the Johannstadt suburb with its prefabricated tenements; directly below him the continuation of the slope of Arbogast's garden cocooned in marshy darkness, the Blue Marvel with its filigree double tent stretching so elegantly across the river, a number 4 tram was crossing it, Meno could see the conductor as a patch of shadow in the yellowish light of the carriage. A white smudge was dangling from the power cable over Schillerplatz, a fraying banner hanging down limply like a dead squid preserved in formaldehyde. When there was some movement in the air, bringing back currents of stench, he thought he could smell the decay away over Körnerplatz and the wooded slopes of the district on the edge of which Arbogast's property stood. It was the smell of ash from the Mitte and Löbtau combined heat and power stations by the Brücke der Jugend, the chimneys of which looked down on the city with red Cyclops eyes. He heard the babble of voices from the conference room, he also had the feeling his name was being called. His tiredness increased, at the same time he felt a strong desire for a cigarette. He watched, saw the Elbe like a spine of tar below him, the houses a gangrenous black, like decomposing flesh, shimmering movements in it, as if gleaming white trichinae had bored into the rotting stone flesh, ready to lay their eggs. There was a play of searchlight beams on the Käthe-Kollwitz-Ufer, fleecy arms of light feeling their way, with the movements of helpless swimmers, over the dark-lying cellular systems of the buildings in the sector of the workers' housing cooperative; sometimes they were struck, as if by an indignant, hostile glance, by the gleam of a distant window, so there must still be life there. What kind of life, Meno wondered, what is life like down there? A ship with an orchestra on board could run aground, the cracks of light along the curtains wouldn't get any wider. The Blue Miracle was deserted, only the Schillergarten restaurant on the opposite bank of the Elbe seemed to still be open. There, too, the curtains were drawn but a door opened now and then and a customer staggered out into the fresh air, either to go off in the direction of the bus stops on Schillerplatz or to disappear behind the restaurant. It was not the only such establishment to have problems with the sewerage system, Meno remembered the Bodega in Leipzig, a favourite meeting place during the book fair that possessed no conveniences, one had to use the back yard there as well . . . Now the Elbe was a bluish shade, then sea creatures seemed to crawl past, milky, misshapen beings made to look leprous by the water. The stench came, rolled up the slopes, Meno knew it from his tongue, it was the taste of a match that has been chewed too long, to which something like a dash of sauerkraut was added: the effluent from the Heidenau cellulose works that was let out into the water at night.

'Do you smoke? There's a hell of a stink again.' Judith Schevola tapped a few cigarettes out of a Duett packet and offered them to Meno when he nodded. 'Impressive the way you described the ways these venomous tropical spiders have of killing. I must read that again later.

I bought your *Old German Poems*. The Old Man of the Mountain spoke to me about it just now. I think he has a pretty high regard for you. Although immediately afterwards he told me you'd rejected one of his projects.'

'That wasn't me, that was the publishing section in the Ministry. I hope he told you that as well.'

'I understand. How stupid. I've no matches on me.' Schevola went through her pockets, the cigarette stuck between her lips.

'Just a minute.' Meno lit a match. She bent over his hand that was shielding the flame. He lit one for himself as well, took a deep pull, blew out the smoke with relish. 'Oh, wonderful. Thanks. I left mine at home.'

'I hope you like it. What do you usually smoke, when your memory doesn't fail you?'

'A pipe. Orient when I'm outside.'

'My grandfather used to smoke a pipe . . . I've always liked the smell. – In the afterword to your book you twice omitted the subjunctive; as far as I know "as if " is followed by the past subjunctive so you should have written "as if it were" and "as if it were to start".'

'Oh dear.'

'Yes,' Schevola said cheerfully, 'it was a pleasure to pick out those mistakes after you pointed out that kind of nonsense in my first manuscript that I sent to Dresdner Edition. You rejected it because of those minor slips!'

'Just a minute, that must be a mistake.'

'But your name was the one at the bottom of the letter of rejection.'

'Oh, I see. That does happen. Let me explain. We have pre-printed letters we sometimes have to use for that kind of communication because we're short of normal writing paper. It can then happen that someone will sign without correcting the name on the pre-printed letter. In your case it was probably Herr Redlich, our senior editor.'

'The signature was illegible, an "R" was recognizable. I thought of you at once. But surely you're not going to slip away now. Perhaps you're afraid I'll strangle you?'

'Then the cigarette was an offer of reconciliation?'

Schevola blew out a cloud of smoke, stared out into the garden. 'Have you seen the dogs? He's got kennels down there. A funny guy. Sometimes I wonder whether he believes what he says. Or whether he's only here because they gave him an institute. – Do you like bullfighting?'

'Only in Hemingway and Picasso.'

'Do you find it too brutal? Too bloody?'

'Too cruel. The crowd bawls because a living creature is being slaughtered.'

'Slaughtered? How melodramatic. The torero and the bull are equal opponents. Each of the two has a chance and the one that dies goes down fighting and in full public view. Neither the torero nor the bull can hide anything, neither a moment of bravery nor one of cowardice. That's honest and it's a good death.'

'Maybe. But I still find the ritual repulsive.'

'You can't bear the thought of death. And that we have to fight if we want to live. That is the idea bullfighting makes clear and I find that honest. But many people refuse to face up to that truth. And get outraged instead. And never ask themselves where the leather for the shoes they're wearing comes from while they're getting outraged.'

'It may be honest to accept death and display it. But it isn't great.'

Schevola looked up and surveyed him in surprise. 'Then for you to lie is great?'

'Send me your manuscript.'

Her expression darkened abruptly. She broke out into an ugly laugh. 'Tell me, do you think I'm chatting to you in order to palm my stuff off on you?'

'I'm sorry, I didn't mean it like that.'

Schevola put her hands to her temples and started to massage them. 'You're tired and I'm being a nuisance . . .'

'May I join you?'

'Of course,' Meno said, 'Herr Doktor Kittwitz, physicist – Frau Schevola, writer.'

'We know each other from previous Urania meetings,' the physicist said. He'd brought three glasses and a bottle of champagne. 'Crimean champagne, the very best. The old man's really pushed the boat out. No expense spared. Don't you want to eat something, Herr Rohde? You've earned it and people are already asking where you are. Herr Altberg and Herr Sperber would both like a few words with you, your boss as well. You've got a little interview list already. Cheers, Judith, Herr Rohde.' They clinked glasses, drank. 'In cases like this Arbogast takes off his watch, puts it down where he can see it and says: Please excuse me but I can't give you more than four minutes and thirty-one seconds.'

'You seem to like him a lot again, Roland.' Judith gave one of her ugly, grating laughs. 'How's your project going?'

'I really do like him. You could say he's got his little quirks, but you have to give him one thing: he takes trouble. We handed it in for publication. Two weeks later they called to say they couldn't print it at the moment since their paper allocation is limited and they first of all have to see where they can get some for the next issues. How does this sound to you: In the Institute here we make a fundamental discovery . . .'

'Oh, my dear Roland's getting modest in his middle age and says "we"?'

'Judith . . . please don't. A fundamental discovery! But only something that gets published is recognized, Herr Rohde, and the priority goes to whoever is published first . . . And do you know what's happened? There's a group in Bremen. A few days ago Arbogast took me to one side and told me he'd spoken to a colleague there. They've made the same discovery as us, four weeks after us, but it will be published sooner . . . Just because there isn't any paper in this country again . . . I really hit the roof, believe you me.' He hastily gulped down some champagne and poured himself some more. 'It was our, it was . . . my discovery, Judith. And it's being taken away from me.'

'Didn't he tell them, on the telephone, that you were quicker?'

'Of course he did. Answer: My dear Arbogast, we know the equipment you have at your Institute and, by and large, we know your colleagues . . . Surely you're not trying to dispute our right to priority. Of course we'll have to accept it if you publish your results before we do! Arrogant arseholes! We can't do any top-level research here, this is the useless Zone . . . And do you know what we get told here? Funding? For flow research? Of what concrete benefit is that to the national economy? We're sorry, but we can't see the benefit. Huh.' Kittwitz went to the edge of the balcony and grasped the balustrade. 'D'you know what I'd like to do? I'd like to get away.'

'There's supposed to be a billion-mark loan from the Bavarian State Bank coming. In return we're to drop the minimum currency exchange requirement for children.'

'How incredibly humane. Yes, our state was always good to children. Franz-Josef Strauss, the arch-imperialist, loans us a billion in hard exploiter's currency. Suddenly the road to the promised land goes right through Catholic Bavaria . . . So that's what their principles are worth!'

'Moreover they say they're going to make it possible for citizens of the GDR and foreigners to marry, also for them to make a complaint if that should be refused. Now if that isn't progress!'

'Then you can hook yourself a capitalist millionaire at the Leipzig Trade Fair. Shouldn't be difficult with your charm, Judith. And if you don't get your class enemy, you can write a complaint. Or how about a gunrunner, buying supplies for Iraq from us. Cheers.'

'You're drinking too much, Roland. Just remember: "But scarce those words my lips had 'scaped –"'

'"I wished I'd kept them in my breast." Schiller, or something like that. As Herr Rohde knows. No offence meant.' With a black look, he raised his glass and drank to Meno.

'Oh, there you are, Herr Rohde. Do come in, you'll get cold out there.' Frau von Arbogast waved from the study window. 'And Fräulein Schevola and Herr Kittwitz. Young people stick together, of course. But do come and join us, otherwise they'll be talking of nothing but politics, cars and prostate glands in here.' She closed the window.

'Fräulein!' Judith Schevola muttered indignantly. Kittwitz laughed. 'For some reason she seems to like you. Come on, we'll finish this bottle together.'

'My God, lilac-coloured hair. Do you know what she asked me, Roland? Why I didn't have mine dyed. Whether it was some disease. Of course I said it was just that there was too much ash in the air.'

Inside, Frau Knabe, a tall woman with short black hair, morello-cherry lipstick and a necklace of blue wooden beads slung several times round her neck, was talking about the advantages of matriarchy and the Feldenkrais method. Her husband was standing beside her, head bowed, fingers intertwined, staring at a pineapple that Professor Teerwagen and Dr Kühnast had approached to within a few fractions of an centimetre. '. . . all it comes down to is the oppression of women, for centuries and centuries, oh, since the beginning of time. And of course it's a woman we have to *thank* for the expulsion from paradise and there's this rule I've learnt: *mulier tacet in ecclesia*! Women are to keep silent in church, it says that in the Bible. The cheek!'

'Perhaps the prophets will have had their reasons?'

'Your smile doesn't improve your joke one bit, *Herr* Däne. What do you have to say about it, Frau Schevola? Isn't it about time to put an end to the rule of men? Especially of old men!'

Judith Schevola raised her glass.

'Aha, and there is Herr Rohde. We were just talking about connections and breaking through the barriers between me and thee. As you were saying earlier on, about those nerve spiders or whatever:

something is injected. It makes me think of anaesthetizing the nervus mandibularis. – Open wide, a little prick, wait five minutes and all quiet in the upper storey. But this in-ject-ing' – Frau Knabe drew the word out, eyes wide – 'this sting, pleasant pressure then something from outside dribbles into us, the bitter or the sweet poison . . . Toxic! I couldn't help thinking about sex when you described it.'

Those around grinned.

'Not with you, Herr Rohde, you're too skinny for me and you've had too much of a classical education. Do you know that some patients find the sharp pain, when you use the three-finger grip and gently push the needle into the mucous membrane, energizing?'

'I have to say that I recently read something like that by a doctor, Georg Groddeck –'

'That's right, Herr Däne, so did I.'

'*The Book of the It*, Herr Dietzsch?'

'Yes! And I thought it was interesting what he had to say about successful treatments, every treatment of patients is the right one, they are always and under all circumstances correctly treated, whether according to science or the method of a shepherd skilled in the healing arts – the cure doesn't come from the prescriptions but from what our "it" does with the –'

'You'd be the ideal doctor for our medical services here,' said Frau Knabe, returning to the fray. 'But, you know, recently I got terrible twinges from my musculus latissimus dorsi and unfortunately my "it" made absolutely nothing of it! It demanded painkillers and a correction of the wrong motion grid that caused it . . . Grid's an interesting word, isn't it? A *mot juste*. Thought grid, experience grid and motion grid, of course. Which takes us back to Feldenkrais. You interrupted me.'

'But there's always an incalculable element to humanity, Frau Doktor Knabe. Science can't count or measure everything or even mark it on a grid.'

'Who is saying it can, Herr Däne? But Feldenkrais doesn't simply put forward unproved assertions. All it comes to in the end is that they say "it" – is a man.'

Meno went to the buffet. Judith Schevola was standing, laughing, in a group of scientists in white coats from the Institute, Sperber, the lawyer, was nearby talking to the Baroness and Teerwagen. Slices of cold roast meat, ham, Hungarian salami cut wafer-thin, several kinds of cheese, all appetizingly set out on plates with a garnish of lettuce leaves, hard-boiled egg halves, caviar and tomatoes, crispy fried chicken, Margon mineral water, beer, wine, Crimean champagne and bread giving off a nice smell. In addition, large bowls of fruit salad, Waldorf salad, grapes, bananas, fruits Meno didn't recognize.

'Not bad, is it?' That was Malthakus, with a faint smile. 'What you've got in your hand there's called a kiwi fruit. Comes from New Zealand.'

'Never seen one before, Herr Malthakus.'

'Me neither, not until this evening. That is – just a minute. On a New Zealand stamp . . . Or was it a bird on it? You have to peel them or spoon them out. Have you tried the potato soup yet? A treat, really herby. Those are the things I like best. Simple dishes. Ones you even get in wartime. Bread, jacket potatoes, cream cheese, stew, potato soup. Though I suppose bananas aren't to be sneezed at either.' Putting his hand over his mouth, he laughed a quiet, bubbling laugh. 'I've already polished off five and purloined a few more.' Malthakus gave Meno a sly look. 'For the kids. There's nothing in the dump down the road.' The 'dump down the road' was the greengrocer's on the corner of Rissleite and Bautzner Strasse, across the road from the Binneberg café-cum-cake shop, and 'nothing' was Golden Delicious, salsify, sugar beet, beans, carrots, cabbage and a large tub of dirty potatoes. There was also juice, a red fizzy drink known as 'Lenin's sweat'.

'It's genuine Malossol caviar, by the way. Would you like a bagful? I always take some back with me when I've been to Arbogast's. He's on the supply programme of those over there. The Michurin kitchen complex. It completely bypasses normal shops.'

'I know.'

Malthakus glanced up in surprise, a look of suspicion flitted across his face. 'Oh yes. I see . . . My girls were friends with Hanna, when they were little. Later on they weren't allowed to be with her any more. Haven't seen her for ages.'

'She's in Prague, working as a doctor in the embassy.'

'In Prague is she, and a doctor in the embassy . . . ? Yes, well, tall oaks from little acorns grow. I can still remember you and Hanna coming to the shop and buying picture postcards. You of Prague and London, Hanna always of Paris. Always of Paris, yes, yes.' Malthakus adjusted his glasses, surveyed Meno reflectively. 'You quoted a poem just now. That kind of thing doesn't usually mean much to me, most of it's above my head. I'm sure our modern poets are all very cultured and advanced but I'm sorry, I just don't understand them. A simple line by Eichendorff or Mörike, that's my limit. But the one you quoted –'

'A Japanese haiku. "Oh, this sultry heat! / The spiders' webs hanging hot / on the summer trees." The poet was called Onitsura, he lived in the seventeenth and eighteenth centuries.'

'Aha. Don't you think it's terribly hot in here? But that's what I can't get out of my mind: the hot spiders' webs. You'll have to forgive me if I couldn't concentrate properly on the rest of your talk, it was going round and round in my head all the time. You get taken in by this Mr, what did you say? – Mr Onitsura. You believe in his hot spiders' webs. Until you realize that it's only a body that can get hot. But a spider's web doesn't have one, so it can't get hot! . . . And yet you trust the fellow, somehow the line makes sense and that irritates me. Oh, I think the Baron would like to talk to you. In the meantime should I . . . act on your behalf?' Malthakus looked round quickly and pulled the corner of a plastic bag out of his pocket. 'We have the same way home as far as Wolfsleite – then the hand-over of the goods in question.' Meno had to laugh at the stamp dealer's innocent blue-eyed look, the words whispered behind his hand.

'Well, Rohde, my friend, have you thought over my offer? Your boss would have no objection.'

'I need a little time, Herr von Arbogast.'

Schiffner raised his champagne glass and drank to Meno. 'We also have to have a talk about the Association conference, my son. The regional office has already been on the line asking where our response to the meeting on the election report is. And there's some work coming your way soon. From our talented up-and-coming young writer.' Schiffner nodded in the direction of Judith Schevola. Arbogast and he exchanged glances, grinned. Sperber and Altberg came to join them. 'She wants to publish a book with us. Have a look some time. I mean at the book.' Arbogast, Sperber and Schiffner began to laugh. 'And just you be careful, my son, talent can be infectious.' The three of them laughed even louder.

'My God, Knabe's shooting her mouth off again. How can you stand her, Ludwig, her and her feminist twaddle?' Sperber rocked up and down on his toes and looked across at the dentist, who, gesturing all the time and rolling her eyes, was arguing with Däne, Jochen Londoner and Kittwitz.

Her husband was standing there, disconsolately holding the stalk which was all that was left of the pineapple. 'That limp-dick Knabe really ought to give his old woman one for once.'

'D'you think that's what she needs?' Schiffner stuck his hands in his pockets and began to rock on his toes as well.'

'No, she swings the other way. She does it with that Julie from the riding school, that's why they don't have any children.'

'The woman who lives on Rissleite, where Heckmann, the carter, used to have his business?'

'The very one! She once gave one of my physicists a good thrashing because he'd had the audacity to pick a cherry that was hanging over the fence of her property.' Arbogast tapped his walking stick, rocked on heel and toe. 'Pity about Knabe, really. Tall woman, splendid hips . . . Junoesque. Or what do you say, Heinz? You're the specialist here.'

Schiffner stroked his face, his habitual gesture for introducing a joke. 'Dear ladies, if you only knew how gladly we see you among us and that it is our greatest pleasure to dwell in your midst . . .' The three of them giggled, Meno turned away. The Old Man of the Mountain drew him aside. 'Let's have a drink, Herr Rohde. What is it to be?'

Meno shook his head.

'Oh, come on, Rohde. It's terribly hot in here . . . That power cut just now, during your talk, perhaps it has something to do with that . . . But in here' – Altberg placed his hand on his chest – 'it's freezing. And that brandy warms you up, I can recommend it. VSOP – yes, in that respect he really does splash out.' Altberg poured three glasses, held one out to Meno, downed the other two as if they were water, filled them again. 'You beware of Arbogast. – Come on, let's walk up and down, Sperber and Dietzsch are watching us . . . I think he's a spy.'

'Dietzsch?'

'Sculptors can write reports too. Especially when they're short of money – and of the success other sculptors enjoy . . . And this bottle's coming with us, this warming, coppery liquor, it'll be a corpse by the time we've finished, we mustn't let something as good as this go to waste. – I had it from Malthakus and he heard it from Marroquin . . .' Altberg emptied the fourth glass, gave Meno a horrified glance, suddenly started to breathe heavily. 'You think that's just rumour and conjecture? Do you know what? You'd be right! You'd be absolutely right! Pure supposition, that's all . . . the imagination of a man whose business is literature has run away with him. I've spoken to Schiffner again, he actually does reject the book . . .'

'Don't you feel well? Would you like to sit down? Or get some fresh air?'

'No, no, I'm all right, Rohde. Thank you for your letter. One has to be a bit careful with you . . . Do you know something? There's no harm in a bit of gossip. After all, we make a living from that delightful fare.'

'Please forgive me, Herr Altberg, I didn't mean to, er, tread on your toes –'

'That's the problem! No one wants to tread on anyone's toes, everyone's polite and quiet and keeps their distance. I'll make a start, for I have to admit . . . I love gossip.' He took a sip and laughed. 'Don't use that against me if I should . . . well, crop up among your lot. As an old brandy spider, for example, heheh.'

Meno felt uncomfortable and yet he listened in fascination to the stories the old man recounted with relish – without appearing to be drunk; Meno had noticed his slight swaying before, during his visit to him at 8 Oktoberweg, it could just as well be ascribed to weakness or tiredness. Against his will he was gripped by the old man's halting and disjointed delivery, soaked up his words with a craving previously unknown in himself, at least not in this connection, and it surprised him; he really ought to have withdrawn at once with some polite but empty phrase. Was Herr Rohde aware that Judith Schevola had had affairs with several of those present? She'd already been married four times – and was only thirty-five! She literally hunted men down, which didn't necessarily do them any good. She must have had some bad experiences. 'Do you know what her first husband said when he found her after she'd attempted suicide? – "Oh, then I'll soon get my collection of prints back." There was blood everywhere, the bathtub was full of it –'

'Now then, Georg, talking scandal again?' Teerwagen, the low-voltage physicist in his mid-fifties with heavy horn-rimmed spectacles and an imposing belly, over which a watch chain stretched, took a sip of a glass of red wine, his other hand casually stuck in the pocket of his elegant suit. 'Are you coming along afterwards as well, Herr Rohde? – To look at the stars. From midnight onwards. It's fairly clear tonight and astronomy is one of the main points of our social evenings. Arbogast will have the large observatory opened. We won't, however, he able to see the Spider constellation. If you'd been here on 15 December you'd have been able to observe a relatively rare spectacle: an eclipse of the sun.'

'Oh, come on, Heiner, it was only a half-eclipse. What we deserve, heheh, in this country with its half-people.'

Teerwagen slowly twisted his glass one way and the other. 'Today we're going to look at Pisces.' He gave Altberg a swift glance; by this time the old man had emptied the bottle.

'Yes, Heiner. The mute fishes,' Altberg murmured.

'It's good that we've got to know each other a bit better, Herr Rohde. There we are, neighbours, but we don't have a real conversation until we meet here. Funny. I quite often see you taking your evening walk, you're pretty unmistakable with your hat. My wife wants me to ask you where you got it.'

'Present from my sister. The Thälmannstrasse Exquisit, delivery from Yugoslavia.'

'My wife thought it must be something like that. Lamprecht, the hatter, is still off sick, who knows if he'll ever go to our heads again, so to speak. His son doesn't seem interested in taking over the business. – But you need the right face to go with it. Mine's too round. By the way, I'm also one of your readers. Our librarian gave it a blue card. I have to say that his feeling for quality is seldom wrong, at least for my taste. – Oh, thank you.' Alke had come and, eyes lowered, was holding up a tray with ice cream.

'Do you like ice cream, Herr Rohde? I'm mad about it. And it's excellent here.' Altberg rubbed his hands in delight and took two tubs.

'Yes' – Teerwagen loosened his tie – 'the ice cream – and the heating.'

Meno was tired and wanted to leave. He gave Alke a surreptitious sign and she responded with a slight bow. He saw Malthakus attempting to slip out of the conference room with a bulging bag and the Baroness, who was close by, turning away at precisely that moment to take the person she was talking to by the arm and stroll away, chatting, as the stamp dealer grasped the door handle.

'The Herr Baron wishes to speak to you,' he heard Ritschel's equally emphasizing voice murmur behind him. They went into the study. 'I really would like to have longer to think your offer over,' Meno said as he went in. Arbogast raised his hand, nodded to Ritschel, who closed the door. 'Don't worry, my friend, I don't want to press you. Just a few formalities. A receipt for your fee. Sign by the red cross please.' Arbogast handed Meno the form and an envelope across the table.

'A thousand marks?!'

'That is what our speakers generally receive. Good pay for good work. The reverse is true as well, something that is unfortunately too little understood in this country. I beg you to excuse the little power cut, there have been more and more recently. I don't think it will have distracted you too much; you were speaking without notes anyway. Oh, and there's one more thing . . .' Arbogast opened a drawer and handed Meno a heavy, leather-bound tome. 'Our visitors' book.' He picked up a fountain pen and slowly unscrewed the lid. 'With a joke if possible, please. You should know that I collect jokes.' There was a knock at the door. Alke came in, whispered something to the Baron.

'Oh yes.' Arbogast drummed his fingers on the desk. He drew the visitors' book to him, leafed through it, took the pen, looked at Meno reflectively. 'In the garden, you say?'

'Yes, Herr Baron.'

'Has anything been affected? The heating plant? The greenhouses?'

'As far as we could tell, no, Herr Baron.'

Arbogast screwed the lid back on the pen, stroked the visitors' book. 'Herr Londoner asked me to tell you that he and his wife would be delighted if you were to visit them again. Once more, many thanks for coming, Herr Rohde. We're going to the observatory now, but you'll be tired.' He stood up and shook Meno by the hand.

20

Dialogue about children

'To have children is a great responsibility . . .'

'They aren't toys one can acquire when one feels like it and throw away when one doesn't like them any more.'

'One has to think about these children. Wouldn't one be prepared to give them everything? To do everything for them? So that they are brought up to be decent people. Can blossom out?'

'Well, Herr Doktor, I'm not telling you anything new there, although it's difficult to be a good father to all one's children at the same time.'

'You don't know what I'm talking about. But we know where you go . . . On Thursdays. – Your wife, does she know too?'

'We were talking about children. Do you smoke? Would you like something to drink?'

'We want to try and keep this conversation calm. Calm and matter-of-fact. Part of that, however, is that in future you must be more careful with our invitations. When a letter's left opened, it does invite people to read it, however ordinary it might look, it's the way things are, a natural human instinct.'

'Some nurses, some colleagues are interested in whom their senior doctor corresponds with. And a secretary's job is to deal with letters, opened and unopened ones . . .'

'Are you a hundred per cent sure of your secretary? – We are talking calmly, perfectly calmly, Herr Doktor. – Look, among other things I'm responsible for the hospitals in this district. The health services are – you know that as well as I do. But how can one improve something?'

'That is the question. Grumbling and grousing will get us nowhere, your boss is absolutely right there. That's something else you know just as well as I do. But perhaps there are disruptive influences?'

'I'm a qualified electrician, you know, and if one thinks of one of these hospitals as a complex circuit . . . You only need *one* break and the current stops flowing.'

'The current is still there, the circuit is the right one, but somewhere in this complex network there's a blockage, whether it's arisen by chance or not . . .'

'Do you think that hospitals that work, factories that work are not in our interest? There was a time when you thought differently about these things – about interests. Once you were completely on our side. Oh, no, no. As a student one is no longer an child, no longer a silly little boy . . .'

'At nineteen one is grown up, responsible for one's thoughts and actions . . . You studied and were active in Leipzig, we know that. And you knew that lip service is not enough, that fine words are nothing in themselves.'

'You were ready for more. May I show you something . . .'

'That's right, Herr Doktor. With your declaration of commitment. And reports. Most of them are rather wordy, in that I agree with my colleagues in Leipzig. But these reports definitely contain substantial information.'

'At nineteen . . . you were a good observer; at nineteen others were officers in the war, partisans, I knew one person who at nineteen was a commander in Budyonny's army . . . How angry you could get! What a low opinion of the workers you had, in nineteen fifty-three . . . And by then you were twenty . . . And a fighter, Herr Doktor, fully on the side of our cause. If you had had your way, Herr Weniger would have been thrown out of the university.'

'Fortunately my colleagues were rather more circumspect than you and have kept a good gynaecologist for our country. You hated him, him and his secure position, him and his defeatism, that wasn't consistent, since Herr Weniger stayed here after all, his naked realism that refused to believe in anything . . . Just as much as you adored his girlfriend of the time. But then you didn't write anything about that, about the four times you went to see her . . . If you should happen to be interested in what Herr Weniger was doing during that time . . .'

'Quite right, he was being questioned. Not for his diploma. That was the version his girlfriend told you. – But we digress. If these children have particular talents, it would be negligent of a father not to support them to the best of his ability. Just suppose your sons were musically gifted, wouldn't you do everything in your power to obtain the clarinet or cello for which they show such talent? See that they have lessons?'

'And then it is often the case that children who are musically gifted have talents in other areas as well, they're not stupid, they have no problems at school.'

'Perhaps they could become outstanding scientists. Engineers. Technologists.'

'Or doctors. Of which our country has such great need. – You would like what? Well we do need a little light, Herr Doktor.'

'But that kind of university course costs money, a lot of money. And the senior high school beforehand. Money that belongs to our state and that it generously disburses for those who, through their qualifications and profession, will at some time in the future occupy privileged positions. Does our state not then have the right to find out who it is who wants to go to university, where they come from and so on?'

'Whether he intends to employ the knowledge he has acquired here and, as I said, at the state's expense for the good of that state and in the service of the people who, by their work, have made his studies possible. We consider that a legitimate interest.'

'So we ought not to be in such a hurry to close your file as our colleagues in Leipzig believe. Your wife seems to have diverted you from our course . . . Think my proposal over, sleep on it.'

'Take your time. Oh, and one more thing: as you know, doctors are needed in *our* country. It would be a betrayal of the patients in your care. – Comrade Sergeant, show the Herr Doktor out.'

21

Caravel

The *Santa Maria* had lateen sails with red crosses, the *Nina* was fat-bellied, curving over the waterline like a Turkish sabre, Robert said: It's floating on its hump, and then came Magellan's ships, sea spray splashing up at the bow, yards torn off in the horse latitudes, the Roaring Forties, masts eaten away with salt and rigging leached dry; Magellan with his telescope on the afterdeck and it was the void into which he was staring, the void explored by Spain and Portugal, wave-torn rocks, dead bays, black holes that kept on swallowing up horizons, suns, moons, signs of the zodiac over the wind-creased sea, and despite everything Magellan looked like a man who had time, that struck Christian as odd and he would spend ages observing the Commander as he circumnavigated the world on a poster opposite the bed. His journey was a string tied round the globe, the equator a cord holding the world together at its fattest place; once right round, from then on there were borders. And beside the bearded seafarer, Gagarin was waving, a man in a space capsule and that, too, had encircled the earth with an invisible string. The colours were slightly faded already, how old was the photo, had they cut it out of a copy of *Army Review*, out of *Sputnik*? Ornella Muti and Adriano Celentano next to them, photos from *Film Mirror*, *Boot Hill* with the, as Ina said, 'incredibly' blue-eyed Terence Hill; Captain Tenkes, the heroic Hungarian freedom fighter. For a moment the ticking of the alarm clock on a shelf above Christian's head was as loud as the click of a metronome, tock, tock, tock, or was it the wooden leg of a buccaneer walking up and down on the deck of his death-trap of a ship, staring at Tortuga, a sharp-tongued parrot on his shoulder? . . . It must be hot on Tortuga, the mysterious island off Venezuela, as hot as in this bed: Christian threw back the quilt and put his arm over his forehead. Doctor Fernau had come on Sunday afternoon, had auscultated and percussed him with fingers flattened by a hundred thousand percussions, the pleximeter middle finger on the left, the percussion middle finger on the right, as Richard explained (and no one understood), and all of Fernau's fingers had bristly hair, they had felt or, rather, kneaded Christian, which hurt quite a bit on his muscles so that Fernau had frowned, told him to Shut His Trap, and continued to knead unmoved, to examine his lymph glands, which he did unexpectedly gently so that Christian, who had anticipated being short of breath, swallowed in astonishment. Then Doctor Fernau scratched his unkempt, iron-grey hair, put his hand to his left breast but found nothing, since he wasn't wearing his white coat but a loose jacket to go with his grey flannels with the broken zip and coarse felt slippers: he lived not far away from the Hoffmanns, on Sonnleite, the road that wound its way down the steep slope on the east side of the district. Keeping two fingers between Christian's jaws, he rummaged round in his worn doctor's bag that was coming apart at one of the seams, growled, 'Right', when he found a wooden spatula and rammed it, grunting 'Aah', into Christian's mouth. 'A bit furred, the lingua. But, my God, as long as it's not festering . . . What have we here . . . ?' and screwed up his right eye, the left turned into a blue eyepiece behind the lens of his glasses, peered down his throat, the look presumably microscoping round his uvula, that was jiggling up and down apprehensively; Fernau tapped the spatula on his tonsil: 'Out with the rubbish!' Christian gave a rasping cough, saw Fernau's gigantic eye as a monster's and laughed on the doctor's lenses, the Cossack moustache widened and slanted: 'What we have here – clearly nothing at all. Spots of irritation, Waldeyer's ring inflamed, but what of it, no need for the hospital, the lung's rattling a bit, is there an important class test in the offing, young sir?' Dr Fernau said, handing the spatula to Anne. 'The lad has a bit of a temperature, it happens at his age, hormones sloshing round, you know, and so on. Keep him in bed, if you like, Frau Hoffmann, the compresses on his legs were a good idea, tea with honey, yes, something to bring his temperature down, yes, has he been sick? Well there you are.'

Influenza infection, Fernau had written, two or three days in bed on a light diet. 'Could I have an appointment with you, Herr Hoffmann. I've got an ingrowing toenail that's bothering me.'

'A bit of a temperature?' Anne asked in a quiet voice once Fernau had left. 'He's got forty point three. He calls that a bit of a temperature? Shouldn't we get them to examine him at the clinic?'

'Fernau's been a general practitioner for thirty years, I think he knows what he's doing,' Richard replied. – The grandfather clock chimed: a quarter past ten. Anne had let the blind down, but arranged the slats so that a dim light seeped through into the room, pale grey and dismal, in which the heroes of the sea on the wall lost their attraction and Tortuga all its mystery; no ship's hull bobbing along lethargically in a lagoon with the brass of a sextant glinting on the seabed, no roar of the waves against the prow of the building, as he had sometimes imagined he could hear on windy nights, no navigation lights to starboard or port; and the expressions of Robert's football heroes said that Italy against Germany, Mexico '70, had not been a truly world-shattering event, just a football match, in the days when Italy didn't just play defensively; Uwe Seeler's expression was blank, not that of a folk hero; World Cup, '74: Paul Breitner's hair looked like an electrified feather duster.

Christian got up, put on his dressing gown, staggered into the kitchen to have a drink of the tea Anne had set out for him in two Thermos flasks. In the larder he found an opened packet of Hansa biscuits, he tried one, the biscuits were damp and tasted like soggy cardboard. In Waldbrunn they would be having physics with Herr Stabenow. He didn't look much older than the pupils with his boyish face and metal-rimmed glasses that kept on slipping down his nose; he would push them back up with the middle finger of his right hand, to which the class, despite its closeness to the gesture of giving someone the finger, paid less attention than to the set-up for the experiment: two chromium-plated spheres on slanting rods, a rubber band and a crank-handle, and when Stabenow turned it, sparks crackled between the two spheres – middle finger, metal-rimmed spectacles; magnets the size of ice-hockey pucks, Stabenow scattered iron filings between them that formed patterns of the electromagnetic field and glittering sheaves at the poles – middle finger, metal-rimmed glasses; but at some point or other they forgot the gesture, forgot their grins and followed, spellbound, Stabenow's operations that never seemed uncertain; his experiments, which he set up and tried out meticulously in the little preparation cubicle next to the physics room, always worked and that naturally impressed them, for they could put themselves in Stabenow's place and sensed their own cruel sharpsightedness that no teacher's idiosyncrasy could escape, they knew that he could well be thinking that they were secretly waiting for him to make a mistake. Christian drank Anne's strong fennel tea, annoyed that he was here in bed, sick, while the others could do experiments. At the high school he hadn't liked physics, it was a subject that had too much maths for his taste; it was only when they got onto nuclear physics that he sat up and took notice, but only as long as it didn't involve calculations – and when Arbogast, as patron of the Louis Fürnberg High School, had come and talked about his own life and about leading scientists he knew. With Stabenow it was different. He was passionate about his subject, the pupils could feel that. His whole body doubled up when he explained the principles behind the construction of a radio and, almost incoherent with enthusiasm, followed the tortuous route of the human voice through all the tubes, transistors, coils and resistances. At the end of the lesson his tie had slipped out of place – one of the so-called 'bricklayer's trowels' you could buy in Waldbrunn and which, so it was said, his landlady chose for him as she did his socks: Herr Stabenow rented a room in one of the lanes leading off from the market. The blackboard was covered with sketches and formulae in his genius's scribble and the remnants of several pieces of red and white chalk were scattered at an exuberant distance around the classroom. He had sparked off a real fever for physics among the boys, they all suddenly wanted to go in for splitting uranium, do great things in the field of microelectronics, invent pocket calculators with a hundred functions . . . first of all, however, to learn to smoke a pipe, for all the physicists of genius they saw in the photographs Stabenow brought smoked pipes: Einstein, Niels Bohr, Kapitza . . . Max Planck had smoked a pipe . . . or was it Heisenberg? The Nobel Prize at thirty-one . . . that left them fourteen years, that was piles of time, they'd surely manage it too. They just had to smoke a pipe all the time and learn to be significantly absent-minded, like the physicist who one morning leapt onto his bicycle and, eyes fixed, pipe in his mouth, started to pedal, until someone asked him: Where are you going? – I'm going to the Institute. – Without a chain?

The fennel tea tasted horrible, Christian poured it down the sink. He looked out of the window, at Griesel's garden, which was still in bare hibernation; Marcel, the Griesels' black poodle, was jumping up and down in his kennel, barking, because the neighbours' fat, grizzled tomcat, Horace, accompanied by his feline lady, Mimi, white with black paws, happened to be sniffing at the tomato sticks in the bed in front of his run and Mimi was elegantly licking her rolled-up right paw; Marcel howled and savaged his toy, a long roll of rags, but it had no effect.

Briquettes were being shovelled in the coalyard behind Griesel's garden, familiar noises: shovels digging sharply into the pile, metal rasping over concrete, then the coal clattered into large metal scales, the shovels, briefly tapped to clear them of dust, scraped up slack, took a slithering run-up, dug sharply into the coal again, a little angrily, a little deviously, a little obsessively in the self-assured horny hands of Plisch and Plum, as the labourers were generally called in the district, after Wilhelm Busch's mischievous pair of dogs, Christian had never heard their real names, one was tall and spindly, the other short and square, a suitcase on two legs, as Aunt Barbara said; and when there was a full hundredweight, the briquettes rumbled down the shiny chutes into gunny sacks that Hauschild, the misshapen, gnarled coal merchant with watery blue eyes shining in his blackened face, would lug round to the shed at the front, on Rissleite, where the customers were waiting.

Christian went back to bed. The light had moved on, the cloud-loom that since Saturday had been weaving a blanket of grey wool over the sky tore open in one place, sending sunbeams into the room: there was Robert's table, the scattered football pictures, the Olympic photo books he'd borrowed from Niklas, beyond it, placed at a right angle to the window, his own table with the sloping writing top on it he'd made himself from left-over bits of wood and two drawing boards he'd bought from Mathes's, the stationer's on Bautzner Strasse, and immediately behind the table the case with his books, hardly three feet away. The tall, solid wood-veneer cupboards, standardized house furnishings, the RUND 2000 model from the state-owned Hainichen furniture works, five of which stood along the walls, leaving just enough space for a sofa, the desks and the bed – Robert's had to be pulled out – weighed down on the room in their dark solidity. He didn't like the room, consisting as it did of these heavy cupboards arranged square-on to each other and the carpeted void between them that could immediately be seen into from the door; there was something of a cage about it, the contents of which could be grasped at a glance. The posters on the wall seemed like foreign bodies, tolerated rather than welcomed by Anne, similarly the net with footballs, handballs and Robert's football boots hanging from a hook over the end of the bed nearest the door. Christian closed his eyes, listened, must have fallen asleep, for he woke with a start when the living-room clock struck the hour. The garden gate slammed and immediately the Griesels' bell rang: that was Mike Glodde, the mailman with the squint and the hare-lip who was

engaged to the Griesels' middle daughter and brought their mail to
their apartment, but only theirs, for the others there were the central
lockers at the far end of Heinrichstrasse that the Post Office had set up
to make their delivery men and women's route shorter; anyway, who
wanted to be a postman now, in this phase of transition, according to
the law of dialectical materialism, from 'Soc.' to 'Comm.'? Christian
smiled when he heard Glodde calling for 'Mar-tsel'; eleven o'clock:
the physics lesson was over and Stabenow would be closing it with his
standard concluding exhortation: 'And just think all this over – why!
Why! Why!'

Music was fluttering round the building, a tune full of melancholy
and bold sentimentality, sung by male voices: that was the 1930s
close-harmony ensemble, the Comedian Harmonists. The tenor's voice
swept upwards, Ari Leschnikoff's supple timbre, smooth as silk; Christian leant over, put his ear to the wallpaper, now he could hear the
lower voices better as well. That was the Stenzel Sisters' gramophone
and at the same interval the record always made a little swerve, soft as
butter. Steps and thuds mingled with the music, probably the Stenzel
Sisters doing their gymnastic exercises . . . In their younger days they'd
been acrobatic bareback riders in Sarrasani's Circus. My little sea-green
cactus – out on the balcony – hollari, hollari, hollaro . . . He lay down
again. The fever had come back, the weakness in his limbs. Two of
the three Stenzel Sisters lived upstairs, the third, the oldest, had a room
with the Griesels, and that was something that made Griesel disgruntled: that he, as the officially appointed block superintendent, had had
one of his rooms allocated to another person and the Hoffmanns hadn't,
and because there'd been telephone calls about it and remarks about
square metres per head and number of children, a few months ago
Richard, after a discussion with the Rohdes in the Italian House, had
attached a sign, 'Ina Rohde', to the door. 'She only pretends to live
here, she never gets any letters,' Griesel objected. Anne said, 'Young
girls nowadays just get their love letters slipped to them, Herr Doktor

Griesel.' Will we be going to the Baltic again this August, Christian wondered, together with the Tietzes as we did last year? Ezzo had been given a new, one-piece rod, made of very soft fibreglass and with a Rileh 'Rex' fixed-spool reel. The Tietzes would presumably go to Rügen again and if Ezzo was lucky the fishermen would take him with them to the lagoon off Greifswald, where there were the biggest pike. Only recently he'd sent a card to Christian in Waldbrunn, telling him he'd bought a spoon-bait, a wobbler and a cod-wiggler from Press's, the specialist angling shop down in the Neustadt district, as well as some fifteen-pound line, green, they could try it out on the Kaltwasser some time.

Veroonicaa, Veroonicaa . . . The Stenzel Sisters were small and shrivelled, like old princesses, in the summer they always wore short skirts so that you could see their white calves with the angular lines of their muscles, their thick hill-walkers' socks rolled down over their ankles. The sisters' heads were covered in fine, soft hair that was so thin their parchment-pale scalp shone through; they braided it into buns the size of tennis balls on the back of their head, holding them together with hairnets, green, blue and red, that had shopping lists, reels of thread and safety pins stuck in them. They would greet him with 'Krest-yan!' when he went up the stairs to look at the photographs behind the glass door; and there was Magellan again, on the landing outside the two second-floor apartments, and his ship, this time on the Hoffmanns' floor, a caravel with a high afterdeck, lateen sails and gossamer shrouds etched on the frosted glass of the door, the waves under the ship's hull snaking back like a Malay dagger or Poseidon's locks, dolphins swimming transparently to the walnut frame of the door that separated the landing from the cylindrical stairwell; and when it was dark and the apartment door was open, the lines of the ship were filled with the corridor light, it was as if an etching needle were engraving constellations on a black sheet of metal: the Ship, the Dolphin; in the glass door of the upper ground floor there were a wind rose and a

Hanseatic cog; a windjammer and a relief etching of the Atlantic and South America with a fine broken line running round Cape Horn as far as Chile on the floor of the Stenzel Sisters and young André Tischer, who had moved in only recently . . . and alone, at that, a lad who was hardly twenty and his own apartment already, no wonder that there were rumours about him going round. He was the son of a high official, people said, who had gone off the straight and narrow, which you could tell from the fact that he had a boxer that he took for walks without a lead or a muzzle, always wearing black leather and his hair either close shaven or long and shaggy – a drop-out! Aunt Barbara declared, I tell you: he's a drop-out! – a studded belt and cowboy boots, that made Robert green with envy, for where, 'damn it all!', was there even the least hint of boots like that in the whole of Dresden – so there! He'll be one of the 'Firm', Niklas opined, he can't even say hello, that in itself's a symp-tom! – On top of that every Sunday an opera singer came to see him, cleaned the stairs for him with a steaming hot cloth that slapped on the steps like a great big eel, then went up, at which there was some crashing followed by a profound silence, a silence that Anne tried to fill with an embarrassed expression, a loud clatter of crockery, the noise of the radio and the abrupt observation that there wasn't enough coal, at which Robert said, 'If you insist', and went to fetch some coal; a silence in which, slowly and irrefutably, the asthmatic creak of a bedstead arose, to be joined by the intense quivering of the Hoffmann's hall light and, finally, the urgent cries of a female voice that sounded as if it belonged to a coachwoman who, thrown to and fro on the box seat of a carriage by wild horses and a bumpy road, still managed, screaming, to hold her course, accompanied by the yowling of the boxer and the rhythmical groans of the mattress springs, intermingled with the grunts of a coachman from a rival firm, 'Last orders', 'Closing time', the cry of the nightwatchman, and sometimes the opera diva would squeal because the dog was trying to rescue its master. Some thought André Tischer was a mysterious West German because he didn't speak in dialect, but Richard waved that away and told a quite different story: young Tischer was the son of a couple who were both doctors and had lived in Blasewitz; one day, about a year ago, when the parents were sleeping after a strenuous period on duty, André's younger brother had been playing with matches and set the house on fire, André had been away with friends; the neighbours, a violinist in the state orchestra and the aforementioned opera singer, had noticed the fire and tried to put it out; in vain. At first André, who had no relatives, had been taken in by the opera singer, but then the city had allocated him this apartment. He was currently working as an ambulance driver at St Joseph's Hospital.

Voices, upstairs: sometimes the Stenzel Sisters would sing in their husky soprano voices, O take my hand, dear Father or All glory be to God on high, it sounded like cautiously establishing contact with a child and when the windows were open it could happen that Griesel would take the electric cable out of the cellar that gave onto his garden and attach it to the frog-like lawn mower. He might be thinking of the quotation about the shepherd feeding his flock, and if the shepherd looked like Pastor Magenstock, it could be all the more unforgivable for little lambs to put their hands together and pray, accompanied by mellifluous tones and blue-eyed unctuousness from the pulpit; for grown-ups to turn childish. The Stenzel Sisters went in armour-like clothes to hear Pastor Magenstock's Sunday sermon, having taken off the rusty brooches – orchid flowers studded with paste gems, cranes' crests dotted with red glass beads – they usually wore on their much mended crêpe-de-Chine blouses: It is a sin to enter the Lord's House adorned with anything other than His Sign, and raised their wrinkled and gnarled rheumatic fingers according to that strict and chaste command that impressed Christian; and the Stenzel Sisters went to church with, on their breast, just a large, plain silver cross that would softly tap their blouse buttons to the rhythm of their energetic steps. With peaceful smiles on their faces, they nodded to those who came towards them then swung away to avoid them. – Yes, Saxon melancholy, it does exist! Christian heard Aunt Barbara say in a whisper, when they encountered the sisters, and her fingers would open like the seed capsule of old woman's purse; she silently nodded her head and could be thinking of neglected duties, of opportunities beckoning from the sisters' flat hats, from the veils of wide-meshed muslin with white spots the size of moths, under which their red lipstick blazed, from their hairnets and their mauve-gloved hands raised in greeting; Aunt-Barbara-secrets smouldering in the teeth-revealing smile, in the sketched nod of the heads. The sisters would straighten the pictures on the staircase with delicate, touching carefulness, as if they came from lovers or brothers in spirit; on Saturday mornings, once they'd finished their exercises – Kitty, the oldest sister, would do her 'Müllers', as she called her exercises after a gymnastics teacher from before the war, in the Hoffmanns' garden – once their down pillows and quilts were airing on the windowsills, they would go down the stairwell to clean the paintings and display cases; for that they used dusters made of ostrich feathers ('the best there are, Krest-yan, from Renner's old department store'), that were discoloured and felted from forty years of trapping bits of fluff; it was only when it came to cleaning materials that the sisters were more modern, they would let one drop of Fit plop into the cleaning water, that was sufficient for the elaborate frames of bronzed limewood irreverently riddled with wormholes which, after washing, were rubbed with bergamot oil – as were, on the top floor, the leaves of a dieffenbachia, which was turning a palish green from lack of light, and the frames of the signed photos – and Christian sometimes wondered, when he was fetching coal, for example, and saw one of the Stenzel Sisters dusting a picture, whether she was interested in what was to be seen inside the frame, or whether the important thing for her wasn't to dust, to look at the frame, but to immerse herself in memories for a while, for which she wanted to be alone, away from her sisters for an hour.

Christian had asked Malthakus, who collected not only stamps and postcards but also stories about the houses up there and the people who had lived in them: Caravel had belonged to Sophia Tromann-Alvarez, who was a native of Dresden; her husband, Louis Alvarez, had worked for the African Fruit Company in Hamburg, which was in partnership with the Laeisz shipping company, and had developed banana plantations in Cameroon, but later he had set up independently in the tropical fruit trade; after his early death in Africa, on an expedition with the Swedish entomologist Aurivillius, Sophia Tromann-Alvarez had returned to the city of her birth, had acquired Caravel and had spent her years of widowhood in memory of her husband and their time with the African Fruit Company; he could remember her well, she was tall and wore clothes made from floral cloth in exotic colours and went for walks with an umbrella and her three basenjis on a long lead, tapping the road audibly with her stick; her dogs bared their teeth and growled at every passer-by. There was a butterfly in Louis Alvarez's display cases that Christian particularly liked looking at: *Urania ripheus* was written in Roman capitals underneath it and how delighted he was when Meno was with him and said, 'Let's practise a little.' That meant something was going to be demanded of him, but that wasn't what he was pleased about, for to describe to Meno something he'd observed was often to answer a question that had not been specifically asked, but indicated clearly enough with gestures: a wave of the hand, a raised eyebrow, the lower lip stuck out, and sometimes, as now when he was thinking about it in his unpleasantly warm sickbed, Christian wondered why he didn't resent Meno's demands, why he didn't get angry with Meno when he gave him to understand, in a friendly but uncompromising way, that he was a poor observer and didn't put his impressions into words precisely enough. He could feel resentful at school, even in subjects that didn't attract him: he often got angry at the arrogant indulgence with which Baumann regarded his, admittedly poor, performance in mathematics; the feeling could be directed at classmates,

for example recently when Svetlana Lehmann had rubbed his nose in
a spelling mistake he'd made. Not with Meno, strangely enough – when
Meno criticized him, it spurred him on to take the criticism to heart
and correct it, he didn't retreat, sulking, into a corner or harbour dark
thoughts, as he had with Svetlana, who, though, had made sure as
many as possible had heard what a howler the oh-so-self-assured Christian Hoffmann had made. With Meno it stayed in the family and his
criticism was the admonition of his own inner voice, which Christian
had suppressed in the hope of getting by without having to make an
effort, spoken out loud. The point was not just to say: this is a
medium-sized butterfly wing, but to respond to Meno's question as to
what that 'medium'-size was related to by being more precise: this
butterfly wing is matchbox-size. Then Meno said: Check your ideas
of beauty; but when he told Christian with scientific coolness that it
was a beautiful thing to be able to measure colours with a ruler, to fix
something as softly ephemeral as this cyclamen-coloured moth from
the central Congo in an inscribed circle and on a millimetre scale, then
Christian felt reservations about following his uncle, a withdrawal, a
loss of clarity: it was as if he were seeing a clear geometrical figure
sharply drawn by thousands of quartz fibres focused in a beam, but
suddenly some of those light fibres had broken off, giving the figure
a slim parallelogram, frayed edges, jagged contours, and for a few
moments Christian wasn't concentrating on the moth any more but
on Meno. At the sight of these butterflies in the display cases Alvarez
had had constructed simply, but out of lignum vitae – they even had
locks, but the keys had evidently been lost, none of the tenants had
them – he was often caught up in a dream-like experience: he regarded
the neatly arranged butterfly mummies and saw not only them, the
specific outlines arranging themselves into the sense impression 'moth',
the pigments, shades, patterns on the wing scales gleaming in the colours of scrap metal, but perceived, the longer he observed them, a kind
of liquefaction in the area round the creature that seemed to him more

exciting than Meno's intention to describe here and now the butterfly, *Urania ripheus*, the Madagascan Sunset Moth, as exactly as possible. If Meno had said: to label it with words, Christian's mind would perhaps not have needed to stray, but as it was, at the concepts Meno let fall with measured deliberation he was thinking of the pins the assistant preparing the butterfly had used to fix it, saw him in his mind's eye place them with the delicacy of a precision engineer; but that was little in comparison with the delight Christian felt when, at a term such as 'to impair', which the tongue of his memory suddenly spoke, the Veronese green on the wings of the Urania moth suddenly started to move. This patch of Veronese green on an African butterfly, a diurnal moth, as Meno explained and Christian didn't quite understand. His dictionary described moths as 'night-flying butterflies' so if this moth was diurnal, how come it was a moth and not a butterfly, but the scientists would presumably have their reasons for this apparent contradiction. A particular light at a particular moment, Meno's face in profile: that was the experiment set-up that remained motionless as long as the catalyst had not been added; a state of expectation dripping with possibilities and Christian was excited by the idea that for precisely this chemical – as you might say – combination it was, of all words, the somewhat out-of-the-way 'to impair' that was the catalyst that, as if drip-fed from a pipette, released his state of inertia in a flash and made it pour into something new, which immediately, mysteriously, like the process of the coagulation of blood, calmed to form a new constellation. Dead-dry bodies behind display-case glass were transformed into prisms before widely varying realities: *Urania ripheus* was a symbol admonishing him in the darklight of a jungle, sleepy from treetops transliquefied with airglow, and 'to impair' was firmly sewn with threads of association to the green of the guiding wings, a colour of which Meno said 'drunk to the last drop' and Christian, remembering a visit to the Army Museum, 'powder green' because he couldn't see anything moist about it, which it would have needed if it was to be connected to 'drunk to the last drop', at which Meno tilted his right hand, which had been reflectively under his chin, and held the palm horizontally upwards, which was as if to say: accepted, not bad, you could see it like that. This 'you could see it like that' was a touch different from the 'if you say so', which he expressed with the same gesture, but with a more slackened body, containing sadness that one couldn't get through, perhaps only on that day, to the other person, that something seemed to have been confirmed, unfortunately, something that one had felt but had tried to banish from the temperature of the conversation, to stop the premonition from turning into the feared reality. 'If you say so' was, in the usage not just of Meno but of most of the Tower-dwellers Christian knew, a polite way of shutting oneself off, though initially only one door among many that were kept open, and even that door, if one had a closer look, was still ajar, the latch hadn't clicked shut; and the perhaps politest form of these restrained little burials, expressed with a momentary lowering of the eyelids, was enthusiastic agreement. Magic was a word Meno did not like. He was in awe of what it stood for and what it expressed, only inadequately in his opinion and somewhat helplessly, 'a label on a preserving jar in which the things are, if we remember', as he said when Christian, furious at his own wordlessness and tortured by the effort to meet Meno's demand for descriptive precision, tried to short-circuit it by using that word to characterize something that fascinated him in a way he still couldn't explain. 'You use it like a flyswatter, of course, walloping something on the head is one way of exorcizing it,' Meno would comment, 'but in doing that you just go round and round your own helplessness, as bad writers do who are not capable of generating a phenomenon – which would be the actual creative act – but are only able to talk about the phenomenon; to say "magic", that is, instead of making something out of words that has it.' At such moments Christian was overcome with a feeling of alienation and it oppressed him, he didn't know why Meno had to be so strict and he couldn't see the affection in the relentlessness with which Meno kept him and his thoughts, which yearned to be elsewhere, tied to this display case, the contents of which, during the hour or more of Meno's drill, no longer transmitted to him the breathtaking contact, the sense of a hunt, that he felt when he walked past and let his eye wander over the colourful pharaohs. That silent flash which hit him as he was about to walk past but something opened up, making a large gate sucking into it everything he'd been thinking of at that moment: school, a football match, the Tomita disc, his application for a place at medical school after he'd completed the eleventh year, sometimes the shape of a drop of milk that had been spilt or the figures on the numberplate of Tietze's Shiguli. All that was drawn out of him, leaving him with eyes wide and mouth open – and even forgetting to breathe. Christian did sense that Meno wanted to get beyond this phase with him, the invisible lips that were whispering to him were to be sealed once more, the images invisible, but he saw no sense in letting the colours go dull and the little symphony of shapes go flat. Often it was Meno who broke off. In that second, when his uncle let his head drop and rubbed his closed eyes with his thumb and index finger, the affection returned all at once, as if it had just been pulled away, like a piece of elastic, and let go again. There must be something other than just being overpowered by a commander of the moment and that was what Meno appeared to be looking for with the instruments of his precision. It seemed to Christian to be a deliberate distancing of himself from deeply rooted convictions, precisely because they were deeply rooted convictions. Perhaps they could no longer bear their load, or Meno wanted to progress and saw it as greatness, not as capitulation, to pay any price for it. He sensed that the reason his uncle was so unrelenting with him was that he saw those convictions in him, Christian, as well, something that came back, unconcerned, and that he knew all too well himself and had long wanted to combat, from the perspective of a different conviction. Which, because it wasn't innate, took on something of a heroic air. And could contain suspicion of the 'language of the heart', as Meno, wooden-lipped, called it, pronouncing the quotation marks as well. Perhaps it was an occupational disease of scientists and editors, for to Christian the 'language of unsentimental observation' that Meno wanted to set against it – did he really want that? – seemed alien, even though he sometimes thought about it, for 'as big as a matchbox' was indeed more vivid and more accurate than 'medium'-sized. Yet what always fascinated him first were the colours and not the tones, what was apparent burnt its mark into him first and not what was obscure, and that seemed logical, for what was obscure would not have been obscure if you had perceived it immediately, so what mattered to him was what made an impression on him and the rarest and, of its kind, strangest moth that looked unremarkable left him unmoved if he saw one beside it that looked like a flying paintbox, even if, as far as its frequency was concerned, it was the cabbage white of the tropics. Meno criticized his attitude, he was less fond of those specimens that, as he put it, 'have all their secrets, if they have any at all, stuck on their coats'. He preferred the unremarkable ones, of which Alvarez had also collected a few; they were hung in a second case outside the Stenzel Sisters' floor, where the staircase came to the glass door. It was a place of grey brightness that diffused through the high window over the stairwell: a seven-petalled glass flower in the middle of which hung a candlestick like an excessively stretched stamen. It was a row of moths, wood-coloured saturniids with eyespots on their wings; 'from the race of the God of Lead and there: those are their watermarks' – Meno pointed to the grain of the paper-thin wings, which reminded Christian of the rings of ripples after a stone has been thrown into a calm pond. They seemed to continue across the individual butterflies, combining them into a larger picture, of which they were only a part, as if they were pieces in a jigsaw puzzle. They looked very alike, only when you looked closer did the tiny differences between the individual moths appear. 'Those are the orchestral parts over which the composer took the greatest care, even though the audience hardly hears them; but they are the ones that are particularly important to him, and you can pay him no greater compliment than to listen carefully, for what is the point of music if not to be listened to. These patches of crimson, moss-green and lilac, this blue that's so intense it could appear on a lemon: these are high points, such as Italian bel canto composers love, as do the average opera-goers, who don't go to the theatre to listen but to see, to promenade during the intervals, to get annoyed at the prices of the sandwiches and cocktails, and to be seen; who know in advance the "famous passage" where the tenor gathers all his strength to weightlift the top C and what comes after it; but what I'm interested in are the inconspicuous tissues, disguises, transitions; camouflage and mimicry; the construction of the beds in which the motifs, those "beautiful", sometimes all-too-beautiful princesses lie. I'm not just interested in the *bel étage*, but in the coal cellar as well, the kitchen and, to extend the image, the servants in the composition.' Thus far Meno. Christian thought about it. In the same way as, all those years ago when they'd been visiting the painter, Vogelstrom, in Cobweb House, and he'd heard the names Merigarto and Magelone and not forgotten them since, something of these conversations with Meno stayed with him, continued to have an effect on him, he could feel it like a foreign body that had penetrated him and was changing him, and at times such as these he searched in order to isolate, feel, observe it, to see if it would be harmful or useful.

The Stenzel Sisters' gramophone had fallen silent. The Westminster chimes sounded four times, then two strokes: two in the afternoon. Anne would be home from work soon and Robert back from school. Then there would be voices, noises, unrest; Caravel would drift back into a far-off dreamland, memories in Magellan's telescope. Christian closed his eyes. He thought of Verena.

22

Enoeff

In the evening the Rohdes came over. 'Ill, are we?' asked Ina, bringing a whiff of Koivo deodorant with her and Christian felt ashamed that he hadn't aired the room. Ina sat down on the edge of the bed, ran her eye over Robert's footballs, Terence Hill and Ornella Muti, crossed her legs, jiggled her foot. She was wearing high-heeled court shoes, fishnet tights and a miniskirt. 'And how are things?'

'Not bad. And you?'

'Lots of stress at the university. Useless room.'

Christian was sweating but he pulled the blanket up over his chin because he had a spot there. Voices sounded in the corridor; Ulrich came in. 'What's that Fernau prescribed for you, the drunken wretch?' Ulrich stretched out his hand, his left hand, and, as so often, Christian fell for it and grasped the back of his hand; Ulrich liked that kind of joke.

'Dad.' Irritated, Ina raised her eyebrows, which had been plucked to thin arches. 'That's defamation, you know.'

'Who cares . . . that schnappshound . . . I'm furious with him, furious, furious! I can't tell you how furious I am. Look.' He showed Christian his inflamed right index finger. 'He treated it as a "swelling of unknown origin", differential diagnosis: "result of an unremembered hammer blow" – does he think I'm off my head?'

'Well, you should have gone straight to Uncle Richard.'

'And now it hurts, it's throbbing and I can't get to sleep. I've put some aluminium acetate on it, but it's not done any good . . . And I'm furious!'

'Dad.'

'It's all right for you to talk, you've no idea what it's like when you're this furious . . . and your finger's this sore!' Ulrich slapped his right hand across his face, which was fleshy and dark blue from his heavy growth of beard. Ulrich was bald on top; lower down, his head was wreathed in thick, rampant Latin curls that Wiener, the barber, cursed because they blunted his scissors; he had hair on his back and on his impressive belly, which Christian knew because in the winter Ulrich liked to stomp around in the snow wearing bathing trunks, to fall down, howling, and make an angel, though he preferred to call it an eagle, that is to make fan-shaped marks in the snow with his out-stretched arms. Afterwards he would have a toughening-up shower with the garden hose, if it wasn't frozen. His eyebrows were so thick they shone like two slugs; his only similarity to Anne and Meno was in the colour of his eyes: brown with green speckles. 'Unremembered ham-mer blow, have you ever heard such a stupid diagnosis . . . Especially as I'm not left-handed.' Ulrich started to stride up and down the room. 'That lousy puffball, I'm furious. I've got this great fury inside me and I'm not going to let it go to waste!' He looked for an empty space on Robert's desk and slapped it several times with the flat of his left hand, accompanying it with strangled cries. 'Out with it, out, out!' He grasped the tops of the table legs and shook them, at the same time moaning with pain, for he was using his swollen index finger, squeezing the table leg as if it were one of the long Borthen potatoes he was determined to squash; he went red in the face from the strain of trying not to break anything while at the same time giving free rein to his fury, like a ber-serker whose frenzy threatens to increase because it is not allowed to be really frenzied and therefore provokes laughter.

In his mind's eye Christian could see the impression in the iron balustrade on the Brühlsche Terrasse that was supposed to have been made by August the Strong with his thumb . . . Bored, Ina jiggled her feet. Ulrich seemed to have calmed down, for he was staring at the football pictures on the table, arms akimbo. Now there would be a special footballological quarter of an hour: Ulrich could always talk about football and knew simply 'everything' – at least he knew as much as Robert, and that was saying something.

'What's this, Chrishan? Laid up again, are we? In Fernau's firm hands? And feeling more bitter than better, closed now those songster's lips of yours?' That was Aunt Barbara, known to the family as 'Enoeff' – she pronounced the English word 'enough' as if it were Saxon and used it, together with a determined karate chop, to indicate that some matter had been decided once and for all. 'How are things at school, apple of my eye?' Robert was the potato of her eye. Christian didn't answer at once and Barbara was immediately worried, sat down on the bed and waved Ina and Ulrich away.

'I was just going to have a chat with him about football, Bubbles.'

'Enoeff!'

'Dynamo against BFC!'

Christian shot up. 'When?'

'Enoeff, I tell you! Out!'

Ulrich gave Robert's net of footballs an appreciative thump with his fist. His face twisted. 'You'll have to get a move on, Cuddles.'

'Don't call me that, Dad,' Ina protested, 'how often do I have to tell you?'

'Out you all go. There's a sick guy here, he needs some peace and quiet. – Did he lose his temper again? He's impossible. And I'm married to him. Shows no consideration whatsoever and here you are, ill in bed. Men! . . . I tell you, Chrishan . . . You're young and foolish and you meet them and before you know it, whoops! you've got a bun in the oven! I'm only telling you this because I hope you're not like that. And don't start something with Ina, that . . . wouldn't be a good idea. Where would it lead, cousins . . . ? I recently read an article about the risks with incest. You mustn't let it go any farther, believe you me. I've already had a hint of the odd disaster. God, I've lost any influence over that child. She does what she wants and the guys she brings home, they've all got long hair and smoke! And listen to that horrible music.

Chrishan' – she took his hand and leant over him, her blue-grey eyes with the fine mascara lines round them looked like porcelain discs – 'listen to me. You know what I always say . . . you mustn't be a pipsqueak in this world. No, definitely not. We're not big shots, no, not by a long chalk. But we're not pipsqueaks either. – So, how are things at school?'

'Quite good –'

'You're saying that out of modesty, aren't you? You Hoffmanns have a tendency to keep things in a low key. Quite right too. What do you think of my new hairstyle? Sorry for putting you on the spot like that, but no one ever tells me anything. – You don't have to say anything if it embarrasses you. I have great sympathy for the male psy-kee. You know that. And you read such a lot and people always say the more a person reads, the more problems he has with words. If you think my hairstyle's good you can, for example . . . just give my hand a squeeze.' Barbara smiled and shook her head proudly.

'Were you at Schnebel's?'

'What an idea! I don't go to that cheap hairdresser. Chrishan – it can't look that bad, can it?' The expression on Barbara's face was the one she had when she stroked Chakamankabudibaba's back and said, 'You looovely cat', as if she were checking what part of the coat she was working on at the moment its soft fur could be used for. 'You do give a person a fright! I went to Wiener's, of course. He's the only one who understands women's hair. It's so difficult to get an appointment with him . . . Even those women from East Rome want to go to him, despite the fact that in '56 . . . I think he even went to jail, down there in dear old Hungary. If only they knew? But I'm sure they do know, those . . . tarts. Yes, that's the word. Wiener's an old charmer and a bit eucalyptical as well – I mean, that toupee! He really shouldn't, especially one that's as black as liquorice – and he's sure to be well into his fifties. And the hairnet as well. I mean – a man! And a hairdresser into the bargain. With a hairnet and that hussar's moustache! At his prices . . . And then he walks in such a lah-di-dah way' – Barbara had got off the bed and was imitating Lajos Wiener's gait – 'his hands raised as if he had to waddle along on them, and then he wiggles his hips and lisps, "I hope we shall see you again soon, dear madam." My God, with his waiting list?! Then he gives you such an outrageous wink, screwing up the whole of his cheek, you have the feeling there must be a gypsy band lurking in the background and someone's going to start hammering with those thingies on the what-d'you-call-it . . . You know, those little hammers that look like the spoons in the milk bar and those . . . zithers. Yes. Those boards with strings over them on which they . . . magyarize!' She sat down again, stretched out her fingers with their generous complement of flower-rings, regarded her nails with their raspberry-coloured paint. 'You know, Chrishan, I'm not just asking you for fun. The women at work are just jealous, you can't talk with them about that kind of thing. They don't tell you whether it looks good, for if they say that, they'd say it would've been better if they hadn't said that. Of course Ina thinks: the aged parent's gone off her rocker. And of course I could ask Snorkel' – that was what Barbara called her husband – 'but he'd just mutter, "That's really great, Bubbles", but wouldn't even look up from his *So We – Soccer Weekly* or whatever the magazine's called. But you: I can ask you. I know that. You have an honest opinion and eyes in your head as well. Wiener, the man who won't admit to fifty, just tells you what you want to hear because he wants you to come back. – I can see you're too embarrassed to tell your aunt how much you like it. It's nothing to cry over. After all, we're all going to end up in communism and then we'll have to cut off our hair anyway. Enoeff, my dear. You mustn't talk so much, it'll just tire you out. Have a good sleep.'

23
Breathing

Richard went into the cellar, to the workshop he'd set up in the old laundry. It was quiet down there. He was going to switch on the light, but then he didn't bother; the twilight in the room calmed him down; the outlines of the objects had already blurred into the darkness, which seemed to be spreading out from the unpainted walls. It smelt of damp, mould and potatoes. He knew that it wasn't a good idea to stay down there too long, especially not now, at the cold time of the year; in the spring and right through to the late autumn, on the other hand, when you could leave the window open, there was a smell of turpentine and dry wood, of paint and benzine. He had to change when he came to work down here, his clothes absorbed the acrid cellar smell and it was difficult to get rid of it. Despite all the disadvantages of the room, Richard liked being there — apart from the fact that it was a privilege to have extra space available for his hobby; he would have been happy with the smallest of attic rooms and would even have let Griesel have a corner. In his study he could be undisturbed — down here, on the other hand, he was alone. As in the operating theatre, the language was not that of words, but that of hands, which was familiar to him and in which he felt secure. He turned on the light, enjoying the clack as the black Bakelite rotary switch engaged; the carbon filament bulb that some predecessor had left cast an ochre tent over the room. His tools were his pride and joy and when he thought of 'possessions' then the first thing that came to mind was not a bank statement, the furniture in the apartment, the record player, the paintings by Querner or the Lada, but the wall cupboards with their rows of ring spanners, open-jawed spanners, the sets of cylinder wrenches, thread cutters and screw-stocks, the chisels. Not rubbish from some state-owned factory, but heavy, pre-war steel goods drop-forged in the Bergisches Land south of the Ruhrgebiet. He saw the thirty screwdrivers in the canvas roll with the broad leather straps, a present from his boss when he'd completed his apprenticeship as a metalworker, hexagonal bars, one blow from which could kill a man, forged from a single piece, the toolmaker's seal punched into the handle; he saw the old drillbits made of solid brown iron, greased for the winter and wrapped in oiled paper as well, sitting in their birchwood case, in the compartments made to size for the thinnest to ones as thick as your finger. Meno often talked about poetry and Richard couldn't always follow him, at such times Meno seemed to have gone off into regions that had nothing to do with Richard, had nothing to say to him, but one thing he did understand: when Meno told them that it was hard work and that something like the poems of Eichendorff – deeply moved, he recited them enthusiastically – couldn't be tossed off in a day, that behind them was an intimation of something that Meno called completeness. And when Meno went on to say that in his experience simple people only rarely had access to that realm, though he begged those gathered there not to misunderstand him, he didn't want to sound arrogant, but it was a fact that everyone knew but didn't dare to say out loud because then the Party would be faced with the question as to whether their cultural policy, their image of the reading worker, was not based on false assumptions, Richard simply couldn't go along with that, he didn't like what his brother-in-law was saying about workers' relationship to reading. He knew of enough counter-examples, and Meno's assertion denied their sense of beauty and quality, and thus of poetry in another but not shallower sense. Oh yes, he understood very well what Meno was saying, even if his brother-in-law would not always accept that. The same feeling of profound satisfaction, of happiness perhaps, and perhaps also of release – that here for once there was a product of the human mind and the human hand that could not be bettered – this feeling that he could see in Meno's face was something he, Richard, knew as well, only it wasn't a poem that set it off but this workbench, and for his father it had been the inner life of a mechanical clock from the great period of clock-making in Glashütte, a testimony to craftsmanship and a meticulous technical ingenuity. Meno might well mock and think him a philistine who seriously dared to see poetry in a set of screwdrivers, but his brother-in-law was an odd guy, stuck in his world of the mind and letters but not seeming to know much about people. Hid himself away behind his desk and researches – then talked about workers and their appreciation of higher things . . . nothing but waffle, waffle. Richard felt tired, went over to the washbasin in the corner, behind the huge tub in which the washing used to be done. Now potatoes were kept in it. He washed his face, then stayed leaning over the washbasin, listening to the drops of water falling from his face and plopping onto the enamel of the basin – like bubbles bursting, unreal in the growing sound of his breathing. He felt so drained that he couldn't understand how there could ever have been anything inside him: his childhood, his experiences during the war, the bombardment of Dresden, getting burnt, Rieke, his apprenticeship, university, Anne, the children. Perhaps we had a receptacle inside us that gradually filled in the course of our life but his, now, had sprung a leak and everything had run out. He washed his face again. The water was so cold his forehead and temples ached, but after he'd dried himself off with his handkerchief he felt better. He looked at the workbench, which went back to Alvarez's time, the smooth wood of the work surface, polished by the touch of countless hands. It was so hard the woodworm didn't attack it. He didn't know what kind of wood it was, it was a coppery red, unusually solid, unaffected even by damp and mould. On it he'd made the table for Meno, the desks for Christian and Robert, the hundred-drawer cupboard in the study that had even earned the approval of Rabe, the singular, cigar-smoking cabinetmaker, tough as old boots, who, as he would say, couldn't stand 'amateurs'. Richard had made the cupboard from the two plum trees that had died during the autumn gales two years ago. What great pleasure the work had given him: planing, cutting to size, fitting the joints, and before that the laborious, detailed design work, repeatedly based on errors, for which he'd studied plans in museums and the Department for the Preservation of Historical Monuments. How he loved the resiny smell, how he'd been delighted when his plane had revealed the strong grain of the plum-wood, the look on Rabe's face when he'd bought some bone glue that was bubbling in a washpot on an open fire in the cabinetmaker's workshop – and how Rabe's expression had brightened when he saw the cupboard and examined it, how the look of suspicion and contempt had turned to appreciation; that was something he would never forget.

There was a knock. Anne came in. 'What's the matter with you, Richard?'

'Nothing's the matter with me,' he replied irritatedly.

'But I can tell there's something the matter. You're not yourself, you're running around like a bear with a sore head, hardly have you got home than you disappear into your study . . . you yell at Robert for some trifle, you're grumpy . . .'

'Problems at the hospital, that's all. The usual stuff, for God's sake. They've got this idea about the collective of socialist work, Müller's demanding overtime from the assistant doctors, and from us as well, of course, the senior doctors are to set a shining example . . . And then the never-ending struggles in the hospital management meetings, we're not doing enough to influence our colleagues to bear society in mind in their work and then it's the Karl Marx Year and we're supposed to "seize" some stupid initiative with our students –'

'It's not that. I know you. You're different when it's that kind of thing.' She went up to him. He was turned away, leaning over the workbench, closed his eyes when she took his hand.

'Is there something you're keeping from me?'

*

They'd made it a rule not to discuss serious problems in their own home but on a walk. These walks were a general custom in the district. Couples were often to be seen walking in silence and with heads bowed or in a discussion with hurried gestures – one could only assume it was being held in a whisper, since it immediately broke off as soon as others came within hearing.

'Is it another woman?'

'No. What makes you think that? No.'

'So it isn't another woman?'

'No. No! I've just told you.'

'You hear this and that. People pass rumours on to me.'

'Rumours, rumours! Are these rumours worth anything? It's just people making things up.'

'A colleague of mine has a sister who works in the Academy, another was recently a patient in your orthopaedics department –'

'Stupid gossip!'

'So it's not another woman.'

'How often do I have to tell you: no!'

These problem walks seemed to have become more frequent recently. There were days when it seemed to him as if all the inhabitants apart from the children had left their apartments and were walking round the streets, murmuring, so that the whispered conversations were constantly being interrupted to say hello, raise your hat, wave. How grotesque it was! He couldn't help laughing – broke off. That he was still able to laugh! Anne gave him a disturbed look. She had wrapped up warm and was grasping the collar of her coat with her hands.

'And you believe this scandalmongering! They're trying to pin something on me, perhaps out of jealousy –'

'They? Who're they?'

'Not your colleagues.' Richard leant against a fence. 'They've dug up the old business. When I was a student. Back in Leipzig.'

He started to tell her about the discussion, at first hesitantly, disjointedly, by fits and starts, then more and more urgently.

'But what reason could they have . . . ? After all these years . . .'

'I don't know.'

Sometimes several couples could be seen leaning against a fence, sometimes Arbogast turned up; he had a strange sense of the comic, would greet them silently with his stick and if it was a fence on Holländische Leite he would have chairs brought up from the Institute.

'This old story . . . did you tell me everything back then?'

'Yes, I did.'

'And Weniger . . . does he know about it?'

'No. No he can't know about it.'

'He's your friend . . . The way you treat him, pat him on the shoulder, sometimes I watch you and –'

'Do stop it!'

'And I'm afraid. You can't tell, not at all. Perhaps you're deceiving me, perhaps you've been deceiving me all these years, just as you've deceived Weniger –'

'Anne! Can't you understand? Can you really not understand? I . . . I was *different* then, the fifties in Leipzig, you never went through that, the mood there was then, and I was honestly convinced as well –'

'So honestly that you shopped your friend to them. My God, I've been living with –'

'Anne!' Richard had gone white as a sheet. He grasped her by the shoulders, shook her. 'We've talked about this already, talked until we're sick of it, right down to the very last detail, don't throw it at me again now. That's what they want! They want it to drive a wedge between us, they want to use it to destroy us because . . . because they're afraid of love, yes, that's it. Because they're afraid of people sticking together and . . .'

Anne burst out into a shrill peal of laughter. 'Afraid of love . . . What

nonsense you're talking. You ought to hear yourself, how . . . sentimental and ridiculous you sound. That isn't you at all and I don't want
to hear any more of your pseudophilosophical analysis . . . My God,
Richard.' She raised her hands, shook them at him, burst into tears.

He embraced her. They stood like that for a while. Richard stared
at the street, shadows moved and came nearer. He closed his eyes,
opened them again, the shadows had disappeared. Treetops and hedges,
their branches still dead and bare, were hanging over the fences; there
was a mild breeze and a smell of grass trailing through the air that smelt
of coal. In his mind's eye he saw the sheet of paper with the figures on
that Lucie had given him for his birthday, the seven wearing a hat, the
five smoking a cigar. He tried to repress the image but he couldn't, it
kept coming back, the figures seemed to be alive, malicious creatures
that kept on bouncing back up. Lucie coming in through the door,
carrying her teddy bear, complaining she had tummy ache. The smiling
dolls in the hall. Then he felt as if Josta were looking at him. He shook
his head, but that image wouldn't disappear either. 'Let's move on.'

They headed for Turmstrasse, walking in silence for a while. He
observed Anne. She wasn't crying any more, was staring straight ahead.
Again he remembered one of the evenings when the whole district
seemed to be on the move. People embracing each other had been
standing, silent and motionless, out in the streets. The lamps cast a
pale light, which suddenly went out, it was dark in the houses all round
as well. A power failure. Then something grotesque had happened:
Julie Heckmann, generally known in the district as Julie-the-horses,
standing with Frau Knabe, had burst out laughing, a hoarse male laugh,
swelling into a piercing screech such as he had never before heard; it
had gradually infected all those out there, even the ones embracing
each other, and set off an outburst of laughter that seemed strangely
liberating, vital, now sobbing, now roaring, spreading down the streets;
you could hear windows in the houses all around being opened, suddenly someone shouted, 'Bureaucracy!', in response someone else

shouted, 'Individualism!' and another, 'Socialism!' – 'I'm frightened,' a woman cried, another, 'Me too!' and still the laughter echoed round the whole street, interrupted by shouts of 'Shh!' and 'Be quiet'; 'Soon there'll be zilch left to scoff,' someone brayed in a disguised voice, 'There's no meat left in Wismar,' came a squeak out of the darkness; 'Is there a war on in Poland?' – 'Don't tempt fate, for heaven's sake!' – 'Are they frightened as well?' roared a female voice Richard thought he recognized as Frau Knabe's. – 'Sure they are! Of us!' and once more the street shook with laughter, and it came from the buildings as well. 'Marx-isn't!' – 'Stalin-isn't' – 'Hey: generalism.' The barking of dogs could be heard, immediately the laughter died away and the people quickly dispersed. Someone came towards Richard, stopped close beside him, scrutinized him, hesitated; it was Malthakus, he tipped his hat with his cane, whispered with his sly smile, 'Well, neighbour, and what's your problem?' then quickly disappeared in the darkness.

Richard pulled his coat tighter round him, the memory of the incident had made him uneasy.

'So they're trying to put pressure on us,' Anne said; he was grateful for the 'us', but she didn't take his hand. 'We must think what we can do.' Her voice was firm again. That gave him back the power to think clearly. 'There are two alternatives, either I play along with them – or I don't play along with them.'

'It's not a matter of playing,' she replied quickly and tersely. 'Exit visa. We have to get out of here. We can ask Regine about making an application.'

'What are you going to ask her? How to fill out the form correctly? It won't work. They made it quite clear to me that they won't let me go. Doctors are needed in *our* country . . . it would be a betrayal of the patients in your care . . .'

'They can't simply hold us here!'

'That's precisely what they can do. Then we'll be stuck here and

I'll be chucked out of the clinic – it wouldn't bother me, but there's Robert and Christian to think of . . . We wouldn't have got anywhere.'

'But we don't have to report people!'

'And the price we'd pay would be our children's future?'

'But spying on people, is that a price we want to pay?'

Richard didn't reply.

'One possibility is that *we* stay here – and Christian and Robert can apply. As soon as they reach maturity.'

'Do you know what you're saying, Anne?! What would happen? Christian would be chucked out of the senior high school and Robert wouldn't be accepted for it.'

'Christian will be eighteen this year, Robert in two and a half years. They'll lose time anyway. In the army. So if they have to wait for this or that –'

'You're assuming everything will work out the way you imagine. And if it doesn't? If they don't give them a visa? If the boys can't leave the country? Do you know if they want to, anyway? We're talking without taking what they think into account, it might just be too much for them?'

'And perhaps not. We should discuss it with them.'

'And what are they to do while their applications are being processed? Regine's been waiting for two years and you know what a state she's in. Sacked from her job with the city administration, branded as an agent of imperialism in front of all her colleagues –'

'– and now she's an unqualified secretary at St Joseph's and she only got the job because you're acquainted with the medical director. I know that.'

'And the boys? They'd take their revenge on us by leaving them to stew much longer, you can be sure of that! Then they'll be stuck here, no school-leaving certificate, unable to go to university; they'd have to do an apprenticeship . . . Christian – what trade could he learn?

And perhaps they'd never get out anyway. Stuck here, their lives thoroughly mucked up . . . Do you think they could forgive us that?'

'One of my colleagues has an application being considered. Despite that she's still working with us and her daughter can finish school.'

'They treat some people this way, others that way, but you can't guarantee anything. I think it's pretty unlikely we would be dealt with in the same way as your colleague. Do you want to try and see what comes of it?'

They walked beside each other, heads bowed.

'What about Sperber? Couldn't he do something?'

'I don't know. I don't know him particularly well. And I don't trust him either, to be honest. We'd be taking a huge risk if I were to go and tell him everything. What would happen if he's one of them . . . or collaborates with them? Don't you think he must have one foot in their camp? Perhaps he's a kind of front man, a lure they set out for us?'

'Meno says there's a few authors he's helped.'

'Could be. But even if he's not one of them, would he help us? Who knows which authors he's helped and in what kind of situation? At the least inconvenience to any reasonably well-known author, the press over there screams blue murder. But for us? For a doctor and a nurse no one's ever heard of? Do you think Sperber can do anything if they give him to understand there's no interest over there?'

'I'm tired . . . Shall we sit down for a moment?'

Richard nodded. They'd walked as far as the 'October View' as the little circle surrounded by a pergola in Mondleite Park was officially called; the locals still called it by the old name of Philalethes' View, after the nom de plume of King John of Saxony, the expert on Dante. In the middle of the flat hilltop was an obelisk with the names of people from the district who had died in the world war.

'Should we drop in on your brother?'

'No . . . I don't want to. He'd think there was something wrong right away. – And there's one thing we have to sort out: how do we tell the family?'

'We have to think very carefully about whether we tell them at all.'

'For me there's nothing to think about. Of course we must tell them.'

'Even at the risk that we can't be sure whether Ulrich for example . . .'

'He may be in the Party but he's not an informer!'

'What makes you so sure? Didn't you warn me against him yourself? You remember, when we were walking home from the Felsenburg.'

'But he's one of the family . . . He wouldn't go *that* far!'

'Because he's your brother – and my brother-in-law? Because he likes the boys and takes them to football matches?'

'I don't know. I just can't imagine he would be capable of informing on you. Still . . . Yes, perhaps I can't imagine it because he's my brother. Father brought us up to be neither moral cowards nor informants. Do you know what he used to say? You know what's the lowest form of life? A man who'd inform on his friend or his wife.' She quivered, slumped forward, started crying again. Richard sensed that she didn't want him to comfort her and went to the edge of the paved area, which had a wrought-iron balustrade with a stylized nautilus, eaten away by rust, worked into it. Beyond it the park fell away steeply. There were lights on in the House with a Thousand Eyes and in the Elephant opposite, at the Teerwagens' a window was opened. Scraps of music, voices, laughter. There seemed to be a party going on. How carefree . . . Richard suppressed the thought. 'Shall we go and see Regine?'

'No . . . not now,' Anne murmured. He rummaged round in his pockets, found the twenty-pfennig piece he kept for emergencies. 'I could call her. There's a phone booth at the crossroads there.'

'It's kind of you to try and distract me but . . . no. I want to go home. I'm very tired.'

He went over to her, sat down beside her on the bench. 'Anne, it might be helpful to talk to her. Perhaps she can see possibilities we've overlooked. And we can trust her.'

'Her, I agree, but not the bugs in her apartment. – Are you going to tell your colleagues?'

'No. At least not for the moment. I can't trust them any more than I can Sperber. Most of all Wernstein, but who knows, sometimes it's the most trustworthy . . . I can do something else before I confide in my colleagues. I can accept.'

'You really want to do that? You want to work for those bastards?'

'Anne! – I'll only pretend to. Give them trivial stuff, play stupid – and I'll go on like that until they realize they've got a poor catch in me. I have to be no use at all to them, perhaps that will give me a chance.'

'Don't you think they'll notice?'

'I'm sure they will notice. But what can they do? Even a senior doctor doesn't get to hear everything that goes on in his clinic. And isn't it logical that the assistant doctors will hold their tongues in my presence?'

'And if they set a trap for you? What if one of your operating-theatre nurses says something incriminating and you behave as if you hadn't heard it, but that nurse is one of them and the next time they ask why you've been withholding information?'

'That would be a mistake on their part, don't you think? Then I'd know that nurse was one of them.'

'And if they don't ask you about it? But quietly draw their own conclusions . . . Then one day they present you with the bill –'

'If, if, if! Do you see any other alternative?'

'Get out of the country.'

'Don't be stupid, Anne. Surely you're not serious. Even the attempt is a punishable offence. They'd nab us straight away and we'd end up behind bars . . . Getting out! How do you imagine we'd do it? With the boys? Or would they stay here? Should we dig a tunnel? Swim across the Baltic –'

'Your student friend managed it.'

'He was a serious swimmer, Anne, took part in competitions. He

lived alone and knew exactly what he was taking on. If he'd been caught
he would have been the only one to take the consequences. Do you
know that they falsify our maps? A patient told me recently. According
to our maps, you think you're in the Federal Republic – in reality you're
still in the GDR. Rivers don't go where they're supposed to go according to the map, in the border area the roads and paths aren't marked –'
    'Yugoslavia –'
    'Anne.'
    She burst into shrill laughter. Richard looked at her. 'Let's go home.'
    They lay next to each other, awake, in the beds they'd put together
when they were first married; each listening to the other's breathing.

24

In the clinic

He was still fascinated by the noises in the building; sometimes he
would open the door of his office to listen and the gap would seem to
him like the bell of an ear trumpet, like the connection between the
middle ear and the pharynx, lined with mucus and cilia (it reminded
him that he ought to get the paediatrician to have a look at Lucie, she
kept swallowing and complaining that it hurt; protracted inflammation
of the middle ear was dangerous); once he'd opened the door, he would
close his eyes and listen, for you could not only tell the things that
were going on in the clinic from the noises, but also the mood in which
they were taking place, what the atmosphere was like and how, as if
the clinic were a collective organism like a swarm of bees, it would
change with the slightest disturbance, the least excitement. It was the
time when the clinic prepared itself for the evening; an in-between
time: the day's work was now largely over; the patients who had been

operated on were back in their beds, had been examined during the afternoon rounds and had had the attention they needed, the early-shift nurses and the patients' visitors had left; there were no more lectures or seminars at this hour either. The solidly built carts that looked like cabin trunks, with the insulated boxes for hot meals, and that the nurses pushed from room to room to distribute the food to the patients, were not yet clattering along the PVC of the clinic's corridors. The castanet click-clack of head nurse Henrike's clogs doing the evening inspection tour of her realm could still not be heard. She lived alone with her mother, who needed looking after, and her son, who had broken off two apprenticeships, in a cramped apartment on Augsburger Strasse, not 500 metres from the Academy, a chubby, maternal-looking woman who had shown childlike delight at the Hufeland Medal that had been awarded her on 'Health Service Day'. Phones rang, washing carts rumbled along in the bowels of the building; the doors of the offices beside his banged open and shut. Most of his colleagues were still there, they'd finished their visits to the wards and would now be going to the laboratories, to the libraries, or writing assessments or reports on operations. Richard had gone to his room to have a rest, it had been an exhausting day. He had been in the operating theatre from seven in the morning until five in the evening and had had no more than three cups of coffee and the sandwiches Anne made for him in the morning. He was on duty but he wouldn't be called for every minor matter; Dreyssiger and Wernstein were experienced specialists, he could rely on them.

He lay down on the examination couch, rolled over and over. Then he lay on his back and stared up into space. Ambulances arrived, sirens wailing, he heard an ambulance of the Emergency Medical Services thunder up the hospital ramp: cries, hurried steps, the clatter of trolleys. They'd call him if he was needed. He couldn't relax, stood up. He felt dazed with dizziness and tiredness, he went over to the window for a breath of fresh air. He grasped the window latch and leant his forehead against the glass. Then he tried some knee bends, perhaps his tiredness came from a lack of movement, the unhealthy posture in which one was frequently obliged to carry out an operation, recently he had often become exhausted very quickly. He sat down at his desk, on which a few specialist periodicals lay open. He was interested in an article on a new method of operating on Dupuytren's contracture, a progressive condition affecting the tissue of the palmar fascia; he had intended to study it thoroughly, since the disease seemed to be increasing in frequency. In the last three months alone he had had fourteen outpatients suffering from the condition. Eventually it could lead to the hand being completely deformed, nodules developed in the connective tissue, causing it to shorten; in the final stage of the illness the hand cannot be opened. Who were the authors of the article . . . Of course, the Hamburg group under Buck-Gramcko, the high priest of hand surgery. He could have bet it would be him. It was the fifth publication since January he'd seen by that team and it was still early in the year. And what did they do here, in this country? Mostly they just copied what they did over there, they evaluated the developments but didn't determine them themselves, they thought about how other surgeons' results could be applied *creatively* to conditions over here; that is: they *improvised* . . . He read the few sentences from the abstract of the study. When he'd done so he knew that they'd be unable to use any of the results because they lacked the technical resources. The old story. And they were surprised that people got out . . . Why hadn't he got out while there was still time? He couldn't concentrate any more, pushed the article to one side. How tired he was, he couldn't even be bothered with his hobby, hand surgery. He couldn't be bothered with anything since his discussion with Anne . . . But he mustn't let himself go, he'd always abominated that. If the world consisted entirely of people who let themselves go as soon as things got difficult, they'd still be living in caves as hunter-gatherers . . . A couple of coffees and a decent meal would be enough to perk him up again, he decided. As

he went to close the window, he saw Weniger coming from the Gynaecological Clinic.

'Richard.' Weniger waved. 'We're both on call, great! Perhaps we
can chat for a bit.'

'Aren't you going home?'

'Then the duty assistant would be left on her own. We've got a few
difficult births due. Once it starts they'll fetch me anyway, so I might
as well stay here.'

'Are you coming over for a bite to eat?' The suppers that the nurses
made for those on duty in the Surgical Clinic had a good reputation
in the Academy.

'That's exactly what I was going to do, old chap.'

'I just want to go round the wards first –'

'I'll join you, if you have no objection.'

They told Casualty they'd be doing a round together. These rounds
with colleagues from other clinics were standard practice in the Academy; in that way you learnt the most important innovations and
problems of the other field from an expert, as if in a private lecture. In
general the hospital routine didn't leave enough time to keep staff
informed about the state of things in neighbouring disciplines.

First of all they went round the general surgical wards, for Richard
hardly knew the patients there at all. If he was called during the night,
it was useful for him to have at least a rough idea about them. From
the duty rosters he saw that capable nurses would be on night duty.
He gave the late-shift nurses a routine and preoccupied 'Good evening', got them to show him the files of the tricky cases and studied them
while Weniger joked and chatted. 'Well then, Karin, how's the house
coming along?' The nurses emptied the medicine basket, set out the
evening doses.

'How do you think it's coming along, Herr Weniger? If only you
could get some decent craftsmen. Recently I called the electrician
because the geyser wasn't working. "Payment in Forum cheques, is

it?" And he wouldn't come after six in the evening anyway – at that time he'd be enjoying his well-earned rest.'

'He wanted a Forum cheque from you? The scoundrel!'

'Or Western currency, Herr Weniger, which comes down to the same thing.' The deputy ward sister on South I shook her head in outrage. 'Recently my neighbour had the plumbers in to install wash-basins and when they heard he couldn't pay in West German marks, they tipped concrete into his drains!'

'They ought to be reported to the police, the whole lot of them!' Weniger thumped the table.

'Then you wouldn't get another tradesman for the rest of your life.' Sister Karin sighed. 'That's the way things are. The only solution would be – aren't you feeling well?' She looked at Richard, concerned; he waved her question away. 'It's all right now. Perhaps I should eat something. And a coffee wouldn't be a bad idea either. No, that's all right. I'll get some in my own ward, thanks all the same. Shall we go, Manfred?'

He could feel their eyes on his back.

In North I they had a coffee; the nurses had put Richard's mug out ready, an extra large tin mug with his name and the transfer of a laughing swordfish on the enamel; the coffee revived him, it was lukewarm and bitter (everyone he knew thought that was revolting); it was his favourite way of having it because he didn't have to waste time waiting, he slurped the coffee down, like a drug, in a few greedy gulps. Weniger observed him, taking little sips, very precise, very practised, Richard found it slightly affected.

'Problems?' Weniger asked as they were going round the ward.

'The usual, you know. On top of that I've had an exhausting day.'

'Müller?'

'No, no. You mean our jokes at the birthday party? Water under the bridge. We've other worries.'

'Should I stop bothering you?'

'I didn't mean it like that. Come along, I'll show you something.'

They went into a room; there were eight beds, each with a white-haired woman in it. A nursing auxiliary was just taking one of them off the bedpan; there was a smell of urine, faeces and Wofasept disinfectant. The women didn't look up when the two doctors came in, they lay there, apathetic, staring into space or sleeping, their wrinkled hands on the white blankets. The auxiliary cleaned the woman with a few energetic wipes, picked up the bedpan, nodded shyly to them and scuttled out. That patient seemed to notice them. 'Herr Doktor, Herr Doktor,' she cried in a thin, pitiful voice, stretching out her arms. They went to her bed, sat down. Richard took her hand.

'Herr Doktor, is my daughter going to come?'

'She will come.'

The woman sank back into the pillows, gave a satisfied nod, leant forward again and, with a roguish smile, waggled her index finger at them. 'You doctors are always telling fibs. Can't I phone my daughter?'

'When you can get up. And you can only do that when your broken thigh has healed properly.'

'Oh, if only I could walk, Herr Doktor –' She turned her head to the window, began to murmur; her fine, silver-white hair was like spiders' webs round the old woman's face.

'Your daughter will come, I'm sure of that,' Weniger said.

'God bless you, Herr Doktor, God bless you. You know,' she whispered with a sly smile, 'I'm not mad, as they say in the old folks' home, I . . . I'm just so thirsty.'

'Sit up now.' Richard picked up the feeding cup from the bedside table and gave her a drink, Weniger supported her.

'Such a long life . . .' She felt for Weniger's hand, put something in it. He shook his head. 'Keep it. You have greater need of it than I do.' He put the mark coin on the bedside table. 'It's very kind of you, but please keep it.'

'Thank you, gentlemen. Will you come again. Oh, it's not good when you're old and alone.'

'We have to go. Here, take this, in case you need anything.' Richard put the bell in her hand and attached the cord to her sheet with a safety pin.

'They come from the care homes,' Richard said outside. 'They fall over when they're going to the toilet during the night, break their femur, are operated on and have to stay in bed here until the break's healed. Two to three months, depending on how quickly it heals. Then they lie in bed and get pneumonia. And that's what they die from.'

'Just like in our wards,' Weniger said. 'Women from the care homes, with bedsores, undernourished, confused because they're thirsty. They're dismissed as old and senile but they're not, all they need is a bit of liquid. Here they're looked after, revive – and go back to the care home.'

'It's the natural cycle,' said Richard. 'They come to you as young women and give birth, they come to me as old women and die. They haven't got enough staff in the care homes. There's never anything about that in the newspapers.'

'Is there no method that makes it possible for them to put their full weight on it and stand up immediately after the operation?'

'Not yet. Various teams over there are looking into it. I read something interesting recently. The idea is a kind of oversized nail inserted between the head and the neck of the bone. I showed the article to the technical director of the factory that supplies our equipment. Just out of interest, a general inquiry, no obligation. He phoned me: "Impossible. We haven't even got the machines to make the machines that could make this thing."'

Weniger went over to the window, stuck his hands in the pockets of his white coat. 'Cancer's on the increase, significantly. Breast and the neck of the uterus, and the patients are getting younger and younger. – By the way, are all your patients so docile?'

'She was a communist. Worked on the *Red Flag*, then, after the Nazis came to power, was active underground, went to Spain, to support the Popular Front. Emigrated to Mexico just before the end. Came back fairly late, when those returning from Moscow already had everything under control. Then she helped with building the Republic, once departed from the official Party line and was transferred to a subordinate position in the transformer and X-ray factory. And then she grew old.'

Weniger nodded, gave Richard a sidelong look; he noticed it, but avoided eye contact.

'Let's see what your famous supper's like.'

The start of his spell on duty was unusually quiet. 'No acute cases?' Richard asked in Casualty.

'Not so far.' Wernstein spread his arms wide. Dreyssiger was looking after a sprained ankle, routine. The nurses were making swabs.

'Slack tonight.' Weniger replaced the telephone. 'My difficult births are – asleep.'

'Then let's go over to my place,' Prokosch, a senior doctor in the Eye Clinic, suggested; he'd been eating in the corner and filling in forms. He was another of the old Leipzig students at the Academy, though he'd qualified two years before Weniger and Richard. He was a brawny, stocky man who looked more like a wrestler than an eye specialist. No one could believe his short fingers, fat as cigars, had the sensitivity and delicacy of touch needed for operations on the eye that often enough, as Prokosch used to say, were as exacting as cutting a tuning fork out of a hair.

'I've got a few cases that'll interest you two. And we can always get some sleep.'

'The god of night duty willing,' said Wolfgang, a male nurse with thirty years' service behind him. 'What's rule number one after it gets dark? Get as much sleep as you can. And be wary of those minutes of quiet – they're the calm before the storm.'

The three doctors walked together in silence, deep in thought – what was there to discuss? They'd known each other for a long time and at work it was not usual, unless you were friends like Richard and Weniger, to cross a certain boundary in conversation. Private matters were kept out of it, not through lack of interest but through a sense of tact that appeared as fellow feeling which, according to an unwritten code, would have been violated by too confidential a conversation between colleagues. You knew whom you were dealing with, you knew who you were (or appeared to be), gave a silent nod and that was all, that was sufficient.

They heard hurried steps behind them, Nurse Wolfgang waved to Prokosch.

'Where?' he asked.

'Ward 9D. Your on-call presence is required in Dermatology. The god of night duty doesn't like sleep.'

'There's no point in kicking against the pricks.' Prokosch shrugged his shoulders in resignation. 'We'll see each other later, I should think. Off we go, then.'

An ambulance was approaching from the Academy gate, but without its blue light; they watched where it was going; it turned off to the right beyond the car park, heading for the Stomatology Clinic.

'Not for us,' Weniger said. They walked slowly back along the road.

'May I ask you something, Manfred?'

'Go ahead.'

'Have you sometimes thought of leaving?'

Weniger gave Richard a quick glance, then carefully looked all round. They moved to the middle of the road.

'I imagine we all have. – At the last Gynaecological conference I was offered a post.'

'I didn't mean that.'

'They're not good thoughts.'

'But you get them.'

'Every person's different. I don't think you can live with them.'

'Did you never think, when you were a student, what it's like to be a father, to have children with a woman, bring them up –'

'I can't remember. I don't think so.'

'To love one woman in all –'

'You know that.' Weniger stared into the darkness.

'And –' Richard broke off. A woman was approaching; even from a distance he could tell it was Josta. His first impulse was to turn off onto one of the side paths, but she was looking at him and Weniger had seen her as well. 'Still here this late, Frau Fischer? Is there something special going on in Administration – something we ought to know about?'

'No,' she said tersely, not using his name or saying good evening. 'Just a lot of work. But nothing special. Construction plans and applications, Herr Doktor.'

'How is your daughter?'

'Oh, she's in the middle group in kindergarten. She loves drawing. I think she ought to go and see the paediatrician, she keeps complaining about earache.'

'Who are you with?'

She named a name. She avoided looking at Richard.

'Are you happy with him?'

'Well, it's a general hospital, there are long waiting lists and I don't want it to drag on –'

'I'll have a word with Professor Rykenthal, if you're agreeable. Give me a call tomorrow.'

'I'll do that. Thank you, Herr Doktor. – But I won't hold you up any longer. I wish you a quiet night. Goodbye.'

'Pretty woman,' Weniger said when she'd gone. 'If only I were twenty years younger – and' – he ran his hand over his bald head – 'wasn't as hairy as an ape. God, I can still see her little girl, umbilical cord cut and wrapped up warm, and her face when the midwife gave her the baby. That's always the best moment.' Weniger looked at his hands. 'Then you know why you're here and what these paws are for. I'm sure it's the same with you.'

'Was it a difficult birth?'

'Yes, pretty difficult. But she didn't say a word. You don't often get that nowadays. You used to, out in the country.'

'We were interrupted.'

'You want to stick to the topic? – We really ought talk about it some other time, not while we're on duty and can get called away any moment and have to break off things that would be better made crystal clear.'

'Agreed,' Richard said after a cautious glance at Weniger.

'No, no, that's OK, no one's calling us yet,' Weniger replied with a faint smile, 'and we've known each other long enough to be able to set what's being said against the situation in which it's being said.'

'You're right there, of course.'

'I should think so!' Weniger exclaimed cheerfully. 'But to go back to what you were saying . . . You can think about it, but that's merely theoretical. Thoughts don't have consequences; you can play with them, like children with building blocks, and if you build a house with them that you don't like, then you change it . . . Tell me, aren't you getting cold? I can lend you my coat.'

'No, I don't feel cold . . . It's fairly warm.'

'I saw it was eight degrees on the thermometer just now. – You can change the house any way you like, and with no consequences.'

'Which isn't possible in real life.'

'It's perhaps possible, Richard, but some people have the problem that they're never satisfied with the houses they build, they keep building houses and discarding them, they do it their whole life long and never have a house that's finished, while their neighbour, to whose house they paid no attention because it's crooked and perhaps not very distinctive, because it's made of cheap materials, lives in a house that's finished –'

'A nice way of describing renunciation.'

'No, I wouldn't say that. He's made a decision, a decision to make the best of what he's been given – and not to waste his time looking for things he can't have.'

'How does he know he can't have them?'

'By a sober assessment of his situation.'

'How do you bring up your children?'

Weniger didn't answer immediately. 'I tell them they're free.'

'Free? In this country?'

'In that sense I don't think people are free anywhere. What I mean is free to find out about themselves – and to build their house. – I have to say, you don't look well.'

'Could be. I've not been sleeping very well.'

'It happens to all of us,' Weniger said with a smile.

'For example, when something happens to you that makes you furious; something that, let's say, gives you the impression you're pretty helpless –'

'Has something given you that impression?'

'No, I just mean . . . As an example, purely as an example to put these thoughts in context. So, if something like that happened to you, would it be better to hit out at once – or to wait and see?'

'It depends very much on what kind of thing has happened to give you that impression. And what you mean by "hit out". In this country the opportunities for "hitting out" must be limited. If you aren't one of them.'

'Just a minute, I've probably not put it very well. "Hit out" really does sound a bit over the top –'

'Another time, perhaps,' Weniger said calmly.

25

The Leipzig Book Fair

Philipp Londoner lived in a seventy-square-metre apartment in a working-class district of Leipzig. The building bordered on a canal, the water of which had been turned gelatinous by the effluent from a cotton mill. Dead fish were floating in it, slowly decomposing, flakes of white flesh sliding off the bones; single fins, blind eyes were swept against the bank where they bobbed on the grey foam with the bare elm branches stretching over it, occupied by thousands of crows that found rich pickings there. The inhabitants of the district had a name for the factory: 'the Flock'; within a radius of several kilometres the streets were covered in cotton flocks that were trodden down, forming a slimy, decomposing crust in which the smell of all the dogs of Leipzig seemed to be concentrated. Drifting cotton got caught in the undergrowth, blocked the chimneys in the summer, floated up in the breezes warmed by the extracted air, formed whirling veils over the roofs, drifted down into puddles and onto railway lines, so that passengers could tell with their eyes closed when the train entered the district: suddenly the sounds were muffled and the general murmur of conversation in the compartment stopped.

Meno went to the Leipzig Book Fair every year. Philipp put him up for those days and continued to do so after Hanna and Meno had separated, for the two men felt a liking, a quiet respect, for each other, what Hanna had once called 'a kind of awkward friendship'. The crows were still there, their numbers seemed to have increased over the years until there were legions of them. Worse for Meno than their squabbling and squawking, their sputtering and chattering, was the moment in the evening when the gates of the cotton mill opened and the workers went home: then the crows fell silent, you could hear many shuffling steps, rhythmically interrupted by the sound of several time clocks punching cards, now and then by the grinding of a tram going round a bend or accelerating. When the wind in Leipzig turned to the north, bringing the fine brown-coal dust from the open-cast mines of Borna and Espenhain that slewed in broad sheets round the houses and dust devils the height of a man – the 'cypresses' – appeared in the streets, the crows would sit, silent, in the jagged black trees that were like veins of ore against the brighter sky, and look down on the workers, most of whom ignored the birds and made their way, head bowed, with sluggish gait, to the bus stop or the central bicycle racks outside the mill. Sometimes a woman would raise her fist and scold the crows in the silence or a man would throw a stone at them and swear, at which a raging, discordant swarm, an avian giant consisting of clamorous take-offs, cries of fury and the clatter of feathers, would swell up over the factory in pulsating rings that circled round in the sky, screeching, and then slowly sink, appearing to be sucked into funnels that gathered together in a thin swirl, like a storm spindle, back down into the elms; individual birds separated from the fraying downflow, folded their wings, came to rest. Meno would observe all this from the window of the little room Philipp had given him, the cotton mill was opposite; in the morning, as he was getting ready for the Book Fair, he could see the workers of the early shift at their machines, silhouettes with swift and measured movements under fluorescent lights.

Meno unpacked his suitcase. In the study a young woman was sitting beside Philipp.

'This is Marisa.' Philipp lit one of his cigarillos, Cuban; perhaps it was the only privilege he took advantage of. 'I've already told her who you are.'

'You haven't shaved your moustache off,' Meno replied.

'She says it's modern in Chile nowadays. One for you too?' He handed Meno a silver case.

'Not something we get every day. With pleasure.'

'When your Spanish is a bit better,' Marisa said, winking at Philipp, 'we'll accept you as a *compañero*. I'll go and make some tea.'

Philipp waved this away. 'No, don't bother. I'll make it.'

'No, you'll stay here and talk to him. Talking is men's business. I'll make the tea. That's women's business.'

'Nonsense.'

'When the time comes to fight, I will fight. Fighting is women's business as well. But now it's time to drink tea.' She lifted up her head proudly and went out.

'Don't think I support that. But lots of our Chilean comrades are the same. These remnants of bourgeois attitudes –'

'They're not bourgeois . . . whatsits. You'd be surprised how many members of the bourgeoisie in our country have long hair like you! If I go for you to bring you the tea it is out of *emoción*. And *la revolución* needs warm hearts and not the one most German comrades have –'

'*Corazon del noviembre?*' Philipp tried out his Spanish.

'November hearrts,' said Marisa.

DIARY
Discussion between Schiffner, Schevola and me before leaving for the Fair. We still have to discuss the title, The Depths of These Years. *A title like that claims something that the text doesn't yet match up to, it's trying to meet the specification and sometimes that just doesn't happen because the book has different ideas about itself from the author. I don't know who it was who said that a book should be named after its 'hero', anything else was mere journalism – the longer I've been in this profession, the more I'm persuaded by that statement, though it does have its problems too, for who can say for certain that this method avoids 'mere journalism' and that where 'Anna Karenina' is written on the cover, Anna Karenina is also inside it. So Schevola's book is to be published by us, something that was a surprise to me. Usually when Schiffner decides on a book, he puts detailed*

instructions in our pigeonholes – and doesn't remain silent, as he has done in this case. Everything's still vague, of course – as always with printed stuff in general, especially with Schiffner and especially especially with the PLAN. *Frau Zäpter, his self-assured secretary – she makes the decision on unsolicited poems – was noisily making coffee as Schiffner sat down opposite Schevola and invited me to join them. He regarded his fingernails, the manuscript in front of him with two pages sticking out that, as the kettle started to whistle, he tried to tap back in. Madame Schevola seemed calm and reserved, she had put her fingers together, was staring at the table and was pale.*

　'*So you've written something here and now you want to publish it. Well, I'll explain the philosophy of our publishing house, my child.' I hate these moments – and enjoy them at the same time, strangely enough, for how an author feels when they're greeted with stuff like that as the very first sentence – not even a 'Good day', that's what the outer office is for, Schiffner just stands up, straightens, briefly runs his hand over his hair, glues the author's wandering gaze firmly to his fatherly publisher's gaze, extends his right hand and, with an inimitable waggling gesture, mutely indicates the penitential chair at the conference table opposite his imperial throne studded with yellow upholstery pins the size of coins – how Schevola, who looks controlled, is feeling is something I can appreciate.*

　'*We publish authors, not books. We don't even just happen' – he raises his chin and gently waves his left hand – 'to publish a book, my child. No.' The way he shakes his head as he says that! The way he says that 'No', not with emphasis, not with a dismissive raising of the voice, he lowers his chin and shakes his head, forbearing, as if he were talking to a badly behaved pet, his hand comes down, flat, like a seal's flipper, gently through the air, as if there were nothing more to say apart from that soft 'No', and as he does this he purses his lips. Tasting the effect. And when he then raises his left eyebrow, Frau Zäpter knows it's time to serve the coffee, with a little bobble of cream for him that sputters out of a vigorously shaken syphon, and then, after he's taken a sip, raising his eyebrow a little higher, it's the time for: 'Just come over here, my child.' Now he shows her the prints and paintings on the walls between the shelves, portraits of writers, all done by renowned figures from the Artists' Association. He flicks out his right index finger, which has a ring with a green stone on it, stabs it in the direction of the first picture: 'Who is that?' – 'X.' Second picture: 'Who is that?' – 'Y.' Third picture: 'And that?' – 'Z.' He pats her cheek and says, 'Wrong, it's A.' Then he takes a mirror off the shelf, holds it up to the baffled Schevola's face: 'And who is that?' – 'Another one?' – 'That's an author who can't write.' He watches her closely, waiting for her response, eyes slightly screwed up, his tongue feeling its way along his left teeth; he spins the mirror round as he puts it behind him, then pauses, like a gunslinger slipping his Colt, still smoking, into its holster, then he places the mirror, carefully, precisely, as if it were a precious object, back on the shelf.*

'If that's your opinion why did you even bother to ask me to come here?'

'Ah, my dear, it's good that you're furious. In general the talent of authors who can get furious is capable of development.' He contemplated his finger-nails, then looked at me: 'That is a task Herr Rohde will undertake; you are already acquainted with him. An experienced editor of great tact and sensitivity. One more thing.' He took a book down off the shelves: 'You make inflationary use of the semi-colon. Here is a book by Gustav Regler. Do you know Gustav Regler? – Well you ought to. You'll sit down now and study the way Regler uses the semi-colon in chapter four. It is' – index finger raised, the green stone flashes – 'a substitute for a full stop! One can also discuss the rule for using it before "but" with a following main clause. Study the old grammarians. And nota bene: German is a complex language with some features that don't appear to make sense, but when you look more closely there is a good reason for everything. Come and see me again in an hour.'

She does so. In the meantime Schiffner has made a telephone call, leafed through folders of prints, ruminated out loud on the three rules about starting a complete sentence after a colon with a small letter, eaten an ice cream from the office freezer with great relish and freshened up by rubbing his temples with eau de Cologne. He takes the book from her and puts it back on the shelf. He looks at her breasts, gives her a pile of books worth a thousand marks and dismisses her.

We spent weeks preparing for the Leipzig Book Fair. We didn't go there just to pick up a few books, open then close them; we went to look through a window into the Promised Land. The window could be in sextodecimo, octavo, quarto and folio format but most often it measured 19 × 12 cm, had no hard cover, but three fishes or 'rororo' on the front, was in a rainbow-coloured row, or was white and had drawings in pastels: then Niklas or someone would say, we're in the right place; then the covers were by a man called Celestino Piatti and the books with his scrawl on it became the subject of many a plan. 19 × 12 cm: paperback format. The measurements were established with a ruler and Barbara used them to tailor the inner life of Book Fair coats, for paperbacks needed a pocket into which they fitted snugly.

DIARY

Today I, as a zoologist, learnt something: the African desert locust has an East German relative, the book-grasshopper (Locusta bibliophila), a two-legged species wearing Wisent or Boxer jeans, hand-knitted roll-neck pullovers and olive-green or earth-brown 'habits' (parkas) that come down over their calves (special models from the Harmony Salon furrier's on Rissleite, undertaken during free time or by arrangement with the boss – he too has preferences in his reading – after which Barbara and, depending on demand, a colleague are diverted from their contribution to the realization of the socialist to that of the individualist plan). Locusta bibliophila feeds on books, though only on those from the Non-Socialist Economic Area. Locusta bibliophila's attack is planned like a military operation weeks before the Leipzig book-feast and I, happy to be the advance guard in the cyclically recurring paper comet, was given strict orders: 'Where are they? When are they coming? You must prepare them. For us. You must take lockers at Central Station. We have to think about a system of signals. Perhaps a handkerchief on which you blow your nose at the approach of danger. What d'you mean, it's the time of year when everyone gets a cold. Of course you have work to do there as well – but you can do that once we've left.'

The book-grasshopper's combat gear (the aforementioned parka-style Book Fair coat) is subjected to a thorough examination about two weeks before the campaign; right interior: two parallel rows of five pockets each, sewn in from breast-top down to about the knee (partly overlapping), size: 21 × 14 cm, the ease of insertion is checked using the Harmony Salon's copy of Heinrich Böll: 'Wanderer, kommst du nach Spa . . .', which has to go 'smoothly'

'fully covered'

'with minimal bulge'

into the pocket. The habit is two sizes too big and not fitted with the standard Solidor zip (the zip gets stuck at the bottom too often, also in this version of the habit it is so low down that the wearer would have to bend, which might perhaps be detrimental to the desired minimality of bulge), but with snap fasteners that can be closed more quickly – and at different points. On the left-hand side are two large pockets for coffee-table books or others of unusual format. On the outside of the Book Fair coat there are more large snap-fastening pockets and, in addition, over each hip a snap karabiner attached to a sturdy leather loop: they are to take the many plastic bags into which it is intended to slip ballpoint pens, brochures, books, chocolate, catalogues, bananas, even more ballpoint pens, Western cigarettes and even more books – leaving the hands free and the bags can't be appropriated by fellow citizens and sufferers.

The approach of the book-grasshopper takes place in carpools: Anne and Robert in Rohde's Moskvitch, Malthakus and Dietzsch in Kühnast's Škoda, Prof. Teerwagen and his wife take the Knabes, whose Wartburg is being repaired, Trüpel, the owner of the record shop, with the Tietzes. Conversations: Oh, look at that magnificent opera book, oh, and that magnificent Picasso book (Däne, the music critic, and Adeling, who arrive by train); the strategy for outwitting the people on the doors (the 'fall-guy' system:

one starts bellowing and the others take advantage of the subsequent con-fusion to get their spoils out). I've prepared things for my colleagues, I've managed to lease two (!) lockers in Leipzig Central. – 'Only two?' Däne's despair comes from ignorance, even after all these years of attending the Book Fair. He should know that lockers in Leipzig are handed down from one generation to the next.

The attack of the book-grasshopper comes in waves, a keen observer will recognize that it is about to begin from the way its eyes, which have a greedy look anyway, narrow to hungry slits. Its hunger is mainly for colours. The more colourful its booty, the better. And the more of it there is, even better. What most arouses its lust are red covers. They spark off the suspicion that it must have something to do with us. Once the hunger-slit has noted the name of a dissident, action must follow immediately. The editor on sentry duty is to be engaged in strategic conversation by book-grasshopper B while book-grasshopper A, heart pounding, breaking out in a cold sweat and blind with courage, trots like lightning over to the shelf (the claw must embrace the book like a soft caress, then comes the decisive pause, the moment of happy fear: I'VE GOT IT! My fingers are enclosing it, the cover is smooth, it's from the West), now:

release studs on Book Fair coat

glance upwards elegantly, wet dry lips with tongue

feign coughing fit

bend down

intensify coughing

open Book Fair coat

close eyes and

one

two

three –

('Hey, you there, what d'you think you're doing?' – 'But you . . . usu-ally always look the other way?' Uproar. Form a barrier. Take care not to be recognized as a unit, otherwise a Book Fair ban. Book Fair ban =

catastrophe. Catastrophe = drive home with 'You could have got it if you hadn't been so stupid!' Barbara cries out, sinks to one side. Emergency. 'Thank you, I'm all right now.' Malthakus and Teerwagen slip away. Spoils: Isaak Deutscher: Stalin. *Alexander Solzhenitsyn:* The Gulag Archipelago, *Part 1. An anthology of writers against atomic weapons. Friedrich Nietzsche:* Why I am So Clever. *Outside. End of round one. Tranquillizers from the first-aid kit in Ulrich's car.*

'A close-run thing, Professor.' – 'Worth it, though.' – 'Have you a list of who gets to read what when?' A mouthful of tea from the Thermos. A comparison of the contents of the plastic bags. Check the coats. Take a deep breath. Back for round two.)

It was the year of the apocalypse. Almost all the books on display dealt with global catastrophes. The forests were dying. Rockets were being deployed, Pershing and Cruise missiles, there was SALT II and a programme for a war of the stars; the total of explosives in the world was sufficient to blow up the Earth several times. The mood at the Book Fair was gloomy – editors, publishers, authors: all were grimly determined to perish. One raised his glass, hoping he would at least see the end of the world in the evening glow outside his cottage in Tuscany: You don't feel so afraid then.

When editors from Western publishers came to the Hermes stand, Schiffner would wave them over, give his enterprising smile and whisper, pushing the intimidated Judith Schevola, whom he'd summoned to the Book Fair, forward, 'One of our most talented writers. We're going to hear a lot more from her.' But the editors would just lower their heads sadly and sip the red wine resignedly. Schiffner would pat Schevola on the shoulder and tell her it meant nothing. But the apocalypse made people hungry, the bars and restaurants were crowded, no places left in Auerbachs Keller, Zills Tunnel, the Paulaner restaurant. It was only when they tried the Jägerschänke, not far from the Fair building, that the members of an important Frankfurt publishing house managed, with freely convertible arguments, to persuade a waiter to release the regulars' table with the 'Reserved' sign, in the corner next to a stove, surmounted by a stuffed capercaillie. Hermes-Verlag had been invited: Schiffner was a friend of the Frankfurt publisher Munderloh; they'd both written theses on Hermann Hesse and in a letter to Munderloh, which mainly concerned typographical errors and two passages with incorrect German in a book from their autumn programme five years previously, he had told him that his whole Frankfurt publishing house was nothing other than the *Glass Bead Game* writ large. The two men formally opened the Book Fair drinking session.

Schevola, taking nervous puffs at her cigarette, was grateful to Meno for offering her a chair next to him. Eschschloraque, the playwright, came in, giving Meno the opportunity to observe him. There was a certain unproletarian grandeur about him. Despite the cool conditions in Leipzig at that time of the year and despite the air that was dirty from the exhaust fumes and brown-coal particles, which was the reason why one seldom saw people in light-coloured clothing in Leipzig, Eschschloraque was wearing a lightweight cream suit of a cut and quality that made its bespoke tailoring apparent. He had a trench coat over his arm and a red cashmere scarf wound several times round his neck, the ends of which, with their long fringes, hung down elegantly, enveloping the writer's slim figure in a way that was both becoming and discreet. Enveloping – the word seemed appropriate. No, the ends of his scarf did not 'flatter' and certainly did not 'bring out' Eschschloraque's slim figure. He took off his hat, stood in the half-light of the large chandelier at the entrance, upright, proud, not part of the noisy, beer-drinking, cutlery-clattering tavern-throng. He scrutinized one table after the other, calmly but with the swift assessment betokening the alertness of an experienced observer. He was still holding his hat in his hand, his right arm half raised in a gesture characteristic of distinguished petitioners or actors who have grown old and know what success they have had but not whether the person they're facing does, and now, with this politely nonchalant gesture, are attempting to conceal the fact that they have to beg for a part less from the other person than from themselves and, since their internal commentator is not open to bribery and makes ironic remarks, at least execute the gesture perfectly: futile but perfect – they owe that to themselves. Eschschloraque stepped back a little, perhaps he felt the spot where he was standing was too bright: it could be indiscreet to draw attention to oneself in that way, it was platitudinous to say the least; a gentleman does not intrude and it would have been an intrusion if Schiffner or Redlich had felt obliged to leap up and greet him, the author of dramas and poems in the classical style (What does the 'classical' style mean here? Meno wondered, for him there is no other style, one ought to say: the author of dramas that have style), profusely and with attention-drawing ceremony. At the same time Eschschloraque could see better in the gloom, wasn't dazzled. Slowly he lowered his hat. It was a brown Borsalino, an expensive hat scarcely obtainable in shops in this country; Meno remembered having seen a similar one in Lamprecht's hat shop, it cost 600 marks and was reserved for Arbogast. A waiter jostled Eschschloraque and the way he stood there at that moment: trench coat over his left arm, hat in his right hand, a look of uncertainty in his eyes for a few seconds, Meno felt a sudden upsurge of sympathy for this man who was surrounded by a known but well-glossed-over aura of loneliness. In order to give a reason for his movement (that it was 'giving a reason' seemed indisputable to Meno), he gently tapped his hat with his left hand to dust it, accepted that this made his trench coat waggle rather a lot (the unsatisfactory gesture would distract attention all the more because of its unsatisfactory nature), shook his hat as if there were raindrops or snowflakes on the brim, but since it had been neither raining nor snowing and a possible observer would know that, he once more corrected his improvised gesture by rubbing his fingers over the hatband, as if he'd just noticed dust on it. At that moment he seemed to sense that he was being observed, not seen but observed, by someone who knew him, for he abruptly looked across at Meno's table and, as he passed through the light, he made no attempt to conceal himself: to conceal himself would have been the reaction of an inexperienced person who thus betrayed his suspicion. He went to the coat stand and hung his hat on the hook beside Meno's, stopped short, looked round quickly, took the other hat, read the name on the inside. His head shot up, Eschschloraque eyed Meno coolly, slowly hung the hat back on the hook. There were no seats free at the table and Meno waited eagerly to see how Eschschloraque would solve the problem. He strolled over, compensating for his uncertainty with exaggerated body movements, staring at an imaginary point – as if he didn't want another's eyes to meet his, arousing embarrassment, shame, perhaps even annoyance at their discourtesy in failing to give the dramatist Eschschloraque preferential treatment. The people from the important Frankfurt publishing house had their backs to him. Munderloh was holding a glass of raki, thumped it on the table in the course of an argument with Schiffner, licked the drops off his wrist. Schevola and Josef Redlich had noticed Eschschloraque, Redlich nudged Schiffner, he waved. Now Eschschloraque was at the table, in a kind of stand-to-attention posture, no one stood up. The conversations died away.

'Could you possibly move up closer?' Eschschloraque asked with a smile, a smile he managed very well, Meno thought. It was slightly sceptical, with an admixture of modesty and dignity, with no hurt pride and no condescension. Room was found for him on the bench, in the corner where Meno and Schevola were at right angles to him, beneath the carved figure of the nightwatchman with his lantern, French horn and eyes eaten away by woodworm. Schevola leant over to Meno, whispered, 'Have you read the article he published about your book?'

'No.'

'No?' She seemed to be astonished. 'He attacked you. You, Altberg and I, he said, are a dubious Romantic faction.'

'No. For him it's medicine, for me it spoils my day. So why should I read it. I'm not a masochist.'

'But if you have to deal with the things he writes?'

'Then I can't avoid it. But only then.'

'And you can bear sitting at a table with him?'

Meno gave a pained smile. 'That's the way things are in this little faculty, you see. Jousting by day and in the evening you have a beer together. You'll have to get used to it.'

'And that doesn't bother you?'

'Who says it doesn't bother me? But –'

'You've a family to feed,' Schevola said with a dismissive wave of the hand.

'You're rather quick to jump to conclusions.' Meno finished his beer. 'Beware of that, if I may give you a piece of advice. It's very attractive in moral terms and gives you a good strong heartbeat, but it's not good for literature. We must talk about that when we discuss your manuscript.'

'What's not good for literature?' Eschschloraque's voice was hoarse, perhaps it was the thick cigarette smoke filling the room. He had a silk cravat that he had tied in a dashing knot in the open collar of his white shirt.

'Moralizing,' Meno replied and looked at Eschschloraque. 'To put it another way: knowing all the answers.'

Eschschloraque gave him a searching look, gently rubbed his carefully shaved cheeks. Munderloh leant forward.

'I'm interested in you, Herr Eschschloraque.'

'I call that a chivalrous lifting of the visor. I thank you for that and for your courage in admitting your shyness with such a direct approach,' Eschschloraque replied, raising his glass to the publisher. 'Fräulein Schevola for example, about whom our friend Schiffner had such nice things to say to you, is not at all shy. That's why her black thoughts are initially hidden. And I will be bold enough to make a further psychological leap: the problem, my dear, is the censor, who is right. – Incidentally, Herr Munderloh, what about me? Your publishing house, so full of wit and without me?'

'I meant it personally – if you've no objection. Stalinism and *esprit*, how can the two be combined?'

Eschschloraque smiled. 'Sleep quicker, comrade, your bed is needed. Well, Herr Rohde, memories of your days living in a *kommunalka*?'

'But surely you can't . . . all those who were killed,' said the Frankfurt press officer, incredulous.

'People have to be killed,' Eschschloraque replied coolly. 'Don't behave as if people didn't die on your side too. Enemies have to be eradicated, that is a sensible, tried and tested custom of ages that achieve great things. And it is definitely better to die for a great cause than to live for a mediocre one. The genuine democrats among you should protest before the main course; sharp wits avoid the digestive process.'

'Let's talk about football.' Redlich squinted across at the Frankfurt press officer, but he refused to play along.

'You are trying to be polite, my dear Redlich, and to save us embarrassment. Look, the way it is with enemies is this: Herr Rohde, whom I respect, is a subtle wag and recently permitted himself a – let's say – employee's joke. As an editor who knows what's right and proper, he marks up a manuscript in pencil; however, when he encounters a passage that is ambiguous, he inserts a red comma. You' – Eschschloraque smiled – 'have put a red comma after socialism. Is that supposed to mean something? That socialism is perhaps not the last word.' Eschschloraque gave a short lecture on monks who commented on the works they were copying out in an equally subtle way, by emphasizing certain letters, over several pages and chapters, so that in a collection of noble love songs the Latin for 'Troubadour thou art a dead loss' was hidden, though clearly visible to the philologist's practised eye.

Schiffner took out his genuine buffalo-horn comb and ran it through the white quiff over his striking features, bronzed from holidays in the Crimea. 'That's why you sounded so terribly calm on the telephone.'

'Rossi was great! He more or less won the World Cup for the *Azzurri* on his own,' Redlich cried.

'You can write?' Munderloh leant over towards Judith Schevola.

'I try to,' she replied, jutting out her chin defensively.

'She tries to!' The publisher slapped his hand on the table. 'Could you kill a dolphin?' Once more the conversations round the table fell silent.

'That would depend on the situation, Herr . . . What was the name?'

Munderloh stared, first at her, then at Schiffner, who was enjoying himself. Eschschloraque clasped his hands under his chin, observing, alert to every nuance, his expression that of a scientist waiting for the result of an interesting experiment that is immoral but unavoidable.

'The name is Munderloh. I like you. Though your answer that it depends on the situation was all too predictable. It always depends on the situation.'

'I hate dolphins,' Schevola said coldly. 'They're always so nice and kind, they save shipwrecked sailors and come to the help of the poet Arion, they dance round Bacchus's boat and bask in the early light of the sun . . . but I don't trust them.'

'There is a school of evil dolphins,' Redlich muttered. 'Black dolphins who are not favourably disposed towards us –'

'What are you on about, Josef?' The Frankfurt press officer waved his hand in displeasure.

'I'd like to kill a dolphin once, just to see what the other dolphins do. Whether they're still so nice and kind, whether the cliché's correct – or whether they'd then show their true character,' Schevola said, not avoiding Munderloh's hard look – from eyes that seemed like light-blue stones, a look like a rod, like a surgeon's blunt probe, Meno thought.

'I will read your manuscript,' Munderloh said after a pause during which the table had been silent, the only sounds coming from the front of the Jägerschänke. 'I will read it if Hermes will let me have it. – Do you like swimming?' He took out a visiting card, scribbled something on the back and pushed it across the table to Schevola.

'Only against the tide,' she replied after she'd read what was on the card and given Munderloh a long, hard stare.

'Great. – So it's not just slaves you produce in this country.'

'Don't say that, Herr Munderloh, please don't.' Redlich was leaning forward. 'They have dealings with the darkness, Lichtenberg, *Waste Books*, notebook L. And feel the pressure of government as little as they do the pressure of the air, notebook J.'

Munderloh nodded. 'Perhaps you have the wrong idea of conditions in our country. Perhaps I have of conditions here. Let us drink a toast to what unites us.' He raised his glass, which he'd filled with red wine, and drank to Redlich.

'We, who know what a valuable thing truth is . . . And it is also a truth to present language in its purity . . .' Redlich sank back onto the bench, his chubby face with the moustache and puffy eyes that reminded Meno of Joseph Roth's face was in shadow again. Schiffner placed his hand on his arm.

'However that may be, you, all of you' – Redlich indicated the row of Frankfurters with a sweeping gesture – 'are much better dressed than we are.' He laughed, put his hand over his mouth.

'You don't like swimming, with or against the tide, is that right?' Munderloh leant forward, clasped his hands. They were strong, peasant's hands with hair on the back of the fingers; Meno was sure Munderloh would be able to crack walnuts between his thumb and forefinger. He would survive the camp – that angular head, the nose that looked as if it had been hewn with an axe, that lumberjack's back, the liberators would see all that when they opened the gates; he's a man that survives, Meno thought and frowned because he was irritated at connecting Munderloh's appearance with the camp; it seemed a perfidious thought. Redlich didn't reply to Munderloh's question. The party broke up. Philipp Londoner was waiting outside the Jägerschänke and greeted Eschschloraque and Schiffner familiarly, Schevola had disappeared.

It was warm at Philipp's, Marisa had turned the heating up; Meno and Eschschloraque soon took their jackets off. Philipp seemed to feel cold, he walked up and down restlessly, rubbing his hands, occasionally doing a knees bend when he stopped beside the little Azerbaijani copper table in front of the wall with the thousands of light-brown, blue, white and red spines of Reclam paperbacks. Eschschloraque knew about Meno's relationship with the Londoner family but had still expressed surprise that he was spending the night at Philipp's place. Meno had said nothing and on his part was wondering why Eschschloraque was there. Jochen Londoner knew him, Meno also knew that he was a frequent guest in the house on Zetkinweg in East Rome but was surprised at the familiar relationship between Philipp and Eschschloraque.

'That nightwatchman,' Eschschloraque said, slowly turning the glass of tea Marisa had given him round and reflectively watching the particles floating in the red liquid, 'that nightwatchman in the Jägerschänke. Anyone who can write about spiders will notice a nightwatchman as well. What do you think, Philipp, does communism need nightwatchmen? I'm sure friend Rohde here would say yes, he relies on the immutability of certain affairs, especially those of humans – but who knows?'

'Nightwatchmen? Rubbish. We've other problems.'

'But it would be a rewarding question for your institute. It's not as humorous a one as you might think.'

Philipp shrugged his shoulders, started walking to and fro again. Marisa came in, made herself comfortable on the sofa beside Eschschloraque, lit one of Philipp's cigarillos.

'Tell me instead what the evening was like, with the people from Frankfurt.'

'A pretty mixed-capitalist soirée. They look on us with both pity and envy. Pity because we are so terribly naive and refuse to give up our belief that the written word can change the world. Envy because, at least in this part of the Fatherland, we are absolutely right. There's also an element of fury. They don't like it when we catch them slackening off. Their manufacturing conditions are not determined by the state. The fact that they keep going on about our generally mediocre paper confirms your thesis that under free-market conditions the spirit is like a cow grazing on superficialities. How are things at the Institute, anyway?' Philipp worked as a lecturer at a Leipzig branch of the Institute for Social Sciences.

'Nothing special. I'm not getting anywhere.'

'Because you're too young?'

'No, that's not the problem.'

'Didn't you apply for a professorship?'

'I'll probably get one but . . . the Institute's losing its influence, it's hardly taken seriously any more.'

'Then go into politics.'

'It's a good thing to know your limits. I'm better off on the theoretical side.'

'Which doesn't necessarily say anything against you. Which doesn't necessarily say anything for the practical side either.'

'Yes. Theories can be powerful agents of change. And I'm not a demagogue, as old Goatee was, despite everything.'

'A little more respect, if you please. He wasn't that bad a politician, taking everything into account. Much better than him up there.' Eschschloraque jerked his shoulder at a portrait of the General Secretary on one of the shelves.'

'As a politician – maybe. As a human being . . . My department's being cut back a little.'

'What's the reason?'

'My name, I think, paradoxical as it may sound. And probably also because we were in England.'

'Do you think so? A bit simple, if you ask me. Still, it is possible. They're not exactly philosemitic, the comrades in the Politburo.'

Philipp broke off. 'No more of that.' He looked across at Marisa, who was calmly smoking and staring out of the window. 'What did you mean with that about the nightwatchman?'

There was something of the clown about Eschschloraque's face when he smiled. His wrinkled cheeks and the clearly defined bags under his eyes seemed to be part of a mask behind which cunning features were just waiting to leap out like jacks-in-a-box and perform somersaults in the momentarily clear space; also Meno had the impression that, for all his fine speeches, Eschschloraque's greatest desire was to get up and do a backflip over the table. 'So he's made you think, has he, our nightwatchman? Well I've got one in the play I'm working on at the moment. I believe a nightwatchman is an idealist out of despair. There's no one out in the streets any more – at least not officially – apart from him and the darkness. I don't know, perhaps I'll have a cat appear as well. His lantern is the only light in the dark. For it is dark, of course, – and not some cosy fairy tale in which the stars turn into silver thalers – and he's awake. He carries his lantern through the darkness. And has to make do with that. He denies nature, more than that: he hates it – in his official capacity.'

'Is that another of your defences of classicism against Romanticism?'

'Why should I defend classicism against something that was cooked up by the English secret service? Unfortunately stupidity seems to be . . . a metaphor for immortality.'

Philipp burst out laughing. 'Do you still keep dossiers on your enemies?'

'That doesn't concern friend Rohde,' Eschschloraque replied. 'Thank you for the tea, madam.' He stood up and bowed to Marisa.

26

Clouds in April

'Do you believe truth exists?' Verena adjusted the pullover that she'd tied across her chest by the sleeves. Siegbert took his time replying. It was warm, April seemed to have taken out a loan from May. They were lying in the grass on a slope above Kaltwasser reservoir, Christian was watching the changing characters inked on the apple-green of the dam by wind and waves. A train of the Erzgebirge railway, small as a model train, was chugging along the opposite bank, steaming up the fir trees along the line.

'Hey, Verena, I believe in Pink Floyd,' said Jens Ansorge in bored tones, pulled one hand out from under his head, took the blade of grass he'd been chewing out of his mouth and inspected it suspiciously. 'You know everything, Chrishan, can you tell me what that is? Tastes as bitter as anti-fever pills, yeuch.' He pulled a face and spat out.

'You watch what you're doing, you mucky pup! Your slobber almost landed on me.' Reina Kossmann threw back her head in disgust, Jens smirked, bursting imaginary balloons with this forefinger. Falk Truschler let himself fall onto his back and laughed his soft, hoarse, shoulder-twitching laugh. His movements were so shambling Christian felt as if Falk had only borrowed his body for a while; Christian tried to think of the *mot juste*: clumsy came to mind, and then he remembered sports lessons and Herr Schanzler directing a green-and-white-clad horde round the sports hall with geometries of Prussian precision; Falk's angular movements as he drew back to throw the Indian clubs for hand-grenade practice, his way of running: legs sticking out side-ways like a girl's, his expression, wavering between despair and self-mockery, at the moment of releasing the club, his hands and fingers waggling, as now at Jens Ansorge's little joke. Ungainly, he thought, that actually describes him even better than clumsy. But, as Meno said, 'actually' is a word to be avoided.

'Truth,' Siegbert said, drawing the word out, 'I don't know. Just watch out that you don't turn into a blue-stocking. Intellectual women don't get no men, then no children, my old mum always says, an' then they're unhappy. There's a truth for you.'

'You arrogant male chauvinist pig!' Verena exclaimed indignantly. 'It's *my* mother who's right: what this country needs is a women's movement.'

'Ooh, no one's got anything against women's movements,' Jens Ansorge interjected coolly, 'as long as they're nice and rhythmical.'

Grunts of laughter came from Falk and Siegbert.

'Stick to the point for once.' Christian felt himself blush as Verena looked up, immediately turned his eyes away and stared at his shoes. 'What do you understand by truth?'

'Certainly not Schmidtchen Schleicher's class standpoint –' That was what they called Schnürchel after a character in a pop song: Schmidtchen Schleicher with the ee-lastic legs . . .

'Ansorge showing off his cynical side again,' Reina Kossmann mocked, 'it's just courtship display, Verena. What was it Dr Frank told us about peacocks fanning their tails?'

Jens Ansorge leant up, gave Reina a worried look, puckered up his lips. She slapped her forehead and blew a kiss back.

'So there you are,' said Jens, satisfied.

'Have you heard? The commitment rigmarole is going to start up soon. Fahner wants it done before 1 May. Then we'll get a heavy roll-call –'

'And turn into nice and tidy, frigging statistics,' said Jens, cutting Siegbert short. He frowned, threw the blade of grass away, suddenly serious. 'Three wasted years . . . God knows how awful it'll be, guys. "Every male graduate of this school commits himself to voluntary service in the National People's Army,"' he said, imitating Fahner.

'Not me,' said Falk.

'It'll be good for your muscles.'

Christian was surprised at how coolly merciless women could be, especially since Reina then pinched Falk's biceps. Women for whom we did everything – oh the heroes in books, in films! – who mourned us when we fell in battle, who before that wept handkerchiefs full of tears for their beloved on the famous platform to the hiss of steam from the engine preparing to depart – and then this callousness from Reina, whose pale, delicate features with the mouth turned down slightly to the left, he liked looking at –

'Hey, you look horrified,' she said, brushing back her hair in a challenging gesture. 'We don't often see you look like that. I must have been really good.'

'She's keen on you, Chrishan,' Jens drawled, holding up his hand for a high five with Falk.

'Get lost, you idiot,' Reina snapped, throwing up her arm. 'I don't want to catch pimples.'

A thrust with a bare bodkin; Siegbert and Jens surveyed Christian, he had the feeling his face had been set on fire, tried a smile.

'You can leave my muscles out of it,' said Falk. 'I'm not going to enlist. Three years . . . I'd have grey hair by the time I got out. And then . . . all those tanks and guns . . . I'm not going to shoot at anyone.'

'Just let Chief Red Eagle hear that,' Reina said quietly and Christian realized she'd said it to him as a kind of offer in the group that had fallen silent, an offer he rejected because he didn't see why he should make the effort to break the silence; he stared down at the bay below them, wondering whether it would be worth coming fishing here with Ezzo and Meno, he'd have to join the local section of the German Angling Association; funny, these nicknames. They had inherited the name 'Red Eagle', as they called Herr Engelmann, their civics teacher and principal of the senior high school, from long-departed generations of pupils and accepted it unquestioningly. Did that indicate their lack of imagination or the aptness of the name – Christian decided in favour of the latter. It was true that when Engelmann spread his arms wide and told them, his lips moist with enthusiasm and his fiery red jug-nose shining above them, about the Great Socialist October Revolution, in which his father had taken part under Trotsky's leadership, when he started to wave his hands, his eyelids behind his thick lenses drooping so he could immerse his gaze in the great times of the past, at such moments Engelmann did resemble an old, ponderous eagle that swept round the class dictating April Theses with words appearing to fall out of his colourless, bubbling chain-smoker's voice and plop like early plums on the pupils' cowering heads.

'First Red Eagle will put the squeeze on you, then Fahner . . . I'm going away for four years anyway.'

Verena stared at Siegbert in alarm; he was picking up pebbles and, unmoved, flicking them up into the bright blue sky.

'Four years . . . Are you crazy?' Jens scrutinized Siegbert as if he'd been wearing a mask all the time that had now slipped to reveal the face of a monster. Siegbert smiled coolly.

'Just realistic. I want to be a naval officer. I was in Rostock last summer. They don't take anyone who hasn't done a period of service in the People's Navy.'

'I thought you wanted to join the merchant navy?'

'Unfortunately that doesn't make any difference, Montecristo.'

'The Count of Montecristo.' Her lips pursed affectedly, Verena imitated Christian's habit of brushing his too-long quiff out of his face: she put her head on one side, turned her eyes up and, with an exaggeratedly camp gesture, pushed back an imaginary quiff, a kind of habitual tic that he had and that he would have to get rid of immediately if it looked the way Verena had demonstrated. 'What an appropriate title for His Dresden Highness –'

'Shut it,' Christian growled. The two girls snorted with laughter.

'Take it easy, old man,' Jens said soothingly, 'the women are going through puberty and the nickname won't last anyway. Much too long and too much trouble to say. – But, my God, Siggi: four years!'

Siegbert shrugged his shoulders. 'I want to go to sea. They want four years in the navy. So I go into the navy for four years.'

'Oh, great,' Verena said. There was a touch of contempt, it seemed to Christian, in her voice, a touch of anger. He thought about Siegbert's answer, as the others appeared to be doing, they'd fallen silent. He imagined Fahner, who summoned the boys one by one to the principal's office, which was guarded by his wife at a heavy Optima typewriter; Fahner would definitely be – as he always was when you turned the handle after he had barked 'Yes!' – sitting at his desk, writing without looking up, so that you had plenty of time to observe the light cut into strips by the Venetian blinds on the highly polished PVC floor, the severe, shadowed faces of Wilhelm Pieck, Walter Ulbricht and the female Minister of Education on the wall over Fahner's head, not knowing what to do, for Fahner didn't say 'Come in' or 'Sit down'; Fahner said nothing at all, just sat there writing, in his elegant suit with the silk oversleeves in the blue of the Free German Youth that he would eventually, with measured movements of his fingertips that spoke of conflicting thoughts, take off and place on the table beside the needle-sharp pencils arranged precisely according to size. In the music class with Herr Uhl they'd recently talked about the English composer Benjamin Britten, and Christian had been amazed at the similarity between Britten's head and Fahner's: the same profusion of caterpillar-like locks, the same boyishly soft features; the similarity was so pronounced that Christian had done some research to see whether Britten had had a son in the Erzgebirge . . . his research had produced no result.

Verena broke the silence. 'You could just as well say: I want to go to sea, they demand that I kill a person – so I'll kill a person.'

'Gentlemen,' said Jens.

'Just a minute,' Siegbert said. 'I'm the one this is about, I'm the one taking on the four years. Anyway, it's easy enough for you to talk, Verena, it's not a problem for you, there's no military district command awaiting you.'

'Killing people . . . that can happen to you in the forces . . . They say the army units on the border are still on high alert and if you end up there . . . Enlisted today, invading Poland, gun in hand, tomorrow . . . Or in Angola. My father says Castro's troops are supposed to be there, the Russians as well . . . You can count me out,' Falk said.

'You'll stick to that? And if they throw you out?'

'Now wait a minute, Verena,' Jens said pretty sharply. 'It was pretty good recently when you handed in an empty sheet of paper, but you did back down eventually –'

'You must be out of your mind, Ansorge!' Reina tapped her forehead. 'Come on, Verena, what are we doing here?'

'You're right,' Verena said after a while. They looked at each other in surprise, for she'd said it to Jens Ansorge.

Three years in the National People's Army. Christian knew he would never forget that moment, that 24 April 1983; the day before yesterday. The three of them had been waiting outside Fahner's office, Jens Ansorge had tried to cover up the situation with jokes, for Falk had come out, a touch paler than usual, his right hand clutching the worn, imitation-leather briefcase with VEB GISAG Schmiedeberg on that he'd got from his father; he nodded and smiled his way past them into the light-grey corridor of the senior high school that was decorated with flags and pennants for the 'Karl Marx Year 1983'. Jens remained silent, Christian avoided Siegbert's eye that was trying to make contact with his, none of them called after Falk, asked him to stop, to tell them what had happened; they just watched him, the way he walked: it was a little less shambling than usual, he kept close to the banister, suddenly a fissure seemed to open up between Falk and them, the ball of his hand pounding the rubberized stair rail, the thrumming noise echoing round the stairwell, the trousers that were too big for him with the green plastic comb in his back pocket and its curving handle, shaped like a drop of water, sticking up cheekily over his belt, his angular shoulders under the Free German Youth shirt: it was something they'd let go of, all three of them, though probably each in his own way, and the fissure Christian sensed came from the fact that he felt no pity. It wasn't just because of the discussion that he would never forget that day.

It had gone differently from the way he'd expected, in an almost friendly atmosphere. Perhaps Fahner had been in a good mood because Siegbert had gone before Christian and signed up for four years, proof of the peace-loving attitude of young citizens with their consciously progressive outlook; once more there was the performance with paper and pencil and silence, the irresolute wait by the door until Fahner, not looking up, murmured 'Hoffmann' and, a few seconds later, as if he'd only just remembered his first name, 'Christian' and, again after a pause, 'Sit down.' Then he'd stretched out his hand and abruptly looked Christian in the face but, with the same motion, pointed to a chair, as if he'd made an error with the gesture, that could be interpreted as impermissible, or at least incompatible with his position as overall principal of the Maxim Gorki educational complex. Christian was embarrassed because Fahner looked good with his tan from holidays in Yugoslavia, his blue eyes and Benjamin Britten hair. 'From what I hear about you, Hoffmann, you don't seem to be making a particular effort,' Fahner had said, his hands clasped over a sheet of paper, at the top of which Christian deciphered his name, below it notes, some typed, some handwritten; among them Christian recognized Dr Frank's illegible scribble. 'Medicine,' said Fahner reflectively, 'the most sought-after, the most difficult subject. Your marks are good, apart from mathematics. It looks like you're heading for a disaster there. But grades alone don't make the medic. What use to us are traitors, who attend the senior high and the university at our cost and then have nothing better to do than to think only of themselves and get out? A sense of social responsibility, Hoffmann, that's important too. Indeed, it's more important than anything else. The committed standpoint. The people here make it possible for you to acquire knowledge free from worry, and we have an obligation to those people: you, by doing your best – and me by helping you, if you show goodwill; and by recognizing those who turn out to be parasites, who cannot or will not comprehend what our Workers' and Peasants' State is doing for them, by recognizing them as that type of character and treating them for what they are. Our nation invests hundreds of thousands of marks in your training. You must show yourself worthy of that trust and that generosity. That is why I expect your assent to three years' service in our armed forces, by which you will give back to it a little of what it is doing for you. Especially since, as agitator, you have an exemplary role for your class collective. Your response, please.' Fahner put down the pencil, the point of which he'd been stabbing at the desk to empha-size what he was saying. Christian had intended to make some objection, to dispute at least one of Fahner's points, to make it less easy for him, but he couldn't, he had to agree with Fahner. He could sense that there was a decisive error in Fahner's arguments, but he couldn't pin it down, however hard he tried; a discussion would end up with the question as to how he could deny this country a right that all other countries probably demanded, how he could – and at this point the discussion would have become dangerous – make a distinction between the defence of the country over there and here, between the Bundeswehr and the National People's Army. In his mind's eye he could see the horrified expressions on the faces of his parents, who had rehearsed this discus-sion and possible lines of argument over several weekends; he had mentioned the undemocratic character of the armed forces over here that earned him, for the first time after many years, a clip round the ears from his father. You hold your tongue, Christian, understood! And for a moment Christian had hated his father – even though it was Fahner he ought to have been hating; but he didn't hate him and wondered about that as, sitting in front of him on the edge of his chair, he looked past Fahner with understanding at the faces of the comrade rulers; he didn't feel hatred, instead he felt a need to agree with Fahner and to do so not only with lukewarm words that the principal would certainly have already heard a hundred times over, their emptiness forming a repulsive combination with the zealous promptness with which they were produced; a kind of bimetallic strip, the fear flowed through it as a current, created warmth, the metal curled and the bulb of the lie lit up. Christian felt the need not to disappoint Fahner, to cooperate with him, to support him. So he avoided the empty phrases and started to lie honestly.

Pale with conviction, he said he'd been going over these arguments ever since he'd applied for a place at the senior high school during the ninth year in Dresden; he knew of a similar case there had been at the time in his class that had aroused controversy among the pupils and then it had been suggested at a school parade that a pupil's position on that case should form part of all applications for a place at senior high school and he, Christian, had not changed his opinion since then. There'd been pro-peace demonstrations in Dresden in February – Fahner looked up, Christian had no idea why he'd mentioned this, that was taboo in Waldbrunn, why he even went on and brought in the situation in Poland – he said 'the People's Republic of Poland' – and in Afghanistan, Fahner clasped his hands and frowned; given, Christian went on, that the socialist system was threatened by revanchist forces, here Fahner slid the document for the declaration of voluntary enlistment across the table, however Christian didn't pause to sign, but suddenly found arguments for the three years' military service that hadn't even occurred to his father: it was good, he said, for anyone involved in an intellectual profession to live together with simple people for a while and thus get to know them better, what he learnt by this would be especially valuable for someone who wanted to study medicine, for how could one be a good doctor for people if one behaved in a snobbish, superior and condescending manner towards them; at this Fahner looked at the clock for the first time. He had been born here, Christian went on, in this country, twenty years after the war caused by Hitler's fascism, which had annihilated so many people and had been financed by money from industrial magnates. Never again must there be a repeat of such a terrible war or the criminal regime that had brought it about; medicine was a humane science, the socialist state was humane and humane its army, which was serving peace with its armaments, as could be seen in Wilhelm Busch's poem about the fox and the hedgehog, fully armed yet bent on peace: once you've had your teeth pulled out, I'll shave my spines from tail to snout. Fahner frowned even more and gave the clock a second glance at the moment when Christian finally looked up, took the pen and signed; the furrows disappeared from Fahner's brow, his eyes expressed, Christian wasn't sure whether it was right, a strange mixture of feelings: friendly repugnance. 'You can go, Hoffmann, I'm proud of your conviction. Send Ansorge in.'

Later Christian remembered again how they'd watched Falk leave; he could still hear Jens's stale jokes as he lay in his bed in the hostel, staring at the ceiling criss-crossed by the lights of the long-distance lorries on the F170; he could hear the murmur of voices from next door, where the twelfth-grade boys had their room, there was a clatter in the corridor, Frau Stesny was still there helping the others prepare their supper and again he saw Falk in his mind's eye, his hand thumping the stair rail, his green comb in his back pocket and he, Christian, had just realized that he had *crawled* to Fahner, had betrayed his principles in the most nauseous way . . . And yet he hadn't felt that way about it in the principal's office, he hadn't lied to Fahner, as he sat facing him he'd been *convinced* of what he'd been saying. And as Falk gradually disappeared from sight, none of them made any effort to follow him and ask how the interview had gone, they'd not asked him later either, and so far he'd said nothing. Christian could see himself standing outside the office not feeling any pity for Falk. That was the second surprising experience of the day. What he felt was contempt, even hostility. He didn't know whether Falk had had the courage to stick to the convictions he'd declared to them by Kaltwasser reservoir, that was probably what had happened and what really shook Christian was that that was precisely why he felt contempt for Falk. To stand upright, even and especially when things got tricky, was that not the way his parents had brought him up? At the same time they practised lying with him . . . Christian recalled another day he would never forget. It was one of the last days of the holiday before he transferred to the senior high school. His father had brought Erik Orré home with him, Tietze's neighbour and a colleague of Gudrun's at the Dresden State Theatre. He had been a patient of Richard's and had come to express his gratitude in an unusual way, by teaching Christian and Robert the art of lying convincingly, which Richard thought was necessary, especially for Christian; the large mirror was brought in from the hall and the actor had thus practised praising enthusiastically with them – and, at Niklas's request, Ezzo – had corrected their gestures, showed them how to deliberately turn red or pale, how to flatter someone with a certain amount of dignity, how to say stupid things with a serious expression, to drape them like a disguise over your true thoughts, how to churn out compliments that are empty but intelligently flattering, how to dispel suspicion, how, in some cases, to recognize other liars. Anne had gone out during these rehearsals. Christian had heard her crying in his father's study. Richard, pale and severe, had watched them, later he'd told Anne that it was hard but unfortunately necessary, especially for Christian. The boys, he said, could only profit from these skills, life was a tightrope and he'd wanted to make it easier for them to keep their balance, to see that it was there, even. At the end Erik Orré had expressed the hope they would recommend him to others, he could well imagine there could be 'further need for his skills in that district' and he was sure Herr Doktor Hoffmann knew his neighbours better than he did.

From the other side, from the common room, the voice of singer-songwriter Gerhard Schöne could be heard; he was very popular with the girls. He, too, was singing about honesty . . . Christian lay there, motionless, tormented by his thoughts. Should he not have felt sorry for Falk? Especially when he wanted to be a doctor – a doctor for whom the feeling of contempt should not exist? Did he really want to be a doctor? Would that be just following the family tradition or did he genuinely want it of his own accord? And why had he felt contempt for Falk? He couldn't say. He could find no answer to all these questions, no explanation.

He listened in the darkness to see if the others in the common room had gone to eat, then he could go and have a shower in the gymnasium. He'd have to hurry because Frau Stesny would certainly notice his absence and knock at his door to call him for supper. He had to wait for the short period when there was no one in the corridor, then he could slip out of his room and have the showers to himself. It was risky and he had to be quick, quick with his shower as well, he always had to be aware that someone might come, even though there was no sports group using the gymnasium that day. He'd copied out the 'Gymnasium Schedule of Use' and learnt it off by heart.

27

Music en voyage. All our strength.
The Writing Fairy

On one of his walks Christian saw Siegbert waiting outside Verena's house. He was looking up at the as yet unlit windows in Lohgerbergasse, which was behind the church. Christian, wrapped in thought and tired from hours of schoolwork, had not noticed him at first and

almost walked straight into him; but he suspected Siegbert wouldn't
have welcomed that and turned off into the shadow of the church in
time. He observed Siegbert, who seemed impatient, nervously smoking
a cigarette. The shops would soon be closing, people with shopping
bags were hurrying to the market square, Christian thought he recognized Stabenow in a man wearing a scarf and beret pushing a bicycle,
and shrank back farther into the shadow of the protruding wall. Darkness fell quickly. There were no street lamps in Lohgerbergasse, light
flickered on in the Winklers' and some of their neighbours' houses,
scattering dull brightness over the cobbled street. Verena came out,
nodded to Siegbert and the two went off together. Christian would
most likely have followed them but at the end of the street they turned
off along the Wilde Bergfrau; they would soon have noticed him on
the long street by the riverbank that ran straight as far as the castle and
allowed clear views. They were probably going to the cinema or the
Vostok Youth Club, which was in a dilapidated building beyond the
castle. It had a discotheque where they played a remarkably free range
of music, even though it could be seen from the Party district headquarters. Or perhaps they were heading for the 'Halls of Culture',
where Uhl, the music teacher, doggedly tried to open the eyes and ears
of the citizens of Waldbrunn to the Serious Arts.

Uhl, Christian thought, and again in his mind's eye he saw Verena
coming out and setting off with Siegbert. Uhl was a strange person,
at odds with himself, liable to fits of rage, selfless, obsessive. With his
glossy black hair, his sickle eyebrows and Wagner beard he looked like
a Flying Dutchman from the opera. The pupils were afraid of him
because of his unpredictability, his furious outbursts. A restless, often
cynical person who could expose a pupil's inability to sing until they
were in tears. He was an excellent pianist, but his lips expressed his
disdain for those before whom he had to perform, for their deaf ears.
Music was everything to him, he loved it, so it seemed to Christian,
more than he did some people; perhaps because everything it said was

clear, a language in which there were no misunderstandings. He contorted his face when someone sang out of tune and smiled when, during
a lesson, he put on one of the records he guarded like a treasure and
Sviatoslav Richter played a piece from the *Well-Tempered Clavier*.
Then another Uhl appeared, softer, milder, a wounded, aware man.
In the 'Halls of Culture' there was, beside the big hall, another room,
which Uhl called the 'closet', where, 'in an intimate atmosphere' as it
said on the posters, there were performances of chamber music, illustrated talks – a few years ago Christian's grandfather had been there
to give an illustrated talk on Amazon Indians – and readings organized by the Dresden District Writers' Association. These cultural
evenings, above all the concerts and performances of chamber music
organized by Uhl, enjoyed a good reputation, attracting people from
the depths of the Erzgebirge and as far away as Karl-Marx-Stadt; the
Waldbrunners were often in a minority in the audience. Subscriptions
and tickets for individual events went out to Glashütte and Altenberg,
the border towns of Zinnwald, Rehefeld and Geising, even hopped
over the frontier to Teplice in the ČSSR, from where a married couple,
fanatical concert-goers, regularly came, were posted to Freital and
Dresden, from where season-ticket holders came by car and bus, went
to Flöha, Freiberg, Olbernhau, to the Western Erzgebirge as far as
Annaberg-Buchholz. All that was the result of Uhl's efforts. During
the school holidays there was an agreement with Waldbrunn's city
transport services that put a bus, a rickety IFA model that was no
longer in service, plus a driver at his disposal to 'undertake cultural
work' in the Erzgebirge district. Uhl never went on holiday, no one
had ever heard him talk about the Baltic or Lake Balaton, of a Free
German Trade Union hostel in Graal-Müritz or the Rest Home for
Outstanding Teachers, no one had ever had a picture postcard of the
Island of Rügen or the Müggelsee from him. In the summer holiday
months and also in the autumn holidays Uhl and his wife, who was a
music teacher in Glashütte, rattled round Erzgebirge villages in the

IFA bus, generally known as 'Oswald Uhl's Music Bus', also called 'Music en voyage' by more poetic humorists, 'making Classical Music accessible' to the children there. But Uhl would have mentioned it to Christian if there'd been a concert in the 'Halls of Culture', for he had not only grown fond of Christian because of his cello playing but also immediately included him in various of his ventures. Also Siegbert and Verena had been too casually dressed to go to a concert. Christian stood motionless, breathing for a few seconds as if he'd just done some heavy physical labour, then held his breath, only realizing he was doing so from his accelerating pulse.

He was on his way to the library. Feeling strangely troubled he left his hiding place, went across the market square, past the church on the other side and the Luther memorial, turned into Seifensiedergasse, at the end of which was the town library, which was in a half-timbered house with maxims written on the gables, a weathercock and the bronze figure of Hans the Soapmaker over the door; it had previously been the guildhall of the soapmakers. He still had twenty minutes, the library shut at six. In the lobby, where they had the issue and return desk, the grey-haired librarian was talking to an apprehensive young member of the Thälmann Pioneers, who had brought back a series of 'Digedags' comics in what, from the sharpness with which the librarian was expressing her disapproval, must be a terrible state: 'chocolate stains' and 'dog-eared pages' she groaned as she leafed through the copies. She made a note on the boy's file card and Christian knew that that was it for him, he'd never be allowed to borrow 'Digedags' comics from the library again. Sabine Winkler came and took the books Christian had brought back. She didn't resemble her sister at all, no one who didn't know would have associated the two of them. Sabine had blonde hair, hidden at the moment under a batik headscarf, outside she'd take it off and show everyone her Mohican hairstyle. She wore studded jeans, a biker's jacket one of her father's patients had given her in exchange for an invaluable ABBA disc and a less valuable one of Oscar Peterson

from the Amiga jazz series with the orange 'J' on the sleeve, and a pair
of men's boots a couple of sizes too big she'd bought in the 'For the
Young Man' section of the Centrum department store in Dresden.
Sabine Winkler called herself the 'first punk in the Godforsaken dump
of Waldbrunn'. For her Christian, just like her sister and her parents,
was a 'bornor', a 'boringly normal person'. She called him Chris, which
for him was the most horrible of his nicknames; it made him think of
Chris Doerk, a pop singer of the 1960s who, with her 'canned-roses'
voice, sang with the state-certified heart-throb of schmaltz, Frank
Schöbel, and acted in two DEFA film comedies. Summer film festival
on the Baltic coast, wicker beach chairs in orderly rows, the half-mast
red ball of the storm signal. A tent cinema, food counter, buffet consisting of plastic dishes with limp cucumber salad. A provincial group
playing in the communal dining room and in a book, *Sally Bleistift in
Amerika* by Auguste Lazar, from the holiday-camp library he'd found
a love letter . . . His memories were interrupted by Sabine: 'Hey, Chris,
we close in fifteen minutes and I'm buggered if I'm going to stay on
later, like I did last time, just because you can't get your arse in gear.'

Christian nodded and went off to the farthest corner of the library,
where the philosophers were sleeping. He tried to repress thoughts of
Verena and Siegbert by forcing himself to study the titles of the books;
they were extremely boring- and dry-sounding titles with lots of Latin
words in them; he found what he was looking for, in a dusty corner
with especially boring- and dry-sounding titles, but he needed a few
of them to prepare for a big class test in civics in which they would
probably be unable to 'waffle', but would have to 'present facts'.

'Hey, Chris, what's up with you, you're not yakking on at me the
way you usually do!' Sabine slammed the issue date on the stuck-in
sheet inside his books. 'My god, what dusty tomes we have in here!'

On 1 May the flags were out all over Waldbrunn. A member of
parliament and representatives of the district Party committee and of
the local base of the Soviet armed forces were standing on the platform

that had been set up in the market square; row upon row of the pupils of the Waldbrunn schools marched past the waving representatives of the people. The gigantic Karl Marx head, on which the Association of Young Artists of the Maxim Gorki schools had been working up to the very last minute, was shining on the canvas sheet rising several metres above the platform, a totem skull made from five kilograms each of gold and silver paint, a mythical ancestor on a sail, the sail of Thor Heyerdahl's *Kon-Tiki*, Christian thought, who was walking in a row with Jens and Siegbert. A raft floating towards the sun. They swore at the weight of the banner, ten metres long with the slogan: 'We dedicate all our strength to building up our socialist Fatherland' and supported every two metres by a pole. When the wind freshened, the five pupils had to lean against the poles with all their strength, the banner billowed out and flapped like the wings of an unruly dragon. Drums rolled, at the front there was a band of cymbals and shawms with drummers and their oompah-oompah, Christian could see the staff whirling and gleaming. Now fanfares sounded beside the platform; Fahner shouted orders into the microphone and the praise of the future, in which there would be no more exploitation and oppression, never again, brightness for evermore, burst from a thousand young throats. Fahner proudly announced the statistics, the loudspeakers hummed; unmoved, as if separated from the procession by a glass wall, the church bells suddenly rang out; the schoolchildren were sweating.

Now every lesson seemed to consist of demands. Frau Stesny looked at her charges with concern as they devoured their supper in silence, running their forefingers up and down the text of books on the table beside them. When she ordered lights out at ten o'clock, they switched off the lights in the rooms of the eleventh-grade classes and counted to a hundred, by which time Frau Stesny would be too far away to see that they'd switched them back on. Schnürchel demanded essays on Soviet films, sometimes they watched one in class: they were always about the Great Patriotic War, about patriotic women partisans, who, duty-bound, resolutely took up their rifles; about soldiers in an almost hopeless situation that they still managed to overcome thanks to their truly superhuman determination and their unwavering class consciousness. Engelmann fluttered and ploughed his way round the class, checking dates of the Comintern, the differences between absolute and relative truth, the role of productive forces in developed capitalist and socialist society. Uhl demanded they learn to sing 'The Peat Bog Soldiers' and 'I Heard a Sickle Sweeping'. Dr Frank demanded presentations about the reproduction mechanism of ferns. Only Hedwig Kolb, who taught German and French, seemed not to demand anything. She would come into the classroom like an absentminded elf, stand wrapped in thought, her hand still on the door handle, unconcerned by the noise of the pupils hurrying to their desks, look in delicate puzzlement, the class register and material for the lesson clamped under her upper arm, at a patch of brightness on the floor, a little sunlit plate on which she'd perhaps discovered a few goblins sticking out their tongues at her; then she came to again, checked the distance to the teacher's desk – she made Christian think of a gazelle that some magic spell had placed on a frozen lake – put down her books and took out a handkerchief with crocheted edges to clear her ever slightly runny nose. This was no explosive snort, no trumpet blast such as that made by Engelmann, who didn't use a handkerchief of normal size but a red-and-white-checked flag that made his trouser pocket bulge as if he had an apple in it; with Hedwig Kolb it was a gentle clear-out, quiet and dry; there was a blue giraffe embroidered on the handkerchief that seemed to be begging their forgiveness. Christian recalled the different ways in which the class would fall silent: with Schnürchel abruptly, a silence that came after murdered noise; with Frank at first the noise grew even louder when he came in because as class teacher he was bombarded with questions and problems; Uhl mowed down the conversations with a thunderous 'Silence!' and it was only with Hedwig Kolb that it was a silence that opened up, as if the voices were a tangle of woodland plants that drew back as she stepped forward. The Writing Fairy picked up a piece of chalk and wrote the topic for the class on the board. The class waited; Hedwig Kolb turned round and let her clouded gaze tap along the rows of pupils, as if she had to ascertain whether the class was the same as at the previous day's lesson, whether a few students had not suddenly changed into grown-ups who would stand up and, instead of talking about delicate things like poems that had to be treated with care, turn to serious activities of direct use to the national economy – hammer a nail into a piece of roofing felt, for example; her eye paused here and there, lingered reflectively above the head of a pupil, as a watering can pauses over flowers while the hand holding it hesitates: one more, two more, or even three more drops? Will they help or harm? Then the eye moved on, concealing its doubts in undifferentiated, though not indifferent, friendliness. Although Hedwig Kohl did not adopt an authoritarian pose, she possessed authority and was respected by the pupils. Things were different, however, with Frau Kosinke, the equally gentle, absentminded, forbearing English teacher. No one took her seriously, the pupils imitated her quirks behind her back and laughed at her. In the other subjects hierarchies had quickly established themselves within the class: Verena and Hagen Schlemmer, a taciturn, gangling beanpole with metal-rimmed glasses and skin that looked as if it was only just out of the home laboratory, were the best in mathematics, Schlemmer and Falk Truschler in physics, in which Verena seemed to have no interest whatsoever, Siegbert and Christian in English, Svetlana in Russian and civics, Reina Kossmann in chemistry, Heike Fieber was the pride and joy of the art teacher, Herr Feinoskar. With Hedwig Kolb, however, all the pupils showed a desire to shine; to write the best essay was difficult, there was a lot of rivalry, to be praised by Hedwig Kolb was like receiving an accolade. Christian's essays had twice been adjudged the best, perhaps that was what had led to Verena's allusions to his supposed snootiness. The first time

was when they had to write about Büchner's play *Woyzeck*; Christian
had put the class-war interpretation to one side and showed himself
more interested in power and impotence in the play, setting out his
essay as a dialogue in blank verse to be acted out. Hedwig Kolb had
asked him if she might keep the essay and put a hectograph copy on
the noticeboard, which made Christian very proud. Verena, Svetlana
and Siegbert too had been annoyed at this and made tart comments on
his essay, especially on the lines that didn't quite work . . . Siegbert
had also twice had his essay adjudged the best; Verena once ('Repro-
ducing impressions', she'd written about a picture in the IX Art
Exhibition, 1982, in the Albertinum in Dresden; Heike Fieber once,
who in German and art woke from the trance-like daze in which she
flowed through the other subjects. Like a large, velvet-fingered seaweed, Christian thought, like something transparent spreading out in
a clear lake. Fluid, like the paint in a watercolour. Heike fascinated
him, her thoughts seemed to run along different tracks from the usual
ones. It occasionally happened that she put her hand up; Hedwig Kolb,
taken aback by this unusual activity, immediately called on her to speak,
but Heike ignored the question set and said, 'I've just been wondering
what the consequence would be if everyone had blue ears.' Then her
arm slowly sank down, she shook her shock of hair back into place, a
characteristic gesture, as if she wanted to get rid of something, recur-
rent troubled dreams, something that ran counter to her snub nose and
the hundreds of freckles on her face, she looked earnestly and thoughtfully at Hedwig Kolb, who, equally earnestly but with a hint of
astonishment, looked back: 'Yes, Heike . . . but is that possible, have
you read something about that?' In this essay Heike had taken the
option of choosing a topic of her own and written: 'Everything comes
through juices. If something goes wrong, then it is because there is
something wrong with the juices. Blood is a quite special juice, Goethe
said. There is a vertical juice axis and a horizontal juice axis. Then
there are the juice shops and there are also crimes against juice.

WE LIVE IN THE AGE OF CRIMES AGAINST JUICE.'
There followed, in the middle of her essay, a drawing, a brilliant tangle
of coloured lines, snakes with arrowheads pointing at each other – in
the distance the scribbles resolved themselves in a sad bearded face.
'We must fight against the crimes against juice' was written underneath.
Hedwig Kolb asked to be allowed to keep that essay as well. She had
marked it 'quite outstanding' but didn't put it on the noticeboard. In
brackets she had added, in red lily-of-the-valley handwriting: 'Unusual
combination of word and image.'

28

Black and yellow

Revolving record, Meno wrote, *for a few seconds Niklas Tietze's hands
remain over the bobbing undulation of the disc (and I heard the musical
clock: Dresden . . . in the muses' nests / the sweet sickness of yesteryear
rests), it's dark in the room, only the spotlight over the turntable is on and
is dispersed, spun together and dispersed again by the rippling rotation, as
if a manikin were sitting at a spinning wheel spinning straw into gold;
Niklas takes the needle over the edge of the record, it still pauses, a tiny
stiletto ready to strike, a little hook that would grab the music, as I imagined
when I was a small boy, by the scruff of the neck, peel it, as I still sometimes
think now, out of the groove like a copper engraver's burin cutting hair-lines
out of the metal plate; shadows wandering over the photographs on the
music-room wall in Evening Star, where I'm visiting Niklas; photos: time
captured in shade and light, pre-war Dresden, the interior of the second
Semper Opera House, the chandelier seems to be covered in snow, the Belle
Époque sitting in the boxes; then, framed and mischievous, his lady-killer
dimples frozen in silver bromide, Jan Dahmen, the Dutch conductor of the*

Dresden State Orchestra; portraits of singers, Martha Rohs and Maria Cebotari, young, misty-eyed, Torsten Ralf in costume as Lohengrin, the Knight of the Swan, Mathieu Ahlermeyer as Don Giovanni, Margarete Teschemacher, all the photos signed in faded old German handwriting, we will hear their voices over the surge of the orchestra, over the rustling curtains of dust and oblivion that have settled on the moment of performance, music from the sound archives; voices, Magelone in the well of time; doors open in the faded wallpaper, stained from burst pipes, of the music room in 10 Heinrichstrasse, I remembered: the steam engines in the Museum of Transport were unmoving, the cars and railway carriages and the sedan chair of the town council sedan bearers, Anne and I holding father's hand, he said: Come on, we're going to practise our seeing; the Reichsbahn loco-motives with their empty tenders and red-painted wheels, the wheels must keep on rolling for victory, the connecting rods spun no more yarns of speed and singing rails, the Blériot aeroplane was gathering dust in the wire fet-ters by which it was hanging from the roof of the hall, melting in the hiss of the record —

Niklas Tietze was a strange man. He was a doctor, one of the rare GPs with their own practice; it used to belong to Dr Citroën and was on Lindwurmring, next to the Paper Boat, Bruno Korra's second-hand bookshop, and the Roeckler School of Dancing. After deportation, which he was the only member of his extensive family to survive, and the end of the war, Dr Citroën had returned to Dresden and taken Niklas on as his pupil; he revered his teacher and had not changed anything in the practice after Citroën's death, with the result that it quickly became old-fashioned. Meno hardly ever heard him talk about medical matters. His interest was in music, especially the Dresden Opera. There were hundreds of photos of singers and musicians, many with personal dedications to Citroën and Tietze, who were known throughout the city as music-lovers, hanging in the rooms of the prac-tice and, like Citroën, Niklas preferred to play opera arias to his patients rather than listen to their complaints. For him the present seemed to be one possibility among others in which one could live, and not the most pleasant; for which reason he avoided it. He possessed a lot of books, they were mostly slim volumes and bore the sign of a ship under full sail in a finely inscribed circle which made Meno wonder why the publishing house, if it had chosen the ship as its sign, was called 'Island' publishers: was the ship the island? the island a ship? did the island consist of books the ship was carrying as cargo? Niklas didn't ask those questions, for the books were something different for him than for Meno: time capsules, their presence alone seemed comforting. In the evening, as the clocks struck and night had fallen, Niklas could sit on the chaise longue and take one of the Insel volumes out of the bookcase that was kept specially for them: *Mozart's Journey to Prague*, with a cover of pale-blue silhouettes, Gothic script, the pages yellowed and with the mild smell of bread that old paper has, then he would leaf through it, get caught up in the story here and there, nod, adjust his large glasses with the square lenses, read in a murmur a few favourite passages he almost knew off by heart; no one was allowed to disturb him, not Gudrun, who was in the next room reading *Leben-Jesu* pamphlets or watching television, nor the children who were occupying themselves at the other end of the corridor.

Mused and listened, Meno wrote, *sat leaning forward, his aquiline nose cut out of the darkness, a musician's posture, attentive and at the same time waiting as if, instead of the notes he had anticipated in his inward ear and often played before, different passages had suddenly come, smuggled into the score on a whim of the demons of the opera, scattered over the familiar melodies as a goblin might drop sneezing powder over a devout and quiet congregation, in his mind's eye he could see the conductor, Furtwängler, writing his cloud-quiver-script with his baton in the electrically charged air, tagged with treble and bass clefs, drum rolls and harp glissandos, over the heads of the orchestra waiting, spellbound, for their entry; the entry*

melted out of his loops, somewhere in his conjurations a drop formed, ran
into the musicians' fingers, made the contact for the circuits, which were
charged up to trembling point: that is, the entry was accepted, the leader
decided to harvest it from Furtwängler's arabesques: to pick it, and he, the
leader who, like a herd stallion, had shaken off the paralysis, pulled the
whole pack along behind him in a mighty, sonorous chord, the audience,
deeply moved, nodded, put handkerchiefs to eyes, hands over left breasts,
held its breath: Furtwängler! The way he's done it again! The way he gets
the orchestra to blossom out, inimitable, that softly cushioned precision, the
severely delicate sound, hallowed German profundity! Who has mastered
the violin bows, tamed the trombones, encouraged the viola and its often
misunderstood elegies, knows the vagaries of the oboe reed, of the horn player's
plight when the water level rises in his French horn, Furtwängler reaching
the moment of free will and with it the breath of the orchestra, sound comes
into being: gauged with the fineness of precision scales –

When Meno came it could happen that a conversation would develop
about the book, which Meno thought overrated, and Fürnberg's *Mozart-*
Novelle, which he thought underrated and better written than the story
by the more famous writer. 'Fürnberg,' said Niklas in his sonorous,
slightly husky voice, '"The Party, the Party, the Party's always right"'
and nodded reflectively. Meno gave him one of the eight copies of the
little book that he'd bought before they disappeared off the shelves.
Niklas leafed through it, praised the drawings by Prof. Karel Müller,
Prague, conventional pen-and-ink vignettes, expressed appreciation
of the classic Garamond type, was taken with the oval of faded green
surrounding the silhouette embossed on the linen cover: Nice, very
tastefully done, really: fine – they put their love into the books – and
put it away 'for later'.

However, Meno wrote, *is it Furtwängler? Doors in the walls of the music*
room (and heard the musical clock: Dresden . . . in the muses' nests / the

sweet sickness of yesteryear rests); there: the 'Starvation Line' after the war, the *11* as it pants its way up the Mordgrund laden with firewood and horse fodder, with double basses for the State Orchestra concerts in the 'Culture Barn' in Bühlau, the 'Starvation Line': like each one of its predecessors, shadows swallowed up in the whirlpool of time that set off up the hill from Neustadt Station pulling goods wagons full of washing, a weary animal, groaning under the burden, to whom the driver shortly before the summit of the climb mutters curses, encouragement, threats, his right hand on the control lever, his left on the brake wheel, his view restricted by the musical instruments lashed to the luggage van, the passengers travelling on the footboards, the musicians, who, in a tight cluster, are clutching the rail of the luggage van, the 'Starvation Line' on which it stinks of sweat and sour breath from rumbling stomachs, which won't be silent in the 'Culture Barn' either, admission one briquette, the audience, hungry for culture, emaciated faces marked by deprivation, squeeze up close together, shivering in their uniform coats, in their often-mended trousers, made up out of rags or potato sacks, in Bruckner symphonies the trombonist is so weak his breath gives out; the record surges on, voices from the past will wake, already stained with the rust that has crept over the vinyl disc during the decades it spent resting 'with the treasures' – in Niklas's record cabinet under the Gothic clock, we called it that because the little pendulum looked as if it was swinging in a tiny abbot's parlour; 'with the treasures': hoarded in Trüpel's archive, under the Philharmonia record shop or with Däne, the music critic of the Sächsisches Tageblatt, who every week in his apartment on Schlehenleite, in which music and paper had grown rampant, played samples of his discoveries to the Friends of Music; the rust in the voices the rose-rust fungus of the Dresden Opera and perhaps that's Schuch, in a sea-green fantasy uniform, raising his baton, perhaps Hofmannsthal is sitting in the semi-darkness of one of the boxes in front of which reality has put on colourful clothes and a ship with huge yellow sails glides past the window of childhood, where the shadows play –

*

'For later.' After that Meno would sometimes go home depressed, hurt, telling himself that his gifts of books were basically unwelcome to Niklas, at least that was the impression Meno had; Niklas seemed never to read them and they didn't talk about them the next time they met. He's not a book person, Meno thought as he made his way home in the dark, he's only interested in books as beautiful objects, things to fill up his bookcase, in precise rows and nice to look at behind glass, and what is important is that they must have a good binding and fine paper – not the content. Goethe is the most important author for him, but only because he's the most important one for everyone up here and he's the most important one for them not because they've grappled with him, studied and examined him, measured his sometimes hack-neyed aphorisms against their own reality and experience, but because he's recognized and sanctioned, because he's the favourite yes-man of the bourgeois, which, deep down inside, is what everyone up here is, their chief councillor, generalissimo of opinion and prince of sentiment; because he's king of their hoard of quotations. Basically, Meno thought, Niklas is only interested in music and in historical recordings of that music. The deader the better! And that's what they're all like up here, most of all they'd like to live in old Dresden, that delicate baroque doll's house and pseudo-Italian wedding cake. They sigh, 'The Frau-enkirche!' and 'The Taschenberg Palace!' and 'Oh, the Semper Opera House!' but never 'Outside toilets! Those magnificent, cholera-friendly sanitary conditions!' or 'The Synagogue!' or 'What liberating living conditions they used to have, ten people in a tenement apartment!' They never say 'the Nazis' but 'the low-flying bombers' and they love to quote Gerhart Hauptmann telling them it was a 'morning star of youth shining on the world' and that 'anyone who has forgotten how to cry will remember at the destruction of Dresden' and then Meno would thump a tree with his fist in exasperation. It was true and yet he was being unjust. How terribly vain you are, he thought. Just because he didn't sufficiently appreciate the book you gave him. How very

seriously you take yourself . . . Not good at all, vanity impedes observation and doesn't serve truth, Otto Haube used to say when we were
using microscopes. When Meno encountered the Kaminski brothers
he bade them an exaggeratedly cheerful 'Good day' and ignored their
nods and smiles. He extended his return to his book- and silence-filled
living room, made long detours in order to call up his hours with
Niklas – Gudrun was seldom there, nor Reglinde or Ezzo – again.

And in writings about the depths of the ocean, Meno wrote, *strange creatures appear outside the windows of the houses, Gempylus, the snake
mackerel with eyes that look like metal discs staring in at the window;
creatures with blind, milky spheres instead of eyeballs and long beards
dangling like dead men's bootlaces; the shadow of the thousand-armed
creature, which writes the depths grey, Architeuthis, the giant that Poseidon
chained and whose sucker-armed tentacles wrap themselves round the houses
like tamarisks, penetrate the plaster and masonry like ivy, embrace them
in order to suck, tie themselves on tighter with each year's growth ring, edge
forward with the same intensity that builds up the silence, scale by scale,
into something else and with which the needle comes down after Niklas has
wiped the yellow cloth over the disc one last time then turned the lever beside
the counterbalance, and I had the feeling I saw a counter-movement at the
same time, as if the needle over the revolving record were aspirating the
air, which looked like a surface, deepening it to a navel, to a funnel the sides
of which continued to grow the deeper the needle went, that had perhaps
already stopped but, since the sides of the funnel were curving up and
the gyrating current had already reached the part of the room beyond the
little Moorish table, on which the record player stood, was touched by the
counter-revolution of the disc, an electric fluid out of which single sparks
flew; trickling neurotransmitters, as if there were a dam between two bodies
which, if they approach within a certain distance of it, comes under immense
pressure, cracks and begins to sweat out what it contains; the surface tension*

of the water bending towards the approaching foreign body, an anticipated contact, the needle was swept away by the disc as it grew into a wave, a moment that Niklas awaited with bated breath, his hand still over the tone arm in a beseeching gesture, ready to intervene swiftly, while my eye was drawn by the intensifying hiss into the room, this beautifully cut room with the green wallpaper that went back to the woman who had built the house, a singer at the Dresden Opera; the wallpaper could well be as old as the century, the submarine fauna worked into the pattern showed glints of cop-per in the cloudy light that was feeling its way from the record player, Niklas never asked me about the animals I was familiar with from Ernst Haeckel's Art Forms in Nature, *how often as a student had I stood in the Jena Zoological Institute looking at the paintings, done with academic precision, delighting in the colours, the shapes of all the siphonophores, Portuguese men-of-war, of the* Desmonema annasethe, *which looked like a Belle Époque headdress floating behind the glass-fronted bookcases with bound volumes of specialist journals; the sapphire slipped into the track and, in the spark-spinning of the disc, in the travelling ripples of the light, all the Radiolarians and Amphoridea on the walls began to move, the crys-talline floating monstrances and spiky little Gothic chapels deepened, as I was familiar with from Malthakus's postcards, when the bell over the door had fallen silent and Malthakus, whom it had summoned, had returned to the back of the shop to bend over a catalogue and a stamp collection, his special magnifying glass, sometimes a watchmaker's lens, over his eye, to estimate its value, London and Prague again, Herr Rohde? he asked when he greeted me, or would Rapallo do? I've recently acquired some decent stuff – and he would leave me by myself with half a dozen sepia picture postcards, a bay, Mediterranean vegetation, at the side a house with an oriel window on pillars with an ancient-Greek look, a statue in the gar-den, I still had snow on my hat and coat, felt I could still hear the street noises, the snow melted and as it liquefied the lines of the house, of the statue, melted too, the sails of the schooner in the bay began to flap, the waves, which looked as if carved out of marble, broke and rolled foaming onto the beach – waves that swell with the orchestra's first note ringing out from the nightshades of the music room –*

Meno crossed Turmstrasse at Lindwurmstrasse, which, running parallel to Bautzner Strasse, bounded the district on that side and bordered the wood on the slope going down to the bridge over the Mordgrund, on which the tram set off for the climb up to the district. On the right, in a dilapidated corner building, was the Steiner Guest House; as with most houses, its plaster was cracked and large patches had fallen off; the red bricks that were exposed looked inflamed, all that was left of the mortar between them was individual lumps, you could pick it out from under the bricks with your finger. The bricks themselves were riddled with holes, as if tiny insects had been eating their way through them, porous as rusks, some gave off gas escaping from leaking pipes, making the plaster that was left bulge and blister, and where dampness seeped through, mould spread like leprosy. There was scaffolding on the Turmstrasse side of the building, it had been there for months, no workmen had ever been seen on it. There was a lot of scaffolding like that round the city and the rumour was that this was a cheap way of supporting the buildings. In the summer the windows of the Steiner Guest House were open, you could hear the clatter of typewriters on the first floor, where there was an office dealing with commercial correspondence, a branch of the Council for Mutual Economic Aid. On the fourth floor, above the rooms of the guest house, Frau Zwirnevaden had two rooms, in one of which she ran a silhouette atelier where she made little figures for the Dresden Cartoon Film Studio. There were rumours about the old woman going round the district, the children were afraid of her and she was rarely seen. She wore black clothes and slipper-like shoes that turned up at the toes, went rat-tat-tat on the road with her boxwood stick with a lion's head, stopped at the shop windows and now and then would crook her finger enticingly.

One of the rumours, put into circulation by the two clockmakers in the district, was that all the clocks would start to chime when Frau Zwirnevaden went past and everyone agreed there must be something to it, for the two clockmakers, Pieper and Simmchen, known as 'Tick-tock Simmchen' because of his delicate health, were deadly enemies and had no time for each other. But Simmchen, whose cousin of the same name had a jeweller's on Schillerplatz, had raised his hands in fervent protestation as he said to Barbara, 'I swear to you, Frau Rohde! All the clocks at once and it was only five to twelve!' When she passed this on at the furrier's, Barbara did point out that Simmchen's nose had been as red as a live coal, but added that during their conversation Simmchen had had to blow his nose several times. Another rumour came from Frau Zschunke, who ran the greengrocer's, popularly known as the 'dump', on the corner of Rissleite and Bautzner Strasse, a woman of around forty, pink and chubby, single and entirely devoted to the extraterrestrial theories of Erich von Däniken, and who was always dropping things because, with an 'Ooh!' and 'Aah!', she would be ter-ribly alarmed by something and, gasping for breath, clutch her imposing bosom. The young folk of the district took full advantage of Frau Zschunke's nervousness with plastic jumping spiders, which could be bought for ten pfennigs in König's toyshop on Lübecker Strasse, pref-erably when Frau Zschunke was taking fruit out of a basket to put it in a metal pan to weigh it with weights that were kept in rows in a wooden box. One day Frau Zschunke had come running into Bin-neberg's cake shop across the road, where, evidently distraught, she had kicked up a great fuss among the customers queuing up for their cake and coffee: 'that Zwirnvaden' had 'prodded' all her cabbages with her spider's fingers, muttering angrily about their poor quality (at which some of the more cold-hearted ones waiting by Binneberg's collection of Dresden custard pies nodded), then handed her two cab-bages, one white, one red, at which she, Frau Zschunke, had first gone to the white-cabbage till, then to the one for red cabbages – but suddenly saw faces in the cabbages! One of them looked like the son of Herr Hoffmann, the toxicologist from Wolfsleite! – Dr Fernau recommended she didn't restrict her diet to Golden Delicious since that kind of apple only contained certain vitamins.

In the winter the blinds on the windows of the Steiner Guest House were kept lowered. When you came from the tram stop the lamps were shimmering like green and yellow eyes through the venetian blinds, which were crooked and rattled in the wind, behind them shadows went to and fro. An officer who'd been on the general staff of the Afrika Korps lived in the guest house, next door to a stocky man with a thick moustache dyed black and a shaven head who called himself Hermann Schreiber; rumour had it that in reality he had a Russian name and when he was young he'd been a spy for the Tsarist secret police, the Okhrana, and at the same time for the Red troops that were still operating underground. Romanians, Poles and Russians often stopped at the guest house on their way to the Leipzig Trade Fair; the parties they held with the foreign-language secretaries of the branch of the Council for Mutual Economic Aid, the Russians sometimes also with officers from the hospital of the Soviet forces, formerly a sanatorium, were notorious. Opposite the Steiner Guest House, on the other side of Turmstrasse, was the Central Depot for Automotive Spare Parts. On days when a delivery was rumoured, long queues formed outside. Meno knew nothing about cars but he'd once joined one of those queues on a kind of heroic impulse, having been gripped by the lust for possession. Among those patiently waiting he'd seen Dietzsch, the sculptor, who'd asked him whether he'd registered an application for a car. That was indeed the case – 'But you're never going to drive, are you, Herr Rohde? Sell me your application – I'll pay five thousand marks!' For that was the first thing many GDR parents gave their children when they reached the age of confirmation or the secular youth dedication: to register them for a car that they would be able to buy after a wait of fifteen years, when they'd long since finished school, an

apprenticeship or a degree and would be earning enough to buy one . . .
A registered application such as Meno's, which dated back to the
early seventies, was worth its weight in gold. But Meno was suspicious (moreover his application was to go to Christian) and in a fit
of acquisitiveness had joined the queue and purchased two exhaust
manifolds for a Polski Fiat, a Wartburg shock absorber and three complete sets of windscreen wipers for a Saporoshez. After that there was
'Nothing left', Herr Priebsch, the sales assistant, raised his arms apolo-
getically, not even one of those wires twisted into a tube with a sucker
on it in which an artificial flower from Sebnitz in Saxon Switzerland
could be attached to the dashboard of a Trabant or a Wartburg, of
which there had actually been a delivery that day. Herr Klothe, who
lived above the Rohdes in the Italian House and was next in the queue,
took it with the composure people had developed for such cases: 'I
presume you haven't got any beds left?' – 'No,' replied Herr Priebsch
in his blue-grey overalls, 'we only have no winter tyres here. You'll
get no beds in the furniture shop. And you won't do any better over
there either, since we don't make beds here any more.' – 'You don't
say. And why is that?' – 'Simple, they're not necessary! The
army's on peace watch, for the intelligentsia life's a bed of roses,
the politicians sleep abroad, the pensioners in the West, the Party
never sleeps – and as for the rest of us, who wants to sleep on a bed of
nails?'

Meno had stored the treasures he'd bought in the cellar. They'd
turned out to be hard currency, for Stahl, the engineer, had managed
to exchange the Wartburg shock absorber for a new mixer tap for the
communal bath of the House with a Thousand Eyes.

– And as the needle, Meno wrote, *lifted the music out of the record and
Niklas's expression changed, the tension, the strain giving way to a happy
calm, coloured photographs, woven from the fiery threads of the music,
began to appear inside my head, slid up with jellyfish-soft outlines, stayed*

there for seconds in which I saw them clearly, like pieces of a retina filled with life, consisting of life; a tide washing up things, the sea's furnishings: round pebbles ground smooth, stones with holes in them, a seaweed-entwined lump of amber with an insect trapped inside it, a drowned moth, the swell rises, rolls up its gifts, rears into a glassberg and when it reaches its peak the movement stops, the projectionist presses a button and the breaker curdles; and then I saw the musicians moving, the spider made of violin bows going up and down simultaneously, saw faces, pockmarked with the wine-scale of time, drifting among the Amphoridea and medusas of the room, listened, on another evening as we sat over a hectographed booklet in landscape format, to Niklas putting names to the faces and recounting anecdotes: 'the one with the long neck, standing with his double bass, that's the Parlour Giraffe', 'that one, a ring with a big stone on every finger, in the orchestra they called him Jumbo-Jewels', then the 'flautist, Alfred Rucker', out of whose silver stick the furies of music thundered, 'the greeeat Alfred Rucker, called Typhoon, he blew everything away', and at the word 'great' Niklas was already leaning back, extending his chin, half closing his eyes behind his square glasses in order to give the adjective, which came from the depths – of his voice and the history of music – that dreamy quality that I heard from the Tower-dwellers when they wanted to characterize some achievement as unrepeatable and superb, as irredeemably lost in the past, in more glorious and perhaps also more sublime ages, as a 'marvel'; and I sometimes thought that the Tower-dwellers themselves moved through time in a similarly strange and typical way: their future led into the past, the present was merely a pale shadow, an inadequate and stunted variant, a dull rehash of the great days of yore, and sometimes I suspected that it was good when something sank into the past, when it expired and perished, that the Tower-dwellers secretly approved of that, for then it was saved – it was no longer part of the present, that they shunned, and often it was precisely once something was dead that it suddenly shot up into the heaven of their esteem, while they hadn't even noticed it while it was still living. – The music seems to be flowing out of the tips of Niklas's fingers, which are white

*because he wears gloves; I can see the signed photograph of Max Lorenz
on the wall over the piano, his arm pointing, the knight is looking into the
distance, his voice, revelling like a bare blade, ascends, makes its thrust,
the disc spins, heavy with cobwebs, sparks crackle, the label in the middle
a yellow magnet, and as the music rose, I saw Niklas growing restless again,
a person for whom it was the elixir of life, who would not be capable of
breathing for long without it, and I thought it would be the end of him, of
his world, if some circumstance should cut him off from music, from his life
of longing to be in music; the fishes in the room surged up and down, moved
like handkerchiefs on a line the wind was plucking at, the rose under the bell
glass seemed petrified –*

The old houses with their crumbling plaster . . . The outlines began
to fade, the goods wagons full of ash from the hospital heating plant
rumbled; the deep throbbing noise, the origin of which he couldn't
explain, started up, perhaps it came from a transformer or a ventilation
system; he had heard it often before on his evening walks.

'Still out this late?' It was Judith Schevola. He started and automatically took a step out of the thin light a street lamp cast over the
Lingwurmring/Mondleite junction. 'You gave me a fright. – What
are you doing up here?'

'And if I were to say, I live up here?'

'I'd reply: In that case I'd have noticed you.'

'Aha, people know each other in the gold-dust district.'

'What did you call it?'

'It was my grandmother's name for it. Sometimes she would take
me by the hand, we'd come over here and she'd say: When you grow
up, girl, you must marry someone from here. From the gold-dust district. Where the professors, doctors, musicians all live. But today I've
just come for a walk. I take the 11 up here, breathe a few lungfuls of
the bigwigs' precious air then buzz off back home. – I bring greetings
for you.'

'From Herr Kittwitz?'

'Your tongue's shedding its needles, be careful when you swallow. Herr Kittwitz lives in Gruna. – No, from Herr Malthakus.'

'You've been to see him. He's married, as far as I know,' Meno said with a smile.

'Now you've got that I-don't-think-that-would-interest-you expression.'

'And you the men-are-all-the-same look.'

'Malthakus and I are just in the process of making friends with each other. A nice old bird. He's very precise, but his clocks have a heart, if I can put it like that.' She took out a packet of cigarettes, offered Meno one. He declined, gave her a light. 'May I accompany you to the tram stop?'

'Thanks but I'd prefer to walk with you a while, if you've no objection.'

He accepted that Judith would now be walking beside him without a flicker of emotion and didn't look back when she went on ahead to the junction, stopped and listened, her face turned towards him, though he would have liked to look round to see where she had so suddenly appeared from; in his mind he went through the building entrances he had passed, but at this hour they were usually closed and he would surely have heard a door creaking; of course, he had been deep in thought, and perhaps she had come silently from farther away. The outlines of the buildings had now been erased, the few lighted windows were patches of yellow hanging in the darkness. Meno crossed the road, the hats in Lamprecht's shop window, on which the greasy light from the lamp at the junction cast a faint glow, looked like the visible part of beings that had a rendezvous with the wigs in the Salon Wiener but it wasn't quite time yet. Schevola held her nose: 'Rotten eggs, yeuch!'

Past Lukas, the tailor's, past the Roeckler School of Dancing and the drizzle of tremolos from a piano worn to a state of thin-skinned irritability.

It must have had a toothache, Meno wrote, *that piano in the dance hall on the first floor, it sounded so out of tune and out of humour, and beside it the Nosferatu fingers of a cellist, carved in stucco from feet to elbows, were twined round the fingerboard of his snuffling cello, the pianist's bald head glinted in rhythmical harmony with the palm-court-soft upanddown of the violinist's bow; he was standing apart from the cello and piano, in bib and tucker, in the metallic shimmer of formality, beside a Monstera with mustard-yellow leaves, sending tangos slithering across the chessboard dance floor to the sandpapering steps of the beginner's course, his left hand churning out vibratos, which elicited from the pianist, with a paper flower in his dinner jacket, blank looks at the ceiling where putti and winged hippopotamuses, which only admitted to being angels at a second glance, were playfully teasing each other amid rosy clouds; the music from* Tannhäuser *sprouts over the decor and I could touch Niklas now, only his body is present, it's frozen and would perhaps not feel anything, the spell is upon him and the second Niklas, the one only he knows, that inhabits his body, has gone.*

This tremolo at the peak of tunes that had become dull from repetition aroused in Meno memories of his schooldays and of dancing classes he had attended in vain. The fog that had come up from Grünleite, a blind alley off the Lindwurmring beyond the junction and where Arbogast's chemical laboratory was situated, was now creeping past Guenon House and down Mondleite in the direction of Bautzner Strasse.

'Shall we go on?' Meno indicated the fog.

'Why shouldn't you smell of rotten eggs when you get home?' Schevola replied. 'What do they actually produce there?'

'No one knows that apart from the Baron and his colleagues. As far as I'm aware it's being kept secret. There are all sorts of rumours.'

'Well let's walk on. – Tell me about yourself.'

'There isn't much to tell.'

'You're very reserved. You don't say much and observe a lot. People like that often have a lot to say.'

'That's your opinion.'

'You don't seem to be particularly adventurous,' she commented when he stopped as they approached Grünleite. Now it was stinking like a rubbish tip.

'It all depends where you'd look for adventure.'

'I bet you won't seek one here and now.'

'Don't bet too much on it.'

'How about there?' She pointed down Grünleite, to the steaming building of the chemical laboratory.

'And if there are guards?'

'Then I could have bet quite a lot on it.'

'We have to be cautious, I don't know what'll happen if we get caught.' He had a quick look at what they were wearing. 'You're too well dressed for what we're about to do. And your coat's too light-coloured, people will see you.'

'No they won't. This is a reversible coat. Just a mo.' She took it off and turned it inside out so that the dark lining was showing. 'Do you know your way round here?' She put on a provocative smile.

'We'll soon see.'

Grünleite was lit by the faint light from a few houses that belonged to the military hospital, Soviet officers and doctors lived in them. One of the windows was open, radio music spilling out of it. Schevola crossed over to the other side of the road that was in the shadow of a high wall. The masonry was badly affected. Meno took out his penknife and stuck it in the mortar to see what it was like. The blade went in right up to the handle without him having to exert much pressure. There was barbed wire running along the top of the wall, but in some places trees stretched out over it. They must be part of the woodland the Kuckuckssteig passed through from Arbogast's chemical laboratory down to Bautzner Strasse and Mordgrund. Fabian Hoffmann, the son of the toxicologist from Wolfsleite, had explored it together with his gang, to which Ina Rohde and Fabian's sister, Muriel, belonged, he'd told Meno about weathered statues and an impenetrable wall of overgrown wild roses separating Kuckuckssteig from the wood of the Chemical Institute. Schevola turned to the wall and stifled a cough. The fog was like damp cotton wool pouring out of the laboratory entrance, which, like that to Arbogast's house, consisted of an elaborately wrought gryphon, here surmounted by a steel arch with black and yellow bands. With that stench Meno wondered how anyone living here could leave their window open, they couldn't have very sensitive noses or were used to much worse. Schevola peered through the gate. 'No one to be seen. Best down there,' she said, pointing to the end of the blind alley where there were a few garages with dustbins beside them, 'if we roll them up to the wall we ought to be able to manage it.' The yellowish fog, which now stank of fish soup, came up to her knees; the expression on her face was both alert and eager, and she seemed to see it reflected in Meno's look: immediately the expression vanished, as if she had let it drop and run a fine, swift eraser over it. 'Just look at this.' She held up her fore-finger, showing Meno a black blob on the tip. 'What do you think that is? Tar?'

He rolled the shiny black blob between his thumb and forefinger, it was pliable, like the plasticine from which he'd made models at school: cosmonauts or Young Pioneers, Laika, the dog in the space capsule, the cruiser *Aurora* after a model in *Komsomolskaja Pravda*. When Meno wiped the blob off on the wall, it left a black streak. 'Pitch,' he said, trying to rub out the streak with his shoe. 'Be careful, there seems to be more of it.' He drew Schevola away from the steel arch. The pitch was running over the projecting wrought-iron feathers of the gryphon, dripping in viscous threads down from its beak, which looked like an oozing, upside-down gondola, onto its lion's claws, filling the gaps in its wings, joining up in braids that in the thinning mist spread out on the ground in puddles that made contact, paused briefly, as if they had to communicate with each other, then merged, seeming to be in constant, searching motion, supplemented from the gate-arch where the black substance was now pouring down in long stretching sheets that tore off with a soft 'plop'. Schevola regarded her shoes, frowning, gave Meno a disgruntled look.

'Well?' he said. 'We'd better get a move on.'

'Hmm,' she replied.

'You suddenly don't feel like it any more?'

'My lovely shoes . . . from the West, genuine Salamander, they were expensive! Judith, you're . . .' She gave herself a light slap on the face. 'No more of that. They're ruined now, so let's get on with it.'

'You can manage it?'

'Now you sound like your boss. All you need is the mirror and comb.' She gave an amused snort. With the supple swiftness of a cat she was on the garage roof in seconds. Picking up a few pebbles, Meno followed, he too without a sound, which drew a soft whistle of appreciation from her. 'To be honest, I was going to ask you the same question. I seem to have underestimated you.' They lay down flat on the roof and stared into the darkness in front of them.

'Watch out,' Meno said; they took cover behind a tree beside the roof. A searchlight flared up, scouring the terrain, they squeezed into the shadow of the tree trunk when it went across them.

'We can use the tree to get back out,' Schevola whispered.

'Keep down.'

Once his eyes had adjusted to the darkness again, Meno threw a pebble. 'If they've got dogs out there, they ought to come now,' he whispered. Nothing happened. He couldn't hear anything apart from the distant throbbing and the goods wagons carrying ash from the hospital heating plant; the radio had fallen silent.

'They just chuck their ash down the hill,' Schevola whispered. There was the hiss of a boiler, the slam of a door shutting, otherwise it was quiet.

The searchlight felt its way back, boring a tunnel of dazzling brightness in the dark, rolled over the garage roofs, abruptly shot up into the treetops, whitewashed the walls like a decorator painting a room systematically, suddenly jerked upwards, came back down in unpredictable swerves; cautiously Meno and Schevola raised their heads once the tunnel of light receded.

'Did you see that?'

'Yes,' she murmured. 'Let's turn back.'

29

Blue vitriol

The record turns like a ship's screw, the steamer Tannhäuser *casts off, taking me into different times (and I heard the musical clock: Dresden . . . in the muses' nests / the sweet sickness of yesteryear rests), on deck Captain Tenkes and Sinbad, Osceola and* Four Men and a Dog – in a Tank, *films we'd seen in the Round Cinema, in the Faun Palace, in the Schauburg in Neustadt, where it smelt of alum, where the fumes of Chlorodont toothpaste from the Leo Works mingled with the chocolate aromas from the factories on Königsbrücker Strasse; the curses of the coachmen with the disgruntlement of misunderstood wits ('Shall I tell you what Dresden is? This emirate of floor polish and rubber plants?'), cinemas with threadbare seats and display cases with film posters and reviews cut out of* Eulenspiegel *that only I studied while Niklas had just a dismissive wave of the hand for them, and the boys, Christian, Robert, Ezzo, Fabian, had already joined the queue outside the cinema, they knew all these posters, Belmondo's boxer's face, attractive, cold depravity in Alain Delon's handsome features, Lino Ventura's sly, brawny correctness, which went with inspectors who, earlier on, before they were inspectors but honest criminals in their prime, had been made an offer, people who couldn't give up smoking because they had seen things that went beyond the parting in their hair, their employee's overalls, their briefcase; they have no illusions about the fact that the past will catch up with them and make them pay for what they've seen; they know that any dream they've put down will never be carried through, even if it's wait-ing unchanged, even if they can take off their jacket, touch it and look for the point where it was interrupted; cinemas that had a supporting programme and the DEFA* Eyewitness *flickered across in front of us, a black-and-white sun, in earlier years the UFA* Newsreel *and different people in the cinemas to whom the wordsmiths spoke, they seemed to be providing the soundtrack to a law, those voices in the Olympia Picture House, in the Capitol on Prager Strasse, in the Stephenson and UT Picture Palaces, the law that the world is eternally divided into friend and foe, that there will for ever be command and betrayal, victory and defeat, and that the light is with the common people, the cruiser* Tannhäuser *put out to sea, radio location finders and beams of light probed the night-dark waters, villas under the Soviet star where the toxic roses grew, and sleep and brown snow came down on the town and acid rain from the brown-coal heating plants, glue crept into the river from the cellulose factory, and Pittiplatsch waved from the television tower and the Sandman scattered oblivion, the Bols ballerina danced at the apprentices' celebration in the slaughterhouse to folk songs on a hurdy-gurdy and the tinkling of a dulcimer, and they shouted 'pisspot' beside the blood-channel, the bolt still stuck in the head of the wriggling pig, and 'piddlebowl' at the steaming dishes on the table where, following ancient custom, the master slaughterman adds meat dumplings to the caul-dron of gruel; fiddles and friction-drum on the Titanic-, panic-deck (and I heard the musical clock: Dresden . . . in the muses' nests / the sweet sickness of yesteryear rests) . . . benumbed, perhaps that's what it was, Niklas sat motionless by the record player on evenings when the snow sank down or the light of a summer's day made the pear tree outside the window glow, I had the feeling that the music sucked him dry and at the same time filled him with the delicious essence of oblivion, the record was a spindle with nettle threads that flew out and clung fast to him with barbed hairs, twined themselves tighter with every revolution and pulled his inner being over: where to? there, there . . . I asked myself how it was possible for a person to live so much in the past, to be able to wipe away the present with an inner flap of the hand – I didn't see one outwardly, Niklas didn't position himself in front of me and raise his arm in a theatrical condemnation of everything that was in the light and shade of our day and that we summed up as 'now' – a gesture that was a brusque 'no', made with all the unmitigated fury with which a grown-up capitulates in the face of their fear; how could he declare this 'now' non-existent – was he a fool who'd made an agreement and would pay for it and could do as he liked until then? – I sometimes thought he'd met the Mistress of the Clocks and that she had granted him a clock face that went differently from those she had allotted us . . . but what was he doing there, in the past? What was it for him? What was it for the Tower-dwellers? Was he present when I thought of him, visited him, imagined him sitting alone at night in the music room listening to opera voices from long-ago recordings that he preserved and perhaps Trüpel or Däne as well, perhaps this or that person we knew nothing about (but one day they would join Däne's Friends of Music, it had to happen, and Däne suspected there were these still undiscovered connoisseurs, that was why he liked to put special recordings, rare performances, hidden works on his programme in order to lure them), and when Niklas was going home from Lindwurmring, his worn midwife's bag in his hand, his beret pulled down sideways over his cheek, the way he approached with dignified steps, gently waving his hand up and down (the echo of music from a performance?), his expression one of strict absorption, still not having noticed me, then I thought: Yes, that's him, one from up here, one of the Tower-dwellers: who spoke of the past as of a Promised Land, surrounded themselves with its insignia, heraldic badges, its postcards and photographs, what was that past to them? A constellation of names, a Milky Way of memories, a planetary system of Sacred Writings and the holiest, the Sun, was called* OLD DRESDEN, *written by Fritz Löffler (and I heard the musical clock: Dresden . . . in the muses' nests / the sweet sickness of yesteryear rests) . . . and I remember evenings in Guenon House: you went in through the scratched swing door, walked down the wall-to-wall carpeting, time-bleached to the colour of ailing rosewood and fraying at the edges, that daily roused Herr Adeling's displeasure, past potted plants at the stair corners that reminded me of nicotine-yellow octopuses sulking away for years in the formalin jars of zoological collections, felt crumbling plaster decorated with scenes from the* Mastersingers, *had accustomed yourself to the panes of glass in the corridor doors held together with Ankerplast adhesive tape – and ended up facing an index finger, pale as a fish and knotted with arthritis, over which a conspiratorial smile appeared: 'Come in, Herr Rohde, we're just looking at it.' There it lay, on a damask-covered table, on a carved lectern, polished to a shine with walnut oil and meticulously rubbed dry, spreading its paper pinions like angel's wings: the book; come all ye that are heavy laden and refresh yourselves and find rest in the unalterability of my dwelling, come and restore your souls. Open at: the Zwinger, photograph of the Cabinet of Mathematical and Physical Instruments. 'It was built between 1711 and 1714 as the first of M. D. Pöppelmann's pavilions during August the Strong's period as Imperial Regent, as is proved by the use of the imperial eagle in the decoration of the pediment frieze.' Voices, at first husky but then lubricated by coffee with cream, cherry brandy and Dresden custard pie, reading out, forefinger sliding along the lines, fingernails boring into individual letters, reading glasses telescoping up and down over the paper: 'Proved, Herr Rohde, did you hear: proved. You will recall the little discussion we had in our circle here on that very topic. Herr Tietze and Herr Malthakus were both here then and agreed with me while you, Herr Pospischil, were a little wide of the mark, as we can see.' Herr Sandhaus ran his tongue between his teeth, a soft slurping noise could be heard, executed a slight turn of his upper body to the left where Ladislaus*

Pospischil, born in Vienna, stranded in the chaos of a chaotic century in Dresden, hotelier, wine waiter, dealer in second-hand goods, briquettes, agent for concert artists, presently manager of the Schlemm Hotel on Bautz-ner Strasse, scrutinized one of Frau Fiebig's exceedingly brightly polished silver spoons: 'Proved, Herr Pospischil. It's in Löffler, I've also taken it out of one of my older copies for you. We also talked about it with Herr Knabe.'

Herr Sandhaus handed the hotelier some sooty typewritten carbon copies, with precise references to place of origin, page and line number added and, as far as the appearance of the imperial eagle in the pediment frieze of the Cabinet of Mathematical and Physical Instruments was concerned, an enlarged photograph. 'There you are. Herr Löffler has also personally confirmed everything to me. I always say: in the next edition he must improve the appearance of the imperial eagle. Just a little. But there it is. It does indeed appear in the pediment frieze, does our much-lauded bird. A drop of liqueur, perhaps? That custard pie's delicious as usual, Frau Fiebig, tell me, where d'you get it?'

'What d'you think, from Wachendorf's, of course, and all through personal connections, y'know. What'd we do without 'em, as my late husband used to say.'

'You're absolutely right there, my dear Frau Fiebig, ab-so-lutely right. You get out of your car, which doesn't exist, go across to the shop and buy till your bags are bursting from the shelves creaking under the load of goods on offer, that's life, isn't it? I think we can regard that topic as closed, your very good health, Herr Pospischil, and no hard feelings, I hope.'

'A company of ghosts,' Hanna called the inhabitants of Guenon House, 'I hope you're not going to be part of it.' The yellow fog drifted through their rooms, leached the substance out of the houses, made the Dresden sandstone porous, left a crust on the roofs, ate away at the chimneys, made the putty round the windows crumble, but the Tower-dwellers listened to Tannhäuser *in seven different recordings and compared them to each other in order to argue about which was the best, the greatest, the most beautiful, the standard recording; they went over the measurements of the destroyed Courland*

Palace, in thought and on paper, while their apartments were decaying, the
wood of the roof beams rotting, and that was something I knew from the whole
city, this bullet-riddled baroque boat in the bathtub of the Elbe valley, this
shimmering foetus trapped in the womb of its own, parallel time; everywhere I
went it was the same: coffee morning, custard pie, OLD DRESDEN

Tannhäuser's ship sailed away and Frau Fiebig made roses bloom just as
others light candles, they were made of fabric, these roses, clouded in aromas
of eau de Cologne, dust, furniture polish, the delicate pink had only survived
in the shadow of the innermost petals, it was the colour of dancing shoes
you find in the loft beside bundles of letters, pastel-coloured paper in lined
envelopes held together with dried-up silk ribbons; the gesture of invitation
with which Frau Fiebig showed her guests into the apartment made the
flowers in the room burst open, made the crocheted antimacassars less dis-
tant, brought out the sweetness of the little porcelain chimney sweep, the
flirtatious looks of the fake tomes in the bookcase beside the little cupboard
in which Frau Fiebig kept her late husband's war medals and chocolate
sweets, they twined round the scores on the piano, their covers decorated
with roguish little cherubs and arbours where kneeling huntsmen were sing-
ing their hearts out, they budded round the canaries' cage, these fabric roses
from the fancy-goods department of Renner's store, where Cläre Fiebig had
worked as a sales assistant; the guests were shown into the parlour, Herr
Sandhaus, who worked on Coal Island for the council of the East District
and perhaps therefore felt obliged to provide the Party newspaper, put a
whole week's copies of Neues Deutschland, *neatly folded and smoothed*
out, tied across and down with string, on the part of the table intended for
them, straightened up after a moment's pause for thought, looked to see
whether the chocolate girl in the reproduction over the cupboard was rousing
herself from her motionless repose, stepped aside to allow Herr Adeling to
place a week's worth of Sächsische Zeitung *on* Neues Deutschland, *the*
edges and folds perfectly lined up, then came Niklas with the slimmer

Sächsisches Tageblatt, *Lukas the tailor and his wife with the* Sächsische
Neueste Nachrichten, *Herr Richter-Meinhold with the even slimmer redtop*
Junge Welt*; one kilogram of newspapers; 's that everything? Frau Fiebig
asked, concentrating as she checked them on her fingers while Herr Adeling
put on his waiter's gloves, straightened the stack of paper, tied it up, lifted
the pile between thumb and forefinger and went over to the window, which
Frau Fiebig opened, Herr Adeling's outstretched arm, his left hand with
the white glove, the package could be seen in the gathering dusk over the
Lindwurmring, with hands joined at the fingertips and heads inclined, the
company waited for Frau Fiebig's grandfather clock to strike, ding dong,
six o'clock, at the last stroke Herr Adeling's fingers snapped open, the pile
of newspapers thudded into the open dustbin outside the house, Frau Fiebig
took off the tablecloth, Herr Adeling sketched a bow to the neighbours,
patted his gloves to clean them before picking them off by the fingertips and
putting them away, followed Frau Fiebig and the others as they went to
wash their hands, filled glasses with liqueur and turned his attention to the
geometry of the pieces of cake on the Meissen plate shimmering under the
glass cover on the little cupboard, assessing their respective weight with a
silver cake-slice; Herr Sandhaus brought the lectern ('genuine Bieder-
meier!'), waited for Frau Fiebig, who put a lace cloth over it; she opened
the Löffler and said, with the syllable-sculpting emphasis with which the
Dresden bourgeoisie distinguish contempt from esteem, low from high,
garbage from roses: Right. And no-w. We COME. To cul-chure.*

The Tannhäuser *caravel,* Tannhäuser *radio, echo-sounding the depths
of time, black-and-yellow the record spindle.*

*Winter 1978/79: the central heating fails in Johannstadt and threatens
to burst in the severe frost, people mock the confidence shining out of the
black-and-white faces in the newspapers, curse the* subbotnik, *the work
for the benefit of the community on Saturdays. Teams of the Free German
Youth go out to open-cast mines in the Lausitz and help units of the National
People's Army bring in coal for Dresden.*

'They're supposed to have three wagonloads. They say they're supposed to come first. Specially to heat the Palace of Culture. Have you heard anything, Herr Tietze, after all you are involved?' Herr Sandhaus rubs his hands. 'I've actually managed to get two tickets.'

Niklas leans over the table, lifts his spoon over Black Forest cake and whispers, 'Böhm's going to conduct, his first public appearance with the State Orchestra here since forty-three. How humiliating if they can't manage to heat the Palace of Culture.'

Frost patterns spread all over the stairs. Sleep. Sleep in winter, the cold sleep at the revolving records on which the hoar frost crackles. The lamps grate, they're old, from before the war, the wires are worn and oxidized, in some houses in Neustadt they leave the bulbs on because they might not go on again if they're switched off, a faint, flickering light in winter, and the whirr of the fan heaters, cubes swathed in cast-iron in which a wire twisted into a snake heats up until it's red-hot, later there are the orange heaters from Hungary in the city's bathrooms, kitchens, book-rooms smelling of ash.

Tannhäuser's ship sailed away,
    and Herr Richter-Meinhold, a gaunt man in his seventies, formerly a producer of maps, walkers' maps among others (yellow-and-red covers, the paper mounted on linen, geographies you never heard about at school: the Hultschin country, the Iser mountains), that people guarded like treasures and that never stayed long in second-hand bookshops, especially when they showed the territory of the GDR ('the only ones that aren't falsified, you know!'); Herr Richter-Meinhold raised his hand (that Dresden gesture, that 'that's the way it is, I'm afraid, everything passes, we can't do anything about it') and said, 'It's really cold, like all those years ago, during the bombardment. By the way, Herr Tietze, Hauptmann's later writings are full of hidden emeralds. Not necessarily diamonds. But certainly emeralds. I knew his secretary, Ehrhart Kästner. He was a librarian in the Japanese Palace and he lived up here. No one remembers.'

'*No.*'

'*I actually met Hauptmann. It so happened that my aunt was in the Weidner Sanatorium, from where he observed the air raid. I visited her and saw him. Unforgettable, that Goethe noddle he had.*'

'*Anyone who has forgotten how to cry will remember at the destruction of Dresden.*' Sandor, on a visit from Ecuador, ten years old at the time of the bombing, turns away in silence. They remember. '*Everything used to be quite different up here. Nothing's what it used to be. No comparison. No, no. Today it's Dresdengrad. A province of the UGSSR: the Union of the German-Speaking Soviet Republics.*' Ruins are still standing after years and years. Electrification along with bombsites, ugly dual carriageways, draughty tenement blocks, fifteen-storey blocks rammed into the famous, now gap-ridden Canaletto skyline. And in the old days: '*We used to be a capital. A royal capital! Yes, well . . . in the old days . . .*' They sigh. Photos are taken out. The view of the Frauenkirche from the Brühlsche Terrasse. A lamp with needles of light in Münzgasse. The conjurations began, the Dresdeners' longing for Utopia, a fairy-tale city. The city of alcoves, of quotations from Goethe, of music-making in the home, looks back in mourning to the world of yesterday; their tiresome, eroded everyday life is supplemented with dreams: shadow Dresden, the illusion behind reality flows through its pores creating hybrid beings à la E. T. A. Hoffmann. Double exposures. Tannhäuser sang, sang of the Army Museum, where needle-guns were aimed at Napoleon, Saxony's days of splendour and soldiers marching to '*Preussens Gloria*', uhlans' lances and cuirassiers' helmets of the Belle Époque (and I heard the musical clock: Dresden . . . in the muses' nests / the sweet sickness of yesteryear rests), wraiths groping their way in the gas war of the trenches, the blue-cross gas of Ypres, the sappers danced, Verdun, Doctor Gottfried Benn, a poet going round the morgue, Otto Dix painting animals in human form and the shattered glass of the photo of the old Frauenkirche, Dresden . . . '*I will give this pearl the setting it deserves*' . . . The Synagogue burnt.

*

How does one drink wine in Dresden, the city with the guilty smile? Tann-häuser's ship sailed away, to Canaletto's archipelago . . . Bells sound on 13 February. From all parts of the city people pour to the centre, place candles by the devastated Frauenkirche, two great ruined walls stretching up into the sky like arms begging for help. The boys' choir of the Church of the Holy Cross sings Mauersberger's Requiem. *Driving home at night, in the Hoffmanns' Lada or the Tietzes' Shiguli: in this perspective the 'Woda' indicator flashing across the dashboard is as big as the birch tree on the gloomy bulk of the ruined castle and looks like a phosphorous needle rest-lessly scanning the sooty remains of the stepped walls where by day suites of rooms and the lines of paintings burnt into them can still be made out.*

'The Great Hall in the castle, what splendid concerts there were there. And kings ate from the swan dinner service, at a table with a thousand pieces of finest Meissen china,' Frau von Stern, a former lady-in-waiting, would tell them. 'Chandeliers hanging down like coral reefs of light! They tumbled down, lumps of glass on the floor, melted and fused over people, the faces, the faces.'

'Florence on the Elbe, such an Italian softness, a smiling city!'

'And the social situation? How did people really live back then? A beau-tiful façade for a lot of misery? Weren't there 100,000 out of work in 1933? Weren't the murderers among us?'

'Oh, that's enough. If they hadn't elected the Nazis, it would still be smiling.'

'You can't be a proper Dresdener if you can say things like that, you don't love your city.'

'For you love's glossing over things, is it? Come off it! Sometimes I think you need a bit of that. Basically you wouldn't even be happy if the old Dresden were suddenly to reappear!'

'I'm not going to say one more word to you!'

Who is talking? The Tower-dwellers, they talk at the soirées and Frau Fiebig's roses bloomed, had the fragrance of dust, eau de Cologne and furniture polish, shining clean silver spoons dipped into the Dresden custard pie from Wachendorf's bakery, outside the frost patterns grew, creeping over the river and the stairs and the clocks; in the evening the Tower-dwellers would sit in their apartments telling each other stories, they told each other about chandeliers found in the loft or in forgotten chests ('somewhere out on the prairie'), covered in soot and unsightly – for the layman, but in their eyes immediately valuable for the engraved detail that careful, expectant rubbing had brought to light; the Tower-dwellers were familiar with every screw of these chandeliers and if they weren't, they became uneasy, for they had to know where every screw came from, had to know every hand that had worked on the chandelier and I sometimes asked myself: What's the point? as I watched them. What did it give them, what adventurous form of satisfaction, to know the name of the master craftsman who had cut that tiny screw? Was it despair at the incompleteness of the world, despair at a missed detail that might cause everything to collapse?

Target coordinates N51°03′/E13°36′. At 9.55 p.m. a radio announcer in the Albertinum cellars reports the approach of large formations of Lancaster bombers of the Royal Air Force . . . 'I will give this pearl the setting it deserves!' The first marker bomb falls on Ostragehege, the grounds of a slaughterhouse in a bend of the Elbe between Friedrichstadt, Übigau and Pieschen. At 10.13 p.m. the first bombs explode in the centre of Dresden

to collapse, to destruction, to loss, was it despair at the passage of time?

and hear the voice of a Dresdener whose right hand, as if suffering from compulsive checking, keeps running up and down the fastened buttons of his coat: 'I loved my city but . . . I survived because it was destroyed,' said Herr Rosenbaum after a long silence.

The Tower-dwellers . . . Do they want a hermetically sealed world? Was their god the god of the sphere, of clock faces, of ships?

Star of the Sea Evening Star sank, the needle went into an idle loop, the fishes and Amphoridea on the wallpaper froze, doors closed, the

photographs on the walls clouded over, Max Lorenz lowered his sword, the
roar of the waves of time died away, the good ship Tannhäuser *ran aground*
  Niklas remained in his frozen posture, I stood up to turn the record over
(and I heard the musical clock: Dresden . . . in the muses' nests / the sweet
sickness of yesteryear rests)
Meno wrote

30
Young woman on a windless evening

Calm: the day seemed to be drifting like a boat after one last stroke of
the oars, no longer straining, not yet at its goal, the sky, in which only
a few light-as-a-feather cloud-eyebrows were raised in astonishment,
expanded to balloon-blue, into which the roofs of the old Academy
stuck up like sail-fins; in the park beneath it watercolours of green, the
white and purple rhododendrons, were already submerging into twilight. For one moment, when a shimmering burst of swallows had
dispersed in the saffron-yellow above the treetops in front of the Dermatology Clinic, there seemed to be an equilibrium of all the balances in
which the sense impressions of the late afternoon had risen and fallen:
the clitter-clatter-clump, clitter-clatter-clump of a nurse's hurried steps;
the metallic pink and white of coats and caps; patients in bathrobes
strolling round the park with X-ray photos under their arms; doctors
with their hands buried in their coat pockets, in which they moved
them impatiently as soon as a nurse came within greeting distance;
the scent of apple flowers drowsing down from the gardens on
Händelallee; the whine of the electric carts; cars puttering past
on Akademiestrasse.

Then it returned in waves and orders, only for moments, his weary body, the piercing brightness of a lamp aimed at him, demands, a student who nodded to him and, as if he wanted something from him, stopped as if uncertain what to do; it lopped off the threads back to childhood that had fluttered out for a long second, Josta's letter, that Richard felt for. He had stood up and left without having given the student an encouraging look; he hadn't been in the mood for discussions about lectures, for proposing a topic for a thesis or whatever else the young man might be concerned about. They were always coming with requests, these young people, and they were always similar, and if they wanted to be surgeons then they had to be neurosurgeons or, even better, heart surgeons; and if they had questions, they were almost always complicated and almost never simple; they didn't seem to be interested in why a violin bow was able to produce a certain note, why all rivers flowed when the Earth was round and consequently there ought to be some rivers that were faced with an uphill course. Or why you could carry a letter from a woman round with you and not know whether you should be pleased or afraid, and why a letter, nothing but a piece of paper, could weigh so heavy.

He didn't read through the letter again, he knew it almost off by heart. Why don't you come, why do you stay away from me, why do you avoid me when I'd like to see you and our paths cross in the Academy, Lucie's asking after you, we have a right to you as well, I don't know how long I can stand this, you'll have to make up your mind some time or other, or have you had enough of us already, of me, is this your 'just going out to get some cigarettes'?

Richard went back to the clinic. He'd arranged for an operation and had some appointments in the Outpatients' department for hands. After the operation he went to the ward to have a coffee and something to eat. His secretary was still there. 'You go home,' Richard said, 'you can just as well do the operation reports tomorrow.'

'Frau Fischer from Administration rang. She'll call again.'

'I'm not in.'

'She said it was important. It's about Doctor Wernstein.'

'I'll be in hand Outpatients in five minutes. She can call me there if she likes.' Outpatients was full and he let the telephone ring. He would have ignored it but the nurse assisting him picked up the phone. 'For you.'

'Can we meet, Richard? Have you read my letter?'

'Good afternoon, Frau Fischer, what is it?'

'Can I wait for you, outside Administration today? It's less notice-able than in the park, if anyone should see us,' Josta said quickly, perhaps expecting him to object in the hackneyed phrases concealing the secret language they'd worked out for telephone conversations when others were present; 'It's a bit awkward at the moment' meant '8 p.m. at the place you suggest.'

'It's a bit awkward at the moment.'

'Or you can come to my place. You can always say things took longer than expected in the clinic.'

'Could you ring me again tomorrow? Thank you.' That meant: no. He hung up.

It was still light when Richard left the clinic. He had taken his time changing, even though it was getting on for eight when he finished with the last outpatient; he had even wondered whether to have a shave, but had put his razor back in the cupboard when it occurred to him that there was a discrepancy between a long day at work and a smooth chin smelling of aftershave that might arouse doubts and further sus-picion. He recognized Josta from a distance, she was standing on one of the forsythia-framed paths by the Eye Clinic talking to a few younger doctors who were pulling in their stomachs. He was furious that she hadn't stuck to their agreement, at the same time he felt a sudden spurt of jealousy when he saw her coquettishly playing with her ponytail, throwing back her head, sniffing, as if casually, at the forsythia twig she had in her hand when one of the doctors went up and down on his toes as he spoke. Of course, she saw me ages ago, Richard thought, and now she's making it clear to me that she only needs to snap her fingers. Josta left the doctors and headed, about fifty metres in front of him, for the Administration building. She was wearing a light dress and had her coat over her arm. He knew that the picture would stay in his memory for ever: a young woman on a windless May evening, the folds of her dress swaying to and fro, a slow-motion image amid the blurred brightness of the other passers-by.

'Why are you so late? Why did you make me wait? Have you any idea when we last saw each other?'

'You shouldn't phone me at the clinic.'

'Is it asking too much that I'd like to see you?'

'Josta . . . they know about our relationship. I'm having my arm twisted. They'll make it known, if –'

'Who is "they"?'

'– if I don't collaborate with them.' He swallowed, exhaled audibly. 'Write reports, gather information.'

She frowned, looking past him. He observed her out of the corner of his eye and was astonished at how differently from Anne she reacted; the expression on her face swung between arrogance and coolness, as if she had not so much feared as hoped for something like that, as if, he thought with alarm, she had wished for it.

'One day you'll have to make a decision.' Her voice broke. 'If you leave me, I'll kill myself.'

'Really?' That was the cynic speaking that every surgeon recognized inside himself, the sceptical, brutal detachment to which no one was immune after a few years in the profession. He regretted it immediately. 'What's this about Wernstein?' he said, incapable at the moment of finding any way of apologizing.

'He's going to have problems,' Josta replied icily, 'perhaps because of you? How did you put it? Reports, information –'

'Josta –' He felt for her hand, she pulled it away. 'I didn't mean it like that. Please. I'm sorry.'

'Kohler and your Clinic Party Committee have submitted a complaint. Disparagement of socialist achievements,' Josta said after a while.

Kohler. Müller's favourite from the General Department. Very efficient as far as clinic management, as it was now called, was concerned. Apart from Müller and Administration, no one seemed to like him.

'What nonsense is that now?'

'I don't know. But it's on the Rector's desk.'

'What is he proposing to do? Call a meeting, the Arbitration Commission? Dismiss Wernstein?'

'I just wanted to warn you in advance. It could be that this time he's going to have recourse to drastic measures, recently there've been a lot of people from the District Committee here and even from Berlin. There were nasty arguments and one of those characters, you could smell where he came from at ten metres, threatened him openly. Suggesting he was perhaps out of his depth as principal.'

'Come, let's walk on a bit. I don't want people to see us here together. They might think you were letting out secrets. What is it this Kohler actually wants? Have you seen his complaint?'

'Only the reference and a couple of lines of the letter, they were clear enough. – He wants to get on. Next month he's being transferred to your section and Wernstein's in his way there. They're suggesting he be taken out of the rotation system and transferred.'

'They want to get him out of the clinic?'

'Müller's already talked to the head of Orthopaedics in Friedrichstadt.'

'And I know nothing about it. Damned schemers. – Will you wait for me outside? I'll fetch the car.'

He parked in a side street not far from her flat.

'Won't you come up? At least for a few minutes?'

'You know I can't'

She said nothing and stared at the street. Some girls were playing

Chinese twist, a three-wheel lorry loaded with barrels lurched past. 'Do you love your wife more than me.'

'Leave it.'

'Why can't we be together . . . Always having to hide, always "You know I can't" and "Leave it" and "Goodbye" . . . Recently Lucie was talking about you in the kindergarten, that you always go away in the evening when you've been to see us. "You've got a funny dad," the other children told her.'

'But I told you she was to keep her mouth shut!'

'I can't forbid her to talk, I can't control her all the time.'

No, she couldn't. After all, it was quite natural for a child to talk about her father; what would he have said if Josta had told him that Lucie never spoke about him. 'Give her my best wishes.'

Without looking at him she squeezed his hand and got out. He wound the window down. 'Josta!'

She stopped but didn't turn round. 'Please forgive me.' She nodded. The girls playing Chinese twist raised the elastic. A window was opened above them, a man in braces over his vest put a cushion on the window seat and scrutinized the girls.

'Another thing I wanted to say –' He fixed his eyes on the man's unshaven face; she didn't react. 'A lovely dress you've got on.' She stayed there for another second, then slowly put on her coat and walked off. The man stared after her. On his way home to Anne, Richard stole a branch of forsythia from a garden.

Next day was the consultant's round, a white-coated gaggle swept through the North wards. The duty assistants held X-rays for Müller and his senior doctors to see, the ward-doctors murmured explanations, nurses took the bandages off the cuts with sterile tweezers and gave gloves to the doctors inspecting them. Müller kept looking at his watch, snatching the X-rays out of the assistants' hands, stabbing at them with his forefinger and throwing them down on the beds. Even the patients could feel the tense atmosphere, lay there rigid, arms along their sides, looking back- and forward between Müller and the doctor reporting to him. By one of the patients' beds there was a glass bedpan with a splash of urine left in. 'Is it beyond the bounds of possibility for the nurses with responsibility for this room to empty the piss out of the brandy snifter when the consultant is doing his rounds. What kind of slovenliness is that, Nurse Lieselotte?' The nurse in charge of North I turned pale. 'But there's that proverb about master and man,' Müller went on. 'Herr Wernstein can't find the charts for two patients, lab results are missing, the abscess in Two is merrily gathering pus . . . What a casual approach to medical treatment in my clinic!' Richard raised his hands in protest. 'The man in Two has been put back by the anaesthetist, we are aware of the problem, but he's on Falithrom –'

'Since when,' said Müller, cutting him off, 'since when, Herr Hoffmann, does an anticoagulant stop us performing our duty as surgeons and lancing an abscess?'

'Herr Professor' – Trautson nodded to Richard – 'I had arranged for the operation, but the anaesthetist flatly refused –'

'Then we'll administer the anaesthetic ourselves, goddammit! An abscess on the thigh doesn't require a general anaesthetic and you're surely not going to tell me the man risks bleeding to death from having an abscess lanced!'

'He's at risk of sepsis if we don't operate,' Kohler pointed out.

'Well, then you do it!' Richard burst out. 'The coagulation is poor and so far the antibiotics have kept his temperature under control –'

'So far,' said Müller. 'I'm not happy, Herr Hoffmann, I want to see you this afternoon.'

No one had ever heard such criticism, in front of all the doctors and nurses, of the senior surgeon. Richard felt like a schoolboy who had been given a dressing down. The gaggle went on to the next ward. Trautson drew Richard aside. 'What on earth can have got into the old man? He knows perfectly well that the anaesthetists are right. And all that fuss just because two patients' charts are missing and, anyway, they're already being operated on . . .' Trautson shook his head. 'Oh, great, we've got something coming. In your place I wouldn't take it to heart, Richard. Who knows what's really behind it?'

'Can I have a word, Herr Wernstein?' Richard asked. They went to the ward day-room. 'Now will you for God's sake tell me what you've been up to. If I'm going to get hauled over the coals because of you, I need to know why. It's Herr Kohler's complaint I'm talking about.'

Wernstein told him. As so often, it was about reality and what one made of it – and the barbed-wire fence between the two.

'And then I told him to mind his own business.'

'Told him?'

'In so many words. That smart-arse – we know what sepsis is as well.'

'And he said?'

'That he'd been observing me for a long time, I was a troublemaker.'

'And you said?'

'That the troublemaker was of the opinion that political bunkum never cured a patient.'

'Hmm.'

'Well, something to that effect.'

'Instead of bunkum you –'

'. . . said something else, yes.'

'My God, Wernstein, have you gone mad?' Richard got up and started to walk up and down the room. 'You know the old man's relationship to Kohler. And anyway.'

'I know,' Wernstein growled. 'Them and their fucking Karl Marx Year.'

'The question is, what do we do now? I've been told that the complaint against you is being considered. Kohler's being transferred to North I next month and Müller's spoken to the head of Orthopaedics in Friedrichstadt.'

'In other words . . . they want to get rid of me.'

'Perhaps not only you, Herr Wernstein. I'm afraid I won't be able to protect you. I suggest that for the time being we wait to see what happens at the meeting this afternoon. Perhaps I can get the Rector to do something.'

'I'm sorry, Herr Hoffmann. And thank you.'

'Off you go now – and keep up your good work on the operating table.'

Richard called Josta. 'Hoffmann from the Surgical Clinic, Frau Fischer, could I have an appointment with Professor Scheffler? It's urgent.'

'What is it about, Herr Hoffmann?' Josta's voice was cool, she sounded businesslike and uninvolved; it cut him to the quick.

'It's about a colleague in the clinic, Herr Wernstein.'

'Are you in the ward? I'll call you back.' For a few moments he could hear her breathing before she hung up.

The afternoon meeting with Müller was cancelled. Richard went to Administration, where he'd been given an appointment for five o'clock. He had to wait and went out because he was afraid Josta would watch him and try to catch his eye, despite the other secretary working in the office. But he was even more afraid that she wouldn't try to catch his eye. He attempted to concentrate on the discussion facing him, to imagine what direction it might take. He didn't know Scheffler particularly well, the last time he'd spoken with him was about the Christmas lecture. Richard seldom attended the meetings of senior surgeons that were held in Administration and that Scheffler chaired; Trauma Surgery was formally part of General Surgery but almost had the status of a separate department. 'Almost'; it was undetermined, sometimes Richard was sent an invitation to a meeting, sometimes not, and when he was invited Richard found himself with conflicting attitudes to Müller: on the one hand he didn't want to go over his head, on the other, that made him feel like a little boy who had to ask permission for everything. Moreover it annoyed him that, when reading these invitations, Müller would turn away from him and give him irritated responses such as: he couldn't see the point of Administration keeping two senior surgeons in the Surgical Clinic away from their work.

Scheffler was a pathologist and, like all pathologists Richard knew, interested in the arts. He had quite often seen him with his young, attractive wife in the theatre, cautiously applauding so-called problem plays or closing his eyes at arias from Mozart operas. Scheffler smoked, which was unusual for a doctor, especially for a pathologist, who saw the smokers' lungs; he smoked Cuban cigarettes, which, despite the fraternal socialist economic relations, could hardly be bought in local shops. The Rector must, therefore, have his own special sources and he seemed, like many pathologists, to be a hedonist. Dermatologists, psychiatrists, clinicians liked beautiful women, could distinguish good from poor wines, read the latest literary works, quoted Goethe and Gottfried Benn, and loved classical music, especially the piano, which they could often play themselves. Moreover they grew to be old. Surgeons loved beautiful women and beautiful cars, and died at sixty-five when their retirement started. Scheffler, Richard hoped, would be open to discussion.

'I've come to see you about a colleague, Rector.'

'I know. It's about Herr Wernstein, Frau Fischer told me. Yes. Shall we sit down?'

Richard saw that the portrait of Brezhnev with the black ribbon had disappeared and been replaced by one of Yuri Andropov. Scheffler noticed his glance. 'Can I offer you a coffee? Some mineral water?'

'No, thank you. I wouldn't want to take up more of your time than necessary, Herr Professor. Herr Wernstein is –'

Scheffler gave a weary wave of the hand, asked for coffee and mineral water over the intercom. Then he got up and stood, with his hands clasped behind his back, looking at the photos. The telephone rang, but he ignored it. His shoes were of fine, perforated leather and certainly hadn't been made in a state-owned company, his suit was of an elegant cut, Richard wondered if he had things made by Lukas, the tailor on Lindwurmring; Scheffler too lived in one of the villas up there.

'Are you interested in politics?' he asked abruptly, half turning to face Richard. Only now did Richard see that Scheffler wore the Party badge in the buttonhole of his elegant suit. Why not, he thought, Ulrich's in the Party too and Scheffler, as Rector, has no choice. Does he always wear it? I certainly didn't notice it at Christmas.

'I believe one ought to be, Comrade Rector.' Scheffler had turned back to Andropov's smile and gently raised his hand, like a conductor for a *piano* entry. 'Oh, let's stick to academic titles, Herr Doktor Hoffmann, I believe that is what you prefer. – Do you know that they say Yuri Vladimirovich' – he pointed to the picture of Andropov – 'loves jazz? He's also said to enjoy watching films from the West and to read a lot. I haven't asked him myself and you can't believe everything you read in the press.'

Richard wondered where in the press it could have said the General Secretary of the Communist Party of the Soviet Union was supposed to love jazz and liked films from the West. Certainly not in *Neues Deutschland*. Josta brought the coffee – although he had declined there were two cups – and mineral water. Richard drank the coffee after all.

'Thank you, Frau Fischer. Tell the gentlemen from the Ministry I'll call back immediately. – We talked in German, by the way, he speaks it quite well. I believe he can't stand medals, in the past the jingling in the sacred halls was considerably louder.'

'I agree with you, Rector, that the younger doctors as well ought to show more interest in politics, it's just the fact that –'

'– Herr Kohler is the chairman of the Party organization in the Surgical Clinics,' Scheffler broke in mildly, going back to his desk, 'one of the idealistic hotheads among our young comrades, who are always on the attack. But we must win over the doubters, as Yuri Vladimirovich indicated in his last communiqué.' Scheffler scribbled something on a piece of paper, showed it to Richard but didn't give it to him. It said, 'I can't promise anything. But I would like to point out that I'm not a careerist member of the Party.'

'I thank you.' Richard stood up, Scheffler tore the piece of paper up into tiny bits and let them trickle down into the wastepaper bin.

Now Josta wrote lots of letters without worrying that Richard only collected them from the hiding place they'd agreed on – behind a loose brick in the labyrinthine subterranean passages of the Academy – at very irregular intervals; he once found four letters there that had been written in one week. She avoided complaining and making demands, concentrated on everyday matters and little expressions of affection, but Richard sensed that this cheerfulness was forced and felt worried. He wrote that he wanted to see her, on one Thursday before he went swimming, she replied that it wasn't necessary, that he had been right when he'd said she lacked self-control and was taking things too far. She was, she said, too impatient and demanded too much of him, she had let her fears run away with her and through that was endangering their relationship, her excessive fear of her fears was making them come true, like a self-fulfilling prophecy. He didn't believe that reasonable tone. Josta was many things, but reasonable wasn't one of them except on rare occasions. The language of the letters seemed to be a protective sheet, supposedly fireproof, but beneath it there were fires waiting for the whiff of oxygen that would be enough to fan the crazy smouldering white between the lines into a blaze. Once, on a Wednesday, he went to her apartment and rang the bell but she didn't open the door, even though he was sure he heard a noise inside. He wrote a few lines and pushed them under the door. In her next letter Josta reproached him for his lack of caution, on that very day, she said, she'd given her key to an acquaintance who was to look after Lucie because she was being sent home early from the kindergarten; by chance Daniel had found the piece of paper and pocketed it, he'd just happened to go up to get a lemonade out of the fridge, Lucie had come along only a few minutes later with the acquaintance, who would surely have read it. But then I would probably have seen them, Richard thought, I waited by the door for a while and it would have been Daniel who'd made the noise I heard. There was something not quite right about it. He found all this disturbing, and on top of it came the trouble with Müller, who rearranged their meeting, first of all asked him, all innocent, about the Querner painting and then rebuked Richard again, though not for the postponed operation this time – the anaesthetists were unmoved and had supported the trauma surgeons – but because he didn't set a proper example for the political attitudes of his junior doctors. Wernstein had to apologize to Kohler in front of all his colleagues and the nurses but was not transferred to Orthopaedics in Friedrichstadt.

Suddenly the tone of Josta's letters changed, despair, reproaches and fear returned. Richard was up to his eyes in work, there was a doctors' conference coming where he had to give a paper on techniques for operating on the hand; Robert was having difficulties at school, he was now in the ninth grade, the results of which were used to apply for one of the much-sought-after places at the senior high school, and Anne said something wasn't right with Christian; but when Richard tried to discuss it with him, Christian became evasive. Richard put it down to puberty when his son didn't come home at some weekends. At least his marks were all right, Richard had checked with his class teacher. Josta was once more demanding he leave Anne, she had started calling him 'Count Danilo' again, which he didn't like precisely because he was aware that there was something true about the nickname; he didn't believe Josta had the psychological insight and judgement of character to give him the name of the character from *The Merry Widow*; he assumed Josta had only given him it because of some vague similarity to a singer from the State Operetta in Leuben, that she had hit the bull's eye by mere chance and he held that against her. The singer could just as well have played the hero of any other operetta and Josta would probably have chosen the name of that character. He believed she wasn't very observant but secretly he knew he was wrong. Towards the end of May a letter came in which she threatened to turn up at his door some time in the near future and force him into a decision, she wrote about his cowardice, about holidays together, about Lucie and Daniel, then about gas and sleeping pills. Richard didn't take that seriously, the letter had too obviously been written in the heat of the moment, people who actually committed suicide didn't threaten to do so but acted; he'd seen too many such cases in his years in hospitals. And still saw them – at this particular time of the year, in May, the loneliness, the despair, the pain seemed to become unbearable for many people. Josta asked for a meeting, he agreed, but something intervened, he was late and when he reached the place of their rendezvous, she'd already gone. She had no telephone at home; for such eventualities they'd agreed that she would leave a sign indicating where she'd gone: a ball of paper that had apparently rolled under a park bench said – gone home; two crossed twigs – waiting for you at Holy Trinity Church; in the winter they arranged snowballs in various patterns. This time he couldn't find anything. He waited, perhaps she'd gone away for a moment. She didn't come.

'Oh, Herr Hoffmann, are you waiting for someone?' That was Heinsloe, the senior manager.

'Me – N-no. Just getting a breath of fresh air.'

'And quite right too, Herr Hoffmann. Now is the month of Maying . . . You feel a new man, don't you?' Heinsloe rubbed his hands.

'I had a letter from Herr Arbogast a few days ago. Do you know him? He wrote to say that he'd like to work together with the Surgical Clinic, more specifically with your department. I'm sure he'll write to you as well. – As far as your application for funding is concerned, I'm afraid no decision has been reached yet. Have you a moment?' Heinsloe took Richard's arm and drew him along with him in the direction of the Clinic for Internal Medicine. Richard was not at all in the mood for discussions about budgets, equipment or funding for a special room for operations on the hand that he had requested a long time ago and that was presumably what Heinsloe was talking about.

'I really haven't got time, Herr Heinsloe, you must excuse me –'

'You have to go back to the clinic?' He was so unprepared for the question that Richard could do nothing but nod. 'That suits me very well, I was going to come and see you anyway, I can deal with it now. Let's walk along together, it'll save you having an appointment with me.' As he went to the clinic, with Heinsloe's chatter filling his ear, he was silently cursing the chance meeting there, of all places, with the senior manager, of all people. He only got rid of him in Outpatients.

'Oh, and congratulations on the award of "Medical Councillor".' Heinsloe gave him a conspiratorial wink. Richard had no time to reflect on the broad hint, Nurse Wolfgang was waving to him. 'Herr Hoffmann, they've been looking for you. Phone call for you.'

Richard went to his ward. 'A Daniel Fischer, sounded pretty young,' said the nurse who had taken the call.

'What did he want?'

'He just said that his mother had been taken into hospital.'

'Aha. And to which one?' Richard asked, leafing through patients' charts.

'He didn't say.'

'Thank you. Have a nice shift.' It was only with difficulty that Richard managed to control himself and not to dash off. He called Rapid

Medical Assistance from his office and was told that Josta had been taken to Friedrichstadt.

'Why?'

'One moment.' Richard could hear the man wheezing as he got up and rummaged through some papers. 'Suspected of having taken pills with the intention of suicide. I shouldn't actually be telling you this, but since it's you, Dr Hoffmann.'

'How long ago?'

'A good hour.'

Richard held down the cradle, closed his eyes. He stood like that for a few seconds, then he could think clearly again.

'Hello, Anne, I'll be late today. – No, a meeting in Administration. I met Heinsloe, it's about the hand operating theatre. – I hope you do too.' He was surprised he'd managed to sound calm. He went to the washbasin, washed his face, looked at his dripping reflection and spat at it. As he was wiping away the spit with a towel, he noticed a single hair on his cheek that he'd missed when shaving. He went to the cupboard where he kept a full toilet bag for when he was on duty at night, took out his razor and shaved off the hair.

Josta was in Ward 4, the intensive-care unit, of Friedrichstadt Hospital. Richard knew it, he'd often enough had to take patients there in the doctors' emergency car when he'd been the duty doctor. Moreover he had done his clinical practice there when he'd been a student. 'Four', as it was called, was on the top floor of one of the Friedrichstadt clinics that had survived the war. As in all hospitals the strong smell of Wofasept disinfectant, and doctors running upstairs and downstairs. He knew the pale, freckled Nurse Markus with the red beard from the days when he'd been a student nurse on this ward, now he was the nurse in charge of the ward. Because of his beard, which had been impressive even in those days, they'd called him the 'Evangelist'. Richard had admired him, for when it was a matter of taking a blood sample and everyone failed, they called Nurse Markus . . . All that went through his mind as he tried to look past Markus and get a glimpse of the resuscitation room. 'I'd like to see Frau Fischer. We had a call in Outpatients.'

Markus pointed to one of the rooms at the back. 'She was lucky. In a stable condition now. Her stomach was pumped out, twenty Obsidan tablets. Is she from your clinic?'

'No. Rector's senior secretary.'

'Good grief!'

'Can I see her?'

'Five minutes. She's still under observation.'

'Nurse Markus –'

'Hmm?'

'If our big shots should turn up –'

'Yes?'

'Please don't mention that I was here.'

Markus gave him a swift glance.

'Can I rely on you? – I ought to be at a meeting.'

Markus looked past him, nodded. 'We have a duty of confidentiality as well, Dr Hoffmann.'

'Thank you. Can I phone you? She is your patient, isn't she? – And it's brought us together again, hasn't it?' Richard concluded weakly, hoping Markus would accept the gesture. He felt uncomfortable, had the feeling all the nurses hurrying hither and thither at the beck and call of the ringing and buzzing of the drips were giving him questioning and reproachful looks; also he didn't want to run into any colleagues.

'I'm on early tomorrow morning,' Markus said, 'you can phone me.'

'I can still remember your number,' Richard said in a further attempt to revive old acquaintance.

'Do you know her family? Someone who could bring a few things?'

'As far as I know she has a son. – Have you put her on a pacemaker?'

'Temporarily. You can go in all the same.'

'Perhaps it would put too much of a strain on her.'

'Is there any message I can give?' Again Markus gave him a swift glance.

'Best wishes . . . from Dr Hoffmann.'

He ran down the stairs. He was so embarrassed he wished the ground would swallow him up. Markus had seen through him, he was pretty sure of that. Best wishes . . . from Dr Hoffmann! In the crumbling, ash-grey plaster of the wide façade of the R-Building, as the clinic in Friedrichstadt was called, many of the windows were open. Crows were croaking in the trees in the middle of the hospital, which was arranged in a square, patients were walking on the paths in the park. The wail of a siren came from the direction of the Yenidze cigarette factory, Richard broke out in a sweat and looked for a bench, his hands over his ears. When he took them off, the siren died away, the bells of Marcolini Palace, in which the hospital Administration was housed, and of the Old Catholic Cemetery on the other side of Friedrichstrasse rang out. It occurred to him that he ought to check on the children. Perhaps they were at home, waiting, perhaps Daniel was running round the streets and Lucie was alone in Josta's apartment.

He drove on automatic pilot, streets and rows of houses flickered past, he almost missed the signal of a traffic policeman, starting when he whistled and swung his baton round vigorously. He rang at Josta's door, no one opened. He waited, tried again. Finally he knocked and shouted for Daniel through the gap in the door. 'Open up, it's me.' The door to the toilet on the half-landing opened to the sound of the lavatory flushing, Josta's neighbour, Frau Schmücke, a divorced assistant in a fish shop who often seemed drunk, came out. 'An ambulance came earlier on. Must have been pretty serious from all the noise they made. I think the boy's there, I heard his voice. He called the ambulance. Are you the uncle? Frau Fischer told me about you.'

'Yes,' Richard said after brief hesitation.

'I haven't got a key.' She went to the door and knocked loudly. 'Daniel, your uncle's here. Open up.' She turned back to Richard. She was wearing shabby jeans, a paint-smudged jersey shirt, under which her nipples stood out, and a crocheted stole that had slipped down. Noticing his glance, she drew the stole over her cleavage. Her hands were covered in paint.

'Bye,' said Frau Schmücke. He looked at her hips. The door to Josta's apartment opened a crack.

'So it's you,' Daniel said.

'I've been to see your mother,' Richard said. 'Are you going to let me in?' Reluctantly Daniel let him through.

'How is she?' A flicker of fear went across the boy's face, which was strangely ugly: ears that stuck out, the head with almost no neck in between his shoulders. Like Dwarf Longnose, Richard thought. He had no idea why that occurred to him, why he was in the mood for such observations, why his eyes presented them to him in that pitiless fashion. As shame welled up inside him he stroked Daniel's hair, but the boy drew back.

'All right. She'll be well again soon.'

'Can I go and see her?'

'No. – Where's Lucie?' Richard peered into the living room.

'Still in the kindergarten. Josta didn't collect her.' Daniel always called his mother by her first name. Richard didn't like it and had once told him off, but Daniel had replied, 'I don't take orders from you, part-time-dad.' – Was that the love the boy was supposed to feel for him? Josta had calmed things down. 'Leave him alone. I don't like it when he calls me Mummy. Or Mum. Why not Josta. After all, that's what I'm called.'

Suddenly Daniel turned to him.

'Now, now, son, now, now . . . It'll be all right.'

'The gas was on as well, I turned it off and aired the apartment as it says on the notice downstairs,' Daniel said calmly.

'You did well.'

'I've still got your penknife.'

'Let's see it.' They went into the living room, where the television was on without sound. Richard switched it off. Daniel unclasped the knife. 'All the blades, and there: the scissors. It's even still got the two pairs of tweezers.' Richard took the knife, Daniel stood there, arms hanging down.

'Now, Daniel, I'll go and collect Lucie. You can stay here – no, you'll come with me. Yes, that's what we'll do. We'll go and collect her together.'

Daniel nodded. 'I can always wait outside the kindergarten,' he said, not looking at Richard.

'No, that won't work. I'm the one who has to wait outside. I'm only your uncle, I don't think they'll give Lucie to me. But they will let you take her, you're her brother. Do they know you? – Good. Let's go.'

Lucie had been completely immersed in her play, happy that for once she had all the lovely toys to herself. The teacher was relieved that Daniel had come, fortunately she asked no questions. She hadn't been able to get in touch with Josta; no one answered at the emergency number she'd been given, that of Josta's hairdresser. Lucie enjoyed the drive in the car; when they stopped at a crossing, she waved to the passers-by, some of whom waved back, amused. By now Richard couldn't care if he should be seen by anyone who knew him; he was whistling to himself, broke off when he saw Daniel's face in the rear-view mirror.

Josta had been shopping, he found cheese, bread, butter, cold sausage in the refrigerator, there were meat and eggs there too. 'Should I cook something for you?' Too late it occurred to him that he would smell of cooking fat and his excuse that he'd been in a meeting would sound implausible. Fortunately Daniel shook his head. 'Not hungry.'

'But you must eat something, my lad.'

'Where's Mummy?' Lucie asked from the living room. She'd switched the television on, Richard heard the signature tune introducing the news, shortly after there was a burst of gunfire, she'd presumably changed channels and there was a Western or something on.

'Lucie, what would you like for supper?'

'In the evening Josta just gives her something light, otherwise she can't sleep and gets tummy ache.'

'Something light, aha. And – is that something specific.' He didn't even know what his daughter had to eat in the evening. Daniel sighed. 'Oh, I'll do it. And she has to be in bed by eight at the latest. Usually after the *Sandman* programme. And she has to be told a story.'

'And you, when do you have to go to bed?'

'Ooh . . .'

'Hey, my lad, that's not on! – I could tell your grandparents.'

'Do you know where they live?' Daniel asked suspiciously.

Richard didn't and he didn't manage to conceal the fact.

'Well, you're going to leave after this anyway. Otherwise your Anne will give you hell. And Josta's in the hospital, so I can do as I like,' Daniel replied defiantly and with a malicious grin that alarmed Richard. 'Listen, Daniel, you have responsibility as well now. So far you've been great, like a grown-up. But until Josta comes back, you have to look after Lucie. And the apartment. Do you understand? Perhaps Social Services will send someone.'

'Are you coming back tomorrow?'

'Yes, tomorrow's Thursday, I can come and check up on you. Will you promise you'll be sensible?'

'Will you promise me something too?'

Richard hesitated, the look on the boy's face confused him. It was a mixture of hatred, sorrow, fear. 'What?'

But Daniel said nothing, suddenly ran out.

Richard wasn't happy with the idea of leaving the children by themselves. It could be a fortnight before Josta was discharged from hospital. Until then he had to find someone who could check up on them regularly. Daniel's father? He'd never seen him, knew neither his name nor address; whenever he'd asked, Josta had been evasive. Her hairdresser? She'd only have time in the evening and, anyway, hairdressing salons were hives of gossip. And even if by now his carefully maintained cover had probably been blown, he shouldn't do anything himself to attract attention. Would Nurse Markus hold his tongue? Whether he did or not, Josta's attempted suicide would stir up a commotion, people would be wondering what had driven her to it, make enquiries, the Arbitration Commission or some other of the organizations in the Academy that made the welfare of individual employees their concern would take her under its wing. 'Take her under its wing.' He said it quietly to himself and as he did so, he realized what that might mean for the children: who would have looked after them if the ambulance had arrived too late; what if Josta should attempt to repeat what she'd done that day, but then –

Had she not thought of the children at all? He couldn't believe that. No mother would do that. At least he'd never met a mother like that. Had she hoped he would take care of the children? Had she told someone? He searched the apartment for a farewell letter but couldn't find one. In the drawer of her bedside table there were vast amounts of sleeping pills and tranquillizers, including further packets of Obsidan. Where had she got them? Beta blockers were only available on prescription, someone must have prescribed them for her, or had she acquired them illegally? But these medicines were registered . . . Had she a heart condition she hadn't told him about? How thoughtless to keep this stuff here, the children could get at it and Lucie at least was still at an age where she put everything in her mouth. He threw all the pills away, she'd get the Obsidan back if she really needed it. Then he

searched through Josta's clothes and bags in the wardrobe – nothing.
So, a knee-jerk reaction. He sat down on the bed, where the crumpled
sheet still showed the outline of her body. On the bedside table there
was the mark made by the bottom of a bottle, the ambulance men
would probably have taken the bottle to the hospital with them, along
with the packet of pills. What should he do now? How were things
going to work out with Josta, with him, with Anne and the children?
For a long time he sat there without moving. The television was on in
the next room. Lucie was clearly quite happy, he heard her laugh, clap
her hands now and then. Perhaps Daniel was sitting with her, examining his penknife . . . Or wondering what he would do once his 'uncle'
had left. That brought Richard back to the unsolved problem of who
was to keep an eye on the children.

Frau Schmücke had changed and seemed to be drunk again, she was
waving her left hand, but then he realized that she had just been painting her fingernails, clearly she was about to go out. Richard was
astonished at her profusion of uncontrollable hair, he hadn't noticed
it before.

'Can I . . . I'm sorry, I've disturbed you. Could I speak to you for
a moment?'

'Come in,' she said after a short hesitation.

'Thank you, but that's not necessary, I don't want to –'

'Look, it may be May already, but I've still got the heating on and
the warmth all slips out when the door's left open. I'm sure it's about
next door and we shouldn't discuss that out here. Moreover' – she
leant forward a little, her voice dropping to a whisper – 'the people
like to have an ear out in the hallway, and not only there, I think.' She
went back into her hall and he followed her hesitantly. This woman
aroused him, it was grotesque, but his heart was pounding as he went
into the stranger's apartment and, to his astonishment, that made him
curious. She walked smoothly and had no shoes on, a little chain round
her left ankle, her toenails were also painted. The sight of her bare feet

with the red nails and the chain aroused him even more. In the hall and the living room the walls were covered with paintings hung side by side; there was a smell of paint. He found the paintings disturbing, death masks with sharp contrasts, screaming blue mouths, yellow birds with black and green heads could be seen, painters' palettes had been nailed to the living-room ceiling and, on an easel, in the corner where most apartments of this type had the television, there crouched a picture in a brutal red that coagulated in streaks, wound into fat whorls, had suffered yawning cuts in the top-left corner, smouldered in the middle round a darker spindle. All the pictures were powerful and gripping, but that one in particular; Richard was impressed but ignored that, he hadn't come to view paintings. 'By you?' he asked hurriedly and more out of politeness.

'Do you want a drink?'

'No, thank you.'

'You need someone to look after the children.'

'Forgive me for coming to you with . . .'

'No problem.' She poured out two glasses of brandy. 'I've quite often helped Frau Fischer. I know where everything is, what they eat and what they don't, I can take the little girl to the kindergarten.'

'That's good of you.'

'You wait and see.' She came over to him with the two glasses. He was so baffled that he took the glass she handed to him. 'How do you mean?'

'Do you smoke?'

'N-no –' He'd almost said: Of course not – and she'd have responded with: Of course not? Why? and perhaps guessed he was a doctor. Perhaps she knew that anyway. He wondered how much Josta had told her.

'Have a sip, it calms you down.'

'Don't you work in a fish shop?'

'As a sales assistant, true. It's not so bad there. Now and then you have to kill a fish. You've got something to exchange, to bargain with, as a painter I was worse off in that respect. – You're not a person who tries out different things?'

'I'll go now. Please, you must see that I'm not in the mood for a chat at the moment. I'm sorry. Another time – with pleasure, but not just now.'

'So what are you in the mood for.' She gave him a rather challenging look. He avoided her eye, stared at her feet. 'To be honest, I don't know.' He held the glass away from him, as if it were infectious, clutched his forehead nervously. What a stupid answer. I must have gone completely mad.

'You'd like to sleep with me.'

'What?'

'Did you think I didn't notice you looking? In the hall and in the mirror just now?' She emptied her glass. 'You were horny and I am too now.'

'Are you . . .' Richard gave a disbelieving laugh. '. . . are you mad?'

'No. Just alone.'

He took a mouthful of brandy after all. It was good brandy. He hated himself for noticing that.

'I've sometimes been listening when you and Josta . . . She seemed to be pretty happy.'

'Oh come now, that's –'

'Enviable. I'd like to be like that again for once.'

'. . . completely mad –'

'And now I have the opportunity. You can take off your "uncle" mask.'

'Are you trying to blackmail me?' Richard couldn't help laughing.

'Call it what you like. I call it seizing the occasion. I don't want to die an old maid regretting missed opportunities.'

'You don't want to . . .' He still had to laugh. 'Are you drunk?'

'Not at all. And certainly not from this bit of brandy. I have that effect on people, I know. I'm a bit . . . what do people say? – woozy. I've always been like that. Grew up in the uranium mines. We were called "the sleeping village".'

'What would you say if I told you I couldn't care less about your blackmail threat?'

She took his glass and threw it on the floor. 'I would say: You don't know what you're missing.' She came over to him, treading in the splinters of glass.

But then they sat there, silent. After a while she lit a cigarette, drew on it, held it out to him, he waved it away. Her feet were bleeding. Splinters of glass in the feet were difficult to find if they weren't stuck in superficially, you couldn't see them on X-rays.

He left the apartment. Said goodbye to Daniel, who had put Lucie to bed, where she was sleeping with her mouth open.

31

Vanilla and indigo

The girls trotted along a bit behind them and were less mocking than usual, perhaps because Christian had invited them: they were to spend the night in Meno's apartment in the House with a Thousand Eyes, Meno was in Berlin. Perhaps it was because of the voices from the gardens, the scent of jasmine that was overpowering in the evening, cutting through the other smells: resin on the plum trees, warm asphalt, all the bubbling ferment coming out of the open windows that subsided with the twilight and the blossom-inflamed slope above the Elbe with its whispering – Niklas said: balsamic – delicacy. Christian and Falk did handstands but only Siegbert managed to keep going to the advertisement pillar at the Mondleite–Lindwurmring crossroads, to the shouts and applause of the Russian officers who had been playing volleyball outside the Villa Clair, where they lived. The piano in the Roeckler School of Dancing repeated 'The Blue Danube' with mindless patience. Heike had brought her drawing pad and Christian was amazed at the swift sharpness with which she caught Siegbert's triumph: his precarious balance as he crossed the road on his hands in front of a honking car, his trousers slipping down to reveal his brown, brambly calves and tennis socks, his jacket that had turned inside out like an umbrella, his face as he tried to look casual and breathe calmly when he stood up and brushed the dirt off his hands, then Heike drew a halo over him and Reina's and Verena's faces with expressions between the craving for an autograph and an approaching swoon. The history and geography exams were behind them.

'Hey, Christian, it's really great that you've arranged this with your uncle,' Reina said. 'What did you say for question three? I thought it was pretty beastly and I don't know –'

'Hey, no more about school, you'll just have to wait and see what you get, you can't do anything about it now.'

'Was it you I asked for your opinion, Falk Truschler, or Montecristo?' Reina retorted pertly.

'Can't you give up these stupid nicknames?'

'We mean it in the nicest way,' said Reina.

'It looks good, your blue dress,' Falk said when Christian didn't reply. They made a detour along Wolfsleite, Christian wanted to pick up Fabian and Muriel; when he rang at Wolfstone, no one came.

'I think they've gone already,' said Herr Krausewitz. He was weeding and paused a moment to wipe the sweat from his brow. 'We're going to have a summer like we haven't had for ages,' he said, more to himself than to Christian, 'I bet it'll be even crazier than last year. – Where are you off to?'

'To the Langes', we're spending the night at Uncle's.'

'He's gone to the Association congress, so I heard. Give him my best wishes.'

There was a fountain in the garden of Dolphin's Lair, a stone dolphin reared up over the mossy rim, a jet of water came out of its mouth and splashed into the basin, the rippling bluish water of which reflected the five-fingered leaves of a horse chestnut. The girls stopped and listened, Heike drew the scroll ornament over the cornice, the door flanked by sandstone pillars with the bee lily above it, and Christian dug up secrets about Frau von Stern, the former lady-in-waiting who had known Kaiser Wilhelm and the last Russian Tsar, going into raptures about her apartment and her souvenirs when he saw he was making an impression; only Verena remained suspicious and asked how he came to be familiar with her apartment. Christian told them about the evenings, with the invitations to the soirées written by hand or on typewriters, when they would gather together, when ice-patterns spread over the windowpanes and Plisch and Plum in Hauschild's coal store were only weighing out damp brown lumps that didn't heat the apartments at all; when they all sat together in Guenon House, in Roeckler's School of Dancing, in Elephant opposite the House with a Thousand Eyes or at Frau von Stern's listening to a talk by the music critic, Däne, on Weber's oboe concerto or by Hoffmann, the toxicologist, on poisons; when they discussed the latest rumours from town and country over sandwiches and mineral water. But only Reina was still listening when he looked up, Verena had gone on ahead to join Falk and Siegbert, and Heike was immersed in the perspectives of a shoe dangling from a rhododendron by the remains of its lace. Ina was standing outside the Italian House with a few of the 'long-haired individuals' Barbara complained about, one was holding a stereo recorder to his ear that was emitting the boom of tender, brutal music. Ina waved. 'Hey, cousin of mine, what are you doing here?'

'Celebrating the end of exams. We're going to the Bearpit, sleeping at Meno's. What's that you're listening to?'

'Yeuch, the Bearpit,' one of the long-haired group drawled, giving Christian's summer suit a disparaging scrutiny. ''s called *Feeling B*.' The one with the stereo recorder turned it up louder. Christian introduced the others.

'Hi, pretty man,' Ina said brightly. 'Siegbert's something different, most of the ones I know are called Ronny or Mike or Thomas. – Your girlfriend?' Verena put her hands behind her back.

'Perhaps we'll see you later, you never know. You're going to the Langes'? I like the old geezer with his sailor's yarns, haven't seen him for ages. – The Bearpit's a waste of time today, we're heading for the Bird of Paradise.'

'Heading's good, getting in's the problem,' muttered the one with the recorder and he pressed stop.

'We'll make it, you can trust me. I know the bouncer, I just have to let him see a bit of leg. – If you make it there, pretty man, I'll reserve a dance for you.'

Siegbert put on his most unfathomable smile. Falk raised his hand but one of the long-haired lads pushed it back down: 'She says for him, not for you. Right?' Falk blew out his cheeks. As they went on, Christian heard laughter and 'Village clodhoppers' and 'Hey, guys, look at him, home-made gear.' Siegbert, who was a few paces in front of Christian, turned round. 'Does that bother you?' He grabbed the youth, who gave a yelp of surprise, by the hair and pulled him towards him, grasping his earlobe with his free hand and twisting it, the other dropped to his knees, Siegbert thumped him. It all happened very quickly; Ina was the first to recover. 'Hey, we didn't mean it that way. – I like you even more, pretty man.'

'Stupid bitch,' Verena, who had come to stand next to Christian, fumed. 'Are all your relations that arrogant?' Ina said nothing, looked her up and down, seconds during which the two groups subjected each other to hostile scrutiny. 'She'd be the one, cousin dear.' Ina burst out laughing; it wasn't malicious, it was like spraying water by holding the end of the garden hose tight on a hot day, the long-haired youths laughed as well, even Reina and Falk. Siegbert shrugged his shoulders. Verena and the one he'd thumped didn't laugh. He checked his trousers, switched the recorder back on.

'Sorry,' Christian apologized when they reached Mondleite, 'that's just the way she is.' He nodded to Siegbert. 'And what was said about your things isn't what she really thinks, her mother makes clothes as well herself. I'd be glad if I could do so,' he added. Siegbert didn't respond.

'We have to wait for Heike, our slowcoach.' Reina was being nasty: Heike hadn't seen anything of what had happened and was surprised when the others exchanged glances.

'How's your application going? When will you hear if they're taking you?'

Heike squinted at Falk, rolled her shoulders, blew a lock of hair out of her face. 'No idea.'

'What was it you had to draw?' Verena asked.

'A shoe –' She leafed through her sketchpad and showed them the shoe she'd discovered in the rhododendron. 'They wanted it from all possible perspectives. Stupid but int'resting.' The sketchpad was handed round, they admired the strictly naturalistic drawings of the shoe. Seen from the front, it had blue eyes. Siegbert was now walking a few paces ahead of them. Christian closed his eyes and opened them abruptly, as if they were the shutter of a camera, as if he wanted to retain snapshots of Siegbert in his memory: a slim young man in light-coloured clothes such as a ship's officer or a member of Louis Alvarez's entomological expeditions could have worn, had it not been for the bizarre details: Siegbert had sewn a purple button on the left leg, at the calf, triangles of green cloth under the armpits and a zip running diagonally across the back. Eyes open-shut, open-shut, on the inside his eyelids were orange, Christian saw Siegbert kicking away a stone, Siegbert raising his head when a tug's siren boomed from the Elbe,

Siegbert throwing a stick to knock an apple, wrinkled by the winter frost, off the tree and lobbing it to Verena; Siegbert and Verena, who was walking beside him and placed the apple on a fence after one bite and dropped back to Reina and Falk, walked on in front again, looking at the street through a monocle of green glass she carried on a string round her neck. The windows in Elephant were open, Frau Teerwagen was putting a bowl of punch on the balcony table. Doctor Kühnast was washing his Škoda. Heike was looking at the rose hedges, covered all over in blossom, of the House with a Thousand Eyes and shaking her head.

'What is it?' Christian asked, ringing the Langes' bell; Meno had left the key with them.

'No, no, I won't paint that, that's kitsch,' Heike declared.

'But it is there,' Falk said teasingly.

'That there is there.' Heike pointed to the copper beech that was breathing like a rust lung.

The Langes had laid the table out in the garden, had set up the round iron table, which hibernated in the garden shed with flower pots, the chopping block and sawing horse, in the overgrown lower part as they did every summer; the round iron table at which the ship's doctor and Meno, sometimes Libussa and Niklas Tietze, would tell stories.

In Meno's apartment it smelt of books, tobacco and plants. He'd left the door with the pointed arch open for Chakamankabudibaba. Reina went out onto the balcony, leant into the climbing roses growing in profusion on the trellis from the conservatory up to the windows of the Kaminski twins. There was a sheet of paper stuck in the typewriter: 'Greetings, make yourselves at home. If anyone happens to have forgotten their toothbrush, there are two new ones on the top shelf of the bathroom cabinet. Light bulbs (should one go, it's been happening quite often recently) are in the hall cupboard. I've put out towels and soap. If there aren't enough, ask Libussa Lange. Two can sleep in my bed; there are loungers in the shed, also a pump for your air beds.

Please don't forget Chakamankabudibaba, there's ground beef and mackerel in the fridge, in the newspaper with the smiling Secretary General. Have a good time. Meno Rohde.'

The ten-minute clock chimed. Siegbert examined the engravings on the signs of the zodiac, Verena perused the titles in the bookshelves, Falk peeped down the microscope.

'Pity we're not going to meet your uncle,' Verena said. 'Great books.'

'Just have a look at those floorboards.' Heike was drawing again: the grain of the larchwood, knots, patches of sunshine.

'I think they're waiting for us,' Reina shouted. When Christian went out he saw Libussa by the garden shed, waving. He held up both hands: ten minutes. Libussa nodded. Reina leant over the balustrade, Christian was amazed at all the freckles on her arms.

'Do you go there often?' She wasn't looking at him; shading her eyes with her hand, she pointed at a pale blue mountain in the hazy distance.

'The Wilisch,' Christian said. 'Not often any more.'

'Sorry about what happened at Kaltwasser reservoir.' She looked away, there was a scar on her neck.

'Where did you get that?'

Reina brushed her hair over it. 'Accident.'

'Just a minute –' He picked a dog rose and put it in her hair. It didn't stay there, he tried again. Then he felt alarmed, looked down at the city, the curve of the Elbe by Blasewitz, a glider was slowly circling in a thermal. Reina didn't say anything; he went back into the room.

'Is that your uncle?' Verena and Falk were standing looking at the photos and pointed at the one with Kurt Rohde and Meno on a botanical expedition.

'My grandfather. The boy's my uncle.' He picked up the photo of Hanna. 'His divorced wife, my Aunt Hanna. And on this one here there's my mother, Meno and my other uncle, Ulrich. The father of Ina we met just now. – If you like I can show you round the house.'

But he told them nothing about the djinn, as they walked round the corridors, nothing about the secrets of the runner in the hall and the leaden shadows that appeared in the mirror in the evening when Meno's living-room door was open. Heike described the toucan as 'wicked'. The ten-minute clock struck.

'We ought to go down.' Christian saw that the key to the door in the salamander wallpaper wasn't in the lock. Verena avoided his eye, he decided to say nothing about the spiral staircase and the conservatory, nothing about the photos; though Falk and Siegbert seemed to have discovered them, for they were calling out to the others from the stairs that they really ought to see this. Reina had stayed in the living room.

Fabian and Muriel were sitting between a lantern and a paper moon in front of the dog roses that completely obliterated the other garden smells in that part; they had presumably sat there deliberately, opposite Libussa and Alois Lange, whom they knew: for as long as he had known them there had been something formal, an element of studied affection, in their behaviour towards each other that they didn't want to expose to the hurried looks of strangers for a casual judgement. Whenever he saw Fabian, his long hair and the unusual shirts he affected – with frills and much-too-long cuffs that he turned back – Christian thought: All he needs is a wig, a sword at his side and a three-cornered hat to go with them and he'd be a vicomte from one of those epistolary novels full of perfume and poison from the second half of the eighteenth century; Barbara had grown thoughtful at one of their Sunday lunches, because Ina's expression had darkened at Fabian's name, had said 'enoeff' and that in her opinion Fabian was 'on the other side', of which his shirts – theatre props, fancy dress – were more than just a cautious indication, and she thought that his parents ought to talk to him about it even though in their place she wouldn't have been overly worried, after all, that kind of thing did happen and Fabian was only fourteen or fifteen, nothing was finally settled yet. At that Ina had bent her head over the bowl of stewed fruit and snorted. Moreover, she went on, in his own way he had taste, as did his sister. Then Fabian raised one hand to rest his chin on it elegantly while with the other he gave his sister a caterpillar and closed her hand over it. They wanted to be artists; 'Yes,' Meno had said without smiling in response to Barbara's look of exasperation, 'that's the result of a youth spent among aromas, poems and conversations about Chopin's nocturnes, that's what one dreams of after reading a passage in which Hermann Hesse meditates on evening clouds in the Ticino. Perhaps Hans talks about poisonous plants too much as well.' – 'But Iris Hoffmann's an engineering draughtswoman with Pentacon.' – 'True,' Ulrich had said in response to Barbara's interjection, 'but you have to admit that there is something about those theatrical evenings in their house, and Cuddles only forgot her lines twice in the role of the almost-mute; they were great, those evenings, and the beer was good!' Muriel was sitting with her legs crossed, she was wearing button boots from the days of Lucie Krausewitz's youth, saved from the wardrobe of the Albert-Theater, which had been destroyed during the bombardment of Dresden, together with a peach-yellow double-breasted suit with black stripes that could have been worn in *The Importance of being Earnest* or by Maurice Chevalier in one of his roles, a beret right on the back of her head. They went to school dressed like that and were the strangest pair in Robert's class; but since they were twins and Muriel held the school record for the sixty-metre sprint and Fabian saved penalties spectacularly as goalkeeper for the Fürnberg High School handball team, they were left in peace. And Robert told them that some pupils secretly envied them their things: it was the period of Wisent and Boxer jeans, status-symbol clothes from 'the other side' or from Exquisit, compared with which there was a certain odd dignity about the things Fabian and Muriel wore. Siegbert scrutinized the pair of them and they scrutinized him; Fabian's eye kept coming back to the purple button,

Siegbert's to Muriel's hair, gleaming black like a wire coil. Lange pulled a yarn out of his sailor's kitbag, it was about conserved hydrangeas and their use as an antidote to seasickness, at which Siegbert remarked that that was new to him.

'Christian,' Alois Lange said, 'be a good lad and get my logbook from the conservatory. – I'll prove it to you.' Lange had spent a quarter of an hour talking about classes of cruisers and types of submarines with Siegbert, to the annoyance of the girls, who had helped Libussa with the punch she had started with strawberries from Hortex; the glass bowl cast an elliptical shadow on the table, the fermenting sweetness attracted wasps and moths; Reina was afraid of the hornets from the nest in the garden shed.

The Kaminski brothers were sitting in the conservatory by the light of a miner's lamp, they were chatting quietly, windows open, smoking, gave Christian a friendly grin to which he didn't respond. 'Hello, how's your application for university? Are you looking for something particular?' He saw that they were leafing through Lange's logbook, went over, without looking at them, stretched out his hand wordlessly.

'Later, young man, it's our turn now. The stories are massively exaggerated, but not bad otherwise, he should discuss them with your uncle.'

Christian went to the window: 'Herr Lange?'

'Oh, no sense of humour.' They gave him the book. 'It's OK,' they shouted into the garden.

There was a ring at Meno's door. 'Oh, he's got visitors,' Judith Schevola said when Christian opened the door. 'You are –'

'His nephew.'

'Herr Rohde and I – we're working together. He's my editor.'

'Do come in.'

'I don't want to disturb . . .'

'Aren't you Judith Schevola?' Verena came from the house and, when Judith Schevola nodded in surprise, said, 'I've read everything of yours, pity I haven't got a book with me or I'd have asked you to sign it.'

'There's punch in the garden,' Christian said.

'What are you celebrating?' Schevola asked, following the two others. 'Is it someone's birthday?'

Verena kept talking to her, full of enthusiasm, Lange had no chance with his sailor's yarns and made a gesture of cheerful resignation. Siegbert and he withdrew with the logbook and lantern, and soon the smoke eddies of Copenhagen vanilla tobacco were feeling their way to the iron table where the others were sitting bombarding Schevola with questions.

'How does a conference like that go?'

'Do you really want to know?' Schevola smiled. 'Rhubarbrhubarb . . .'

'I think I've heard that before.'

'And: whisperwhisperjeerjeer. – What do you like reading best?'

'At school? *The Adventures of Werner Holt,*' Siegbert shouted. 'At last a book that's fun to read.'

'That doesn't surprise me. And Hermann Kant: *Die Aula?*'

'Dishonest shit!'

She laughed. 'That was clear.'

'And you're a real writer?' Reina wanted to know.

'I write books, yes. But whether I'm a real writer . . . Sometimes I think I'll never be one.'

'Well I enjoyed your books,' Verena said. 'You can really get into them, and the people you describe . . . it's as if they're alive. – I think you like them a lot, even the awkward ones,' she added quietly. Schevola rummaged round in her handbag, fished out a packet of cigarettes. 'May I?' she asked Libussa.

'Of course, child. Meno thinks a lot of you and, believe me, he has his opinions about authors.'

407

'I can imagine.'

'Do you often suffer,' Verena hesitated, 'I mean . . . You're so successful, my sister works in a library and your books are frequently asked for and everyone I know likes you –'

'Self-doubt? – Yes, I do. It's an affliction, success and praise make no difference. You know, in the evening you're alone in your room and the great authors, the masters, are watching you from the walls, their books are silent on the shelves and you're sitting over a sheet of paper, scribbling away –'

Verena's face lit up. 'I like you, may I say that to you? And I thought I was the only one who always had such thoughts.'

Schevola glanced at her, blew smoke at the paper moon. 'Nice here.'

'Sometimes I think of this as Eichendorff's garden,' Christian said. 'The one in his story about the good-for-nothing, near Vienna, the Countess's castle and it all ends happily ever after?'

Ina arrived, they could see from afar that she was frustrated. 'Damn, damn, damn! We didn't get in. It was a different bouncer. And d'you know who's on? *Neustadt!*'

'That's why it's so full today.'

'Is it the Bird of Paradise Bar you're talking about?' Schevola asked. And when Libussa nodded: 'Could I use your telephone?' Schevola stubbed out her cigarette and went up with Christian. Five minutes later she came back down. 'How is it then? Who's coming?'

'Wow, how did you manage that?' Falk said in astonishment.

'Vitamin C. Right then?'

Ladislaus Pospischil's Bird of Paradise Bar was living off its earlier reputation. In the sixties the notoriety of disrepute had shone over its parquet dance floor that bands with acceptable names, gawky youths in crocodile-yellow shoes and suits from VEB Herrenmode, authenticated by string ties, had filled with Bill Haley's and Elvis Presley's incendiary music, after two or three numbers the mirror wall was showing nothing but smears of colour and the outlines of bodies, was sweating condensation among the smoke from Karo cigarettes and the exudations of 500 squealing, wildly jigging bodies and warm champagne stirred with the finger. Cheap beer went flat as excited conversations were held on table telephones with pulsating red lights. In the men's toilet there were glasses of sugar water for dishevelled duck's-arse haircuts, between the mirrors was a warning about sexually transmitted diseases and couples that spent two hours over the same cocktail wanted mostly to listen. Representatives of order and rebels had subjected each other to hostile scrutiny across Sprelacart laminate tables, many a Dresden marriage had been arranged by the cigarette spirit in the private booths that could be closed off with bird-patterned curtains made by Tashkent weavers. Since it had been nationalized, it had gone downhill, Pospischil was no longer its owner but senior employee; the smugglers' cave in the Schlemm Hotel ran out of smugglers.

Christian had never been there before. The deafening noise that suddenly enveloped him like a rubber wall, the screaming, laughing stream of people, drifts of smoke and beer fumes in the air that lay on his skin like a warm, damp nappy, the cramped, claustrophobic room with the throng heaving like heavy, dark water in a tank with a few lantern buoys drifting on it; the jerky movements of the dancers on the small floor in front of the band that seemed to him like the desperate flounderings of non-swimmers: all that repelled him and he was glad to find a seat in the corner of the bench Schevola had reserved. Beside them were soldiers in their uniforms, squinting longingly at the girls, glasses of cheap champagne in their hands. 'Poor sods,' said Muriel pityingly, after a glance at their epaulettes, and asked the ugliest one to dance; a flush immediately twitched across his face, spreading a few fractions of a second later to the others, as if there were a connection between them, the hope of a similar piece of good fortune; but Verena and Siegbert were already on the dance floor, Ina had dragged

Fabian up and Reina, after a glance at Christian, Falk; Heike simply shook her head when one of the soldiers attempted an awkward bow, and Schevola was at the bar, flanked by a man with a ponytail and a big bushy beard and a woman in a sari-like dress.

The music was booming out of the loudspeakers; when the drummer sent his sticks flashing over his skins the impact of the sound was physically painful, Christian would really have liked to put his hands over his ears. He wondered whether the others felt the same, no, they were dancing and laughing in high spirits, expressions of liberation on their faces, and enjoyment. Libussa and Alois Lange stepped onto the floor, the bandleader smiled, leant over the mike and announced, 'Grandad and Grandma Lange' – a real cheek, Christian thought, and how did the guy know them – as 'twist legends from the lejjen-derry days of the old Bird of Paradise', then the rhythms of 'Let's Twist Again' ripped out and, urged on by cheers and raised arms, Libussa and Alois put on a brilliant twist that no other couple on the floor could match; we can't dance any more, Christian thought, and: This just can't be true. He'd never seen the pair of them like that before and yet he imagined he knew them well. Instinctively he dismissed what he was seeing, two white-haired people who, at a click of the fingers and a few bars of rousing music, had cast off their age like a straitjacket that had nothing to do with them and into which an abusive, imperious power had forced them. Christian was shocked to observe them and began to sense that we only knew as much of other people as they were prepared to reveal. This observation hurt him, made him jealous – after all, it was 'his' people who were showing Verena, Siegbert and the others something they'd never shown him; they were seeing them for the first time, and in a light they had no idea was new. New for him – suddenly he couldn't help laughing: You're behaving like one of those artists Meno sometimes talks about; they imagine people belong to them and feel insulted when they behave differently from the way they'd assumed in their plans.

Christian emptied his glass. It was some cocktail for young people, tasting vanilla-ish and excited at its own alcohol content; it made his tongue sticky. Verena and Siegbert were jumping about, waving their arms as if they had a fit of the shivers. Silly! Christian thought. What was the point of looking like that? Verena's feverish eyes; a flush creeping over Reina's usually pale face, like red wine spilt on a tablecloth. It fascinated him. It disgusted him. The hooch tasted revolting, but what could he do except drink it. Heike was observing him, he could see her out of the corner of his eye, he couldn't bear being observed, gave her a glinting stare but she wasn't bothered by it, compared him with her drawing, stared back, unmoved, dissecting. He thought the music was terrible, but it was just loud, not bad, it was good. That was the stupid thing about it: it was good. Not a twist now, a take on the state-approved *Lipsi* dance, the cellar was filled with roars of laughter. Guitar riffs with eyes closed and rapt open mouths. That was as filthy as a dustbin, not the music they taught you at school. Music that bared its teeth, a thermometer bursts in your arse. Yes, right there, in your arse, in your arse! Christian greedily repeated the word. The lads on their instruments knew what they were doing, even if they weren't playing the cello or piano. Five lads, at a guess just a few years older than he was. At a guess, Christian thought, perhaps I should simply take the drawing pad away from Heike? 'You OK, Heike? You're drawing the whole time,' he said boorishly, grabbing her cocktail. She didn't object, simply nodded. So he just downed it. His skin was burning. The cigarette smoke was like a smouldering shroud hanging from the ceiling. Christian imagined the drummer, with his violent up-and-down gesticulations, as a wind machine that would suddenly blow away the smoke, the voices and the laughter bubbling up over the tables, above all the laughter, it sounded like paper tearing. He checked whether anyone could see him. Heike had found other subjects. The soldiers were interested in skirts and female bottoms in jeans, he moved deeper into his shady corner, under the foggy light of a circular neon lamp from the sixties, nothing had changed, he couldn't loosen up. He imagined playing his cello in a cathedral, the congregation frozen in devotion, Bach forcing them to their knees, these very people here, with a nervously trembling hand Libussa would change the hymn numbers on the board, the ship's doctor, head bowed in contrition, would do penance on a hard bench, the laughter on Siegbert and Verena's lips would die away. Silence, church-cool eternity, Bach's harmonies, not this home-slaughtered howling with its cheap texts . . . Falk threw his head back joyfully and gasped for air like a carp. In his mind's eye Christian could see him walking away after his interview with Fahner, comb in his back pocket, the dripping quiet on the stairwell, and he'd felt no pity as he watched Falk leave, his angular shoulder blades and his arms that, as Reina had said, were really too skinny for a boy. Now he was dancing like crazy and a week after the interview in the hostel room he'd still had difficulty concealing his fear: 'He ranted and raved a bit, not actually very loudly, but . . . You know him. Nothing's happened . . . so far. Perhaps the worst is still to come, you never know with them, and he'll chuck me out of the school.' That was what Falk had said, his words merged with the voices in the bar, the music. Rock ballads now. Good, good, good. Yes. He ought to get out. Perhaps go to the toilet. No, better stay here, otherwise his place might get taken. Christian observed Judith Schevola, who appeared to be having an agitated discussion with the woman but during the pauses in the conversation peered over at the tables. Make sure you don't get under her magnifying glass, he thought. The band leader had an Armenian cap on his cropped head, a leather coat with shoulder straps and belt, and a 'Swords into Ploughshares' badge sewn on. Theatrical, honest gestures, so allergically sweeping that those playing guitar kept at arm's length from him. The drummer in a Russian shirt streaked with sweat; hovering like a misty halo above his wildly jerking head was the tail of a bird of paradise made from pieces of coloured glass and illuminated from behind.

'So, what d'you say?' Ina flopped down beside Christian.

'What's the guy waving his arms around called?'

'The front man? André Pschorke. Hey, wouldn't you like a dance?'

'Pschorke,' Christian said meditatively. 'International careers start with names like that.'

'You can be pretty arrogant at times, has anyone ever told you that?'

'Her over there,' Christian said with a weary nod in Verena's direction. 'I don't care. Never-ending boom-boom-boom –'

Ina made a dismissive gesture. 'Oh, you are a wet blanket, Cousin. You really are going to come a cropper one of these days. Your classical music is something for the old fogies. You can stick it up your arse. Uptight aesthetes, huh, to hell with 'em.' She lit a cigarette.

'Hey, Cousin, lighten up.'

A guitar chord cut off Ina's reply, she shook her head and, as those on the dance floor separated, went over to Siegbert. Now Muriel was dancing with Falk, Verena with Fabian, the soldiers were skipping round Reina, who was dancing alone with her eyes closed. Neustadt sang about cobblestones, about mail inspector Alfred going to his night shift along dark dreary stree–heets with his briefcase and sandwiches, about the bit of sky above the back yard as blue as Milka chocolate – the dance floor bawled along – they sang the 'Ash Song'. 'No, it's not what you think,' André Pschorke shouted to the soldiers, 'it's about . . . Ash lies over the streets / People have it in their hair / Ash that's the colour of sleep / Ash of the things that were . . . // Tell me, where has the dream gone / Everyone had at dawn / Did they all get rid of it / Like a baby that never gets born . . .' Christian was impressed by the words, he scribbled them on a beer mat, making it obvious so that no one would get the wrong idea about him. They sang 'Your Eyes', a slow number with a lot of keyboard.

Schevola came, behind her the woman in the sari. 'We've seen you've been drawing away industriously, may I have a look?' she said to Heike. She opened the drawing pad, examined the drawing with brief glances, like a craftsman checking the contents of a tool chest, turned over the pages. 'You're still at school?'

Heike jutted out her chin and twined a lock of hair round a finger, the woman in the sari presumably took it as a yes. 'What do you want to do, after school?'

'Paint,' Heike said. The woman in the sari nodded. 'If you want, you can come and see me. My name's Nina Schmücke, during the day I sell fish, on Friday evenings we look at each other's pictures and discuss them.'

'You had the red picture in the art exhibition,' Heike said.

'For one day.' Nina Schmücke handed back the pad. 'Then someone with influence didn't like it and it was taken down.'

'It was very powerful,' Heike said. 'May I really come and see you?'

'Have you something to write on?'

Heike turned the block over, Nina Schmücke wrote her address on it. Then the two of them sank into their own universe of painters' names and pictures and painting techniques.

Schevola sat down beside Christian. 'Shall we have a chat,' she said to him in amused tones. She pointed vaguely in the direction of the steps. Neustadt were strumming furious protests.

'What about?' was the only thing that occurred to Christian. He said it no louder than normally, Schevola couldn't have heard.

'I presume you don't dance?'

He shook his head, then he picked up another beer mat, wrote, 'Would you tell the others I've left. The door's open.'

How quiet it suddenly was: as if a space full of noise had been shut off and was no longer in operation here, dispersing and dissipating in the smells Christian once more perceived: from the park where a large bird flew off, startling him, from the garden, from the House with a Thousand Eyes. Bats were flitting between the treetops, visible as angular shadows against the muddy sky. The barometer at home was on 'set fair' and Libussa had said there wouldn't be any rain. Chaka-mankabudibaba emerged from the sweet briar beside the path, briefly touched his calf with his bottle-brush tail in a kind of condescending greeting noting his arrival, licked a front paw, sniffed at the depths of the garden, disappeared as silently as he had come. The Teerwagens were sitting on their balcony, a trickle of pop music was coming from open windows, perhaps it was *Here's Music* with Rainer Süss, a popular show on Channel 1. Half past eleven, no, it wasn't on at that time. It was unusually warm, he wondered about sleeping outside, then he remembered he still had to get the loungers out of the garden shed and pump up the air beds, he decided to do it right away. Everything was dark at the Kaminskis' and the Stahls', but when he went to the balus-trade, below which the garden fell away steeply, he saw the Stahls sitting in the light of the coloured bulbs they strung up over the iron table in the summer. He went down, the engineer asked whether Sylvia had been quiet; Christian hadn't heard anything, Sabine Stahl said she sometimes secretly watched television when they were down in the garden, the glow of the screen couldn't be seen from down there. Christian said there could be problems with washing in the morning but Stahl replied that there were things young people had to put up with, he'd filled the tin bathtub in the garden. 'Are you staying longer?'

'A little.'

'Meno told us you and your friends will have to go to the pre-military training camp soon?'

'Yes.'

'Keep your chin up. – Good night, Christian.'

'Good night.'

The Stahls got up. Christian noticed the bulge in Sabine Stahl's stomach. She smiled. 'Meno will soon have to let us have the bedroom.'

They slowly made their way upstairs. Christian watched them leave, two patches of brightness going up the steps to the house. The slight feeling of intoxication he'd had from the cocktails had gone; he poured himself a glass of punch, it tasted flat, he abandoned his glass. He switched off the lights, put out the lamp, sat down in the chair where the ship's doctor had been sitting, stared up at the Chinese lantern swaying in the currents of air, a white sphere with a clown's grin in red drawn on it in which burnt insects were to be found in the mornings. At night the garden was a mysterious realm, the crickets sawing their soporific 'tsik-tsik' into the distant noises of the city and the whispering of the trees, everywhere there seemed to be eyes opened, everywhere a hunt was on. A bug crawled onto the table, it had long, backward-curving feelers that seemed to be sieving the air, Christian, startled, stood up: that was something for Meno, not for him, Meno would certainly have had a Latin name ready at once and told him something about the habits of the bug. Christian was afraid of it, for him the creature was one of the night spirits, an eye with which nature looked at humankind.

He went to fetch the pump from the shed. Stahl had placed a lantern beside the tin bathtub, a yellow pinhead in the darkness dappled with the white moth-attracting plants: narcotic vibrations; he suddenly felt the need to dip a hand in the rainwater butt beside the shed; then the other hand: he was amazed how unpleasant it was if you only wet one. The hornets' nest was empty, he remembered that Meno had told him that hornets lived for just one year and that the queens built new nests after they'd overwintered; also hornets, unlike wasps, didn't go for human food; he could have told Reina that. When he looked up, the pinhead had gone. He found candles in the shed, matches as well, Meno probably used them when he worked out there. On a shelf were some apples from the previous year, on the windowledge cardboard cylinders of greenfly killer; there was a smell of fertilizer and rubber boots. The tin bathtub was in the lowest part of the garden, on a terraced piece of lawn with tomatoes and raspberries where Libussa toiled to keep them clear of dog roses and the maple shoots that landed in the autumn like invading propeller troops from the mother trees below the end of the garden – beyond a rotten wooden fence there was a drop of several metres, the neighbouring plot was overgrown and didn't seem to belong to anyone. Glow-worms whirred across the path Christian was slowly going down, twigs kept scratching his face; here were gnarled fruit trees, the Cellini apples Lange used to make cider and puree, Boscs, Russets and Orange Pippins; Lange's particular pride, the old pear trees: Beurré Hardy, Gute Luise, one tree with Christian's favourite variety, the red and yellow Comice, Meno preferred the cinnamon-red Madame Verté and the spherical Grüne Jagdbirne; in the cellar there were hundreds of jars of bottled fruit.

He waited. One woman's and one man's voice, then splashing and when they burst out laughing he recognized Ina and Siegbert; he squatted down and only stood up again when his legs started to hurt. The splashing again, they were laughing in the drawn-out way drunks laugh, Christian crept nearer and saw their milky bodies in the bathtub, they separated, murmured, came together, touched each other gently, as if they were two doctors sounding each other with the warmed membranes of their stethoscopes.

Yes, he thought, yes. You ought to be somewhere else. But he waited, avid and sad.

Then he went upstairs, fetched the loungers, put them up in Meno's living room and saw to the air beds. His thoughts wandered hither and thither and the chirping of the crickets coming through the open balcony door was excessively loud. The desk lamp would attract insects, he switched it off, went outside for a breath of fresh air. All at once the garden was alien, the frothy, dark-blue tree shadows threatening, there was still pop music coming from somewhere, suddenly cut through by squealing, as if someone were being thoroughly tickled. How boring, how meaningless! And all these blooms and plants, pushing against each other like forces in a polite and unfair game, existed just as well without him; this insight filled him with such consternation that he could no longer bear it on the balcony. The door opened. Verena switched the light on, started. 'You gave me a fright. I didn't know you were here –'

'Where are the others?'

'Still at the Bird of Paradise. Siegbert went off with Muriel and Fabian. Have you seen Reina?'

'No.'

'She left shortly after you. Christian . . . may I say something to you?' She looked past him, he had to swallow. Verena wanted to go into the garden, to the iron table, but he said no, even though, for a moment, he felt a desire for revenge because he was expecting reproaches.

'OK then, we can just as well stay here,' she said.

'No, I . . . Would you come? I'd like to show you Caravel. Just from outside –'

He hesitated, he turned away. 'We won't need to ring, I don't want to go in . . . it's not far,' he said quietly.

They walked along Mondleite, deserted at night, it was dark now at the Teerwagens' too. For a long time Verena said nothing and he didn't urge her, recalled the walk with Meno in the winter, before the birthday party in the Felsenburg, how mysterious and full of stories the district had seemed, now it looked closed. There was something ghost-like about Verena's dress over the streets that were like grey ribbons, she was wearing soft shoes, he couldn't hear her steps. 'I don't think it was right of you simply to leave like that,' she said when they'd already reached Heinrichstrasse, where the only lights were at Niklas's and in number 12, the house with the wisteria, the scent of which mingled with that of the elderberry bush outside Caravel. 'We'd so looked forward to this evening and then –'

'This is where I usually live.' Christian pointed over the arched gateway to number 11.

'You mustn't be annoyed with me for telling you this.'

'No.'

'I don't know if you realize yourself, but you have a way . . . We're dancing, you sit in the corner. We're enjoying ourselves, you're pulling a face.'

'Of course. My arrogance –'

'You don't need to be cynical. Please, you must understand, I don't have to tell you all this –'

'Well don't do it then.'

'Actually you're pretty immature,' Verena retorted softly. 'Pity.'

'But Siegbert, he's mature.'

'Let's go back. You've gone into a huff just like a peacock. Won't you listen to me for once! Or can't you stand being criticized?'

They walked back in silence, not by Wolfsleite, where Muriel and Fabian lived; he didn't know whether they'd given Verena their address or not.

He couldn't leave it at that. 'Out with it, then. What was it you wanted to say to me?' he said when they reached Mondleite again.

'Yes, that is arrogance,' she said reflectively. 'You call us into question, for to you everything we do's too stupid . . . All the fun of a dance, how common; then the look on your face, like, Oh God, how I must suffer, no one loves me, I'm all alone in this world full of cheap rock music and stupid jigging about, no one understands me, I'm so mis-understood, in such a bad way!'

'It's certainly not Bach those guys are strumming –' Christian was shivering with rage.

'Yes, that's what I'm talking about. This disparagement. And the arrogant twist of your lips when you express it, I don't need a lamp to see it. But I like what they do ten times better than your spoilt –'

He broke in. 'Oh, leave off.'

'I think you're a coward,' Verena called after him.

32

East Rome II. Barsano

'I'm not interested in what Fräulein Schevola thinks!' Schiffner stood up and began to walk agitatedly back and forth. 'I would like – no, I demand that that scene goes. We're both just back from the congress, you heard the directives just as well as I did and now you present me with this!' Schiffner threw the pages up in the air, they floated down slowly to the floor.

'We'll destroy the book if we insist on cutting that kind of scene,' Meno replied quietly.

'So what! Then she'll just have to rewrite the stuff. Why else did she become a writer? Do you know how many drafts Tolstoy made for his books? Tolstoy! And Fräulein Schevola and you rabbit on about "destroying the book" . . .' There was a knock at the door. 'Come in,' Schiffner roared. Frau Zäpter appeared in the doorway, small and apprehensive. 'Barsano's office have rung to say it starts at seven tonight.' Schiffner nodded and waved Frau Zäpter out with a rough gesture. 'What do you have to say about this, Josef?'

Josef Redlich lowered his head and nervously played with a ballpoint pen. 'But it's true, Heinz. Such . . . incidents did actually happen, we all know that, and our friends better than anyone –' Schiffner cut him short. 'Truth! As if literature had anything to do with truth! Novels aren't philosophy seminars. Novels always lie.'

'I don't share your view on that,' Josef Redlich ventured to object. 'You know my opinion: literature that capitulates in the face of reality is not literature but propaganda. We're not making propaganda, Heinz. Rohde let me have the manuscript, I agree with him. If we take that passage out we'll be castrating the book. And it's not the days of the Eleventh Plenary Session any more.'

'That's clearly your opinion too?' Schiffner leant over to Stefanie Wrobel, who avoided his eye. 'I only know that passage, not the context –'

'But I gave you the manuscript,' said Meno, astonished.

'I didn't get round to it. Herr Eschschloraque has priority.'

'All right, then, let's try it,' Schiffner said in conciliatory tones. 'But on your head be it, Josef. I will make my objections known if Central Office rings up and there are difficulties. I bow to the will of the majority of my editors. But I can tell you both right now' – Schiffner leant forward with his hands on the table and fixed his gaze on Josef Redlich and Meno in turn – 'it's your necks that are on the block. Of course the event Fräulein Schevola thinks she has to write about did occur. But the question is, to whose advantage is it if she does write about it? Our country has problems enough as it is, our friends as well, and she comes along with this old stuff. My God, who was it who started the war! That's just the counterclaim, and she's moaning and wailing just because a few Nazi women –'

'They weren't just Nazi women,' Meno said even more quietly. 'She portrays quite ordinary people.'

'Do shut up, Rohde. It was these very people you describe as "quite ordinary" who elected the Nazis in 1933! They sowed the whirlwind and were surprised to reap a hurricane. The scene ought to be cut precisely because your objection is possible, but have it your own way, and don't say I didn't warn you. – I want three external reports, then it must go to the Ministry first of all; I want a translation for our friends and that has to go off before anything's decided. This evening is the report on the congress; you'll write it again please, Herr Rohde, and show it to me.' He went over to his desk and handed his paper back to Meno. The pages were covered with corrections in red ink.

Meno looked back from the middle of the bridge to East Rome: a yellowish haze hung over the town, fed by the smoke from the factory chimneys; the outlines of Vogelstrom's house and the funicular creeping up the rise shimmered in the air; the slope above the Elbe drifted into the falling twilight like an island hedged round with a proliferation of roses. A smell of decay wafted over, perhaps the wind came from Arbogast's Chemical Institute. Judith Schevola was waiting on the Oberer Plan. She told Meno about the evening in the House with a Thousand Eyes and the Bird of Paradise and he let her talk; his thoughts were already at Barsano's reception that was being held in Block D, on Karl-Marx-Weg; it was the headquarters of the Party, the Schneckenstein, the former castle of an expropriated prince of the Wettin dynasty. Judith Schevola fell silent and surveyed Meno with furtive glances, Josef Redlich and Schiffner would have made the most of the situation and kept her on tenterhooks a while longer; Meno didn't like these little games they played with authors, the revenge of those whose hard work in the background went unheeded and drew little thanks; he told her about the editorial discussion.

'Three external reports,' Schevola said quietly after a while, 'and a translation for the Russians . . . That'll take for ever. That means the book is dead, it won't get through.'

'I promise I'll do everything I can.'

'And what can you do?' Schevola retorted in irritation. 'You know just as well as I do how things work here. It'll end up with you paying me an advance of ten thousand but the book won't be published.' That was common practice, Meno didn't dispute the fact: the publishers would pay a so-called difficult author for a bogus edition of, say, ten thousand copies, but in reality only a few hundred were printed, to be locked away in the collections of non-approved books in a few libraries – and the author, although cheated, couldn't even complain.

'I'm prepared to go a long way,' Meno said. 'You're very talented and I . . . I'm grateful that you trust me as your editor. Your writing is unusual. Very French. Elegant, light, roving, not ponderous like that of many German authors, especially those over here.'

'It's the first time you've said that to me.' Schevola turned away.

'I'm not trying to cheer you up. It's going to be hard work getting your book published. You've got enemies.'

'Why?'

Meno accepted the naive astonishment he saw in her expression as genuine. 'Why? You're lively. You're vivacious and passionate. You understand people, you express yourself in language that is worthy of the name. Put together, all this means that when people read you they have the feeling they're reading something true. Not intended as propaganda.'

'Something true, my editor says! That won't buy me anything. I have the impression that that's not what the reading public wants at all. They want entertainment, something to take their minds off things, otherwise stuff like Hermann Kant's *Aula* wouldn't have had such a success.'

'You want to write best-sellers? You won't. And in my opinion that's not something for you.'

'But the others are praised and courted, I'll have to bow and scrape, suck up to VIPs . . .'

'Listen,' Meno broke in, 'none of them is capable of writing a scene like the one in which your heroine says farewell to her father. You complain about your lack of success. Lack of success makes one sensitive. Sensitivity, along with background, is a writer's great asset. Don't let yourself be corrupted.'

'Said the man with the steady income. It's easy for you to talk of lack of success. True, I've got talent, as you say, but no one will know.' He sensed she was tired and didn't reply. They turned into Karl-Marx-Weg. At the gate to Schneckenstein they were stopped by soldiers who checked their identity cards and Meno's briefcase. A sergeant phoned the castle, Meno and Schevola waited, there was no point in getting worked up about the process and pointing out that the check and phone call had already been carried out by the sentry posts when they'd gone onto and left the bridge. The gate, a steel wall several metres high on rails, opened like a theatre backdrop and closed again behind them.

The drive was tarmacked, in earlier times carriages would have driven up the serpentine road, lit by spherical lamps, to the castle building. It was in the shadow of tall trees and noticeably cooler; Schevola was shivering and Meno gave her his jacket. 'Do you know Barsano?' he asked to prevent her from refusing it.

'Only from a distance. And you?'

'I've been up here a few times.'

'You were born in Moscow, weren't you?'

Meno looked at her in surprise. 'How do you know that?' She winked at him. 'I like to know about people I have to deal with. – Did you know that Barsano's father was one of the founders of the Comintern?'

'And of the German Communist Party, together with Rosa Luxemburg and Karl Liebknecht. The family emigrated to Moscow in thirty-three, they lived in the Hotel Lux, Barsano attended the Liebknecht School. His father died during the purges.'

'I didn't know that,' said Schevola.

'And never mention it. His mother and his brothers and sisters were arrested and he, as the son of an enemy of the people, was expelled from school and banished to Siberia. He slaved away in the mines and lost his left index finger. When we get there, behave as if you haven't seen it.'

'How long were you in Moscow?'

'I don't know exactly, I only have hazy memories. Sometimes I remember fragments of children's songs. My brother was born in thirty-eight, he knows more. My sister was still in kindergarten when we came back. – Can you speak Russian?'

'Only what I learnt at school, *Nina, Nina tam kartina* . . . and a little that has stuck in my mind from travels. – Why?'

424

'Because up there' – he pointed to the castle – 'they sometimes only speak Russian. Almost all of Barsano's people are ex-Muscovites, and they send their children to school and university in Moscow.'

'The Red aristocracy,' said Schevola. 'The ones in the West go to Paris and London and New York, here they go to Moscow. Paris . . . That's the city where all the women wear gloves and white dresses with black spots. Oh well. Mustn't it be great to be cured of your clichés. I'd still like to go there one day.'

'You might perhaps be disappointed.'

'Yes. The grapes will surely be sour. There's one single reason I'd like to go there. In his novel *The Man Who Watched the Trains Go By* Simenon has his central character, Kees Popinga, write a letter to the police chief: ". . . he deliberately used paper with the letterhead of the bar". So there are bars there that have their own writing paper! I think that's wonderful. It sounds so matter-of-course . . . As if it often happened that people wrote letters in bars.'

'You're a dreamer and pretty trusting,' Meno warned her with a smile. 'You don't know where I belong.'

'No, I don't know that,' Schevola said after a while.

The castle was a neo-classical fort, the main building flanked by two octagonal towers, the Soviet flag flying on the left-hand tower, on the right-hand one the flag of the Workers' and Peasants' Republic. Meno and Judith Schevola crossed the gravel of the square outside the entrance; a head of Lenin in reddish stone was like a meteorite lying on the ground, the Tartar face staring with a faint smile at the trees in the park; Schevola couldn't resist tapping it with her knuckles. 'Solid,' she said in surprise.

'What did you think?' Meno said, even more surprised. 'Just imagine if it sounded hollow.'

They waited in the foyer. The dusty brass hands on the clock clicked onto seven. Max Barsano could be heard laughing from some way away, immediately the group of people waiting relaxed, the faces of the Comrade General Secretaries in the two window-sized portraits on the walls either side of the entrance assumed encouraging expressions. Barsano stopped at the foot of the stairs, surveyed the assembled guests with a swift glance and, with an 'Excuse me, comrades', went up to Judith Schevola and clasped her right hand in both of his. 'You've had your feathers ruffled, so I hear,' he said to her in a sonorous bass voice that didn't seem to go with his delicate figure, 'doesn't matter! That means it's some good. Keep writing, tall oaks from little acorns grow and you're someone who's got what it takes to follow on from our great writers of the older generation.' With that, he went past Meno to the author Paul Schade, who was proudly wearing his anti-fascist-resistance medal on his chest, and to Eschschloraque, who gave a thin smile and elegantly sketched a bow of the head as they shook hands; Schiffner, whom Barsano greeted next, looked embarrassed after the praise that had echoed round the foyer, Josef Redlich glowed with pleasure. 'Just don't get carried away,' growled Paul Schade, the author of the revolutionary poem 'Roar, Russia', lengthy extracts from which were in the school readers of all their fellow socialist nations with the exception of the USSR, 'we'll deal with you later.' Schade, who held an important position in the Writers' Association, gave first Schevola then Meno a threatening look. Barsano turned to the two Londoners, father and son; Philipp in an elegant cream summer suit, still wearing his hat over his hair done up in a ponytail, something probably only he could get away with there. 'Well, Herr Professor,' Barsano cried cheerily, 'I'll send my barber round to you tomorrow. In the war those splendid locks would have been full of lice! – That's young people for you,' he said to his deputy, Karlheinz Schubert, who, at least a head taller than anyone else there, was doing the honours after Barsano in the cautious, slightly bent posture of people who are too tall. Barsano patted the Old Man of the Mountain on the shoulder, a gesture that would have seemed too hail-fellow-well-met and falsely jovial had it not been for the moment of hesitation that seemed to beg his complicity, to ask whether the restrained pat on the shoulder was acceptable; not everyone saw it as a mark of honour, for some it was crudely chummy familiarity, others perhaps even felt it marked them out. Barsano greeted Meno; he put his left hand in the pocket of his poorly cut jacket – how much more elegantly dressed were the Londoners, Eschschloraque and Schiffner! – then took it out again as if he realized that things one hid attracted interest, tried to smile but broke off immediately when the conversations of the others, conventional as they were, just filling in time, died away. 'How's your father? Haven't seen him for ages. Making preparations for a journey, is he?'

'He's giving illustrated talks. Most recently in the Magdeburg House of Culture.'

'Aha, in the Magdeburg House of Culture. Just needs to go down the Elbe. I wouldn't put it past him. Kurt Rohde gets in a canoe and paddles to Magdeburg.'

Schubert and Josef Redlich were the first to laugh.

'You're the spitting image of your mother,' Barsano said, subduing the laughter with a wave of the hand. 'Brave Luise. I've lots of memories.' He turned to Paul Schade. 'Do you remember her facing Nadezhda and showing her Vladimir Ilyich's letter?' Schade's leathery face brightened. 'And the hand grenade she threw back into the train, a real partisan!' As he spoke he gave Meno a disparaging look.

'Let's go into the film theatre,' Barsano said. 'Communal viewing of *TV News* at half past seven, the reports at eight.'

Meno and Schevola were the last to go in. Once they'd left, the foyer filled with members of staff from Party headquarters. A secretary attempted to breathe fresh life into three ceiling-high yellow rubber plants with water and peat. Voices could be heard from the offices again, one after the other lights gradually went on in the telephone booths underneath the picture of the General Secretary of the Communist Party of the Soviet Union.

'Probably government lines,' Schevola said. Black telephone receivers were painted sloping diagonally across the glass doors, below them was the yellow glow of the letter T engraved on the frosted glass. 'Do you know the man with the ponytail? And could you introduce me to him?' Schevola hadn't turned to Meno but addressed the air between him and Philipp Londoner, who was in front of them; she'd spoken loud enough for Philipp to slow down until he and Schevola were side by side; she tried clearing her throat, which Meno discourteously cut through with a 'And how is Marisa? Did you leave her in Leipzig?' and an innocent expression, at which Philipp muttered that she was still tired from a trip to Moscow as a member of the Chilean delegation to celebrate Yuri Vladimirovich's appointment. The film theatre was a box-shaped, wood-panelled room on the first floor. After impatiently shooing his guests to their seats, Barsano pressed a button; blinds came down over the windows, televisions slid out from the walls, immediately followed by the signature tune of *TV News*. 'Lower Jaw' was reading the news. That was what the newsreader was popularly called; with sparse hair and square spectacles, he sat stiff as a poker on the screen, like a mummy, holding a sheet of paper from which he read the news without making a single mistake and emphasizing each syllable equally – Lower Jaw had never made a slip of the tongue, the whole Republic seemed to be waiting for that unheard-of event to happen; only the lower half of his angular face moved, grinding out news item after news item at the calm, steady speed with which a cable is unrolled from a cable drum . . . *moving purposefully towards the realization*. Schevola and Philipp Londoner were sitting in front of Meno, on Schevola's left was Barsano's deputy, Schubert, who'd squeezed into the row at the last minute . . . *comprehensive exchange of views . . . in a constructive atmosphere*. On the screens combine harvesters advanced in formation over the wide grain fields of the Uckermark . . . *impressive testimony . . . all-round strengthening*. Barsano pointed to the screen, a jubilant sea of waving hands as *the General Secretary of the*

Central Committee of the Socialist Unity Party and Chairman of the State Council of the German Democratic Republic, Comrade . . . shook the hand of the *Chairman of the Praesidium of the State Great Hural of the Mongolian People's Republic, Comrade . . . matter of prime concern . . . unshakeable foundation.* Now the bottling plant of the state-owned Wine and Preserves Combine was shown, muted clinking of glass as bottling forewoman Comrade . . . spoke of the overfulfilment of the plan's targets for gooseberry juice . . . *the assent of millions.* The next picture showed tanks in the course of a NATO exercise, Paul Schade roared 'Imperialist swine!' . . . *indestructible relationship based on mutual trust.* Aeroplanes thundered across the sky, rockets jutted out their noses threateningly. Cut: a major in the 'army service uniform/summer' of the land forces of the National People's Army in a steel helmet, binoculars to his eyes, scanning the horizon: . . . *impressive testimony.* Eschschloraque took out his handkerchief and quietly blew his nose. Now the reporters of *TV News* were visiting the Agricultural Cooperative 'Forward' that had harvested the largest pumpkin in the Republic. "s already been on *Unique or Freak!*' Paul Schade crowed . . . *worldwide recognition . . . dynamic growth.* Three of the four televisions suddenly went dark. Barsano pressed a button, there was a knock at the door, Herr Ritschel in an Arbogast Institute lab coat came in and inquired, emphasizing each word equally, what Barsano's wishes were . . . *far-reaching change* came from the television, which was still on; the General Secretary flapped his hands at the three sets and told Comrade Ritschel to repair them immediately.

Barsano had chairs taken to his office, a sparsely furnished room at the end of a corridor with a grey PVC floor that swallowed up the sound of their footsteps; the murmur of voices behind the doors with the official signs, the sound of roll-fronted cupboards being opened and closed, the clatter of typewriters seemed to fade away in the puddles of light left by the fluorescent tubes with yellowing protective strips. While Paul Schade arranged his manuscript on the lectern and started to speak when Barsano gave the nod, Meno looked round: wood-panelling, a few veneered cupboards, a wide desk with a pennant on the right and a signed portrait of Lenin, which Barsano was very proud of, on the left corner, photographs of his wife – she was a doctor at the Friedrich Wolf Hospital, one of the few wives of senior functionaries who still went out to work – and of his daughter, about whom, as far as Meno knew, Barsano never spoke. Paul Schade's voice grew higher, the worker-writer's cheeks were flushed bright red and what had happened at the congress was about to happen again: one of his feared fits of rage, foaming with coarse venom, that the audience let wash over them with closed eyes and stony expressions and that in Berlin had come to a ghastly and grotesque end: Paul Schade's false teeth had come loose and, rattling like those of a ghostly skeleton, shot out between his lips, which had brought a horrified expression even to the face of the chairman of the Writers' Association. Meno shuddered as he recalled the urge to laugh welling up inside him, like a poisonous liquid boiling over in a hot saucepan, at the sight, at the icily embarrassed silence of the gathering: woe to anyone who lost control of themselves; the corners of Judith Schevola's mouth had twitched, as they did now when Schade raised his left forefinger to castigate 'parasites, formalists, scribblers out of touch with the people and the real world', during which, remarkably, he did not look at Meno, the Old Man of the Mountain or Schevola, as he had in Berlin, but at Eschschloraque, who was sitting in the front row beside Barsano, legs crossed, and was giving his fingernails all the more bored and weary looks the more enraged Paul Schade became. Judith Schevola had assumed her insect-researcher look again, the cold, stone-grey interest in a man with medals and decorations bobbing up and down on his chest as he continued his vulgar vituperation. What was she thinking? Was she reflecting on the fact that Paul Schade had been in a concentration camp, had experienced the Gestapo's torture chambers? Was she thinking of his book in which he described his childhood in a working-class district of Berlin and with which he had made his name until no one read him of their own free will any more since 'Roar, Russia' and various novels in which Stalin was portrayed as a father and the Germans – with the exception of those who had emigrated to the Soviet Union or communists working in the underground – as a wolfish race of incorrigible fascists? Josef Redlich was squirming restlessly in his seat in the second row beside Schiffner. Was it just that he couldn't stand the shouting or was he thinking of Paul Schade's editor, whom no one envied . . . Art was a weapon in the war between the classes, Schade bawled, today it was no longer enough to sit quietly in one's attic room, turning well-crafted sentences, the world was once more threatened by the old enemy, by imperialism and its accomplices, literature had to go on the offensive, novels had to be like MIG fighters and articles like a salvo from a MIG and he demanded that agitators be sent to the schools to practise revolutionary poetry with the children; he had noticed that bourgeois ideas were creeping back into the teaching of literature and music, formalism, defeatism, recently he'd discovered poems by Eichendorff in a school reader, that was pure reactionary ideology. And by other Romantics! In earlier days people like that were strung up from the nearest lamp post. Eschschloraque nodded.

Schiffner, who followed Schade at the lectern, drip-fed his audience with figures and tables, dwelt on Dresdner Edition's overfulfilment of its Export Plan norms for the non-socialist economic area and on the acquisition of hard currency. After him Josef Redlich reported on the political-ideological training of Dresdner Edition's authors, especially the younger ones; at this point Judith Schevola stood up, cried that she couldn't bear any more and left the room, slamming the door behind her. 'Don't worry, my dear, we won't molest you, you're as white-hot as ice,' Eschschloraque mocked at her departing figure. 'Oh, isn't she sensitive,' Barsano said, 'and yet what Comrade Redlich is demanding is correct, only too correct. We've slackened the reins too much recently.

That always takes its toll. Reactionary elements immediately stir like the nest of vipers they are. Think they can make something of it. We must be vigilant, comrades. The young are always at risk. They must be given a firm grounding in ideology.' After Josef Redlich had returned to his seat, Meno didn't dare get up to read his paper; it was about the 'Role of the Author in a Developed Socialist Society', of all things, and had already been criticized in Berlin; he looked across at Schiffner, who gave a quick shake of the head, even though he'd cut the most provocative passages, and stood up to leave, to see how Judith Schevola was, which Paul Schade misinterpreted, and said, 'There's no point in you dumping your shit again here, Rohde, your mother would have given you a good box round the ears for stuff like that', which had Barsano, Schubert and Schiffner slapping their thighs in amusement.

Meno went out. Judith Schevola had opened the window at the end of the corridor.

'There's a balcony at the front,' he suggested. She nodded. 'I need some fresh air. I just have to get away from here.'

Their footsteps echoed in the empty corridors. The sound of voices and the clatter of typewriters could only be heard from a few rooms. In the rotunda the murmur of conversation drifted up from the telephone booths on the ground floor, the service lift for food in the shaft beside the stairs started to move, one of the beige microphones of the intercom crackled, someone cleared their throat, then all was quiet again. Curtains from the sixties, printed with grey flowers, hung over the wide double doors.

'One for you?' He offered her his packet of Orient, she mechanically took one, didn't move when he gave her a light.

'May I ask you something?' She turned her face towards him, without looking at him. It looked pale and tired but perhaps that was an illusion created by the faint light that came to them from the searchlights in the park directed at the castle. 'What are you actually doing here?'

He remained silent, smoked. 'And you?'

'Typical. You're as cautious as . . . well, as an editor. – There was a time when I believed in all that. The better social order . . . But with them?' She pointed vaguely over her shoulder. Meno leant his ear forward, which made her smile. 'Oh, I don't care if they do hear! They know anyway, don't you think? All those clichés . . . it makes me want to puke! And most of all Schade would like to lock us up, like in Stalin's days. Or simply *whisht*.' She made the gesture of having her throat cut.

'Do be quiet,' Meno whispered, 'just smoke your cigarette but keep your mouth shut.'

'Shall I tell you something? I can't be bothered.' She laughed her ugly, gritty laugh. 'My grandmother always used to say, "You're nowhere so safe as under Old Nick's hams, child."' She waved her hand, drew on her cigarette. 'And afterwards we'll be good as gold and play along with them, say nothing and get drunk. That's it, not a word more.'

'It's not just for me,' Meno said after a long pause. 'My mother . . . oh, let's forget it. Later, perhaps, if you're really interested. Schade's just chucked me out with a verbal box round the ears.'

'You're a funny person,' Schevola said reflectively. 'I never know where I am with you. Despite that, I trust you.'

'We should go back in,' said Meno, changing the subject, 'you can't simply leave one of Barsano's receptions as if it were a birthday party where you've had an argument.'

'And what comes after the insults?'

'Drinks, a film and singing revolutionary hymns. He seems to like "Vetcherniyzvon".'

'Then he's moved to tears?'

'That kind of thing.'

'I'll stay for that.'

They finished their cigarettes. In the distance dogs could be heard barking and for the first time Meno noticed the overpowering smell of henbane that grew rampant on the castle walls; the park must attract lots of nocturnal insects.

433

'Calmed down, have we?' Barsano asked with a cool ironic expression when they came back. 'You shouldn't be so touchy, everyone says what they think here, you have to be able to take the odd jab.'

'A conspiratorial meeting!' Schubert gave a suggestive smile.

'The following's on offer, comrades,' said Barsano, counting the items off on his fingers. 'One: watch a film, *Chapayev* or *Vesyolye rebyata* –'

'Have you got the whole series?' Paul Schade broke in.

'The lot. Or Sergei Eisenstein's *Oktyabr*. Two: we can have some food. Three: go down to the White Pavilion and see how Comrade Vogelstrom's getting on with the panorama of revolution. Four: something special. I'll show you some documents from the time of struggle. So, what d'you think? – Right, we'll have a bite to eat and then communal viewing – of? *Oktyabr*. Great. A good choice.' Barsano pressed a button, the doors of a cupboard opened, a control desk with hundreds of buttons and levers came out. There was a knock at the door after he'd pressed a button, a man in forestry uniform came in. 'No, no,' Barsano told the man, 'I want the comrade duty cook', pressed another button, a man with a grey beard in the uniform of German Railways appeared. 'Not you either, isn't it possible –' He searched, scratched the nape of his neck, pressed the next button, this time it seemed to be the right one, the duty cook from the Ivan V. Michurin restaurant complex pushed in a trolley with dishes and a canister of kasha, a mini-bar on the shelf beneath them.

'Buckwheat groats,' Philipp Londoner groaned to Eschschloraque, whom he'd asked how his play was progressing and the nightwatchman question was developing.

'You're all far too spoilt,' Paul Schade snapped. 'During the time of struggle we old revolutionaries sometimes roasted rats and in Spain we lived on dry bread for weeks! And in the concentration camp we'd have been glad of a bowl of buckwheat groats, I can tell you. You of the Young Guard should be carrying the revolution forward!' His reproachful look took in Philipp Londoner and Judith Schevola, who were in front of him in the queue.

'A very valuable pedagogical hint,' the Old Man of the Mountain agreed, filling his bowl with a portion indicating either genuine appetite or his openness to memories. Paul Schade turned away contemptuously and fished out a bottle of Żubrówka vodka. 'Don't think you can butter me up like that, Comrade Altberg. Spare me your comments and honour us with your presence at an Association meeting for once instead. – And you, *Herr* Eschschloraque, been travelling in the West again?'

'*Comrade* Eschschloraque . . . I'm ap*paul*ed to be so misunderstood.' With that Eschschloraque turned away and started to mix a long drink, a 'Gentle Angel', for himself and Philipp Londoner: one part curaçao, one part champagne, one part orange juice. Karlheinz Schubert poured himself a glass of vodka, *Sto gramm*, murmured, 'Na zdravje' and downed it in a few appreciative gulps. The Old Man of the Mountain told him he'd regret it on an empty stomach but Barsano's deputy just pulled a face and poured himself another glass. Barsano gave the control desk a kick, telling those around that Arbogast had installed the thing, it was getting worse and worse, he'd completely forgotten which was the button for the projectionist, but he was already at the door waiting for Barsano to say what he wanted.

The kasha smelt and tasted of wall filler, the Old Man of the Mountain was the only one who hadn't finished when Barsano went round personally pouring vodka he'd spiced with ginger and nutmeg, a little sugar and cinnamon, the 'concertina' mixture, of which Meno had unhappy memories from previous visits. Barsano grinned as he filled Meno's glass to the brim. 'Y'spend too much time at y'r desk, comrade. Can't take a drink. Well, I'll treat you to a real one. Y'r mother could take her drink, a revolutionary through and through she was. There you are, get that down you and you'll see splendid . . . whatsit.' Meno had little desire to see splendid 'whatsit', the last time it had been a porcelain oval in Barsano's personal toilet; at least that had revealed to Meno that the District Secretary must be a great fan of the 'Digedags' and 'Abrafax' series of children's comics, huge piles of which were stacked on a ledge in the middle of the glazed tiles with the panorama of 'Our World of Tomorrow': blond children were sitting on the arms of full-bosomed tractor drivers waving to their fathers, who were zooming across the cloudless sky in jet aeroplanes; on the left-hand side was a lab full of microscopes and retorts with well-known scientists in gleaming white coats bending over them; magnetic suspension railways, an underground chicken farm, viaducts on several levels with futuristic cars gliding along them; deserts and steppes were transformed into blooming landscapes by canals; on the right-hand wall star-cities on distant planets were to be seen, orbited by spaceships and glass-roofed island resorts; and on the floor was a Lenin quotation, in the original Russian: 'So let us dream! But on condition that we seriously believe in our dream, that we observe real life most precisely, that we connect our observations to our dream, that we conscientiously work to realize what we imagine! Dreaming is necessary . . . VLADIMIR ILYICH LENIN.'

'To the Great Socialist October Revolution,' Barsano cried, raising his glass. Schubert and Paul Schade uttered a 'Gorko, gorko', as was usual in the Soviet Union – 'Bitter, bitter – and downed with good cheer / as if it were water clear'. Judith Schevola didn't seem to be bothered by the 'concertina' either. After his glass had been filled, Meno had quickly gone over to the cabinet with the presents from delegations of friendly governments; there was a carpet from the Frunze Military Academy on which the heads of Marx, Engels and Lenin had been sewn with tiny glass beads beneath crossed Kalashnikovs; a model of the Moscow television tower in malachite; a Bulgarian wine cask Young Communists had made by sticking halves of clothes pegs together and with folk designs burnt into it, and a 'Cup of Friendship between the Nations' in the form of a brass amphora, from Greece; that was what Meno was heading for; he didn't want to make the acquaintance of Our World of Tomorrow again; pretending to suffer from a coughing fit, he poured his 'concertina' into the Friendship between the Nations; it swirled round in it. 'To the memory of our great Comrade Vladimir Ilyich Lenin', '. . . to the good health of our great Comrade Yuri Vladimirovich Andropov', '. . . to the Party', '. . . to world revolution'.

Judith Schevola wasn't even swaying when all the toasts had been drunk. Paul Schade gave her a tap of appreciation on her shoulder, 'Great girl! I'll venture a dance with you', and Schiffner, a beatific smile on his face, patted her cheek.

By that time Ritschel had finished his work in the film theatre. The projectionist, with several rolls of film over his shoulder, went up some stairs into the projection room; behind a little window the size of an embrasure in a castle wall was an ancient Ernemann projector, as Meno knew from the Londoners, whom Barsano quite often invited to his film evenings. The film theatre was not solely used for Barsano's personal hobby, films were previewed there, decisions were taken as to whether a film could be shown to the general public or not. The light went out once the District Secretary and those he wanted with him in the front row had dropped into their seats, the machine began to rattle, a shaft of light with motes of dust floating in it cast the opening images onto the screen, which had risen as if by magic; at first a white pane with rounded edges was to be seen with black scratches scurrying over it, figures appeared in cross-hairs, a crackly, quivering countdown, Barsano and Paul Schade shifted expectantly from side to side in their seats.

33

Pre-military training camp

Garden smells, the fragrance of the rhododendrons, of jasmine opening, pale-faced, in the evening, white mouths of the murmuring twilight, and blue, ochre, water-tinted currents, fanned by the breeze; the secrets of the cuckoo-striped grass that deepened to purple at the edges, suddenly the call of a bird from the top of a maple full of trickling green, elderberry, its whispers sounding as if someone were pouring sand,

a leaf, a gleaming paddle, carried up by a thermal, it whirled back down and stopped on the branch from which it had fallen off, so that you looked at the street to make sure the passers-by weren't walking backwards, as in silent films; the sudden flash of bicycle spokes as a boy turned a bike propped up on the curb; dissonance: a thistle in a meadow with fruit trees,

cats slumbering on stacks of wood behind sheds, first two, then three, then another grey one, a brown one stretching on brown wood and there: a tabby, dozens of cats sitting in the sun, at a stubbornly respectful distance from each other, no cat looked at another, none was lying parallel to another or behind another's back, they looked past each other at angles that seemed precisely calculated, however minimal they were, and more and more kept appearing, as silently as outlines on a developing photograph, some might be touchable, some not; as if the colony were made up out of different June days and through a disruption of the normal course of time all the cats that had sat on this spot over the last hundred years had become visible,

then summer came.

'We would prefer not to see you for the time being,' Josta had written after her discharge from hospital and it was that 'we' – which included

Daniel and Lucie as well, who didn't understand what had happened – that disturbed Richard and increased the melancholy that often, after the peaceful enticement of spring, its vulnerable and non-assertive green, befell him in the hot months. The summer was demanding, driving, everything was going full throttle, a hectic, sweat-soaked hustle, the sky seemed to be turning like a millstone, weighing down on treetops and roofs, honing the river to a shining blade; the blossoms didn't calm down at all, they had no time, or so it seemed, and burst open, pumping aggressive white out onto the streets that, around midday, beneath a pebble-grey sun scratched like old films, was swirled up into streaks of heat then withered and, when the blossoms, crackling, fell onto the paths, billowing up like clouds of plaster dust. Richard went swimming on Thursdays – despite the heat he preferred the indoor to outdoor pools – circled round Josta's house, found the shop where Frau Schmücke sold fish. 'The boy'll be on holiday soon,' she said in response to his cautious enquiry when the shop was empty and the tench in the glass tank sank lethargically back down to the bottom, 'it looks as if they intend to go away. The little girl doesn't laugh any more. By the way, someone came for the children, I didn't need to look after them. – A woman,' she added, 'I don't know her. From the city's Family Welfare Office, she said.'

The boys from the eleventh grade went to the training camp. Christian brought home a light-green uniform and a gas mask he'd been given and had a pair of black boots over his shoulder. 'It's only two weeks,' he said to Anne, who was concerned. The uniform came from a depot, stank of mothballs; Robert, who was unhappy that his brother was back in Caravel for the holidays, threw the windows wide open: 'That stuff's stinking out the whole pad! And by the way, bro, some tart keeps calling, is she the one from Waldbrunn? Reina, she says she's called, Reina Kossmann.'

'You mind your own business,' Christian said. He went to Wiener's to have his hair cut short. 'Might as well go the whole hog' – he went in his uniform and boots, his cap under one of the epaulettes. Wiener said nothing as he worked and the customers fell silent, avoided his eye. Only when Colonel Hentter, formerly an officer on the general staff of Rommel's Afrika Corps, stood up and put his hand on Christian's shoulder did Wiener and his assistants look up. 'We thought we'd paid,' Hentter said, 'I saw lads like you die like flies at El Alamein. And then you turn up here in that outfit. Go home and only put it on when you have to.'

Christian was disappointed that the colonel hadn't understood. He wasn't wearing the uniform out of pride but because he wanted to be pitied, perhaps out of defiance too, a masochistic 'look-at-me' feeling, the public exhibition of suffering. The Russians were still in Afghanistan. Poland was still under martial law. He couldn't bear the idea of running around free with the uniform lying as a reminder in the room. The moment he'd been given his kit, a shadow had fallen across his freedom, the days until he was to leave had been poisoned – and he felt a need for dignity: outwardly he conformed, inside himself he said, 'I'm wearing these clothes, I even have short hair, I'm doing more than is required and despite that you have no power over me.' He covered up the real reason: he put on the uniform earlier in order to make the moment of departure more bearable.

Richard saw Christian when he came back from the barber's, could that lanky beanpole with the bright red scalp, blond hair shorn to shoe-brush length, really be his son? Anne, who'd been working in the garden and had just put the watering can down by the rose beds next to the gate, cried out, lifted up her hands, the doors of Tietze's Shiguli slammed shut, Richard saw Niklas in a white coat, waving, the watering can fell over, running slowly in flowery patches over the paved path. Christian waved back, stopped in front of Anne, spoke to her shaking his head, she didn't react, he picked up the can and watered the roses, which rustled in the heat like crêpe paper.

*

The carriages were crammed full, the Railway had only put a few special compartments at their disposal, in which schoolboys in light green from Dresden and the surrounding area were sitting squeezed up together, supervised by their teachers. The embracing, the shedding of tears and the surreptitious passing of love letters was over, doors slammed, a conductor blew a piercing whistle and raised his baton for departure, slowly, like a steamroller inching its way between the ash-grey platforms, the train began to move, leaving behind the people – waving, running alongside, blowing kisses, reaching for the flailing arms of particularly delicate boys still tied to their mother's apron strings – who so clearly fell into the categories of 'parents' and 'girlfriend' that Christian couldn't accept this concentration of sentimentality and angrily refused an apple Falk offered him; he didn't like these farewells, they didn't make it any easier, tear-stained faces didn't make the inescapable any less inescapable. For the first time in his life he'd forbidden his mother something: to drive him to the station; he'd done it so curtly that he was now suffering pangs of conscience. Anne had slapped him, the first time for many years, he'd seen her horrified expression but had still gone out slamming the door behind him. Pigeons flew up, Christian squeezed into his corner and looked at the glass arch at the end of the beer-brown station concourse, there were reefs of bird droppings hanging from the steel girders. After Siegbert and Jens had gone on enough about Christian's haircut, they invited him to play cards, they played for eighths of a pfennig and Christian lost a few ten-pfennig pieces. Sitting opposite were boys from the School of the Cross, whispering to each other, watching them sleepily. Their school had an elitist reputation, the choir, under their choirmaster, Rudolf Mauersberger, had become famous all over the world, its classical curriculum made exceptionally high demands on the pupils; recently the school had been decried as 'Red' and, so it was said, its singing had also suffered. Still: to be a Crossian was special, it counted for something in Dresden; the ladies at their coffee mornings raised their eyebrows, grandmothers clasped their hands and exclaimed, 'Oh no, oh no!' with happiness if their grandchild had made it through those august portals. Meno was an Old Crossian, as was Christian's Uncle Hans, and both Muriel and Fabian were down to go to the senior high school there. The Crossians frequented the Café Toscana, where they displayed the bored-blasé expression that had been characteristic of them for generations and that, as reliably and incestuously as a transfusion with your own blood, as Meno said, established them in the bourgeoisie of Dresden Island. Christian envied them their self-assurance. Siegbert ignored the boys in the other compartments, he'd brought a stack of 'Compass' adventure stories and started to read one as soon as they got bored with cards. Falk took his guitar out of its case. Now the Crossians perked up. 'Hey, that's great, shall we play something together?' With an elegantly casual gesture a sun-tanned boy with shoulder-length hair indicated an accordion on the luggage rack. 'And you can get your horn out, Fatso.'

'D'you think I'm a queer, or what?' The one addressed as 'Fatso', fair-haired and thin as a rake, grinned and shook his fist at him.

'That's not the one I mean, blockhead!' The sun-tanned boy took his accordion down. 'Crossians – *viva la musica!*' Raising an eyebrow, he turned to Falk. 'Can you play?'

'Can you read music?'

'Can you do irony?' the sun-tanned Crossian replied to Christian.

The Crossians wanted to sing the Latin 'Carmina Burana', but had to do it by themselves since no one else knew them. Falk accompanied them on his guitar, the fair-haired Fatso blew his trumpet with feeling. The only ones they all knew were the hymn of the Italian labour movement, 'Bandiera rossa', and the German equivalent, 'Side by Side We March', and as no one wanted to sing those, the Crossians once more started on part-songs. The sun-tanned boy played his accordion and conducted with nods of the head.

The train meandered through Lusatia, a landscape of stone houses with half-timbered upper storeys, the palatal 'r', sleepy villages and gently rolling fields stretching away to the horizon; here potatoes were called 'apern' and many of the place names on the signs were in two languages, German and Sorb. When the train travelled slowly you could hear the skylarks singing over the pale yellow of the wheat; there was a smell of sweat and dust and sweetened rose-hip tea. From the front compartment came the clack of the conductor's revolving ticket punch, Christian leant forward, Stabenow's youthful voice could be heard, he was giving an enthusiastic lecture on something or other and sitting round him were Hagen Schlemmer and a few more of those keen on physics whose eyes still lit up at names like Niels Bohr and Kapitza. Stabenow too was wearing the training-camp uniform. Dr Frank supervised the civil-defence course for girls at the senior high.

The camp, two and a half acres with huts, flagpoles and parade ground, was on the edge of the little town of Schirgiswalde, surrounded by green hills high up on which were detached houses with closed roller-shutters and single miniature spruce trees; they looked artificial, like the scenery for a model railway. The Waldbrunners were greeted by a corporal who showed them the hut they'd been allocated: two communal rooms, each for ten boys, double bunk beds, reveille at six, exercises, at the double to wash in the central washroom, bed-making and cleaning of rooms, breakfast at seven, then training.

'Any free time?'

'Name?' The corporal drew himself up to his full height in front of Jens Ansorge, who was standing in the doorway chewing gum. 'And take that chewing gum out when you're talking to me.' – 'Ansorge.' The corporal wrote it down. 'You're not on holiday here, just you remember that. You're on toilet duty first, Ansorge. Report to me afterwards. Understood?'

Jens said nothing.

'Have you understood, knucklehead?'

'Uhuh.'

'Heels together, hand at your cap and: Yes, Comrade Corporal. – We'll be practising that.'

The days began with an ear-piercing whistle followed by Corporal Hantsch's bellowed, 'Platoon Nine – Up! Prepare for morning exercises.' Then one or two morose, tousled heads would appear, yawns, sighs, grins of disbelief at not being woken at home, in their own cosy bed, by a loving mother to the smells of tea and breakfast but by him, the corporal who'd been seconded from a motorized infantry unit to Schirgiswalde and thought this was the direct extension of a National People's Army barrack square where he could drill the arrogant, pampered senior-high puppies with their affected airs to his heart's content. During morning exercises, which consisted of running at the double interspersed with bunny hops, press-ups and knee bends on the parade ground, Christian observed Hantsch: for the first time in his life he had encountered a person who took obvious pleasure in ordering others about, demonstrating his power by trying to find their weaknesses and, when he'd found them (Hantsch seemed to possess an unerring instinct for that), by exposing them for his own satisfaction and his victim's torment. It was brazen and it disturbed Christian that Hantsch didn't seem to know (or didn't want to know) the limit beyond which humiliation began. Naturally Hantsch realized that Christian, after morning exercises, when they had to run, bare-chested, to the washroom, tried to drape his towel round him like a toga in order to hide his acne – which didn't work because the towel was much too short – that he always tried to find a place at the back of the row so that the others wouldn't see his bad skin. Hantsch made the platoon halt, came up to Christian, looked him up and down with an expression of surprise and

444

disgust and said, 'Christ, no woman's going to want to fuck you. Platoon about turn!' All the boys turned round, Christian closed his eyes, but he could feel the eyes of the others burning into his body. 'Hey, now he's so red the pimples are almost invisible. It's really revolting, man, don't you wash yourself properly, can't you do anything about it?' Putting on a concerned expression, Hantsch ordered them to turn back and move on. In the washroom he stood behind Christian, watching how he washed. 'And your willy?'

'In the evening, Comrade Corporal,' Christian said through clenched jaws, giddy with rage.

'You leave the thing stinking all day, you dirty dog.'

'Leave him in peace,' Falk muttered. Hantsch slowly turned his face towards him, everything went quiet in the washroom. Hantsch shrugged his shoulders. 'What do I care? Senior-grade students, huh!' He blew down his nose in contempt.

The heat made the drill, the mind-numbing marking time in highly polished boots that, after two or three about-turns on the dry paths, were covered in dust, the 'Left turn!' – 'Right turn!' – 'Right, left wheel – marrch!', the field exercises, in which only Stabenow let his platoon rest in the shade of the brambles and the fringes of the woods, and the assault run, a combination of press-ups, squats and flying jumps in the camp's Werner Seelenbinder Stadium, into sweat-soaked torture. Only Siegbert seemed at ease, at least his only response to the daily programme was a shrug of the shoulders. 'Oh, that's nothing,' he said with a touch of contempt to Falk, who kept getting out of step when they were marching and was therefore characterized as an 'uncoordinated idiot' by Hantsch. Siegbert grew impatient. 'Just pull yourself together and concentrate. I don't want you to spoil our points score, we have to get one over those idiots from the School of the Cross.' On the way to the canteen there was a board showing the daily points score of the various platoons; Siegbert was determined to finish first.

'This isn't a war – and you're not Gilbert Wolzow either,' Falk objected.

'Oh what the hell. Reina was right, you're just too sissy.'

Christian stood in front of Falk. 'You must be out of your mind, Siggi.'

The camp was commanded by a former major of the National People's Army, a stocky man with a wrinkled face and sunburnt complexion, his fat belly made his uniform stick out over his belt. In the evening he would stride up and down the tarmacked camp road, swollen with pride and affable, examining the things the boys bought from the camp shop (vanilla ice cream for twenty pfennigs, pink strawberry ice that tasted of water and strawberries that were on the way towards strawberry flavour); clicked his heels as he welcomed 'his' (as he put it) platoon leaders back, and Christian sometimes watched him as he stood, hands clasped behind his back, looking over to the houses with the shutters down. 'His' platoon leaders, 'his' property (the training camp), 'his' soldiers as Major Volick called the boys at morning roll-call and talks in the canteen; his favourite word was 'immaculate'. A jovial, affable man who seemed to be at one with himself and the world – and one who could have run a corresponding camp with the same joviality and affability fifty years ago, or so it seemed to Christian. He didn't discuss his impressions with anyone, didn't write either. Siegbert replied to Verena's letters, which came almost daily; Christian recognized them from her characteristic spiky handwriting; he himself had a letter from Meno, who told him there was little worth telling: the heat in Dresden, the stones on the bottom of the Elbe were visible, dead fish were floating in the branches of the river; two girls by the names of Verena Winkler and Reina Kossmann had sent him a thank-you letter for 'your hospitality and the wonderful time we had in your house'. Then he mentioned the Kaminski twins, who were becoming more and more free and easy in their behaviour, then that he had managed to find a precise adjective for the colour of one of the saturniid moths on the stairs at Caravel. Typical Meno, Christian thought.

Now Richard had said it; he turned away from the table around which Barbara and Ulrich, Niklas and Gudrun, Iris and Hans Hoffmann were sitting, turned his shoulder towards Anne, who kept her head bowed while the ticking of the grandfather clock grew louder and louder in the living room of Caravel, and Meno, who was sitting next to Regine, felt a profound sense of shame, he couldn't say why, and sympathy for his brother-in-law, who had always seemed so strong and uncomplicated to him; the usual clouds life brought, certainly, but basically a sunny character, a practical person little given to introspection whose nature seemed to say, What d'you expect? You can live life in a different way, be more cheerful, more open to the simple things that are amazed at you worriers anyway – what you make out of them, how you manage to festoon a breath of fresh forest air with complexes.

'You have to tell your colleagues.' Barbara let out a long breath.

'But the children' – Anne raised her tear-stained face – 'the children . . . What do we do if they carry out their threat?'

'Things are never as bad as they seem,' said Gudrun, trying to look on the bright side.

'You think so?' Richard stood up, walked to and fro. 'They're not your children. Would you risk it?'

'My God, it'd just mean they don't go to university . . . Do you have a problem with that? I love my child just as much whether she goes to university or not . . . But with you lot it absolutely has to be something special. I think it would be much more important for them to be able to go through life with their heads held high, if you make a clean breast of it; then you'd have a clear conscience too.'

'What high-sounding words!' Richard said, mocking Barbara's

contribution. Ulrich tried to calm things down, took Barbara's hand, which was flapping indignantly. 'Don't get worked up, Bubbles. You may well be right but I can understand Anne and Richard. It's their children's future that's at stake and even if it makes no difference to you whether Ina goes to university or not – it makes a difference to her.'

'The lads *want* to go to university,' said Meno, who so far had taken no part in the discussion, 'at least as far as I'm aware. Anne and Richard want the best for them and that, I think, involves studying at university –'

'At the price of Richard spying on his colleagues?' Hans Hoffmann leant forward; he'd gone pale. 'I wouldn't have thought that of you, Meno. You're an opportunist.'

'Now listen here . . .'

'You mustn't provoke them,' said Gudrun.

'We have problems with Muriel, but do you think we'd be prepared to spy on people? Not provoke them! What nonsense! They're the ones who provoke us!'

Niklas raised his hands. 'I can remember a similar case in the State Orchestra. Then it was a question of whether the daughter could go to university. After a while he admitted it. He'd only told them unimportant stuff. By that time his daughter was at university and was still allowed to stay on.'

'How do you know he only told them unimportant stuff?'

'What are you suggesting, Iris?'

'There's no need to shout.'

'Stop it! We been through all these pros and cons already. What if they take a different approach with me?' Richard was walking up and down again.

'And if they don't?' Barbara asked challengingly.

'It's all right for you to talk, it's not you who're taking the risk. It's not Ina's future that's at stake,' Anne interjected.

448

'They say that Security only approach certain people . . .' Gudrun gave Richard a suspicious look.

'You take my breath away. Do you think this can't happen to you? A word from you in the ear of the high-ups . . . Well, just you wait and see,' Richard shouted with malice and desperation.

'How about asking Christian and Robert what their opinion is? We're going over their heads and yet they're the ones most immediately concerned –'

'You're being naive,' Richard snorted. 'Can you imagine the pressure we'll put them under if we invite them to join us and ask them what they think of the matter! Eh? Take pity on your parents, that's what they'll feel's being demanded here, so then they'll yield and give up the idea of going to university, to their own disadvantage. Is that your idea of responsibility? If we did that we'd be delegating it, to boys still going through puberty who can hardly assess the consequences of decisions. Moreover that would be cowardly. No, Meno, I'm sorry, but that question's outside your competence.'

'That's enough!' Ulrich thumped the table. 'We have to do something.' Now they all started talking at once. Regine sat, mute and dejected, beside Meno, who also remained silent.

'Give it here.' Siegbert stretched out his hand. Jens threw him the frog he'd taken off one of the cherry trees, large numbers of which grew round the camp. During the first rest the boys had stuffed themselves with the yellow cherries, Hantsch had waited patiently, then ordered gas-mask training; Falk had torn the mask off his face and, even though Hantsch threatened to make him do extra training, dashed off into the bushes – afterwards Hantsch had silently offered him a water bottle.

'A nice frog,' Siegbert said. He thought for a moment. Hagen Schlemmer was lying, arms outstretched, on the forest floor, Christian was watching Falk, who, red in the face, was gasping for breath. Siegbert felt in his pocket, took out his penknife, placed the frog on a piece of bark in front of him and cut off its legs.

'They really do keep thrashing,' he observed. Falk opened his mouth; Hagen Schlemmer said, 'Yeuch', Jens looked round – Hantsch had gone off to the side somewhere, they'd been wondering how to pay him back for this or that (stinging nettles? a push so that he landed in a fresh heap of cow dung? but he'd have seen them); it was too soon, it wasn't the right occasion, they'd agreed that something like that had to mature. Christian saw the frog's body slowly separate from the blade and therefore from its detached legs, that were still mechanically open-ing and closing, the animal was croaking softly and its arms were still going to and fro like windscreen wipers; Christian couldn't understand it, looked up to where the branches were shimmering, then back down again to the alert, interested expression on Siegbert's face; then he stood up, took the knife, which was sticking in the piece of bark between the frog's body and legs, and stuck it in Siegbert's thigh; it didn't go in very far. Siegbert said nothing.

Christian twisted the knife to the left and the right. Only now did Siegbert seem to understand and protested in surprise. Christian pulled the knife out and threw it into the bushes. Then he looked at the frog; Falk also tried to do something for the animal; they exchanged glances and Christian looked for a largish stone. Now Siegbert really did protest. Hantsch came. 'What's going on here?' He looked from one to the other, his eye finally coming to rest on Christian. 'What have you done, Hoffmann?' He went over to Siegbert, saw the blood. 'Are you crazy? You've –' he shook his head, then he seemed to under-stand something and couldn't help smiling – 'you've had it, man. You're finished. I quite clearly saw you throw something away, that will be the weapon, vital evidence.' He seems to read detective stories, Chris-tian thought.

'That's not true,' Siegbert said, groaning. 'That's not true Comrade Corporal. Christian didn't . . . have anything to do with it. He was trying to help me. I fell over . . . right on something sharp. Too stupid.'

'And what was that?' Hantsch bent down over the ground, eagerly scouring it. 'Can you stand up? You two carry him out of the way.' He pointed to Jens and Hagen. 'Nothing to be seen. What was it you say you fell on?'

'That was before, I crawled a short way.' Now Siegbert's face was waxen. 'The others are witnesses.'

Hantsch straightened up, stared from one to the other. 'If you give false evidence here there'll be consequences. We'll get to the bottom of this. Form two groups, look for the knife.'

'I don't have a knife,' Siegbert said.

'But I saw it in your hand myself, you were slicing an apple, yesterday. What's this nonsense you're telling me, Füger? Hoffmann stabbed you and out of misconceived comradeship –'

'That's what you say,' Siegbert replied wearily. 'I borrowed the knife from someone.'

'From whom? His name!'

'I don't know, I can't remember . . . A damn nuisance to fall like that. I can't walk.'

Hantsch ordered them to make a stretcher and had Siegbert carried to the medical station. Falk found the knife. He buried it and they had to keep searching until the evening. Since Siegbert stuck to his version and no one gave any evidence to the contrary, Hantsch could only report an accident to Major Volick. The injury wasn't serious, but from now on Siegbert was on indoor duty.

What irritated Meno and made him think rather than amusing him – amusement at certain aspects of life, the Old Man of the Mountain had told him, also presupposed a certain kind of inhumanity: a taking-things-lightly that drifts like a balloon, beguiling, rootless and weightless, above the days and so having nothing to do with them at a deeper level – what seemed so strange to him that he didn't simply find it entertaining was the fact that scenes he had been through could be repeated, at the same hour on a different day, at the same position of the sun (again it was in Caravel), with the same smells and the same seating arrangement; even Regine had come after her work in St Joseph's Hospital, again she had chosen to sit next to Meno on the black leather couch, opposite Querner's *Landscape during a Thaw*, next to the Hoffmanns' Junost television and the grandfather clock with the Westminster chimes; again the same arguments about Richard's revelation and again Richard had paced up and down like a big cat. Irregularities in the picture didn't abolish the correspondence with the evening two days previously; indeed, they seemed to emphasize it, as if the scene were just being mirrored and the mirror admitted: I could be precise, if I wanted, but I don't feel like it, for in that case everyone might notice me and that's no fun; my efforts are to remain something for the better observers. Now Richard and Meno were standing on the veranda, drinking beer and looking out of the open window at the garden.

'I see you like Wernesgrüner,' Richard said.

'I find it lighter, more hoppy and leafy than Radeberger,' Meno said. – Why did he tell us? Was he afraid one of us might find out before he admitted it; does he think one of us might know something?

'Particular kinds of men always go for particular kinds of beer, I've noticed that,' said Richard. – Keeps out of everything, does my brother-in-law. Unfathomable. Do I like him? Yes, I do, somehow or other. He's not a windbag, he knows how to keep his mouth shut. Why hasn't he got a wife? Could he be . . . ? Anne ought to know. But what do brothers and sisters know about each other? What do I know about Hans? And he about me? Perhaps Meno's a ladies' man? But still waters sometimes just run still.

'Top-fermented or bottom-fermented guys? Those that prefer

dark beer and those that drink light beer for preference?' – Perhaps he's trying something out? Perhaps he's trying to see how far he can go? He said they wanted information about things inside the hospital from him. He didn't say they wanted information about his relations and if he's kept quiet about that, his revelation to us is meaningless. Or is it? Does he suspect one of us is an informer? Have his doubts about me? Ulrich as well. Party member, director of an industrial combine and both of us born in Moscow, the sons of communists. He wants to be able to tell himself that he's done everything possible without bringing himself into danger. He wants us to be in the situation of sharing his knowledge.

'Wernesgrüner's drunk by artists and people who don't really care for things that are centralized, accepted, popular, but have retained their scepticism: can something that is generally recognized and the centre of attention for the general public, as Radeberger is among beers, really be the best of all? Your Wernesgrüner men look for what is hidden, they look for the *éminence grise*. They're often *éminences grises* themselves – or think they are. In musical terms Wernesgrüner men are those who're sceptical about the Berlin Philharmonic and put the Vienna Phil. at the top. Niklas is a Wernesgrüner. They also believe in conspiracies. And Wernesgrüners will always prefer an Erzgebirge landscape to any far-away country, however exotic it is.' Richard raised his glass to Meno. 'The country of quiet colours. That's what they love. It's just the same with me, I only need to look at the Querners. Even though I'm a Radeberger guy.'

'Well I prefer the State Orchestra.' Meno emptied his glass. The beer tasted fresh as a mountain spring and was cold as an old key.

'The amethyst looks good in front of the Insel volumes. – So in mineral terms the Radebergers would stick to diamonds, the Wernesgrüners to emeralds?'

'Yes, because deep down inside they believe emeralds are the real thing,' Richard said. – Basically, Ulrich and Meno are Reds. The only thing that surprises me is that Anne is completely free of that. Or seems to be. What do brothers and sisters know of each other? What do husbands and wives know of each other? He is a bit unworldly, my brother-in-law, with his insect research and his writing he doesn't show anyone. Can't be any good, otherwise he'd be reading some of it to us from time to time, they're all supposed to be vain, are authors. Spends his days at the publisher's poring over paper with writing or printing on, what difference does it make whether they use commas in this way or that? But everyone's made the way they are. 'Tell me, Meno, there's something I've wanted to ask you for ages, you know the Faun Palace, there's a plant in the foyer I call a snake plant because it has striped leaves. Do you know what it's really called?'

'Have you any idea whether Christian's all right? I wrote to him but he's not answered yet . . . They could still conscript me, you know. My last spell with the reserves was only three years ago.' – Richard with his calculations: practice prevails, theorists are cripples who know nothing of life and the world. And yet we all have our feet firmly immersed in our dreams. What he's saying is that Wernesgrüners don't really count. What nonsense. And just because doctors are important. Demigods in white, huh! They make people healthy again, so what? If a patient's stupid, he's just as stupid when he's well again. And if I were to suddenly start drinking Radeberger beer, so what? 'Do you happen to have a bottle of Felsenkeller?'

'He has to see the training camp through, we told him that. We can't get him out of it and if he wants to go to university, he can put up with the two weeks,' Richard said.

'It could be a *Vriesea splendens*, a bromeliad,' Meno said.

One evening in the pre-military training camp Christian was reading a book, an autobiographical account with the cover wrapped in the newspaper of the Party's youth organization. Gothic print on foxed wood-pulp paper; someone shouted: 'Attention!' Stools were shifted and before Christian could react the book was snatched out of his hand. Christian stared at Hantsch's triumphant expression. He wanted to jump down from his bed and take the book back but he couldn't move. The book was called *My Way to Scapa Flow*, written by the U-boat commander Günther Prien. Naturally Hantsch opened it at the last picture: Hitler awarding Prien the Knight's Cross; Hantsch closed the book again, lifted it up. 'Who did you get this from?'

Christian said nothing even though fear clutched at his throat. It had been a serious mistake to read that book, especially there, and he wished he could turn the clock back to the moment when Siegbert had given it to him and say 'No', to refuse it on the grounds of the uneasy feeling he'd had and that he'd ignored.

'I'm asking you who you got this book from.' Hantsch went out into the hall and called in the boys who were outside cleaning their boots.

Christian said nothing. Siegbert, standing by the door, pale, said nothing, avoided looking at anyone. Hantsch said, so quietly that Christian thought he might be dreaming and his classmates would dissolve into thin air like an apparition, 'So it's yours, as I assume from your silence. You will pay dearly for this, Hoffmann. You read Nazi books, you who are studying to qualify for university. At a socialist senior high school. That's something I've never encountered before. – All of you here' – he gestured right round the room – 'are witnesses to this. There will be an investigation. This time you're not going to get away with it, Hoffmann. You two' – he designated Siegbert and Jens – 'are to make sure Hoffmann doesn't run off or do something stupid. I will report this to the Commandant.'

'Herr Hoffmann? – Frank, Christian's class teacher here. Can I have a word with you? – A private word. It's about your boy, something's happened.'

Frank had called him at the clinic, in the ward. Richard sat down.

'On the telephone there was talk of him having read a Hitler book. I've tried to speak to my colleague who's in Schirgiswalde but they're still all with the Commandant. They've set up an investigation.'

Richard listened as Frank made a suggestion but it was only after some seconds that he realized he was being asked to go and pick up Frank and drive with him to Schirgiswalde.

He called Anne at work but couldn't get through to her. He called home, but when Robert answered he immediately put the phone down again, he hadn't worked out whether it would be wise to tell the boy something to pass on to Anne; he'd picked up the phone without thinking and now he had doubts whether it would be right to inform Anne, she might perhaps crack up; then he saw her in his mind's eye and thought he could hear another voice inside himself telling him that he just had to get through to her, it would be better if she came with him; he looked up and saw the nurses eyeing him and thought, Where's your decisiveness, surgeon? Then he rang home again. 'Listen carefully to what I'm saying, Robert', and he told him that he was going to Schirgiswalde with Christian's class teacher; 'Tell Anne. I'll call back as soon as I know what it's about.'

Frank was already waiting for him in Waldbrunn; he told him that in the meantime Stabenow had called and given him the details; not a Hitler book but one from the Hitler period; he felt it was a serious matter. Richard drove like a madman; the inhabitants of Schirgiswalde didn't respond to questions about the training camp; only when he stopped two policemen in a patrol car by waving and honking was he told the way, not without first being asked to show his driving licence and to take an alcohol test. Now Richard would have liked to have had Anne with him, for he felt capable of killing the policemen; Frank tried to calm things down, showed them an identity card that, however, didn't impress the two policemen.

*

Christian saw his father come out of Major Volick's office with Dr Frank, his short, sandy hair still showing the mark of the scrub cap; the dark-blue eyes didn't look at him.

'Come with me,' was all Richard said. They went outside. The flags on the parade ground were fluttering in the wind. A platoon of boys from the School of the Cross were practising the goose step. Christian observed his father, suddenly the fear returned that he hadn't felt during the interrogation by Volick and Hantsch. 'You've really got yourself into a mess,' Richard said wearily, turning to look at the gate, where two guards were letting a few pupils in on the camp road; laughing and babbling tipsily, they strolled off towards the huts.

'Been allowed out,' Richard said, with a nod in their direction.

'They were in Wilthen, where the brandy comes from.' If Anne and Richard had come to visit him on a normal day, Christian would have felt ashamed for the drunken schoolboys, now he felt nothing but indifference.

'Didn't we tell you not to do anything stupid?'

Christian hunched up, made himself as small as possible; he was determined not to say anything. Richard raised his arms, mentioned Erik Orré, saying his efforts must have been pointless, a pure waste of time; he dropped his arms. 'How could you, my lad . . . you know very well what kind of place this is.'

'Yes.'

'So? Why did you do it? My God, there's a swastika in the book! I sometimes wonder –' Richard clasped his forehead. 'I've never seen you with a book like that, but what does that mean? Where did you get it from?' This seemed to represent a hope and he clutched at it, suddenly grasped Christian's shoulders, shook him. 'Where from? From Lange, that old fool? Did someone lend it to you? You can't be that stupid. I just can't imagine that.'

Christian remained silent, hunched up even more.

'And we're left to get you out of it. I've got into this mess, now you get me out of it. You're not just stupid, you're selfish too. What d'you think Anne'll say? She doesn't know yet, or perhaps Robert's telling her at this very moment. Did you think of that? – Of course not. My son doesn't think, he just acts without thinking. Have you any idea what all this means?' Richard shook Christian again. 'No, you haven't. They were talking about the military prosecutor, about a juvenile court. They believe we haven't brought you up properly and you'd be better off in a reformatory. Your class teacher has persuaded them to agree to let your case be dealt with by the school. They'll call a staff meeting.'

'Yes,' Christian said tonelessly, he had to keep hold of himself.

'Now you just listen to me, my lad. We have to work out a strategy. You'll say you read the book because you wanted to find out about the fascists' way of thinking. Because you wanted to understand how it was possible for Hitler to seize power. You hoped you would get some information about that out of it. Have you understood?'

'Yes.'

'Did you say something different before?'

'No.'

'Did they want to know why you read it?'

'No.'

'Good. That's the version you'll tell them. And you'll stick to it whatever bait they put out for you. They'll definitely want to try and pin something on you. You'll use the Red Front argument. Have you understood? – I'm asking if you've understood!'

34

The Ascanian Island

For expulsion: Schnürchel, Kosinke, Schanzler, the two principals: Engelmann and Fahner. Against expulsion: Frank, Uhl, Kolb, Stabenow, Baumann. Five–five. Christian's case was to be brought before the District Schools Officer.

'Did you manage to find anything out about him?' Ulrich asked when Barbara, Anne, Meno and Richard met before leaving for Waldbrunn. It was a Saturday. Christian's grandfather was going to come by bus from Glashütte; he knew the Schools Officer, who also came from Glashütte.

'He's building a house,' Richard replied.

'Good. That means that in the first place he'll have trouble getting supplies and, in the second place, problems with the tradesmen. Anything else?' Ulrich had turned up in his Sunday best and with the 'sweet', the Party badge, in his buttonhole; Barbara had been to Wiener's and was wearing a flamboyant white dress with large black flowers on it. After the meeting with the District Schools Officer they wanted to make the most of their outing together and go for a meal.

'He drives a Saporoshez.'

'Then he'll need dates with a garage – and any amount of spare parts. Anything else?'

'He's sixty-four.'

'So he'll be retiring next year at the latest. Firstly that means he won't want to saddle himself with another difficult case. He'll want to make it short and to cover himself. He'll probably pass Christian's case on up the line. Minus point. Secondly that means that he'll be all the more interested in help with building his house. What use is a retired Schools Officer to anyone? That's what the tradesmen will be telling themselves. Plus point.'

'And if the house is finished before next year?' Barbara objected. Ulrich gave a knowing smile. 'What are you thinking of, Bubbles. We're living in a planned economy.'

DIARY

Sunflower wallpaper, hardboard table, beige telephone, on the wall the Comrade Chairman of the State Council, the grim-faced likeness of the lady Minister of Education, opposite a portrait of Makarenko. We were sitting in a semicircle facing the desk and the fact that the Schools Officer stood up to lower the blind over the only window could be an escape mechanism on the part of the short, tubby man, perhaps also an attempt to gain time: six pairs of eyes staring at him expectantly, narrowly, anxiously, restlessly, disparagingly, six times bodily odours on this hot day, which had not yet reached its zenith; Barbara's heavy and Ulrich's light perfume (eau de Cologne, he'd soaked the handkerchief in his breast pocket with it and kept taking it out to wipe his bald head, a damp patch on his jacket pocket slowly grew larger) in competition from either side, and when the Schools Officer, who had fished a sign with the name Röbach out of a drawer, sat down again, Richard said, 'My son', Ulrich said, 'My nephew', Arthur Hoffmann said, 'My grandson'; then for a while no one said anything and Anne started. – I sat and waited to see how she would proceed. I was interested in that. The researcher into spiders, Barbara would have said, if at that point she'd felt like a diversion: observing me instead of the Schools Officer. They were being a little mean and Anne alone wasn't aware of it (I'm not entirely sure of that but my sister's never been devious); that's why they let her speak – also, of course, because they knew it would make a greater impression if it was the mother who spoke: she who was generally reserved, at least when faced with all these men present, sitting on the edge of their chairs, just managing to control their inner urge to speak; even Arthur Hoffmann, sitting upright like a retired officer who has to balance the weight of the medals on his chest, seemed to be waiting impatiently for Anne to finish, as if the mother were not the best person to speak up for her child; as if he, the experienced officer, were watching the young folk using playground tactics against a hard-boiled enemy interpreting gifts brought by Greeks. Richard and Arthur Hoffmann had greeted each other briefly: cheek-to-cheek embrace, short discussion of the table reservation in the restaurant, no 'How's things?' or 'Not seen you for ages' (a Christmas card, that was all, as I knew from Anne, pre-printed with angels and gold lettering, Arthur's signature neat and precise, the dent made by the pencil still visible under the letters); no 'Hi, my son', or 'Hello, Father', just the terse assurance that there was no problem with the table reservation; then Arthur shook Barbara's hand, ignoring for the moment Ulrich's proffered hand, gave Barbara a charming, ceremonious, friendly nod, and yet with a touch more emphasis than his greeting for Anne, hat and umbrella in his left hand. I hadn't seen him for two years, he didn't seem to have changed at all: the thick, cropped, snow-white hair with the whorl Richard and Christian also had, the gold-rimmed spectacles, big blue eyes behind the ground glass, a coolly friendly cornflower gaze; the deliberate, measured gestures, the slender hands that Richard had inherited and that dealt with clocks without sentimentality yet appropriately: without kid gloves such as people wore for whom clocks, especially valuable ones, were just highly prized ornaments; without the thoughtless roughness of those who saw clocks as mere objects of practical use and who couldn't care less what kind of ticking thing they wore on their wrist as long as it performed its function of measuring time as precisely as possible and as reliably as possible. Röbach didn't interrupt Anne, even though he must have been familiar with the case. He'd put a file with Christian's name on the table, nodded at Anne's halting explanations that, with many repetitions and tear-choked assurances, begged him to regard Christian's deed as a silly, childish escapade. – He was sorry, Röbach said, but that was precisely what he was still in doubt about. Principal Fahner had sent him Christian's file and in it there was this and that element that indicated that . . . Röbach was sweating and gave Ulrich's handkerchief ploy a long look. 'You're welcome to open the window, if you want,' Barbara said. Röbach declined;

no, no, he said, that would just mean the hot air from outside would come in and it was the same with the fans, they just swirled the warm air round the room, did nothing to cool it down. – 'Yes, at this time of the year it ought to be cool in a room, in an apartment!' Ulrich exclaimed. The people in the Dresden apartment blocks were really sweating, that was the way it was with concrete slabs and asphalt joints and tin roofs and you couldn't remedy it just with eau de Cologne . . . 'Although,' he went on brightly, that was worth thinking about, he'd have to have a chat about it with his colleague, the Technical Director of the Karl Marx Combine, man-to-man, one director to another: eau-de-Cologne atomizers in every newly built apartment. It wouldn't do much good though, might even just encourage allergies, joking aside: anyone who had a house could consider himself fortunate, with the new methods of insulation it was on the one hand pleasantly warm in winter and on the other refreshingly cool in summer, even our forefathers with their clay-brick buildings had known that and in the Combine they'd partly relearnt it, partly developed something new, just have a look at this. Ulrich took a piece of paper and with a This-is-the-house-that-Jack-built, he'd drawn a house that looked like a lantern in a single line: 'Very simple when you know the principle.' – Yes, of course, you had to know that: Röbach seemed to be sweating even more, 'that you can do it just like that, off the cuff, so to speak, I presume you have experience of this?' He was familiar with the game, he said, there were several methods of drawing a house in one line; he was building a house, a real house, and in that case it wasn't, unfortunately, just a matter of a pencil and paper. Ulrich nodded: 'If you could draw the workmen' – he picked up the pencil and doodled a few, one was even pushing a wheelbarrow – 'who simply just do what they're supposed to' – 'If only!' Röbach's face was shining. 'But where on earth can you find them? And modern insulating materials as well?' Yes, if everything was as easy as on the sheet of paper where you could draw a line from the matchstick man to the house-that-Jack-built with a pencil! – 'Yes,' Ulrich said with a laugh, 'like that', and drew an arrow. – But insulating materials weren't the only *thing, Barbara said, when Röbach slid the file back and forward a bit, then left his hands above it without touching it. True, they were important, but there were other kinds of insulation, and not purely theoretical, she just happened, as a furrier who was also a qualified dressmaker, to have a few samples of lovely insulating material with her, 'Just feel', and she handed Röbach a swatch card of materials across the table. — 'But I'm sure we've taken up too much of your time already,' Arthur Hoffmann said; the effect was like a blade cutting the air between Röbach's hand (still close to the file) and Barbara's swatch card; it was Saturday, the Schools Officer reassured them, glancing at his watch, he'd no other appointments until twelve; now, as he turned his wrist to look at his watch to see the time, he picked up the swatch, felt the materials between his fingers; above all now, in summer, Barbara went on, they said it was going to be a hot summer, you could sense it already and her customers sensed it too, and the ventilation that was possible in suits made from that quality of cloth; according to his watch there were still twenty-two minutes left, the Schools Officer said, nodding; Arthur Hoffmann pulled back the left sleeve of his jacket, two watches could be seen, pieces from his collection that was known in other countries as well; he took one off, handed it to the Schools Officer, 'Nineteen minutes precisely, if you would like to check it for yourself . . . forgive me for speaking frankly, yours is by Poljot, not too bad, designed for everyday use in Russia, but . . . that cosmonaut on the face.'*

They waited.

'Right then.' The District Schools Officer gave a deep sigh, pushed the drawing, the cloth samples and the watch away from him. 'I'll have to pass it on to the Regional Schools Officer.'

Downriver, enclosed by arms of the Elbe, was the Ascanian Island. That was where Richard and Meno were heading after a fruitless meeting with the Regional Schools Officer. He had turned out to be a timid, indecisive man who dropped Christian's file like a hot potato. 'Oh God, oh God, what's this that's being loaded on me again, always these difficult cases, Herr Doktor Hoffmann. You've no idea of the stuff that arrives here every day. Only yesterday we had a similar case . . . What's the matter with our young people? What's going on? I can't do anything, anything at all. It has to go to someone higher up. I'm sorry but I can't make a decision on this.'

That left the lawyer, Sperber.

'Thanks for arranging this,' Richard said to Meno. They were standing at the entrance to Grauleite, part of Arbogast's Institute behind them. 'Did it take a great effort to persuade him – I mean, was he annoyed? After all, I'm not part of the family and you aren't married to Hanna any more.'

'He picked up the telephone right away.' Meno lit his pipe with the spherical bowl and glanced through the papers again. 'Can we trust Sperber, what d'you think?' Richard seemed nervous, they were already within sight of the guards in Grauleite, one could see them both from Sibyllenleite and from Buchensteig, which met the road there. The streets were empty, apart from a few children playing football in the square outside Rapallo Castle and the Sibyllenhof restaurant, but the funicular would soon be bringing up people who were coming home from work in the town. But it was already starting to get dark, the implacable July sun was sinking; by day it was like a disc of boiling milk in the stone-white sky, recognizable only by pressure marks, circles of waves pulsing out; as if the air were a body that had been gashed by the low-lying rays, it had been covered with lines of reddish metallic discoloration, light rubbed raw: haemoglobin that was dispersed and deposited in layers on the fences, the shiny surfaces of dark car roofs hot enough to fry an egg on, the cracked asphalt of the streets, that surrendered its living red first and the iron molecules, glittering rust that remained.

'Of course, he has contact with them.' Meno nodded in the direction of the grey concrete block on Grauleite. With all its aerials it looked like a larded roast that had gone wrong, left mouldering in the deep terrine of the ring of walls. The clatter of a typewriter could be heard from one of the windows. 'Londoner says if anyone can help us, it's him. He called Joffe as well, but he declined: no accused, no defender. Such affairs had no business in a lawyers' chambers.'

'They're all hand in glove with each other. There's no lawyer in the country who isn't in cahoots with them. We simply have no choice.'

The guard at the entrance patiently checked all their papers, made a few telephone calls and let the two men through with an imperious nod. At the end of the road was a black-and-yellow-striped sentry box with a barrier, the soldier on duty glanced briefly at their identity cards and gave them two one-quarter permits. If it was Sperber who had arranged for that, they had a long discussion to look forward to. They set out across the bridge.

'Have you been here before?' Richard asked; he was walking in front of Meno, there was scarcely room for two people side by side on the bridge. It was made of iron and its railings were closed off with wire netting; a weathered sign said 'Grauleite' with 'Min njet' beneath it in Cyrillic characters that the soldiers of the Red Army had put on buildings after the war.

'Once with my senior editor and an author, once with Hanna,' Meno replied, 'but each time we went to see Joffe, not Sperber.' Joffe, the bald lawyer with horn-rimmed glasses whom many people knew from television: with heavy rings on his fingers, that he spread out to emphasize his measured speech, he presented the fortnightly programme *Paragraph*, during which he discussed difficult and spectacular cases and answered viewers' questions. Joffe also wrote in his free time and had published two love stories with Dresdner Edition, brilliant pleas, the response to which had in many cases been a deafening silence. Eschschloraque and Joffe hated each other, the relationship between Sperber and Joffe was said to be difficult as well.

'You know Joffe?' Richard looked at Meno with an expression of surprise and suspicion.

'I was just thinking about him. There aren't many lawyers in the country. He sometimes comes to the office.'

'A professed communist with a predilection for capitalist sports cars,' Richard said.

Meno looked at his watch. 'We'd better hurry up, we've still quite a way to go.'

They were above the Rose Gorge; beside it a few turrets and battlements of Arbogast House peeked out of the web of trees, some flat ground with a swing hammock and Arbogast's observatory not far away. There was no one to be seen, the bridge empty as far as it stretched; the windows of Arbogast House caught the late rays of the sun and threw them back in warm copper tones. There was hardly any wind at all, the Old Man of the Mountain would have said the air was rummaging round in its pockets a bit; there were currents, the warm evening air rising, a strong marshy smell from the Rose Gorge with its thousands of flowers looking inflamed in the darkness.

The inflamed body of a giantess lying on her side, legs drawn up half modestly, half lasciviously, Meno wrote, *she seemed to be leaning on one arm, snuggling up against the curve of the bridge; white and red islands that had burst open on her body, and this could be heard: an unceasing, deep humming, like the drone of a transformer but without the crackle as it switches on and off; thousands of bees were scouring the roses, stopping them from congealing, as would have been right and proper for them in the falling twilight, the red, the white liquid, the extract of flower heads woven from hundreds of petals: delicate material, membranes that seemed to consist of old fragrances expressing themselves in fragments: spikenard, battlefield sweetness, forming thin braids, as it were, in the marshy smell and attaching themselves to the brown decay of the pillars, climbing up like vetch – an advance guard of roses was already on the way, exposing tendrils as thick as bell clappers – strengthened by clusters of blossom deepening their red into crimson in their centres, covered with a transparent, glutinous substance, like the sticky traps of pitcher plants, that they released in the no-longer-hot, not-yet-cool phase of evening, in the expectantly trembling stage shortly before being touched, all a-quiver under the tiny engravings of insect legs of which the humming faun of the bees consisted; and suddenly, when the flowers – replete with red, resembling wounds dripping red, magnets sucking in swarms of insects – showed patches of white, white roses a wind we could not yet feel had touched and opened, I was made to think of one of my old teachers, a chemist showing the prospective zoologists the shelves of his laboratory: stuffed vixens; regina purple 'is a term for three coal tar dyes known since 1860'; rose-chafer paint: which tipped over the blossoms rustling in the wind from the country and set windows of fire a-glitter; rokzellin, an 'azo dye close to true red', with which the oscillating rays, like brushes dipped in it, painted the pulsating hedges; again, when the wind turned, splashes of white among the tumour-like clumps of red roses; picrotoxin, a 'poison obtained from the berry of Anamirta cocculus, it forms a fine, white, crystalline, extremely bitter-tasting powder or crystal needles arranged in a star-form'; or was it the up-and-down of the bees, dusted all over with pollen, that created the impression of a swirling flow, repeatedly discharging white –*

'Look, over there.' Richard pointed to the bank of the Schwarze Schwester, which, now visible, was winding its way along the Rose Gorge like a snake gleaming purple and tar-black.

'The statues?'

'Yes. I'd like to know who this wilderness belongs to.' Richard took his jacket off and slung it over his shoulder.

'Arbogast, I assume. At least, it's below his Institute. As far as I know it was supposed to have been a rose nursery.'

'As far as I know, it still is. – I once had a patient who worked here. An accident at work with interesting consequences for the insurance. Got a thorn in his forefinger and it festered, eventually we had to amputate. – It stinks of petroleum here. I wouldn't be surprised if

Arbogast's chemical laboratory didn't discharge into the stream. Everything's dead down there.'

'Who knows?' Meno replied. The marble statues, green with age and neglect, were on the bank of the Schwarze Schwester, up to their waists in nettles and asphodel; here and there the face of a stone warrior could be seen entwined by roses; Amazons with bows and arrows that on his last visit Meno had seen with their breasts clear of foliage had been almost completely swallowed up by the hedges.

'Anne told me you were doing a book with Arbogast?'

'His autobiography, I'm helping him, sifting through material, listening to him. He's very much in favour of oral expression.'

'What does he say about the time he spent in Sochi? There's all kinds of rumours.'

'Not Sochi. Sinop.'

Richard nodded. 'Yes, you know more about that, having been born over there.'

Meno seemed not to notice the jibe. 'So far we haven't talked about it and you know how it is – that phase might be left out. It doesn't depend on us.'

'He wrote me a letter, he wants to work together with the clinic. Medical projects on combating tumours.' Richard had let the little dig slip out without giving it much thought and now he wanted say something friendly to Meno, who seemed taciturn and subdued; it couldn't be him or Christian's problem that was bothering him, perhaps it was just the heat. 'By the way, those string quartets you gave me – top class. The Amadeus Quartet play outstandingly well. Those guys at Eterna must know what they're getting for their limited resources of hard currency.'

'Nothing but the best.' Meno smiled. 'What has Niklas to say about them?'

'Benchmark recording. He's got it, of course, though not the Eterna but the Deutsche Grammophon original. He hinted that I should note the difference.'

'Oh' – now Meno made an effort to speak in a serious tone – 'so you've already checked which recording had the better sound mixer?'

'Impossible to say, our man as well as the one from over there are both masters of their art but Grammophon have the better microphones and speakers, that's just the way things are, we can't do anything about it. And the better vinyl, of course.'

'But you have the better record player?'

'The very idea! Not even the better needle. Niklas is fair, I have to give him that. It would be no problem for him to decide the matter once and for all by bringing stuff back with him. But that would be like the high jump on the moon – only the Americans can get there, so they'd only be defeating themselves, in the long run it's no fun.'

'It's self-irony, is it? I thought music was sacrosanct, especially German music.'

'Well, we're not exactly the norm, I can see that.' Richard laughed. The last time Meno had seen him laugh was at the birthday party, when he'd been given *Landscape during a Thaw*. Meno remembered Christian and fell silent. He looked across to the ruinous pseudo-baroque town house that used to belong to a manufacturer of photographic paper but now housed the rules committee for the game of skat; four flags were hanging limply from the flagpoles outside the building: the ace of clubs, the queen of spades, the king of hearts and the ten of diamonds; there were lights on, they seemed to be pondering over enquiries.

The DEFA film studios were beyond the Rose Gorge, in the valley of the Schwarze Schwester, the sheds and the rails, on which scenery was moved backwards and forwards, could be seen. The studio grounds were fenced in, there were watchtowers, tall street lamps curved like cobras mingled their dull light with that of the searchlights from the towers. A gigantic Sandman waved, his helicopter was slowly coming towards him from the far end of the valley, the sleepy-time sand was in a third car, Richard and Meno observed it squashed in a corner that the roses from the gorge had already taken over. The bulbs hanging from a chain over the bridge went on but only about half lit up, some were making rasping noises, would soon go out.

'Odd that you can't see anyone,' Richard said, 'the scenery cars seem to go of their own accord.'

'Remotely controlled, perhaps?' Meno raised his hand, music came from one of the studios: 'First we-he wa-a-tch our bedtime sho-how, then ev'ry chi-i-ld to slee-eep must go-ho . . .'; the familiar ditty of the *Sandman* programme, which started at ten to seven. They continued on their way. Settings for Westerns could be seen, on a poster a larger-than-life-size DEFA Indian was brandishing his tomahawk. Beside it were rows of garden gnomes, next to them an arbour, probably for the popular programme *You and Your Garden*. A searchlight caught the Weather Fairy at the entrance to the site, a cardboard eagle perched on an aerial, the emblem of the Monday-evening programme of carefully selected clips from Western TV, *The Black Channel*, by and with Karl-Eduard von Schnitzler, known as 'Sully Eddy'. That's where Frau Zwirnevaden works, Meno thought.

The closer they came to the Ascanian Island, the more nervous Richard grew, imagining scenarios of what would happen to Christian if Sperber couldn't find a way out or, contrary to Londoner's assurance, refused to take on the case. 'What else could we do then?' He went through lists of names. Could Londoner himself not do something, after all he was a close friend of the Chairman of the State Council; would Meno ask for an appointment with Barsano or perhaps with Arbogast? He was an influential man, valued by the high-ups, an important earner of hard currency.

Meno tried to calm him down. 'First of all let's see what Sperber says.' But he too was wondering what they could do if Sperber held back. 'And Christian? Has he written that essay?' 'That essay' had been Anne's idea, Christian was to present his view of the affair, explain why he'd read the memoirs of a U-boat commander in Hitler's navy.

'Yes. It's been sent to the Regional Schools Officer and to the Schools Committee.' Again Richard started thinking, found new names, examined and accepted or rejected them.

'Has he recovered a bit by now?'

'He is, let's say, reasonably approachable once more. By now he seems to have come to understand what he's done. Anne and I have discussed the matter: if all goes well, it would be best if he didn't come on holiday with us this year but has the chance to think things through, get over it by himself. He'll stay with Kurt. You can go and see him, of course, that will certainly do him good. He should be free for a few weeks and have time to reflect on what's happened. Perhaps he has a girlfriend? The boy never tells me anything.' Richard looked at Meno, Meno shrugged and raised his hands.

The bridge ended with a sign warning, in four languages, that unauthorized persons were not allowed onto the island. There was dense woodland either side of the well-trodden path, only sparse light came through the tops of the trees, Meno and Richard started when a guard suddenly asked to see their papers.

'Pass,' the man said in an expressionless voice, waving the two men on in the direction of the ferry. There was a smell of decay, yellow-and-black flowers were slumbering in the twilight, fields of henbane in delicate, fimbriate movement, as if sucking, even though there wasn't a breath of air. The forest floor was covered in pine needles, the atmosphere was like a hothouse, stifling, deadening all sound. Meno coughed, a brief sound without echo, immediately smoothed out by the syrupy air. He was surprised that no birds were to be heard, nor any other woodland noises: the creak of branches, the warning cry of a jay, the leaves quietly foaming in the listless evening breezes that made thousands of branches, moving up and down at leisurely pace, shade in the darkness with the soft, silent strokes of pencils on paper.

Richard put two ten-pfennig pieces in the coin box by the jetty,

Meno pulled the lever, the two coins clicked out of the slots in the revolving disc; a grey-bearded conductor came out of the shed with geraniums on the window ledges that was the ferry waiting room, gestured the two men wordlessly to the ferry, a rusted flat-bottomed boat with bulwarks and wheelhouse. The man started the engine, the ferry pushed out into the pitch-black arm of the river by the banks of which, a radiance of metallic white in the sluggish current, masses of water lilies proliferated. Neither Meno nor Richard spoke during the crossing, each looking round with rapt attention.

One of Sperber's assistants was waiting for them on the island. He led them along a lighted path; soon, between clumps of milky green, the baroque castle came into view; it had been built on the island by one of the successors of the Ascanian dynasty.

'He wants to speak to you by yourself,' the assistant said to Richard.

'What should I do in the meantime?'

'You can wait in the secretary's office with a cup of tea, you can have a walk anywhere in the park, just as you please, Herr Rohde.'

'Then I'll take a walk. – All the best, Richard.'

Richard followed the assistant. Sperber's chambers were in one of the pavilion-like outbuildings flanking the Ascanian castle, the seat of the regional high court. The corridor floors were covered with grey PVC that muffled the sound of their footsteps, fluorescent tubes cast the unhealthy-seeming pus-yellow light typical of official buildings. The assistant rang the bell at a door with the plain sign 'Dr Sperber Lawyer', after a brief pause there was a buzz, the door opened. It was padded. They passed the secretary's office, where there were a telex machine and several black typewriters, and went into Sperber's office. The assistant, aiming his words at the ceiling, said, 'Herr Doktor Hoff- mann', and withdrew. Sperber, sitting at his desk writing, did not look up. He pointed to the chair opposite him. Richard smoothed his jacket and sat down.

'You must excuse me, this is urgent, it won't take a minute.' The lawyer still didn't look up. Behind his desk, on the wall and on a shelf, a collection of clocks were ticking, all good pieces as Richard, with the practised eye of a clockmaker's son, could tell. A few framed prints by the painter Bourg, spidery drawings with heavy cross-hatching; Richard recalled the *Black Plants* in the corridor of his brother's house. Above a washbasin a little mirror at tie-knot level. A comfortable-looking sofa with a table and chairs, probably reserved for important visitors, or for Sperber himself when he was reading the newspapers: there were stacks of the *Frankfurter Allgemeine*, *Die Zeit* and the *Süddeutsche Zeitung* on the table; clearly Sperber belonged to the restricted group who were permitted to subscribe to Western newspapers – and who could afford to. A Querner was hung over the sofa. Sperber seemed to collect Russian nesting dolls as well, one of the wall shelves, otherwise packed with files, was kept free for them. A tiled stove, the tiles with blue windmills in the Delft style. Framed diplomas and letters of thanks in free spaces on the wall beside the clocks; a certificate for the Patriotic Order of Merit in gold.

Sperber waved what he'd been writing dry, put it in the outbox, took two loose-leaf files out of a drawer. 'I don't want to waste either your time or my time, Herr Hoffmann, so let's get down to business right away. I have two cases here. I can do something for one of them. Our system of justice is remarkable. It is rare for two similar cases – such as that of your son and this one here – to be judged in the same way. If I win one, I will lose the other. That has often happened to me. So I will pass on the case I don't accept, that is only sensible. A different lawyer – another chance. Unfortunately not all my colleagues have my experience; which is why – there's no point in beating about the bush – so many clients turn to me. So which case do you think I should pass on?' He put his splayed fingers on each of the files and looked at Richard expectantly.

'Not my son's,' Richard replied after a while.

'You see, the other father gave me the same answer. Put yourself in my position . . . What should I do? That father wants your child to lose, this father wants the other's child to lose . . .'

'If it's a question of your fee –'

'It's not a question of my fee, Herr Hoffmann. It's a question of time.'

'But couldn't, I mean . . . your time, isn't that a question of your fee . . . you love clocks.'

Sperber smiled. 'We're not even going to start talking about that kind of thing. I became a lawyer because I love justice. Where would we be if the dispensation of justice went with those who are able to pay more. No. I decide this in my own way.' He took out a coin. 'Heads or tails for your boy?'

'Are you being serious?'

'Certainly,' Sperber replied. 'And before you condemn me, I would ask you to put yourself in my place. I have time for one case – given that, how do we choose in a way that is reasonably fair? So, heads or tails?'

'May I . . . go out for a moment?'

'No, stay here. In the first place I haven't unlimited time for you and in the second all the thoughts and fundamental considerations you will go through outside won't make it any easier. Heads or tails?'

'Heads,' Richard murmured. Sperber tossed the coin and it was as if through a veil of mist that Richard saw it fall back down onto the table, onto the rubber pad, bounce up, come to rest balanced on its edge, slowly roll down the table, tip over and disappear.

'Shit,' Sperber said. 'That doesn't count, of course. We have to find it, though, I always use that one for tossing a coin.'

Richard remained seated, unable to move, while Sperber crawled round the desk looking for the mark coin. 'So there you are!' he cried, after a certain amount of crashing and banging, and appeared, red and panting, from under the desk, triumphantly holding up the coin. 'Right then. That's not going to happen again.' The coin spun, this time Sperber caught it and slapped it onto the back of his other hand. 'Heads,' he said, 'so you have got me for your boy. – Would you like to know the name in the other case? – I can understand that. Though it would have been more honest if you had wanted to know.' Sperber seemed to be wondering whether he should tell him the name anyway but changed his mind, put the other file back in the drawer. 'I think Christian has a good chance of coming out of this unscathed and I don't imagine it will have much effect on his prospects of going to university either.'

While this was going on, Meno was exploring the island. Beyond the park, which was well tended – agaves and orange trees in tubs, fountains, gravel footpaths – a wilderness began: spruce and beech trees were wreathed in creepers, lepidodendrons grew closer and closer together the farther Meno went, masses of leaves tumbling on top of each other, tangled lianas round moss-encrusted giants, tree ferns, leguminous species: it was the vegetation of past geological periods; he was in a brown-coal forest. How quiet it was; it was so quiet that it struck him that there were still no birds calling, no mosquitos buzzing, that he could hear his watch ticking. The ferry terminus was on the other side, to the north the arm of the river widened out into a lake. When Meno went to the shore he saw pipes under the surface, on the opposite bank, amid a wall of swamp cypresses with their high aerial roots, they curved upwards, supported on pylons, they'd been coated with camouflage paint. Meno put his hand in the water – bathtub temperature – before listening again and watching the almost imperceptible tug of the river, the silent forest of swamp cypresses. Rays of the sun slanted down on the surface, like lancets of light operating carefully and filling the water with metallic fire; the edge of the woods merged with the sky to create an active osmotic layer with an iridescent greenish tinge – smoky flowers, steaming waters – ferns, bloated horsetails seemed to sit up, like sleepers awakening, on the ground of more distant alluvial islands. On a tree stump jutting out into the water not half a metre away from him Meno saw a cocoon, a horned butterfly larva the size of his hand, shaped like a sea snail and, to go by the movements that could be seen, the occupant must be close to emerging. Meno stood there, fascinated and confused. The cocoon burst open, feelers groped, twitched in the currents of air, the olfactory stimuli, the scents of danger, then the body pushed its way out, the eyes appeared over the edge of the pupa, little baskets gleaming like tar, then the front legs, still uncertain, the wings, still tied up and folded like umbrellas half out of their covers. The lines of the tracheae could be distinguished, one wing broke out. Veronese green, moonspots, motes of rusty red on the body: a uraniid, a day-flying moth from the tropics. Cheered up, Meno walked back.

Outside the court building he met Joffe. The fat lawyer recognized him, looked in the direction from which Meno had come and waved him over. 'You mustn't talk about that, Herr Rohde,' he said in his guttural voice, oiled by elegant addresses to the jury and countless *The Law and You* programmes, 'there's an explanation for everything. You'll have seen the pipes. Well, they're for district heating. They leak a little, the heat gets out, that's all. In winter the snow doesn't lie here – and we have some rare birds among the winter visitors. – You've come with Herr Hoffmann?'

'I've just had a little walk. Herr Hoffmann has an appointment with Sperber –'

'I know,' Joffe broke in. 'By the way, since I've happened to run into you – before long Herr Tietze will be going to Salzburg with the State Orchestra as their accompanying doctor. He shouldn't take on any errands for Frau Neubert, make that clear to him.' Surprised, Meno said nothing. The lawyer seemed irritated by his incomprehension. 'Herr Neubert intends to meet Herr Tietze in Salzburg and to give him money for his wife, with whom your brother-in-law is on friendly terms, as I know. Herr Tietze should leave the money where it is if he wants to avoid getting into trouble.' Joffe gave Meno a searching look, seeming to enjoy the effect of what he'd said. His expression became friendly again. 'About that little business with Herr Eschschloraque, has he' – Joffe waved his hand as if to ward off annoying insects – 'that nonsense with the comma he wanted to foist on you, you know what I mean?'

'He hasn't said any more about it to me.'

'Oh, good, very good. I heard about the matter and thought that one should do something to prevent Herr Eschschloraque from doing anything rash. Vindictiveness is ugly, I think, and unworthy of a communist.'

'Thank you.'

Joffe laughed, making his shoulders shake. 'Ah well, my dear Rohde, one does what one can. A very good evening to you.'

35

Dresdner Edition

When Meno got up for his lauds he felt tired, washed out. At night the temperature only fell by a few degrees. Sultry air was hanging over the garden, virtually no cooling breeze came from the river. A marshy smell was loitering on the slopes above the Elbe. Sometimes Meno could hear the Kaminski twins laughing, the heat didn't seem to bother them, in the evenings they would walk up and down by the parapet with the eagle, spick and span in their white cotton slacks and white shirts, murmuring, perhaps they were revising for an exam. When the sultry heat became unbearable, Meno would sleep in the summerhouse, wash in the rainwater butt and run naked, with rubber slippers on his feet, round the garden to get dry. Water was starting to be rationed; the city council had posted notices that curled up on the trees like the locks of a wig: no washing with running taps, cars to be washed with a bucket only, gardens only to be watered with a watering can.

He took the 11 to work. In the morning, when the passengers were squashed together, the tram stank of sweat (nylon shirts, the fabric of the future) and over-applications of perfume, all the sliding windows and vents in the roof were wide open, the airstream was cooling; on the stretch between Mordgrundbrücke and the Pioneers' Palace, where the road was lined by the outliers of Dresden Heath, you could breathe fragrant air. Meno got out on Dr-Kulz-Ring and walked to the Old Market; the Dresdner Edition offices were in the block beside Holy Cross Church – gambrel roofs, historicizing architecture from socialist town planning; you went in by a hall lit by 1950s lamps with cone-shaped shades and smelling of Frau Zäpter's coffee, Josef Redlich's tobacco and the used air from the office refrigerator. Josef Redlich suffered during those dog days. With a morose expression he would stick manuscripts in the editors' pigeonholes, close the window in his little room, which looked out onto the Old Market – too much noise, too much pitiless light on typescripts, he wanted nothing to do with dissecting rooms, microscopes, halogen lamps, shook his head at Meno's activities. 'Aren't you going to put your stethoscope on as well, Herr Rohde?' And he would point to stacks of paper, chalky white under the lampshades, which seemed to be projecting X-rays. At that time of the year the Old Market shimmered like a layer of salt with dead car-fish strung out along it; the oddly skiddy noise of the trams in Ernst-Thälmann-Strasse interrupted the rumble of traffic between the post office and Pirnaischer Platz in an unpleasantly irregular rhythm. Josef Redlich wanted the blinds shading his room before he sat down to his literature – and before the telephone, a black toad squatting on a tray on an extending shelf, started to disturb him. On some mornings the temperature had already risen to over thirty degrees, then even Oskar Klemm, the proofreader, would loosen his tie, the consumption of ice cream, of which there was always a supply in the refrigerator, could lead to shortages and Josef Redlich would cover the floor of his room with colourful plastic tubs that he filled with cold water and walk up and down with bare feet – clasping his hands behind his back and puffing away at his cheap cigars (Meno could never find out what brand they were, Redlich took them out of a leather case; Madame Eglantine said: railway-embankment harvest), sometimes contemplating a corn on his left middle toe, thinking, 'The things it's seen, all the countries its walked round with me', and musing in the dreamily abstracted Josef Redlich manner with its Lichtenberg quotations. Sometimes he would lean back in his chair, his waistcoat stretching over his potbelly, though without a single button flying off, his pocket watch, still on its chain, lying open on the table in front of him, the cuffs of his white starched shirt with the impeccably smooth sleeves (he had them ironed, he had been a widower for a long time and had two wedding rings on his right ring finger) turned back, the veins stuck out on his hands dangling down, over his spherical head he'd draped a wet handkerchief, the corners of which protruded like a flying squirrel. At moments like that he looked as if he'd had a stroke, but when Meno came over, a look of concern on his face, he would wave him away wearily, 'Oh, Herr Rohde, I still have some prose to order around, but just look at me . . . rarely can a mind have come to a standstill more majestically.'

Josef Redlich would never have given his personal taste the status of objective authority. That was what the West German tsars of the arts pages with ambitions to educate the nation did – for example, the great panjandrum of critics, Wiktor Hart, whose articles Josef Redlich read with fixed cigar, on which the ash grew to a structurally ominous length; then he would put the pages (numbered copies) aside, tap the ash off his cigar and declare, 'We ought to take him seriously', or 'His argumentation is ringfenced, if you'll forgive the expression; a fence is made by its fundamental component, the slat, being repeated time

and time again; it is unclear whether the desire for variety is out of
place here', or 'He doesn't understand poetry at all, he confuses it with
the exclamation marks in the margins of our biographies', look across
at Meno, happily expecting contradiction, which wasn't long in coming, for Meno enjoyed reading the reviews, which were written with
fervour, and were knowledgeable and positively obsessed with the
desire to champion literature; Hart made no concessions as he delivered
judgement, an advocate of common sense (that did not, of course,
always produce the desired results in literature, that vague art of feelings, contradictions and dreams: half-mad authors had created half-mad
immortal works; this or that representative of the most socially committed realism nothing but crystal-clear whimsies); he was a weather
god who could cut up rough at a neglected nuance and stood guard
before his holy place – though he himself never used that expression,
nor a word such as soul, he would mock it, reject it, put it in inverted
commas, scenting waffle. He understood a lot, it seemed to Meno, and
he possessed the chief virtue of the born critic: he didn't enjoy panning
a book (though such reviews were enjoyable to read) and he disposed
of the whole palette of praise. Hart was vain, but he was vain for literature and he was capable of putting his vanity on one side and leaving
some matters unmentioned out of tact or discretion; and Meno always
felt that, basically, he didn't want to make a fuss about himself, there
was an unspoken 'That's not done' and much quiet knowledge of
human nature. Everyone who was able to get his reviews read them
immediately, but not everyone in publishing enjoyed that privilege,
copies went to Schiffner, the senior editors and Party secretaries, at
Dresdner Edition to Kurz alone among the editors; Meno owed the
fact that he could read them to the sympathy Josef Redlich clearly felt
for him (that, moreover, was mutual). Everyone who read Hart either
nodded vigorously or vented their feelings with gestures of outrage,
no one remained indifferent to him, especially not the authors he dealt
with. Eschschloraque wished for Moscow conditions 'in which I could

have had this individual taken care of'. The Old Man of the Mountain thought Hart was 'magnificent, he panned one of my books, you know, but I can see that he was right', and Schiffner said, 'An important man, unfortunately. He helps our work, when he praises us, he helps our work, when he pans us; we are dismayed he doesn't come to our aid, when he ignores us.'

The typographer, Udo Männchen, suffered from the heat more actively than Josef Redlich; he would emerge from his graphic studio at the end of the corridor more frequently than usual, tear at his shock of fuzzy hair, hold up his glasses to the light, then dangle them resignedly. Fanning himself with one of his outer garments (Indian-Hawaiian-Buddhist – shirts they were not) that had the look of the theatre about them, he would shout down the corridor, 'Dante! I'll use the Dante Antiqua, since it's sizzling.'

'Quiet!' the proofreader, Oskar Klemm, cried from the office diagonally opposite.

'Or perhaps not the Dante after all.' Udo Männchen put his glasses back on, let his arms hang down.

'Eschschloraque, king of the ornamental fish, is a classicist; but the decline began with Dante. – What do you think, Herr Rohde, should we, as men of profound feeling, not use Dante, of all fonts, for him?'

'He'd notice,' Meno said with a smile.

'Notice, oh yes, he would that. And he'd grab me and rumple me, he'd curse me – Männchen, he'd say menacingly, you did that on the wings of wrong! Intellectually speaking, the solecism you managed to perpetrate there is elementary, my dear Männchen. As far as I'm concerned, your reputation – O editor! Now something bad is coming. A dirty word, a non-literary word. Impossible to represent graphically – is shit.'

'He wouldn't use it, Herr Männchen.'

'No, I have to agree with Meno there.' When she heard Männchen, Stefanie Wrobel liked to go and fetch a cup of coffee or an ice cream.

'We have it on good authority that a single so-called four-letter word can take him two to three hours.'

'Vulgar expression,' Josef Redlich corrected. 'If you must quote Lichtenberg, then please stick to his terminology. Notebook F, note 1155.'

'How can it be so hot? Or should I use the Walbaum . . . a fine font, a beautiful font, Goethe's collected works in the Insel India paper edition are set in Walbaum. He'd notice that . . .'

'Herr Männchen, there are still people in this office who are trying to work,' Oskar Klemm growled, 'and, anyway, what do you know about Goethe?'

'Or should I rely on the delicate timelessness of Garamond? But Eschschloraque avoids italics and Garamond is the king of italics. We ought to print nothing but books in italics, don't you agree, Herr Rohde? Italics were derived from the monks' handwriting, eternity begins with the monks. More eternity in literature! Or a Bodoni? A Bembo, that Antiqua typeface, matured like an old cheese? It bears the name of a cardinal . . . Perhaps we ought to be truly radical?' Männchen rolled his eyes and did some shadow karate chops. 'A sans serif font, bare and clear and unadorned, like a meat axe . . . Courier, that's the typewriter font. A serif again, true. Remind him of a golden age . . . ? The typeface for a summons and no one will laugh, no one dare to say a thing . . . Anyway, Herr Klemm, you know nothing about the Beatles.' Udo Männchen started to whistle the tune of 'Yellow Submarine'.

Meno and Madame Eglantine exchanged horrified glances. Oskar Klemm remained silent for a while. He was seventy-five and should have retired years ago, but the pension he would get, after almost sixty years working, would be ridiculously small. Schiffner wasn't pushing him out. Oskar Klemm was a legend; there was no one waiting for him at home, his wife had died in the Dresden air raid, his children had long since moved away. The publishing house was his whole life, Goethe his lifelong love, horse-racing, which he followed at the Seidnitz and Berlin Hoppegarten racecourses, his passion. His deepest feelings and well-concealed tears were for Mozart; he could be standing in the corridor, of an evening, when the hustle and bustle had died down, the record player playing the adagio from the *Gran Partita* with its fragrant, elysian writing for wind and, if Meno should come, he would put his finger to his lips, take off his glasses and stay there, face turned away, eyes closed. Herr Männchen belonged to a different generation; young philistines who could see no farther than the flared bottoms of their trousers; one had to make allowances.

'You know' – by now Oskar Klemm was standing in the doorway – '"Yellow Submarine" is very popular but it seems to me that, from a purely musical point of view, "Lucy in the Sky with Diamonds" or "A Hard Day's Night" are more profound. And, of course, those immortal songs "Penny Lane" and "Yesterday". And even at my age there is no doubt that "She Loves You", for all its simplicity, makes a very important statement.'

Oskar Klemm walked slightly bent but no one had ever seen him without a tie. When he wasn't at work he liked to spend his time at the races and in the various antiquarian bookshops in Dresden, especially Dienemann Succrs. and Bruno Korra's Paper Boat on Lindwurmring. Should he find a mistake in a manuscript that had already been edited, during the afternoon meeting he would lean over the conference table and look along the row of editors, a sorrowful expression on his face – apart from Madame Eglantine, Meno and Kurz, the Party Secretary, there was also Felizitas Klocke, known as Miss Mimi, an oldish spinster with a liking for hard, action-packed melodramas, samurai swords and Alain Delon as a youthful, angel-faced killer: she grew cacti, wore bobble hats, liked snakes and conspiracy theories, and couldn't stand the sight of blood. Melanie Mordewein had the desk opposite her; she was known as Frau Adelaide, was in charge of the Romantics and dreamt a lot; she looked so gossamery it was as if she hadn't been born, but crocheted. After Oskar Klemm – who had seen Hofmannsthal in the old Insel Verlag and in Kippenberg's, the publisher's, villa, and whom Stefan Zweig had shown Goethe memorabilia, whom a misplaced comma, an inadequately checked term, would cause sleepless nights – had nurtured his sorrow in silence for a while, he would whisper, 'Please . . . ladies and gentlemen . . . Please bear in mind . . . It's . . . It's supposed to be . . . literature . . . language, that is. A living being of words . . . There is a saying that poets are like freebooters, they live from robbery under the open sky. The poet is free. But we are bound . . . so, please . . . bear that in mind. The poet is the composer. We are his musicians . . . We have to play what is in the score. That is how it has to be. Please be correct.'

After that Kai-Uwe Knapp, the managing clerk, reported on the situation at the printer's. Because paper was short and the plan's targets sacred, because printing presses were in short supply and printer's ink had been short before now, because, in addition to all that, time was short and coordination with Central Office in Berlin difficult, the long and the short of it was that the manuscripts of Editorial Office 7 would be printed when there was a shortage of these shortages. The class standpoint, which was expressed vehemently by Ingo Kurz, an editor and Party Secretary, was no help. Despite that, he did know something about literature. During the reports of Kurz and Knapp, Oskar Klemm sat with his head bowed. He had been through the bombardment of Dresden. He always left his door ajar.

36

First love

Green water splintering off the paddle-wheels, atomizing into spray that drifted along the steamer, swirling into the wide channel at the stern in which the wake of the grinding, pounding boat fanned out and gradually disappeared. Christian was standing by the rail in the bows, holding his face up to the wind, which smelt of grass and cellulose – the industrial area of Heidenau, with its factory chimneys and effluent pipes from which grey sludge sloshed into the Elbe, slipped past. The boat was full of people on a day out, the excited chatter of children from school holiday camps and the irritated admonishments of those in charge of them; walkers with rucksacks who kept to one side, as did the few inhabitants of the Elbe Sandstone Hills: recognizable from their faces worn from hard work, their unfashionable clothes; the women wore headscarves, the men flat, brown leather caps.

The windows glittered in the newly built district of Pirna-Sonnenstein, huge concrete blocks that had been rammed into the foothills of the Elbe Sandstone range above the little market town with its church. After Pirna the wind freshened and the broad valley of the Elbe narrowed, hemmed in on either side by steep hills. The sandy yellow of abandoned quarries mingled with the light green of the birches and the dark green of the conifers in the Elbe woods. Now it smelt of summer: dry air, cow dung, wild dill in the meadows, diesel and grease from the boatyards, sun cream mixing with sweat into an oily film. He tried to stop thinking about the training camp. He'd sent off his application to do medicine in Leipzig, there'd been an interview at the university. One of the three examiners, a GP, had leafed through his file and asked why he wanted to be a doctor? The question didn't catch Christian unawares; outside was Richard, who had prepared several answers for him. Christian wanted to decide between them himself. Because I would like to be a famous medical scientist, he'd thought, and for a moment he felt a great urge to say it just like that, the truth and nothing but the truth. 'Because I would like to work in medical research eventually,' he'd said.

'Aha, so you want to become famous,' the second examiner, a psychologist, had replied with an ironic smile.

'. . . That too. Yes.'

'Well, at least you're honest, young man,' the third examiner, a professor of Internal Medicine, had commented. 'Do you know what we mostly get to hear? – Because I want to help people. Sometimes even humanity, then it becomes interesting again. If you'd said something like that, and with your file, we'd have rejected you. As things are, we'll support your application. – How's your father, by the way? We were at university together. Off you go, now, and tell one of those silly geese who want to help people to come in.'

He closed his eyes, listened to the thump of the engines for a while. He shivered when the steamer entered the shadow of the cliffs. Cumulus clouds were building up. The blue skies of summer, the blue skies of air raids, he recalled; Grandfather Kurt's words.

Above Wehlen the rocky pinnacles of the Bastei rose up from the river; parties of tourists pushed their way to the stern rail, pointing up, waving. Christian didn't wave, there were countless sparks flitting across the cliffs, he had to screw up his eyes and shade them with his hand. The Elbe passed Rathen in a wide curve, cut like a steel blade between Lilienstein and Königstein, the bases of the hills wooded, above them sandstone bluffs with steep, cleft walls on which myriads of swifts nested.

He reached down for his suitcase, suddenly feeling the need to test out the strength of his grip on the straps; it was with satisfaction that he felt the crumpled resistance of the leather that he couldn't squash beyond a certain degree however much effort he put into it. A dragonfly landed on the handrail hardly a metre in front of him. He was fascinated: how these creatures, invisible in flight, could come to an abrupt halt and be as if switched on: blue needles with a double pair of transparent, filigree wings, and Christian would have liked to catch the dragonfly to see if the spurs of skin felt like cellophane, whether you could cut yourself on them. It shot off, with no preparation, like the tick of a second hand.

Schandau came in sight, the bridge, the dusty station, the rails and electric cables seeming to shimmer in the heat, an engine was puffing

away below the signal box, sleepers stacked up on trestles and overgrown with weeds. The spa promenade with hotels, pennants from
the regatta and chains with lanterns along the bank by the car park,
behind it, hidden by the houses on the market square, the domed tower
of St John's. Christian breathed out. No one was waiting for him at
the quay. A brass band greeted the passengers, gleaming on the terrace
of the Elbe Hotel between blue-and-white sunshades and waiters calmly
serving and clearing away food and drink. He weighed the suitcase in
his hand. He hadn't been expelled. He had the second-best results for
his year and had even managed to congratulate Verena.

Lene Schmidken had seen him as he put his suitcase down and looked
up at the house: the curtains were drawn, the skylights in the shingle
roof closed; Pepi, Kurt's Alsatian, came whizzing round the corner
and sat down in front of him, panting, giving him a man's-best-friend
look.

'So you still remember me, you old rascal. How's things?' He fondled
Pepi behind the ear. The dog bounded over in great leaps to Lene
Schmidken, who came hobbling along leaning on a stick; she seemed
to be a head shorter than at his last visit. 'D'you want something to
eat, lad? Or take your case up first?' She rummaged round in her apron
pocket and took out the key from where it would have been refusing
to acknowledge the presence of clothes pegs, eucalyptus sweets, rubber
rings for preserving jars.

'How long you staying for?'

'Don't know for sure. Two, perhaps three weeks. Depends when
Grandad's coming back.'

'The beginning of September's what he told me.' She took a sweet
out of her apron and he put it in his pocket, just in case.

'It'd be nice if you could look after the rabbits. And Pepi. Come
over for lunch, my lad. There's *guvech*. An' Hussar's toast tomorrow.
You like that.'

'Thanks, but I'm not hungry just now.'

Holding on to his arm, Lene Schmidken sat down on one of the steps, shaking her head at the heat and the anti-thrombosis stockings the doctor had prescribed for her. '*Ischtenem!* They look like stuffed vine leaves. And – have you got a place at university?'

'We're only told when we go back to school. Some friends might come to see me. Grandad doesn't have to know. Please?'

Lene Schmidken nodded, stood up with a groan. 'He'll find out anyway. If you need a bath I'll get the tub out of the wash-house. Kurt should have filled the water tank, the old wood butcher. Keep the *priculic*, that black vampire, away from me.' She jabbed Pepi with her stick.

'Did Grandpa leave any other messages?'

'No. All he could think about was his journeys. A real bundle o' nerves, 'e was. I thought 'e'd drop down dead when they sent 'im that letter refusing his application. Like a bear with a sore 'ead, 'e was, the old spindleshanks. Few weeks later the acceptance came.'

'He didn't say anything about that.' Surprised, Christian turned back to Lene.

'He still didn't have no passyport, 'dentity card, *papuci* for trav'lin' in. Keeps it all locked up inside hisself. Then came another refusal. The Amazon's out, Danube delta's OK. And now 'e's down there with the *Lippengabors*.'

'With the what?'

'Polenta-guzzlers. Total goulash. With the gyppos.'

'But they're not all gypsies, Lene.'

'Oh, leave it, lad.' Leaning her head a little to one side, she shuffled off to her house, where for years she'd lived alone in a Transylvania of the mind – and speech.

He was afraid of the death masks, the garishly coloured, roughly carved faces, then he would turn the television on or the radio, go to places out of their reach: the rabbit hutches by the compost heap, the earth closet in the yard at the back – it housed fly-demons and photographs of Baltic flatfish that did nobody any harm. When twilight fell with the smell of meadows and blue shadows, the things in the house seemed to conspire against Kurt's travels and to go back; clay figures, a spatula for flatbread, crowns of bird feathers went back to the Cayapa Indians in Ecuador, copper bowls and blowpipes with curare-tipped arrows back to the Amazon, straight into the murmuring of a tribe planning a hunt. Christian had brought a biochemistry textbook with him, but in the house it became ineffective, his interest died away with the hours that he heard the voices from the colourful lips. The house, the summer in the Elbe Sandstone Hills, carried him away from the events of the previous months; he drifted away from them like a boat and they remained on the shore. Kurt seemed to be there when he went up into the loft, rummaged round in the boxes that stood there, dry and dusty among fragilely balancing stacks of junk. He could hear Kurt commentating on the rolls of film on the shelves: rain dance of the Crao Indians, 16 mm camera. Stories of travels in a folding canoe on Norwegian fjords, long before the war. Adventures hunting in the polar sea. In his mind's eye Christian could see Kurt's gnarled hands, his sparse gestures accompanying the stories in the smoke of the garden fire and cigars, he could see Ina, who had embarrassed Fabian and himself with her daring summer dresses, made in the Harmony Salon workshop, Muriel with her eyes closed, Meno poking the fire.

After a few days Christian stopped shaving. Lene said nothing about the light-brown woolly tufts on his cheeks, the brigand's moustache, the stubbly hair gradually turning shaggy again. A week later the others arrived: Reina with a rucksack and a case full of cosmetics that made Christian laugh, at which she recoiled; but perhaps it was his unkempt hair that had startled her and not the washbasin he handed her, nor the earth closet he pointed out in the yard. Siegbert and Falk immediately started fooling around, both grabbed masks that immediately started emitting jungle roars; Pepi came jumping up at them, yapping angrily, Verena squealed, she was frightened of dogs.

The days blurred at the edges, turned into time. The sun cut up across the sky over the mountains. The tips of the bracken flushed red, the hollows were haunted by misty ghosts until the August heat drove them away. Cocks crowed from the village but Christian was awake before them and listened to the breathing of the others, who slept more soundly than he, even though it was hot on the air beds and the air in the room, unmoving despite the wide-open windows, was stifling. He looked at the girls, sleeping there before him, Verena in her nightdress despite the heat, Reina stripped to the waist, she was lying on her front, the sheet had slipped down to her waist. Then he got up and went out, the alarm clock said four, ten past four; Pepi wearily raised his head when Christian went past his kennel, decided he could nudge him with his nose and wag his tail: Bit early for food, he seemed to be trying to say as the meat flopped into his bowl, but OK, since it's you. Christian filled the bucket Kurt had left by the water tank, washed himself, pouring the water over his naked body; that was what Kurt did, what Meno did and what he had done for as long as he could remember. In the winter it was an icy whiplash, tearing his tiredness apart; now the water was lukewarm and smelt of cress. He warmed it up for the girls with an immersion coil.

Meno came, bringing provisions, and settled in his old room in the attic, where, on a desk made of bare planks, there was a Fortuna typewriter, clunky as a Konsum cash register, surrounded by phials of liquid ammonia, a microscope, a bowl with 'Carlsbad Insect Needles', entomologist's collecting jars: this was where he retired to when he was free and wanted to do his own work. His birthday wish had been for quiet and company, so Verena and Reina took him some flowers as a late present: the eighth of the eighth had disappeared somewhere in the far blue yonder down the Elbe. Christian waved away questions about the pre-military training camp and the possibility of being expelled from school. They were drifting. Spreading out their arms they drifted on the compressed light glazing the hills and only disappearing in the gorges. After they'd breakfasted Meno said, 'You must be both plant and animal. Be alert, keep your ears and eyes open. A body has boundaries but they will dissolve if you wait and trust.' They went for walks early in the morning. The Falkenstein was obscured by haze. The jagged Schrammstein cliffs were still dark as lead, beyond them rose the Grosser Winterberg then, to one side in the distance, the regular cone of the Rosenberg: Růžová hora, Meno murmured; that was already in Bohemian Switzerland. Leaning over the rocks, they looked down at the curve of the Elbe below Schandau. In those early hours the river seemed to have to expand, at the bend it was wrinkled, bright as a newly minted coin in the middle alone; barges engraved lines on it. Verena and Falk were each trying to outdo the other in finding names for the varying shades: liquorice, pitchblende, mocha, chemist's-bottle brown, with a shimmer of oil and splodges of purple when the sun had risen a little higher. Once, from the Postelwitz bank, they saw dead fish floating down the river, so many it looked as if the Elbe had been paved with metal bars. With a stick Meno pulled a few over, they were roach, unnaturally large. 'Cadmium.' They flaked to pieces when Meno pushed them back into the current. The girls turned away.

The clefts were fern-dark and full of a stench that only the midday heat would disperse. The cliffs were mossy, covered in brown iron stains and yellow patches of sulphur, as slimy as a toad's skin. Sometimes Meno's 'Careful!' came too late and Christian, who wanted to show off a bit to the others, watched in alarm as the scree tumbled down into the gorge. They didn't take marked routes but followed Meno, who walked in front, silent and avoiding tourist paths and popular viewpoints: the Bastei, from where one could see far out over the countryside, the fields dotted around, the plain with its wide-open spaces in which the jagged-backed table mountains – Königstein, Lilienstein – seemed to be like prehistoric animals resting. At first they couldn't manage more than ten to fifteen kilometres a day, came home too exhausted to follow Meno's explanations. He was different here, no longer the calm, pipe-smoking publisher's editor from the House with a Thousand Eyes who listened to music with Niklas and Richard in the evening, went to talks in the Urania group, gossiped about literature with Josef Redlich or Judith Schevola. This was where he had grown up, where he once more assumed the swift, sinewy gait of the mountain-dweller, the keen senses that Christian admired: there were the tracks of a pine marten that Meno was puzzled no one else had noticed; here the remains of a pine cone but they couldn't tell which animal had nibbled at it; strange noises came from a tree plantation, outside which they waited, with ants crawling all over them, so long it was like torture: in the twilight a bird, black with a bright-red crown, was settling on a branch, a black woodpecker that no one, apart from Meno, had seen before.

After a week even the pale-skinned Reina was brown. They now managed to keep up with Meno without collapsing, half dead, onto their air beds in the evening. Lene did the cooking, the girls the shopping, the boys chopped wood for the winter. Ravenous, they fell on the Transylvanian dishes with the strange-sounding names like wild animals. In the evening Meno went out alone or typed on his Fortuna in his room; they stayed close to the house, just once Reina and Christian went back into the woods at twilight. They took Pepi with them and torches.

'The way you toss your hair back, it's so affected,' she said, imitating him to his annoyance.

'I'm not doing it out of vanity but because the quiff irritates me. I don't like it when it falls down over my forehead.'

'Then cut it off.'

'So my hair all sticks up.'

'It does that already. Doesn't look bad at all. I'd leave it, if I were you.'

'Why?'

'Verena likes it better too.'

'How do you know?'

'Do you really not like being called "Montecristo"?'

'Not particularly.'

'But it sounds so serious when I say "Christian". And when it sounds so serious I can't help laughing and I don't really want to do that. – Have you heard whether you've got a place at Leipzig yet?'

'No. What about you?'

'I don't know whether chemistry's right for me,' Reina said after some hesitation.

'But you like it so much. Frank thinks very highly of you. You're the best in chemistry, by a long chalk. It annoyed me.'

'Really? Well, I think that's great.' Reina laughed, exuberantly kicking away a pine cone. 'You're so ambitious and always studying . . . do you know what they said about you?'

'No. But I'm sure you're going to enlighten me.'

'Svetlana says you've got a screw loose. Verena thought the way you shut yourself off was a kind of immature reaction, compensation for some family traumas or other . . .'

'I thought she wanted to be an art historian, not a shrink.'

'Today Verena wants to be this, tomorrow something else. That tender butterfly with dark brown eyes. She should be glad you got her Siegbert out of trouble.'

Christian ignored that. 'And you? What did you think?' He gave Reina a suspicious look.

'Do you really want to know?'

'That's why I'm asking.'

'I thought you were afraid of girls. You really ought to see yourself when you're talking to a girl. Always half turned away, always in a defensive posture. I thought . . . you were gay. That was my first reaction. Then I thought: I wish I could be as disciplined as that.'

'Gay, you said?'

'You asked me for my honest opinion. Anyway, my brother's gay. A very nice guy, I think you'd get on well together.'

'Hey, are you trying to pair me off?' A smell of dry wood, sweet woodruff, if the heat continues, Meno had said, we'll have an infestation of bark beetles. Fireflies drifted ghostlike across the path. Pepi came back.

'No one's ever given me a flower.'

'Not even for your birthday?' Christian asked sceptically.

'We don't celebrate them at home. My father says, why should I congratulate you just because you're a year older? If anything, we should be congratulating each other. And if you're happy to be here you should be the one giving us a present.'

'Sounds logical,' he said, teasing.

'In that case I'd rather have unlogical parents. – What will you do if you don't get a place at university?'

'I'll go to the hospital, work as a nursing auxiliary. You can apply every year, eventually it'll work out.'

'Christian . . . What exactly happened at the camp? Will you tell me?'

'Why d'you want to know?' he replied coldly.

'There's too many rumours about it and that bothers me.'

Now she might well be thinking: Christian the hero. But he felt nothing when he thought back to the training camp. He saw Siegbert and Corporal Hantsch, his father's expression of despair; he heard himself reply to the committee of inquiry. Mechanical, lying answers. The fear of being expelled. Fear of something worse: what did one know? Barbara had feared the worst, talked about being arrested, going to prison. Barred from going to university: nothing had been decided yet, it wasn't over and done with. Reina walked along beside him, meditatively twisting and turning a twig. Fahner came to mind, and Falk, the way he'd gone down the stairs in the administration block.

'Perhaps later,' he equivocated. 'What d'you want to do, if not chemistry?'

'Dunno. Perhaps I'll do it after all. Or medicine. But for that I'd need a better average grade. Perhaps I could do something in foreign trade, I'd be interested in that as well. – Does your father talk to you about that kind of thing? What you want to be and what you have to do to get there?'

'All the time. He even checks my homework. He rewrote an essay for my brother because he hadn't formulated things cautiously enough.'

'My father wouldn't give a tuppenny fart for all that. My parents couldn't care less what my brother and I do or don't do.'

'You poor thing. I feel *so* sorry for you.' All at once he felt the need to mock; perhaps she was getting too close to him, the others might already be talking, would exchange meaningful glances when they got back.

'Not half as sorry as I feel for myself.' Reina laughed merrily, suddenly took his hand and he was too late withdrawing it.

Was this it, then? Was this what first love was like? A profound, quivering emotion turning his whole world upside down such as he'd read about in Turgenev? Reina his Juliet and he a Romeo out of his mind with passion? – When he looked inside himself he was disappointed. This wasn't what he'd imagined. Reina had simply taken his hand without asking. (What would his response have been if she had asked? One of his snubs, probably.) And now they were, as the saying was, to go with each other. (What did you actually do when you 'went' with someone? He couldn't imagine it as anything but boring.) Reina was to be the woman with whom he'd be his whole life long, have children? Children: from the pure chance that Reina and he were in the same class, that she was here now and had plucked up the courage to take his hand. And that was to lead to something as irrevocable as children . . . And what if Verena had taken his hand? (But she hadn't, which meant that her children would have Siegbert's solitary-seafareresque figure, the bright eyes of Corto Maltese, and perhaps also a cruelty before which Verena would shrink back in trepidation.) And, anyway, what was it about love – had he not been afraid of it, did it not keep you away from your studies, turn men who could have been great scientists into narrow-minded, sofa-bellied home birds?

He didn't mention Reina's gesture. He decided it hadn't happened. Reina didn't remind him.

Mosses stayed cool in the hollows. Giant hogweed appeared, raising its threateningly thorny bell-tiers, Falk made a bow. Meandering conversation, banter about Reina, who had fallen silent and kept away from Christian. Siegbert was wearing frayed home-made togs, more and more, Christian thought, resembling a sailor stranded on some foreign shore for whom homelessness, banishment, a war was over.

'Shall we be friends, Christian?' he asked one evening. Meno and Falk had both gone their own ways, the girls were watching TV with Lene. 'You and me, both at sea, that would be great. Me as an officer, you as ship's doctor. The two of us. As blood brothers.'

'And Verena?'

'Women on board is bad luck stored, the old sea captains used to say.'

'Then there's nothing between you, between Verena and you?'

'Who says there is something between us?'

'Oh, come on, we're not blind.'

'You saved my skin. I'll never forget that. If ever you want or need something – you can count on me.'

'Promise?'

'Cross my heart and hope to die. – Can I say something else?' Siegbert seemed embarrassed. Christian waited, unsure what was to come. 'I don't know what's going on between Reina and you –'

'Nothing at all,' Christian said brusquely.

*

They watched timber being stacked in the Grosser Zschand valley. At twilight they went to the Affensteine to observe the pair of eagle owls that were still nesting in the cliffs there. They took a short cut to the Nasser Grund, a damp valley where the signposts were in disrepair and fallen trees blocked the gorge. At a bend in the path there was a crow that didn't fly off when they went past it, only a few metres away. Christian felt frightened of the animal. Afterwards Meno, laughing and shaking his head, told them it must have been a sorcerer, for he'd never before seen a bird that could turn its head so slowly, like a human being. To observe! The animal's eyes had been full of malice as well. — She had no idea zoologists, scientists with a materialist view of the world, were superstitious: Verena's surprise was expressed without irony. — There were still certain matters; no gynaecologist, for example, knew what seemed the most simple thing: why a birth came about, Meno replied after a while.

Spiders hunted moths. Ground beetles, wasps, assassin bugs, ants pursued insects. Bats snatched at twitching life. Tachinid flies laid their eggs in caterpillars. Ichneumon flies drilled thinner-than-thin ovipositors into the soft, protein-rich bodies, laid their eggs. Meno explained: a bottling plant, for apple or gooseberry juice for example, the automatic out-and-in movement: thus they pumped their eggs into the hapless caterpillar, which became a walking placenta and was eaten away from inside by the maggots. The pupae of braconid wasps were stuck like grains of rice to their future food, ground beetles, gleaming metallic black, dragged their prey into the darkness. — Never pick up a hairy caterpillar, Meno warned them. Verena said she didn't want to move to the coast.

The larvae of some kinds of caterpillar had up to 600,000 stinging hairs between their bristles; they broke off, causing allergies, rashes, asthma. Reina coughed, Falk scratched himself. The oak processionary moth made caterpillar nests; Meno showed them the crackling, glittering shape made of cast-off skins, held his fingers up in the air, there was no wind. The wind blew the stinging hairs away, he told them, they could irritate the skin for years. Gypsy moth caterpillars were like extra-terrestrial warriors: black, with poppy-seed dots and red warty bumps (a forest of spears, darning mushrooms full of tiny splintered lances) commanded by a yellow head. Burnet moths flew, showing their red petticoats. They learnt how to distinguish fritillaries from tortoiseshells, ringlets from graylings: camouflage brown drew doors on the beeches.

Reina took the salt down from the shelf; Christian saw that her armpits had been shaved.

'Does God exist, what d'you think?'

'Christian wants to be a great research scientist, but he starts out with God,' said Falk, still high from singing along, they'd been listening to Hans Albers records; 'La Paloma' had twisted the summer out of shape, homesickness and blue eyes had softened into musical pasta dough swirling round the full moon. 'I've got another idea. Just imagine that at the end of the war Hiddensee – the whole of the island – had been made into a prison camp. Around five million prisoners. They'd have crapped in the Baltic every morning. That would've meant the Baltic'd be a sewage farm now and you could walk across it to Denmark.'

'Why bother with a sewage farm, you can get to Denmark on the water just as well.' Reina tapped her forehead at Falk. 'Just imagine you and Heike got married. All you'd have would be latchkey children.'

'A sewage farm becomes firm in the sun,' Falk said, unimpressed.

'And you think they wouldn't arrest you while you were crossing your firm sewage farm?'

'You've not got the point, Siggi. There wouldn't be any border patrols with the stench. No one could stand it.'

'I believe in him.' Verena was sitting with her legs drawn up, staring at the ground. 'We get born and we live – but what's the point if God doesn't exist?'

'God rhymes with clod.' Siegbert twisted his lips contemptuously. 'And my mother used to say OhGodohGod when I'd done something wrong. OhGodohGod, leave me in peace with your God-squad twaddle.'

'Red Eagle would say that God is an invention of the imperialists to stultify the people. How does it go? Religion is opium for the people. – What do you say to that, Herr Rohde?'

Meno, who had listened to the discussion in silence, glanced at Reina, shook his head. 'I'm going out for a bit. I'll take Pepi with me.'

'Religion is opium for the people,' Christian repeated after Meno had left, 'how do they know that, actually?'

'They spent a long time thinking about these things and they were a bit cleverer than you,' Reina sneered.

'Other philosophers thought about these things long before Marx and Lenin, and perhaps they were greater than Marx and Lenin,' Christian replied in irritation.

'Funny that you never dare to come out with things like that in class. Only to us. But when Red Eagle or Schnürchel are there you chicken out.'

'And you – you don't chicken out?'

'Why are you suggesting they're teaching us nonsense?'

'Because –' Christian jumped up and walked up and down excitedly. 'Because they're lying to us! Only Marx, Engels and Lenin are right, all the others are idiots . . . And their slogans? All men equal? Then all philosophers must be equal and therefore at least as smart as those three,' he concluded with a malicious smile.

'Sure people are equal,' Siegbert bellowed, 'all men've got a dick and all women've got a pussy.'

'Hold on a minute – there's transsexuals and hermaphrodites as well,' Falk chortled.

'Do you have to drag everything in the mud? You're just like little children, can't take anything seriously.' Christian was still speaking calmly. 'You say you're my friend, Siegbert, but your language is . . . tasteless. Cheap and disgusting. How can you sink so low?'

Now Siegbert stood up as well. 'Tasteless . . . disgusting . . . how can you sink so low?' he mocked. 'You're in for a big surprise, my friend, when you see how things are outside. You were born with a silver spoon in your mouth. But not everyone's had one of those to suck, *mon cher*. You're pretty snooty for someone who wants to be a doctor, I think someone needed to tell you that.'

For hours Christian blundered about in the woods, thinking of Reina's armpit.

Reina seemed to have been looking for him, for she came to meet him as he returned to the house by a roundabout way.

'Why did you contradict me? Is that what you really think?' he asked her.

'Yes.'

'And why did you speak up for Verena after the class test? You know it was all lies, that about her period and the rest.'

'Christian: just because individuals don't behave as they ought doesn't mean the whole idea's bad. Why should I say Verena's lying? Schnürchel's a bootlicker, however much of a communist he is.'

'You like living in this country?'

'You don't?'

Now things were getting dangerous. Christian surveyed Reina with an alert, suspicious look, mumbled something she could take for agreement.

'This country allows you to go to school and university for free, the health service is free, isn't that something? Don't you think we should give something back?'

'You sound like Fahner, Reina.'

'It doesn't have to be wrong just because Fahner says it.'

Christian snorted. 'Your free health service crams old people in retirement homes, your noble state gives those who built it up a pension that's barely enough to keep body and soul together.'

'How d'you know that? Where did you get that information from?'

'Where from, where from!' Christian exclaimed, furious at Reina's slow-wittedness, furious at himself for getting so worked up, for opening up like this. 'From my grandparents, for example. And from my father.'

'He has his subjective point of view. Other doctors are of a different opinion.'

'So you say.'

'No. I know. My uncle's a doctor too and he's not one of those who only see the negative side or are only in it to earn money.'

'What are you suggesting about my father!' Christian cried angrily, waving his hand as if he were trying to mow down whole swathes of grass. 'Oh, forget it. – Do you think it's right that boys have to spend three years in the army?'

'They don't have to. Eighteen months is what they have to do, anything beyond that is voluntary.'

Christian dropped his arms. He couldn't believe Reina really was so naive. 'Fahner "suggested" we think about volunteering for the three years – the file with our assessments and what we want to go on to study was very visible on his desk. And they call it volunteering!'

'The American soldiers have to go to Vietnam. They have to kill people for the interests of the ruling classes, of capitalism. Or do you think they're there for humanitarian reasons? And what about the Falklands War?'

'The Russians have to go to Afghanistan. That's just as much an invasion. And they have to kill people there too. Can you tell me what business the powerful Soviet Union has in poor Afghanistan?'

'That's Western propaganda. I don't believe that's correct. You've got it from West German radio, that's just imperialist propaganda.'

'So, in your opinion, what are the Russians doing in Afghanistan?'

'Responding to a request from the government, for help against the counter-revolution.'

'Of course. Just as in '68 in Czechoslovakia. They also asked the Russians for help. Funny that the population wasn't of the same opinion.'

'That's Western propaganda again. The people cheered the Soviet soldiers, we saw that on TV. Christian, you really ought to think about what you're saying.'

It didn't sound threatening, just puzzled, but it brought him back down to earth at once. But he was interested in the topic, he couldn't leave it just like that; there was also the urge to be right, so he changed the subject. 'You told me your brother's homosexual. He doesn't have any problems?'

'My father threw him out. And for Mother he doesn't exist any more. She says she never had a son. Otherwise – not as far as I know.'

'There used to be a law according to which your brother would have had to go to prison. Just because of his nature. He can't help it.'

'The Yanks have racial discrimination. Anyway, that law was abolished. – And my brother's going into the army for three years.'

'Because he believes in it?' Christian asked dubiously.

'What are you suggesting?'

He had to laugh. 'It wasn't meant as a suggestive remark.'

'I'd wait for you,' Reina said.

Turgenev's pounding heart after all; he knew he'd blushed and stuck to the dim light of the path; Reina's armpits, her body the sheet had slipped off, how simple it would be to touch her now, to seek the lips of her wry, freckled face, to stammer the usual things, but he resisted: her fingers, stroking the pus-capped bumps of his acne, would say: a nasty rash; a shudder of nausea, I don't want to catch acne, then, out of consideration for him, she'd murmur something soothing, yet still feel nauseated: a lead balloon the whole thing; what would it be like to sleep with Reina, he longed for it, feared it.

'Would you stick to your convictions whatever happened?'

'I'd try to,' Reina replied after a while, without looking at him; the distance between them was more than her outstretched arm; his hand would have had to do its bit.

'Even if you were blackmailed or tortured?'

'If I say yes, you'll think I'm bragging or overestimating what I'm capable of resisting. Who can know that? – Do we have to talk about this?' Reina was getting irritated, he could tell from her voice and yet he continued to provoke her, now because it gave him a certain pleasure. 'And if they didn't torture you but someone you love?'

Reina took a deep breath. 'Who should torture you?'

'Beware of Reina,' Verena said one evening, 'I think she's one of them. Be careful about what you say.'

A magnetic needle swinging round the compass, indecisive fluttering, floundering movements; Verena seemed out of reach, she now openly held hands with Siegbert, and Christian could stare at the musical-instrument brown of her hair for so long that he noticed streaks of sweat and a powder of dandruff on the shoulders of the dark velour pullovers she wore; he could bear her looking at him without feeling he immediately had to make a contribution to the ongoing discussion or conceal the directness of this exchange of looks with some fidgety gesture – clenching his fists, scratching his head – firmly push everything away from him. Suddenly the magnetic needle had come to a halt.

Beware of Reina.

*

But now he had to be where she was; he hated it when she lost her balance going downhill and Siegbert or Falk grasped her flailing hand; when they had a rest he stared at the down on the nape of her neck, that vulnerable hair bent in bright whorls that exuded a dangerous attraction: several times already he'd stuck out his finger because there was a mosquito on them or he needed to check something, he also thought that the scar must hurt and the pain would go away if he touched it. He remembered in time that Falk was keeping an eye on his movement and it was only a matter of seconds before the conversation would die away and Reina sit there, mortified; in the evenings he wished she were still on the mattress next to him and he could decide where she should feel the shudder of his first kiss – but she'd moved to a different place well away from him. On her back, the side of her shoulder, the spot with the whorls of hair (too predictable, he told himself, perhaps she'd have forgotten later on when he asked her: Where was my first kiss, do you remember? or another boy had already kissed her there, immediately he assumed that must be the case, probably on the scar, that's what happened in pirate films – he didn't even know whether he'd be Reina's first boyfriend; it was unlikely, there must have been crushes in her earlier years at school; did she actually have a boyfriend? he decided to give him a good thrashing, the swine); perhaps on the scar after all or, better still, a point on the line the sheet had made, where her back merged with her pelvis; her earlobe (the right or the left? both were well perfused), her navel (at the thought of that he gave a soft cry of pleasure: just before the kiss her stomach would draw back as if electrified, as if an ice cube had been dropped on it, would slowly come up again, as when you breathed out, and he would hold his lips precisely over that rising movement so that her navel would touch his lips, not the other way round), her elbow (unusual, but dry, the way he imagined model-railway enthusiasts kissed), the tip of her nose (but she wasn't a cat after all), or better still her ring-toe, the one next to the little toe (no one ever placed a kiss there, but would she realize that? perhaps that was too far-fetched, too complicated?), her breasts (sure, where else? he went on walks feverishly visualizing the colour of her nipples, whether they were pink or light brown like milky coffee, whether he could nibble at them delicately without hurting her, whether they would respond to his tongue, his lips, possibly even his nostril – that when he snuffled particularly lasciviously), or the back of her knee?

No.

He would kiss her armpit. Of course there was always her mouth as well but that was out of the question for his first kiss, he'd go there later. His first kiss, he decided, would be on her armpit, that shaven, sweating, bread-roll-white dove-bellied cove under her left arm.

Kurt didn't have a telephone, invitations came to him by post; Lene didn't have one either; Christian went into the town to ring Barbara. He didn't want to worry Anne and he could well imagine what Richard would say. As he dialled the number, he could see the dilapidated balcony of the Italian House in his mind's eye, the staircase windows with the dame's violets he and Meno had admired during the winter, the night of the birthday party. It was Friday, Ina would be out; it would have disturbed him very much if she'd answered. Barbara often came home earlier on Fridays, she'd probably be in the kitchen, cooking. She answered. He told her about Reina.

'And you're asking whether you should fall in love with the girl? Tell me, have you gone soft in the head? Now you just listen to me. Do you think we were interested in politics when we were your age? Do you think Ina gives a damn about the politics of whoever's her latest?'

Perhaps she ought to, Christian thought.

'But that's something you get from your father. Just between you and me, Christian, your father's a bit . . . well, how shall I put it? Inhibited? Recently we were talking . . . oh, but now I remember it's something you're not to know about. Enoeff. You need a girlfriend, a boy of your age without one, if I were your mother I'd be wondering. – Why haven't you rung Anne?'

'I don't want her to worry, Aunt Barbara. Please don't say anything to her.'

'No, enoeff. Silent as the grave, that's me. You know how a girl kisses and what else comes after . . . Red roses, sure, etc. etc. – all that has nothing to do with politics.' Barbara sighed and in his mind's eye he could see her splayed fingers with all the rings, he heard her bangles clunk against the receiver. 'You're only young once.'

Meno warned him. Christian had never seen his uncle so exasperated. He would have liked to talk to him about Hanna but no one in the family seemed ever to have asked why Meno's marriage had failed.

'If she informs on you? – From what you've told me you should be prepared for that.'

'You really think she'd inform on me –'

'Even though she's in love with you, you mean? That kind of romantic stuff is Barbara's cup of tea, not yours, Christian. What do you know about love? What do you know about what's possible?' Christian felt hurt; Meno seemed to sense it, he said, 'They kiss you and they betray you. Both in the same breath. It doesn't have to be like that, but sometimes it is and you can't take any more risks. Perhaps Reina's an exception. But only perhaps. What if you try it out, just to see, and walk straight into the trap?'

'I like her very much . . . The way she walks, the way she moves and . . .' Christian hesitated, watching his uncle out of the corner of his eye. '. . . her armpit,' he concluded with a trusting smile. Meno burst out laughing. Christian felt as if a machete were cutting apart the flesh between his forefinger and middle finger.

'Her armpit? And you call that love? That's just sexual. It's about time you started to learn that in this country you can't behave like a little child.'

'Now you sound like Father,' Christian retorted indignantly. 'Just because you and Hanna –'

'Don't talk about Hanna.'

Christian was sorry but he refused to apologize, he felt hurt.

'We want the best for you, especially your father, but he won't be able to help you any more if something else like the training-camp business should happen. If you let Reina know what you really think and she tells others . . . She doesn't even have to do it with malicious intent. Perhaps just out of pride in you, out of naivety, or simply to get over an awkward pause in the conversation . . . Lots of things happen out of boredom. Do you want to risk your future for this girl? Have you absolute trust in Reina? Do you really know her that well, how she will react, what you mean to her? Does she know herself?'

'So in your opinion I have to make a dossier on a girl before I can fall in love with her?'

'That's the way things are,' Meno said coldly. 'I understand your feelings better than you perhaps think. No, this country's not the place to be young. I wouldn't be talking to you like this if I didn't know someone who'd gone through what I'm warning you against.'

'Who was it?'

Meno prevaricated. 'Later perhaps.'

'No, now,' Christian insisted.

'Your grandfather Kurt,' Meno said after a long hesitation.

'Oma informed on him?'

Meno shook his head, started to speak then broke off. 'No, the other way round. It was in the Soviet Union, at a terrible time. He told us children on his seventieth birthday. I don't want you to talk to anyone about it.'

Interlude: 1984

In the evening doors into the dream opened. In the evening the cast-off skins of the body were left behind after the magic word 'Mutabor' had been spoken. In January '84 the dustbins were overflowing, ashes had to be tipped out on the snow beside them, sometimes the Tower-dwellers, on the initiative of a citizens' meeting, would heave the dustbins up onto a lorry that took the ashes out into the woods. Newspapers piled up, were torn to shreds in gusts of wind sharp with frost. The District Hygiene Inspector's office recommended putting a layer of lime over the garbage. The lime was distributed to designated individuals in each street from whom the inhabitants filled their buckets: 'Causes severe eye damage. Keep out of reach of children.'

Andropov died.

'So what now?' the Tower-dwellers asked while they were queuing at the butcher's, the baker's or outside the Konsum. 'The next juvenile lead will take the stage,' they whispered with an apprehensive shrug of the shoulders.

Cigarette smoke, aquarian swirls of incense, eyes on the ceiling in the dim light of a guttering candle in an apartment somewhere in the Prenzlauer Berg district of Berlin. Shutters with the paint peeling off, cracks plugged with newspaper, putty rock hard and crumbling; the tiled stove is doing its best but plywood, fenceposts, mouldy coal are only enough for a few hours' heat a day. Men in woolly pullovers with biblical beards, workers' hands, beer mugs in their nicotine-stained fingers and a Karo or an F6 between their lips, are listening to a poet

509

reading out poems typed on wood-pulp paper, hastily, making mistakes, deliberately avoiding pompous declamation, they're all friends together, highfaluting stuff is not what's required here. Judith Schevola is listening, observing, smoking. She has introduced Meno to this group, to which you only gain admittance after passing through several rear courtyards with bullet holes from the last war, after giving a password at the cautiously opened door with no nameplate, after submitting to partly furtive, partly openly aggressive scrutiny the newcomer has to accept: there are too many spies and instinct is not always infallible. Meno senses that he is a foreign body, but his presence is accepted, no one seems to be holding back in what they say because of him. The poet reads. They are poems with turned-up collars and flat caps pulled well down. He's been published in one of the magazines lying on the table in the middle of the room, where the air is so thick with sweat and tobacco smoke you could cut it with a knife. Without the *Communist Manifesto* under one of its legs the table would definitely wobble; the *Communist Manifesto* performs this service alternately with a brochure about venereal diseases after protests from members of the audience committed to grass-roots democracy. The magazines all give off the fresh air of insubordination, have titles such as *POE TRY ALL BUM*, *bones of contention*, *AND*, *POE TRY ALL bang*, and are screen-printed on thin Czechoslovak copy paper at ten crowns per 2,000 sheets – solely for the church's official use, thus avoiding the need to apply for permission to print. They lack a stapler that can reliably staple more than fifteen pages. There's a lack of paper: the entry fee to the reading was a certain amount of writing paper that can – for the church's official use – be stapled or folded into little booklets and filled with controversial articles on environmental issues in editions of between fifteen and fifty.

'My hand for my product.'

And then? the Tower-dwellers ask.

Sarajevo calling, a wolf-cub waves to the viewers watching

television. Skyscrapers, bare mountains surrounding a basin, a dreary urban landscape that is not sought out by any reporter accredited to the first Winter Olympics to be held in a socialist country nor recorded by the camera that cannot lie. Here is the ice rink, there the tracks of the cross-country ski run, the ski jump where Jens Weissflog from Oberwiesenthal flew on strictly parallel skis to gold and silver. Did people recall a summer's day seventy years previously when a student was waiting on a street corner for the car of the heir to the Austrian throne? The Ice Queen sets out on her free programme. Her trainer stands behind the barrier, stony-faced, while her protégée, with fluttering miniskirt and Kirgiz eyebrows, inscribes flowing cursive periods on the ice. The exclamation marks of a triple toe-loop, pirouette flourishes, bouquets of roses in cellophane, Heinz Florian Oertel wallows in tulle and taffeta. Torvill and Dean dance to Ravel's *Bolero*, a Swede runs up the slopes with skating steps. There is a smile on the fairest face of socialism.

It was Christian's winter holiday from school. He had been accepted for medicine at university. Oddly enough, he hardly felt delighted at all, relieved rather, also weary; a guilty conscience for those who had been rejected. Becoming famous didn't seem that important any more after his experiences at the training camp and with Reina. He'd hardly done any school work since the start of the twelfth year, his marks had got worse, which was a matter of concern to more than just Dr Frank – there had been discussions in the staff room: he'd stopped singing in Uhl's choir, had resigned from the Free German Youth committee without giving any reason, cut himself off more and more. When Hedwig Kolb set an essay on the essential characteristics of socialist literature, Christian wrote a single sentence: 'It lies.' Hedwig Kolb didn't give his essay a mark, took him on one side and told him that she had to insist he did the essay: couldn't he? As he knew, his acceptance for university was still provisional, so couldn't he? He was kept in for an extra hour, under the surveillance of Herr Stabenow, who was still full of enthusiasm for physics, a critical attitude to research and the unprejudiced pursuit of the truth, and he put together some rubbish with the usual platitudes that Hedwig Kolb returned to him without comment but with a two minus mark. He avoided Reina. Verena was in Dresden a lot now. Siegbert had to find another career, since he'd been rejected for the merchant navy because of a lack of social commitment. He still didn't know what to do. When Svetlana started a discussion at the supper table in the hostel, Christian would silently drink his soup, and when Falk started fooling around and set Jens Ansorge off as well, he went out for a walk, stood for a long time on the bank of the Wilde Bergfrau or Kaltwasser reservoir, where there were just a few ice fishers with Mormyshka rods, sitting staring gloomily at the holes they'd made. He often went out for walks when he was at home, which made Richard remark that the lad had been ruminating and brooding over things too much recently, perhaps a regular work-out would do him good, a girlfriend; he, at Christian's age . . . Anne said that with all those walks at least he got out in the fresh air and if he didn't want to talk they ought to respect that. Christian neglected his cello. In his pocket he had Reina's letters. There were long queues outside Hauschild's coal store, the conversations of those waiting cut across by the sharp sound of the shovels with which Plisch and Plum removed the swiftly diminishing mountain of briquettes. It was the time of theatre productions, of Erik Orré's Recitation Evenings, Adeling's (the waiter) and Binneberg's (the pastry cook) 'Chocolate kitchen for children and those who want to become one' in the foyer of the Felsenburg: cooking chocolate was melted in pots and pans to a dark brown molten mass with a Christmassy smell and poured into baking moulds from Binneberg's cake shop: chocolate caravels stuck out their curving bows that Binneberg, an obese man with a network of burst veins and cheeks like a bulldog, provided with frosting sails and a sweet dribble of rigging from a piping bag; Pittiplatsch with his tongue sticking out and a white fondant cowlick multiplied on the edge of the table as if in a hall of mirrors; heads of Napoleon and culverins attacking the fortress of Königstein delighted the fathers. For each chocolate moulding Binneberg and Adeling charged one mark, which they put in a money box on which 'Solidarity' was written; they used the money to buy toys in König's toyshop on Lübecker Strasse that they gave to the children in the Arkady Gaidar children's home on Lindwurmring: an extensive, dilapidated building in the Swiss style beside the villas requisitioned by the Russians.

Once the cold season begins the heating levels are announced daily on the radio. The heating levels apply to firms and institutions with buildings and plant that do not have functioning output regulators. They set maximum heating times: heating level 1 means the heating is on for at most four hours a day with the proviso that the room temperature must not exceed the limit – for offices, schools, cinemas and other social institutions that is 19–20°C. Heating level 0: no heating for any firms or institutions, special arrangements are in operation for certain buildings or spaces (e.g. hospitals). The date at which space heating starts (heating level 1) is determined by the director of the energy combine after consultation with the chairman of the District Energy Committee.

'Learning from the Soviet Union means learning to freeze' is the joke going round the queues outside Hauschild's coal store.

In the spring Josta broke up with Richard. She wrote him a letter: since he refused to divorce his wife, she had drawn the obvious conclusion; moreover there was another man now. She was going to get married. She and her fiancé would take action to prevent any attempt by Richard to see Lucie again, to influence her or to challenge their right to custody of the child. Her fiancé had connections. 'Farewell.'

One evening Christian saw his father come round the corner of Wolfsleite into Turmstrasse. Richard had dug his hands into his coat pockets and his eyes were on the ground. Christian's first impulse was to hide behind one of the parked cars and wait until his father had passed, but Richard had already seen him. 'Well, lad,' he said, raising his shoulders like a large, skinny bird that felt cold. He seemed tired, he didn't have his usual coolly searching look. 'Problems?' Richard went on, prodding Christian gently with his elbow without taking his hand out of his pocket.

'Nah.' Christian made an effort to make his voice sound unconcerned. 'And you?' He was alarmed at his familiarity, the forced joviality hung in the air. He'd never talked to his father like that before, as an equal, it just wasn't done. He drew his head down into the collar of his parka.

'Keep everything bottled up, hm?' Richard said with a soft laugh. 'Keep everything bottled up, that's the way it is. The Hoffmanns and the Rohdes – we keep our mouths shut.'

'Meno says, "A wise man –"'

'"– walks with his head bowed, humble like the dust." A Chinese proverb. He's good at following it. The art of lying . . . You might perhaps find it useful some day, who knows?'

'Are you going home?'

'Not yet.'

'Can I walk along with you?'

Richard looked up, then he suddenly went to Christian and embraced him. 'I have to walk a bit by myself, my lad. – Sorry I couldn't do anything about the army. The guys at district headquarters promised they'd conscript you into the medical corps.' But that hadn't happened, Christian had been conscripted into an armoured division.

'I'll survive.'

'You go that way, I'll go this.' Richard pointed in either direction along Turmstrasse.

It's a time for reading: Orwell is read, circulates in laboriously typed copies – transcripts by hand, such as the monks made, would be too easily recognized, cases were known in which State Security had sent registered mail to every household in one district in order to have a sample of handwriting on the receipt they could use for comparison, checked dictations done by children at school, students' test papers, documents written by the spouse who hadn't signed the receipt. It's the time of the chain letters, of transfers, the time when poetry albums go from hand to hand in the classrooms and boys whose voices are breaking fill them with sparks of genius such as: 'There's no place like home' or 'Roses are red / violets are blue / sugar is sweet / and so are you.' It's busy at the post office: beside the buzzing long-distance booth – Herr Malthakus calling a philatelist who lives abroad; beside the booth for local calls – the mother of Frau Zschunke, the greengrocer, has been admitted to hospital; there's a queue at the parcel counter to send solidarity parcels to Poland. Outside the church Pastor Magenstock has put up a list of items that are most urgently needed, which should be sent to make the long journey (because they fetch the highest prices on the Polish black market, though that reason doesn't feature on the list, of course); addresses have also been attached to the notice. People have little trust in the officials of the German and Polish post, border control and customs, in dark hands in the interior of the People's Republic of Poland. Coffee, sugar (whole shopping-bagfuls of one-kilo packets at 1.55 marks each are lugged there from HO Lebensmittel or Holfix), children's clothes, cigarettes, flour. In the furrier's section of Harmony Salon the clippings of fur are collected; 'It's all going to Poland,' Barbara informs the children who ring at the door; the dressmakers do extra shifts to make the scraps into winter clothes that they proudly deliver to the parcel counter, where the assistant, wheezing asthmatically and wearing DVT-stockings and slippers with furry pink mice on them, is heaving weighty string-tied blocks up onto the scales with a regularity that usually only occurs at Christmas, writes the postcode on the wrapping paper with a blue wax crayon (zeros the size of hot-water bottles), brushes the completed dispatch form with glue and slaps it onto the parcel. There's a smell of glue in the post office. There's a smell of wet umbrellas drying in a plastic stand in the entrance; there's a smell of Postmaster Gutzsch's St Bernard, who's lying, like a calf, on a blanket in the passage behind the counters. The special stamps to mark the forthcoming thirty-fifth anniversary of the founding of the Republic only have a faint smell of glue, and of Gutzsch's extinguished cigar – he sometimes puts it down on the edge of the sponge used for moistening the glue on the stamps when he's checking that both the recipient's and the sender's address on the envelope are written correctly; he draws one of the narrow-gauge railway series with the fine edging past his cigar across the wet sponge or takes a statue from Balthasar Permoser's seasons series of stamps out of a folio-sized post office file and measures the space up meticulously before sticking down 'Spring' and 'Summer', then picking up the rubber stamp and thumping it down twice: pa-dum, first of all on the rich black of a pre-war Pelikan inkpad, then, joyfully, on the virgin stamp.

Regine waited. Under the ricepaper lamp in the living room that Jürgen had made and decorated with pictures of flying fish, in the garden of the house in the street in Blasewitz that was named after a resolute woman who fought for socialism, by the woodland park where the children tobogganed and skated in winter and in summer the ice cream and lemonade vendors sold colourful refreshment – in the garden, surrounded by the statues Jürgen had carved out of the sandstone from the Lohmen quarry: a frieze of cubes with children beneath fruits, a female torso, two boys based on their children, Hans and Philipp, she sat and waited. She waited beside the telephone when Richard and Anne left the living room in Caravel to leave her alone with Jürgen's voice, which, from the hubbub of the great light-spattered city of Munich far away at the other end of the crackling, hissing line, would say, accompanied by a further crackle, 'Hi'; when they went for a walk so as not to hear Regine sobbing, not to witness the silence that could arise after four years of separation and that everyday matters could never quite cover over: How are the kids? Are they doing OK at school? Is there anything you want, what should I send you? – And you? Have you found a job yet? An apartment? My God, all that's incredibly expensive. Regine waited when the lamplighter took his metre-long pole with the hook on the end off his black bicycle, inserted the hook in an eye in the grubby glass hexagon of a gas lamp, blew up a ball of light, one after the other in the streets of the district; she waited on the Thursdays when the ice cart came, drawn by two apathetic Haflinger horses, when the iceman's attention-demanding loud bell rang out, as if hurt, through closed windows and undrawn curtains along the summer-quiet street, to announce with its shrill 'Here I am!' the delivery of fresh blocks of ice that the iceman took down from the cart with a cramp-iron – shimmering like fish, glassily smooth, the hunks were put into the kitchen icebox, where, within a few days, they melted onto bowls hung underneath them; pre-electric chilling for butter and meat, milk and jam.

It is the month of the workers' celebrations. 'Everyone out for the first of May' was the wish expressed on a placard on the wall of the Dresden-Tolkewitz city graveyard.

It is the time when every Wednesday at 1 p.m. the wail of a siren can be heard over the city, practising for the real thing, when at night the rattle of machine-gun fire from the Soviet training grounds all around the city penetrates their sleep, when by day the vapour trails of fighter-bombers circle round the blue sky, followed a few seconds later by the roar of jet engines. And what point is there in ignoring the fact that the coconut, well-known for its ability to migrate across oceans, is able to find its way up the Elbe and seems to exist in reality and all its fibrous hairiness, the size of a cannonball, on some of the fruit racks in Frau Zschunke's shop one cold afternoon in May? The widowed Frau Fiebig first looks at Frau Zschunke, who lowers her eyes and nods. Then she looks at the other customers: long-suffering housewives, pensioners kept supple by all the running around, Herr Sandhaus, an ally. Ignoring the fact that they don't stand a chance not to be, they decide to be fair: first of all the widow Fiebig secures two of the phenomena of existent reality for her basket and impresses on Herr Sandhaus that he's not to take his eyes off it. Then she runs out into Rissleite, right in front of Binneberg's café, where Dresden ladies indulging in nostalgia along with their cream cakes have already registered her hurried behaviour, makes a megaphone of her hands round her mouth and shouts three times 'COCONUTS!' out into the depths of the life of a socialist district that has no choice but to be the mode of existence of protoplasm (as Friedrich Engels wrote), which consists essentially in the constant renewal of the chemical constituents of that substance. The widow Fiebig's cry does not go unheard and, since consciousness is a developmental product of matter, it is followed by the realization of the necessity of transferring one of the fibrous, tropical, travelling cadres in Frau Zschunke's 'dump' from property of the people to private property. Meno, happening to be in the right place at the right time for once, has already secured one for the Hoffmanns in Heinrichstrasse and one for himself (that is, for the Stahls and their few-months-old baby) when Frau Zschunke, with an insistent, 'One nut per nut, no more', asks him to replace the excess specimen. As Meno bears the Hoffmanns' coconut in the direction of Heinrichstrasse past a hundred-metre queue, from which dark looks speak of layers of consciousness that have supposedly been long since overcome, he has, for the first time for years, the feeling of having performed a solid, truly useful, unqualifiedly good deed deserving of praise – Judith Schevola's book is subject to delay at Dresdner Edition, assessments cause ideological stomach ache; Meno is powerless to do anything about it. That evening the coconut, cleaned, defibred (Barbara: 'Don't throw the stuff away, Anne, who knows what we might be able to use it for?') and scrubbed, is standing upright on the kitchen table before the disbelieving looks of the whole family. It's a small kitchen, they're crowded together, it's stuffy. There are candles burning all round the coconut, another of Barbara's over-the-top ideas, Meno thinks as he quietly enjoys his triumph.

'Come on, Richard, crack the nut,' Ulrich says teasingly. Robert is holding the Kon-Tiki book by the Norwegian ethnologist and adventurer Thor Heyerdahl, in case anyone should have any doubts that coconuts have eyes, which have to be bored out if delicious milk is to flow. Anne has put out bowls. A sip for each one of them. Richard picks up the corkscrew and digs it into one of the darker spots that could be one of the 'eyes' Heyerdahl talks about. Richard manages a few twists, pulls with all his might, the nut between his feet, and retrieves a fibrous plug and a bent corkscrew. The milk refuses to flow. Hesitantly Robert points out that Heyerdahl was talking about green nuts when he described himself and his men drinking coconut milk on the Marquesas. Barbara shakes the nut; it is as it was: round, compact and mute. The nutcracker from Seiffen beside the samovar, a carved wooden figure of a miner with a hinged lower jaw, is too small and breakable; more brute force is required, but Anne's steak hammer is no use either, it just chips a few splinters of Sprelacart laminate off the work surface and Ina puts her hands over her ears because Ulrich is hammering away at it in blind fury. Richard goes out with Ulrich onto the balcony, where he keeps some tools and, using an anvil as a firm base for the nut, raises a claw hammer, the nut slips off to one side and hits Ulrich on the shin. Hasn't Richard got a sledgehammer, he's had enough now and he's not going to let himself be beaten by a damn coconut, even if he has to drive the Moskvitch over it! Richard doesn't have a sledgehammer. Neither the Stenzel Sisters nor their neighbour, Dr Griesel, own such a weighty argument but André Tischer has a cutting torch with which Ulrich threatens the coconut as a last resort. Richard has a vice. They tighten it until the spindle starts to bend. The nut, a tough nut to crack, has no intention of giving up. 'We could throw the thing down from the balcony onto the pavement, really slam it down.' – 'But then the pieces would go all over the place and I'd like, no, Snorkel, I *want* to have drunk something like that for once in my life. Just imagine there's some milk still in it and it goes all over the pavement flags.' They try with a saw, but it won't grip, keeps slipping off the smooth surface. 'Perhaps it's got a screw top and you just can't see it,' Robert ventures to suggest.

Summer came. The twelfth grade have their final exams. Final parade: We wish you all the best for your future in our socialist society. Flowers, handshakes, one last visit to a disco together, booze and cigarettes, partying.

Muriel was sent to a reformatory. She had been warned but she still insisted on saying what she thought in civics classes.

Hans and Iris Hoffmann are accused of having failed in their upbringing, they are stripped of their parental rights. The guidelines say: 'The aim of a reformatory is to overcome individualist personality developments, to smooth out peculiarities of thought and behaviour in children and young people, thus creating the basis for normal personality development.'

BOOK 2

Gravity

37
An evening in Eschschloraque House

Jolting and creaking, illuminated by the murky light of the upper station and a few lamps in the interior of the car, the suspension railway left the passenger bay and sank on its rail under the horseshoe steel supports into the open and down towards the valley. It was a cool evening in late autumn. Judith Schevola was shivering in her thin coat, Philipp Londoner had lent her his scarf, which she had wound round her neck like a ruff so that only the tip of her nose and her coolly observant eyes were visible; with an oversized flat cap, such as UFA film stars used to wear with knickerbockers, her head threw a bat-like shadow.

'If the guard at the top had asked to see my identity card one more time –'

'– you'd have exploded.' Pulling down the scarf, Schevola gave Philipp a mocking glance. 'Perhaps he could tell that and decided not to risk it. Who knows, perhaps that's a reaction that's become more frequent recently from people who've been to see Barsano.'

'They dismiss these things as if they were nothing. Barsano didn't even look at the document. As if he were getting that kind of stuff daily now. He smiled and gestured towards the buffet like a . . . bourgeois old fogey. And you . . .' He nodded at Meno. '. . . hang back, say nothing and keep your head down when one of your superiors –'

'You know very well you're talking nonsense, Philipp,' Meno broke in calmly. 'What is there I could say about your theses and figures? I haven't even read them.'

'I must speak up for him. He really stood up for my book and just because Redlich supported him doesn't make that any less courageous. You came barging in with your position paper.'

'Came barging in my arse! I'll tell you something. The meeting was actually arranged to discuss points that came up in the Institute's paper. What you writers had to do with it is a mystery to me; perhaps he just invited you out of cowardice, as a let-out . . . After all, one or other of his reptilian secretaries will have prepared him on the subject.'

'Philipp . . .' Meno nodded a warning in the direction of the conductor sitting, motionless, at the controls at the other end of the car. Philipp was unimpressed. 'OK, if you insist, they're not reptiles, just toadies, jellyfish! – And that's a standard answer anyway: I'm not familiar with this, I don't understand it, submit it to those whose responsibility it is.'

'Is it Barsano's responsibility?'

'Don't you realize what's at stake here, Judith?'

'You call her Judith, aha,' Meno broke in, surprised. 'You're getting loud,' he hurried to add when he saw the two of them exchange glances.

'Eschschloraque would have a witty response ready for that. Something like: Beethoven is still Beethoven no matter at what level the volume control is set,' Philipp said in a fairly arrogant tone of voice. Schevola breathed on the window, wiped it, tried to see out. 'And you think he'll be happy to see us. Not everyone likes unannounced visitors. Especially not here in East Rome. Perhaps he's an evening type and is working on one of his plays in which nightwatchmen are chairmen of the State Council in disguise.'

'That I'm coming, he knows, that you're coming, he doesn't. Surprises stimulate him, he says. – And you haven't answered my question, sweetheart.'

Philipp, Meno thought, had a peculiar sense of humour now and then. Judith Schevola seemed amused by the nickname and the use of the familiar '*du*', perhaps she'd heard them more than once already. 'We'll continue the discussion outside, Comrade Professor, we'll be there in a moment.' Lifting up her face, she mimicked the hard-boiled vamp: 'Baby.'

Philipp rang the bell when Kosmonautenweg came in sight. The car slipped into the stopping bay, shuddered as it came to a halt; the car going in the opposite direction had stopped on the other side. Meno saw two passengers sitting in it; they nodded to him: Däne, the music critic, and Joffe, the lawyer, who seemed to be having an animated conversation. Perhaps about the Semper Opera House, which was due to be reopened on 13 February, perhaps Joffe was asking Däne about a composer for an opera since he'd written a crime libretto from which Erik Orré had performed some gory street ballads the previous winter. The doors creaked open, Philipp gave Judith his hand to help her alight, one of his inconsistently bourgeois courtesies, as Marisa would have said; Meno was tempted to ask after her but decided not to. After a short wait, during which no other passengers appeared, the conductor set off again with the empty car. Gesticulating vigorously, the critic and the lawyer glided on uphill.

'Since we're talking about modes of address, shouldn't we use the "*du*" to each other?' Judith Schevola sat on the handrail and tried to slide down but the drizzle had made it tacky. Philipp Londoner laughed, gave Meno a friendly, condescending pat on the shoulder, 'Want to bet he says no, Judith? With me he was as coy as a young virgin even though I'm the brother of his ex-wife. I'll never forget what you said to me: "There's nothing we've been through together that would justify such a step, we haven't fought together yet, we don't yet know what we should think of each other." Meno, our little warrior. What made you say that?'

'As long as it doesn't give you another opportunity to mock me – experience. I don't like being disappointed, that's all. And I don't like disappointing other people either.' He turned to Judith Schevola. She was watching the other car disappear like a brightly lit bathyscaphe in the tangle of the steel supports. 'I don't want you to feel insulted but I think it's better if a certain distance between author and editor is retained. What would you do if, while addressing you as "*du*", I tore one of your chapters to pieces?'

'I'd say, "You arsehole" – using the familiar "*du*" – and bear it with a smile.'

'Why don't you give it a try, Meno? Vain as she is, she certainly won't laugh.' That evening Philipp was clearly enjoying provoking her.

'Vanity's when you can say to your image in the mirror: so you had a bad night too? What about it?' she said, turning impatiently to Meno.

'I'd prefer to sick to the more formal "*Sie*". You just wait and see, you'll be grateful to me for it one day. Moreover I never want to see you as a moaning minnie. There's something off-putting about wailing geniuses, they lose status, and familiarity leads to the sight of rooms with dog ends and mouldy biscuits lying all over the place. Not something for me.'

'Well, that's that sorted out then,' Judith Schevola replied, somewhat put out.

'I suspect a man's never refused you something in such a matter-of-fact way before.' Philipp grinned. Suddenly his expression darkened again. 'Let's get on. If we're going to surprise Eschschloraque, then at least let's do it punctually.'

Kosmonautenweg was a series of steep winding bends, ending at steps that led through romantic woodland, held back by walls, down to Pillnitzer Landstrasse. In winter the steps were slippery, anyone going up had to pull themselves up laboriously by the rail, carrying the shopping they'd had to do in the town on their back, like a mountaineer, in order to keep both hands free. In the summer there was a smell of moss, it was damp and cool as a gorge on the steps that cut

through between Eschschloraque's house and a guarded property, the
entrance to which was blocked by a broad iron gate; the park had been
allowed to run wild. Rumour had it that Marn, the right-hand man of
the Minister of Security, would come here to recover from the stresses
and strains of his responsibilities in the capital. A further set of steps
linked Kosmonautenweg with the higher parts of East Rome, they
were hardly wide enough for one person on foot and now, when the
autumn rains had begun, full of rotting leaves on which it was easy to
slip; the wooden handrail was rotten and longish sections had completely broken off.

'How's your nephew doing?'

'Not particularly well, I assume. He's got to go into the army soon.
Three years.'

'I have pleasant memories of that evening in your garden,' Schevola
said after a while. 'I thought your nephew – he's called Christian, isn't
he? – was, in a strange sort of way, nice.'

'What d'you mean, in a strange sort of way? Are you going in for
baby-snatching now?' Philipp laughed but it didn't sound genuine.

'Very charming you revolutionaries are. But for you lot revolution's
a male thing anyway.'

'When it comes to fighting, yes.'

'While your wives are at home warming your slippers. By nice in
a strange sort of way I mean that normally I can't take a man I call
nice seriously. Your nephew's nice but I still take him seriously, that's
what I find strange. He seems to know a lot. Perhaps a bit too much
for his age. And he's attractive to women. Interestingly, he doesn't
seem to be aware of that.'

'I hope you're not going to put that idea into his head,' Meno warned
more brusquely than he intended.

'Don't worry,' Judith Schevola replied, 'I don't believe he's unthink-
ing and carnal enough to climb into bed with a woman who's twice
his age and could therefore be his mother. There are men who, in

a certain way, always go to bed with their mother and others who hate that. He probably belongs in the second category.'

'Young things belong together.'

'How tactful you are, Philipp. From mature women young men can learn what sensual fulfilment and discretion are. And they'd soon lose the desire to play war games.'

'You have an uncomfortable way of assessing other people,' Philipp remarked, hurt. 'You often base it on mere outward appearances.'

'Don't you start getting profound with me, Comrade Professor. – Revolutionaries! You only have to scratch the surface a bit and the home sweet home appears. And a kitchen with a stove and a red-and-white-checked tablecloth with a cosy samovar making heart-warming drinks to go with the cake.'

'You're accusing me of that? Me? Of being a bourgeois old fogey? I think you need someone to knock some sense into you.'

'Don't worry, my friend, there are lots who're trying to do that. By the way, you're welcome to bring your little Chilean woman along. I was never particularly taken with middle-class morality.'

'Here we are,' Meno said.

Eschschloraque's house was built into the slope. A dilapidated-looking bridge, with cannonballs in iron baskets and chains between them as a guard rail, led from the wrought-iron gate, a bent bee lily at the top, to the first floor of the foreign-looking building set amid gloomy firs. The street lamp on the steps down to Pillnitzer Landstrasse cast a faint light over the gable and part of the roof that, with its ornamental shingles, looked scaly, like dragon's skin. 'Cinnabar House,' Judith Schevola murmured, reading the inscription written underneath a rusty culverin between half-timbered gables.

Eschschloraque flung the door open, surveyed Philipp, who still had his hand stretched out for the bell push, then Meno and Schevola. 'We're busy with glue,' he said, nodding for them to come in. 'For the more advanced part of the evening we had thought of lectures on repetitions and preservatives. Anyone who has something to contribute to that should not be shy and raise their hand; and it would make the quality of the Michurin dinner seem forgivable should anyone urgently desire to correct something even while chewing. Albin!' he cried to the smiling young man waiting behind him in the hall who seemed to favour the same pastel-colour suits as Eschschloraque, although Albin's was an iridescent lilac and Eschschloraque's the silvery shade of fishes' fins. 'We have visitors.'

Albin was wearing a monocle and introduced himself with a bow, sketched a kiss on the hand for Judith Schevola. 'Albin Eschschloraque, whether pleased to meet you remains to be seen. I'm – the son. My father gave me strength and height, my lack of application. My mother, I beg you, nothing at all. Welcome.' He pointed to a row of sandals and through the barely furnished hall into the living room. It was like the spacious cell of Japanese monks that seemed to receive them with a severely elegant mien; a sparse room, not made for putting your feet up in the evening; two desktops on roughly hewn sections of tree trunk stood facing each other, some distance apart, like proud, unapproachable chieftains, a plank, sticking out into the room from a bookshelf, like a springboard, held a few little bonsai trees up to the bright white of a spotlight. On the sofa under it Vogelstrom, the painter, was sitting with a sketchbook on his knees; he'd torn out several pages and placed them down in front of him on the low wooden table with the clearly defined wavy grain. The 'Michurin dinner' kept its head down in a stainless-steel cart. The most striking thing in the room was an aquarium where, in pleasant, slow motion, colour-coordinated choreography, a wide variety of tropical fish alternated in the dreamy oxygen bubbles of its clarity.

'Philipp, my friend, before you reveal to me how understanding Barsano was of your, I'm sure, polished, trenchant report, sparkling with figures, I'd like to ask you to cast your eye over my aquarium. Can you tell what heinous deed this individual' – he pointed to Albin, who was still standing by the door, arms folded – 'committed against my darlings, against their Mozartian weightlessness? And you, Rohde, you who are usually slitting allusions with red commas, can you see it? Ah, Fräulein Schevola, you who have Schiffner piping like a billy-goat, demonstrate your gift for observation undimmed by that fine bottle of Scheurebe, the label of which you were just examining.'

'You have to admit,' Albin explained, detaching himself from the door frame and approaching, theatrically limp-wristed, 'that it can't have been easy. The slipperiness of fish in general and of their tail-fins in particular, thin and gossamery as they are, resists the adhesive power of even the best glues. And then glue is water soluble-ollubel-wollubel, oh yes.' He giggled extravagantly. 'But in this country many things are possibul. Even special adhesives. A spot on every tail-fin, slight pressure in the hollow of your hand – they wriggle like butterflies – then straight back into their element. See, it sticks, they're heading point-lessly in different directions.'

'You've stuck the tails of my most valuable fish together,' Eschschloraque retorted, taking a ham sandwich from the Michurin cart. 'Was it an ideological test? This way or that? What were you up to?'

'Science, Father. The gentlemen wanted a report.'

'Science! That is a deity to whom I will gladly make a sacrifice.' Eschschloraque picked up a net and took out the two fish that had been stuck together. 'I'll show you, Albin.' He waved over his son, who adjusted his monocle suspiciously. 'You're going to do me ill, sir. Even Vogelstrom has noticed and is covering the caricature, which is not me, in tinder and fungus.'

'Oh, just come here.'

With one bound Eschschloraque was with Albin, who had stepped towards him, grabbed him by the cheeks and tried to stuff the fish in his mouth. Albin didn't spit them out but bit into them and chewed, stretching the second fish like a rubber toy animal and tearing it off. He threw it back into the aquarium, where the fish, injured and with only half a tail-fin, swam behind a stone. 'I need something to help me digest it. Are there no bitters there?' Albin rummaged round in the cart. 'Typical, they always forget them.'

'You misbegotten son of mine.' Eschschloraque calmly lit a cigarette. 'If you want to be a dramatist and outshine me, you'll have to think up better things than that. Although I do admit –'

'– that I'm making progress? Have you any idea, dearest Father, what it cost me to acquire that special glue. I had to make serious sacrifices.' In a pretence of indignation Albin let his monocle fall out. Judith Schevola leant over to Meno – while all this was going on they'd sat down on the sofa beside Vogelstrom, without his either uttering a word of greeting or looking up from his sheets of paper – 'Albin resembles a castrated seal, don't you think? The apples on his tie are so . . . tasteful. Should I get you a bowl of peanut puffs?' she whispered. Meno looked at her out of the corner of his eye, she seemed determined to enjoy the scene to the full. 'How do you know what castrated seals look like?'

'Do you mind if I smoke, Herr Eschschloraque? – I have inclinations of which you know nothing,' she said to Meno, letting the first smoke dribble out of her nose.

'Would it perhaps not be better if we left?' Philipp asked; the expression on his face had become cold.

'Why the hurry, my dear guests? Are you not enjoying yourselves?' Eschschloraque gave a mocking smile. 'So what did it cost you, sonny? By the way, I suggest you check your gestures in the mirror. I know that it's a cliché that pooftas make poofish movements, but you're doing it like the worst possible actor.'

'I must get it from you.' Albin slurped his coffee with relish. 'Always Goethe, Goethe, Goethe and nothing else . . . And then the most you get is amusement, a bite with your false teeth. A couple of jokes snatching at the Holy Grail when in fact it was just a cake tin floating past. Raspberry sauce instead of blood . . . The fate of the clown.'

'Do you know what it is that he holds against me?' Eschschloraque flicked cigarette ash into the aquarium. 'The fact that I've seen through him, right through to the aqueous humour of his expressionless eyes. He's so desperate, deep down inside he loves me, that's the problem, but he would rather the floor swallowed him up than descend to sentimentality . . .'

'It was you who called me Albin! Albin! Only ducks or penguins are called Albin. How can one be taken seriously with a name like that!'

'Yes, that's it. Can you imagine that a dramatist who's called Albin can be really good? Talented fathers almost never have talented children, they say. But does that mean that talented fathers should deny themselves the joy! of having children? That was what occurred to me at the moment when I . . . hmm, let's say: set you off on your journey. I should have acted in a more responsible way.' Eschschloraque scrutinized his son's face, which he held in the harsh light under the bonsai shelf, to see what effect his words had, innocently opening wide his long lashes, silky like a woman's. 'The pleasure was at best moderate, anyway.'

'Even wearily fired cannons can hit the mark.' Albin was white as a sheet, though his movements were calm and measured, not even the flame of his lighter trembled as he lit himself a cigarillo.

'That's enough, the pair of you.' Philipp stood up, waving his position paper. 'We've more important things to talk about.'

'If you think so,' Eschschloraque replied.

'Damn it all, no one's listening to me. Here you are, indulging in your private quarrels, which, I have to say, I find in pretty bad taste, especially in front of –'

'– your guests?' Albin broke in, unimpressed. 'So what? Let them learn how far admiration can go. Guests? They don't bother me,' he went on with a smug pout.

'I think the way the pair of you are behaving is not only in bad taste but immature. Surely in a family it must be possible to treat each other normally, naturally –'

'Normally! Naturally!' Eschschloraque sounded amused. 'Two pathologists are discussing their clientele. "He was an artist. He died a natural death," one says. "So he killed himself?" says the other. My dear Philipp –'

'Eddi –'

Albin burst out in a fit of squealing laughter that Eschschloraque cut off with the remark that it sounded silly rather than genuine, that people who had imaginary complaints often laughed in that way. – Complaints! Albin laughed even louder. Then he suggested they should listen to Philipp at last, for what would become of revolutions without position papers. Passing over the comment in silence, Philipp, head bowed and hands clasped behind his back, raising his fingers to emphasize his succinct exposition, started to explain the ideas his planning staff had come up with. They concerned the reform of economic policy, a topic that clearly bored Judith Schevola, for she started peeking over Vogelstrom's shoulder. The artist was sketching Philipp's face in various stages between indignation and fervour until Philipp concluded, 'You're no more interested than Barsano was', and dropped his arms in resignation. 'If not even you, for whom socialist ideals still mean something, will listen to me . . .'

'For which of those here do socialist ideals mean something?' Eschschloraque asked, jutting out his chin imperiously. 'Rohde's a mere opportunist, inscrutable and taciturn, a mole perhaps; Fräulein Schevola's interested in anecdotes and striking episodes for her sassy novel; Vogelstrom in his doodles; and that one over there –' he pointed at Albin sprawled out in a free corner of the sofa with a grin on his face, sucking like an addict at his cigarillo – 'is no socialist. He's an enemy, a counter-revolutionary, worse still, a Romantic. Perhaps he's even a Wagnerian, that would be worst of all. He desires our collapse, Philipp, one ought to –'

'Yes, yes, I know what "one" ought to do. "One" ought to inform on him, that's what you were going to say, wasn't it? As was the accepted thing in the era you think of as golden. You'd have handed me over without hesitation, a father his own son. Come on now, how many did you grass on?'

'What a way to speak, you young whippersnapper!' Philipp broke in angrily. 'After all he is your father.'

'That's all right,' Eschschloraque said with a wave of the hand, 'I'm not afraid to answer that. I reported – to use a term I consider more appropriate – those who were against the system –'

'Really against or only apparently? Or did you "report" them to save your own skin? By the way' – Albin turned to Philipp – 'I can't remember having suggested you call me "*du*". I'm not a child, you know, and we're not poets or underground musicians, among whom it's customary. For my part, I prefer the distance of the formal "*Sie*" since it opens up unknown territory. Anyone who uses the formal mode of address sees poetry and underground music as a country of vast, uncharted landscapes rather than a provincial place where everyone knows everyone else and no one can see any farther than the walls of their own back yard. A person who uses the formal mode of address is insisting on the dignity of his own specialism because he is thus saying that it is by no means exhausted, and anyone who cannot see that is simply demonstrating that he is on a lower level, a lower level of thinking, of understanding others.'

'Sounds familiar. Is that irony?' Philipp asked in an ironic tone, nodding to Meno.

Eschschloraque surveyed his son with an indulgent look. 'You know the word impertinence, you look through the lens of contempt but you do not honour the word investigation and you do not like the word improve, my son. What do you know about those times . . .? I didn't need to save my skin, as you put it. I was and am a professed supporter of the order established by Stalin and I've never made a secret of it. – And "secret" in that expression,' he said turning to Meno, 'is a neuter noun, not masculine as I read recently in one of your publications. The corruption of the times is increasing, for it is the corruption of morals, and morals, like vegetables, start to go bad in little details.'

'Details, is it? Nicely formulated. Always nothing but words, Father. What's your opinion of the murders, to mention one of those, er, "little details"? Or do you deny them? The *chistka*? Did it never happen? All imperialist propaganda?'

'No. In the big picture, the murders were necessary. Desperate times must not leave you desperate for means. The Soviet Union was surrounded on all sides, what should the Moustache do? What would you have done in his place? Waited until civil war had torn the land apart? Waited until the fascists conquered Moscow?'

'I would have thought about whether the good things that were written on the standards were worth the evil they were starting to cost. He had the old Bolsheviks killed, his comrades from the revolution. He wasn't concerned about the country, about the well-being of the people, all he was concerned about was power.'

'He trampled the idea of socialism underfoot!' Philipp exclaimed in agitation. 'Are you out of your mind, Eddi? Am I in the company of madmen?'

'Ah, now we're back with the repetitions,' Albin said. 'You said that the last time you were here.'

'Trampled the idea of socialism underfoot . . . Huh, that's the way children talk who know nothing of the harsh hand of time, who do not know that the gap between weal and woe crushes those who hesitate indecisively.'

'Just listen to my father! So strong the iron hand of time that right can only flourish in the land if we do wield the baneful sword of wrong, of wrack and ruin . . .'

'How sharper than a serpent's tooth it is to have a thankless child.'

'Should I thank the hand that strikes me?'

'You hate the hand that feeds you.'

Albin stubbed out his cigarillo, lit a new one, at the same time offering his finely tooled leather case around but only Judith felt like trying one. 'England hath long been mad, and scarred herself; the brother blindly shed the brother's blood, the father rashly slaughtered his own son, the son, compelled, been butcher to the sire. – I have a letter. A charming, truly informative letter, a carbon copy of it, to be precise; I always carry it with me, although that's not necessary, since I know it off by heart. A document. Listen.' Albin leant back, blew out smoke and began to recite: '"My son is the offspring of a musician and a writer and will therefore, as far as genetics allows us to judge, also seek to make his mark in the world of art and it was thus my duty as a caring father not only to show him my love, to assert it with words, but to prove it by (the uncomprehending majority will have little sympathy but we have drunk of dragon's milk) – by doing something that was designed to make a life beside my shadow possible: I have disowned him, he will have acquired injuries but that has not, as far as I can tell, killed him; pain and sorrow: that is the propitious foundation for an artist; now he has something to write about, he does not need to live from hand to mouth, as would probably have been the case had I made things too easy for him. But that is the most important thing for an artist: his works. So as a good father I had to see to it that he had something to work on. He has strength and needed something he can fill with that strength; that I have given him, and to say that doesn't look like a father's love is a petty-bourgeois way of thinking and suggests the lack of a sense of particularities, also the lack of a sense of the laws that determine one's fate that I, in less high-flown Romantic fashion, prefer to call the shape of one's life. You may rest assured, my esteemed friend, that I do not willingly lay bare these confessions, but recently you adopted a posture such as certain heroes do in certain melodramas when they brandish their swords and mostly wish to find out what their names are (as if that would change anything). Selah."'

Eschschloraque waited, no one said anything. He calmly spread his arms. 'So? What am I? A pipe-smoking jackal?'

'But you smoke cigarettes. No, no. You're right.'

'You say I'm right?'

'Why not? I wouldn't like to have a son like me. I'm in favour of the death penalty, but I hate Stalinism.'

'My God,' Philipp murmured. 'You're both mad.'

'That is the remark of someone who doesn't know life and doesn't know it because he doesn't know himself and he doesn't know himself because he has never been compelled to get to know himself.' It wasn't clear whom Eschschloraque was addressing, his son or Philipp. Both stared into space.

38
National Service

... but the tram set off, leaving behind it Simmchen's clockmaker's shop, Matthes's stationer's, the ticking wall clocks at Pieper's Clocks, 8 Turmstrasse, the babble of voices in Wiener's hairdressing salon, where Colonel Hentter fought out old battles with polystyrene heads and curlers for little boys waiting for a fifty-pfennig haircut and ladies under the hairdryers leafed through yellowing copies of *Paris Match*; Christian did not turn round and look back at the street, he thought, I'm coming back; Malthakus bent over his stamps, photographic series from the former German colonies on New Guinea: names such as Gazelle Peninsula and Blanche Bay, Empress Augusta River and Bismarck Archipelago, which Siegbert, looking up from his comic books of seafaring adventures, had told him was where Corto Maltese and Captain Rasputin had met Lieutenant Slütter; Christian closed his eyes so as not to see the children, satchels on their backs, trotting along to Louis Fürnberg High School, past the recycling depot, the clink of empty bottles in plywood boxes, the blue one-ton scales you weren't to rest your hand on when the tied-up bundles of newspapers were being weighed, a wooden flap separating the customers from the blue-coated woman in charge of waste paper; in his mind's eye Christian could see the chemist's and Trüpel taking a record out of its sleeve and showing the silky black disc to a customer, shiny as a top hat and recommended by the Friends of Music; the train set off, on the right the Schlemm Hotel disappeared – there Ladislaus Pospischil would be serving widows sticky, richly coloured liqueurs to go with their memories of pre-war splendours, all Viennese elegance as they spooned up their cake; the bus stop kiosk was left behind with its numbers of *Filmspiegel*, under-the-counter copies of the magazines *Für Dich* and the *Neue Berliner Illustrierte* with a black-and-white photo of Romy Schneider, beside *Deutscher Angelsport* and *Sputnik* and *FF Dabei*, in which Heinz the 'awkward customer' told amusing stories about the Night of the Celebrities in the Aeros Circus; the Tannhäuser Cinema disappeared on the left, at that time of day there was no boy standing looking at the posters for *Once upon a Time in the West* and *Sinbad and the Eye of the Tiger* that Robert and Ezzo were to go and see again and again until they could join in the dialogue, until they knew what Hyperborea was where the mysterious people of the Arimaspi lived and until they gave up trying to be able to reproduce Sinbad's fabulous throw – his dagger nailed the mosquito that had been swollen by Zenobia's magic juice to the doorpost of the cabin – with their penknives; the sanatorium was left behind, the Soviet soldiers strolling around in bandages, hobbling along on crutches, Lenin's silver-plated plaster head in the middle of the spa gardens, the heating plant with the conveyor belts spilling ash, the Kuckuckssteig path below Arbogast's chemical laboratory

. . . but the tram was travelling, and his father had said, 'Goodbye', Ulrich, 'Keep your chin up, lad', Ina that he just shouldn't start to cry;

only Anne had said nothing and made him a mountain of sandwiches and had *been all over the place* for treats, and Kurt Rohde had scribbled a couple of lines on a postcard that Christian knew was in the bag round his neck, a card from the Danube delta, a melancholy hoopoe was sitting on a tree staring out over water and reeds: in the first place life is short and in the second it goes on; Meno had said, 'Come what come may, time and the hour runs through the roughest day' . . . day, day echoed in his memory like a bell tolling; Christian dug his hands in the pockets of his battledress and slipped forward to expose a greater area of his body to the underseat heating, pulled his case in out of the corridor: it had stopped raining, the window was covered in strands of watery hair, the passengers getting on and off left moisture on the grooved surface of the floor; he felt for the box of books with the tip of his toe: Reclam paperbacks, stories by Tolstoy, Gorki's *The Artamanovs*, Meno's *Old German Poems*, a few volumes from the Hermes-Verlag's 'Black Series', he wouldn't turn into a cabbage, he wouldn't forget language, that was what he feared most – that they would manage to cut out part of his brain

. . . but the tram was travelling and he had a strange experience, he was sitting in a place where he was not yet present, he was still walking along Wolfsleite and Mondleite and was on the way to the House with a Thousand Eyes; he could still hear the Stenzel Sisters' gramophone tunes in Caravel, watch Kitty doing her 'Müllers', enjoy the quietness in Wachwitz Park, where October made furious peace with the clay court outside the Roman Villa and its windows that couldn't help the light casting itself on them so lavishly, the bushes looking like waiting cats spattered with honey and the fire of the rhododendrons already dying in the afternoon; he was still walking round the park, seeing the gardening implements, wheelbarrows, bottles of propane gas, and thinking of fleeing: *to stay here, to be here*, screwed up his eyes: the world in orange, opened them: reddish brown and ochre flitting through the tops of the beeches, leaves tilting like the visors of tiny sentries, speckled with rust and definite, there were still gossamer threads of spiders' webs floating through the air and he tried to catch them with outspread fingers, as if they were tissue hanging down from the cloud-steamers and he could unravel them or fly along with them like a little boy; but he couldn't, he was sitting here on a grey seat in one of the red-and-white-painted Czech Tatra trams – and was yet still there; it was as if he were the shadow and the other Christian the man of flesh and now congealed blood (do I have everything with me? Conscription papers, military identity card, in a moment of hysteria he pulls out the bag round his neck, Kurt's card is already dog-eared), and he, the shadow, were attached to the other at every point of his body by thousands of untearable but enormously elastic threads that were tearing him off, molecule by molecule, and filling the shadow (like swimmers who were attached to the edge of the pool by rubber ties and tried to swim a length, did thirty or forty metres then fought to at least touch the other end with their fingertips, their arms going round like the sails of a windmill, whipping up the water into foam, then the swimmers gave up, pretended to be dead and floated back, face down – but he was torn off)

. . . for the tram was travelling, he looked at the Elbe opening up in a wide curve on the left, on the other bank was the Käthe-Kollwitz-Ufer, the three high-rise buildings before Brücke der Einheit, blocks made with prefabricated concrete slabs stuck into the silhouette of the Old Town, he walked round the Old Town once more, as he had done the previous day: the Academy of Art seemed to be letting its shoulders droop in the blinding white sun, cranes were revolving over the Semper Opera House, the ruins of the Frauenkirche stretched the stumps of two charred arms up to the heavens, the Catholic Church of the Royal Court of Saxony lay athwart the river like a portly duck and seemed to be baked in sleep amid the agitation of the morning traffic; the Elbe, covered in grey-brown scales, resembled a dinosaur lethargically creeping forward and at this moment the other, the more real Christian was sitting with Niklas on the chaise longue in the sparkling brightness of the music room, his parents, Lothar Däne, record shop Trüpel, Ezzo and Reglinde, Gudrun at the table with the filigree Meissen place settings, Gudrun's father, bearded, morose and ignored in the armchair by the veranda: guests at a birthday party, musicians from the State Orchestra were standing in the hall recounting gossip, Robert was looking over Ezzo's angling equipment in the children's room, Christian was sitting beside Meno, who, as always, was quiet and observing the others; the tiled stove twittered softly, Niklas was fussing about with the arm of the record player, brushing the sapphire needle, checking the speed setting, he was going to play Weber's *Freischütz*, with which the Semper Opera House was to reopen on 13 February, it had been the talk of the town for months.

. . . but the tram only stopped briefly on Rothenburger Strasse, allowing commuters heading for Sachsenplatz and Äussere Neustadt to alight, picking up schoolchildren and their teachers with their exhortations, office workers with briefcases under their arms, Christian thought of Muriel, the news that she was being sent to a reformatory had got round the neighbourhood

. . . and didn't stop at Platz der Einheit, at the Transport Services' high-rise building nor at Otto-Buchwitz-Strasse with the light-blue Central Post Office, he felt like simply getting out and walking down Strasse der Befreiung, past the memorial to the Soviet army with its heroic Red Guards and past the Schiller stele, past the four-ball clock and then going on to the Golden Rider, simply leaving his suitcase in the tram, let whoever wanted take care of it; to run away, yes; why could he not simply run away (because they'll catch you), why did he have to be here (because you want to study medicine), but aren't there people who managed to get to university even though they only did a year and a half (perhaps, but there's that law saying you can only go to university after you've completed your military service . . . what if they don't conscript you for years?); he wanted to see the Golden

Rider, now, to wonder about the circular hole at a particular place on August the Strong's horse (where was the thingy kept, was it really made of gold?); he wanted to walk over Dimitroff Brücke to the Brühlsche Terrasse and he remembered at that moment, as the doors of the 11 closed and also singing could be heard from the other carriage, making a few passengers lower their newspapers and shake their heads, the apple his mother had placed on a white porcelain plate, the last apple from a, as Anne put it, priceless gift in kind Richard had been given by a patient in thanks for good treatment: a basket with old varieties of apple, priceless because unavailable in the shops; Star Rennet, English Strawberry Apple, Red Warrior, Mohrenstettiner (Meno used a regional name, Chimney Sweep, Richard knew it from his father's garden in Glashütte as Red Eiser), which had given Robert stomach ache because they weren't quite ripe; Yellow Bellefleur, Pomeranian Crooked Boot, Lemon Apple; they still grew on the slopes above the Elbe, but they were guarded by their owners, kept for their own consumption; boys who tried to steal them had to watch out for fierce dogs and even Lange only rarely gave away some of his treasured fruit (Meno got some in exchange for books); fragrance, the crackle of leaves when the autumn drizzle came, shiny green, full, harlequin-striped fruits on the branches, Christian remembered the clear, almost brazen red of the apple on the plate, a shallow, slanting oval of shadow licked like a tongue across the porcelain in the angora light of a November morning, the harsh, glazed-looking red, beside the living-room door was a jug with the same red bleeding down from its rim in decorative dribbles; now he was going out of the kitchen into the hall and listening, stepped on a place in the parquet flooring that creaked because all was quiet in the house, no Stenzel Sisters' gramophone sketched gestures made of starch and melancholy, neither lawnmower noise nor doleful poodle slurped at the windowpanes, Plisch and Plum weren't shovelling either, no stove-stirring plumbed the silence; he thought of cutting a slice out of the apple and placing it on the toaster – or holding it in a spoon over the flame of the gas stove, as Robert sometimes did with honey substitute that he scraped out of a cardboard tub (the honey tasted of sugared wax), but he put the apple back on the plate and decided to walk round the house once more before eating the apple; he still had plenty of time

... as the tram took the Otto-Buchwitz-Strasse/Bautzner Strasse crossing and approached Neustadt Station, he was walking round Caravel thinking about the apple on the plate that was as red as a billiard ball and would be just as cool, and also too refined to tip its fragrances on demand and without exception into his greedy mouth, the flesh would crunch as he bit into it, perhaps there would be a trace of blood along the edge of the bite; the apple would taste of pride, of autumn or, to be more precise: of the frothy concord between the zenith and the calm of descent in which that *raphe* had pursued its course – he had found the term in the Leipzig anatomical atlas that medical students, as was recommended in a letter from the dean's office, should purchase before their military service or their year of work experience, Richard had acquired the lavishly illustrated book with the orange binding for him from the duplicate copies of the library of an out-of-the-way academy – that *raphe* (Christian loved the word), the force with which, just for moments, the tidal waves of September and October collided, that point in time (but it wasn't that, Stabenow had spoken of ellipses of time and blobs of time), this blob of time, then, would suck the essence of the autumn out of immense aromas: it was smells (for Christian autumn, October, the month of his birth, began with smells: the scent of the leather of old wallets that came from the gills of mushrooms, the smell of horses that came from wet foliage, the impotent sweetness of the fruit in the Anker jars that were heated in the preserving pans), it was haste going hither and thither, crossed by the lines of a great crested grebe in the shiny, sleepily quivering calm of the castles of Pillnitz, it was images furiously popping up and down (lemon sticks, spiders' stars in the trees, moist wood washed up on the banks of the Elbe, decay, moss-green in forgotten sewer pipes and in the joins in the wall on the lower section of Rissleite, the coral red of the rowan berries, peacock butterflies on the greying, sun-warmed wood of a window seat, the fine-pored stillness, slightly loosened at the edges, of a watering can in the corner of a garden, little, transparent camels of warmth slipping away from the radiator fins past chairs and sofas in the direction of cracks in the doors); and yet the apple had blemishes and 'stocking marks', as Barbara called them, scaly notches caused, perhaps, by some parasite or abnormal growth, so he wouldn't bite into the apple but cut it with a Japanese blade, would delight in the moisture on the cut (the steel would turn blue from the malic acid and taste pleasantly bitter), he didn't divide the apple into four pieces, as everyone else he'd watched eating apples did, instead he cut the apple across in slices as thick as your finger (Reina said she'd never seen anyone cut an apple like that before),

Reina

tired and lame, I sought an inn, my host was wondrous kind, a golden apple was his sign . . . he murmured as he went up the stairs to the attic, lines from his school reader that had stuck in his mind, Uhland was the name of the poet who had refreshed his parched throat with an apple,

don't think of

Reina

he thought, having taken up the struggle with the loft, suddenly he hated the quiet and the coppery red of the purlins, the clay pots and the Stenzel Sisters' cork swimming belts that helped them when they went swimming – they also wore bathing caps decorated with rubber roses – in the Massenei baths, felt fury rising up inside him at the rusted, heavy radiators next to Griesel's attic room, that they could listen to the memories of the dust here and needed nothing; he unlocked the door to the Hoffmannesque room, opened the suitcase with the film magazines, took out his penknife and stuck it right in the face of the girl on Fanø, sharply lit in momentous black-and-white on one of the programmes, saw an abandoned wasps' nest and thought of the apple, the hungry red that seemed to suck at the other objects in the kitchen, broke off, went down into the apartment, gathered his things together, left the apple untouched

. . . and for a few moments couldn't understand why Neustadt Station had come into sight, why the 11 was slowing down and stopping; even while he was some way away he could see the people waiting on Dr-Friedrich-Wolf-Platz, a motley crowd that was fed by cars driving up and suitcase-bearing young men such as he was; it blocked the entrances to the station and when he got off he could even hear the cries and raucous shouts from the tram stop, which was separated from the station by the wide square reflecting the blue of the sky.

39

Pink is the colour of your weapons

Comrade Soldier, Comrade Sailor, a new phase in your life
lies ahead – active service in the National People's Army.
With your work and your study you have already helped
to shape our socialist society. Now, as a soldier, you are
exercising a basic constitutional right, you are fulfilling your
duty to defend peace and socialism against all enemies.

What It Means to be a Soldier

Training Centre Q/Cadet School Schwanenberg,
9.11.84

Dear Parents, 1,000 days, but the first ones are over. We were driven from the station in Schwanenberg to the barracks in several batches of 30. There were only 2 lorries so we had to spend 4 hours standing by the loading ramp on a cobbled square outside the station, we sat down on our cases and bags, the corporal accompanying us forbade us to go under cover. I was one of the last batch, it was already dark and we were silent (we should never let an opportunity to be silent pass ungrasped, the corporal said with a knowing smile); I was sitting by the tailboard and could have a look around. On the horizon the reflected glow of industrial areas, blast furnace tappings licking at the sky, the land is flat, there are just a few stunted trees like frozen sentries on the edge of the open-cast mines. The lorry drove out of the town, there was less and less traffic on the road, then I saw Schwanenberg disappearing like a space station (it was us who were moving away, of course, but it felt as if the lorry were standing still and the populated areas were being pulled away from us), a few lights here and there, navigation lights for the brown-coal excavators that lumber along like prehistoric animals, grazing mastodons in the dark. There's a metallic hum in the air, interrupted, when the excavators are moved, by the squeal of their rusty joints, you have to get used to it, it reverberates across the countryside, breaking at night on the concrete of the living quarters of the cadet school. Then smells: the soil smells of metal, the air of flints being struck against each other; there's a large sweet factory in Schwanenberg and when they're pouring chocolate into moulds the smell drifts into our corridors and rooms, you can even tell the different liqueurs they use to fill the chocolate sweets. Then, depending on the wind direction, cocoa dust settles on the tables, stools, beds, in such fine layers you can't collect it.

The school is in the middle of the brown-coal district, no houses, no trees in the vicinity, bushes just along the drive. It covers an extensive area, light-grey, almost white roads made of concrete slabs that are swept by squads with brushes made of willow twigs. That scraping noise, the hum of the excavators, the croaking of the crows, on Sundays music in 4/4 time from the loudspeakers along the roads of the facility and the barked commands are our daily music. Accommodation boxes, a hectare of parade ground right by the entrance (here they call it the CEG – controlled-entry gate), a few low cubes in the background, watchtowers at the corners, barbed-wire fence, a flowerbed outside the staff officers' building: Welcome to the Hans Beimler Training Centre Q. After we got off the lorry we had to fall in, a different corporal took us into a hall where they went through the general attendance check. After each name, the unit and the number of the building where we are quartered were bawled out; I was assigned to Block 1, an oblong with hundreds of windows in the long sides and with 100-metre-long (132 metres to be precise, they were measured generations ago) corridors floored with granite slabs spattered with black and white spots and polished till they are smooth as glass. The black and white spots are distributed more regularly than on a Great Dane and therefore don't look very nice. We had to go by ourselves. Not a person to be seen. Fluorescent tubes, in the middle of the corridor a plain table and two stools, above them a wall newspaper on red cloth with the title 'Subject area: Tanks/Fiedler Unit', underneath that a large-format daily schedule, a calendar for birthdays and a slogan: 'The stronger socialism, the more secure peace.'

Right in front of me a door flies open, a man in camouflage uniform comes out and shouts that I'm to pick up my bag and follow him. He takes me into a bare, not very big room, table in the middle, at it another man in camouflage uniform with strikingly Mongoloid features and a bespectacled man in ordinary uniform, pale, fishlike, Unpack bag, Fish orders. The Mongol grabs my bag, probably because I'm too slow, and empties it out. Underwear, a cardboard box so I can send my civvies back, my case of books. Whazzat? Fish asks. There's books in it, I say. – Open. He even gets up off his chair and kneels down, the Mongol's scattered the books all over the place, which doesn't endear him to me. At Lev Nikolayevich Tolstoy, Fish grasps his spectacles. Send back home, at once. The case is against regulations. You can't read all those books anyway. Or d'you need them when you have a crap? Sergeant Rehnsen (that's the Mongol), report to me when the package has gone. Name? – Christian Hoffmann. – What trade have you learnt? – None. Completed senior high. – Hm. What do your parents do? – Father doctor, mother nurse. – Hm. Hobbies? – Reading, angling, art, history. – No sport? – Chess. – Trying to be funny, eh? the Mongol rasps. – It can get tiring if you keep sticking your oar in, Rehnsen, Fish says. You'll have your work cut out here, he says to me. Delicate blossoms need watering. Corporal Glücklich! (The man who shouted for me to get my bag comes in.) Get him kitted out. Glücklich bawls that I'm to get my stuff together: Move! Move! You're not in the kindergarten here. Glücklich has brown skin like stretched rubber and looks like an Inca; we cadets (also known as 'day-bags', 'dishcloths', best of all, I think, is 'furniture': 'You, furniture, need a good shellacking, eh?') pretty soon agreed on the nickname. Inca pushes open a door diagonally opposite the corridor table – Your room! Bag in there! We go to another door, which he opens gently: the clothes room. He pulls down a flap, chucks me a panzer cap, a sealed package, a water bottle, underwear, two brown terry towels plus a white linen towel, army socks, an olive-green woollen pullover, gas mask, steel helmet, protective clothing and two field packs. Shirt off, green pullover on, he says to me, the furniture with two arms. Come on, come on, don't stand around like that, you're not here to fatten yourself up. Grab your kit and dismiss to your room. At one whistle you come out. The room (no. 227): small, bright, a big window facing the door, one table, two stools, along the left wall two steel bunk beds with blue-and-white checked sheets and one grey blanket at the foot, on the right four plain lockers, brown with age, a broom cupboard by the door. No nameplate on one of the lockers, so there are just three of us in the room. I looked out of the window; a dull evening, below the main facility road to the CEG, underneath the window a strip of grass, across the road a row of corrugated-iron sheds. To the right the road bends and goes out of sight, at the crown of the bend there's a sentry box by an exit gate with a barrier, beside it a guard post with the sign 'DO' (Depot Officer/technical depot). Beyond the barbed-wire fence, the brown-coal zone. I shut the window, switched the light on. My things were still lying where I'd put them before donning the pullover. I was going to tidy them up but I didn't know if there was any point. After a while I heard steps – the others were coming. A sharp whistle: Everybody out!

My comrades are queuing up at Corporal Glücklich's clothes room. He throws them their things in the face, bawls, Next! C'mon, move your arse! The Mongol walks up and down the line. Now listen to me, you lot. After this each one of you will be shown his room and locker. You just place your things by the locker and come back out again immediately and line up as you are now. Right then, off you go, Corporal Glücklich. Corporal Glücklich takes a sheet of paper out of his breast pocket and bawls, First platoon, first group – Schnack, Krosius, Lahse: 225. Müller, König, Rusk. (He pauses, exchanges glances with the Mongol, Rusk? – One of them shouts, Here! – Freshly toasted, eh? Inca says. Very tasty too.) Ress: 226. Hoffmann, Irrgang, Breck: 227. First platoon, second group . . .

Have to stop now, I'm too tired. More soon. Best wishes, Christian.

TC Q/Schwanenberg, 11.11.84

– continuation. The masked ball, as the kitting-out ceremony is called here. Whistle: Everybody out! The Mongol has the red DS (duty sergeant) armband. Corporal Glücklich will now lead you over to the Central Regimental C/E room (C/E: Clothing/Equipment) where you will be given your remaining things. Once you are ready you come back under your own steam to the unit. Take over now, Corporal Glücklich. Off you go.

At the double – quick march!

Hundreds of cadets were waiting outside the Regimental Clothing

Room, an orange corrugated-iron shed. Light in the entrance that only shone on those at the very front. At regular intervals the searchlights of the watchtowers passed over the queue that went right round the parade ground. It was quiet, most seemed occupied with their thoughts (that is, assuming they had any). Noise came from inside the shed, a knocking, clattering, rumbling, thrumming and humming, now and then a few bars of the 'Radetzky March', loudspeaker crackle. The hall seemed like a gigantic open maw swallowing up the queue. At a few places in the queue they were doing knee bends, at others jogging on the spot; the smokers in our platoon, which was right at the back, clicked their lighters and held the flames to each other's hands; the army pullovers hardly kept us warm at all and it was over two hours before we got into the shed. Inside it smelt of washing powder. The noise thumped our ears, there were sounds like those of boxing gloves on sandbags, the soft trickle as they sway back. Steel shelves several metres high, little spotlights attached to them, oddly enough always in motion, as if they were flying saucers or spinning tops. The light didn't move in time to the 'Radetzky March', which they were playing from a tape, sometimes it started droning and jolting, as when an ignition key's trying to get a recalcitrant car to start, then I thought of muscles, a biceps doing unending pull-ups until all its fibres gradually snap. The steel shelves angular, their arrangement unclear, crammed full, as far as I could see, with uniforms, boots, groundsheets, belts, caps, next to a bundle of belts was a packet of lemonade powder, which I stuck in my pocket. In front of each set of shelves was a table onto which assistants, who were climbing all over the shelves, threw things down after we shouted the size of the item up to them. Kit orderlies were dashing hither and thither. Always batches of four; we were pushed to the boot shelves, there was a cardboard sign: ISSUE POINT 1. The orderly whispered (that's what it looked like, I couldn't hear anything because there was a 'Radetzky March' loudspeaker right above us), I bawled out my shoe size, sweating and bright red, he clambered up a ladder and chucked two pairs of boots straight at me. Irrgang, who has the bed next to mine, pointed up: there were bathtubs with claw feet hanging there: the chips in the white enamel were like a flurry of stars merging in the black of the bottom of the tub. I dropped one of the pairs of boots, they were tied together with string, bent down, one of those pushing from behind stumbled over me, taking others down with him, there were five or six people on top of me, I could see arms, the weight became heavier, perhaps even more were falling on top of me, then I saw Irrgang give a few a good kick in the backside, making them crawl away. The orderly shouted, Hey, you're holding everyone up, come on, come on, get along, follow the chalk line, I pulled myself up by the shelf struts, saw the red line and staggered on. ISSUE POINT 2: groundsheet, winter uniform, coat. The orderly there waved us over to the table, slapped four groundsheets down on it, pack your stuff in that, scrutinized me, dropped two stone-grey uniforms and a heavy military coat on me, coarse cloth, felty, here there was an even stronger smell of washing powder, the things had probably been dry-cleaned. I felt revulsion, someone or other's worn them before me, I thought, they've been soaked in someone else's sweat and God knows what other exudations. Your stuff in the groundsheet, you've to tie it into a sack, there are buttons along the sides, and don't form a coral reef, on you go, on you go. ISSUE POINT 3: gym shoes, dress shoes, caps, carrying frame, a few things thrown in my face. ISSUE POINT 4: sports kit, brown tracksuit, yellow gym shirt, red shorts, the colours of the Army Sports Association. ISSUE POINT 5: black overalls for working on the tank, combat uniforms. Size! – M 48. The black overalls, two lined and one unlined combat uniform flutter through the air like woodland birds. That's the way out and get your arse in gear, cadet. A corridor, hollowed out by two floodlights, there was still the dadadum, dadadum, dadadumdumdum of the 'Radetzky March', this was where the smell of washing powder was most powerful, Irrgang pointed to another bathtub, only this time it was on the floor, assistants were dipping lavatory brushes in it and giving the cadets a good scrub as they hurried past, shouting 'Earholes, earholes' and 'It comes out through your arsehole', jiggling with laughter. Then off we go to join the company. All line up. Preparing kit for inspection! Inca snarls. A corporal we haven't seen yet comes. That, we are told, is the 'assdusarge' ('assistant to the duty sergeant'). The assdusarge holds up a piece of cardboard with a standard locker drawn on it, as he barks he stresses every syllable so that when he turns round I automatically look between his shoulder blades to see if there's a key to wind him up. We fill our lockers: shirts with the edges flush, ties with the edges flush, valuables and service identity card in a lockable drawer, cutlery and brown mug into the compartment with a ventilation filter, uniform on hangers, steel helmet, tank hood, gas mask (called protective mask here), field packs (called monkeys) and protective suit (called a jumbo) on top of the locker. The Mongol walks along and inspects the lockers. Most have everything wordlessly tipped out; do it again. Your locker's like a pigsty. Do it again. Get a move on, there is a standard time, Comrade Cadet! Whistle. Everybody out! Masked ball, Inca snarls. Clothes back out of the cupboards that we've just laboriously transformed into standard lockers, the Mongol grins, the assdusarge bawls down any moaning. Now in front of each cadet is the cardboard box in which our civvies, including handkerchiefs, socks and shoes, are to be sent home. Beside it is the groundsheet with our army things. The assdusarge holds up cardboard signs each showing a standard AM (army member). It must be three in the morning when we squat down. First command: Item: steel helmet. Stretch out right hand, grasp helmet! It's not precise enough for the Mongol, Everyone up! Stand to attention! Thumbs on trouser seams! Down! Kneel down. Item: steel helmet. Stretch out right hand, grasp helmet! Second command: Present! Stand up, present the steel helmet with arm outstretched. One is starting to droop, the Mongol bawls, Did I say anything about putting it down? Inca walks along the row, very slowly, the steel helmet gets heavier and heavier. Finally: Put down! So kneel down again. And that happens with every item. Knees bends alternating with changing clothes: Standard time, comrades! There are too few epaulettes, every time we change uniform we have to unbutton the epaulettes from the one we've just taken off. We change clothes, transferring the epaulettes with the pink stripe. Irrgang, who's next to me, gets tangled up because the sleeves of his overalls are sewn up, all part of the fun. The wind-up assdusarge breaks wind noisily a lot. Perhaps he's furious since he can't get to bed because of us. We're like a colony of brooding albatrosses with the flutter of sleeves and trouser legs all over the place. Check. Stand to attention. One of the Group Two cadets has a beard. The Mongol, who, as we now know, wants to be an actor and doesn't just wake us for early-morning exercises by kicking the bed but likes to brighten our start to the day with dramatic monologues, grasps the cadet by the chin and says, Itchie, kitchie, razor blade, beardies never make the grade. The cadet pulls back, doesn't quite know what's happening to him. Dismiss to scratch your beard, Gorse-face!

Haircut. That's in the swimming pool, it's empty so the hair can be swept up. A couple of surly soldiers wield the rattling electric clippers. Conk down! Keep still! Beside each stool there's a so-called 'standard noddle' stuck in a flag-holder on a broom handle. The standard noddle is a grinning papier mâché private's head with the hairline drawn by a felt tip. So I didn't need to go to Wiener's before I left. Breck, who also rooms with me, screams. 's only a wart, dogface, the Comrade Barber says, taking a cotton ball soaked in antiseptic out of a tin of Carlsbad wafers and slapping it on the bleeding spot.

Next stop the photographer, right next door. We go behind a headless dummy that's been sawn open vertically and has a dress uniform with epaulettes, shirt and tie stuck on the front. Stand inside the dummy, your neck in its neck! Photo. Proceed! At the Med Centre we get a tetanus jab in the upper arm. The medical orderlies can hardly keep up with the crush and groan that these batches of cadets that keep coming every six months ought to be gassed. Back to the company. By now it's a quarter to six. By the time we've washed, put on our pyjamas and dropped into bed it's four minutes to six. At six Inca whistles. Company Four – rise and shine! End of night-time rest! That was the first day. Today is Sunday, we have some free time.

Love, Christian.

TC Q/Schwanenberg, 12.11.84

Dear Parents, The package with my civvies ought to have arrived by now? Please check the outside wrapping paper, there's a note hidden in the folds.

Today was our 'beginning of Carnival'. We were woken at 5, followed by the usual 10 minutes for washing, dressing, putting things away, falling in. Marched off, destination unknown. We marched along a road at speed, suddenly the order, 'Gas!' was given. (Masks on, and they stayed on for 3 km.) We were loaded down from head to toe with: rifle, belt (loaded with a belt, oh yes, Pa, didn't you tell me not to exaggerate, it was un-Dresdenish? Herr Orré also taught us that, ask Ezzo), water bottle, bayonet, combat pack, ammunition pouch. After the 3 km some simply keeled over. But that was only the start of the exercise; it was followed by 1: moving on the field of battle – we spent one and a half hours elbowing, crawling and jumping our way across muddy ploughed fields (there was drizzle all day) and were frozen through, chatterchatter. Then came 2: camouflage. That meant we had to burn a newspaper to smear ash all over our face and neck, a filthy business. And elbowing, crawling etc. etc. as well. I had intense pain in my joints from the constant contact with the ground. (It's no longer constant, the contact with the ground, I mean.) And my face nice and black. Our clothes were as cold as the Heart of Stone and truly impregnated with dirt. But then came 3: digging out a battle station. While lying down we had to dig out a hole, 1.80 m by 60 cm and 50 cm deep in 30 minutes; and it has to have a specific shape. No picnic with the heavy baggage. Digging out a firing hollow made me think that being a gravedigger's not an easy job.

The afternoon was entirely occupied with cleaning our rifles, drying and brushing the mud out of our things as well as the usual being hustled to and fro. Now I'm sitting writing by the light of my pocket torch (it's night-time rest); my room-mates are doing that too. Night-time rest is the only time during the whole day when the whistle doesn't go. Unfortunately it's all too short: 3,000 m in full uniform is already on the horizon. At the moment I'm constantly getting a pain in my heart and dizziness. I might be imagining it though. When we're ordered to wear our steel helmets I quickly get a headache from the hulking great thing. But then I just think it away (you don't have to think much while marching).

13.11. Some easy diver training for us, Company 4. At the double, march! to the facility swimming pool (as they call it here); we got undressed, sat for four hours in the cold on the edge of the pool. Then we had a breathing mask and a heavy, sopping-wet uniform put on and had to walk round the pool for a quarter of an hour, completely wrapped up in that revolting stuff. It was a quarter of an hour of gasping for breath. Then into the water, that was icy cold. If you let some water get into the breathing tube (you only needed to smile), you could even die, despite the safety line, for the clothes were heavy, moreover we had lead plates on our feet so that the instructors wouldn't have been able to pull us out that quickly (it was about 6 m deep). Well, perhaps we wouldn't have drowned. The sight of us under water was grotesque, hopping round on the bottom of the pool like big, black embryos on long umbilical cords; I felt like a puppy that was being trained to do some trick retrieving things.

How's Robert doing at the senior high? How did his German homework assignment go? Has Reglinde got into music school for organist/choirmaster? There's an MTO here (Military Trading Outlet that's open for cadets on Sundays); I saw some roofing felt there, you can tell the Tietzes. Didn't Niklas want to seal the leak over the music room? If I'm to send some, he'll have to send me packaging that's big enough to take it, since there isn't any here. By the way, I get 225 marks a month. With love from Christian.

TC Q/Schwanenberg, 15.11.84

Dear Parents, Many thanks for your parcel that arrived yesterday. It was just at the right time, we couldn't have lunch because we were in training. The apples above all were important, we've already made quite an impression on them (sometimes I think of 'Tired and lame, I sought an inn, my host was wondrous kind', but no one here reads Uhland). We only rarely get vegetables and no fruit at all, but otherwise life here is very healthy (lots of sporting activity). So if you should be sending another parcel at some time, Ma, then if possible just apples, carrots, a bit of soap, a salt cellar. And please don't let Barbara send me a radio (I was going to write to her but I've only time for one letter), radios are forbidden in our rooms. I could perhaps find another way of compensating for the lack of music – in the company copy of the regulations for internal service I have found none that forbids a cello. But it would have to shrink, the problem's the small locker and even in the tank the cello would stick out of the hatch. However, if I could put the tank hood on Mr Violin Cello and teach him to salute, he could easily pass for me since I'm sure he could manage the grunting and mumbling to the tank mike.

Today we marched for 6 hours, exercise training, everything in the 'rococo style' (we have to stretch our legs out and lift them at least 30 cm above the ground and make very, very little loops). Right about turn, left about turn, get on with it, hey, Gunner Arsehole in the last rank, lift up your trotters. After that we were on fatigue duty, from 1 in the afternoon until 9 in the evening scrubbing, painting tanks, scraping off rust, the corporal standing behind the cadet whistling on his whistle. The area round the facility is particularly beautiful, bare as a Cossack's head, no trees growing, cranes on the horizon, factory chimneys, shed-like structures. Here are the words of our marching song that we have to learn, because it's our song, the 'Song of the Tankers': 'Bright shines pink the Tankers' colour, / I so proudly bear. / Pink too is a dress of yours / I love to see you wear. // From the fields pale hands are waving, / one is waved for me. / In my thoughts I fondly kiss you, / together soon we'll be. // Oh the joy that now awaits us / at the dance tonight. / You the fairest of them all, / pink dress shining bright. // *REFRAIN:* Through the little village march, / the Tankers two by two. / Nevermore will I forget / the path that leads to you.'

We sing it every evening when we march to dinner, the tune doesn't matter, everyone bawls it out however they like, the main thing is that it's loud. The other companies sing the same song but change the colour, instead of pink (Tanks) they put green (Chemical Services), black (Engineers), red (Artillery), white (Motorized Gunners), gold (Intelligence). It doesn't really flow but it still comes out nice and loud.

The answer to your question about the swearing-in ceremony, Ma, is unfortunately no. Our tank unit can't invite any family members, the accommodation available in Schwanenberg couldn't cope with the numbers, they say. You'll just have to wait until I get leave, I'm afraid. Have you heard anything from Muriel? And is it true that Ina's got engaged? Keep me informed. Love to all, Christian.

Hans Beimler-TC / Schwanenberg, 19.11.84
Dear Tietzes, There's a smell of chocolate, the Schwanenberg sweet factory's making chocolates. Our company's cleaning the rooms and the rest of the building and above all that means sweeping up cocoa powder: the wind blows the brown dust over from kilometres away. But I'm sitting on the loo quickly writing this letter to you.

The bottled pears arrived safe and sound, many thanks for your gifts in the parcel my parents sent. The kidney warmer you knitted for me, Gudrun, will come in useful when I'm on guard duty or camping out; I just hope it doesn't get stolen or forbidden as being against regulations.

At the moment we're being instructed in the subtleties of communication within the military sphere, especially saluting and swearing. It's done by a sergeant we call the 'Mongol'.

Permission to speak, Comrade Rank, sir.

Permission to go past, Comrade Rank, sir.

Permission to dismiss, Comrade Rank, sir.

Permission to join you, Comrade Rank, sir.

My room-mate Irrgang puts up his hand. I've a question there, Comrade Sergeant. What if I need to go and the Comrade First Lieutenant's sittin' next to me on the toilet? Permission to join you, Comrade First Lieutenant?

The Mongol's reply: Cadet Ammofeed, Cadet Irrgang, will never have a shit next to the Comrade First Lieutenant. Never ever.

Irrgang puts up his hand again. There's another question I have. If I meet the Comrade First Lieutenant and the comrade doesn't give me permission to speak, how can I ask for permission to go past?

The Mongol shrugs his shoulders, continues with the lesson. We practise saluting.

Irrgang raises his hand again. I've an important problem there. 'f I meet the Comrade First Lieutenant an' along comes another Comrade First Lieutenant, that is two comrades at the same time, one on the left an' one on the right, should I put both hands up to my thinkpot at the same time.

At the moment Cadet Irrgang is busy on the obstacle course.

Dear Niklas, Have you been to the Semper Opera? What does the building look like? Best wishes, Christian – who's looking forward to receiving letters.

TC Q/Schwanenberg, 24.11.84

Dear Parents, Ina's engaged to Herr Wernstein?? How did that come about! Thank you for all the news and the parcel. You must have put yourselves to some expense for that, I don't know how we're going to eat it all up in our room without getting really fat. If you want to send me some books, Ma, then please wrap them in the paper I showed you (incoming parcels have to be opened for checks).

Today was the day we were sworn in. After the official ceremony (I crossed my fingers when taking the oath) I had, on the order of the company commander, to propose a toast in the 'House of the National People's Army' in the barracks (before I did, he read through it for mistakes and ideologically unsound remarks); after that I went back to our block and not into Schwanenberg with the others, so at least I had a quiet afternoon, I locked myself in the lav and wrote replies to a few letters. Anyway, I saw Schwanenberg a few days ago when I went with a corporal to buy stuff for the company staff officers in the store there. Schwanenberg's a garrison town, mostly bare and rect-angular, qualities my 'noggin' also possesses since the 'Masked Ball'; but my hair's growing again. Send my love to Aunt Iris and Uncle Hans, to Fabian as well. And to you, of course. Christian

TC Q/Schwanenberg, 25.11.84

Dear Parents, Robert thinks I'm exaggerating when I write that we only have three hours' free time on Sundays. Our daily schedule is, with minor variations, as follows: 06.00 hours: wake, put on red/yel-low tracksuit in 2 min, 06.02: go out, early-morning exercises until 06.30: return to building, wash, dress, put sports things away by 06.40: fall in, at the double to canteen, breakfast until 07.00: at the double back to the company, 07–07.30: make beds, clean room, 07.30–15.00: training, lunch jammed in somewhere (bolt it down, what else), 15.00–16.00: 'big' cleaning of rooms and building (each of us has his own patch that he has to keep clean), 16.00–18.00: parade practice and extra physical training (on top of the morning 3,000 m comes the obstacle course, 500 m with 22 so-called chicanes, plus weightlifting with the 50 kg weight, standard 6 times, exercises with the tank-track weight); return at the double, no time to wash, 18.05–18.20: supper, after that daily cleaning of rifles and care of personal protective equipment (protective mask and protective suit), 19.30–20.00: communal viewing of *News Camera*, 20.00–21.30: outdoors work (cleaning the tanks, painting fences, cutting the grass, with nail scissors if the Mongol feels like it, brushing facility paths), 21.30–22.00: cleaning rooms and building, make up sports pack, wash, check rooms, 22.00: night rest. I can only write letters during night rest or on Sundays. There's only one time during the day when we can relax a bit: *News Camera*, which we watch in the club room, where we're not allowed otherwise. At least we see something civilian once a day. Once a week we have showers, we go into the shower hall in sections, 200 men under 150 showers and we have 10 minutes to soap ourselves and wash everything off – that's assuming the NCOs in charge of the showers don't amuse themselves by turning off the water or only letting cold through. They're discharge candidates and can do as they like; we're the new boys, we're 'order-receivers', that's why they call first-year conscripts 'earholes'. Love to all, Christian, on the way to an ARDSP (All-Round Developed Socialist Personality)

PS: Of course, I'm exaggerating, otherwise you might end up believing me.

Schwanenberg, 25.11.84

Dear Frau Doktor Knabe, Many thanks for your letter of 23 Sept., the metre-long parcel with the brochure on 'Keeping Your Teeth Healthy' that you and Prof. Staegemann have edited. Odile Vassas and Dr Vogel from the Museum of Hygiene have put a lot of work into it. Sensi the dwarf is easily recognizable, likewise his enemies Dirtfinger, Stinkifoot,

Nosedrip, Blackear and, of course, Lazitooth. Whenever they invaded the socialist kindergarten, Sensi was there with his toothpaste machine gun and face-cloth-grenade. I think every Dresden class must have seen the cartoon with the dwarf; I remember that he checked whether his exhortations were really being followed – he watched the lazy children on his surveillance monitor, had a telephone to inform the primary school teachers and a magic telescope. If he were to focus it on our Training School, he could study our feeding habits. We go (but to go means to run, going at the double is the natural mode of progression for members of the armed forces) to the 'Interhotel'. At long, Sprelacart-topped tables, on stools, after the polite invitation to sit down and 'proceed with the meal', we bend over the *Komplekte*, savour the finest unsugared tea with its faint hint of peppermint which, under the nicknames of 'bromide' or 'Impo-tea', is said to have a certain calming effect and which waiters with grey coats and choice manners heave onto the table in tubs; on Sundays, if you are quick (and who isn't?) there's hot milk and 1 piece of cake for breakfast. Ah, *Komplekte* . . . How should I describe it? O delicious mixture of atomic bread and cosmonaut's groats and steadfastness against the aggressor! As yielding as dough, you stick, O friend from the Soviet Union, to the soldier's teeth, making him replete and sending him to ride the porcelain bus. Let me embrace you, tastebud, you cry from a distance and, rest assured, we love you too. How fine it must be to lie there, round, sharp and contented as a peppercorn, then to gradually turn into a balloon, to sing your backfiring song as you dream, simply releasing all ballast with a sound like thunder, then bray no more. Everything is in motion, but *Komplekte* is so through thick and thin. Even its fragrance gilds our noses, does not splash around pointlessly in dromedary rumens, plunges through cackroaches, swirls round strips of sandpaper, twangs the balalaika carved out of knackwurst, trills its lovelorn song through the exhaust of a Trabbi – only in the end to drop nothing but flour bombs; but it dances on the congresses of Vienna steak, sweats attar of roses and swings, as it dips its Big Toe in the water of a smile, the propeller of our hunger. Complex is *Komplekte*, a true miracle, and no cook worth his salt will ever reveal the recipe to you . . .

The roofing felt will be sent off to you in your cardboard box, also included is 1 packet of roofing nails they also had in stock. My father told me about the death of Prof. Staegemann's son; my brother Robert has Prof. Staegemann to thank that he can still play the clarinet after his skiing accident on Untere Rissleite. His shattered incisor was reconstructed using a technique from the West (a transparent liquid that hardens under a lamp; I can still remember how astonished you were). What you wrote in your letter about Muriel and her family sounds ominous. My father told me that a joint letter is to be sent to the Minister of Education. Best wishes to you, to your husband (perhaps I'll have time for a visit to the Zwinger when I'm on leave, I haven't been there for ages), to the Krausewitzes, Herr Dietzsch and Herr Marroquin – he came to mind during our kitting-out ceremony, they call it the Masked Ball. Christian Hoffmann.

TC Q/Schwanenberg, 28.11.84

Dear Parents, Your parcel arrived safe and sound yesterday, thanks for sparing no effort or expense. The apples have all gone already. Please don't put anything in your parcels that has even the slightest hint of the West. The parcels have to be opened and the quartermaster-sergeant (the man who deals with clothing, equipment, mail, food requirements etc.) confiscates anything that has the slightest hint of feelers 'the enemy' might be putting out for innocent military cadets, even if it's a midge from the other side. Could you perhaps get me a bottle of aftershave? But not Dur that you can get in the store here – or, rather, can't get any more since one of the regulars told us that Dur has 'revs' (= high-percentage alcohol – well, he is a driving instructor). That evening Irrgang and Breck were both drunk and they've been put on extra guard duty as a punishment. In the chemist's recently I saw a few bottles of Tüff aftershave, that might do.

Yesterday I was the 'cookroach', that is I was on kitchen fatigues. I ended up in a dark place, the so-called 'pot-sink', the centre of washing-up as an existent reality. It starts at 6 p.m., you're given so-called hygienic clothing (a grey coat that has strange powder-burn holes, perhaps from an unknown species of moth? and is used as a handkerchief by the cooks now and then). You keep at it until 10 p.m. The next day it starts again at 4.30 a.m. and continues until 6 p.m. The pot-sink is a place of true feeling. Pots look like officials who've burnt their behinds, they have that leather-trousered look that Meno once hinted at, they have ears as well, floppy as a marzipan flag, steam comes pouring out and they flutter when you're scrubbing them. The pot-sink knows all about the mixed-fruit vat that comes back from the 'Inter-hotel' (the canteen) empty and that we cookroaches had previously filled.

Take:

150 jars of preserved mixed fruit

a tin trough of 1 m³ capacity

the 'crocodile': a gigantic multifunction whisk, held by two cook-roaches, with a handle on the drum to which two whisks are attached and which has to be turned by a further two cookroaches. The croco-dile gives the preserved mixed fruit in the preserved-mixed-fruit trough that mushy consistency that is so sought after in mixed fruit and for which the cookroaches who lug the trough into the Interhotel are rewarded with sincere compliments, to which they generally respond with a cautious raising of the middle finger. The pot-sink knows the merits of the steam-jet hose, also known as the 'cobra', that yellow-and-black something that now and then feels an uncontrollable desire for freedom and, with a whistling release of steam, goes its own way. That means that we, the two pot-sink cookroaches, have to 'become fakirs' and 'teach the cobra to play the flute', that is: slip through under the wildly wriggling, boiling hot snake dance and turn down the steam valve at the entrance to the pot-sink until the manometer beside it once more indicates tamed levels. The pot-sink alone allows the observer the sight of *Cacerlaca superdimensionalis*, known for short as 'Super Roach', searching through pots and pans, tubs and vats for the remains of the *Komplekte* – and that without epaulettes and hygienic clothing! Anyone who sees this member of the army has to shout 'Mooncalf'. Mooncalf is the kitchen ghoul, a regular NCO, who had long since served his 10 years but couldn't manage outside, repented and returned to the environment he was used to. He regularly throws pieces of snot in the stew pan, is stooped and carries the hygiene knapsack, on the side of which is a lever that sprays 'some stuff'. Normally we have to ventilate the room for an hour after that and aren't allowed in the pot-sink. But Mooncalf only does the spraying for form's sake, the cockroaches lie on their backs and laugh. Christian.

TC Q/Schwanenberg, 2.12.1984
Dear Meno, Today is the first Sunday in Advent and the candles will be burning at home. Thank you for your offer, but please don't send me any books. In the little free time we get I write my letters or catch up on my sleep. I brought a box of books with me but had to send it back. It's not advisable to be seen with a book in your hand too often. Then you're looked on as a 'professor' and 'professors think they're superior' and they're fair game for special treatment. Fish (that's what we call our platoon commander, a Comrade First Lieutenant) likes to give 'professors' extra individual drill on the obstacle course in the evening after *News Camera*. And he wears glasses himself, which puzzles me (are glasses a sign of stupidity?). There are even some among my fellow cadets who have something against books. Special treatment comes from above and from below; the latter is seen as 'internal training' and connived at by our superiors. Cadet Burre was the object of some 'internal training' only a few hours ago. He's not in Company

4, where I am (tank commanders), but in 3, tank drivers, whose rooms are one floor lower down. My room-mate Irrgang and I heard some noise and rushed down. One of the prospective tank drivers was standing facing the assembled squad reading out a love poem Burre had written. It was kitschy and I felt like laughing along with the others. But I didn't feel like laughing when Burre grabbed the reader by the throat. With a couple of blows the reader knocked little, fat Burre to the ground (an odd sound, quite different from in films where the sounds are added on), then Burre was grabbed by four of them and debagged while the one who'd been reading fetched a pair of work mittens and a so-called 'bercu' ('bear's cunt', it's what the chapka we wear in the winter's called) and, to the jeers of those around, shouted, Bread-roll (clearly Burre's nickname) – now we're going to play at Sigmund Freud. Father and you are always telling me I should observe carefully, should try to describe what I see as precisely as possible. But I couldn't see Burre's face, just heard his breathing. Burre was thrashing about, trying to jerk his lower body up and down, but the four held him tight. The one who'd been reading grasped Burre's penis with the work-glove, held up the piece of paper with the poem and recited, 'O Melanie, could I but kiss you by moonlight . . .', all the other cadets in the corridor were urging him on. (Toss him off! Let's see if Bread-roll can get it up. Come on, where is it? God, Fatso, you stink like a pole-cat!) The reader pressed the bercu against Burre's penis and started to 'milk the chicken'.

I went up to the reader and said, Stop it. He stared at me as if he couldn't understand what I was saying. Irrgang supported me, That's what I want to tell you as well, my friend. Leave him in peace. The others just laughed, the reader as well, then he went on with his 'milking'. He's a great hulk, I'm more of a shrimp. Then Burre suddenly said, Ooh, I feel great, let the idiots carry on. At that they laughed even louder. – Please don't tell my parents about this letter. We probably won't get leave over Christmas since a 'Guard Complex I' week of SST ('Social Science Training') has been arranged. How's the Stahls' little boy? How are things at Dresdner Edition? Are you still working on the Schevola book? *Salve*, Christian.

armed forces rate/Schwanenberg, 4.12.84
dear pa, birthday greetings+++unfortunately couldn't get present+++moving out to camp+++letter follows+++love christian

TC Q/Schwanenberg, 16.12.84
Dear Parents, Today you will have lit three candles and I'm writing you the promised letter. Many thanks for yours that was delivered to me out in the field camp. Dear Ma – I wasn't thinking, please excuse me. I should have realized what would be going through your mind when you saw the telegram boy at the door. But I wanted to wish Pa a happy birthday and didn't have time for a letter.

It could well be that they read our letters but I don't care. I know it's forbidden to write so openly about things here. If you complain and are asked where you got the information I would probably get into trouble. As if thousands didn't go through the same thing and talk about it at home some time or other.

Field camp. It started on the 4th at 3.30 a.m. with 'Action stations'. Whistles, shouts, people rushing all over the place. Be ready to move off within a set time, grey blanket lengthwise over the bed. Proceed to a designated assembly point, where we wait. Suddenly Fish orders, Division – about turn! We do a 180-degree turn. Fish comes and stands alongside us, points to the horizon: Just look at that sunrise – something like that's rare. You may never see such a magnificent one again! When the duty officer appears, the company is divided up into groups. Irrgang, Breck and I are part of the ammunition group. Off we go to the technical depot, 60 tanks, approaching from Godknowswhere, are to be shelled up. Lugging cases of ammunition. When in action, one tank has a complement of 43 shells, each weighing 50 kg. $43 \times 50 = 2{,}150$ kg. There are ten of us, so $2{,}150 \times 60 \div 10 = 12{,}900$ kg of shells for each of us to lug to the tanks. The shells have to be thrown to the tanks 'in chain' where a driver fits them into the racks. After that exercise I caught myself doing 'straight-ahead-staring', what they call 'breathing'. You stand there and breathe. Nothing else.

The tanks that are to go to the field camp with us are loaded onto wagons at the goods depot. We travel in cattle trucks, where the Mongol allows us to lie down on the chopped straw, in the direction of Cottbus, spend hours shunted into a siding, then continue on towards Frankfurt/Oder. The field camp is in the vicinity of the Polish border, the Oder isn't far away – as we marched into the camp we could hear the ice floes drifting down the river. The camp's in the woods, 20 railway carriages from the war years arranged in a square, behind them a stone building for the driving instructors and the officers; the wagons are for us. In them are one table, one stove (all with the stovepipe missing); we sleep on planks of wood across both ends. There are 16 of us, 4 on top, 4 below, the same at the other end, a bare 1 metre space for each one. Where I was to sleep there was a dead stag beetle (female), unfortunately I had nothing to keep it in and didn't know what to do with it and couldn't put it in the letter (it would get damaged when they stamp it). Irrgang said, Give it to me, at least it's a bit of protein and who knows, we might be dining on just *Komplekte* here. Frozen dust everywhere, it's hanging down from the ceiling like a forest of dirty crocheting needles. At least there's electricity, 1 bulb casts 1 circle of light. First of all we put our kit away, then dig the company latrine. Every year's intake has to do it again. For washing there's an outside tap, frozen, of course, but the driving instructors have thought of that and unfreeze it with a flame-thrower. The water is pumped out of the forest floor (and is naturally not drinking water). So washing is a true pleasure: every morning we line up in gym shorts, otherwise naked apart from our boots, in a refreshingly cool winter wind, and move off at the double: march! through the powder snow to wash in the troughs, in which the water is naturally frozen, chop away the ice with the tank axe and enjoy the plunge. What is the difference between a skunk and an army cadet after a few days at the field camp? The cadet doesn't have any eau de Cologne. Every morning we're woken at 5, then 10 minutes for washing, 10 minutes to put the room in order, breakfast: 'O-tins' (O for operations). Then march off for training, it lasts from 6 a.m. to 8 p.m. Shooting practice with the barrel inset (it's stuck into the tank gun so it can take smaller-calibre shells), with the tank MG. Practise with live hand grenades. We march off with the 'lemons', as they're called, in the pockets on our trouser legs to a burnt-out T34 here in the forest, climb in, pull the ring on the grenade, briefly emerge from cover and throw the grenade at a class enemy made out of sawn-off pines and already in a bad way from the lemon effect. Irrgang asks, What do I do, Comrade Corp'ral, 'f the grenade drops on my paw? – 've y' already pulled the ring? Corporal Glücklich asks. – Think so, Comrade Corp'ral. – So what're y'worryin' about. Y'won't have to wash it again.

Tactical training: for that we go to the Tiktak range, for tactics are as refreshing as Tictacs. And everything so near, only a few kilometres through the winter woods. Crawl, pulling ourselves along by the elbows, to the horizon, aim, crawl back, running, creeping, sliding, crawling, hauling, sprawling, oh, aren't we having fun in mock fights with a wooden gun. Driving practice with tanks. What I was really born for. I'm the son of a time-served metalworker, I'm the son of a trauma surgeon, I'm not a 'professor', I tell myself again and again. I'm furniture, a dishcloth, has a dishcloth ever driven a tank badly? Right then: there's the gas, there's the brakes, there's the gears, to start the engine turn up the oil pump, prime with oil then press the starter button, engine up to 500 rev/min, to steer it you have the two steering levers, one on the right, one on the left, to see there's the observation slit. We practise on an army training course, the tank bounces up and down like a rocking chair, the driving instructor, who's up in the commander's hatch, roars over the intercom that's plugged into your tank hood, Listen to the engine, you dud, put your foot down, can't you hear it's labouring? Double-declutch. Brackish water comes in through the hatches, the MG slit is closed, on the end of the barrel the 'elephant's condom', a rubber cap for protection. Russky on the right! the instructor suddenly bawls. Have I misheard? Russky? Aren't we fighting side by side with our comrades-in-arms of the Warsaw Pact? The tank spins to the right. Rattatatat! the instructor shrieks, he's had it! After driving there's cleaning and oiling the tank. Each metal part is rubbed clean and, as is well known, a tank consists entirely of wood. And of course it's the furniture that does the scrubbing while the instructors gather round a stove drinking coffee.

Guard duty. At night the winter constellations glitter, more beautiful than on Meno's ten-minute clock. The moon looks like a 1-mark piece, you stand guard for 2 hours, the cold creeping up from your toes to your bottom, your back (I've got Gudrun's belt round my kidneys, it keeps them warm), makes your muscles start quivering, there's a razor on your nose, and the guards' urine forms stalagmites sticking out of the snow like bizarre yellow flowers. On the third day there was an SI ('Special Incident'): Cadet Breck was on guard and became nervous when there was a rustling in the plantation opposite the guard post. When, after he had called out several times, the rustling grew louder (enemy agent! parachutist! NATO advance guard!), Breck raised his Kalashnikov and fired half the magazine of tracer bullets into the plantation. (Normally he should have let off a warning shot into the air first, but before going out on guard duty Cadet Breck had been at the soldier's comforter, Dur.) Now there was a dead wild boar. Our CC (company commander), Captain Fiedler, swore at this Special Incident – after all, you can't simply gun down a wild boar in a state forest. But Fish said, Well, since the beast's dead, we can eat it. – Fiedler: Have you done that before, Comrade First Lieutenant? – Fish: Nah, but there's bound to be a cook among the cadets. (There wasn't.) – Sergeant Rehnsen: We sh'd stick it on a spit. – Inca: How? I've had a look. Its arsehole's closed and where're you goin' to find a spit? – Rehnsen: We'll dump it in a cauldron and boil it. – An' where're you goin' to find a boiler? And the pig's still got its bristles on. Breck, you swine, you'll scrub the swine, it that clear? And you two, Hoffmann, Irrgang, take those stupid grins off your faces and make some sensible suggestions.

So how can a wild boar be frizzled out in the woods by people who're hungry but completely clueless? Cadets dig a pit, chop wood and stack it in the bottom of the pit. Then tanks drive up and park, one on the right, one on the left of the pit. Breck, Irrgang and I put on heavy-duty mittens and try to scrape off the bristles. It doesn't work, they're too stubborn. So Fish uses the flame-thrower on them. The pig now looks like a roasted doormat. A steel-wire noose with a hook is put round its neck. A steel hawser, such as every tank has, is fixed between the two 'trestles' that have been parked beside the pit, the hook is hung on the hawser. Then the fire is lit and the pig roasted, after half an hour the hawser's glowing. The pig's full of smoked parasites. Fish sticks his bayonet into the flesh and prises a few out. I don't know who ate any of the roast pork, I'm on guard duty again, listening to the ice breaking up on the distant Oder.

No Christmas leave. We've been detailed to 'Guard Complex I', that means guard duty and Social Science Instruction (irradiation with red light) alternately, until New Year's Eve. Here in our quarters cocoa dust is gradually accumulating on the filthy things from the field camp that are scattered around (despite the cold and the wind coming from the wrong direction we've got the window wide open). I'm sitting in the middle of the mess finishing this letter with love from Christian.

40
The telephone

The telephone rang and for a long time the Old Man of the Mountain said nothing; it was Londoner on the line, as Meno deduced from various signs: Altberg automatically straightened his back after he'd picked up the receiver and mumbled his name, something he didn't do when he was speaking to Schiffner or a colleague. On the contrary, on such occasions he seemed to slump down even more, his face crumpling as if he were anticipating both a reproach, or an attack disguised as a reproach, and the annoyance that would cause him; he was, so to speak, building up a reserve of annoyance so that the actual unpleasantness that came out of the receiver would be as nothing compared with what he had anticipated. To put it in its limits: for anyone who mentally prepares himself for three hours of torture, when about to go to the dentist for example, the half an hour during which the whine of the drill often becomes intense but also often dies away, is a mere fleabite. Taking a sledgehammer to crack a nut, Meno thought, though it wasn't a nut you wanted to be faced with too often, it was a pretty tough nut. As far as calls from Schiffner or out-of-favour colleagues were concerned, the old man would murmur his 'Yes' or 'Yes, yes' or 'Yes, yes, of course' or 'Yes, yes, yes, that's quite clear' into the receiver like spells to ward off evil, would turn his profile to Meno, but wave him down if Meno was about to go out of the room; he even seemed to get angry at the gesture, would push down with his flat, outstretched hand like a press and shake his head vigorously, which Meno interpreted as a kind of order to remain seated, with which he complied, though reluctantly and uncertainly. The old man would not even let Meno, if he wasn't allowed to leave the room, walk round, at least putting some distance between them and thus being able to occupy himself with the books on the shelves along the wall, rustle the pages audibly and stare at the paper intently, as if enthralled, so that he would at least not make a bad impression on the housekeeper, should she come in. Meno had once tried this manoeuvre, at which the old man had immediately put his hand over the receiver and glared at Meno suspiciously; close to the bookcases was the desk with the thick pile of the manuscript, a battery of paste pots and a bowl for snippets of paper, and the old man's 'That's nothing for you, editor, sir', had sent Meno scurrying back to his chair. When Schiffner called, Altberg would wind the telephone lead round his finger, sometimes forgetting what he was doing and pulling the plug out of the socket. If it was a fellow writer who had called, Altberg would walk up and down restlessly, ducking down a little lower at every turn, as if punches from the receiver could hit him in the solar plexus until he was creeping, as far as the telephone lead would allow, round the room as though stalking an animal. Why Meno had to remain present during these telephone calls became clear when, with a conspiratorial smile, the old man once took a large brown medicine bottle off the shelf with utensils from the chemist's. 'The stopper, my dear Rohde, fits to a hundredth of a millimetre, so precisely has it been ground, but you can move it – look', and he began to twist the stopper in the neck of the bottle, which made a terrible, jarring screech, that Altberg skilfully and with a knowing grin screwed up to a shrill squeal. 'If I should give you a sign, please begin to make the noise. Stand right next to me and start turning it to the left'; and when the call had come that Altberg wanted to be treated in this way, Meno had set up a nerve-jangling 'shreeek, shreeek' while the old man, with a expression of intense concentration, as if it were an actor's swansong, had imitated the sound of a faulty sewing machine, slurping his tongue against his cheek, making soft snoring noises and hollow metallic grunts, repeatedly interrupted by a despairing, 'Can you hear me? Hello? Are you still there?' aimed at the ceiling, before finally, with a satisfied though exhausted look, tapping the rest.

If it was Londoner on the telephone his 'not saying anything' would, after a long minute, be cut off by a 'Good' or 'Interesting' or 'Did you get that from him? From him personally? Oh, on the upstairs telephone' that startled Meno out of his reflection – at the second or third of these calls, after he'd been able to gather observations and allowed them to precipitate into a conclusion – about how he knew that it was Jochen Londoner talking to the Old Man of the Mountain: during other calls the old man might well straighten up, hold the receiver to his ear for a long time without saying anything, during other conversations he might well nervously pass his hand over his dressing gown or, if he was wearing a jacket, pat the pockets to check the flaps, put the receiver to his left ear when he first picked it up but transfer it to his right ear one second later; perhaps this habit they shared – Londoner also changed ears after picking up the phone when he was taking an official or even just semi-official call – was just one of a number both men had when answering the telephone and that led Meno to the superstitious conclusion: if each used the telephone in the same way as the other then the one, if he showed the same characteristics, must also be talking to the other – which wasn't logical but, to Meno's astonishment, was true in the case of the Old Man of the Mountain. Allowed them to precipitate into a conclusion: Meno used this technical term from chemistry for himself, for he liked the parallel between observing and concluding and the arrangement of an experiment in which a substance was carefully and gradually concentrated so that it could form a compound with a second substance – with another observation – which, once a certain degree of concentration had been exceeded, would appear – be precipitated – in the solution. The Old Man of the Mountain had put a small telephone table, clearly visible, a little away from one wall of the room; at Londoner's the telephone, that is the one the family called the 'downstairs phone', was similarly prominently placed in the hall. There were two sides to this prominent position and Meno wasn't quite sure which Londoner had in mind when he decided to put the little table so well to the fore in the hall that was crammed with vast numbers of books, so that many a visitor, especially if they'd spent some time sampling Londoner's excellent collection of sherry and port, had stumbled against the table – which did no damage to the telephone, it was a heavy official one with a protruding dial that in such cases would land on a cushion the lady of the house had had the foresight to place there. That was the custom at the Londoners', the table was never moved out of the way.

It wasn't out of vanity, Meno wrote, *at least not that alone, since most of the guests who made the acquaintance of the telephone in that way had a similar one and shook their heads at Londoner's strange custom, and even if I in no way underestimate my ex-father-in-law's talent for acting – he enjoyed every kind of theatre, loved vaudeville and Shakespeare, whom, an English pipe clenched between his teeth, he would study in the original, with the tendency to systematization, to create order, and the courage to attack impregnable-seeming bastions that had won him a certain celebrity in the country and gave his often printed words, which lingered in the minds of the powerful, specific gravity; even though he liked to declaim dramatists' iambic pentameters, with his eyes pouring out the searing flash of passion or the velvet of ingratiation, and would invite Eschschloraque, the classicist and socialist marshal of moderation, not only to one of the inevitable East Rome binges but also to private sessions to refresh the inner man with a joint play-reading – I do not rate his acting talent so highly that he could make his guest believe he felt embarrassed, even slightly ashamed, in view of the fact that he, Jochen Londoner, was privileged to have his own tele-phone, if he hadn't felt the least bit embarrassed; he did feel embarrassed and that was precisely why he put the telephone in such a visible place in the hall – just as a nouveau riche shows off his money – though hardly out of embarrassment – put it in the hall as if to say, That's the way things are, yes, I've got a telephone, sorry; but since you would be more likely to discover it if I'd discreetly put it in a corner – for you'd say, Aha, having a telephone is such a matter of course for him that he can afford to ignore it – I might as well stick it right under your noses; so please excuse me for having been allocated the damn thing. For his embarrassment to be feigned he plucked at his top lip too often when they had visitors and Irmtraud was busy putting coats and scarves on the coat stand; put his hand to his fore-head too often – reflecting on something, remembering something? – thus leaving the telephone in the shadow of his tweed jacket that Lukas, the tailor, had measured up and made, with several others exactly the same, out of Harris tweed. Perhaps the prominent position away from the wall taken up by the downstairs telephone was meant as a kind of decoy that hungry observers, greedy for sensations, were to swallow, concluding that Londoner was consumed with vanity and simple-minded pride: So he's finally made it to a telephone, and to put it properly on display he's stuck it out in the hall where you trip over it. What a way to behave! – a decoy to distract attention from the much more important second telephone in his study that wasn't on the same line as the one downstairs – otherwise if he'd wanted to make a call from upstairs he'd have had to take the cable of the downstairs one out of the connection box – but had its own line and tele-phone number that was known to a few alone. He was, it seemed to me, hiding his light under a bushel and he became nervous and indignant if the upstairs telephone rang while he was talking to someone; he had given us – Hanna, Philipp and me – strict instructions not to call him on private matters on the upstairs telephone. That was what the telephone in the hall was for. It belonged to Irmtraud's territory, she was the one who answered, whose voice one heard; if it was for Jochen Londoner, he would get her to call him or, depending on his mood or the name she would tell him with her hand over the receiver, say he was out. I hesitate, having read the pre-ceding lines again, uncertain whether I'm not overestimating Londoner, whether the psychological pirouettes that are trying to encircle him are in truth going round and round a phantom, for why can a scholar such as he, member of various academies, valued contributor to daily newspapers and widely read weekly magazines, why can he, who is familiar with the*

*subtleties of the sonnets of the Swan of Avon, he who has, behind his warm
brown eyes with the remarkably pronounced bags under them, so much
Marxism and so much English style – why can he not simply be vain?
Don't go looking for fish in trees, Father used to say. For the way Londoner
bundled up the newspaper when the characteristic ringing tone of the green
RFT phone sounded, the way he struggled to get out of his rocking chair,
in which, wrapped up in a blanket, he'd not so much read the articles as
mutter his way through them, making comments and extensive digressions,
reading out to the others in the room, whether they wanted him to or not,
examples of journalists' bad German for minutes on end, the way he threw
down the newspaper – rocking forward in the chair, having to throw out his
arms like a swimmer diving into the water – and dashed upstairs as if
electrified, as if the world, even Dresden perhaps, depended on the call: all
that spoke of the craving addicts have for the object of their addiction, an
astounded craving, perhaps even alarmed at itself; the way the chair went
on rocking backwards and forwards for a while, until it was too much for
Irmtraud or Hanna: the stagey way the hand appeared out of the semi-dark
of the room and halted the rocking chair, so that the silence deepened,
became slightly oppressive, Irmtraud's worried look that she tried to disguise, Philipp's challenging clearing of the throat and gleeful 'By the way,
Meno, have you heard this one?' joke-telling at the precise moment when
the silence was deepest and, as I felt, at its most vulnerable, as if it were a
white surface on which a verdict would appear – Irmtraud didn't even dare
continue reading the Party's Study Year brochures or one of Philipp's publications; she didn't touch anything during the phone call, as if the sherry
were a reward to which she was possibly not entitled, something of which
she had been reminded by the ringing of the telephone and, set off by that,
by some complicated psychological impressions that had sunk into oblivion
in her day-to-day life like bad dreams that you shake off on waking, calm
and happy at the prospect of the day that is beginning until you discover
an object from your dream on the tallboy in the hall –; the way Jochen
Londoner came back, his expression inscrutable, his look indifferent, the*

way he went into the kitchen to pour himself a glass of water that he drank in several gulps garnished with sipping, tasting, judicious observation of the drops slowly forming on the spout of the tap, the way he came back into the living room without bothering about the silence around Irmtraud, who'd put her sherry glass down, around Hanna or Philipp, who were joining in the game – but was it a game? – which was something that always amazed me; Hanna was staring at the table, Philipp was jutting out his chin, and the jokes – splendid Jewish jokes that always, despite Irmtraud's reproach-ful look in the time of silence, made me laugh, which Irmtraud probably felt as a slap in the face; but these jokes, especially the ones with rabbis, had delightful punchlines – Philipp firmly swept these jokes aside, as if annoyed at himself, when his father came back into the room; and the way Londoner came back to the table, didn't sit down in the rocking chair again but next to his son on the couch, deliberately, letting his legs fold, his broad hands on his knees: one could definitely, I felt in cooler moments, call that vain, and all the following clearing of the throat, the play of his facial muscles, indicated that the conversation he had just had was of immense importance –

In contrast to Londoner and his wife, the Old Man of the Mountain gave his name when answering the phone. When she picked up the downstairs telephone, Irmtraud Londoner would say, 'Speaking', noth-ing more, and Meno wondered how she could know that the person at the other end of the line knew it was she who was saying, 'Speaking'; when he answered the upstairs phone Jochen Londoner said nothing, as Meno knew from Hanna, simply picked up the receiver and remained silent. Meno had never been able to find out what the reason for this behaviour was; both Jochen and Irmtraud as well as Hanna and Philipp had avoided answering his question. No names on the phone, no slips of paper with addresses on. Certainly no slips of paper with addresses on left lying round the house. Letters are headed with the address of the Institute, the Administration, the Academy, and are written on the most widely available model of typewriter, there are as good as no handwritten notes and they are treated as a sign of great confidence, Meno thought; the sole handwritten note I received from him was when he invited me for Christmas: You're one of the family. Hanna is in Prague, Philipp will be here and we've invited Altberg, who appears to be alone. He's promised us a surprise.

'You really want to invite me over for Christmas? I didn't know, Herr Londoner . . . Oh, then I'm in your debt,' Altberg said and Meno was irritated by the formal way Altberg had suddenly started to address Londoner until he realized he was talking to Philipp, 'but then has your father . . . aha. However, please understand me . . . can I speak to him? Hm. I find that a little embarrassing, I have to say it comes as a surprise, of course I'm very grateful, you can . . . What? You're right there again . . . Would you pass on a message to your parents from me?' Then Altberg expressed – Meno hadn't intended to observe him but he felt a strange satisfaction to see Altberg in this situation, so he remained seated – Altberg was trying to express something, was struggling to find the right word and, since it didn't occur to him immediately, cast a number of rhetorical nets to try and fish it out: Would Philipp be so kind as to inform his parents of his, Georg Altberg's, decision . . . no, 'decision' sounded inappropriate, too familiar, Philipp would know what he meant and should remember how condescending . . . At the moment he was working on a story that had a beggar in it, not anything that took place here and now, of course – where were there beggars in our country? – but there happened to be one in his story and what a nice discordant note it would strike if he were to make this beggar decide to accept the alms the other had been so kind as to offer; was his father working or had he been urgently called to the Academy? – However that might be, he wanted to inform him of his intention, 'Hm' – Altberg smiled, scratching his head, which he held on one side as he walked up and down – 'hm . . . my intention, good God, please forget that slip of the tongue, my dear Philipp', when you thought about it the telephone was a really strange business, you were speaking into the mouthpiece to another person who was nothing but a voice and whose physical appearance you had to imagine to go with the voice, which didn't always work satisfactorily, naturally Philipp knew that it wasn't his, Altberg's, intention, that was, it was that of course, only he didn't intend with the self-confident overtones that went with the word, 'intend . . . my God, Altberg, you're in highfalutin mode again today', stretched out his hand and fanned the air round the receiver as if in that way he could reduce the unpleasant word, which had unfortunately been spoken and heard by the other, to fragments that would make their original shape unrecognizable; 'that means quite simply, I want to, that is, I'd like to . . . Would you tell him I'm coming?'

Meno was too much taken up with his reflections to see Altberg's look and silence, after he'd put the telephone down, as aimed at him; it was one of those searching looks behind which thoughts are going round and round seeking something, and suddenly present it as a possible answer to the unspoken question; it was the silence that knows it is the final barrier before something possibly ill-considered is said – ill-considered because spoken in too hasty confidence – the silence before the uncertainty about to what extent the other person is what he appears to be, about whether one will come to regret it bitterly if one says the word that at the moment is still well-guarded in the depths of the complicated machinery that is needed to put a stamp on it, to turn it into the currency of language and speech; one doesn't know whether one's initial impulse, to let the word slip out right away, is really worth following or whether the word, once and therefore irrevocably spoken, will turn into a coin that will bribe the sentry guarding the other's silence or blood money for the unknown Judas inside oneself that for one brief, dangerous moment abandoned its excellent camouflage. In his mind's eye Meno could see Londoner, sitting at his desk copying down extracts from something, beside him a slip of paper with names on it that he weighed against each other and against considerations you go through as you contemplate your fingernails; could see Londoner, on coming to Altberg's name, perhaps reach out for his telephone but leave his hand hovering and then call Philipp and tell him to convey the invitation to Altberg; and after Philipp had left the room Londoner had, perhaps, sat there, legs crossed, tapping his chin with the rubber on the end of his pencil in cool calculation for a few seconds before tearing the slip of paper into little pieces on which not even the letters of the names were legible any more.

41
Leaving the country

Touching the glass. Sticking a knife into a kilo packet of sugar full to bursting. Breaking the bird's egg they'd taken from the nest when they were children. First clear white, the yolk on glassy threads, then yellow, soft as a Dali clock, spilling over the jagged edge of the shell and into his mouth. Dreams like that.

When he couldn't sleep at night and Anne was at work, Richard wandered round the living room. He woke up quite often now, would lie awake for a while then put on his dressing gown. When she was on night shift and he wasn't on call, Anne took the car. If it was parked outside, he would get dressed and drive somewhere or other. He didn't stay out for long. When he got back she didn't question him, just asked him to be quiet and not to wake Robert. Sometimes he would wake up bathed in sweat and with cramp in his hands, stare round the room, in which a street lamp cast a pale silver veil, feeling afraid. The contours of the bedroom wardrobes, the washing basket, the candelabra with the light discs were drawn in thin lines; the wardrobes were blocks, darker than the rest of the room, at the foot of the two beds, which had been pushed together and seemed to him like a rectangular island, a raft on which he and Anne had found refuge. It didn't move. The town, the country were asleep, sometimes the distant sound of a manoeuvre could be heard from the Russians' firing ranges. Anne slept well, he no longer did, a consequence of the nights on duty, riddled with telephone calls, knocking at the door, the disturbance. Sometimes he would feel for Anne and she reacted, murmured in her sleep, which moved but didn't calm him. When she wasn't there he had the feeling figures were coming closer, that the blocks were not wardrobes but secret doors through which they came in. He opened and closed his hands, in these hours of wakefulness the right one with the healed tendons felt as if it were under a sewing machine, the needle of which was slowly, as if the current transmitter were being cautiously tested out, piercing the jagged suture.

Sometimes he took out one of Christian's letters, which Anne kept in a file with the things that had to be immediately to hand should there be a fire (an air raid, as had happened to Emmy and Arthur; an arrest, as with Kurt and Luise). He would read one or two and then put them back. He would have liked to tear them up or given the boy to understand, in a way that didn't hurt him or cast him down, that he shouldn't write any more for it pained him to see the way they made Anne suffer. He had no idea whether it was all true or whether the lad was exaggerating for some particular reason – a desire to attract attention, a need for tokens of love, a certain emotional extortionism, a masochistic tendency (look how I'm suffering)? Because of his injury, Richard had not been conscripted, Ulrich and Meno had spent their time stuck in orderly rooms, Niklas had been called up to the reserves and had spent eight weeks sweeping the runways of a military airport.

He was probably being unjust to the lad.

When he heard the sound of an engine he would start and wait. The front door was locked, Griesel made sure of that, but that wouldn't bother them, they could get through any door. They came at night, when everyone was asleep, like their fellows in their bomber jackets and sharply creased trousers everywhere on the islands of the socialist archipelago.

He'd heard no more from them since Josta had separated from him. No summons to a meeting, no confidential communication, no telephone call in which the caller did not give his name and you only heard his breathing; no one who folded a newspaper and followed him when he left the clinic, until a car drove up to the pavement and a door was opened with the engine still running. They seemed to be waiting. But for what? Were they taking it out on Christian? The post of medical orderly he'd been definitely assured by the husband of a former patient who worked in the army district command had been postponed in a rather suspicious way . . . Were they planning measures against him? Against Robert? Anne? Would they get their claws into Lucie? The thoughts went round and round inside his head. Sometimes, when he didn't put the light on in the room and watched the street, he had the impression he could see the glow of a cigarette outside the house opposite . . . That meant that they were watching him as well, knew that he couldn't sleep. Was afraid. And they wanted him to notice them, they were keeping the area under surveillance, making that clear to him and not even being particularly discreet about it. If they were showing themselves, they could afford to . . . Then he went to the hall and quietly opened the wardrobe by Robert's door, where, without telling Anne, he'd hidden one of his doctor's bags. He'd packed everything in it he thought was necessary and if they came, he'd be ready. Sometimes he felt he couldn't bear it any longer and would most of all have liked to go out into the street to challenge the spy, to tell him to go to hell. But he didn't know whether he was imagining the spy, the glow of a cigarette could be an illusion, his view was restricted by hedges and trees. And even if it wasn't just his imagination, there might be someone having a cigarette there who wasn't interested in him.

Perhaps they'd even given up on him, in silence, without informing him . . . Josta had left him, that couldn't be used as blackmail any longer. And he assumed that by now Anne knew, or at least suspected, everything: an anonymous letter, delivered when she was at home and he at the clinic, would, like damp powder, not spark off any response. But who knows – he'd better have a chat with Glodde, the cross-eyed postman.

He waited, stared at the grandfather clock with the heart-shaped tips to the hands, the bulbous glass over the face. The top hook on the pendulum door, which had to be opened to wind up the three lead weights, mustn't be closed: there was pressure on the glass, his father had said, it could crack if the hook were closed and variations of temperature in the room changed the elasticity of the glass. Richard went over to the clock. The glass drew him to it but it would crack the moment he stretched out a finger, of that he was convinced.

Christmas came and went and the mood in the household was depressed. Anne cried because Christian wasn't there, was stuck on a watchtower in icy wind or had to drive out to the field camp with horrible people. 'If something should happen to the boy . . . He has no idea about these technical things. Those awful tanks, I can't imagine Christian inside one and then he's training to shoot at other people . . .'

After an unfortunate fall (on Sundays he wound up all the clocks in his collection, he had to use a ladder to reach the cuckoo clocks) Arthur Hoffmann was in hospital with a broken ankle. He didn't want Richard to operate on him. 'Your hand will tremble when it's your father and, who knows, perhaps now that I'm defenceless you'd like to get your revenge for this or that,' he said with morbid humour. 'Moreover, I don't want special treatment. I've never needed it. I refuse!' Since it was way off on the outskirts of the region, the supply situation in the district hospital in Glashütte was distinctly worse than in the clinics in the regional capital. Richard talked to the chief surgeon and, by bribing the Academy pharmacist with a few Hermes books given by Meno, at least managed to arrange for a few important drugs to be passed on from the Academy stores to those of the ward where Arthur Hoffmann was.

Emmy spent the whole of Christmas Eve wallowing in gloom and neither the music of the spheres from the Holy Cross choir nor the present of a shopping trolley with a tartan cloth cover could stop her insisting that soon everything was going to blow up and that the woman next door was a witch, a jealous cow who was plotting against her and was out to kill her. 'Yes, really. It's as true as I'm sitting here. She's after my living blood, she is, the storm-hag!' Moreover her neighbour 'kept on' finding money, something that she, Emmy, had never managed to do. But her neighbour had her nose to the pavement all day, her ear to the wall and her fingers in other folks' letter boxes and on other folks' fruit, even if it didn't hang over the fence into her garden. When Robert, at Richard's insistent request, played a sequence of lively pieces for clarinet, she shook her head morosely, adding that the lad would never get anywhere, he was a Hoffmann and Hoffmanns always got stuck. And besides, Arthur had abandoned her.

Snow fell in large, soft flakes, hanging in the trees like semolina pudding, covering the ash-smeared streets. The Stenzel Sisters brought their steel-edged skis down from the loft; they had spring bindings and had glided over the snow in Innsbruck, in the Norway of the Telemark and Cristiania turns, on the cross-country runs of the Oberwiesenthal and Oberhof, where Kitty, with the carefreeness of a recent pensioner and the bravery of a bareback rider in the Sarrasani Circus, had secretly gone down the ski jump.

In the evening Meno would sit at his typewriter or microscope in the House with a Thousand Eyes wearing his coat and gloves with the fingertips cut off, puzzling over reports or Judith Schevola's prose, studying zoological preparations Arbogast had lent him. Something seemed to be happening in the country, the rigidity, the inertia were

now only a thin layer beneath which something was moving, an embryo
with as yet unclear outlines developing in the womb made of habit,
resignation, perplexity, sometimes the people seemed to sense the movements of the foetus, the pregnancy of the streets, of the smoke-clouded
days. Spurred on by Ulrich, Meno had started to read books about
economics, a subject that had never particularly interested him and
whose number-juggling precision, mathematical modelling and apparently irrefutable self-assurance repelled him just as much as the
matter-of-fact way human traits, that is fallibility, favouritism and
illogicality, were pinned to the ice-cold drawing board of the laws of
nature. But he began to suspect something . . . People's fear that this
crystal-clear science, its axioms that society in his country had been
resisting for years, might be right . . . The per-head coal allocation
had been reduced. As a bachelor who only had books to bribe people
with (the car spares had to be kept for darker times) he had no pull
with Hauschild. And you couldn't go and buy the extra hundredweight
you needed from another coal merchant – the coal merchants worked
according to the district system and had lists of the registered inhabitants. Meno burnt wood that he and Stahl, the engineer, had cut down
illegally in the forest; they were committing a punishable offence, but
Stahl said he didn't care – if the state couldn't manage to supply its
children with sufficient fuel then he, Gerhart Stahl, had to help himself.
The Kaminski twins noticed these woodland excursions, waited, hands
in their trouser pockets, in the hall and asked if they could be of any
help. Stahl was still suspicious of them, but they could certainly use
two pairs of extra hands and ears. Busse, the forester, and his dog were
faced with a difficult task, for of course the large sleigh covered with
a tarpaulin on which the men from the House with a Thousand Eyes
transported their spoils was observed by thoughtful eyes, even in the
dark.

On New Year's Eve 1984 an inspection team from the Communal
Housing Department arrived. They established that Meno Rohde and

the Langes had too many square metres of apartment and that the Langes' use of Meno's bedroom for their son Martin was unauthorized. A new apartment, with the right to use the Langes' and Rohde's bathroom, was set up, consisting of the bedroom, the cabin and Alois Lange's study on the corridor side, that is of rooms in different parts of the house. In the basement, beside the laundry room, was the former scullery (where Libussa preserved her fruit); that too was allocated to the new apartment. The Stahls, Langes and Meno protested, but it was futile, the Housing Department was not open to reason and insisted on its right to allocate living space. At the beginning of January a middle-aged married couple moved in and caused even greater disruption to the lives of the other tenants than the Kaminski twins had done with their uninvited appearance in the conservatory.

In the middle of January, Regine received a letter from Coal Island. In plain terms she was informed that her application to leave the country had been refused.

'What are you going to do?' Anne asked. They had gathered at Niklas's to discuss the situation.

'I've renewed my application every two weeks and I intend to continue doing so.'

'Then you'll be committing an offence,' Richard said. 'I talked with Sperber, the lawyer, who strongly advises you not to make any more requests. Your request has been refused and they can arrest you, if you start again.'

'The bastards,' said Ulrich.

'But what happens next?' Regine covered her face with her hands. She was emaciated and had dark shadows round her eyes. Gudrun went out to make her a cup of tea; it wasn't warm in the living room, she was wearing knitted cardigans over several pullovers or waistcoats she had made herself out of scraps of fur from Harmony Salon; Ezzo was practising in the next room. Reglinde, in gloves, woollen scarf and bobble hat, was ill in bed, in her little, icy-cold room beside the Tietzes' second toilet, which froze over in winter.

'If they send you to prison, they'll take the children away, perhaps even beforehand,' Anne said. She was pale, her nose sharp; Christian had been writing fewer letters.

'It was good that Jürgen simply stayed over there. I know someone in the orchestra whose brother took their social security card with him; it meant his wife couldn't prove she'd known nothing beforehand; she was accused of complicity and her son ended up in a children's home.'

'Shh!' came from several sides. Index fingers pointed at the walls.

'Oh, don't exaggerate.' Niklas waved away their warnings.

'I have to sell the car. The pittance I can earn as an untrained secretary . . . Over the last year I've sold a few pieces of furniture, we managed, more or less. Hans is getting on for sixteen and grows out of everything so quickly and Philipp needs new things all the time . . . Pätzold will give me twenty thousand for the car.'

'For a Wartburg with less than a hundred thousand on the clock? And it's in good condition, Jürgen looked after it really well. Don't you want to put an ad in the paper and wait for a better offer. I've been to Pätzold too . . . the crook!' Niklas exclaimed indignantly.

'The Valuation Section sent me to him. And I have to give the state half the money. Anyway . . . Pätzold gave me an advance on the car, in January, I needed the money. Five thousand marks.'

'Why didn't you ask us?'

'Money and friendship don't go together,' Gudrun reminded Anne, putting a cup of tea down in front of Regine. 'You may sneer at me, but it's true all the same.'

Richard pointed to the *Sächsisches Tageblatt* that was lying open on the table at a picture of a confidently smiling Barsano beside the General Secretary of the Central Committee. 'Have you read the stuff they've been spewing out again. I heard Chernenko's supposed to be in a pretty bad way . . . Why's Barsano in Moscow, I ask myself. By the way, it's true that his daughter has an application to leave the country being considered. The way she ranted and raved! I can still see it as if it were yesterday. Did you notice anything?'

'No,' Regine said, 'she was quiet in the room. Perhaps it was a put-up show?'

'I can't see that.' Niklas said. 'Why should the daughter of the First Secretary dress up as a punk just to intimidate all you in the queue? There are easier ways of doing that. No, the bigwigs' own children are running away from them. They don't believe in it themselves any more.'

'I know someone who knows her,' Meno said. 'A colleague is a close friend of her boyfriend – her boyfriend, by the way, is the same one who got Pätzold's daughter pregnant, you were talking about that at the party in the Felsenburg . . . Now he's living with Alexandra Barsano. She was also friendly with Muriel, did you know that?'

The abbot's clock struck clear as a little bell.

'How are Hans and Iris?' Gudrun asked Richard.

'Can't say, we hardly see them. If we do happen to meet, it's just, Hi, Hans – Hi, Richard. They don't open when we knock either. And if we call them they're rather brusque, won't talk.'

'We still haven't had an answer to our letter.'

'We won't get one, brother-in-law. – Have you got a cold? You sound blocked up.'

'But you did pinch plenty of wood, you rogues.' Niklas gave an approving laugh. 'But just you make sure they don't catch you. Do you think no one notices? Kühnast asked me about it recently, while we were queuing for sparking plugs at Priebsch's.'

'We must think about how we can help Regine,' Anne said, changing the subject to help her brother.

'For me there's not much to think about. I'll keep turning up there . . . I've applied for family reunification, Jürgen and I have been separated for four and a half years . . .'

'And the children? Remember Sperber's warning,' Gudrun said.

'I know how to proceed.'

'How?' The question came from several mouths simultaneously.

'Don't get me wrong. But it could be that . . . I mean, Niklas, can you be sure? And Richard, you have at least admitted that they . . .'

'You think I'd tell on you?'

'Sorry, that wasn't how I meant it. My nerves are all to pot.'

Pedro Honich was a man for whom order was all-important. The day after he moved into the House with a Thousand Eyes he asked who it was who kept the house register: Lange, who had neglected to keep it for ages.

'But that can't go on, Herr Doktor Lange. Rules are rules,' Honich, who was the commander of a paramilitary Combat Group of the Working Class, told the ship's doctor, and offered to keep the register himself in future. 'There are no entries for Herr Rohde and yet he often has visitors.'

'Yes, you know Herr, er, Honich –'

'Comrade Honich. I am a member of the Socialist Unity Party.'

'I'm not. We're not spies and whether Herr Rohde has a visitor or not, and who it is and how long they stay, is his business alone, that's my opinion.'

'That's your opinion, is it?' Herr Honich went on about bourgeois arrogance and loopholes that had to be closed. A few days later he called a meeting of the house community.

'Do we have to go along with this?' Stahl asked. 'What does the fellow actually want? Does he take us for members of his combat group?'

'Let's listen to what he has to say,' Lange said.

Because of the lack of a room big enough, the meeting took place in the upstairs corridor. Frau Honich had put out some liver sausage sandwiches, beer and mineral water that only the Kaminski twins touched.

Herr Honich, in his combat group uniform, stood up and declared the meeting open with an attendance check. Sylvia Stahl was excused, she had an evening in the Schlemm Hotel with the work team sponsoring her class. Then he introduced his wife and himself. His wife was called Babett, came from Karl-Marx-Stadt and was the new head of the Pioneers at the Louis Fürnberg High School. Herr Honich, as he emphasized, came from a working-class family in the Micken district of Dresden. His wife's hobbies were the garden and the Timur group providing assistance for old and handicapped people; he himself was passionately fond of motorbikes, was a great fan of Dynamo Dresden and liked playing football himself. He intended to form a street club and hoped many, especially young people, would join; if others followed his example they could have street championships that the women could support by organizing solidarity tombolas, handicraft activities for the little ones and a field kitchen for the players. It was his ambition to win the 'Golden House Number' for the House with a Thousand Eyes in socialist competition.

'For God's sake,' Stahl whispered to Meno, 'what have they lumbered us with here?'

'That's all very well,' Sabine Stahl broke in, 'but, as you know, we all go out to work and in general have little time for that kind of thing. I'm more interested in practical matters, for example how we are going to organize use of the bathroom. With just Herr Rohde it was manageable, but now there are nine of us who want to use the bathroom morning and evening and our boy is still completely unpredictable. How are we going to sort that out?'

'I suggest we work out a plan of who should use the bathroom when, Citizen Stahl. As a mother you will of course have priority.'

'Plan, plan! Do you think we can go to the bog according to plan? As you will have perhaps noticed, the toilet's in the bathroom as well, so what about that?'

'We have noticed that, Comrade Stahl.'

Stahl, infuriated, pulled up the lapel of his jacket and waved it to and fro. 'Can you see a badge there? No? I'm not a comrade.'

'What is that supposed to mean?'

Frau Honich gently patted her husband's hand. 'We noticed that too,' she said calmly. 'Perhaps we can share your toilet?' she said, turning to the Kaminskis, who raised their hands in horrified protest.

'We have an application for a new bathroom that has been under consideration since 1975 without any progress at all having been made. Instead the Housing Department have added you to the inhabitants of the house. Scandalous! Also, since as a comrade you are in favour of speaking openly, I find it just as scandalous that you, hardly have you moved in, have been given your own telephone line while Herr Rohde and I have been waiting for years for one.'

'But that is not our fault, Citizen Stahl. I have to be available twenty-four hours a day. I can well see that there's a problem. Perhaps I can do something for you,' Herr Honich said in conciliatory tones.

'You have connections?' Libussa croaked. She had a thick scarf round her neck and was sipping at a glass of warm milk with honey.

'Well . . . You know we were directed to a bathhouse in Querleite, it's supposed to be in one of the villas that used to belong to the sanatorium.'

'That's right, it's the house called Veronica. Yes, go there. But be careful not to step on the grids without flip-flops – athlete's foot!' Stahl cried irascibly.

'Oh, come now, Gerhart, that's no permanent solution,' Meno said, trying to calm things down a little. 'We all have to make the best of it we can. We'll find some solution. We could take it in turns to use the bathhouse, then the bathroom would be available for two groups each day. As for the toilet, we still have the earth closet in the garden.'

'You're welcome to get that working again,' Sabine Stahl said angrily. 'I wish you joy of it, especially now in winter.'

591

'I could see to that,' Herr Honich said.

Stahl threw up his arms in fury. 'Say what you like, you're not getting me on that . . . cavity! And how do you think that business with the bathhouse in the morning's going to work? Are Sabine and I to trot over there with the children and let them catch their death of cold in this freezing weather?'

'I'll speak to the Housing Department, Citizen Stahl, and see what I can do.'

'And stop all this "Citizen Stahl" nonsense. I'll send in a formal complaint. Conditions here are beyond belief.'

'Strange things are going on in Moscow, strange things,' the newspaper vendor whispered to Meno one morning when, from the window of her kiosk, she handed him the copy of *Izvestia* she'd just been reading, while he was waiting, his nose red and bunged up with cold, at the 11 tram stop.

At 8 p.m. on 12 February – Richard and Anne were visiting Regine – a messenger rang the bell and delivered notification that Regine was to report to Coal Island, second floor, F wing, the next morning. 'Call us straight away and tell us what they want,' Anne said. 'I'm free tomorrow and if you need the car I can drive you.'

'I'm obliged to leave the territory of the GDR by midnight,' Regine murmured on the telephone the next day. Richard had just come out of the operating theatre.

'Is it bad news, Herr Hoffmann?' one of the nurses asked, concern in her voice. 'You've gone quite pale.'

Richard waved her away. 'I can probably finish at the normal time today, Regine. Give Anne a call, she's got the car. I'm on duty at the theatre this evening.'

'Oh, lucky you,' the nurse exclaimed. 'My husband would have paid you five hundred marks if he could have had that shift.'

Regine hung up. For a few seconds Richard sat there without moving.

After he'd finished at the clinic he took a taxi to Lene-Glatzer-Strasse. Meno and Hansi were packing suitcases in the Hoffmanns' Lada. The door to Regine's apartment was open, there was a light on in the hall. Someone had emptied out their ash pan in Philipp's pram. On the Neuberts' letter box was a strip of adhesive plaster with 'Traitor' written on it in felt tip. Richard tore it off.

Regine and Anne were sitting in the living room, crying. Meno had obtained some capacious, solidly made Vietnamese tea chests for Regine that Hermes used to send large quantities of books. After Richard, Hansi came in, sixteen by now and almost as tall as Richard. 'We have to get a move on, Mum, the train leaves at ten p.m. and they warned there might be black ice,' he said.

'Have you got the snow chains?' Richard asked Anne, who shrugged her shoulders. Richard rushed outside. The snow chains were still up in Caravel, in the cellar. 'Are you going with them? Great. You'll make sure Anne drives carefully, won't you?' he asked Meno. Hansi came with some luggage, they'd packed thirteen suitcases for the journey, some had to be strapped to the roof. The day had been spent going through the list of things to be done: the State Bank, certificate to say Regine had no debts, Housing Department, Education Authority, expatriation with certificate of identity.

'Well, Hansi, your violin isn't a cultural object of state importance,' said Richard attempting a joke. It fell flat, the boy was looking nervously at his watch. 'We still have to go and say goodbye to Grandad –'

'I'll say goodbye now then, Hansi; I have to go soon.'

'You're going to the Semper Opera House today?' The boy looked at him with a mixture of melancholy and incomprehension.

'Couldn't swap the shift.'

'So goodbye . . . May I call you "Richard"? "Uncle" just sounds stupid and isn't right anyway.'

Richard went up to the boy and embraced him awkwardly. 'Farewell, Hans. And all the best over there.'

Regine came with two suitcases. 'Quick and painless . . .'

'Yes, quick and painless, that's always the best.'

'Thank you for everything, Richard. And if things go on as they are, you'll be following us . . .'

'And today it's all over,' Richard said.

'I just hope nothing else goes wrong. Have you got everything, Hansi?'

'You'll be seeing Jürgen again today –'

'I don't know whether to laugh or cry,' Regine said. 'The way things are! I was furious and then I couldn't help crying . . . Tell me about the opera, how it was, what they played, what people said . . . The Pegasus medallions above Wallenstein and Iphigenie there are by Jürgen.'

'Call us,' Richard said.

'I'll write,' Regine said.

Hans tapped his watch with his fingernail.

42

Iron Curtain

Richard raised his arms. The bodyguard frisked him. 'I must ask you to get undressed, Herr Doktor.'

'Are you going to go through this with everyone in the audience?' Richard asked, astonished more than annoyed as he was examined in a room beside the cloakroom, first by a member of East German then of West German security. They even shone a torch in his mouth, looked through his hair and, despite his protests, inspected his intimate areas.

'Do you think I've hidden a poison capsule up my backside. It's monstrous the way I'm being treated here.'

The bodyguards were unimpressed. 'Weren't you briefed?'

'Not about your methods.'

'We have our orders. As a doctor you could come into contact with people under our protection. Be prepared for an inspection after this. Together with you, the two personal doctors will check out the sickbay, medicines and doctor's bag. – That's all right, you can get dressed now.'

For the premiere Richard had had to be at the Semper Opera two hours before the performance began. Furious at the undignified examination procedure, he tossed his coat onto the cloakroom counter. Like a criminal, he thought. And then they're surprised when people run away . . . He thought of Regine and Anne, who must be on their way by now. If the road conditions were reasonable, they could be in Leipzig in an hour and a half.

'If you want, you can look round the house for a while, Herr Doktor. You'll get a walkie-talkie and we'll call you when the advance convoy arrives.' The bodyguard's radio telephone rang. 'Aha. Good. – That was it. You are asked to confirm by telephone that the appropriate hospital wards in the city are prepared. You're asked to call back.'

'By the General Secretary?'

The bodyguard scrutinized Richard's expression. 'By his personal physician, of course. Tell me when you're ready and I'll make the connection.'

'Where can I phone from?'

'Over there.' The bodyguard pointed to the room next to the examination room. 'Direct lines have been set up.'

'Müller here.'

'Hoffmann.'

'Yes, I'm ready. How many more times am I going to be phoned this evening, dammit all,' Richard's boss growled.

'Sorry but I've been instructed to check the connections.'

'Hmm. OK then, they seem to be working. – And?'

Richard didn't reply. He didn't know what Müller was asking.

'What does it look like, the Opera?'

'Haven't got round to looking at it yet.'

'Hm. I expect a report from you tomorrow, Herr Hoffmann, if I have to provide background cover for my senior physician. Have you enough batteries for pacemakers with you?'

'Haven't got round to checking that yet.' Richard had to laugh.

'I'm just eating a piece of cherry cake, your wife's recipe,' Müller growled. 'It's very good, but I'd rather be at the opera. Well, enjoy yourself.' He hung up.

Richard called the Internal Medicine Clinic, Reucker gave him a few tips as to what to do if there were strokes, or heart or asthma attacks. 'But you'll have been briefed, I assume, Herr Hoffmann? I mean if Traumatology's taking over theatre duty . . .'

'There are a few in-service training courses for first aid I've –'

'– screwed on? Like your Christmas tree last year? Well, let's just hope nothing happens.'

My God, Richard thought, are they crabby! Were they jealous of him because he was on duty at the gala performance? Great! He thumped the table, making the telephones jump up and down. He'd have liked to see the look on Reucker's or Müller's face if they'd had a torch shone up their backside!

Urology. Professor Leuser's easy-going drawl boomed out of the receiver. 'If they've got a kidney stone get 'em to jump off a chair; phimosis ain't an emergency, and if their joystick's itchy either it ain't been washed or there'll be some wild life crawling round on it. Not an emergency either, Herr Hoffmann. An' if the piss comes out in sev'ral jets, I recommend op'nin' their barn door. There'll be a catheter there, I s'pose, my Gawd, what a palaver.'

Even the Gynaecological Clinic had been put on alert; they'd been told a woman in the retinue of the ex-Federal Chancellor was pregnant. Richard informed the bodyguard that the lines were operational and all the doctors on stand-by. He called the advance convoy in which were the East and West German personal physicians. The area round the cloakroom was now full of people gesticulating, telephoning, trying to look important. Richard went to the foyer. When he saw the red-carpeted stairs up to the dress circle he felt like dashing up two or three steps at a time, tugging for pure joy at the red cord they'd put on either side as a handrail, bursting out into a cry of jubilation, so overcome was he by the magnificence of the building that for a few precious minutes, perhaps only seconds (he could hear steps and the murmur of voices), was his own to enjoy. What he was familiar with was the ruined opera house that, with collapsed gable, burnt-out auditorium, walled-up doors and overgrown with trees, had for decades dominated the view of Theaterplatz. He stood on the stairs, open-mouthed, and looked round. Then he ran back down the stairs again to take in once more the splendid perspective of the staircase, ran up, stroked the marble pillars and with greedy looks devoured pictures, ornamentation that in the light of hundreds of lamps, effervescent as champagne, opened their eyes freshly washed and reborn. Here was this picture, this blue, there a scene with Knights of the Holy Grail, winged Madonnas and swans; bucolic landscapes in the lunettes; names of operas glittered in gold leaf, competing for his attention with busts of composers, dark and light rippled marble (much of it imitation, as Richard knew from the newspapers) gave him the feeling that he was at the centre of a dazzling, high-quality, at the same time dangerous force, of a fire, tamed by strong willpower, that was sending out tongues here and there, fanning the flames of the chandeliers, mirrors and polished ledges, shattering into a thousand beautiful shards on the windowpanes of the gallery. He had the feeling he was being borne up, charged to his very fingertips by this great, sun-like force; he rocked on his toes, laughed, turned this way and that like a spinning top, drinking in everything with his eyes, couldn't feel his shoes any more. He felt like dancing – how he would have loved to execute a waltz with Anne there! He put the walkie-talkie in his pocket, looked round.

Arbogast was standing beyond the curve of the gallery; Richard sashayed along towards him. The Baron smiled, 'It makes you young again, Herr Hoffmann, doesn't it, when you see all this? Is it the first time you've been in here?'

Richard nodded, still a little breathless and abashed. Arbogast mentioned the letter he'd written to Heinsloe, the senior manager at the hospital, that Richard had put on one side then forgotten. Arbogast talked about oxygen and the healing of wounds. 'Breathe, Herr Hoffmann! Anyone who wants to live must breathe!' he declared, clearly in jovial mood, giving Richard a cautious and comradely pat on the back. 'Perhaps we can tackle cancerous tumours with oxygen. People at my Institute are working on the problem . . .' He went to the window, waving Richard over. A large crowd had gathered in the square. A platform had been set up, the police had drawn a cordon round it. Barsano was speaking but no one seemed to be listening to him, the eyes of all those gathered there were fixed on the Opera, admiring the richly decorated, flame-catching building.

'Oh yes, our dear Dresdeners,' Arbogast mused, 'they only want to go back. Neo-Gothic, Neo-Renaissance, Neo-Monarchies. Their greatness is when they can have something "back", can rebuild it . . . Their style is a purloined mishmash, eclectic, not primary . . . and yet overall it does have something of its own and it's charming too. Perhaps that's the way art will go in the future: doing something again, though paying tribute to time, thus making what has been into something secretly new, its depths perhaps now revealed, something, therefore, that can be truly appreciated. An art of translation, so to speak . . . You understand? Translators are the most precise readers, or so your brother-in-law has told me. Who's interested in reality when we can wish . . . This whole opera house here's a dream: something that has no purpose, no necessity, given shape in bricks and mortar. And, as ever, not cheap at that. Hundreds of millions for – bubbles . . .'

'But very beautiful bubbles,' Richard ventured to object.

'Yes, very, very beautiful' – Arbogast cleared his throat – 'bubbles.' Then, with a nod of the head, he left Richard on his own.

What a strange guy! He watched Arbogast go. The Baron's walking stick rat-tat-tatted on the floor, as if he were checking the soundness of what was underneath.

Anne was tired, Meno poured her a third cup of coffee from the vacuum flask; she gulped it down, impatiently flashing her headlights when cars coming in the opposite direction left it too long dipping theirs. The regular 'ba-bum' every time the Lada went over an asphalt join between the concrete slabs had sent Philipp to sleep, he had his head in Regine's lap and didn't even wake up when they jolted over one of the many potholes, each time making Anne quietly swear.

Meno felt restless too. He felt oppressed by the dark countryside all round, the occasional lights in the villages seemed like periscopes from undersea zones staring out over a leaden, misty ocean; but they were abandoned, or so it seemed to Meno, they were part of a fleet drifting in the darkness of the polar sea, the crews, stuck like Cartesian divers to breathing tubes, benumbed with sleep. What had happened to this country, what illness had infected it . . . ? The hands on the clocks trundled the hours along, time seemed to flow like cold treacle. Philipp Londoner was worried, there were vague and contradictory rumours coming from Moscow, the Kremlin seemed to be in turmoil, the General Secretary of the Soviet Communist Party was said to be in his death throes in the government hospital . . . Meno came to with a start when Anne hooted the horn: they were driving behind a convoy of timber lorries, the overtaking lane was blocked by a motorbike escort.

After a few minutes they were waved past imperiously. A motorbike escort for timber lorries? Meno had a closer look as they drove past: cylindrical shapes, tapering at the front, could be made out under the tarpaulins; at the wheel of the articulated lorries were soldiers of the Soviet army.

'Rocket transport,' Hans said, breaking the silence, 'those are SS-20 rockets, camouflaged as loads of uncut timber.' He knew that from a friend at school, he said.

'*Davai, davai,*' one of the motorcyclists shouted.

They overtook and lapsed into silence again. Meno was thinking of the Honichs, who had brought strife and something like nudist-beach easy-going ways into the House with a Thousand Eyes . . . Things were certainly pretty noisy. Herr Honich did early-morning exercises with the window open to booming folk music ('I love to go a-wandering . . .'), knocked at Meno's door to invite him to join in the keep-fit session (as soon as he switched the radio on that was the end of Meno's ability to concentrate), he needed it, he said, spending all the day in a sitting position; morning exercises strengthened one's concentration and woke one up . . . Herr Honich seemed unconcerned at Meno's rejection that grew more pointed with every day. But the woman got on Meno's nerves even more. She claimed to be entitled to use the balcony, rang at the most inconvenient times and protests could not stop her flinging the balcony door open, thus allowing the warmth in his living room to pour out. Meno had rearranged the furniture and bookshelves to compensate for the reduction in space in his apartment but the little nooks and crannies that created aroused Frau Honich's curiosity, no muttered curse could keep her away; she knocked on the bookcase, squeezed through, asked if she might come over when she was already standing by his desk, smiled at Meno, who, with a pained look, quickly hid his manuscripts. What was he doing, she wanted to know. Working. But what on? On poetry perhaps? Oh yes, on poems, of course; but he didn't need to hide them from her, she thought poems were suuuper (she drew out the 'u' like a rubber band; at this adolescent expression Meno had to bend down to keep his fury under control), perhaps he could . . . Oh yes! she exclaimed, he was an expert, he knew all about that, she was sure he could teach her how to write poems! It was something she'd been longing to do for ages and now she'd met someone and someone who lived right next door into the bargain, if that didn't mean something, she said teasingly, shaking her finger roguishly at him. She wanted to learn how to do it.

The next day Meno rang Coal Island and complained. However: according to such and such a regulation, they explained, Citizen Honich had the right to use the balcony in his apartment and he could not lock her out of his apartment if she wished to make use of that right. Why were the tenants of 2 Mondleite always making difficulties? They had no time for that kind of thing.

Stahl thought they should fight back and regularly took out the Honichs' fuses. Then they sat in the dark and the pop music (Oberhofer Bauernmarkt, Regina Thoss, Dorit Gàbler) died away. Herr Honich countered this by threatening to report Stahl because he listened to West German radio and had repeatedly responded to repeated requests that he participate in socialist competition with comparisons from the animal kingdom; his wife Babett was a witness.

'Penny for them, Mo.'

'Oh, this and that.'

'Problems?'

'Not particularly. How about you?'

'They've lengthened our shifts. One doctor and one nurse have left the country. There are intrigues going on in Richard's section. One of the doctors, the Party Secretary, seems to be spying on him. He has to train him. They don't like it when knowledge is beyond their control and in hand surgery they'd have problems finding someone to replace Richard, at least in Dresden. Robert has a girlfriend. He's a bit young, I think. But he does know all about the birds and the bees.

Barbara has her head full of wedding preparations. Ina already has something on the way, it seems. Look, over there.' She pointed to a line of windmills, turning in the empty countryside in front of a blue-green strip of bright sky, as if in slow motion, with flocks of crows silently drifting up and down round them. Regine said nothing. Meno looked out of the window.

'May I?' Sperber, the lawyer, pointed to the empty chair beside Richard that was usually reserved for the theatre doctor's partner. 'Your wife's not coming, of course.'

'How do you know?'

'One knows one's cases, one knows one's colleagues cases,' Sperber said with a smirk. 'And one's friends' problems. You discussed Frau Neubert's case with me . . . Oh, that's not a breach of client confidentiality. A certain exchange of information is necessary, we have to work together if we want to have material we can use against the prosecuting counsels – what do you think of it?' Sperber's gesture took in the whole auditorium, which was gradually filling up; people were standing at the balustrades, craning their necks in the stalls, expectant faces filled with pride; many had handkerchiefs in their hand. 'Is that not something special our little country's managed to achieve?' Sperber asked without waiting for an answer. The standard expression was 'our state' or 'our socialist GDR' (an odd adjective, Richard thought, as if there were another one); at 'our little country' Richard pricked up his ears.

'If you like, you can come and visit us sometime. The invitation includes your wife too, of course,' the lawyer hastened to add. 'We would be delighted to have the opportunity to get to know you better. One moment.' He fished a visiting card out of his little leather handbag and pressed it into the right hand Richard, nonplussed, held open. 'The *Freischütz* isn't really my thing, all that Romanticism and merrymaking at the shooting competition on the village green. A beautiful dream for which we're gathered here and every one of us will understand in their own way. But the music's admirable and for our lord and master' – Sperber nodded cautiously in the direction of the official box – 'it's probably just the right thing. Only last Saturday he shot a twelve-pointer. Will you excuse me for a few minutes.'

Sperber went off, appearing up in the VIP box a few moments later, where a prolonged session of handshaking began.

The train was late; now, after all the rush, they were standing on the platform, waiting. This would have been the time to say farewell but the station announcement had talked of an hour's delay. The light in the Mitropa café was pale, slimy; cockroaches scuttled across the tables as if caught in the act. On the menu was soup as green as weathered copper, mixed-vegetable stew, schnapps and beer. Hans felt nauseated, wanted to go out again. Meno bought a packet of Marie biscuits. 'Do you like reading?' he asked Hans outside.

'It all depends. Most of all Karl May.'

'Here, take this. You might get bored on the journey.' He handed him a volume of Poe's stories, illustrated by Vogelstrom.

'I'm sure I won't, but thanks.' Hans took the book and stuck it in the inside pocket of his coat.

'Isn't it cold?' Regine moaned when they came back. 'I hope nothing goes wrong now.'

'Do you know why there's a delay?' Meno asked. Regine, in tears again, turned away.

'Frozen points. The train's coming from Rostock,' Anne replied. They'd made a kind of bed on the suitcases for Philipp, covering him with various articles of clothing, but he wasn't asleep, he was staring up at the arched ceiling with little spikes of crusty ash hanging down, intestinal hairs of a Gulliver in the land of Lilliput; hundreds of pigeons were roosting on the crossbeams, heads under their wings, packed close to each other so that none could be a danger to the others during the night, Meno thought, they probably kept each other warm as well. The loudspeakers over the platform crackled, a woman's voice in broad Saxon extended the delay into an indefinite period. Regine put her hand over her mouth and leant forward, it looked as if she were covering a yawn, but she was screaming into her hand. Hans took Regine to one side, they walked up and down. There was no one apart from them waiting on the platform. Railway police were checking a few drunks on platforms some way away.

'Scream, if you want,' Anne said, 'it won't bother me, let people hear it.'

'So that they can arrest us after all?'

'Hans,' Regine begged him softly.

'I didn't mean it like that.' There was steam coming out of Anne's mouth, Meno looked at his sister closely. She'd pulled her orange scarf right up to her eyes, perhaps out of embarrassment; she was wearing a chapka Barbara had made and buttoned down the earflaps. Meno filled his pipe. Now Anne took Regine's arm, they were walking round and round, discussing how to deal with her effects. The Vietnamese tea chests could be sent to Jürgen's address in Munich; Anne was to take the money for it from the sale of the furniture Regine had had to leave behind.

'What did you have in mind?'

Regine turned to face Meno, who was sniffing the strong vanilla smell of his tobacco. A suspicious expression appeared on Hans's face, though Meno had only asked out of curiosity and to pass the time. 'Doesn't matter.'

'Richard thinks that as soon as you're over there you should bring an action against the state for confiscating your paintings, even though there's no chance of success, of course.'

'The paintings have gone, Anne, and Jürgen's sculptures too. That's the price we had to pay.'

*

'Ebony.' Sperber examined the grandfather clock beside the lacquered door and the two delicate chairs where Arbogast and Joffe were sitting chatting. 'What do you, as an expert, say?' he asked, turning to Richard, who was standing beside him, glancing uneasily now and then at the door with the shining 'Box' over it. 'I often went to see your father in Glashütte. He has an excellent collection and was so kind as to advise me on the purchase of various pieces. You admired some of them the last time you came to see me.'

The door was opened, the General Secretary let Barsano and the ex-Federal Chancellor go in first. Richard looked at the buffet, there were servants in ceremonial livery, frozen in bows. On the tables with damask cloths were butter knives with rounded blades. Looking at the butter knives, then the Comrade Chairman's brightly shining face and his neck, stiffened by a snow-white, starched collar, Richard started in horror as it occurred to him how well suited to being cut through or hanged such necks seemed, even those of the ex-Chancellor and Barsano; yet they consisted of the same substance – vulnerable human flesh – as the necks of so-called ordinary people and Richard automatically started looking for a mark that branded them. Perfidious, forbidden thoughts!

'I'm familiar with that look you have on your face at the moment, half pleasure, half horror,' Sperber whispered. 'It's the expression associated with crime.'

'Is that intended as a joke, Herr Sperber?'

'I like to think I have some knowledge of human nature' – the lawyer gave a brief smile – 'and you get a thrill out of taking risks. There's some attraction in having a conversation like this here. And I have to say such thoughts are not unknown to me. It's the fear of the crime they might commit that drives young people into my profession. I'm interested in the depths people can sink to. I have quite a collection.'

'How do you collect them?'

'Not in the form of deep-sea charts or sections of the seabed, as you might assume. – Don't shake his hand, if you're introduced to him. He doesn't particularly like that, and he's the one who determines the degree of familiarity.'

'You feel sorry for them.' Anne nodded in the direction of soldiers standing guard by a tank transport train.

'What are you going to do?' Regine asked as Anne looked in her purse.

'Take them something to eat.'

'But they're Russians.'

'They get cold too. Come with me, Mo, I can't carry it all myself.'

They went to the Mitropa café, bought tea, potato soup with sausage and rolls; Meno and a grumbling waiter with cigarette burns in his snow-white jacket carried the teapot. The soldiers were standing by an outside track on the other side of the station. Suspicious, almost fearful, they felt for their Kalashnikovs when Anne showed them the bowls they'd brought. Meno said in Russian that they'd brought them something to eat, tea to warm them up. The soldiers, children's faces with shaven heads and caps pushed back, looked longingly at the tea, but were hesitant about coming closer; one ran to the front of the train where an officer had jumped down from a carriage and was knocking the dust off his flat-peaked cap. They conferred. A second officer appeared, clearly of a higher rank than the first, for he reported to him. The second officer took his cap off, scratched his head, turned his hat in his hand for a while, went back, knocked on the carriage. After a while a third officer appeared, to whom the second reported this time.

'Well, I'll get back to my place of work,' the waiter said. 'I simply can't believe it. And anyway, I've just got over a cold. No offence meant.'

He stuck his hands in his pockets and strolled off. The three Soviet officers exchanged glances. The soldier facing Meno and Anne stood, motionless, with neutral, apprehensive expressions, now and then giving the bowls, Anne's coat, Meno's shoes a quick glance. The waiter returned, walking between two tracks. 'What's going on here, citizens?'

Silent and unannounced, a train arrived at Regine's platform. Anne put the bowls down on the ground and was about to run over.

'Stop!' one of the policemen shouted, fiddling with his revolver belt. 'Where are you going, citizen?'

'Our friends are over there . . . the train –'

'That's the through train to Munich,' the other policeman said. 'What business is it of yours?'

'We were accompanying our friends –'

'And were going to try to emigrate illegally, I presume.'

'What?!' Meno exclaimed, completely baffled. The superior Soviet officer went over to the policemen and pointed at the bowls, the pot of soup, the tea.

'What a load of nonsense!' The waiter threw up his hands in despair.

'We must ask you to follow us.' The first policeman went in front of Meno and Anne, the second grasped the arm of the waiter, who was laughing. Across the station Regine and Hans were shouting and waving. When a whistle sounded they set off running, stumbling and encumbered with their thirteen pieces of luggage, Hans stopped once to put Philipp, on his shoulders, who, as far as Meno could tell, was merrily directing them with his little arms.

'We will investigate what your true intentions in the vicinity of the Soviet armed forces were. Move!' the first policeman ordered.

43

A wedding

The Hoffmanns' barometer indicated 'changeable'. The first three days of May were cold. There was hail and snow, then the sun appeared, pale and still half asleep; suddenly, as if it had come to an abrupt decision, it climbed out of bed, full of energy. On the fourth the bees started to swarm. Waves of dandelions broke over the gardens on the slope above the Elbe. Bird cherry and sweet cherry blossomed. On the thirteenth Meno entered plum and pear in Libussa's spring calendar, two days later the Cellini apples. When Meno looked out towards Pillnitz from the Langes' conservatory, the white blossom covering the still winter-dark trees was like down from thousands of torn pillows.

One Sunday in the middle of May a wedding party was standing outside Pastor Magenstock's church waiting for the bride and groom to appear. After a glance at her watch, one at Pastor Magenstock's calming gesture, one at the sky, Barbara wailed that there was a jinx on the wedding: where were the two of them? And now the first drops were starting to fall, thick and soft as slugs, on Ulmenleite.

'Doesn't matter,' Niklas said, opening the Tietzes' family umbrella with demonstrative casualness over Gudrun and Reglinde; his own aristocratic pepper-and-salt thatch, still giving off the scent of Wiener's birch hair lotion (it made Meno think of a Russian track across the fields with exultant larks and the obligatory horse-drawn cart), he sheltered under the porch, from which a blob occasionally spattered down. Pastor Magenstock was proud of the birds' nests and all the spiders' webs. They were all God's creatures, he'd insisted to Barbara, to which Barbara had retorted that the Lord would do better to think of the dressmakers and their wearisome wedding preparations and did it not bother him that the stuff stuck to the soles of your shoes and was

thus trodden in all over the church? His Reverence had made a slight
bow. Pastor Magenstock, as Meno was aware, had his own ideas about
caring for his flock and what it meant to be a shepherd in difficult times.
The ship of Christianity was heading for dangerous depths and sometimes when, in the dark of the night, Pastor Magenstock turned to the
picture of Brother Luther – his countenance afire, the hammer of the
fenceposts, lion of the Scriptures and flail of disputes – seeking a draught
from the spirit of his strength, all he could hear was the familiar clatter
of the loose shutters and the breathing of his seven loved ones.

Ulrich shook back the sleeve over his wristwatch, spread his arms
wide, startling Josta and her husband (a fellow student of Wernstein's,
Richard had learnt, who was staring at a saint looking up in improb-
ably mild ecstasy in the aisle of the church), rubbed his chin that, like
all the male chins in the wedding party (even Robert's and Ezzo's,
Ulrich had insisted because of the photos), had been shaved by Lajos
Wiener himself with a heavy, blue-ground Solingen blade, stropped
on Russia leather. All Ulrich said was 'Oh, for Heaven's sake' (he
wasn't wearing his Party badge, Meno had established) spat out through
clenched teeth, at which Barbara's teacher Noack, the white-haired
furrier from the Brühl, exchanged looks of concern with Barbara's
brother, Helmut Hoppe, a pastry cook at Elbflorenz, and pointed to
the sky as a first rumble of thunder was heard.

'But it's true' – Ulrich looked up at the sky with a shrug of the
shoulders – 'can't stand criticism, eh?'

'But surely Herr Kannegiesser will make it?' Anne's question sank
into the unfathomable discretion of Pastor Magenstock's face. Who knew
whether the organist/choirmaster's F9 could still manage the climb from
the Mordgrund, past the Soviet army hospital and up to Turmstrasse?

'I'm going to get in the car and go to meet them.' Ulrich, furious,
jutted out his chin and squeezed his key ring in his fist. 'They must be
somewhere. But I don't suppose it would occur to your daughter and
our son-in-law to find a telephone kiosk and call us?'

'You never give us a call when you're late. – Perhaps they've secretly run off.' She'd seen a thing or two herself, Barbara said in horrified tones, in her life in and around Dresden.

'Of course.' Helmut Hoppe took out a hip flask. 'Just you have a sip of egg liqueur, sister. Made it ourselves, it tastes better than the stuff from the other side. The eggs come straight from the farmer to our Rationalization Department and if it's a long day, and it's always a long day in the Rationalization Department, they rationalize this tasty little sauce.'

'Here they are,' Christian said. The fact that he was there was due to a promise he'd been able to give, after correspondence with Meno, to the sergeant in his new unit who dealt with requests for leave. 'Private Hoffmann,' Staff Sergeant Emmerich, known as Nip, said, 'you're an earhole in the second six months of your term and earholes don't actually go on leave, but if you happen to have a Polski Fiat exhaust manifold . . .' Meno had provided one.

Ina got out of the car, laughing. Wernstein and Dreyssiger, his best man, looked like dyers; both were stripped to their vests and shivering, despite the heat; their arms were smeared black up to the elbows. Ina was carrying their white shirts and tails.

'For Heaven's sake, child, what's happened?'

'Engine fault, mother-in-law.'

'How stupid can you be! You should have left the car and taken a taxi.'

'We tried, there were none available. And hitching a lift didn't work either, there weren't any cars to hitch.'

'And what do you look like?! Can the pair of them get washed here, Herr Magenstock?'

'We've only got cold water in the church. We'll slip over to my house.'

Christian watched Ina as the three of them, followed by Magenstock, came back out of the parsonage; she still hadn't calmed down and had to hold on to the fence to give her exhausted body a few moments to gather strength such as happens in ripples between contractions or after the relief of vomiting in cases of gastroenteritis. Then she lifted her head and looked Barbara in the face: in moments of great agitation it resembled a horrified jackdaw. Limp and groaning, she raised her right hand and put it to her forehead, then she was once more shaken by convulsive laughter. Wernstein and Dreyssiger each hooked an arm under hers, Pastor Magenstock tried to hold an umbrella over the bride. The organist's wife had rung up while they were in the parsonage to say her husband was ill, Dr Fernau, who was still with her, had said he must stay in bed, but she'd spoken with Herr Trüpel, who was already on his way to the church with a selection of records.

'And there he is now, our sunshine man.' Ulrich grinned.

'A good thing we've got these excellent umbrellas. Do we feel smug! Magnificent.' Helmut Hoppe licked a drop of egg liqueur off the rim of his hip flask and observed with interest Rudolf Trüpel as he fluttered along towards them in the now pouring rain like a water rail, bent under the weight of his case of records.

Many times before when Kannegiesser was ill, the owner of the Philharmonia record shop had helped to provide a solemn setting for weddings, baptisms and funerals. Meno remembered Christmas services with toccatas and fugues struck up by a player who sought release in music and showed no consideration for a parish choir on a Silbermann or Arp Schnitger organ in a hurricane of thunderous sound that aroused sinners' consciences the moment Rudolf Trüpel, with quiet satisfaction and educational aggression, let them resound from the Japanese hi-fi equipment donated by members of a twinned parish in Hamburg with a concern for quality. Meno recalled his father telling him when he was a child about the Abode of Rest, as if Rest were a woman with a tenancy agreement and a list of the house rules, and when he remembered the domes of St Basil's Cathedral on Red Square, he thought that was where she lived and not in the Arbat district and not in the office of the director of the Lubyanka where a telephone screamed even when silent. The onion dome of St John's in Schandau had had the same effect on him; now, however, in Ulmenleite the chain of associations broke off. The wedding party outside the church was getting restless (Barbara with discontentedly furrowed brow), for one of Bach's funeral chorales after another was ringing out with the force of an alpenhorn blown next to the ear of a sleeping infant.

'Great choir,' Niklas said, 'could be the Thomaskirche. It's the Gewandhaus orchestra, the violins speak Saxon, but not that of Dresden.'

A further attempt brought melancholy, obstinacy and God with open arms.

'Some marriages are like that,' Helmut Hoppe said. 'Anyone it makes think of egg liqueur is a rogue.'

'You and your suggestive remarks,' Helmut Hoppe's wife Traudel sighed. 'Can't you keep them to yourself, at least at your niece's wedding.'

'Nah. It'd be nice if the wedding could get going. Oh look over there now. There's a man shrugging his shoulders and spreading his arms. I know that from work. It means we'll just have to improvise.'

The congregation was waiting inside the church while Herr Trüpel conferred with Pastor Magenstock. As far as Meno understood, Trüpel's son must have swapped the contents of the record cases (baptism, wedding, funeral) round. Magenstock nodded, thought, adjusted his spectacles. Reglinde shook her head categorically. She had graduated from the school of church music but not taken up a post as organist/choirmaster. At the moment she was working in the zoo as an assistant keeper. Robert had an idea and as the wedding party entered the church, after the bride and groom and Pastor Magenstock, a choir, singing in canon, improvised Mendelssohn's 'Wedding March' from the gallery: Trüpel conducted, Niklas's bass imitated the organ, Gudrun the high voices, Ezzo and Christian hummed delicate arabesques while two of Ina's fellow students and Robert intoned the melody. Pastor Magenstock welcomed the bridal couple, family and friends. 'We now begin this service in the name of the Father, the Son and the Holy Ghost.'

'Amen.'

'Let us pray with the words of psalm thirty-six: Thy mercy, O Lord, is in the heavens and thy faithfulness reacheth unto the clouds . . .'

'So there's nothing doing under water, you can lie as much as you like down there,' Helmut Hoppe whispered to Barbara, who was sitting in front of Meno.

'I don't believe in it myself, but enoeff. Blaspheming in church brings bad luck.'

'. . . in thy light shall we see light. Glory be to the Father, and to the Son, and to the Holy Ghost. As it was in the beginning, is now, and ever shall be, world without end.'

'Amen.'

Pastor Magenstock gave the choir a sign. A safe stronghold our God is still, a trusty shield and weapon – Trüpel conducted with feeling and zest. The voices of Noack, the furrier, and the Stenzel Sisters rose up, thin and quavering. Richard kept his eyes on the ground. Meno knew that he only went to church services as a favour to Anne and, that day, his niece. Kurt Rohde would come later and wait outside for Malivor Marroquin, who was to take the wedding photos. The hymn began to die away in embarrassed tatters; Trüpel brought the choir in again to bolster up the tailing off in the pews below and bring it to a conclusive end. Pastor Magenstock went up into the pulpit and began his sermon on the text chosen for the wedding ceremony. 'But he that doeth truth cometh to the light, that his deeds may be made manifest, that they are wrought in God.'

Richard observed Lucie. She had scattered flowers with other children. Now she was sitting between Josta and the husband he didn't know, surreptitiously dangling her legs. Daniel was lounging next to

Josta, blowing bubbles with his chewing gum, and kept turning his head round.

'What a badly behaved boy,' Anne whispered. 'Why does he keep grinning at you? Do you know him?'

'No. Perhaps a patient's son.'

Richard listened to the sermon for a while, then let it go in one ear and out the other when Magenstock brought in his third parable: the kingdom of heaven was like unto a net that was cast into the sea, and gathered of every kind; the good were gathered into vessels, the bad were cast away. That made Richard think. Wasn't there a hymn that said: Whatever thou may be, come to Him and He will welcome thee? So the kingdom of heaven had to fish out its own inhabitants . . . Did that mean the little fish felt no desire to swim into heaven and had to be dragged up out of their stupidity and into paradise? But if it was so splendid up there why did the fish not go of their own accord? All that seemed familiar to him. He watched Magenstock, who was in the pulpit, preaching with joyful fervour. It also brought back the scene in the forest when Wernstein, Dreyssiger and he had tried to steal a Christmas tree. A hymn started, he didn't join in; too proud to pretend. He didn't know any of these hymns and Ina, he thought irritably, hadn't thought of making copies of the words for those who didn't know them. And, of course, there weren't even enough hymn books. Ulrich seemed to be able to keep up pretty well . . . Interesting. The Stenzel Sisters didn't need a hymn book. They stood up straight in their row giving those beside them, doctors from the Academy, their noses plodding along the lines of a shared hymn book, looks of restrained puzzlement. As Ina Wernstein was putting the ring on her husband's finger (with a grin, as Richard could tell from his view diagonally behind her: Wernstein's fingernails were still dirty from the engine oil), Barbara shouted for help, scrabbling around wildly in her cleavage; a scorpion had fallen on her, she said, running out of the church, Ulrich behind her. 'An earwig,' he whispered when they came back.

'Our father, who art in heaven.'

Richard resolved to ask about Wernstein's family; the wedding party seemed to consist of just the Rohde wing and a few of Wernstein's colleagues from the Academy and his student days.

'Plizz lukk at liddel gold-finsh, plizz sink she fly naow, you smile.' Outside the church door, in the damp light of a returning sun, Malivor Marroquin was adjusting their positions for the photo. Kurt Rohde kissed Ina on both cheeks, looked Wernstein up and down, turning his face either way as he did so, gave him a brief but hearty pat on the shoulder; Meno thought: he likes him, all the rest is embarrassment. Typical Tower-dweller. They do have the big emotions but they play them down, they prefer to make them look ridiculous rather than admit to them; to show them all too openly would seem like an affront to them, indiscreet, an infringement of the inviolable inner sphere. To speak the secrets out loud is to lose them, anyone who is lavish with the big emotions doesn't respect them; they avoid kitsch and prefer to tone down the grand gesture; they are afraid of the things that are important to them being sold off cheaply. Marroquin held up his light meter, adjusted the three thumbscrews on the wooden tripod legs that looked like propellers which were about to join forces to lift the scratched, bulky camera case with its brass-bound lens and black cloth up into the air, leaving the baffled photographer standing there with the torn-off cable release in his hand. Marroquin had closed off the street with two warning triangles ('Photography in progress'). He wasn't put off when cars started to hoot, waggled a warning index finger at them as he threw his red flag of a scarf in a challenging gesture over his coat, the pockets of which, added by Lukas, the tailor, according to Marroquin's instructions, were crammed with pieces of photographic equipment and accessories that might turn out useful in the usual kind of session ('What do you think, how is it to be? – No idea, you're the expert'): false noses, paper chrysanthemums, for children a Makarov cap-pistol. Marroquin wore a beret with a badge pinned to it over his long white hair that was engaged in philosophical discussion with the bewitching May breezes; on the badge were the words '*No pasarán*' between exclamation marks, one inverted, one normal, that looked to Meno like two quarrelling fists and had a strangely ironic effect (why two exclamation marks, wasn't one enough?); at least he couldn't repress a smile when he imagined Party slogans between the belligerent punctuation marks.

'Do you want peepul to see liddel gold-finsh or not?' Marroquin came out from under the black pharaoh's cloak and pointed to Ina's belly. 'Then plizz lukk at home of stirrup of imperialism.'

Magenstock's response was a bored raising of the eyebrows.

'Hold breath. Ready . . . Two liddel brrats have stuck tongues out – once more? But that will cost extra.' Wernstein and Ina declined with a wave of the hand, despite Barbara's objections and the fact that Traudel Hoppe hadn't been able to repress a sneeze. The bride's posy was caught by Kitty Stenzel.

The party was to be held in the House with a Thousand Eyes. Two days before the wedding, demijohns with kvass that Ulrich had started had burst in the house; he had been impatient, had placed heaters beside them, the pressure of fermentation had sent circular discs of glass, that looked as if they'd been cut with a glazier's diamond pencil, shooting out of the bottles. The Afghan rugs, the Tibetan runners and the big Persian carpet from Vietnam, Barbara's walking tour of distant lands and daily vacuumed pride, were soaked through and sticky; Meno and Ulrich took them out into the garden and dipped them in tin bathtubs filled with hot water. The kvass had seeped through into the apartment below – they had to get a device to draw the dampness out of the walls (Herr Kothe, who was sitting on his balcony dunking a biscuit in a glass of tea as the carpets splashed about in the garden like colourful seals, knew someone who knew someone); a team of painters had to be arranged and courage screwed up for a contrite ring on the bell of a firmly closed door: would the Scholzes be prepared to accept an invitation to the wedding as interim compensation? Now Herr Scholze was standing on the washing area in front of the balustrade with the eagle exchanging tips about the preparation of sucking pig with Pedro Honich. He favoured *le porcelet farci* but Honich could not find a butcher who could supply the ingredients for stuffing the piglet ('Boiled ham? A hundred and fifty grams? No chance!'), a shop that had fifty chestnuts in stock in May, nor a dairy that sold Parmesan or mature Comté cheese, and you couldn't get saffron, not even in Delikat shops. Pedro Honich stuck by Serbian (he said 'Yugoslavian') sucking pig. Helmut Hoppe and Noack joined them, made wise comments and bore the responsibility as Honich prepared sausage meat, sliced peppers, rubbed salt on the inside of the piglet, warmed up Puszta sauce and beer. Meno kept apart. The Kaminski twins were away and had locked their apartment, otherwise all the doors in the house were open. In the shed Meno and Stahl had set up one table with bread and one with a cold buffet from the Felsenburg; Adeling, the waiter, and Reglinde's friend who now had a job in the Felsenburg were serving dumplings in Danish sauce.

A smell came from Arbogast's chemical laboratory, at first of peaches, then of slurry. Christian looked for Fabian and Muriel but couldn't see them, their parents weren't there either, but had sent a camera (K16 model, Christian knew it from his period of work experience with Pentacon) that was on a table with the other wedding presents in the summerhouse; Alois and Libussa had put them there in case it rained. Records, books (historical pigskin-bound medical tomes from Ulrich's collection, a complete *Treatment of Fractures* by Lorenz Böhler, all the surgeons present envied Wernstein for it); then a dkk refrigerator with a two-star freezer compartment from Anne, Richard and Meno; from the Hoppes a perambulator and baby clothes ('A Baby-Chic nappy makes any mother happy'); Barbara had made both a winter and a summer suit for her son-in-law; Kurt and Ulrich had given a voyage (on MS *Arkona* to Cuba, Ina had been beside herself with joy); Christian saw a washing machine, vouchers for furniture (the Tietzes; Niklas had added one of his St Petersburg stethoscopes); from Noack, the furrier, a marten fur muff 'for Madame' (a suggestion of a kiss on the hand), a lambskin coat collar 'for Sir' (sketching a bow); a canoe from Wernstein's colleagues.

Compared with all these useful things, his present . . . Christian, not knowing quite how to put it, recalled the hours looking at the saturniid moths in Caravel with Meno: an awkward, somewhat clumsy but touching child in the company of grown-ups – that's what the green jug he'd bought, without a long search, in a potter's studio in Neustadt seemed to be; he'd only had two hours between arriving at the station and the start of the marriage ceremony in the registry office and he'd wasted a good hour, desperate and undecided, in a second-hand shop, nudged by greedy elbows, jostling his way from an unusable tailor's iron to a television set in need of repair (and still priced with three zeros after the 2). The jug had been surrounded by rolls of wallpaper and buckets of emulsion paint, brushes were being kept soft in it. – 'No, that jug, if it's for sale,' he'd said to the potter, who was wiping her hands on her apron in astonishment and was offering to show him what she had on display. The jug wasn't one of hers but she wasn't insulted, even though Christian had expressed a desire to buy it without hesitation; perhaps she was impressed by his insistence, his spontaneous decision, perhaps by his explanation that he was going to his cousin's wedding (he was wearing walking-out dress); she took the brushes out of the jug, washed it and wrapped it up in a smudged copy of *Union*; Christian had paid the price she asked without hesitation. Most of all he would have liked to keep the jug for himself. The green was the green of holly leaves, the rich, dark tone immediately appealed to him, also the simple, ancient jug shape with subtle asymmetry; there was something about it that had said, I'm for you, I'm a part of you in another world. Christian was struggling with himself; when the houses on Lindwurmring were already in sight he recalled that Meno had once said to him that presents you give should be precisely those you can least bear to be parted from. He had handed the jug to Ina exactly as it was, still wrapped in the smudged newspaper.

'The disadvantage would be that we'd have to accept any dump we're offered. A fellow student knows someone in the accommodation directorate and says teachers are supposed to get preferential treatment. We'll see. At least it's in Berlin and you suggested Thomas's prospects might be better there than here.'

'Yes, that's something I wanted to discuss with the pair of you. I can say "*du*" to you now, can't I?' Richard gave a playful tug on the sleeve of Wernstein's tailcoat, which Barbara had altered; you could tell from the cut that it must have been handed down and all the oil of lavender from Barbara's secret stock couldn't overpower the smell of mothballs coming from the swallow tails and shiny lapels enclosing a pink bow tie with black dots on a white frilled shirt. 'As long as Müller's head of surgery I can't imagine you're going to get anywhere. Grefe's the assistant in South One and that's where the real careers have started ever since I've been with Müller. I can offer to put in a word for you with Orthopaedics or in Friedrichstadt; Pahl's a man you can get on with, one of us.'

'I'd still only be an assistant there, I wouldn't be any farther on,' Wernstein said after a few moments' thought.

'If they separate trauma from general surgery, as Pahl tells me they've been working towards for some time, he'll become head and you could apply for a post as senior physician. Of course, there's always the possibility they've already earmarked the post for an internal candidate. And you said you don't want to move into orthopaedics.'

'You could take the job in Buch?'

'I'd be stuck there, my dear spouse. I wouldn't be able to develop.

Their main focus of research is in different areas and I want to do my post-doc qualification in traumatology. We've already talked about that and we don't need to go through it all again. Especially not today.'

'You'd be earning considerably more than at the Charité Hospital in Berlin.'

'Maybe. But I'd be at the Charité . . . Sauerbruch, Brugsch, Felix, Frey, Nissen . . . I could continue my research there. Here Müller won't let me get on.'

'You'll soon be a father, let me remind you. Even if your wife isn't that important to you, you ought to be able to give your son something. – Yesyes, we're coming,' Ina shouted to some of the guests in the lower part of the garden.

'When is it due? Do you already know –'

'It will be a boy,' Ina said emphatically.

'No, it'll be a girl.' Wernstein laughed. 'By the way, we're with Weniger. – What d'you think of him, Herr . . . er . . . Richard?'

'One of the best gynaecologists I know. One of the old school.'

'The fifth of July,' Ina said. 'It will be a boy. You may have your clinical wisdom, but I'm the mother, I know it's going to be a boy. Uncle Richard, would you write a reference for Thomas?'

'Yes, of course,' Richard said, nonplussed by Ina's direct approach.

'May I ask you something? What do think of him as a surgeon?'

Richard gave her a searching look. Wernstein had flushed bright red and tried to wave away her question; she shook her head. 'I know it's tactless of me but I'd really like to know. I want you to give me an honest answer and if you think it's not for his ears, we'll send him away. – And, by the way, Christian doesn't look too good. Perhaps he's exaggerating? He's always tended to overdramatize a bit.'

'I don't think he's exaggerating. He's in the army, in Grün, it's just a little place.'

'He gave me a jug. It's really nice of him.'

Richard clasped his hands behind his back. He could sense that both Ina and Wernstein were curious, which he found embarrassing, he felt it was a little improper; he was also disturbed by the eagerness, the hint of calculation, in Ina's question, as if she suspected that under these circumstances – alone with the newlyweds – it would be impossible for him to avoid answering. 'I wouldn't answer your question if I had to lie because it's your wedding day. I'd have managed to wriggle out of it, believe me. But since it won't spoil your day, as I hope, I can give a straight, honest answer to a straight, honest question. I think your husband's a born surgeon and expect great things of him. I'd be proud and happy if my boys had his abilities. I can also say that I regard him as a kind of son. What I was actually hoping, Thomas, was that you'd succeed me but, as I can see, you have other plans. If you want my opinion: in your place I'd do exactly what you intend to do. Unfortunately Müller's allocated Kohler to me as assistant, not you.'

'Him!'

'Not a bad surgeon, but not a patch on you. I'll have to see what I can do for you. I know a few people at the Charité. Though, of course, you could always wait and see, Müller's retiring next year – though that doesn't mean things will be any easier. – Perhaps we should discuss this later, or another time, your friends are getting impatient already. What did you think of the sermon?'

'You shouldn't be intransigent, Uncle Richard. Pops was also against a church wedding, but I wanted it. For a man who has to preach the word of God in the middle of atheism, I think he does it very well.'

'Certainly, certainly,' Richard said in placatory tones. He watched the pair of them go as they headed for the summerhouse. They exchanged a few words with Josta and her husband; Josta was holding Lucie's hand, not letting go, and Richard turned round and quickly left before his daughter could look at him. She'll be starting school this year, he thought.

*

Meno puzzled over the custom of sawing a tree trunk at a wedding. Two people joined together in marriage and affirmed this union by, of all things, putting a frame saw to a trunk the diameter of a telegraph pole and starting, as Ina and Wernstein were now doing to the encouragement and raillery of those around, to heave it back and forth. Ina soon wearied and, with a laugh, begged for someone to replace her. Helmut Hoppe shouted that that was the beginning of infidelity and she couldn't have a replacement for the birth, 'So keep sawing, child', otherwise what they'd just heard was the bride herself calling for her rival.

'You've got things completely wrong again, Meno. To get through a trial together, that's what it means. You always insist on spending so long thinking things over until they get distorted and a cat suddenly becomes a dog. Which is more or less the case with your Chakababa or whatever he's called, the name's completely unpronounceable. I'm sure even Arbogast's monsters are afraid of him. And isn't it outrageous to stink the street out with toxic gases. Yes, toxic gases, I know exactly what I'm saying. A very shady character, that Baron, they say that with the Russians . . . I can believe anything of him. Toxic gases. It stinks – and that when we're celebrating a wedding. After all, we did put up notices spelling it out clearly. It's criminal, the stench the people in that dubious Institute of his make. Enoeff.' Barbara waved away any possible objections Meno might have with a vigorous gesture. He was standing beside Gudrun, trying to keep both bride and groom in sight while Barbara took out a clothes' brush and wiped the dandruff off his jacket. 'What d'you think of him? Isn't he a fantastic man? So attractive! And he's got a head on his shoulders, too, a doctor, a surgeon, he'll never starve and Ina won't want for anything.'

'As long as he's faithful.' Gudrun insisted on putting a damper on things. 'In Ina's place I'd have made him have his palm read. A colleague of mine does it, doesn't cost a lot.'

'Do you really believe in that?' Barbara's bracelets tinkled as she

let go of Meno and ran her fingers through her hair, one of Lajos
Wiener's experimental creations of impressive stability (Western
all-weather hairspray, one of Ulrich's barter enterprises he'd been pursuing surreptitiously and pretty successfully recently); her look swung
from one of Gudrun's eyes to the other, but Gudrun took her time
selecting a sausage kebab from her plate before answering, 'You can
believe in it – or in something else, it all comes down to the same thing.
At least it was a point that could have been taken into account so that
you wouldn't need to reproach yourself for having neglected it later
on. And so far my colleague has always been right.'

'Really? Well I never! And does she read palms in general or just
for weddings? Could I, for example, ask her how long I'm going to
live?'

'I imagine you could, though I think she has specialized in
fidelity.'

'Aha . . . And you say it doesn't cost a lot, Gudrun? People say that
dark-haired men with blue eyes are unfaithful. Robert, for example.
Don't you think it's terrible how quickly young people develop these
days? On the other hand there is a definite positive side to it. I always
thought Ina would bring home one of those long-haired types, but no,
she's my clever daughter, she's inherited my instinct. One day she
turned up at the door and said, "Mum, this is Thomas, we've made up
our mind." And I hadn't noticed a thing, not a thing! I must have been
ill, that's the only explanation.'

'Black-haired men with blue eyes are unfaithful? In an article on
Alain Delon in *Paris Match* I read at Wiener's it said he was very faithful. He and Romy Schneider –'

'That's just newspaper nonsense, Gudrun! They just want to keep
his female fans happy. Faithful? With his looks? I ask you. Anne says
Robert has a girlfriend already – but I can't see her, he hasn't brought
her. He must have a new one already. And how faithful is Richard . . .
True, he has blond hair, but his eyes are pretty blue. I mean, what does

he see in Anne, she's let herself go a bit recently, she should look after herself more. Richard's still in his prime, has a good job, has an air about him, the children are gradually moving away, that's when you become open to certain offers . . .' Barbara made an apologetic gesture to stop Meno from walking away. 'I know she's your sister and what I've just said might sound insulting, but that's not how it was meant. I think it's worse when no one says anything and then one day you're picking up the pieces – and everyone else is nodding, they'd all known about it, had seen it coming ages ago. People are saying all sorts of things about Richard; I had a long conversation with Thomas . . .'

'Saying what kind of thing?' Meno asked.

'You see, now you're curious, you've lost that disapproving look. They say this and that. So what, Dresden's a small town. And you know yourself what he admitted to us.'

'I think exposing those who peddle such rumours is the best way of putting a stop to them. I have to stand up for Richard.'

'That's not quite the way you were talking back then, Gudrun. You said State Security only approached a certain type of person . . . and that one shouldn't do anything to attract them. I remember it very well. Look, there comes the wedding cake. Isn't it a beauty? The idea of the amputated hand was Ina's, she thought it was somehow – surgical. They used red jelly for the blood. Or was it ketchup? Well, you'll soon find out.'

'And the ruler stands for education? Is it made from frosting? I have to say I don't think it's very nice the way you confront me with the things I've said – or am supposed to have said. There's something insidious about it, as if you were secretly noting down everything we say just so that, years later, you can accuse us of contradicting ourselves, make any development or change of opinion seem stupid. How would you react if, years later, I imitated your shriek in the church at every opportunity?'

'I'm sure you'd do it very well. It's your speciality.'

'Enoeff, Barbara, enoeff.' Gudrun got the tone exactly right and for a while Barbara didn't know what to make of it. Then, closing her eyes, she flapped her hand.

'They're a lovely couple, don't you think? He doesn't idolize her, that'd be quite wrong, he'd be disappointed and take refuge in booze, work or affairs. It's not that particularly pretty women, and that's what Ina is, have no faults. She is a bit of a spoilt princess, perhaps we weren't strict enough with her and once the child's arrived and he's spending the whole day at work, perhaps even working on his post-doctoral dissertation in the evenings as well, she'll look round and realize what a family means. They're planning to go to Berlin. She'll be the one who'll have to deal with the move as well.'

'I think the best thing is to book a few appointments with a good beautician right away. Giving birth and everything that follows, a little mucky pup getting on your nerves all hours of the day, isn't exactly good for your complexion. Ina's pretty, I give you that, but I think she's one of those who fade early . . . There's something dry about her skin. And she has a tendency to cellulite, as far as I can see, which indicates weak connective tissue that won't have regained its elasticity after birth. Not exactly what men want. For women with weak connective tissue in particular the first child can often be a disaster, they get fat like Russian women, and Ulrich was born in Moscow, as you know.'

'Look, the bridegroom's going to say something,' Meno said, in an attempt to change the subject.

Wernstein made a short speech, thanked the guests for coming, took Ina's hand and kissed it. Adeling brought in trays with Crimean champagne, Ulrich wiped his forehead with his handkerchief and tapped his glass with a spoon.

'A pleasant lad, doesn't think he's superior.' Barbara didn't give Gudrun, who was craning her neck, the chance to hear any of Ulrich's speech. 'And such a tragedy! Has no relatives at all left. His whole

family were from the uranium mines. Thank God I didn't need to ask
him whether . . . enoeff. Snorkel and I had set an afternoon for it, it
should have been his business, really, between two men, but he couldn't
bring himself to, couldn't sleep the whole night for thinking about how
he should go about it . . . God, the ways of putting it. The next day
Ina came with the positive test from the gynaecologist.'

'Tell me, Barbara, there was something I was going to ask – why
kvass of all things? Or was that what Ulrich wanted? Does he sometimes dream in Russian? Or do you, Meno?'

'Meno won't know that. There's no one beside him in bed to tell
him the next morning. Pity, really. Why don't you get married again?
Hanna just wasn't the right woman for you, I could have told you that
from the very beginning. She didn't even know how to prepare a boiling fowl. If you ask me' – Meno didn't ask but still listened with
amusement to Barbara – 'you need a woman who'll tell you what's
what. A woman who knows something about practical matters. I mean,
you don't even have a car. Can you even drive? But where on earth
are you going to find one with the pittance you bring home. Snorkel
said they could take you on in the firm right away, they're looking
for – what did he say? – a coordinator for the combine. You'd get at
least twice as much. – The kvass was my idea, Gudrun. I like a tot of
it myself from time to time and it would have been something different
for a wedding. We just started it too late, Snorkel said the heaters would
make up for that . . . and I did insulate the demijohns with coconut
fibre. – Enoeff, now it's the toasts: to the bride and groom.'

Christian was standing at the window of the summerhouse listening
to the sounds coming from below and out of the house, a drizzle of
voices, bursts of laughter, music from the gardens on the other side of
the park. The rain had freshened the colours and restless waves of the
still-new green of the beeches and maples mingled with the blossom
of almond trees and rhododendrons at the upper edge of the steep

park. Soft, loud; wedges of melancholy in between. He wanted to be alone. If he closed his eyes he could see images of the barracks in Grün, hear the tread of boots in the endless corridors, listen to the slow, mournful dance of the polisher's barbels that, at the turn just before they hit the walls, made a characteristic noise: the bearings at the end of the rods clicked against the cross-guides of the polishing brushes, pulling them back; again and again he was astonished at this crudely controlled elegance, similarly at the regularity with which the arched ceiling of the corridors reappeared in the evening, in the light of unshaded bulbs, strip by strip in the wooden floor, after all the boots that had trampled on it during the day. Down below someone must have told a joke, he heard Adeling's bleating laugh, Alois Lange said in a clear voice, the Danish sauce was very good. Noack's white hair was sucked into a cloud of plum blossom as he bent over the buffet to insert his fork into the glittering knitwork of all the other forks, the faces over them had hungry expressions, the eyes commanding the hands to perform swift, begrudging thrusts. Suddenly all these things had nothing to do with him; the house, the people: everything seemed alien to him. The civilian clothes he was wearing seemed something forbidden, something he wasn't entitled to – it would never have occurred to him to judge others according to whether they were worthy to wear civilian clothes; yet earlier on, when he had been standing next to Herr Honich, watching the guests toasting the bride and groom, he'd caught himself automatically assessing each one according to whether he or she was worthy of being there, of laughing, eating, enjoying themselves with the others and wearing clothes the choice of which was entirely dependent on them (and on what the stores had in stock), they didn't have to account for them to anyone. If his mother approached, he slipped away. Ezzo and Robert, Niklas and Ulrich, were talking about football, Wembley, the final at the Wankdorf Stadium; Ulrich explained a Fritz Walter goal, the famous Leipzig shot, the overhead backheel; it seemed trivial to Christian, he couldn't

627

understand why Ulrich tried to copy it and shot the previous year's Golden Delicious past Herr Adeling into the shed (Ulrich supported himself on his hands and slipped down, face first, into a bed of rhubarb); Christian walked away sadly. Children were playing by the tin bath, supervised by Babett Honich; the Stahls were sitting at the iron table and waved him over, but he shook his head. Now he was here, in the conservatory, touching the plants as if they might disappear, looking for Chakamankabudibaba in his hiding place in the sago palm, bending down, placing his hand on the chessboard floor, which was cool. Motes of dust in the light, the shadows of leaves like grey fish swimming through it, the slow movement of currents, that calmed, pleased him. Before anyone could come, he went into the park.

One of those Ulrich things, Meno thought as his brother wiped his face with a handkerchief dipped in eau de Cologne and spread his arms wide, beaming with delight: shot on target, he would later say, holding Malivor Marroquin's photo; the Chilean had been standing around patiently with his finger on the shutter release of a Praktika and had caught both the flying Golden Delicious and Ulrich's landing; his plate camera was keeping an eye on Meno's balcony. Another thing was that Ulrich was thinking about sending his dentist a card on New Year's Eve. 'No one wishes their dentist a Happy New Year. But then no one knows how much he suffers. I always say, give a flower seller flowers and a dentist a smile for New Year. Why not? Even if it's one of his own. And even if he's called Frau Doktor Knabe.' When, as now, he had sat down at the head of a table laden with good food where there was a big enough audience, he liked to impart, in tones of utter conviction, knowledge that was at best patchy and would not have withstood serious examination; but although doubt would appear on some of the faces, Ulrich's self-assured body language, his expression of certainty that suggested that there was more to what he was saying, was convincing enough to keep any scepticism unexpressed. People withdrew into themselves, were no longer quite sure, were afraid of making fools of themselves – how could one dare to cast doubt on an authority such as the eldest of the Rohdes, the Technical Director of one of the most important firms in Dresden (making typewriters, low-power engines and springs, the latter everything from mattress springs to coach springs for railway carriages), a 'Hero of Work' (Ulrich had spent part of the 10,000 marks that went with it on their trip to Cuba) with intimate knowledge of the ups and downs (and, above all, the to-ings and fro-ings) of the planned economy; they didn't dare and held their tongues, but checked up when they got home, smirked or slapped their thigh, annoyed with themselves and determined to expose Ulrich the next time. Gudrun, however, did not remain silent. 'That's interesting, Uli. You sound very convincing, you could easily take the part of a director in a play about, let's say, a socialist high-speed bricklayer. It's almost a pity that your rock-solid certainties are mistaken. For example, the Garrison Church in Dresden is called just that, the Garrison Church and not the Garrison's Church, even though to be correct it ought to be called that. Otherwise it would be a church in the form of a garrison, wouldn't it? But good for you, Uli, you've got a natural gift for it, we have to grant you that, and you'll go far, perhaps even as far as a high-speed bricklayer.'

At that Ulrich would pause for thought, check the effect her intervention had had on his audience, make some remark about the notorious unworldliness of workers in the cultural sphere, then just carry on. As well as that there was Uncle Shura. Neither Anne nor Meno had ever seen him, Kurt would just shrug his shoulders when asked about this dubious uncle; Ulrich insisted he had known him since childhood and even now (he was a very influential man in Moscow, he said, but one who worked behind the scenes) 'did business with him'. It was from this Uncle Shura that Ulrich claimed to have all sorts of recipes that he described as 'truly authentic' and as coming to us 'from the depths of the Russian people', for example instructions on how to make pickled cucumbers that Uncle Shura had from his babushka, who had been given them by the witch Baba Yaga herself. His babushka had given Uncle Shura the recipe on her deathbed, as she breathed her last, her voice scarcely audible, after she'd kissed the icon and crossed herself; and Uncle Shura had then passed it on to him, his friend from his earliest years, under the seal of strictest secrecy and to promote friendship among the nations (if not on his deathbed). Similarly a recipe for kvass and the 'ultimate method' of repairing bicycle tyres. The vodka too, under the influence of which Helmut Hoppe was gradually becoming merry, had its source in the unfathomable depths of Russia, with which Uncle Shura was in mysterious intuitive contact.

'Come on, Uli boy, tell us.'

'It would be a sin, if I were to reveal it to you. It comes from Grandmother's deathbed, that's an obligation you accept, you don't give it away.'

'I can unnerstand that. But we're your relatives, yer own flesh an' blood! You refuse to share it with us, you wanna keep it all for yersel', shame on you, my friend, shame on you. I'd never have thought it of you, no I wouldn't.'

'All right, then, since it's you. I don't want people saying I was stingy at my daughter's wedding.'

'Nah, you've never been a penny-pincher, have to give you that,' Helmut Hoppe said, his Saxon accent becoming thicker and thicker. 'How long did it take to put all this stuff together, eh? An' what did y'use t' grease their palms, the bastards? I s'pose a few mattress springs must've changed hands. But you're tryin' to wriggle out of it, Uli boy, you're changin' the subject again. I don't think the old geezer would've liked that, him bein' a friend of all the nations, like. Now out with it, the recipe f' this voddy. By the way, chief' – Helmut Hoppe turned to Herr Honich – 'your suckin' pig's great, I c'd gorge myself on it, I really could.'

'Right then. You take spirit, ninety-six proof, to which you add distilled water to the desired amount. Add one sugar cube and three drops of pure glycerine. Seal the bottle.'

'Thass all?'

'Then some blackberry leaves picked in the spring.'

'Why picked in the spring?'

'That's when they're full of juice, I assume. You put them in a little bottle with pure alcohol. Close the bottle and leave it in the warm sun on the windowsill for ten days.'

'An' what if it rains for ten days? Y'll be left wi' no'hing but vinegar.'

'You put three drops of that extract in the big bottle.'

'Jus' three drops? Sounds a bit acupuncturic, 'f y'ask me. An' then?'

'The vodka's ready.'

'Ready?'

'Ready.'

'Don' b'leeve it.'

'It's true.'

'Reelly ready?'

'Really.'

Helmut Hoppe regarded his glass. 'Well yeh, now y'say so, the taste of a few blackcurrants does come through. Did y'hear Weizsäcker's speech?'

'No.'

'I did.'

'And?'

'Hm. More'n three drops o' blackcurrant in there. Great guy, a real Fed'ral Prezeden' he is. Looks impressive, no' like the bigwigs here. I wonder what's goin' t' happen in the Soviet Union now. They'll have t' keep off the blackcurrants now, so t' speak. Y'r uncle Shoe-ra 'll be drinkin' water 'stead o' vodker. Hey, look, the dancin's startin'.'

*

Richard, sitting beside Niklas at a table at the far end, only heard snatches of what people at the top were saying. He observed Josta, who, to his relief, was sitting a long way away from Anne, with Wernstein's friends at a table under the blossoming pear trees. Lucie didn't look round at him. The man cut up her food for her, wiped her mouth, raised his forefinger two or three times, at which she nodded and lowered her head. Richard would have most liked to get up and knock the guy flat, it took a great deal of self-control to appear uninvolved, to sip his wine and feign interest in what Niklas had to say about the re-election of Ronald Reagan, Michel Platini's goals at the European Championships, the sudden disappearance of touch-up spray for cars from the stores (there'd been a film called *Beat Street*, following which trains had been sprayed with graffiti). Anne threw him a glance now and then, which made him even more annoyed, and when Herr Scholze and Alois Lange appeared, telling jokes, he excused himself and got up. As Richard was heading for the iron table, someone pulled him into the bushes. It was Daniel.

'Awkward situation, isn't it?' The boy grinned. He'd shot up, at fourteen he was almost as tall as Christian. 'How about a little deal?'

'What kind of deal?'

'Well, I won't go up, tap my glass with a spoon and tell things about you and my mother – and you shell out a hundred marks for that.'

Richard said nothing.

'I'm serious,' the boy said with a smile. 'I really feel like going up to your wife and whispering things to her.'

'You do, do you?' Richard looked round.

'Don't worry, there's no one here. Apart from a damn tomcat perhaps. Your wife would be delighted.'

'She already suspects something,' Richard replied, weary and horrified.

'But you're not sure. Are you willing to take the chance? It'd be great to drop a bomb like that in the middle of a wedding.'

'So Lucie's got a louse of a brother.'

'Hey, don't you dare touch me! Come on, let's get this over with before someone comes. I get a hundred marks or –'

Richard looked in his wallet. 'I've only got a fifty with me.'

Daniel looked surprised, seemed to become uneasy, then he noticed Richard's wristwatch. 'Then give me that.'

'No.'

'Hand it over.'

'No. It's a family heirloom, my oldest son's going to get it.'

'Lange and Sons,' Daniel read, tilting his head to the side. 'Now I'm going to have it, otherwise in two minutes you're a dead man, I promise.'

Richard stared at Daniel. 'Can't we discuss this?'

'Not interested.'

'We could meet some time.'

'Give me the watch.'

'OK, my friend. But what do I tell my wife when she asks me where it is? She saw me putting it on.'

'I don't care. Think something up. Tell her it was stolen.'

'Which would be more or less the case.'

'In the Sachsenbad, for example. When you went swimming one Thursday.'

'And I put it on today, before her very eyes? Come on.'

'Then it was stolen here. Perhaps by the bridegroom before he sailed off to Cuba.'

'Then I'd go straight over to her and we'd turn everything upside down. She'd probably also suspect you've got it. She was watching you before, in the church. And do you really think I wouldn't notice if someone stole the watch off my wrist?'

'Then you can bring it to the Sachsenbad for me next Thursday, then you could say it was stolen there.'

'In that case that's the end of your blackmail here. And if your attempted blackmail comes up, I might have to get divorced – but you'll end up in the juvenile court.'

Daniel hesitated, broke off a twig, twisted it into little pieces. Richard's anger had gone, now he felt sorry for the lad. 'Why do you need the money?'

'I did something stupid,' Daniel said after a while.

'Does Josta know about it?'

'No. Nor her new guy either.'

Richard observed the boy. There was something funny about a blackmail attempt from someone whose voice was breaking. Suddenly Daniel took a step towards him and threw his arms round him.

'There I am, walkin' in Saxon Swizz'land, and su'nly I'm under this huge rock, a real whopper. An' I says to myself, if that comes down you won't be able to catch it all at once. Have a drink, Meno, then we'll go an' dance.' Helmut Hoppe swayed slightly when he stood up. He went to fetch a bottle, checked the glasses on the table, as if he were trying to work out the course of an obstacle race, looked at the label, then the metal spout in the neck of the bottle, pulled it to one side, like a flag being kept away from enemy hands, and sent clear, curving jets of schnapps spouting over glasses, trousers and shoulders.

'I've been reading your books,' Meno said to Ulrich, who raised an ironic, wait-and-see eyebrow as he licked a few splashes he'd wiped off his suit, 'and, as I see it, in the final analysis everything's a question of energy. Brown coal's our primary source of energy. But you have to be able to get at it. If I've understood the tables in the paper correctly, it costs more to clear away a unit of overburden than the same unit of brown coal brings in?'

'Economics –' Ulrich started to reply, but Honich broke in. 'Where'd you read that?'

'In a memorandum from the Economic Secretariat of the Central Committee.'

'An internal document,' Ulrich said. 'It mustn't go any farther.'

'But they'll have reserves of which we here know nothing.' Honich nodded earnestly. 'Some things are difficult to understand, but the comrades on the Central Committee are no fools and so far we've overcome all difficulties. The unity of economic and social policy –'

'– costs more than we can afford,' Ulrich said.

'Surely you don't mean that seriously?'

'I do, and it's no secret, ask in your organization. Ask the men with whom you do your exercises. Only recently I was at a meeting of the Planning Commission and people were speaking just as openly.'

'Aha, private tuition again, is it?' Gerhart Stahl asked, seeing their looks of dismay, also fear, as he walked past. 'Just be careful what you say, the sky isn't blue, even if that's the way you see it, but red, and Moscow's a long way away.'

'Please refrain from these constant hostile remarks, Herr Stahl. I warn you, there'll come a time when you suffer the consequences.' Pedro Honich turned back to Ulrich Rohde and Helmut Hoppe. 'You're right, there are shortcomings. I'm not blind, even if Herr Stahl thinks I am. But just think what we're aiming for, what our country has achieved so far, what ruins had to be cleared away, and what it could achieve if our people . . . These childhood diseases could be eradicated, we could work together on building a future where truly socialist life could blossom –'

'D'you know what an economy is?' Helmut Hoppe downed a schnapps. 'I need a dustpan – an' I can choose one from half a dozen, even if it looks like my wife. And d'you know what a planned economy is? When there's not even any dust.'

'Excuse me, but it's always the same old story. Are things really that bad for you? If I look at the spread set out here, the presents for the couple, and compare it with what we used to have – What are you complaining about?'

'OK then, y're right there. That's true. When I was young I

sometimes didn't have a car; an' my Traudel an' me couldn't go sailin' off to Cuba either, all we knew about Cuba was the Cuba crisis.'

'I'm pinning my hopes on Gorbachev,' Pedro Honich said. 'I think he's a good man.'

'Openness, glasnost. If he's for openness, great, but what's being opennessed? That brown coal makes a mucky mess? You know that anyway, you don't need to read about it in the paper as well. And perestroika an' perfume both begin with a P, as my Traudel says.'

'If all members of the working class were to talk like you . . .'

'Oh, knock it off. I come from a firm that's an existent reality. And the way things go there's as follows: people go to work and after work there's nothin' left in the shops. So they do their shoppin' during work hours. And I'm the foreman, am I to forbid them from doing that? 's what I do masel'. We make things that aren't there, an' if there is something there, we make a queue. An' even the Comrade Chairman of the State Council said there's a lot more c'd be got out of our enterprises.'

'That's why we have the problems we have,' Pedro Honich replied. Malivor Marroquin slipped past, taking photos. Hoppe put his schnapps glass calmly down on the table. 'I've been awarded the "Activist of Socialist Work" medal several times,' he said, slowly and emphatically, his strong dialect disappearing, 'and as for Uli, he's even got the "Hero of Work". Are you trying to tell me what things are like in my firm?'

'Over here,' Kurt Rohde shouted from the balcony. 'The king of the dance floor gets a kiss from the bride, the queen one from the bridegroom.'

Josta and her husband left, Richard went into the summerhouse. In one corner Robert was kissing one of Ina's fellow students. Richard was taken aback for a moment, then said, 'Don't mind me, I'll be gone in a minute.' He checked the foot pump for the air beds. When he looked up he saw that the girl's blouse was undone. 'Is this something serious between you? I mean, I'm going to have to change the name-plate on our apartment door anyway. – Are you on the pill?'

'Are you always that direct?' The girl, flabbergasted, was smoothing her hair. Robert put his hand in his pocket and held up a packet of Mondo condoms.'

'Hm, I didn't want a practical demonstration,' Richard muttered. 'Just be careful, sometimes the things burst.'

A yellow leather glove atop a fencepost, beside it a note wrapped in cling-film: 'I lost the other one here. Reward for the finder: this left glove', a pair of scissors on a garage window ledge, the rusty nautilus at Philalethes' View. Christian looked up at the sky, which was turning a darker blue from the south. A few boys were preparing to play football and were arguing about names: 'I'm Pelé.' – 'Rubbish, you're Zoff and you're in goal.' – 'But I'm Beckenbauer.' – 'OK, then I'm Rummenigge.' Some men had lugged buckets of water out to wash their cars and were discussing the look of the sky, arms akimbo. Others were standing in their slippers by the street letter boxes nodding, waving away remarks, tapping the newspaper they'd brought with the back of their hand. The elms along Mondleite drew in their green, then released it, like old ladies letting out their breath after the tensest moments of a tragic opera; the wind died down, freshened again, sending blossom and winter ash swirling up in fine sashes – undecided, like a child playing with sand and getting bored. The first raindrops spattered the brightness of the street with blots of slate-grey. Christian went back to the House with a Thousand Eyes, while the sky looked like a swimming pool of ink edged with flailing treetops; in the gardens tables were hurriedly cleared away or covered with plastic sheets, portable radios and children brought under cover. A little dog came running down a garden path yapping angrily, whirling round at the gate on its tiny paws. How mysterious it all was.

The dance; without interrupting a single number, the band from the Roeckler School of Dancing retired, instrument by instrument, to the shelter of the tarpaulin under the canopy of oak leaves: first the cello, then the violin; last of all the grand piano, together with the pianist on his chair, was rolled under the trees. Then the rain fell so heavily that the paper streamers over the sweet briars tore and there was a moment of uncertainty. But Herr Adeling stayed standing in the doorway, ramrod straight in his tails and white shirt, which was gradually becoming transparent, in his left hand a tray with champagne glasses, over his right a napkin hanging down like a dead stoat. Gudrun held Niklas tighter; Herr Honich, the best dancer, stuck it out with Traudel Hoppe; Barbara and Ulrich threw off their shoes, for puddles were already forming. 'Kalimba de luna', 'Über sieben Brücken musst du geh'n', 'Goodbye, Ruby Tuesday'. Meno watched the rain gradually taking over from the champagne in the glasses until the contents were like clear water. To whoops and cheers Gudrun Tietze and Pedro Honich were crowned the best dancers. But they went unkissed: Ina and Thomas Wernstein had gone.

44

Be like the sundial

From now on proving yourself as a socialist in the National People's Army, always thinking and acting in the spirit of the working class, means subordinating yourself to the rules of military life.

What It Means to be a Soldier

'Yes?' came the surly grunt from the tank commanders' room when Christian knocked.

'Permission to come in, Comrade Sergeant.'

'Oh, look, our earhole's come back from leave.' Sergeant Johannes Ruden, senior soldier in the barrack room, was a 24-year-old man with grey hair. 'Before he has to, even. He gets leave, the lucky bastard, and then he's stupid and doesn't stay out until the very last minute. Get this into your thick head: a dogface don't give the army nothin'. Don't just stand there like an idiot, put the wood in the hole. What d'you think, Rogi?' Corporal Steffen Rogalla, like Ruden in the sixth half-year of service and therefore a discharge candidate, put his thumbs under the braces he was wearing over a civilian T-shirt and thought while Christian put his bag on his bed and went to his locker to change his walking-out uniform for fatigues.

'First of all hand over that bag.' Rogalla let his braces snap back. 'Let's see what the earhole's brought from home.'

'Permission to speak, Comrade Sergeant.' Christian, who had learnt to get changed in no time at all at the cadet training school, stood to attention before Ruden, who, with a wave of the hand, graciously granted permission. 'My leave was sanctioned by Comrade Staff Sergeant Emmerich.'

'In exchange for a Polski Fiat exhaust manifold, yes, we know. And here it is.' Rogalla held it up then continued to rummage round in the bag he'd put on the table. 'An earhole doesn't get leave for that. You could've written a letter and had the thing sent. Instead you get leave and go home to Mum while your elders and betters have to sweat away for you.'

'Took over your section, junior,' squawked Thilo Ebert, a lance corporal in his third half-year, playing with the locknut on his key ring. It was Ruden who allocated nicknames to crew members in their first two half-years. Since he wanted to study classical languages, they were Greek and Latin; Thilo he'd dubbed Musca, the fly, since only someone with the brain of a fly would think of swigging anti-freeze. 'That is, arsehole, if you're going off on leave you don't do it secretly, on the quiet, like you did, only after we've given you permission to dismiss.'

'Oh, boy,' Rogalla whispered, delighted, 'was that Musca wafflin' on about junior? Hey! Apples! And cake!'

'You've only been here for fourteen days, earhole, and for twelve of those you've had to manage without us, which I'm sure you thought was a great shame.' When he laughed Ruden exposed a broken front tooth. 'Because we were off on those shitty manoeuvres. We were workin' our arses off while you were stuffin' yourself. You were sharp enough to slip away, of course. You knew well enough we wouldn't have let you go.'

'God, I can't stand smart-arses,' said Corporal Jens Karge, known as Wanda, fourth half-year of service. 'You can take those fatigues off again, Lehmann.'

'Hoffmann,' Christian ventured to correct him.

'Lehmann, I said. Black overalls on. You're to go with this ignoramus – what's this useless sod called?'

'Irrgang,' Rogalla, who had tipped the whole contents of Christian's bag out on the table, told him. 'But this Burre's even worse. He really has a screw loose.' He took a piece of paper out of his trouser pocket. 'Just listen.' He struck a pose and began to declaim in orotund tones. '"WERE IT NOT –"'

'Eh? Werrit?' Ebert put his hand to his ear.

'"Were – it – not." And all in capital letters. It's poetry, you philistine. "WERE IT NOT FOR LOVE, THERE WOULD NOT BE / ANY VENEREAL DISEASES / WERE IT NOT FOR LOVE WE WOULD HAVE / HARDLY ANYTHING TO SAY / WERE IT NOT FOR LOVE / I WOULD NOT BE / AND THAT WOULD BE / A FUCKING NUISANCE."'

Ruden went to the door. 'Popov!'

'Wassit?' came a weary voice from the driving instructors' room.

'Burre's been at the grass again. Special treatment.'

'Again?' shouted Corporal Helge Poppenhaus, fifth half-year and therefore number two.

'Now to you.' Ruden took a drink from the brandy bottle they called a 'tube', which was on Rogalla's place at the table. 'We have to check whether you're smuggling booze.' He took a knife and began to cut up the apples. 'There are the most incredible hiding places. I knew a guy who'd discovered that exactly sixteen tubes would fit in a tank barrel. And in such a way that they didn't get broken when it was driven. He was a clever lad and that set him up for the rest of his term.'

'I knew a guy, was called Johannes Ruden, and he let helium balloons with returnable bottles hanging from them float up to the ceiling,' said Rogalla. Ruden tapped Christian on the forehead. 'You say you want to study medicine. The titless nurses at the med centre are drunk all the time. They smuggle in booze in those horse syringes before they ram them in our arses with anti-tetanus.' He handed round the apples, which were eaten with relish.

'Well he didn't inoculate mine,' Lance Corporal Ebert moaned. 'Dry as my granny's tit. A real dimwit he is.' He dropped the core, giving Christian a disappointed look. 'We're your comrades, we share everything. You could've thought of us. In your place I'd 've baked a cake that was at least fifty per cent.'

'Guys like you'll drink tank juice anyway.' The next moment Ruden hit out, Christian slumped down, couldn't breathe for a moment, then there was excruciating pain in his liver, the room started to turn golden. A kick from a boot brought him back to consciousness. 'Pick up the cores!' Ruden pulled Christian up and hit him on the ear with the flat of his fist. It was like an explosion, an eruption of red. 'What's that you said? I can't understand a word.'

'Yes . . . Comrade Sergeant.'

'I can't hear anything.' Again Ruden's fist hit his ear. Christian, staggering, tried to resist but Ruden was an ox of a man, the muscles stood out like cords on his forearm.

'Yes . . .' Christian threw up his arms to ward off the blow. Rogalla and Karge put on whiny voices, 'Please don't hit me, Daddy.'

'We can't hear anything! Bucket practice!' Ebert bawled. Rogalla and Karge grabbed Christian and dragged him into the toilets. A few soldiers, who were smoking by the company ashtray, watched. The duty NCO was writing, the duty NCO's assistant was demonstrating polishing the corridor floor to a group of rookies who were doing their basic training there. Ruden lifted a lavatory lid and pushed Christian's head down.

'Yes, Comrade Sergeant!' Christian shouted as loud as he could. Karge and Ebert were leaning against the wall laughing. Rogalla pulled the chain.

45
The paper republic

'We'll get round to you, Fräulein Schevola, never fear. As you are trying to interrupt me again, I would like to point out that general courtesy, not only among colleagues, demands that we listen to each other and allow everyone to finish. I will continue with my report. – I call it *The Screw*. Now, many of our colleagues did not grow up with a pencil in their hand, even less a silver spoon in their mouth, but holding a mains tester, a mason's trowel, a wrench. Now I'm sure you'll agree with me when I say that to be "in work" doesn't just mean you are in a works but also that you are working on something. The writers of our country are in work; they are laying foundations, raising structures with the mind and only some of them, who do not know – or have forgotten – what axle-grease smells like, who do not know what the honest handshake of the team leader or the heat from the run-off of a blast furnace feels like, some colleagues, that is – and there are only very few of them – seem to be no longer aware what this our country is, what it stands for and who the people are who are building it up. We writers are respected in this our country. We are not at the mercy of the lying capitalist press that poured out its venom over my last novel, *The Silent Front* – claiming I was a dubious character who took liberties with the reality of our times and merely spread propaganda, who put clichés in the mouths of allegedly cardboard comrades, if not one of the tribe of the bores, as Herr Wiktor Hart put it . . . Our reviewers are not paid puppets of Springer and Co., our reviewers are members of the working class, for whom we write, to whom we owe the privilege of following the trials and tribulations of our times in our writing . . . The screw, then, that inconspicuous but interesting component of construction without which we would not be able to meet in this fine setting, without which this lectern, with the manuscript of my talk in the middle, would not be a lectern but just a pile of planks; the screw that holds together the chairs on which a few of our colleagues are tilting back precariously, it is the screw, small but beautiful, that I want to look at more closely . . . it is also there in the postbox, where letters are posted, love letters, dead letters, letters of condolence, letters to the editors of the Western press that concern us, but did not come to us beforehand. Letters from four colleagues whose literary achievements, though varying, have always been recognized by us, who could have no complaints as far as the publication of their books is concerned, for which ways of producing second editions were always found, so that the idea of censorship, that keeps popping up in letters from colleagues, became an all-too-frequently touted commonplace that even the expressive pen of our esteemed colleague David Groth could not render less ill-fitting . . . He hides behind generalized accusations, distorts what I say – your turn will come, Herr Groth – and with the publication of his letter places himself outside the laws of our state. He infringes the statutes of the Association to which he belongs and omits to mention the advantages he enjoys from it in his letter that was printed by the vociferously anti-socialist Springer Press . . . Not a word about the journeys for which he was granted permission, but loud protests at the cancellation of a journey by a colleague that would have resulted in a reading in the Bavarian parliament, where the worst attacks against us come from . . . You are trying to give me a lesson in morality, Herr Groth, while you publish your novel *Trotsky*, the literary quality of which can at best be described as dubious, in which you twist facts from the history of our Soviet friends in the worst possible way and which authors of undoubted literary quality such as my friend Eschschloraque and our colleague Altberg have described in letters to me as muckraking trash, in the West, circumventing the laws of the land! Yes, circumventing the laws of the land – you know the address of our copyright office as well as we, the members of the Association committee and all our other colleagues here present do. And it is not at all scandalous – you should choose your words more carefully – if I object to your insinuation that our colleagues Rieber and Blavatny have only been "dragged" here to face this "tribunal", as you choose to call our annual general meeting, because they are communists who have not abandoned rational thought . . . In a letter to me – to return to the postbox – Blavatny called a lady colleague a "blood-and-soil bardess" because grass and soil appear in one of her poems. Is it your opinion that I may not describe that as the shameful nonsense, as the slanderous calumny it is? Where are these standards, Herr Groth, that you demand of us? Censorship? Oh dear. Anyone who calls the state planning and direction of publishing censorship should not let the words "cultural policy", which he is supposedly so concerned about, pass his lips. The truth is that he rejects the very idea. Critical voices among our writers are being silenced? I look round and see so many familiar faces, not one of which does not belong to a critical voice. But there are critical voices that want to work effectively in our country and for our society, and do not feel, at every trifle, that they have to pass on a "subversive piece" – or whatever it's called – to some has-been Western correspondent, because otherwise they wouldn't be noticed . . .

Herr Blavatny, who came to us from Nuremberg, got nowhere at home, then nowhere here, because you don't get anywhere in a publishing house with your Party membership card but with a manuscript that is worth something. Rejected by the experienced editors of Hermes-Verlag, he immediately thought up some story of repression and state despotism, used it to dress up his feeble product and offered it for sale on the other side, where they of course also recognized its inferior quality but were, as ever, interested in news from the supposed darkness over here. A screw can be large or small and, as I remember from my apprenticeship, the very small ones are called grubs. We on the committee are not the kind of people to hurl abuse. We do not shy away from debate or openness. Our Soviet comrades show us the way and, although we do not have to follow them in everything, for now and then conditions are different, now and then a Moscow nut doesn't fit one of our screws, we are united in matters of principle. Hölderlin says, "To be gentle at the right time, that is good, to be gentle at the wrong time, that is ugly, for it is cowardly.' And in a further letter, in which he thanked me for bringing to his attention, in a review in *Neues Deutschland*, the dangers threatening his undoubted talent, Herr Rieber wrote that he felt strengthened by my honest remarks for, as a solitary desk worker, who did not always sense the homely presence of the Association, one was all too often desperately groping in the dark . . . And you, my esteemed colleague, write in another place that without the West writers here would find no response? There I must charge you with untruth. In this our country sensibly expressed questions receive sensibly expressed answers, that is in the nature of our society. It is also in the nature of our society to handle screws properly, for it is the society of the working class that is familiar with tools and the means of production. Here, in contrast to other social systems, they are turned to fasten things together, but not warped or stripped. We are building according to our plans.'

'We thank you for your firm, clear exposition, Comrade Mellis. I

645

would also like once more to extend a particularly warm welcome to our guests: our Minister for Books, Comrade Samtleben, and Comrade Winter from the Cultural Section of the Central Committee of the Socialist Unity Party. But before I invite Comrade Schade to speak in his function as First Secretary of the Regional Association, perhaps I may be permitted a few words. The class war is intensifying. There are voices making themselves heard in Federal Germany saying: the class war is a thing of the past and we belong in a museum. In a museum, comrades! And colleagues. But it is precisely these pernicious tirades that prove that it is not at all wrong to talk of class warfare. The achievements of our Republic are under attack, the very existence of our Republic called into question. But what do these attacks on us mean? I did an apprenticeship with a forester and one thing I learnt was that when a tree is dying, it puts all its remaining strength into producing its fruit, its seed. And what we have here is a social system that is going to seed, and the things that are thrown at us are the blossoming fears of the last stage of imperialism, the fruits of anger at being part of a social system in terminal decline, the seeds of death. They dig and dig and are not satisfied until they have found some defect. And this poison keeps seeping through the gaps of our tolerance, our friendliness! Certain people and forces give the impression that their so-called concern for the development of our Republic is in truth nothing other than the untiring and, as such, actually pathological search for defects and things that call that development into question. You don't need to shake your head, Herr Eschschloraque, and you, Fräulein Schevola, should stay in the hall so that when it's your turn you will not twist our words. Our policies as a whole, and thus our cultural policy as well, have stood the test of time. The cultural policy in this country is not subject to fluctuations, to temporary changes; we are not riders of the boom-or-bust wave who spread their lies according to the law of the capitalist jungle. There are certain people who are always talking about truth. Pointing accusing fingers at us. But what is the truth we are talking about? About the large number of copies of the books of our colleague, Herr Groth, that are published thanks to our tireless commitment – commitment not only to his well-being but to the well-being of all members of our Association? And that both here and on the other side? Is he not allowed out of the country? Last year you, Herr Rieber, applied for six journeys to non-socialist countries – were any of them turned down? I am saying that because there were certainly serious misgivings about allowing you to travel. Your appearances over there were dominated by clichés and feelings of resentment; you kept repeating the old story of the repression of art and artists over here. And you were so repressed as to be able to do that with our hard currency, armed with a visa that is popularly known among writers as a "flying suitcase" . . . Is that not hypocrisy? But to put it in a nutshell: all our decisions, all assessments of political events should be based on one fundamental question: who against whom? Bertolt Brecht, "The Song of the Class Enemy", the last verse, yes, let us stand, comrades, improvisations are not on the agenda but they refresh us; I'm sure most of us can join in Brecht's words: "However much your painter paints / The gap will open anew / One must yield while one remains / And it's either me or you / Whatever else I may learn / This simple lesson will be / Never will I share anything / With the cause of the class enemy / The word has not been found / That can ever unite us two: / The rain falls down on the ground / And my class enemy is you." Now Paul Schade has the floor.'

'That was clear, Comrade Bojahr! You almost took the wind out of my sails a little. But only a little. Ladies and gentlemen, colleagues. I spent this morning drying out the manuscript of my latest long poem, "Buchenwald", sheet by sheet with the hairdryer. The heavy showers yesterday meant I had a rude awakening. The rain had come in through the window with the floral pattern in my study, made its way tortuously but unerringly to my poems and dripped on them. As I set about clearing things up I was immediately struck by the uncanny symbolic meaning of the event: on the one hand there was my window with the flowers – my political illusions that could not withstand the storms of socialism as an existent reality; on the other my poems – my own past and that of many comrades. I had written them in Barock iron-gall ink, for I didn't want scholars two hundred years hence to be irritated at my faded manuscripts and was, as I read the soaked lines, more deeply moved than usual. How could the mishap have occurred? I established that the rain, instead of coming as usual from the west had, exceptionally, assailed my poet's cell directly from the east. What a mess! What did the rain think it was doing to my manuscript? Did Moscow have a hand in it? West German television, that I am parodying so perfectly here, would certainly have asked how the poet, Paul Schade, could show such a lack of character and still not curse the rain. I say: in the interest of the flowers in the garden. In the interest of the rhubarb and cabbage beds. Of my wife's beds with pansies. In the interest of my outdoor cucumbers and tomatoes. Joking aside, colleagues, I didn't choose this introduction to my topic by chance for, truly, I feel more like crying than laughing. As if we hadn't experienced that several times already. As if the methods of our internal and external enemies were new. As if we didn't know how we have to counter these methods. You know me, I was never in favour of a few half-hearted words of encouragement for dangerous animals. "Buchenwald" is the name of my poem. We who were there know what fascism means and we know that it is the siren tones of monopoly capitalism that keep making the eternal snake of Nazism raise its venomous head. We who survived fascism and the concentration camps swore an unbreakable oath with the comrades of the Red Army of liberation never again to allow such a crime. But the womb out of which it crept is still fertile. That is my clear standpoint, the standpoint of a communist who has dedicated his whole life to the fight against revanchism, revisionism and the manifold endeavours of the aggressor to destroy us – armed with a weapon that spits out cartridge shells and with a weapon that planes out pencil shavings. Oh, I understand very well what the aim is of some of those present even if they have attentive and apparently friendly expressions. They want us to take a decision that fits in with the cliché people have of us; to do something today that we are forced to do but that for certain people in the Western media will only confirm the things they impute to us anyway. Should we really make it so easy for these individuals? On the other hand, should we make it easy for ourselves by leaving things as they are? Sometimes we must have the courage to do what is expected of us. Sometimes we must have the strength to be predictable. For that reason I propose that, after our discussion, our meeting agree to the following resolution –'

'How is it that the resolution comes before the discussion, Herr Schade?'

'That is only a draft resolution, Herr Blavatny. The resolution is: "The annual general meeting of the Writers' Association discussed the behaviour of a number of members who have contravened their duty as members of the Association and impaired the reputation of the Association. In so doing the meeting accepts the proposal of the Central Committee of the Writers' Association to have, on the basis of the constitution of the Association, a fundamental discussion about their positions with those members mentioned by Günter Mellis in his report. The facts presented by Comrade Mellis in his report prove that these members have acted contrary to their duty, anchored in the constitution, to work positively to further our Developed Socialist Society, have found it right and proper to attack, in a foreign country, our socialist state, the cultural policy of the Party and the government, and our socialist system of justice. By so doing they have served the anti-communist campaign against the GDR and socialism. By so doing they have clearly contravened the Association constitution, in particular articles I.1, II, III.2 and IV.2, and shown themselves unworthy of membership of the Writers' Association of the GDR. The meeting therefore sees itself compelled to draw the necessary consequences from this behaviour. It passes the resolution to exclude Judith Schevola, David Groth, Karlheinz Blavatny and Jochen Rieber from membership of the Writers' Association of the German Democratic Republic."'

'Colleagues, we have heard the resolution, that is, the report, the draft resolution the committee has put before the general assembly. Now we come to the discussion. A number of members have indicated their wish to speak, so I would ask you to keep your contributions brief. We are happy to allow others who wish to do so to speak. First I call upon David Groth.'

'Herr Mellis's report with its attacks on my colleagues and me was in *Neues Deutschland*, our national newspaper, below a letter our esteemed colleague Lührer addressed to the Comrade Chairman of the State Council in which he chose to call his colleagues Schevola, Blavatny, Rieber and Groth harmful pests and damaged individuals. I hereby demand that the Association committee see to it that my voice and the voices of our colleagues who have been attacked with me are also printed in *Neues Deutschland* and that we can defend ourselves just as publicly as we have been attacked.

'In this country we, the critical voices, are subjects on sufferance. Critical means that we dare to contradict the one and only true Party in places where it, in our opinion, does not tally with reality. You, my dear colleague, say that it is entirely possible to speak one's own opinion in our country. Yes, that is what it says in article 27 of the Constitution, which grants all citizens, and therefore authors, the right to express their opinions freely. But what I am asking is whether this corresponds to reality. Unless one is completely corrupt or blind, the answer to that can only be no. It is unfortunately the case that certain problems we have are not discussed in the media here, that certain books are not published. Do you dispute that? Do not make yourself a laughing stock. Not one single time have I been able to read in one of our newspapers a response to the kind of abuse Herr Lührer deems necessary, not one single time have I seen on *T V News* a report on actual conditions in our factories, on environmental problems, the increasingly brutal nature of our society. Or is it your opinion that all that does not exist? Then you're looking with your blind spot and all I can do is congratulate you on that skill, it is unheard of in the history of science. You, my dear Herr Mellis, object to my seeing a connection between censorship and criminal law. Now it is true that any author who would like to publish a book that has not been authorized in our country must automatically run up against the currency laws. Fräulein Schevola and I have committed an offence by seeking a publishing house in the West for our books that were not allowed to appear here. I think it is criminal that our actions are criminal offences. The purpose of such an interlinking of censorship and criminal law can only be to muzzle authors who will not acquiesce in lies and will call them lies. Or will they at last allow authors in the GDR to write about subjects that have always been – or are now once more – considered taboo? Will they, instead of hauling critical authors in front of a tribunal and heaping insults on them, deal with the conditions that have been criticized? – And may I conclude with a personal comment. It is not my business nor is it in my character to try to teach you a lesson in morality. You suggest it is immoral to want to publish in the West. All I have to say about that is that there is no other way left to authors who are to be silenced here. Our tormented colleagues in the Soviet Union or Romania do not have that way. It is not being published over there that is immoral, it is being censored here. Furthermore, anyone who ended up in the wrong uniform, under the wrong flag, in the wrong camp would do well not to go on a crusade against people who, in those days, fought in the right uniform, on the right side, for the right cause. I do not need to be ashamed of my past, it was not because of my "Jewish" nose alone that I was persecuted. No, the truth is that this is not about currency fraud or the like. It is about preventing writers from producing a certain kind of literature, namely one that will have nothing to do with rose-tinted spectacles. Today the annual general meeting has to vote on the expulsion of some colleagues from the Association. You are all aware that before this meeting many of you were brought together and it was made very clear what depended on the way you voted: trips to the West and bursaries, publications and performances, film versions and prizes. I will not hold it against anyone if, in consideration of such advantages, they vote in favour of the expulsion of our other colleagues and myself from the Association.'

'That's beyond belief! What do you think you're saying? Stop!'

'I will do you and myself that favour in a few moments. May your sense of shame and guilty conscience when you get back home not make you feel too depressed. Just remember, when you cast your vote, that there is such a thing as time and that what appears to be fixed and unchangeable can change, sometimes more quickly that you would think possible. It could be that one day you will have to account for your actions to your children; or to people in whose name some of our colleagues here claim to be speaking. It could be that you will be asked, "What did you do, master of the word, when the time came to stand up and be counted?"'

'I call on Karlfriede Sinner-Priest to speak.'

'Thank you, colleague. David Groth: I remember a man who came through the gates of Buchenwald, in American uniform, and who looked into the faces of two colleagues here, Paul Schade's and mine, into my ugly face, I had no hair and hardly any teeth from scurvy and the beatings. He looked into the faces of the prisoners, sat down and took off his helmet. David Groth: I remember an author who wrote moving books, full of life, about the difficult beginning of the new times and some of the contradictions that marked them. The times that were as a little child and have still not properly grown up yet, for social processes do not count in human years. Forgive me for introducing this personal note into the discussion, but I wonder what time, and perhaps also fame, have made of the David Groth I used to know as an ardent champion of our cause, as a man who fought for a better, fairer world, against fascism and imperialism. Yesterday I sat down and went through letters he wrote to me, read articles in old newspapers, read passages from his earlier books. I will never forget the author of *Soldiers* and *Dawn*, the advocate of the "Bitterfeld Way" and of harsh but appropriate words against forces I will not name so that they will not pollute the minutes of this meeting. The author of *Trotsky* is, as has already been said, a writer of muck-raking trash for whom no calumny, no trick is too cheap if it promises to serve his purposes; what these purposes are I do not know, I avoided them when I read the book for I simply could not believe what I was reading and checked the title page several times to see whether it was just a nasty joke and someone had submitted a trashy novel under David Groth's name. Unfortunately certain stylistic vanities and infelicities, which were always there but compensated for by the substance of his books, taught me otherwise. Not everyone who beats the moral drum is a good writer; not everyone who plays the honest dissident in the West is, looked at honestly, an author worthy of that name. I compared the times after the war to a child. Most of us will probably have children. Do you tell your child all the time that it's ugly? Do you only see what is ugly in your child? Or are you simply proud and happy at that great gift? There are things that are wrong and ugly about the child that is socialism but it doesn't need moaners and misery-guts rubbing its nose in it all the time: its legs are too bandy, its arms too short, its body too thin, its voice is husky, its lips are twisted and thin, its intellectual abilities weak . . . Those are the glasses that only let you see what is bad and ugly in everything, dismiss the good things as trivial or unimportant. The fact is, we have our constitution and one has to stick to it if one wants to remain a member of the Association. David Groth, you and a number of other authors, including Fräulein Schevola, with whom I am above all disappointed, I would have expected better of her – you do not stick to it. You complain that you are not allowed to speak but bring in the

Western media before contacting us. We made allowances about that and proceeded on our side according to the requirements of the constitution in article III.7: that the committee should have discussions to see if the qualifications for membership still obtain. You say that you are so profoundly concerned about our socialist cultural policy that you no longer regard the Western media as the instrument of the class enemy but as assistance in changing these allegedly terrible conditions. You say you want to express your criticism but you don't come to Association meetings where you are free to do so. David Groth: it was not an easy decision to take. I have had sleepless nights. Yet everything has already been decided. By you and by those other authors who decry us. It is not we who are withdrawing from you – you are withdrawing from us. You and your colleagues: you have excluded yourselves.'

'Thank you, Karlfriede Sinner-Priest. The next speaker is Herr Altberg.'

'Ladies and gentlemen, I have not brought a prepared speech with me since I only became aware of the subject of our annual general meeting here and the same could be the case for most of you. True, the unusual firmness of the invitation caused me agitation and a sense of foreboding. Seeing many faces among you that I have not seen in our Association before, I wonder whether they belong to authors and, if so, what they can have published. I have a suspicion it's about obtaining a majority in a vote. Is it about literature as well? Literature is not the maid of politics, the illustrator of what happens to be the current mode. Only idiots or people making malicious insinuations equate a character's opinion with that of the author – well, there are characters out there in the world that I don't like but whom I must interest myself in, if I don't want to portray the world solely through characters that are acceptable to me. Only simpletons think that Judith Schevola's grey hair or the number of hairs on Georg Altberg's nasal wart would say anything at all about their books. It doesn't, does it? Literature is poetry, drama, the essay, the novel; it is not the interview. There are some colleagues whose interview activity far outweighs their literary production, and often not merely in volume. They know about anything and everything, they have no inhibitions about expressing an opinion on space flight and disarmament, women's rights and cultural policy; but their novels and poems are thin affairs, lacking in life, in world. We, whose task is with language, with words, should not climb on the colourful merry-go-round of opinions. That is for actors, politicians and sportsmen. Please do not misunderstand me. It is a popular exercise in this country to dismiss those who work with words as publicity-mad jack-in-the-boxes when they address certain problems that, in the opinion of certain officials, should be swept under the carpet and left there. That is denunciation. But it is in my opinion also denunciation, my dear David, to respond to Herr Mellis with – just a moment, I've noted it down – "anyone who ended up in the wrong uniform, under the wrong flag, in the wrong camp". You said, "I do not need to be ashamed of my past." I say: I do. And I think Günter Mellis does so as well. We have both had to pay dearly for the errors and delusions of our youth, and the nightmare of the past is something that haunts me every night. Every one of us has to cope in his own way with what he has or has not done, every one of us has skeletons in the cupboard – and should refrain from confronting others as someone who knows best or even as one entitled to judge them. We will all be judged – but in another place.

'Toleration – the word that, I believe, has remained unsaid today. There is the law and there are people, but the law is made for people, not people for the law. I know that my words will fall on deaf ears for some, they are those who believe the losses are unavoidable and at times – some of these people, I hope it is not too many – perhaps even hope it will happen because they think their own reputations will rise if others are out of the running. You don't have to like Judith Schevola but she is one of the most talented writers in the East, along with one who is working clearing the tables in a restaurant out in the country. Do we have so many talented writers that we can afford to drive them away? Are defamation, intolerance, narrow-mindedness the appropriate way of dealing with talented people? Does our society not have to learn, if it is to remain attractive to people, to tolerate its critics?

'Colleagues, I call on you, I implore you, not to vote for exclusion. It would be a disaster with unforeseeable consequences if our colleagues were to be excluded. You all realize that they would lose their livelihood, that it would be almost impossible for them to continue working in their profession here. Exclusion would not be the end of our problems, just the beginning of the next turn of the screw.'

'I call on Eduard Eschschloraque to speak.'

''Tis hard to speak the truth when / falsehood rules the world. / Who would seek the sun that scorches? / Desert with no shade and no oasis, / the pure and unresponding slate, / the mirror whose reflection's just a void? / One thing alone is meaningless and sad, / two it takes for question and response, / each to fortify the other's weakness. / Now I will play the devil's advocate / and in this gath'ring pose some awkward questions, / such as: What is freedom / when all barriers fall? / For does not Goethe say about the law: / That it alone can give us freedom? / What is our constitution that, like a ring of iron, / binds both tongues and human flesh, / that ages and expires? / What is the boundless ocean for the ship / that's guided by the hand / of the figurehead atop the prow?'

'Wow! Off by heart.'

'"They are bad people – and yet good musicians," / Brentano said, inverting the set phrase in *Ponce de Leon*. / And did we not begin / to get on with each other / but then: "What do you think of him . . . between ourselves? / A gem-encrusted toad but decomposing. / There he is, watch out. – Eschschloraque, my friend, / it long has been my wish to tell you how / deeply I admire your sh— . . . shows, / your bravery as well to see / the spirit of the age as water in the loo / and all that floats thereon worth being flushed away." / – Hypocrisy, for instance. / In my hands you see a catalogue / of class enemies and nicely printed / by a nasty publisher in the West. There / among them is our dear own Günter Mellis / and others of the fauna of our state. / They should be punished, yes. / But I demand the same for Mellis and his ilk / for swine are those who call another swine / and have themselves their snouts deep in the trough.'

'Outrageous! Off! Off!'

'The time is out of joint / but faithful I remain unto our fathers' ways, / hold close to the laws, which makes our dreams unbounded / and people in accord. / Sweet honey often comes from bitter combs! / Order must have order of its own, / discord ne'er was by discord o'erthrown. – By the way, Herr Schade, you should check your German. "A weapon that planes out pencil shavings" – language like that is a monkey with fleas picking at it.'

'Herr Rohde, Herr Groth, as chairman of this meeting it is my duty to point out that it is our minutes secretaries who are taking everything down in shorthand. After Herr Eschschloraque's contribution, that was, as ever, both witty and helpful, the last person to speak before the break will be Judith Schevola. After that the buffet will be set out at the rear entrance.'

46

Hispano-Suiza

Dietzsch, the sculptor, kicked the lock, one of the rifle-brown, bug-shaped pieces 'from the good old days' such as were occasionally available for special customers from Iron-Feustel's by Rothenburger Strasse; a lock with a shackle as thick as your finger that only snapped open after the fourth or fifth blow with a cross-pein hammer, 'like a crocodile's jaw that has just overcome the resistance of some chewing gum,' Dietzsch said; Richard thought the comparison childish and enjoyed it; the painter clicked the lock open and shut a few times, it must be a good feeling, security, quality, parts that smoothly fitted together; some people became prison guards for that feeling. Stahl had gone back a little way, which surprised Richard – wasn't he interested in what Dietzsch wanted to show them and that they'd driven several kilometres to see? The quarry was in Lohmen, a small place near Pirna. Dietzsch had made a great fuss about it and adopted the expression of someone who decides he's really going to show people something; 'I know about your hobby, Dr Hoffmann, and you did a great job operating on that carpal-tunnel thing; I think I've got something for you.' Now Stahl was watching two sculptors working at the other end of the quarry. 'Jerzy, our Pole, and Herr Büchsendreher,' Dietzsch called out to him, pointing to a rock above them on which bearded faces had been painted.' Jerzy's work, art is a weapon, but he wouldn't harm a fly.'

Stahl shaded his eyes with his hand, surveying the rocky outcrops, the thick brushwood above them. 'Tell me, is there only the one way in here, through the gate at the front?' Stahl didn't turn round to Dietzsch, but studied the dumper trucks, tackle on stands over sandstone blocks, rails leading from the gate to a few goods wagons brooding forlornly in the sun, lowered his hand, then put it back to shade his eyes when Dietzsch replied; the sun was pouring its dazzling light over the unworked blocks lying around and the separate sculptures.

'Yes, and normally it's locked. We're not particularly keen on having visitors, you know, especially not unannounced ones. Sometimes children come in and have even managed to wreck some sculptures. They climbed over the gate. We've welded barbed wire onto it and since then we've had no problems.'

'How do we get in, then? Through the bushes?'

'There's no way through. Jerzy tried but couldn't get farther than a couple of metres. – If we do the deal, you'll get a key from me. You could get in at the weekend as well, usually there's no one here then. We've got electricity, water you'd have to bring yourself; we are connected up, but it's shut off at weekends.' Dietzsch slammed back a bolt, opened the shed door, ushered Richard and Stahl in first. Their eyes had to adjust to the dim half-light. The sculptor shooed away a few hens that had presumably got in through the dilapidated roof. The large space was partitioned off into separate areas in which there was a jumble of sculptures, orange boxes, petrol cans, tools, at the side on the left bales of straw, horse collars and a shapeless something underneath a tarpaulin. Dietzsch pulled it off. 'It's yours – for five thousand marks, I thought.'

'Hispano-Suiza.' Stahl leant over the radiator.

'One moment.' Dietzsch tugged at a shutter, the light suddenly pouring in dazzled them.

'A vintage car.' Stahl slowly walked round it. Richard stood behind the sculptor, always behind the seller, that was Arthur's tactic when he was going to buy or swap a clock; never be the first to say something about the goods on offer, if you have to speak, then a vague, casual remark to get your voice under control, to disappoint expectations, reduce tension, no give-away gestures, no indifference that could be seen as feigned.

He could go on and on for hours about bodywork, Meno wrote, *mere covers – though of course he would never have called them that – for technology that meant nothing to me and which (like most of his guests, I assumed, especially the women) I found boring; what I didn't find boring was the way he, a surgeon, raised his hands and indicated shapes, tenderly and bashfully as if it were women's bodies that the doctor in him was looking at, with a professional eye and yet receptive; names rained down on our poor heads, only Robert seemed to be really taken with the subject, returning the names to his father like table-tennis balls. 'Saoutchik – did you hear that, Meno? Isn't that a name, a sound that sends shivers down your spine? Maybach and Duesenberg, Rolls-Royce and Bugatti – don't they sound like extinct gigantic beasts? This construction drawing, look at the interplay of the lines, so elegant and clear, if you ask me what poetry is, Meno, this is it! If I were a painter, I'd paint construction pieces like that. Gerhart Stahl, I'm calling you by your full name because you understand me. We use all these things every day but hardly anyone apart from a professional reflects on them at all. What, for God's sake, is a brake? Do you think it's a matter of course that the steering wheel's on the left? Can you imagine that there were coachbuilders who covered the bumpers in leather. Do you know how it is and what it means to touch a bumper like that? I have heard that in a museum in Washington there's a piece of stone from the Moon and no one can go past without touching it – does it feel the same as stone from the Earth? Oh my God, am I going to get some extraterrestrial disease, are there unknown rays in this thing? A leather-covered bumper, that's the skin of an animal on a machine that is going to vibrate with power. Forged muscles, veins of copper, joints of stainless steel. A giraffe-skin pattern on a bonnet, tough dark-blue paintwork on a Horch, a Daimler-Benz, a Bugatti La Royale, an Isotta Fraschini Tipo 8B with Landaulett-De-Ville bodywork from the Milan coachbuilder Castagna. And what do we have? A hat on wheels by the name of Dacia, a sardine tin transformed into a frog by the name of Saporoshez, a petty-bourgeois's dream with the aerodynamics of a snow plough by the name of Wartburg; we have a stuttering loaf of army bread by the name of Polski Fiat, a whining abomination by the name of Trabant, known as the cardboard racer, a two-stroke with steering-column gear lever, with jolts and toxic exhaust, but non-standard the earmuffs we ought to be wearing when we're rattling at 70 kph to the Baltic coast with the feeling we're inside the throat of a screaming baby!' That, said Richard, was the theme of his Christmas lectures to students. Only Robert and Ulrich showed any interest, Christian, arms crossed, stared at the floor as if he*

*found it embarrassing to see his father in the role of an enthusiast, Barbara
picked fluff off the sleeves of her blouse, Niklas and Gudrun examined the
colour pictures of cars Richard slid across the table, then returned to the
pieces of cake on their plates –*

'A vintage car, yes,' Richard said.

'Not any old vintage car,' Dietzsch said, 'a Hispano-Suiza H6B, 1924,
right-hand drive, six-cylinder engine with 6.5 litres cubic capacity,
rear-wheel drive and a top speed of a hundred and thirty kph.'

'Mechanical servo-brake back-up,' Richard said.

'Doesn't work all that well in reverse,' Dietzsch said. 'Rolls-Royce
improved it. Basically normal drum brakes. The inner drum is linked
to the drive shaft by a worm shaft.'

'And thus gives torsion to the whole system,' Richard said. 'The
shaft rotates anti-clockwise, thus moving the cable drums for the front
wheels and the levers for the rear.'

'One cable drum is missing,' Dietzsch said.

'The car's yellow,' Stahl said.

'The leather's black,' Richard said.

'Double-quilted leather from Provençal cows, tanned with plant
extract and upholstered with horsehair,' Dietzsch said. 'That yellow's
interesting, I had to rack my brains about it. For grapefruit yellow it's
too rich, for banana yellow the scent's lacking, neither cadmium nor
Indian yellow, sulphur's too loud, it's not the shade of gamboge or
buttercups, not nankeen yellow, not Naples yellow or Hansa yellow,
not egg yolk yellow, not saffron yellow.'

'But?' Stahl said.

'The closest is Vatican yellow,' Dietzsch said. 'Vatican flag yellow.
Papal yellow.'

'What kind of bird is that?' Stahl tapped the figure on the bonnet;
it was attached over a sideways-on rhombus with a winged Swiss cross.

'A stork,' Richard said.

'Aha, a stork,' Stahl said.

'Have you anything against storks?' Dietzsch said.

'No,' Stahl said.

'Oh yes you have,' Richard said. '"Aha, a stork" – it sounded like: all animals with wings are blackbirds, if they're flying at twilight they're bats, if they've a splash of red on their breasts they're robins.'

'There are two tyres missing, the exhaust's hanging loose and can I have a look at the engine?' Stahl said.

'There's a story to the stork,' Dietzsch said.

'Obviously,' Stahl said.

'Then I won't bother,' Dietzsch said.

If a museum, then the Museum of Transport, Meno wrote, or an art gallery; at Anne's insistence he went to the 1984 Klee Exhibition in the Albertinum, outside which the Dresdeners formed 200-metre-long queues in the winter slush; with Ulrich to the Francke Foundations in Halle to see a collection of medical preparations. Richard knew every nook and cranny of the Museum of Transport. Sometimes he went there with Father, the Museum of Transport was one of their common interests. Kurt would say, 'Look over there, Richard', Richard would say, 'Look over there, Kurt.' Both would say, 'Oh come on, Meno, look around.' Richard would talk about spark plugs, something that lasted despite the great strain put on it, as far as one could talk about earthly things lasting. No misfiring right up to the end, at least not in the West. Standing by the Benz, he talked about the first long-distance journey in a car, ironically the first car driver of all had been a woman: at the crack of dawn on an August day in 1888 Bertha Benz, the wife of the man who constructed the car, climbs into the rattling vehicle resembling a horseless carriage with her two sons, not before leaving a note for her husband that they had no intention of abandoning him, and sets off from Mannheim for Pforzheim to visit her mother. Climbing the hills of the Black Forest, Bertha and fifteen-year-old Eugen have to get off, leaving thirteen-year-old Richard to steer. Downhill they go with smoking brakes; the leather brake linings get so worn Bertha has to have them replaced en route by cobblers. A blocked petrol feed is cleared with a hatpin, an ignition wire insulated with a garter after a short circuit. Petrol is bought at the apothecary's. Everywhere people stand and stare, in one inn two peasants almost get into a fight over an argument as to whether the carriage is driven by clockwork – but then where's the key to wind it up, it must be huge – or by supernatural forces. They reach Pforzheim before it gets dark. That was the start of the triumphant progress of the car. We went to the Museum of Transport, saw aeroplanes, ships, trains, the array of vintage cars in the glass-roofed yard; as Richard went round, more and more adults and children stopped to listen to his explanations – I had the feeling he was talking deliberately loudly to show off his knowledge, at least he had no objection to other people listening. After a few minutes he was accompanied by an entourage of visitors eager for information and anecdotes, attendants included, as long as they could remain within sight of their exhibits –

After he'd bought the car, Richard went to Lohmen as often as he could. Stahl had more time; he worked in a department for rationalization and innovation and most of his suggested rationalizations and innovations were not accepted by the management. On weekdays when he wasn't on call, Richard would drive out in the evening, at weekends at dawn. He left the money for Daniel with Nina Schmucke.

47
. . . count the sunny hours alone

Therefore you must never shut yourself off from your group,
crew or unit. It is only among your comrades that you can
develop and maintain a socialist soldier's character.

What It Means to be a Soldier

He couldn't stop thinking about the frog Siegbert had cut the legs off
at the training camp. The animal struggling desperately in the darkness
of its lack of language, its slow, as if indifferent movements of
resistance – was that any concern of his, could one not say: it's only a
frog? And who knows whether it does actually feel pain? Christian
could hear the voices in the block, the coarse laughter when they were
chasing someone again. Burre didn't lack language. Burre wrote poems.
Weak, sentimental poems, but he did express himself. He would actually be someone to be friends with, Christian thought. Would be. For
he didn't want to be friends with Burre. Burre was weak and he thought
about why that gave him a low opinion of Burre. And he, what was he
himself? Couldn't they do what they wanted with him? But Burre was
submissive. Or so it seemed. They tormented him because there had
to be someone to torment. They had to find a release for their own
torment. But for him, Christian, that wasn't necessary, and they knew
it. To torment Burre was necessary.

They went out to the field camp and came back, they hadn't washed
for ten days and to clean your teeth there was dew from the pines or
drops of water, mixed with diesel, from the tank of the tank-tractor,
the commander of which, a grumpy lance corporal, called them a load
of dirty buggers he wouldn't give his precious water to. They bashed

him about the face a bit, did a bit of *sursum corda*, as Ruden called it, and Christian smiled as he recalled his contorted face when Ebert, 'in order to improve abilities and skills', twisted the guy's nose with fingers like a vice; he did look funny, the grotesque way his flabby cheeks twisted, and the noise they made when Ruden and Rogalla hit them – poff, botch, gump – made you want to laugh . . . Christian discovered it could be fun when someone was beaten up; God, the absurd way their eyes rolled, their mugs twisted, the way they grunted like little pigs as they wailed, the way they stumbled along in the poor light made you snort with laughter . . . Power. When the tanks started up, when the driver closed his hatch, pushed the lever down to lock the hatch, the sheer power you needed for that movement – at the cadet school, deafened by the bawling of the driving instructor in the command tower, they'd hardly been able to do it with both hands and pushing down with their whole weight – when the oil pump could be heard, the driver pressed the starter, the thunder of steel, then the twelve-cylinder engine would give a roar, a dark beast, ready to attack; when the caterpillar tracks made the ground sing and they *ripped* along over stump and stone, through hedge and ditch: that was power. *Smash it in the face.* Sometimes a tree got in the way that looked just ripe for shooting. A fish flapping terribly on dry land. A buck with so many points on its antlers that, a monument to horribly useless virility, it could hardly take a step for the weight. What could one do with a buck like that? It was screaming for a Kalashnikov. Safety catch off your automatic and fire, *shoot the buck to pieces*. Buck, buck, he chewed on the word. It had a hard, harsh sound. Like *fuck*. He would never be allowed to say a word like that at home. He would never have said a word like that at home. Now, here, almost everyone used it, by now he'd got used to it. It cropped up in every second or third oath. A woman, he learnt here, was not loved or kissed or simply left in peace, a woman was fucked. Go and fuck your old woman, you filthy ponce. Yes. Get fucked to hell. Go and fuck yourself, you little shit. I don't talk like that. It's not me, Christian thought. All the things that aren't me. Shooting. Until the ground around you's spattered with cartridge cases. At the windowpanes. The whole magazine. And the one taped to it, as the Russians had taught them, after that. Sustained fire. Until the whole damn' barracks was in ruins. *And to fuck. Need to fuck a woman*. Sleep with her, he thought. Go out with her. Talk to her.

They loaded ammunition onto the tanks, they unloaded ammunition off the tanks. Did guard duty in the heat, listened to the rustling of the pinewoods when the wind got up. They slept in tents they erected on black sand. At night it was so hot the hands of the older soldiers slipped off the mouths of their victims and the whimpering, the cries, could be heard, panting and desperately relieved groans of relief. Christian kept his knife beside him. Musca drank Dur, Rogalla Tüff aftershave. The Russians, with whom their battalion was on manoeuvre, had vodka and coolant. They didn't use the ramp to unload the tanks from the goods wagons but turned a steering lever until the tank was sideways on, stepped on the throttle and let it flop down backwards. Crash bang, went the axles. Eat dirt, went the Russians. *Parni*, they said to their GDR brothers-in-arms, spat and waved, a tank doesn't need all its axles. *Konechno*. When they were drunk they took out their Makarovs, stuck them in a pile of sand and proved that they could fire even then. *Ochen horosho!* Then they sang, danced round the fire, tossed tracer bullets onto it, were delighted at the sparks flying up. There were problems with the local farmers, the Russians were starving, you could tell from the way they looked. They took food wherever they could get it. For example, from the field kitchen of their brothers-in-arms. They were very skilled at plucking chickens. They danced like crazy. One of them challenged Ruden. Ruden was good, but not as good as the Russian. He taught the German *parni* close-combat tricks from Afghanistan. How to bump off a guard with a knife when you were on reconnaissance. Christian was translating. He didn't know the word for 'bump off'. How to 'take out' a village, sparing the women as far as possible. A gesture was enough for 'fuck'.

Talk to her.

They sang well and then all the bad words, the filth, simply vanished. Lots of them could recite Pushkin by the yard; afterwards it got dangerous; once one of them emptied the magazine of an anti-aircraft MG into a pile of ammunition boxes. The soldiers only managed to contain the forest fire that followed the explosion because they leapt into the tanks and flattened wide breaks round the blazing pines. At night, when the wind was calm or in the right direction, we could hear talking, then laughter, then sounds of intercourse from a nearby campsite by a lake. Musca said he reckoned he could get a bite of a cherry or two. The others said he should keep his trap shut, they couldn't hear a thing. 'Don't let me catch any of you tossing off here, you goddamned filthy bastards,' Ruden, who was mounting guard, bawled.

Ruden. Who wanted to study classical languages. Who knew Nietzsche. Praised be whatever makes us hard. What does not kill me makes me stronger. Ruden had a girlfriend who left him in the summer of '85. He stood there looking at the photo in the 'personal compartment' of his locker, the tall, brawny discharge candidate, sergeant, possessor of the sports badge in gold and various shooting awards, holding the letter in his hand and saying nothing. He wanted to go on leave, there was an exercise coming, the company commander cancelled his leave. Ruden ranted and raved a bit, out in the corridor. The company commander kept his cool. To *bawl out* Ruden in front of the soldiers would have meant that all the other DCs would have immediately downed tools: farewell top mark for socialist competition. Ruden read Caesar and Xenophon, descriptions of battles. 'What are you called?' he asked Christian during 'baptism'.

'Christian Hoffmann, Comrade Sergeant.'

'No. You're no one. Nemo, that is. From now on you're called Nemo.'

The drivers had prepared slices of bread for their *earholes*: one had been spread with mustard, another with shoe polish, Burre's with excrement. When he refused to eat it, they held him and pushed the slice of excrement bread into his mouth. 'Eat shit. You're in the army now, comrade.' They baptized him Nutella, after the spread from the West.

'Baptism': Irrgang was Aquarius. He was given a teaspoon. There was a bucket full of water on the ground floor of the battalion, an empty one on the second floor in headquarters company.

Christian's turn came during the night, when he was already asleep. He was tied up in a blanket, dragged out into the depot and laid down in front of a tank. Popov started the engine and drove over Christian, who was unable to move. He watched the tank pass above him, saw bolts, the emergency exit flap. The game was called 'hot dog'. Then Rogalla untied him, handed him a water bottle. 'Have a drink, comrade, we all had to go through it. They made Ruden lick the company corridor and once almost knocked his eye out. And for me there was piss in the bottle. Oh, by the way, you get clean bedding in a fortnight's time.'

Talk to her.

Lars Dieritz, known as Costa, the rib, was the saddest soldier doing his penultimate six months Christian knew. He was wretchedly thin, like a baby bird, though tough and with great stamina, only Christian was a match for him at the 3,000 metres. Costa, the rib, had all the privileges of his status but none of the higher ranks respected him. 'You're a milksop,' Ruden said, 'you're not a warrior, you're just a mummy's boy. And something like that's in the cavalry! We're the vanguard of the army. I'd chuck you out if you were younger.'

'Oh, shut your trap.' Costa just wanted to get it over with, just wanted to go home. He couldn't stand Ruden and Rogalla's muscleman boasting, he had no time for playing the hero.

'So why did you sign up for three years, then? Nemo did it to get to university, me too. But you? No one was forcing you.'

'I believed their promises. I had a soft spot for the state, can you imagine? And no idea how lousy things are here.'

'Hey, Rogi, when we've gone, everything will collapse here. Costa in his final six months . . .' Ruden made a dismissive gesture. 'Can't imagine how he's going to maintain the proud tradition, the rights and privileges of the discharge candidates. Ah well, Wanda'll sort things out.'

Costa liked music, best of all Leonard Cohen's melancholy ballads; since he was in his final year of service he was allowed a record player. 'My God, Ruden, you are limited. Aren't you going to go to university? Always coming out with bits of Latin and Greek . . . I'm just an electrician but it could be I've got more candlepower in my upper storey than you.'

In political education they were told about the clear ideological position of socialist members of the army, the danger of an atomic war threatening the existence of humanity caused by imperialism, of the tasks facing them, the comrade NCOs and privates. Socialism needed class-conscious, well-trained and steadfast men who were ready to fight for it and to fulfil their military duty at any time, thus assuring the peaceful future of mankind and victory over war even before it broke out through the strength of socialism. They sang. Sang 'The Song of the Foe'. The Political Officer had asked who could play an instrument. Costa and Popov could strum a guitar a bit. 'Soldier, you hold a gun in your hand, / And a worker it was who gave it you. / You carry your gun for the Fatherland, / So the workers' life stays safe and true. / Our foe is ruthless, crafty, vile, / He took some comrades from us through the years, / He has no thought for love, for wife and child, / Nor for the tears they shed, such bitter tears . . .'

In their free time they sat in the company recreation room for a communal viewing of *TV News*, made tanks out of matches for the solidarity bazaar for a Pioneer group the company was sponsoring, wrote letters. Musca had to stand in posture with all his gear for one of the soldiers to do his portrait for the battalion diary: 'The Tanker'. In the Free German Youth group the achievements of the comrade army members were evaluated. Christian, who was still inexperienced and couldn't control the tank properly yet, was delegated to the technical circle run by his platoon leader. After their duty was over, the technical circle went out into the depot. 'There's only one guarantee / The aggressor can be contained / To be better equipped than he, / Better armed and better trained.'

Staff Sergeant Emmerich, known as Nip, swayed as he distributed the mail and when he read out the names, when he gave out orders, he didn't articulate correctly, his voice scraped over the outlines of the words, grunted out the short ones and stirred the polysyllabic ones into a linguistic mush, out of which the soldiers' attuned ears fished what he, the sergeant, wanted. Nip had the dull, lifeless hair and stretched-looking skin of heavy drinkers and the blackheads in his large, slanting pores sat deep and inaccessible as wasp-grubs in their breeding cells. He had been in the army for fifteen years and been given an honourable discharge but he hadn't known what to do with himself at home, in a flat in a new development in the little town of Grün. The company had been his empire, the soldiers the charges in his care, and morning, noon and night he had dealt with clean underwear, requests for leave, repairs, had the boilers heated, organized tea and sandwiches for his men when they came back, tired and filthy, from field camps to the barracks. He could no longer say how many field exercises he'd taken part in. He'd been at the legendary 'Comrades-in-Arms' manoeuvres, he knew Kapustin Yar in Kazakhstan, where battalions of Tank Regiment 19, 'Karl Liebknecht', in which Christian was serving, were going with artillery units of other regiments; he knew all the training areas of the Republic, knew about the little difficulties of their shooting and driving ranges. He handed out the wax for polishing the corridors, he sanctioned radios, he had the cassette slots on cassette recorders sealed, he marked with felt tip the tuning for the permitted radio stations. Subordinate to him were the duty sergeant and his assistant, whose attention he personally drew to 'crud' in the rooms (Christian learnt that that was what dirt was called, another word was 'gunge'), whom he personally instructed as to how the two stoves in the battalion staff office – when the trees along the roads turned yellow – were to be stoked; he carried out the inspection of rooms and lockers personally, searching for alcohol, magazines from the West or secret radios; when the day's work was done he personally pressed the aluminium seal into the crown corks filled with modelling clay on the doors of us soldiers, the bearers of secrets. And he personally saw to it that before the visit of any bigwig even the trunks of the birch trees outside the battalion building were washed. At morning roll-call he checked the tunic collar binds and gave a look of disgust when he found a dirty one. He, as did the officers, knew very well how the young soldiers were treated; complaints dragged on and on until they fizzled out or were dismissed, Nip believed the unofficial privileges exercised by the senior recruits were part of the men's psychological training. One of his favourite amusements was to come into the barracks secretly at night. When Christian was on duty he could smell the reek of schnapps before Nip came stomping up the steps. According to regulations he should have reported his arrival but Nip would put his finger to his lips and pat a bag that was hanging from his shoulder. In the bag was the 'drake', Staff Sergeant Emmerich's personal hand-siren. Drunk and happy, Nip staggered along the unlit corridor, and after having unlocked the armoury turned the handle of the 'drake' like a hurdy-gurdy man and bawled out, 'Comp'ny Four – action stations!'

One day Nip ordered Christian to come to his room. He ran his thumb over a bundle of postcards. 'This letter is confiscated, Hoffmann. It has marks from a non-socialist country. From the class enemy! In a facility of the National People's Army!'

Christian recognized Ina's handwriting on the envelope. 'Cuba is a socialist country, Comrade Staff Sergeant. My cousin was there on her honeymoon.'

'It's been franked in Hamburg. There are two alternatives. We make a fuss about it, you complain . . . or the letter disappears. You should be grateful. According to regulations . . .'

Christian stared at Nip's collection of pot plants. Anne would have advised him to let the matter drop. Meno, with his coolly observant scientist's manner, would presumably have waited to see what his nephew would do. Robert would have said, Sell him the letter, you can see how keen he is on it, the poor slob. Try to get something out of it. Only Richard would have lost his temper.

Richard, from whom Christian had inherited his mania for justice, as Barbara put it. But his father wasn't there. Christian was certainly interested in what would happen if he insisted on having the letter. The Hoffmanns' daredevil recklessness. Spin the ball and see what turns up on the roulette wheel. 'Yes, Comrade Staff Sergeant.'

48

ORWO black-and-white

Chug-chug-chug and put-put-put, rumbling and grumbling, baboom, baboom,

'Something's rattling, shut the door, Robert.' – 'It is shut.' – 'I said something's rattling', baboom, baboom,

crawling (the traffic jams on the Berlin ring road) and jolting (the hot Pneumant tyres over asphalt bulging out of the joins in the concrete slabs) lip-smacking (hard-boiled eggs, liver sausage on bread, Golden Delicious, peeled cucumbers and carrots at the concrete tables of the autobahn picnic areas) pissing (as Niklas said, there was no other word for it when you had to go into the scraggy pine trees beside the picnic areas where plastic bags, empty bottles, swarms of flies round the traces left by your predecessors – for the women there was a path leading deeper into the little wood – tons of toilet paper all seemed to say, Oh God, how happy we were) baboom, baboom,

Plastics from Schkopau baboom,

Faster – higher – further baboom,

Plastics from Schkopau babang (pothole),

Forward to the XXth Party Conference baboom,

Plastics from Schkopau badong (deep pothole),

fill the tank (*VK 88 the fuel that takes you further*) boom

(bomb crater – Niklas drove onto the shoulder and checked – the bumper was still attached),

and give thanks (survived it once again, Gudrun groaned in Stralsund, as we straightened ourselves out):

thus one drove away on holiday across the German Democratic Republic.

Stralsund was a sad town. No proud Hanseatic flags any more, no noble regattas. Störtebecker, the pirate, was dead. After being beheaded he walked until he stumbled over the leg of one of the officials. Crumbling brick, dilapidated roofs. The sun was grey, enveloped in clouds of rubbish, hung low over the Sound. They parked the car but left Meno's luggage in it. He was going to travel on alone. There were a few hours before the ferry for Hiddensee left. Gudrun suggested they wander round the town; Anne and Niklas wanted to go and see the churches; Christian, Robert and Richard were hungry; Meno wanted to go to the Museum of the Sea. The market square was belly-up like a dead fish, gleaming in the fatty air rancid with kitchen fumes; all that was left of the light was some brownish dross that stuck to the walls like traces of tartar. The few people in the market square, which no longer seemed to be the centre of town, kept their heads down and disappeared hurriedly along side streets, as if they were being pursued. The town hall with its pointed Gothic gables seemed glaringly alien; the town was being eaten away by mould and acid discharge from brown coal. There was a long queue at an ice-cream stall offering vanilla ice in a wafer for fifty pfennigs and a cone for a mark; those queuing had the poor, pale skin of holidaymakers from inland before their holiday. Christian and Robert joined the queue. Meno, who had last been in the town as a student – youth hostel, excursions to the Museum of the Sea – wanted to go round by himself.

'Back at the car in two hours,' Anne, who seemed to distrust his sense of direction, told him.

In the side streets yellowing curtains were raised and lowered. The window frames had splits, cracked panes were held in place by screws or replaced by plywood. Meno stopped outside a butcher's; there were two sides of bacon and one sausage hanging in the window, he couldn't understand why there was still a queue outside. As soon as he bent down to look in the window, where a poster with 'Long live Marxism–Leninism' hung over piled-up cans of meat, a woman started to scold: he should kindly join the queue at the back like everyone else. 'Tourists!' he heard someone else moan. 'Probably from Berlin, eh? Buy up everything here then put on airs!' – 'Clear off.'

The way to the Museum of the Sea was signposted. Meno slowed down once he could no longer hear the vituperation. He thought about Judith Schevola. He hadn't seen her since the events at the annual general meeting; she was probably at some machine doing a job no one else wanted. After she'd been expelled from the Association there was hardly anything else left for her. Perhaps Philipp knew more details. At least the book had been printed, in the West, by Munderloh's publishing house. A few smuggled copies would certainly already have found their way through customs and be passed round the nomenklatura or as typewritten parts stapled together like school exercise books in the Valley of the Clueless. Those in the senior ranks of the Party and favoured officials of the various associations had no need of such subterfuges, they could acquire books from the West quite legally. Perhaps Jochen Londoner had the book and could lend it to him.

An odd idea, housing a museum of the sea in a former monastery. And equally odd that the brickwork of the monastery and the aquariums harmonized, that disciplined drawing, a Gothic silver pencil and unfettered painting, the play of colours, soiled by reality and never to be found in an entirely pure state, should live together so peaceably. The skeleton of a finback whale with a gigantic shoe-shaped mouth and jawbones as thick as your arm hung down from the vaulted ceiling. Children, probably from a holiday camp, were making a racket under the shrill-voiced supervision of two teachers. That, Meno felt, was the unpleasant aspect of natural-history museums: there were always children scurrying around, especially when there was no school, shouting and playing the fool with no consideration, no feeling for the fawn-like stillness, waking the corals from their sleep, making even snails moulded from plastic or alone in jars of formalin pull in their horns. Why could people not stand silence? Zoology was a quiet science and as he walked past preserved dolphins and aquariums bubbling with oxygen, he recalled scenes from his student days in Jena under Falkenhausen, the fraught and taciturn interpreter of the world of central-German spiders who called his predecessor, Haeckel, a fool, though a commendable one, and the Phyletic Museum in Jena a Planet Goethe. *Art Forms in Nature*. Dried plants, dust-encrusted chandeliers in the shape of jellyfish in blown glass, drawings of diatoms the size of a saucer, Radiolarians, Amphoridea: a stranded kingdom gradually fossilizing.

No more noise, the children had gone; there was no one to be seen, apart from an attendant dozing in a chair. Someone licked Meno's hand; in the aquarium by which he had stopped there appeared the guileless, panting face of a black dog.

'Do excuse me. Kastshey's still rather rude. It's difficult to teach this breed anything, but they're good watchdogs. And anyone they've taken a liking to . . . Good afternoon, Herr Rohde.' Arbogast tipped his cap with the stick with the gryphon handle. The Baron looked fresh and healthy; his usually grey face, which his steel-rimmed spectacles gave an extra touch of coolness to (now he was wearing glasses with tinted oval lenses, a Western pair), had a deep tan. The skin where his watch and ring had been was still white. Arbogast noticed Meno's glance and, inviting him to walk along with the gesture of an expert guide, explained that that year, contrary to his habit, he had not taken off his watch before going on holiday, nor his ring, which he now hardly noticed during his everyday business; however, it did bother him while sailing. At the moment his boat was in Stralsund harbour. Had Herr Rohde received – 'as promised', Arbogast smiled – the packet of pencils? 'No? Then it's on its way, or arrived after you left. You've moved up, so to speak, there have been some changes in our Institute. I presume you've heard that already from Fräulein Schevola?'

Meno said no.

'Some of my physicists, including Herr Kittwitz, have not come back from a conference in Munich. It caused quite a stir. I spoke up on their behalf to make sure they could go, but they abused my trust. That requires a certain lack of imagination or, to put it better, a fair amount of selfishness, just to clear off like that. They want to go to India. There's a lot of poverty in India. And they shouldn't think that all that glitters in the West is gold.'

You can talk, Meno thought but said nothing. He was surprised to hear that Kittwitz had left the country and he felt a stab of pain, for although he had only met the physicist once, he had sense of loss. Contemporaries form a cohort; they watch out for each other, even when the years pass and no one drops a hint.

'You'll be thinking I don't practise what I preach.' Arbogast pointed to a room with aquariums arranged according to themes, one was 'The Baltic', one 'Symbiosis', one 'Poisonous Sea Creatures'. Kastshey was attracted to the 'Harbour Basin' aquarium in which wrasse and butterfish, codling with barbels on their lower jaw (they made Meno think of Lange's goatee), turbot and mackerel were swimming round.

'I don't want to sound impolite, but for my part I'd love to travel and I think I'm not the only one who feels like that. I'm sure lots of people would like to see what the world outside is like for themselves, instead of getting it at second hand.' Meno watched a cuckoo ray with dark blue spots rising up with calm shimmering movements.

'Of course, there's no disagreement on that, my dear Rohde. The people in charge should accede to those wishes. Privately I advised the General Secretary to do just that but I fear he's forced to ignore the suggestion. Unfortunately. In their greed people would take the West for paradise and not return.' Arbogast pointed to some sea anemones and their iridescent colours. 'From our own cultures. We've had great success at trade fairs.' He took Meno by the arm and walked on a few steps, as a ruler in affable mood might do with one of the 'ordinary people' when it's politically opportune and there's a camera nearby. 'The country would empty, as it did before '61. The time it took for people to realize their mistake would be enough for the useful and meaningful experiment of socialism to collapse. How are your affairs in Thomas-Mann-Strasse?' That was where the Hermes offices were. Meno hesitated. Arbogast took a glasses case out of the inside pocket of his elegant, white-linen summer suit, swapped spectacles and, leaning forward, mouth slightly open, observed a red lionfish that was languidly fanning its fins. Its antennae, red-and-white-striped like a stick of candy, were erect.

'We've been sidelined.'

'Hmmm' – Arbogast tapped the glass, the lionfish turned away – 'that's not the way to go about original projects. – You're on holiday? In this area?'

'On Hiddensee.'

'Kloster? I guessed so. I can take you there.'

'There are seven of us,' Meno lied.

'A nice number. Usually one too many and quarrels break out. No offence meant, you know I like jokes. There's one they ought to put in the quarantine basin.' A weever fish with half its tail-fin missing limped past. 'Taking seven people wouldn't be a problem on my boat.' It was a proper yacht, Arbogast explained, and, of course, not only meant for pottering along the coast. His wife was there too, they were heading across the Baltic to the Soviet Union, he had authorization to enter their territorial waters, to sail at night and PM 19, permission to cruise to the land of their socialist brothers. Meno hesitated.

'I can see I've caught you by surprise. But you must come to one of our evenings again. People are already asking if you're coming. We have an interesting programme.' Arbogast waved Kastshey over.

Hagstones warded off misfortune. There were some threaded on a faded clothesline over the door of the waiting room in the holiday season doctor's bungalow, with dazzling white shells with holes bored in them between the stones. To take one off and keep it for later was to steal good fortune and that didn't count; neither Christian nor Robert touched the chain. Genuine stones with a natural hole were difficult to find. In the grey-yellow sand of the lagoon they found empty ink cartridges, shards of glass, dried dog shit and, if they were lucky, a rusty key; but the white flints, smooth and round from the sea with a hole you could thread a string through, were rare. Mostly a hollow of varying depth had been ground into the stone. Boring it through didn't count. The hole had to go right through, a talisman-eye for the view from Fuhlendorf beach across Bodstedt lagoon to the Darss, for the pearl-white balls enclosing the bathing area, the jetty with its boathouse, the fish-traps further out with cormorants and seagulls perching on them; to see through to the Baltic sky, to the reeds cradling the August of bleached hair and freckles. Anne thought the lagoon was too warm, too shallow, too unsavoury. Children with brightly coloured buckets built messy sandcastles, threw mud as they waded in the water while their mothers dozed under sunshades, paddled on air beds, dreaming they were on the Kon-Tiki, below them the 5,000 feet of the Humboldt Current full of bonitos and snake mackerel, above them clouds driven by the trade winds, before them South Sea islands. In the lagoon there were ruffe, roach and occasional eelpouts. For zander you needed a boat. Robert had brought his angling equipment and went for non-predatory fish, Christian took the spinning rod, attached a 0.35 mm green line and cast spoons and blinkers. Ruffe bit, little spotted guys with spiny fins and huge appetites, some were shorter than the blinker lure that they'd taken for their prey.

The summer season doctor – for three weeks in August that was, alternating daily, Richard Hoffmann and Niklas Tietze – lived with his family in the bungalow on the village street. A white flag with a red cross was unrolled and placed in the mounting beside a bug-plastered lamp. As soon as the inhabitants of Fuhlendorf, nearby Bodstedt and the communities as far as Michaelsdorf saw the flag they remembered various infirmities that couldn't stand the long journey to the hospital in Barth and, silent and within their rights, occupied the plasticized-linen waiting-room chairs. There were four rooms in the bungalow, one of which served as the doctor's surgery. Two WCs (private and patients'). The rooms each had two bunk beds at right angles to each other, two cupboards and a washbasin with a cold tap. If you wanted a shower, you packed your flip-flops, picked up your toiletry bag and went through the German Mail holiday camp, to which the bungalow belonged, into the shower shed beside the canteen kitchen, where you hung your things under one of the clouded mirrors in the corridor and waited on bleached duckboards, a potential source of athlete's foot, in the cabins open to the corridor, surrounded by cheerful and cursing voices, for warm water to come.

The Hoffmanns had been going to Fuhlendorf since 1972; Richard shared the practice with colleagues (for a long time Hans had joined them), which allowed him to give his family holiday on the Baltic, which were much sought after, and also earn an extra month's salary. Only once had the family managed to get a holiday that wasn't associated with Richard's work: at a German Trades Union holiday hostel in Born, on the Darss lagoon. The food was poor, the weather even worse and that year the lagoon had been full of jellyfish and seaweed. A bell in the corridor to wake them and a radio that couldn't be switched off. They preferred Fuhlendorf, even if the bungalow beds had horse-hair mattresses that were turned over from one doctor to the next, and steel springs on which Richard, who slept in the lower bunk, regularly tore his scalp when he got up. The Tietzes had Room 1, the Hoffmanns Room 2. That room looked out onto the village street and Christian knew it was a disadvantage, for often drunks coming from 'night angling' in Redensee Café would go past the bungalow bawling, hammer on the door demanding nurses and booze. Some years previously a soldier from the Soviet forces had appeared and, Kalashnikov at the ready, demanded the practice motorbike, an elderly Zündapp, and zoomed off on it, lurching from side to side, only to be brought back several hours later, bound and held on either side by grim-faced officers in order to have various broken bones seen to.

Christian immediately felt at home again in Fuhlendorf. The storks' nest on the reed-thatched cottages. The continuous barking of the spitz next door. The light-blue dovecote full of snow-white doves whose cooing and fluttering the Tietzes counted against the risks of the village street. The holiday camp: the dozens of bungalows in rows down the slope with children's faces looking out of the windows. The gravelled paths edged with white stones, lit by welded toadstool lamps. Wakey, wakey at six in the morning from the camp loudspeakers. Once a week the siren was tested. Roll-calls, the clatter of cutlery at set times in the camp canteen. Socialist competition: races, games of football, volley-ball, table tennis on concrete tables, the nets could be collected, after having been signed for, in the camp office. Flags fluttering in the summer breeze.

Christian was on leave, much longed for by members of the army. He didn't talk very much. What did it smell of in the bungalow? Dry air, aniseed drops from the shop in the Mail holidaymakers' canteen, twenty pfennigs a tube, the drops always stuck together. There was the smell of the toilets that always had daddy-longlegs sitting on the cistern. Vita-Cola didn't smell, but tasted good, ice-cold from the humming refrigerator in the recreation room. There, as in the previous thirteen years, was the Junost television with the irrevocably faulty aerial, showing GDR 1 and 2 plus a semolina image of West German Channel Two that suffered additional interference from the military's Baltic transmissions. It smelt of the wood lining the outer walls that was badly affected by the winter weather, of Florena sun cream, sand, heather: beside the bungalow, shut off from it by a chain-link fence, was a path going to a little pinewood. Floor polish, insect repellent, medicines. Acetate of alumina for wasp stings, Ankerplast spray as a substitute for plasters, Panthenol for sunburn, Sepso tincture. The glass syringes tinkled in the enamel kidney bowls, sweated out strepto- and staphylococci in the cylinder sterilizer. The very sight of wooden spatulas made you feel sick. Scissors and scalpels were submerged in disinfectant solution. Bandages, Gotha adhesive plaster, the smell of rubber: the brick-red, washable sheet on the examination couch, the enema bags, the footplate of the scales, gloves drying off to be used again, dusted with talcum powder. It smelt of brackish water, the air from air pumps, the lemon mist that Gudrun sprayed to combat all the other smells in the bungalow.

'Hiddensee!' Lange had exclaimed in both envy and appreciation. 'We've never had a holiday there. Send us a card.'

Without the offer from the Association's trade union, Meno would have gone to Saxon Switzerland again, would have taken his little room, inserted a sheet of paper in his Fortuna typewriter; but this year, he had been informed, it was his turn to have one of the rooms in Lietzenburg, the Association's rest home, 'for the purposes of vacation' as it said in officialese; attached was a three-page list of house regulations. Meno knew that this was probably the only time he'd have the privilege of staying in Lietzenburg. It was offered in rotation over a cycle of thirty years. Meno's application had originally been made in 1974, so he'd been lucky. Especially since married couples were given preference. Editors were the lowest of the low in the Association. Only the head of Editorial Section 1 in the central office of the publishing house was said to have managed to get to Lietzenburg twice.

The ferry chugged its way north from the Sound of Strela, above which the needled outlines of St James's, St Mary's and St Nicholas's rose up into the leaden sky, past Altefähr on Rügen, meadow-flat Ummanz. For a while Arbogast's ship kept alongside with shortened sail, then the wind freshened; the Baron, at the wheel, nodded to Meno, who was standing by the ferry rail watching the manoeuvres that Herr Ritschel, a bosun's whistle between his lips, piped up to the sailors climbing the rigging with even movements. The sails caught the wind, billowed out, the black-caulked yacht cut across almost silently and disappeared in the haze. Meno filled his pipe, staring at the bottle-green waves flickering with phosphorescence, offered his Orient cigarettes first to Judith Schevola, then to Philipp Londoner, listened to the stories, scratched by loudspeaker noises, that the grey-bearded captain was telling about the steamer, the *Caprivi*, the author Gerhart Hauptmann had brought to Hiddensee, about Gret Palucca and her longing for dance in the flaxen light of the north that they greeted at dawn, naked and worshipping the sun. Between announcements of lentil stew with sausages, the captain asked if all the passengers had a coin in their pockets, for the deceptive glitter on the waves could be the golden roofs of Vineta, the lost city that emerged every hundred years, seeking deliverance. It had appeared to a boy called Lütt Matten, offering him all its treasures for a mark, a ten-pfennig piece, any coin at all, but the boy had been wearing his swimming trunks and had no money on him at all, so the town had sorrowfully sunk back down.

'Perhaps our General Secretary ought to go diving here.' Philipp had spoken to Judith Schevola but she remained silent, lips pursed, blowing smoke rings that the wind blew away. Streaks of cloud, tinged with ochre and pink, announced the approach of the island.

It was evening by the time the ferry berthed at Kloster. Philipp Londoner and Meno carried their cases to the Lietzenburg handcart. They waited until the last day-trippers had gone on board, the few visitors who were staying on the island had disappeared inland. The ferry cast off, turning into the channel for Schaprode. Judith Schevola did a handstand on the harbour edge.

'Risky,' Meno said when she dropped back down. 'I wouldn't have fancied fishing you out.'

'We've already had a conversation about risks.' Judith Schevola frizzed her hair until it stuck out like the bristles of a bottle-brush. 'The gentlemen will pull my luggage.'

'How is it that you got a place? If I may ask.'

'Socialist bureaucracy. The Association threw me out but I'm still a member of the trade union with a right to a vacation place. And since I had nothing planned anyway –'

'How are you making a living now?' Philipp asked rather brusquely; perhaps he was just annoyed because he had to struggle with the handcart, the tyres of which dragged slackly over the paving stones. Of the ten pieces of luggage, six belonged to Judith Schevola.

'You won't believe it. I'm a nightwatchwoman now.'

'What hare-brained idiot appoints a woman to a job like that?'

'Someone who can't even get pensioners to do it. – At a crematorium and graveyard. "Too much future, too many acquaintances," my seventy-year-old predecessor said as he gave me the keys.' Taking off her shoes and socks, she threw them into the cart, which Meno was helping to pull, rolled up her jeans and splashed though a puddle. Horse-drawn carriages came in the opposite direction. Cyclists rang their bells for them to make way. It was getting cool, the wind came off the sea. The mosquitos buzzed, with an oath, Philipp slapped his neck, examined what he'd killed with an expression of disgust. The old chestnut trees along the main street of Kloster mingled their scent with that of cow dung and hay coming from the extended meadows between Kloster and Vitte. A Schwalbe moped approached, stopped the three of them; the section representative demanded to see their room confirmation. When he read Lietzenburg, he reminded them that no kisses from the muses were allowed after 8 p.m. The road became a sandy track when they turned off north from the main street, past Kasten's bakery. Holidaymakers came towards them, bronzed creatures from another age. Women in flowing batik dresses, lots of wooden ornaments, bangles made from coloured leather straps, sandals with strings of glass beads; pipe-smoking men with artists' locks, the Jesus look, less often short hair and proletarian donkey jackets à la Brecht. Reed-thatched houses beneath the spreading chestnuts, the first lights flashed on.

He could have gone out and perhaps Anne wouldn't have followed him. Christian sensed that she wanted to talk to him but he hated sentimentality: tears, confessions of weakness, despair – all that women's stuff, he thought; he imagined his mother on a walk like that, softening him up with sobs and moans or, even worse, with nothing like that, just with *sympathetic silence*: why? What difference would it make? They were sitting outside the bungalow with a lantern but not enough light for Regine's letter that Richard wanted to read out; Niklas switched on the light over the door.

Christian didn't go. He was tired, it was nice that no one asked him anything, it was a mild evening, crickets were chirping sleepily, it was comfortable lying in the lounger. Gudrun suggested they visit Ina on their way back to Berlin, little Erik was over the worst, visitors weren't a nuisance any more. Anne had made some tea. The shrill of a whistle chopped up the calm of the holiday camp, children came out and stood in two rows in front of the bungalows. Richard didn't read any louder.

'. . . the door was slammed shut from outside. The train was already setting off. We stowed the luggage away. No embraces before the frontier, we were superstitious. The train stopped between stations. Outside there were little men in uniform running up and down, I thought, they're Russians: lots of scurrying and pattering, already there was one in the compartment. "Passports and customs", in the Vogtland dialect. The fear returned: is everything going to be all right? First of all he rummaged round in my handbag. "What's this then?" It was Philipp's wish list, I'd written it out for him. It said: Papa. A peach as big as a football. The uniform put the piece of paper in his pocket. "And this?" I'd made a driving licence for Philipp with a pass-port photograph and a stamp drawn on it for his Liliput three-wheeler (he was a master on his scooter, could park backwards better that I can in the car). I stammered out an explanation, I was pretty overwrought. He shut the little folder, put it back in my bag, handed it to me. "Have a good journey", and he was gone. For a while longer there was noise out in the corridor, clattering, disgruntled voices. Then the train started again. Hansi was annoyed that the guy had stolen the wish list. Philipp slept calmly through everything. We were so exhausted we both dropped off too. The screech of brakes, "Landshut", from outside, Bavarian dialect this time. Around 11 o'clock the family was reunited in Munich Central Station.'

Robert went into the bungalow; he wanted to do some night fishing in the lagoon. The lantern crackled with diving, fluttering insects. The toadstool lamps lit up, one after the other, each one pouring out bright-ness, Christian thought, like milk out of a jug in a girl's hand. There was a vortex in the wall of pines beyond the holiday camp, a frenzy of dissolution on the sky that was being dragged into darkness. Christian felt uneasy. Niklas lit his pipe. Gudrun gargled with tea, leant back, both arms on the arms of her deckchair, began to recite, lines Christian didn't know:

'"Sleeplessness. Homer. Taut sails. I read
The catalogue of ships but halfway through:
That youthful brood, the cranes in retinue
That Hellas saw, once long since, overhead."'
Said, 'Mandelstam.'

Now Niklas took his pipe out of his mouth and declaimed:
'"A golden frog, the moon's bright ring
Floats in the lake's dark night.
Like apple blossom in the spring
My father's beard is turning white."'
Said, 'Yesenin.'

Said Anne:
'"Like that wedge of cranes to distant lands,
Your princes' heads becrowned with godly spray,
You sail. Had Helen not been torn away,
What would Troy be to you, Achaean band?"'
Said, 'Mandelstam.'

Said Robert, 'Now I'm going fishing.'
Christian said nothing.
Richard fetched his accordion, sang:
'"Goodbye, my friend, no hand nor word,
And let not tears your cheeks bedew.
To die is nothing new, I've heard,
And living, yes, that's old hat too."'
Broke off, said, 'Yesenin.'

Said Gudrun:
'"The sea and Homer – both by love impelled.
Which shall I listen to? Now Homer's fallen silent,
And the black sea, with its heavy swell,
Breaks on my pillow, thunderously eloquent."'
Said, 'Mandelstam.'

Christian said nothing. Anne cried.

49

On Hiddensee

Was that not one of the grey sisters, as Falkenhausen had called them, floating down? Common spider to you, garden spider to me. Or was it a winged fruit from one of the shady trees that surrounded Lietzenburg, only allowing the sun to tiptoe in? The spider scuttled up the window frame, paused, raised its rear end (now it was presumably releasing its gossamer thread, you couldn't see it), waited until the pull told it that it could let go – and off it went. Meno looked up at the sky: clear, cloudless days, a dry blue, Our Lady's weather as the old people in Schandau used to call it. Summer's surface scraped away, hot days paid for with chilly nights; already an extravagance of blossom and insect activity, a burden pulling down upward-striving forces. He thought of the cliffs at the north end of the island. There the god Svantevit vented his swirling fury, boiling current and mud, flowing over sticky loam, the smooth-washed, putty-white flesh of the beach, turning potters' wheels in the swell, grating on water-organs, binding fast wave-frisbees that swept every swimmer along, sharpening the breakers into knives that cut deep into the island's body, clawing up shingle and clay, tirelessly paring away, in ever-new upswings of rage, grooves, tunnels and caves in the steep faces that were sagging, eroding, crumbling; sappers' trenches edged forward between two projecting rocks that marked the line of terra firma, long since gnawed away, and, heralded by trickling, rolling rubble and clouds of dust, collapsed into the sea or onto the remaining narrow strip of sand. Meadows tore off from the overhang like wet paper. Pines, brave and tenacious in the carousels of wind and hurricane, tumbled over. The sparse vegetation on the cliff flanks was scraped off. The tidal runnels gurgled, raged, lashed, sobbed, fizzed, drummed, pounded, depending on the strength and direction of the wind; in the autumn squalls, said the Old Man of the Mountain, who had the room opposite Philipp Londoner's at the end of the corridor, it sometimes sounded like a ship being wrecked: creaking wood, splintering masts, drowning bodies whirled down into the gullet of the sea surrounded by the howling, growling tarantella of the storm orchestra. A garden spider on the fan of the spokes. So they were already flying, the young spiders. The Indian summer was early this year. For Judith Schevola just one more reason to borrow other people's clothes (despite the half-dozen pieces of luggage – 'I always find someone to lug my stuff'), to wear Meno's pullover with Philipp's suit when they were sitting round the hall fire in the evening. There was a knock at the door.

'Are you coming? We're going for a swim.' Judith Schevola, a rainbow-bright beach bag, made from strips of cloth sewn together, hanging from her left forefinger, came into the room without waiting for Meno's answer, pushed the carriage of his typewriter until it went 'pling', opened, after having hung her bag on the line-space adjuster, the cupboard and started to rummage through Meno's things. 'I would have bet you'd have several of these things. One to dry, one to use, one as replacement. What did I say?' In triumph she held up three pairs of swimming trunks. 'How can you sit in here in weather like this – doing what? Don't tell me you're writing? Poems?' Her gravelly laugh had become less husky, the sea air was obviously doing her good and she seemed to be smoking less. 'You can't write in here. These crocheted lampshades, these tablecloths, one square red, one square white, the same on the bedspread, red square, white square and always tiny little squares.' She switched on the room radio. 'You can hear the sea!' she commented on the froth of noise interspersed with a swirl of hissing and crackling, occasional deep-sea Scandinavians and snatches of Tchaikovsky, abruptly clear then breaking off, coming from the loudspeaker grille under the faded photograph of the chairman of the trade union. Meno looked at Judith's bare feet, which, as she walked, no: tripped, produced cheeky facial expressions at the back of the knees of her frayed jeans. She went over to the washbasin, smelt the Fa soap (a present from Ulrich), sniffed at his aftershave, peered at his bushily splayed shaving brush, unscrewed the top of his toothpaste tube, squeezed out a blob onto her index finger and quickly rubbed it round her mouth, not seriously cleaning her teeth. Then she gargled, spat out, said 'Big nose' to her mirror image, stuck out her tongue at the fascinated and flabbergasted Meno. 'Come on, then. What are you waiting for? For the house dragon to come and give us a lecture on socialist morality?' From Lietzenburg there was a path through dog roses and thickets of sea buckthorn. There was a smell of henbane. Lizards were sunning themselves on broken steps and only gave way hesitantly to a cautious foot. Philipp Londoner and the Old Man of the Mountain were already on the beach. Philipp had built a stockade of sand and put a windbreak between the walls. Now he was busy making the names of the users by laying pebbles in the sand, he'd already done SCHEVOLA and ALTBERG. He was sitting there, naked and tanned, immersed in this, as Judith Schevola declared with a laugh, very German activity, wearing a straw hat underneath which his long hair was blowing in the wind. The Old Man of the Mountain was naked too. Meno had some objections to naturism, and even more to the uninhibited way Schevola went about it. With a few quick movements she was undressed, just keeping her rubber sandals on; the beach was stony, as everywhere along this stretch of the coast. Meno observed her. Her lips curved in a malicious grin, she smeared sun cream all over herself with obvious pleasure. Was one not exposed to enough indiscretion in this country? The naked body was a mystery and should remain so. The same naked body was untouchable when bathing, when flirting it haunted your imagination; he thought you lost something when it was presented unveiled, however attractive it might be. It had been seen, there was no room for the imagination any more. In the House with a Thousand Eyes, alone in the thick foliage of the garden on a warm summer morning, nakedness was something different. Meno stared at Schevola's beach bag, Philipp at his pebbles, the Old Man of the Mountain pursed his lips and occasionally pretended he had to shake his ears out.

'Would one of you gentlemen be so good as to rub oil over my back?'

Philipp threw his pebbles on one side, Meno avoided the Old Man of the Mountain's eye; he scratched the silvery mane on his chest, put his head on one side and, with intricate excuses and verbose self-irony, did it himself.

The water was cold, light green in the shallower areas, with a slight peppermint flavour. Meno put up stoically with Judith Schevola's attempts to splash water all over him. She seemed to be disappointed that he didn't squeal. The water in the tank at home in the Elbe Sandstone Hills wasn't any warmer. Philipp was a good swimmer, he wanted to go out to the Cape and beyond, the Old Man of the Mountain warned him that there were unpredictable whirlpools and the coastal police – he nodded at the concrete tower on the Dornbusch hills – didn't like to see swimmers heading out for the open sea. So for a while they played with Lührer's dark-blue Nivea ball.

Meno went for a swim, did the crawl with long, regular strokes. The sun had the sharp clarity of a burning glass. He saw the Cape. There was a cordon of stones round it to break the waves, the spray was thundering against them. Once long since. The Mandelstam lines came back to mind, he and Anne had learnt them off by heart; he'd come across them again in a Reclam volume called *Finders of Horseshoes* that Madame Eglantine had lent him; the book was printed on poor paper and came armed with a whole battery of afterwords against expected objections. He died in 1938, in the gulag. Now there was Gorbachev and no one had forgotten. To distant lands you sail. The ball splashed in the water beside him, Schevola shouted something to him; Meno punched it back in the direction of the shouts. He propelled himself gently backwards with his arms, sensed he was getting into deeper water, it was darker, colder. '*Bessoniza. Gomér. Tugije parussa,*' he murmured to himself. Lay with his face down, saw the ripples in the sand, finely ribbed, as if drawn with rakes or sculptor's combs, at an enticing depth already, he was surprised he didn't feel afraid. They shouted, he wanted to go a bit further. He suddenly felt his pulse accelerate and that made him go a bit further. He felt himself being pulled down, as if by filaments, caressingly, blue-washed hair, then slender, delicate fingers; for a moment he was disorientated, he struck out and only realized from the rising wall of water that it was in the wrong direction; he dived, the mountain thundered over him, carried him back into the light green of classical antiquity, now he was swimming frantically, for it came back from the beach, mingled with the breakers heading for the shore, forward and back were struggling against each other, on the surface waves grabbed him by the neck, pushing him towards the beach, below currents heading out to sea had taken a fancy to him; he wasn't making any progress. He dropped into a vertical position: no bottom; the lumps of rock stuck in the clean sand, the seaweed and shells looked deceptively near.

Once he was out, he hoped no one could tell what he'd felt. He waved away Philipp, who'd had his suspicions. Felt Schevola's mockery at his back and was grateful to the Old Man of the Mountain for interrupting his 'philosophical sandwalk' (shoulders hunched, bronzed, slightly paunchy stomach, ribs sticking out and duck-like flat feet with toes marking the sand well in front of the rest of the foot) and starting to argue about the conditions for a game of volleyball; Schevola, Meno could see over his shoulder, seemed to go along with that, at least she still possessed some tact, then. Meno wrapped a towel round his waist, stuffed a towel under the towel, checking that his skirt was unlikely to fall down. His trunks were hanging over his skin like a sodden nappy. He shivered in the wind, which had become sharper, crumpled briefs, shirt and trousers up into a balanceable bundle and slipped over towards the dunes. No volleyball after all, he saw out of the corner of his eye. The Old Man of the Mountain had returned to his reflective walk, Schevola, Philipp and Lührer were stretched out on beach towels by their sand fortress, looking to the right and left, Schevola down; but now – the rubber strap of Meno's left flip-flop had slipped to a painful position between his longest toe and his big toe – she raised her head. Meno skipped up the dune. The place where the marram grass was particularly tall and thick was already occupied by a courting couple. Skipping was strenuous, he tried to run, but with the tightly tied towel he was holding with one hand while the other was clutching the bundle of clothes he could only manage little, ridiculous waddling steps. By now Schevola was openly devoting her full attention to him. That annoyed him. He wasn't a specimen to be studied. Now he was skipping again, jumping without looking. Too late it occurred to him that he could have used their sand fortress. He was so annoyed that he didn't pay attention to the stones stuck in the sand, brown, smooth and rounded, like darning mushrooms. His foot slipped. Meno folded at the waist, stuck out his free leg behind him, obstinately holding on to his towel with his right hand and waving his left to compensate. But the bundle made him unbalanced, for a while he whirled it around in the air, finally dunked it in the sand. As he struggled to right himself, he found himself performing a gymnastic position on one leg, wobbling, his arm and other leg forming a downward slanting line and the towel flopped over, allowing the sun to shine on the Herr Editor's derrière, pale as two white loaves. 'Oh, spiders!' he muttered, using the favourite curse of Mr Fox from the children's *Sandman* television programme.

DIARY

(Tuesday)

By now her hair is more ash blonde than grey. Kim Novak's hair in Vertigo. *Hydrogen peroxide. Don't think Judith uses that. She asked me about*

Christian – and whether I'd brought my Dawn alarm clock with me. Then we talked about plums (the Old Man of the Mountain's brought some Zibarten schnapps, a delicious speciality). I told her the Zibarte was a wild plum variety from the late Celtic period. She shrugged her shoulders. Me: 'Best of all I like plums when they're young and still almost green; they're already juicy, plump but without grubs.' She: 'But when they're ripe they're sweeter, heavier, more intense. These young things, don't they give you stomach ache?' Me: 'Only when you're insatiable.' She: 'You're not insatiable – as far as plums are concerned?' I continued my lecture on the Zibarte plum, an interesting excursion into botany. Judith turned away, bored (?). And round here there are cherry plums, bigger and lovelier than I've ever seen on the slopes above the Elbe. As a name 'cherry plum' shows an odd lack of imagination; I would have called Prunus cerasifera *a peach. The Old Man of the Mountain shook his head slowly from side to side, explaining that one did not rechristen something that bore the name* myrobalan *from the depths of time. – How does Judith know I have an alarm clock?*

(Wednesday)

One word about breakfast, for all I have to say about early-morning exercises that here (I have to be fair) are recommended rather than compulsory is: since so far I've still managed to get up at five for my lauds and snip off a bit of the day's work with the scissors of my willpower, I can observe the gathering of keep-fitters on the sports field behind Lietzenburg with an easy eye. You can borrow the army tracksuit – you have to sign for it, of course. Later on in the day the man in charge of Fun and Games (as the official name has it) is the house electrician – they say Günter Mellis, when he's staying here, is generous in his offers of help – caretaker, messenger and boilerman in winter as well. I spent ages wondering where I'd seen him before: when I met Arbogast on the way to see the Old Man of the Mountain. The man leading the students from the House of the Teacher. Our F&G leader insisted he'd nothing to do with him, he'd always worked here, at Lietzenburg. Similarly Frau Kruke, housekeeper, charwoman and watchdog, Judith's 'house dragon'. She insists she's never heard of Else Alke, even though she's the spitting image of her. A dwarf shuffling along in slippers. – To get back to breakfast, which she's in charge of. As Judith takes her plastic plate with the standard two slices of Tilsiter cheese, two slices of blutwurst, two slices of bologna, one little slab of hotel butter, two slices of pumpernickel (Saturdays rolls from Kasten's bakery, Sundays a piece of cake), Lührer, the writer, who's in front of her in the queue, says, 'Enjoy your meal', and apologizes that 'recently' he voted for her expulsion, she must understand that he had four children to provide for. – That's all I needed! (Judith) Breakfast starts on the dot of eight. At the moment there are thirty-three of us in the house. In the canteen eight tables, each spread with a red-and-white-checked cloth and decorated with a light-green, transparent plastic vase, stand silent. In each vase there is water rising to a line marked one centimetre below the rim and pierced by a single artificial flower, style: red marguerite, from the workshops in Seibnitz. All the stems are ground like a cannula and slightly curved, inclined, as seen from the canteen door, to the right, so that the blooms all look to the east and at eight o'clock on the dot they all (assuming it's a good day) don a little cap of light the size of your thumbnail. On every table the latest copies of Neues Deutschland, Junge Welt *and the* Ostsee-Zeitung, *in aluminium napkin holders in the shape of a half-sun, await the guests; in addition, on the men's tables there is* Magazin *and on the women's* Für Dich *and* Sowjetfrau. *The copy of the satirical weekly* Eulenspiegel *is chained and on such a short chain that it can only be read at the occasional table by the entrance. There is a board with slots for strips of paper (blue and pink, typewritten) and each morning you have to check where you're sitting. In order to make us mingle as much as possible and to 'assure the maximum communicative contact' (quoted from house regulations) the men and women – always separate – go from table to table. But what is the use of that when the Old Man of the Mountain spreads out his personal napkin, Philipp brings his own cutlery, Judith responds to Karlfriede Sinner-Priest's comment that Fräulein Schevola actually had no right to be there by sweeping her plate off the table and strolling out of the room, and Lührer, the writer, all too pointedly places a jar of Nutella between himself and the poor editor, Rohde?*

(Wednesday evening)

Notions –

Prague '68. The third way. Stony monumental faces on the canyons of Sacred Theories. The bare You or I that, like everything unavoidable, is not without its comic side, nor without its boring side. There, in '68 in Czechoslovakia, a humane society seemed possible, a society that does not forget that it consists of individuals. Democracy and open discussion. Criticism, publicly expressed but not simply for its own sake.

Schevola: 'A dream, Herr Rohde. Crushed by tanks.'

The Old Man of the Mountain: 'Perhaps Dubček and his friends were just lucky.'

Philipp: 'You a heretic? Go on.'

The Old Man of the Mountain: 'The most radiant dreams are those that never need to become reality. Do you, Herr Londoner, seriously consider a capitalist socialism a possibility? Freedom of production, of reaction to the market, demands freedom of thought. Your father had something interesting to say about that recently.'

Philipp: 'Thought does not have to be unfree in socialism. Unfree socialism isn't socialism. A genuinely socialist society will develop by openly naming and overcoming its contradictions.'

Schevola: 'That means we're not living in socialism.'

The Old Man of the Mountain: 'Don't say that so emphatically, my dear. – Dubček has become a martyr, Prague '68 a legend. It could become a myth because it was spared failure. That was the fault of the fraternal states and we're left with a fairy-tale flower that never had to prove in the

695

soil of reality that its bloom would be as beautiful as promised. — You think me an opportunist. Maybe that's what I am. Maybe I'm a coward. I'm on publishers' advisory boards, now and then the Minister for Books listens to me — and I didn't dare to speak up loudly for your book, Judith. I'm even prepared to look inside myself and to admit I found a nasty little piece of envy down there. I'm a censor, and not an easy-going one. I was in the SA. I was a soldier in the Wehrmacht. I was in the camp. Despite everything I saw, I believed in the good in people. I've remained a child. I'm afraid. For this country as well. I'm no longer young and my life's consisted of broken dreams, day after day. I don't believe in anything any more.'

Schevola: 'Amen to that.'

Philipp: 'You're old, that's all. Indigestion, itchiness, you've seen it all before . . . the whole business! But you're making things difficult for us. There are lots of people like you in this country and, unfortunately, often in senior positions. Waving things away, weary hands, weary blood — but we need strength, encouragement, it's not easy —'

Schevola: '— to be a revolutionary? Da-da-da-da! It's so difficult to bring happiness to mankind.'

The Old Man of the Mountain: 'And to stay polite as you do so. I don't hold it against you for dismissing me as an old man. But itchiness . . . that's tactless, my lad.'

Philipp: 'Judith Schevola: cool, cynical, ironic. Go on, open your big mouth and make fun of us. We still believe in something. And what do you believe in? Nothing! Like you, Herr Altberg.'

The Old Man of the Mountain: 'Yesyes, I've said that already. It used to be called defeatism. Carried the death penalty by firing squad.'

Philipp: 'Then resign if you can't do anything any more. Your generation is hanging on to power, they'd rather die than let someone else take over. And what use to us is all the hullabaloo about young people, the reserves of the Party, if we stay just that: reserves . . . Oh, what the hell, that's not really the problem. The problem is that the gerontocracy's leading this country to rack and ruin! We have new data, the economy's heading for disaster – and no one seems concerned about it!'

Schevola: *'A priest was murdered in Poland. Popieluszko he was called. That concerns me.'*

Philipp: *'You think that now you can say whatever you want.'*

Schevola: *'For a while I'll think about what I'm saying. All that's left is to lock me up or kill me. Well, Herr Altberg, however long you look at them, the chestnut leaves above us don't look like ears.'*

The Old Man of the Mountain: *'Oh yes they do. Dachshund's ears. All that is left us is precision.'*

Schevola: *'How do you imagine your world revolution? A bit of playing Che Guevara in the jungle? You'll only catch simple-minded girls at the university with that.'*

Philipp: *'Make fun of us, if you like. What does it matter? – By the way, Marisa's coming here.'*

Schevola: *'Your Chilean whore.'*

Philipp: *'Oh, yes. She's neither simple-minded nor a student, so what else is there left for you to call her? What was it you said when we were going to Eschschloraque's?'*

The Old Man of the Mountain: *'Can you explain this garden spider's nest to me, Herr Rohde?'*

Schevola: *'You're welcome to stay here, we've nothing to hide. It'd be a pity about the juicy bit of gossip you'd miss.'*

Herr Altberg: *'Don't worry, back then I just happened be in the vicinity; Herr Rohde is as discreet as* Pravda.'

Philipp: *'"I was never particularly taken with middle-class morality . . . you're welcome to bring your little Chilean woman along."'*

Schevola: *'Quack, quack, quack.'*

We saw the bay, in the haze the cliffs of Møn. Sunlight settled over the clear depths of the bay; an endless shimmer over the slow slapping of the water: as if swarms of grasshoppers were making their wings buzz. Beside it, scenes as peaceful as a jar of night-cream.

697

(Thursday)

Writers need training! But the tutor, who had come with the ferry from Stralsund bringing ice cream, sections copied from Apprentice Year in the Party *and a social science periodical, was shot down by Philipp ('a hit', the Old Man of the Mountain said gleefully afterwards, 'a palpable hit'), who highlighted his errors of logic and misquotations — most of what the tutor was spelling out painfully slowly from typescripts he knew off by heart, precisely, even down to the occasionally old-fashioned spelling of the original; so there the young professor sat, a strand of his long hair in his left fist, a pencil tapping out point-end-point-end in a semicircle in his right, his feet in their openwork slip-ons jogging up and down in time to the click-clack of his pencil on the Sprelacart tabletop until, fed up to the back teeth and examining his fingernails, the tutor suggested: 1) Comrade Smart-aleck should please take over and 2) what did people think of transferring the study of the classics to the beach? Philipp leapt up and wrote on the blackboard:*

Petty bourgeois	*(Educated) Middle class*
Cabinet with display shelf, budgerigar, knick-knacks, doilies	Telephone, Insel series of books, pipe collection
Visitors: remove shoes (slippers for guests)	Can keep their shoes on
Toilet roll in car with crocheted cover, pine-tree air freshener over dashboard, head-wagging dachshund, Smurfs	Leather cover for gear lever, 'No smoking' sticker 'A heart for children' on the dashboard
If a dog: Alsatian, Pomeranian, mongrel	If a dog: poodle, Afghan hound, Great Dane
Invites to barbecue party	Invites to coffee or tea

Petty bourgeois	(Educated) Middle class
Works team party, punch with inhabitants of apartment block	Solitary walks (with wrist bag)
Watches football (with team scarf)	Talks about football, quotes from the legendary Zimmermann commentary on 1954 World Cup
Forward to Majorca	Back to nature
The wife cooks, cleans, goes out to work, looks after the children	The wife cooks, cleans, goes out to work, looks after the children
Garden plot, swing hammock, garden barbecue, water butt, stock of beer, portable television	Dacha
Puts his hope in the Federal Chancellor	Puts his hope in Gorbachev
The world of early rising	The world of coming home late

I belong to the working class, the tutor said icily, I stick to Marx, Engels and Lenin. He demanded, 'Your name, comrade.' Philipp expressed regret that fewer and fewer cadres had a sense of humour, took a brochure from the Institute of Social Sciences off the desk, searched through it briefly, twirling the ends of his moustache into the curving-up ends of a sleigh, and gave the comrade tutor an autograph.

(Friday)
Choice of activities ('the house management recommends'): an excursion to Warnow shipyard in Rostock (5 votes), a sightseeing tour of Sassnitz and the smallest museum in the Republic (the goods wagon in which Lenin, a spark on a long fuse, travelled to the powder-keg of pre-revolutionary Russia, 4 votes). Beside it some joker had scribbled BATHING (19 votes).

So it was the Warnow shipyard. I wrote a card to the ship's doctor (the maritime theme of the new development at Lütten Klein outside Rostock seemed appropriate), then I called Libussa. Arbogast's consignment of pencils has arrived. She said Frau Honich was snooping around my apartment and suggested I threaten to go to the police. I've given my manuscripts to Anne for safe keeping so told her to avoid confrontation even though I find it hard to bear the thought of that bitch's fingers on the ten-minute clock – how familiar, how comforting the gong I heard over the phone – perhaps even breaking it: some people cannot stand other people's happiness, the dignity of aristocratic and defenceless objects makes some people want to cripple them. Libussa said Chakamankabudibaba had brought up a poorly digested mouse on my copy of Schelling.

(Saturday)

Who wears white gloves nowadays? Marisa's seem to be of deerskin, so finely tanned that when Marisa closes her fingers to make a fist, shiny infant's noses form over her knuckles. She wore them with khaki drill trousers, the top of a toothbrush sticking out of the right front pocket, a bright-blue T-shirt with orange flamingos printed on, and a jean jacket casually thrown over her shoulder and held with her little finger. She arrived without luggage. When she saw me (I happened to be listening to some trees with a stethoscope, decaying ones especially are acoustic cathedrals, elms grow with different noises from beeches), she pulled off her soldier's cap and waved it round and round, as if she were trying to swing an aeroplane propeller. I'd just had a little argument with Judith about reality – Judith's response to my explanation was to pull up a nettle and show it to me, an impassive expression on her face: 'That, for me, is reality'; then, still with the nettle in her hand that already had a rash and atolls of itchy spots, she saw Marisa joyfully waving her cap. Philipp was behind us, leaning back against a bent elm branch as thick as an elephant's leg and rocking to and fro, at the same time leafing through a Reclam volume on utopian socialists

(Babeuf, Blanqui); the Old Man of the Mountain was strolling up and down the west side of Lietzenburg, admiring the architectural mixture of art nouveau and English country house, the fairy-tale windows with wide-spread arms; now and then he would declaim some lines out loud: 'As when the budding flowers, half dead and half alive / In the cellar's darkness struggle there to thrive.' – Judith saw Marisa, went up to her with a smile, embraced her, holding up the hand with the nettle.

'Oh, it's you,' Marisa said. By now her German was almost accent-free.

'Yes. Lovely T-shirt you've got on, Frau Sanchez.'

'From Santiago de Chile. May I go and clean my gloves first? I was stupid enough to eat a sticky ice cream. Hello, Herr Rohde.' I took the stethoscope out of my ears.

Judith: 'I've got a knife.'

Marisa: 'A good one?'

Judith handed it to Marisa, who unclasped it and examined it with an expert eye. 'A good knife,' she said, giving it back to Judith, 'where did you get it? And do you also know where your thrust should go?'

'Where it hurts, I assume. It's a genuine French Laguiole, a present from a reader.'

'Please – give it to me. You don't know how to handle it.'

'I'd love to give you one now. There.' Judith raised her fist and stopped just short of Marisa's cheekbone.

'Not very effective, even though it looks spectacular. Don't deceive yourself, most people find it more difficult than they think to hit someone in the face. I'd be quicker than you, ward the blow off upwards, like this' – Marisa demonstrated how she would do it – 'and then hit you there.' Marisa stopped her little fist in its white glove short of Judith's Adam's apple.

'First the man, then the knife.' Judith regarded the open, stick-insect-slim blade.

'You'd use it for Philipp?'

Judith looked round at Philipp, who'd put his book down and, sitting

astride the branch, had started to cut his fingernails. Now and then he cried,
'Stupid', pushed his cream hat back but didn't come any closer, and I looked
for the Old Man of the Mountain, who was now sitting at his typewriter
in the sun, glue pot, draft paper and scissors beside him, working away at
his mountain project and not looking up. Judith said, 'You can have the
knife. Your demand is so outrageous that I'm beginning to like you again.
I like it when a balance clearly tips down on one side. If I have to lose, then
properly, the other pan says. At least it's empty and free.'

'You want to stab from outside but that's quite wrong. Come on, I'll show
you.' Marisa took the knife out of her hand, linked arms with Judith and
they headed for Lietzenburg, deep in conversation, their heads close together.

The Old Man of the Mountain started when the clock struck; there
was no one in the library of Lietzenburg apart from himself and Meno.
He took off his reading glasses, stood up, groaning, put the Apollodorus
book back on the shelf beside the stack of *Sibylle* magazines from
which, in the evenings when the watchtower on the Dornbusch sent
segments of light feeling their way over land and sea, Karlfriede
Sinner-Priest read out stylistic bloomers; they were hours pampered
by the tick-tock of the grandfather clock and, since it was already
getting cold when evening fell, the approving puffs of the stove with
the windmill tiles. Two censors sitting together, she in a crocheted
stole, he in a knitted cardigan, both with flushed cheeks, for when her
rocking chair went 'creak', his rocking chair went 'croak'.

'Time, Herr Rohde. One doesn't keep Barsano waiting.'

Marisa and Philipp joined them on the beach. They had guitars
slung over their shoulders on brightly coloured, folksy woven straps
and looked like adventurers with their hair stiff with salt under straw
hats casting frayed star-shadows on their feet that, as they waded along
the back-and-forth of the water's edge with its unconsciously stumbling
shells, they let glittering hands run over. They were heading for the
Cape, the cliffs of which were already gathering the red of sunset,

climbing one of the steep paths leading up from the shore. Agrimony and yarrow, black mullein and woody nightshade grew along the path; to Meno's surprise the Old Man of the Mountain identified them without having to think for long. 'A pharmacist's son, Herr Rohde, ought to have sufficient botanical knowledge –' The rest of the sentence was drowned out by the roar of engines. Beyond the Cape, beach buggies were tearing through the waves and up the dunes that sandslips had rendered less steep there. Philipp shaded his eyes. Meno recognized the Kaminski twins, in the other three buggies were members of the Central Committee of the Socialist Unity Party of Germany. One of the twins roared up the slope, stopped in front of Philipp. 'Well, Herr Londoner, in which column of your table does this activity come.'

'Impudence,' Philipp said without thinking; Meno grasped his arm.

'Watch your tongue, Master Londoner, we've told you that before. Ah, Herr Rohde, you've been invited too? How are things at home? Frau Honich will be sorry you're not there.'

Kaminski – Meno still couldn't say which was Timo and which René – grinned, glanced briefly at Marisa, ignored the Old Man of the Mountain.

'I thought motor vehicles were forbidden on the island?' Philipp stared at Kaminski, who was coolly taking off his suede openwork racing-driver gloves. 'Fancy a ride? I'm called Timo.'

'Thanks, but no, *compañero*.' Marisa tried to get Philipp to move on but Barsano was already waving them over. Timo Kaminski put two fingers to his baseball cap in salute. With a roar of the engine, the buggy shot back off towards the beach. Philipp swore at his departing back. His father, he said, was a highly placed cadre in the nomenklatura, a genuine fighter still, but his spawn, Philipp said, spitting on the ground out, were betraying the ideals of the revolution; they were wastrels, exploiting their connections. 'An apartment – who gets one at that age, single students, huh!'

'You too,' Meno ventured to object, but that only exacerbated Philipp's rage.

'It's different with me. I got my flat through people I know . . . by fighting for it. Yes, you can certainly call it that. Moreover I'm not a student any more!' Philipp's tendency to fly off the handle, to become obstreperous; Philipp's blindness for parallels (that he shared with Hanna); Meno said nothing, he was thinking what Judith Schevola had said on the way to East Rome: the Red aristocracy.

'I can well imagine what you're thinking.' Philipp gave a bush, quietly dreaming of the peak of its aspirations, a kick. 'And I'd like to remind you that without Father's intervention you'd never have got the apartment on Mondleite. No question about it. But these guys . . . they're gangsters, they have no scruples and belong to our Party – it's been totally corrupted by bastards like that!'

'He might be able to hear you, Philipp,' Meno warned, nodding towards Barsano, who had got out of his buggy and was climbing up the dune. The Old Man of the Mountain whispered that it was impolite to stand around when the First Secretary was approaching, especially from below; he stooped and went to meet Barsano.

'*They're* the ones who have power in the Party, not the honest comrades who're pinching and scraping at the base in order to preserve at least something . . . Now, don't tell on me,' Philipp said abruptly, outwardly composed again. They followed the Old Man of the Mountain, but Philipp held himself proudly upright.

'A few toys' – the First Secretary made a dismissive wave – 'Father Kaminski had them delivered to the Central Committee's holiday house. Wouldn't have thought it was such fun to drive them. Where've you left Schevola? We don't want to see her any more. We can forget her. Pity, we don't see pretty women that often,' he said to Marisa, holding out his gloved hand to her with a remark on the work of the Chilean Solidarity Committee. 'They're from the Federal Republic, those things. We ought to build them here too. Perhaps Arbogast can manage it. – Off you go up there now, comrades, there's something to drink at the top.'

50

And if you have worries or problems

Class comrade – give the order. Class comrade – carry it out.
The same desire. A common goal. That leads to trust.

What It Means to be a Soldier

When autumn came, the ash came. When November came, the rains and the new recruits came to Grün. During the last ten days of their service anyone who tried to rouse Rogalla and Ruden from their cheerful and yet, in the afternoon, impatient and despairing drunken rest was shown an aluminium spoon that had been rolled flat and made to look like a railway baton, holding up first the side painted red, then the one painted green: Stop. Departure. The discharge candidate's 'measure' of his last months of service, self-made out of a brass grenade case containing a 150 cm tailor's tape measure sticking out through a slit (was there not a VEB somewhere, Christian wondered, that could proudly announce it had realized its planned targets for these tape measures?) was shortened by one centimetre each day.

Sometimes, when the room and section cleaning was over and the polishing brushes were no longer clattering along the corridor, Christian, together with Burre, would go to fetch coal, that was one of the earholes' tasks. Burre, whose first name was Jan – Christian never used

705

his nickname – would lumber along, a clumsy bear cub in his black
overalls, grasping the rubber handgrips firmly in his work-mittens,
muttering and humming, trundling the wheelbarrow with its pneumatic
tyres over the cobbles of the road that, years ago, had been tarmacked,
past the med centre, from which the bedridden soldiers in brown camouflage uniforms shouted snide comments, the maintenance unit, the
tailoring workshop, and swung round, singing by now, towards headquarters, behind which, screened off by a few low-rise sheds and the
swimming pool, lay the regiment's coal supply. The piles were covered
in rampant weeds – the coal had to be ordered far in advance and
was delivered in the spring; skinny cats had dug out hollows for themselves (the coal was mainly slack, tiny lumps and dust rather than
briquettes), crows were arguing over scraps of food: the kitchen dust
bins, which never shut properly, stood, immersed in their own kind of
melancholy, next to the piles of coal. Whenever Burre and Christian
saw men with wheelbarrows from 1st and 3rd Battalions they would
start to run and, if no one had got there before them, choose the best
places and begin to shovel like mad – those who got the best coal had
the hottest stoves and boilers. The full wheelbarrows weighed a good
hundredweight and Christian would never have thought that he, the
spoilt son of the educated middle classes who'd stayed on at senior
high school, would be able to lift such a weight, never mind push it
forward over greasy wooden planks between the grassy mounds and
obstacles that made the coal in the cart, which looked like an upturned
dissected frog, bounce merrily up and down. In addition to that, it was
impossible to keep the load in the optimum position, on their tyres that
weren't properly pumped up the barrows wobbled this way and that,
and those pushing them staggered like drunks; Christian had the feeling he was trying to transport an ox on a ruler. On the way back Burre
would sing even louder, his muttering would become a droning and
rhythmical 'da-da-da'. At such times Christian felt so sorry for him
he had to stop for a moment to fight down the sadness that swirled up

inside him like an unrestrained garden hose. The birch trees shimmered, from the square in front of headquarters they heard the officer shout, 'Mount guard!' Squirrels, fiery red, weightless little fellows, scampered along the barracks wall, overhung by elms. And yet, at such moments Burre was perhaps happy; he seemed to be in a world of his own, kept his head bowed, singing and muttering to help him forget the obstinate wheelbarrow, the evening noises of the barracks, his dripping nose that was a shining black from the coal dust. Christian thought of the slug-yellow paste full of gritty bits they'd have to rub all over their face, neck and hands; he didn't want to but couldn't help thinking of the lumps of black snot the size of broad beans they'd blow out of their noses, followed by a dry cough and shivers of horror at the things coming out of their bodies and into the washroom outflow. Burre was staggering and there was a regular occurrence when they drew level with the repair shop of the maintenance unit: there was a speed bump he tried to take at a run – the shovel lying across the barrow jumped up and to one side, lumps of coal squirted up and fell onto the road. Burre, trying to keep his balance, swerved like a figure-skater fighting the centripetal force of the ice in order to prepare another jump, braced himself, still singing, ever more desperately against the wheelbarrow's determination to topple over and finally jumped aside to let it have its own, mindless way. Then Burre would start to laugh and Christian suspected that at that moment he saw himself from outside, that he burst out laughing at his own uselessness and the film-cartoon-like inevitability of the overturning, in a wobbly fit of shamefaced amusement that was as much a mystery to Christian as the fact that Nip would never allow them to fetch the coal before cleaning the rooms and section. They had to take it up the stairs and for that there was nothing apart from the 'pig trough' as they called the sledge, originally painted army green and presumably constructed from an ammunition case resting on two stringers, between the scraped planks of which, irrespective of the panting, the cursing, the gasped instructions from the 'earhole' in front and the 'earhole' behind, brown coal powder trickled out, leaving a trail on the stairs and the freshly polished wooden floor of the corridor.

Burre came from Grün. He and his mother – his father had walked out on them when Burre's little sister had drowned in the emergency water pond one winter – had two rooms in one of the tumbledown half-timbered houses behind the market; one evening he had pushed some photos under the dividing wall in the toilets: there, in one of the four stinking WC bays with their iridescent flypapers, was the only place you could have time for yourself, undisturbed, although naturally the more senior soldiers were aware of this and Musca liked to jump up the door, as if it were an assault wall, to see what was going on behind it.

Burre's mother worked shifts as an adjuster in the Grün metal works. Every two weeks she sent her son a parcel, a tedious (the post office was at the other end of the little town) and expensive way of circumventing the unreliable guards at the barracks checkpoint, to whom she had at first given the parcels – Burre was never given a pass, Nip didn't like him because, as the staff sergeant indicated, he was one of those who 'ruin the company's record'.

'Injustice is the spice of life,' Tank Driver Popov said, regarding his toes, which needed some attention, calmly sticking his cap on his head and a turnover in his mouth: Company 4 was on guard duty, five days before the discharge of the soldiers in their third and the NCOs in their sixth half-year. Christian saw Burre's mother sitting with Musca, Costa and a few drivers who were not on duty; she spoke falteringly, mumbling, Christian was amazed at the similarity in timbre to her son (Burre also had that colourless voice of indeterminate register), the similarity in their features, while at the same time finding it depressing, and as he handed his machine pistol to Ruden, who locked it in a weapons cupboard, as he took off cap and belt (a minor pleasure every time), he tried to remember something that was connected with that feeling of depression; but it only came back to him when he ran his fingers through his shorn hair: 'The Hoffmanns' hair whorl,' his clock grandfather had said, 'my father had it, I have it, your father has it and if you have children, Christian, you'll find it on them, as faithful as ever . . . perhaps you'll soon understand how funny and sad that is, you laugh and feel resigned. – Upbringing?' He made a dismissive gesture. Christian had remembered that, although its meaning had remained unclear. Burre's mother was dressed up in her Sunday best and Christian quickly realized she had come to plead for her son.

Ruden strolled over, said nothing. Rogalla explained it was nothing to do with him any more; Ruden, who probably had been going to say something, nodded, happy at this neat solution that relieved him of responsibility; he followed Rogalla out, holding up the spoon with the green side showing.

'They were the worst,' Costa said, 'they're leaving in five days' time. Then he'll be over the worst.' Burre's mother didn't respond, she hadn't taken her headscarf off, was still sitting there in her trench-coat, one of those putty-grey ones with buttons the size of pocket watches, which were still available in the shops alongside green and forest-brown parkas, the sole difference between the men's and women's styles being (Barbara claimed) that the women's buttoned on the left, the men's on the right.

After a while she turned to Musca. 'Haven't you got a mother?' she asked.

'No,' he replied. 'And if I did have one she wouldn't come strolling in with five hundred marks in an envelope.'

'You have no mother?'

'No, I haven't! I come from a home, you see, my old lady drank herself to death. I drove her nuts, when I was little she put red wine in my bottle. I was quiet once I'd had it. But you – you just come barging in here with your money and fine words: *a sensitive boy* – I'm sensitive too, gentlemen. If you only knew how sensitive I sometimes am and how my comrades here sometimes really piss me off –'

'Heeheehee.'

'Shutyertraparsehole. – So, what do you have to say to that?'

But Burre's mother didn't answer, for her son had come in. At first he didn't seem to understand, looked irritatedly from one side of the table to the other, then, when he saw the envelope, he abruptly turned round, lowered his head, as if to think, fingering his pack frame with the pockets for his reserve magazine and his water bottle that, against regulations, he'd hooked on to it. 'You shouldn't have come here, I asked you not to. And certainly not with money, have we got a golden goose?' He didn't turn round, spoke agitatedly, shoulder raised, to an uncomprehending spot on the floor, from which his mother's answer could reach him by ricochet.

'But you told me he wouldn't come,' Burre's mother murmured to Costa in a weary, monstrously sad voice.

When autumn came, the DCs left. Not after having given advice: Keep your tank water bottle clean. Your field pack in order. Tell the new ones they should get some material for slings and motorbike goggles.

The new 'earholes' arrived, stuffed with rumours, from 'outside' and from the cadet schools; they approached with trepidation, panting under the weight of the packed groundsheets, driven by a taskmaster with his hands behind his back, and dispersed into the various companies, like one of those lines of ants that resemble a procession of walking leaves – with one exception: Steffen Kretzschmar, who, because of his baker's hands, his round face, his short, wiry black hair and ears that stuck out like handles, was immediately dubbed 'Pancake'. Pancake was pulling a handcart in which he had his things (only the more senior servicemen had sailor's kitbags, diverted from navy stores): a Weltmeister accordion with cracked mother-of-pearl buttons, a barbell and a box of juggler's balls. When Musca exulted, he did it with childlike openness, he pushed his cap onto the back of his head so that his protuberant eyes formed a lilac-blue centre in a face creased with laughter lines: widened by knowledge or ideas that were still in the state of chortling anticipation and only after a few seconds would send out shudders all over his skinny body, like a kind of nettlerash.

'Just look at that dogface! Pullin' a handcart, have y'ever seen anythin' like that before!' He went to his locker, put on his belt, aimed a cherry pit, still a pleasing red, at Karge on his bunk. 'Hey, Wanda, get your finger out, the virgins are coming and one we can show what's what.'

Even Christian was actually too tall for the tank, the limit was one metre eighty; but Pancake was at least one metre ninety. 'The hatch's goin' to knock his head into his shoulders,' Popov said, 'well, perhaps that's why they put him in the cavalry. How's he going to park those spindle-shanks of his between the gear lever and the brakes . . . and a cap to fit that noddle just don't exist.'

Musca drew himself up to his full height in front of Pancake, which looked rather ridiculous: he was a whole head shorter and looked like a buzzing insect that, in order finally to attract the attention of the giant explorer – Christian observed Pancake looking down on Musca, at first puzzled, then with increasing interest – had transformed itself into a dancing spider, a raving frog, a double-bass player during the 'Flight of the Bumblebee'; except that after a while Pancake asked, 'What d'you want?'

'. . . anyway!' Musca was waving his hands about; Pancake lifted him up with one arm, over his head, popped a cigarette between his lips with his left hand, lit it with the long flame of a red Bic lighter (Musca squealed, the flame was licking round the crotch of his trousers), waited until Musca's boots had fallen off, then gently put him down in a November puddle, skilfully avoiding his fists flailing round in the air. Karge almost died laughing. 'Great balls of fire!'

Costa said it served the bigmouth right. Irrgang came from the

depot and shouted that if that was one of the privileges accorded discharge candidates, then count him in.

Pancake accepted his nickname, even seemed to be happy with it
and look on it as flattery, for he didn't object to it, on the contrary,
sometimes when he was on duty he would report as 'Private Pancake',
grinning maliciously at the confusion he caused. During the first few
days, Christian thought, he was trying things out, giving the officers
a look-over: he respected Nip, who, giving him a look from his
yellowed sclerotics, breathed out an alcohol-reeking, 'Imtheonewho-
decidesonthefunnybusinessizzatclearcomrade', looked the battalion
commander, Major Klöpfer (whom all the soldiers in his battalion
thought totally incompetent), up and down, listened to the political
officer with half-closed eyes, observed Christian, who was his tank
commander. Pancake seemed to possess an intuitive knowledge of
human nature that came to rapid conclusions, a cool ability to see
through bluster and poses and assess people as 'useful' or 'no use',
'dangerous' or 'harmless', a crude but probably tried-and-tested classification on which he based his behaviour. He seemed to have problems
fitting Christian into this classification for more than once Nemo, as
Pancake also called him, felt the grey-flecked eyes under their sleepy,
heavy lids on him. After a few days Pancake had declared poor Burre
his 'slave' (what surprised Christian was that none of the other drivers
protested; perhaps the performance he'd put on with Musca had convinced them?); Nip's 'humming top' he dismissed with a twitch of his
fleshy lips; the company commander did not interfere in the business
of the lower ranks and Pancake was in the platoon leader's good
books because he was the best driver the battalion had ever seen. He
was better than Popov, for Pancake had the confidence to reverse into
the tank shed in the technical depot at full throttle (and without a guide,
that was the game when a fractional movement on the steering lever
could decide the fate of a Double-T carrier); on the old Wehrmacht
practice course, which had been adapted to Russian conditions, he

lowered the company record that had been set by a legendary reserve officer in the early seventies; in Pancake's fist the right-angled steel hook to open the hatch bolt looked as delicate as the handle of a lady's hatbox.

There was no baptism. Five of them tried to overpower Pancake; Christian, who was duty NCO, woke from his doze with a start when they flung open the door to the drivers' room; the first Pancake threw out of the open window (a coarse-voiced loader who was ready for any brawl or booze-up, even when it was an NCO — otherwise the various ranks were strictly separated); then Pancake put on a knuckle-duster, sat down at the table, an open clasp-knife in front of him, had a drink of tea and calmly asked if there was anyone else who wanted a go. He seemed to be thinking while the others stood, uncertain what to do, in the doorway, then, smiling, he raised his forefinger and pointed to his locker, letting it circle round a block wrapped in silver foil, gave the bed in which Burre slept a kick and bellowed, 'Up you get, Nutella, serve us the steaks.'

The new arrivals: among the commanders a man whose cheesy, acne-ridden face creased like a glove puppet when there was something he didn't like and who was running off all the time to the political officer, who dampened his ardor with a variety of commendations. A taciturn goldsmith, who used a serviette when eating and folded it before throwing it away. There was an argument about the allocation of areas to be cleaned, Burre wanted to keep the toilet. Christian knew it wasn't the filthy enlisted men's toilet he was concerned about but the officers' toilet, which could be locked. But Pancake said he just wanted to get out of the way there and it would be enough if he stayed at the personal disposal of the drivers.

'But I want to do the toilet,' Burre insisted. A short, stocky driver refused to give in as well.

'Aha, you slaves *want* something. OK.' Pancake put two dolls on the table, carved from wood, one red, one green. 'I see things this way.

There are basically two kinds of people: those at the top and those at the bottom, those with dough and those without. Those who give orders and those who receive them, and if one wants something and the other doesn't, God, what happens then? If two want to scrub the loo but only one can do it, they'll have to fight for it.'

'We could get them to compare dicks,' Karge suggested. 'But that would be unfair. Nutella's is swollen from all those hand jobs.'

'It has to be fair,' Musca crowed. 'Clever Dicks always have small ones! And who knows whether this mucky pup here will polish my loo seat as well as Nutella does?'

'Oh man,' Popov sighed, 'that I should live to see this. Two earholes sluggin' it out over who's to scrub the shithouse. Right, I want to see blood.'

'They're to lift weights. A fair competition.' Pancake went over to his bed, rolled out the bar with the two 50 kg weights. He came from a circus dynasty, his ancestors had bent iron rods, juggled with 25 kg balls, wrestled and taken part in eating competitions; he himself had worked as a smith with the Aeros and Berolina circuses; there had been an argument, 'some business, sorted out', as he put it with his malicious grin; for some time he'd been dealing in cars and it was said he'd gone to ground in the army for three years because of some shady affair (there were targets here as well, what did a recruiting officer care about the past if he got a useful recruit because of it). Pancake lifted the weights with no problem. The driver tried first; his head wobbled like a baby with a weak neck but eventually he got his arms stretched. Burre stepped forward and as he bent down Christian knew he'd never lift the weights. His thin arms dangled over the barbell, then Burre put his glasses on the table, spat on his hands and made a show of jogging about a bit, a kind of voodoo or conjuration; perhaps it would help; at last with a vigorous jerk he lifted the weights up to his chest – Christian would never have believed the chubby, clumsy Burre capable of it; it was followed by a shout, like those made by weightlifters on *Today's*

Sport, then a sidestep to the right, his knees still bent, he puffed, his hands turning white under the bar, concentrated, his right leg, stuck out at an angle, began to tremble, Musca said, 'Just no one laugh now'; Burre closed his eyes, struggling, his face went red, then he uttered a dull cry, it sounded like casual disappointment, mixed with surprise, this 'Oooh', damning his own limited body and weakness, from Burre, whom, at the moment of the change of grip, of the decisive effort to lift the weights, all his poems did nothing to help.

At night, before going to sleep Christian had the feeling his body was floating away, was breaking up in the area where he took breath, something was fraying (he thought of his cello, only briefly, pushed it out of his mind: dead, dead, *what are the old ghosts to me*, to his inner eye his cello seemed to be smouldering like a hot strip of celluloid film); a bridge collapsed and dark water swept away the voices (Verena's, Reina's), the warming memories of Dresden, which might at the moment be as mysteriously and richly filled with conversation, music, old plays as Ali Baba's cave with treasure; open sesame. But the catfish on the fountain outside Vogelstrom's fortress wouldn't take off its mossy cloak of silence, the sound of a porcelain coffee cup being put down on its saucer in Caravel, cut in two by the to and fro of the pendulum of the grandfather clock and the constant violet glow of the amethyst druse, wouldn't change. He thought of home, had difficulty calling up the images. Did they exist at all, Caravel, the House with a Thousand Eyes, the Rose Gorge, from which at that very moment sleep could be flowing over the city, Evening Star, where Niklas was cocooned in music and voices and his archives, sick with longing for the Nuremberg of the Mastersingers? Christian moved and was back in his bed in the tank commanders' room of the 2nd Battalion of the 19th Armoured Regiment, which would likewise disappear as soon as he closed his eyes.

The company was sleeping. Dreams and visitations had taken hold of them. Those with a pass wouldn't come back until shortly before seven, when duty officially started, they would be sitting in the Dutch Courage, the only bar in Grün that didn't shut at midnight. The worn-out women who hadn't got married went there after the second shift in the metal works, the late girls of the town, ready for a drink and with ready tongues: they didn't say 'a man' but 'a guy' or 'a dude'. And Christian heard; listened: there was the quiver of the flower water in the plastic vases on the bar tables, two or three waves of a napkin got rid of the smells, the crumbs, the food-filled presence of the previous customer before the waiter gestured with his thumb at the still-warm seat of the chair, next please, dealt with at thirty-minute intervals, only the regulars' table with, in the middle, the carefully painted sign with a border of oak leaves, was left in peace; and if in Schwanenberg it had been the noises of the brown-coal excavators, the distant screech (or was it cries? Squeals? Feeling hungry? Being tortured?) of skeleton-armed primeval giants that performed their lumbering sumo wrestler change of stance against a sky ranging from burgundy-, piano-, chocolate-, fire-hydrant-red, flamingo- and tongue-pink, islands of matchstick- and vaccination-drops-red, close-your-eyelids-orange to cat's-paw- and love-letter-rosé; animals buried beneath chains of buckets, burrowing in the treadmills of the open-cast mines, the sounds of tortured creatures that Christian couldn't forget – here in the small town of Grün it was the shimmering whistles of the goods trains that mostly travelled through the provincial station at night, rumbling tapeworms of carriages filled with the products of the metal works, with coal, with wood from the surrounding spruce monocultures, eaten away by acid rain, with ore from the mountains out of which the people in the works to the west of the town still managed to boil a few grammes of nonferrous metal, with chemicals, an indigestible brew drawn by a landlord lying in a coma. He thought of the Danube delta and the hoopoe on a postcard Kurt had sent him that he had pinned up in the private compartment of his locker, where others had a picture of their wife or girlfriend, a photo from *Magazin*. He thought of the constellations on Meno's ten-minute clock, the Southern Cross that he would never get to see, nor the sky into which it had hammered its silver nails.

The senior high and its problems, the final exams preceded by weeks of revision, their fear of the teaching staff in overheated classrooms when they were called in for an oral exam, the discussions with Reina, Falk and Jens by Kaltwasser reservoir all seemed to be in the distant past; his sense of time said: in another life. Had he ever passed the school-leaving exam? Sat in a classroom, in civilian clothing and wearing slippers, bent over a book or a sheet of paper? In another life. A barrier had come down between there and here. Even though he was tired, it hurt when he closed his eyes; a salty pain; but out of habit the inner drive inside his body that was ready for, thirsting for sleep rolled on, could not suddenly halt. In his mind's eye he saw Burre, his reserved expression, trying for dignity; he was tormented by the way they treated Burre. It wasn't fair . . . Fair, fair! came the mocking echo from the dark corner of the room where Musca and Wanda had long been gathered into the claws of a wheezing but in its way caring night deity. What could one do? *What can I do?* –

Write a report. Describe everything, the conditions here, the reality. Submit it to the Minister of National Defence or, even more effective, straight to the First Secretary personally. They said that such reports were considered . . . But the postboxes were under observation, especially here in the regiment. And if his complaints were actually checked, Nip would build a pretty Potemkin village, the inhabitants would have snow-white collar binds, clean fingernails; they would all be entirely satisfied comrades ('I am serving the German Democratic Republic,' was the prescribed formula) and on that day a soldier like Burre would have been sent on leave. And once the inspectors had left, shaking their heads at the completely unfounded, slanderous accusations of that Private Hoffmann . . .

The sound of caterpillar tracks from outside, at the entrance to the technical area: the 3rd Battalion returning from an exercise. Was that someone coughing outside? Nip, perhaps, with his 'drake'? Christian felt restless, got up again. The corridor was empty, gleaming from the evening exertions of the floor-polisher's barbels; the duty guard's table was floating, like a tiny island with a yellow position light, in the darkness by the stairs; Costa was sitting there reading.

There was no light on in the toilets. Christian could feel that there was someone there, he had a sixth sense for it, could tell by looking at them whether postboxes were full or not (an 'aura', something or other left over from the postman, a change, no greater than an eyelash, in the resonance of the postbox interior, the echo of the clank of the flap?); he could tell by looking at an ice cream whether it contained too much milk fat and he wouldn't like it; he sensed that someone was sitting in the cubicle by the window, motionless, probably holding his breath, his eyes scouring the tiny gloom over the top of the door; and he sensed that it was Burre. He went into the cubicle next to it, waited.

'Christian?'

'I wanted to ask you something, Jan. – Can I do anything for you? I have an uncle, he knows people.'

'Why don't you ask him for yourself? I don't need help.'

'So you don't want me to?'

'I can look after myself. – Makes you feel good, does it? Why do you laugh at my poems?'

Pause; but Christian didn't want to chicken out. 'Because they're not very good – I think. I don't laugh at them.'

Burre remained silent, there was a rustle of paper, a streak of brightness stabbed across the floor. 'I know they're not any good.'

'My uncle's a publisher's editor, perhaps he can help you?'

'But they're all I've got.' When boots were heard outside, Burre switched off his torch. Then it was quiet again, Costa must have been stretching his legs. 'I'd like to be your friend.'

Christian, only wearing his thin pyjamas, started to shiver with cold. 'This Pancake . . . perhaps we could make a complaint somewhere?'

'Perhaps I'll kill him, one day,' Burre mused. 'As his "slave" I get to know him better than he does me, and eventually, perhaps, when he's asleep . . . I don't care. I'm fed up to here, sometimes I just can't take any more . . .' Burre was speaking rapidly, in a strained voice, full of hatred. 'And at the works they work themselves to the bone, everything to meet the plan's targets and when my mother comes home she's so exhausted she falls asleep in front of the television . . .'

'Jan, I won't tell on you, but be careful.'

'Yes, I thought you wouldn't do that. – Go now, I'd like to be on my own for a bit. – Thanks.'

Christian didn't ask what he was thanking him for. On one of the next days there was PNP – preparation for a new period of operation: tank tracks were lying on the ground outside the shed like the dried-up skins of a colony of dragons – he saw Burre outside the regimental office, looking round hastily. He seemed not see Christian, went into the building.

51

In the Valley of the Clueless

November: in the evening, after periods on duty, the operations, Richard began to be more aware of his body than usual. His arm and hand were sore, also the spot on his thigh where the skin transplant had been taken from. Something inside him seemed to slip out of position on these short, waxy days that turned over sluggishly, in a flat trajectory, not properly born and heading for an early, rain-pale death; he didn't like this *epoch* of grey skies (even if the days themselves were short, the time they added up to was not, and the year seemed to have two clocks: a small one for blossom, spring and summer – and a big one with the slow, dream-damp November numbers on its face); he became morose in the atmosphere of ill-temper and keeping one's head down (would they ever disappear, these brown and grey coats with turn-up collars and pockets your arms went into up to the elbows, making him feel impolite when he encountered an acquaintance and held out his hand to him); and in contrast to Meno, who particularly liked going for walks at this time (hat, pipe, scarf, sniffles and memories), the town held no attraction for him either, the slimy streets, houses deadened by catarrh. He was depressed by the ruins, the Frauenkirche, the castle, Taschenberg Palace, Rampische Gasse, which was tumbling down, all said out loud that Dresden was a shadow of its former self, destroyed, sick. The weeds grew rampant on the huge, wind-blown patches of waste ground in the city, in the new districts the pavements and roads were unrecognizable under layers of mire and mud. Rain . . . In the seeping damp, soaking the finest pores, sieved by the roofs and strained into metronomic drips, the Neustadt houses were like rotting ships. The façades broke out in a pre-winter sweat, the cold sweat of a moribund town, with no official approval . . . In the art gallery it clung to the walls in a greasy film, removed Giorgione's *Venus* to an inaccessible distance, overlaid the joys of the flesh in the Rubens scenes with melancholy, gave Heda's blackberry pie a withered look, even the roguish faces of the chubby-cheeked cherubs below the Sistine Madonna suffered that too. Mist hung over the meadows by the Elbe. The side roads in the Academy were sodden, the fountains switched off. When Richard came back from a consultation, he looked up at the Academy buildings in Fetscherstrasse, wondered what the sandstone volutes on the roofs reminded him of (the wigs of English judges – he kept on forgetting and that annoyed him!), looked at the lamps, which were on all the time now, like metabolizing leucocytes appearing or disappearing in the glassy-thin, creeping blood vessels of the park trees.

Wernstein was at the Charité Hospital in Berlin, he hadn't been replaced.

'You're always demanding staff, more staff!' Scheffler, the Rector, raised his hands after Müller had stated his case. Gorbachev's plump peasant's face, friendly and unretouched, looked down on the meeting from the place where Andropov and Chernenko had previously hung. Josta brought documents; in the sixth or seventh month, Richard guessed after a look at her stomach.

'We have none! You know that as well as I do. The planning of requirements –'

Rykenthal, the head of the Paediatric Clinic, broke in, scornfully repeating 'planning of requirements'. The Paediatric Clinic was falling down, the roof was not watertight; on the top floor the damp patches had now joined hands by their amoeba-like finger processes; black mould was sprouting like a strong growth of beard in the rooms closed down by the authorities. Naturally Rykenthal, a stocky man with the aura of a hippopotamus, a magician's bow tie and butterfly-blue paediatrician's eyes, demanded that an end should finally be put to this deplorable state of affairs ('I don't know, colleagues, how often I've had to make this point already'); at that Reucker became restless and emphasized the, in his opinion, more urgent problems in Nephrology; Heinsloe, the head of Administration, was asked for his opinion but all he could do was, as usual, spread his arms regretfully. 'The funds, gentlemen, we lack the funds. And the building resources, where do we find them!' Material, gentlemen, he couldn't wave a magic wand.

'There has been an application for a room for hand operations for over five years now,' Richard broke in, furious when he noticed the looks of pleasure following Josta. 'It's surely not possible that in the whole of Dresden we cannot find the means for that minor matter.'

'All due respect for your private ambitions, Herr Hoffmann, but I have to remind you that the Ear-Nose-and-Throat section has had an application for a new operating theatre in for thirteen years –'

'What are you calling private ambitions?'

'You can continue to do operations on the hand in Outpatients, as you have until now, Herr Hoffmann, but it's preposterous that my patients have to have their dialysis in the ward corridor, because the extension, which was promised years ago –'

'Please, gentlemen! Our resources are limited. Let us think what is the best use we can make of them. Most urgent, it seems to me, are the repairs to the Paediatric Clinic. My grandson was in there recently, there are drips from the ceiling on the top floor, the nurses have to put bowls underneath them . . .'

Clarens was sitting quietly in a corner, stroking his beard; he said nothing and was asked nothing. A frail man, Richard thought, whom people automatically wanted to do something for, give him an orange, for example, less in order to be friendly than from a feeling of embarrassment and in order to be noticed by him – Clarens, sitting there as if he were counting their sins, found it impossible to fight, almost disappeared beside the broad-shouldered representatives of the various surgical fields, all fully convinced of their own importance and of that of their requests. Leuser's urologist's jokes seemed to cause him physical pain, his hands and ears went an indignant sky-grey, then paled to the colour of synthetic honey when the full-time Party Secretary of the Medical Academy spoke. A humorously down-to-earth workaholic, more interested in doing than talking, who liked to see everyday detail from the perspective of a Party youth camp morning ceremony, whose *Chto delat?* – What is to be done? – and *Kak tebya zovut?* – What are you called? (difficulty or enemy) – had stuck with him from a reservoir construction site in Siberia where, during his ('heart-stirring! heart-stirring!') days as an official of the Free German Youth, he had had hands-on experience of communism.

'Always the same,' Richard moaned outside, 'lots of talk, nothing done.' Having left the Administration building, Clarens and he were walking down the Academy road. Clarens talked about suicide. He was an internationally renowned expert on suicide and sometimes said he was lucky to be able to pursue his passion in this country, only the old Austro-Hungarian Empire had had more plentiful material. 'Oh to be a Viennese psychiatrist,' Clarens sighed. The suicide cases in the Austrian Empire had shown greater imaginativeness, a tendency to grotesquely droll and out-of-the-way methods, while the Germans mostly 'ended it all', at which Clarens put his hand to the back of his neck, jerked it up and stuck his tongue out as he made the death rattle. There were those who used gas, of course, with their peaceful expressions and delicate cherry cheeks; peaking in May and at Christmas; sleeping pills, of course, mostly women, men preferred harder methods. A hammer drill, for example, straight into the heart. Richard remembered the case: the man, a railwayman with long and honoured service, had turned up in Outpatients the night after his retirement party, with all his medals on and the drill in his chest; like all the others, he'd waited at the duty sister's desk and, when his turn came, made his request. Or the foreman at the garden centre who for his supper one day ate a bowl of chopped-up dieffenbachia with salad dressing and ended up in Intensive Care the next day with his stomach pumped out. Clarens's enthusiasm suddenly turned into frustration: he was respected throughout the world – at home, on the other hand . . . plenty of material, true, but also plenty of obstacles and hurdles. Above all when he wanted to pursue research into the causes. Abruptly he changed the subject. 'Are you still in contact with Manfred?'

'For a while now we haven't seen very much of each other.'

'He seems to hold something against you. He doesn't have a good word to say for you. – Oh, this November weather! It makes you quite melancholy. And what use is a melancholy psychiatrist to my patients? And they say there's going to be a frost.'

Richard didn't respond. He was thinking about the contradictory nature of his companion: sparse appearance – and robust joviality when he got onto his favourite topic . . . Clarens had other favourite topics as well, he loved the fine arts, sculpture less than drawing, which he called the 'chamber music of the visual arts', he was a regular visitor to some studios, knew Meno's boss very well, also Nina Schmücke and her circle. A further favourite topic was the history of Dresden, in pursuit of which Clarens, who lived in Blasewitz, would often cross the Blue Miracle on foot to go up on the funicular or cable-car to the Urania meetings or Frau Fiebig's soirées in Guenon House.

'Did you get a new geyser?' he asked, clasping his arms round his body. On their way to the meeting in Administration they still hadn't been able to see their breath. Electric carts clinked and clattered past, shivering students headed for the canteen.

'No. I know an engineer who improvised something.'

'The one you're tinkering at your vintage car in Lohmen with?'

Richard looked up in surprise. 'How do you know about that?'

'I recently went to see Dietzsch and bought a little print. Money well invested, I should think.' Clarens told him that a kind of second market had grown up among a number of artists. Now gallery owners from the Federal Republic regularly visited the studios, looked at this and that, bought this and that. And had no inhibitions about talking to other ladies and gentlemen who also looked at this and that and, by now, were also buying this and that.

'What is it Manfred's saying about me?'

'Oh, it's not good, not good. I thought you were friends?' Clarens breathed in deeply and, as it seemed to Richard, with relish. He refused to say what it was that was 'not good'. Was he slandering Weniger? What would happen if he grabbed Clarens by the tie and shook him . . . what would appear? A hideous face, a goblin with features distorted with malice? If only one could see behind the masks, explore the mines inside people.

'Just sounding brass,' Richard muttered.

'And a gold tiepin,' Clarens murmured, taking Richard by the arm and pointing to the rowans along the road, which were being covered in hoar frost before their very eyes.

'I found the meeting pretty wearying,' Clarens said. 'Difficulties, jealousies, constant psychoses . . . Leuser's coprolalia, and the full-timer a *blindissimus realitensis totalis*.' The psychiatrist made a dismissive gesture. In such situations he preferred to go to the laundry, he said, there were always some overalls or other to be collected, the steam reminded him of his childhood and the busy little irons were so sooth-ing. God, the suicides, the lunatics, including Party secretaries and other psychiatrists!

Richard went to the wards. Nurse Lieselotte was waiting with the cart for the rounds. 'Your son's here.'

'Christian? What's happened?' – The alarm of the trauma surgeon whose thoughts immediately go to broken bones, blunt-force traumas, traffic accidents and injuries from machines.

'No, it's only me.' Robert came out of the nurses' room with an expression of gentle consideration well beyond his years.

'Coffee?' Nurse Lieselotte turned her searching look away from Richard's face, which was gradually recovering its normal colour; he nodded, still confused, shyly embraced Robert. Patients at the other end of the corridor, in dressing gowns, taking little steps as they pushed stands with infusion bottles, stopped.

'The nurses say you're doing your rounds; can I come too? I've got a coat.' On his index finger Robert held up a dissecting-room coat that closed at the back, threadbare from washing; they kept some on the ward for forgetful students.

'I thought you were at school? Have you no classes?'

'Finished. Came back on the bus, thought: let's have a look at what Richard does.'

Like the time when Josta was in hospital in Friedrichstadt and Daniel had called her by her Christian name; it must have become general by now, Richard thought. Oh well. Nurse Lieselotte brought his mug with the coffee, a stethoscope, reflex hammer and protractor for Richard.

There were eight patients in the first ward. As they entered they were hit by the smell of sickness, a smell Richard, since his student days, had inhaled more often than what people call 'fresh air'; the smell of sickness: that mixture of urine, faeces, pus, blood, medication and serum in the bandages and drain bottles, the smell of cold sweat on unshaved skin (they were in a men's ward, with the women the smell was more of urine titrated with the sickly sweet, over-camomiled efforts of a cosmetic industry that had the humility of a poor relation), of cognac, a breeding ground for bacteria, medicinal spirit and vinegar (the dusting water in which the student nurses and nursing auxiliaries dipped their cloths to clean bedsteads, strip lights, bedside tables); the smell of PVC, wiped with Wofasept; of something age-old that seemed to incubate in the walls of the wards, in the white, washable oil-based paint with an olive-green stripe chest-high – where the arms are bound during arrests, where the respiratory trees branch, where the heart is. Seven of the eight patients had tried to sit up in their beds and had remained in this stand-to-attention position, as the nurses called it, one hand on the bar of the bed trapeze, rusty steel painted tooth-yellow and sagging under the weight; the eighth patient was in a body cast, his arms and trunk immured in the white suit of armour that had square windows over his wounds to allow drains (perforated plastic tubes as thick as your finger and bent like a shoemaker's awl) to draw off the secretions from the wounds. His left leg, also in plaster, was held up in the air on the stirrup of a Kirschner wire bored into the ankle bone and pulled down, via a cord and pulley, by iron discs, the white paint of which had completely flaked off. His head, from which a pair of eyes looked with quiet anxiety at the nurse and Richard, was in Crutchfield tongs that, fixed in the skull above his ears, were stretching his cervical vertebrae, also via a pulley and weights. The optician, second bed on the left, immediately repeated his offer of marriage to Nurse Lieselotte, who, he said, would never lack for spectacles; moreover, he went on, it was pointless wasting time and money on the poor guy with the skull-hoops, who, he added with the crude humour of some patients, was going to kick the bucket anyway. His own leg, on the other hand, healed? when? And from Nurse Lieselotte, whose stony looks were clearly the visual equivalent of a thumbs-down, he ordered a sledge-hammer so that he could finally smash the eternal brass band music of the sky pilot (second bed on the right, a priest, pale as a fish fillet, who had broken his lower leg while removing two bugs, one from the confessional and the other from the Saviour's crown of thorns) and the revolutionary hymns of the comrade community policeman (third bed on the right, midfacial fracture, at the moment he was on the bedpan behind a screen; on his bedside table were the two Karls, May and Marx), he couldn't stand any more of their ideological warfare.

'Well, young man, fresh out of college?' First bed on the right, a professor of Slav linguistics, emigrated from the Sudetenland to escape the Nazis, emigrated from the Sudetenland to escape the Czechs. Two lacerated arms laboriously emerged out of the white cover made from guinea pig skins: injuries from sabre-slashes (long-established jealousy between long-established rival sword collectors).

'My son. He simply came straight from school in Waldbrunn to the ward here, wanted to see what kind of thing I did.'

'Really proud of him, our doc. Start 'em young, my old man used to say,' the riverboat engineer in the fourth bed on the right cried, closing a catalogue of toupees and waving two mangled fingers; he was twenty-two and still wore his hair long, even though a considerable part of it had been caught up in the rotor of his engine and a patch of scalp the size of his palm had been torn off. The light went out.

'Good night.' Third bed on the left, a forklift truck driver from Kofa, the Dresden canned food factory; craniocerebral trauma after falling, drunk, from the dam of Kaltwasser reservoir. In the ward room the late shift were sitting in the dark, a nurse lit candles; in the light of the flame her face looked calm; the objects in the circle of brightness had an unreal, rapt, Christmassy air about them. Nurse Lieselotte hurried to the end of the ward and unlocked the medicines cupboard, where she kept some torches and replacement batteries. The Intensive Care Unit! Richard thought, but already Kohler had come running in through the door followed by Dreyssiger, beams of light moved over the walls of North I. Dreyssiger cried, 'The operating theatre, they're down there, nothing's working. The heart–lung machine's stopped.'

The telephone was still working. Richard called the ICU. No one answered. 'What about the anaesthetists, can they keep the oxygen going?' he asked Dreyssiger over his shoulder.

'No.' Just 'no', it was Kohler who had said it in an expressionless, impassive tone. 'If the emergency generator won't start up'

'– if it starts up'

'– they'll have to insufflate with a bag valve mask'

'– why's it not starting up'

'Just like in the war,' said one of the nurses anxiously; it was Gerda, who was almost seventy.

'Africa.'

'And what do things look like in the operating theatre?'

'Like Africa. I just told you.'

'– it's just not starting'

'Bananas, jungle.'

In the ward room it smelt of eucalyptus oil, Kohler had knocked the medicine basket off the table.

'– more like Russia. Russia, so'

'Africa.'

'Oh do shut up.'

'– or can you hear something? It's not starting up.'

'The emergency plan will come into force.'

'Funny that the telephone's still working.'

'Comes via a relay station, low voltage. Everything can be dead all round, they'll still get a tone,' Dreyssiger said.

'Africa. Central Congo.'

'We must go to the ICU,' Richard said. 'Nurse Lieselotte, will you please call in all available staff. Robert, you're coming with us, we can use anyone who can give a hand now.'

They ran to the Intensive Care Unit. Cones of light blazed up, stamping meal carts, nurses' legs, distraught faces out of the deep-sea darkness of the clinic, somewhere a bedpan clattered onto the floor. Someone was thumping on the lift door, ghostly footsteps echoed in the stairwell. The Medical Academy was a concentrated mass of black stone; there was still light on in Nuclear Medicine, as there was in Administration. Shadowy figures could be seen dashing to and fro. In the ICU a string of torches was hanging over the insufflation beds, candles had been lit. The duty anaesthetist was just switching to pressurized oxygen, the compressor for room-air insufflation, which came out of the walls, had stopped working, as had the monitors over the patients' heads. 'An unstable patient, Herr Hoffmann.'

'Still no current in the emergency generator sockets.' One of the nurses was transferring cables. 'What a mess.'

Richard looked at the noradrenaline drip. The patient attached to it seemed peaceful, like a figure in a painting by one of the Old Masters: a scene in a cave. One nurse was constantly measuring his pulse, another his blood pressure. The slightest bit too little or too much and his condition would be up and down like a roller coaster, they had to take countermeasures, that tied staff down.

'CVP?' the anaesthetist asked, pressing one of the patient's fingernails, checking the recapillarization time. One nurse bent down to the venotonometer that measured the central veinous pressure.

'We could use a man,' the anaesthetist said. 'It could take some time until ours get here. Most don't have a telephone.'

'What's it like in the operating theatre, have you heard anything?' Richard asked.

'Your boss's broken off the operation. Insufflation's continuing manually. One patient in the recovery room – another doctor who can't get away. And the neurosurgeons want to start on a tumour. Haha.'

Kohler stayed at Intensive Care; Richard, Dreyssiger and Robert went to the A&E. The corridors, also lit by strings of torches, were jam-packed with moaning patients on stretchers; ambulance sirens wailed and died away. No one seemed to be coordinating things, doctors and nurses were rushing to and fro. Porters brought more and more new patients; doors were flung open and slammed shut; exasperated voices from the treatment rooms called for bandages, nurses, drugs. The waiting area by the desk, behind which Nurse Wolfgang was dealing with complaints and demands with a stoical expression on his face, looked like a field hospital. Faintly lit by the candles on the desk, injured people were sitting on the floor, rocking to and fro; a young girl had been laid on a blanket, pale, she endured the lamentations of two older women in silence. Forcefully and with words of comfort, Dreyssiger pushed his way through to the desk. Patients in A&E wheelchairs were either sitting in silence or waving their arms around, most probably with ankle injuries; as he passed Richard glanced at the swollen joints, trying to repress the wave of images, memories of his injuries during the 13 February air raid, the screaming, whimpering wounded who were waiting with him amid detonating bombs, the machine-gun rattle of an isolated Wehrmacht unit, the heat from the burning surgical and paediatric clinics; at that time the Academy had still been called the Gerhard Wagner Hospital, after the Reich doctors' leader.

'Have you seen any of the technical guys?' Nurse Wolfgang called to Dreyssiger. 'It'd help if they got a cable laid.'

'X-rays possible?'

'No. No CAT scanner either.'

'Then close down,' said Richard. 'We can't deal with all this. We can't operate.'

'I've called regional headquarters, Herr Hoffmann. They say all the Dresden hospitals want to close down.'

'But not all of them can have a power cut?'

'They're not sending us any multiple traumas, that's all I managed to get out of them.'

'Who's coordinating things?'

'Grefe. But he can't get out of the plaster room.'

'Are there any beds at all?'

'No.'

Dreyssiger went into a treatment room. Richard picked up the phone. 'I'm sure the boss will turn up soon, until then I'll coordinate the surgical clinics. – The line's busy.'

'Eddi!' Wolfgang shouted, waving vigorously to a brawny man in the blue overalls of Technical Services. Eddi was its head, he was a former boxer, there was a punchbag in his office and on the walls, between bunches of boxing gloves, were photos of famous welter- and heavyweights. Eddi panted, 'The diesel! Someone's siphoned off the diesel from the emergency generator.'

'Nonsense.'

'I'm telling you, Wolfgang. And there's no reserve, it's enough to drive me mad.'

'There must be a few fuckin' litres of diesel somewhere in the hospital! People are stuck in the lift.'

'It's being seen to. We'll have to jack it up. Internal and Gynaecological've got diesel but they need it for their own generators.'

'Dad,' Robert said, he'd squeezed himself into a corner behind the desk, 'there's some people from the Western Channel 2 out in the car park. Four big diesel lorries, I saw them when I came up to your ward.'

Eddi said, 'Touch wood', and he and Robert ran off.

'Are you just standing around or is someone going to see to us?' a man in a leather hat said in a querulous voice through the sliding window of the enquiry desk. 'Oh, Herr Hoffmann.' Griesel took a step back. 'I'd no idea it was you, neighbour. I can't believe how long we have to wait here.' Suddenly his expression changed. 'Wouldn't it be possible . . .'

'All patients have equal rights,' Richard said, a bit too loud for Griesel's liking.

'It caught me out on the way home from work, you see . . .' Griesel went on in placatory tones and bowing in an ingratiating manner. 'Our house hasn't been hit, by the way.'

Emotions a doctor couldn't afford to permit himself bubbled up like boiling milk inside him as he watched Griesel push his way through the patients back to his chair; hatred and contempt for that man, the conditions, the whole system. To pay them back in their own kind, to be able, just once, to retaliate to power with power, to have an outlet for the impotent rage piling up inside him day after day! He goes to the back of the queue, Richard felt like saying, Wolfgang would have understood and probably approved. The deep-rooted, feared esprit de corps of health professionals. Richard didn't say it. All patients have equal rights. The welfare of the sick is the final law, that was what was written in Latin on a board in the entrance to Accident and Emergency: *Salus aegroti suprema lex*.

A commotion outside the entrance, floodlight beams flashing to and fro, powdery snow coming in through the door. Eddi and an auxiliary brought in Robert, who was holding his arm.

'I slipped and fell. Stupid.' Robert shrugged his shoulders. 'It's all frozen outside. But we've got the diesel.'

His wrist was swollen but his hand didn't show a bayonet deformity, as with a fracture in a typical position. Robert gave a quiet cry when Richard examined it.

'Volar radial fracture, the non-typical type.'

'Meaning?' Robert asked in a deliberately calm voice.

'Prickling in your fingers? Any numbness?'

'A bit, yes. It's cold outside.'

'We'll have to X-ray it. If that confirms what I think, it means an operation. You can wait in there.' Richard pointed behind the desk. Once Robert had gone, Richard couldn't control himself any more and swore. If the lad had fallen with his arm outstretched a plaster cast would have done the job.

'Smith-Thomas?' Wolfgang, who'd watched Richard examine him through the desk window, asked, using the technical term for the fracture.

'It'll need an operation, yes.' Richard stamped his foot in his fury, a ridiculous sight and, for the patients waiting, not one to inspire confidence.

Müller came in, behind him the man with the floodlight, followed by one carrying a microphone on a long boom like a fishing rod; three other men, in sharply creased trousers and bomber jackets, had over-powered the cameraman and were dragging him out of the flurries of snow, where a second cameraman was coolly filming the scene, into the crowded waiting area. They stopped short for a moment when they saw all the patients. The cameraman who'd been detained took advantage of that to free himself and protest loudly. The floodlight dug a dazzling white tunnel though A&E.

'There will be no filming in my clinic and certainly not by your lying station,' Müller cried angrily.

'But you take our fuel!'

'The diesel has been confiscated,' announced one of the three men in bomber jackets. 'This is an emergency, as we've already explained to you.'

'The fuel taken will, of course, be replaced, Citizen Capitalist,' shouted the second of the three in the silence that had arisen all around;

even the two women beside the young girl had broken off their lamentations.

'We need everyone we can get.' Müller pointed to the three in bomber jackets. 'You are to help charging the room sterilizers. No, gentlemen, we have no time for discussion. You will do what I, as head of this clinic and of the emergency team, tell you until the Rector and your immediate superiors arrive. No sterile material means no operations. The central sterilizer isn't working. You' – he pointed to the West German television men – 'can make yourselves useful transporting patients and clearing paths. Have them shown what to do, Nurse Wolfgang. Will you please come with me, Herr Hoffmann.' Müller waved Richard out through the swing door into the corridor to the vestibule and wards. 'A word in your ear. A difficult situation within a difficult situation. I've just had a phone call.'

When Richard said nothing, he went on, 'A call from the top, Barsano himself. His daughter is on her way to us, he claims. With these African conditions out there . . . He's asked me to have our most experienced trauma surgeon operate on his daughter, should an operation be necessary.'

'My son's been injured, Herr Professor.'

'Oh.'

'Volar radial fracture, the nerve has probably been compressed.'

'Hm. But you can reset it and put it in plaster, Herr Hoffmann. I know it's not a permanent solution but it'll do until the morning and then you can take your time over it.'

'I'd prefer not to wait until the morning. The results don't get better if you leave it.'

'I know that,' Müller, exasperated, replied with a sweeping gesture. 'I have a suggestion: when the generator starts, we'll at least have power in the ICU again and then Herr Kohler can join us. Never operate on a relative, you know that. And you've trained up Herr Kohler very well.'

Richard, alarmed, didn't reply. That possibility had never occurred to him. The maxim he had followed in training Kohler was not in the Hippocratic Oath: If you have to instruct your enemy, teach him just enough to make sure he won't harm the patients, but not enough that he can replace you.

'All patients have equal rights,' Richard muttered. There were sounds of the jacking-up operation from the lift shaft, metal on metal, someone calling for pliers.

'I can understand you, believe me. But Barsano has protected you. There are those, and not only here in the clinic, who are unhappy with the opinions on certain things you often express quite openly.' A fragment of the pocket-torch light from South I slipped into the stone in Müller's signet ring. Beautifully cut, Richard thought. Does he take it off when he's doing an operation? It wouldn't fit under the gloves and disinfection to a surgical level wouldn't be possible either. Why not operate on Robert, take the reprimand and resign?

'And suggest you have to prove yourself. Nonsense, if you ask me. As if you hadn't proved yourself here.'

Not a threat, more a plea for understanding. Richard sensed he was getting nowhere the way things were. 'So far we've no power, no X-ray, we can only use one room, if any at all.'

'The CAT scanner's working again. Tellkamp has been informed, he's waiting. The technicians are running a cable from Admin and Nuclear Medicine to us. We'll be able to operate and X-ray again, even if we don't have mains current very soon – which I reckon we will. For the moment the generator ought to be enough for the ICU. I'm only halfway through my operation too.' Müller suddenly spoke in an unusually understanding tone: 'We'll manage. You never know, Fräulein Barsano might arrive immediately and you'll be able to operate on both. Lord alone knows what's wrong with her: sent with multiple traumas, arrives with athlete's foot.'

'But why here, of all places. Can't she be treated up there in Friedrich Wolf?'

Müller nodded. 'I'm sure they won't have a power cut up there, but I've no idea, Herr Hoffmann. – Thank you for your cooperation.'

Accident and Emergency did not empty. The doctors from the various surgical areas had formed teams (no one there said 'collectives' any more, Richard thought), those from Internal Medicine went to and fro between the wards, Endoscopy and Outpatients. Whenever Richard thought the stream of patients was slackening off, the outside door would swing open and Rapid Medical Assistance, a taxi driver or a relation would bring more people with injuries. They also brought news of how things were in the city outside. From what they said, which was immediately passed on by the nurses rushing in and out, by doctors, porters, waiting patients, the situation outside must be chaotic. Trams were stuck on Platz der Einheit, the power was off there too, passengers had forced open the doors, the people who lived in Neustadt didn't have far to go and could trudge home through the snow; anyone who wanted to get across Marienbrücke to the city centre tried to hitch a lift from one of the cars crawling past; worst off of all were those who had to go up to the high residential area: with no possibility of hitching a lift, they were faced with several kilometres on foot. The Elbe was covered with a sheet of ice, a Czech tug had been squeezed against the Blue Miracle, the bridge had had to be closed. None of the ferries between the north and south bank were running any more. When Richard went out to get a breath of fresh air, the Academy looked like a darkened honeycomb: the roofs waxy with ice, the snow on the paths and roads knee-deep. In many of the ten-storey buildings in Johannstadt, in the new developments of Prohlis and Gorbitz, the central heating wasn't working; the people there were shivering in their beds, envious of those on the slopes of the Elbe with their tiled stoves that devoured coal and produced ash but also – and that was the important thing – warmth.

In Outpatients no one seemed to know who had already been treated and who still needed treatment, who could be transferred to a ward and where which of their colleagues was occupied with which case. Wolfgang was still ensconced behind the desk, flanked by sheets of paper on which he tried to provisionally record the details of the arriving and departing patients, telephones were ringing, always someone wanting to know something: patients when they'd be treated, family members where their relations had got to, staff where there were supplies of syringes, bandages, admission forms – and couldn't someone finally make a decent cup of coffee, after all the emergency generator was working now!

'Yes, in the I C U and the patient lift to the operating theatre, clever Dick.'

'Clever Dick yourself! Then they can just make the coffee up there and send it down to us!'

'And when's the light going on here again? Oh, sorry, nurse, missed again. But you can hardly see anything here.'

'I'm sorry to have to put it so frankly, but you're an old goat.'

'You've completely misunderstood me, nurse. It must be this pitch darkness. Goats have two horns.'

'Where's the testicle?' Frau Doktor Roppe, a urologist, called across Outpatients, arms akimbo. 'The strangulated one. – You've called me away from a septic catheter, Wolfgang, you'll be sorry if it's a false alarm.'

'Here,' a faint voice said shyly, 'here, Herr Doktor.'

A National People's Army tanker was expected but still hadn't arrived. Scheffler, the Rector, had formed a crisis committee and inspected the clinics. Walkie-talkies were taken out of the Administration safe, important telephone calls, listed in a sealed plan, were made in the prescribed order. The Intensive Care Unit in Internal Medicine was supplied by the emergency generator there, the one in Gynaecology was working too. The idea of transferring urgent surgical cases there was dropped: moving there with all the equipment would be too much of an upheaval, and beside that Eddi and his men were already in the process of laying cables through the Academy's system of tunnels to supply Outpatients and the operating section. A simultaneous 'Ah!' rang out when the lights flickered back on. The heavy X-ray machines started to hum again, the coffee maker in the rest-room sputtered water over the coffee powder, X-rays appeared on the lightboxes, nurses who had been holding torches over lacerations and scalp cuts in Minor Surgery could return to other tasks. Richard helped Grefe with the resetting of broken bones and subsequently putting them in plaster, between the cases (a wearying, mildly comic coming and going between fractures of the radius on the left, fractures of the radius on the right) he went to the enquiry desk, impatiently looking for Alexandra Barsano, telephoned Intensive Care but Kohler couldn't be spared yet.

Richard had aspirated the haematoma on Robert's wrist himself and given the anaesthetic that made resetting bearable for the patient. But that he had asked Dreyssiger to do, that brutal-seeming bending up and down over the broken wrist; then they'd put it in plaster, done an X-ray (Dreyssiger had done the resetting excellently, but Richard insisted on the operation; that type of fracture mostly did not stay stable), and put Robert in the duty doctors' room. Kohler arrived an hour later.

'I will not operate on your son, at least not immediately.' Kohler didn't wait for Richard to respond. 'All patients have equal rights, you've always told me that, Herr Hoffmann, should we disregard it today of all days?'

'He's my son, he wants to be a doctor . . . his hand, he needs his hand.' Richard was so taken aback by Kohler's attitude that he didn't ask him but Müller, who came over, 'Would you not give your son preferential treatment?'

'My father's sitting out there,' Kohler said calmly. 'Wolfgang gave me the patients' names in order of arrival. Others come before him, I don't want to give anyone an unfair advantage, nor put them at a disadvantage.'

Richard flew into a rage. 'Strictly according to the rules . . . like a blockhead!' How dare the fellow, he'd given him a formal order! 'Head down and follow the plan, head down whatever the cost, that's the way it goes . . . You're leaving your own father sitting there for the sake of your convictions?' Richard asked, suddenly interested.

'I give others the same rights as him. And do you know what?' Kohler adopted an impatient, hostile tone. 'He even approves of it. That's the way he taught me to be. As a convinced communist. Which you are not.'

'Gentlemen.' Müller stepped between the two of them, for a moment Richard was surprised he wasn't furious, that he seemed to have ignored Kohler's open refusal. 'Gentlemen,' he repeated, a pointless, plaintive request, 'gentlemen!'

'It is against my beliefs as a doctor to give anyone preferential treatment.'

'Herr Kohler –' Müller ushered him out.

'Herr Hoffmann,' Wolfgang called from behind the desk, 'Frau Barsano's here.'

But it wasn't Alexandra Barsano coming towards Richard as he went out, but the wife of the Regional Secretary. She was standing, very upright, by the door of her Wartburg. Richard plodded over to her, the blizzard had died down a little, beyond the entrance to the Academy snow-clearing teams could be seen, a lorry, perhaps the impatiently awaited army tanker, was flashing its indicators. The even blanket of fine powder snow seemed to gather the light and reflect it back onto the paths as high as the hips of the passers-by. Frau Barsano's expression looked reserved when Richard shook her hand. The interior light flickered, he could see Alexandra Barsano, she was staring into space and holding a discoloured bandage round her left wrist.

'We're colleagues, of course,' Frau Barsano said, getting straight down to business, 'and you have problems here. My husband tells me they're pulling all the stops out to resolve it and you should have power again in one hour, at the latest two.' She lit a cigarette, blew out the smoke, looked at the glowing tip that lit up her face when she drew on it. 'I suggest I treat my daughter in our place, I mean at the Friedrich Wolf Hospital. Herr Müller –'

'– informed me. – As you wish, Frau Barsano.'

'That's also what my daughter wants. We have everything necessary there.'

'You don't owe me an explanation. Nor your daughter.'

'We have even acquired magnifying spectacles and a operation microscope. – Good. I would like, and my husband would also like' – she inhaled then threw the cigarette away – 'nothing of this conversation to become more widely known. Can we rely on that? Thank you. Goodbye, Herr Hoffmann.'

'Goodbye.'

The Wartburg slithered off, Richard watched it go. A few minutes later a figure emerged from the shadow of the park, spoke into a walkie-talkie. The flurries of snow were thicker now. For a few moments the man stood there, irresolute, then raised his arm in an awkward salute. A car drove up. When the chauffeur opened the door, the man bent down to get into the seat; the interior light revealed Max Barsano's face.

52
Keep the record and needle free of dust

The wind had died down, the Party secretaries fallen silent, in the living rooms there was the flicker of the evening programmes: *Potpourri*, *What's It Worth?*, *Portrait by Telephone*, a cowboys-and-Indians film with Gojko Mitić. Meno felt he could almost hear it, the whole country breathing a sigh of relief: at least we've made it, a comfortable run-up to Christmas with festive roasts, warm stoves, slippers and enough beer. The provision of pretzel sticks and peanut puffs for the New Year was guaranteed, as long as people didn't go crazy. The masters of entertainment, of giving the people a thrill, calming them and lulling them to sleep, had taken up the baton, Willi Schwabe, in his velvet smoking jacket, white hair neatly parted, went up to his junk room to the tinkling doll-like strains of Tchaikovsky's 'Sugar-Plum Fairy' and chatted, once he'd hung his carriage lamp on a hook, about the Land of Smiles that had been set up in the UFA studios of Potsdam-Babelsberg or of Wien-Film . . . an old charmer, a soigné *esprit* from the world of yesterday sashaying elegantly in front of a backdrop of black-and-white photos and theatre curtains, leaning against the curve of a grand piano with a lighted candle on it. Meno loved the programme, *Willi Schwabe's Junk Room*, he was annoyed when he missed it, and when, sometimes on a Monday, as he came home late from the office, he could see in many windows of the district the simultaneously changing pictures of GDR TV 1 and imagined he could hear through the glass the well-modulated tones of the presenter reminiscing about Hilde Hildebrandt, Hans Moser, Theo Lingen, 'the great Paula Wessely'. Once, once there was . . . and the silent snow, goose-white, downy flakes with grains of soot, more like organisms (starfish, children's hands) than lifeless crystals, floated through the even tenor of the days. Once, once there was . . . but the clocks struck, the ten-minute clock signalled the hour with softly resonating strokes; in the evenings the theme tune of *TV News* crept through the houses, made its way through the apartments on Lindwurmstrasse without upsetting the creations of Lamprecht, the hatmaker, without making the apprentices in Wiener's hairdressing salon pause in sweeping up the day's production of fallen hair, rummaged round the premises of Harmonie, the furrier's, where the manager was still sitting, bent over accounts, with a dutiful sewing machine humming away on fur waistcoats or mittens (no, Meno knew better: at this hour no one was sewing for the people), ignored Dr Fernau's curses with which, in camel-hair slippers, an open bottle of Felsenkeller-Bräu in his hand, he would toast the newsreader with the lower jaw faultlessly grinding out reports of successes for the annual accounts, made Niklas Tietze, when he stopped below the windows of the Roeckler School of Dancing on his way home from his practice to listen to the out-of-tune piano, the slurred waltzes of the violin and cello, open his bag and pull out his tattered diary: for it was the time, the signal swirling in uncertain outlines from the windows and through vestibules, that reminded him of the time: was it not already Thursday today, which meant he was invited to the *regular hour* at Däne's, the music critic's, on Schlehenleite, had Gudrun asked him to do something that he might possibly have forgotten, were there still house calls he had to make, Frau von Stern, for example, who had an iron constitution but also a will of iron that insisted on her weekly examination by Dr Tietze, who, 'as always', ordered cold affusions that did her, the 'old lizard' (Frau Zschunke) of over ninety, no harm, prescribed 'as always' cardiac drops and digitoxin tablets, that she regularly collected from the pharmacy (one shouldn't let them go to waste, should one?) and equally regularly (as Meno knew) mixed into the food for her ageing cats, that she called by name to prevent the young ones from snatching their food . . .

. . . Atlantis, the contours of which Meno saw returning behind the rooms, a kind of parallel displacement, a flickering projection; the planks, uprights over the Rose Gorge, with a scab of barnacle-like rust, Grauleite was listening in with slowly rotating parabolic dishes, at that hour, when the wooden snow shovels had cleared the paths between the banks of dog roses and been knocked clean beside the snowed-in cars, pupils of the Louis Fürnberg High School were going to the funicular, throwing snowballs onto the roof of Arbogast's little observatory, at the elegant black numerals of the white enamel oval house numbers – and Meno could hear, when the 11 wasn't running and he had to use the funicular to go into town, the pupils in the car cheerfully prattling about football (Dynamo Dresden, BFC Dynamo): they were going to Helfenberg Manor Estate for a day's 'Instruction in Technical Production', where they would assemble K-16 cameras, trying to match the standard time and get a good mark. And the elephant-backed dustcarts of the City Cleansing Department were grinding along the streets again, leaving snakes of ash beside their tyre-tracks. 'Rice pudding with cinnamon' the Dresdeners called it, glad that the dustcarts, with the coarse-mouthed dustmen on the boards under the dumping device, who were so good as to bowl the dented dustbins out of the yards – cleared and sanded, *if you please* – were running again; they were said to be the best-paid workers, supposedly earning more than a professor at the Technical University. Lange, wreathed in the smoke from his pungent cigars, muttered his lack of understanding for the overtones of envy in those rumours, reflected out loud on the due reward for hard work, before ringing Guenon House to see whether he should take a 'decent bottle' to Frau Fiebig's rummy evening.

On the Wednesday after Richard's birthday Meno decided to ask Madame Eglantine to remind him that on Friday he intended finally to start on his long-postponed winter washing. The winter washing! He dreaded the sight of the linen basket full of used sheets, and bed and cushion covers, which in the summer he could give to Anne and sometimes, if the washing machine was working, to Libussa – now in the winter that wasn't possible, the women had enough to do with hunting for Christmas presents, baking biscuits, getting New Year firecrackers and sparklers. Madame Eglantine grinned as she reminded him and on Friday Meno went home with an uneasy feeling that he was faced with an impossible mountain to climb. Just his bad luck that that year the steam laundry wasn't taking any more orders! The linen basket, woven out of willow with strengthening hoops, capaciously rotund, was sitting in one corner of his bedroom, brooding and full of malice. Meno dragged the basket over, tried to empty it out, but the washing was stuck as fast as a deep-lying boil. Once he'd managed to pull out the top layer the rest of the washing burst out onto the floor, spreading itself with a sigh of relief. Meno went down to the laundry room, a spark of hope still glowing, even as he opened the door, that Libussa's washing machine had been repaired, but its place was empty, the Service Combine had been fiddling around with it since the summer washdays. Meno looked round. How he hated this subterranean chamber! He hated it with the hatred of the bachelor who wants to read and smoke a pipe on the balcony before strolling back to his warm living room, at ease and relaxed, at one with the world, sniffing the scent of fresh linen promising a night of sweet dreams. What was it Barbara had said? The washing would turn out whiter if it was soaked overnight. So, take hope and a few spoonfuls of Schneeberg Blue, and off you go into the lye, you children's ghosts.

He woke at around four in the morning after a terrible nightmare: an incubus was squatting on him, a sheet-demon that kept calling for more and more linen to come flying through the air and, with a grin, piled it up on its back – though all that had happened was that Chakamankabudibaba had crept into his bed and stretched out on his stomach. There were fern-patterns of ice on the windows. Meno went down to the laundry room. The water in the tubs had frozen over. Taking the dolly, he smashed the layer of ice: the sheets floated round in the solution like frozen lumps of dried cod. Too early to light the stove; with weary, leaden steps, Meno went back to bed, even though he was tempted to pay his new neighbours back for their lack of consideration in knocking others up, for the repulsively triumphal radio music accompanying Honich's bending and stretching before he slammed the front door to go out for his early-morning exercises. But even a combat group commander was exhausted by the winter; and after the Kaminski twins had also quarrelled with him Honich at least showed some consideration at weekends. Meno dreamt of being able to sleep . . . but Chakamankabudibaba was prowling round the bed, mewing, and

upstairs Meno could hear Libussa, already busy with the coal scuttle
for the bathroom stove. He dreamt of the laundry room . . . Saw the
ox-like, hoop-bound washtubs, made by a cooper in a past age, quality
workmanship the soap-manufacturer presumably thought he owed
himself. They stood menacingly on their wooden stands over the drain
that kept blocking. Then the male inhabitants of the house had to poke
round in the darkness beneath them with long wires, hoping that the
suds stuck there would find their way out to the pipes going down the
garden slope . . . the toilets of the House with a Thousand Eyes also
drained there and they, too, tended to get blocked. Stahl had explained
that to Meno: if such pipes went down too steeply then the fluid quickly
ran off but solids remained – and they had to rod them. For that purpose there were iron rods, about five metres long with hooks and eyes,
and when Hanna and Meno had moved into the house the ship's doctor
had given them a short introductory course in the problems and peculiarities of life in an old building that hadn't been renovated for decades.
At the sight of the laundry room Hanna had just shaken her head in
disbelief, until she'd got married her mother had done the washing for
her and she knew nothing of unreliable 'fully automatic' washing
machines, nothing of the tiny spin-dryers that consisted of a drum
standing on end that was full with two towels and, when it was switched
on by a plastic bow sticking out over the lid like a record arm, developed
such dynamic imbalance that it started to move across the floor, the
water came out of the drain-spout beside the basin and the spin-dryer
pulled the plug out of the socket, thus switching itself off. Meno remembered Hanna going round the laundry room. The stove, made of bricks
with a zinc tub let in, had to be fired up, each tenant taking the wood
and briquettes out of their own allocation. There were a table, chunky
slabs of soap, packets of powdered Schneeberger Blue that, according
to the theory of complementary colours, was added as a whitener to
washing that had yellowed. When clothes were being washed there
was vapour, that warm, lethargic, cottony steam, saturated with

moisture, that made your clothes stick to you, made breathing a struggle and the laundry room a tropical cavern, vapour that billowed up
out of the boiler piping hot when, protected by rubber gloves, you
lifted the wooden lid in order to use the dolly (Libussa called it a 'butter
paddle') to stir the 95°C sludge that had a steel thermometer, long,
thin, as beautiful as a tailor's yardstick, stuck in it. There was a wash-
board for shirts and underwear; Meno dreamt of scrubbing hands that,
instead of soap bubbles, had plectrums growing out of their fingers,
making the rasping rhythm for jazz . . . The inexorable chainsaw screech
of his *заря* alarm clock bit into his benumbed mind.

One week later the washing was done and dried in the loft of Caravel. Meno and Anne had managed to get a slot on the wringer that was
beside the steam laundry, an eighty-year-old fossil in Sonnenleite.

'Well now, Herr Rohde,' said Udo Männchen at Dresdner Edition,
'are you going to need another day off for spring cleaning?'

'It's all very well for you to talk,' said Meno, irritated by the typographer's obvious pleasure, 'living in a three-room all-comfort apartment
and with a wife who looks after your, er, fabrics.'

The typographer had taken to wearing wide-sleeved jackets with
cuffs at the wrist, self-cut and self-sewn, silk and linen combined and
as colourful as the flags of developing countries.

'How is it that the people in Central Office always go for this Garamond? Why not Baskerville for once, as in the Insel edition of Virginia
Woolf? Three-room all-comfort! Are you pulling my leg? During
the recent power cut it was three-room blind man's buff! The maternity
hospitals in this city have something in store for them, I can tell you.'

'Persitif, persitif,' said Miss Mimi, boldly and determinedly putting
a ring of cactus spines round French yearnings.

'A day off for doing housework? I assume, Herr Rohde, that you're
not a married working woman, so you have no right to a statutory day
off for housework,' Josef Redlich said. 'Look, I too, wrinkled work-
horse that I am, have to take leave when the washing gets too much

for me. "The tablets of chocolate and arsenic upon which the laws are written", Lichtenberg, Volume D.'

A distant creaking in the morning twilight mixed, as Meno and Anne turned from Rissleite into Sonnenleite, with the clatter of the coal the apprentice at Walther's bakery was shovelling into his wheelbarrow, with the hum of a transformer, the rasp of ice scrapers on windscreens. The creaking was approaching radially from Lindwurmring, Rissleite and lower Sonnenleite; soon Meno perceived dark patches laboriously trudging closer: the women of the district who, like Anne, had the day off for housework and were bringing their washing to the steam laundry in handcarts. They approached through the grey undulations of snow, the brighter patches of their faces gradually separating from the darker ones of their bodies (their coats came down below their knees, their clumpy boots sank into the frozen snow that the few lamps with their white glow made to look like paper; the snow clearers and the winter morning shift would start work later), of those broad-shouldered, warmly wrapped-up, non-gender-specific bodies that, heading, as if drawn by a magnet, for the point of intersection of their tracks (it seemed to be Walther's bakery, which sold rolls after 7 a.m., there was already a queue), would form an arrowhead aimed at the laundry. The women nodded greetings, but weren't speaking yet. The creaking was an acoustic foreign body in the morning quiet, Meno thought: a rusty bar rubbed through a pelt; unpleasant, as if it were dragging bad dreams out of the night and into the day. It was the sound of the handcarts in which the women were bringing their washing, the wooden wheels scraping against dry bearings; the wheels had iron rims, on many of which quarter or half circles were missing, or the heavy square nails fixing them had loosened, causing the carts to bump and jolt; it was the screech of the shaft in the pole arm, the rumbling of the stanchions over the front wheels and the knock of the supports over the rear wheels; a medley of sounds, grey as driftwood like the colour of the carts bleached by rain and sun.

'I just don't know whether Richard can trust Stahl,' Anne went on. 'They spend whole weekends out there in Lohmen. And it's all "Gerhart" and "Richard". It's not for my own sake that I'm asking and Robert often stays the weekend out in Waldbrunn . . . despite that we could do something together again.'

'Go to Saxon Switzerland the way we used to,' Meno said, 'with Enoeff dishing up the gossip, getting annoyed she can't find any mushrooms, that she's got the wrong shoes on because she thought we were going out dancing, and Helmut merry and sliding into a crevasse? And once we've lugged him out, Enoeff says, "But we're not over the hill yet, over the hill we're definitely not yet."'

'Reserving seats in the wrong restaurant, Niklas bawling out opera arias, Gudrun going on about Bach flower therapy, returning via Schandau . . .'

'. . . where we all pile into Lene's,' said Meno, completing her sentence as Anne burst out laughing. 'Good old Lene Schmidken. Have you been out there recently?'

'Ulrich wanted to go but now, just before Christmas, they've got the Plan Commission on their backs. — They're not showing their old car to anyone. But you're Stahl's neighbour.'

'I don't believe he belongs in that street,' Meno replied. 'But what does "believe" mean and "I can't imagine"? The Stahls are certainly having problems with the new tenants.'

The 'new' tenants: the Honichs had been living in the House with a Thousand Eyes for almost a year now, but that was the way things were up there: hardly anyone moving in or out, many of the people had been living in the houses with the strange names for thirty or forty years and someone could still be 'the new inhabitant' when they'd only managed a quiet decade, hardly enough to acclimatize.

'They must be uncouth people. Do they at least leave you more or less in peace now?'

'A bit,' Meno replied with a grin — had the atmosphere rubbed off on Anne so much that her childhood language had been swapped for the more discriminating mode of expression up here. Meno had noticed that even in everyday conversation they used words that some authors even avoided in written German, 'Kunigunde-speak', he called it, 'uncouth' where 'coarse' or 'boorish' didn't seem precise enough.

'Perhaps they don't mean to be importunate, perhaps they think their homespun pleasures are everyone's idea of happiness – and are baffled when they come across people who see things differently.' Meno pulled their handcart past the queue, which stretched from the steam laundry to the rotting fencepost. Halting conversations, dirty looks that only cleared when Meno opened the door with the inscription 'wringer' in Gothic letters. They'd been given a slot for 7.30.

'Oh well, perhaps I'm being too demanding as far as Richard's concerned. He's pretty overworked and that worries me. You know I was so happy when he came back from that terrible time when he was on duty during the power cut. With Robert in tow! He ought to have been at school! He grasped the lad by the shoulders and pushed him into the apartment. I've never seen him so proud of Robert. Of Christian, yes. But he's quieter about that, doesn't show it that much. At least not to me or the boys. – Perhaps we should prepare our washing a bit, the ironing-woman's a real dragon. We mustn't overrun or she'll kick up a fuss.'

'Morning, Herr Rohde,' came the croaking voice of Else Alke from the door into the laundry. Clouds of steam and squashed transistor radio music poured out of the door. 'The Baron's waistcoat over here,' she ordered one of the assistants. 'And count the buttons again.' The red of the waistcoat, the gleaming steel buttons were a refreshing sight.

'The Baron will be sending you an invitation,' the old woman rasped before handing the Arbogast handcart over to the assistant with a haughty nod.

749

53

The laundry wringer

The ironing-woman, full-bosomed with piggy eyes and reddish down
on the backs of her fingers and her upper lip, brusquely instructed them
in how to operate the machine, after she'd checked their time in a notebook and ticked them off with a sharp pencil stroke. Neither Anne nor
Meno were there for the first time and the woman probably recognized
them, but the repeat of the instructions was according to regulations,
as any observant customer could see from the exclamation-mark-spattered
section of the typewritten sheets of paper in the glass frame by the
door connecting the wringer-room with the steam laundry, where the
ironing-woman was also in charge of the button replacement department (mostly braided buttons for bed linen). The rest of the sheets of
paper, printed in Gothic script and not yellowed, presented adages to
do with washing and had been left behind by the previous owners,
who, expropriated, had long since disappeared westwards: 'A bar of
soap, no more, no less, / brings healthy skin and happiness.' 'On linen
white / we start and end our life.' 'What smooths out our wrinkles, /
what can we rely on / to keep our faces young? / The wringer and
the iron.' Meno, fascinated by these reflections, would have most liked
to have started thinking about them immediately; above all he felt the
urge to check the substance of these axioms presented as folk wisdom
(and therefore infallible): on linen white . . . Ulrich and he had been
born in a Moscow clinic, had they had white sheets there? And for
those born during the war? Anne was pointing to the clock suspended
on two struts over the table, an octagonal model with hands ending in
a heart shape and curved numerals on a face that was now grey; she
wasn't smiling, as she so often was when she roused her brother from
one of his abstractions (a touch, an insistent look), she seemed

nervous – Meno knew she was afraid of the monster in the room. Even in the clear 100-watt light of a bare bulb the wringer looked like a tarantula that had been forced onto its back and gagged; one of the giant specimens with wolf's hair such as can be seen, modelled in synthetic material, sucking at Tertiary insects in the dioramas of museums of natural history (the stalked eyes in the woolly carnivore's face sticking out like a binocular periscope) or circulated at research conferences on arachnids in the form of copper engravings, such as those made for Brehm's *Life of Animals*, both praised for their technical skill and dismissed with a smile. Meno recalled Arbogast's 'our friend Arachne' as he opened the safety grating to pick up the three beechwood rollers off the sliding table in front of the wringer box, which had returned to the starting position – first of all he stretched out to get the one farthest away, prepared in case the box, which was filled with boulders weighing tons, should shoot out towards him like a vicious prehensile claw to drag him into its gullet (in fact there wasn't one, all that there was behind the mechanism was a black-and-yellow-striped wall, but he was haunted by the idea that there were digestive organs hidden in the casing); Meno grabbed the two remaining rollers with exaggerated speed and handed them to Anne, who silently and with the same exaggerated speed took them off him and went with them to the set-up table. She wrapped the washing, which had to be dry for this machine, round them. Now came the more difficult part of the preparation: Meno placed the three rollers with sheets and bed covers round them on the sliding table the way the ironing-woman had demonstrated (in a whiny, scarcely comprehensible voice and without switching on the wringer); rollers at a precise right angle to the direction of travel, only in that way was free rotation in both directions possible, only in that way would nothing get jammed – the wooden rollers could move freely under the box – holes wouldn't be rubbed in the washing, as would happen should the sliding process be disrupted by a wrong angle. The difficulty lay in the precision with which the wooden cylinders had to be aligned; Meno felt less afraid offering the gagged tarantula full rollers than he had removing the empty ones previously – he stepped back, let the safety grille down, anxiously watching the box that, when Anne pressed a button, started to hum forward on a toothed rail and slowly moved onto the rollers that smoothly took up the motion. Anne nodded, pressed a second button and now it sounded as if someone – or something – were being tortured, torment and pain were flying over the solid beechwood, worn by decades of use, of the wringer, shuttling to and fro, the boulders in the box thundering and rattling, a convulsive tremor from the transmission belts running over driving wheels on the side of the machine, obeying the blind, unfeeling voltage commands of a motor. For the moment there was nothing to do. Meno looked into the laundry through the little window in the wall: steam was rising from the huge vessels, resembling autoclaves, with rod thermometers stuck into them that an assistant in grey overalls kept his eye on (his other one was, as could be clearly seen, made of glass); now and then the one-eyed man pulled over a kind of brass shawm that went into an endoscopically flexible tube, and grunted something down it, probably telling a stoker hidden in the cellar to regulate the steam pressure in the boiler. – The ironing-woman appeared right on time.

54

Be at home

. . . but the clocks struck, it grew colder, it grew warmer, for days on end it seemed as if that year we would have a green Christmas but on the third Sunday in Advent the sky's pillows were shaken, the arched wooden candle-holders in the windows, the illuminated Moravian stars on the balconies, in the tops of the trees (Stahl had hung one up in the copper beech, despite Pedro Honich's protest), disappeared in the hazy snow; the lamps, when Meno strode round the streets in the evening, his Yugoslav hat pulled well down, his pipe filled with Copenhagen vanilla tobacco, were like jellyfish hanging below the branches of the elms on Mondleite and Wolfsleite with gelatinous haloes of light. In the kitchens there was a smell of gingerbread dough and cinnamon; Holfix and the grocer's on Bautzner Strasse were both out of icing sugar and hundreds-and-thousands and when Meno stopped at the door of Caravel, his hand already on the handle inside, he could see the winged shadows of a revolving wooden pyramid from Seiffen moving across the ceiling of the Hoffmanns' living room. In Evening Star the light was on in the Orrés' bathroom (Erik Orré was in the habit of learning his lines in the bath), the lights were on in the Tietzes' music room, the yellow glow was seeping through the dilapidated veranda, half hidden by a spruce tree. Meno could see a shadow bow dancing up and down the ceiling of the children's room: Ezzo was practising. Was he using Anne's chin rest? It was still too early for Niklas's music hour. At this time, if Gudrun didn't have to go to the theatre and Niklas had no more house calls to make, the music room was filled with the delicate aroma of baked apples; the tiled stove beside the mirror and chaise longue had a warming compartment in which Niklas steamed rather than baked the deep-red Consinots, Cox's Orange Pippins, Rheinische Krummstiefel, Winterstettiner from the gardens on the slope above the Elbe – with incomparable results, Meno had never eaten such tasty baked apples as at the Tietzes'. When, a few minutes later, he went down Heinrichstrasse, he was often roused from his reflections by a loud 'Watch out!' – toboggans with curved-up horns, flat, wooden Davos sledges or ancient metal ones with tubular runners and seats of plaited strips of leather were on their way to the steep Dachsleite, where a merry crowd was enjoying skiing and sledging, unconcerned about the darkness and flurries of snow.

For Christmas the fathers put up the family Christmas tree that they'd bought at the Striezelmarkt or from Busse, the forester (they were the better, though of course dearer, ones), brought the stands down from the loft, the angels and coloured glass balls to decorate it, hung tinsel over the branches.

Niklas still had strips of silver foil and decorated the tree in traditional style with wooden ornaments from the Erzgebirge that had been handed down from generation to generation, and with genuine candles, for which he pinned on pine-cone holders. Green, red and silver balls, on the topmost sprig the star, between them the crinkled aluminium fringes that the Christmas department of the Centrum store sold under the name of 'lametta': thus decked out, the standard Dresden fir tree (that was, if truth be told, a blue spruce) stood in its place of honour in the living rooms and shed its first needles even before its owners had gone to the watchnight service. Meno spent Christmas Eve with the Londoners; Jochen Londoner had invited him: Hanna was busy at the embassy in Prague, he'd said, Philipp and his 'companion' (as Londoner put it after a moment's pause for thought) would 'bring their youthful joy and colour / to light the smoky grey of our days'. Meno didn't buy a present; Libussa cut some roses for Irmtraud Londoner and stared wide-eyed in surprise when he said they weren't a present, just a small token he'd take along, even though he knew how much Irmtraud Londoner loved flowers. With a lovely bouquet of flowers in her hand she could even become prickly towards her husband, something that never happened otherwise: Do you see, Jochen, you study economy and the whole house is full of scholarly treatises, but it's this young man here who's brought me roses in the winter. Libussa didn't feel hurt, she knew Meno would pay her back for the roses by chopping wood and bringing up coal, four bucketfuls, Pedro Honich was going to see to the rest as 'Timur Assistance'. Frau Honich promptly brought some wrapping paper, and a creamy smile spread over her face when she enquired: Londoner – had she heard correctly? – She had. – The famous Jochen Londoner who wrote for the weekly magazine *Horizon* – and a book now and then?

Now and then: Londoner's output was notorious; he had no compunction about making use of left-over scraps, reworking things that had been printed long ago and passing them off as new; Meno responded to Babett Honich's smile (even if suspiciously); he remembered that they were Londoner's own words – 'and now and then we write a little book' – which he had the habit of repeating in his countless interviews, from which no one dared to edit out that 'we' – the royal 'we'? Londoner as the head of a capitalistically enterprising business concern? – But then Herr Rohde must be an important person if he counted Londoner among his friends! Babett Honich was quite carried away. She'd realized at once that Herr Rohde was made from finer stuff, well, who was called Meno anyway, he had a 'certain something' about him ('but that you write about spiders of all things, my God, yeuch!'); could he not invite Herr Londoner to tea here? – Herr Rohde had to go now, he was in a hurry and as far as *she* knew, old Jochen didn't drink tea.

On Turmstrasse, waiting for a parade of Father Christmases to march past (Grauleite had taken over special shifts for the children of East Rome), Meno was still chuckling at Libussa's presence of mind and her casual, saucy 'old Jochen' that had left even Babett Honich speechless. The guard in the sentry box subjected his papers and invitation to a thorough check.

'Purpose of your visit?' The first lieutenant had become a captain. He waited, fingers on the typewriter keys, for Meno's answer.

'To spend the Feast of Hanukah with Comrade Jochen Londoner.' Meno couldn't have said himself why he suddenly felt his oats. The Feast of Hanukah! The duty officer, who would certainly have a wife and children and had to be on guard here instead of spending Christmas with them, would probably not know what he was talking about.

'Hannucker? Are you pulling my leg?' The comrade immediately got worked up. 'We'll soon see about that.' He picked up the telephone. The Brezhnev portrait had been removed from the guardhouses, it hadn't been replaced by one of Gorbachev but by a sour-faced black-and-white likeness of the Minister of Security. 'Aha.' The captain remained sceptical. 'A full pass? That has recently been forbidden for visitors, Frau Comrade Londoner. – I've no idea why. Instruction from the top. – Correct, Frau Comrade Londoner, if he gets a half-pass he'll have to report on the Oberer Plan tomorrow morning. – No, we're not allowed to do that. Two one-third passes, that's the most I'm allowed to do.'

He put the phone down, typed, put a second sheet into the typewriter. 'Sign here.' Meno picked up the ballpoint pen and form off the revolving tray and while he was signing he could hear the captain muttering, 'Hannucker, Hannucker' to himself. 'The things there are. Didn't it use to be called Christmas? Is that official now?'

Meno tipped his hat, turned up his collar and left the captain without replying. The gusts of wind were making the bridge hum, the bulbs, of which only a few were working, were swinging between the parapets; Meno stuck the roses inside the lapels of his coat. The mule is trying to find its way in the fog, he thought; the deep snow on the bridge seemed like mist, the tracks of the Father Christmases had already been blown away. With every step Meno sank in up to his knees so that he was only making slow progress, holding on to the railing. Cobweb House loomed up black in the smoky white air in which swirls and twists of snow were dancing over the steep valley; perhaps Vogelstrom was working on the panorama of revolution or was communing in the dark with the painted garden scenes, perhaps he was away, spending Christmas with his children, though the painter never talked about them. 'Doesn't mean anything!' Meno forced the words out against the assaults of the wind. Recalling Meyer's poem, he addressed it, 'Thou heavenly child.' This wind was an unruly child with a mind of its own, a raging brat. Sometimes the child paused, seemed to be wondering how it could get the better of the solitary man plodding across the bridge, scurried on ahead, whirled back over his hat and dropped down in a flurry of snowflakes to try it from behind, came whirring at him from the right and the left, only, after blustering blasts, vengeful rattling of the bridge's cables, to collapse, as if its fury had earned it a click of the fingers from up there, out of the air: then, soothingly bronchitic, the hoarse roar of the Weisse Schwester could be heard. Meno hurried up. True, Jochen Londoner had not stated a time. Even though in East Rome they were prepared to tolerate Christmas as an obviously ineradicable relic of Christianity, until there would no longer be a place for it in the period of transition from socialism to communism, even though they were prepared to remain silent, to conform to the code of conduct requiring a Christmas tree and window decorations, to sit back and, after the presents had been handed out to wife and children on Christmas Eve, enjoy the television programmes with the family, Jochen Londoner was and remained an East Roman and one who frequently indulged in mockery of that evening: so they had a family Christmas and Jochen insisted that both Irmtraud and the children first of all respected the customs, then 'celebrated Christmas critically'. He called it the dialectical approach. That is: he took care about the decor but treated the ritual, of which the decor was, after all, an abbreviated symbol, with an indifferent shrug of the shoulders, even with disdain and dismissive pride, pride in half-recognition, in a freedom that for him might lie in not fulfilling a cliché and the demands concealed within it. He, the 'merry Marxist and Mr Rigorous' as he called himself, half ironically, half threateningly, took the liberty of coming up with laissez-faire where others didn't expect it, where they would react with dismay to the stereotyped thought thus revealed or 'at best' (sometimes he would say 'at worst') with curiosity: '*The Jew*,' he would then growl irritably, 'was in exile, and *the Jew*, who was in exile, must know the Jewish customs, mustn't he? And if he knows them, surely he must follow them? That's what you always think, isn't it? For how can *the Jew* take the liberty of ignoring customs that cost so many fellow sufferers their lives?' And when Meno remained silent, horrified, he went on, 'But I take (a), the liberty of deciding for myself who or what I am; I'm not a Jew, I'm a human being and as such I also take (b), the liberty of determining which customs are important to me and which not, which I do or do not *have to* follow.' So he lit a Hanukah menorah and the lights on the Christmas tree, baked with Irmtraud and Hanna, when she was at home over Christmas, ginger-bread and sufganiyot, the tasty jelly doughnuts, fried latkes that Philipp called hash browns, hung up lametta and little toy spinning tops on the Christmas tree. 'We're having Chrisnukah!' And instead of 'Maos zur jeschuati' the sound of the Beatles echoed round the house at 9 Zetkinweg, a cul-de-sac at the end of Krupskaja-Strasse.

Chocolate and wood – that was the smell of books and Meno knew of no house where it was such a commanding and inviting presence as at the Londoners'.

'Chanukah!' Irmtraud cried when she opened the door, grasped Meno by the shoulders and touched him 'cheek-to-cheek', a greeting he loved because of its discreet, delicate intimacy. 'You really gave the poor guy a fright. I had to explain it to him. He'll be telephoning now. – But you know Jochen doesn't like that sort of joke, don't say anything about it; he thinks it's no one else's concern how we live. Be at home.'

Be at home, not 'make yourself at home', Meno had always found that simple greeting moving; he felt slightly ashamed at having to take the roses out of his coat in such an unceremonious manner since he'd forgotten to unwrap them before ringing the bell – and since he wanted to conceal how moved he was, he held out the budding Maréchal Niels to Irmtraud, who had his hat and gloves in her hands, with an awkward firmness that was nothing other than embarrassment, which he had never managed entirely to shed at the Londoners'. Jochen knew that. Meno took his time fiddling with his shoelaces, drips or dirt from the streets made Irmtraud furious. At his first visit, to be introduced as Hanna's 'boyfriend', before which he had given himself Dutch courage with three miniatures of bitters from Lange's stock, the 'old connoisseur of life' (as the 'Herr Professor' that Jochen Londoner had been for Meno at that time put it with an understanding nod and ironically crossed fingers) had not found anything to dispel his embarrassment: neither a tour of his personal library, taking down first editions of Kant and signed copies of Brecht and leafing through them at length, nor the table loaded with delicacies, the celebrated scholar's markedly homely attire of cardigan and tartan slippers or his amiable questions, going into detail and offering a wide range of interests. On the contrary, the wealth (both material and intellectual) of the Londoner household had intimidated Meno even more and Londoner could well have sensed that, for on future occasions he changed his 'tactics', as he said: since then it was Irmtraud who greeted him with 'be at home' and called him 'Menodear' or 'my dear', which for a long time he assumed was a bizarre term of affection, softened in the Saxon manner, until he saw it at the beginning of a letter and realized she was speaking English.

But he recognized the bat-cap on the clothes stand, and listened for what was being said in the living room instead of to Irmtraud singing the praises of the roses, and since it was what he expected to hear, it wasn't long before it came: Judith Schevola's gravelly laugh. Philipp was showing off, Meno heard that as well; Irmtraud now, with a mute and conspiratorial gesture to the stairs down to the basement kitchen, left him to his own devices. A brief, warm greeting, a gesture of invitation and then the guest could, if he was a friend of the family, spend the time until the official part of the invitation (the beginning of which was announced by a dinner gong or a little bell, such as the chairman of the television *Professors' Forum*, of which Londoner was a member, rang) doing as he liked: sit in the wing chair in the living room and browse through one of the magazines set out there (among them *Literaturnaya gazeta* and the *Times Literary Supplement*), leaf through the books or, if there were two of you, play a game of ice hockey on the slot machine in a niche in the basement; there was always a supply of ten-pfennig pieces there; if you put one in you could use a wheel to make the red or blue lead figures, with sticks that had been bent by the steel ball, revolve. You could also go home again, as Eschschloraque had once done: immersed in a book-covered wall on the stairs up to Londoner's sanctum ('The Haunted Chamber' it said in English and in cursive letters on an oval pottery sign), the dramatist had been gripped by a scene, glassy-eyed and waving his arms about (Meno had quickly put a pencil in his hand) he had drifted down to the little tele-phone table, where, without success and ever more desperate, he searched for a sheet of paper (he didn't find one; there were printed sheets of paper by the million in the Londoner residence, blank ones the old man stored in the 'Haunted Chamber' and kept a strict watch over where they were left; do not leave anything handwritten lying around in the house, no addresses, no notes that might be misunderstood – a maxim from the time when he'd been active in the underground), until Meno, who always put some in his pocket when he went to see Londoner, gave a sheet to Eschschloraque; in a world of his own, the Marshal of Moderation had picked up the phone, rolled out iambic lines and belaboured an imaginary public with the receiver; at that moment Londoner had come down the stairs, he too glassy-eyed, he too with accumulations of word, thought and deduction within reach, had shuffled over to the telephone, where instead of the receiver he took the pencil from Eschschloraque, nodded, stared at it intently and, shaking it in his raised hand, carried it off, leaving Eschschloraque staring uncomprehending at the receiver before leaving the house without a word and still wearing the house slippers he'd put on.

They were discussing things that were often discussed at the Lon-doners': the history of the working class, economics, appropriately for the occasion the history of the Christmas roast, dates and events in the history of the Communist Party. Judith Schevola was sitting, an amused expression on her face, beside Jochen Londoner, who, in his rocking chair, had got so carried away that he kept losing one of his tartan slippers, which Philipp fitted back on his foot, addressing his father, as did Hanna, by the familiar form of Josef: 'Seppel' (Irmtraud was called 'Traudel' by her husband and children). Jochen Londoner would certainly have preferred not to be repeatedly reminded of the mortality of euphoria (let the slipper fly wherever it wanted!); in Judith Schevola there were unknown ears that had never been exposed to the Londoner fount of knowledge, at least not the old man's one that delighted in the world around. A glass of port, filled while rocking in the middle of an extensive drilling-core analysis of the 'main task' and handed to him with neither comment nor eye contact was sufficient greeting for Meno; out of amazement at Schevola's presence and a creeping feeling of discontent at the elegance and self-evident pleasure with which Philipp basked in the splendour of the house, bobbing up and down like an excited schoolboy, Meno had already poured the glass down his throat and was now perched like a tawny owl, limed to the heavy wash of the wine, in the wing chair opposite the old historian. Now 'Londoner-speak' flew between three points round the room, giving Meno the feeling he was sitting by the edge of sparkling electricity; Irmtraud asked when dinner should be served: 'When kenn I servier ze roast herr, my dear?' And Seppel, deep in a description of the starvation conditions created by the beasts of prey in the Manchester cotton mills, spread his arms interrogatively, indicating democracy – which Philipp took up instead of Judith Schevola, who was snorting with laughter, and Meno, who, assuming Londoner's son had a bad conscience, sat there in silent ill-humour, with 'We love you dermassen, Traudel, you are ä Heldin, denn I sink there's not matsch fun in de Kittschen?'

'You really don't have tomatoes on your eyes,' said Traudel, confirming his observation. 'Bleib sitting, my dear' (that to Judith Schevola), 'de patätohs are alle geschält bei now, än I sink de Rosenkohl is quite reddy.'

'Okäh,' the paterfamilias decreed, 'zänn I sink we take sammsink zu nibbeln in de Zwischentime.'

A call on the upstairs telephone and the trucks of the Michurin complex on Gagarinweg were on their way with a selection of snacks. Irmtraud hadn't wanted that, even though Jochen had made the offer several times, as Meno knew from Philipp, who by now was casting revolting sheep's eyes at Judith Schevola. As at the time when they'd been going to see Eschschloraque, Meno felt like inquiring about Marisa; perhaps she was having Christmas with fellow Chilean exiles or playing with Judith Schevola's knife in Philipp's room opposite the cotton mill. Meno observed Philipp: did this man have any idea at all what he wanted? Surely you're not jealous? He waved the idea away with a vigorous gesture that set the hand with the ring on the index finger in motion, offering Meno a bowl of pretzels; without interrupting his flow of speech or taking any notice of Meno's reaction (perhaps Jochen Londoner took it for acceptance), the scholar continued his Manchester speech. Philipp had put a Gorbachev badge on the table in front of him, the head with its birthmark on a red background; the tin disc had a pin on the back, ironically it came from the West; Philipp had brought it back from Berlin, where these 'sweet liddel provocations' (as Jochen Londoner called them, he had examined it closely, praising the quality of the soldering of the pin) had been on sale for several months.

Philipp, the child of heroes. Who wanted to keep the Party pure and to uphold the ideals for which his parents had fought and suffered one (Meno could not imagine the pair of them separately) of the terrible destinies of that century: all of Irmtraud's and Jochen's relations had been murdered in the Nazi death camps, they themselves had escaped by hazardous routes to England ('mit nothing in de pockets and hunger, my dear, immer hunger'), where he had worked for the British Museum Library and she as a cleaner in Guy's Hospital before they had been interned as 'enemy aliens'. Philipp, who attacked corrupt officials and believed in socialism as something sacred – in discussions he would never be prepared to go beyond a certain limit, to call the whole system in question, as Richard did (and Anne? had she not been brought up in the same way as Philipp and he, Meno Rohde, the bearers of a proud name in the hierarchy of communism? . . . at that moment she was probably in church to hear Pastor Magenstock's sermon and see the nativity play); Philipp never doubted that socialism had the better, the more hopeful future. Everything for the welfare of the people . . . Philipp donated a significant part of his salary to a workers' retirement home in Leipzig; while a student he had worked on the Baikal–Amur railway. And his science? It served the people, for whom socialism had been thought up and planned; Meno was convinced that Philipp regarded his science, his professorship, as a contribution to the strengthening of socialism and would have relinquished them without hesitation had that seemed necessary for the defence of the 'just cause' (as people here liked to call the dictatorship of the proletariat).

The whistle of Black Mathilda was heard, at which Jochen Londoner, taking a sip of sherry, interrupted his peroration and made Meno prick up his ears with a drawn-out '. . . by the way . . .'; mostly this preceded an important tip about everyday matters, as was the case this time as well. It had struck him, he said, that the energy-saving programmes on the Republic's television had been on the increase again, Meno 'and you too, my dear' (Judith Schevola came back with a start from the contemplation of the many original prints on the walls between the rows of books) would be well advised to order more coal in time; if necessary he could help them in that, they only had to ask. And if there was anything else . . . ? This offer was to be seen as a 'liddel advance' on the presents that were to be distributed later. Meno took it up, he had thought of doing so before setting off and asked whether Jochen could do anything for Christian, transfer to another unit, for example, a post as headquarters clerk; Londoner said sorry, that was the army, he could do nothing there, nothing at all, he had enough to do sorting out Philipp's idiotic petty bourgeois/educated middle class comparison on Hiddensee, the comrade had played the stool pigeon and reported him; dangerous, Jochen Londoner said, but it could presumably be sorted out. And, by the way, was the telephone working again? Groaning slightly, he pushed himself up out of his rocking chair; the expression of intent listening returned as Londoner grasped his chin between thumb and forefinger. Irmtraud raised the stick of the dinner gong and said, 'The gong is gonging.'

Meno watched as Londoner shuffled over to the telephone, hesitated a few moments before lifting the receiver and, with a concentrated expression, put it to his ear. 'Oh, could you come round some time. Yes, I can't get a connection when I dial. It would be a pity about all those conversations, wouldn't it? If I can't talk to people on the phone, you'll have nothing to record, don't you have your plan targets too? Goodbye and a merry Christmas.' He remained standing while Irmtraud served up the roast hare. 'Let's have a liddel feastolos,' he said in Londoner Greek.

After the meal, the presents: Meno watched Schevola, who spoke less than usual, maintained her reserve even at the old man's sly compliments; they weren't suggestive; Londoner liked talking and liked listening to himself ('with crit'cal love, not that I can't see through myself'), well aware that monologues can hold people's attention, but not for long. Schevola was watching Philipp and the old man, as she ate her assessing gaze went from Irmtraud's pearl necklace to the Meissen porcelain, the serviettes with monograms (all that vaguely illuminated by the first candle, lit too early, on the menorah); Meno suspected that, like himself, Judith Schevola was waiting for the moment, the 'characterology of moments', of which the moment would consist: the translation of the old scholar from professed revolutionary (who served the juiciest portions of the roast to his wife and Judith) into property-owning bourgeois. Would the smile on the Liebermann portrait above the settee be any less fierce, would hints of forbearance, of weariness even, an awareness of the darker side, cross the painter's wide-awake, pitiless expression with its glint of wit? – A clearing of

the throat, embarrassment, reluctance. Jochen Londoner stood in front
of the tree and invited the family (his heavy eyelids pushed the word
'guests' aside) to join him, passed his hands, searching, over the tweed
of his jacket, found a pair of glasses and, with appeasing words, much
furrowing of the brow and 'So – for you' and 'There – for you', handed
out envelopes that, as Meno knew, contained cheques for considerable
sums of money. 'No, no' – Londoner raised his hands to wave away
objections that hadn't even been made – 'warm hands, children. / Not
with cold hands should you give your gifts, / the young need wings
like these to fly. No, no, take it, forget it, buy yourselves sammsink.
You know you shouldn't give us presents. We don't want any. Not one
word more. But there is something' – he nodded to Irmtraud and
turned to Judith Schevola – 'we would like from you.' Irmtraud opened
Judith's novel, *The Depths of These Years*, with the mark of Munderloh's
publishing company that was so familiar to Meno, and asked for a
dedication. Judith Schevola was not in the least embarrassed. Jochen
Londoner read it out in a disheartened voice, 'Since you've decided to
be a horse – then pull.'

'Let's go for a walk,' Irmtraud Londoner suggested.

'What have I done wrong?' Schevola whispered to Meno in the hall.

'Touched on a sore point,' he whispered back.

'How stupid of me, how tactless,' she said.

'Child' – Irmtraud Londoner plucked her sleeve – 'you couldn't
know. Don't let it worry you. If you're going to be part of the family
it would be best if you got used to these swings of mood now. We are
all very unstable,' she went on, switching to English. 'Isn't that so,
my son?'

'It is so, my sunshine,' Philipp agreed, helping his mother on with
her coat.

Outside Jochen Londoner tried to divert attention away from the
scene, discussing the book, praising its dense atmosphere, the figure
of the father, applying the 'you don't have to be long-winded if you

vant to say sammsink ernsthaftly' that hung, in Londoner English, over his desk, to Schevola's novel – Meno recalled reviews Londoner had written for *Neue Deutsche Literatur* and *Neues Deutschland*, in which he indulged in high-sounding phrases and empty grandiloquence without having more than sampled the books; Schevola seemed to feel that his praise was honestly meant, for she pushed it aside with a reaction Meno had seen in other authors (and they weren't the worst): she pointed out weaknesses, played the novel down by not simply mentioning parts of the plot she felt were not quite successful, but showing them in a critical light (in East Rome the street lamps worked) in order not to appear presumptuous. What did Meno as an editor have to say to the book, Londoner asked cautiously. – Meno replied that he really couldn't say anything since he didn't know the book, at least in its printed form. Meno behaved as if he were having difficulty lighting the tobacco he'd tamped down in his pipe. – Had he not received it? Schevola asked in alarm. She had asked for a copy to be sent to him.

'We read good books,' Londoner said, waving a shopping bag and lending Meno a box of matches, 'with a sense of security.' He regretted that it hadn't been possible for it to appear in the country. If it was any comfort, if it gave her any encouragement, he too knew what a muzzle felt like, he'd had to wait six years for permission for what was probably his most popular book, *A Short Critique of Soap*, to be printed. Did Meno know ('by the way') that after the book had appeared Ulrich Rohde had sent him a whole carton of the substance? After a lecture on astronomy in the Orient at Arbogast's place. 'You know' – Londoner merrily hit himself on either side of his chest with his unencumbered left hand – 'here the medals – and here the Party's punishments, that's the way things are; don't imagine people like Barsano or even our Friedel Sinner-Priest can do their work without receiving such correction for their own good.'

Meno was surprised at what Londoner had said. Some of the passages he'd remembered from Schevola's book contained strong criticism of the Party, a few were even openly aggressive . . . There it was again, the schizophrenia he was familiar with from Kurt. If they ever talked about such matters at all, it was the Party that punished but those it punished fell to their knees and would not say anything against the Great Mother. Even when facing the firing squad, condemned men had shouted, 'Long live Stalin, long live the Bolshevik Party, long live the revolution.' Meno recalled what a shock it had been for him when Irmtraud, who hadn't worked for ages now, had talked in a casual conversation about her previous job. She had been a censor for 'books of philosophical content', she had even rejected Philipp's dissertation for 'deviant readings'. They were both, as Philipp put it, 'coldly curious' as to whether their children would 'make it' and at the same time well-disposed towards their dreams: 'We will help, but you must do your fighting yourselves.' And now they were both praising a book that Irmtraud would have rejected and Jochen Londoner, had he had to speak in an official capacity about it, would have classed as 'ideologically unclear', perhaps even as 'harmful'.

'"The world's abuzz with rumour, / The truth they would deny. / Hearts may lose their way, / We have climbed so high!"' Judith Schevola broke off; for a moment, so it seemed to Meno, Londoner was about quote another verse of Becher's *Tower of Babel* himself, but remained silent instead. Philipp and Irmtraud were ahead of them, Philipp gesticulating.

'May I ask you something? – Ernsthaftly.'

'Go ahead, my dear, if I can answer it.'

'Philipp often says I'm not interested in the problems in this country – I mean the economic problems. That's not true. I do keep my eyes open. Do you think –'

'Lennin,' Londoner broke in with a sweeping gesture of his right hand; he seemed to move away from Schevola slightly. 'As soon as the war was over Lennin introduced a capitalist economy into Soviet Russia; he always used to say, capitalism is our enemy but it is also our teacher.' He gave her a suspicious look, perhaps he thought he'd ventured too far. 'And it was Lennin who said that, the man who taught *us all* our trade.'

Meno permitted himself a quiet grin at this 'Lennin'; it sounded like Lennon with an 'i' and Jochen Londoner was a professed fan of the Beatles.

'And since it's Christmas I'll just add this, my dear: Lennin's theory of the necessity of grassroots democracy. Lennin at the head of the October Revolution, ten days that changed the world – and we're part of the Soviet Union, we couldn't survive alone. I leave it to you to draw your own conclusions, in regard to current politics as well.'

They regrouped; Irmtraud and Jochen Londoner fell behind. They were holding hands, looking at the road, saying nothing. Philipp would probably not have been allowed to ask his father such a question; from Meno's experience problems of that kind were not discussed in the nomenklatura, at least not between the generations. No addresses in the house, except in the safe, no doubts that threatened to become matters of substance in their own four walls, no deviancy, unquestioning loyalty to the Party. Meno recalled Londoner's malicious subtlety in getting Philipp to invite the Old Man of the Mountain; what a humiliation – and what a strange reaction from the old man. He had been furious with the Londoners for inviting him; he thought that in such a way they had exposed his loneliness, which – and this made it worse – must be so great 'that it was not even possible for me to decline the invitation in a friendly way'. 'Act-u-al-ly a substitute invitation,' that was what he had called it, 'the way they used to issue a kind invitation to lackeys or the children of the servants to the table with the Christmas presents from which they were allowed to take home a few crumbs.'

'Do you want to go along with this?' Meno asked Judith Schevola softly. Philipp was in full flight, Meno was familiar with it, Hanna had also had these ecstatic states; it was something that was alien to him but that he admired, something he'd loved Hanna for. On Philipp's lips words such as 'world revolution', 'a community in which everyone has a good life, in which no one goes hungry any more and no one is oppressed' didn't sound like hollow phrases, as they so often did from the hardliners. Philipp believed in the future. It belonged to socialism – and it belonged to them, the children of heroes, the children of people who had gone through unimaginable suffering for the realization of their ideals. When Philipp's eyes shone, as they did now, when his enthusiasm at being able to take part in the struggles of this age, which according to the law of history would lead to a tomorrow without exploitation and want, put a flush on his cheeks, he was beautiful and, with his long hair, though with a hat instead of a beret and star, he did resemble his ideal, Che Guevara, a little. At this point usually a different tone broke through, for he, Philipp, and others of a similar background, were the children of the victors of history, of genuine revolutionaries that was, who had not stuck to theory but put it into practice – 'while the petty bourgeois, the shit-scared and all the riffraff, for whom men and women like my parents put their lives at risk, had kept their heads down and betrayed everything they had worked for'. Meno bit back the question of whether the 'riffraff', whom Philipp dismissed with a disparaging wave of the hand, did not also belong to the people, to the working class whom he and his comrades wanted to stand by; when he was in one of these 'states' Philipp no longer seemed open to critical arguments.

'Go along? You mean into the jungle? Where the true revolutionaries live? – Why not?' Meno remained silent after this reply and with a shrug of the shoulders Judith Schevola went on, 'It's for a better world, I once went to Prague for that . . . however often Altberg might try to decry it. In the end we all have to die, and live . . . better to burn short and bright like a firework than to spend a long time poking around in cold ash.' Hostile tones! Meno dropped back, flabbergasted at the way Judith Schevola had spoken, sickened by the smitten sidelong looks she was giving Philipp; it offended him, he recalled their

conversation when they were going to see Eschschloraque, the part
about calling each other 'du' and about wailing geniuses – smitten
geniuses were at least equally disappointing.

'Well, lad' – Jochen Londoner took his arm – 'is she the right one
for Philipp, what d'you think? You know, I'm starting to get old, this
morning Traudel and I were talking about how nice it would be if we
had grandchildren and could play with them under the Christmas tree.
Grandfather ambitions! Don't you think a pair of old bracket funguses
like us have the right to let the world go hang and just concern ourselves with happy smiling children? We had so hoped that Hanna and
you . . . that you would get back together again. No *fnuky*, as my Polish
friend calls the pleasures of being a grandfather, from those in front
either. – Oh well, enough of that.' But Londoner hadn't finished yet –
Meno, he said, still didn't seem to realize what he'd lost. 'Your country,
lad, your real home!', the things that would be possible if . . . days
spent reading in the West Berlin State Library, there were visas for
personal and for official travel; he, Londoner, had the ear of the General Secretary; with a document like that one could dip into one world
and then another, like an amphibian, unchecked, and if Meno felt that
went against his conscience ('which I could understand'), then the
'Archipelago' would still be open to him, the Socialist Union, a continent of unsuspected richness that people 'over there', arrogant and
with their Atlantic fixation, had absolutely no idea about . . . the Crimea,
the Adriatic islands off Yugoslavia, Cuba, Vietnam, China, the
mind-numbing oriental part of the Soviet Union . . . Dushanbe was
wonderful; Bokhara, Samarkand awaited you on the Silk Road, you
could sense the very breath of history . . . after all, Meno, like Hanna
and Philipp, was a 'child of heroes' (Meno was grateful that Londoner
had become ironic again); he was respected ('oh, definitely') by the
leaders of Party and state, by some, 'as I have it from a reliable source',
even very highly regarded! 'You could have a very easy time of it, my

dear boy. If you only wanted. That subordinate post in Editorial Office Seven . . .'

'The roast hare was very good,' Meno said when Londoner fell silent. Irmtraud Londoner said nothing.

'Edu Eschschloraque told me that you all went to see him once.' Londoner's voice was firm again; the scholar, measured and well-disposed, had returned to his body. 'It gave him much food for thought. I think he likes you.'

Meno had to laugh at that. 'Altberg thinks Eschschloraque hates me.'

'Oh yes, the red comma. That's a sensitive matter with him. Like Siegfried, we all have our vulnerable spots. – Georgie Altberg, hm. What do you think of him?'

'A brilliant essayist, supports young writers like no one else in this country.'

'That's not what I was asking.'

'A man in the depths of despair.'

'An opportunist, I think. A censor, an author but out of the limelight, an old pal.' Tapping the fence with his signet ring, the old scholar slipped into his bizarre English again. 'We are stränsch. Really stränsch.'

They were approaching the limit of East Rome, below them was Block A. The sound of dogs barking came up to them.

'I go for a walk here almost every evening and they still always bark. Real brutes they are, I wouldn't like to meet them when they're running free. Or is it this here?' Londoner raised his shopping bag.

'Where are we going actually?'

'You just wait and see,' Londoner said with a sly grin. By now a special lamp was burning beside the statues of the 'Upright Fighters' outside the House of Culture, Eternal Flames were flickering in the pylons, guarded by two sentries either side of the avenue leading to Engelsweg.

'Look.' Following Londoner's eye, Meno looked over to Coal Island, lying like a wreck dotted with yellow Argus eyes in the snowy twilight. 'That's where the listeners-in are, they're even busy on Christmas Eve.'

They walked along the path that the street had become until a searchlight was turned on full beam and someone shouted, 'Password?'

'Roast hare.' The searchlight was turned down, Londoner signalled to Meno to follow him. They walked slowly up to the barrier, which consisted of a concrete wall with barbed wire pointing outwards on top; there was a watchtower every fifty metres. From the nearest one a rope was let down in the beam of a torch; Londoner tied the shopping bag to it, gave it a brief tug, the rope was pulled up. Meno went up to the wall. Where he could reach the stone it felt greasy and warm; there was no snow here, the brambles, which were growing all over the concrete and barbed wire, which had climbed up the watchtower and started to wrap it in a cocoon, to catch on to the tops of trees, shimmered like oiled metal.

'We always do it, my lad. At Christmas something is smuggled up to one of the guards on the watchtower,' Londoner said, rubbing his hands with a conspiratorial wink. They walked back. The old scholar proudly reported his illegal mercy mission to Irmtraud, who, with an indulgently loving smile, guided him round potholes.

. . . but the clocks struck, snow dribbled, swirled, fluttered down on Dresden, became firmer, became softer, then grey like flakes of kapok, crusts of snow formed at the crossing points of gutters, swelled up, inflamed by ash, grew into brownish coral outcrops. Between the years Meno heard the carpet beaters again, saw the 'Persian' carpets from Vietnam and Tashkent, the rugs from Laos and the People's Republic of China, saw fathers and their sons brandishing carpet beaters from Zückel's workshop (behind the little City Hall Park with its weathered statue of Hygieia, savings bank and woodland café, which had ice cream in the summer and hot sausages and grog in the winter, and the 'Reading Room' inviting one to peruse the newspapers), working off, beating off, thumping off, knocking down, thwacking down, battering down the rage that had built up over the year; they pounded, they struck with the elegant weapons, with the rococo loops that sat neatly in the hand and, with a crunching, willowy blow, got rid of dirt, fluff and carpet beetle larvae; Zückel would contemplate them meditatively 'in action' when he walked round the district . . . but the clocks struck, inside, in the living rooms heated with difficulty, struck at Ticktock Simmchen's and Pieper's Clocks on Turmstrasse; in Malthakus's stamp shop, on the counter with the picture-postcard albums; in Trüpel's record shop; on Postmaster Gutzsch's table in the post office; in Binneberg's café; in Frau Zschunke's greengrocer's; and in the pharmacy: inside –

outside, however, outside the wind got up again and snowstorms danced across the country.

55

The underwater drive

Life with your comrades-in-arms will give you unforgettable experiences

What It Means to be a Soldier

Whistles like that are a fatal stab to sleep.

'Company Four: Stand to!'

Costa's clock with the luminous dial moved on to 3 a.m.

'Go and jump out of the window, Nip, you measly rat.' – 'How I hate it! How I hate it!' – 'You corpsefuckers, trouser-hangers, fart-arses!' – 'You Bunsen burners, shit-for-brains, scumbags!' – 'Tossers, douchebuckets, cockburners, shirtlifters!' the commanders growl, desperately trying to get dressed (underpants, field coverall, protection pack, gas mask, belt, tank hood) in the gloomy chill of their room –

'Dear Mum, What gives you the idea I might do something silly? Because the dear comrades I share the room with keep the radio on all the time? Basically Costa's a poor soul, his mother died from cancer at 42, she came from the "sleeping villages", his father worked for Wismut, was retired at 45 on health grounds – bone cancer. Big Irrgang swears like a trooper – but that's what we all are here – gets on our superior officers' nerves with his absolute refusal to use the dative and is a real sly fox. Recently he smuggled in litres of "stuff", his father, who works in refrigerator construction, inserted a false bottom in his travel bag, lined with metal foil, into which they poured several bottles of some sugary Romanian hooch called Murfatlar that turned an honest tank crew into seamen on deck during a storm and doubled the company. Musca, the fly, needs a girlfriend, that's all, but here there's only the regimental cultural officer, 130 kg of model worker, and those left on the shelf in the Dutch Courage, and even they don't want to know. Which goes to show that aftershave is *not* for internal use. Pancake was on a charge of manslaughter but they couldn't prove anything and now he's my driver. Recently he waylaid the company commander, put on his lopsided grin and said, "If you want a car, Comrade Captain . . . you earn peanuts. All you need to do is to tell me, I just have to make a call and you can take your choice. What would you like? A Lada, a Dacia, a Wartburg – or would you go for something more high-powered? No problem." Our CC merely laughed and said, "You're after something, aren't you, Kretzschmar?" – "Yes, well, it won't be completely free, Comrade Captain; if I could just make that phone call?" A few hours later the cars drove up outside the barracks for him to have a look at. Guys in leather jackets and shades, drinking apple juice and shouting, "Why're you running round in that uniform?" to Pancake. He put on his grin again. "Well, Comrade Captain? For you I'll make a special price." – why should I "do something silly" when I've the chance of seeing expressions like that on the face of our CC at that moment?

'Well, well, Reina Kossmann wants to go and see you, does she?'

A whistle: 'Company Four – fall in to receive weapons!' Nip had unlocked the grille, waved the men of the first platoon into the armoury; this time the alert (the siren in the corridor started to wail) wasn't one of his little jokes; Nip was stone-cold sober and really pissed-off and had stuck a steel helmet on his head; Christian took his AK-47 out of the cupboard, signed for it with the duty corporal in the armoury, dismiss, c'mon, c'mon, down the stairs at the double, Company 4 and 5 gathered outside battalion headquarters, staff officers running to and fro, gesticulating wildly; it had been raining, a mild April night, the smell of the smoke from the metal works mingled with the scent of flowers, line up, number off, march off to the technical depot –

'Dear Reglinde, I almost envy you that you can now enjoy the view from Father's study. I know how important it is to him, but Anne told me that it was only by concluding a tenancy agreement with you that they could avoid having someone quartered on them. Griesel set something in motion, probably to show the Herr Medical Councillor that you can't ignore your neighbours with impunity. And now you're working with the apes. Congratulations. At least you'll be seeing some human faces. I remember the gorilla sitting behind the glass with a grumpy expression on its face, morosely poking round in carrots and lettuce leaves, now and then picking something up off the ground; it particularly seemed to enjoy eating vomit. We sometimes play at "zoo" as well, though to be more precise it's called "Alfred Brehm House": the drivers mimic chimpanzees, soldiers bound down the company

corridor like chamois, traditionally the commanders are rhinoceroses
or elephants: stretch out one arm, bend the other back and hold your
nose and then "toot, toot". – Thanks for the postcards you got from
Malthakus, that was a really nice surprise. I have a set of Constantinople
postcards and when I was on leave I also bought some of the South
Sea islands – expensive, but I earn a decent amount here. Tahiti and
Nouméa, New Caledonia . . .'

Whistles, shouts, the stamp of boots, searchlights wandering over the
concrete tracks, the startled faces of the soldiers, the platoon leaders
with map-holders hanging round their necks hurried over to the company commander, who, expressionless, broke the seal on a little folder,
took out a document, glanced over it in the light of a torch, then gave
the platoon leaders brief instructions – Christian saw his lieutenant
make windmill movements with his right arm: start engines; the sound of
the oil pump, Pancake pressed the ignition, Christian plugged his helmet
into the radio, adopted the commander's position: standing on his seat
above the gun pointer, chest behind the secured hatch cover, the loader
wailed, 'It's war now, dammit, now war's broken out', the gun pointer
said, 'Shut your gob, you over there, you've more days of service left
than the Eiffel Tower has rivets, my time's almost up and now this –
d'you know anything, Nemo?' Christian's answer became a stutter as
the tank seesawed its way through the depot gate: 'The orders the CC
had were to wait', then, as per regulations, he had to trot along in front
of his tank and behind Musca's, hatch spotlight on so that the red and
yellow guide flags were visible to Pancake; along the stretch of road,
it was on the edge of the town, lights splashed on in the houses that
were rundown, supported by scaffolding and eaten away by brick cancer; shadows in the windows and Christian wondered: What do they
think of us, do they hate us, do they not care either way (that was
unlikely at that time in the morning), do they admire us or pity us with

our Afrika Korps outfit: goggles on our tank helmets, a sling such as medical orderlies use to immobilize broken arms over our faces, like a bank robber's mask, and we're sneaking out at dead of night and along the edge of the town – going where? Alternative concentration area, the platoon leaders ordered –

'Dear Barbara, Your package has arrived, thank you very much. Uncle Uli's soap is particularly useful, of course, and since the Military Trading Outlet here has been closed "for technical reasons" for several weeks, the eleven tubes of toothpaste are also very welcome. Little Erik's nine months old already . . . True, he's crying in the first photo you included in the package but at least he's standing on his own two feet, and the way he's gnawing the bear in the second – I assume the blobs at the side are its entrails? – shows he's at least starting to develop a capacity for empathy. You asked about two things: leave and a girl-friend. The situation with leave is that I can't say what the situation with leave is. If you apply, then you get the notorious 6×D: derided, dealt with, declined: squaddie due for deployment. In the army leave is the great unknown . . . I hope I can get back in the early autumn, perhaps in September or the beginning of October, by then we'll have the summer field camps behind us. By the way, I know what it was Gorbachev said that you and Gudrun quarrelled about. The political education here is strict, the notebooks we keep are checked. It was the report to the plenum of the Central Committee at which they were discussing calling the XXVII Convention of the Soviet Communist Party; there was no word he used more often or more emphatically than "acceleration". Heated political argument under cold damp patches, with an opera in between that no one apart from Niklas and Fabian, perhaps Meno too, is interested in: such are the "family musical evenings" as I see from your letter. I'd give a lot to hear one of those operas. I'm glad Niklas could repair the water damage over the

secretaire with the roofing felt I sent; despite that, sometimes when
I'm lying awake at night in my bunk I think there'll soon be underwater
plants growing in the music room, that mermaid sopranos and an
orchestra of fishes will emerge from the photos on the wall.

a restricted area full of ammunition boxes and covered vehicles in
which the men were loading up, switching from the exercise rounds
to the live ammunition that was here; new orders were given, by now
the regimental staff had arrived; the order that it was to continue, that
from now on radio messages were only to be sent in code; Christian
told his crew to relax, he knew what lay ahead of them: hard work
driven on by bellowing officers running to and fro, shells out, shells
in without a break, camouflage the tanks, leave for the freight line at
Grün station, load the tanks onto goods wagons, then transport to an
unknown destination –

'Dear Christian, Your parents have given me your address, I also learnt
from them that you are in a tank regiment and things aren't that great.
That's why I wanted to write to you and I hope you're not annoyed
with me because of that. Now I'm in Leipzig, doing medicine – nothing
came of chemistry, but medicine's not that far away from it. I often think
of that evening at your uncle's in the House with a Thousand Eyes, of
the Bird of Paradise Bar. By the way, I've made some tapes, Neustadt
have been on DT 64 recently, if you want I can send you one. The way
you sat at the table in the garden when the others were in the bar and
I couldn't go over to you because you were completely self-absorbed
and I had the feeling you didn't need other people, at least not at that
moment. I have a room in the student residence, sharing with three
other students, one of them's Hungarian, she's very jolly, I get on best
with her. It's the evening now, the others have gone out, I ought to be
studying but by chance I happened to see the title of a book one of the
others is reading, *The Count of Monte Cristo*, and all at once I could

hear our conversations again, the walks in Saxon Switzerland, your voice. Your father sounds similar, it gave me a start when he answered the phone, and he also takes sudden breaths in through his nose like you if there's too long a pause in the conversation. I can tell that this letter's getting stupid, I keep jumping from one thing to another and all I wanted to do was to make contact again. On the card I've put in it's meant to be a female flamingo staring at an empty postbox. I can't draw as well as Heike. I didn't put the card in with the letter as a reproach to you but because the empty, lifeless postbox simply doesn't express for me what I feel when I read your letters. You wrote three to me, I've read through them again and again. It isn't very easy finding the right words to express what fascinates me so about your letters. Under philosophy I've always imagined Chief Red Eagle or something supernatural. Or screwballs. It was your letters that have made me want to know more about the subject – but not because I feel I have to keep up with your interests. I haven't failed to notice with what loving care your letters are written, in contrast to mine, but I didn't know how to reply, to make my letters more confiding, more personal. Reina shy? That's what you might perhaps be thinking now. I know that's not the way I seem but actually I'm quite a reserved creature. Sometimes I'd really like to say something but can't get a word out. And in Saxon Switzerland I finally had the chance to take a "risk" and put aside the characteristics of my quiet type. My fear of being rejected, of perhaps not finding the right words, has its origin in my partial lack of self-confidence. There are people who think they have to show something and so develop into "pushy" types. Probably one of the reasons why I feel affection for you is that you're not like all the others but have something individual about you. I'm well aware that your free time will be very limited; it's all right if you can't write very often. Perhaps I think too seriously about many things. I'm sure that makes it more difficult to find answers and I tend to see the situation as more critical than it really is. Can we meet some time? There is a train from

Leipzig to Grün. I would really like that. (Please answer this letter.)
Reina.'

a grumpy railway inspector held up his lantern in front of the tanks,
no, he knew nothing about this, yes, there were goods wagons ready
but they weren't for the army; and while the staff officers got on their
walkie-talkies, turned the handles of their field telephones, Christian
felt for Reina's letter, for his Constantinople and South Sea talismans;
lamps were hanging like white-hot pots over the station tracks, most
of the railway clocks, encrusted in fly-shit and ash, weren't working,
had shattered glass, bent hands or only one; on the passenger platforms
a few drunks were staggering round, waving bottles of beer and, as
soon as they saw the soldiers, flying into a rage; they shouted and
swore, just about managing to stand upright, upper bodies tilting forward, shaking their bottles, until Pancake, who was looking out of the
driver's hatch, said, 'Hey guys, they're not angry, they want to sell us
some hooch!' and scurried across, unnoticed by the bearers of the silver
epaulettes, quickly did a deal and ran back, crouching, to the tank,
where he threw the spoils, a shopping bag full of beer bottles, to the
loader, who stuffed it under the machine gun on his side of the tank –

'Load tanks!' a voice ordered brusquely, torches made circles,
the sign of 'start engines', the tanks moved forward to the loading
ramp.

Christian and Pancake changed places, the better driver gave the
instructions, the worse one drove; Christian raised the seat, he hadn't
driven since cadet school, the tank moved off, Christian let in the clutch
far too quickly, straight as possible up the ramp, the gun above his head
threw a dark shadow, a halogen spotlight on the left was dazzling, now
the slope of the ramp, the tank had to be precisely aligned with the
wagon, Pancake had to get the timing of the turn exactly right, a tank had
no radius of curve, it turned on the spot and on the goods wagon the
tracks would stick out a good way on either side, Pancake gesticulated

with the flags, Christian tugged at the s̶ ̶ ̶ow Pancake was
waving 'Stop', Christian realized he wa̶ ̶ ̶fast but couldn't
stop, suddenly found he couldn't reach the ̶ ̶s and gear lever, his
uniform trousers had got stuck, as had his upper body between the
edge of the hatch and the driver's seat, 'Stop!' Pancake roared, appearing and disappearing in the sharp whiteness of the halogen lamp and
the shadow beside it, 'Stop, stop!'

Christian tried to switch the engine off with the lever above the
knurled section but he was paralysed, could see the lever, the brown,
oval plate of hard plastic you pulled down and pushed from side to
side to regulate the revs but couldn't reach it; now others were shouting, 'Switch off, you idiot' and 'Down', he saw the soldiers leap off
the goods wagon; their task would have been to wedge the hefty steel
chocks with the spikes into the wooden floor of the wagon in front of
and behind the T55:

He pulled the steering levers into the 'second position' but the tank
didn't stop, as it ought to have, an old Russian thing, Christian thought,
and:

I might not be able to answer Reina's letter at all

and:

What shall I say to Mum?

and:

This thing's tipping over –

Growth; a moment, gentle as a pinprick at the beginning, a break, a
tear, Richard could see the shed, Stahl's bent back and, when he turned
round again, the overgrown quarry in the sudden and alarming second
of an explosion after which there were smells all at once: sun-warmed
stone; plants keeping their flowers at the ready, like crazy archers desperate to start shooting, a bundle of ten arrows on their bowstring; of
axle-grease, chicken shit; the light swivelled like a cutting torch, hitting
his face full force: it made you want to suck in the fresh spring air, fists

clenched, get *drunk* on the colours (a postbox-yellow oil can on a black shelf) – the way all that was growing and sprouting and bursting and splitting rotten husks, the way the sap was returning to the trees, making them vibrate and the leaves, like a thousand green fingers that touched and wanted to be touched, swell out, branches hummed with bee electricity; and how it was growing, his 'baby', as he called the Hispano – that wasn't a car, wasn't a lifeless machine, it had eyes that looked now happy, now sad, it was a living being with nickel veins and character.

'Damned useless rubbish.' Stahl threw a wrench on the ground.

'I can't join you, Gerhart. They've got me in their sights anyway.'

'I know, you explained that.'

'But are you really going to do it? With an aeroplane?!'

'Crazy, yes. But there's method in my madness. That's exactly why it'll succeed. They won't be expecting something like that. And it will work, I tell you. With two MZ motorcycle engines. Fuselage wooden planks, covered in plastered fabric. Very easy to make, despite that warp-resistant. Plastic for the cockpit, I was thinking of the windscreen of a Schwalbe motorbike.'

'Four of you!'

'Martin will be at the back, all of us lying down. The engines ought to produce the power, I've done the calculations. – The only question is – can I trust you?'

'And if you can't.'

'Then it's just my bad luck. It's not possible without outside help. And you've told me about your problems yourself. That wouldn't have been very clever of you if you were going to report me.'

'For God's sake, I could still do it now.'

'Like hell you would. I think I know you better than that.' –

tipped, and Christian said, 'Nono', screamed:

'No!'

felt the tank, the steel hull weighing tons, slowly sink down, so slowly that it probably looked as if it were making itself comfortable, and Christian, in the oddly uncertain light on the ramp, had time to look at everything again and take in all the details: the distressed but interested expressions of the soldiers watching, a few officers who had become aware of what was happening, Pancake's expression that seemed to be saying, stupid, you don't turn like *that*, the searchlights, the flat goods wagons along which he should have driven:

The tank fell on its track, which, since the engine was still running, dug into the ground beside the rails. Christian saw a spot of gold on a puddle, perhaps a reflection of the turret searchlight, the tank came to a stop on its side, its barrel pointing in the direction of the town, Christian felt someone grasp his shoulders and pull him out through the hatch and just let it happen, it was pleasant and the guy who'd grabbed him by the scruff of the neck would know what he was doing, it would be what was necessary; Pancake's face, turned into a huge, black puffball by the shapeless helmet, the white side-pieces, the sheepskin of which had a bizarre glow – phosphorescence? could it be? – dangling like a dachshund's ears: 'Man, you could be dead!'

another voice, 'The turret would have squashed him flat, like a mashed potato. He was sitting right at the top. Funny, a machine like that turning turtle.'

'Must've been out of his mind, mustn't he?'

'An SI . . . That's an SI . . . as perfect a Special Incident as you could hope to see that Hoffmann's managed to cause . . . 's he still alive?'

'– or drowned. It probably wouldn't've squashed him but drowned him in that puddle there. I waded through it earlier on, it was deeper than I thought. Shit, I've got some of it in my boots.'

'You mean head down?'

'Head down and he can't get out. I mean, who's going to heave a tank up just with his feet and nothing to brace himself against?'

'But don't y'think it could've squashed him anyway? First of all snap-crack and then glug-glug.'

Then Christian was standing to one side, like an Untouchable, recalling a lesson at school when he was a child and the teacher, when there was no other way, had made him stand in a corner of the classroom ('Facing the wall and there'll be trouble if you move'), recalling the whispers and the quiet laughs, the idea, which made him break out in a cold sweat, that something might be wrong with his shoes, stockings, trousers, with the seat of his trousers: could he have . . . had his shirt gone threadbare at the back and split open, did he look funny from behind (for the first time he was made aware that others could see him from behind, could see a Christian Hoffmann he himself didn't know); over there they were dragging the tank, the tracks of which were still going round and round, back into its normal position, organizing hawsers and the tank recovery vehicle – What's going to happen now? Christian thought. What will they do with me? He whistled a tune. Would there be birds' nests in this station? He'd seen a lot of bird droppings. Pigeons. He rummaged round in his pockets felt his penknife, box of matches, army ID – and something that rustled, something granular and yielding: a packet of lemonade powder, already much the worse for wear, he tore it open, tipped the contents into the hollow of his hand, spat on it, making it foam up, licked and ate the lemon-tasting powder until there was none left apart from a thin film of food-colouring on his hand that couldn't be licked off. –

Richard waited until it was dark. On the mezzanine floor of the building, one of the typical Striesen-Blasewitz 'coffee-grinder' houses, the light was on, illuminating the path from the garden gate to the entrance; that would make it more difficult. Richard put on the work-jacket that he wore out in Lohmen, tightened the laces of his trainers, pulled the buckle of his belt round to the side (he'd heard that electricians working on pylons did that). It occurred to him that it would be better to creep up from the back. He climbed over the garden wall, swung himself hand over hand past an arbour, jumped down onto a concrete path. He avoided the dark, loosened soil of the flowerbed beside it, there was a shimmer of early flowers (crocuses? narcissi?) in it, pale ghosts. A trellis was no use to him, the bevelled posts were too thin and the soil below it had also been dug over. He felt the ground with the tips of his toes at a point on the wall that seemed suitable; a paving slab would provide a firm enough base for him to push off from; the slab was granite, vaguely lit by the light in the room above the window ledge: children's room? bedroom? he didn't know; often in this kind of house the rooms of growth and sleep were at the back, giving onto the garden. Strange how the silence seemed to fill with sounds, like a funnel sucking them in but letting too few pass through; as if the sounds were like him, waiting in the dark for a movement, but losing patience sooner since their time was limited: the crunch of a car driving out, clocks striking from the lungs of the house, garden whispers, the Sandman's evening greeting from the television. Now a baby was crying, sobs of tired protest, it seemed to come from the other side of the apartment. Josta's little one, Richard thought. Off we go! He jumped up but couldn't reach the window ledge. The impact of his soles on the slab sounded unexpectedly harsh. Take off his trainers? And if he had to run for it . . . ? You'll be doing that anyway, he joked. What did it matter? He took his shoes off and tried again. This time he jumped higher, reached the window ledge, dangled there. Immediately his right hand, his forearm weakened from his old injury, started to hurt. What was worse was that the window ledge was sloping and was made of smooth tiles. Richard, holding on with four fingers, started to slip. One sock got stuck on the trellis when he scrabbled with his feet on either side to try and find support; in the pale light his bare foot looked like an anaemic flatfish with fringes, the house wall was icy cold. He jumped down, his bare foot landed on a piece of gravel which made him hop around in silence for a while. The sock had been pulled off by a splinter of wood precisely between his big toe and second toe. A piece of luck. He tried again with his shoes on, hung there, swaying, couldn't manage to pull himself up. He thought of rock climbers on an ascent but that made him feel weak all at once. In an access of rage he flung up his left leg, his foot, clenched in the trainer, stuck on something, fairly high up, fragile; Richard pulled himself up; centimetre by centimetre, his fingers trembling with the effort, until he could see in through the window. He was breathing stertorously, it sounded like a faulty compressed-air valve, his right hand found something strangely flexible to hold on to (radio cable? lightning conductor?), just at that moment he felt the urge to laugh. Daniel was sitting in the room, applying dubbin to a football; Lucie, opposite him, was sitting at a children's table wearing a white coat and a cap with a red cross, with, above it, an examination mirror such as ENT doctors use; she was bent over a naked doll, cutting a leg off with a bread knife.

unload, travel, pine twigs, parts of puzzles, bizarre, unsolved. The Elbe at Torgau was awake, Christian had never seen an awake river before, large clock face numbers were drifting down it. Could Muriel hear it? The reformatory was somewhere round here. Fields, filled with surf, bursting, crackling. Swill? Wind? Ready to pounce. The wind was grimy, heavy, little slowcoaches of graphite grease in it. 'Alight!' was ordered. Searchlights. Playing at knitting. The Elbe at Torgau was an awake river, a livingmost giant, no: it was whispering, shivering: a 'listening-post giant'. With rotting boots. Yes, precisely, that was it, Pancake swirling piss-flowers over the ground covered in bird feathers: a bed linen factory (cambric; he knew the word from Emmy) in the vicinity. The river had eyeballs, one after the other. Then none again. Colour? Shoe-polish black. Keep a tight hold on it. Streaks of rotten-apple-brown, there where the crêpe-paper-grey fairy rings are dotted down. Forest honey, ever so glutinous. Just don't try it.

Flapping, swallowing: nightingale-box paint, that black. Swish, swish: trees crumbling in the star-swell, on the downriver bank where the company's taken up position. Listen. A river like that is alive, sleeps, dreams, digests, tosses and turns, lives its giant's life. What has it got to say?

It's talking of the wheat.

Whispering of the ships it's seen.

The haulers that pulled the barges upstream on chains. There were still milestones. The burlaks sang, the singsong of the barge-haulers, on the Elbe, the Volga. He recalled a picture by Ilya Repin, men in tattered clothes, greybeards and downy-faced youths, in broad harnesses dragging the ship upstream. They said, What do you want? – Music. To be alone in silence. The music of the river, the throaty murmuring down the ages. 'To walk until you're free, that is what you want,' Christian chattered, unconcerned whether anyone could hear. The river wanted nothing. The river was a molten magnet, a baroque ship was stuck in it, wanted to sail on but the algae, the filth, the garbage from the towns made a slick round the bow, twisted round the throttled propeller. It couldn't move forward, it couldn't drift back. It was full of people, it was a city, you could see houses, electric cables, the entrails of the city. Dresden . . . the sigh went through the air, Dresden . . . a stranded ship, stuck in the past, clinging with every fibre onto the past that had never been as beautiful as the raptures you go into. Dresden . . . Christian took a mouthful of water. Am I a human being? What do you want? No one's interested in what you want. Now orders will come and you will have to obey them. Now orders will be expected and you will have to give them. What is an order? How is it that there are orders anyway?

The river didn't know. It stank of cellulose and sewage farms. Of solid glue and burnt animal skins, of shampoo from Wutha, yellow as marzipan, washing powders from Ilmenau and Genthin: IMI, Spee,

Wofalor: don't forget anything. Don't forget anything. At Torgau the Elbe was a dead river; the water was rusty and if you threw a pfennig in, it floated for a long time.

Christian looked for a flat pebble and had a go at skimming: he heard the stone hit the water four times. It should have been five since seven times for a first try (and he hadn't done it since he was a boy) would have been unrealistic. One too few, Christian thought. One too few is a broken leg: as the saying Anne had brought from childhood went.

The most disagreeable thing about a tank was that it gave you the feeling of being safe and sound. The company commander was pacing up and down in the preparation area, checking with the platoon leaders, the crews that were making their T55s ready for the underwater drive, known as a UD. Christian had been on one twice, for Pancake it was something new, he kept running over to the machines beside theirs. The Elbe at Torgau was wide and it was also more than a metre deep, the tanks couldn't get across without assistance. The two underwater drives Christian had been on had been in daylight; this time they were to cross the river by night, an exercise everyone was afraid of. The preparation area was lit by several floodlights, it was a sandy clearing in a pinewood. The crews were working hurriedly, the commanders had to report their tanks as ready for UD in thirty minutes. All the things that had to be done! There was a lot Christian had had to learn; he had to know this, to be able to do that; he was the commander for whose orders the crew would wait if they didn't know what to do next. He had to know what came next. He bore the responsibility for the crew and he would never have dreamt of being in such a tricky situation: hating the tank, the noise, the drill, the military life – but having to have mastered it because he was the commander. Technology, the principles of operation (why can't I start a tank cold, why must the driver pre-heat the diesel and, if there's an alert, why must I run to the tank hangar, in my pyjamas if necessary, in order to switch on the pre-heating battery?), writing surveys on tactical and strategic problems. Here as well, in the army, he was part of a Great Plan, of a great computation of mankind; here as well they used the words 'collective' (his crew was a 'combat collective') and 'main task'.

He worked mechanically, starting in alarm when he lost concentration. He forced himself to think systematically, to go through everything step by step. Seals on the hatches exchanged for the sponge rubber ones? The loader and the gun pointer were sharply delineated shadows heaving the packed anti-aircraft machine gun onto the turret. Pancake had dropped down into his driver's hatch, Christian heard the hum of the course indicator starting up – the device that made it possible to drive in a straight line under water. He climbed into the forward area, closed the drain of the mantlet over the cylindrical mounts, checked whether the breech wedge of the gun was closed, lashed down the turret and tightened the seal of the turret ring, which had turned out to be one of the trouble spots during previous underwater drives. Inspected and closed the filter fan next to the gun. Checked and closed the overflow slide on the rear wall of the forward area, below the heavy fragmentation and hollow-charge shells. He heard the voice of his platoon leader asking, 'Why do we need that, Lance Corporal Hoffmann?' – 'In order to divert water that's got in the drive into the forward area and pump it out from there, Comrade Lieutenant.' – 'And why must there be no water in the drive?' – 'So that it doesn't get into the engine, Comrade Lieutenant.' – 'And why mustn't any water get in? Irrgang?' You're the pupil and they're the teachers Christian had sometimes thought during these instruction periods – only that here they ask about seventeen-disc dry clutches and epicycloidal gears; a school, the whole country's a school! 'Hey, Pancake, batteries charged up?'

'As charged up as a sailor on shore leave. I've been thinking. I know the Stenzels. Trick riders from the circus.'

'Checked lower compressed-air cylinder?'

'One thirty kPa, enough. – Course indicator working, Comrade Mummy's Boy.'

'Level, earhole?' Responding in kind, Pancake was probably grinning. Christian inserted the bilge pump.

'Track cover plates secured, changed elephant's rubber,' the gun pointer shouted down the turret hatch. Elephant's rubber – the muzzle cap on the gun. Funny words you learnt here. Close ejector plate, open dividing wall fans. What was the point of that thing there? A window between the forward area and the engine room that looked oddly like the black radiation trefoil printed on yellow: a diesel engine guzzled air and under water it couldn't get it in the usual way through the slats in the drive-cover – they were sealed – but drew it in through the periscope tube, which was like a snorkel fixed on the loader's side.

'Fuel three-way tap set to interior container unit,' Pancake reported.

'Checking driver guide system.' Christian pressed the buttons to activate the device with which he could guide the driver should radio contact fail. Port red, starboard green, as on a ship.

'Left. Right.' Pancake repeated Christian's commands.

'Right then. Shitting yourself?' One of the driving instructors had stuck his head into Pancake's hatch.

'I've never drowned yet.'

'Keep an eye on the auxiliary transmission. Forgot the cover plate last time, just a tiny leak and it poured in like a mountain stream. Hey, Nemo,' the driving instructor shouted. 'Pancake's to go over, to One, the CC's driver's unwell.'

'And who's his replacement?'

'Nutella.'

Christian switched on the command frequency, on which the CC could communicate with the tank commander, and the recovery frequency, which called the recovery tank. The next tank, Irrgang's, hooted twice, a diesel engine roared into life. Christian looked across: the gun pointer was controlling the fuel with the Bowden cable through the closed driver's hatch, the driver watched the manometer, Irrgang, holding a stopwatch, raised his arm. They were already on the low-pressure-leak test – and had come through it to go by Irrgang's expression. They had hardly anything to do with each other any more; each went his own way and tried as far as possible to get the upper hand . . . Say nothing, keep your head down, be invisible. Lie. Christian had not told Anne the truth in his letter. The art of knowing how to lie – how to praise enthusiastically, how to keep a serious expression when saying stupid things that are empty of meaning but please the person you're flattering, how to encourage illusions. Herr Orré had taken great pains. And Irrgang had lost his witty repartee. After duty he mostly lay on his bed, staring at the ceiling and listening to Costa's melancholy music that he'd copied onto cassettes before Costa was discharged. If he had a pass, he came back drunk. That was presumably what was meant by being brought into line. Big Irrgang, never at a loss for a quick saucy response, now jumped smartly to attention for every officer, didn't argue any more, said what was expected in political education, secretly cut the monthly seal off the string of seals the more junior soldiers used to count the days until they were due for discharge . . . Leak test OK, they continued. Thirty seconds had to pass before the pressure fell from 1,200 to 200 mm of water. Since he had been commander Christian's tank had never managed that; like most of the tanks in the regiment, his T55 was an 'old banger', a 'rust bucket' and the best servicing could do nothing about it. Tank 302 remained watertight for twenty-five seconds, despite the layers of UD putty that had been smeared over it, actually five seconds too few for the forthcoming exercise, but what did they say: Actually the sun's shining, you just can't see it for all this rain.

Burre. All the sympathy Christian felt for him couldn't alter the fact that he was a lousy driver.

He reported for duty: 'I'm to join you.' He attempted a grin, tilted his head, climbed aboard the tank.

'C'mon, c'mon, time's passing,' the platoon leader urged them. 'The drive's still open, shut the thing, get your finger out.'

Burre disappeared down the driver's hatch.

'Slats position five,' Christian ordered, shining the hand lamp. Moths flew out, the pines smelt of resin. 'Position two!' The gun pointer and he stamped the lock on the drive unit shut. 'Lock!' Check the lugs – the drive unit was closed. Musca had already collimated the UD pipe, transferred the recovery hawsers, tied on the floating buoys, white in front, red at the back. During the first UD exercise Christian had put them the wrong way round and had had to suffer the bawling-out of the tug commander: should there be an accident, a tank was pulled out by the stern hawser to which the red buoy was tied – 'if you'd got stuck I'd 've had to drag your bow round 'n people 've drowned when that happens, dickhead!' –

'Dear Christian, Comet fever has broken out here, everyone's humming Halley, Halley; even Herr Honich, whom we know as a dyed-in-the-wool materialist, had none of his dismissive remarks based on scientific dialectics for the Widow Fiebig in the queue for rolls recently – it was so impressive in the night of the comet (I spent it in Arbogast's observatory with the Urania group, Ulrich was there, Barbara and Gudrun came along later) the way, just at the moment when the sky cleared and such a wealth of constellations appeared, that we felt like Babylonian astrologers – the way that at that moment the clocks all struck, all at the same time it seemed, from near and from afar; a jingling, tolling, tinkling, pealing, gonging, Westminster-chiming, as if all their hands were in collusion and all that despite the fact that this time the comet couldn't be seen in the northern hemisphere; only the Widow Fiebig refused to believe it, craned her neck and shouted, "There, there! That's it's sulphur tail!" But it was only one of Herr Malthakus's jokes, he'd set off an anachronistic New Year's rocket from the roses below Arbogast's Institute. We also thought it was a joke, something we couldn't really take seriously, when Professor Teerwagen was arrested recently. He was supposed to be a spy, it was

said; dubious dealings in Mexico; his wife seems to have known nothing at all about it and now she's in the Academy, being treated by
Dr Clarens. – Lange's turning strange. On the evening of the comet,
after the talks (Stahl spoke about reservoir dams, Ulrich about the
Babylonians) Arbogast organized a guided tour of his estate, as smiling
and inscrutable as ever, and Lange suddenly groaned and started to
ramble, pointed to a sealed bottle, saying, "Lead, it's made of lead,
and the seal on top, encrusted with gold – King Solomon's bottle!" – "But Herr Lange," Arbogast laughed, "who believes such fairy
tales? That's an eighteen-twelve cognac trapped in ethyl alcohol from
Kutusov's supplies, he took it from the French general staff as they were
retreating across the Beresina." Sometimes Libussa comes down and takes
me to one side. Alois, she says, is spending all their money on sailing
ships: photographs, ships in bottles, books; sometimes in his sleep he
mutters the names of the captains of the Laeisz Line, the names of the
ships, he knows all the legends, every one of their sails – and that when
he's never been on a sailing ship himself. And what does he say to her?
"My little Brunetka," he replies, "I have to know all about it for when the
great hell-ship comes and the press gang tell me to join the crew . . ."
That's the latest from up here. Let me know if you need any books.
Libussa's just shouted for me to send you her best wishes. She's going to
make up a package of preserves for you. Frau Honich has started a Timur
Assistance project for the elderly here, does the shopping for them, deals
with the authorities (commendable, you can't deny), her husband's carrying coal, also has a package to take to the post office. Perhaps it'll include
socialist greetings for you. You have the honour of guarding the peace
for us. You should look on it as experience, Libussa's just shouted. Worth
recording, says Adeling the waiter, alias Skinny. Best wishes, Meno.'

Twenty-five seconds for the leak test, the platoon leader had called the
company commander over, he waved the objection away, 'Drive on.
They'll be on the other side before the tank's full.' Christian was

sitting on the loader's side, from now on it was radio traffic over the command frequency of the UD route; he was worked up, he could only see an occasional gleam of light through the periscope, perhaps from the regiment in the woods, perhaps from the Elbe already, from the recovery armoured personnel carrier, the engineers' boat or the motor tractors. They'd passed the initial checkpoint and were travelling along the line of departure, Musca's tank in front of them, the goldsmith behind; Burre accelerated too much and didn't steer smoothly enough, the UD tube, which was now extended, scraped against twigs. The direction indicator, a gyro compass, added its hum to the crackle of the radio. He hoped Burre was familiar with the direction indicator – if not, the tank could veer off course if Christian couldn't manage to guide it by the periscope. Vision: a disc the size of a saucer, no more. Across there, on the other side of the Elbe, floodlights had been set up, he had to focus on them before the serious business started.

Checkpoint. Musca stopped. The other tanks continued steadily on their way. Christian heard shouts, someone closed the shutter valve on the exhaust; footsteps, stamping, flap 6 over the drive was closed. 'Idle at eleven hundred revs,' Christian ordered, Burre repeated.

'Line up on floodlights.'

'Is lined up.'

'Unlock direction indicator.'

'Is unlocked.'

'. . . foor-ward!' Christian heard the company commander order over the radio. So now the serious business was starting. His diving goggles were pinching. Was the glass misting over? That ought not to happen. Gun pointer, loader, driver – they all wore diving goggles over their padded helmets. The black life-saving equipment over their chest so that the loader, who was on Christian's seat above the gun pointer, could only twist and turn with the greatest difficulty. The light filled the forward area with a misty ochre. Was the turret really lashed tight? Burre let the clutch in gently, the shutter valve made a snort of irritation. That wasn't the earlier noise, the one they'd listened for with tense expressions during the leak test; the sucking in of the outside air at the turret race ring, almost ending in a slurp. The company commander wasn't replying; the noise floor of the radio, a crackling, as if from slight electrical discharges. The tank tipped forward. Christian could see through the periscope that they were nicely lined up on the floodlights, were going down the UD track. The river was known there, but not on either side of it. Musca's tank was already in the middle of the river. No one knew anything about underwater obstacles. Nip had told them a story from his time as an ensign: when recovering a T54 that had got stuck, a motor tractor had struck an unexploded bomb. It was here at Torgau that the Americans and Russians had met; the Elbe was silent about what had been before. There were channels and potholes in rivers, Christian knew that from fishing, treacherous deeps, wash-outs made by the current where the old fish liked to stay. There were shoals, places where the bank had been undermined, others where the river bed would give way, inner and outer banks at bends. He switched over to internal radio. Burre was muttering, the gun pointer was muttering.

'Coolant temperature?'

'Ninety.'

'Brief report, Jan.' A hundred and ten degrees was the maximum temperature for coolant, more than that and the tank could be damaged. A slight draught – the diesel engine was taking in air from the cockpit. Woe betide them if the UD tube went under water. Water from above, the air sucked out from behind.

'Report, three-zero-two,' it crackled over the radio. Christian switched over, then the radio went off. The internal radio too. Christian guided the driver via the driver guide system. 'To the left. To the right. Not so far! To the left!' Burre made the correction. Christian could hear him talking. The tank creaked, the struts at the back were being wrung by hydraulic forces, the wind got caught in the periscope tube, swirled up and down making an odd rumbling noise, perhaps there was sand in it, as the ship's doctor had told him about the old sailing ships: in a storm the captains would stay on the poop deck and if they felt sand scouring their face, they would know the ship was in danger of running aground, there must be land or a sandbank out there. He couldn't see anything. The navigation light on the other bank had disappeared.

'Report direction indicator.'

No reply from Burre.

'Position!' Christian bawled. The loader raised his head that he was apathetically leaning against the gun pointer's shoulders, as if the latter were giving him a piggyback; his eyes were large dark splodges.

'Ze-hero,' Burre sang out. He was actually singing. Anything that occurred to him, it seemed: the 'Internationale', the hymn of the German Socialist Party, a setting of a Goethe poem and the song of the Thälmann Column in the Spanish Civil War. The sound of flowing water changed, suddenly the tank slipped to the right, sank down, took a knock.

'What are you doing, arsehole?' The gun pointer stamped down but his boot caught in the MG cartridge holder; he stamped down again, directing a stereotyped 'arsehole, arsehole' at the space between the optical periscope and the cylinders of compressed air, where Burre's back must be. And now water burst in. Before that the tank had been sweating, Christian had observed drops swelling up in the join of the turret race ring, thinking, OK then, it's sweating as well, it's pretty hot in here. A sauna. Warm sweat from his feet was going through his grey military socks into his boots, where it sloshed about for a while; sweat dripped from the extensor side of his thigh to the flexor side, built up, dribbled down when he moved, mingling with the sweat from his feet; sweat was trickling down from his back into the groove between his buttocks, he was sitting in warm soup. The cover plate of the intermediate transmission, Christian thought. He hadn't checked it. Pancake had climbed through to the back but shortly afterwards the order to change drivers had come. Criminal, really, Christian thought, you don't split up a crew used to working together and certainly not just before a night UD. The loader caught some drips and rubbed them between his hands. Christian looked at the gun pointer. He didn't even know his full name, only his surname and that he came from a village in Thuringia and was a mechanic for farm machinery. 'Pump out.' The bilge pump began to spin, bubbling, smacking noises, reassuring. Funny that a tank had similarities to a U-boat. The bilge pump couldn't cope with all the water, by now it was also coming from the drive into the forward area, Christian was surprised the engine was still running. The radio still wasn't working. The water was rising. It was up to the gun pointer's boot. Burre must be right in it. And the smell: a mixture of burnt rubber and fossil hen's eggs. The tank tilted further down. Christian tried the periscope, found a floodlight far to the left. They must have come off the route. They'd be doing something up there – if they'd noticed, which Christian hoped they had. 'Left, left,' he shouted as the tank went further to the right. His diving goggles were gradually misting over and his view of the others was blurred. And then the stupid tank hood with its fleece getting wetter and wetter. Where was all the water coming from? The bilge pump couldn't cope with it –

'Dear Christian, There's not much that's new to tell. I hope you can read my "gentian script" (as Gudrun calls it); I prefer phoning to writing, but since you haven't got a phone I'm sending you these brief items of news. Please excuse the "case history" sheet, I'm writing this between seeing two patients. Our veranda's almost completely rotten by now, perhaps Meno told you. It's also sunk so that the windows are squint and the glass has cracked. The glazier cut the new ones to fit the slanting frames. We had to supply the material ourselves. We went all round the town. The leak in the roof hasn't got worse, thank

God – the roofing felt you got us is worth its weight in gold. The roofer said, Have you got an allocation for roofing felt? One for adhesive? No? Then let the rain come in, pal. Not long ago I was sitting in my favourite chair with a pipe and *Tannhäuser* (Max Lorenz, State Orchestra, Fritz Busch) and there was a crack! then plaster crumbling, one of the wall ties had come out. I thought: well, to sink slowly down into the spruce tree along with the veranda, listening to *Tannhäuser* (and that recording above all), having just got my pipe going and enjoying a nice little glass of liqueur, that could definitely be a source of new insights. For three and a half months now, since the severe frost in January, it's been like living on a farm here, both toilets were frozen up, only the water in the kitchen was still working, we have to get water from there to fill the buckets we use to flush the lavatories. The Schwedes below us have this ingenious water-pipe-heating-ring (one of Herr Stahl's brilliant inventions) that has just the one disadvantage – it's dependent on electricity. If there hadn't been a power cut the pipes wouldn't have frozen. The Communal Housing Department immediately wanted to copy the water-pipe-heating-ring – but, God, who's going to do that? The next time you're here, pop in to the practice to see me; I'll take you with me on my rounds. Or to the Friends of Music, we've managed to find some more lovely records. Since Chernobyl old Frau Zschunke's been stuck with all her vegetables. The accident to the reactor's the big topic of conversation in the town. Officially it's played down, but the Valley of the Clueless borders on the hills that can receive Western television. See you soon. Best wishes, Niklas.'

then the engine stopped. The bilge pump gurgled on for a while then that fell silent too. The light made a rasping noise but stayed on. Christian could just make out the outlines of the others. The lashing bar of the gun had an unnatural white gleam. The water was rising more slowly, a dark mass that looked as if it had crackling cellophane stretched over it; it calmly started to swallow a fragmentation shell.

'Jan?' He didn't answer. 'Jan!' Christian bellowed. The gun pointer shook his head. 'Can't see him.'

'Restart!'

No one answered. The characteristic rumbling start of the engine after the explosion of the compressed-air ignition didn't come. 'Switch on recovery frequency.' Nothing there either. It was quiet, the warmth was pleasant now. If they had to get out then it must be the way they'd practised in the diving bell, enclosed in a flooded steel chamber. Swimming goggles and life-saving equipment on, breathing, the others panicking but not him, Christian Hoffmann, the son of a metalworker and trauma surgeon. Under water the sounds came with a delay, echoed sleepily, taps with a wrench were used for communication. Unlock hatch, calmly climb up into the water-filled cylinder – don't panic, that was the most important thing. Panic destroyed everything, made an ordered sequence of actions impossible. An algorithm, Baumann, the apple-cheeked mathematician from Waldbrunn, would have said. Why did that occur to him now, of all times? What was the matter with Burre? Why wasn't he replying? Christian signalled to the gun pointer to go and check. He pointed to the rising water. But then the light did finally go out.

'RG-UD on.' The instruments gradually took on a phosphorescent glow: infrared sighting mechanism, radio dial and the stupid thermometer the gun pointer had brought that wasn't part of standard equipment. Sixty-eight degrees in the tank. They had to get out. He thumped the turret walls, perhaps someone from the rescue boat would hear, perhaps the tug commander was experienced enough to realize what had happened. White buoy at the front, red buoy at the rear. Put the hawsers on the downstream side, otherwise they'll be pressed against the turret and could twist. It was dark but he could breathe. At this moment a verse by Goethe occurred to him. 'White as lilies, candle-pure, / Starlike, bowing modestly, / From their centre, from their hearts, / The fire of love is glowing brightly.' *The Chinese–German Book of Seasons and Hours*. He murmured to himself. He heard the boat, someone was tapping the U D tube. Christian tapped a response; wait. 'The water roared, the water rose, / A fisher sat beside it.' If Burre had tried to climb out of the exit hatch at the bottom of the hull, the tank might crush him when the tractor pulled the recovery hawser.

'Dear Reina, Thank you for your letter. Perhaps we can see each other. There's been an accident. My driver was injured during an exercise and died in hospital. I did something stupid, I attacked my company commander. Now I'm back in the barracks with no idea what they're going to do with me. It's possible I might get a pass since almost the whole of the regiment is still out on the exercise; officially I'm confined to barracks but I know the company clerk who's in charge of the passes that have been signed but aren't filled in very well. Please don't say anything to my parents. Best wishes, Christian.'

56

Perhaps you repeated often-said words, pointed out things you'd often seen, and drew attention to things you knew anyway

'There's no salt.'

'My weak side. Here. Sorry. I'm always forgetting it. I've made three cups of coffee for you. You can leave them, if you like. I'm on the afternoon shift.'

'Do you need the car? It'd be nice if I could have it. When I've finished I could go to the plumber's, they've finally got some instantaneous water heaters in stock again.'

'If you'd finally got your Süza working you could go in that.'

'Suiza.'

'It seems a bit fishy to me what the pair of you are doing out there. Are we ever going to get to see the car?'

'Why don't you come out there. Bring Robert with you, he's interested in it.'

'He's to concentrate on his work for the school-leaving exam. – And Stahl's helping you just for the sake of it, with nothing in it for him? Because, as an engineer, he loves the Süza?'

'Are you suspicious?'

'There's just one thing I ask: don't get involved in anything. Think of the children.'

'Morning, Reglinde.'

'Morning. Can I use the bathroom?'

'I just need to wash my hands, then you can. Would you take the rubbish when you go? Do you need anything from the chemist's? I'm going shopping when I've finished.'

'Just some toothpaste, Anne. I'm starting a bit later today, I can give you a hand, if you like.'

'My God, who can that be at the door at this time in the morning?'

'I'll get it. – Morning, Niklas. Something urgent?'

'Morning, Richard. Switch on West German radio. Our radio's on the blink.'

'The one from Japan? The one you brought back when you were abroad with the State Orchestra?'

'Morning, Anne. Yeah, the Sharp. And who's going to repair it for me now? Just listen. – It's a disgrace. And they don't tell us, the devious swine. Think we won't cotton on. They'll end up blowing us all sky high. A nice breakfast there. I wouldn't say no to a cup of coffee.'

'Do sit down.'

'Morning, Lindy.'

'Morning, Schmoops.'

'And what have your monkeys to say about that?'

'They're radiant.'

'They'll poison us, I tell you. Sell us down the river, down the toxic river. Bastards. – What have you on today, Richard?'

'As per schedule.'

'Aha, routine, eh. For me too. There's a bit of flu about again. Meno's going to drop in later on, the poor soul's got a bit of a cough. Well, I'll be on my way again. Thanks for the coffee. But it's a funny business with Teerwagen, don't you think? Was supposed to have secret papers on him. Rockets or something of the kind. A U-boat the like of which has never been seen before. Oh God, when I go back I'll have all the stoves to do . . . It's nice and warm in here. Well, Ezzo has to do the stove in the children's room himself. But the living room, the music room . . . The one in the living room's on its last legs. Fibrosis of the lungs, the final stage, I'd say. When I think I'll have to let a stove fitter loose on it, oh horror! The dirt, the noise!'

'Do sit down, Niklas, you're getting on my nerves going up and down like that.'

'Thanks, Richard, but I'm off. Though if you have another cup of coffee there . . . One has to keep awake. Any news from Christian?'

'His regiment was on an exercise, night alert and so on.'

'Now then, Anne, don't take on. The lad'll get through. Takes after Richard as far as his constitution's concerned – I'd like to know how you can stand it all, mate, operating for hours on end, then writing reports and your outpatients. By the way, I've got some more great records. Great records, I tell you. We must listen to some again. State Orchestra, Rudi Kempe, Strauss. Terrific. Simply terrific.'

'Won't you have something to eat?'

'Well, if you insist. I wouldn't say no to that piece of cherry cake. It's a real miracle is your cherry cake. – Tell me, Richard: Müller, he's retired now, isn't he?'

'Officially from the first of May but he's already had his leaving party.'

'And you're the boss now?'

'Whatever gave you that idea! Trautson's the temporary head of the clinic until the appointment procedure's completed. I haven't applied.'

'You just be careful you don't get sidelined. That sometimes happens after change-overs. – It's an absolute disgrace, this Chernobyl, I'm really getting worked up about it. The dirty liars, that gang of criminals, no, no. Where's it all going to end? You tell me, where's it all going to end? There's a little space here, Lindy.'

'You know Sperber, don't you, Niklas?'

'Not personally and not particularly well. Why?'

'He's invited us round. To his house.'

'Tricky business. A dubious character, if you ask me. A go-between – and he doesn't get stung by either side, as my teacher Rudi Citroën used to say. – Y'know what? I wouldn't mind a cup of coffee.'

'I'll make some more.'

'Oh, I'm bein' a nuisance, putting you to all this bother. I'll toddle along at once. If things go on like this we'll have to get out, Richard. 's not the money, you know. But you have the feeling . . . as if you're slowly being drowned. But wouldn't that be betraying our patients?'

'That keeps on cropping up: the doctor as a bastion of morality. There are patients on the other side as well.'

'Yes, but you're here to make the patients here well again.'

'With what? What should I do if the health service is ailing itself? Use empty syringes? Is that moral?'

'I didn't even get any more plasters the last time. You're right, y'know, it's all very well for them to talk about it being morally unprincipled for a doctor to skedaddle over there. You never hear anything about how morally unprincipled it is to be a doctor with nothing to give your patients here. I've been havin' to prescribe Julie from the riding school cold-water treatment that she doesn't even administer to herself. It wouldn't be 'cause of the money. That's jus' what they say it's about. An' then havin' to tell your children to lie so they don't get into trouble. An' to tell the "firm" what you hear from your patients. Oh yes, that'll be moral all right, won't it? Not that I do that, though.'

'Dad.'

'OK, OK. But that's the way things are. You get drowned here, slowly and thoroughly. Y'have to breathe through y'r ears, keep y'r trap shut with y'r eyes, an' you're s'posed to stay here into the bargain. All right, all right, I'm on my way.'

57
Suspended matter

'Reina?'

'Richard?'

'— I do too.'

58
Sing and be happy

You will include the woman or the girl you love in all these considerations, wishes and dreams. You will write to her and receive mail from her. Through her love she will help you to meet the high demands and master the strains of military life.

What It Means to be a Soldier

He stood on the platform, between two dustbins that were full to over-flowing, thinking. He was thinking about how it had come about that he was stuck here and had had to steal a pass. Reina would arrive on the 4 p.m. train from Leipzig. Philosophy. It was about power and nothing else. You're to go there and there, and if you don't do that we'll lock you up. And then two men will come and arrest you and if you kick out with your legs you'll get a thump on the head. And if you knock the two of them down, four will come. And even if you can deal with them, a fifth will appear. Christian was sweating in his walking-out uniform but didn't roll up the sleeves of his blue-grey shirt – the mili-tary patrols carried out checks here at the station above all, and presumably first and foremost on soldiers with a pass who were not dressed according to regulations. He felt like smoking, he'd allowed himself a cigarette now and then, to relieve the pressure, but he'd stink of it and he didn't have enough mints to cover the smell. Moreover, when he smoked he could see Ann's worried expression in his mind's eye; it spoilt the pleasure of smoking and he was annoyed at that.

Officers came and went, passenger trains stopped with a squeal of brakes, no one waved to him. Perhaps Reina looked different – a new hairstyle, her face no longer that of a girl, a year and a half could be a long time. He was twenty-and-a-half years old and when he thought back to their conversations by Kaltwasser reservoir, to his mania for learning as much as possible, his delusion about becoming famous, he felt he could smile like an old man. He'd had light work during the day, Nip had chased him round the company a bit, tidying up, polish-ing floors, cleaning weapons, heating the bathroom stove (for four men: himself, Pancake and two sick soldiers on barracks duty). Breath-ing space. Burre had died in the military hospital, there had only been a brief interruption to the exercise, during the initial questioning by the military prosecutor; Burre's mother had only been informed after the death of her son. That was the 'Burre case', the 'Hoffmann case' was still pending. But that was a dream, it couldn't be anything else.

All that just wasn't right. Burre's slack body, still half stuck in the hatch while the recovery tank was already pulling. The gurgling darkness, the gun pointer helplessly flailing round above him until he gave him a kick: Get out of the way, crawl over to the loader's side or behind the gun, open the hatch and climb out, but let me get at Burre. If that was true, then how could he be out here on Grün Station waiting for a train from Leipzig in his walking-out uniform? People stared at him. You couldn't wear these things, even in a small garrison town like Grün, without getting hostile or contemptuous looks. But I'm not one of them! he wanted to cry out. I hate these things just as much as you do. Surely you must realize that, lots of you have done military service. The blue-grey shirt made of poor-quality material with the dull aluminium buttons and the 'Monkey's swing', the silver braided marksman's cord, dangling down; some, who had shown greater ambition than he, had the military sports badge, the marksman's bar, pinned to their chest; the cap with its stiff plastic peak and cheap cockade, the grey felt trousers and the black shoes; the plastic arch of the sole had to be polished – an old Wehrmacht tradition, as Christian had been told at cadet school: there were seams on the arches of their military boots and woe to thee, Russia, if they hadn't been greased. You had to have your sewing kit with you as well: torn trousers, always a possibility, would be detrimental to the dignity of the member of the army and therefore to the armed forces as a whole, so had to be mended immediately.

The train, a grumpy voice that sounded as if it were made of felt announced, was delayed. But now the light was falling, withdrawing, seemed to be saying, Come on, it's up to you now, to the twilight. This was the hour of the day Christian liked best. He used to like the early morning just as much, when the air was still fresh and had a silky dampness, like a sensitive photo that had just been taken out of the fixative; but those hours no longer belonged to him, for eighteen months now they had been the hours of whistles and shrill shouts, of the start of terrible days. This wilting, this hardly perceptible waning was something different. The station, with its grubby concourse, the sleepers with their dusting of ash, the smell of toilets, Mitropa snack bars and coal, seemed to be drinking in the thinning light, gradually filling itself with it until, with its rusty red dusting of ash, it had entirely become non-poisonous copper bloom. At this moment it would be enough to spread your arms to be able to fly – as he knew and it filled him with joy and satisfaction. The other people on the platforms seemed to feel the same, he saw workers throw out their chests, stride up and down with a bouncing gait, then, when they once more became aware of being watched, pluck at their overalls in embarrassment; he saw the down-and-outs hold up their bottles of beer assessingly to the light; and all at once the two men in the uniform of the transport police were casually swinging their batons. And he – he had cyclamen. Bought at Centraflor on the station forecourt where a supply had just been unloaded from a lorry; hundreds of pots of cyclamen; no cut flowers.

Reina alighted from the last carriage of the train that had just arrived. Christian gave an embarrassed wave, waited, set off hesitantly; he suddenly felt this meeting was inappropriate, the pot of cyclamen, which he was holding like a basket full of bees, ridiculous; the purple, turned-back flowers waved dementedly in the evening breeze. For a moment Christian thought of Ina in Berlin, of his wedding present for her and the awkward gesture with which he'd put it in her hand. He lifted up the pot, at the same time Reina also lifted up her present; unlike him she'd unpacked her cyclamen and as they exchanged their 'Hello, Christian' and 'Hi, Reina', they also exchanged their pots of cyclamen. Reina raised her shoulders, scratched her upper arm, looking for an insect bite, and Christian couldn't think of anything to say; he searched desperately for some compliment but what occurred to him, of all things, was that the scar on her neck brought out the delicacy of her skin, the lovingly scattered freckles. But he didn't want to say that, just like that. It would have made her even more confused, more inhibited than she seemed to be: standing there, uncertain what to do, for now she was there and that left the question of what they should do, in a strange town that Christian too only knew from its station – barracks, metal works, chemical smells, the Dutch Courage were none of them the kind of place one knew because one was at home there.

Reina was there; he had no expectations. She'd changed in the eighteen months since the senior high, the woman she was becoming shimmered through her still girlish features, her hair was done differently: Christian found these changes strangely arousing and since he immediately began to reflect on that, he trotted along beside Reina in silence, head bowed, sensing the torment that she was trying to cover over with words that didn't get to him. He wasn't quite sure but he felt for a moment that he wanted to annoy her a little – that was when she was at her prettiest. She hadn't put on very much make-up, for that he was grateful. Her new hairstyle, yes, that did look a bit dolled up, that would be the effect of the big city. That and the womanliness in her features made Reina strange beyond what he had expected and imagined, and that was precisely what aroused him, not her smell, her voice, not the glances of the others on the platform that awoke from their torpor as they passed over Reina and drew back into contempt, perhaps just indifference, when they looked at Christian. I don't belong to you any more, the womanliness in Reina seemed to be saying and aroused desire, the instinct for possession. She fell silent; immediately he withdrew into himself, even more than he had already done with his discourteous silence that made their encounter hard work for her, an exhausting search for ways of getting a conversation going, leaving the approach to her; and now he felt bitter, decided it had been a mistake to meet Reina, especially in his situation.

Christian sought out the shade, looked nervously to the left and right, taking on the skipping gait, ever ready to flee, to manoeuvre, of those who believe they are being followed. Sometimes he quickly ducked, clenched his fists (he'd stowed the cyclamen in the knapsack he'd brought with him) as if there were something in the empty air between them that he could only ward off in that way; sometimes he abruptly took one step back, which, as he noticed, Reina at first found irritating, then merely awkward, it seemed; but he was only avoiding an anticipated burst of light, an as yet invisible punishment that he didn't know and couldn't have explained but was sure to come, perhaps already had a face and was observing him; whatever he did, it would encounter him, and differently, in a different form from the one he expected. But he too could behave unexpectedly, not avoid a patch of brightness here, there take fifteen paces straight forward and suddenly swerve to the right because the punishment was thinking, right, I've got you now, at the sixteenth pace you're mine – but that was precisely when he'd gone off to the side, the spear had been thrust into empty space! Christian realized that Reina had stopped.

'You're being very odd, what's wrong? I think you're not even listening to me.'

That was true. Like a euphoric sower on his field, the neon sign over the station concourse kept on casting a cheerful 'Welcome to Grün – the pearl of the West Erzgebirge' over the floor, unconcerned that it was pale from carefully torn-up newspaper. Reina wouldn't start to cry now. The shy Reina, as she'd written in her letter; she began to dissolve into the mocking Reina who could turn into the hurtful Reina; he felt sorry about that and yet incapable of making things any easier for her. He felt paralysed, he would have known what words to use, but they refused to roll off his tongue, it was lumpy and too steep a climb and they just couldn't make it.

'Your letter, have they . . . I did receive your letter.'

Yes: he just nodded, briefly observed the way her fingers were tapping the edge of the cyclamen pot, then he gave her a bag that she accepted with a thoughtful look. There was a cupboard on the station forecourt and Christian would have thought it quite natural if the door had opened to reveal a skinny, white-eyed girl. 'They haven't decided anything yet. There'll be a hearing. Military court. We should talk about something else.'

'I went to see your parents.'

'You said so in your letter.'

'Should I go back? You're so negative.'

'No. No.' And then another word that took a great effort to say but for that very reason he wanted to see what would happen when he did say it: 'Sorry.' It came out fairly easily and made him think of Wald-brunn, his walk along the Wilde Bergfrau, his arrogance that was directed at Verena.

'Where are we going?' Reina looked round, didn't seem to like what she saw.

'Dunno. Have you any suggestions? I don't really know my way round here. Cinema?' he said, in the hope that they would sit there next to each other, watch some film or other, remain silent. Silence was what was best. Each close to the other, just close, without words. But Reina said no. 'We can't talk there. Perhaps . . . perhaps that sounded too challenging: Where are we going? It was just . . .'

They passed the cinema, it was the only one in the town. It was showing Soviet fairy-tale films: *The Scarlet Flower*, *Gharib in the Land of the Djinns*. Christian liked to go to the cinema when he had a pass. It reminded him of the Tannhäuser Cinema. The roof was damaged, on fine days the sunlight came in through a gap, rain on wet days – on sunny days a black umbrella with balloons tied on and guided by a string was floated up underneath the hole, on wet days a bucket placed under it.

'You always called me Montecristo. My real name made you laugh.'

'I didn't say anything to your parents, just as you told me. But don't you think . . . Your father could do something for you.'

'No. They have enough worries as it is. Especially my mother. – We could go and have a meal. My treat.'

'Verena's made an application to leave. She's in Leipzig too, I some-times see her.'

'That could harm you.'

'I've already had a discussion in the dean's office. It was two of them who conducted the discussion. – But she's my friend, they can't forbid me to see her.'

'Oh yes they can. They have ways of doing it. The guy who died offered to spy for them if they saw to it that he was transferred. They said: It's where you are now that we need you, Comrade Burre. Of course we'll protect you, we know what military ethics means. They can do as they like.' They crossed the marketplace to the fountain. Jets of water came from a four-headed gryphon in black sandstone. 'And Siegbert?' Christian asked.

'They've separated.' That wasn't the self-confident, sometimes haughty Reina he'd known any more. She seemed apprehensive, cau-tious, often looking round, scrutinizing the passers-by, the policemen strolling across the marketplace. 'You know, I always wanted to write to you, but I didn't dare. So much has changed. We left school and . . . well, perhaps it sounds odd now . . . so naive. Perhaps that's the way we were. I mean, I knew I couldn't say everything, not to Schnürchel nor to Red Eagle and certainly not to Fahner. And I asked myself: why not, actually? They're communists, they claim to be honest . . . And us? Why do we talk one way at home and quite differently at school . . . just churn out what we know's expected of us so as not to get into trouble? But why should you get into trouble when you have an opin-ion that's counter to other opinions? And why is there this contradiction: on the one hand reality – on the other what's written about it and they're completely different? I was so blind . . . I didn't know anything. Sometimes I would sit in my room in the school hostel and think of you and that you probably despise me for my cluelessness. But you . . . you were fortunate –'

'Siegbert sometimes accused me of that.'

'I'm not reproaching you for that, far from it. It's just . . . upbring-ing. I was brought up to believe in the country, in the ideals, the system. Well, brought up . . .' Reina laughed nervously. '. . . there were so many things my parents couldn't care less about. Apart from: as long as you expect us to support you –'

'Can Verena continue her studies?'

'She's been kicked out. Before that she was one of the best, people couldn't do enough for her – then her application and she was dropped like a hot potato.'

'This tender butterfly with dark brown eyes.'

'You were in love with her.'

'Don't think so.'

'She wasn't worth it!' Reina declared in a sudden outburst of hatred.

'She was so. – How's her sister?'

'She and their mother both still have their jobs. Her father was dismissed immediately she made the application. Apart from me all her friends have turned their backs on her. Siegbert already had prob-lems of his own and one of them told him that if he didn't break off his relationship with Fräulein Winkler they couldn't guarantee any-thing any more.'

'Does he still want to go to sea?'

'Yes. That's why they've got him where they want him. He's study-ing education now, sport and geography.'

'Siegbert a teacher! And his enlistment for four years?'

'He's withdrawn it. – All her friends have turned their backs on her. As if she were a leper. And me? What should I do? They tell me straight out that I should break off the relationship.'

'Then do that. Eventually she'll be over there. And what use will it be to you if Verena's gone and you're not allowed to go to university?'

'Do you really think that? You?'

'I don't know what I think. I just know the way things are.'

'You can't really think that. Siegbert yes. But not you. And you know that. It's only for the sake of argument that you're pretending to be so cynical. But you're not like that.'

'Why not? There's something to what I said. Anyway, I don't know myself what I'm like. But you claim you do know. We haven't seen each other for ages and there was a time –'

'What d'you mean by that – you don't know yourself?'

'There are situations, decisions you have to take . . . But things turn out differently and you're surprised. Perhaps you were more of a coward than you thought. Perhaps you thought you were an honourable person who knew what was right and that there were certain things you wouldn't do – and then you find yourself secretly reading somebody else's diary. – What was it like at my parents'? Why did you go to see them?'

'I'd done this work experience year, in a clinic. A small clinic. I saw things there . . . We had no syringes. Then we did have some: there were patients who'd gone to the West and brought back syringes and bandages from there. They go to the West and buy their insulin syringes, their cannulas, there so that we can give them to them. We did Socialist Aid in a care home. There were no nurses there, the old people were lying in their nappies that no one had changed. There was one male nurse, he went round the wards and said he'd wipe up the shit of anyone who had Western money. Said the oldsters can travel over there, I can't. There are beds and whole wards you can only get in if you can pay with hard currency. Your father confirmed that. He explained: the health service doesn't bring in foreign currency, it's funded by the state, which urgently needs foreign currency and therefore has to sell what's available –'

'Yes, we weren't told about that at school.'

'Svetlana's gone to the Soviet Union. There's no fire here any more, she said, only ashes. She couldn't bear it any longer, the weariness, the bureaucracy.'

'And now she's looking for the fire in our friends' country. She might be lucky enough to find some. There was a splendid one in Chernobyl recently.'

'You've become very cynical. That's not like you. I know Svetlana . . . was special. I felt more sorry for her.'

'I believe she would have thought nothing of reporting Jens or Falk if they'd been careless enough to say what they really thought when she was listening.'

'Do you know Svetlana?'

'Go on, tell me she wouldn't have done that.'

'She was in love with you.'

Christian said nothing.

'You often used to study in the school library.' Reina smiled. 'You were as arrogant as a turkey-cock. And condescending. Svetlana wrote a love letter to you on the blackboard on the easel, I was to check it for spelling mistakes. I thought the letter was somehow . . . unsuitable. Unsuitable for her. So self-abasing and at the same time schoolmarm-ish . . . She wiped it all off shortly before you came.'

'And now she's in the Soviet Union hoping for less bureaucracy. Oh yes.'

'Schnürchel got her a university place in Leningrad, for Russian teachers. She must have met a man there. I respect her despite every-thing, for her it wasn't just an empty word, socialism. And that everyone should have a decent life. Did you never wonder why she was a boarder – when her family lived in the next village? Her mother was an alcoholic, her father the same – and he used to beat them. She had six brothers and sisters, and Svetlana was a mother to them.'

'And why are you telling me all this, what am I supposed to do with that sentimental story? What are you trying to prove? That I'm an arsehole? Funnily enough, Verena tried that. That I'm too quick to judge people? My uncle's hinted at that already. Are you trying to teach me how to behave? – That's what they're trying to do all the time – teach people how to behave!' Christian cried. 'Teach yourselves!' A fit of rage was coming on, a crust was bursting open, heat fizzed through his veins, a generator seemed to be pumping dark electricity into his fingertips, loading them with manic power, sharpening his eye for some target he could demolish with one slash of the knife or punch of the fist or blow of the axe – Christian had raised the tank axe at his company commander. He could feel the fit coming on, that too part of his Hoffmann heredity, Richard was liable to frighteningly violent outbursts of fury, Christian had seen his grandfather Arthur, half-crazed with rage, smash the living-room window with a meat-grinder, raving, roaring, he'd bombarded Emmy with clothes pegs. Christian dragged Reina into an entrance hall, bit her hand, then kissed the place he'd bitten. Her armpit! he thought. You wanted to kiss her armpit first. Now that had come to nothing. There was rubble in the hallway, plaster had trickled down to form bright cones of dust on the floor. He had to laugh when he heard Reina protest. How soft she was, her arms, her cheeks – so soft. Splinters of sunshine came in from the back yard, where the dustbins were, but only as far as a rusted bicycle. He was in a blind rage of desire. Go out with her. Talk to her. Reina was crying. He noticed that he was pressing the bag with the cyclamen against her. A door shut somewhere on a higher floor. He pushed Reina away, she let herself slide slowly down the wall, crouched there, face turned away though not crying any more. He could see himself the way he'd looked at himself, naked, in the mirror, his nauseating skin, covered in pimples, that longed for a touch and feared it. He flattened a little pile of plaster under his shoe, waiting, uncertain as to what was going to happen. He'd have to say, Sorry, please, again, and then go, but he really didn't feel like that at all.

59
The crystal apartment

When Richard was on night duty, the telephone rang and he set off
with an orderly and a driver, he recalled the apartment in which his
retired boss had given a farewell meal for the doctors and a few nurses –
the long-serving workhorses, as Müller used to say; the apartment that
seemed to consist entirely of crystal, even the front door greeted the
visitor with palm trees and a bird of paradise engraved on the frosted
glass, followed by glass hall-stands, crystal-clear mirrors, display cases
with glass flowers by Blaschka & Blaschka of Dresden, who had supplied their fragile, handblown works of art to zoological and botanical
collections from Harvard to Vienna, the dandelion-clock weightlessness of Eucalyptus globulus,
the telephone rang, the nurse in Casualty held out the phone to him.
'Frau Müller, for you, Herr Doktor',
or volvox algae, enlarged until they were clearly visible, fragile radial
sketches, Richard was reminded of the microscopy courses when he
was a student, 'Eucalyptus globulus, habitat Australia and Tasmania',
Müller, shaking a glass of water with ice cubes, had explained,
'Yes? Hoffmann',
'Yes,' said Edeltraut Müller,
and while Richard was looking for a formulation that sounded less
off-hand than What's wrong, What can I do for you? she said,
'Come. Now',
after taking a sip of water Müller had patted his lip with his signet ring and
Richard had been confused by the opulent clarity, the single-minded trans-
parency of the apartment, confused that Müller was something like a
representative of the Blaschkas, he spoke for them, and for Richard the
two things didn't fit together: Müller's choleric rule in the clinic, the

contemptuously violent cut with which he opened up his patients' abdominal walls, his silent, vigorous advance into the depths, passing by, uninterested, anything that wasn't *relevant* – and these glass anemones, freshwater polyps, cacti with cat's-tongue flowers, irises in ballet poses; preparations of hardened, unhearing delicacy in the flexible, aerosol-light fluid that came spurting out of the lead crystal chandeliers and wall candelabras as if out of atomizers, and Müller, Richard recalled, turned away in embarrassment, perhaps also fearful, at compliments, raised-eyebrow assessments of the cost of this crystal druse, as if his self-confidence in the clinic had only been outward show, as if a man's ability to assert his will, his decisiveness, were called into question if the one who possessed, or claimed to possess, those qualities lived in an apartment filled with watery light, burgeoning silence and glass flowers, and perhaps Müller was sorry he'd invited his colleagues, had quietly regretted not having satisfied the custom of giving a leaving party by holding it in the clinic – or did vanity and the need to show off outweigh caution; this Now-I-can-be-myself, ladies and gentlemen, this So this is me the way I never wanted you to see me while I was still in employment, but now everything's different, now I'm retired, now I've escaped from you and can do as I like, can even brag unpunished, and out of relief at that I request the pleasure of your company to enjoy your little, agreeable defeat?,

when Richard set off and they were speeding along in the Rapid Medical Assistance van to Schlehenleite on the Elbe slope above the Blue Miracle, he could still hear the words of Grefe, the junior doctor, who had come out of one of the patients' rooms in Casualty in the fluttering, already somewhat tatty white habit of the duty doctor, still traces of plaster on his forearms and the backs of his hands: 'The surgeon's illness, Dr Hoffmann, pensioned off – and that's it?',

'Come. Now',

but her voice had sounded calm, controlled, not strained, not trying to maintain her composure for the emergency response physician, as often happened when they were on call,

Richard recalled the long table with the, now emeritus, professor at the head, his relaxed, inviting gestures, and the way Trautson had tapped a glass with his fork to request silence for a speech, below the one painting in the apartment, the picture of a loaf of bread,

'I don't know, Dr Grefe, your aunt just said, "Come. Now", is there someone here who can replace you?' But Dr Grefe was already being called for the next urgent case,

amid the sound of the engine's rpm angina, its whooping-cough chug-chug when the driver changed gear on a climb and double-declutched, Richard recalled that loaf painted in oils on the wall over the top end of the table, creaking (so immediate it seemed) like a carriage wheel, with a casual dusting from the lavish excesses of flour piled up beside it, partly in absolutist pointed cones, partly in churned-up heaps, as if the painter (strangely enough one didn't think of the baker) had dug his fists into it; a loaf with its crust burst open in the form of a starfish with, coming out of the cracks, the soft, nutritiously steaming dough, giving the brown (chitin-brown, acorn-brown, double-bass-brown, tree-trunk-brown, rock-brown) crust stuttering outlines, jagging out ridges, here raising a plate that would splinter when you bit on it, there a tumour of crust swelling in a thin network of pores surrounded by the crumb that recalled the growths on gnarled beeches,

'Bread, Herr Hoffmann. The man painted nothing but bread, bread all the time. It was his speciality, so to speak, and even if there's something odd about obstinately sticking to one single subject, at least he achieved genuine mastery in that, as you will admit. The King of the Loaf',

'But a king at least,' Dreyssiger broke in mockingly,

'A king who is truly powerful, you never experienced the war, young man',

Richard recalled before Niklas Tietze opened the door to the Müllers' apartment or, rather, dragged it open across broken glass that crunched and crackled under his feet,

Richard saw Niklas's stethoscope through the gaps between the splinters still left in the front door, then his face, serrated by fragments of the bird of paradise and palm leaves hanging down like icicles, saw, silently observed by neighbours, Niklas's hands, his bow tie, his Sunday suit that he wore when going to Däne's Friends of Music,

'Yes,' Niklas said, 'she came to fetch us, we'd been listening to Mozart and . . . it's not far for her, we were still chatting',

'What happened?' Richard saw the ruins, the smashed mirrors, the clothes stands in pieces, the thousands of glints shooting up from fragments of glass in the light of the few remaining bulbs,

'He was sent a letter demanding he declare everything,' Niklas said, waving the orderly and driver, who'd pushed their way with the stretcher through the rapidly growing crowd of onlookers, through to the back,

Joffe, the lawyer, came out of one of the rooms, hesitantly and with much shaking of the head – he was wearing checked slippers – seeking gaps in the piles of broken glass,

'The police and forensic have been informed, everything will have to be cordoned off here, I couldn't do more than that, Herr Hoffmann, this kind of thing isn't my field',

'Thirty-nine ampoules of regular insulin, Dr Tietze immediately injected some glucose intravenously but I fear we were too late,' Edeltraut Müller said, tapping a needle then pumping up a blood-pressure sleeve round Müller's right arm, feeling in the crook of his arm with the stethoscope and slowly releasing the column of mercury with the knurled screw while Richard checked the pupil reaction with a torch: both pupils fixed; checked breathing, pulse, circulation and examined the two kidney dishes, in the one on the left the broken ampoules and two ampoule saws, a compress; in the one on the right the glass syringe with the injection cannula still attached,

'He knew I was going to the Friends of Music, Dr Hoffmann, and that I'd be away for several hours; the neighbours above us were also away

and the noise wouldn't have been very audible on the floor above them,'
she said, pumping up the blood-pressure sleeve again
'the letter,' she said,

'Dear Dr Hoffmann, The ampoules of regular insulin come from the
stock of the Surgical Clinics, please sort that out with Administration
and with Senior Nurse Henrike.
Dearest Edeltraut, I thought they shouldn't have the apartment. Please
don't go to any unnecessary trouble as far as the funeral's concerned.
I've made the necessary arrangements with Herr Pliehwe of Earthly
Journey, the undertaker's in the Service Combine. For your widow's
pension apply to Administration, Herr Scheffler will help you. I have
done forty-one years of good work. As a communist and as a doctor.
This isn't the socialism we dreamt of.'

turned the membrane of the stethoscope, pulled out the earpieces with
one hand, making them collide, pumped up the sleeve, made the column of mercury in the pressure gauge contract, but had forgotten to
put the earpieces back in, pumped again, the hooks holding the sleeve
had loosened so that it swelled asymmetrically,
'And,' Niklas said, his eyes fixed on the broken display cases, the
smashed glass flowers, the hammer with which Müller had reduced
the crystal pendants on the chandeliers to fragments,
'Thirty-nine ampoules,' Edeltraut Müller said, 'he drew them up into
a urology syringe, look',
certainly with a raspberry-coloured pout of his lips, certainly his eyes
concentrating as he scored the ampoules, broke off the necks with the
compress between glass and fingers, certainly with his owl-like eyebrows knitted, his fingers lifting, cool, professional actions, regular
insulin worked quickly,
'They waited until he retired,' Edeltraut Müller said,

Police stomped over broken glass, the duty forensic doctor nodded to Richard, who caught Edeltraut Müller before she fell onto the splinters of glass beside her husband's corpse.

60

Journey to Samarkand

Should I ever / break this my solemn oath of allegiance /
may I suffer the harsh punishment of the laws / of our
Republic and the contempt / of the working people
Oath of Allegiance of the National People's Army

'At the double!' Nip gave a sharp nod; Christian and Pancake followed him along the empty, polished company corridor. Their footsteps echoed. Musca was on duty, saluted, his blue eyes wide. Far away, Christian thought, for him we're already untouchable. He hummed quietly to himself. 'Shut it, Hoffmann,' Nip ordered. The battalion building was deserted, the companies were out on a training exercise. Outside the light was so bright it made Christian sneeze.

'At the double!' Nip pushed him forward like something at which he felt revulsion, which filled him with unutterable disgust. He didn't need to tell Pancake. He had gone quiet, his lopsided grin had vanished. He too had said something. He had taken the axe out of Christian's hand and said, 'But he's right.' Among other things. There were grinning faces at the windows of the medical centre. There was a smell of spring; the fresh green on the trees did his eyes good. On the parade ground it was 'Left about turn! Right about turn! Right wheel – march!'

with the new recruits, the sound of engines came from the technical depot, containers of food were being loaded outside the kitchens.

Inquiry. Handed over to a duty officer in headquarters. On the first floor they waited at a barred door. Christian and Pancake were interrogated separately by a man in civilian clothes.

'You have not yet found your place in society, Hoffmann. You're still young.'

'The problem is not what you did, but what you said. You have betrayed the trust put in you. It is not the death of Comrade Lance Corporal Burre that we are dealing with here. That is regrettable. We will investigate it, of course. But that is not at issue here. That is a completely different case. We will investigate that separately. No, Hoffmann, you and your crony Kretzschmar, with whom we are already acquainted, very well acquainted, made remarks. You defamed us. Openly attacked our state! But we know all about that . . . harmful pests. Both of you. You have betrayed our trust, made subversive comments. To defame our state! That is the worst.'

'You made disparaging remarks about us in public, Hoffmann. That will have serious consequences.'

'We know you as well, oh yes, you and your fine family. – Oh, you don't know? Well, you have a sister. Your fine father cheats on his wife in his free time. You don't know that. But we do. He's screwing your girlfriend, Fräulein Kossmann. But your sister isn't hers. Half-sister, to be precise. Thunderstruck, eh? Have a look here.'

'You think we don't know you? Came to our notice through a particular incident at the pre-military training camp. Got out of it through the legal tricks of your lawyer. Already called attention to yourself at high school. Said the following at senior high school . . . But that's clear. Morally degenerate. And we allow something like you to go to university, something like you that betrays our trust! I can't even bring myself to repeat what you said. There, read it out yourself. Come on, don't be shy. Coming the prissy little middle-class mummy's boy, are we? And then one incident after another . . . We've got it all down in writing, confirmed by witnesses. Go on, read it out.'

'Something like that's only possible in this shitty state,' Christian read out falteringly.

'So, found our tongue again, have we? – But you're still young. There's still hope. At the senior high school you and a certain Heike Fieber made a great portrait of Karl Marx, in the Karl Marx Year. That shows that there is some good in you, deep down inside. That's the influence of your mother, who comes from an illustrious family. That's the legacy of your revolutionary grandmother, who fought and suffered for the just cause. There's goodwill there, your blood has not yet been entirely corrupted.'

Penal Code, section 220

PUBLIC DISPARAGEMENT

1. Anyone who in public disparages the state's system of government or state bodies, institutions or social organizations or their activities and measures taken is liable to a sentence of up to three years' imprisonment or a suspended sentence, a prison sentence, a fine or a public reprimand.

The guard led Christian towards a checkpoint. He didn't go out of the barracks, he was taken to the guardroom. One of the detention cells was unlocked. Christian saw: a rectangle, the rear left corner of which was cut off by sunlight, a tightly made up bunk bed, a stool. Christian turned round to the guard but he shook his head: Don't speak. The guard locked the door behind Christian, taking care not to make too much noise. Christian sat down. The walls had been painted with mud-grey gloss paint. UNDER CONSTRUCTION, he thought. What will they do? What will happen? They're not saying anything. He could hear the voices of the instructors coming from outside: 'Right turn! – Left turn! At the double – march!' The thud of boots, now and then a bellowed command: 'Regiment atten-shun!' The regimental commander had come and the duty officer made his report. The rumble of engines. From outside, from the guardhouse, the usual rhubarb, rhubarb before and after the changing of the guard, the clunk of metal as they took off their machine pistols, belts and mess kit. In the evening drunken soldiers bawled at him from the neighbouring cells, 'Hey, pal, why'd they lock you up?'

'UA.' Unauthorized absence, Christian thought. Unauthorized. Absence. Morally degenerate. You have a sister. 'And you?' That was to Pancake.

'Hey – can't you open your mouth?'

'Shut your trap.'

'And you, mate?' That was to Christian. He was sitting on the stool and heard it as if it came from far away. He didn't reply. The soldiers swore. Pancake and Christian stayed in the detention cell for three days, Friday, Saturday, Sunday. They were given their food in the guard-room, in their mess tins. A piece of cake on Sunday. If they needed the toilet, they had to shout. The sun moved across the cell in thin stripes from left to right, towards evening the stripes became longer, thinned out, leaving one stripe that disappeared over the edge of the folding table. Christian spent most of the time sitting on the stool, by the evening he couldn't bear the precise awareness of the slight dips, lumps, cracks in the wood, the places smoothed by the clutches of his predecessors (hands under their thighs). Despite that it was important for him to get to know this small square on which he sat, on which after a few hours sitting he felt sore – look closely, Meno and Richard had taught him that.

He couldn't lie on the bunk during the day. The bells rang from the tower of Grün church at 6 p.m.; Christian had never registered the peal before. Then he would lie down on the floor, as close as possible to the radiator and its lukewarm fins. Five fins: ivory on the colour of the silicon stove-enamelling (silver). It had flaked off in 117 places, none of them triangular. The window was accessible.

Transport. 'Hoffmann, Kretzschmar, I warn you that I must use my gun if you resist.' Nip tapped the pistol on his belt. 'Get in.' A converted, military-green Barkas van, folding seats, bars between the driver and loading space.

Examining judge. 'The examining judge is waiting for you.' They didn't go across the bridge, across the courtyard with the monument and the guard in front of it; they approached Coal Island from the restricted area. A civilian official waved the van through with a friendly gesture after she had *taken down* their personal details and *passed them on* over a black telephone.

'Prisoners' escort.' A first lieutenant took over. The barrier opened at the checkpoint. Coal dust from the pithead frames drifted through the mild spring air. A large yard, concrete slabs, pansies in tractor tyres painted white, pansies had *come into bloom*, as the lieutenant pointed out to Nip, whom he addressed by his first name. 'So what have you brought for us today?'

'Two two-twenties.'

'Problems?' The lieutenant tapped the handcuffs he had on his belt.

'Nah. Kretzschmar here' – he prodded Pancake, who was trotting along apathetically, head bowed, in front of Christian, in the ribs – 'has already got quite a record. A big mouth but nothing behind it. A good driver, though, pity to lose him.'

'Aha,' the lieutenant said as the shrill whistle of Black Mathilda was heard. The yard was surrounded by a barbed-wire fence. There was a blossom on one of the concrete slabs. Christian bent down and picked it up: from the apple trees on the slope across the Elbe, from the

Italian-looking gardens. He was punched and doubled up, gasping for air. 'Do that again and there'll be trouble,' the lieutenant said. Corridors like catacombs. Christian smelt the stale air – not a window anywhere. The echoing tramp of boots. The clink of metal, harsh orders, sticks hitting bars rhythmically, challenges shouted out across distances – signals? – regularly, as if separate transports were trying to avoid each other. The corridors had been painted black on the lower half, yellow above. There were buttons on the walls at regular intervals. The ceiling was cross-vaulted, bare bulbs hung down from the intersections of the ribs.

'Halt!' A steel door with a number.

'The comrade major has gone for lunch,' the secretary said.

'Then you two will take your nourishment as well,' the lieutenant told Christian and Pancake. 'Open ration bags!' They had been given the ration bags before setting off on the transport, the guard had whispered to them, 'Eat the lot, the examining magistrate can take a long time.'

While they were still eating (standing up) a major came out of the door. The army judge, not the examining magistrate.

'Atten-shun!' the lieutenant roared. Christian and Pancake didn't know what to do with their food as they tried to stand to attention. The judge took it good-humouredly. He read out their names. After that they were called *the accused*. 'The accused are suspected of having committed offences according to section two hundred and twenty of the Criminal Code.' He read out the relevant section. 'After detailed examination of the facts in the case the investigating officers recommended the accused be taken into custody on the grounds that they might attempt to abscond.'

That made Christian laugh: attempting to abscond. He was wearing the uniform of the National People's Army. Well, yes, if he could fly. Then he found he was flying, saw a rubber truncheon raised.

'Comrade First Lieutenant, I must ask you to treat the prisoners according to regulations.'

The examining magistrate strolled back from lunch chatting with two colleagues about gardening, the problems of growing pumpkins. Not looking at anyone, he indicated with a nod that they should go into the room. Christian had to stand behind a wooden barrier with a view of greying curtains, a standard government-issue desk, filing cabinets. Instead of the smiling portrait of the Comrade First Secretary the grim one of the Chairman of the Ministerial Council was hanging on the wall above the examining magistrate's chair with, beside it, a certificate for an 'Exemplary Combat Collective in Socialist Competition'. There was a seedling rubber tree on the window ledge with a little copper watering can beside it. The examining magistrate listened calmly to Christian's stammering Sorry, won't happen again, I didn't say it like that, I didn't mean it like that.

'You have the right of appeal. You will be remanded in custody while further investigations are carried out.'

Trial judge advocate. Stairs, corridors, bare light bulbs. This part of Coal Island seemed not to be linked to the administrative offices unless by secret tunnels. Christian had already been in Central Registration with the counters with the letters of the alphabet above them, and then in the rotunda with the statues before, on the day he'd handed in his identity card and received his military service identity card in return, that grey document with the pease-pudding-yellow pages – these corridors, however, along which the lieutenant had led them unerringly, seemed to be from a previous age. On the surface, in the daylight, the blocks made of prefabricated slabs hadn't suggested this labyrinth, it must branch off deep into the mine and sometimes, when the lieutenant ordered them to stop after a challenge from a guard, Christian thought he could hear the clunk of hammers and the sound of distant explosions. And then something was ticking, regularly, it sounded like a metronome set at slow, the walls of the basement corridors seemed to bring it from afar. Or were they cellars? He'd lost his sense of direction some time ago. The corridors had no windows. Then they went even deeper, down a spiral staircase that made Christian dizzy; now and then there was a barred door at which the lieutenant ordered them to halt and shortly afterwards a guard would appear. The guards wore dark-blue uniforms that Christian had never seen before. He thought, the Navy? what's the Navy doing here? They reached a vault that must have been very extensive, the light from the bulbs didn't illuminate the whole of it. There was another major sitting at a desk not far from the entrance, he seemed to have the same seniority as the other two majors: promotion-according-to-years-of-service, sitting-your-way-up-the-ladder, as per regulations. As per regulations, Christian thought. Things are clearly as-per-regulations here. The lieutenant reported to him. The major nodded, put a sheet of paper in the black Erika typewriter. Nodding to Christian, he pointed to a spring folder in front of him on the desk. 'I have studied the documents. I disapprove of your behaviour. I have to institute preliminary hearings against you.' He nodded to the lieutenant and Nip, who took Pancake into a room by the bottom of the stairs. The major read out a statement. 'You are supposed to have said that. Now we all know what witnesses are sometimes like, so my lad, what was it really like. After all, we want to get at the truth.'

The major typed out Christian's answers as he spoke, slowly, with two fingers. To correct mistakes he used some white paste he smeared over the mistyped letters with a little brush. 'Right then, to begin at the beginning, my lad, we have this sentence: "You bastard, you damn' bastard!" Is that what you said?'

'I said, "You bastard, you lousy bastard", Comrade Major.'

'– l o u s y bastard,' the major typed. 'It has to be correct. Right, then, that was point one. Point two: "You've killed him. It's your fault, there were five seconds too few."'

'I can't remember exactly, Comrade Major.'

'Come on, try. It's important.'

'I didn't really mean it . . . It just slipped out, the situation, Comrade Major . . .'

'Now you don't need to start crying. I can understand. We were all young once. And we're not without our feelings, are we? But – the class standpoint, young man, we've always been right about that. That's the difference. We've occasionally had one too many, we've liberated eggs from a farmer, we've chased women. That's being young! Did you say that in those words, Hoffmann? Come on, calm down. I want to get home today and you're not the only one I've got to deal with.'

'I think . . . I think . . . I didn't mean it like that.'

'I'm not interested in what you think or don't think, I want to get at the truth, the correct wording of your statements.'

'I said it in those words.'

'There, you see. You can do it. We'll get this done, we'll go through it step by step, I'll read each sentence out to you and you'll think about it carefully. At least you're cooperating. Right. That was point two. Point three: "Something like that's only possible in this shitty state."'

Remanded in custody. The major had one of the doors unlocked. Christian was handcuffed and taken down long corridors. Aluminium doors at regular intervals at which the lieutenant reported: press the button, a buzz, little loudspeakers out of which voices sounding like angry cranes croaked. Christian felt nothing, not even afraid. Of course this couldn't be a dream, for that the lieutenant was too grumpy. Sometimes they encountered other delinquents. Always one officer to one prisoner – the prisoners in handcuffs. The lieutenant ordered him to wait outside a door with the state symbol painted on it. Once more report arrival. Wait. A buzz as the door was unlocked. This was the prison. To the rhythm of their steps Christian thought: prison, prison, it's a mistake. He was led down a wide corridor. Dark-blue uniforms, men in grey-green clothes. Civilian clothes, for many the trouser legs were too short; the clothes had been mended, fluorescent strips had been sewn onto the trouser legs and sleeves in the form of large question marks. He had to stand against the wall, hands raised, to be searched.

'Trousers down. Legs wide apart.' The man in uniform shone a light up his arse. Christian saw Pancake further ahead, a tied-up blanket on the floor in front of him.

'Turn round. Pull back foreskin. – Shut your trap!' The rage flaring up in the face of the man in the blue uniform, his raised hand: We don't hang about here, sonny. The echoing voices. A windowless vault, Christian could make out: steel staircases in the middle, either side of them gratings in the ceiling, on them, on top of each other, the outlines of boots walking slowly.

'To Effects!' That was a boxroom with clothes. A woman behind a wooden barrier said, 'Possessions here.' Yes, he actually had possessions. Someone had carved their initials in the wood of the barrier, which was worn smooth and round like a tiller. Possessions: watch, handkerchief, comb, military identity card, purse, the photo of the hoopoe on the Danube delta, Reina's letter, washing things, his uniform. The woman checked them, indicated what Christian was allowed to keep, recorded the rest in a list that she *countersigned* with initials. Christian was given a bundle of blankets and an often-repaired uniform with fluorescent stripes, the trousers were too short. Then he was taken to a cell. Behind him the key rattled in the lock, three times, four times, very loudly, a special lock, a special key. Christian stood in the cell and realized he wasn't alone. First he had to adjust to the dim light. He said, 'Hello.'

The Tram. Christian saw: two benches opposite each other along the walls, on them around twenty men scrutinizing him, some with calm, some with hostile looks.

'Informer,' one said.

'Nah. It's the first time he's been sent up, you can see that right away. Let's see your mitts.'

Christian held out his hands.

'Nah. He's never worked. A student.'

'University entrance,' Christian muttered.

'No use to you here. D'you know where you are now? In the tram and it's heading for the slammer. The slammer's better. In your case I'd put my money on shit in the forces.' The detainee pointed to Christian's uniform. 'Number?' Christian didn't understand.

'What section?'

'Two hundred and twenty.'

'Oh yes, public disparagement. A tip: when you're in the glasshouse, read the laws. You're allowed to.'

'Pretty boy,' one said.

'Yeh. Almost like a girl.'

'On the nail.'

'Mm?'

'I get a cigarette for that tip,' the man who'd asked him what he was accused of said.

'Haven't got any.'

'Y'll have to buy some. You owe me one cigarette. We'll see each other again, don't you worry.'

'Someone let some air in.'

A metre-long rod raised the window. Bars outside cut the light into seven strips. The door was flung open, the door was slammed shut. New detainees arrived, others were called out. Always the same words: At the double. Or: Move your arse! Or: Get your finger out! The key was like a hammer being driven into the lock. At the sound the inhabitants of the cells started, even the older detainees with brutality written all over their faces. Then the key pushed some soft metal resistance aside, three or four times, each time sounding like the bolt of a machine gun being engaged. Christian, squeezed into the farthest corner of the room, observed the others without moving, not even daring to give way to the itch that was tormenting him all over his body, like the precursor to an allergic attack. He stood motionless and when he breathed out he did it when there was movement in the room, also switching the leg he was standing on at the same time. After a long time (his watch had remained at Effects) he was taken out of the cell. Up the stairs in the middle of the vault.

At Registry. 'At the double, at the double!' Four floors up; he was told to wait at a wooden barrier worn smooth. Other detainees arrived. Out in the middle of the neighbouring room was a piano stool with a red-leather seat that could be screwed higher or lower.

'Sit down.' The photographer busied himself, adjusted floodlights, took photos of Christian from the right, left and in front.

'Hold out your hands.' The guard took Christian's fingerprints, he gave his thumb a light tap with his fist. There was hardly any ink left on the pad.

Christian didn't go back to the tram. The guard unlocked one of the grey iron doors on the fifth floor. The cell number had been sprayed on with black paint using a stencil.

'Detainee Hoffmann, you're to stand one metre away from the guard when the door is being opened and shut!' the man in the blue uniform bawled. He pushed Christian into the room. Two others were in there already, they shot to their feet, thumbs on trouser seams; the older one said, 'Custody Room five-zero-eight, two detainees present, nothing to report.'

Christian was given his bundle of blankets, a sheet of paper and a pencil. He was to write his CV. Mother, father, when did I join the Young Pioneers, the Thälmann Pioneers, when did I become a member of the Free German Youth. Hobbies, school career, job preferences.

The Custody Room. In the cell there were three bunks, two hanging cupboards, a washbasin, a mirror, a table folded down, beside it a lavatory bowl with a pipe and a chain made of white plastic links, a black plastic handle at the bottom.

'The bed at the back's yours, lad. I'm Kurt and this is – oh, tell him your name yourself.'

'Korbinian Krause,' the younger man said.

'Christian Hoffmann.'

'Your number? By the way, you can call me Kurtchen.'

'Two-twenty.'

'Him over there' – the older man nodded at the younger one – 'is in here for two-thirteen. IE – illegal emigration. And me – well, this and that.'

'Kurtchen's a murderer,' the younger man with the odd name of Korbinian muttered.

'Now let's not exaggerate. I did kill someone, true. But that was in anger, that's something different. When you're angry, you don't know what you're doing. First everything goes red, then black, y'know.'

'Because you haven't found the way to God, because you shut your ear to Him, brother.'

The older man grinned, jerked his thumb at Korbinian, who didn't look as if he'd been joking. 'That's his thing, y'know. He's a preacher, y'see.'

'I studied theology but I'm not a preacher. Preacher's what the Methodists and Baptists call it; with us it's pastor or minister. You haven't made confession yet, Kurtchen.'

Kurtchen nodded, grinned. 'I do it as a favour to him, y'know. Keeps him quiet. And sometimes – yeh, it really does help. Get everything off your chest.'

'The one he killed was his own brother. Kurtchen was a cabinet-maker, Arnochen was a cabinetmaker. Their workshops were opposite each other, they lived a cat-and-dog life. And one day they went for each other with axes. Arnochen's axe went in Kurtchen's sideboard, Kurtchen's in Arnochen's noddle.'

'Nah. It went in his neck. Thou shalt not bear false witness, or whatever they say. – But you' – he turned to Christian – 'where're you from? What did you do?'

'Dresden . . . senior high,' Christian stammered.

'Senior high . . . that's good. You'll be educated, imagination . . .'

'Kurtchen needs someone to help him masturbate,' Korbinian said.

'Don't condemn me!' Kurtchen wagged his finger. 'I've not had a woman for ages and I'm a man with strong physical urges. An' if you think up something good, it's a relief for me an' y'get three tubes for it. But it has to be really horny, with lots of diff 'rent bits, know what I mean? Best of all with film stars, then I know who you're talking about.'

Waiting. The words had vanished, they only came back slowly, like fish letting themselves sink back down lethargically after a net had lifted them up into deadly brightness and a hand found them too light. Kurtchen, whom Christian now also called by that name, found the waiting difficult. He was impatient for his trial so that he would finally get to the proper jail, where things were better (he confirmed the opinion of the man in the tram whom Christian owed a cigarette) than on remand. Better because clearer. A clearer situation. The POs (that was what the guards were called, it was the abbreviation of Prison Officer) had no doubts or scruples. They didn't have any here, either, as Kurtchen said, but there, in the proper jail, everything was clear – and since everything was clear and you had proper time as well, it wasn't just waiting for something else any more, the POs could behave as regulations required. Even the trusty, who brought their meals and the book cart once a week, did so. The detainees were allowed to read. Christian borrowed the autobiography of the Comrade General Secretary. The familiar face looked up at him from the photos, familiar from the sky-blue pictures in classrooms, government offices, placards at the First of May processions and celebrations for the anniversary of the Republic. The familiar face had once been that of a child, in a house in the Saarland, oppressive conditions, large families, child mortality, hunger, having to earn money when young, father old before his time, mother a woman who seemed caring but had a frozen smile. Conditions in the factories. The Communist Youth Organization. Fanfares, shawms. The war, post-war inflation. *Little Man, What Now?* '33. Underground, arrested, Gestapo, interrogations, prison. Christian had always hated these stories (they were repeated, with minor variations, in the biographies of the Leading Representatives of the Republic); he didn't want to know about them. Had always switched off the war films on Thursdays, GDR TV Channel 2; Katyusha rocket launchers with subtitles, heroes on the quietly flowing Don, overblown emotionalism hardly different from that of the Nazis. He thought of Anne. 'Good night,' she'd said when he was a child far down, it seemed to him, in the abyss of time. He recalled things said, he tried to make Anne say those things – then the words, then Anne would disappear. Exhortations, touches, surreptitious. When she'd touched him and Robert it had always been surreptitiously, as if the tenderness didn't become her. Now and then a present put out unobtrusively, something 'they needed', clothes from Exquisit, a can of pineapples from Delikat. A book he'd mentioned in passing that she'd managed to get hold of.

The trusty brought their food. It was the same every day: indefinable jam that sometimes had little spots of mould growing on it: then Kurtchen would point it out and Korbinian speak the words 'detention complaint'. Then a PO would appear and, with a look of contempt, place a new pot of jam before the detainees. Everything had to *be in order*. It had to be *as per regulations*. They had to do everything *at the double*. The spyhole in the door, a little window with a steel shutter on the outside, was opened once every hour, but at a different minute of each hour. The shutter squeaked as it was opened and shut with a click. What Kurtchen had called tubes were *papirossi*, cheap tobacco rolled in newspaper. After a week Christian overcame his revulsion and, lo and behold, they didn't taste bad. Glue and printer's ink, often *statements* from the Comrade General Secretary or one of the Leading Representatives, gave the tobacco an additional slightly burnt taste. As children Christian and Robert had tried to smoke ivy stalks from the garden wall of Caravel, they'd had a similar taste to these *papirossi*. Christian borrowed the tobacco from Kurtchen. He had no money, here that was called *having purchase*. Kurtchen gave him generous amounts, he thought he would soon have purchase; the people who'd graduated from senior high that he'd got to know on Coal Island had always been afraid and worked hard; you were paid, though not much.

The exercise yard. For their *free hour* in the mornings they go out at the double (keeping one metre away from the guard) and run at the double. There was a square asphalt yard bounded by a cobbled path and high concrete walls with barbed wire sloping inwards. The sky above the yard was patterned by a grid of bars. In the middle of the grid was a gap through which the trunk of a lime tree towered up. The lime gave off an overpowering scent, but there were no flowers on the ground; there was a net under the top of the tree that collected the leaves and flowers that fell; there were also birds' nests in it from which came contented twittering. There was a bench round the tree trunk, but no one ever sat on it. The detainees ran round in a circle, always to the left, at the double, without talking. Tobacco changed hands and one day Christian managed to pay his debt of one cigarette when the man from the tram suddenly but unobtrusively appeared behind him. Sometimes the guards would bellow. They were bored.

The knives they were given to eat with were blunt. The stapler Christian had to use to keep documents together was so made that the slot where the staples were inserted could only be opened by a little key the guard kept. When all the staples were used up Christian had to wait until the spyhole was opened and he could make a sign. The waiting time did not count towards the time allowed.

*

Visits. Christian received a letter. Sperber, the lawyer, wrote that, at his parents' request, he would take over his defence.

Visits. A visitor for Kurtchen. Kurtchen had a girlfriend. His girlfriend was making difficulties. She wanted to be screwed, Kurtchen explained, and he wasn't there, of course. Kurtchen had had an idea and asked Christian's advice, for he had been to senior high and had imagination. Christian didn't want to advise him, he was sick of the evenings when Kurtchen used the word 'imagination'. At that Kurtchen frowned and explained that he didn't want to get angry.

'Should I let her get laid by my best friend, what d'you think?'

Christian avoided a direct answer. 'Perhaps . . . but there must be other possibilities to consider first.'

'Nah, not any more. She has a dildo, from over there. But now she wants a guy on the end of it, an' there aren't any batteries for it either. An' just using her imagination's not enough any more, she says.'

'Well, if it's your best friend –'

'Keeps it in the family, yeh. 's what I thought too. Then I'll tell her that, since you say so. You get a tube for that. Should I give her your best wishes?'

Lawyer's visit. Sperber was well dressed, shiny suit, lilac-coloured shirt, slim gold wristwatch that he wore with the face on the inside of his wrist and now and then shook round to the outside. The 'sweet' was in the buttonhole of his left lapel. Limp handshake, it felt to Christian as if he'd squeezed a raw chop instead of a hand. Sperber gave Christian some cigarettes. He'd been told by his father, he said, that he didn't smoke, but they were the common currency in there. Christian wasn't paying close attention. He was fascinated by the lawyer's smell. It came from outside. He hadn't realized that the world outside had a smell that was clearly different from the one inside the jail. After all, it was the same air that came in through the window and at night sometimes even the scent of the lime tree. But that belonged in there – its smell was so strong it mocked them.

Sperber had *examined* Christian's files but at the moment, he said, apart from the cigarettes there was nothing he could do for him.

'We must wait for the indictment. You will be indicted, young man. And until then you will continue to be remanded in custody. – Your parents are very worried.' His tone changed to one of fatherly concern, then of mild reproach. 'They know where you are. How could you get carried away like that? Your father taught you how to avoid that. Remember Herr Orré's lessons. Are they to have been so much wasted effort?' So the lawyer knew about that. Now he was smiling, anticipating Christian's question. 'Word gets round, Herr Hoffmann. But you've done something very stupid. In fact you quite often, so it seems to me, do stupid things.'

'I didn't mean it like that.'

'How you meant it is neither here nor there. What matters is what is in the files and you signed the transcript.'

'But the situation –'

'Courts don't concern themselves with situations,' Sperber broke in, giving his arm a friendly pat, 'but with verifiable facts. I feel sympathy for you, certainly, but sympathy gets us nowhere.'

'Herr Doktor Sperber.' Christian found he suddenly had to fight back the tears, which seemed to embarrass the lawyer, his expression cooled. 'What's going to happen to me?'

'We'll have to wait and see. It doesn't look that bad. Don't worry about that for now. – Have you always wanted to study medicine?'

'N-no,' Christian said, surprised.

'Good. So you do have alternatives. It's better not to get too set on one thing. Well, chin up, young man. Things will sort themselves out, I'm doing my best.'

Waiting. Christian was getting fatter, his skin was pale and puffy.

'That's the food and the lack of exercise,' Kurtchen said. At some point Christian stopped being bothered at using the toilet in the cell. It did bother him if the door was flung open at the moment when he was squatting down on the seat and the PO ordered a room count. In the evening Christian sometimes recited poems, Once more the valley quietly fills / with your misty glow . . . Twilight spreads its wings once more. Korbinian leant against the window and recited psalms. Kurtchen would stay silent then. If Korbinian became too loud the key would crash in the lock and the guard take Korbinian out of the cell: 'At the double!'

The trial was set for 6 June 1986. It was a sunny day. After breakfast Christian was given a food bag.

'We'll see each other again,' Kurtchen said.

'You think so?'

'You're not going to get out of here,' Korbinian said cheerfully. 'The Lord be with you. Farewell and forgive us.'

'Farewell and forgive us,' Kurtchen cried as Christian went out of the cell door. He was taken to Transport, but first to Effects. Christian was shown his possessions, had to check them, sign that they were all there.

Handcuffs. The long corridors lit by bare bulbs and smelling of floor polish. The light outside hit Christian like a blow in the face. He lifted up his hands, the movement alarmed the accompanying officer, who immediately drew his pistol. The Black Maria drew up.

The Black Maria was grey. The door was opened, Christian pushed in. A guard took over. There were little cells inside the Black Maria, each with room for one delinquent. Tip-up seats, no windows. The Black Maria set off, cell bolts clanking; Christian listened to the slow resolution of the clink-clank of the bolts that were outside the basic rhythm, after a while all the bolts were in time with each other, a vigorous metallic ringing, comforting and oddly full of the joy of living; then it dissolved again, in a mirror image of the synchronization, into individual rhythms.

'Get out.'

Remanded in custody. Once more he was taken down long subterranean passages. The walls were sweating, damp had left patches on the ceilings, some looked like the clouds of smoke at the mouths of cannons that had just been fired. Christian and the other detainees from the Black Maria went 'yoked', their handcuffs had been chained together.

'Halt!' They waited by the wall in a corridor, hands raised. Christian was put in a custody room in the basement. There were six bunks, four already taken. The door slammed shut. The toilet was under a barred window.

'Welcome to Ascania,' one of the detainees muttered. 'What are you in for, then?' By now the answer came automatically to Christian's lips.

'Food for the national economy,' the detainee replied with a grin. His front teeth were missing. No questions, that was something Christian had learnt by this time. It wasn't his place to ask questions, the others, the older ones did that, not him.

During the night he heard shouts. At first he thought he'd been dreaming but the man on the bunk next to his was restless, grunting, perhaps in his sleep. The air was cold, the cell bathed in the bluish glow of the nightlight. Christian lay there, motionless, arms along his body, under the blanket. He suddenly sensed that no one else was asleep. The light sleep of prisoners . . . That wasn't true. In the tram in the first detention centre, on Coal Island, most had slept a deep, snoring sleep. Even Kurtchen had slept well and wasn't so easily disturbed. Not even by the shouts, which had always woken Christian, or so he thought.

'Quasimodo,' one of them in a more distant corner of the room said.

'Yes, on his rounds again.'

'Could be on the fourth, above us, from the echo.'

'He's got a dimpled cosh.'

'How d'you know that?'

'My arse tells me.'

'Pull the other one! You're just having us on.'

'Italian job, he showed it me, very proud of it he was, before using it. 's got little bobbles on it – doesn't leave any blue marks.'

'A rubber truncheon that doesn't leave any weals, did you ever hear the like of it?'

'Just arrived.'

'And they pay hard currency for that . . .'

'Have you ever seen his daughter?'

'They say she's in a wheelchair. Our PO told me he's supposed to be a good father. Looks after her, that kind of thing.'

'He gives his wife flowers on her birthday and International Women's Day.'

'Hey, sonny!' That was Christian. 'If he gives you flowers as well – keep your back to the wall.'

'Otherwise those cyclamen – might turn into a lily wreath, haha.'

'And your mother gets a telegram . . .'

'Exactly!'

'But you can bribe him.'

'Nah, y'can't. I've tried it. Thought, even a PO needs winter tyres. Was against his honour . . . He refused to go along with it.'

'And?'

'Well, cyclamen.'

'We ought to do him in. Just a little bit.'

'What with? All you've got here's the toilet chain and the plastic stuff would break. And blunt knives.'

'If I ever meet him outside . . .'

'Then you've got a long wait.'
Shut it! Saw some logs.'

Lance Corporal Christian Hoffmann
8051 Dresden, Heinrichstrasse 11

SUMMONS

In the criminal proceedings against you, you are required to attend the
Dresden Military Court on
Friday, 6 June 1986, 8.00 a.m.
Also invited to the proceedings are:
Dr Sperber, Lawyer, Dresden and Berlin.
Representative of the Collective . . . Witnesses . . .

Ascanian Island. Handcuffed, Christian and Pancake were taken into
a round domed room. It bore some resemblance to a lecture hall, there
was even a blackboard. Christian saw his parents and Meno; his parents
were pale; he avoided looking at them. The guard pushed him and
Pancake into the front row of the benches that had been set up facing
the table with a red cloth over it. On either side of a grooved column,
from which the ormolu was flaking off, there were windows with pot
plants on the window ledges. Hung high up on the column was the
coat of arms of the German Democratic Republic. Sperber gave Christian's parents an encouraging smile.

The court entered. Christian and Pancake were jabbed in the back:
Up! They got up, Christian stood there even though he couldn't put
his weight on his right leg and, clearly visible to the court (a colonel,
an assessor with the rank of captain, a clerk), was wobbling to and fro.
The colonel nodded to those present. The representative of the
Collective – it was the taciturn goldsmith, who, Christian now realized,
was a member of the Socialist Unity Party – read out an assessment

of the two accused: Lance Corporal Hoffmann was a suspiciously taciturn member of the army who, despite that, could argue eloquently once he had been drawn out; he liked reading in his free time, once poems by Wolf Biermann. Several times he had described the practice of sealing up the cassette compartment on the radios as 'daft'; several times he had swept the copies of *Junge Welt* put out in the day-room off the table in a manner suggesting contempt. As far as performance of his duties was concerned, he had done nothing to draw attention to himself apart from the two incidents during the last military exercise. The judge waved this away impatiently: these were not a matter for the court, would the Comrade Lance Corporal please stick to the matter in hand! Nip was called and took Ina's letter from Cuba out of his briefcase. Hoffmann had been stubborn, they had frequently had to take *corrective measures*. Next the evidence was heard. The witnesses stepped forward: Musca, Wanda, the driving instructor who had passed on the company commander's order to Christian. They were asked about the precise wording of the things Christian and Pancake were supposed to have said. Every one remembered something different. The judge became annoyed. He ordered the interrogation transcripts that the witnesses were to confirm to be read out.

Then the accused were called up to *state their case*. First Christian, then Pancake. Christian apologized, he'd been confused, in an exceptional situation. Most of all he would have liked to scream, to mow down the whole lousy lot of them (he had to be careful not to let that expression slip out) with a machine gun, if he'd had one with him. Out of the corner of his eye he saw that Sperber was unhappy with this. Pancake spoke, head bowed, in a low, halting voice. Just like his comrade, he too had not meant it like that. He bitterly regretted his misdemeanour and wanted to make up for it. There was no one there for Pancake, it looked as if he had no relations or, if he did, they didn't care. The court ordered a recess.

They were taken, handcuffed, to a room where there were two cells in the form of barred cages. Each was given a cage and they had to wait. Christian's handcuffs were too tight, he pointed it out to the guard. The guard informed the officer in charge, who loosened them a little. Then he asked if they were all right like that. Sperber arrived. 'You almost did something stupid, Herr Hoffmann, when you pointed out the special situation you were in, I thought we'd discussed that? I told you that that's my business. Control yourself, otherwise you'll just make things worse.

'Herr Doktor Sperber . . .'

'I know what you want to know. Are you always so impatient? Have a smoke first, calm down.'

'Will I be acquitted?'

The lawyer looked at Christian in disbelief, then at Pancake, who couldn't repress a grin.

'It seems you still don't really understand what you've done, Herr Hoffmann. You said something very bad. I would just advise you not to panic, panic's always an inappropriate response. From my experience I would say that things aren't desperate. It's the breakfast recess now; at lunch I'll have another word with the judge advocate, we know each other from our student days.'

'Then I'll be convicted? Prison?'

'Don't keep trying to anticipate decisions. It's not a question of detention but of the terms.'

'And . . . my place at university?'

'Herr Hoffmann' – Sperber seemed seriously exasperated – 'you can't really be that obtuse.' Shaking his head, he lit himself a cigarette. 'There's one thing I have to tell you. As I've already explained to your father, appeals' – he blew his cigarette smoke out of the window, it wasn't barred – 'are as good as never successful. They're just a waste of paper and can cause you trouble. Accept the verdict as it is. From the outset the courts make their decisions on the principle that the punishment must fit the crime. In your case, in both your cases'

– Sperber nodded across at Pancake, who was immediately roused from his apathetic state – 'the plain facts constitute an infringement of the laws cited and you, Herr Kretzschmar, must be very careful as to how you act; you will know why.'

In his *summation* Sperber described the mental state of the accused at the time of the offence as 'diminished'. He disapproved of what had happened, but at least in the case of Herr Hoffmann it could not be a question of a consistently hostile and negative attitude to 'our state'. After all, he had been the agitator in the group council of the senior high school and had received the certificate 'For good study in a socialist school' several times. He was socially active, had, for example, been editor of several wall newspapers at the high school and the senior high school. And he begged the court to remember his mother's maiden name.

The judge advocate expressed his disapproval of the behaviour of the accused. Everything was a question of attitude. In this case ingratitude was to the fore – after all Hoffmann owed his place at university to the generosity of the Workers' and Peasants' State. He had betrayed the trust put in him. He was guilty of a gross violation of his duty as leader of a military combat collective. Had disappointed the trust placed in him. He demanded twelve months' confinement. Sperber frowned, tried to get it reduced to ten months.

The next morning the judgment was *pronounced*:

In the Name of the People

In the case against
Lance Corporal Christian Hoffmann
b. 28/10/1965 in Dresden,
single, no previous convictions,
at present remanded in custody for crimes against
Section 220, sub-section 1, Public Disparagement,
on the basis of the hearing of 6/6/1986

*the 1st Division of the Dresden Military Court,
represented by . . .*

has delivered the following judgment:

*The accused is found guilty of Public Disparagement of the State according
to Section 220, sub-section 1 and sentenced to a punishment of*

twelve months' detention in the military prison.

*The period spent in custody will be taken into account. The period spent in
prison will not count towards his period of military service. His place to
study medicine at Karl-Marx University Leipzig, planned entry 05/10/1987,
is cancelled. Lance Corporal Hoffmann has to bear the cost of the
proceedings.*

*By law
signed*

Then Pancake: also twelve months' detention. The assessor read out
the grounds for the judgment. The court left the room. Christian and
Pancake had to sign the judgment and the grounds for judgment. The
clerk kept her hand firmly on the paper while they signed.

Transfer. Again a lorry arrived with VEB Service Combine written
on it. From Dresden they went to Frankfurt an der Oder. 'Right along
the wall,' Pancake joked, as he came back from Effects with Christian;
both had their kitbags with their possessions over their shoulder. Pancake was annoyed that he couldn't take his accordion. 'No amusement,'
the guard snapped, pushing them into the lorry. They travelled in
handcuffs. At some point during the hours on the road there was thumping on one of the cell doors. 'I need to go.'

'Sniff it up and spit it out,' the guard told him. Then he

asked, 'Anyone else?' A few put up their hands. The lorry stopped, a short discussion with the officer in charge. Go one at a time. Christian was chained to the guard. The toilet was at a provincial station that remained nameless for Christian; they went along subterranean passages and through back doors. In the toilet he urinated against the blue-tiled wall they had instead of a urinal; there were cigarette butts in the drain, metal ashtrays at chest height on the wall, the man next to him put his cigarette down on one. He asked no questions and finished as quickly as he could. The guard stood, half turned away, smoking, glanced at his watch. 'Get a move on, man, can't you pee quicker?'

The *remand detention centre* in Frankfurt an der Oder was small and dilapidated. The men who had been sentenced were taken to a custody room, where Pancake and Christian couldn't stand up straight. It was damp, in places the paint was flaking off the walls, the legs of the stools had mould on them. The bunks had been let down, the cell was overfull, they had to take it in turns to sleep. Christian lay on a bunk watching a drop of water growing like a bright pupil in the middle of a damp patch. Cockroaches rustled along the floor, ran across the walls. The other half of the night, when Pancake demanded his place, Christian sat at the table staring into the darkness with the shimmer of floodlights outside.

The next morning they were sent to the barber. The doors were low, you had to be careful not gash your forehead. The staircases were narrow, steps were missing, you had to make sure you didn't fall, that might have looked like deliberate disobedience. Men in handcuffs were waiting to have their hair cut. The barber was a little old man with gaps in his teeth and his hair combed straight back, giving him the look of an arctic loon. Christian remembered a book from his childhood: *Germany's Birds* it had been called, a green cigarette-card album that his clock-grandfather had given him. He'd seen a picture of the arctic loon in it. Christian's hair was shorn off with electric clippers, it didn't take a minute; the arctic loon knew what he was doing.

Transfer. Now the military detainees were separated from the other prisoners. The military detainees boarded the *Schweden*, as the vehicle was known, which took Christian and four others. At first they went northwards, through the Oder marshes, where the birds screeched and the flapping of their wings sometimes drowned out the clatter of the bolts on the cages, there was a smell of rushes and fish and kerosene. Then they turned off to the east, towards the Polish border.

Schwedt. A name of terror, murmured in the army with your hand over your mouth, familiar to every soldier, to hardly any civilians; Schwedt an der Oder: a new town established in the countryside, like Eisenhüttenstadt in the south, the place where the Friendship oil pipeline from the depths of the Soviet Union terminates, high-rise buildings made of prefabricated concrete slabs, a windswept plain, the gigantic petro-chemical combine. They got out. Christian saw: a barred gate with sentries, a road coming out of a forest, industrial pipelines along one side of the road, beyond them a field, in the distance the colourful rectangles of a mobile bee-house. Schwedt an der Oder Military Prison. From all the rumours about it Christian had imagined it would be more grandiose. But that? It looked small, unassuming, cramped. They were taken into a low concrete building, into a room that was bare apart from a portrait of the Minister of National Defence, a table and a few chairs.

'Put out your things,' the guard ordered. Christian and Pancake emptied their kitbags while the other prisoners waited outside in the corridor. The guard made a list of their possessions.

'Pick up your things. Fall in. Follow me.' With their kitbags over their shoulders Christian and Pancake followed the guard. In a flat-roofed shed, still outside the actual camp, they had to take everything out again. A guard threw them each a set of fatigues, they had to take off their detention clothes and put on the uniforms, which had no epaulettes. The guard read out the prison regulations.

'To the governor.'

That was a colonel. He was in the farthest shed. On the way there Christian was instructed as to how he was to report.

'Military prisoner Lance Corporal Hoffmann reporting for instruction, Comrade Colonel.'

The colonel, a stocky, fatherly-looking man, remained seated, leafing through Christian's file, and didn't look at him as he spoke. He talked of remorse, of necessary punishment, of trust and re-education. That word was the most frequent one in his speech. Re-education: for two-twenty meant that he, Hoffmann, was a very bad case. He'd soon lose the taste for that here, he, the governor, could promise him that. He, the governor, would turn him, Hoffmann, into a contrite member of the army and a well-educated citizen of our Republic. He could promise him that too.

The reception block, where the new arrivals were, was separated from the actual camp by a wall with barbed wire on top. There was a barred gate in the wall through which the guard led the new arrivals. There were watchtowers at the corners of the wall on which visibly bored guards were pointing light machine guns into the camp. The concrete wall was only the outer boundary, between the reception block and the camp, inside it there was a barbed-wire fence. Between the wall and the fence was a strip of gravel where dogs were sleeping.

Christian was taken into a shed. The air in the room and the corridor smelt musty. There were eighteen beds in the room, six bunks with three beds each. The guard showed Christian his locker and ordered him to stand there. The guard went out, Christian stared out of the window through which dusty light came. The window was barred, you could see one of the watchtowers and a strip of gravel with the dogs, of which two had now woken up. Only now did Christian understand what had happened to him and that this was his foreseeable future: Schwedt an der Oder Military Prison, one year, one irreplaceable year of his life. And that Here, Here you stand was burrowing itself deep into him, like a screw, he needed to distract himself and started to count: with the years of service that he still had to complete he would be discharged in the autumn of 1989, five years in the National People's Army and he'd no idea what would happen after that, perhaps Meno would help him. He couldn't stay standing but already the guard was back ordering him to do just that.

'We'll see to it that you're re-educated.'

The daily routine began with being woken at four in the morning. The prisoners jumped out of their beds, where they'd been sleeping in cotton vests, the genital area naked. Morning exercises and washing. In Christian's company there were forty-seven military prisoners sharing one washroom with ten water pipes. The water points had no taps, the taps were kept by Staff Sergeant Gottschlich and had to be screwed onto the pipes. They were usually issued.

After breakfast there was either *training in the facility* (drill training, putting on and taking off protective clothing, instruction in fire protection, march with extra-full pack, assault course) or work. For the disciplinary units – soldiers who had not been through a military court – work was mostly in the cellars of the sheds. Christian and Pancake were serving a sentence handed down by the court and were driven out to the Combine every day. There they sandpapered doors, repaired or made pallets, smoothed the edges of plastic furniture or screwed screws into screw-holes. Work lasted eight hours, after that they were taken back to the facility for training. After cleaning the room and their section, 8 p.m. lights out. There were no doors on the toilets, everyone could watch you doing your business.

'So you don't do something stupid like committing suicide,' Staff

Sergeant Gottschlich said. Hanging from the ceiling of the company corridor was a grotesquely bizarre object: a toy train made by earlier prisoners out of scraps of plastic from the Petrochemical Combine for the company commander's fortieth birthday. The train had thirty-six goods wagons in different colours. Because the wagons were so brightly coloured it was called the 'Orient Express'. There were coloured cards in the wagons and names on the coloured cards. The position of the name indicated the level of fulfilment of targets. It was an advantage to have your name in one of the first ten wagons. If you were in the middle, there were *drills*. One of these was to be woken at midnight and spend two hours standing in full rig. If your name was in the last or next-to-last wagon (Staff Sergeant Gottschlich wasn't entirely consistent in that) for more than a week, you were sent for a spell in the *U-boat*, where you also ended up for *recalcitrance, insubordination, failure to accept one's errors, uncooperative attitude, doing something stupid*. Doing something stupid could be not to sit *absolutely motionless, but ready to learn* during political education or on Thursdays during the communal viewing of Karl-Eduard von Schnitzler's *Black Channel* on TV2.

The official name for the U-boat was Detention. Detentions were announced at roll call. Before Christian went to the U-boat he had to go and see the doctor 'to determine suitability for detention'. The doctor was a young but weary man in a white coat but with no stethoscope. He asked Christian whether he was taking any medicine or had any illnesses.

'Acne vulgaris,' Christian said.

'That blooms even in the dark.' The doctor put a weary scribble on the detention-suitability-assessment form.

The U-boat was dark, since there were no windows, and Christian spent a long time there, a week, he guessed. During that time he had felt his way round every nook and cranny of the cell. The bucket beside the table for him to relieve himself had an enamel lid with two wire guide brackets; Christian learnt to use his sense of touch like a blind man, the writing on the lid was slightly raised and said 'Servus'. The blankets smelt of Spee washing powder and – it took him a while to work this out – of the lamas in Dresden Zoo, of lamas in the rain to be more precise. For a long time in the even longer darkness of the cell Christian could not get rid of the idea that he had reached the innermost point of the system. He was in the GDR, the country had fortified frontiers and a wall. He was in the National People's Army, which had barracks walls and guarded entrances. And in Schwedt Military Prison he was stuck in the U-boat, behind walls with no windows. So now he was entirely there, now he must have arrived. But more than that he must, Christian thought, be himself. He must be naked, his self laid bare, and he thought that he must now have the great thoughts and insights he'd dreamt of at home and at school. He sat naked on the floor but the only thought he had was that if you sat naked on stones for a while you got cold. That you were hungry and thirsty, that you can count your pulse, that in darkness you also get tired, that for a while you can hear nothing but dead silence and that then your ear starts to produce its own sounds, that your eye is constantly trying to light little cigarette-lighter flames, here and there and there, and that you go mad in the darkness, however many poems you know, novels you've read, films you've seen and memories you have.

Now, Christian thought, I really am Nemo. *No one.*

On a hot day in July, Christian, Pancake and twenty-eight other prisoners were sent to Effects. They were being transferred, they were told, to the Orient, as the chemical area round Leuna, Schkopau and Bitterfeld was known because of the colourful effusions from the factories. The chemical industry brought bread, prosperity and beauty and for it they needed workers. Handcuffed, they followed the Friendship oil pipeline that went from the town on the Oder, whose high-rise buildings were bright in the distance, to the Orient of the chemical industry in its main area, Samarkand, in the south-west of the Republic.

61

Carbide Island

Apart from crows, there were no birds there. As the summer twilight began to fall in the garden of Caravel the yearning, melodious lament of the blackbird could be heard; here, on Carbide Island there were no bird calls apart from the ugly, coarse croaking of huge flocks of crows that seemed to feel at home on the foam-washed banks of the Saale, the bend of which could be seen from the window, and gathered every evening in the pale skeletons of trees for sleep and for the stories of the day, the poet's 'day that has been today' . . . They chattered and cawed and fished around in the scum for edible matter, which was presumably washed up in sufficient quantities, and sometimes, when the lights went out in the cells on Carbide Island, they seemed to be laughing, giving voice to their gratingly repulsive mockery. Like a cloak of invisibility, the colour of their plumage, that shining coal-black, blended with that of the river, which flowed sluggishly and, almost every evening now, in August, illuminated by an iron-red sun, through the landscape of the chemical industry over which, fixed to the platforms at the top of the furnaces, the flag of Samarkand fluttered: a yellow flag, the yellow of the quarantine flag for ships, with a black retort on it. Christian and the others had been sent from Schwedt to Camp II, which took up a separate corridor on the fifth floor of the prison. On the corridor wall, beside the table for the guard on duty, was a 'daily schedule of work', abbreviated to DSW. It was similar to the one in Camp I: the early shift was woken at four (though here it was by the rising and falling wail of a siren, as if an alert for an impending air raid), followed by morning exercises and washing. Here the taps over the basins were fixed, but there wasn't always water – when Samarkand was 'on a lift', as they put it, when all the machines, filtering installations, cooling systems, works conduits were demanding water, it was a dribble that came out of the washroom taps. Also it wasn't drinking water that came out of the pipes but a liquid that was sometimes rusty, more often as yellow as soup, and smelt of floorcloths and rotten eggs. People said the smell came from carbide, from 'the other side', from across the Saale on the bank of which, connected to the prison by a bridge that looked as if it were coral-encrusted, there was a carbide factory. From the bridge, which the company approached at an easy march, it looked like an old steam locomotive that was bending down for a drink from the Saale. Pouring out of a cyclopean chimney were clouds of light-grey smoke that, below the clouds, mingled with the discharges from the coking plant, the chlorine works, the power stations lower down the Saale, creating a dark, unmoving swirl that widened out at the top like a flower head.

Christian and his companions went in with the early shift along a passageway barely lit by fluorescent tubes, past a porter's lodge with flowery wallpaper, through a barrier with a 'No smoking' sign over it. Conversations ceased, silent and hunched up, driven on by Staff Sergeant Gottschlich's 'At the double', the prisoners hurried into the factory. It was already light, the air already oppressive, it was going to be a hot day. The company waited in a yard that the tall grey-dusted buildings on either side turned into a well-shaft. Cylinder drums, running diagonally across the yard, turned slowly, workers in blue-grey clothes and hard hats were running to and fro on gratings above the drums. Water was pouring over the drums, it seemed to come directly from the Saale. The drums boomed and rumbled as if boulders were turning round inside them. Strange noises came from the buildings – a shrill, dangerous-sounding hum, as if a special kind of stinging insect were being held captive; as if there were a new breed of long-extinct Meganeura dragonflies or carboniferous hornets behind the closed doors. The buildings were grey: mud-grey, the colour of lead dust, carbide dust that had settled in thick layers on pipes, walls, stairs, even on the windows, simple openings with flapping rags made in the walls. What Christian saw was a coral reef of muck and in every second during which the rust-brown cylinder drums turned and smoke from the chimneys crept up under the clouds, darkening the sky, dust was trickling, falling, crackling in fresh layers on the old ones hardened by wind and weather. Christian looked across at a woman parking her red Simson moped by a furnace and heading off towards a square brick tower at the back – he saw the outline of her shoes in the dust, at first cut sharply into the yielding layer but soon powdered over with the dust drifting down, the sharp edges blurred, gradually the footmark filled in, became invisible. After a ten-minute wait there were epaulettes of grey powder on Pancake's shoulders, their caps, boots were snowed up; Staff Sergeant Gottschlich wiped his wristwatch clean. The dust got between their teeth, in their eyes, making them inflamed, rubbed against their groin until it was raw. And then there was the wind. The wind, ferreting round, bringing unrest, the blind marshal of the weather. Like a dark-grey djinn rising out of an unsealed bottle, a spiral of dust swelled up over the carbide factory; at ground level, where clumps of grass stuck up like the mops of hair of people buried in the carbide powder, the spiral was as slender as a boa, rising up, against the wagons on the goods line behind the factory, like a trombone that twisted and turned, spreading out its bell above the furnaces lining the top of the locomotive.

Pancake accepted it with a shrug of the shoulders. He'd heard that work in the carbide factory was well paid and when a foreman came to instruct them in their work he brightened up and started to haggle. Gottschlich was occupied elsewhere and the prisoners were left to themselves and the carbide people. Christian saw the bars on the windows of the furnace shed where the foreman took them. Here, not far above the ground, the windows were of glass, wiping them had left bright smears, like bull's-eye glass, slim triangles of dust had built up in the corners.

'But you can pay me extra.' Pancake smiled. Aha, so he'd only kept his self-assurance hidden. He was a smart lad, knew when it was better to keep your head down and say nothing. To play the repentant: Christian hadn't believed his 'reformed character' act. In the evening he would often talk about prisons he'd been in. There were people, even ones as young as Pancake, who saw the country from the prison perspective, with 'bars before their eyes'. They'd been round the prisons of the Republic, knew the guards, their preferences and weaknesses, knew whether you could bribe them and what with. Pancake didn't know Schwedt and Carbide Island, but they knew him, as Christian discovered. Pancake had immediately come to an understanding with Gottschlich, each sensed a 'brother' in the other. Chance, sometimes just the accident of birth, could decide what dress you wore: dark blue or striped. The only difference in expression was whether you hit people as per the law or not. That was something Christian had had to learn: that you didn't waste words. A punch was quicker than a word and who was right was not sorted out by discussion, at least not by oral discussion. *Do you want it in writing? To get something in writing*. That meant something different in there from *outside*, that had to be learnt as well.

'We'll see,' the foreman said. Pancake raised his head, had a quick look round.

'You can look after it for me. I'll collect it when I'm out again. You won't lose out on it.'

'For the moment you get your seventeen per cent.' The prisoners were entitled to 17 per cent of the normal wage, if they reached their targets. If the foreman was open to discussion like that, the situation regarding the workforce must be bad and with that their prospects of reaching the planned targets. Christian was put in the Gustav furnace shop.

Carbide. He had heard of the substance, seen the film *Carbide and Sorrel*, knew that Grandfather Arthur's Wanderer bike had a carbide lamp; but he had no idea exactly how it worked. That was now explained to him by Asza Burmeister, the tapper of furnace 8 in Gustav furnace shop, an oldish worker who had been 'in carbide' for twenty-two years, had trained as a carpenter and had also been to sea. He took a piece of carbide and poured some water over it. 'Y'see, Krishan,' (he called him the same as Libussa, which pleased him) 'now that makes acetylene. It's welding gas, that is, welding gas. An' now when I hold my cigar against it,' (he smoked Jägerstolz cigars) 'there's a bang an' it lights up. That's the way a carbide lamp works. Only no bang, it shouldn't go bang.' Asza spoke very quickly, it was difficult to follow him, he often repeated individual words, rolled his 'r's in a dialect Christian had never heard before. 'I'm a Sudeten lousewort,' Asza said, avoiding a direct answer. Asza: an unusual name, but Christian didn't ask. He couldn't ask many questions. Questions were forbidden. Conversations were forbidden, fraternization. The workers and the prisoners should have as little as possible to do with each other, but the prisoners had to be trained, that was where the problems started. Gottschlich was supposed to keep a check but, as Christian soon realized, appeared only rarely. That had two reasons and they were: heat and dust. What is heat? Asza, if he hadn't been so taciturn while working (during the breaks he would sit, left leg over a chair, with his Jägerstolz and a bottle of rhubarb juice, which was available to the carbide workers at a reduced price, muttering 'Piraeus, Faroes, Bordoh' – the harbours he'd seen), Asza could have said, heat, brother, you can't explain it. The furnace has a white heart and each heartbeat comes flying like a red-hot iron. The shift lasted twelve hours. That had its good side for afterwards the prisoners didn't have to go to the ploughland as they called the training ground: drill, assault course, tactics, instruction in protection. On the other hand it was twelve hours in an atmosphere Christian would not have thought imaginable. When Ron Siewert, the Free German Youth secretary of the Thälmann work team, came over from the furnace next to theirs Christian would only see him when he was two or three metres away. Along with Asza, King

Siewert, as he was known, was the best furnace tapper: no absences, no dawdling, no boozing at work, no negligence. *Negligence* was bringing carbide into contact with water; negligence was not wearing a hard hat; negligence was working without wearing welder's goggles. Siewert would appear out of the greenish haze of dust (hanging lamps on completely encrusted wires that looked as if they were inside the wreck of the *Titanic*), open his beard and shout to ask Asza how the furnace was to be run.

Carbide. The word pursued Christian into his sleep, for here he didn't dream. When he got back from his shift, he was *all in*. He flopped onto his bunk and fell asleep. Pancake had to shake him awake when Gottschlich did his rounds.

Carbide. What was it? Trees (there were meadows along the banks of the Saale that were reduced to ash) were living beings, they felt heat and cold, growth and decline, they blossomed and withered. But this, this grey stuff, this carbide? Time consists of water, the future of carbide, they said in Samarkand. The furnace was several storeys high and it produced carbide, carbide, always the dazzling white melt when Asza burnt a hole in the skin of the viscous carbide with the flame cutter, directed along caterpillar tracks, so that it would run along the 'fox', as Asza called the tapping spout, into the 'walrus' (the water-cooled cylinder drum). Christian thought, I can't stick this out. Christian thought, Meno would say, There, you see, that's completely unironic. Christian thought, if only you were like Pancake. Keep your head down. Always fall on your feet. Take things as they come with a shrug of the shoulders. He doesn't get worked up about being locked up here but about the fact that he earns so little money. What sticks in his craw is the 17 per cent wages, not the hundred per cent Carbide Island. Still, Christian had *become smarter*. To be smarter meant keeping your trap shut. A few of the others in the cells still hadn't become smarter, still talked about *error* and *misfortune*, wanted *consultations with their lawyer*, and *appeals* and *visits*. But no visits were allowed on Carbide Island.

They moaned instead of sleeping. They were *damaged*. They ended up in the U-boat. There everything was as per regulations.

Carbide. When the wind turned to the south, it blew the dust onto the island. Roses grew against the southern wall. Christian would have liked to know what colour they were. They had no scent. The flowers looked as if they were made of plaster. Even the leaves and shoots had a light-grey dusting, a stucco-like beauty heavy with sleep.

Asza said, 'Anyone who sticks it out for a whole summer in the carbide will stay.' Carbide. What was it, what did they need it for? Christian learnt: it needed coke and quicklime, the mixture was called Möller. A round furnace was charged with it. Christian had assumed the furnaces here would work in the same way as the stove at home with coal on a grating through which the ash fell into the ash pan underneath. But he had never seen – never mind heard – a stove anything like this furnace. Three Soderberg electrodes, several metres high and arranged in an equilateral triangle, jutted down into the furnace, were electrically charged and, since the material from which they were made formed resistance, became hot, creating an arc with a temperature of up to 3,000°C. In it the Möller reacted to produce calcium carbide. The arc was dazzling white and hummed in the furnace opening that Asza called the nostril of hell. The hum was accompanied by the thump of the coke-crusher, since, before they were put in the mixing tower to be made into Möller, the coke and limestone had to be of a certain particle size. It sounded as if a herd of bison were stampeding across the shed, a knocking and rattling, sometimes a deafening clatter, as if goods wagons full of sheet metal were being tipped out. The furnaces used an immense amount of electricity – so much that on some days in Halle-Neustadt the lights went out when the early shift started and high-rise blocks stood there in the semi-dark like angry mountain trolls. Furnace 8 was a vicious dragon. Asza knew it well and respected it. When Asza burnt open the carbide crust, it sounded like a record arm being pulled right across the record, potent and dangerous, and it wasn't always carbide that shot out into the 'fox', there were impurities, residues of quicklime and coke that ought not to be there. The shift supervisors knew that and kept quiet about it; they were under pressure from the targets and twenty-two tappings per shift were the norm, twenty-two times the white-hot snot had to pour out of the dragon's nostrils. But the god of industrial processes had blocked them with lumps. Even at 2,200°C the molten mass of the Möller tended to form lumps and the chemical reaction threatened to come to a halt. Preventing this was Christian's job. With iron poles several metres long that they called rods he poked around in the glowing mass. What did such an iron pole weigh? Enough for it to be too heavy after half an hour. There was a steel thermometer beside the steps up to the top of the furnace, over the years it had been covered by more and more layers of flue dust and now looked more like a stalactite than a thermometer. When he was standing at the furnace using the rod, Christian had the feeling he was being smelted into a new kind of creature, a cross between an otter (sweat, the side away from the furnace) and a broiling fowl (facing the opening). The heat made you tired, despite that you had to be alert. Sometimes hot oil would spurt out of a leaky pipe, land on your tough cotton clothing and sparks would spray out from the burner, setting the cloth alight. Once Asza was in flames but Ruscha, the second tapper (they worked in fours per furnace and shift), calmly threw a blanket over him and smothered the blaze. Pancake, working the rods with Christian, had leapt aside in alarm. The dust made your throat scratchy and this was soon followed by the cough, a never-ending retching and barking to clear out the dust; it was worse over in the chlorine works, Asza said, over in the chlorine works they exceeded the officially permitted level of air contamination by 100 per cent. The heat made you thirsty.

'Some time ago,' said King Siewert, 'they used to give us vitamins, fresh fruit, oranges – but now? Rhubarb juice! Rhubarb juice all the time! Nothing but rhubarb juice every day!'

'But you're in the Party,' Ruscha said, 'you tell those up there what it's like here. Where's Monkeydad?' Monkeydad was what they called the departmental Party Secretary. 'Sitting at his desk but never gets his arse off it. Polishing up his speeches . . . You tell him, King.'

'I do, I do! But they never tell you anything. I'm none the wiser when I come out than when I went in.'

'They're driving the furnaces to rack and ruin. If one of them should blow up, then Yuri Gagarin here'll be in the landing capsule; some red-hot communists at last.'

For their thirst there was rhubarb juice, pressed by VEB Lockwitz-grund. The juice was brought on a cart by a woman, 'Rhubarb-juice Liese'. Of indefinite age, though already a pensioner, she sold the juice throughout Samarkand in order to supplement her pension. She was thin and bent as she walked, probably from the advanced stages of osteoporosis, and Christian never saw her other than in the same old-fashioned black dress, to which the yellow hard hat with the retort emblem of Samarkand formed a jarring contrast. People said that Rhubarb-juice Liese was not quite right in the head, she had lost her husband and her son in the war and had been raped, not by the Russians but by a Canadian unit. She had worked in 'the chlorine', which had left her with a rusty laugh that could be heard during the breaks, when the furnaces (contrary to regulations) were shut down and the noise fell to a bearable level. With a trembling, claw-like hand she gave out the bottles of rhubarb juice and took the money, which she kept in a leather conductor's bag, giving it a long and thoughtful look. She stopped in front of Pancake, who was resting next to King Siewert, and felt his face, which confused him; he frowned in irritation.

'She fancies you,' Ruscha joked.

'Oh, shut your gob.' Pancake stood up, walked away from Rhubarb-juice Liese.

'You just be careful, she's got the evil eye,' Asza said. 'I once went to see a fortune-teller in Piraeus, she had just the same look.'

'So that's why you're still here! Twenty-two years!' Ruscha tapped his forehead. 'Only a nutcase would stay in carbide for so long.'

'And you?' Pancake had come back and looked Ruscha up and down contemptuously.

'I'm not here to improve my mind, chum, but to make money. I do my twelve hours –'

'And all the rest can go to blazes, eh?' King laughed.

'There's fire everywhere,' Ruscha replied, shrugging his shoulders.

Christian sat on one side in silence, listening to their stories, mostly about carbide and women, and trying to get some rest. He sensed that he wasn't taken seriously. Pancake, the former blacksmith with the strength of an ox, they did take seriously. Not him. He was one of the 'white collars' as the workers contemptuously called the management. He worked like them, they didn't make things easy for him, they didn't help him. Despite that, he wasn't one of them, there remained an insurmountable barrier. He hardly took part in the conversations at all, perhaps it was his silence that made the others so reticent. One day, however, Ruscha stood up and strolled over to Christian, who was drinking his rhubarb juice. 'What I wanted to ask, mate – you don't happen to belong to the firm, do you?'

'Sit down, Ruscha,' Pancake said.

'Wouldn't be the first time they'd dumped a stoolie on us,' he said threateningly.

'Not everyone likes shootin' his mouth off like you,' Asza said. 'Just be happy we've got the lad, or do you want to do extra shifts again?'

'If the dough's right . . .'

'The class standpoint can go to hell . . .'

'Rhubarb juice, rhubarb juice, I've got the very best rhubarb juice,' said Liese, praising her wares.

Once Christian had settled in, he began to observe Asza, Ruscha and the other workers and spent a lot of time thinking about them. Ron

Siewert lived in a high-rise block in Halle-Neustadt, which was cut through by a four-lane motorway connecting Samarkand with the rest of the Orient. He got up at four for the early shift, went to bed at eight in the evening. His apartment was tiny, he and his wife had one child; his grandparents lived in a little room. Dumper trucks were going round and round the building day and night, the paths consisted of wooden planks. The children played on the piles of rubble or in the rubbish containers by the huge central shopping mall. White and decked out with flags, it was stuck in a sea of mud. Asza dreamt of going to sea again, as he had done when he was young. He wanted to go round all the harbours he'd been to again, in an ocean-going yacht with a four-man crew. He lived in Halle-Neustadt as well, Housing Complex 2, Block 380, House 5, apartment 17.

'And if you come to visit me, Krishan,' Asza said, 'and can't find my apartment, 'cause it's a bit difficult, difficult – it's the one with the red flowers on the balcony, all the others just have white ones.'

When they sat on their chairs during the breaks, silently smoking, silently sitting with their heads leaning forward:

(because there'd been an explosion: because there was a fault in the water-cooling system, water had come out of the cracked rubber hoses and combined with carbide to produce acetylene, which was spreading,

because acetylene was inflammable and exploded in the temperatures in the furnace,

because the carbide in the air, the dust fairies, also combined with the moist air to produce acetylene so that sometimes ball lightning seemed to be zooming round the furnace shop,

because molten carbide could suddenly shoot out of the furnace and hit the tappers and rod-men,

because impurities could be deposited on the furnace shell and gradually eat their way through the fireproof masonry of the furnace wall then be hurled out of the furnace like lava surrounded by tongues of flame, because the dust-removal vent hadn't been built,

because the effluent from the process was spewing out of open pipes as a toxic slick into the Saale,

because carbide was an indispensable component of plastic, artificial fibres, synthetic rubber,

because Samarkand urgently needed the long-overdue investment for other parts of their operations so therefore nothing would change,

because the hum of the furnace transformers, the interconnected single-phase transformers with an output of 53 MVA, and the rotary current transformer that, in order to increase output, was in parallel with the neighbouring carbide furnace, caused headaches, unbearable throbbing headaches,

because these transformers had a tendency to short-circuit and in the shower of sparks Asza would start to pray that the Lord would let them all get home safely, because there were planned targets and therefore 'blanking': at the times of peak demand, during the day, when there was often less power available, the furnaces were cut back, working like pumped storage power plants as buffers for the public network – but operated at full power during the night and on Sundays, when there was power available, to make up for the loss of production,

because there was not only carbide in Samarkand, there was the vinyl chloride department, electrolysis, where the workers inhaled toxic gases and died at fifty, the lime works where the carbide factory got its quicklime from, the fibre-spinning mill, the ball crushers, a conveyor belt with capsules the size of spaceships revolving on rollers, which ground the brown lumps of carbide to dust,

because retirement at sixty had once more been cancelled,

because the cars on the four-lane urban motorway drove and drove on and drove past)

they sat in silence, seeming to Christian like damned souls.

*

He observed Pancake. He'd driven Burre so far, he and others.

'Why did you do it? Support me?'

'Because it wasn't right, Mummy's Boy.'

'And Burre?'

'He was weak, that's all.'

'You think that's right?'

'The weak have to serve the strong, that's the way things are.'

'No, it's the other way round. The strong have to support the weak.'

'Well, yes, if it's a matter of your own turf. Everyone has their own turf and anyone who belongs to your own turf has to be protected. Even if he's weak. That's what it's always been like.'

'But that's why I still don't understand why you supported me.'

'You have a home, you have someone who comes to visit you, you have a place where you belong.'

'You haven't?'

Something strange happened: the resistance Christian had long felt inside himself – to society, to socialism as he experienced it and saw it – disappeared, gave way to a feeling of being in agreement with everything. It was right that he was there. He was an opponent of the army and of the system and that was why he was being punished. No country in the world handled its opponents with kid gloves. Christian sensed that here, in the chemical empire eaten away by brown-coal open-cast mines and poisoned rivers, he was in the right place for him. He had found his place in society, he was needed here (he could see the despair, the quiet pleas behind all the severe masks). He did what he was told to do and if he wasn't told to do anything, he did nothing. And when he was doing nothing, he took pleasure in little things: a dandelion in postbox yellow, the clarity of a line of migrating birds (as autumn began, the greylag geese passed over the Orient). It was so much simpler to let go and not resist. If you did exactly what was demanded, the punishments passed you by, you were left in peace. Why struggle? What use was it knocking your head against a brick wall until it was bleeding? A wise man, he remembered, walks with his head bowed, humble like the dust.

In the evening he sometimes looked out of the cell window. By that time the swirling wind had mostly died down; across the black Saale and beside the coke-drying plant, which let off its soot now, sending housewives dashing out in their aprons to save their washing, you could see the housing estate where Asza, King Siewert, Ruscha and many of the other carbide workers lived. New blocks surrounded a square, in the middle was a windmill, its sails turning against the chemically inflamed sky of Samarkand.

62

Nu ʒayats – pogodi

If you wanted to know what was new in the district, the place to go to was Veronica, a building in Querleite where a communal bathhouse was run for those who didn't have a bathroom of their own or, as in the House with a Thousand Eyes, where there was only one used by too many tenant families. At the beginning of the winter of 1986 three events caused a stir: the return of Muriel Hoffmann from the reformatory, the strange operation of the Minister of National Defence and the story of the exchanged child. Meno went to the bathhouse once a week, as the water allocation and usage plan allowed, showered, observed, listened. Herr Unthan, who was in charge of the bathhouse, was blind. He made his way round the cellar of 12 Querleite, where the baths were housed, with its atmosphere of steam and spray, dimly lit by Schuckert bulbs, from its time as a popular sanatorium, whose contacts could still withstand the damp, with the sureness of a sleepwalker. The cubicles were approached along duckboards with pimpled rubber

mats; two still had the good zinc baths with the wind vane symbol of
the Erzgebirge firm of Krauss that had originally been installed there;
two others were wooden tubs and the last two injection-moulded plastic
baths with original enamel signs above them on which was written, in
black Gothic letters: 'O Krauss, O name of fearful chime – I never
bathe, I love my grime' (the sarcastic advert was by Joachim Ringel-
natz), as well as, presumably, to deny the boys of the district any excuse:
'This rule holds true for ev'ry house: you need a bath – you need a
Krauss.' The cubicles were secured with brass padlocks that hung in
the gloom like greeny-gold jewel beetles; since, however, the wood of
the doors had become so rotten with the damp and mould you could
easily put your hand through them, this security measure was like
trying to keep jewels in cardboard boxes with strong metal locks.
Beyond the baths, farther back in the cellar, there were shower cubicles
with brown plastic swing doors that reached from the knees to the
shoulders of an average adult and sounded like a Jew's harp when
opened or closed. Herr Unthan had a grandfather who had played the
violin and since Herr Unthan senior lacked both arms, he'd done it in
a circus, with just his toes; Herr Unthan junior had a shellac record,
'incontrovertible proof', that he never played to anyone, even though
when the Tietzes came to have a bath Ezzo would, by his expressions of disbelief as far as his grandfather's skills were concerned,
provoke Herr Unthan to statements such as 'He died poor, but with
rich eyes.'

Niklas too would have liked to have had the record for the Friends
of Music but Herr Unthan junior's response to all offers was silence,
as he lugged bucket after bucket of hot water to the baths and showers
using a yoke decorated in folk-art style. The communal baths had only
two cold-water connections, which were linked by pipes to a tank over
a stove, for which there was a significant pile of briquettes in the back-
yard of Veronica, tipped out there in the summer by Plisch and Plum
from their boss's Framo pickup truck and, if the winter was long, Herr

Unthan very busy and the deluge 'after us' cool, people stole without compunction.

'Well, Meno, too much ink on your fingers again?'

'And you, Niklas? Washing off the rosin?'

'Oh well, you know how it is.'

'Frau Knabe, I've forgotten my bath salts, could you pour me some over?'

'But it's from over there, Frau Fiebig.'

'But that's what I meant, Frau Knabe. Could you pour me some from your cubicle over there into my bathtub. If you would be so kind.'

Laughter, the hum of voices. Curses and jokes. Gossip and scandal from the district and the town. Sometimes someone would start singing and mostly others would join in. Herr Unthan slaved away with the water (it never occurred to anyone to help him) and Meno listened:

'You still haven't told us the story of the minister, Herr Tietze.'

'Ah, this is how it was, Herr Kühnast.'

The Minister of Defence, who naturally took a military approach to matters, was, as happens to men of a more advanced age, visited by a problem in a place where orders are no use. The Minister of Defence thought about it and called his adjutant.

'Find me the best specialist in the Republic!'

'The best specialist for the task in question, Comrade Minister, is in Dresden, St Joseph's Hospital.'

Surely he wasn't trying to tell him, the Minister growled, that in the whole of the capital of the German Democratic Republic there was no specialist for that manoeuvre of the same rank!

'The specialists were unanimous in naming that name, Comrade Minister.'

'All right, then. Make the necessary preparations and have the comrade brought here.'

Dr Focke, the Chief Urologist at St Joseph's was, like many

urologists, a man with a tendency to fly into a rage and express himself very directly.

'Then I'll just have to fly to Dresden,' the Minister told his adjutant. 'I have to check out things at the Military Academy there anyway. See to it that everything's prepared in that hospital and have the helicopter on stand-by. I want this Dr Focke to operate on me the day after tomorrow.'

Dr Focke said he was willing to do that. He asked for all the documents to be sent to him immediately. He had reserved a single room for the Herr Minister, but he refused to have the crucifix over the bed removed.

The Minister, who had led many companies, battalions and regiments, been in command of many attacks on the Eastern front as a young officer and spent time in the Nazis' prisons, was a man with a tendency to fly into a rage and express himself very directly.

'And so,' Niklas Tietze explained, as he knocked the long-handled wooden back-brush against the cellar ceiling, making the brush head, which could be hired from a whole collection for twenty pfennigs, come off and drop into the next shower cubicle, 'and so a compromise was agreed.'

It did not, as every sensible person would have imagined, consist of moving the operation to another Dresden hospital. Dr Focke wanted his tried-and-tested team around him, wanted to be able to concentrate fully on the task in hand and not be 'stuck in an alien atmosphere', as he explained to the adjutant on the telephone. But it was the Minister they were talking about! The latter, listening in on the second receiver, was, Niklas told his amazed audience in their bathwater or under dripping showers, *in the picture*; first he had gone bright red then, with a grim smile and crushing the receiver in his hand, stomped up and down muttering '*Nu ʒayats – pogodi*.' Just you wait, hare.

'Then he had a look at a map of Dresden and tapped a large patch of green with his finger. The large green patch close to which, on the other side of the busy Stübelallee, St Joseph's lay, was the Great Garden. Just there, on the meadow that had been hurriedly reconnoitred and declared suitable, even though already attacked by hostile, negative hoarfrost, a tented camp was erected by the 7th Armoured Division, which was stationed in Dresden and had been put on unscheduled alert, and the officer cadets of the Friedrich Engels Military Academy. The Dresdeners were probably wondering why on that day there were diversions in operation on the busy Stübelallee, the equally busy Dr-Richard-Sorge-Strasse and the Brücke der Einheit, why the open-air Junge Garde stage, the exhibition centre on Fučikplatz, even the Zoo on the other side of the large patch of green, remained closed. Only the little narrow-gauge railway carrying cheerful schoolchildren through the fresh morning air had been forgotten, at which the Minister's adjutant flew into a rage. The whistling might disturb the doctor, it was to be stopped at once! The adjutant, a far-sighted man, had even taken into consideration the fact that the operating area, since it was situated in an open meadow, might be liable to instability, which was confirmed by a call to the department responsible: there was a plague of voles that had long been out of control. Several companies of soldiers with torches had therefore spent the night emptying standard cartridges of carbide down holes in the ground; on the morning of the operation they had managed to blow away the oppressive stench by means of an aeroplane propeller mounted on a lorry.'

'And Focke?' Herr Kühnast asked.

'It took him four hours. He told me he *enjoyed* it.'

'Poor Gudrun,' Meno murmured.

But Gudrun started to sing, first of all a folk song, then 'A shower bath, a shower bath, to wash those blues away, Annie's got a new sweetheart, the handsome Johnny Grey.' She sang alone, for they were lines she made up while scrubbing the children, Niklas and herself in the shower. Then something of the merriment would return that she must have bubbled over with as a girl and that reappeared at rare moments, sometimes for no reason at all. Then it could happen that Gudrun would put a washbasin on her head, shout something to Herr Orré, if he was in the neighbouring cubicle, at which the actor would leap out into the corridor, naked apart from a washbasin on his head and holding an elderly umbrella, which was used to keep the spray from the first shower out of the bathtubs, and perform a flip-flop-slapping tap dance with Gudrun Tietze to the accompaniment, bawled out rather than sung, of the other bathers: 'We were often stony broke, / bein' broke it ain't no joke. / But now I've got a new hat / an' I feel much better for that. / Life has its ebb an' its flow, / you get tossed about to an' fro, / sometimes you're here, sometimes there / but now I'm a millionaire!'

Herr Unthan had difficulty getting past the two dancers. The buckets had to be emptied – into the zinc storage tanks that, like lavatory cisterns only higher, were hung from the cellar ceiling to provide the necessary water pressure. In order to get the water out of the buckets and into the containers, there were rails fixed to the sides of the shower cubicles up which rope hoists ran; they had tipping handles, to which the buckets were attached, and when Herr Unthan pulled a lever that worked via the rope hoist the bucket, just three metres above the floor, tipped forward and emptied the water into the storage container that could take enough water to shower a family of four. Since there were only two buckets, it didn't make sense to accelerate one's shower, as some intelligent observers had wanted to do, by simply pouring the contents of a bucket over one's head. In the first place that wasn't a proper shower and would have hurt Herr Unthan's professional pride; in the second a safety regulation indicated that such a procedure was not permitted.

'Good day, Herr Rohde. I hope you don't mind but Herr Unthan's put me in the *banja* with you.'

'Hello, Herr Adeling. No water for you at home either?'

'Oh, water, yes, but the stories, Herr Rohde, the stories. May I put my soap beside yours. There's a cat winking on yours, quite unmistakable.'

Frau Knabe, the dentist, was telling the story of the exchanged child. And while she was talking, in his mind's eye Meno could see the Roecklers, the couple who ran the dance school of the same name on Lindwurmring, to whose daughter the unbelievable event, which had been a topic of conversation in the town for months, had happened.

'One day Silke Roeckler, their youngest daughter, went to the shop of the military hospital. You can go in, the guards let you through and sometimes they have things you can't get from Frau Zschunke's or in Sweet Corner or Konsum.'

Meno heard the click of the abacus that Frau Knabe was imitating, making her majestic bosom press against the plastic door, to the delight of the men in the shower cubicle opposite. Frau Roeckler was small with a pale, waxy complexion in the white pleated dress she wore with the gold lamé shoes for the dancing lessons partnering her husband in his black tails. In perfect posture, with doll-like make-up, as graceful as one of Kändler's Meissen figures, she would float, her still-black hair swept up in a shiny 1950s style, across the chessboard floor of the dance school on the first floor, accompanied by the drizzle of the grand piano beside the pale-leaved Monstera, on which, when the central paste chandelier was lit, the shadow of a stuffed hobby from the Bassaraba pet shop, which was hanging from the stucco ceiling, would fall.

'I think she went to the shop because, unusually for August, they had oranges there, and when she came out, she found a different child from her own in her pram.'

—Pliés, pirouettes, complicated tango steps: Eduard Roeckler seemed born to do them, even though dancing had not always been his profession; it was his passion, as was art in general; he was deeply moved by the passion and beauty it can convey. He wanted to be a painter and did a course in microscopic drawing at art college and that saved his life during the war, in which he ended up in Königsberg and Riga; he met a woman, that same floating Magdalene Roeckler, who came from a dynasty of dance teachers; after that war he too wanted to do nothing but dance. Hundreds of pictures on the walls of the dance school bore witness to his continuing passion for painting and microscopic drawing; he thought the large mirrors, such as they had in other dance schools, pointless. 'If you have to have a mirror, let it be a face close to you,' he used to say.

'The guard called for a doctor; on that day the microbiologist of the military hospital, a Romanian called Doctor Varga, was there. He gave her an injection and she came round. They established that the child had had many operations. Silke Roeckler screamed, she was completely hysterical.'

'How can you say that, Frau Knabe?' Herr Kühnast objected. 'You have no children of your own. Put yourself in the poor woman's situation, simply terrible. – What happened next?'

'There was an immediate investigation, of course. The whole complex of the military hospital, all the Russians' houses on Lindwurmring and Grünleite were cordoned off.'

And Meno remembered how he had been called upon as an interpreter, for he too had heard that there were oranges in the shop there, and had gone home early on that day, a hot Friday in August, to get a little present for Anne; he'd called Barbara, and she had come from the furrier's; a woman had looked at him and said, 'You're another of these stooges of the Russians', in a quiet but clearly audible voice. The commander of the military hospital was in despair, he promised to do everything in his power to clear the matter up and get the stolen child back.

'But to no avail, they still haven't found the child.'

'How old was the boy?' Herr Kühnast asked.

'Eight months. The other child was about the same age.'

'But they ought to be able to find out about it. The child must have been operated on by a specialist, surely he can be found, Frau Knabe. And he would know who the mother was.'

'I heard that the trail goes cold somewhere on the Russian border.'

'A cover-up. And the Roeckler lad's growing up as a Russian, with no memory of his real parents, unable to speak their language. But you can't leave an eight-month-old child by itself like that. I don't understand it.'

'Yes, and then there was that solidarity bazaar, on Lindwurmring. The commander of the military hospital was devastated; although it's not certain it was someone from the hospital, or a Russian at all, there were visitors there as well, it still happened on his patch. You can't imagine what went on . . . they turned everything upside down and the guard who was nearby's been arrested.'

'Oh, God, yes, that solidarity bazaar with the matryoshka dolls, chai from the samovar and accordions . . . the stuff they happen to have.'

'That's rather condescending, don't you think, Herr Kühnast? It's not their fault,' Meno said.

'All right, Herr Rohde. We all know where you come from. And you don't have any children either.'

Meno remembered: the Russian women had cooked some food, a whole cauldron full, and stood there waiting, anxious and embarrassed. A lot of local people had come to the solidarity bazaar. They had walked up in silence and spat into the cauldron one after the other.

'Yes, and then Magda Roeckler went over to the Russians and said just the same as you, Herr Rohde. "It's not your fault." And then she said to the others, "Please, please don't do that."'

While the story was being told the blind Herr Unthan wound bucket after bucket of warm water up into the storage tanks.

63

Castalia

Meno wrote,

rooms, one above the other, linked by thin bridges and the cables for clunky, black Bakelite telephones. Father said, 'Beware of countries where poems are popular. Places where people recite lines in the trams, others join in until eventually whole compartments are echoing with rhymes, office-workers with tears running down their cheeks, holding on to the strap with their right hand, in their left their ticket for the conductor, who keeps reciting to the end of the poem before he clips the tickets', he doesn't miss either a line or a ticket and manages to issue penalty notices while weeping at the beauty of Pushkin's lines, 'places where, before the teams line up in the ice-hockey stadiums, Mayakowski is recited', the stadium announcer reads it out and the crowd chants it after him, 'everywhere in that country there is cruelty and fear, falsehood rules. Beware of the country where the poets fill stadiums . . . Beware of the country where verses are a substitute.' Truth, truth . . . the choruses echoed across the Elbian river, Scholars' Island came in sight. The major educational project . . . The enlightenment had been brought in, the structure grew, layer upon layer. Many years had passed since the building of the wall that enclosed the country and divided the capital, the Copper Island of the government. For many years the roses had grown, slowing down time, and when I stepped onto Scholars' Island, the paper republic, where Hermes-Verlag was going to one of the weekly editorial and committee meetings, the speed with which the water was dripping from the leaking pipes, the undiminished effect of gravity, which made the contents of the ashtrays from the smoke-ridden rooms of Editorial Office II float down into the oily puddles covering the inner courtyard, seemed unreal to me, as unreal as the figures moving with measured tread in the oddly dry, sepia light, my colleagues, my superiors; specialists who wrote a report;

staff of the institutes that give us backing against the demands of the censors, against the ideological stomach ache of strict comrades, the narrow-mindedness, the pitfalls, the unpredictable twists and turns of the Book Ministry. It was in the depths of Scholars' Island, only accessible with a special card, an escort who knew his way around and nimble surfing of the paternosters. Creatures I found interesting from an anthropological point of view, categories of cave-dwellers, pale as plants grown out of the light, pawing at the world above ground with knuckles that were the jangle of telephones, muffled voices that seem to be creeping up out of sealed rusted catacombs and reprimanding us for hiding pieces by Musil, Joyce, Proust in an anthology in the hope that they wouldn't notice this trial balloon, no bigger than a lemon, so that we could say, when we applied for permission to publish À la Recherche, Ulysses, The Man without Qualities, *that these were authors who had long been in our list . . . They were, we were informed, the spearhead of Western decadence, inappropriate for 'our people' (they mostly said 'our people') . . . We devised afterwords that were like waybills declaring the harmless nature of the goods on 100 pages; we wrote blurbs like lead palisades to ward off the arrows of the unfathomable attackers; we sent one well-loved caravel floating along in a phalanx of battleships, staring apprehensively at the telephone that would announce the discovery of our ploy, order the destruction of the caravel and an increase in the number of battleships . . . Creatures like hermit crabs in rooms with the acoustics of screw tubes, twitching feelers at every deviation, seismically sensitive antennae running over the lines of text; clown fish in sea anemones, darting through their tentacles, afraid they're no longer able to produce the semio-chemical that camouflages them and keeps them safe from the voracious appetites of their host plant; hammerhead sharks furiously after blood, tearing to pieces everything the food-providing hand tipped in front of their mouths; sea cucumbers that never come to a decision, slithery and glassy, like conserved fruit; electric eels and moray eels in the reefs, lying in wait for their prey; remoras holding on tight with their suckers to the great whale shark called Socialist Realism . . . Hermes-Verlag wasn't a publisher, it was a literary institute. In the silence of smoke-filled lamps, of cigarettes flaring up and dying down, in the galvanic crackle of the aquarium of reading eyes in which pieces of paper catch the light like the white bellies of fish drifting past, the geographers of horizontal and vertical planes pursued their researches, let down plumb lines into the voices of the past, plucked at meridians and waited for a response. We gave the people bread for the spirit; we were a window on the world . . . The wall wrapped itself round Scholars' Island, this socialist Castalia, triply secured: inwardly, outwardly and against smiles; the barbed-wire roses sprouted up the building, only the birds didn't get caught; searchlights scanned the wall, dogs on long chains prowled the no-man's-land between the circular walls. Everywhere relics of lost cultures, signs waiting to be deciphered, seamarks on mouldering maps, but the old captains were dead, the astrolabes or sextants, with which the signs could have been read, sold or lying forgotten in the storerooms of the museums beneath the city. At the Hermes offices there was a sign in the vestibule, a left-over, like so much else in the houses of Atlantis, that read: '"The bourgeoisie has squandered the literary heritage and we must bring it together again carefully, study it and then, having critically assimilated it, move forward." A. A. Zhdanov at the 1st conference of the Writers' Union, 1934'; 'Education, education,' was the whisper in the corridors, the crackle from the telephones, the repeated message from long-abandoned archives of discs that seemed to be fed by electric leakage from sources above ground level, so that they were able to continue revolving endlessly and, perhaps illuminated by the gleam of 'on air' lamps, keep on sending the sound pickup into the scratch from which the old principles came like the same workpieces filling box after box as they dropped down from a punch that couldn't be switched off. But we enjoyed making discoveries; knowledge was our food and we couldn't get enough of it; books were sacred and there was nothing we feared more than the heat smouldering in the cellar, the sparks that could suddenly, without advance warning, without anyone being able to foresee them, fly out from the heating appliances that were still under control, from the steaming valves, the butterfly nuts screwed down tight on tow sealant and plain washers, the cracked welds and mangy fire-clay, the worn-out threads and filthy chimneys, their bricks eaten away by the acid smoke; we were afraid of fire, some of us had already seen books burning. In the editorial offices there were people playing the glass-bead game, they had set up telescopes that looked out through mildewed portholes, through well-disguised hatches in the barbed wire, at the culture of foreign countries; periscopes that saw manuscripts when they were still drying on the writers' desks; with extreme love and care we selected what seemed important, right and valuable . . . A drifting head, a Jupiter head, floated across the paper republic on a tour of inspection. We anchored in Weimar, our umbilical cord attached in the house on the Frauenplan, where our sun, a disc of placenta, was rising, Goethe our fixed star . . . People imbued with the love of literature, of language, of the well-made book (endless discussions over tea and Juwel filter cigarettes about the disadvantages of staple binding and the advantages of sewn binding, print space, ligatures, the colour of cases and endpapers, the quality of linen for bindings), sat in the cabins of Scholars' Island and spent years bent over Romanian and Azerbaijani poetry, translations from Persian, Georgian, Serbo-Croat, the quality of which (only that of the translations) had been checked by editors, wondered with specially appointed style editors whether someone could enter literature on 'Jesus flip-flops' or rather on 'Christ sandals', while behind them, in the walls, in the radiators with steam being let off in their wrinkled, rumbling pipes that brought up strange digestive noises from the depths, in the antique typewriters, the busy manufactory of glue pots, scissors, bone folders and pots with Barock iron-gall ink (sometimes I thought I could hear the scratch of goose-quills on their paper from the VEB Weissenborn paper factory, but it was only the standard ATO nibs with which the glass-bead-game players scribbled notes or the draft of a report), the clocks scraped away in the grinding and, depending on the season, slurping noises of the river, measurable time, terrible and submarine, fermented, while the pendulum of the other time, which gives things development and change, slowly swayed to and fro, like a metronome rod with the weight at its highest point . . . Whom did we reach? Sometimes we had the feeling we bounced off people or, worse still, threw things that went right through them; saw not them but ourselves, when we tried to look out of the windows of the island into the apartments of Atlantis. Who were the others? How much of the things that we considered important reached them? Philosophers in scholar's studies high above the wall pursued research on utopian socialists, I thought of Jochen Londoner, who spent his exile in England, to whose daughter Hanna I had been married, now he was brooding in his institute, which resembled a baroque wooden screw, over the history of the working class, reflecting on the problems of a planned socialist economy, specialist workhorses were producing commentaries on the canonic works, were connected up to the system of blood vessels –* The Complete Works of Marx and Engels *– helping to make the sun of the Only Ideology rise. The working party of professors meets. The working party of verbal erotomanes meets. They talk themselves up into a state about a decisive, indispensable, life-saving aspect of existence in Atlantis: the colour of house walls – was it floorcloth-grey or dishwater-grey? Which dishwater? That of the Interhotels or of works canteens? Of nationally owned or private ones? Were the charred caryatids on palaces in Leningrad the colour of window putty? Fauns' ears, stone plants, the plaster pockmarked by bullet lumps (lymph nodes, cancerous growths from the last war) – what shade of grey was it that they had taken on over decades of decay? We thought of grisaille painting. Of worry-grey. Grisette-grey. Argus-eyes-grey. Prison-inmate-grey. Of men's-fashion-grey, snail-grey, groschen-grey, oyster-grey, tree bast, wolf-grey, pencil-grey, elephant-grey. This colour, wasn't it a brown? Ash-coloured. Powdery-clayey, flat, wooden, produced by time, exhaust fumes, acid rain; the plaster looked flea-bitten like a camel's rusky fleece. We were getting into the zone of justification. What was the Great Project? The reconstruction of reality so that we would be able to shape it according to our dreams . . .*

64

Optional: needlework

Herr Pfeffer took off his gold-rimmed spectacles and, eyes narrowed to slits, scrutinized Christian. His glasses had left a dark-red impression on the bridge of his nose. 'Let's see what your boss has sent me. You graduated from senior high school?'

Christian said yes. Pfeffer wiped the lenses of his glasses with a crisply ironed white silk handkerchief.

'You wanted to study medicine?'

Again Christian said yes. Pfeffer checked the lenses of his glasses, rolled up one corner of his handkerchief into a cone the length of his finger and used it to clean the fine streaks along where the bevelled edge of the lens ran under the gold frame. 'I'm not all that fond of medics. Arrogant, in general artistically inclined and therefore in general of the mistaken opinion that artistic ability comes from, or is the same as, laissez-faire. Though admittedly there are different specimens of the species. Perhaps you're one of those different specimens. We will have the opportunity to establish that. I've had really good experiences with philosophers and modelmakers, with many artists of the Saxon school. What does precision mean to you?'

In the middle of the harsh winter of '86/87, during which he was to be transferred to a different job, Christian had no answer to that question.

'Precision, young man, is love. I will give you a chance, even though it's likely that the carbide will have completely ruined you for the kind of work that is done at my place.' He breathed on his spectacles, checked and polished them until they were gleaming and spotless.

Traugott Pfeffer, formerly in a managerial position in the Republic's Mint, now a foreman in VEB Phalera, which some quirk of fate had made part of the consumer goods production department of the Chemical Combine, had his own methods of convincing himself of the 'outstanding quality of work' that was done in his company – the certificate was hung over his desk in the foreman's office, a bird's nest of corrugated iron that allowed an all-round view of the shed. Below him, sitting at a circle of workbenches that allowed a view of the barred windows of the shed, were the ten men of A shift, all in the faded but spotlessly clean prisoners' dress supplied by VEB Phalera – the state coat of arms the size of a saucer sewn on over the heart – busy making decorations, medals and badges from unfinished metal or polyester workpieces. In order to keep a close eye, both clockwise and initial-wise, on his men, one of whom Christian now was, Traugott Pfeffer, former master craftsman in the Mint, used a swivelling telescope suspended on gimbals, like a ship's chronometer; it was made by the nationally owned 'Enterprise with outstanding quality of work' Carl Zeiss Jena, and belonged to him personally, which fact was lovingly engraved on it. A second method of control, the unspectacular one, as Traugott Pfeffer, for whom the unspectacular was as much a part of art as bread is of our daily diet, lay in the examination of the workpieces. For that he took a special gauge out of the right hip pocket of his grey overalls, which were always neatly ironed, placed the scale, which measured in hundredths of a millimetre, along the diameter of the Medal for Exemplary Service on the Border, the Clara Zetkin and Hans Beimler medals, checked the distance between the awns of the three ears of grain on the medal for Distinguished Inventors, counted the rays of the rising sun of the pin for Outstanding Service to the Union, on which, right in the middle, there was a very bushy ear of wheat, checked the number of radiating needles of the ten-pointed star of the Patriotic Order of Merit.

Christian's tasks included the following operations:

Mondays: take unfinished Grand Star of the Friendship between Nations, version for wearing on the chest, from palette of materials on right, check quickly, take bronze pin from VEB Solidor from palette of materials on left, check briefly, pick up soldering iron, solder pin to Grand Star of the Friendship between Nations, check, polish five-cornered star, polish coloured enamel coat of arms of the Republic in the middle, shine and deburr curved oak leaves between the points of the star using polishing awl, clean dove of peace stamped on top point of star.

Tuesdays: take unfinished Faithful Service medal of the German Post from palette of materials on left, briefly check. Take Solidor steel pin from palette of materials on right, briefly check, pick up soldering iron, solder pin to clasp-bar of Faithful Service medal, polish front, especially post-horn and two jagged electric flashes sticking out either side of the horn's cord. This medal was one of Traugott Pfeffer's favourites and he urged Christian to work carefully, for: 'Always remember, young man, it's mostly older people who get medals and decorations, their whole life is symbolized by the piece of metal, so you ought to get yourself to solder the pin on really straight, not everyone likes to see their life engraved crookedly or hanging askew.'

Wednesdays: Christian was standing at the cutting and embossing presses where the unfinished medals and decorations were produced from little sheets of tombac, brass and aluminium.

Thursdays: Christian washed the grease and oil left over from embossing and deburring off the medals with a solution, used a brush to apply enamel to the indentations – pulverized glass that was mixed with distilled water and adhesive and then fired. After the lunch break Christian moved either to the mordant bath, where the scale left over from firing was removed with acid, or to electroplating, where the medals and decorations were lowered into baths of electrolytic gold beside Traugott Pfeffer's Solingen *oak leaf* control spoon that, at the end of the procedure, had to be covered up to the handle with a clear layer of gold; only then did Traugott Pfeffer go for lunch.

Fridays: Christian was back at the workbench, mostly occupied with making Sailor of Outstanding Merit decorations, in bronze, gilt, edge smooth; Sailor of Outstanding Merit, in bronze, edge milled; the Decoration for Outstanding Achievements in Fire Protection; the Golden One children's decoration; membership badges for the Association for Sport and Technology, Pigeon-Racing Section; the Drop of Blood badge of the German Red Cross for giving blood; the Free German Youth Harvest Pin; the Pin of Merit for Workers in the Administration of Justice, bronze, enamel and gold versions, coated with polyester.

Every day pins of the attachment systems from VEB Solidor had to be filed sharp with a triangular file. Using a doll in uniform which, for the purposes of demonstration, had decorations in the correct position, Traugott Pfeffer explained, 'The uniform, which is the clothing with which phaleristics in this country is mostly concerned, is made of coarse material and the pins of our decorations must penetrate it easily despite that. Just imagine if the Comrade General Secretary could not attach the Karl-Marx Medal to the chest of the man or woman receiving it, or not in the time allowed, because the pins, which are unfortunately often blunt when supplied by our partners at Solidor, bent out of shape.'

The A shift had to complete 150 per cent of the planned target every day; Herr Pfeffer only put 100 per cent in the account book. Christian learnt the reason three months later.

Traugott Pfeffer did not like fog; he liked knots and Marcel Proust. Christian had worked 'satisfactorily', he could – having practised with the ship's doctor – tie knots and he had at least heard the name of Proust.

'Good,' Traugott Pfeffer said, 'I can see that you're ready for the B shift.'

On the B shift, which worked at night, neither medals nor decorations were produced, instead the seven volumes of the Rütten & Loening edition of Proust's *Recherche* were read. 'Sometimes you have to force people to do what's good for them,' Traugott Pfeffer said. 'This is my realm and all those who, one after the other, go through my night shift, read the *Search* – page by page, volume by volume. Sleeping is not allowed. I will test you, to see if you are worthy because you are thorough. With this.' Out of the left hip pocket of his overalls he took a case, from which he extracted a tiepin, gilded in the electrolyte bath and filed sharp till it shone. Traugott Pfeffer, Christian learnt from a philosopher on the B shift who had been sent on probation to work in industry, would stick this pin into *Lost Time*, open it at that page, read and start to ask questions. 'It's best if you make notes,' the philosopher said. 'Anyone he finds worthy of reading Proust doesn't come off the night shift until he's read the whole book.'

There were five of them; the other four on B shift were all philosophers, though from different schools, and would spend the whole night in silent but bitter arguments, hastily scribbled in pencil on rough paper, about alienation in a Developed Socialist Society.

65
In our hand

'Richard.'

'Anne.'

'Can I have a word with you?'

Richard stepped back from the vice, in which there was a part for the gas water-heater, *improvised* and filed to size from a constructional drawing Stahl, the engineer, had made for him. 'Shall we go out?'

'Not necessary. The people who're listening to us know just as much as we do. Or would you like a breath of fresh air? I couldn't last ten minutes in the stuff you breathe in this cellar.'

Upstairs, in the living room, she said, 'I can't take any more, Richard. For a long time I've watched and said nothing. But this Reina, this student . . . it's too much. We' – Anne suddenly laughed – 'ought to have an argument now but, you know, I don't want to, I . . . I just don't have the strength.'

'Yes, Anne,' Richard murmured. He touched a few things, sofa cushions, the edge of a cupboard. 'Is Reglinde in?'

'She's gone out. The letter on the table's from Robert.'

'I know, I . . . I've read it. He seems to be doing quite well.'

'Better than Christian. But you always say that Christian tends to exaggerate a bit, with his, what d'you call it . . . bragger, braggerdosho, I can't get the word right.' Again she laughed.

'Robert, yes, he's never had that many problems. And yet – perhaps he doesn't say anything simply because Christian's already, in a way . . . that's Christian's style and perhaps Robert doesn't want to be the same.'

'The grandfather clock, Richard, can't you stop it? I can't stand the tick-tock, it hurts. Shall I get you something to drink?'

'I can do that.'

'You won't be able to find anything. What were you going to say?'

'It meant nothing to me, Anne.'

She nodded and went out. Richard heard her busying herself about the kitchen, there was a chink of ice cubes in glasses, he stopped the pendulum of the grandfather clock. It resisted, started to get back into rhythm with micro-oscillations, Richard had to take off one of the lead weights, he put it down carefully inside the clock case. He heard a clatter in the hall, the dull thud of a fall. Anne's right hand was full of splinters of glass.

'We'll have to go to the clinic.' He thought for a moment, then rang Friedrich Wolf Hospital.

'Barsano. Yes, you can use the room. I'll have everything made ready.'

'You gave yourself away back at the wedding, you know,' Anne said. Richard was driving the Lada, wasn't concentrating, thought it would have been better to take a taxi – No, taxis were rare, they might have had to wait hours for one. Oddly enough, it had never occurred to him to call an ambulance. Anne was staring at her bandaged hand. 'When I asked you whether you knew the boy, you said: No, perhaps the son of a patient. How did you know he wasn't the son of Wernstein's friend?'

'She's our senior secretary,' Richard replied wearily. The red needle flickered restlessly over the the the elongated numbers on the speedometer. He was driving on automatic pilot, as if another being inside him were doing it, a matchstick man made of a few nerves and linked muscles. How alien and yet important all this was: the dashboard, the trees along the street, the key in the ignition.

'Then you shouldn't have said *perhaps*. By the way, I've seen Lucie. Pretty girl, there's a lot of you about her.'

Everything was ready at the hospital. Frau Barsano offered to assist Richard.

Anne's hand. My wife's hand, he thought. White and bloodless (a nurse had taken the bandage off), it lay in the dazzling, mocking light of the operating lamp.

A hand – what it does is one thing. A piece of body, a body itself, an assistant at performances; eloquent, undisguised truth. What it prevents, perhaps simply by not moving, is another. He found both interesting. He loved hands. Hands were stimulants, gave him pleasure. He had studied hands: the sea-lily femininity of Botticelli's women's fingers (they were fingers, but weren't they what made hands?); hands that were obstinately convinced of something; hands as if in despair at their size and at their incessant, steady moving away from childhood; creamed and uncreamed hands, alluring and mossily unfathomable hands; the hands of women gardeners, tanned by sap, and of stokers in which coal dust has lodged and can't be washed off; he had seen the hands of a butterfly expert (who had called them feeble fools); his father's hands examining a clock: all these (now ghostly-seeming) hands with the trace element of tenderness. Hands that had gone numb, fingers as fragile as a quail's bones, and had transformed cities. Hands of peasant women, gnarled, a weave of harshness and cold and a life of hard work, Querner had painted them: they seemed to be made more of wood than of flesh, the fingers were crooked with gout and arthritis and blows: blows warded off and blows handed out. At the same time Richard thought hands were sometimes curious, the fact that there were two of them seemed to take away something of their value, of their gleaming precision. Why do Cyclops have only one eye? So that its look is more threatening, so that there's less distraction. One hand, two hands: around another person's body – or neck – to clasp from both sides, to caress in stereo; to murder. Lines of bitterness. Some looked restless from unchangeableness. There, that scar – do you remember? On our honeymoon, it was the way the travels of our youth were: no great distance, Rheinsberg and Havel, reachable on our Berliner motor scooter: apples lit from behind, grainy with the nocturnal dew, pumpkins in the windows, the size of grapefruit, striped like the trousers of Turks in operas, some beige with green growths, some like fluffed-up turbans, others pear-shaped, yellow and dark green, a sharply drawn boundary between the colours. The breakdown on the way, Anne letting the second screwdriver slip.

'You've made yourself unsterile, Herr Hoffmann. The edge of your hand was on the tap.'

He'd found *reading* hands satisfying even when he was a junior doctor; others might see it as a challenge, tormenting, abrasive, for him it was taking something that was packed, carefully and willingly encircling it, peeling off its coverings, full of inhibitions, fear of nakedness – but it was there, softly throbbing, demanding to be known. And no one had explained what cutting into a hand meant (oh, that word: 'to grasp'). To cut into one's own wife's hand; five fingers, the constriction where the wedding ring had been (the nurse had had to use soap and a silk thread to take it off); the ball of the thumb; the pulse of the two main arteries, that couldn't be felt now; the palm of the hand with lines and grooves and a cloud of superstition; pale, brittle-looking nails; so that the hand on the green sheets looked like an anaesthetized stoat with its winter fur, ready for dissection. No one told you how to deal with the irrevocability, the absence of irony at the moment of the cut: Here I am, the hand seemed to say, there's no turning back, I have to trust you. So make me well again. What you are capable of will have to be enough. Of course there was experience, but there was always something lurking in the background, always the suspicion that with this patient it didn't necessarily have to work the way it had in a 'similar case' the previous day; always the fear that the 'knowledge' would vanish at an abracadabra. As in any task without an escape hatch.

If you looked at it long enough a hand seemed to be sending out watchwords from the hidden depths – they remained motionless, still beneath the surface that presented an unambiguous exterior but their outlines could be made out, could be filled in by interpretation. Hands mostly did quite sensible things. Tied shoelaces in the morning, spooned up soup at lunchtime, cracked open a bottle of beer in the evening and rested. The life of a hand consisted of clenching and stretching for sensible gestures. Richard remembered a patient he'd had many years ago, at the time she'd been fifteen, both her forearms had been torn off in an accident. One night, he'd been on duty in A&E, the neighbours had rung up. She'd gassed herself.

'I think your wife will be able to be treated as an outpatient. Save us a lot of paperwork. Would you like to operate yourself?'

He nodded. Hands trained you to be economical, at least the operating surgeon. There was no surplus skin. You couldn't, as was otherwise usual and possible, cut out a generous area round the wound. Microscope. Magnifying spectacles. The hospital was excellently equipped. Frau Barsano was aware of that, which, Richard thought, was why she said nothing. The silence during an operation, thirsting, sucking you in. Absolute concentration; consciousness focused and sharpened to the point of attention, picking out tiny indentations of interest like a diamond drill. In between: slumps, demands on energy, rallying, a spatter of distractions. You could give way for a while, for a while you could leave the burning glass to your cooperator as it crawled maddeningly slowly over the situation, mercilessly revealing, followed by the blade exploring the wound. Hands had their own kind of slumber, but also of ecstasy. That was mostly connected, Richard thought, with the word 'to attain': food and light, skin and control-panel knobs, silence, apprehensiveness and prophecies, things made tangible by a child's drawing.

'Glass,' Frau Barsano said, picking up a splinter.

Anne's hand. If I cut this here, she'll have no feeling any more there, in this lobular area on the short muscle that bends the thumb. Responsibility. Power. Sometimes he enjoyed, sometimes he feared that power, the thoughts that it seemed to suggest to him and that he found unworthy of a doctor. But they were there, whispered by thin, venomous lips and he had to employ a valuable part of his forces to repress them. Did that happen to other surgeons as well? They didn't talk about it. Perhaps out of fear of being seen as a bad doctor, without a vocation. One who didn't correspond to the cliché most patients had of a noble person in a white coat. It depended on what one did. He recalled his conversation with Weniger: to be free. They were free to do what helped people. He looked at Anne's hand, it was injured, slender and thus, in a discreet way, pleading; a hand that insisted: That's the way it is, a commitment, startled at its irrevocable nature and yet in the secret of dignity: This is it, my hand (and to hold back the shadows with it); Anne's hand: small from grief and time, unique . . .

He felt incapable of continuing the operation. Emotion, sentimentality, despair: overpowered by a mixture that repelled him, he asked Frau Barsano to continue on her own.

*

It was still light when they stopped outside Sperber's house on Wolfs-leite. With astonishment Richard heard the intoxicatingly sweet, hallucinatory calls of the blackbirds, free of tribulation, somehow selfish in their calm, their self-assurance, he thought, also . . . merciful. As Anne raised her hand to the bell without any explanation – Richard now felt that sense of shame that disputes one's right to explanations – raised it, the hand with its dressing that she hardly felt the need to protect any longer, there was something about the white of the plaster, from which Anne stuck out a comical-looking finger (a hard shaft piercing its way through the air, silent and saucy) to press the bell for an absurdly long time, something indocile that didn't belong in the evening even though it passed through it amazingly close – now, as Anne let her arm drop in front of the trunk of an elm tree, conscientiously slowly yet casually – a white that rendered down its dryness and took on another quality: the indocile, shrewd white an electric socket would have had in the black bark of the tree. Richard walked up and down. When Frau Sperber opened the door, Anne asked him to wait. 'And please don't behave badly in such a . . . theatrical manner. It'll take half an hour, perhaps an hour, depending.' The lawyer waved to them from the front door, came towards Anne, arms outstretched, a *serious smile* on his face (it didn't even seem disagreeable, Richard thought), looked at her hand, appeared to be considering, took the silk handker-chief out of the breast pocket of his suit (it seethed a lemon yellow and breathed a sigh of relief), dipped it in a barrel of rainwater and washed Anne's fingers clean with obscene care. Then all three went in without paying any attention to Richard. After a few minutes he rang the bell.

'It's nice you're still here,' Frau Sperber said. 'Won't you come in?'

'Where are they?' Richard forced the woman up against the row of coat hooks where Anne's coat was hanging.

'In the cellar. Please don't disturb them. It's locked anyway. My husband doesn't like being disturbed when he's doing it.'

'In the cellar?'

'It's dry, it's been converted, with a bar and a fire. My husband loves that cellar.'

'Will you tell my wife at once that I'm waiting for her and want her to come up.'

'Would you help me?' Frau Sperber waved Richard into the kitchen. On the worktop was a large bunch of carrots. 'There's going to be carrot salad, my husband really likes that. And I can't manage with these peelers. If I have to cut up more than two carrots, my hands go numb.'

'Spare me all this nonsense and tell my wife. At once.'

'I can't do that. He's the only one who has a key to that door.'

'Then I will call the police.'

'I don't think you should do that, Herr Hoffmann. In the first place you wouldn't have a chance against him. Secondly, your wife, as it appears, went with him of her own free will.'

'And you?'

'We have a modern marriage, Herr Hoffmann. Enlightened and tolerant. We have our arrangements, I don't want you to think me the injured wife. And I must add that I prefer it if I know the women; it means I can more easily work out whether they'll do him good. Your wife's very nice, a really pleasant, likeable person.'

'You don't say.' Richard tried in vain to sit down on one of the bar stools round the centrally placed worktop. 'Where did you get that huge extractor hood?'

'No problem for my husband. He actually wanted to buy a new one and give this one to your wife, who also admired it, but your kitchen's too small. – And I'd like to say I'm delighted to see you, Herr Hoffmann. My husband has great respect for you. Shouldn't we call each other "*du*"?' She wiped her hands on a tea towel with windmills on it. 'Evelyn.'

'Oh, don't try that on me.' Richard went out of the house. He wandered round the streets, happened to end up in Ulmenleite. The church was still open. Pastor Magenstock was skipping. Richard watched for a while. Magenstock, eyes closed and seeming not to notice him, was turning slowly, with quick, low hops to and fro, the rope swinging fluently and making a whistling sound. Meditating, Richard thought. And even though the sound of the skipping behind him didn't suggest it, he found the offertory box by the door and felt the need to make a donation but, when he searched through his pockets, could only find the twenty-pfennig piece he kept for emergencies. He put it in.

'Ah, Herr Hoffmann.' Sperber, seeing Anne out, bowed to her. 'I have some good news for you. My efforts to get your son's place at medical school reinstated will very probably be successful.'

'Well, then, brother mine?'

'Robert.'

'Is there anywhere we can go in this hole? For an ice cream?'

'There's a bar here. If you'd like a beer.' Robert drinking beer, little Robert – that's the way it had always been, but not any more. Robert flicking his windproof lighter open with a resonant click and letting the flame that shot up play over the tip of a Cabinet.

'Later perhaps.'

'It's . . . great that you've come.'

'Hey, you'd never have said that before. Being conscripted must have done that to you. Not bad at all.'

'Shut it, earhole.'

'If you insist.' Robert joked about the army. He'd been sent to join the medical orderlies in a barracks outside Riesa. 'A real cushy number. My God, that really is a ridiculous outfit. Right turn, left turn, loaf about, wait, end up as a fat cabbage. You can't take it seriously.'

'Depends where you are.'

'You must be doing something wrong to get caught like this all the time.'

'How about passes?'

'As many as you like,' Robert boasted. 'And my physical needs are well supplied too. I've got a nice little girl in Riesa. What about you?'

'What d'you say to the old folks?'

'Well parried, brother mine. They're OK, there are others who're much worse. It's great that they've gone away on holiday. At last I can do as I like there. You don't know how long I've wanted a place to myself and when I get one it's at the same time as a sister, and I've been called up. You don't smoke, right?'

'Half-sister.'

'Don't take it to heart like that, brother mine. It happens. She's called Lucie. Have you seen her?'

'No.'

'How would you, shut up here like this? I've not seen her yet either. But I am keen to see her. Really. And to be honest, in a way I'm look-ing forward to it as well. I've always wanted to have a little sister.'

66

After this interruption the days . . . passed

781 years of Dresden: in 1987 one could see stickers with that number on the rear window of many cars; often next to the 'L' that officially stood for 'Learner', unofficially for 'Leaver'. The number was a revolt against another number: 750 years of Berlin, an anniversary that was to be celebrated on a grand scale, a spasm of joie de vivre, pride that no one believed in any more; the tired, ailing body of the Republic was to be squeezed dry once more in order to extract from the putrid juices a cup of hemlock that, dribbled into the arteries of the capital, was supposed to transform sickness into life, exhaustion into hope and vigour . . .

Now Judith Schevola was no longer working at the cemetery in Tolkewitz, she had been sent to work at VEB Kosara, where she made hectograph copies of brochures in alcohol baths and by the Ormig process. Whenever he could, Meno, drawn in a way he couldn't explain, would drive out to the factory and watch her. He recognized her from a distance by her bat cap as she came out of the factory gates with other workers. She swayed, kept close to fences along the paths and looked for something to hold on to in the streets, drunk from the alcohol fumes coning from the baths for the pieces that were being copied; passers-by frowned when they saw her, presumably thinking she was a drunk and once when she fell into the slush on a grey winter's evening, no one went to help her until Meno, who had heard her muffled cries for help even from a distance, finally managed to pull her up out of the puddle. Judith didn't recognize him, staggered as she resisted; no one took any notice of the two people despondently fighting with each other.

Meno took her home. She lived in Neustadt, in a one-and-a-half-room apartment giving onto a back yard; the corridor was created by the backs of cupboards, the half-room ended at a wall; she shared the plaster rosette for the chandelier. There was a screw across the larger room with cigarettes and cut-out poems and stockings hanging from it. The screw had a fine thread with (Judith had counted them) 5,518 turns, passed through the masonry and, braced with straps and pieces of wood outside, held the storey together.

'What do you want from me?' Judith muttered, dropping onto the bed.

'Is there anything you need? Can I help you in any way?'

'I'm beyond help. Oh, how self-pitying . . . Have you brought anything to drink? Thank you very much for accompanying me, Herr Editor, and now adieu.'

She was quickly getting clearer, Meno turned to leave.

'If you could fill the jug, there's a tap in the kitchen . . . Since you're here, you can stay if you like. I've a record with Indian music, written for the living and the dead, just the right thing for you and me. Are you hungry?'

'Yes.'

'How stupid. I only asked out of politeness. So here's my suggestion: first we eat nothing at all, then we go dancing.'

'I can't dance very well. – How are you? Are you working? Writing?'

'We aimed so high and look at us now,' Judith said after a while.

'I find that too sentimental. You must write, times are changing and I don't think your exclusion's going to last long.'

'I want something to drink.'

'No.'

'Are you trying to forbid me to get drunk?'

'It won't change anything and you not an immature kid any longer.'

'Yes, Daddy.' Judith Schevola felt under the bed, pulled out a half-full bottle of Kröver Nacktarsch and drank the wine in large swigs. She threw the bottle into a cardboard box beside the little stove where it broke on other glass things. Judith gave a hoarse laugh. Then she stretched out on the bed like a big cat. 'Do you never feel you have to explode? To shake the stars down from the sky? Don't you ever want to taste all the dishes at once, dance till you drop, drink till everything goes black, blow all your money at the casino, be stony broke, come back after a terrible hour and win everything and more back again? Do you never want to make a river flow upstream?'

'I'm happy with a bath that works,' Meno replied coldly.

'To be able to fly, to be free, to be great, to be full of untamable power that can compel the elements . . . like the revolution.'

Meno remained silent.

'But revolutionaries are always timid,' Judith said bitterly.

The cocoons grew thicker and thicker, deeper and deeper the years. Whom were the clocks calling? In the evening the magic word 'Mutabor' was spoken, town and country set up dolls that looked outwards but the Tower-dwellers had long since gone down the stairs to their interests . . . A Urania evening had attracted a large audience for a talk on Mesopotamia; the lecturer, who had come specially from Berlin, from the Pergamon Museum, had used a slide projector to cast coloured shadows on a screen in the darkened lecture room of Arbogast House that had roused not only the widowed Frau Fiebig to enthusiastic astonishment. The lecturer signed a few square blue books and left, but his subject remained and ramified and, as if it were tinder, set off discussions and quiet studies in the evening drawing rooms. But the books left behind by the lecturer were also beautiful to look at: there was a reproduction of a relief of the Ishtar Gate on the cover. White lions strode over a frieze of daisies against a timeless azure background; Frau Fiebig said it gave you a shiver, 'the eternities since then and what has remained'. Suddenly never-heard names appeared, forming little white clouds at the mouths of those waiting for rolls outside Wachendorf's bakery; Ashurbanipal, Ashurnaspiral I, Ashurnaspiral II and Hammurabi buzzed to and fro, and anyone who did not want to be 'behind the times' had to know something about them. In Guenon House research into old Dresden was broken off and they turned to those ages full of mythical men clad in animal skins and with long, rectangular beards, bracelets, hairnets and war-smocks that left their calves and upper arms free and more than once caused Frau Fiebig to exclaim, 'Those muscles, my God, what muscles those men had', to which Herr Sandhaus retorted, 'Yes, my dear, and with them they quite happily cut their enemies' heads off.' 'Yes, but what de-cisive virility, what a proud, lusty culture, a culture with *muscle*,' Frau Fiebig replied, 'and don't you think there's something both delicate and muscular about this cuneiform script? When I imagine our newspapers written like that, I'd immerse myself in them more. I think even fibs would be diff'rent in cuneiform script, they'd be quite diff'rent, I think.'

After the talk all four copies of the blue book that had been peace-fully sleeping their life away in Bruno Korra's Paper Boat second-hand bookshop on Lindwurmring were sold, even though the sly bookseller, recognizing the signs of the times, had immediately upvalued them from ten to 100 marks, and were now being photocopied by all the inhabitants of the district who had not had the good fortune to get hold of a copy; some of the secretaries at the offices of the Council for Mutual Economic Aid typed the books word for word on their machines, with up to five layers of carbon and writing paper that Matthes's stationery shop put at their disposal, as it did the coloured ribbons from their allocation of black ones. The eyes of the Tower-dwellers, accustomed to grey, to the finest gradations of everyday grey, thirsted after colours, were exhilarated by the strange reliefs, the sun and star signs, the sea-blue of the glazed tiles of the procession street, which bore the name 'May the enemy not cross it' and went from the Marduk Temple through the Ishtar Gate, one of the eight gates of the inner city of Babylon, to the Akitu Temple. They turned the pages of the book reverently, and if they had one of the carbon copies, stapled and bound in Arbogast's own printing and binding shop, that had had to do without the illustra-tions, they didn't take less care, on the contrary, these had demanded people's work, people's time, and that of people they knew and saw every day. There were phone calls at late hours, a network connecting telephone receivers grew up in the district; people pointed out espe-cially beautiful features, discussed the location of the Hanging Gardens in the city of Babylon; the women asked what kind of clothes Semiramis might have worn, whether the Nofretete cosmetics salon could manage to discover and exploit the refined secrets of Babylonian beautification; the men wondered whether Herodotus's claim that the outer wall was so wide that a four-horse carriage could turn on it was not perhaps just a legend. The lights in the rooms stayed on, outside the acid, black-grained snow of a winter heated with poor-quality coal was falling and brows, smooth, lined, enthusiastic and down to earth, were bent over the colours and shapes of that long-vanished age, buried beneath sand and flood.

It disappeared as quickly as it had arrived. Hardly had a trip to Berlin, to the Museum Island, been organized than the imposing ziggurats crumbled, the charioteers on starflower wheels, the sun-kings in gold and lapis lazuli vanished; Herr Sandhaus, who had gone to the trouble of making the arrangements, stood on the station platform, bewildered, but apart from Meno only Herr Adeling arrived. 'Is it all over with Assyria now, Herr Sandhaus? But, you know, for me it's only just beginning, here in our Niniveh.'

The Babylonian fantasies faded away after the visit to the Museum of Ethnology in the Japanese palace. The thirst for knowledge of the Tower-dwellers demanded new material . . . Quietly amused, Meno watched the fashions change. After Mesopotamia they discovered the Phoenicians and Carthage; the ship's doctor was in demand because of his ability to transfer plans of the ships of that seafaring nation with the most delicate of pens onto sheets of Polylux film, filigree masterpieces of the art of drawing ships of which Arbogast, from his antiquated alderman's chair in the semi-dark, expressed his approval with nods and smirks of satisfaction. If only one could do that! Sail across the wide Mediterranean from Cyprus to Gibraltar and out into the open sea that the ancients feared. Model ships were made out of pinewood chip and balsa wood; Stationery Matthes didn't know what was happening to him and where he could find all the materials that were in demand. You could use cork for balsa, the handles of fishing rods were made of cork – so sharpen your knives and get out your razor blades. Certain television programmes now enjoyed widespread popularity; Meno could tell that from the synchronized switch-over in the windows as he went home . . . films about heroes of the sea and explorers, bold privateers and adventurers; programmes such as *She & He & 1,000 Questions*, *By Educationalists – for Educationalists* and, popular with the Harmony dressmakers, who met for a hen party at Barbara's, the advice programme for home sewing: *From Head to Toe*. Joffe, the lawyer, invited people round to an evening with *Sandokan, the Tiger of Malaysia*, whose smouldering eyes set not only Frau Fiebig's heart on fire, and the Schlemm Hotel showed a video of *Paul and Virginia*, set on Mauritius, a shallow colonial love story that the men couldn't watch without a bottle of beer and sidelong glances at their wives and their watches; afterwards people talked about Joffe's privileges.

Meno pursued his own researches. It was the cell that occupied him, the smallest unit of life, a highly complex piece of organic machinery that Arbogast put at his disposal in the form of model blocks the height of a man, examples of Herr Ritschel's skill. It was even possible to simulate a few chemical reactions . . . He wanted to write poems about them, hoping that would save Romantic poetry, which seemed stuck between antiquated rhymes on the one hand and rapturous effusions about nature ('Beauty is truth') on the other . . . There had been impressive publications from Hermes, an admirable essay on Georg Trakl by the Old Man of the Mountain that had brought a venomous attack from Eschschloraque . . . The union of science and literature (an old, rather humanist idea), a line of tradition, thin and often almost completely submerged, indicated by the names of Empedocles, Strabo, Rabanus Maurus, Jakob Böhme, Novalis, Annette von Droste-Hülshoff, Jakob Philipp Fallmerayer and Carl Ritter down to Jean-Henri Fabre and Gottfried Benn, had become a quiet fixation with Meno that took up his whole desk, by now shielded from prying eyes by metre-high bookshelves. The guiding star of these endeavours was called Goethe, as so often . . .

In 1987 Meno didn't spend his summer holiday in his father's house in Schandau but in the Museum of Zoology, which, as he discovered to his astonishment, hardly anyone in Dresden knew. There, in dusty cupboards with trays of butterflies bequeathed by Saxon collectors, on microscope tables covered in petri dishes, piles of periodicals, stuffed birds looking out sadly at the Elbe, in the fauna library, extensive but suffering from damp and degradation due to acid, Meno found a profusion of material for his investigations. Since his student days he hadn't felt the initial joy of the good researcher – to look at nature without questioning or examining it, only differing from the way children see it in that the response is not astonishment but perplexity – so strongly as in the flow of those August days that already had a touch of autumnal clarity. The town was empty, the children were on holiday, even the cinemas, yawning with the melancholy of hot days, didn't seem to believe the magic that flickered across their screens, caught in the dusty light of grumpily creaking projectors. The Elbe was grey and lethargic, like an elephant taking a bath. The spider manuscript and his university card for the Biology Department in Leipzig had opened the door to the collections for Meno and thus he sat, undisturbed by the staff, in the brooding quiet of a place behind untidy shelves full of the researchers' silent dreams, which at night, after he'd gone, might possibly start to whisper about him – he sometimes thought – for uncatalogued collections, cases full of butterflies, of which one is 'wrong' because it's been wrongly placed or catalogued, are like restless revenants thirsting after the neck of a scientist so that they can be released. There Meno sat and studied the cell. *Cella*, he read, the smallest unit of organisms that retain the fundamental properties of life, metabolism (Meno recalled a saying of his tutor, Falkenstein: metabolism is an investigation of different forms of gratitude), response to stimuli, ability to move and reproduce; most human and animal cells have a size of about 20–30μ; the human egg cell, on the other hand, was a giant of 0.2 mm, even visible to the naked eye. This egg cell rose out of the corpus luteum, a sun in the lunar cycle, guided by a complicated interplay of hormones (the word means 'to stir up') and wiped free by the fimbrias of the tubes, sucked into the Fallopian tube, the ovum headed off in the direction of the uterus, from where the counter cells, the flagellated combat swimmers of the sperm, were to be expected. What did all these things mean, what was their

significance, organelles within the membrane that formed the boundary of the cell, serving as vascular skin? There was the endoplasmic
reticulum, it looked like a layer of potato fritters hastily stacked on top
of each other with the biosynthesis of protein going on between them,
a bewildering multistorey, thousand-track space launch centre with
deliveries and dispatches, construction, customization, repairs and
dismantling; then there was the Golgi apparatus, the so-called internal
network consisting of several double-layer membranes, folded con-
vex/concave and stored behind each other, some extended to form
caverns and vacuoles whose purpose was to package the secretions
that they welded, so to speak, into vesicles that were sent out of the
cell along special canals; there were the mitochondria, the tiny power
plants in the cell protoplasm, compact smoked sausages, some also
resembling rugby balls; and there was the mystery of how the egg
knew about the seed (for that seemed to be the case, the egg cell seemed
to emit attractants and control agents, indeed even sought out the seed
cell by which it wanted to be fertilized; Meno had read in *Nature* that
the principle of 'first come, first served' was clearly not unreservedly
valid; the egg cell seemed to have some say in who for her came 'first' –
not always the robust woodcutter who, as a muscle man, immediately
set his drill to work to penetrate the membrame, sometimes she even
let him do the work, only to pull in the soft good-for-nothing, the
Bohemian, the charming lady-killer at the last moment, slamming the
door in the hulk's face); there was the mystery of connections, of meaning, that was beyond language.

At times there was a coffee percolator snorkelling away somewhere
in the depths of the Museum, at times there was a knocking in one of
the painted, uncovered heating pipes running along the wall, at times
a drop of water, falling from the damp patches that spread like parasitic
flowers on the pale yellow ceiling with its root system of decades-old
craquelure, went 'plop'. When the snow was melting or there was
heavy rain, Meno was told, the water didn't just go 'plop', it poured

and streamed, cheerfully babbling, through the damaged roof and down the walls of the building that had formerly housed the Saxon Parliament. At times he also fell asleep, for in the cubicle where he was working the midday temperature on a sunny day was 40°C. And yet he was still as strangely moved by these living beings (even when they were dead they weren't just things) as he had been as a child: musing on the ravages of time, he stood looking at Steller's sea cow, which was just as extinct as the Tasmanian wolf, the Carolina parakeet, the passenger pigeon, the huge flocks of which Audubon had described so impressively and that once used to darken the sky over the fields of American farmers; he didn't dare smooth the turquoise feathers of one of the European rollers he had seen as a boy on expeditions with Kurt and Anne in Saxon Switzerland. Now it had long been extinct in the country, as a card beside it said.

But it was the fate of a fish that moved him most of all, though he couldn't say why: the Saxon sturgeon, the Latin name of which, *Acipenser sturio*, he murmured to himself like an incantation. Recorded on the Elbe as far up as Saxony and Bohemia, the sturgeon had long since vanished from the region's rivers; the Zoological Museum possessed the only remaining specimen and even in the lodge of the Association of Elbe Boatmen, where Hoffmann's barometer came from, they would have looked on it as a tall story, had there not still been an old document over the bar listing their privileges that included the right to fish for sturgeon. – So Meno sat there in the silence, surrounded by little colourful pharaohs stuck on pins, the remains of long-forgotten expeditions to nearby and distant tropics, read, his heart aching with a yen for faraway places, where the lantern flies and other beetles were found (the Museum had an important collection of weevils, Curculionidae, nailed up in stubborn sleep), studied the little maps for the birds lined up in drawers, murmured the names: Philippines, New Guinea, knowing he would never get there; he tried to decipher the regular characters, which looked as if they'd been drawn with a fine brush and seemed to speak of light and bright matters, of shells from Andaman, New Caledonia (or could it be a sound-scanning system, music?), as he searched for a language that expressed what he felt at the sight of these treasures washed up on the shore of time. Thus he lived in those days. Thus he dreamt.

Christian was back with his unit in Grün. He'd been in the army for over three years now; in normal circumstances he would have been discharged in the autumn and would have started to study medicine in Leipzig. Now he was a soldier, had his school-leaving certificate and nothing else, was doing the extra service that was part of his punishment and that would last until the spring of 1988, to be followed by another year and a half of regular service: discharge autumn 1989. Apart from Pancake there were none of his old comrades left; he saw unknown faces; Nip and the regular officers remained. Nip greeted them with 'Hoffmann and Kretzschmar – one more incident and you're back where you've just come from. Understood?' Christian was now squad-room leader, the others looked on him with a mixture of shyness and respect; he had the feeling he was out of synch, a living anachronism, as Meno would have called it. No one asked about Schwedt or Samarkand; he'd had to sign a document that he would say nothing about them. Talking had become foreign to him, if it was unavoidable he restricted himself to what was absolutely necessary. He had signed. He didn't want to go back. He liked the bread. His comrades were nice, especially the goldsmith. The tanks were good. The sun was lovely.

In the winter of 1988 the theatre evenings started again. It was freezing in the rooms, in the ramshackle buildings, and what better way to get warm than with a glass of grog or a cup of tea while watching a play put on by Erik Orré or Joffe in the Schlemm Hotel, the Tannhäuser Cinema or a private house? Christian was granted extended leave.

Before he went, he had to show Nip his fingernails, his tunic collar bind and sewing kit. It was already dark when he arrived at Dresden Central and he stood waiting for an 11 at the tram stop in his walking-out uniform, his patched kitbag over his shoulder, freezing. The wind was playing in the lamps suspended over the rails, ruffling the edges of poorly stuck posters on the advertising pillars. Country buses went from Leninplatz out to Waldbrunn, Zinnwald, the Westergebirge; the 11 approached from the hill on Juri-Gagarin-Strasse outside the Russian Church and buildings of the Technical University, a bobbit worm with two chemical antennae. Christian sat in the single seat on the right in front of the middle door, it was his favourite seat in the tram: it was good for observation, no one could sit next to you, there was underseat heating that usually worked. The lights were flashing on Prager Strasse. People were rushing past the Lenin memorial in both directions. *Robotron*, the fluorescent writing on the multistorey factory building on Leningrader Strasse promised. The Round Cinema, left behind. 'Drink Margon Water' a neon sign on Dr-Külz-Ring recommended. Left behind. Left behind: the Ring Café, Otto-Nuschke-Strasse, Postplatz with its after-work bustle, Thälmannstrasse with the House of the Book. A white banner was hanging from the theatre on which it said, in red letters: 'ANATOMIE TITUS FALL OF ROME'. 'Socialism will triumph,' neon writing on a high-rise building proclaimed. The Zwinger Crown Gate, the wing with the Porcelain Collection were mourning in the brash light of a few construction floodlights, there were gaps in the row of putti on the Long Gallery, there were schnapps bottles and disappointed-looking swans on the Zwinger moat. Rome, Christian thought. No, Troy. This here is Troy. The city seemed cold and alien as never before, the people going home sat there in the unpadded seats, heads bowed, worn out by worries and their days of work, the cardboard signs with the names of stops clattered, knocking against the scratched Plexiglass windows; get on, get off, a swill of lights, of

human exudations, regularly interspersed with the expressionless voice
of the driver announcing the stops.

Christian slept in the House with a Thousand Eyes. He had the
apartment to himself, Meno was in Berlin for committee and editorial
meetings, contentious points in Hermes's annual programme and outline programme for the future had to be fought through, one of the
books Meno had prepared for the acceptance procedure was threatened
with being cancelled. The living room was cold, the ash pan hadn't
been emptied; Christian lit the stove, fed Chakamankabudibaba; he
purred round his legs, he'd grown old and infirm. The television was
on in Libussa's apartment. Christian wondered whether to go up, but
he wanted to be alone. The Stahls' little girl was crying, the engineer's
powerful voice arguing with the Honichs could be heard on the stairs;
the woman's voice sounded shrill and outraged. When Christian had
said hello, Stahl had responded with a curt and, as it seemed to Christian, indignant nod. 'You'll have to go to the Querleite bathhouse for
a shower, Meno's registered you with Herr Unthan. Our bathroom
and toilet have a schedule of use.' The last words he shouted upstairs,
his hand beside his mouth. The ten-minute clock struck. How soothing
the sound was, like something in a dream . . . In the pool of light from
the lamp on Meno's desk were periodicals (*Sinn und Form*, *Neue Deutsche
Literatur*, *Reichenbachia*), the two Schelling books, two of Plato's dialogues, the *Timaeus* and *Critias*, and, open in the middle of the literature
wing of the desk, Judith Schevola's *The Depths of These Years*. Christian
carefully closed it after he'd read the handwritten dedication to Jochen
Londoner on the title page. Perhaps the ship's doctor is in the conservatory, Christian thought, leafing through books about sailing ships
and puffing away at a pipeful of Copenhagen vanilla tobacco. Christian
went up through the concealed door but found not Alois Lange but
the Kaminski twins smoking and watching a colour television. 'Aha,
young Hoffmann. The conservatory's no longer accessible to all. It's

now part of our apartment. But if you feel like watching a James Bond video we'll make an exception this time,' said Timo or René, casually taking his feet off a chair and offering him it with a gesture of invitation. Without a word Christian went back down the stairs. There was a ring at the door.

'Evenin',' two furniture movers mumbled. 'We're supposed to be collecting Herr Rohde's ten-minute clock.'

Surprised, Christian said nothing.

'It's all right. It's for the play. It's being put on tomorrow. Herr Rohde said you'd been informed.'

'One moment, please.' Christian went to Meno's desk, found a sheet of paper in the typewriter. A few notes and comments such as Meno always wrote for his guests when he wasn't there. A PS mentioned the furniture movers. The only strange thing was that, contrary to his habit, Meno had not left a telephone number where he could be contacted. The men waited.

'Have you any papers?'

The driver handed down a folder. 'Don't make difficulties, young man, we have other things to collect. It's been arranged with your uncle.'

'I simply can't imagine my uncle would leave his grandfather clock in the care of complete strangers,' Christian said. 'I'll call him and check.' He went back in and waited a while. When he came out, the men and the lorry had disappeared.

In the house the noise rose and subsided, there was the clatter of footsteps, a kettle whistled in the Langes' kitchen, the scratching and scraping behind the walls moved up and down. Herr Honich seemed to be calling someone who was hard of hearing, in his powerful voice he kept bellowing, 'What? How?' into the receiver. Christian decided to go for a short walk. Light rain had started, making the black of the copper beech shine, whispering in the gutters. The Bhutan pines were giving off a tangy scent. From the depths of the park came the 'too-wit' of an owl. Christian set off for Caravel, went down Wolfsleite, crossed

Turmstrasse, where, grunting and squealing, accompanied by regular chanting of individual syllables by a few of the staff from Arbogast's institute, a procession of fluorescent fire salamanders the size of crocodiles was going down the street.

'Well, well, Herr Hoffmann' – startled, Christian turned round to see Sperber dressed as a weather-glass seller. 'Have you been given leave? As you can see,' he went on, nodding towards the salamanders that crunched past on wooden wheels and shouting 'Good evening, Herr Ritschel' to one of the figures accompanying them, 'Joffe's play's made a big impression even before it's started. We're doing *The Golden Pot*. Your cousin Ezzo's playing Anselm and Muriel the snake Serpentina – I've even seen her laugh again. But now you must excuse me, I have to go to the rehearsal. Ah, our Archivist. Good evening, Herr Lindhorst,' he said to a man in a long black coat. 'How was your flight in this weather?'

Falling in with the joke, Arbogast spread out his arms; the material of his sleeves was ribbed, like a bat's wings. 'Herr Marroquin had to dig deep in his props box and what he didn't have the Institute ordered from Herr Lukas and Harmony Salon. The scenery comes from Rabe's, the joiner's. Worked out well, hasn't it? In another place they call it sponsoring. I'm really looking forward to our little play.' Arbogast waved his stick cheerfully. 'Best wishes to your father,' he called out to Christian before he and Sperber, the clink-clank of whose weather glasses was quickly swallowed up by the rain, disappeared in the gloom of Turmstrasse; the yellow patches of the salamanders still glowed in the dark.

Christian turned back. Caravel would be dark and deserted, perhaps there'd be a light on in the Griesels' living room, on the garden side, or at André Tischler's; the Stenzel Sisters went to bed early. Anne and Richard were away, Robert in the army, Reglinde at the Tannhäuser Cinema, where the play was to be put on.

*

Summer 1988 began with red spots. Shaking his head, Herr Trüpel wiped them off the record sleeves. In Binneberg's café they crawled over the Black Forest gateau, custard pies, marzipan slices and cream puffs, ruining the old ladies' coffee morning, and formed a crust on the bottles of syrup in the greengrocer's. They squatted on the picture postcards in the window of Malthakus's philately shop, lay, weary unto death, between the covers of Postmaster Gutzsch's books of stamps, crept across his pre-war Pelikan inkpads and sent his St Bernard into itchy spasms. They buzzed in through the open windows of the Roeckler School of Dancing, found Korra's Paper Boat and Priebsch's stock of spare parts, hid under Lamprecht's gentlemen's hats, sprinkled spots over the cloth at Lukas's, the tailor's, were squashed under the characters of the secretaries' typewriters, ruined Lajos Wiener's wigs (Meno had never seen the Hungarian in a frenzy of rage: red as a beetroot, hairnet askew, he was holding the fair and dark toupees in both hands and smashing them down again and again on a fire hydrant). They made Pastor Magenstock's cassock look as if it had scarlet fever. Gave choirmaster Kannegiesser's organ pipes sore throats. The Rose Gorge below Arbogast House vibrated with dry rustlings and cracklings, like short-wave interruptions to hair electricity, became an infected system of blood vessels; fat bunches of red were stuck to the rose buds and stems: Frau von Stern had never, she said, not even with the Tsar in the summer of '17, seen so many ladybirds. 'Where you have ladybirds, you also get greenfly,' said the pest controllers as they fanned out but could not get the plague under control.

Christian's unit was to contribute to the national economy, was put on work detail. It was Samarkand again, but this time the open-cast brown-coal mines and he wasn't there as a convict. The company was allocated a shed in the treeless lunar landscape churned up by excavators and lorries. The beds were made with fresh lemon-yellow linen. Christian's job was as an assistant on a power shovel. The soldiers were collected from the shed by a lorry and, when the shift was over, brought back from the shovels and slag-transporters. Christian had been put on night shift, that was where they were most short of workers.

The summer drew on, the ladybirds disappeared as suddenly as they had arrived. The City Cleansing Department swept up the remains of the seven-spot beetles, whole tons of red wings and black bodies. The eating and cooking apples ripened, there promised to be a good crop of Gute Louise, even though that year the pear trees on the slopes of the Elbe from Loschwitz to Pillnitz had been attacked by rust. Herr Krausewitz stood in the garden of Wolfstone, chin in hand, a look of concern on his face, unable to agree with Libussa what could be done about it: water mixed with crushed walnuts and poured round the trunks of the affected trees did nothing to get rid of it, nor did any of the pesticides from the chemist's. Clouds of Wofatox enveloped the trees, leaving a grey deposit on the leaves.

The message in Meno's typewriter had been a forgery.

In September Ulrich was fifty, Niklas in October. The parties were held at home, with just family and friends.

And on one of the sunny, almost windless days in the late autumn, filled with calm warmth, like an Anker glass with cider, Richard took the postbox-yellow oilcan off the black shelf, went over to the Hispano-Suiza, poured a drop here, smeared some over a running part there, while Stahl, his hands in the pockets of his work overalls, stood staring up at the sky spread out over Lohmen quarry like a silk parasol, said, 'Finished. Really, it's finished, Gerhart. Can't wait to see how it works.'

Sputnik magazine, a digest of the Soviet press, was banned.

And on another late-autumn day, which would turn into a sunny, almost windless late-autumn day, there was loud knocking on the door of the House with a Thousand Eyes at four in the morning. Still half asleep, Meno groped his way into the hall, where he was pushed aside by a squad of men in uniform demanding to see Herr and Frau Stahl.

Stahl came out of their bedroom, bleary, his sparse remaining hair tousled, Sabine behind him.

'Herr Gerhart and Frau Sabine Stahl?' He was arresting them, in the name of the Republic, for the intention of leaving the Republic illegally.

'You,' another of the men in uniform said, turning to Meno, the Honichs and the Langes, who, wakened by the noise, had appeared in the landing, 'will also be questioned and are to report for questioning at Grauleite at nine this morning. Your employers will be informed.'

'Well, all this you've been telling us is a bit mysterious, Herr Doktor. Just think: a man builds an aeroplane in the same shed as you. A real, live aeroplane, not one of those radio-controlled things like I've made for my boy that can go whizzing round the pond, no – a real flying machine, our experts have said it's actually capable of flight. And you say you didn't notice anything. Come on now, I don't believe even you believe that yourself. So you just tell me about it, one step at a time. – My God, Herr Doktor, you do have a talent for getting into difficulties. So this Stahl was working on the plane without your knowledge? And he must've tried it out too, mustn't he?'

67

Brown coal

If you say open-cast mining, you say wind. The wind was always there. It came from all directions, bringing the smells of Samarkand, the yellow fog, the carbide dust and the quicklime from the lime works. When the cloud was low, the slim-waisted funnels of smog would swing like umbilical cords between rust-red placenta zones on the ground and lazy, genie-in-a-bottle cloud-foetuses; it would start at the edge of the mine, where even the weeds didn't thrive, jump down, elegant and self-assured as a paratrooper, onto the lower, churned-up terrace, turn into a child splashing contentedly in the bathtub, push and shove the W50 and Ural lorries, making the tarpaulins billow out and, where they'd been attached too casually, tear off the hooks and flap up and down like the wings of trapped prehistoric birds; or it would blow buffers of dry soil at the lorries that were so fierce the drivers had to step on it even when going downhill. And they couldn't see any farther than the inside of their windscreens, in front of them the brown grit, already containing coal, swirled, easily swallowing up the light of the headlamps so that vehicles coming towards them, now pushed by the wind and grabbed by their tarpaulin collars, emerged abruptly, immense, out of the booming darkness. To the roofs of their cabs the drivers had fitted special horns that reminded Christian of ships' fog-horns (he didn't ask, perhaps that was what they actually were), but even the bellow from these throats, which could normally be heard kilometres away, broke off when the wind decided to swing round uphill. The wind would hop down exuberantly from terrace to terrace, but patiently spend time on each one of them, chewing and biting into lumps and bumps, smoothing out the track, a spiral going down in tighter and tighter hairpins, that the lorries, with the shifts on the lurching, bone-shakingly shuddering wooden benches on either side of the open back, slithered up and down. At the bottom, on the circular floor of the crater of the open-cast mine, the wind would sometimes pause for minutes on end. An almost arrogant pause, Christian thought, raising his head and listening in the gaseous darkness with its wash of white from the lights on the machines. The wind was waiting. Was it gathering its strength for an attack on the excavators as they moved with stolid finality? They pushed the wind up onto their shoulders, unconcerned. But the wind seemed at last to have found a challenge to clear the fun out of its rage (it reduced its strength), to hand out and receive the blows of a worthy opponent that make victory triumphant, radiant (like the cut through a valuable, incredibly irreplaceable early-Victorian sideboard that has been handed over to the circular saw); the wind returned, keeping, since for the moment it couldn't get the better of the excavators, close to the ground, over which, if they wanted to shift their position, they had to move and needed to be as flat as a tabletop. Brutal as they were in the way they ripped into the layers of gley and seams of coal (the bucket chains ate into them as if they were Trinkfix cocoa powder), they were powerless to resist an incline: however ungainly it looked, an excavator, Christian had learnt, was a finely balanced system, even the slightest slope of the underlying surface could cause it to tip over. The wind dropped, ceremonially (somehow the idea of spats came to Christian in his seat high up on the excavator), and opened out like a Swiss army knife, only the tools the wind exposed were cudgels or, to be more precise . . . flails. On the one hand the furious and, in some respects admirable, choreography (only human beings were capable of the ruthlessness and obsessiveness with which the wind declared certain areas of the ground, and not always the most suitable ones, a threshing floor) made Christian feel like laughing (he suppressed it, he was afraid of this wind), on the other it stimulated, surprisingly for him, his boldness in a fit of vitality that was rare, but for that all the more violent and, because it was not free of cruelty, frightening: he jumped down from the excavator as quickly as he could and stood in the middle of the fight between the wind and the ground surface, lifted up his head to the bolts of air falling down from the night sky, as heavy and quiet as chandeliers, and screamed. That relaxed him. He thought of Burre, of Reina. And couldn't resist singing out his own modest happiness against the deafening vehemence of calamity.

He was the third man on the excavator. His job was to clean the bucket wheel. The soil above the coal was systematically removed, starting with the top edge of the overburden in which a channel a good

metre deep, the length of the extended bucket-wheel arm, was cut out
from right to left and, on the next level down, from left to right. Did
one cut last twenty minutes, half an hour? Christian couldn't say, he
wasn't allowed to wear his watch on the excavator. The bucket wheel
stopped at the highest point and Christian, as nimble as an orang-utan
once he had become accustomed to the work, would clamber up the
struts, gratings and railed walkways to the front of the boom at the
end of which, about fifteen metres from the body of the excavator, his
work began: knocking off the clumps of soil stuck to the wheel. For
that he used a pickaxe that the driver, at the beginning of the shift,
sharpened in the crow's nest of a workshop in the top storey of the
excavator, as well as a butcher's cleaver that was not a piece of standard
equipment, brought for him by the second 'man' (a giant of a woman
of indeterminate age in men's work clothes, who kept her mittens on
all the time, even while eating during breaks, and didn't say a word),
who demanded it back with a sullen grunt at the end of the shift. Christian hacked away like a murderer, on his back he could sense the eyes
of the driver, who, from the lower cab, was examining the darkness
above the calm glow of his cigarette; as a joke, the driver would switch
on the wheel after precisely ten minutes, sometimes sooner, just for a
try-out and 'to wake him up', as he said. Christian tried to stick to the
interval between the chimes of the ten-minute clock but he couldn't
summon up the period of time that he thought had become part of him.
When it wasn't freezing, the soil that had been rolled flat against the
bucket-wheel cover had the consistency of cork; the pick and cleaver
bounced back off it and more than once the implement had slipped out
of Christian's hand and landed below, beside the crawler tracks, like
a pathetically thin toy. When it was freezing the soil, in the minute it
took him to get from the recreation room to the bucket wheel, became
as hard as a tree trunk, and then Christian could only hack and split
and cut the dark brown mass off in shavings and splinters, working as
hard as he could, driven on by the fear of being caught by the wheel

as it suddenly started to turn. Up there the wind went to work roughly, without the cajoling and, when they paused, hypocritical blandishments of its ground troops, without the boxing gloves of its dust-welterweights, which gave a muted sigh as a punch was landed, without the air cushions beneath their flat-footed leaps onto the conveyor belts for the overburden, above which tin lamps swayed like drinkers who had tried to slip out without paying being shaken by a strapping landlord. The ship's doctor had told Christian about sailing ships in a storm, how the sailors were hanging on the yards, the raging sea twenty or thirty metres below them, balancing on footropes, clinging on to a recalcitrant sail that was furiously trying to burst its bonds and they were trying to reef, 'one hand for the ship, one hand for your life'. That's overdoing it, Christian thought, you're not on a ship. But the idea helped, forced a breach in the reality, made it in an uncomplicated way more bearable. Water . . . and rats. The water gathered at the bottom of the open-cast mine, clearing it away was a task that was almost beyond the pumps, whose groans the wind occasionally released, a sound that seemed to Christian like the death throes of creatures that were active in the machines (enslaved and imprisoned by some modern curse) and for which Christian felt sorry because they had to drink just water all the time – which he took as further proof that there was also a gradual side to the tortures. The rats were fat and uninhibited and had the slippery suppleness of animals you had to hold tight between your two hands (feral cats, polecats, old toads); when the bucket wheel swung into the hillside and started its work as a mechanical mole, the driver, whose name Christian never learnt, only his nickname ('Schecki' or 'Scheggi' depending on the degree of alcoholic merriness), liked to shoot at them from his cab with an air rifle, his ambition being to hit them with a 'clean' shot – in the eyes or, which counted for more, in their slimy, pink, bare tails that would then 'come to life' as a whip with St Vitus's dance – Schecki said in one of the few conversations he had with Christian; it had started with a vague wave of the hand in the direction of the top of the slope and a grunted 'There used to be graveyards up there', after Christian had found a half-decomposed foot in one of the buckets. Schecki grinned, took a sip of the rosehip tea the management distributed free to the workers, pressed the switch on the excavator radio and shouted 'Food' at the diaphragm; the reply was an irritated croak from Schanett's (that was the name of the woman unloader) cab. Schanett left the wagon she'd just filled, slammed the cab door, bent over the boom and gave a shout confirmed by a panting whistle from the locomotive in front of the spoil wagons. She stomped into the recreation room, where it was Christian's task to lay the table with four of the scratched plastic plates, with 'Property of the Brown-Coal Combine' on the back, and three sets of aluminium cutlery (Schanett ate with a butcher's knife of her own) and to switch on the frying plate that stuck out from the wall next to the locker with Schecki's change of clothes. When the plate was red-hot Schanett stood up, skewered a cube of margarine on the end of her butcher's knife, slapped it down on the plate, which was bent up at the sides, where the margarine fizzed round (the surplus dribbled into a rusty Wehrmacht helmet Schecki had found in the spoil and fixed under the plate), took (without removing her mittens) four gammon steaks wrapped in news-paper out of her rucksack, let the blood drip off, chucked them angrily onto the plate, turned them, scattered pepper, salt and garlic over the sizzling meat out of a tin containing all three spices together and, when the steaks were ready, nodded Schecki and the engine driver, who were exchanging dirty jokes that were going round the mine, over with a contemptuous gesture. She would serve Christian herself, hesitating for a moment before giving the plate a push in his direction, sending it slithering across the table with sauce and blood splashing over onto the oilcloth fixed to it with steel clamps. They mostly ate at two in the morning and the plate cooled down as they did so. They all lived *in the coal*; the open-cast mine was only one of many that belonged together and formed a conglomerate of churned-up ground, mud,

spoil heaps, coal seams stretching to the horizon with the excavators
squatting on them like grasping treasure-seekers and the bloodsucking
insects of the dumper trucks buzzing round. *In the coal*: somewhere in
the darkness, which came either from above (the quickly turning sky)
or from below (clay, gley, the oily shimmering puddles it was best to
avoid), were the remains of a small town: fire walls, rotten fences,
houses torn apart at an oblique angle, scraps of wallpaper with the
shapes of furniture still visible, a Konsum branch, no longer open
(Schecki, Schanett and the engine driver were self-sufficient, had a few
cows and pigs, grew what they needed). Schanett lived on a farmstead,
left over from a village, alone with her bedridden father, the former
village butcher, with no electricity, no running water, not even one of
the mine railways went out there. For the last hour of the night shift
Christian took over the unloader. Schanett went, guided by her sense
of smell and precise knowledge of the constantly changing tracks in the
working area, past the palely lit wagons and the kilometres of conveyor
belts, in order to be able to feed her stock at daybreak. Beside the window
in the unloading cabin there was a poster, green islands in a green sea.

Finale: Maelstrom

*Time fell out of time and aged. Time remained time on a clock with no
hands. Time above was its passage, the sun shone on dials, indicated morning, noon, evening, indicated the days on calendars: past days, the present
day, days to come. It leapt, it circled, it hurried off, a marble rolling down
a narrow spiral track. But time below pointed to the laws and didn't concern
itself with human clocks. A country with a strange disease, young people
old, young people not wanting to be adults, citizens living in niches,*

retreating into the body politic that, ruled over by old men, lay in deathlike sleep. Time of the fossils; fish were stranded when the waters receded, flapped mutely for a while, submitted, died motionless and fossilized: in the house walls, on the mouldering landings, they fused with documents, became watermarks. The strange disease marked faces; it was infectious, there was no adult who didn't have it, no child who remained innocent. Truths choked back, thoughts unspoken filled the body with bitterness, burrowed it into a mine of fear and hatred. Hardening and softening were the main symptoms of the strange disease. In the air there was a veil through which one breathed and spoke. Contours became blurred, a spade was not called a spade. Painters painted evasively, newspapers printed lines of black letters; however, they weren't what promoted understanding but the space between them . . . the white shadows of words that were to be sensed and interpreted. In the theatres they spoke in ancient metres. Concrete . . . cotton . . . clouds . . . water . . . concrete . . .

but then all at once . . .

Meno wrote,

but then all at once . . .

68

For technical reasons. Walpurgis Eve

Dances, dreams . . . Sleep became mushy, the early shift came and went, doors banged, from the rooms at the farther end of the corridor came Nip's babbling, sending the duty NCO or his assistant to the nearest shop to get some schnapps (over in Samarkand, an hour on foot through mud and the proud lifelessness of no-man's-land) . . . 'To be *sloshed* for a whole week,' Nip had said, 'and then to get up as if nothing had happened, simply to *lose*, forget a whole week. Seven empty pages in the calendar and despite that you're still there.' – 'That's too much of a luxury, boss,' said Pancake, who enjoyed the privilege of being allowed to sit on the edge of the mine crater playing tangos for the excavators; he took the right to address him by that title from the deals he set up with Nip. But the sergeant seemed to be taking him for a ride, threatening him with a 'you know what, Kretzschmar', so that Pancake had started to make a list that he added up now and then. Too much of a luxury: not to know what was going on for a week, then just to smooth out your uniform, 'not even kings can do that. And anyway, I'd be there. I like shirkers. Boss.'

Between the shifts, on the lemon-yellow linen that made the soldiers' quarrelling somehow cosy, amid tobacco smoke, the clatter of dice, bored-frustrated card bids, Christian spent a lot of time thinking about things.

'Do you think Burre was an informer?'

'Course I do. What else could he do, Nemo?'

'You're not calling me Mummy's Boy any more?'

'No one who can stick out a summer in the carbide is that. Simple fact, simple conclusion. – That makes you feel good, does it? Applause is our food, as they say in the circus.'

'I saw him outside the staff building. – You see a lot of people there, but not like that. It's hard to say why, but I could imagine where he was off to.'

'If I'd been him I'd have done just the same. You tell them this and that and you're left in peace. It must be difficult to pin something on you after that.'

'So what would you have told them about me?'

'That you think too much for a convinced socialist brother. That makes you dangerous. A clever Dick who can keep his trap shut as long as you, who quietly observes and isn't close to anyone, will never be satisfied with some provisional solution. He wants more. Freedom or justice, for example. And they're always the ones who make difficulties.'

'Perhaps you're an informer?'

'I'd get nothing out of it. Would ruin my business. I depend on my reputation and something like that always comes through, like damp through the wall.'

'Still.'

'Anyone else would have had that stuck in his ribs by now.' Pancake pointed to the crowbar propped against the shed wall.

Up to 29 December the winter was unusually mild; the cold arrived suddenly, Christian could see the puddles freezing over from the excavator, the rain abruptly turning into hail. The wires of the mine's electric locomotives crackled. The wind blew cold dust at them.

'Oh, brother' – the foreman in charge of the shift adjusted his hard hat and looked in concern at the flurries of snow – 'this really looks as if it's going to be something. And that just before New Year's Eve.'

'Four o'clock sharp, Meno.' Madame Eglantine's cigarette-hoarse, guttural laugh drew one's gaze to her eyes, which were as wide as a startled animal's and had the vulnerable-seeming shine of chestnuts fresh out of their spiny shell, to her dress (natural-green linen with red felt roses sewn on with exuberant irregularity), to her melancholy gait, which didn't appear to go with it, in cheap trainers or (in the winter) hiking boots that had been handed down to her, the laces of which she liked to leave untied: just a big girl, Meno thought as he followed her into the Hermes conference room, where another editor, Kurz, had already switched on the television for the live transmission of the 'Ceremony of the Central Committee of the Socialist Unity Party to celebrate the seventieth anniversary of the founding of the German Communist Party'. But the picture vanished a few seconds later, the radiators crackled and went cold, the hum of the refrigerator in the hall ceased and Udo Männchen, the typographer, standing by the window, said, 'Our life overall here is – underinstrumented. The whole of Thälmannstrasse's dark. We ought to be publishing books in braille.'

'You suggested that last time and the joke doesn't improve with age,' growled Kurz. Frau Zäpter brought in candles, a Christmas stollen, home-made gingerbread. 'I was just going to make tea anyway.'

'Why else would we have a spirit stove?' said the managing clerk, Kai-Uwe Knapp. 'I'd even filled it – man is a creature that can learn from past experiences.'

'How romantic,' Miss Mimi and Melanie Mordewein, who was sitting next to her, sighed simultaneously; Miss Mimi had got the tone so exactly, so caustically right that the laughter came slowly and remained just an expression of admiration.

Putting on white gloves, Niklas tipped the record, a flexible EMI pressing given him by one of his State Orchestra patients, out of its sleeve and the paper protective covering lined with foil, held the disc between middle finger and thumb (his index finger supporting it on the red label with the dog listening to his master's voice coming out of a gramophone horn), started to stroke it with extra-soft carbon fibres, which looked like a collection of seductive women's eyelashes, in an aluminium brush from Japan (another present from a musician patient), which was said to remove the dust more gently and yet more thoroughly than the yellow cloth that VEB Deutsche Schallplatten put in with its Eterna albums, slowly and pensively combed the fine sound track until Erik Orré, who was free that evening and had been talking to Richard about duodenal ulcers, said, 'That's enough, Niklas, I think you've gained its trust now.' The Schwedes (she, an operetta singer squinting with charming helplessness through lenses as thick as the base of a bottle; he, with handsome Clark Gable looks, Richard thought, a toothbrush moustache, a cardigan, worked in the branch of the Council for Mutual Economic Aid on Lindwurmring; the women there, as Richard knew from Niklas, called him by his first name, Nino) were standing by the window, both holding a tulip glass of beer; Nino said, 'If it keeps snowing like this we'll be switching on our water-pipe heater again, Billie.'

The whole town seemed to be in motion, pushing and shoving, things quickly breaking out in the darkness, violence kept under control by the street lamps, perhaps also by the civilizing power of other people's looks (violence, Meno thought, that grew remorselessly since you couldn't see the eyes of the people you were swearing at, elbowing, jostling, hitting); groups formed but only to disperse within the next few minutes; the streams of people seemed to be following the most cautious changes in conditions, perhaps just a murmured rumour, a correction in the magnetism (pushing, hoping), and at the same time to be moving aimlessly, disturbed bees whose hive had been taken away. Screaming and groaning, shouts across the dark streets, the tinkle of broken glass: had looting started already? Meno wondered, trying to keep his composure. Clinging on tight to his briefcase, he crossed the Old Market, heading for Postplatz, where he hoped to find a tram that was working. There were still a few lights on in the Zwinger restaurant, contemptuously called the 'Guzzle-cube' by Dresdeners, as also in the House of the Book and the fortress-like Central Post Office, built by Swedish firms. Meno was caught up in a rapidly growing swarm of people who seemed to be drawn, with moth-like instinct, to the lights, heliotropic creatures that would perhaps have been better off in the dark. A blizzard started. The theatre was in darkness, the 'Socialism will triumph' sign on the high-rise building had gone out. The trams had stopped, marine mammals, frozen in a ball of snow.

'Replacement bus service,' one of the conductors kept shouting resignedly, carefully wrapping himself up in a blanket, to the people crowding round. The bus for the 11 route left from the Press House on Julian-Grimau-Allee and was crowded; Meno saw Herr Knabe, the Krausewitzes, Herr Malthakus in his good suit with a bow tie, even Frau von Stern, who waved her senior citizen's pass in sprightly fashion as Dietzsch helped her onto the bus and to a seat that had been vacated for her. 'The opera, the theatre – all shut down,' she shouted angrily to Meno. The bus took them as far as Waldschlösschenstrasse.

'And the rest of the route? Are we to walk?'

'Yes,' the bus driver replied with a shrug of the shoulders. 'I have my instructions.'

After walking for a few kilometres the little cohort that was left halted at Mordgrundbrücke. The hill before them wasn't steep but, as they could tell in the strange brightness of the driving snow, covered with a milky sheet of ice. Halfway up a tram was stuck, frozen fast up to the top of its wheels; long, bizarrely shaped icicles were hanging down from the wires and the steep slope on the Mordgrund side of the hill.

'A water main must have copped it,' Malthakus said in an appreciative tone. 'The question is, how are we going to get up there. Given that no one's going to pull us up –'

'A belay such as they have with roped parties in the mountains,' said Frau von Stern. 'We had that during the war when it was icy.'

'– otherwise we'll all have a nice slide and they can hack us out of the stream in the morning.'

'I'm not going up there with my instrument anyway,' a double-bass player from the State Orchestra declared; a French-horn player agreed. 'Our valuable instruments.'

'Why didn't you leave them at the Opera, then,' Herr Knabe asked exasperatedly.

'What a . . . excuse me, but I have to say it: stupid question. I'm sure that even in these conditions your Mathematical Cabinet will be well secured, but our miserable artists' dressing rooms?! Do you think I'd leave my instrument by itself?'

'OK then, but have you another suggestion?'

'We'll just have to go up by Schillerstrasse.'

'But the water mains run along there too. They could well have burst as well . . . And Buchensteig is even steeper. But don't let me stop you going to reconnoitre. Or you can simply stay here with your valuable instruments,' Herr Knabe said scornfully.

'What the hell, we can just turn round and go to a hotel,' said Herr Malthakus. 'I've got a few marks on me, perhaps they'll let us stay in the Eckberg with a down payment.'

'You'll be lucky,' Meno said, 'they're already full with evacuees from the Johannstadt district.'

'Look – a snow blower.' The French-horn player pointed to the stretch of road before Kuckuckssteig.

The cold bit deeper, the cold crushed up the white clouds from the cooling towers of the power station that usually bloomed like a drunken dream: finding heaven here on earth and swelling up, with explosive clarity, thrillingly, fantastically into short-lived atmospheric mushrooms; the cold gave the iron of the pickaxes a different sound; the power station cables, usually buzzing with electricity, whispered like the strings of instruments with mutes on, seemed raw and sensitive to pain under the coating of ice; made by humans. Christian had been working for seventeen hours continuously. The trains bringing brown coal were lined up outside the power station, but the coal was frozen fast in the goods wagons and had to be blasted out; the detonations briefly drowned the rattle of the power hammers that had been hurriedly brought from the Federal Republic. It wasn't pleasant to be one of the squad whose job it was to move the wagons out of the way when the explosive charge hadn't detonated.

'We've two candidates,' Nip said to the drivers, who were getting their bachelors to draw lots.

'Hoffmann or Kretzschmar, who's going?' He tossed a coin, said, 'Kretzschmar.'

'Stay here,' Christian said, 'I'm going.'

'Why?' Nip asked, flabbergasted.

'Things'll go wrong with him.'

'All right then,' Nip said, 'it doesn't bother me. I've nothing against heroes.'

'Don't fool yourself, Nemo. Your knees are trembling.'

'Yes, but you're staying here all the same.' Nothing was going to happen, Christian decided. –

A helicopter landed, letting out a few big shots, who went here and there, waving their hands about nervously, clicking walkie-talkies, talking with the crisis committee of the Brown Coal Combine (plans were unrolled, held their attention for a moment, then there was something new and the plans, hurt, rolled up again and just stayed there); *decisionmakers* whose movements in front of the power station and the setting sun behind it seemed to Christian like a ritual dance of Red Indians. Before the *decisionmakers* climbed back into their helicopter, they stood motionless, arms akimbo, by the coal wagons, a collection of sad, impotent men.

30 December: the evacuees came out of the town on army lorries labouring up the track that had been chipped free up the Mordgrund; more water kept running down the hill and freezing; gravel and ash didn't stop the route from turning into a dangerous skid-pan. Richard saw companies of soldiers and some of the staff from Grauleite swinging pickaxes to keep the way clear; some acquaintances were spreading grit. Where was the water coming from? The power cut – it was the south of the Republic that was said to be affected, the capital with its special fuse protection was still bathed in the pre-New Year glow – had allowed the water to freeze in many of the pipes, causing them to burst. But that was ice? Richard thought, as he strode through the snow beside Niklas observing the water flowing over the road; more kept bubbling up and quickly turned to ice, those spreading grit couldn't

keep up with it. Niklas was pulling a handcart with bandages and medicines they'd taken from his practice. Richard was quietly cursing, he'd thought he was going to spend a relaxing New Year with punch, conversations, some post-Christmas reflections, a walk to Philalethes' View to watch the blaze of rockets over the city and to drink to the New Year . . . Anne was still at Kurt's in Schandau and of course there were no trains running; they'd arranged for Richard to phone the pastor of St John's (Kurt still wasn't connected) but the line was dead – that too, then. Now Anne was stuck in Schandau and he was trudging through ice and snow with Niklas to attend to the sick – and there were probably some waiting there already. They were going to the military hospital, that was where Barsano and his crisis team had set up their base, people were being evacuated there from the new developments: Prohlis, Reick, Gorbitz, Johannstadt.

'Have you noticed that your sense of touch seems to get duller if your hearing's worse?' Niklas, Richard thought, was aware of the seriousness of the situation. 'Ezzo must be stuck in the Academy of Music, Reglinde was going to see the New Year in with friends in Neustadt, Gudrun was supposed to be on stage – Meno! Hey, Meno! Have you seen Gudrun?'

Meno, who was getting off a lorry, shook his head. 'She wasn't on our bus. – You're going to the military hospital?'

'Herr Rohde!' Barsano called from the gate with the red star and waved. 'Come and help us – you speak Russian. I've got enough to do coordinating things. We can use you as an interpreter. Herr Hoffmann, Herr Tietze, will you please report to the duty doctor.'

A Forbidden Place, a place of dust, Meno thought, going through the gate that a confused sentry was trying to guard. NATURA SANAT was the greeting from the former ladies' pool, in front of it, with a Kirghizian smile, the silver head of Lenin. The suspended walks were dilapidated, windowpanes shattered, art nouveau decoration faded, wind and rain had gnawed at the roof. From the eaves, off which many of the projecting rafters had broken away like teeth off one of those hand-sawn beauty-salon combs anointed with good wishes and promises, a proliferation of icicles was hanging down, heavy and dirty, as if they wanted to silence a music box, the gracefulness of which would have enlarged the cracks in the buildings and amplified the throb of the conveyor belts from the heating plant on the slope. On the covered walks outside the former patients' rooms were the old tubs, crammed full of sticks of wood and newspaper. Spiders' webs, like the ornaments on Tartar helmets, hung down from the carved wood, black, glittering with frost. But were they spiders' webs? Meno thought he had been mistaken. None of the spiders' webs he was familiar with were shaped like that, not even ones made over decades and with many layers, only to be destroyed in moments. They were lichens, long mossy growths, hanging down, sucked into the flesh of the arms of the trees at the outpost; felty beards of indefinite colour on the roofs that the woods seemed to be trying to draw back into their kingdom in a slow embrace. Barsano waved Meno over to join his deputy, Karlheinz Schubert, who led the way to Heinrichshof, a half-timbered villa that had belonged to the former owner of the sanatorium and now housed the hospital headquarters. The gentlemen's massage room and the kitchen were empty, boarded up. Blocked gutters, missing roof tiles, clouds of dry rot building up on the woodwork of the corridors that had once been glazed, black mould creeping across the ceiling. Schubert said nothing, marched on with long strides that ate up the ground, as if he were afraid of missing his footing with short ones, past piles of dead leaves and snow that had been blown in, doors marked with Cyrillic letters and meticulously drawn numbers; glassy-eyed, he silently greeted the occasional patient they encountered, who glanced at the two men apprehensively. The musty smell of the corridors, the greeny-blue gloss paint that had been plastered over the walls to counter the damp and the pests that had taken up residence in them; the mosaics that had been shamelessly taken up from the floor where corridors crossed, only the odd pale tile left to suggest ancient Roman bathing scenes; on the other hand the dust-swathed chandeliers dangling in the fluctuating draughts over smashed windows were untouched; wall newspapers with the current editions of *Pravda* and the satirical magazine *Krokodil* – both present impressions and old memories that awoke many things in Meno's mind. In a faltering voice Schubert asked Meno to wait; after a few minutes he came back, shaking his head: the lavatory basins had all been torn out, packed up and addressed to be sent home, and two soldiers were squatting over holes, a camp stool with the board on it between them, playing chess . . . But Karlheinz Schubert seemed to pull himself together and, pressing his lips into a thin line, reminded Meno that it was allies they were talking about, brother socialists. In Heinrichshof, where they had to wait, Meno looked at a framed silhouette hanging in the vestibule; it was, as he could see from the fine cut-out signature, one of Frau Zwirnevaden's, showing scenes from Goethe's poem 'The Sorcerer's Apprentice' in which the apprentice himself, who was usually portrayed (by the author too) as in despair at his unbiddable creation, appeared to be waiting for his master's return with cool interest.

The open-cast mine looked like an army camp. Soldiers had been transferred, were camping in hastily erected tents. To go by the rapid-rumour network, power supplies were unaffected in the north of the country and the capital. To the south of a line corresponding roughly to the course of the middle Elbe between Torgau and Magdeburg, the excavators were at a standstill, the houses in darkness, the supply chain collapsed; Samarkand no longer received its most important raw material and the huge power stations, coal-consuming tumours pumping energy into the life around that had knotted themselves with an abundance of veins into the lunar landscape, remained dark, unnourished, unexpectedly starving.

The soldiers went out on twelve-hour shifts – there weren't enough tents, one shift could sleep while the other was working. Christian's room now housed sixty men, the ten bunk beds had been given a third storey (for those on the top the gap between body and ceiling was so narrow that they couldn't turn over) and there were only twenty lockers for the sixty men – some now had three padlocks on them, which didn't contribute to the quiet in the room. Pancake and Christian shared bunk and locker; Pancake threatened to beat up anyone daring to claim room in the locker and the former circus blacksmith's physical strength and violent temper made an impression on even the toughest types. A piece of soap, a cigarette, a letter not handed out on time could lead to a punch-up, and since the men came from other units and their officers were far away, Nip had no power over them. 'Oh, go to hell,' they said to him when, lying drunk in his room, he pointed to the mail (forgotten letters that should have been sent out, forgotten letters that should have been distributed) with a mournful, apathetic gesture; before his very eyes, which had taken on the dull this-ness of hard-boiled eggs, they wrote their names in the exit log, stole his schnapps and underpants, which, bawling and shouting, they hung on poles they stuck into the pile of spoil beside the shed – where they fluttered in the wind, exposed to everyone's pity – or soaked them in miner's hooch the brown-coal engine drivers sold to them, then roasted the spirit-infused item over a fire.

A shower tent had been put up, ten showers for a hundred filthy bodies, with the water coming in dribbles and ice-cold from the nozzles; the crudely chopped-up slabs of soap made no foam. Christian was revolted at the idea of fighting for a few jets of water in a cramped space, he hated the enforced removal of the last bit of privacy remaining to those who had managed to keep an individual self alive in the uniform and tried to keep it out of the compulsory 'us' of the army. Recalling the winter water from Kurt's tank, he washed himself far away from the shed in one of the puddles that were steaming with cold.

On New Year's Day the water in the tanker that supplied the units in the camp was frozen and there wasn't enough to eat, a lorry with the meals had got stuck somewhere, the *Komplekte* had all gone long before Christian and Pancake arrived; to his astonishment Christian discovered that hunger existed. He'd never gone hungry. Not in Schwedt, not on the Carbide Island, certainly not at home, where everyone he knew *groused* but strangely enough had *everything* . . . acquired, of course, through *contacts* and *endless chasing round*, but bread cost onezerofour, a roll one groschen, milk had gone up from sixty-six to seventy pfennigs, but all that had always been available . . .

'We need something to eat, Nemo.' Pancake wondered whether to take the *Komplekte* from one of the younger, weedy soldiers who had been in front of him in the queue, but others in the line of waiting soldiers behind them were doing that already, the tough ones were taking the food away from the less tough ones, the faster pursuers from the less fast ones running away, and whenever anyone protested against this law of the jungle, it was fists that decided who was in the right. 'Any ideas, Cap'n?'

'The woman who does the unloading on my shift,' Christian said after a while spent searching hungrily through his memory, 'lives on a farm somewhere in the coal. There's sure to be something there.'

'D'you know where it is?'

'Not exactly,' Christian said hesitantly. Schecki had pointed vaguely in a northward direction. 'Torch and compass, perhaps we'll find it. We could ask one of the railwaymen.'

'Better not, Nemo. If we want to get something, then we don't want anyone else in the know.'

'We could knock.'

'We could. But if she lives the way you say, she won't open. – We have to be back before the shift starts. I don't fancy being put away again.'

Doctor Varga lifted up the lamp, shortening the shadows on the walls of the cellar passage. The water on the floor didn't seem to be getting any higher, it still hadn't risen up the legs of the rubber boots they were wearing; also it was starting to freeze over so that the rats, which showed no fear in following them, had to go under water in some places; the dark bodies with the pointed noses covered in bristles paddled under the ice and didn't panic even when one of the soldiers accompanying Varga and Meno tried to crush them under his heel. 'Air-raid shelter,' Meno read, a red arrow pointed to a steel door, the handle of which was draped in spiders' webs. Notices in old German handwriting with Cyrillic scribbles over them on the cellar walls. The water started rising again.

'Here, I think,' Varga said, but he spread his arms out in front of the doors. 'I don't know exactly, I've never been down here before.'

'*Voda — otkuda?*' Barsano's deputy asked. The soldiers shrugged their shoulders. With the butt of his Kalashnikov one knocked the padlock off one of the doors; the rats scurried towards it and vanished, it was impossible to see where. The soldiers dragged the door open, Varga said, 'Let's have a look', and clicked on a rotary switch, light shot out of ceiling lamps encrusted with spiders' webs only to be swallowed up by the darkness again with a muted 'fatch' that was reflected back from the depths of the room as a distorted echo – the teeming darkness filled with pecking and scraping noises into which Varba pushed his pit lamp. Meno thought: the ticking of thousands of clocks; but it was the legs of the brown rats, some heading purposefully, though with comical slithering, stumbling and waving of legs, for the depths of the room, while others were trying to recover their balance with desperately clutching claws; thousands of brown rats; there were so many black button eyes caught in the smoky light that they looked like a shower of sparks leaping across the room. It seemed to be very big, the far side couldn't be seen. None of the men ventured inside, the soldiers grasped their rifles tight – the rats kept going towards their goal. The water wasn't coming from there, although the floor was covered in a thick layer of ice. Meno took Varga's lamp (the microbiologist had frozen, likewise the deputy, though he had managed to turn his head); by the faint light Meno could make out marks, lines forming a circle, the ice sounded as hard as porcelain; the strange ticking noise of the thousands of tiny feet had grown louder. But there was a goal there! A handball goal with a torn net, beside it posts and climbing ropes, wall bars, a pile of rubber mats – the gymnasts were there too. Frozen stiff in the ice, orthopaedic models were standing on the court in bent and contorted postures; they were carved from old wood that gleamed darkly in the light of Meno's lamp, as if it had been rubbed smooth by the hands of generations of interested pupils.

The torches were kept off, Pancake waited until the grey of first light began to change objects back out of the cellar darkness: a chopping block with the axe sticking out, jars that the blanket of snow had cemented together, making them look like dully glittering molars in a white shimmer of swollen gums. He broke out one, a standard jam jar with a plastic lid, examined it in the meagre light, cut out a cone of the waxy pale contents, smelt it. 'I don't think anyone would conserve poison in jars,' he whispered, holding out the cone to Christian. 'Though time can poison many things.'

69

A storm brewing

'When I saw you for the first time I never thought you'd be giving me lines of verse. – That's honey. Frozen honey.'

'Artificial honey?' Pancake wondered as he tasted it. He broke more jars out of the snow and put them into their bag. The jars seemed to have stayed airtight. 'We've got to clear off. It's too quiet for my liking.

I'm surprised they don't have a dog. I'd have one if I had to live out here.'

The dog jumped up on Christian in silence, pressed him against the wall by the cellar door, stayed on its hind legs, panting and flapping its chops, its front paws on his shoulders. A scythe blade curved round Pancake's throat, drawing the alarmed blacksmith up the steps. Schanett crooked her index finger, beckoning them into the house, the scythe she hung on a peg over the door. The house was cold, the windows crooked, covered with fern-patterns of ice. Schanett led the way with a lantern, leaving it to the growling dog to push the two surprised burglars forward. More dogs appeared but Schanett shooed them away. The touch of the soft muzzle Christian could feel on his behind was like that of a rubber truncheon – a sign from stick to cloth, individual, biding its time; Christian was horrified at the thought that Schanett might report them and thus send them back to *there*; in that case, he decided, he'd try to take the quick way out. They probably didn't have a telephone here and of course there was no electricity . . . They seemed to be going down, there was a cellar smell to the air. The circle of light from Schanett's lantern no longer reached the ceiling, a black vault with meat hanging down in pieces from the size of your finger to that of a man, all frosted over, some entirely encased in ice that seemed to be waiting, motionless, for contact with the floor; presumably the weight of all this and the yielding ground of the open-cast mine were making the house gradually subside. But that didn't explain the vast height of the room that nothing suggested from outside – perhaps the house had been torn in half, the lower storeys were sinking while the roof stayed above ground. Meat; Pancake kept his head down. Dark-red flesh, with sinews running through, embedded in white fat; ice-bound kidneys; pig's heads, glittering with rime, their open eyes giving them a strangely ironic expression; hearts close together, dotted with white lumps.

*

'Come.' The proofreader nodded to Meno. 'Redlich,' Klemm murmured, 'as every year honest Josef Redlich faithfully bears the yoke, prepares for the Fair and . . . oh, Fräulein Wrobel, I didn't think you were still here; the Beethoven quartets have fallen silent.'

'You're . . . going to the events?'

Instinctively they moved out of the light from the street lamp and as answer Oskar Klemm, a gentleman of the old school, offered his arm to Madame Eglantine – which she took even though, as Meno was aware, the 'Fräulein' annoyed her. Her face was pale, her eyes dark with doubts and fear; but her coat, her grandfather's loden coat that had been altered to fit her, had felt patches of various colours in the form of soles of the feet, the toes of which were cheekily splayed. 'May I tie your shoelaces? Just think of the consequences of a stumble, my dear.'

'Rosenträger's going to speak,' Meno said cautiously.

'It's good to hear something different for once. Schiffner's forbidden us to go but, my dear colleagues' – Klemm stopped and lifted up his face – 'I for my part have finally decided to start being brave.'

The Church of the Holy Cross, a programme of music by the choir's former director, Rudolf Mauersberger. The people were so tightly packed that a middle-aged woman close to Meno fainted but didn't fall down. The motet: 'Now is the town laid waste'. But (and that was characteristic, Meno thought) the terrible things had to be beautifully expressed, resolved in euphony – the transparent tongue of the boys' choir started to beguile their ears – and harmony, within a framework of elegant proportions and established modes; people then called it traditional, even though it could well be something different. Ethereal voices, the simplicity of the burnt-out church a contrast, the roughcast walls, in the candles' halo above the boys' heads the measured gestures of the conductor evoking mourning, negotiating hurdles, which the choir's veil of transfiguration around the supporting tones of the Jehmlich organ followed with childlike innocence.

Rosenträger entered the pulpit. A perceptible movement went through the people who had been gripped by the music, upper bodies leant forward (like the ominous, tumescent turn of a carnivorous plant towards a potential prey that has unknowingly touched the outer signal circuit), necks were craned, hands nervously felt prayer books, fingered the brims of hats as if they were prayer beads; the clouds of breath from their mouths became invisible and passed, when the clearly articulating voice of the preacher was at last heard, like a sigh of relief through the flickering gloom of the nave. He spoke about the thirteenth of February. Meno sensed that that wasn't what people had hoped for – and what Madame Eglantine had perhaps meant with the hesitantly spoken word 'events'; they had expected memories of the air raid, war, devastation and the past, but had hoped for words about the present. When they did come, it was as if a flash of lightning went round the galleries, so quickly did the congregation lift up their faces to look at Rosenträger, whom Barsano, as Meno recalled, had designated a 'main enemy'. The lean man with the straggly, casually combed hair calmly said things people would previously only have dared to whisper in private or have kept to themselves. Meno kept being made physically aware of the way people froze when Rosenträger spoke of 'aberrations', of the sole and indivisible truth that could only be found in God and not in political parties; when he used the comparison of a mirror that didn't reflect fine wishes but realities people would prefer not to see (out of ingrained habit Meno was not sure whether the image worked). The man, Meno decided after some time observing him, was neither a gambler carried by the wave of presumed gratitude beyond the sands of inhibition necessary for survival, nor a self-important windbag for whom, when he mounted the pulpit as God's representative in ecclesiastical dress, a little sun of vanity rose. He expressed simple truths in simple words. That he was doing it here, in Holy Cross Church in front of an audience of a few thousand, was a necessity and it was by no means merely the way of seeing things of an 'isolated clique', as

Barsano called those who attended services in the church. Here some-one was breaking through the barrier of silence, of looking the other way, of fear; Rosenträger was afraid, Meno could tell that from the pastor's movements, which were more agitated than might in the long run be good for his authority in the eyes of cool observers – but the people, as Meno could see, sucked in his words in greedy silence. Per-haps it was precisely the fact that Rosenträger's bearing was not that of a Party official crudely and dictatorially handing down judgments from the clouds of the laws governing the progress of history; Rosen-träger adjusted his spectacles, spoke without notes, searching for words, in an upright posture, the people heard no empty words; he was afraid – and still spoke.

Richard had asked Robert to stop before the bend to the quarry. He wanted to do the last few metres on foot, with Anne's sarcasm behind him, true, but, to make up for that, in glorious anticipation of enjoying a long eye-to-eye; and he also wanted to amaze Robert, his seen-it-all son (being overwhelmed was good for people). How clear the air was – spring sketches; a bird on a branch shook its feathers, sending down a shower of alarmed drops of water.

Jerzy, the sculptor, was hanging from a pulley, busy on the ear of his giant Karl Marx, and waved to Richard. From the other end of the quarry came the sound of furious hammering: Dietzsch was shaping his 'work in progress' as he called it, 'The Thumb', but didn't wave back to Richard. The shed was in the lovely disorder of children's games. Stahl, in reflective and self-ironic mood, had once commented on work that was done with enthusiasm and for its own sake because it was being done by grown men disguised as boys; brightness threaded in through the gaps in the planks. His car was waiting under the tar-paulin. 'Hispano-Suiza,' Richard whispered, the very sound delighted him. Repeating the name, his eye fell on some pliers Stahl had used. Nothing was left of his aeroplane, the 'SAGE' as Gerhart had christened it after the first letters of 'Sabine' and 'Gerhart', but a few chalk marks, partly washed away by the rain that got in, partly scuffed by Richard's shoes, indicating the former places of tools and material. The children had been sent to children's homes, in different towns, that much Richard had learnt from Sperber. Which towns? Embarrassed, Sperber had looked away and shrugged his shoulders.

For a few seconds Richard enjoyed the sight of the postbox-yellow oilcan on the black shelf. The way it shone. How immediate it was and how calm its immediacy. Then he went to the car and pulled off the tarp.

The Hispano-Suiza had been demolished with professional precision. The leather seats had been slit, the steering wheel, the column sawn off, had been stuck into the upholstery of the driver's seat. Richard opened the bonnet. The leads, the copper arteries that seemed so alive, the nickel-plated fuel veins, had been hammered flat and cut up – with enjoyment, oh yes, one could sense that. The engine – concreted in; lying in the solidified mass as if in a stone case – Richard could take them out easily – were the bolt cutters he'd lost when they'd tried to steal a Christmas tree. Dangling from them, neatly attached between the two blades as if they were a birthday present, was a note on which 'With socialist greetings' had been typed.

Splints, padded protection for legs, leather straps: even though it was an old-fashioned version, Christian had already seen the seating along the tiled walls during his periods of practical experience in hospitals, similarly the glass cases with neatly arranged instruments: steel cylinders of various sizes cut off at an angle, dressing forceps, kidney bowls, clamps. From the next room, the warmly heated kitchen gleaming with copper, came the rich sweet smell of cakes. The honey extractors rattled and rumbled as Pancake and Christian turned the cranks to remove the wax. Towards evening Schanett let them go with a shoebox full of vanilla slices topped with caramelized almonds.

*

One April evening, there were more people than usual out for a walk, Pastor Magenstock put up the call to action of an environmental group in the glassed-in board outside the church, a bright orange notice, a magnet to the eye, between quotations from the Bible and another one about donations for the Third World. Meno stopped and watched Herr Hähnchen, the district policeman, reluctantly approach, looking down at the ground and up at the sky fading in floral colours, placing his hands alternately behind his back or over his imposing stomach, thumbs in the Adidas braces visible under his uniform jacket. 'You know that you shouldn't do that,' Herr Hähnchen said after he'd read the notice thoroughly through the spectacles he'd made heavy weather of unfolding. By now Herr Kannegiesser, the organist, his face bright red with alarm, had come to stand in front of Pastor Magenstock, taking deep breaths as he protected him; the tall, fat district policeman and the short, skinny church musician looked each other up and down in amazement for a while.

'I suppose you want to be a hero?' Hähnchen asked, sadness in his look.

'The word "hero" does not occur in the New Testament, Herr Hähnchen. It is my duty to my parishioners and to my own conscience no longer to remain silent,' Pastor Magenstock said.

For a moment Hähnchen said nothing, then admitted he could understand that. Nevertheless it was his official duty to request the removal of the notice.

'But you have children as well,' cried Herr Malthakus, who had come over with the Kühnasts and the Krausewitzes and stood by Magenstock's side. Herr Hähnchen replied that that was true.

'There's no point shutting your eyes,' Frau Knabe declared. She was carrying several shopping bags and also came to stand at Magenstock's side, together with a few members of the emancipation group she'd recently set up.

'Herr Rohde, come over here,' she commanded.

'Herr Hähnchen,' said Meno, 'perhaps it's possible that you haven't seen anything?'

Herr Hähnchen said that in principle such a possibility always existed, only –

Staff from the Grauleite barracks approached. 'Disperse!' an officer bellowed. But the people stayed where they were. Frau Knabe slowly shook her head. The officer looked aghast, seemed confused. Other people out for a walk saw the gathering and instead of quickly going past, heads down, with eyes that saw nothing, as had been the case in confrontations with the power of the state so far, they came over, more and more of them, followed by observers from the gardens along Ulmenleite and stood beside Pastor Magenstock.

The officer remained silent. And never had Meno seen such a lonely man as District Police Officer Heinz Hähnchen in the middle of the open space between the two groups.

Nina Schmücke's circle was mixed. Richard, whom she greeted like an old acquaintance with kisses to the cheeks right and left (probably so that Anne would see, he started on an explanation but she waved it away), nodded across to Clarens and Weniger, who gave him a surprised and hostile scrutiny, at the same time whispering something to one of the bearded men in check shirts and jeans, who, as far as Richard could tell from a quick assessment, ran the show. Anne was confused by the pictures on the walls, on several easels whose crusts of coloured drips were at war with the aggressive tones on the canvases. From one of the few windows of the studio that weren't pasted over or nailed up with cardboard or plywood, Richard looked out over Neustadt: broken roofs in which naked men bowed before the setting sun; eroded chimneys, the boards below them for the chimney sweeps all taken: a fat man was sleeping on his back, arms and legs hanging down. A gaunt person in black latex clothing walked up and down, a woman was checking her angling equipment. Richard got a drink for Anne, put a chair by the window for her – after the man with the full beard had taken Nina Schmücke aside and clearly been calmed down by her, the discussions, which had been interrupted by their entrance, continued with frequent striking of matches and clicking of lighters. Sluggishly, slowly, sluggishly. Richard knew a few of those present: two women who were medical technical assistants from the Neurological Clinic, the former junior doctor from Internal Medicine who had spoilt their Christmas-tree triumph, Frau Freese stared at him with uncomfortable directness – he lowered his head, was furious with himself at his cowardice and stared back defiantly, at which Frau Freese ducked behind the shoulders of two men who worked on Coal Island. Richard recognized the attendant who had leafed through his documents in melancholy fashion before Regine had emigrated and let him stay in F corridor; he had had dealings with the other about the gas waterheater. Rapid looks that slipped off faces and waited between them. Fear that was afraid of fear. Hands that didn't know what to do with themselves. An engineer was talking about his life that, as he concealed rather than revealed in evasive descriptive loops, could no longer be 'sufficiently' distinguished from the mundane . . . tedium. The Great Tedium had his existence in its grip! One agreed. One shared the experience. One asked for suggestions. – One ought to start with a sit-in straight away, said a woman with a pirate's headscarf and a linen dress that had embroidery in the shape and red-and-white colour of a traffic cone on it that Richard found as beautiful as it was unusual. Something must finally change in the country, too many had gone already, half the multistorey building where she lived, for example – how was it all going to end?

'Perhaps our guest could tell us something about that,' said Weniger pointing at Richard, 'he has contacts not everyone has –'

'That's a malicious insinuation, Manfred, you'll take it back, please.' Anne had stood up.

'Great, the way you stand up for your husband. – You should have told us you were inviting him, Nina. I can see too many unknown faces anyway.'

'When we talk and want to get beyond our little circle, then we have to go outside. You agreed with that, Manfred,' the bearded man replied.

'Maybe, but I would like to have been told whom you're inviting. If he stays' – Weniger avoided looking at Richard – 'I'm going. The risk is too great.'

'Sit down and eat your cake,' Clarens begged him.

'We have to take risks,' said a man with a shaven head. Richard knew him, one of Gudrun's colleagues at the theatre. His leather coat came down to the ankles and was very scuffed. He folded his arms (rich creaking of leather), licked the cut end of a cigar. Two young women sitting cross-legged, both wearing keffiyehs as neckcloths, spoke up. – 'I'm Julia,' said one. – 'And I'm Johanna,' said the other. 'We think what Annegret's just suggested is a good idea. And I'm sure Robert in Grünheide would also –'

'And would Robert in Grünheide also have known where the sit-in's to take place?' Weniger broke in. Did they seriously believe they could compel them to introduce reforms with methods like that?

'Absolutely,' a man in a suit and tie replied in measured tones, 'in general yes.'

The man beside him, wearing a jean jacket with a 'Swords to Ploughshares' sew-on badge, argued that they should read Bonhoeffer.

'No, read Bahro,' someone on a settee under an acrylic Stalin with a black eye demanded.

Richard could see the woman with the fishing gear waving. Police burst into the room. The interest in art had suddenly become widespread.

'Identity card check! No one is to leave the room.'

70

Walpurgis Night

'Ah, there you are.' Arbogast leant back against the window, looking at the butterfly on the tip of his forefinger. He handed it to Herr Ritschel, who put it in a net and left, walking carefully.

'It's no small matter you're asking of me, Herr Hoffmann.'

'You have published something before.'

'Our Assyriologist's blue book, yes. But that was entertainment. Your piece is about politics. To accede to your request would be to give them pretexts.'

'So you won't help us?'

'Who is "us"?'

'A group of people who are more than just concerned about the situation. Who are determined to do something about it.'

'– are determined, aha. There's something direct about determination, that could well be seen to correspond to the principles of my institute. Why don't you approach a newspaper, Herr Hoffmann? The best place for multiple copies. There have been many interesting reports recently and not all editors are blinkered.'

'Herr von Arbogast – no newspaper in the country will publish such an appeal. You know that just as well as I do.'

'That's something we must discuss . . . As you wish. Did you get my letter? I thought of calling you several times. – I suspect you have other things than my project to worry about at the Academy.'

'I'm sorry.'

'Moreover I share many of the views expressed in your piece, Herr Hoffmann. I'll think the matter over.'

'The fee –'

Arbogast smiled. 'Oh, you know, that wouldn't be a problem, Herr

Hoffmann. A few jokes . . . you know perhaps that I collect them? Possibly the Bier/Braun/Kümmell surgical manual you have? Your brother-in-law from the Italian House told me about it. – Let's both think it over. Will I see you at the Sibyllenhof afterwards? – Pity.' Arbogast stood up, smoothed down his red jacket as, on the horizontal face of a desk clock behind the forest of sharp-pointed pencils, a dancer, an ivory Thumbelina, began to turn to the strains of a waltz.

A fancy-dress ball! The foyer of the Sibyllenhof restaurant was decorated with Chinese lanterns and garlands with streamers dangling down, flickering coloured bulbs had been hung over the window bays, a banner across the ceiling announced, 'Dance your way into May'. Meno showed his invitation, took his old zoologist's overalls and microscope out of his rucksack and went to the cloakroom, where a Red Riding Hood attendant hung up his hat between the Borsalinos of the two Eschschloraques. Karlfriede Sinner-Priest, dressed as a lady-in-waiting from the baroque period in Saxony, was standing next to Albert Salomon (August the Strong) by the Sibyllenhof telephone booths, which could be opened with a Allen key you were given after your name had been entered in the house telephone book at reception, and seemed to be in animated conversation with several writers – Meno recognized Lührer (embarrassingly also dressed as August the Strong) and Altberg (as a miner, who raised his hand in a half-wave of greeting). The main room of the restaurant was bathed in bluish-purple light that, coming from disco spotlights, ran down the wall like veins of ore. Albin Eschschloraque was wearing a nightwatchman costume and sitting, looking quite forlorn, with his lantern and nightwatchman's horn, at one of the tables with white cloths; he waved to Meno. 'Well then, man at the microscope, how's things?' he called out gloomily; Meno replied evasively but in markedly friendly tones.

'Things might get quite lively tonight.' Albin Eschschloraque pushed a bowl with pieces of Brockensplitter chocolate across to Meno but was dipping into it so frequently himself that Meno felt obliged to tear open one of the triangular packets from VEB Argenta and refill the bowl. Stewards in white that the Sibyllenhof, short of staff as were so many businesses, appeared to have borrowed from Arbogast's personnel (by the entrance Frau Alke was occupied making last-minute adjustments to the buffet), were putting out carafes on the tables; Albin filled two glasses with the juice of a reddish tinge: 'Rhubarb juice,' he announced with a look on his face that still appeared undecided whether it was to express appreciation or displeasure. 'They urgently need to make an inventory of the drinks in East Rome.' The Sibyllenhof had hardly made any contribution, it didn't have an allocation for such events; that was a Michurin product or one of the scientists' little jokes to celebrate the day, as was, for example, the punch, brewed in Arbogast's laboratories in Grünleite. 'Have you brought your excommunicated sphinx, Herr Rohde, the grey-haired Roman lady?'

'She doesn't need to get me to escort her.'

'Do I detect a note of bitterness? That's true, she's once more held in esteem and dread, as Papa, for whom the dread a person arouses is definitely part of a mature personality, would say. It's the same with paternosters as with this guy here.' He felt inside his costume and held up a ballpoint pen, the barrel of which was filled with a transparent liquid in which a little figure floated up and down when you turned the pen. 'A Cartesian diver, quite nice. They're handed out free as advertising in West Elbia, usually by pharmaceutical firms. The guy over there' – Albin jerked his thumb at the barman, reputedly the tallest man in the Republic – 'sells replicas. Of course, they can't copy the reservoirs. Instead of pills, promotion of our little town in its little hills, and instead of the Argonauts there's a daughter of the winds dancing here. – Here come the others.'

Malthakus had simply hung a Beirette round his neck and gone as a photographer, Record-Trüpel as a chimney sweep with ladder and top hat, Frau Zschunke wore bundles of radishes as ear-rings; Frau Knabe, in her overalls and carrying a molar on her shoulder, was beside Frau Teerwagen and the Honichs, who had hardly made any effort (Babett in a Young Pioneers blouse and a blue cap; her reply to Meno's nod was rather silly: she put her hand up vertically to the top of her head in the Pioneer's salute; Pedro in his combat group uniform with a full row of medals). Behind them came Joffe, rather amusingly dressed as a red taper, in lively conversation with Frau Arbogast; in that light the Baroness's blue rinse looked metallic, the leather tan of her face contrasted sharply with the Dalmatian fur she had draped over her shoulders more for decoration than for warmth. After her, Guenon House arrived, led by a merrily laughing Widow Fiebig as the witch Baba Yaga on the arm of Herr Richter-Meinhold, who was dressed in yellow-and-red, like the covers of his maps.

'Look, here come the balloonists.' Albin Eschschloraque pointed to the terrace outside the main room that was now lit by floodlights. Alke and some of those in white overalls opened the French windows, where a crush of curious onlookers was growing.

'Why don't you come over here if you want to see something?' a slim figure with an ass's head, whom Meno recognized as Eschschloraque senior, called out to them. 'You look surprised, Rohde – and would be justifiably so: not everyone has the self-irony to discover this grey fellow within himself. Most don't even look for it. And imagine they're lions and eagles. – They're landing.' A balloon came down, steered by Herr Ritschel, who was wearing a sailor's peaked cap and had a bosun's whistle. Beside Arbogast in his black cloak, Meno saw Judith Schevola – in a balloonist's jaunty leather outfit; she'd even managed to get hold of a pilot's leather helmet – and Philipp Londoner, he in the picturesquely ragged costume of a buccaneer.

'The Flying Dutchman.' The mocking comment came from the ass's head. 'Through the thunder and storm, from distant seas. And that on the eve of the day of the working class. He's also got his steersman with him. Together with Senta in leathers. – *Fatigant*, *hideux*, and, above all, by no means fair. What do you think, Albin?'

'I think she should beware. The sea is cold and deep.'

'Your colleagues' – the ass's head nodded to the entrance – 'Heinz Schiffner in a toga, laurel wreath round his brow. And in his hand a thistle, probably even a real one. That must symbolize clauses in a contract. What do you say to your boss appearing in his true colours, Rohde? That's going over the top. It really shakes you up, doesn't it, Rohde?'

'Fräulein Wrobel as the Chocolate Girl,' Albin said, licking his lips, 'a delicious child, all at once I have a yen to see that sharp girl's sweeter vein. A pair of scales she has as well, the pans say come then go again. – I'll keep your seat for you,' he shouted after Meno.

The nomenklatura of Dresden's Party rolled up. They rolled up in the rubber-tyred horse-drawn charabancs from Heckmann's carriage business; Julie-the-horses was on the box of the first one, cracking her whip merrily as she drove the two draught horses. The funicular brought more guests and locals, directing furtive glances at the Party secretaries dressed as knights who were toasting each other in loud voices. Their wives, in the costumes of high-born damsels, were quieter. The passers-by kept their heads down and quickly continued on their way.

When Meno returned, Judith Schevola looked through his microscope. 'I hope those aren't infectious.'

'What are you talking about?' Meno asked irritatedly.

'About those pretty things on your slide, of course.'

'Well, they're certainly not things,' said Albin, who was also peering through the eyepiece. 'Do enlighten us, Herr Rohde. All I can see is full stops, dashes and commas.'

'I didn't bring a preparation with me,' Meno said, bending over the microscope. 'Cocci stained with eosin, I'd say at a glance. Someone must have stuck it in.'

Eschschloraque senior's ass's head suddenly came alive again: 'Eosin, what a poetic name in the cool realm of tissue science. Eos, rosy-fingered dawn, Aurora in Latin. And that shot in the year of seventeen that made a breach in the gate of time. What I wanted to ask, Fräulein Deepyear: what is it like flying with the Chilly Councillor? – But silence, comrades. Our prince is about to have a shot at addressing us.'

Barsano spoke poorly but kept it brief. It was the same empty catch-phrases as ever and Meno wondered whether Barsano believed in what he was saying, whether there was a man behind the public figure as he knew there was with Londoner, who spoke quite differently at university staff meetings and on other occasions from how he did among friends and family at home. There were rumours about Barsano going round, Londoner had told Meno that for some time now their First Secretary had no longer been so highly regarded in Berlin, he was too close to 'our friends' in Moscow, too sympathetic towards certain ideas of the Chairman of the Supreme Soviet. There had been 'visits'.

That evening old Londoner was ill at home on Zetkinweg, but only yesterday he had enjoyed a play-reading with the parts cast, corrected Meno's English pronunciation and joined in at favourite passages, so joyfully carried away that his absence through illness gave Meno pause for thought. But at the very least, Meno was convinced, Londoner would have advised Philipp, Judith, the Eschschloraques and himself not to attend Barsano's party if it had been dangerous. Perhaps though, Meno reflected, Londoner had deliberately not given them such a warning since it increased the credibility of his own excuse if he didn't attend himself but those closest to him did; in that way Barsano wouldn't suspect anything. The balance of power seemed to be changing . . . Barsano had been attacked in *Neues Deutschland*, which *Pravda* had found 'disconcerting', which in its turn caused deflections on the seismograms that alarmed even less experienced quake-observers.

An emcee took over, he had the same red tie as the pianist, who appeared with arms outstretched and eyes closed, groping in the dark (the piano had had to be turned round); the other members of the dance band were also sporting red ties, which resulted in a barrage of algal up-and-down cross-beats when they began their tasteful manipulation of a few evergreens; a routine that made Meno think of the sales assistants at the Christmas market who showed the same matter-of-fact efficiency in packing the balls to decorate the trees as these instrumentalists in playing their way through their musical comfort food. Judith Schevola leant over to him. 'One, two, three, another bar *fini*. The socialist work ethic applied to dance music. So silent, Herr Rohde? Actually your name ought to be Kibitzer. May I beg one of your Orients?'

. . . but then, all at once . . .

Else Alke brushed against flowers as she went past, the flowers withered. Malthakus and Frau Fiebig and the Guenons were drinking punch and started to twist and turn on their chairs as if they could hardly hold themselves back; their legs twitched in time to the music.
click,
Meno heard, beside him, the flame of a cigarette lighter lit up Judith Schevola's features, Altberg was giving her a light. From Barsano's table came the feverish laughter of the high-born damsels, vodka, punch, schnapps trickled down throats, eyes glistened as if blackened by deadly nightshade. Meno heard dogs barking, heard the wind carrying voices to him through the dreamily slow movements of the guests, across the tables and the brushed-aside chords of the dance band; howling and wailing; but it might have been an illusion like the two men in green at the window, like Eschschloraque's voice, quiet but distinctly audible through a hubbub of voices, as he said to Philipp, 'I've looked through your papers; as far as I can understand it we're heading for bankruptcy. That's explosive stuff, if the figures are right, and I can't understand why they're shutting their eyes to it.'

The emcee threw his head back like a stallion, his mane, fixed with Dreiwettertaft hairspray, looked frosted in the disco light, his moustache lifted on one side, revealing long teeth. 'The floor is yours, ladies and gentlemen.'

Heinz Schiffner, his eyes on Babett Honich's cleavage, searched in vain for a comb in the folds of his toga.

. . . but then, all at once . . .

'They're not interested in that kind of report. D'you know what he says? "For me that's of no value whatsoever. That's exactly the same as what's in the Western press." That's why it doesn't bother him.'

'Since that which must not –'

'– cannot be. I would start to wonder if people on Grauleite were saying the same as *Der Spiegel*. In that case there might be something to it. But those at the top think in exactly the same way and that's the problem.'

'Recently the Politburo was looking into the panties problem. There are no panties, neither in Berlin nor in the unimportant rest of the country,' Albin Eschschloraque said, 'so they were trying to develop a panties-problem-elimination plan. But the Women's League had already started a newspaper campaign with patterns for making your own panties.'

'The two Kaminskis have come as angels! God, if only virtue could be taught.'

'But don't listen to that Eschschloraque, Rohde. We'll deal with him soon enough. That count with the slick, Frenchified tongue – who's only in favour of communism because it means everyone will have time to go to his plays.'

'Oh, Paul. Don't say you're jealous.'

'And you, Lührer? Wherever you go you're gabbling on about journeys to the West and hard-currency royalties.'

'Herr Schade, there's something I've been wanting to say to you for a long time –'

'Oh, are you still around, Fräulein Schevola?'

'As you see.'

'Yes, OK, things can change. And what is it you want to say to me?'

'You're useless.'

'What?'

'Completely. You're a functionary but not a writer.'

'I tell you . . . I tell you, the Jews . . . they're back in power again. They're stirring things up against us in America, getting our loans blocked . . . We've come to an agreement with Japan. The Japanese are helping us. There are certain traits of character, national . . . whatsits.'

'You're drunk, Karlheinz. You . . . revolting.'

'Just grin and bear it, Georgie Altberg. Like Comrade Londoner. Don't get worked up. My God, this is pretty strong stuff. Almost as bad as the boss's accordion playing.'

'Ladies' panties? Let them tie Pioneer neckerchiefs round them – like that Honich woman. There's no shortage of them.'

'Karlheinz, I've always kept my mouth shut when you go on like this, but now I'm asking you to apologize to Philipp and Judith.'

'Hey, what's got into you? Have you got something you want to get off your chest now, Georgie? Usually you're the best at keeping your trap shut. You're finished, I mean – dead.'

'You may well be right. But being dead's not that bad. You can get used to anything. If you refuse to apologize I will pass on what you said to the Party Control Commission.'

'Oh, you're going to inform on me, are you? All I can say is: best of luck. You'll hear a quite different tune from those birds.'

'Virtue, virtue! I'm asking you about virtue, my dear Altberg, and you come back to me with – virtues. Don't keep making one thing into many – like people who break something.'

'And what is it, in your opinion, my dear Eschschloraque? By the way, may I congratulate you on your costume. The ass's head suits you down to the ground.'

'I knew you'd allude to it. Well, not everyone will go down – or should one say sink – so low as you . . . To take pleasure in beauty and to have it at your command. That is what the philosopher says. So this is what I understand by virtue: to be able, full of desire for beauty, to acquire it for oneself. – Herr Ritschel, over here. Please. Surely our table gets its turn. I'd love to try the marbled electric ray looking up with such a resigned expression from your fish board.'

'According to your logic, my dear Eschschloraque, every punter who buys a pretty whore is a very virtuous person. He's full of desire for beauty and presumably he has enough money in his pocket.'

'You're cynical, Altberg. That's not you. A cynic starts to die during his life.'

'Excuse me if I laugh, my dear Eschschloraque, but, you and a paragon of virtue! That's ac-tu-al-ly something for Arbogast's joke collection.'

'I'm a paragon of virtue as long as virtue is something useful. Come on now, Altberg, I've often been occupied with useful things.'

'Useful but not good!'

'Good because useful! Dig, miner, dig deep.'

'And always with the mighty, my dear Eschschloraque: eat and carouse with the high and mighty, sit with them, be agreeable to them.'

'Ah, but there's more. You will permit me to continue, my dear Altberg? From the good alone will you learn what is good, the bad will rob you of what wits you have.'

'Panties? Pioneer neckerchiefs?'

'My husband, well, you know. In the morning I always think I'm married to a walrus. His hair stands on end, he takes the toothbrush glass, whips the toothpaste up into foam and gargles like nobody's business. Then he blows out the whole lot through his stubble into the basin. I watch him and think: you're wedded to something like that, cooped up in this marriage for thirty years. And then the constant changes of address. Free German Youth study year, extension course, advanced study in Moscow, Party Secretary in provincial holes, and I'd promised myself that we'd go to Berlin sometime . . . My friends have all got a house out in the country and a dacha and a car as well, most even two cars. And us? A three-room dump in a new development because he didn't want to be in Block A and because a Party member has to set an example and he can't stand the corrupt guys who can call themselves comrades and damage the Party's reputation . . . Which means I'm sitting there asking myself, what have you made of your life, girl?'

'The eye has a very simple anatomy, my dear Rohde. It's as if you were to write something, in a letter say, in plain, clear language, as simply as possible, but the other person only reads what someone else's lens system, an optical illusion, places over the sheet of paper as meaning – the one thing is written but the other is understood.'

'Oh, if only I'd taken King Thrushbeard, oh, if only I'd taken that one.'

'Those brain-dead bastards! Ideals? God, they never had any! They wanted to earn money, really live it up, perhaps even get themselves a car from the West, that's the limit of their ambitions! Socialists? All they do is drag the idea of socialism through the mud!'

'Be careful what you say, Philipp.'

'That's the worst thing about it, that you have to be careful what you say.'

'Tell me where you stand –'

'Herr Ritschel, a little more of your chemist's punch, please. I'll tell you one thing, Rohde. That business with the red comma – forgotten. I was even quietly amused by it.'

'– and how you serve the land.'

'I'm a man of the Enlightenment, that is: critical, ironic, an unbeliever perhaps. It's possible I don't even believe that I believe in nothing. You're a Romantic and that means you contribute to capitalism. For longing and homesickness drive the world but the driving force is capitalism. Utopia is being at a standstill. That's why I want the clocks not to chime, that's why I'm for the winter. As a Romantic you think you're renouncing the world, escaping from it. Nonsense! You're driving it on . . . the pursuit of happiness, that's what it says in the American constitution. A Romantic principle. And the motto of the empire of the self.'

'Ladies and gentlemen, especially for you: songs by Karat! For all of you who love the "Rainbow", Karat have lit the "Magic Light": Henning and Bernd have cast a spell on their strings, Micha has drummed out his heartbeat, Herbert and Ed given of their best. And of course, the floor is still there for those who want to dance.'

'I've seen a picture, my dear Eschschloraque, ice floes coming up through the frozen surface of a lake; relics they were, the past in the here and now. Will there at some time be a society consisting entirely of things from the past?'

'Such alarm, Herr Altberg? Don't worry, I've no objection to anyone daring to think that there might be something different coming after socialism.'

'There have been times when you've taken a quite different line, Eschschloraque.'

'Come with me, Judith. It will be a great time, we'll be making history . . .'

'Just stories are enough for me. Break with Marisa.'

'I can't, I simply can't. I love both of you. That's the way it is . . . both of you, each in a particular way.'

'Said Casanova: I have been faithful to all of them, in my fashion.'

'You're accusing me of bourgeois attitudes? And yourself, Judith?'

'And what do you say, Master Kibitzer? Should I go with him? – You remain silent. You always remain silent.'

'He'll have his reasons, Judith. Come with me, I beg you.'

'The floor is yours! Already a few bold couples are dancing their way into May.'

'It is one of the mysteries of nature as well as of the state that it's safer to change many things rather than just a single one –'

'You're suspicious tonight, Trude.'

'Oh, you know, Ludwig, as far as thoughts are concerned, suspicions are like bats among birds – they're always fluttering in the twilight.'

'It's a sickness that always eats away everything. Good evening.'

'Ah, Herr Eschschloraque. How are your two machines coming on? Did you get the pencils I sent you?'

'Clouds the mind, darkens the brow, distrusts sugar, calls it the sweetest of poisons, makes friends part and nourishes the nettle of suspicion. Crawls along beside time bent crooked . . . a forest of suspicion, full of dark creatures.'

'That Eschschloraque – there were times when someone like that would have been arrested. What do you think? He comes from the past, doesn't he? Yes . . . we ought to have been more alert. He's absolutely convinced of his own greatness and immortality . . . Did you know, Rohde, that he's had all his plays engraved on steel plates, from the Freital stainless-steel factory – in case there should be a fire? He has a bunker underneath his house and that's where they're kept.'

'We can rely on the Japanese. They love German orchestras more than anything, above all our State Orchestra. Recently we had . . . perhaps you know this. It wasn't in the newspapers. We had this toothbrush problem. A Russian artilleryman was drunk and fed up. And he – whee! – sent a little artillery rocket on its way. And of all places, it hit the main production plant of our toothbrush factory. There was no one in it, thank God, the workers on the night shift were playing cards.'

'May . . . might I ask for a dance, Comrade Esch . . . sch . . . You do have a funny name, Herr . . .'

'I don't think you should dance in your state, Frau Honich.'

'Ki-king of the f-fancy fish, ha ha. That's what they call you. Come on, you miserable lord, you . . . Bolshy-wigg.'

'Herr Rohde, I think I'll just go out for some fresh air, are you coming?'

'Then you dance with me . . . Nemo . . . Rohde. Another o' those funny names. Oops! My brooch's fallen in your solyanka soup.'

'Unfortunately I can't dance, Frau Honich.'

'Limp-dick . . . you're both the same . . . no toothpaste in the tube . . . you —'

'Don't . . . please.'

'— cocksuckers. The pair of you! Pansies!'

'Yeah, the night shift. And nothing left of the toothbrushes. The news spread like wildfire right across the Republic that there was likely to be a toothbrush shortage in the near future. We had to respond! People started hoarding toothbrushes like mad so that there really was a shortage. But the Japanese helped us. Sent an aeroplane full of toothbrushes at once. In return we sent them some half-timbered houses, from the brown coal, they had to be pulled down anyway. The samurai're very keen on 'em. Rebuild 'em, in authentic style. And we had our toothbrushes — made in Hong Kong, the Japanese import those things as well.'

'Whether it's possible to teach virtue, that's the problem.'

'Just look at the Kaminskis. The Honich woman's just given them a clout round the ear. Does she know what she's doing?'

'Ladies and gentlemen, your attention please for our solidarity tombola. Don't worry, every ticket's a winner! A fanfare for Frau Herrmann, you will all know her from *Tele-Lotto*, where she makes sure everything's done according to the rules . . . Our Comrade First Secretary is drawing the first prize — he unrolls the slip of paper — the furrows disappear from his brow — he hands me the slip of paper — he has won: a sociable get-together over coffee and cakes with veteran workers of the Elsa Fenske Retirement Home!'

'click,'

said the Old Man of the Mountain.

'click,

I hear the lighter strike, the blue light flares up, but the wind blows it out; to the East, to the East, the drummer boy cried and the soldier tightened the straps of his knapsack. To the East the tanks rolled on, the Greatestleaderofalltime cried Deutschland Deutschland; the soldier had a comrade, he opened his darling's letter, laughed as he started to read, a bullet punched a hole in his steel helmet and he fell down, his eyes staring up at the sky. At once another comrade wanted to have his boots

click,

and the soldier was on guard at night when they were bivouacking by the river and he didn't guard them very well for he was reading a book by moonlight and partisans came at night to the bivouac by the river and stabbed the other guards, who had not gone down to the river, and stabbed his comrades while they were sleeping, finally the company commander's dog barked and those who could still see saw the soldier pull himself up, he didn't say anything, didn't shout anything for he could no longer do that; but the others shouted and grabbed their rifles, shots cries fire the red flashes from the muzzles, and he saw the company cook with a carving knife

you bitch you bitch you Russky bitch

cut the throat of a female partisan, and before that her chapka rolled off into the snow and her hair fell down, her soft blonde hair

click click,

an anthem rings out, hands are raised in the white oval, the Greatestleaderofalltime steps up to the microphone, declares the Summer Olympics, Berlin 1936, as open, a grammatical error the young blond man reflects on for just a second, for in a moment the camera up there on the rails with the bold young woman director will swing round to focus on his troop, the youth of Germany will perform gymnastic exercises, the youth of classical antiquity, the youth of all ages below a sky of blue silk with an aeroplane sliding across like a slim flat-iron, the young man's pulse is racing, he senses his movements fusing with those of the others, Gau Brandenburg, Gau Breslau, Warthegau, into something higher, hears the stadium announcer's voice, shimmering with enthusiasm, what a magnificent day, what a magnificent life, then the blond young man seeks out his father's eye, he's in the delegation of the Silesian NSDAP, for the first time he looks proud and the blond young man feels something tighten his throat, go through his veins, into his eyes, a swimmer as free as the bright clouds up above.

Snow. Mother Holle shaking out her eiderdowns. An old woman with a kindly face, they sometimes saw it, slumbering in the lakes, quivering and vanishing among the water lilies when the pike awoke. Snow filling the muddy furrows of Russia, soft, creeping snow. The horses' bodies steamed, the soldier and the sergeant rubbed them dry. They whinnied, fearfully jerked their heads back, shied in their harnesses, their eyes like lumps of pitch. Flakes, hands slowly descending, white, six-fingered hands, stroked his comrades' hair, shoulders, felt the tents, the radio truck, motorbikes, tanks. White hands cut white osiers, wove white baskets round the bivouac. White feather-hands, scattered down, plunging down, no longer melting; outside Moscow the soldier saw the towers, the Spasskaya and the red star on Lomonosov University, the colourful onion domes on St Basil's Cathedral; outside Moscow the winter, cross-hatched by the anti-aircraft fire, tightened its frosty vice, the company was caught in its icy jaws. The snow grew coarser, didn't caress them any more and sometimes the soldier heard scraps of songs or voices drifting towards him, the little mermaid was dead, the red flower was frozen in Malachite Mountain, the soldier thought he could hear the snow rattling, the flakes clinked like little pewter plates. A comrade passed water beside him, it froze up from the ground, he swore and broke it off. Snow packed up the jeeps, the blankets on the horses that nudged the frozen-stiff tents with their frosted nostrils.

Snow blocked the tanks heading for Moscow and then the diesel froze, then the oil froze, and the soldiers of the company saw people hurrying to and fro in the streets of Moscow, saw trams and banners.'

'And swing to the left, then swing to the right, that keeps your eyes both clear and bright. Dance your way into May, comrade ladies and gentlemen.'

'What is it that comes up out of the deep sleep of time,' Meno heard Eschschloraque murmur, 'out of the deep sleep of time and then, Rohde, this melody quivering up, this swan-white melody flickering, yes, flaring up, a star over Moscow, and Levitan spoke, but you know him, don't you know him? You were a little boy, I know, I know your father, I knew your mother, what is it that comes up out of the deep sleep of time?'

71

The main task

'click,'
said the Old Man of the Mountain, 'goebbelstongue crackled from the radio, Lale Andersen sang Lili Marlene and Zarah Leander sang I know some day a mi-hiracle will come, Christmas on the German front line, and Goebbels shouted and the Greatestleaderofalltime shouted and the voices on Reich radio and the Russians shouted. Urrah, urrah, they broke out from Moscow, at first black dots on the white background, pinpricks, intermingling swarms, then lumps, then nests and then the tanks came at us from both sides and ours were stuck there, tracks broken by ice, and had no fuel and one comrade shot a bazooka at the oil tank of a T34 that sprang a leak, the oil a black trail in the snow that caught fire, spiders of flame ran over the tracks, but the T34 drove

on, they could drive without oil, and then over the comrade in his tank-hole, turn to the right first, the soldier emptied his magazine but it just went ping ping ping on the sides of the tank, then turn to the left, until his comrade's cries could no longer be heard, and then across and the soldier picked up a handful of snow and looked at it, he couldn't think of anything else

Hang him

No

It's your turn, so

I don't want to

Hang him, the Jew

I can't

So you've got to learn, you coward, that's an order

that was in the Ukrainian village. The captain drew his pistol and pointed it at the soldier, who saw the black hole of the muzzle aimed at his face. An order, and if you refuse to obey it, I'll blow your brains out. And his comrades said to the soldier Come on. It's only a lousy Jew. And they pulled the thin young man by the hair, he was a lad of twenty, the same age as the soldier, and his hat was lying in the snow and beside it his girl was whimpering, crept over to the captain and tugged at his coat, he pushed her away, she went back to him, he shot, she lay there. Then the soldier said I can't. And the captain Oh yes you can, I'll make you get a move on! Here! and threw the gallows rope over the branch of the lime tree beside the village well, its trunk had no bark any more, the sole lime tree, shot to a white ghost, from which the mayor and the doctor and the rabbi were dangling, it had gone round his comrades in turn, the captain hissed Get on with it, or, chambered a round and pressed the muzzle against the soldier's forehead. And the person beside him threw his arms up and down and clutched at the empty air and tried to get to the captain and sank into the snow beside his girl and gently stroked her sleeve and shook her head. His comrades dragged him up and tied his hands behind him, put a cloth over his face. The soldier picked up the rope, his comrades lifted the lad onto the stool, pulled the noose tight, the soldier climbed onto a stool beside it, the captain made a sweeping gesture with his pistol, the soldier carefully wiped the snowflakes off the man's collar. His breath was blowing the cloth out and sucking it in, and then he heard the man start to bleat, disjointedly and askew like a billy goat, ugly, as the soldier thought at that moment, and as he did his spittle moistened the cloth. That sounds so silly, I want to see his mug, take the rag off, the captain laughed. But then the soldier was already pushing the stool away

click,'

'click,' Eschschloraque murmured,

'. . . up out of the deep sleep of time: the corridors, stream of dark, and the rats not only at night, envy sending its yellow mist creeping out, it penetrates all the cracks, it knows all the doors, in dreams, at night, by day, rolling out travel destinations, lighting magic lamps as the husband of Lady Greed, the Cold Councillor, and makes the whisper-buds grow in the field of thoughts'

DIARY

At Ulrich's place. Richard and Anne there, a party for a few relatives. Ulrich worried. He's aged. Problems at work, difficulties meeting planned targets. Talked about meetings in Berlin, with the Planning Commission. Since the international price of crude oil, and therefore of industrial products based on petroleum, had sunk sharply since '86, the price we had to pay the SU for oil, according to the COMECON agreement, was well above the international level. That made our products more expensive – we could no longer sell them to the West with the necessary profit margin. On which we were totally reliant. At his factory they were compelled to use the wastage produced by their suppliers – which of necessity increased the wastage

*among their own products. Now we were suffering the consequences of not
having released funds for investment. How often had his warnings been
given a dusty answer by the Party Secretary? As a Party member, he was
told, he couldn't use that kind of argument . . . The department with which
his firm had to cooperate for the electronic control units you need for modern
typewriters now had to join in the great microchip madness. Consequently
he had to procure his control elements elsewhere, at the moment from Italy.
Which more or less swallowed up the amount of foreign currency one could
earn with typewriters nowadays. Since, however, his firm was required to
earn such and such an amount of foreign currency he, the managing director
Ulrich Rohde, might possibly be faced with personal proceedings against
him. In September '88 the 1-megabit chip had been presented to the General
Secretary in a grand ceremony – what the population at large didn't know,
however, but that he had learnt from Herr Klothe upstairs: that chip was
a handmade specimen. What, he asked us, could one do with it? Attach
the chip, as an existent reality, to the completely outdated machines, as an
equally existent reality? In the hope that they would then automatically be
transformed into manna-producing, miracle-working cybernetic beings?
The state was subsidizing the 256-kbit chip to the tune of 517 marks per
item, on the world market, on the other hand, it didn't even cost two dollars
any more. 'And now I'm asking you, Richard, Meno, what conclusions
should we draw from all this?' Richard suggested buying bicycles. If everything should collapse, no electricity for trains, no petrol for cars, we could
at least still get round on bikes. We ought to build up stocks of provisions
that will keep and somehow secure them against looting, official raids and
confiscation. Guard one's valuables for which, as after the war, one could
get at least something from farmers. Barbara should set aside material from
which clothes could be made. I was instructed to acquire books that might
be of interest to people from the West, for if our money was worthless and,
as had happened before, subject to inflation, then the West German mark
would be the sole currency. Anne and he, Richard, would see to
medicines.*

'click click click,

the lighter,' the Old Man of the Mountain said, 'the snow covered the plains, covered the villages, Argonauts saw it in Colchis, on Mount Kazbek and Mount Elbrus, over which the swastika flag flew, the soldier caught typhus and his sister's fiancé froze to death at Stalingrad. The frozen body of a wren lay in the snow. Aeroplanes went into a tailspin and fell into rivers that burnt. Scraps of songs, of bagpipe tunes to which the troops of Marshal Antonescu went into battle. Anti-aircraft batteries, artillery, the hoarse bark of Schmeisser machine pistols, the tumbleweed whispered, balls of weed driven by the wind. The taste of sunflower seeds, whores dancing in a front-line brothel, chewing up liquorice sticks between their mouths; horses with swollen bodies in the ditches, their eyeballs screwed into stillness. The slaughtered woman in the fancy-dress shop in the little town on the Narev, chests broken open, splintered cupboards that had been kicked in, one of his comrades laughed, went out into the front garden, shot the tea rose, that was waving in the wind, off its stalk, plucked the petals she loves me she loves me not, oh to hell with it, shit, comrades, stopped laughing, chambered a round in his Parabellum, picked up the woman's cat, which was crouching in the corner, stuck the muzzle under its chin, squeezed the trigger. click,

the torch of the military policeman going round the hospital in search of malingerers. Bullet lodged in the lungs, the doctor said, bending over the soldier. The clatter of instruments thrown into a dish, the smell of tobacco, long missed, a surgeon in blood-soaked overalls, a nurse holding a cigarette out to him in a clamp; the soldier remembers the sweet plant-smell coming from the anaesthetist's mask. Field hospital, shots, Katyushas blotting out the light, a tent for the wounded burning down, screams will make him start from his sleep at night. The clatter of trains being shunted, the steam whistle of an engine cuts through the fever's curtain of heat, Rübezahl's mocking them. Retreat during the *rasputitsa*, the muddy season. Trucks got stuck, wheels spinning until they were completely enveloped in mud, had to be pulled out by horses and men. Yoke and bridle, soldiers and prisoners of war got into harness, tried to heave the baggage wagons out, their axles broke, the swingletrees of the forage carts broke. Mosquitos ate at their faces, crept into their ears, mouths, nostrils, bit their tongues, through their clothes, crept under their collars. Then the frost returns, it comes all of a sudden, the air seems to pause, is stretched, tautened, compressed, starts to crunch, is motionless for a while, then breaks like the neck of a bottle. The mud froze as hard as concrete, the bizarre ridges sliced through truck tyres and soles of boots. Retreat. Villages. Suitcases in the snow, locks forced open, letters, photos scattered

click,

the radio knob

Ideals! Not one, darling! not one

artillery fire, close combat, the white eyes of the Russian, then he's on me, his panting breath and filthy collar tie, I see the sharp outline of a cloud over his knife

Not one was too much for you

the beads of sweat on the Russian's brow, the soldier sees a birthmark and at the same time a scene from the puppet theatre he had as a child, the beautiful, colourful Harlequin's costume, tries to thrash his legs around a bit, senses he's going to succumb to the Russian, who's working silently and is stronger than he is, suddenly the Russian throws his head back, his eyes widen, he opens his mouth

The German soldier's absolute will to victory and fanatical determination will

opens his mouth in a toneless look of amazement, the captain has stabbed him from behind

Every inch of ground will be defended

blood comes pouring out of the Russian's mouth, splashes over the soldier's face

To the last cartridge, to the last man

You owe me a beer, sonny
the captain said, wiping the blade in the crook of his arm'
'click,'
said Eschschloraque, 'the radio knob
click, and in the evening we turned into glass: in Hotel Lux, fragile in
the lips of a telephone, breathless in the creak of a lift: Those footsteps,
where are they going? To your door? The night was an earthly process, we lay, rigid, on the diaphragm of a stethoscope, the night was
Snakekeeper's Empire'

DIARY
*In the evening at Niklas's. Talking about Fürnberg's Mozart story – Niklas
agrees with my assessment, which truly astounded me and made me wonder
about my judgement of him – when Gudrun came in: we were to come and
listen to the radio. We heard: death in Peking. Demonstrations. The Square
of Heavenly Peace. On the Republic's stations: dance music. Ezzo continued
to practise stoically. Beautiful weather outside. Niklas on* Ariadne *under
Kempe, but I left. The smell of wisteria in the street, from Wisteria House,
as Christian calls it – how will he be doing? Shimmering blossom, the whole
house seemed to be engulfed in flames of fragrance.*

'click,'
said the Old Man of the Mountain,
'Six groschen worth of fat bacon
and graves in the snow, iron crosses with steel helmets and a rifle hung
on them, open graves full of staring faces, machine-gun emplacements
with gunners in white camouflage cloaks, arms round each other as if
asleep
Six groschen worth of fat bacon
and in the Ruthenian forests they cut the leather off the bodies of those
who'd been hanged, shot, throttled in order to boil it in snow-filled
steel helmets to make it soft enough to chew and swallow down to still

the hunger, like the lumps of tallow of which the cook still had a supply; boiled leather and tallow candles the soldiers ate, and the thin-stripped bark of the aspens

click,

went the lighter from the Sertürn Pharmacy, setting the torch alight, the soldier shook his head, raised his arm

What are you doing, are you trying to stop me setting this damn Jew-dump alight, sneered the deputy leader of the Buchholz NSDAP, pointing the torch at the Hagreiter House of the Rebenzoll Brothers, the richest merchants in the town, who had regularly invited the mayor, the medical officer, the pastor and the pharmacist to dinner; now the yellow star was emblazoned on the door and on the walls between the smashed windows

Where are the Rebenzolls

Where d'you think, where they belong, in the house there's only the pack of relatives the mayor's been protecting, that traitor to his people, he's just as much of a milksop as you

You will not do it

The way you've always been

You will not do it, or

What

the soldier raised his gun, but the Buchholz NSDAP deputy leader, owner of the Sertürn Pharmacy, just gave a snort of laughter and shrugged his shoulders, on the upper floor a woman's voice started pleading

Stop it, these people

Jewish vermin, loan sharks, they tried to shut me down with their exorbitant interest, so

No

Perish the lot of you!

and threw the torch, the house was set on fire immediately, the flames blazed up to the first floor, where terrified faces appeared, at once

followed by a commotion in the house, clatter, screams, and the sol-
dier looked his father in the face, that he no longer recognized, for a
moment disconcerted by the grey hair and the hands hanging down
helplessly
Would you raise your hand to your father
You set the house on fire
They're only Jews
People! Human beings!
Have you joined the traitors now as well
Human beings!
You're aiming your gun at me
Human beings!
I'll put you down like a rabid dog, you're not my son, you bastard
the soldier shot his father.'

Dresden squatted by the riverbank like an arthritic hermit crab, cocoon
threads ran round the roughened edges of the blocks in the new development, the powdery grey of which fluttered at the almost halting
footsteps of the passers-by and blanked them out as if in an overexposed
photograph. The casing creaked and groaned. Meno stopped but no
fissure rent the air. That returned his fear to him as something serenely
elegant, the teardrop shape of the cross-section of an aeroplane wing
had set off the heavy rotation of the concrete mixers in the town centre,
flexing like the wings of an insect as it takes off into the flow matrices
that for moments traced the air, even though it was so sluggish. He
saw a wrecked boat-shaped pulpit, the viper-needles of the master
compass frozen in the gesture of a sun-worshipper. In the waves of the
heat-surf the monstrous, herpetic lips of the navigators spewed water
lilies over the Old Market and the Zwinger, the syrupy brightness of
Thälmannstrasse (and fairy tales as their almanac, a young fairy in
clothes from VEB Damenmode scattered gladioli over the tower blocks
on Pirnaischer Platz); the water lilies, with flowers boiled soft, swelled

out towards the people so that he looked for the bottom of the sea on the chalky sky and not below, where bunches of cars held up at crossroads resembled flounders gasping for oxygen. The Elbe had laid aside its keel-scratched, wind-hackle-roughened clothes and was sunning its metal body, which he had never seen so smooth and bare. The sun, however, with its quivering scatters of birds electrically magnetized to and fro, was at its zenith; micro-impulses were constantly knocking at the taut quicksilver skin of the river on which circles, as fine as if drawn with dividers, appeared with the abrupt *noblesse* with which the yellow flowers of the evening primrose open at a specific moment of twilight, or the bathyscaph of the moth in which the mysterious, inexplicably immense metamorphosis takes place. While he was remembering that you could accelerate the opening of evening primrose flowers by removing the calyx-lobe from the tip of a bud close to bursting so that the compressed petals, rolled up and under tension, sprang open and the long sepals submitted to the eclosion, became redundant and slackened to a rigidity that was that of sprung mousetraps – while he was remembering that, he saw the eddies heading for encounters, making contact, the parabolas, visible echo waves, splintering into each other with the precision of sections of buildings in architectural drawings. And while he mused on the words of his physics teacher, which came back to him from the unimaginable remoteness of discontented provincial summers and with his musing chipped off a flake from a block of previously unknown nostalgia since his words, nameless, had traversed time, just as buoyant meteorological balloons cross considerable deeps when the lines tethering them to the seabed, eaten away by the mandibles of the zooplankton, the caresses of the sea veils, its own disintegration accelerated by growths and carbonization, finally break – while he heard the voice holding forth over the dutifully lowered heads of the pupils, telling them that even two wardrobes exert attraction on each other and in millions of years would have surmounted the space separating them in a typical bedroom of the

Workers' and 'Peasants' State, while he heard all this, interspersed with the muttered mockery of the boy next to him declaring that, with all due respect, such durability of wardrobes from the VEB Hainichen furniture factory was purely theoretical, he saw the town turn into an ear.

In those sweltering, heat-weakened days Anne decided to abandon caution (for only strangers, Richard thought, could call it timidity or delusion) and to look the various swirling threats in the eye, threats others' hands, mouths (printed mouths that spoke, at profuse length or in silence, on others' behalf), had at their disposal. After the destruction of the Hispano-Suiza, thinking about which during many futile meetings, petty quarrels, the fight against woolly-headedness had made some things bearable for Richard, his rage had given way to depression, rebellion to resignation. Sometimes he went to the cellar and planed away aimlessly at a few planks. Sometimes in the morning he would stare at himself in the mirror and couldn't look away; the water fizzed and bubbled in the basin, he hardly moved when it started to overflow. He bought flowers for Anne, drove round the country looking for something that might give her pleasure; but after she had responded with polite consideration to a water pump he'd painted bright yellow and installed in the garden, and a Steiff teddy bear, all he could think of was household implements. Now she attended the Schmücke group alone, although Arbogast had helped them to duplicate their article.

When the names Hungary, Budapest, acquired a conspiratorial, blue sound of freedom, Anne and Judith Schevola took over the job of duplication; instead of Party brochures, Judith Schevola was now running off copies of dissident articles. Richard observed Anne and was amazed to see how, in a short time, their apartment had become a kind of conspirators' cell. Shoeboxes with photocopies of articles were piling up in the rooms (and were collected by tight-lipped young men after giving a password, once by André Tischer in an ambulance), strange books and strange people appeared; the latter were given food and drink, swiftly threw up their arms to rant on about some ideal social system or other (afterwards the sandwiches were all gone) or listened to others ranting, made intelligent or less intelligent objections, admired the grandfather clock and the remains of middle-class prosperity that a copy of 'Chopsticks', put on the piano for amusement, somehow gave an oppressively alien feeling that was only slowly warmed up by the solitude and quiet once they'd all left. There were break-ins, after which shoeboxes with the photocopied articles were missing and – an odd, primitive way of camouflaging the real reason – whole shelves of bottled fruit. One day Robert's collection of football pictures had gone (photos inserted between the silver paper and the wrapper of a West German brand of chocolate that Alice and Sandor had for years included in their Christmas parcels) and for the first time for ages Richard, who in impotent despair had gone to the police, to Coal Island, finally to Grauleite to complain, fell ill (Clarens called it endogenous depression, he said nothing) and, while outside the almond trees were in flower and from the meadows by the Elbe the nutty scent of summer hay came through the joins in the lockable windows, spent two weeks of profound melancholy in Clarens's clinic, along the corridors of which Frau Teerwagen shambled, a blank look on her face, where Richard saw Alexandra Barsano again with short-cropped hair, following without resistance the instructions of the nurses who accompanied her on her daily routine; where at night the insane screams from the suicide room chopped up the warm sleep of the other patients – until the duty doctor appeared, followed by a Valkyrie with a tray full of syringes, from which he took what he needed, as Richard knew from going with him on his rounds, as others would take spare parts off a conveyor belt; and 'reestablished' quiet – injected it back in, throat by throat. Richard had no visitors. His colleagues said nothing, no one wanted to know anything after he'd been discharged, not even the ever-inquisitive nurses. And Anne? She had no time. Said, 'You're back. Good.' She didn't make many telephone calls (they'd only have been able to exchange banalities), did a lot of organizing, was often out. Richard didn't ask where it was all going to end. Perhaps Anne wouldn't have answered that – so he could still hope he might get an answer from her. At weekends, when he wasn't on duty, he had dinner, waited on by Adeling, in the Felsenburg with the pendulum ticking and the corals of paint on Kokoschka's easel dustlessly gleaming in the foyer. Anne slapped something on a roll and went out to what she called her 'work': meetings somewhere in town, talks with representatives of East Rome and the Schmücke group. She too had packed a suitcase; it was next to Richard's bag in the hall cupboard. The more the exodus via Hungary increased, the more tense Anne was as she sat on the veranda, where she immersed herself in articles copied in purplish print on poor paper. She had arranged contact between the Schmücke group and Pastor Magenstock, who was a friend of Rosenträger; Rosenträger was in a position to offer refuge to those in immediate danger. She talked to Reglinde, telling her she would have difficulties if she continued to live with them – Reglinde began to work as a courier, the zoo was a good, neutral meeting place (presumably no outsider would dare to search the gorilla enclosure); secret messages were exchanged beneath the somnambulistic clasp of the gibbons. What Anne was doing, what Magenstock, the members of the Schmücke group were doing, was illegal, the section in the Criminal Code was number 217. But she, who had previously held Richard back when it was a matter of something 'political', now hesitated no more. She seemed to know exactly what she wanted. He didn't.

72
The magnet

. . . up out of the deep sleep of time,
Meno wrote,

paper: was sucked down grumpily where the fullers were poking their rods, fulling mills felting the raw material, down the arm of the river to the paper republic, SS Tannhäuser *sailed down the avenue of uniforms (and I remembered brass bands and military bands, the wide boulevards of the Atlantic city with winter and clouds sweeping across it like eider-duck nests, polar explorers sailing in the sky: the* Chelyuskin *and Nobile expeditions, greeted by children of October), the river raised and lowered the city as if it were on hydraulic stages, the water, brown, with smears of ice, heated up by remnants of cellulose and engine oil and the loudspeaker horns (encrusted, leaking, dented by body hammers) over the concreted bank that spewed into the effluent drain from a fertilizer factory, the foam: guano white, phosphates, swirling at the sluice, set off a vein of lemon yellow – was it the lemon-yellow Neva, crackling with rouble notes in the frost, was it the Moskva, was it the Elbian river that suddenly became transparent for the ships on the bottom, poisonous honey glowing with blossom? – ice floes creaked as they rubbed against each other, and in the early hours of the morning, when the brontosaurian, weather-beaten, thousand-headed tenements – with the sour smell of rumours and fear, of the sweat of having to hold their tongue, at night holding their breath at the beams of light, the stamp of boots, the corridors with the washing lines and vests frozen overnight into Eskimo salt cod, the blocked toilets in the communal apartments, the Moorish plaster arches in the rigging four metres up, rooms divided up by the backs of cupboards, curtains, trunks – seemed to melt back out of frozen blocks of graphite in the early hours of the morning, when the black lorries with the inscription 'Meat' had done their work, when the crows from the city parks had discussed what was to be done during the day (visit the slaughterhouses, see the frozen fountains of Bakhchisaray, blacken the portrait of Our Beloved Leader over the Admiralty, the Navy Museum), in the early hours of the morning the military marches started up, pumping four-four time out of the loudspeakers onto the main streets, where it lay like ooze, it must be the birthday of one of the bigwigs, one of the high priests from the Palace of Byzantium, red star over the sea of ice, it was going to be a morning full of trolley buses stopping, faces tense with joyful expectation, veterans with chests covered in chinking metal; a morning of the air force, Ulrich, envying the pilots their Poljot watches and the light blue on their peaked caps and collar patches, waved their flag with the propeller on it; I liked the navy uniforms, dark blue with gold buttons, liked the Raketa twenty-four-hour watches the submarine commanders wore, and then, when the commands from the loudspeakers died away, drumrolls and military marches faded, there was a second of silence, Atlantis holding its breath by radio sets in the factories, schools, universities, the inevitable Tchaikovsky melody rang out, played by the Bolshoi, then the Great Procession started to move, drum majors' batons whirled in front of white-gloved drummers and shawm bands, on the gallery of the Red Pharaoh's Mausoleum there was a flash of gold as the fanfares were raised. Mere dots, the royal household, sublimely blasphemous on the red granite blocks beneath which the Great Man lay, waved to the masses of workers marching past, to the electricity works on wheels, to the Taiga, the boreal forest of the rockets, the white-gloved commanders saluting on their tanks that creep past aligned on an invisible spirit level, the MIGs tying colourful birthday bows in the air, I remembered that the houses of Atlantis were rinsed through with military marches and Tchaikovsky, losing grain after grain of an old, half-forgotten substance, like salt being washed out of a level —*

The city was listening. Extremely sensitive stethoscopes kept track, as if they were in the hands of midwives on the bellies of the summer days pregnant with rumours that waddled along the singed Elbe valley, squashed flat beneath the baroque shapes of cumulus, without looking for a place to give birth. They listened to Prague, to Libussa's reports of the things happening in the Federal German embassy there, climbed the stairs of the district, returned, distorted and blown up, didn't come to rest, trickled down Buchensteig to Körnerplatz, scurried across the Blue Miracle, encountered Meno in Fendler's delicatessen, where he was buying foam-rubber cosmonauts, as a conjecture, at Nähter's, where he was doing an errand for Barbara, as a manifest certainty. They were listening to East Rome, where the garden gnomes were smiling and the cuckoo-clock postboxes overflowing with petitions.

Londoner wanted to know what Meno was worried about. During those days he seemed to be in the best of moods, gave his ex-son-in-law a glass of port, crossed his legs with an expression of cheerful satisfaction. Yes, Hanna had told him. Those people at the embassy . . . He was the brother-in-law of a surgeon, wasn't he, they called it lancing the abscess. Where there is pus, make an incision. At that very moment there were unmistakable signs of significant progress; the Secretary for Economic Questions had consulted him, referring to an article he, Jochen Londoner (the old man's face glowed with pleasure), had published in *Einheit*, the Central Committee's periodical for theory . . . There was to be an, oh, what was he saying, there were to be many, rubbish, there were to be *masses* of actions taken by the Free German Youth, for the Max iron works in Unterwellenborn, for example: Max needs scrap iron – we'll take them a hundred thousand tons. That showed what huge reserves we have at our disposal. Meno remained silent, staring at Londoner. In previous times he would have said what an awful joke he'd just made, now he was rubbing his hands, talking about loans from Austria, about secret (how he savoured the word, the gratified smile of one *in the know* on his lips) reserves of hard currency, making Meno wonder what the Londoners father and son would talk about in the evening; Jochen Londoner gave Meno a cheerful pat on the shoulder: his latest book ('perhaps, no, *definitely* my best') had now finally been accepted for printing, moreover he and Irmtraud were going on holiday: to Sicily, Taormina! What did he have to say to that?

. . . but then, all at once . . .

(Schade) 'Oh, do stop going on about the people knowing best, Fräulein Schevola. We've seen what that amounts to once before, we, the communists of the first generation were proved right and the people wrong! We have a truth, we have the truth, just you remember that, and we will defend it again, even against the people if need be!'
(Lührer) 'Haven't you got anything else to say? You sound like a scratched record.'
(Schade) 'And you're talking like my uncle, who was a shopkeeper. You say "my readers", just the way he used to say "my customers". And he did everything for his customers!'
(Schevola) 'Knowst thou the land, where light and shade are clearly distinguished? I long for it.'
(Barsano) 'Something for your joke collection? When Khrushchev was sacked he wrote two notes. To his successor he said, "If you're ever in a hopeless situation, open the first one. If you get in such a situation again, the second." Soon his successor was in such a situation. In the first note it said: Just blame me for everything. That helped. In the second it said, "Sit down and write two notes."'
(Emcee) 'I'm the Whirligig, when wound, I keep everything going, round and round.'

The cry of the thousands of prospective emigrants up to the balcony of the German embassy, where the Federal Foreign Minister had proclaimed freedom, was like a highly infectious splinter in the hearing of the sick and weary body whose fortieth birthday had to be celebrated in a few days' time. Even when the six trains with the emigrants were passing through Dresden, the Prague embassy was overcrowded again. The news that a further train from Prague was to be diverted northwards, via Bad Schandau and Dresden, swept through the town like an infection, beyond the control of the radio and the press, which were trying to play it down, impossible to contain with lies and intimidation, beyond the despairing fury with which the duty officers employed their nautical instruments: despite their delirious tone, the ship they believed they were steering was scarcely obeying their orders any more but, as Meno knew as he made his way home from Barsano's reception for the Writers' Association, the wind, with which the unpredictable, power-hungry force that they thought they had tamed over the years with promises, threats, distractions, sweetness, returned.

The cold built up in the tenements, in the kitchens with the extractor hoods and sliding doors, from which hung little mascots, kitchens in which the mothers grew old at the tiny cookers for baby's milk and dinner, the menu dependent on what was available in the local store: shelves for flour and malted bread, for cabbages, preserves and for 'nowt', at the meat counter gleaming empty hooks and the usual under Plexiglass hoods: blutwurst, brawn, tripe, bacon fat, among them a little aluminium figure of Ernst Thälmann; cold air saturated with particles hung in the hatch between kitchen and living room where the Sandman introduced the children's evening programmes to Young Pioneers sitting staring at the standard wall unit with matryoshka dolls, miners' pennants; the cold in the halls with local wall newspapers, the house rules, the announcements of the Tenement Community Committee ('Tee See See' voices resounded across the river, SS Tannhäuser at the border of Atlantis): The Committee Secretary calls on you to do a day's extra voluntary work. Care for your green spaces, citizens. Not everything should be put down the refuse chute, citizens. Call to participate in the Economic Mass Initiative ('Ee Em Aye, Ee Em Aye,' sang the Minol oriole): Repairing the paths in the area. Cold turned the puddles outside the tenements to ice, made the muddy paths freeze. Wind, the dark foreman, sucked warmth out of the central heating, tore the banners outside the House of Culture, rummaged round in the skips where the children played cowboys and Indians after school

Pale children. Scarred knees, cuts on the head, gashes that are sewn in the local outpatient clinic without anaesthetic; grazes, stinging, at the ice-cold Sepso tincture, while racing round the clothes poles in the back yard, skin scraped off on the wood; freckled, jug-eared children in football shirts made by their mothers with the famous numbers on, the legendary names: Walter, Rahn, Ducke, Puskas, Hidegkuti (difficult to spell! difficult to find someone who knew how to), Pelé. Girls played at Chinese twist, girls read books . . . girls played chess. ('This book prize is to honour your successful participation in the City Spartakiad in the field of chess. We wish you much joy and success in the practice of this mental exercise. Your sponsoring work team.') You couldn't go a hundred metres without names. Freedom for Luis Corvalán. The Bohr, the Rutherford, model of the atom; the Comrade Chairman of the State Council looking up from the light-blue background, his head slightly tilted to one side, with a thoughtfully reflective gaze at ('nah!' 'nah!') 'our young citizens'. Build up, build up: in the physics and chemistry rooms the 'Young Technicians', 'Electronics', 'Young Cosmonauts' study groups –

On 3 October a crowd forced its way to Central Station, to the Kasko advert and the ever-lit Radeberger sign, several hundred men (the women, more cautious, waiting to see what would happen, behind them) on the dull, chilly evening that belonged to a new reckoning since the New Forum had been banned, since the events on castle hill in Prague, something had happened that could no longer be determined by the traditional enclosures, something was happening somewhere in the darkness that was perforated by the rectangular yellows of the tower-block windows on Leningrader Strasse, the reciprocal tunnelling of the headlights of the trams and country buses. The men were young, almost all of them around twenty or thirty, dressed in the ill-fitting jackets, army anoraks with dyed artificial fur and check cotton shirts of the country's garment industry; a few middle-aged men were, absurdly, Meno thought, in their Sunday best, as if they were off for an excursion and a meal at a country inn. Their faces bore the defensive and horrified expressions of people who have been rescued, and are in a place that is for the moment safe, at the sight of a natural disaster. The larger the waiting crowd became, the more police lined up against them. They seemed to have come from all over the country, Meno saw Rostock and Schwerin numberplates on the police vehicles.

'But we've got tickets, we have the right to go through,' Josef Redlich said. He was stopped, a policeman brusquely ordered him to show his ID and open his luggage. Confused, he lifted up his briefcase with the documents for Hermes's autumn meetings, a swift gesture of surprise, the policeman leapt back and raised his truncheon. Meno and Madame Eglantine, who was chewing a frankfurter, stepped between them and were grabbed by several policemen, who pushed them into the station, where they managed to prove their bona fides. More people were waiting there. Most, Meno learnt, had come from Bad Schandau, where they had hoped to take one of the emigrants' trains or get to Prague but had been forced back by police or men in bomber jackets. Since midday, passport- and visa-free travel to Czechoslovakia had been suspended, that to Poland had not been reintroduced. Now the bitter joke in the town was that the only way of leaving the country was feet first.

The police were wearing helmets with visors; they were uncertain and watchful in their movements, like pilots who had made a good landing but in the wrong place and were therefore only half heroes. Punks were camped in front of the station flower shop. A bevy of nuns was following a yellow umbrella waving the message 'Jesus lives' above the heads of the waiting crowd. Outside the telephones near the exit to the tram stops for the 11 and 5, usually, when Meno went to Berlin, an area with bunches of people buzzing with impatience as they besieged the booths, an exclusion zone had formed round a huge patch of vomit, a beige ejaculation fraying outward, still seething with explosive energy, a paint bucket slopped out in a wild, Expressionist gesture. Josef Redlich took off his hat to it. In the Mitropa a crush, tobacco-smoke-filled air, yeasty looks over the red-and-white checked oilcloth covered in splotches of sauce, plastic plates, restaurant cups with a green rim. Outside, clusters of people, the three had difficulty pushing their way through to their platform. Overfull wastepaper baskets knocked down. Pigeons, fluttering, agitated, the whale skeleton of the concourse stretched over a chalk reef given a daily coat of whitewash. Josef Redlich examined the trains, explained details. Electric engines, diesel engines, on the outer tracks fossils from pioneering days expelling smoke from their nostrils like angry buffaloes. The little man seemed uncertain what to do, jiggled his case, kept tugging at his hat. 'What do you think of all this, Herr Rohde?' He stared at the smooth, putty-grey floor covered in beer bottles and crumpled newspapers.

'I don't know,' Meno said evasively. They had to be careful, that was all he could say. He'd always liked Redlich, that 'honest soul' as he was called at Hermes, who 'did what he could'.

'What about you?' Madame Eglantine asked, flicking cigarette ends down onto the rails with the toe of her shoe.

'I don't know either.' Josef Redlich shivered as he raised his shoulders.

'Something has to change, surely you know that,' said Madame Eglantine.

'But where is it going to lead, Frau Wrobel, where, that's the question,' Josef Redlich replied quietly. 'You went to Holy Cross Church, the two of you and Herr Klemm. The boss has put that on the agenda. As if there were still time for such kindergarten disciplinary measures. – Do you play cards?'

On the opposite platform a cloud of paper swirled up, a sweeping machine rattled past like a bug being chased. Immediately the balance of the waiting crowd shifted, a patter of feet, excited shouts, a baby whimpering, a train wasn't in sight yet but one just had to come since the crowd were invoking it so intensely, 'Wishes become Reality', Meno read in an advert torn out of a West German magazine. But all that came was an orange shunter. The driver jerked his head when the crowd's disappointment was expressed in whistling. The police were there at once. Groups of three or four advanced, grabbed protesters, dragged them back, the main force swallowed up those who'd been arrested, here and there a shaking head, arms protesting and thrashing could be seen before disappearing in a hail of truncheons. Suddenly perceptible air pressure, swirls bouncing forward and back, the power cables over the platforms humming like the taut wires of an egg-slicer; protests flickered up out of the acoustic mush of voices, single cries slit the human cocoon of uniforms and civilians outside the exits swelling and subsiding, then swelling again. The Berlin train drew in with a provoking lack of urgency. The cries now splashed over onto that platform, Redlich and Madame Eglantine hopped into the carriage before those dashing along the platform, Meno was pushed away by the panicking knot of people the police were shoving from behind. And more bits of paper falling, a hail of scraps, some descending as if in slow motion onto a bench, Meno could make out 'H. Kästner, condoms supplied discreetly by mail order', exchange requests, outboard motors, laxatives. Redlich's horrified seal's face sank in the compartment window, in front Madame Eglantine's hand stretched out over the platform to Meno, really to me, he thought in the buffeting and tussling, her mouth torn in a strange grimace between the desire to shout and her throat's refusal, the loudspeakers looked blind in the snowstorm of paper that, repeatedly kicked up by furious boots, dodging shoes, was a confetti revue dancing onto the ash-brown stage of the ballast and sleepers. Meno didn't manage to get on the train. Whistles, the guard's baton, a hoarse 'Close doors'. Someone knocked his briefcase over, another man tripped over it, collided with Meno, who was trying to get his case away from the trampling feet. 'Can't you watch

out? Fucking idiot!' the guy shouted and drew his arm back for a punch.
Meno ducked and it landed on a policeman behind him, who, like a fat,
spoilt child who suddenly feels the flat of his mother's hand, clutched
his cheek and uttered a whiny, flabbergasted 'Oww!' Meno grinned.
Two policemen plucked him out of the crowd, he was hit, in the pit of
the stomach (which, since he had a travel chess set in his coat pocket,
wasn't particularly painful), then in the kidneys (at which his
round-bowled pipe broke with a crack of regret), several blows, not
delivered quickly but with a searching deliberation that took his breath
away, then led off, together with the man who made the unfortunate
punch and was bleeding from both eyebrows. There was the clatter of
glass breaking, howling, pigeons shredding the air with their wings.
Meno's briefcase was left behind. A train drew in on the next platform,
clearly the one expected from the Leipzig depot that was to collect
those who'd occupied the embassy; it was stormed with shrill cries of
panic intermingled with the screech of loudspeaker warnings and police
megaphones demanding the station be cleared. In the station concourse
boys were kicking balls of paper at the barricaded Intershop.

'Clear off, man,' the policeman said.

'But my briefcase –'

'Buzz off.'

(Eschschloraque) 'But people, when they're free, what do they do with
their lives? If their aspiration is to be happy, what is then the expression
of that happiness? They go hunting! The favourite pastime of the
aristocracy, which had the most leisure, was to go hunting. And ordinary people have their own ordinary kind of hunting: they go fishing.
What are you going to achieve with your revolution? An increase in
the number of anglers. That's all. The improved lot of the workers
will consist in being able to devote themselves to that simplest form
of hunting. And liberty, equality, fraternity for just that? Gosh!'
(Altberg) 'Now you're the one being cynical.'

(Eschschloraque) 'I'm simply trying to avoid idealizing. Don't make human beings more interesting than they are . . . Things are often too easy in life and art often imitates it as well, so what then?'

(Schubert) 'But there must be hope! You can't live without hope.'

(Eschschloraque) 'I'm afraid we're going to have to learn to do that. – To stand on the Mastersingers' shore, the place of the age-old new melody, everyone remains in his place in the firmly established order, time, the sorceress who is eternally changing everything, powerless!'

(Emcee) 'There he is, part of that power, misunderstood, that ever evil wills and ever works for good, listen now, ladies and gentlemen, to the "Mephisto Waltz" rendered by our enchanting big band from Dresden.'

(Albin Eschschloraque) 'Not do anything at all. I just want to . . . sit here and brood. I wish I were a hen.'

(Judith Schevola) 'You're keeping for yourself the whole repugnance people feel for a former idol.'

(Albin Eschschloraque) 'Should I call you Fräulein Anna Lysis?'

(Eschschloraque) 'You can't stay calm, my son, when the world's revolving round the quiet axis of your room.'

(Sinner-Priest) 'You can imagine what I felt when my boss wanted to proceed according to the principle of that nation I hate. That in superstitious madness actually knocks the noses off statues so that they won't come alive.'

(Barsano) 'We believed that all people were basically good. If we gave them enough to eat, somewhere to live, clothes to wear, then they wouldn't have to be bad any more. An error, what an error!'

But Meno refused to. The case in the station contained manuscripts, including one of Judith Schevola's, with corrections; irreplaceable. A sense of duty, fear, curiosity and adventure: he circumambulated the station, went back in by a side entrance. Since he could show a valid ticket, he was allowed through. Meno's briefcase was under a bench, guarded by an old woman who lived nearby and had come to hand out tea and biscuits. She had seen Meno and the other man being led away.

'Have you ever seen anything like that before?'

'No,' Meno said.

'That only happened during the war and on the seventeenth of June. You're young – in your place I'd go too.'

Meno went home. The tram was full of rumours, people didn't hold their tongues any more, they didn't seem bothered whether anyone who would report them was listening. Dresden lay in the chill shade, heavy with mourning, of the desolation of its autumnal days; the lamps swung over the quiet streets of the district, full of the whisper of swaying branches.

Swirls of wind twisted the treetops on Mondleite, bounced up from the roof of the House with a Thousand Eyes, which creaked and groaned. Pedro Honich had already put the flag in the holder outside his window. The television was on at Libussa's. The scent of vanilla tobacco was feeling its way through the gaps under the doors even though Meno had put cloth draught excluders made by Anne and Barbara over them. Someone was walking restlessly up and down in the conservatory. Meno opened the door onto the balcony and went out, followed by Chakamankabudibaba, who sniffed the misty air. From the park came the smell of decaying wood, which mixed with that of humus and wet leaves in the garden. Meno stared at the city, the visible bend of the Elbe, on which a gently bobbing lighter was drifting: so that, too, was time, someone had to keep an eye open for currents and signs, people needed coal or gravel or whatever the ship there was carrying. He went back into the room. How peaceful his desk was: his microscope and the typewriter with a blank sheet of paper still in it. He sat down, tried to work, but his thoughts kept slipping away. He stood up, he had to talk to someone.

By now Libussa and the ship's doctor, who gave Meno a vigorous wave through the wooden-bead curtain, had switched on the radio.

'Shouldn't you be in Berlin?' Lange asked, surprised.

'Couldn't get through, Central Station's been closed.'

Libussa found a Czech station, translated. Hardly anything new, qualified expressions. The familiar sonorous announcer's voice on Radio Dresden didn't say a word about the events. Libussa switched off and remained silent. Suddenly Meno couldn't say anything any more, he sat, hunched up underneath the collection of knots. He wanted to see Niklas.

'Don't endanger yourself, lad,' Lange called out to him as he left.

The Heinrichstrasse villas seemed to have withdrawn into an ivy-wreathed dream, the few lighted windows were not looking out into the street but at the Land of Yesterday; the rhododendrons and brambles on the fences between the rusted gates seemed to be made of rampant silhouette paper. The light was on in the Griesels' apartment; the first floor, the apartments of André Tischer and the Stenzel Sisters, was dark. Richard was on duty, Anne probably out, at a meeting of some opposition group in Neustadt or over in Loschwitz, in Kügelgenstrasse . . . Or at Matz Griebel's with his more or less anarchist artist friends.

Ezzo came to the door; his violin stuck under his chin, he tightened his bow, tried a few strokes while Meno was hanging his coat on the coat hooks opposite Reglinde's former room. Ezzo left him there. Far away in time the abbot's clock and the grandfather clock in the living room asked the question and the silvery voice of the Viennese clock in the music room replied. Meno waited by the flowers engraved on the frosted glass of the living-room door, careful not to let his shadow fall on them, then he knocked briefly and cautiously pressed the handle down. Niklas, standing by the stove, nodded. *The Oldest German Cathedrals* was centrally placed on the table with a few Dehio volumes round it. Meno tried to say something but couldn't. Art books open, warmth, then some music later . . . Niklas's universe.

*

982

(Barsano) 'At night the footsteps. At night the scuttling of the rats along the corridors of the Lux. A bakery at the bottom attracted them. They were there during the day as well, weren't bothered by us. Lifts went, lifts stopped. At night we lay awake and counted the seconds the lift motor ran. Counted the seconds the footsteps were coming closer.'

(Eschschloraque) 'A time will come when it's diabolic for the rituals of uniformity – I'm being imprecise, Rohde, and you're not telling me off. The concept of ritual contains within it the concept of uniformity. Heheh. Diabolus: the one who throws things into confusion. To put it bluntly: the eternal revolution is devilish, the eternal change of the existing state of things . . .'

(Barsano) 'Mother was taken to be interrogated. The examining judge threatened her with the stick. The other swore. Coarse, filthy swear words. Russian is a language that's rich in swear words. Mother asked whether she was at the Gestapo. The two started swearing at her again. Then she stood up and said, You haven't served in the army, comrade. I'll show you how to swear properly.'

(Eschschloraque) '. . . time, therefore. Time is the devil's work, Rohde, for it is the instrument of change . . . the glue to which we're stuck . . . That is why we're living in a divinely ordained state, for we have undertaken to abolish time. Woe betide us if we fail . . . I see an age of the present dawning in which all change will consist of the eternal recurrence of the ever-same, Diabolus will plunge into everyday routine, his affair will no longer be change but quiescence, uniformity, the mill that grinds all great or would-be great stones to powder on the paths of an eternally unchanging present . . .'

(Barsano) 'Which struck the others dumb and they stopped swearing. They started asking Mother about intimate matters, it had nothing to do with the charge, they wanted to know everything, and that in my presence.'

(Eschschloraque) '. . . which would mean that God had become the devil, had merged with him. God is the devil.'

Order and security:

But the paper, the snow-shower of scraps, falling asymmetrically, colourful as a circus. Meno worked his way through the crowd to the station exit, clutching his ticket and his case; duty called but didn't entice him, here something beyond the usual thesis-and-antithesis games was happening, also beyond the usual answers. Luise, his undaunted mother, would perhaps have said: It'd be reckless not to stay here. The noises in the station: cavernous, with slithery, aimless echoes: was that like the way the outside world flooded into our hearing, the still unfiltered acoustic stream splashing, breaking against our eardrums, making the malleus, incus and stapes vibrate: Morse signals to the endolymph contained within the membranous labyrinth of the tympanic canal? The town was the ear, the station jutted out into the cochlea: the helix, oscillations, particles of sound rolling about, knocking, some as fine as dust, just scratching at the acoustic threshold of perception, others full of themselves, vibratory amplitudes of the authorities. Cinderella's peas, then a clicking, a hailstorm of glass raining down, as if a hole had been punched in the store of a marbles factory, meanwhile a basic rhythm was getting into shape, boomboom! boomboom! the crude, martial, theatrical solemnity of Siegfried's journey down the Rhine to death – perhaps the police had been trained, or was it mere chance. (But did mere chance exist in uniform in this country?) Hitting their truncheons against their plastic shields, they shooed the people in droves out of the station. Meno was carried along with them. The exits spewed out those fleeing the police, at the same time sucking in, as a whale's stomach factory does plankton, a crowd curious to see what was going on, the background body of which was gathering in Prager Strasse and, after crossing the tram tracks on Wiener Platz, headed for the northern entrance to the station. Two forces; they collided under the

Radeberger sign (now mute and dull on this plumage-grey morning), forming a buffer zone of kicking, of gesticulations, of archaic fear and relief, a remarkably soothing ring, bubbling up like batter, with thorny wound ruptures shooting off in places where the stitches burst between the battering wedges, which immediately blunted each other with the force of thrust from behind: as Meno saw in units of time of hallucinatory alertness that had nothing to do with his attempts to keep his balance in the swirling tumult, nor with his ticket that, in mortal fear, like a fish flapping in the air, was a vague promise screwed tight in a grip that was being jogged every moment; that had nothing to do with the thought that he didn't want to leave but to stay there, daring. I'm staying here. I want to see. I want to see (with my own eyes) what is going to happen here. Curiosity? A maternal gene that had so far remained silent, that had started to flash hesitantly on the Rohdes' partisan horizon and wanted to have an effect? Paper, floating, hissing, tramped on, scrunched up out of rage or joy. People trickling to the passageways. Suddenly shouts: the train! the train! Fields of swimmers desperately doing the crawl. The train was said to have arrived. Where! Where? The train! The expected train, from Prague; the train to freedom. The train. Freedom! some cried at the camouflage-coloured turbine that started to throb, greedily and dangerously: batons beat out their rhythmical Clear off! Clear off! The train had not arrived. Immediately the people slipped back into waiting postures, many awake with pain and furious, even more drained and disappointed; backpacks slumped down onto paper-strewn platforms. The train didn't come.

Berlin had called Dresden. The district had called the Administration of the Academy, the heads of the city hospitals, the transfusion centres. The management had called the wards. That was where the instruction had ended, was noted and kept quiet about. Have extra supplies of stored blood ready: the blunt terms of the message. In the breaks between operations Richard walked round the clinic to get his conflicting emotions under control. He went down into the basement, where the nurses and doctors were smoking, whispering, exchanging rumours about the unrest at Central Station, the situation in Prague. He went out into the park, where it was monastic and autumnal, where the statues on the fountain were frozen in remarkably graceful attitudes, which must have demanded a great effort from the sculptor, for their grace was beyond this world and yet was not a lie. It wasn't even kitschy; the statues seemed to feel at ease and that must have cost the greatest effort. It was the grace of lunatics. Christian had written, 'What should I do if they order me? You've always tried to bring us up to be honest, but you lied yourself. What you said about moral cowardice, all those years ago outside the Felsenburg (it was loud enough, perhaps we boys played so happily so that we didn't have to hear everything) – the lessons with Orré, your warnings and reproaches in the training camp, do you remember? What should I do? The barracks is on stand-by, no day-passes or leave, the telephone lines out have been closed down, there are no newspapers any more. If they give me the order: Hit them! – what should I do? I'm giving this letter to the cook in the hope that it will get to you and that your reply, if you should (can?) send me one will reach me.' Richard kept the letter with him. Never before had Christian written one like that to him. He'd avoided the word: father. And Anne? Richard hadn't shown her the letter. What had happened, what had happened to him, to them? Time, time, came the whisper from the branches with the copper-art foliage. The wind smelt of coal.

Someone had thrown a stone, a cube of black-and-white granite from the cobbles that fitted nicely in the hand; there could have been a commentary on its flattened parabolic trajectory, like a ball that even at the player's run-up, at his crisp, explosive shot, the experienced reporter suspects will become the goal of the year, analysed again and again in countless action replays, demonstrated by fathers, who were there, to their sons on male-bonding Sundays (or would there come a time when there were videos in this country?); Meno watched the stone descend over the phalanx of transparent shields, which reflected the clinical fluorescent light, and appear to lose height and its curve turn into a dotted line, as on airline pilots' maps, before it would hit its target and, in a strange reflection, make the line of its trajectory flash up again, the electric-fast click of the bolt again confirming the alignment of the sights

and

shouts, the drumming of batons, sheer lust. Kettling, scurrying, boring. Thousands had come back from Schandau on foot, driven partly by the police, partly by other authorities, partly in resignation after days of camping by the tracks

and

rioters, the scum of every day on their faces cracking open to show the white undercurrent of hatehatehate, they stripped wood off scaffolding, broke bottles into deadly jagged crowns, suddenly had an armful of cobblestones that they hurled at the advancing power of the state, shields cracked, visors split open, windowpanes shattered, glittering theatrically, into splinters that seemed to salt the ground, howling was the response. Meno was standing pressed against a pillar, incapable of moving

and

yet they came closer, the gangs and cordons and rubber truncheons at the ready, Describe the rutting and attack ceremonies of red deer, went through Meno's mind, he still had his case, not his ticket any more, just a scrap of paper, someone had torn it out of his hand

and

the black dogs, barking, their gums very pink, their teeth very white and dripping saliva, pulled on their leads, shaking their handlers with the power of their black haunches, strange engravings of their claws on the smooth, hard floor of the station concourse, loops and scrolls, perhaps flowers, dog roses, Meno thought

and

truncheons came raining, pelting, whizzing down, a thudding like horse chestnuts on the roof of parked cars, the bizarre reality of the screams that answered them, people were kicked to the ground, trampled, hands raised in defence, but the rubber truncheons had tasted

fear and

blood and

blood and

lust

and

there were the toilets, Meno ran with the others, the herd, instinctive, opportunities. The toilets. The vault, blue tiles, the stench of ammonia cutting like a discus through the breath of those rushing in. Meno recoiled, the trap, what will you do if they lock them, ran out, he could see the expressions of the police, the index-finger arms. Out, out, outside the station, get out of the station. Tear-gas cartridges clattered on the ground, people ran away, a yielding zone yawned like a slit in taut skin, then the smoke swirled up. Water cannons squirted paths through the tangles of flight and free-for-all, mashed the paper, pushed it into slimy castles on the edge of the tracks. Meno looked up, saw video cameras, saw smashed station monitors; water was dripping down from the girders, filling the station with spray and gleaming metallic ribbons with which threads of blood interwove in slow motion.

– *paper,*

Meno wrote,

paper, the mountain of paper –

Christian was sitting in the quartermaster's store, to which he now had a key, and roared as he bit his teeth into a fresh pack of soldiers' underclothes. Sometimes he thought he was going mad. That the barracks, the tanks, the transfers from company to company were nothing but a dream, a long, unpleasant nightmare that yet must some time come to an end and he would be in bed, free, perhaps with the Comedian Harmonists singing on the Stenzel Sisters' gramophone. Then he would go to the barracks library, a grotesque place watched over by a fat kindly woman with a granny apron and knitting (she knitted kidney warmers for the 'young comrades'). Pale-gold trees shimmered along the barracks roads. The officers saluted jerkily, tension and fear on their faces. The political education classes had been doubled. The clichés trickled from their lips, covering the ground where they lay, invisible but attracting dust, despised, not taken seriously by anyone. There were exercises, work on the tanks, there were to be manoeuvres in the autumn. Christian was counting the hours to his discharge. Sometimes, even though he'd been in the army for almost five years now, he felt that he could no longer bear the few days of being locked in, would climb up onto the roof of the battalion building, the tar on which was still a malleable summery mass bubbling in the thermals between the black extractor fans, write letters that a kitchen assistant would smuggle out into a civilian postbox, read what Meno sent him (little Reclam paperbacks, Soviet fiction published by Hermes that had changed remarkably, suddenly there were blue horses on red grass). Most of the soldiers were now being sent out to work for various firms in Grün. Christian stood by a lathe, doing shifts as an assistant lathe operator. The soldiers wanted to go home but on the morning of 5 October they were given batons. Pancake laughed and asked Christian what he was going to do. Christian didn't know, he couldn't imagine, he didn't want to imagine. Police came and trained them in their use on the regiment's football ground. Attack from the left, attack from the right. Recognizing ringleaders, advancing in groups. For a while there was a rumour that Christian's unit would be sent out with firearms. The soldiers were a motley crew brought together from companies that were left (sometime in the spring of '89 disarmament had been decreed), from Cottbus, Marienberg, Goldberg, no one could keep track of the streams of transferees any longer. Nip was happy if he could scrape together enough clothes and food for all of them. The kitchen assistant was still allowed through the barracks gate and he brought new rumours, from Grün, where there was unrest in the metal works, from Karl-Marx-Stadt and Leipzig, from Dresden. In the evening they were ordered into lorries. No firearms! Rubber truncheons, summer combat fatigues, body protector, an extra ration of alcohol and cigarettes for each man. Most of the soldiers were silent, staring at the ground. Pancake was smoking.

'I presume you don't care,' the man next to Christian said.

'Get stuffed,' Pancake said. He stuck his head out. 'Nothing to be seen. No signs with place names.'

'If we only knew where we're going,' a younger soldier said, he still had a year to go.

'To Karl-Marx-Stadt,' the man next to Christian said. 'Makes sense, hardly anyone here comes from there.'

'We've already gone past,' Pancake said.

'Have you swallowed a map?' a corporal asked.

'Plus an odometer.'

'So it's Dresden,' the younger soldier said.

'Beat up a few queers, something to look forward to for once,' the corporal said. 'Hey, Nemo, are there many queers in Dresden? I'm sure there's loads of them there.'

'Class enemies,' Pancake prompted; someone gave him a light.

'Do you believe what they told us? That it's just hooligans and that kind of thing? From the West. And counter-revolutionary factions.'

'And you're one of them too, hmm? You just watch out,' the corporal said menacingly. 'Hey, Nemo, lost your tongue?'

'Just leave him in peace,' Pancake said casually.

'I don't let people threaten me, and I don't let people run our state down,' the corporal said.

'Christ, what dark hole did you crawl out of?' growled a sleepy voice from the seats by the driver's cab.

'So you're going to fight,' Pancake said.

'Of course, they're just a load of swine. It's all they deserve.'

'Then I'll whack you over the head. The way you grunt.'

'I'll report you, Kretzschmar. You all heard what he said.'

'You won't report anyone,' Christian said.

'My view entirely,' Pancake said. 'No one here heard anything. *Nichevo.*'

'They're supposed to have hanged a policeman in Dresden.'

'Fairy stories.'

'They say Central Station's closed. More damage than from the air raid.'

'That's what they tell you. And you fall for all that nonsense. Their fucking lies!'

'Who said that? Who said fucking lies?'

'And what if it's true, eh?'

'Can't you lot just shut up,' the sleepy voice said.

The soldiers fell silent, smoked, checked the numbers of the cars that overtook their convoy of lorries.

Dresden. Dismount.

They were in Prager Strasse. Christian saw the lights but they were something alien, unknown, he came from this town and yet didn't seem to belong any more, and the objects, the buildings seemed to have come alive: the Round Cinema had coyly covered up the glass cases with the film posters, the Inter-Hotels stared arrogantly over the heads of the soldiers, the riot police, the trainee officers who were assembling, *instructed* by officers running to and fro, but also by bomber-jacketed civilians: shouts, orders, threats.

Crack down.

Hard.

The enemy.

Counter-revolutionary aggression.

Defence of the homeland of the Workers-and-Peasants.

In front of them people heading for Central Station. The soldiers formed squads of a hundred, hooked arms to make a chain. Christian was beside Pancake in the second row. From the station came a dull rhythmical knocking noise. 'Forwaaard – march!' the officers shouted. Christian could feel his legs turning to jelly, the same feeling as he'd had when judgment had been pronounced in the court, oh to be able to fly, to be able to do something that would put an end to the madness, to turn around and walk away, he was afraid and he could see that Pancake was afraid as well. The station was a gurgling, gobbling mechanism, an illuminated throat that swallowed footsteps, spewed out water, smoke and fever. Over there? Was that where they were going? Trams lay, helpless, like seeds in the swelling flesh of a fruit made up of human beings. A car was turned over and set alight, Molotov cocktails fizzed through the air like burning beehives that burst, throwing out thousands of deadly spikes of flame. The soldiers halted by the Heinrich Mann bookshop, closing off Prager Strasse. Christian saw Anne.

She was a few metres away, one of a group of people outside the bookshop and was haranguing a policeman. The policeman raised his baton and hit out. Once, twice. Anne fell down. The policeman bent down and continued to beat her. Kick her. Was immediately backed up when someone from the group tried to stop him. Anne had put her arms over her face like a child. Christian saw his mother lying on the ground, being kicked, thrashed, by a policeman. Lamps slid by like divers. There was an empty area round Christian, a lost darkness into which all the silence and protection and obedience that had gathered inside him slipped. He took his baton in both hands and tried to rush at the policeman, to beat him until he was dead, but someone was holding Christian, someone had wrapped his arms round Christian, someone was shouting, 'Christian! Christian!' and Christian shouted back and howled and thrashed about with his legs and wet himself out of impotence, then it was over and he was slumped in Pancake's vice-like grip like a puppy that has had its neck broken, they could do what they liked with him, he wanted nothing but to be in the future, he wanted nothing but to be elsewhere, Pancake carried him to the rear, Christian was sobbing, Christian wished he were dead.

He was taken back to the barracks' where the following day he was interrogated by an official of the sealed and barred doors. He studied Christian's file, rested his chin on his hands woven into a loose mat, said, 'Hm, hm.'

Christian had been given an injection, a tranquillizer, from the doctor at the Med. Centre. He said (thinking as he did so of Korbinian and Kurtchen: We'll see each other again. You're not going to get out of here. Farewell and forgive us): 'Schwedt', said it in a matter-of-fact voice.

The other man stood up, went to the window, scratched his unshaven cheek. 'I'm still thinking what we should do with you. But I don't think Schwedt is what is required. No. I think you need . . .'

Christian waited, unconcerned, his nerves weren't much use any more.

'. . . leave,' the other man said. 'I'm going to send you on leave. You have a few days left. Go and stay with your grandfather in Schandau. Though . . . you might do something stupid there. It's better if you go to Glashütte.' He took a pass out of one of the drawers, signed it, stamped it. 'Perhaps you'd better not go via Dresden. There's a country bus from Grün to Waldbrunn and you know how to continue your journey from there.'

Christian remained seated. The pass was on the table in front of him.

'Just say thanks, Comrade Captain. We're not that bad.'

*

Walpurgis-Night's Dream:

Meno wrote,

Climb aboard, Arbogast says, breaking a pencil in two and jamming a piece in the rudder. The airship rises, it's rigid but light and I can see the city, Berlin, the government's Copper Island. In front of it the ships are stuck in the wide, coagulated Liver Sea, their masts wrecked, their keels beyond dreams, on the isle the outline of a mountain becomes visible, a deposit of still-ticking clocks, behind it is the surging, sucking, swallowing Whirlscrew, the spiral, the downward reflection of the Tower. Blue skies over the Republic, real national-holiday weather. If I look through one of the eyepieces of the strange construction – a kind of huge microscope – fixed to the cockpit of the airship, I can see details; it's 7 October, the anniversary of the founding of the Republic, a Pioneers choir is singing the song of the young naturalists: Our land has donned its Sunday best, the dew glints in its hair . . . The fields are full of flowers bright, the trees stand tall and strong, and whisper soft, for our delight – come hear their secret song. We approach. I don't need the microscope to see that the roads are an extensive network of convolutions of a whitish substance, I can see the two hemispheres floating in the Liver Sea; the piece of screen above the brain, a TV weather map with the felt-pen circles of the areas of high and low pressure, has taken on the tent-grey of the dura mater; the cobwebby skin of the arachnoidea is covered with the rusted hedges of the hundred-year-old roses whose scent washes over the smell of fat from the state-owned fried-food outlets. Neues Deutschland, *the organ of the Central Committee of the Socialist Unity Party, has appeared in a special edition, doves of peace, workers' proclamations, flutter up from the paper, smiling, children-kissing soldiers wave. The official route, along which the cars with the foreign delegations will approach the centre with its rostrums and still-empty main streets for the procession, has been swept clean, the buildings freshly plastered up to the maximum height that can be seen from the official limousines and decked out with optimistic slogans. In the eyepiece nerve cells, with an auratic glow from psycho-cocktails, tropical plants spring up on the banks of the Spree, the Palace of the Republic infiltrated by the furtive, lethargic blooms of flesh-red parasitic flowers, other nerve cells appear to have been shut out, avoided by nutrients and neurotransmitters, they decompose and, in a kind of retro-embryonic abandonment, are walled into the rhythm of the clocks on the mountain, layer by layer the calcareous deposit thickens round their cell membranes. The brain is old, an aged brain, the fine blood tubes supplying it crack like puff pastry when searching endoscopes – I am not the only one looking, the system has distrusting members of staff – follow a curve, arteriosclerotic plaques have been deposited, only allowing single red, oxygen-bringing blood corpuscles through. A gala performance! The Sandman arrives by helicopter. The Skat Court of Arbitration, cross-hatched by fibre roses of rising pain tracts, lays its cards on the table, Karl-Eduard von Schnitzler, the bosun of the Black Channel – its offbeat, jangling, vampire-drama theme tune is playing in the entrance hall of the Palace of the Republic, a lamp shop that today has spared no expense with the illumination – has turned into a naval shipworm, his chief propagandist's mouth twisted in a grimace of hatred and torment, we can see him bore into the room of* Make a Wish *where Uta Schorn and Gerd E. Schäfer weave little anecdotes into their cosy chat, but that is not his destination, nor the jolly lads in blue from* Eight Bells, Sea Astern *singing sea shanties to the squeezebox and small talk, he traverses* Kati's Ice Show *and disappears in the depths of the Book Ministry lodged in Wernicke's Centre, the auditory word centre, drills into the crumbling mass of files and log books. Dance the samba with me, Samba, samba the whole night through. Dance the samba with me, For the samba brings me close to you, rings out over Alexanderplatz, the guests at the state reception turn to the culinary delights: ham from Wiepersdorf pigs that fed under the olive oaks there, venison between decoratively crossed Suhl rifles, parsley in the barrels, to go with it Edel brandy, lemonade for the fraternal Soviet delegation, wine from Meissen, pineapples and all the other things the TV chef recommends – Truth! Truth! the Minol oriole cried, and it is printed there, in the Party newspapers, the CENTRAL ORGAN and in the district newspapers, do you see the wires, they're as fine as cobwebs, touch them, a telephone will ring and a trembling editor will reply, and if it's time for the drinking trough, every Thursday after the meeting of the Politburo (Tuesdays) and after the discussions of the Secretariat of the Central Committee (Wednesdays), then gather, you editors-in-chief of all the newspapers of Copper Island in the depths of the copper forest, of the mass organizations, with the head of the government press office, plug the functionaries into the machine, the apparatus: the linguistic punch unrolls its tongue = lingua! white-gloved robot hands pull, the linguistic punch starts up, trial run! there's a clinking on the floor: empty word shells, tin headlines, paper streamers curl: THE MOST IMPORTANT CRITERION OF OBJECTIVITY IS COMMITMENT, COMRADE! TO BE OBJECTIVE MEANS TO COMMIT ONESELF TO THE LAWS GOVERNING THE PROGRESS OF HISTORY TO THE REVOLUTION TO SOCIALISM! The linguistic punch had a red button: the Lenin button that is now pressed: THE TRUE PRESS IS A COLLECTIVE PROPAGANDIST, AGITATOR, ORGANIZER!–*

(Emcee) 'The State Opera ballet will now perform the polonaise from Tchaikovsky's *Swan Lake*. For those of you watching on black-and-white televisions I will describe the pretty tutus of our comrade ballet dancers.'

An embrace here, an embrace there, outside a couple of demonstrators but they're all singing and dancing, because it creates a good atmosphere, the head of the riot police mobile unit, with his office in the House of the Teacher doesn't dare to order a large-scale operation to clear Alexanderplatz. –

(Emcee) 'Now comes the "Awake" chorus from Richard Wagner's *Mastersingers*.'
(General Secretary) 'Today the German Democratic Republic is an outpost of peace and socialism in Europe.'

(Gorbachev) 'Anyone who comes too late . . .'

(The people, in chorus) 'Freedom!'

(Minister of Police) 'Most of all I'd like to go and give these scoundrels a thrashing they won't forget in a hurry . . . No one needs to tell me how to deal with class enemies.'

(The people, in chorus) 'Freedom!'

(Minister of Security) 'Well, once he, Comrade Gorbachev that is, has left, I'll give the order to move in and that'll be the end of humanism.'

Porous zones, the brain switches off awake fields, the alpha waves of sleep can be seen. But this little attachment, the thyroid gland, the control centre of metabolism, never sleeps, a grey concrete palace with reflective or painted-on windows below which the lymph creeps along the slimy lactiferous duct, infested with enemies –

. . . but then, all at once . . .

the clocks struck –

Gudrun said, 'We step out of our roles.' Niklas said, '*Fidelio*'s on at the Opera and at the prisoners' chorus the people stand up and join in.' Barbara said, 'And Barsano's sitting in the royal box, his mind elsewhere, and doesn't join in.' Anne, her face still beaten up, her wrists swollen from the blows with the truncheon, took a candle. Richard and Robert, who had saved up his leave for the last days before his discharge, checked whether the slogan 'No violence' was dry on the paper sashes they were going to wear. They went out into the street.

There were a lot of people out in the streets. All their faces showed the fear of the last few days, grief and unease, but also something new: they shone. Richard could see that these were no longer the dejected, slump-shouldered people of the previous years who slunk along, greeting and cautiously nodding to people but avoiding holding eye contact for too long, they had raised their heads, still breathing apprehensively, but already full of pride that this directness was possible, that they could walk upright and declare who they were, what they wanted and what they didn't want, that they were walking with increasingly firm steps and felt the same elemental joy as children who have stood up and are learning to walk. The Schwedes and the Orrés had linked arms with the inhabitants of Wisteria House, Hauschild, the coal merchant, came out of Ulenburg, the house next door to Caravel, with his wife and many children ('like organ pipes', Barbara said), looking as if they'd lit their whole winter's supply of candles, Herr Griesel with his wife and Glodde, the postman, who'd just come home from work, locked his Trabant, the saw fell silent in Rabe's, the carpenter's, workshop, he whistled to his apprentices, took a candle stub out of the pocket of his corduroy trousers.

For a moment they hesitated – down Ulmenleite to the church or along Rissleite towards Walther's bakery? The queue outside the shop began to precipitate, grew thin, dispersed, the assistants looked out, crumpling the skirts of their aprons in their hands, 'Bring some rolls,' one man shouted, hands waved, cries of 'Join us, we need every man', and Frau Knabe, pushing her intimidated husband forward, added, 'That's right – and every woman.' Ulrich threw his Party badge away. Barbara put off an appointment with Lajos Wiener, who wrote on the door of his salon, 'Closed due to revolution'. Frau von Stern, with a lunch box slung round her neck, thumped the ground with her heavy, gnarled walking stick: 'In case anyone tries to tread on my toes. Oh, that I've been spared to see this, after October the seventeenth.' And for Richard the day, that October day of 1989, suddenly became serious and simple, full of energy that seemed to bring out the hairline cracks in the clouds behind the trees, he saw the potholes, the futile blobs of asphalt, the perfunctorily patched cover of the old roads, which were now about to break out, like a snake sloughing, and even though twilight was already falling there came through the fissures something of the overpowering freshness he'd felt as a boy when they were up to some prank, the sudden flash of one of those splendid ideas that infringed the norm but gilded his inner self with a nimbus of happiness and battlesong. 'Hans,' he said to his brother, who had come from Wolfsleite; 'Richard,' the toxicologist said, and that was all, even though they were their first words for a long time. Iris and Muriel rejected the candles Pastor Magenstock offered them, Fabian too, now a young man with his somewhat ludicrous hussar's moustache, declined; they weren't carrying candles, nor wearing Gorbachev badges, as so many were, they didn't want better socialism, they wanted no socialism at all, and for their hopes they didn't need a sermon, nor a candle chain. The Honichs too, as Richard had to admit, demonstrated courage, unrolling the GDR flag, the mocked and despised flag that here and there, as Richard was aware, had been disarmed by a circular cut; they joined the rest and were admitted, without anyone taking further notice of them.

They rang doorbells. Some didn't come, some curtains twitched and were lowered again, some dogs started to bark and weren't silenced, and Trüpel from the record shop, hobbled – sorry, sorry – past with a conveniently broken leg and an inconvenient plaster cast on it. Malivor Marroquin's fancy-dress shop remained closed, no warning signs out in the street, no photo of the more and more confident demonstrators was taken by the white-haired Chilean.

. . . but then, all at once . . .
the clocks struck:

and Copper Island tips under the weight of the people, who take up position on the starboard side, the red-and-white checked tablecloths slither down to where foam and sea are gyrating in a funnel, the briquettes with a too high water content disintegrate –

*

999

(Emcee, handing out medals from a shoe box) 'There you are. Medals! For exemplary achievements in socialist competition! There you are. Plenty of everything. There's no charge!'

the giants on the Kroch skyscraper in Leipzig let their hammers thunder on the bell, Philipp Londoner sits in silence in the darkened room, the workers in the cotton mill switch off the machines and join the processions of demonstrators, 100,000 people marching into the centre on this Monday, to the rose-wreathed university, to the Gewandhaus, shining like a crystal in the twilight, the people trying out their voice, refusing to be put off, weary of all the lies and barred doors and windows –

(Eschschloraque) 'Mole, blind in the dark earth, morning noon and night, but without time, that was what made him afraid, *without time*. A ship with a mad captain and a mad crew, full of noise and rage between yesterday today tomorrow . . . a journey woven on the Big Wheel, which is still turning in the mist and we the kings at a board on which is marked in blood the rise and fall of empires, the eternal recurrence of what is eternally the same, and for a brief moment the suggestion of a sunbeam and lovers embraced by the executioner's block of the beautiful new world, in which purity is an evil beauty and a black womb gives birth to a black womb' –

'We are the people'

(Eschschloraque) 'Mole dreams the mole's dream of sunlight and an open sky and digs and digs in the darkness, but he is not guided by his dream, only by his forepaws and following his nose, and he dreams he is the Lord of Creation, heaven earth stones created for him alone, Mole is the centre of the world and his burrowing race of blind diggers to whom the Mole-God promised immortality – but suddenly there are doubts, a voice: the Mole is just a mole and nothing else, created the Mole-God as his mirror, a shadow image made of sound and delusion' –

'We are the people'

(Eschschloraque) 'And just as the river doesn't flow upwards, Mole will ever remain a mole, will never leave the tunnel of darkness, never reach the light of the sun: that is his lot as a mole, the universe isn't concerned about it and however much he suffers, struggles and thinks and feels, he won't change anything, he will remain without time' –

'We are a people'

. . . but then, all at once . . .
the clocks struck

the clocks of the Socialist Union, the Kremlin clock stopped with the sound of a broken spring, the red star over Moscow still sending radio signals across the sea to the vassal islands, to the guards on the ridges between Bucharest and Prague and Warsaw and Berlin

(Pittiplatsch) 'Ouch, my nose'
(Schnatterinchen) 'Naknaknak'

the blood, that special juice, clots, Apoplex extinguishes Lenin's lights, now the copper plate sticks up out of the sea like an ice floe, I'm the Whirligig, when wound, I keep everything going, round and round; thyreos, the shield, where ferns crawl and break the monolith, the concrete of Norman castle architecture, into whose rooms with their standard flower wallpaper, veneered furniture, standard ashtrays, standard officials' desks fresh air now sweeps as the people break through; paper swirls up, paper, the old files treated as founding documents, a storm of papers, a riot of papers down the air well, from the galleries with foliage plants and plastic watering cans that, equipped with a surveillance camera, can be used anywhere in the Republic's cemeteries, in the cellars the shredders gobble up paper, gulp the typing down into their voracious maws for as long as they still can, the citizens' committees still have enough to do making sure their amazement, their revulsion is not misinterpreted as weakness: the seal is opened on the room in which the register of smells is kept, the sweat under the armpits of thousands who are persona non grata is taken on a piece of cloth, shrink-wrapped in cellophane, precisely mapped and kept for the dogs, paper crunches underfoot, little scraps of paper make breathing difficult, punch-reinforcement rings, white confetti from the cast-iron hole punches, crumbling files swell up, an indigestible mush from the entrails of the authorities, paper, paper –

And on a November day Christian and Pancake stood outside the barracks, some of the guards at the checkpoint enviously watching them leave while others had already gone back to their duties. The flags along the barracks road, still the black-red-and-gold ones with the hammer, compasses and wreath of grain, the blue of the Free German Youth, flapped listlessly in the wind, as the new recruits reported for duty, uncertain and heads bowed at the fact that here, that now, given what was happening outside, they would no longer have their freedom and would have to wear the hated uniform of the National People's Army. Pancake, in a worn leather outfit, his home-made reservist's sash with the forbidden black-red-and-gold eagle, dog tag, insignia, reservist's badge, a green tank and the ballpoint pen signatures of his comrades between his years of service in Roman numbers casually knotted over his shoulder, turned to Christian, who felt he looked ridiculous in the same get-up (how he had been imagining this day for years, especially since the '99 Balloons' of Nena's song that were traditionally released into the sky above every regiment when discharge candidates only had that many days left in the army), also anachronistic (as if anyone were still interested in that, as if anyone would actually have waited for them, the young men who were now leaving the army, waving the brown tracksuits they'd been given as trophies, bawling and drunk when they fell upon the stations and bars, but getting quieter and quieter the closer they came to the various places where they belonged, where people had other things to worry about and would brush off with a 'So there you are' their stories, which had to remain untold in a nucleus of explosive silence); Pancake turned to him, jerked his thumb at his mates, who had turned up on motorbikes and revved up now and then or let in the clutch to make their bikes leap forward; Pancake said, 'So long.'

'So long,' Christian said.

– Seeking: purity,
Meno wrote,
paper, with writing on and blank, with photos printed on, with the fine and heavy lines of a drawing woven in, paper confirming, pacifying, emphasizing, read between the lines, exultant, cautious, shady, opaque, official, revoking; paper for the TRUTH, the printed mirror, NEUES DEUTSCHLAND, JUNGE WELT, PRAVDA, newspapers washed down the drain, greaseproof paper for sandwiches, cigarettes form raging whirlpools, tickets for CSKA Moscow Sparta Prague Dynamo Dresden Lokomotive Leipzig HFC Chemie football matches, for speedway races and swimming pools, receipts mix with insulating paper; announcements, ukases, books, writing pads trundle along towards the propellers of a turbine in which they are mashed and pulped, scraps of paper trailing down like moss from the propeller blades, paper slush, fibrous sludge being wound into gigantic ropes that are chopped up by the slicers, mowing machines in constant scything movement that clip off the ends of the paper strudel like a string of spaghetti dough; newspapers that are flushed into the water, there are the buckets of the excavator dredgers, the leaking flanges over a

*field of vegetables that is being fertilized with chopped-up paper, there are
the gutters on the archives sinking in patient impassivity under the weight
of paper, the pressure sinters the spring folders, layers forms, makes files
damp, arranges moist marriages between printer's ink and wood pulp and
acid, wing nuts are tightened, drops form, like beads of sweat on the brows
of men arm-wrestling, swell, one layer of moisture curves over another, a
calibration mark is passed, suddenly it starts to run down an incline, two
drops amalgamate with the sound of a chest expander held by too-weak
arms snapping back, make two out of one, pus-white rivulets look for a
way to the pipe openings, which point to pipe entrances, which point to pipe
exits, mouth spews into mouth, and out of the gutters pours the extract, a
liquid as precious as blood and sperm, from the papers of the archives –*

. . . but then, all at once . . .

the clocks struck, struck 9 November, 'Germany, our Fatherland',
their chimes knocking on the Brandenburg Gate:

List of characters

Characters have been listed by first name with the exception of those primarily known either by their surname or by a nickname.

ADELING, 'THEO LINGEN': head waiter, Felsenburg restaurant

ALICE HOFFMANN: from Ecuador, Sandor's wife; Christian's 'aunt'

ALTBERG, GEORG, 'THE OLD MAN OF THE MOUNTAIN': writer of older generation

ALOIS LANGE: former ship's doctor, lives in the same house as Meno

ANNE HOFFMANN, NÉE ROHDE: nurse, Richard's wife; Christian's mother

ARBOGAST, BARON LUDWIG VON: scientist, has his own institute

ARTHUR HOFFMANN: clockmaker, estranged husband of Emmy; Christian's paternal grandfather

ASZA BURMEISTER: furnace tapper in carbide factory

BARBARA ROHDE, 'ENOEFF': Ulrich's wife, dressmaker; Christian's aunt

BARSANO, MAX: General Secretary of District Party

BURRE, JAN, 'NUTELLA': conscript

CHRISTIAN HOFFMANN: senior high-school student, later conscript

CLARENS: psychiatrist at medical academy

'COSTA', LARS DIERITZ: conscript

DÄNE, LOTHAR: music critic

DANIEL FISCHER: Josta's son by her divorced husband

DIETZSCH: sculptor, lives in the same house as Hans Hoffmann

DREYSSIGER: junior doctor in surgery

EMMY HOFFMANN: Christian's paternal grandmother, Arthur's estranged wife

ERIK ORRÉ: actor, lives in the same house as the Tietzes

ESCHSCHLORAQUE, EDUARD: writer, dramatist, Stalinist

EZZO TIETZE: son of Niklas and Gudrun

FABIAN HOFFMANN: son of Hans and Iris; Christian's cousin

FALK TRUSCHLER: classmate of Christian

FIEBIG, CLÄRE: widow, inhabitant of 'Tower' district

GLODDE, MIKE: local postman, engaged to the Griesels' daughter

GRIESEL, DR: engineer, keeps the house register where Christian's family live

GUDRUN TIETZE: actress, wife of Niklas; Christian's 'aunt'

HANS HOFFMANN: toxicologist, husband of Iris; Christian's uncle

HANSI NEUBERT: Regine's son

HEIKE FIEBER: classmate of Christian, artist

HONICH, PEDRO AND BABETT: work in Party organizations, live in the same house as Meno

IRIS HOFFMANN: wife of Hans; Christian's aunt

INA ROHDE: daughter of Ulrich and Barbara; Christian's cousin

JENS ANSORGE: classmate of Christian

JOFFE: lawyer, communist

JOSTA FISCHER: Richard Hoffmann's mistress, secretary in hospital administration

JUDITH SCHEVOLA: young novelist; Meno is her editor

KARLFRIEDE SINNER-PRIEST: 'Mrs Privy-Councillor', official in Book Ministry

KAMINSKI, RENÉ AND TIMO: twin sons of important Party member, live in same house as Meno

'KING' SIEWERT, RON: Free German Youth secretary at carbide factory

KITTWITZ, DR ROLAND: scientist in Abogast's institute

KNABE, FRAU: dentist, lives in the same house as Hans Hoffmann and family

KRAUSEWITZ, HERR AND FRAU: live in the same house as Hans Hoffmann and family

KURT ROHDE: Christian's maternal grandfather

LIBUSSA LANGE: wife of Alois, Czech

LONDONER, JOCHEN: writer on social/political topics, Meno's ex-father-in-law

LUCIE FISCHER: Josta's daughter by Richard

LÜHRER: novelist

'MADAME EGLANTINE', STEFANIE WROBEL: editor at Dresdner Edition

MAGENSTOCK: pastor of the church in the 'Tower' district

MALTHAKUS: owner of stamp and picture postcard shop

MARISA: Philipp Londoner's partner, Chilean, communist

MARROQUIN, MALIVOR: Chilean, owner of fancy-dress shop, photographer

MENO ROHDE: zoologist, writer and editor at Dresdner Edition; Christian's uncle

MÜLLER, PROFESSOR: head of surgery

MURIEL HOFFMANN: daughter of Hans and Iris; Christian's cousin

'MUSCA', THILO EBERT: conscript, lance corporal

NIKLAS TIETZE: GP, husband of Gudrun; Christian's 'uncle' (Richard's cousin)

'NIP', STAFF SERGEANT EMMERICH: professional soldier, responsible for the conscripts

'PANCAKE', STEFFEN KRETZSCHMAR: conscript, imprisoned with Christian

PHILIPP LONDONER: son of Jochen, academic, economist

REDLICH, JOSEF: editor at Dresdner Edition

REGINE NEUBERT: friend of the Hoffmans whose husband, Jürgen, has fled to the West

List of characters